Comhairle Contae
Átha Cliath Theas
South Dublin County Council

LIBRARY SERVICES ONLINE AT www.southdublinlibraries.ie

Items should be returned on or before the last date below. Fines, as displayed in the Library, will be charged on overdue items. You may renew your items in person, online at www.southdublinlibraries.ie, or by phone.

his own world, and armed with the powerful magic of his white gold, Covenant begins a new quest – to heal the stricken Land.

'If there is any justice in the literary world, Donaldson will earn the right to stand shoulder to shoulder with Tolkien.'   *Time Out*

'Magnificently sustained . . . m[...]
the Atlantic rave about this ser[...]

Works by Stephen Donaldson

Voyager

THE SECOND CHRONICLES OF
THOMAS COVENANT

BOOK ONE: THE WOUNDED LAND
BOOK TWO: THE ONE TREE
BOOK THREE: WHITE GOLD WIELDER

HarperCollins*Publishers*

Voyager
An Imprint of HarperCollins*Publishers*
77–85 Fulham Palace Road,
Hammersmith, London W6 8JB

www.voyager-books.com

This paperback edition 1996
19

Previously published in paperback by
HarperCollins Science Fiction & Fantasy 1994, reprinted twice

First published in Great Britain in three volumes:

The Wounded Land published by Fontana 1980
Copyright © Stephen R. Donaldson 1980

The One Tree published by Fontana 1982
Copyright © Stephen R. Donaldson 1982

White Gold Wielder published by Collins 1983
Copyright © Stephen R. Donaldson 1983

This one-volume edition copyright © Stephen R. Donaldson 1994

The Author asserts the moral right to
be identified as the author of this work

ISBN 0 00 647330 X

Set in Meridien

Printed in Great Britain by
Clays Ltd, St Ives plc

Dedications

THE WOUNDED LAND
To Lester Del Rey:
Lester made me do it

THE ONE TREE
To Pat McKillip –
a friend in all the best ways

WHITE GOLD WIELDER
To Bruce L. Blackie
without whose help . . .

CONTENTS

BOOK THREE: WHITE GOLD WIELDER 839

Part I   *Retribution*

Part II   *Apotheosis*

Epilogue   *Restoration*

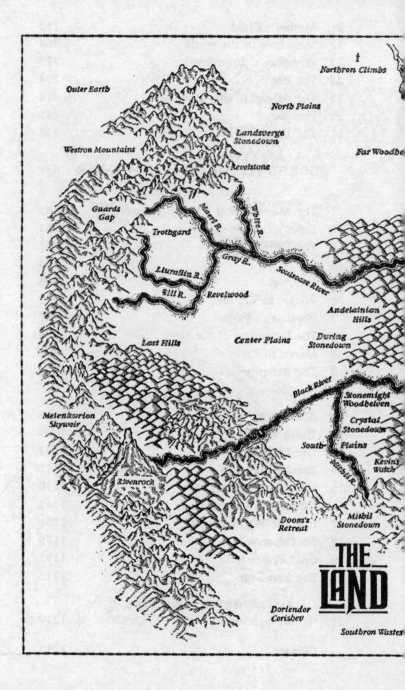

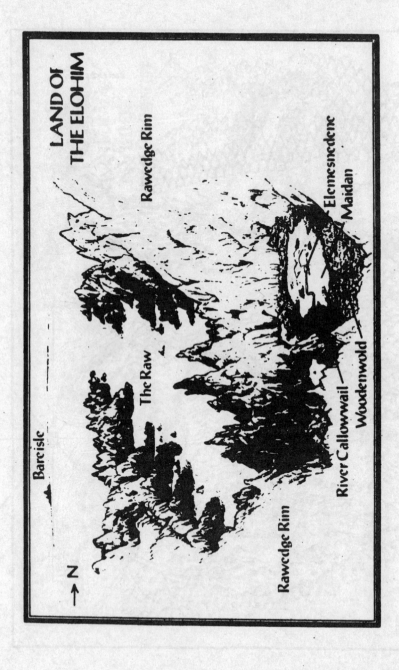

LAND OF
THE ELOHIM

Barcisle

N

Rawedge Rim

Rawedge Rim

The Raw

Elemesnedene
Maidan

River Callowwail
Woodenwold

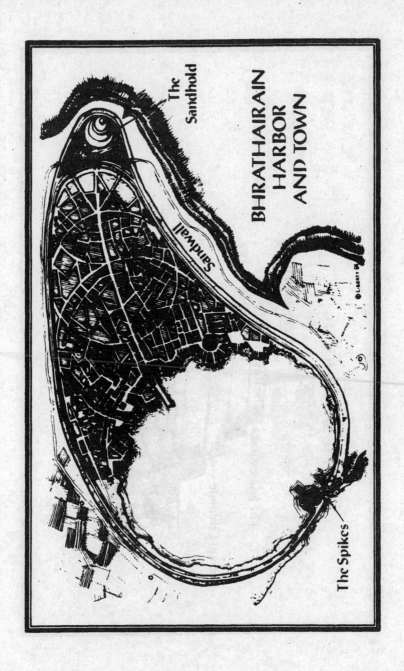

BHRATHAIRAIN
HARBOR
AND TOWN

The Sandhold

Sandwall

The Spikes

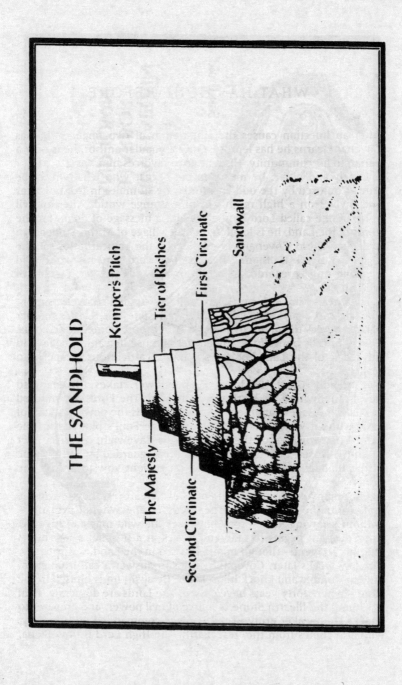

THE SANDHOLD

Kemper's Pitch

The Majesty

Tier of Riches

Second Circinate

First Circinate

Sandwall

WHAT HAS GONE BEFORE

After an infection causes the amputation of two fingers, Thomas Covenant learns he has leprosy. Once a popular author, he is now a pariah to his community. His wife Joan divorces him.

Lonely and bitter, he meets an old beggar who tells him to 'be true.' Confused by the odd encounter, he stumbles in front of a car and revives on a high mountain in a strange world. After an evil voice of one called Lord Foul gives him a message of doom for the Lords of the Land, he is led down to the village of Mithil Stonedown by Lena. There Covenant is considered the reincarnation of the legendary Berek Halfhand, the first High Lord, and his white gold wedding ring is regarded as a talisman of great power, capable of wild magic.

Lena heals him with hurtloam mud. His sudden recovery is more than he can bear, and he rapes Lena. Despite this, Lena's mother Atiaran agrees to guide Covenant to Revelstone, home of the Lords. Covenant calls himself the Unbeliever because he cannot believe in the magic of the Land. He fears it merely a delirious escape from reality.

A friendly Giant, Saltheart Foamfollower, takes Covenant to Revelstone, where he is greeted as ur-Lord. The Lords are shocked at Foul's message that an evil Cavewight holds the powerful Staff of Law, without which they cannot overcome Foul's plot to ruin the Land. They must rescue the Staff from the Cavewight caverns under Mount Thunder. Covenant goes with them, guarded by Bannor, one of the Bloodguard who have taken an ancient vow to protect the Lords.

After many encounters with Foul's evil creatures, they rescue the Staff from the Cavewights. The Lords escape when Covenant – without knowing how – somehow uses the wild magic of his ring. But Covenant begins to fade and wakes in a hospital a few hours after his accident – though months passed in the Land.

A few weeks later, Covenant rushes to answer a call from Joan, only to stumble and knock himself out. He again finds himself in the Land – where forty years have passed. The Lords are desperate. Foul has found the Illearth Stone, a source of evil power, and prepares to attack. The weaker army of the Lords is commanded by Hile Troy, who also comes from the 'real' Earth. The High Lord is now Elena,

Covenant's daughter by Lena. She greets him as a saviour.

A force of Bloodguard and Lords is sent to *Coercri* to ask help of the Giants. But there Foul has possessed three Giants to house the spirits of his ancient Raver lieutenants. The other Giants are monstrously murdered. The surviving Lord destroys one Giant-Raver, and the Bloodguard seize a piece of the Illearth Stone to return it to Revelstone. But the Lord dies before he can warn them of its danger.

Hile Troy takes his army south, accompanied by Lord Mhoram, Covenant's friend. Foul's army is commanded by another Giant-Raver, and Troy is forced to flee to Garroting Deep, a forest protected by an ancient, mysterious Forestal, Caerroil Wildwood. The Forestal saves Troy's army but demands that Troy become an apprentice Forestal.

Elena has taken Covenant and Bannor to *Melenkurion* Skyweir, a mountain near Garroting Deep. Inside the mountain, Elena drinks from the water called the Earthblood, and thus gains the Power of Command. She summons the spirit of Kevin, an ancient Lord, and orders him to destroy Foul. But Foul overcomes Kevin and sends him back to drag Elena and the Staff to their doom within the mountain.

Covenant and Bannor escape down a river, to meet with Mhoram. But again Covenant fades, to come to his own living-room.

Filled with guilt, he neglects himself and wanders the country at night. Then he encounters a little girl endangered by a snake. He saves her, but is bitten. Again, he returns to the Land – to Kevin's Watch where he first appeared in the Land. He has been summoned by a surviving Foamfollower and Triock, Lena's former lover, who has overcome his hatred of Covenant for the good of the Land. In Mithil Stonedown, Covenant again meets Lena – a crazed woman who claims to have kept herself young for love of Covenant, though she is old now.

During the seven years since the Staff was lost, things have grown worse for the Land. Mhoram is about to be besieged in Revelstone, and no place is safe. Only Covenant can destroy Foul with the power of the ring, they believe. Finally, Covenant sets out for Foul's Creche in the far east, accompanied by Foamfollower, Triock and Lena. They seek help from the Ramen, a people who serve the great Ranyhyn, the wild horses of the plains. But the Ramen are betrayed. Lena gives her life to save Covenant, but he is seriously wounded.

He is saved by an Unfettered One and healed. He meets Foamfollower and Triock – but they are captured by a Raver and brought to the Colossus that guards the Upper Land. There the ghost of Elena tries to destroy them, since she has been enslaved by Foul. With his ring, Covenant overcomes her and destroys the Staff she holds.

He and Foamfollower continue down into the Lower Land towards Foul's Creche. They are helped by the *jheherrin*, pitiful creatures of living mud, and finally penetrate the stronghold of Foul. There, with the courage of Foamfollower to help, Covenant discovers how to tap the power of the ring – though still without really understanding it. Whereupon he overcomes Foul and destroys the Illearth Stone.

He seems to be destroyed also. But the Creator of this world – the old beggar who first told him to 'be true' – saves him. After showing Covenant that Mhoram has also triumphed against the forces of evil – by using the *krill*, a sword activated by Covenant's presence in the Land – the Creator sends him back to his own world.

Satisfied that the Land will survive, Covenant willingly faces the challenge of making his way as a leper in his own time and place. And for some ten years, he does face that challenge, with no further summons from the Land.

And now to begin The Second Chronicles of Thomas Covenant . . .

THE WOUNDED LAND

Gallow-fells

PROLOGUE

Choice

1

DAUGHTER

When Linden Avery heard the knock at her door, she groaned aloud. She was in a black mood, and did not want visitors. She wanted a cold shower and privacy – a chance to accustom herself to the deliberate austerity of her surroundings.

She had spent most of the afternoon of an unnaturally muggy day in the middle of spring moving herself into this apartment which the Hospital had rented for her, lugging her sparse wardrobe, her inadequate furniture, and a back-breaking series of cardboard boxes containing textbooks from her middle-aged sedan up the outside stairs to the second floor of the old wooden house. The house squatted among its weeds like a crippled toad, spavined by antiquity; and when she had unlocked her apartment for the first time, she had been greeted by three rooms and a bath with grubby yellow walls, floorboards covered only by chipped beige paint, an atmosphere of desuetude bordering on indignity – and by a piece of paper which must have been slipped under the door. Thick red lines like lipstick or fresh blood marked the paper – a large crude triangle with two words inside it:

JESUS SAVES

She had glared at the paper for a moment, then had crumpled it in her pocket. She had no use for offers of salvation. She wanted nothing she did not earn.

But the note, combined with the turgid air, the long exertion of heaving her belongings up the stairs, and the apartment itself, left her feeling capable of murder. The rooms reminded her of her parents' house. That was why she hated the apartment. But it was condign, and she chose to accept it. She both loathed and approved the aptness of her state. Its personal stringency was appropriate.

She was a doctor newly out of residency, and she had purposely sought a job which would bring her to a small half-rural, half-stagnant town like this one – a town like the one near which she had been born and her parents had died. Though she was only thirty, she felt old, unlovely, and severe. This was just; she had lived an unlovely and severe life. Her father had died when she was eight; he mother, when she was fifteen. After three empty years in a foster

23

home, she had put herself through college, then medical school, internship, and residency, specializing in Family Practice. She had been lonely ever since she could remember, and her isolation had largely become ingrained. Her two or three love affairs had been like hygienic exercises or experiments in physiology; they had left her untouched. So now when she looked at herself, she saw severity, and the consequences of violence.

Hard work and clenched emotions had not hurt the gratuitous womanliness of her body, or dulled the essential lustre of her shoulder-length wheaten hair, or harmed the structural beauty of her face. Her driven and self-contained life had not changed the way her eyes misted and ran almost without provocation. But lines had already marked her face, leaving her with a perpetual frown of concentration above the bridge of her straight, delicate nose, and gullies like the implications of pain on either side of her mouth – a mouth which had originally been formed for something more generous than the life which had befallen her. And her voice had become flat, so that it sounded more like a diagnostic tool, a way of eliciting pertinent data, than a vehicle for communication.

But the way she had lived her life had given her something more than loneliness and a liability to black moods. It had taught her to believe in her own strength. She was a physician; she had held life and death in her hands, and had learned how to grasp them effectively. She trusted her ability to carry burdens. When she heard the knock at her door, she groaned aloud. But then she straightened her sweat-marked clothes as if she were tugging her emotions into order, and went to open the door.

She recognized the short, wry man who stood on the landing. He was Julius Berenford, Chief of Staff of the County Hospital. He was the man who had hired her to run his Outpatient Clinic and Emergency Room. In a more metropolitan hospital, the hiring of a Family Practitioner for such a position would have been unusual. But the County Hospital served a region composed largely of farmers and hill people. This town, the county seat, had been calcifying steadily for twenty years. Dr Berenford needed a generalist.

The top of his head was level with her eyes, and he was twice her age. The round bulge of his stomach belied the thinness of his limbs. He gave an impression of dyspeptic affection, as if he found human behaviour both incomprehensible and endearing. When he smiled below his white moustache, the pouches under his eyes tightened ironically.

'Dr Avery,' he said, wheezing faintly after the exertion of the stairs.

'Dr Berenford.' She wanted to protest the intrusion; so she stepped aside and said tightly, 'Come in.'

He entered the apartment, glancing around as he wandered

towards a chair. 'You've already moved in,' he observed. 'Good. I hope you had help getting everything up here.'

She took a chair near his, seated herself squarely, as if she were on duty. 'No.' Who could she have asked for help?

Dr Berenford started to expostulate. She stopped him with a gesture of dismissal. 'No problem. I'm used to it.'

'Well, you shouldn't be.' His gaze on her was complex. 'You just finished your residency at a highly respected hospital, and your work was excellent. The least you should be able to expect in life is help carrying your furniture upstairs.'

His tone was only half humorous; but she understood the seriousness behind it because the question had come up more than once during their interviews. He had asked repeatedly why someone with her credentials wanted a job in a poor county hospital. He had not accepted the glib answers she had prepared for him; eventually, she had been forced to offer him at least an approximation of the facts. 'Both my parents died near a town like this,' she had said. 'They were hardly middle-aged. If they'd been under the care of a good Family Practitioner, they would be alive today.'

This was both true and false, and it lay at the root of the ambivalence which made her feel old. If her mother's melanoma had been properly diagnosed in time, it could have been treated surgically with a ninety per cent chance of success. And if her father's depression had been observed by anybody with any knowledge or insight, his suicide might have been prevented. But the reverse was true as well; nothing could have saved her parents. They had died because they were simply too ineffectual to go on living. Whenever she thought about such things, she seemed to feel her bones growing more brittle by the hour.

She had come to this town because she wanted to try to help people like her parents. And because she wanted to prove that she could be effective under such circumstances – that she was not like her parents. And because she wanted to die.

When she did not speak, Dr Berenford said, 'However, that's neither here nor there.' The humourlessness of her silence appeared to discomfit him. 'I'm glad you're here. Is there anything I can do? Help you get settled?'

Linden was about to refuse his offer, out of habit if not conviction, when she remembered the piece of paper in her pocket. On an impulse, she dug it out, handed it to him. 'This came under the door. Maybe you ought to tell me what I'm getting into.'

He peered at the triangle and the writing, muttered, 'Jesus saves,' under his breath, then sighed. 'Occupational hazard, I've been going to church faithfully in this town for forty years. But since I'm a trained professional who earns a decent living, some of our good people – ' He grimaced wryly. ' – are always trying to convert me.

25

Ignorance is the only form of innocence they understand.' He shrugged, returned the note to her. 'This area has been depressed for a long time. After a while, depressed people do strange things. They try to turn depression into a virtue – they need something to make themselves feel less helpless. What they usually do around here is become evangelical. I'm afraid you're just going to have to put up with people who worry about your soul. Nobody gets much privacy in a small town.'

Linden nodded; but she hardly heard her visitor. She was trapped in a sudden memory of her mother, weeping with poignant self-pity. She had blamed Linden for her father's death –

With a scowl, she drove back the recollection. Her revulsion was so strong that she might have consented to having the memories physically cut out of her brain. But Dr Berenford was watching her as if her abhorrence showed on her face. To avoid exposing herself, she pulled discipline over her features like a surgical mask. 'What can I do for you, Doctor?'

'Well, for one thing,' he said, forcing himself to sound genial in spite of her tone, 'you can call me Julius. I'm going to call you Linden, so you might as well.'

She acquiesced with a shrug. 'Julius.'

'Linden.' He smiled; but his smile did not soften his discomfort. After a moment, he said hurriedly, as if he were trying to outrun the difficulty of his purpose, 'Actually, I came over for two reasons. Of course, I wanted to welcome you to town. But I could have done that later. The truth is, I want to put you to work.'

Work? she thought. The word sparked an involuntary protest. I just got here. I'm tired and angry, and I don't know how I'm going to stand this apartment. Carefully, she said, 'It's Friday. I'm not supposed to start until Monday.'

'This doesn't have anything to do with the Hospital. It should, but it doesn't.' His gaze brushed her face like a touch of need. 'It's a personal favour. I'm in over my head. I've spent so many years getting involved in the lives of my patients that I can't seem to make objective decisions any more. Or maybe I'm just out of date – don't have enough medical knowledge. Seems to me that what I need is a second opinion.'

'About what?' she asked, striving to sound noncommittal. But she was groaning inwardly. She already knew that she would attempt to provide whatever he asked of her. He was appealing to a part of her that had never learned how to refuse.

He frowned sourly. 'Unfortunately, I can't tell you. It's in confidence.'

'Oh, come on.' She was in no mood for guessing games. 'I took the same oath you did.'

'I know.' He raised his hands as if to ward off her vexation. 'I know. But it isn't exactly that kind of confidence.'

She stared at him, momentarily nonplussed. Wasn't he talking about a medical problem? 'This sounds like it's going to be quite a favour.'

'Could be. That's up to you.' Before she could muster the words to ask him what he was talking about, Dr Berenford said abruptly, 'Have you ever heard of Thomas Covenant? He writes novels.'

She felt him watching her while she groped mentally. But she had no way of following his line of thought. She had not read a novel since she had finished her literature requirement in college. She had had so little time. Striving for detachment, she shook her head.

'He lives around here,' the doctor said. 'Has a house outside town on an old property called Haven Farm. You turn right on Main.' He gestured vaguely towards the intersection. 'Go through the middle of town, and about two miles later you'll come to it. On the right. He's a leper.'

At the word *leper*, her mind bifurcated. This was the result of her training – dedication which had made her a physician without resolving her attitude towards herself. She murmured inwardly, Hansen's disease, and began reviewing information.

Mycobacterium lepra. Leprosy. It progressed by killing nerve tissue, typically in the extremities and in the cornea of the eye. In most cases, the disease could be arrested by means of a comprehensive treatment programme pivoting around DDS: diamino-diphenyl-sulfone. If not arrested, the degeneration could produce muscular atrophy and deformation, changes in skin pigmentation, blindness. It also left the victim subject to a host of secondary afflictions, the most common of which was infection that destroyed other tissues, leaving the victim with the appearance – and consequences – of having been eaten alive. Incidence was extremely rare; leprosy was not contagious in any usual sense. Perhaps the only statistically significant way to contract it was to suffer prolonged exposure as a child in the tropics under crowded and unsanitary living conditions.

But while one part of her brain unwound its skein of knowledge, another was tangled in questions and emotions. A leper? Here? Why tell me? She was torn between visceral distaste and empathy. The disease itself attracted and repelled her because it was incurable – as immedicable as death. She had to take a deep breath before she could ask, 'What do you want me to do about it?'

'Well – ' He was studying her as if he thought there were indeed something she could do about it. 'Nothing. That isn't why I brought it up.' Abruptly, he got to his feet, began measuring out his unease on the chipped floorboards. Though he was not heavy, they squeaked vaguely under him. 'He was diagnosed early enough – only lost two fingers. One of our better lab technicians caught it, right here at County Hospital. He's been stable for more than nine

years now. The only reason I told you is to find out if you're —
squeamish. About lepers.' He spoke with a twisted expression. 'I
used to be. But I've had time to get over it.'

He did not give her a chance to reply. He went on as if he were
confessing. 'I've reached the point now where I don't think of him
as leprosy personified. But I never forget he's a leper.' He was talking
about something for which he had not been able to forgive himself.
'Part of that's his fault,' he said defensively. 'He never forgets, either.
He doesn't think of himself as Thomas Covenant the writer – the
man – the human being. He thinks of himself as Thomas Covenant
the leper.'

When she continued to stare at him flatly, he dropped his gaze.
'But that's not the point. The point is, would it bother you to go see
him?'

'No,' she said severely; but her severity was for herself rather than
for him. I'm a doctor. Sick people are my business. 'But I still don't
understand why you want me to go out there.'

The pouches under his eyes shook as if he were pleading with her.
'I can't tell you.'

'You can't tell me.' The quietness of her tone belied the blackness
of her mood. 'What good do you think I can possibly do if I don't
even know why I'm talking to him?'

'You could get *him* to tell you.' Dr Berenford's voice sounded like
the misery of an ineffectual old man. 'That's what I want. I want
him to accept you – tell you what's going on himself. So I won't
have to break any promises.'

'Let me get this straight.' She made no more effort to conceal her
anger. 'You want me to go out there, and ask him outright to tell
me his secrets. A total stranger arrives at his door, and wants to
know what's bothering him – for no other reason than because Dr
Berenford would like a second opinion. I'll be lucky if he doesn't
have me arrested for trespassing.'

For a moment, the doctor faced her sarcasm and indignation.
Then he sighed. 'I know. He's like that – he'd never tell you. He's
been locked into himself so long – ' The next instant, his voice
became sharp with pain. 'But I think he's *wrong*.'

'Then tell me what it is,' insisted Linden.

His mouth opened and shut; his hands made supplicating gestures.
But then he recovered himself. 'No. That's backward. First I need to
know which one of us is wrong. I owe him that. Mrs Roman is no
help. This is a medical decision. But I can't make it. I've tried, and I
can't.'

The simplicity with which he admitted his inadequacy snared her.
She was tired, dirty, and bitter, and her mind searched for an escape.
But his need for assistance struck too close to the driving compul-
sions of her life. Her hands were knotted together like certainty.

28

After a moment, she looked up at him. His features had sagged as if the muscles were exhausted by the weight of his mortality. In her flat professional voice, she said, 'Give me some excuse I can use to go out there.'

She could hardly bear the sight of his relief. 'That I can do,' he said with a show of briskness. Reaching into a jacket pocket, he pulled out a paperback and handed it to her. The lettering across the drab cover said:

Or I Will Sell My Soul for Guilt
a novel by
THOMAS COVENANT

'Ask for his autograph.' The older man had regained his sense of irony. 'Try to get him talking. If you can get inside his defences, something will happen.'

Silently, she cursed herself. She knew nothing about novels, had never learned how to talk to strangers about anything except their symptoms. Anticipations of embarrassment filled her like shame. But she had been mortifying herself for so long that she had no respect left for the parts of her which could still feel shame. 'After I see him,' she said dully, 'I'll want to talk to you. I don't have a phone yet. Where do you live?'

Her acceptance restored his earlier manner; he became wry and solicitous again. He gave her directions to his house, repeated his offer of help, thanked her for her willingness to involve herself in Thomas Covenant's affairs. When he left, she felt dimly astonished that he did not appear to resent the need which had forced him to display his futility in front of her.

And yet the sound of his feet descending the stairs gave her a sense of abandonment, as if she had been left to carry alone a burden that she would never be able to understand.

Foreboding nagged at her, but she ignored it. She had no acceptable alternatives. She sat where she was for a moment, glaring around the blind yellow walls, then went to take a shower.

After she had washed away as much of the blackness as she could reach with soap and water, she donned a dull grey dress that had the effect of minimizing her femininity, then spent a few minutes checking the contents of her medical bag. They always seemed insufficient – there were so many things she might conceivably need which she could not carry with her – and now they appeared to be a particularly improvident arsenal against the unknown. But she knew from experience that she would have felt naked without her bag. With a sigh of fatigue, she locked the apartment and went down the stairs to her car.

Driving slowly to give herself time to learn landmarks, she

followed Dr Berenford's directions and soon found herself moving through the centre of town.

The late afternoon sun and the thinness of the air made the buildings look as if they were sweating. The businesses seemed to lean away from the hot sidewalks, as if they had forgotten the enthusiasm, even the accessibility, that they needed to survive; and the courthouse, with its dull white marble and its roof supported by stone giant heads atop ersatz Greek columns, looked altogether unequal to its responsibilities.

The sidewalks were relatively busy – people were going home from work – but one small group in front of the courthouse caught Linden's eye. A faded woman with three small children stood on the steps. She wore a shapeless shift which appeared to have been made from burlap; and the children were dressed in gunny sacks. Her face was grey and blank, as if she were inured by poverty and weariness to the emaciation of her children. All four of them held short wooden sticks bearing crude signs.

The signs were marked with red triangles. Inside each triangle was written one word: REPENT.

The woman and her children ignored the passersby. They stood dumbly on the steps as if they were engaged in a penance which stupefied them. Linden's heart ached uselessly at the sight of their moral and physical penury. There was nothing she could do for such people.

Three minutes later, she was outside the municipal limits.

There the road began to run through tilled valleys, between wooded hills. Beyond the town, the unseasonable heat and humidity were kinder to what they touched; they made the air lambent, so that it lay like immanence across the new crops, up the tangled weed-and-grass hillsides, among the budding trees; and her mood lifted at the way the landscape glowed in the approach of evening. She had spent so much of her life in cities. She continued to drive slowly; she wanted to savour the faint hope that she had found something she would be able to enjoy.

After a couple of miles, she came to a wide field on her right, thickly overgrown with milkweed and wild mustard. Across the field, a quarter of a mile away against a wall of trees, stood a white frame house. Two or three other houses bordered the field, closer to the highway; but the white one drew her attention as if it were the only habitable structure in the area.

A dirt road ran into the field. Branches went to the other houses, but the main track led straight to the white one.

Beside the entrance stood a wooden sign. Despite faded paint and several old splintered holes like bullet scars, the lettering was still legible: Haven Farm.

Gripping her courage, Linden turned on to the dirt road.

30

Without warning, the periphery of her gaze caught a flick of ochre. A robed figure stood beside the sign.

What – ?

He stood there as if he had just appeared out of the air. An instant ago, she had seen nothing except the sign.

Taken by surprise, she instinctively twitched the wheel, trying to evade a hazard she had already passed. At once, she righted the sedan, stepped on the brakes. Her eyes jumped to the rearview mirror.

She saw an old man in an ochre robe. He was tall and lean, barefoot, dirty. His long grey beard and thin hair flared about his head like frenzy.

He took one step into the road towards her, then clutched at his chest convulsively, and collapsed.

She barked a warning, though there was no one to hear it. Moving with a celerity that felt like slow-motion, she cut the ignition, grabbed for her bag, pushed open the door. Apprehension roiled in her, fear of death, of failure; but her training controlled it. In a moment, she was at the old man's side.

He looked strangely out of place in the road, out of time in the world she knew. The robe was his only garment; it looked as if he had been living in it for years. His features were sharp, made fierce by destitution or fanaticism. The declining sunlight coloured his withered skin like dead gold.

He was not breathing.

Her discipline made her move. She knelt beside him, felt for his pulse. But within her she wailed. He bore a sickening resemblance to her father. If her father had lived to become old and mad, he might have been this stricken, preterite figure.

He had no pulse.

He revolted her. Her father had committed suicide. People who killed themselves deserved to die. The old man's appearance brought back memories of her own screaming which echoed in her ears as if it could never be silenced.

But he was dying. Already, his muscles had slackened, relaxing the pain of his seizure. And she was a doctor.

With the sureness of hard training, self-abnegation which mastered revulsion, her hands snapped open her bag. She took out her penlight, checked his pupils.

They were equal and reactive.

It was still possible to save him.

Quickly, she adjusted his head, tilted it back to clear his throat. Then she folded her hands together over his sternum, leaned her weight on her arms, and began to apply CPR.

The rhythm of cardiopulmonary resuscitation was so deeply ingrained in her that she followed it automatically: fifteen firm heels of her hands to his sternum; then two deep exhalations into his mouth, blocking his nose as she did so. But his mouth was foul — carious and vile, as if his teeth were rotten, or his palate gangrenous. She almost faltered. Instantly, her revulsion became an acute physical nausea, as if she were tasting the exudation of a boil. But she was a doctor; this was her work.

Fifteen. Two.

Fifteen. Two.

She did not permit herself to miss a beat.

But fear surged through her nausea. Exhaustion. Failure. CPR was so demanding that no one person could sustain it alone for more than a few minutes. If he did not come back to life soon —

Breathe, damn you, she muttered along the beats. Fifteen. Two. Damn you. Breathe. There was still no pulse.

Her own breathing became ragged; giddiness welled up in her like a tide of darkness. The air seemed to resist her lungs. Heat and the approach of sunset dimmed the old man. He had lost all muscle-tone, all appearance of life.

Breathe!

Abruptly, she stopped her rhythm, snatched at her bag. Her arms trembled; she clenched them still as she broke open a disposable syringe, a vial of adrenaline, a cardiac needle. Fighting for steadiness, she filled the syringe, cleared out the air. In spite of her urgency, she took a moment to swab clean a patch of the man's thin chest with alcohol. Then she slid the needle delicately past his ribs, injected adrenaline into his heart.

Setting aside the syringe, she risked pounding her fist once against his sternum. But the blow had no effect.

Cursing, she resumed her CPR.

She needed help. But she could not do anything about that. If she stopped to take him into town, or to go in search of a phone, he would die. Yet if she exhausted herself alone he would still die.

Breathe!

He did not breathe. His heart did not beat. His mouth was as foetid as the maw of a corpse. The whole ordeal was hopeless.

She did not relent.

All the blackness of her life was in her. She had spent too many years teaching herself to be effective against death; she could not surrender now. She had been too young, weak, and ignorant to save her father, could not have saved her mother; now that she knew what to do and could do it, she would never quit, never falsify her life by quitting.

Dark motes began to dance across her vision: the air swarmed with moisture and inadequacy. Her arms felt leaden; her lungs cried out every time she forced breath down the old man's throat. He lay inert. Tears of rage and need ran hotly down her face. Yet she did not relent.

She was still half conscious when a tremor ran through him, and he took a hoarse gulp of air.

At once, her will snapped. Blood rushed to her head. She did not feel herself fall away to the side.

When she regained enough self-command to raise her head, her sight was a smear of pain and her face was slick with sweat. The old man was standing over her. His eyes were on her; the intense blue of his gaze held her like a hand of compassion. He looked impossibly tall and healthy; his very posture seemed to deny that he had ever been close to death. Gently, he reached down to her, drew her to her feet. As he put his arms around her, she slumped against him, unable to resist his embrace.

'Ah, my daughter, do not fear.'

His voice was husky with regret and tenderness.

'You will not fail, however he may assail you. There is also love in the world.'

Then he released her, stepped back. His eyes became commandments.

'Be true.'

She watched him dumbly as he turned, walked away from her into the field. Milkweed and wild mustard whipped against his robe for a moment. She could hardly see him through the blurring of her vision. A musky breeze stirred his hair, made it a nimbus around his head as the sun began to set. Then he faded into the humidity, and was gone.

She wanted to call out after him, but the memory of his eyes stopped her.

Be true.

Deep in her chest, her heart began to tremble.

2

SOMETHING BROKEN

After a moment, the trembling spread to her limbs. The surface of her skin felt fiery, as if the rays of the sun were concentrated on her. The muscles of her abdomen knotted.

The old man had vanished. He had put his arms around her as if he had the right, and then he had vanished.

She feared that her guts were going to rebel.

But then her gaze lurched towards the dirt where the old man had lain. There she saw the used hypodermic, the sterile wrappings, the empty vial. The dust bore the faint imprint of a body.

A shudder ran through her, and she began to relax.

So he had been real. He had only appeared to vanish. Her eyes had tricked her.

She scanned the area for him. He should not be walking around; he needed care, observation, until his condition stabilized. But she saw no sign of him. Fighting an odd reluctance, she waded out into the wild mustard after him. But when she reached the place where her eyes had lost him, she found nothing.

Baffled, she returned to the roadway. She did not like to give him up; but she appeared to have no choice in the matter. Muttering under her breath, she went to retrieve her bag.

The debris of her treatment she stuffed into one of the plastic specimen sacks she carried. Then she returned to her car. As she slid into the front seat, she gripped the steering wheel with both hands to steady herself on its hard actuality.

She did not remember why she had come to Haven Farm until the book on the seat beside her caught her attention.

Oh, damn!

She felt intensely unready to confront Thomas Covenant.

For a moment, she considered simply abandoning the favour she had promised Dr Berenford. She started the engine, began to turn the wheel. But the exigency of the old man's eyes held her. That blue would not approve the breaking of promises. And she had saved him. She had set a precedent for herself which was more important than any question of difficulty or mortification. When she put the sedan into motion, she sent it straight down the dirt road towards the white frame house, with the dust and the sunset at her back.

The light cast a tinge of red over the house, as if it were in the process of being transformed into something else. As she parked her car, she had to fight another surge of reluctance. She did not want to have anything to do with Thomas Covenant – not because he was a leper, not because he was something unknown and fierce, something so extravagant that even Dr Berenford was afraid of him.

But she had already made her commitment. Picking up the book, she left her car and went to the front door of the house, hoping to be able to finish this task before the light failed.

She spent a moment straightening her hair. Then she knocked.

The house was silent.

Her shoulders throbbed with the consequences of strain. Fatigue and embarrassment made her arms feel too heavy to lift. She had to grit her teeth to make herself knock again.

Abruptly, she heard the sound of feet. They came stamping through the house towards her. She could hear anger in them.

The front door was snatched open, and a man confronted her, a lean figure in old jeans and a T-shirt, a few inches taller than herself. About forty years old. He had an intense face. His mouth was as strict as a stone tablet; his cheeks were lined with difficulties; his eyes were like embers, capable of fire. His hair above his forehead was raddled with grey, as if he had been aged more by his thoughts than by time.

He was exhausted. Almost automatically, she noted the redness of his orbs and eyelids, the pallor of his skin, the febrile rawness of his movements. He was either ill or under extreme stress.

She opened her mouth to speak, got no further. He registered her presence for a second, then snapped, 'Goddamn it, if I wanted visitors I'd post a sign!' and clapped the door shut in her face.

She blinked after him momentarily while darkness gathered at her back, and her uncertainty turned to anger. Then she hit the door so hard that the wood rattled in its frame.

He came back almost at once. His voice hurled acid at her. 'Maybe you don't speak English. I – '

She met his glare with a mordant smile. 'Aren't you supposed to ring a bell, or something?'

That stopped him. His eyes narrowed as he reconsidered her. When he spoke again, his words came more slowly, as if he were trying to measure the danger she represented.

'If you know that, you don't need any warning.'

She nodded. 'My name is Linden Avery. I'm a doctor.'

'And you're not afraid of lepers.'

His sarcasm was as heavy as a bludgeon; but she matched it. 'If I were afraid of sick people, I wouldn't be a doctor.'

His glower expressed his disbelief. But he said curtly, 'I don't need a doctor,' and started to swing the door shut again.

'So actually,' she rasped, 'you're the one who's afraid.'

His face darkened. Enunciating each word as if it were a dagger, he said, 'What do you want, Doctor?'

To her dismay, his controlled vehemence made her falter. For the second time in the course of the sunset, she was held by eyes that were too potent for her. His gaze shamed her. The book – her excuse for being there – was in her hand; but her hand was behind her back. She could not tell the lie Dr Berenford had suggested to her. And she had no other answer. She could see vividly that Covenant needed help. Yet if he did not ask for it, what recourse did she have?

But then a leap of intuition crossed her mind. Speaking before she could question herself, she said, 'That old man told me to "Be true."'

His reaction startled her. Surprise and fear flared in his eyes. His shoulders winced; his jaw dropped. Then abruptly he had closed the door behind him. He stood before her with his face thrust hotly forward. 'What old man?'

She met his fire squarely. 'He was out at the end of your driveway – an old man in an ochre robe. As soon as I saw him, he went into cardiac arrest.' For an instant, a cold hand of doubt touched her heart. He had recovered too easily. Had he staged the whole situation? Impossible! His heart had stopped. 'I had to work like hell to save him. Then he just walked away.'

Covenant's belligerence collapsed. His gaze clung to her as if he were drowning. His hands gaped in front of him. For the first time, she observed that the last two fingers of his right hand were missing. He wore a wedding band of white gold on what had once been the middle finger of that hand. His voice was a scraping of pain in his throat. 'He's gone?'

'Yes.'

'An old man in an ochre robe?'

'Yes.'

'You saved him?' His features were fading into night as the sun dropped below the horizon.

'Yes.'

'What did he say?'

'I already told you.' Her uncertainty made her impatient. 'He said, "Be true."'

'He said that to you?'

'Yes!'

Covenant's eyes left her face. 'Hellfire.' He sagged as if he carried a weight of cruelty on his back. 'Have mercy on me. I can't bear it.' Turning, he slumped back to the door, opened it. But there he stopped.

'Why *you*?'

Then he had re-entered his house, the door was closed, and Linden stood alone in the evening as if she had been bereft.

She did not move until the need to do something, take some kind of action to restore the familiarity of her world, impelled her to her car. Sitting behind the wheel as if she were stunned, she tried to think.

Why you?

What kind of question was that? She was a doctor, and the old man had needed help. It was that simple. What was Covenant talking about?

But *Be true* was not all the old man had said. He had also said, *You will not fail, however he may assail you.*

He? Was that a reference to Covenant? Was the old man trying to warn her of something? Or did it imply some other kind of connection between him and the writer? What did they have to do with each other? Or with her?

Nobody could fake cardiac arrest!

She took a harsh grip on her scrambled thoughts. The whole situation made no sense. All she could say for certain was that Covenant had recognized her description of the old man. And Covenant's mental stability was clearly open to question.

Clenching the wheel, she started her car, backed up in order to turn around. She was convinced now that Covenant's problem was serious; but that conviction only made her more angry at Dr Berenford's refusal to tell her what the problem was. The dirt road was obscure in the twilight; she slapped on her headlights as she put the sedan in gear to complete her turn.

A scream like a mouthful of broken glass snatched her to a halt. It pierced the mutter of her sedan. Slivers of sound cut at her hearing. A woman screaming in agony or madness.

It had come from Covenant's house.

In an instant, Linden stood beside the car, waiting for the cry to be repeated.

She heard nothing. Lights shone from some of the windows; but no shadows moved. No sounds of violence betrayed the night. She stood poised to race to the house. Her ears searched the air. But the dark held its breath. The scream did not come again.

For a long moment, indecision held her. Confront Covenant – demand answers? Or leave? She had met his hostility. What right did she have – ? Every right, if he were torturing some woman. But how could she be sure? Dr Berenford had called it a medical problem.

Dr Berenford –

Spitting curses, she jumped back into her car, stamped down on the accelerator, and sped away in a rattle of dust and gravel.

Two minutes later, she was back in town. But then she had to slow down so that she could watch for street signs.

When she arrived at the Chief of Staff's house, all she could see was an outline against the night sky. Its front frowned as if this, too, were a place where secrets were kept. But she did not hesitate. Striding up the steps, she pounded on the front door.

That door led to a screened veranda like a neutral zone between the dwelling itself and the outside world. As she knocked, the porch lights came on. Dr Berenford opened the inner door, closed it behind him, then crossed the veranda to admit her.

He smiled a welcome; but his eyes evaded hers as if he had reason to be frightened; and she could see his pulse beating in the pouches below their sockets.

'Dr Berenford,' she said grimly.

'Please.' He made a gesture of appeal. 'Julius.'

'Dr Berenford.' She was not sure that she wanted this man's friendship. 'Who is she?'

His gaze flinched. 'She?'

'The woman who screamed.'

He seemed unable to lift his eyes to her face. In a tired voice, he murmured, 'He didn't tell you anything.'

'No.'

Dr Berenford considered for a moment, then motioned her towards two rocking chairs at one end of the veranda. 'Please sit down. It's cooler out here.' His attention seemed to wander. 'This heat wave can't last for ever.'

'Doctor!' she lashed at him. 'He's torturing that woman.'

'No, he isn't.' Suddenly, the older man was angry. 'You get that out of your head right now. He's doing everything he can for her. Whatever's torturing her, it isn't him.'

Linden held his glare, measuring his candour until she felt sure that he was Thomas Covenant's friend, whether or not he was hers. Then she said flatly, 'Tell me.'

By degrees, his expression recovered its habitual irony. 'Won't you sit down?'

Brusquely, she moved down the porch, seated herself in one of the rockers. At once, he turned off the lights, and darkness came pouring through the screens. 'I think better in the dark.' Before her eyes adjusted, she heard the chair beside her squeak as he sat down.

For a time, the only sounds were the soft protest of his chair and the stridulation of the crickets. Then he said abruptly, 'Some things I'm not going to tell you. Some I can't – some I won't. But I got you into this. I owe you a few answers.'

After that, he spoke like the voice of the night; and she listened in a state of suspension – half concentrating, as she would have concentrated on a patient describing symptoms, half musing on the image of the gaunt vivid man who had said with such astonishment and pain, *Why you*?

'Eleven years ago, Thomas Covenant was a writer with one bestseller, a lovely wife named Joan, and an infant son, Roger. He hates that novel – calls it inane – but his wife and son he still loves. Or thinks he does. Personally, I doubt it. He's an intensely loyal man. What he calls love, I call being loyal to his own pain.

'Eleven years ago, an infection on his right hand turned out to be leprosy, and those two fingers were amputated. He was sent down to the leprosarium in Louisiana, and Joan divorced him. To protect Roger from being raised in close proximity to a leper. The way Covenant tells it, her decision was perfectly reasonable. A mother's natural concern for a child. I think he's rationalizing. I think she was just afraid. I think the idea of what Hansen's disease could do to him – not to mention to her and Roger – just terrified her. She ran away.'

His tone conveyed a shrug. 'But I'm just guessing. The fact is, she divorced him, and he didn't contest it. After a few months, his illness was arrested, and he came back to Haven Farm. Alone. That was not a good time for him. All his neighbours moved away. Some people in this fair town tried to force him to leave. He was in the Hospital a couple times, and the second time he was half dead – ' Dr Berenford seemed to wince at the memory. 'His disease was active again. We sent him back to the leprosarium.

'When he came home again, everything was different. He seemed to have recovered his sanity. For ten years now he's been stable. A little grim, maybe – not exactly what you might call diffident – but accessible, reasonable, compassionate. Every year he foots the bill for several of our indigent patients.'

The older man sighed. 'You know, it's strange. The same people who try to convert me seem to think *he* needs saving, too. He's a leper who doesn't go to church, and he's got money. Some of our evangelicals consider that an insult to the Almighty.'

The professional part of Linden absorbed the facts Dr Berenford gave, and discounted his subjective reactions. But her musing raised Covenant's visage before her in the darkness. Gradually, that needy face became more real to her. She saw the lines of loneliness and gall on his mien. She responded to the strictness of his countenance as if she had recognized a comrade. After all, she was familiar with bitterness, loss, isolation.

But the doctor's speech also filled her with questions. She wanted to know where Covenant had learned his stability. What had changed him? Where had he found an answer potent enough to preserve him against the poverty of his life? And what had happened recently to take it away from him?

'Since then,' the Chief of Staff continued, 'he's published seven novels, and that's where you can really see the difference. Oh, he's mentioned something about three or four other manuscripts, but I don't know anything about them. The point is, if you didn't know better, you wouldn't be able to believe his bestseller and the other seven were written by the same man. He's right about the first one. It's fluff – self-indulgent melodrama. But the others –

'If you had a chance to read *Or I Will Sell My Soul for Guilt*, you'd find him arguing that innocence is a wonderful thing except for the fact that it's impotent. Guilt is power. All effective people are guilty because the use of power is guilt, and only guilty people can be effective. Effective for *good*, mind you. Only the damned can be saved.'

Linden was squirming. She understood at least one kind of relationship between guilt and effectiveness. She had committed murder, and had become a doctor because she had committed murder. She knew that people like herself were driven to power by the need to assail their guilt. But she had found nothing – no anodyne or restitution – to verify the claim that the damned could be saved. Perhaps Covenant had fooled Dr Berenford: perhaps he *was* crazy, a madman wearing a clever mask of stability. Or perhaps he knew something she did not.

Something she needed.

That thought gave her a pang of fear. She was suddenly conscious of the night, the rungs of the rocker pressing against her back, the crickets. She ached to retreat from the necessity of confronting Covenant again. Possibilities of harm crowded the darkness. But she needed to understand her peril. When Dr Berenford stopped, she bore the silence as long as she could, then, faintly, repeated her initial question.

'Who is she?'

The doctor sighed. His chair left a few splinters of agitation in the air. But he became completely still before he said, 'His ex-wife. Joan.'

Linden flinched. That piece of information gave a world of explanation to Covenant's haggard, febrile appearance. But it was not enough. 'Why did she come back? What's wrong with her?'

The older man began rocking again. 'Now we're back to where we were this afternoon. I can't tell you. I can't tell you why she came back because he told me in confidence. *If* he's right – ' His voice trailed away, then resumed. 'I can't tell you what's wrong with her because I don't know.'

She stared at his unseen face. 'That's why you got me into this.'

'Yes.' His reply sounded like a recognition of mortality.

'There are other doctors around. Or you could call in a specialist.' Her throat closed suddenly; she had to swallow heavily in order to say, 'Why me?'

'Well, I suppose – ' Now his tone conveyed a wry smile. 'I could say it's because you're well trained. But the fact is, I thought of you because you seem to fit. You and Covenant could talk to each other – if you gave yourselves a chance.'

'I see.' In the silence, she was groaning, Is it that obvious? After everything I've done to hide it, make up for it, does it still show? To defend herself, she got to her feet. Old bitterness made her sound querulous. 'I hope you like playing God.'

He paused for a long moment before he replied quietly, 'If that's what I'm doing – no, I don't. But I don't look at it that way. I'm just in over my head. So I asked you for help.'

Help, Linden snarled inwardly. Jesus Christ! But she did not speak her indignation aloud. Dr Berenford had touched her again, placed his finger on the nerves which compelled her. Because she did not want to utter her weakness, or her anger, or her lack of choice, she moved past him to the outer door of the veranda. 'Good night,' she said in a flat tone.

'Good night, Linden.' He did not ask her what she was going to do. Perhaps he understood her. Or perhaps he had no courage.

She got into her car and headed back towards Haven Farm.

She drove slowly, trying to regain a sense of perspective. True, she had no choice now; but that was not because she was helpless. Rather, it was because she had already made the choice – made it long ago, when she had decided to be a doctor. She had elected deliberately to be who she was now. If some of the implications of that choice gave her pain – well, there was pain everywhere. She deserved whatever pain she had to bear.

She had not realized until she reached the dirt road that she had forgotten to ask Dr Berenford about the old man.

She could see lights from Covenant's house. The building lay flickering against a line of dark trees like a gleam about to be swallowed by the woods and the night. The moon only confirmed this impression; its nearly-full light made the field a lake of silver, eldritch and fathomless, but could not touch the black trees, or the house which lay in their shadow. Linden shivered at the damp air, and drove with her hands tight on the wheel and her senses taut, as if she were approaching a crisis.

Twenty yards from the house, she stopped, parked her car so that it stood in the open moonlight.

Be true.

She did not know how.

The approach of her headlights must have warned him. An outside lamp came on as she neared the front door. He stepped out to meet her. His stance was erect and forbidding, silhouetted by the yellow light at his back. She could not read his face.

'Dr Avery.' His voice rasped like a saw. 'Go away.'

'No.' The uncertainty of her respiration made her speak abruptly, one piece at a time. 'Not until I see her.'

'Her?' he demanded.

'Your ex-wife.'

For a moment, he was silent. Then he grated, 'What else did that bastard tell you?'

She ignored his anger. 'You need help.'

His shoulders hunched as if he were strangling retorts. 'He's mistaken. I don't need help. I don't need you. Go away.'

'No.' She did not falter. 'He's right. You're exhausted. Taking care of her alone is wearing you out. I can help.'

'You can't,' he whispered, denying her fiercely. 'She doesn't need a doctor. She needs to be left alone.'

'I'll believe that when I see it.'

He tensed as if she had moved, tried to get past him. 'You're

41

trespassing. If you don't go away, I'll call the Sheriff.'

The falseness of her position infuriated her. 'Goddamn it!' she snapped. 'What are you afraid of?'

'You.' His voice was gravid, cold.

'Me? You don't even know me.'

'And you don't know me. You don't know what's going on here. You couldn't possibly understand it. And you didn't choose it.' He brandished words at her like blades. 'Berenford got you into this. That old man – ' He swallowed, then barked, 'You saved him, and he chose you, and you don't have any idea what that *means*. You haven't got the faintest idea what he chose you for. By hell, I'm not going to stand for it! *Go away.*'

'What does it have to do with you?' She groped to understand him. 'What makes you think it has anything to do with you?'

'Because I *do* know.'

'Know what?' She could not tolerate the condescension of his refusal. 'What's so special about you? Leprosy? Do you think being a leper gives you some kind of private claim on loneliness or pain? Don't be arrogant. There are other people in the world who suffer, and it doesn't take being a leper to understand them. What's so goddamn special about you?'

Her anger stopped him. She could not see his face; but his posture seemed to twist, reconsidering her. After a moment, he said carefully, 'Nothing about me. But I'm on the inside of this thing, and you aren't. I know it. You don't. It can't be explained. You don't understand what you're doing.'

'Then tell me. Make me understand. So I can make the right choice.'

'Dr Avery.' His voice was sudden and harsh. 'Maybe suffering isn't private. Maybe sickness and harm are in the public domain. But *this* is private.'

His intensity silenced her. She wrestled with him in her thoughts, and could find no way to take hold of him. He knew more than she did – had endured more, purchased more, learned more. Yet she could not let go. She needed some kind of explanation. The night air was thick and humid, blurring the meaning of the stars. Because she had no other argument, she challenged him with her incomprehension itself. '"Be true,"' she articulated, 'isn't the only thing he said.'

Covenant recoiled. She held herself still until the suspense drove him to ask in a muffled tone, 'What else?'

'He said, "Do not fear. You will not fail, however he may assail you."' There she halted, unwilling to say the rest. Covenant's shoulders began to shake. Grimly, she pursued her advantage. 'Who was he talking about? You?'

He did not respond. His hands were pressed to his face, stifling his emotion.

'Or was it somebody else? Did somebody hurt Joan?'

42

A shard of pain slipped past his teeth before he could lock them against himself.

'Or is something going to happen to me? What does that old man have to do with me? Why do you say he chose me?'

'He's using you.' Covenant's hands occluded his voice. But he had mastered himself. When he dropped his arms, his tone was dull and faint, like the falling of ashes. 'He's like Berenford. Thinks I need help. Thinks I can't handle it this time.' He should have sounded bitter; but he had momentarily lost even that resource. 'The only difference is, he knows — what I know.'

'Then tell me,' Linden urged again. 'Let me try.'

By force of will, Covenant straightened so that he stood upright against the light. 'No. Maybe I can't stop you, but I as sure as hell don't have to let you. I'm not going to contribute to this. If you're dead set on getting involved, you're going to have to find some way to do it behind my back.' He stopped as if he were finished. But then he raged at her, 'And tell that bastard Berenford he ought to try trusting me for a change!'

Retorts jumped into her throat. She wanted to yell back, Why should he? You don't trust anybody else! But as she gathered force into her lungs, a scream stung the air.

A woman screaming, raw and heinous. Impossible that anybody could feel such virulent terror and stay sane. It shrilled like the heart-shriek of the night.

Before it ended, Linden was on her way past Covenant towards the front door.

He caught her arm: she broke the grip of his half-hand, flung him off. 'I'm a *doctor*.' Leaving him no time for permission or denial, she jerked open the door, strode into the house.

The door admitted her to the living-room. It looked bare, in spite of its carpeting and bookcases; there were no pictures, no ornaments; and the only furniture was a long overstuffed sofa with a coffee table in front of it. They occupied the centre of the floor, as if to make the space around them navigable.

She gave the room a glance, then marched down a short passage to the kitchen. There, too, a table and two straight-backed wooden chairs occupied the centre of the space. She went past them, turned to enter another hall. Covenant hurried after her as she by-passed two open doors — the bathroom, his bedroom — to reach the one at the end of the hall.

It was closed.

At once, she took hold of the knob.

He snatched at her wrist. 'Listen.' His voice must have held emotion — urgency, anguish, something — but she did not hear it. 'This you have to understand. There's only one way to hurt a man who's lost everything. Give him back something broken.'

She gripped the knob with her free hand. He let her go.

She opened the door, went into the room.

All the lights were on.

Joan sat on an iron-frame bed in the middle of the room. Her ankles and wrists were tied with cloth bonds which allowed her to sit up or lie down but did not permit her to bring her hands together. The long cotton nightgown covering her thin limbs had been twisted around her by her distress.

A white gold wedding ring hung from a silver chain around her neck.

She did not look at Covenant. Her gaze sprang at Linden, and a mad fury clenched her face. She had rabid eyes, the eyes of a demented lioness. Whimpers moaned in her throat. Her pallid skin stretched tightly over her bones.

Intuitive revulsion appalled Linden. She could not think. She was not accustomed to such savagery. It violated all her conceptions of illness or harm, paralysed her responses. This was not ordinary human ineffectuality or pain raised to the level of despair; this was pure ferocity, concentrated and murderous. She had to force herself forward. But when she drew near the woman and stretched out a tentative hand, Joan bit at her like a baited cat. Involuntarily, Linden recoiled.

'Dear God!' she panted. 'What's wrong with her?'

Joan raised her head, let out a scream like the anguish of the damned.

Covenant could not speak. Grief contorted his features. He went to Joan's side. Fumbling over the knot, he untied her left wrist, released her arm. Instantly, she clawed at him, straining her whole body to reach him. He evaded her, caught her forearm.

Linden watched with a silent wail as he let Joan's nails rake the back of his right hand. Blood welled from the cuts.

Joan smeared her fingers in his blood. Then her hand jumped to her mouth, and she sucked it eagerly, greedily.

The taste of blood seemed to restore her self-awareness. Almost immediately, the madness faded from her face. Her eyes softened, turned to tears; her mouth trembled. 'Oh, Tom,' she quavered weakly. 'I'm so sorry. I can't – He's in my mind, and I can't get him out. He hates you. He makes – makes me – ' She was sobbing brokenly. Her lucidity was acutely cruel to her.

He sat on the bed beside her, put his arms around her. 'I know.' His voice ached in the room. 'I understand.'

'Tom,' she wept. 'Tom. Help me.'

'I will.' His tone promised that he would face any ordeal, make any sacrifice, commit any violence. 'As soon as he's ready. I'll get you free.'

Slowly, her frail limbs relaxed. Her sobs grew quieter. She was exhausted. When he stretched her out on the bed, she closed her eyes, went to sleep with her fingers in her mouth like a child.

He took a tissue from a box on a table near the bed, pressed it to the back of his hand. Then, tenderly, he pulled Joan's fingers from her mouth and re-tied her wrist. Only then did he look at Linden.

'It doesn't hurt,' he said. 'The backs of my hands have been numb for years.' The torment was gone from his face; it held nothing now except the long weariness of a pain he could not heal.

Watching his blood soak into the tissue, she knew she should do something to treat that injury. But an essential part of her had failed, proved itself inadequate to Joan; she could not bear to touch him. She had no answer to what she had seen. For a moment, her eyes were helpless with tears. Only the old habit of severity kept her from weeping. Only her need kept her from fleeing into the night. It drove her to say grimly, 'Now you're going to tell me what's wrong with her.'

'Yes,' he murmured. 'I suppose I am.'

3

PLIGHT

He guided her back to the living-room in silence. His hand on her arm was reluctant, as if he dreaded that mere human contact. When she sat on the sofa, he gestured towards his injury, and left her alone. She was glad to be alone. She was stunned by her failure; she needed time to regain possession of herself.

What had happened to her? She understood nothing about evil, did not even believe in it as an idea; but she had seen it in Joan's feral hunger. She was trained to perceive the world in terms of dysfunction and disease, medication and treatment, success or death. Words like *good* or *evil* meant nothing to her. But Joan – ! Where did such malignant ferocity come from? And how – ?

When Covenant returned, with his right hand wrapped in a white bandage, she stared at him, demanding explanations.

He stood before her, did not meet her gaze. The slouch of his posture gave him a look of abandonment; the skin at the corners of his eyes crumpled like dismay pinching his flesh. But his mouth had learned the habit of defiance; it was twisted with refusals. After a moment, he muttered, 'So you see why I didn't want you to know about her,' and began to pace.

'Nobody knows – ' The words came as if he was dredging them out of the privacy of his heart – 'except Berenford and Roman. The law doesn't exactly smile on people who keep other people prisoner – even in her condition. I don't have any legal rights at all as far as she's concerned. What I'm supposed to do is turn her over to the authorities. But I've been living without the benefit of law so long now I don't give a damn.'

'But what's wrong with her?' Linden could not keep her voice from twitching; she was too tightly clenched to sound steady.

He sighed. 'She needs to hurt me. She's starving for it – that's what makes her so violent. It's the best way she can think of to punish herself.'

With a wrench, Linden's analytical instinct began to function again. Paranoiac, she winced to herself. He's paranoiac. But aloud she insisted, 'But why? What's happened to her?'

He stopped, looked at her as if he were trying to gauge her capacity for the truth, then went back to his pacing.

'Of course,' he murmured, 'that isn't how Berenford sees it. He thinks it's a psychiatric problem. The only reason he hasn't tried to get her away from me is because he understands why I want to take care of her. Or part of it. His wife is a paraplegic, and he would never consider dumping the problem off on anyone else. I haven't told him about her taste for blood.'

He was evading her question. She struggled for patience. '*Isn't* it a psychiatric problem? Hasn't Dr Berenford been able to rule out physical causes? What else could it be?'

Covenant hesitated, then said distantly, 'He doesn't know what's going on.'

'You keep saying that. It's too convenient.'

'No,' he retorted, 'it's not convenient. It's the truth. You don't have the background to understand it.'

'How can you be so goddamn sure?' The clench of her self-command made her voice raw. 'I've spent half my life coping with other people's pain.' She wanted to add, Can't you get it through your head that I'm a doctor? But her throat locked on those words. She had failed –

For an instant, his gaze winced as if he were distressed by the idea that she did in fact have the necessary background. But then he shook his head sharply. When he resumed, she could not tell what kind of answer he had decided to give her.

'I wouldn't know about it myself,' he said, 'if her parents hadn't called me. About a month ago. They don't have much use for me, but they were frantic. They told me everything they knew.

'I suppose it's an old story. The only thing that makes it new is the way it hurts. Joan divorced me when we found out I had leprosy. Eleven years ago. Took Roger and went back to her family. She thought she was justified – ah, hell, for years *I* thought she was justified. Kids are more susceptible to leprosy than adults. So she divorced me. For Roger's sake.

'But it didn't work. Deep inside her, she believed she'd betrayed me. It's hard to forgive yourself for deserting someone you love – someone who needs you. It erodes your self-respect. Like leprosy. It gnaws away at you. Before long, you're a moral cripple. She stood it for a while. Then she started hunting for cures.'

His voice, and the information he was giving her, steadied Linden. As he paced, she became conscious of the way he carried himself, the care and specificity of all his movements. He navigated past the coffee table as if it were a danger to him. And repeatedly he scanned himself with his eyes, checking in turn each hand, each arm, his legs, his chest, as if he expected to find that he had injured himself without knowing it.

She had read about such things. His self-inspection was called VSE – visual surveillance of extremities. Like the care with which he moved, it was part of the discipline he needed to keep his illness arrested. Because of the damage leprosy had done to his nerves, the largest single threat to his health was the possibility that he might bump, burn, scrape, cut, or bruise himself without realizing it. Then infection would set in because the wound was not tended. So he moved with all the caution he could muster. The furniture in his house was arranged to minimize the risk of protruding corners, obstacles, accidents. And he scanned himself regularly, looking for signs of danger.

Watching him in this objective, professional way helped restore her sense of who she was. Slowly, she became better able to listen to his indirect explanation without impatience.

He had not paused; he was saying, 'First she tried psychology. She wanted to believe it was all in her mind – and minds can be fixed, like broken arms. She started going through psychological fads the way some people trade in cars, a new one every year. As if her problem really was mental instead of spiritual.

'None of it made sense to her parents, but they tried to be tolerant, just did what they could to give Roger a stable home.

'So they thought she was finally going to be all right when she suddenly gave that up and went churchy. They believed all along that religion was the answer. Well, it's good enough for most people, but it didn't give her what she needed. It was too easy. Her disease was progressing all the time. A year ago, she became a fanatic. Took Roger and went to join a commune. One of those places where people learn the ecstasy of humiliation, and the leader preaches love and mass suicide.

'She must have been so desperate – For most of her life, the only thing she really wanted to believe was that she was perfectly all right. But after all those years of failure, she didn't have any defences left. What did she have to lose?'

Linden was not wholly convinced. She had no more use for God than for conceptions of good and evil. But Covenant's passion held her. His eyes were wet with violence and grief; his mouth was as sharp as a blade. He believed what he was saying.

Her expression must have betrayed some of her doubt; his voice took on an echo of Joan's ferocity. 'You don't have to believe in God to grasp what she was going through. She was suffering from an affliction for which there's no mortal cure. She couldn't even arrest the way it rotted her. Maybe she didn't know what it was she was trying to cure. She was looking for magic, some power that could reach into her and heal – When you've tried all the salves in the world and they don't work, you start thinking about fire. Burn out the pain. She wanted to punish herself, find some kind of abnegation to match her personal rot.'

His voice broke; but he controlled it instantly. 'I know all about it. But she didn't have any defences. She opened the door for him, and he saw she was the perfect tool, and he's been using her – *using* her, when she's too damaged to even understand what he's using her for.'

Using her? Linden did not comprehend. He?

Slowly, Covenant suppressed his anger. 'Of course, her parents didn't know anything about that. How could they? All they knew was that about six weeks ago she woke them up in the middle of the night and started babbling. She was a prophet, she'd had a vision, the Lord had given her a mission. Woe and retribution to the wicked, death to the sick and the unbelieving. The only sense they could make out of it was that she wanted them to take care of Roger. Then she was gone. They haven't seen her since.

'After a couple weeks, they called me. I hadn't seen her – that was the first I'd heard about it. But about two weeks ago she showed up here. Sneaked into my room during the night and tried to tear my face off. If she hadn't been so weak, she would have succeeded. She must have come all the way on foot.'

He seemed too exhausted himself to go on pacing. His red-rimmed eyes made him look ill, and his hands trembled. How long had he been without decent sleep or peace? Two weeks? When he sat down on the opposite end of the sofa, Linden turned so that she could continue to study him. In the back of her mind, she began trying to conceive some way to give him a sedative.

'Since then,' he sighed, 'Berenford and I have been taking care of her. I got him into this because he's the only doctor I know. He thinks I'm wrong about her, but he's helping me. Or he was. Until he got you into this.' He was too tired to sound bitter. 'I'm trying to reach her any way I can, and he's giving her drugs that are supposed to clear her mind. Or at least calm her so I can feed her. I leave the lights on in there all the time. Something happens to her when she's alone in the dark. She goes berserk – I'm afraid she'll break an arm or something.'

He fell silent. Apparently, he had reached the end of his story – or of his strength. Linden felt that his explanation was incomplete, but she held her questions in abeyance. He needed aid, a relief from strain. Carefully she said, 'Maybe she really should be in a hospital. I'm sure Dr Berenford's doing what he can. But there are all kinds of diagnostic procedures he can't use here. If she were in a hospital – '

'If she were in a hospital – ' he swung towards her so roughly that she recoiled – 'they'd keep her in a straitjacket, and force-feed her three times a day, and turn her brain into jelly with electroshock, and fill her up with drugs until she couldn't recognize her own name if God Himself were calling for her, and it wouldn't do any good! Goddamn it, she was my *wife*!' He brandished his right fist. 'I'm still wearing the bloody ring!'

'Is that what you think doctors do?' She was suddenly livid; her failure made her defensive. 'Brutalize sick people?'

He strove to contain his ire. 'Doctors try to cure problems whether they understand them or not. It doesn't always work. This isn't something a doctor can cure.'

'Is that a fact?' She did not want to taunt him; but her own compulsions drove her. 'Tell me what good *you're* doing her.'

He flinched. Rage and pain struggled in him; but he fought them down. Then he said simply, 'She came to me.'

'She didn't know what she was doing.'

'But I do.' His grimness defied her. 'I understand it well enough. I'm the only one who can help her.'

Frustration boiled up in her. 'Understand *what*?'

He jerked to his feet. He was a figure of passion, held erect and potent in spite of weakness by the intensity of his heart. His eyes were chisels; when he spoke, each word fell distinctly, like a chip of granite.

'She is possessed.'

Linden blinked at him. 'Possessed?' He had staggered her. He did not seem to be talking a language she could comprehend. This was the twentieth century; medical science had not taken *possession* seriously for at least a hundred years. She was on her feet. 'Are you out of your mind?'

She expected him to retreat. But he still had resources she had not plumbed. He held her glare, and his visage – charged and purified by some kind of sustaining conviction – made her acutely aware of her own moral poverty. When he looked away, he did not do so because he was abashed or beaten; he looked away in order to

49

spare her the implications of his knowledge.

'You see?' he murmured. 'It's a question of experience. You're just not equipped to understand.'

'By God!' she fumed defensively, 'that's the most arrogant thing I've ever heard. You stand there spouting the most egregious nonsense, and when I question you, you just naturally assume there must be something wrong with me. Where do you get the gall to – ?'

'Dr Avery.' His voice was low, dangerous. 'I didn't say there was anything wrong with you.'

She did not listen to him. 'You're suffering from classic paranoia, Mr Covenant.' She bit each word mordantly. 'You think that everybody who doubts you isn't quite right in the head. You're a textbook case.'

Seething irrationally, she turned on her heel, stamped towards the door – fleeing from him, and fighting furiously to believe that she was not fleeing. But he came after her, caught hold of her shoulders. She whirled on him as if he had assaulted her.

He had not. His hands dropped to his sides, and twitched as if they ached to make gestures of supplication. His face was open and vulnerable; she saw intuitively that at that moment she could have asked him anything, and he would have done his best to answer. 'Please,' he breathed. 'You're in an impossible situation, and I haven't made it any easier. But please. At least consider the chance that I know what I'm doing.'

A retort coiled in her mouth, then frayed and fell apart. She was furious, not because she had any right to be, but because his attitude showed her how far she had fallen into the wrong. She swallowed to stifle a groan, almost reached out towards him to apologize. But he deserved something better than an apology. Carefully, she said, 'I'll consider it.' She could not meet his eyes. 'I won't do anything until I talk to you again.'

Then she left the house, frankly escaping from the exigency of his incomprehensible convictions. Her hands fumbled like traitors as she opened the door of her car, slid behind the wheel.

With failure in her mouth like the taste of sickness, she drove back to her apartment.

She needed to be comforted; but there was no comfort in those grubby walls, in the chipped and peeling floorboards which moaned like victims under her feet. She had accepted that apartment precisely because it offered her no comfort; but the woman who had made that decision was a woman who had never watched herself buckle under the demands of her profession. Now, for the first time since that moment of murder fifteen years ago, when her hands had accepted the burden of blood, she yearned for solace. She lived in a world where there was no solace.

Because she could think of no other recourse, she went to bed.

Tension and muggy sheets kept her awake for a long time and when she finally slept, her dreams were sweat and fear in the hot night. The old man, Covenant, Joan – all babbled of *He*, trying to warn her. *He* who possessed Joan for purposes too cruel to be answered. *He* who intended to harm them all. But at last she sank into a deeper slumber, and the evil went back into hiding.

She was awakened by a knocking at her door.

Her head felt swollen with nightmares, and the knocking had a tentative sound, as if the knocker believed the apartment to be dangerous. But it was imperative. She was a doctor.

When she unclosed her eyes, the light of mid-morning pierced her brain.

Groaning, she climbed out of bed, shrugged her arms into a bathrobe, then went to open the door.

A short timid woman with hands that fluttered and eyes that shied stood on the landing. Timorously, she asked, 'Dr Avery? Dr Linden Avery?'

With an effort, Linden cleared her throat. 'Yes.'

'Dr Berenford called.' The woman seemed to have no idea what she was saying. 'I'm his secretary. You don't have a phone. I don't work on Saturdays, but he called me at home. He wants you to meet him. He's supposed to be on rounds.'

'Meet him?' A pang of apprehension went through her. 'Where?'

'He said you'd know where.' Insistently, the woman went on, 'I'm his secretary. I don't work on Saturdays, but I'm always glad to help him. He's a fine man – a fine doctor. His wife had polio. He really should be on rounds.'

Linden shut her eyes. If she could have summoned any strength, she would have cried out, Why are you doing this to me? But she felt drained by bad dreams and doubt. Muttering, 'Thank you,' she closed the door.

For a moment, she did not move; she leaned against the door as if to hold it shut, wanting to scream. But Dr Berenford would not have gone to such trouble to send for her if the situation were not urgent. She had to go.

As she dressed in the clothes she had worn the previous day and ran a comb through her hair, she realized that she made a choice. Some time during the night, she had given her allegiance to Covenant. She did not understand what was wrong with Joan, or what he thought he could do about it; but she was attracted to him. The same intransigence which had so infuriated her had also touched her deeply; she was vulnerable to the strange appeal of his anger, his extremity, his paradoxically savage and compassionate determination to stand loyal to his ex-wife.

She drank a quick glass of orange juice to clear her head, then went down to her car.

The day was already unnaturally hot; the sunlight hurt her eyes. She felt oddly giddy and detached, as if she were experiencing a hallucination, as she entered the dirt roadway and approached Covenant's house. At first, she was not sure of her vision when she descried the dark stain on the wall.

She parked beside Dr Berenford's car, jumped out to look.

Near the doorway, a tall, crude triangle violated the white wall. It was reddish-black, the colour of dried blood. The vehemence of its intent convinced her that it was blood.

She began to run.

Springing into the living-room, she saw that it, too, had been desecrated. All the furnishings were intact; but everything was splotched and soaked with blood. Buckets of blood had been thrown into the room. A sickly-sweet smell clogged the air.

On the floor near the coffee table lay a shotgun.

Her stomach writhed. She slapped her hands to her mouth to keep herself from crying out. All this blood could not have come from one ordinary human body. Some atrocity . . .

Then she saw Dr Berenford. He sat in the kitchen at the table, with a cup between his hands. He was looking at her.

She strode towards him, started to demand, 'What the hell – ?'

He stopped her with a warning gesture. 'Keep it down,' he said softly. 'He's sleeping.'

For a moment, she gaped at the Chief of Staff. But she was accustomed to emergencies; her self-command quickly reasserted itself. Moving as if to prove to him that she could be calm, she found a cup, poured herself some coffee from the pot on the stove, sat down in the other chair at the old enamel-topped table. In a flat tone, she asked, 'What happened?'

He sipped his own coffee. All the humour was gone out of him, and his hands shook. 'I guess he was right all along.' He did not meet her stare. 'She's gone.'

'Gone?' For an instant, her control slipped. *Gone?* She could hardly breathe past the thudding of her heart. 'Is anybody looking for her?'

'The police,' he replied. 'Mrs Roman – did I tell you about her? She's his lawyer. She went back to town after I got here – a couple hours ago. To light a fire under the Sheriff. Right now, every able-bodied cop in the county is probably out looking. The only reason you don't see cars is because our Sheriff – bless his warm little heart – won't let his men park this close to a leper.'

'All right.' Linden mustered her training, gripped it in both hands. 'Tell me what happened.'

He made a gesture of helplessness. 'I don't really know. I only know what he told Mrs Roman – what he told me. It doesn't make any sense.' He sighed. 'Well, this is what he says. Sometime after midnight, he heard people at his door. He'd spent most of the evening trying to bathe her, but after that he fell asleep. He didn't wake up until these people began acting like they wanted to tear the door down.

'He didn't have to ask them what they wanted. I guess he's been expecting something like this ever since Joan showed up. He went and got his shotgun — did you know he had a shotgun? Had Mrs Roman buy it for him last week. For self-defence — as if being a leper wasn't more defence than he ever had any use for.' Seeing Linden's impatience, he went back to his story. 'Anyway, he got his gun, and turned on all the lights. Then he opened the door.

'They came in — maybe half a dozen of them. He says they wore sackcloth and ashes.' Dr Berenford grimaced. 'If he recognized any of them, he won't admit it. He waved the shotgun at them and told them they couldn't have her.

'But they acted as if they wanted to be shot. And when it came right down to it, he couldn't. Not even to save his ex-wife.' He shook his head. 'He tried to fight them off by main strength, but one against six, he didn't have much chance.

'Sometime early this morning, he came to long enough to call Mrs Roman. He was incoherent — kept telling her to start a search, only he couldn't explain why — but at least he had sense enough to know he needed help. Then he passed out again. When she got here, she found him unconscious on the floor. There was blood everywhere. Whoever they were, they must have bled an entire cow.' He gulped coffee as if it were an antidote for the reek in the air. 'Well, she got him on his feet, and he took her to check on Joan. She was gone. Restraints had been cut.'

'They didn't kill her?' interjected Linden.

He glanced at her. 'He says no. How he knows — your guess is as good as mine.' After a moment, he resumed, 'Anyway, Mrs Roman called me. When I got here, she left to see what she could do about finding Joan. I've examined him, and he seems to be all right. Suffering from exhaustion as much as anything else.'

Linden shrugged aside her doubts about Covenant's condition. 'I'll watch him.'

He nodded. 'That was why I called for you.'

She drank some of her coffee to steady herself, then enquired carefully, 'Do you know who they were?'

'I asked him that,' Dr Berenford replied with a frown. 'He said, "How the hell should I know?"'

'Well, then, what do they want with her?'

He thought for a moment, then said, 'You know, the worst part about the whole thing is — I think he knows.'

Frustration made her querulous. 'So why won't he tell us?'

'Hard to say,' said the doctor slowly. 'I think *he* thinks if we knew what was going on we'd try to stop him.'

Linden did not respond. She was no longer prepared to try to prevent Thomas Covenant from doing anything. But she was equally determined to learn the truth about Joan, about him – and, yes, about the old man in the ochre robe. For her own sake. And for Covenant's. In spite of his fierce independence, she could not shake the conviction that he was desperately in need of help.

'Which is another reason for you to stay,' the older man muttered as he rose to his feet. 'I've got to go. But somebody has to prevent him from doing anything crazy. Some days – ' His voice trailed away, then came back in sudden vexation. 'My God, some days I think that man needs a keeper, not a doctor.' For the first time since her arrival, he faced her squarely. 'Will you keep him?'

She could see he wanted reassurance that she shared his sense of responsibility for Covenant and Joan. She could not make such a promise. But she could offer him something similar. 'Well, at any rate,' she said severely, 'I won't let go of him.'

He nodded vaguely. He was no longer looking at her. As he moved towards the door, he murmured, 'Be patient with him. It's been so long since he met somebody who isn't afraid of him, he doesn't know what to do about it. When he wakes up, make him eat something.' Then he left the house, went out to his car.

Linden watched until he disappeared in dust towards the highway. Then she turned back to the living-room.

What to do about it? Like Covenant, she did not know. But she meant to find out. The smell of blood made her feel unclean; but she suppressed the sensation long enough to fix a breakfast for herself. Then she tackled the living-room.

With a scrub brush and a bucket of soapy water, she attacked the stains as if they were an affront to her. Deep within her, where her guilt and coercion had their roots, she felt that blood was life – a thing of value, too precious to be squandered and denied, as her parents had squandered and denied it. Grimly, she scrubbed at the madness or malice which had violated this room, trying to eradicate it.

Whenever she needed a break, she went quietly to look at Covenant. His bruises gave his face a misshapen look. His sleep seemed agitated, but he showed no sign of drifting into coma. Occasionally, the movements of his eyes betrayed that he was dreaming. He slept with his mouth open like a silent cry; and once his cheeks were wet with tears. Her heart went out to him as he lay stretched there, disconsolate and vulnerable. He had so little respect for his own mortality.

Shortly after noon, while she was still at work, he came out of his bedroom. He moved groggily, his gait blurred with sleep. He peered at her across the room as if he were summoning anger; but his voice held nothing except resignation. 'You can't help her now. You might as well go home.'

She stood up to face him. 'I want to help you.'

'I can handle it.'

Linden swallowed bile, tried not to sound acerbic. 'Somehow, you don't look that tough. You couldn't stop them from taking her. How are you going to make them give her back?'

His eyes widened; her guess had struck home. But he did not waver. He seemed almost inhumanly calm – or doomed. 'They don't want her. She's just a way for them to get at me.'

'You?' Was he paranoiac after all? 'Are you trying to tell me that this whole thing happened to her because of you? Why?'

'I haven't found that out yet.'

'No. I mean, why do you think this has anything to do with you? If they wanted you, why didn't they just take you? You couldn't have stopped them.'

'Because it has to be voluntary.' His voice had the flat timbre of over-stressed cable in a high wind. He should have snapped long ago. But he did not sound like a man who snapped. 'He can't just force me. I have to choose to do it. Joan – ' A surge of darkness occluded his eyes. 'She's just his way of exerting pressure. He has to take the chance that I might refuse.'

He. Linden's breathing came heavily. 'You keep saying *he*. Who is *he*?'

His frown made his face seem even more malformed. 'Leave it alone.' He was trying to warn her. 'You don't believe in possession. How can I make you believe in possessors?'

She took his warning, but not in the way he intended. Hints of purpose – half guesswork, half determination – unexpectedly lit her thoughts. A way to learn the truth. He had said. *You're going to have to find some way to do it behind my back.* Well, by God, if that was what she had to do, she would do it.

'All right,' she said, glaring at him to conceal her intentions. 'I can't make you make sense. Just tell me one thing. Who was that old man? You knew him.'

Covenant returned her stare as if he did not mean to answer. But then he relented stiffly. 'A harbinger. Or a warning. When he shows up, you've only got two choices. Give up everything you ever understood, and take your chances. Or run for your life. The problem is – ' his tone took on a peculiar resonance, as if he were trying to say more than he could put into words – 'he doesn't usually waste his time talking to the kind of people who run away. And you can't possibly know what you're getting into.'

She winced inwardly, fearing that he had guessed her intent. But she held herself firm. 'Why don't you tell me?'

'I can't.' His intensity was gone, transformed back into resignation. 'It's like signing a blank cheque. That kind of trust, foolhardiness, wealth, whatever, doesn't mean anything if you know how much the cheque is going to be for. You either sign or you don't. How much do you think you can afford?'

'Well, in any case – ' she shrugged – 'I don't plan to sign any blank cheques. I've done about all I can stand to clean up this place. I'm going home.' She could not meet his scrutiny. 'Dr Berenford wants you to eat. Are you going to do it, or do I have to send him back out here?'

He did not answer her question. 'Goodbye, Dr Avery.'

'Oh, dear God,' she protested in a sudden rush of dismay at his loneliness. 'I'm probably going to spend the rest of the day worrying about you. At least call me Linden.'

'Linden.' His voice denied all emotion. 'I can handle it.'

'I know,' she murmured, half to herself. She went out into the thick afternoon. I'm the one who needs help.

On the way back to her apartment, she noticed that the woman and children who advised repentance were nowhere to be seen.

Several hours later, as sunset dwindled into twilight, streaking the streets with muggy orange and pink, she was driving again. She had showered and rested; she had dressed herself in a checked flannel shirt, tough jeans, and a pair of sturdy hiking shoes. She drove slowly, giving the evening time to darken. Half a mile before she reached Haven Farm, she turned off her headlights.

Leaving the highway, she took the first side road to one of the abandoned houses on the Farm. There she parked her car and locked it to protect her medical bag and purse.

On foot, she approached Covenant's house. As much as possible, she hid herself among the trees along that side of the Farm. She was gambling that she was not too late, that the people who had taken Joan would not have done anything during the afternoon. From the trees, she hastened stealthily to the wall of the house. There, she found a window which gave her a view of the living-room without exposing her to the door.

The lights were on. With all her caution, she looked in on Thomas Covenant.

He slouched in the centre of the sofa with his head bowed and his hands in his pockets, as if he were waiting for something. His bruises had darkened, giving him the visage of a man who had already been beaten. The muscles along his jaw bunched, relaxed, bunched again. He strove to possess himself in patience; but after a moment the tension impelled him to his feet. He began to walk in circles around the sofa and coffee table. His movements were rigid, denying the mortality of his heart.

So that she would not have to watch him, Linden lowered herself to the ground and sat against the wall. Hidden by the darkness, she waited with him.

She did not like what she was doing. It was a violation of his privacy, completely unprofessional. But her ignorance and his stubbornness were intolerable. She had an absolute need to understand what had made her quail when she had faced Joan.

She did not have to wait long. Scant minutes after she had settled herself, abruptly feet approached the house.

The lurching of her heart almost daunted her. But she resisted it. Carefully, she raised her head to the window just as a fist hammered at the door.

Covenant flinched at the sound. Dread knurled his face.

The sight of his reaction stung Linden. He was such a potent individual, seemed to have so many strengths which she lacked. How had he been brought to this?

But an instant later he crushed his fear as if he were stamping on the neck of a viper. Defying his own weakness, he strode towards the door.

It opened before he reached it. A lone man stepped uninvited out of the dark. Linden could see him clearly. He wore burlap wound around him like cerements. Ash had been rubbed unevenly into his hair, smeared thickly over his cheeks. It emphasized the deadness of his eyes, so that he looked like a ghoul in masque.

'Covenant?' Like his mien, his voice was ashen, dead.

Covenant faced the man. He seemed suddenly taller, as if he were elevated by his own hard grasp on life. 'Yes.'

'Thomas Covenant?'

The writer nodded impatiently. 'What do you want?'

'The hour of judgement is at hand.' The man stared into the room as if he were blind. 'The Master calls for your soul. Will you come?'

Covenant's mouth twisted into a snarl. 'Your master knows what I can do to him.'

The man did not react. He went on as if his speech had already been arrayed for burial. 'The woman will be sacrificed at the rising of the full moon. Expiation must be made for sin. She will pay if you do not. This is the commandment of the Master of life and death. Will you come?'

Sacrificed? Linden gaped. Expiation? A flush of indignation burned her skin. What the hell – ?

Covenant's shoulders knotted. His eyes flamed with extreme promises, threats. 'I'll come.'

No flicker of consciousness animated the man's grey features. He turned like a marionette and retreated into the night.

For a moment, Covenant stood still. His arms hugged his chest as if to stifle an outcry; his head stretched back in anguish. The bruises marked his face like a bereavement.

But then he moved. With a violence that startled Linden, appalled her, he struck himself across the cheek with his half-hand. Abruptly, he threw himself into the darkness after his summoner.

Linden almost lost her chance to follow. She felt stunned by dismay. The Master – ? Sacrificed? Dreads and doubts crawled her skin like vermin. The man in burlap had looked so insentient – soulless more than any animal. Drugs? Or – ?

However he may assail –

Was Covenant right? About the old man, about possession? About the purpose – ? *She's just a way for them to get at me.*

Sacrificed?

Oh, dear God! The man in burlap appeared insane enough, lost enough, to be dangerous. And Covenant – ? Covenant was capable of anything.

Her guess at what he was doing galvanized her. Fear for him broke through her personal apprehension, sent her hurrying around the corner of the house in pursuit.

His summoner had led him away from the highway, away from the house into the woods. Linden could hear them in the brush; without light, they were unable to move quietly. As her eyes adjusted, she glimpsed them ahead of her, flickering like shadows in and out of the variegated dark. She followed them.

They travelled blindly through the woods, over hills and along valleys. They used no path; Linden had the impression that they were cutting as straight as a plumb line towards their destination. And as they moved, the night seemed to mount around her, growing steadily more hostile as her trepidation increased. The trees and brush became malevolent, as if she were passing into another wood altogether, a place of hazard and cruel intent.

Then a hill lay across their way. Covenant and his summoner ascended, disappeared over the crest in a strange flare of orange light. It picked them out of the dark, then quenched them like an instant of translation. Warned by that brief gleam, Linden climbed slowly. The keening of her nerves seemed loud in the blackness. The last few yards she crossed on her hands and knees, keeping herself within the cover of the underbrush.

As her head crested the hill, she was struck by a blaze of light. Fire invisible a foot away burst in her face as if she had just penetrated the boundary of dreams. For an instant, she was blinded by the light, paralysed by the silence. The night swallowed all sound, leaving the air empty of life.

Blinking furiously, she peered past the hillcrest.

Beyond her lay a deep barren hollow. Its slopes were devoid of grass, brush, trees, as if the soil had been scoured by acid.

A bonfire burned at the bottom of the hollow. Its flames sprang upward like lust, writhed like madness; but it made no noise. Seeing it, Linden felt that she had been stricken deaf. Impossible that such a fire could blaze in silence.

Near the fire stretched a rough plane of native rock, perhaps ten feet across. A large triangle had been painted on it in red – colour as crimson as fresh blood.

Joan lay on her back within the triangle. She did not move, appeared to be unconscious; only the slow lifting of her chest against her nightgown showed that she was alive.

People clustered around her, twenty or thirty of them. Men, women, children – all dressed in habiliments of burlap; all masked with grey as if they had been wallowing in ashes. They were as gaunt as icons of hunger. They gazed out of eyes as dead as if the minds behind their orbs had been extirpated – eyes which had been dispossessed of every vestige of will or spirit. Even the children stood like puppets and made no sound.

Their faces were turned towards a place on Linden's left.

Towards Thomas Covenant.

He stood halfway down the hillside, confronting the fire across the barrenness of the hollow. His shoulders hunched; his hands were fists at his sides, and his head was thrust combatively forward. His chest heaved as if he were full of denunciations.

Nobody moved, spoke, blinked. The air was intense with silence like concentrated coercion.

Abruptly, Covenant grated through his teeth, 'I'm here.' The clench of his throat made each word sound like a self-inflicted wound. 'Let her go.'

A movement snatched Linden's attention back to the bottom of the hollow. A man brawnier than the rest changed positions, took a stance on the rock at the point of the triangle, above Joan's head. He raised his arms, revealing a long, curved dagger gripped in his right fist. In a shrill voice like a man on the verge of ecstasy, he shouted, 'It is time! We are the will of the Master of life and death! This is the hour of retribution and cleansing and blood! Let us open the way for the Master's presence!'

The night sucked his voice out of the air, left in its place a stillness as sharp as a cut. For a moment, nothing happened.

Covenant took a step downward, then jerked to a halt.

A woman near the fire shambled forward. Linden nearly gasped aloud as she recognized the woman who had stood on the steps of the courthouse, warning people to repent. With her three children behind her, she approached the blaze.

She bowed to it like a dead woman.

Blankly, she put her right hand into the flames.

A shriek of pain rent the night. She recoiled from the fire, fell in agony to the bare ground.

A red quivering ran through the flames like a spasm of desire. The fire seemed to mount as if it fed on the woman's pain.

Linden's muscles bunched, ached to hurl her to her feet. She wanted to shout her horror, stop this atrocity. But her limbs were locked. Images of desperation or evil froze her where she crouched. All these people were like Joan.

Then the woman regained her feet and stood as dumbly as if the nerves to her burned hand had been severed. Her gaze returned to Covenant like a compulsion, exerting its demand against him.

The oldest of her children took her place at the bonfire.

No! Linden cried, striving uselessly to break the silence.

The young boy bowed, thrust his emaciated arm into the blaze.

His wail broke Linden's will, left her panting in helpless abomination. She could not move, could not look away. Loathings for which she had no name mastered her.

The boy's younger sister did what he had done, as if his agony meant nothing to her. And the third waif followed in turn, surrendering her flesh to harm like lifeless tissue animated solely for immolation.

Then Linden would have moved. The rigid abhorrence of Covenant's stance showed that he would have moved. But the fire stopped them, held them. At every taste of flesh, lust flared through it; flames raged higher.

A figure began to take shape in the heart of the blaze.

More people moved to sacrifice their hands. As they did so, the figure solidified. It was indistinct in the flames; but the glaring red outlined a man in a flowing robe. He stood blood-limned with his arms folded across his powerful chest − created by pain out of fire and self-abandonment.

The worshipper with the knife sank to his knees, cried out in exaltation, 'Master!'

The figure's eyes were like fangs, carious and yellow; and they raged venomously out of the flames. Their malignance cowed Linden like a personal assault on her sanity, her conception of life. They were rabid and deliberate, like voluntary disease, telic corruption. Nothing in all her life had readied her to witness such palpable hate.

Across the stillness, she heard Covenant gasp in fury, 'Foul! Even children?' But his wrath could not penetrate the dread which paralysed her. For her, the fiery silence was punctuated only by the screaming of the burned.

Then the moon began to rise opposite her. A rim as white as bone crested the hill, looked down into the hollow like a leer.

The man with the knife came to his feet. Again he raised his arms, brandished his dagger. His personal transport was approaching its climax. In a shout like a moan, he cried, 'Now is the hour of apocalypse! The Master has come! Doom is at hand for those who seek to thwart His will. Now we will witness vengeance against sin and life, we who have watched and waited and suffered in His name. Here we fulfil the vision that was given to us. We have touched the fire, and we have been redeemed!' His voice rose until he was shrieking like the burned. 'Now we will bring all wickedness to blood and eternal torment!'

He's mad. Linden clung to that thought, fought to think of these people as fanatics, driven wild by destitution and fear. They're all crazy. This is impossible. But she could not move.

And Covenant did not move. She yearned for him to do something, break the trance somehow, rescue Joan, save Linden herself from her extremity. But he remained motionless, watching the fire as if he were trapped between savagery and helplessness.

The figure in the blaze stirred. His eyes focused the flames like twin scars of malice, searing everything with his contempt. His right arm made a gesture as final as a sentence of execution.

At once, the brawny man dropped to his knees. Bending over Joan, he bared her throat. She lay limp under him, frail and lost. The skin of her neck seemed to gleam in the firelight like a plea for help.

Trembling as if he were rapturous or terrified, the man set his blade against Joan's white throat.

Now the people in the hollow stared emptily at his hands. They appeared to have lost all interest in Covenant. Their silence was appalling. The man's hands shook.

'Stop!'

Covenant's shout scourged the air.

'You've done enough! Let her go!'

The baleful eyes in the fire swung at him, nailed him with denigration. The worshipper at Joan's throat stared whitely upward. 'Release her?' he croaked. 'Why?'

'Because you don't have to do this!' Anger and supplication thickened Covenant's tone. 'I don't know how you were driven to this. I don't know what went wrong with your life. But you don't have to do it.'

The man did not blink; the eyes in the fire clenched him. Deliberately, he knotted his free hand in Joan's hair.

'All right!' Covenant barked immediately. 'All right. I accept. I'll trade you. Me for her.'

'No.' Linden strove to shout aloud, but her cry was barely a whisper. 'No.'

The worshippers were as silent as gravestones.

Slowly, the man with the knife rose to his feet. He alone seemed to have the capacity to feel triumph; he was grinning ferally as he said, 'It is as the Master promised.'

He stepped back. At the same time, a quiver ran through Joan.

She raised her head, gaped around her. Her face was free of possession. Moving awkwardly, she climbed to her feet. Bewildered and afraid, she searched for an escape, for anything she could understand.

She saw Covenant.

'Tom!' Springing from the rock, she fled towards him and threw herself into his arms.

He hugged her, strained his arms around her as if he could not bear to lose her. But then, roughly, he pushed her away. 'Go home,' he ordered. 'It's over. You'll be safe now.' He faced her in the right direction, urged her into motion.

She stopped and looked at him, imploring him to go with her.

'Don't worry about me.' A difficult tenderness softened his tone. 'You're safe now – that's the important thing. I'll be all right.' Somehow, he managed to smile. His eyes betrayed his pain. The light from the fire cast shadows of self-defiance across his bruised mien. And yet his smile expressed so much valour and rue that the sight of it tore Linden's heart.

Kneeling with her head bowed and hot tears on her cheeks, she sensed rather than saw Joan leave the hollow. She could not bear to watch as Covenant moved down the hillside. *I'm the only one who can help her.* He was committing a kind of suicide.

Suicide. Linden's father had killed himself. Her mother had begged for death. Her revulsion towards such things was a compelling obsession.

But Thomas Covenant had chosen to die. And he had smiled.

For Joan's sake.

Linden had never seen one person do so much for another.

She could not endure it. She already had too much blood on her hands. Dashing the tears from her eyes, she looked up.

Covenant moved among the people as if he were beyond hope. The man with the knife guided him into the triangle of blood. The carious eyes in the fire blazed avidly.

It was too much. With a passionate wrench, Linden broke the hold of her dismay, jumped upright.

'Over here!' she yelled. 'Police! Hurry! They're over here!' She flailed her arms as if she were signalling to people behind her.

The eyes of the fire whipped at her, hit her with withering force. In that instant, she felt completely vulnerable, felt all her secrets exposed and devoured. But she ignored the eyes. She sped downward, daring the worshippers to believe she was alone.

Covenant whirled in the triangle. Every line of his stance howled, *No!*

People cried out. Her charge seemed to shatter the trance of the fire. The worshippers were thrown into confusion. They fled in all directions, scattered as if she had unpent a vast pressure of repugnance. For an instant, she was wild with hope.

But the man with the knife did not flee. The rage of the bonfire exalted him. He slapped his arms around Covenant, threw him to the stone, kicked him so that he lay flat.

The knife – ! Covenant was too stunned to move.

Linden hurled herself at the man, grappled for his arms. He was slick with ashes, and strong. She lost her grip.

Covenant struggled to roll over. Swiftly, the man stooped to him, pinned him with one hand, raised the knife in the other.

Linden attacked again, blocked the knife. Her fingernails gouged the man's face.

Yowling, he dealt her a blow which stretched her on the rock.

Everything reeled. Darkness spun at her from all sides.

She saw the knife flash.

Then the eyes of the fire blazed at her, and she was lost in a yellow triumph that roared like the furnace of the sun.

PART I

Need

4

'YOU ARE MINE'

Red agony spiked the centre of Thomas Covenant's chest. He felt that he was screaming. But the fire was too bright; he could not hear himself. From the wound, flame writhed through him, mapped his nerves like a territory of pain. He could not fight it.

He did not want to fight it. He had saved Joan. Saved Joan. That thought iterated through him, consoling him for the unanswerable violence of the wound. For the first time in eleven years, he was at peace with his ex-wife. He had repaid the old debt between them to the limit of his mortality; he had given everything he possessed to make restitution for the blameless crime of his leprosy. Nothing more could be asked of him.

But the fire had a voice. At first, it was too loud to be understood. It retorted in his ears like the crushing of boulders. He inhaled it with every failing breath; it echoed along the conflagration in his chest. But gradually it became clear. It uttered words as heavy as stones.

> 'Your will is mine –
> You have no hope of life without me,
> Have no life or hope without me.
>   All is mine.
>
> 'Your heart is mine –
> There is no love or peace within you,
> Is no peace or love within you.
>   All is mine.
>
> 'Your soul is mine –
> You cannot dream of your salvation,
> Cannot plead for your salvation.
>   You are mine.'

The arrogance of the words filled him with repudiation. He knew that voice. He had spent ten years strengthening himself against it, tightening his grip on the truth of love and rage which had enabled him to master it. And still it had the power to appall him. It thronged

67

with relish for the misery of lepers. It claimed him and would not let him go.

Now he wanted to fight. He wanted to live. He could not bear to let that voice have its way with him.

But the knife had struck too deeply; the wound was complete. A numbness crept through him, and the red fire faded towards mist. He had no pulse, could not remember breathing. Could not —

Out of the mist, he remembered Linden Avery.

Hellfire!

She had followed him, even though he had warned her — warned her in spite of the fact that she had obviously been chosen to fulfil some essential role. He had been so torn — She had given an excruciating twist to his dilemma, had dismayed and infuriated him with her determination to meddle in matters she could not comprehend. And yet she was the first woman he had met in ten years who was not afraid of him.

And she had fallen beside him, trying to save his life. The man had struck her; the fire had covered her as it reached for him. If she were being taken to the Land — !

Of course she was. Why else had the old man accosted her?

But she had neither knowledge nor power with which to defend herself, had no way to understand what was happening to her.

Blindly, Covenant struggled against the numbness, resisted the voice. Linden had tried to save his life. He could not leave her to face such a doom alone. Wrath at the brutality of her plight crowded his heart. By hell! he raged. You can't do this!

Suddenly, a resurgence of fire burned out of him — pure white flame, the fire of his need. It concentrated in the knife wound, screamed through his chest like an apotheosis or cautery. Heat hammered at his heart, his lungs, his half-hand. His body arched in ire and pain.

The next instant, the crisis broke. Palpable relief poured through him. The pain receded, leaving him limp and gasping on the stone. The mist swirled with malice, but did not touch him.

'Ah, you are stubborn yet,' the voice sneered, so personal in its contempt that it might have come from within his mind rather than from the attar-laden air. 'Stubborn beyond my fondest desires. In one stroke you have ensured your own defeat. My will commands now, and you are lost. Groveller!'

Covenant flinched at the virulence of the sound.

Lord Foul.

'Do you mislike the title I have given you?' The Despiser spoke softly, hardly above a whisper; but his quietness only emphasized his sharp hate. 'You will merit it absolutely. Never have you been more truly mine. You believe that you have been near unto death. That is false, groveller! I would not permit you to die. I will obtain far better service from your life.'

Covenant wanted to strike out at the mist, flail it away from him. But he was too weak. He lay on the stone as if his limbs had been bled dry. He needed all his will to dredge his voice back to life. 'I don't believe it,' he panted hoarsely. 'You can't be stupid enough to try this again.'

'Ah, you do not believe,' jeered Lord Foul. 'Misdoubt it, then. Disbelieve, and I will rend your very soul from your bones!'

No! Covenant rasped in silence. I've had ten years to understand what happened the last time. You can't do that to me again.

'You will grovel before me,' the Despiser went on, 'and call it joy. Your victory over me was nothing. It serves me well. Plans which I planted in my anguish have come to fruit. Time is altered. The world is not what it was. You are changed, Unbeliever.' The mist made that word, *Unbeliever*, into a name of sovereign scorn. 'You are no longer free. You have sold yourself for that paltry woman who loathes you. When you accepted her life from me, you became my tool. A tool does not choose. Did not my Enemy expound to you the necessity of freedom? Your very presence here empowers me to master you.'

Covenant flinched. Lord Foul spoke the truth; he was not free. In trading himself for Joan, he had committed himself to something he could neither measure nor recall. He wanted to cry out; but he was too angry to show that much weakness.

'We are foemen, you and I,' continued Lord Foul, 'enemies to the end. But the end will be yours, Unbeliever, not mine. That you will learn to believe. For a score of centuries I lay entombed in the Land which I abhor, capable of naught but revulsion. But in time I was restored to myself. For nearly as many centuries more, I have been preparing retribution. When last comes to last, you will be the instrument of my victory.'

Bloody hell! Covenant gagged on the thickness of the mist and Lord Foul's vitriol. But his passion was clear. I won't let you do this!

'Now hear me, groveller. Hear my prophecy. It is for your ears alone – for behold! there are none left in the Land to whom you could deliver it.'

That hurt him. None! What had happened to the Lords?

But the Despiser went on remorselessly, mocking Covenant by his very softness. 'No, to you alone I say it: tremble in your heart, for the ill that you deem most terrible is upon you! Your former victory accomplished naught but to prepare the way for this moment. I am Lord Foul the Despiser, and I speak the one word of truth. To you I say it: the wild magic is no longer potent against me! It cannot serve you now. No power will suffice.

'Unbeliever, you cannot oppose me. At the last there will be but one choice for you, and you will make it in all despair. Of your own

69

volition you will give the white gold into my hand.'

No! Covenant shouted. No! But he could not penetrate Lord Foul's certitude.

'Knowing that I will make use of that power to destroy the Earth, you will place it into my hand, and no hope or chance under all the Arch of Time can prevent you!

'Yes, tremble, groveller! There is despair laid up for you here beyond anything your petty mortal heart can bear!'

The passionate whisper threatened to crush Covenant against the stone. He wailed refusals and curses, but they had no force, could not drive the attar from his throat.

Then Lord Foul began to chuckle. The corruption of death clogged the air. For a long moment, Covenant retched as if the muscles of his chest were breaking.

But as he gagged, the jeering drifted away from him. Wind sifted through it, pulling the mist apart. The wind was cold, as if a chill of laughter rode it, echoing soundlessly; but the atmosphere grew bright as the mist frayed and vanished.

Covenant lay on his back under a brilliant azure sky and a strange sun.

The sun was well up in the heavens. The central glare of its light was familiar, comforting. But it wore a blue corona like a ring of sapphire; and its radiance deepened the rest of the sky to the texture of sendaline.

He squinted at it dumbly, too stunned to move or react. *Of your own volition* – The sun's aurora disturbed him in a way he could not define. *Plans which I planted in my anguish* – Shifting as if it had a mind of its own, his right hand slowly probed towards the spot where the knife had struck him.

His fingers were too numb to tell him anything. But he could feel their pressure on his chest. He could feel their touch when they slipped through the slit in the centre of his T-shirt.

There was no pain.

He withdrew his hand, took his gaze out of the sky to look at his fingers.

There was no blood.

He sat up with a jerk that made his head reel. For a moment, he had to prop himself up with his arms. Blinking against the sun-dazzle, he forced his eyes into focus on his chest.

His shirt had been cut – a slash the width of his hand just below his sternum. Under it lay the white line of a new scar.

He gaped at it. How – ?

You are stubborn yet. Had he healed himself? With wild magic?

He did not know. He had not been conscious of wielding any power. Could he have done such a thing unconsciously? High Lord Mhoram had once said to him, *You are the white gold.* Did that mean he was capable of using power without knowing it? Without being in control of it? Hellfire!

Long moments passed before he realized that he was facing a parapet. He was sitting on one side of a round stone slab encircled by a low wall, chest-high on him in this position.

A jolt of recognition brought him out of his stupor. He knew this place.

Kevin's Watch.

For an instant, he asked himself, Why here? But then a chain of connections jumped taut in him, and he whirled, to find Linden stretched unconscious behind him.

He almost panicked. She lay completely still. Her eyes were open, but she saw nothing. The muscles of her limbs hung slack against the bones. Her hair was tangled across her face.

Blood seeped in slow drops from behind her left ear.

You are mine.

Suddenly, Covenant was sweating in the cool air.

He gripped her shoulders, shook her, then snatched up her left hand, started to slap her wrist. Her head rolled in protest. A whimper tightened her lips. She began to writhe. He dropped her arm, clamped his hands to the sides of her face to keep her from hurting herself against the stone.

Abruptly, her gaze sprang outward. She drew a harsh gasp of air and screamed. Her cry sounded like destitution under the immense sky and the strange blue-ringed sun.

'Linden!' he shouted. She sucked air to howl again. 'Linden!'

Her eyes lurched into focus on him, flared in horror or rage as if he had threatened her with leprosy.

Fiercely, she struck him across the cheek.

He recoiled, more in surprise than in pain.

'You bastard,' she panted, surging to her knees. 'Haven't you even got the guts to go on living?' She inhaled deeply to yell at him. But before she could release her ire, dismay knotted her features. Her hands leaped to her mouth, then covered her face. She gave a muffled groan. 'Oh my God.'

He stared at her in confusion. What had happened to her? He wanted to challenge her at once, demand an answer. But the situation was too complex. And she was totally unprepared for it. He remembered vividly his first appearance here. If Lena had not extended her hand to him, he would have died in vertigo and madness. It was too much for any mind to accept. If only she had listened to him, stayed out of danger –

But she had not listened. She was here, and in need. She did not yet know the extent of her need. For her sake, he forced a semblance of gentleness into his voice. 'You wanted to understand, and I kept telling you you weren't equipped. Now I think you're going to understand whether you want to or not.'

'Covenant,' she moaned through her hands. 'Covenant.'

'Linden.' Carefully, he touched her wrists, urged her to lower her arms.

'Covenant — ' She bared her face to him. Her eyes were brown, deep and moist, and dark with the repercussions of fear. They shied from his, then returned. 'I must have been dreaming.' Her voice quavered. 'I thought you were my father.'

He smiled for her, though the strain made his battered bones ache. Father? He wanted to pursue that, but did not. Other questions were more immediate.

But before he could frame an enquiry, she began to recollect herself. She ran her hands through her hair, winced when she touched the injury behind her ear. For a moment, she looked at the trace of blood on her fingers. Then other memories returned. She gasped sharply. Her eyes jerked to his chest. 'The knife — ' Her urgency was almost an attack. 'I saw — ' She grabbed for him, yanked up his shirt, gaped at the new scar under his sternum. It appalled her. Her hands reached towards it, flinched away. Her voice was a hoarse whisper. 'That's not possible.'

'Listen.' He raised her head with his left hand, made her meet his gaze. He wanted to distract her, prepare her. 'What happened to you? That man hit you. The fire was all over us. What happened after that?'

'*What happened to you?*'

'One thing at a time.' The exertion of keeping himself steady made him sound grim. 'There are too many other things you have to understand first. Please give me a chance. Tell me what happened.'

She pulled away. Her whole body rejected his question. One trembling finger pointed at his chest. 'That's impossible.'

Impossible. At that moment, he could have overwhelmed her with impossibilities. But he refrained, permitted himself to say only, 'So is possession.'

She met his gaze miserably. Then her eyes closed. In a low voice, she said, 'I must have been unconscious. I was dreaming about my parents.'

'You didn't hear anything? A voice making threats?'

Her eyes snapped open in surprise. 'No. Why would I?'

He bowed his head to hide his turmoil. Foul hadn't spoken to her? The implications both relieved and frightened him. Was she somehow independent of him? Free of his control? Or was he already that sure of her?

When Covenant looked up again Linden's attention had slipped away to the parapet, the sun, the wide sky. Slowly, her face froze. She started to her feet. '*Where are we?*'

He caught her arms, held her sitting in front of him. 'Look at me.'

Her head winced from side to side in frantic denial. Exigencies thronged about him; questions were everywhere. But at this moment the stark need in her face dominated all other issues. 'Dr Avery.' There was insanity in the air; he knew that from experience. If he did not help her now, she might never be within reach of help again. '*Look* at me.'

His demand brought her wild stare back to him.

'I can explain it. Just give me a chance.'

Her voice knifed at him. 'Explain it.'

He flinched in shame; it was his fault that she was here – and that she was so unready. But he forced himself to face her squarely. 'I couldn't tell you about it before.' The difficulty of what he had to say roughened his tone. 'There was no way you could have believed it. And now it's so complicated – '

Her eyes clung to him like claws.

'There are two completely different explanations,' he said as evenly as he could. 'Outside and inside. The outside explanation might be easier to accept. It goes like this.' He took a deep breath. 'You and I are still lying in that triangle.' A grimace strained his bruises. 'We're unconscious. And while we're unconscious, we're dreaming. We're sharing a dream.'

Her mien was tight with disbelief. He hastened to add, 'It's not as far-fetched as you think. Deep down in their minds – down where dreams come from – most people have a lot in common. That's why so many of our dreams fall into patterns that other people can recognize.

'It's happening to us.' He kept pouring words at her, not because he wanted to convince her, but because he knew she needed time, needed any answer, however improbable, to help her survive the first shock of her situation. 'We're sharing a dream. And we're not the only ones,' he went on, denying her a chance to put her incredulity into words. 'Joan had fragments of the same dream. And that old man – the one you saved. We're all tied into the same unconscious process.'

Her gaze wavered. He snapped, 'Keep looking at me! I have to tell you what kind of dream it is. It's dangerous. It can hurt you. The things buried in us are powerful and violent, and they are going to come out. The darkness in us – the destructive side, the side we keep locked up all our lives – is alive here. Everybody has some self-hate inside. Here it's personified – externalized, the way things happen in dreams. He calls himself Lord Foul the Despiser, and he wants to destroy us.

'That's what Joan kept talking about. Lord Foul. And that's what the old man meant. "However he may assail you. Be true." Be true to yourself, don't serve the Despiser, don't let him destroy you. That's what we have to do.' He pleaded with her to accept the

73

consequences of what he was saying, even if she chose not to believe the explanation itself. 'We have to stay sane, hang on to ourselves, defend what we are and what we believe and what we want. Until it's over. Until we regain consciousness.'

He stopped, forced himself to give her time.

Her eyes dropped to his chest, as if that scar were a test of what he said. Shadows of fear passed across her countenance. Covenant felt suddenly sure that she was familiar with self-hate.

Tightly, she said, 'This has happened to you before.'

He nodded.

She did not raise her head. 'And you believe it?'

He wanted to say, Partially. If you put the two explanations together, they come close to what I believe. But in her present straits he could not trouble her with disclaimers. Instead, he got to his feet, drew her with him to look out from the Watch.

She stiffened against him in shock.

They were on a slab like a platform that appeared to hang suspended in the air. An expanse of sky as huge as if they were perched on a mountaintop covered them. The weird halo of the sun gave a disturbing hue to the roiling grey sea of clouds two hundred feet below them. The clouds thrashed like thunderheads, concealing the earth from horizon to horizon.

A spasm of vertigo wrenched Covenant; he remembered acutely that he was four thousand feet above the foothills. But he ignored the imminent reel and panic around him and concentrated on Linden.

She was stunned, rigid. This leap without transition from night in the woods to morning on such an eminence staggered her. He wanted to put his arms around her, hide her face against his chest to protect her; but he knew he could not do so, could not give her the strength to bear things which once had almost shattered him. She had to achieve her own survival. Grimly, he turned her to look in the opposite direction.

The mountains rising dramatically there seemed to strike her a blow. They sprang upward out of the clouds a stone's throw from the Watch. Their peaks were rugged and dour. From the cliff behind the Watch, they withdrew on both sides like a wedge, piling higher into the distance. But off to the right a spur of the range marched back across the clouds before falling away again.

Linden gaped at the cliff as if it were about to fall on her. Covenant could feel her ribs straining; she was caught in the predicament of the mad and could not find enough air in all the open sky to enable her to cry out. Fearing that she might break away from him, lose herself over the parapet, he tugged her back down to the safety of the floor. She crumpled to her knees, gagging silently. Her eyes had a terrible glazed and empty look.

'Linden!' Because he did not know what else to do, he barked, 'Haven't you even got the guts to go on living?'

She gasped, inhaled. Her eyes swept into focus on him like swords leaping from their scabbards. The odd sunlight gave her face an aspect of dark fury.

'I'm sorry,' he said thickly. Her reaction made him ache as badly as helplessness. 'You were so – ' Unwittingly, he had trespassed on something which he had no right to touch. 'I never wanted this to happen to you.'

She rejected his regret with a violent shake of her head. 'Now,' she panted, 'you're going to tell me the other explanation.'

He nodded. Slowly, he released her, withdrew to sit with his back against the parapet. He did not understand her strange combination of strength and weakness; but at the moment his incomprehension was unimportant. 'The inside explanation.'

A deep weariness ran through him. He fought it for the words he needed. 'We're in a place called the Land. It's a different world – like being on a completely different planet. These mountains are the Southron Range, the southern edge. All the rest of the Land is west and north and east from us. This place is Kevin's Watch. Below us, and a bit to the west, there used to be a village called Mithil Stonedown. Revelstone is – ' But the thought of Revelstone recalled the Lords; he shied away from it. 'I've been here before.

'Most of what I can tell you about it won't make much sense until you see it for yourself. But there's one thing that's important right now. The Land has an enemy. Lord Foul.' He studied her, trying to read her response. But her eyes brandished darkness at him, nothing else. 'For thousands of years,' he went on, 'Foul has been trying to destroy the Land. It's – sort of a prison for him. He wants to break out.' He groaned inwardly at the impossibility of making what he had to say acceptable to someone who had never had the experience. 'He translated us out of our world. Brought us here. He wants us to serve him. He thinks he can manipulate us into helping him destroy the Land.

'We have power here.' He prayed he was speaking the truth. 'Since we come from outside, we aren't bound by the Law, the natural order that holds everything together. That's why Foul wants us, wants to use us. We can do things nobody else here can.'

To spare himself the burden of her incredulity, he leaned his head against the parapet and gazed up at the mountains. 'The necessity of freedom,' he breathed. 'As long as we aren't bound by any Law, or anybody – or any explanation,' he said to ease his conscience, 'we're powerful.' But I'm not free. I've already chosen. 'That's what it comes down to. Power. The power that healed me.

'That old man – Somehow, he knows what's going on in the Land. And he's no friend of Foul's. He chose you for something – I don't know what. Or maybe he wanted to reassure himself. Find out if you're the kind of person Foul can manipulate.

'As for Joan, she was Foul's way of getting at me. She was vulnerable to him. After what happened the last time I was here, I wasn't. He used her to get me to step into that triangle by my own choice. So he could summon me here.' What I don't understand, he sighed, is why he had to do it that way. It wasn't like that before. 'Maybe it's an accident that you're here, too. But I don't think so.'

Linden glanced down at the stone as if to verify that it was substantial, then touched the bruise behind her ear. Frowning, she shifted into a sitting position. Now she did not look at him. 'I don't understand,' she said stiffly. 'First you tell me this is a dream – then you say it's real. First you're dying back there in the woods – then you're healed by some kind of – some kind of magic. First Lord Foul is a figment – then he's real.' In spite of her control, her voice trembled slightly. 'Which is it? You can't have it both ways.' Her fist clenched. 'You could be dying.'

Ah, I have to have it both ways, Covenant murmured. It's like a vertigo. The answer is in the contradiction – in the eye of the paradox. But he did not utter his thought aloud.

Yet Linden's question relieved him. Already, her restless mind – that need which had rejected his efforts to warn her, had driven her to follow him to his doom – was beginning to grapple with her situation. If she had the strength to challenge him, then her crisis was past, at least for the moment. He found himself smiling in spite of his fear.

'It doesn't matter,' he replied. 'Maybe this is real – maybe it isn't. You can believe whatever you want. I'm just offering you a frame of reference, so you'll have some place to start.'

Her hands kept moving, touching herself, the stone, as if she needed tactile sensation to assure her of her own existence. After a moment, she said, 'You've been here before.' Her anger had turned to pain. 'It's your life. Tell me how to understand.'

'Face it,' he said without hesitation. 'Go forward. Find out what happens – what's at stake. What matters to you.' He knew from experience that there was no other defence against insanity; the Land's reality and its unreality could not be reconciled. 'Give yourself a chance to find out who you are.'

'I know who I am.' Her jaw was stubborn. The lines of her nose seemed precise rather than fragile; her mouth was severe by habit. 'I'm a doctor.' But she was facing something she did not know how to grasp. 'I don't even have my bag.' She scrutinized her hands as if she wondered what they were good for. When she met his gaze, her question was a demand as well as an appeal. 'What do you believe?'

'I believe – ' he made no effort to muffle his hardness – 'that we've got to find some way to stop Foul. That's more important than anything. He's trying to destroy the Land. I'm not going to let him get away with that. That's who *I* am.'

She stared at his affirmation. 'Why? What does it have to do with you? If this is a dream, it doesn't matter. And if it's – ' She had difficulty saying the words. 'If it's real, it's not your problem. You can ignore it.'

Covenant tasted old rage. 'Foul laughs at lepers.'

At that, a glare of comprehension touched her eyes. Her scowl said plainly, Nobody has the right to laugh at illness.

In a tight voice, she asked, 'What do we do now?'

'Now?' He was weak with fatigue; but her question galvanized him. She had reasons, strengths, possibilities. The old man had not risked her gratuitously. 'Now,' he said grimly, 'if I can hold off my vertigo, we get down from here, and go find out what kind of trouble we're in.'

'Down?' She blinked at him. 'I don't know how we got up.'

To answer her, he nodded towards the mountains. When she turned, she noticed the gap in the curve of the parapet facing the cliff. He watched as she crawled to the gap, saw what he already knew was there.

The parapet circled the tip of a long spire of stone which angled towards the cliff under the Watch. There were rude stairs cut into the upper surface of the shaft.

He joined her. One glance told him that his dizziness would not be easily overcome. Two hundred feet below him, the stairs vanished in the clouds like a fall into darkness.

5

THUNDER AND LIGHTNING

'I'll go first.' Covenant was trembling deep in his bones. He did not look at Linden. 'This stair joins the cliff – but if we fall, it's four thousand feet down. I'm no good at heights. If I slip, I don't want to take you with me.' Deliberately, he set himself at the gap, feet first so that he could back through it.

There he paused, tried to resist the vertigo which unmoored his mind by giving himself a VSE. But the exercise aroused a pang of leper's anxiety. Under the blue-tinged sun, his skin had a dim purple cast, as if his leprosy had already spread up his arms, affecting the pigmentation, killing the nerves.

A sudden weakness yearned in his muscles, making his shoulders quiver. The particular numbness of his dead nerves had not altered, for better or worse. But the diseased hue of his flesh looked fatal and prophetic; it struck him like a leap of intuition. One of his questions answered itself. Why was Linden here? Why had the old man spoken to her rather than to him? Because she was necessary. To save the Land when he failed.

The wild magic is no longer potent. So much for power. He had already abandoned himself to Lord Foul's machinations. A groan escaped him before he could lock his teeth on it.

'Covenant?' Concern sharpened Linden's voice. 'Are you all right?'

He could not reply. The simple fact that she was worried about him, was capable of worrying about him when she was under so much stress, multiplied the dismay in his bones. His eyes clung to the stone, searching for strength.

'Covenant!' Her demand was like a slap in the face. 'I don't know how to help you. Tell me what to do.'

What to do. None of this was her fault. She deserved an answer. He pulled himself down into the centre of his fatigue and dizziness. Had he really doomed himself by taking Joan's place? Surely he did not have to fail? Surely the power for which he had paid such a price was not so easily discounted? Without raising his head, he gritted, 'At the bottom of the stairs, to my left, there's a ledge in the cliff. Be careful.'

Coercing himself into motion, he backed through the gap.

As his head passed below the level of the Watch, he heard her whisper fiercely, 'Damn you, why do you have to act so impervious? All I want to do is help.' She sounded as if her sanity depended on her ability to be of help.

But he could not afford to think about her; the peril of the stairs consumed his attention. He worked his way down them as if they were a ladder, clutching them with his hands, kicking each foot into them to be sure it was secure before he trusted it. His gaze never left his hands. They strained on the steps until the sinews stood out like desperation.

The void around him seemed fathomless. He could hear the emptiness of the wind. And the swift seething of the clouds below him had a hypnotic power, sucking at his concentration. Long plunges yawned all around him.

But he knew this fear. Holding his breath, he lowered himself into the clouds – into the still centre of his vertigo.

Abruptly, the sun faded and went out. Grey gloom thickened towards midnight at every step of the descent.

A pale flash ran through the dank sea, followed almost at once by thunder. The wind mounted, rushed wetly at him as if it sought to

78

lift him off the spire. The stone became slick. His numb fingers could not tell the difference, but the nerves in his wrists and elbows registered every slippage of his grasp.

Again, a bolt of lightning thrashed past him, illuminating the mad boil and speed of the clouds. The sky shattered. Instinctively, he flattened himself against the stone. Something in him howled, but he could not tell whether it howled aloud.

Crawling painfully through the brutal impact of the storm, he went on downward.

He marked his progress in the intensifying weight of the rain. The fine cold sting of spray against his sore face became a pelting of heavy drops like a shower of pebbles. Soon he was drenched and battered. Lightning and thunder shouted across him, articulating savagery. But the promise of the ledge drew him on.

At last, his feet found it. Thrusting away from the spire, he pressed his back to the wall of the cliff, gaping upward.

A flail of blue-white fire rendered Linden out of the darkness. She was just above the level of his head.

When she reached the ledge, he caught her so that she would not stumble over the precipice. She gripped him urgently. 'Covenant!' The wind ripped her shout away; he could barely hear her. 'Are you all right?'

He put his mouth to her ear. 'Stay against the cliff! We've got to find shelter!'

She nodded sharply.

Clenching her right hand in his left, he turned his back on the fall and began to shuttle west along the ledge.

Lightning burned overhead, to give him a glimpse of his situation. The ledge was two or three feet wide and ran roughly level across the cliff face. From its edge, the mountain disappeared into the abyss of the clouds.

Thunder hammered at him like the voice of his vertigo, commanding him to lose his balance. Wind and rain as shrill as chaos lashed his back. But Linden's hand anchored him. He squeezed himself like yearning against the cliff and crept slowly forward.

At every lightning blast, he peered ahead through the rain, trying to see the end of the ledge.

There: a vertical line like a scar in the cliff face.

He reached it, pulled Linden past the corner, up a slope of mud and scree which gushed water as if it were a stream bed. At once, the wind became a constricted yowl. The next blue glare revealed that they had entered a narrow ravine sluicing upward through the mountainside. Water frothed like rapids past the boulders which cramped the floor of the ravine.

He struggled ahead until he and Linden were above a boulder that appeared large enough to be secure. There he halted and sat down in the current with his back braced on the wall. She joined him. Water flooded over their legs; rain blinded their faces. He did not care. He had to rest.

After a few moments, she shifted, put her face to his ear. 'Now what?'

Now what? He did not know. Exhaustion numbed his mind. But she was right; they could not remain where they were. He mustered a wan shout. 'There's a path somewhere!'

'You don't know the way? You said you've been here before!'

'Ten years ago!' And he had been unconscious the second time; Saltheart Foamfollower had carried him.

Lightning lit her face for an instant. Her visage was smeared with rain. 'What are we going to do?'

The thought of Foamfollower, the Giant who had been his friend, gave him what he needed. 'Try!' Bracing himself on her shoulder, he lurched to his feet. She seemed to support his weight easily. 'Maybe I'll remember!'

She stood up beside him, leaned close to yell, 'I don't like this storm! It doesn't feel right!'

Doesn't feel — ? He blinked at her. For a moment, he did not understand. To him, it was just a storm, natural violence like any other. But then he caught her meaning. To her, the storm felt *un*natural. It offended some instinctive sensitivity in her.

Already, she was ahead of him; her senses were growing attuned to the Land, while his remained flat and dull, blind to the spirit of what he perceived. Ten years ago, he had been able to do what she had just done: identify the rightness or wrongness, the health or corruption, of physical things and processes, of wind, rain, stone, wood, flesh. But now he could feel nothing except the storm's vehemence, as if such force had no meaning, no implication. No soul.

He muttered tired curses at himself. Were his senses merely slow in making the adjustment? Or had he lost the ability to be in harmony with the Land? Had leprosy and time bereft him entirely of that sensitivity? Hell and blood! he rasped weakly, bitterly. If Linden could see where he was blind —

Aching at the old grief of his insufficiency, he tried to master himself. He expected Linden to ask him what was wrong. And that thought, too, was bitter; he did not want his frailties and fears, his innate wrongness, to be visible to her. But she did not question him. She was rigid with surprise or apprehension.

Her face was turned up the ravine.

He jerked around and tried to penetrate the downpour.

At once, he saw it — a faint yellow light in the distance.

It flickered towards them slowly, picked its way with care down the spine of the ravine. As it neared, a long blast of lightning revealed that it was a torch in the hand of a man. Then blackness and thunder crashed over them, and Covenant could see nothing but the strange flame. It burned bravely, impossibly, in spite of the deluge and battery of the storm.

It approached until it was close enough to light the man who held it. He was a short, stooped figure wearing a sodden robe. Rain gushed through his sparse hair and tangled beard, streamed in runnels down the creases of his old face, giving him a look of lunacy. He squinted at Covenant and Linden as if they had been incarnated out of nightmares to appal him.

Covenant held himself still, returned the old man's stare mutely.

Linden touched his arm as if she wanted to warn him of something.

Suddenly, the old man jerked up his right hand, raised it with the palm forward, and spread his fingers.

Covenant copied the gesture. He did not know whether or not Lord Foul had prepared this encounter for him. But he needed shelter, food, information. And he was prepared to acknowledge anyone who could keep a brand alight in this rain. As he lifted his half-hand into the light, his ring gleamed dully on the second finger.

The sight shocked the old man. He winced, mumbled to himself, retreated a step as if in fear. Then he pointed tremulously at Covenant's ring. 'White gold?' he cried. His voice shook.

'Yes!' Covenant replied.

'Halfhand?'

'Yes!'

'How are you named?' the man quavered.

Covenant struggled to drive each word through the storm. 'Ur-Lord Thomas Covenant, Unbeliever and white gold wielder!'

'Illender?' gasped the man as if the rain were suffocating him. 'Prover of Life?'

'Yes!'

The old man retreated another step. The torchlight gave his visage a dismayed look. Abruptly, he turned, started scrambling frailly upwards through the water and muck.

Over his shoulder, he wailed, 'Come!'

'Who is that?' Linden asked almost inaudibly.

Covenant dismissed the question. 'I don't know.'

She scrutinized him. 'Do you trust him?'

'Who has a choice?' Before she could respond, he pushed away from the stone, used all his energy to force himself into motion after the old man.

His mouth was full of rain and the sour taste of weakness. The strain of the past weeks affected him like caducity. But the torch helped him find handholds on the walls and boulders. With Linden's support, he was able to heave forward against the heavy stream. Slowly, they made progress.

Some distance up the ravine, the old man entered a cut branching off to the right. A rough stair in the side of the cut led to its bottom. Freed of the torrents, Covenant found the strength to ask himself, *Do you trust him?* But the torch reassured him. He knew of nobody who could keep a brand burning in rain except the masters of wood-lore. Or the Lords. He was ready to trust anybody who served wood or stone with such potent diligence.

Carefully, he followed the old man along the bottom of the cut until it narrowed, became a high sheer cleft in the mountain rock. Then, abruptly, the cleft changed directions and opened into a small dell.

Towering peaks sheltered the vale from the wind. But there was no escape from the rain. It thrashed Covenant's head and shoulders like a club. He could barely see the torch as the old man crossed the valley.

With Linden, Covenant waded a swollen stream; and moments later they arrived at a squat stone dwelling which sat against the mountainside. The entry had no door; firelight scattered out at them as they approached. Hurrying now, they burst bedraggled and dripping into the single room of the house.

The old man stood in the centre of the room, still clutching his torch though a bright fire blazed in the hearth beyond him. He peered at Covenant with trepidation, ready to cringe, like a child expecting punishment.

Covenant stopped. His bruises ached to be near the fire; but he remained still to look around the room.

At once, a pang of anxiety smote him. Already, he could see that something had changed in the Land. Something fundamental.

The dwelling was furnished with an unexpected mixture of wood and stone. Stoneware bowls and urns sat on wooden shelves affixed to the sidewalls; wooden stools stood around a wooden table in one stone corner. And iron – there were iron utensils on the shelves, iron nails in the stools. Formerly, the people of stone and wood, Stonedownor and Woodhelvennin, had each kept to his own lore – not because they wished to be exclusive, but rather because their special skills and knowledge required all their devotion.

For a moment, he faced the man, bore the old, half-wild gaze. Linden, too, studied the old man, measuring him uncertainly. But Covenant knew she was asking herself questions unlike the ones which mobbed into his mind. Had the Stonedownors and Woodhelvennin grown together, blended their lore? Or had – ?

The world is not what it was.

A raw sickness twisted his heart. Without warning, he became conscious of smoke in the room.

Smoke!

He thrust past the old man, hastened to the hearth.

The wood lay on a pile of ash, burning warmly. Coals cracked and fell off the logs, red worms gnawing the flesh of trees. At intervals, wisps of smoke curled up into the room. The rain in the chimney made a low hissing noise.

Hellfire!

The people he had known here would never have voluntarily consumed wood for any purpose. They had always striven to use the life of wood, the Earthpower in it, without destroying the thing they used. Wood, soil, stone, water – the people of the Land had cherished every manifestation of life.

'Ur-Lord,' the old man groaned.

Covenant whirled. Grief burned like rage in him. He wanted to howl at the Despiser, what have you *done*? But both Linden and the old man were staring at him. Linden's eyes showed concern, as if she feared he had slipped over the edge into confusion. And the old man was in the grip of a private anguish. Fiercely, Covenant contained the yelling of his passion. But the strain of suppression bristled in his tone. 'What keeps that torch burning?'

'I am ashamed!' The man's voice broke as if he were on the verge of weeping. He did not hear Covenant's question; his personal distress devoured him. 'This temple,' he panted, 'built by the most ancient fathers of my father's father – in preparation. We have done nothing! Other rooms fallen to ruin, sanctuaries – ' He waved his brand fervidly. 'We did nothing. In a score of generations, nothing. It is a hovel – unworthy of you. We did not believe the promise given into our trust – generation after generation of Unfettered too craven to put faith in the proudest prophecies. It would be right for you to strike me.'

'Strike you?' Covenant was taken aback. 'No.' There were too many things here he did not understand. 'What's the matter? Why are you afraid of me?'

'Covenant,' Linden breathed suddenly. 'His hand. Look.'

Water dripped from the old man; water ran from them all. But the drops falling from the butt of the torch were red.

'Ur-Lord!' The man plunged to his knees. 'I am unworthy.' He quivered with dismay. 'I have trafficked in the knowledge of the wicked, gaining power against the Sunbane from those who scorn the promises I have sworn to preserve. Ah, spare me! I am shamed.' He dropped his brand, opened his left hand to Covenant.

The torch went out the instant he released it. As it struck the floor, it fell into ash.

Across his palm lay two long cuts. Blood ran from them as if it could not stop.

Covenant flinched. Thunder muttered angrily to itself in the distance. Nothing was left of the torch except ash. It had been held together, kept whole and burning, only by the power the old man had put into it. The power of his blood?

Covenant's brain reeled. A sudden memory of Joan stung him – Joan clawing the back of his hand, licking her fingers. Vertigo reft him of balance. He sat down heavily, slumped against the nearest wall. The rain echoed in his ears. Blood? *Blood?*

Linden was examining the old man's hand. She turned it to the firelight, spread the fingers; her grip on his wrist slowed the flow of blood. 'It's clean.' Her voice was flat, impersonal. 'Needs a bandage to stop the bleeding. But there's no infection.'

No infection, Covenant breathed. His thoughts limped like cripples. 'How can you tell?'

She was concentrating on the wound. 'What?'

He laboured to say what he meant. 'How can you tell there's no infection?'

'I don't know.' His question seemed to trigger surprise in her. 'I can see it. I can see – ' her astonishment mounted – 'the pain. But it's clean. How – ? Can't you?'

He shook his head. She confirmed his earlier impression; her senses were already becoming attuned to the Land.

His were not. He was blind to everything not written on the surface. Why? He closed his eyes. Old rue throbbed in him. He had forgotten that numbness could hurt so much.

After a moment, she moved; he could hear her searching around the room. When she returned to the old man's side, she was tearing a piece of cloth to form bandages.

You will not fail – Covenant felt that he had already been given up for lost. The thought was salt to his sore heart.

Smoke? Blood. *There's only one way to hurt a man. Give him back something broken.* Damnation.

But the old man demanded his attention. The man had bowed his wet grey head to the stone. His hands groped to touch Covenant's boots. 'Ur-Lord,' he moaned. 'Ur-Lord. At last you have come. The Land is saved.'

That obeisance pulled Covenant out of his inner gyre. He could not afford to be overwhelmed by ignorance or loss. And he could not bear to be treated as if he were some kind of saviour; he could not live with such an image of himself. He climbed erect, then took hold of the old man's arms and drew him to his feet.

The man's eyes rolled fearfully, gleaming in the firelight. To reassure him, Covenant spoke evenly, quietly.

'Tell me your name.'

'I am Nassic son of Jous son of Prassan,' the old man replied in a fumbling voice. 'Descended in direct lineage son by son from the Unfettered One.'

Covenant winced. The Unfettered Ones he had known were hermits freed from all normal responsibilities so that they could pursue their private visions. An Unfettered One had once saved his life – and died. Another had read his dreams – and told him that he dreamed the truth. He took a stringent grip on himself. 'What was his calling?'

'Ur-Lord, he saw your return. Therefore he came to this place – to the vale below Kevin's Watch, which was given its name in an age so long past that none remember its meaning.'

Briefly, Nassic's tone stabilized, as if he were reciting something he had memorized long ago. 'He built the temple as a place of welcome for you, and a place of healing, for it was not forgotten among the people of those years that your own world is one of great hazard and strife, inflicting harm even upon its heroes. In his vision, he beheld the severe doom of the Sunbane, though to him it was nameless as nightmare, and he foresaw that the Unbeliever, ur-Lord Illender, Prover of Life, would return to combat it. From son to son he handed down his vision, faith un – '

Then he faltered. 'Ah, shame,' he muttered. 'Temple – faith – healing – Land. All ruins.' But indignation stiffened him. 'Fools will cry for mercy. They deserve only retribution. For lo! the Unbeliever has come. Let the Clave and all its works wail to be spared. Let the very sun tremble in its course. It will avail them nothing! Woe unto you, wicked and abominable! The – '

'Nassic.' Covenant forced the old man to stop. Linden was watching them keenly. Questions crowded her face; but Covenant ignored them. 'Nassic,' he asked of the man's white stare, 'what is this Sunbane?'

'Sunbane?' Nassic lost his fear in amazement. 'Do you ask – ? How can you not – ?' His hands tugged at his beard. 'Why else have you come?'

Covenant tightened his grip. 'Just tell me what it is.'

'It is – why, it is – yes, it – ' Nassic stumbled to a halt, then cried in a sudden appeal, 'Ur-Lord, what is it not. It is sun and rain and blood and desert and fear and the screaming of trees.' He squirmed with renewed abasement. 'It was – it was the fire of my torch. Ur-Lord!' Misery clenched his face like a fist. He tried to drop to his knees again.

'Nassic.' Covenant held him erect, hunted for some way to reassure him. 'We're not going to harm you. Can't you see that?' Then another thought occurred to him. Remembering Linden's injury, his own bruises, he said, 'Your hand's still bleeding. We've both been hurt. And I – ' He almost said, I can't see what she sees. But the words stuck in his throat. 'I've been away for a long time. Do you have any hurtloam?'

Hurtloam? Linden's expression asked.

'Hurtloam?' queried Nassic. 'What is hurtloam?'

What is – ? Distress lurched across Covenant's features. What – ? Shouts flared in him like screams. Hurtloam! Earthpower! *Life!* 'Hurtloam,' he rasped savagely. *'The mud that heals.'* His grasp shook Nassic's frail bones.

'Forgive me, Ur-Lord. Be not angry. I – '

'It was here! In this valley!' Lena had healed him with it.

Nassic found a moment of dignity. 'I know nothing of hurtloam. I am an old man, and have never heard the name spoken.'

'Damnation!' Covenant spat. 'Next you're going to tell me you've never heard of Earthpower!'

The old man sagged. 'Earthpower?' he breathed. 'Earthpower?'

Covenant's hands ground his giddy dismay into Nassic's thin arms. But Linden was at his side, trying to loosen his grip. 'Covenant! He's telling the truth!'

Covenant jerked his gaze like a whip to her face.

Her lips were tight with strain, but she did not let herself flinch. 'He doesn't know what you're talking about.'

She silenced him. He believed her; she could hear the truth in Nassic's voice, just as she could see the lack of infection in his cuts. No hurtloam? He bled inwardly. Forgotten? *Lost?* Images of desecration poured through him. Have mercy. The Land without hurtloam. Without Earthpower? The weight of Nassic's revelation was too much for him. He sank to the floor like an invalid.

Linden stood over him. She was groping for decision, insight; but he could not help her. After a moment, she said, 'Nassic.' Her tone was severe. 'Do you have any food?'

'Food?' he replied as if she had reminded him of his inadequacy. 'Yes. No. It is unworthy.'

'We need food.'

Her statement brooked no argument. Nassic bowed, went at once to the opposite wall, where he began lifting down crude bowls and pots from the shelves.

Linden came to Covenant, knelt in front of him. 'What is it?' she asked tightly. He could not keep the despair out of his face. 'What's wrong?'

He did not want to answer. He had spent too many years in the isolation of his leprosy; her desire to understand him only aggravated his pain. He could not bear to be so exposed. Yet he could not refuse the demand of her hard mouth, her soft eyes. Her life was at issue as much as his. He made an effort of will. 'Later.' His voice ached through his teeth. 'I need time to think about it.'

Her jaws locked; darkness wounded her eyes. He looked away, so that he would not be led to speak before he had regained his self-mastery.

Shortly, Nassic brought bowls of dried meat, fruit, and unleavened

86

bread, which he offered tentatively, as if he knew they deserved to be rejected. Linden accepted hers with a difficult smile; but Nassic did not move until Covenant had mustered the strength to nod his approval. Then the old man took pots and collected rainwater for them to drink.

Covenant stared blindly at his food without tasting it. He seemed to have no reason to bother feeding himself. Yet he knew that was not true; in fact, he was foundering in reasons. But the impossibility of doing justice to them all made his resolution falter. Had he really sold his soul to the Despiser − ?

But he was a leper; he had spent long years learning the answer to his helplessness. Leprosy was incurable. Therefore lepers disciplined themselves to pay meticulous attention to their immediate needs. They ignored the abstract immensity of their burdens, concentrated instead on the present, moment by moment. He clung to that pragmatic wisdom. He had no other answer.

Numbly, he put a piece of fruit in his mouth, began to chew.

After that, habit and hunger came to his aid. Perhaps his answer was not a good one; but it defined him, and he stood by it.

Stood or fell, he did not know which.

Nassic waited humbly, solicitously, while Covenant and Linden ate; but as soon as they finished, he said, 'Ur-Lord.' He sounded eager. 'I am your servant. It is the purpose in my life to serve you, as it was the purpose of Jous my father and Prassan his father throughout the long line of the Unfettered.' He seemed unmindful of the quaver in his words. 'You are not come too soon. The Sunbane multiplies in the Land. What will you do?'

Covenant sighed. He felt unready to deal with such questions. But the ritual of eating had steadied him. And both Nassic and Linden deserved some kind of reply. Slowly, he said, 'We'll have to go to Revelstone − ' He spoke the name hesitantly. Would Nassic recognize it? If there were no more Lords − Perhaps Revelstone no longer existed. Or perhaps all the names had changed. Enough time had passed for anything to happen.

But Nassic crowed immediately, 'Yes! Vengeance upon the Clave! It is good!'

The Clave? Covenant wondered. But he did not ask. Instead, he tested another familiar name. 'But first we'll have to go to Mithil Stonedown − '

'No!' the man interrupted. His vehemence turned at once into protest and trepidation. 'You must not. They are wicked − wicked! Worshippers of the Sunbane. They say that they abhor the Clave, but they do not. Their fields are sown with blood!'

Blood again; Sunbane; the Clave. Too many things he did not know. He concentrated on what he was trying to ascertain. Apparently, the names he remembered were known to Nassic in spite of their age. That ended his one dim hope concerning the fate of the Earthpower. A new surge of futility beat at him. How could he possibly fight Lord Foul if there were no Earthpower? No, worse – if there were no Earthpower, what was left to fight for?

But Nassic's distraught stare and Linden's clenched, arduous silence demanded responses. Grimacing, he thrust down his sense of futility. He was intimately acquainted with hopelessness, impossibility, gall; he knew how to limit their power over him.

He took a deep breath and said, 'There's no other way. We can't get out of here without going through Mithil Stonedown.'

'Ah, true,' the old man groaned. 'That is true.' He seemed almost desperate. 'Yet you must not – They are wicked! They harken to the words of the Clave – words of abomination. They mock all old promises, saying that the Unbeliever is a madness in the minds of the Unfettered. You must not go there.'

'Then how – ?' Covenant frowned grimly. What's happened to them? I used to have friends there.

Abruptly, Nassic reached a decision. 'I will go. To my son. His name is Sunder. He is wicked, like the rest. But he is my son. He comes to me when the mood is upon him, and I speak to him, telling him what is proper to his calling. He is not altogether corrupted. He will aid us to pass by the Stonedown. Yes.' At once, he threw himself towards the entryway.

'Wait!' Covenant jumped to his feet. Linden joined him.

'I must go!' cried Nassic urgently.

'Wait until the rain stops.' Covenant pleaded against the frenzy in Nassic's eyes. The man looked too decrepit to endure any more exposure. 'We're not in that much of a hurry.'

'It will not halt until nightfall. I must make haste!'

'Then at least take a torch!'

Nassic flinched as if he had been scourged. 'Ah, you shame me! I know the path. I must redeem my doubt.' Before Covenant or Linden could stop him, he ran out into the rain.

Linden started after him; but Covenant stayed her. Lightning blazed overhead. In the glare, they saw Nassic stumbling frenetically towards the end of the dell. Then thunder and blackness hit, and he disappeared as if he had been snuffed out. 'Let him go,' sighed Covenant. 'If we chase him, we'll probably fall off a cliff somewhere.' He held her until she nodded. Then he returned wearily to the fire.

She followed him. When he placed his back to the hearth, she confronted him. The dampness of her hair darkened her face, intensifying the lines between her brows, on either side of her mouth. He expected anger, protest, some outburst against the insanity of her situation. But when she spoke, her voice was flat, controlled.

'This isn't what you expected.'

'No.' He cursed himself because he could not rise above his dismay. 'No. Something terrible has happened.'

She did not waver. 'How can that be? You said the last time you were here was ten years ago. What can happen in ten years?'

Her query reminded him that he had not yet told her about Lord Foul's prophecy. But now was not the time: she was suffering from too many other incomprehensions. 'Ten years in our world.' For her sake, he did not say, *the real world*. 'Time is different here. It's faster – the way dreams are almost instantaneous sometimes. I've – ' He had difficulty meeting her stare; even his knowledge felt like shame. 'I've actually been here three times before. Each time, I was unconscious for a few hours, and months went by here. So ten years for me – Oh, bloody hell!' The Despiser had said, *For a score of centuries. For nearly as many centuries more.* 'If the ratio stays the same, we're talking about three or four thousand years.'

She accepted this as if it were just one more detail that defied rationality. 'Well, what could have happened? What's so important about hurtloam?'

He wanted to hide his head, conceal his pain; he felt too much exposed to the new penetration of her senses. 'Hurtloam was a special mud that could heal – almost anything.' Twice, while in the Land, it had cured his leprosy. But he shied away from the whole subject of healing. If he told her what hurtloam had done for him in the past, he would also have to explain why it had not done him any lasting good. He would have to tell her that the Land was physically self-contained – that it had no tangible connection to their world. The healing of his chest meant nothing. When they regained consciousness, she would find that their bodily continuity in their world was complete. Everything would be the same.

If they did not awaken soon, she would not have time to treat his wound.

Because she was already under so much stress, he spared her that knowledge. Yet he could not contain his bitterness. 'But that's not the point. Look.' He pointed at the hearth. 'Smoke. Ashes. The people I knew never built fires that destroyed wood. They didn't have to. For them, everything around them – wood, water, stone, flesh – every part of the physical world – was full of what they called Earthpower. The power of life. They could raise fire – or make boats flow upstream – or send messages – by using the Earthpower in wood instead of the wood itself.

'That was what made them who they were. The Earthpower was the essence of the Land.' Memories thronged in him, visions of the Lords, of the masters of stone- and wood-lore. 'It was so vital to them, so sustaining, that they gave their lives to it. Did everything they could to serve it, rather than exploit it. It was strength, sentience, passion. *Life*. A fire like this would have horrified them.'

But words were inadequate. He could not convey his longing for a world where aspen and granite, water and soil, nature itself, were understood, revered for their potency and loveliness. A world with a soul, deserving to be treasured. Linden gazed at him as if he were babbling. With a silent snarl, he gave up trying to explain. 'Apparently,' he said, 'they've lost it. It's forgotten. Or dead. Now they have this Sunbane. If I understand what I've been hearing – which I doubt – the Sunbane was what kept Nassic's torch burning in the rain. And he had to cut his hand to do it. And the wood was still consumed.

'He says the Sunbane is causing this rain.' Covenant shuddered involuntarily; firelight reflecting off the downpour beyond the entryway made the storm look vicious and intolerable.

Her eyes searched him. The bones of her face seemed to press against the skin, as if her skull itself protested against so many alien circumstances. 'I don't know anything about it. None of this makes sense.' She faltered. He could see fears crowding the edges of her vision. 'It's all impossible. I can't . . .' She shot a harried glance around the room, thrust her hands into her hair as though she sought to pull imminent hysteria off her features. 'I'm going crazy.'

'I know.' He recognized her desperation. His own wildness when he was first taken to the Land had led him to commit the worst crimes of his life. He wanted to reach out to her, protect her; but the numbness of his hands prevented him. Instead, he said intensely, 'Don't give up. Ask questions. Keep trying. I'll tell you everything I can.'

For a moment, her gaze ached towards him like the arms of an abandoned child. But then her hands bunched into fists. A grimace like a clench of intransigence knotted her mien. 'Questions,' she breathed through her teeth. With a severe effort, she took hold of herself. 'Yes.'

Her tone accused him as if he were to blame for her distress. But he accepted the responsibility. He could have prevented her from following him into the woods. If he had had the courage.

'All right,' she gritted. 'You've been here before. What makes you so important? What did you do? Why does Foul want you? What's an ur-Lord?'

Covenant sighed inwardly – an exhalation of relief at her determination to survive. That was what he wanted from her. A sudden weariness dimmed his sight; but he took no account of it.

'I was Berek re-born.'

The memory was not pleasant; it contained too much guilt, too much sorrow and harm. But he accepted it. 'Berek was one of the ancient heroes – thousands of years before I came along. According to the legends, he discovered the Earthpower, and made the Staff of Law to wield it. All the lore of the Earthpower came down from

90

him. He was the Lord-Fatherer, the founder of the Council of Lords. They led the defence of the Land against Foul.'

The Council, he groaned to himself, remembering Mhoram, Prothall, Elena. Hell and blood! His voice shook as he continued. 'When I showed up, they welcomed me as a sort of avatar of Berek. He was known to have lost the last two fingers of his right hand in a war.' Linden's gaze sharpened momentarily; but she did not interrupt. 'So I was made an ur-Lord of the Council. Most of those other titles came later. After I defeated Foul.

'But Unbeliever was one I took for myself. For a long time here, I was sure I was dreaming, but I didn't know what to do about it.' Sourly, he muttered, 'I was afraid to get involved. It had something to do with being a leper.' He hoped she would accept this non-explanation; he did not want to have to tell her about his crimes. 'But I was wrong. As long as you have some idea of what's happening to you, "real" or "unreal" doesn't matter. You have to stand up for what you care about; if you don't you lose control of who you are.' He paused, met her scrutiny so that she could see the clarity of his conviction. 'I ended up caring about the Land a lot.'

'Because of the Earthpower?'

'Yes.' Pangs of loss stung his heart. Fatigue and strain had shorn him of his defences. 'The Land was incredibly beautiful. And the way the people loved it, served it — that was beautiful, too. Lepers,' he concluded mordantly, 'are susceptible to beauty.' In her own way, Linden seemed beautiful to him.

She listened to him like a physician trying to diagnose a rare disease. When he stopped, she said, 'You called yourself, "Unbeliever and white gold wielder". What does white gold have to do with it?'

He scowled involuntarily. To cover his pain, he lowered himself to the floor, sat against the wall of the hearth. That question touched him deeply, and he was too tired to give it the courage it deserved. But her need for knowledge was peremptory. 'My wedding ring,' he murmured. 'When Joan divorced me, I was never able to stop wearing it. I was a leper — I felt that I'd lost everything. I thought my only link with the human race was the fact that I used to be married.

'But here it's some kind of talisman. A tool for what they call wild magic — "the wild magic that destroys peace." I can't explain it.' To himself, he cursed the paucity of his valour.

Linden sat down near him, kept watching his face. 'You think I can't handle the truth.'

He winced at her percipience. 'I don't know. But I know how hard it is. It sure as hell isn't easy for me.'

Outside, the rain beat with steady ire into the valley; thunder and lightning pummelled each other among the mountains. But inside the hut the air was warm, tinged with smoke like a faint soporific.

And he had gone for many days without rest. He closed his eyes, partly to acknowledge his exhaustion, partly to gain a respite from Linden's probing.

But she was not finished. 'Nassic – ' Her voice was as direct as if she had reached out and touched him. 'He's crazy.'

With an effort of will, Covenant forced himself to ask, 'What makes you say that?'

She was silent until he opened his eyes, looked at her. Then, defensively, she said, 'I can feel it – the imbalance in him. Can't you. It's in his face, his voice, everything. I saw it right away. When he was coming down the ravine.'

Grimly, he put off his fatigue. 'What are you trying to tell me? That we can't trust him? Can't believe him?'

'Maybe.' Now she could not meet his gaze. She studied the clasp of her hands on her knees. 'I'm not sure. All I know is, he's demented. He's been lonely too long. And he believes what he says.'

'He's not the only one,' Covenant muttered. Deliberately, he stretched out to make himself more comfortable. He was too tired to worry about Nassic's sanity. But he owed Linden one other answer. Before he let go of himself, he replied, 'No, I can't.'

As weariness washed over him he was dimly aware that she stood up and began to pace beside his recumbent form.

He was awakened by silence. The rain had stopped. For a moment, he remained still, enjoying the end of the storm. The rest had done him good; he felt stronger, more capable.

When he raised his head, he saw Linden in the entryway, facing the vale and the clear cool night. Her shoulders were tense; strain marked the way she leaned against the stone. As he got to his feet, she turned towards him. She must have replenished the fire while he slept. The room was bright; he could see her face clearly. The corners of her eyes were lined as if she had been squinting for a long time at something which discomfited her.

'It stopped at nightfall.' She indicated the absence of rain with a jerk of her head. 'He was right about that.'

The trouble in her worried him. He tried to sound casual as he asked, 'What have you been thinking?'

She shrugged. 'Nothing new. "Face it. Go forward. Find out what happens."' Her gaze was bent inward on memories. 'I've been living that way for years. It's the only way to find out how much what you're trying to get away from costs.'

He searched her for some glimpse of what she meant. 'You know,' he said slowly, 'you haven't told me much about yourself.'

She stiffened, drew severity across her countenance like a shield. Her tone denied his question. 'Nassic isn't back yet.'

For a moment, he considered her refusal. Did she have that much past hurt to hide? Were her defences aimed at him, or at herself? But then the import of her words penetrated him. 'He isn't?' Even an old man should have been able to make the trip twice in this amount of time.

'I haven't seen him.'

'Damnation!' Covenant's throat was suddenly dry. 'What the hell happened to him?'

'How should I know?' Her ire betrayed the fraying of her nerves. 'Remember me? I'm the one who hasn't been here before.'

He wanted to snap at her; but he held himself back grimly. 'I didn't mean it that way. Maybe he fell off the cliff. Maybe Mithil Stonedown is even more dangerous than he thought. Maybe he doesn't even have a son.'

He could see her swallowing her vexation, wishing herself immune to pressure. 'What are we going to do?'

'What choice have we got. We'll have to go down there ourselves.' Sternly, he compelled himself to face her doubt of Nassic. 'It's hard for me to believe we can't trust those people. They were my friends when I didn't deserve to have any friends.'

She considered him. 'That was three thousand years ago.'

Yes, he muttered bleakly. And he had given them little in return except harm. If they remembered him at all, they would be justified in remembering only the harm.

With a sudden nausea, he realized that he was going to have to tell Linden what he had done to Mithil Stonedown, to Lena Atiarandaughter. The doctor was the first woman he had met in ten years who was not afraid of him. And she had tried to save his life. What other protection could he give her against himself?

He lacked the courage. The words were in his mind, but he could not utter them. To escape her eyes, he moved abruptly past her out of Nassic's stone dwelling.

The night was a vault of crystal. All the clouds were gone. The air was cold and sharp; and stars glittered like flecks of joy across the immaculate deeps. They gave some visibility. Below the dark crouch of the peaks, he could see the stream flowing turgidly down the length of the dell. He followed it; he remembered this part of the way well enough. But then he slowed his pace as he realized that Linden was not behind him.

'Covenant'

Her cry scaled the night. Echoes repeated against the mountainsides.

He went back to her at a wild run.

She knelt on a pile of rubble like a cairn beside the hut – the broken remains of Nassic's temple, fallen into desuetude. She was examining a dark form which lay strangely atop the debris.

Covenant sprang forward, peered at the body.

Bloody hell, he moaned. Nassic.

The old man lay embracing the ruins. From the centre of his back protruded the handle of a knife.

'Don't touch that,' Linden panted. 'It's still hot.' Her mouth was full of crushed horror.

Still – ? Covenant kicked aside his dismay. 'Take his legs. We'll carry him into the house.'

She did not move. She looked small and abject in the night.

To make her move, he lashed at her, 'I told you it was dangerous. Did you think I was kidding? Take his legs!'

Her voice was a still cold articulation of darkness. 'He's dead. There's nothing we can do.'

The sound of her desolation choked his protests. For one keening moment, he feared that he had lost her – that her mind had gone over the edge. But then she shifted. Her hair fell forward, hid her face, as she bent to slip her arms under Nassic's legs.

Covenant lifted him by the shoulders. Together, they bore him into his house.

He was already stiff.

They set him down gently in the centre of the floor. Covenant inspected him. His skin was cold. There was no blood on his robe around the knife; it must have been washed away by the rain. He must have lain dead in the rain for a long time.

Linden did not watch. Her eyes clinched the black iron knife. 'It didn't kill him right away,' she said hoarsely. 'It didn't hit him right. He bled to death.' The bones of her face seemed to throb with vehemence. 'This is evil.'

The way she uttered the word *evil* sent cold fear scrabbling down Covenant's spine. He knew what she meant; he had formerly been able to perceive such things himself. She was looking at the cruelty of the hand which had held that knife, seeing the eager malice which had inspired the blow. And if the iron were still hot – He swallowed harshly. Nassic's killer must have been someone of great and brutal power.

He scrambled for explanations. 'Whoever did it knew we were here. Or else why leave him out there? He wanted us to find the body – after he got away.' He closed his eyes, forced some clarity on to his spinning thoughts. 'Nassic was killed because of us. To keep him from talking to the Stonedown. Or from talking to us. By hell, this stinks of Foul.'

Linden was not listening; her own reaction dominated her. 'Nobody does this.' She sounded lorn, fear-ravaged.

He heard the strangeness of her protest; but he could not stop himself. His old anger for the victims of Despite drove him. 'It takes a special kind of killer,' he growled, 'to leave a hot knife behind. Foul has plenty of that kind of help. He's perfectly capable of having

94

Nassic killed just to keep us from getting too much information. Or to manipulate us somehow.'

'Nobody kills like this. For pleasure.' Dull anguish blunted her tone, blinded her face. 'People don't do that.'

'Of course they don't.' Her dismay reached him; but the frailty of Nassic's dead limbs affronted him to the marrow of his bones, made his reply savage. 'He probably decided to take a nap in the rain, and this knife just fell on him out of nowhere.'

She was deaf to his sarcasm – too intimately shocked to recognize him at all. 'People kill because they're hungry. Afraid.' She struggled for certitude against the indefeasible iron. 'Driven. Because someone, something, forces them.' Her tone sharpened as if she were gathering screams. 'Nobody likes it.'

'No.' The sight of her distress pulled Covenant to her. He tried to confront her mounting repudiation. 'Everybody likes it. Everybody likes power. But most people control it. Because they hate it too. This is no different than any other murder. It's just more obvious.'

A flinch of revulsion twisted her face; his assertion seemed to hurt her. For an instant, he feared that her mind was going to fail. But then her eyes climbed to his face. The effort of self-mastery darkened them like blood. 'I want – ' Her voice quavered; she crushed it flat. 'I want to meet the sonofabitch who did this. So I can see for myself.'

Covenant nodded, gritted his own black ire. 'I think you're going to get the chance.' He, too, wanted to meet Nassic's slayer. 'We can't try to second-guess Foul. He knows more than we do. And we can't stay here. But we've lost our guide – our only chance to learn what's happening. We have to go to Mithil Stonedown.' Grimly, he concluded, 'Since the killer didn't attack us here, he's probably waiting for us in the village.'

For a long moment, she remained motionless, mustering her resources. Then she said tightly, 'Let's go.'

He did not hesitate. Nassic had not even been given the dignity of a clean death. With Linden at his side, he marched out into the night.

But in spite of the violence in him, he did not allow himself to rush. The stars did not shed any abundance of light; and the rain had left the floor of the dell slick with mud. The path to Mithil Stonedown was hazardous. He did not intend to come to harm through recklessness.

He made his way strictly down the valley; and at its end, he followed the stream into a crooked file between sheer walls, then turned away along a crevice that ascended at right angles to the file. The crevice was narrow and crude, difficult going in the star-blocked dark; but it levelled after a while, began to tend downward. Before long, he gained a steep open slope – the eastern face of the Mithil valley.

Dimly in the distance below him, the valley widened like a wedge northward towards an expanse of plains. A deeper blackness along the valley bottom looked like a river.

Beside the river, somewhat to his right, lay a cluster of tiny lights.

'Mithil Stonedown,' he murmured. But then vertigo forced him to turn away leftward along a faint path. He could not repress his memory of the time he had walked this path with Lena. Until he told Linden what he remembered, what he had done, she would not know who he was, would not be able to choose how she wished to respond to him. Or to the Land.

He needed her to understand his relationship to the Land. He needed her support, her skills, her strength. Why else had she been chosen?

A cold, penetrating dampness thickened the air; but the exertion of walking kept him warm. And the path became steadily less difficult as it descended towards the valley bottom. As the moon began to crest the peaks, he gave up all pretence of caution. He was hunting for the courage to say what had to be said.

Shortly, the path curved off the slopes, doubled back to follow the river outward. He glanced at Linden from time to time, wondering where she had learned the toughness, unwisdom, or desperation which enabled or drove her to accompany him. He ached for the capacity to descry the truth of her, determine whether her severity came from conviction or dread.

She did not believe in evil.

He had no choice; he had to tell her.

Compelling himself with excoriations, he touched her arm, stopped her. She looked at him. 'Linden.' She was alabaster in the moonlight – pale and not to be touched. His mouth winced. 'There's something I've got to say.' His visage felt like old granite. 'Before we go any farther.' Pain made him whisper.

'The first time I was here, I met a girl. Lena. She was just a kid – but she was my friend. She kept me alive on Kevin's Watch, when I was so afraid it could have killed me.' His long loneliness cried out against this self-betrayal.

'I raped her.'

She stared at him. Her lips formed soundless words: Raped – ? In her gaze, he could see himself becoming heinous.

He did not see the shadow pass over their heads, had no warning of their danger until the net landed on them, tangling them instantly together. Figures surged out of the darkness around them. One of the attackers hit them in the faces with something which broke open and stank like a rotten melon.

Then he could no longer breathe. He fell with Linden in his arms as if they were lovers.

6

THE GRAVELLER

He awoke urgently, with a suffocating muck on his face that made him strain to move his arms to clear the stuff away. But his hands were tied behind his back. He gagged helplessly for a moment, until he found that he could breathe.

The dry, chill air was harsh in his lungs. But he relished it. Slowly, it drove back the nausea.

From somewhere near him, he heard Linden say flatly, 'You'll be all right. They must have hit us with some kind of anaesthetic. It's like ether – makes you feel sick. But the nausea goes away. I don't think we've been hurt.'

He rested briefly on the cold stone, then rolled off his chest and struggled into a sitting position. The bonds made the movement difficult; a wave of dizziness went through him. 'Friends,' he muttered. But the air steadied him. 'Nassic was right.'

'Nassic was right,' she echoed as if the words did not interest her.

They were in a single room, as constricted as a cell. A heavy curtain covered the doorway; but opposite the entrance a barred window let the pale grey of dawn into the room – the late dawn of a sunrise delayed by mountains. The bars were iron.

Linden sat across from him. Her arms angled behind her; her wrists, too, were bound. Yet she had managed to clean the pulp from her cheeks. Shreds of it clung to the shoulders of her shirt.

His own face wore dried muck like a leper's numbness.

He shifted so that he could lean against the wall. The bonds cut into his wrists. He closed his eyes. A trap, he murmured. Nassic's death was a trap. He had been killed so that Covenant and Linden would blunder into Mithil Stonedown's defences and be captured. What's Foul trying to do? he asked the darkness behind his eyelids. Make us fight these people?

'Why did you do it?' Linden said. Her tone was level, as if she had already hammered all the emotion out of it. 'Why did you tell me about that girl?'

His eyes jumped open to look at her. But in the dim light he was unable to discern her expression. He wanted to say, Leave it alone, we've got other things to worry about. But she had an absolute right to know the truth about him.

'I wanted to be honest with you.' His guts ached at the memory.

'The things I did when I was here before are going to affect what happens to us now. Foul doesn't forget. And I was afraid – ' he faltered at the cost of his desire for rectitude – 'you might trust me without knowing what you were trusting. I don't want to betray you – by not being what you think I am.'

She did not reply. Her eyes were shadows which told him nothing. Abruptly, the pressure of his unassuaged bitterness began to force words out of him like barbs.

'After my leprosy was diagnosed, and Joan divorced me, I was impotent for a year. Then I came here. Something I couldn't understand was happening. The Land was healing parts of me that had been dead so long I'd forgotten I had them. And Lena – ' The pang of her stung him like an acid. 'She was so beautiful I still have nightmares about it. The first night – It was too much for me. Lepers aren't supposed to be potent.'

He did not give Linden a chance to respond; he went on, reliving his old self-judgement. 'Everybody paid for it. I couldn't get away from the consequences. Her mother ended up committing a kind of suicide. Her father's life was warped. The man who wanted to marry her lost everything. Her own mind came apart.

'But I didn't stop there. I caused her death, and the death of her daughter, Elena – *my* daughter. Because I kept trying to escape the consequences. Everybody refused to punish me. I was Berek reborn. They wanted me to save the Land. Lena – ' oh, Lena! – 'got butchered trying to save my life.'

Linden listened without moving. She looked like a figure of stone against the wall, blank and unforgiving, as if no mere recitation of guilt could touch her. But her knees were pressed tightly, defensively, to her chest. When he ceased, she said thickly, 'You shouldn't have told me.'

'I had to.' What else could he say? 'It's who I am.'

'No.' She protested as if an accusation of evil had been raised between them. 'It isn't who you are. You didn't do it intentionally, did you? You saved the Land, didn't you?'

He faced her squarely. 'Yes. Eventually.'

'Then it's over. Done with.' Her head dropped to her knees. She squeezed her forehead against them as if to restrain the pounding of her thoughts. 'Leave me alone.'

Covenant studied the top of her head, the way her hair fell about her thighs, and sought to comprehend. He had expected her to denounce him for what he had done, not for having confessed it. Why was she so vulnerable to it? He knew too little about her. But how could he ask her to tell him things which she believed people should not know about each other?

'I don't understand.' His voice was gruff with uncertainty. 'If that's the way you feel – why did you keep coming back? You went to a lot of trouble to find out what I was hiding.'

She kept her face concealed. 'I said, leave me alone.'

'I can't.' A vibration of anger ran through him. 'You wouldn't be here if you hadn't followed me. I need to know why you did it. So I can decide whether to trust you.'

Her head snapped up. 'I'm a doctor.'

'That's not enough,' he said rigidly.

The light from the window was growing slowly. Now he could read parts of her countenance – her mouth clenched and severe, her eyes like dark gouges below her forehead. She regarded him as if he were trespassing on her essential privacy.

After a long moment, she said softly, 'I followed you because I thought you were strong. Every time I saw you, you were practically prostrate on your feet. You were desperate for help. But you stood there acting as if even exhaustion couldn't touch you.' Her words were fraught with gall. 'I thought you were *strong*. But now it turns out you were just running away from your guilt, like anybody else. Trying to make yourself innocent again, by selling yourself for Joan. What was I supposed to do?' Quiet fury whetted her tone. 'Let you commit suicide?'

Before he could respond, she went on, 'You use guilt the same way you use leprosy. You want people to reject you, stay away from you – make a victim out of you. So you can recapture your innocence.' Gradually, her intensity subsided into a dull rasp. 'I've already seen more of it than I can stand. If you think I'm such a threat to you, at least leave me alone.'

Again she hid her face in her knees.

Covenant stared at her in silence. Her judgement hurt him like a demonstration of mendacity. Was *that* what he was doing – giving her a moral reason to repudiate him because she was unmoved by the physical reason of his leprosy? Was he so much afraid of being helped or trusted. Cared about? Gaping at this vision of himself, he heaved to his feet, lurched to the window as if he needed to defend his eyes by looking at something else.

But the view only gave credence to his memories. It verified that he and Linden were in Mithil Stonedown. The wall and roof of another stone dwelling stood directly in front of him; and on either side of it he could see the corners of other buildings. Their walls were ancient, weathered and battered by centuries of use. They were made without mortar, formed of large slabs and chunks of rock held together by their own weight, topped by flat roofs. And beyond the roofs were the mountains.

Above them, the sky had a brown tinge, as if it were full of dust.

He had been here before, and could not deny the truth; he was indeed afraid. Too many people who cared about him had already paid horrendously to give him help.

Linden's silence throbbed at his back like a bruise; but he remained still, and watched the sunrise flow down into the valley. When the tension in him became insistent, he said without turning, 'I wonder what they're going to do with us.'

As if in answer, the room brightened suddenly as the curtain was thrust aside. He swung around and found a man in the doorway.

The Stonedownor was about Linden's height, but broader and more muscular than Covenant. His black hair and dark skin were emphasized by the colour of his stiff leather jerkin and leggings. He wore nothing on his feet. In his right hand he held a long, wooden staff as if it articulated his authority.

He appeared to be about thirty. His features had a youthful cast; but they were contradicted by two deep frown lines above the bridge of his nose, and by the dullness of his eyes, which seemed to have been worn dim by too much accumulated and useless regret. The muscles at the corners of his jaw bulged as if he had been grinding his teeth for years.

His left arm hung at his side. From elbow to knuckle, it was intaglioed with fine white scars.

He did not speak; he stood facing Covenant and Linden as if he expected them to know why he had come.

Linden lurched to her feet. Covenant took two steps forward, so that they stood shoulder-to-shoulder before the Stonedownor.

The man hesitated, searched Covenant's face. Then he moved into the room. With his left hand, he reached out to Covenant's battered cheek.

Covenant winced slightly, then held himself still while the Stonedownor carefully brushed the dried pulp from his face.

He felt a pang of gratitude at the touch; it seemed to accord him more dignity than he deserved. He studied the man's brown, strong mien closely, trying to decipher what lay behind it.

When he was done, the Stonedownor turned and left the room, holding the curtain open for Covenant and Linden.

Covenant looked towards her to see if she needed encouragement. But she did not meet his gaze. She was already moving. He took a deep breath, and followed her out of the hut.

He found himself on the edge of the broad, round, open centre of Mithil Stonedown. It matched his memory of it closely. All the houses faced inward; and the ones beyond the inner ring were positioned to give as many as possible direct access to the centre. But now he could see that several of them had fallen into serious disrepair, as if their occupants did not know how to mend them. If that were true – He snarled to himself. How could these people have forgotten their stone-lore?

The sun shone over the eastern ridge into his face. Squinting at it indirectly, he saw that the orb had lost its blue aurora. Now it wore

100

pale brown like a translucent cymar.

The Stonedown appeared deserted. All the door-curtains were closed. Nothing moved – not in the village, not on the mountainsides or in the air. He could not even hear the river. The valley lay under the dry dawn as if it had been stricken dumb.

A slow scraping of fear began to abrade his nerves.

The man with the staff strode out into the circle, beckoning for Covenant and Linden to follow him across the bare stone. As they did so, he gazed morosely around the village. He leaned on his staff as if the thews which held his life together were tired.

But after a moment he shook himself into action. Slowly, he raised the staff over his head. In a determined tone, he said, 'This is the centre.'

At once, the curtains opened. Men and women stepped purposefully out of their homes.

They were all solid dark people, apparelled in leather garments. They formed a ring like a noose around the rim of the circle, and stared at Covenant and Linden. Their faces were wary, hostile, shrouded. Some of them bore blunt javelins like jerrids; but no other weapons were visible.

The man with the staff joined them. Together, the ring of Stonedownors sat down cross-legged on the ground.

Only one man remained standing. He stayed behind the others, leaning against the wall of a house with his arms folded negligently across his chest. His lips wore a rapacious smile like an anticipation of bloodshed.

Covenant guessed instinctively that this man was Mithil Stonedown's executioner.

The villagers made no sound. They watched Covenant and Linden without moving, almost without blinking. Their silence was loud in the air, like the cry of a throat that had no voice.

The sun began to draw sweat from Covenant's scalp.

'Somebody say something,' he muttered through his teeth.

Abruptly, Linden nudged his arm. 'That's what they're waiting for. We're on trial. They want to hear what we've got to say for ourselves.'

'Terrific.' He accepted her intuitive explanation at once; she had eyes which he lacked. 'What're we on trial for?'

Grimly, she replied, 'Maybe they found Nassic.'

He groaned. That made sense. Perhaps Nassic had been killed precisely so that he and Linden would be blamed for the crime. And yet – He tugged at his bonds, wishing his hands were free so that he could wipe the sweat from his face. And yet it did not explain why they had been captured in the first place.

The silence was intolerable. The mountains and the houses cupped the centre of the village like an arena. The Stonedownors sat impassively, like icons of judgement. Covenant scanned them, mustered what little dignity he possessed. Then he began to speak.

'My name is ur-Lord Thomas Covenant, Unbeliever and white gold wielder. My companion is Linden Avery.' Deliberately, he gave her a title. 'The Chosen. She's a stranger to the Land.' The dark people returned his gaze blankly. The man leaning against the wall bared his teeth. 'But I'm no stranger,' Covenant went on in sudden anger. 'You threaten me at your peril.'

'Covenant,' Linden breathed, reproving him.

'I know,' he muttered. 'I shouldn't say things like that.' Then he addressed the people again. 'We were welcomed by Nassic son of Jous. He wasn't a friend of yours – or you weren't friends of his, because God knows he was harmless.' Nassic had looked so lorn in death – 'But he said he had a son here. A man named Sunder. Is Sunder here? Sunder?' He searched the ring. No one responded. 'Sunder,' he rasped, 'whoever you are – do you know your father was murdered? We found him outside his house with an iron knife in his back. The knife was still hot.'

Someone in the circle gave a low moan; but Covenant did not see who it was. Linden shook her head; she also had not seen.

The sky had become pale brown from edge to edge. The heat of the sun was as arid as dust.

'I think the killer lives here. I think he's one of you. Or don't you even care about that?'

Nobody reacted. Every face regarded him as if he were some kind of ghoul. The silence was absolute.

'Hellfire.' He turned back to Linden. 'I'm just making a fool out of myself. You got any ideas?'

Her gaze wore an aspect of supplication. 'I don't know – I've never been here before.'

'Neither have I.' He could not suppress his ire. 'Not to a place like this. Courtesy and hospitality used to be so important here that people who couldn't provide them were ashamed.' Remembering the way Trell and Atiaran, Lena's parents, had welcomed him to their home, he ground his teeth. With a silent curse, he confronted the Stonedownors. 'Are the other villages like this?' he demanded. 'Is the whole Land sick with suspicion? Or is this the only place where simple decency has been forgotten?'

The man with the staff lowered his eyes. No one else moved.

'By God, if you can't at least tolerate us, let us go! We'll walk out of here, and never look back. Some other village will give us what we need.'

The man behind the circle gave a grin of malice and triumph.

'Damnation,' Covenant muttered to himself. The silence was maddening. His head was beginning to throb. The valley felt like a desert. 'I wish Mhoram was here.'

Dully, Linden asked, 'Who is Mhoram?' Her eyes were fixed on the standing man. He commanded her attention like an open wound.

'One of the Lords of Revelstone.' Covenant wondered what she was seeing. 'Also a friend. He had a talent for dealing with impossible situations.'

She wrenched her gaze from the gloating man, glared at Covenant. Frustration and anxiety made her tone sabulous. 'He's dead. All your friends are dead.' Her shoulders strained involuntarily at her bonds. 'They've been dead for three thousand years. You're living in the past. How bad do things have to get before you give up thinking about the way they used to be?'

'I'm trying to understand what's happened!' Her attack shamed him. It was unjust – and yet he deserved it. Everything he said demonstrated his inadequacy. He swung away from her.

'Listen to me!' he beseeched the Stonedownors. 'I've been here before – long ago, during the great war against the Grey Slayer. I fought him. So the Land could be healed. And men and women from Mithil Stonedown helped me. Your ancestors. The Land was saved by the courage of Stonedownors and Woodhelvennin and Lords and Giants and Bloodguard and Ranyhyn.

'But something's happened. There's something wrong in the Land. That's why we're here.' Remembering the old song of Kevin Landwaster, he said formally, 'So that beauty and truth should not pass utterly from the Earth.'

With tone, face, posture, he begged for some kind of response, acknowledgement, from the circle. But the Stonedownors refused every appeal. His exertions had tightened the bonds on his wrists, aggravating the numbness of his hands. The sun began to raise heatwaves in the distance. He felt giddy, futile.

'I don't know what you want,' he breathed thickly. 'I don't know what you think we're guilty of. But you're wrong about her.' He indicated Linden with his head. 'She's never been here before. She's innocent.'

A snort of derision stopped him.

He found himself staring at the man who stood behind the circle. Their eyes came together like a clash of weapons. The man had lost his grin; he glared scorn and denunciation at Covenant. He held violence folded in the crooks of his elbows. But Covenant did not falter. He straightened his back, squared his shoulders, met the naked threat of the man's gaze.

After one taut moment, the man looked away.

Softly, Covenant said, 'We're not on trial here. You are. The doom of the Land is in your hands, and you're blind to it.'

An instant of silence covered the village; the whole valley seemed to hold its breath. Then the lone man cried suddenly, 'Must we hear more?' Contempt and fear collided in his tone. 'He has uttered foulness enough to damn a score of strangers. Let us pass judgement now!'

At once, the man with the staff sprang to his feet. 'Be still, Marid,' he said sternly. 'I am the Graveller of Mithil Stonedown. The test of silence is mine to begin – and to end.'

'It is enough!' retorted Marid. 'Can there be greater ill than that which he has already spoken?'

A dour crepitation of assent ran through the circle.

Linden moved closer to Covenant. Her eyes were locked to Marid as if he appalled her. Nausea twisted her mouth. Covenant looked at her, at Marid, trying to guess what lay between them.

'Very well.' The Graveller took a step forward. 'It is enough.' He planted his staff on the stone. 'Stonedownors, speak what you have heard.'

For a moment, the people were still. Then an old man rose slowly to his feet. He adjusted his jerkin, pulled his gravity about him. 'I have heard the Rede of the na-Mhoram, as it is spoken by the Riders of the Clave. They have said that the coming of the man with the halfhand and the white ring bodes unending ruin for us all. They have said that it is better to slay such a man in his slumber, allowing the blood to fall wasted to the earth, than to permit him one free breath with which to utter evil. Only the ring must be preserved, and given to the Riders, so that all blasphemy may be averted from the Land.'

Blasphemy? Clave? Covenant grappled uselessly with his incomprehension. Who besides Nassic's Unfettered ancestor had foretold the return of the Unbeliever?

The old man concluded with a nod to the Graveller. Opposite him, a middle-aged woman stood. Jabbing her hand towards Covenant, she said, 'He spoke the name of the na-Mhoram as a friend. Are not the na-Mhoram and all his Clave bitter to Mithil Stonedown? Do not his Riders reave us of blood – and not of the old whose deaths are nigh, but of the young whose lives are precious? Let these two die! Our herd has already suffered long days without forage.'

'Folly!' the old man replied. 'You will not speak so when next the Rider comes. It will be soon – our time nears again. In all the Land only the Clave has power over the Sunbane. The burden of their sacrificing is heavy to us – but we would lack life altogether if they failed to spend the blood of the villages.'

'Yet is there not a contradiction here?' the Graveller interposed. 'He names the na-Mhoram as friend – and yet the most dire Rede of the Clave speaks against him.'

'For both they must die!' Marid spat immediately. 'The na-Mhoram is not our friend, but his power is sure.'

'True!' voices said around the ring.

'Yes.'

'True.'

Linden brushed Covenant with her shoulder. 'That man,' she whispered. 'Marid. There's something – Do you see it?'

'No,' responded Covenant through his teeth. 'I told you I can't. What is it?'

'I don't know.' She sounded frightened. 'Something – '

Then another woman stood. 'He seeks to be released so that he may go to another Stonedown. Are not all other villages our foes? Twice has Windshorn Stonedown raided our fields during the fertile sun, so that our bellies shrank and our children cried in the night. Let the friends of our foes die.'

Again the Stonedownors growled, 'Yes.'

'True.'

Without warning, Marid shouted over the grumble of voices, 'They slew Nassic father of Sunder! Are we a people to permit murder unavenged? They must die!'

'No!' Linden's instantaneous denial cracked across the circle like a scourge. 'We did not kill that harmless old man!'

Covenant whirled to her. But she did not notice him; her attention was consumed by Marid.

In a tone of acid mockery, the man asked, 'Do you fear to die, Linden Avery the Chosen?'

'What is it?' she gritted back at him. 'What are you?'

'What do you see?' Covenant urged. *'Tell me.'*

'Something – ' Her voice groped; but her stare did not waver. Perspiration had darkened her hair along the line of her forehead. 'It's like that storm. Something evil.'

Intuitions flared like spots of sun-blindness across Covenant's mind. 'Something hot.'

'Yes!' Her gaze accused Marid fiercely. 'Like the knife.'

Covenant spun, confronted Marid. He was suddenly calm. 'You,' he said. 'Marid. Come here.'

'No, Marid,' commanded the Graveller.

'Hell and blood!' Covenant rasped like deliberate ice. 'My hands are tied. Are you afraid to find out the truth?' He did not glance at the Graveller; he held Marid with his will. 'Come here. I'll show you who killed Nassic.'

'Watch out,' Linden whispered. 'He wants to hurt you.'

Scorn twisted Marid's face. For a moment, he did not move. But now all the eyes of the Stonedown were on him, watching his reaction. And Covenant gave him no release. A spasm of fear or glee tightened Marid's expression. Abruptly, he strode forward, halted in front of Covenant and the Graveller. 'Speak your lies,' he sneered. 'You will choke upon them before you die.'

Covenant did not hesitate. 'Nassic was stabbed in the back,' he said softly, 'with an iron knife. It was a lousy job – he bled to death. When we left him, the knife was still hot.'

Marid swallowed convulsively. 'You are a fool. What man or woman of Mithil Stonedown could wield a knife with the fire yet within it? Out of your own mouth you are condemned.'

'Graveller,' Covenant said, 'touch him with your staff.'

Around him, the Stonedownors rose to their feet.

'For what purpose?' the Graveller asked uncertainly. 'It is mere wood. It has no virtue to determine guilt or innocence.'

Covenant clinched Marid in his gaze. '*Do it.*'

Hesitantly, the Graveller obeyed.

As the tip of the staff neared him, Marid shied. But then a savage exaltation lit his face, and he remained still.

The staff touched his shoulder.

Instantly, the wood burst into red fire.

The Graveller recoiled in astonishment. Stonedownors gasped, gripped each other for reassurance.

With an explosive movement, Marid backhanded Covenant across the side of his head.

The unnatural power of the blow catapulted Covenant backwards. He tumbled heavily to the ground. Pain like acid burned through his sore skull.

'Covenant!' Linden cried fearfully.

He heard the Graveller protest, 'Marid!' – heard the fright of the Stonedownors turn to anger. Then the pain became a roaring that deafened him. For a moment, he was too dizzy to move. But he fought the fire, heaved himself to his knees so that everyone could see the mark of Marid's blow among his bruises. 'Nice work, you bastard,' he rasped. His voice seemed to make no sound. 'What were you afraid of? Did you think he was going to help us that much? Or were you just having fun?'

He was aware of the low buzzing around him, but could not make out words. Marid stood with arms across his chest, grinning.

Covenant thrust his voice through the roar. 'Why don't you tell us your real name? Is it Herem? Jehannum? Maybe Sheol?'

Linden was beside him. She strove fervidly to free her hands; but the bonds held. Her mouth chewed dumb curses.

'Come on,' he continued, though he could barely see Marid beyond the pain. 'Attack me. Take your chances. Maybe I've forgotten how to use it.'

Abruptly, Marid began to laugh: laughter as gelid as hate. It penetrated Covenant's hearing, resounded in his head like a concussion. 'It will avail you nothing!' he shouted. 'Your death is certain! You cannot harm me!'

The Graveller brandished his flaming staff at Marid. Dimly, Covenant heard the man rage, 'Have you slain Nassic my father?'

'With joy!' laughed the Raver. 'Ah, how it fed me to plant my blade in his back!'

A woman shrieked. Before anyone could stop her, she sped in a blur of grey hair across the open space, hurled herself at Marid.

He collapsed as if the impact had killed him.

Covenant's strength gave out. He fell to his back, lay panting heavily on the stone.

Then a stench of burned flesh sickened the air. One of the Stonedownors cried out, 'Sunder! Her hands!'

Another demanded, 'Is he slain?'

'No!' came the reply.

Linden was yelling. 'Let me go! I'm a doctor! I can help her!' She sounded frantic. 'Don't you know what a doctor is?'

A moment later, hands gripped Covenant's arms, lifted him to his feet. A Stonedownor swam towards him through the hurt; slowly, the face resolved, became the Graveller. His brow was a knot of anger and grief. Stiffly, he said, 'Marid sleeps. My mother is deeply burned. Tell me the meaning of this.'

'A Raver.' Covenant's breathing shuddered in his lungs. 'Bloody hell.' He could not think or find the words he needed.

The Graveller bunched his fists in Covenant's shirt. 'Speak!'

From somewhere nearby, Linden shouted, 'Goddamn it, leave him alone! Can't you see he's hurt?'

Covenant fought for clarity. 'Let her go,' he said to the Graveller. 'She's a healer.'

The muscles along the Graveller's jaw knotted, released. 'I have not been given reason to trust her. Speak to me of Marid.'

Marid, Covenant panted. 'Listen.' Sweating and dizzy, he squeezed the pain out of his mind. 'It was a Raver.'

The Graveller's glare revealed no comprehension.

'When he wakes up, he'll probably be normal again. May not even remember what happened. He was taken over. That Raver could be anywhere. It isn't hurt. You need a lot of power to knock one of them out, even temporarily. You've got to watch for it. It could take over anybody. Watch for somebody who starts acting strange. Violent. Stay away from them. I mean it.'

The Graveller listened first with urgency, then with disgust. Exasperation pulsed in the veins of his temples. Before Covenant finished, the Stonedownor turned on his heel, strode away.

Immediately, the hands holding Covenant's arms dragged him out of the centre of the village.

Linden was ahead of him. She struggled uselessly between two burly men. They impelled him back into their jail.

'Damnation,' Covenant said. His voice had no force. 'I'm trying to warn you.'

107

His captors did not respond. They thrust him into the hut after Linden, and let him fall.

He sank to the floor. The cool dimness of the room washed over him. The suddenness of his release from the sun's brown pressure made the floor wheel. But he rested his pain on the soothing stone; and gradually that quiet touch steadied him.

Linden was cursing bitterly in the stillness. He tried to raise his head. 'Linden.'

At once, she moved to his side. 'Don't try to get up. Just let me see it.'

He turned his head to show her his hurt.

She bent over him. He could feel her breath on his cheek. 'You're burned, but it doesn't look serious. First-degree.' Her tone twitched with nausea and helplessness. 'None of the bones are cracked. How do you feel?'

'Dizzy,' he murmured. 'Deaf. I'll be all right.'

'Sure you will,' she grated. 'You probably have a concussion. I'll bet you want to go to sleep.'

He mumbled assent. The darkness in his head offered him cool peace, and he longed to let himself drown in it.

She took a breath through her teeth. 'Sit up.'

He did not move; he lacked the strength to obey her.

She nudged him with her knee. 'I'm serious. If you go to sleep, you might drift into a coma, and I won't be able to do anything about it. You've got to stay awake. Sit up.'

The ragged edge in her voice sounded like a threat of hysteria. Gritting his teeth, he tried to rise. Hot pain flayed the bones of his head; but he pried himself erect, then slumped to the side so that his shoulder was braced against the wall.

'Good,' Linden sighed. The pounding in his skull formed a gulf between them. She seemed small and lonely, aggrieved by the loss of the world she understood. 'Now try to stay alert. Talk to me.' After a moment, she said, 'Tell me what happened.'

He recognized her need. Marid incarnated the fears which Nassic's death had raised for her. A being who lived on hate, relished violence and anguish. She knew nothing about such things.

'A Raver.' Covenant tried to slip his voice quietly past the pain. 'I should have known. Marid is just a Stonedownor. He was possessed by a Raver.'

Linden backed away from him, composed herself against the opposite wall. Her gaze held his face. 'What's a Raver?'

'Servant of Foul.' He closed his eyes, leaned his head to the stone, so that he could concentrate on what he was saying. 'There are three of them. Herem, Sheol, Jehannum – they have a lot of different names. They don't have bodies of their own, so they take over other people – even animals, I guess. Whatever they can find. So they're always in disguise.' He sighed – gently, to minimize the effect on his head. 'I just hope these people understand what that means.'

'So,' she asked carefully, 'what I saw was the Raver inside Marid? That's why he looked so – so wrong?'

'Yes.' When he focused on her voice, his hurt became less demanding; it grew hotter, but also more specific and limited. As a fire in his skin rather than a cudgel in his brain, it crippled his thinking less. 'Marid was just a victim. The Raver used him to kill Nassic – set us up for this. What I don't know is why. Does Foul want us killed here? Or is there something else going on? If Foul wants us dead, that Raver made a big mistake when it let itself get caught. Now the Stonedown has something besides us to think about.'

'What I don't know,' Linden said in a lorn voice like an appeal, 'is how I was able to see it. None of this is possible.'

Her tone sparked unexpected memories. Suddenly, he realized that the way she had stared at Marid was the same way she had regarded Joan. That encounter with Joan had shaken her visibly.

He opened his eyes, watched her as he said, 'That's one of the few things that seems natural to me. I used to be able to see what you're seeing now – the other times I was here.' Her face was turned towards him, but she was not looking at him. Her attention was bent inward as she struggled with the lunacy of her predicament. 'Your senses,' he went on, trying to help her, 'are becoming attuned to the Land. You're becoming sensitive to the physical spirit around you. More and more, you're going to look at something, or hear it, or touch it, and be able to tell whether it's sick or healthy – natural or unnatural.' She did not appear to hear him. Defying his pain, he rasped, 'Which isn't happening to me.' He wanted to pull her out of herself before she lost her way. 'For all I can see, I might as well be blind.'

Her head flinched from side to side. 'What if I'm wrong?' she breathed miserably. 'What if I'm losing my mind?'

'No! That part of you is never going to be wrong. And you can't lose your mind unless you let it happen.' Wildness knuckled her features. '*Don't give up.*'

She heard him. With an effort that wrung his heart, she compelled her body to relax, muscle by muscle. She drew a breath that trembled; but when she exhaled, she was calmer. 'I just feel so helpless.'

He said nothing, waiting for her.

After a moment, she sniffed sharply, shook her hair away from her face, met his gaze. 'If these Ravers can possess anybody,' she said, 'why not us? If we're so important – if this Lord Foul is what you say he is – why doesn't he just make us into Ravers, and get it over with?'

109

With a silent groan of relief, Covenant allowed himself to sag. 'That's the one thing he can't do. He can't afford it. He'll manipulate us every way he can, but he has to accept the risk that we won't do what he wants. He needs our freedom. What he wants from us won't have any value if we don't do it by choice.' Also, he went on to himself, Foul doesn't dare let a Raver get my ring. How could he trust one of them with that much power?

Linden frowned. 'That might make sense – if I understood what makes us so important. What we've got that he could possibly want. But never mind that now.' She took a deep breath. 'If I could see the Raver – why couldn't anybody else?'

Her question panged Covenant. 'That's what really scares me,' he said tautly. 'These people used to be like you. Now they aren't.' And I'm not. 'I'm afraid even to think about what that means. They've lost – ' Lost the insight which taught them to love and serve the Land – to care about it above everything else. Oh, Foul, you bastard, what have you done? 'If they can't see the difference between a Raver and a normal man, then they won't be able to see that they should trust us.'

Her mouth tightened. 'You mean they're still planning to kill us.'

Before Covenant could reply, the curtain was thrust aside, and the Graveller entered the room.

His eyes were glazed with trouble, and his brow wore a scowl of involition and mourning, as if his essential gentleness had been harmed. He had left his staff behind; his hands hung at his sides. But he could not keep them still. They moved in slight jerks, half gestures, as if they sought unconsciously for something he could hold on to.

After a moment of awkwardness, he sat down on his heels near the entryway. He did not look at his prisoners; his gaze lay on the floor between them.

'Sunder,' Covenant said softly, 'son of Nassic.'

The Graveller nodded without raising his eyes.

Covenant waited for him to speak. But the Graveller remained silent, as if he were abashed. After a moment, Covenant said, 'That woman who attacked Marid. She was your mother.'

'Kalina Nassic-mate, daughter of Alloma.' He held himself harshly quiet. 'My mother.'

Linden peered intently at Sunder. 'How is she?'

'She rests. But her injury is deep. We have little healing for such hurts. It may be that she will be sacrificed.'

Covenant saw Linden poised to demand to be allowed to help the woman. But he forestalled her. 'Sacrificed?'

'Her blood belongs to the Stonedown.' Sunder's voice limped under a weight of pain. 'It must not be wasted. Only Nassic my father would not have accepted this. Therefore – ' his throat knotted

– 'it is well he knew not that I am the Graveller of Mithil Stonedown. For it is I who will shed the sacrifice.'

Linden recoiled. Aghast, Covenant exclaimed, 'You're going to sacrifice your own mother?'

'For the survival of the Stonedown!' croaked Sunder. 'We must have blood.' Then he clamped down his emotion. 'You also will be sacrificed. The Stonedown has made its judgement. You will be shed at the rising of the morrow's sun.'

Covenant glared at the Graveller. Ignoring the throb in his head, he rasped, 'Why?'

'I have come to make answer.' Sunder's tone and his downcast eyes reproved Covenant. The Graveller plainly loathed his responsibility; yet he did not shirk it. 'The reasons are many. You have asked to be released so that you may approach another village.'

'I'm looking for friends,' Covenant countered stiffly. 'If I can't find them here, I'll try somewhere else.'

'No.' The Graveller was certain. 'Another Stonedown would do as we do. Because you come to them from Mithil Stonedown, they would sacrifice you. In addition,' he continued, 'you have spoken friendship for the na-Mhoram, who reaves us of blood.'

Covenant blinked at Sunder. These accusations formed a pattern he could not decipher. 'I don't know any na-Mhoram. The Mhoram I knew has been dead for at least three thousand years.'

'That is not possible.' Sunder spoke without raising his head. 'You have no more than twoscore years.' His hands twisted. 'But that signifies little beside the Rede of the Clave. Though the Riders are loathly to us, their power and knowledge is beyond doubt. They have foretold your coming for a generation. And they are nigh. A Rider will arrive soon to enforce the will of the Clave. Retribution for any disregard would be sore upon us. Their word is one we dare not defy. Our sole concern is that the shedding of your blood may aid the survival of the Stonedown.'

'Wait,' Covenant objected. 'One thing at a time.' Pain and exasperation vied in his head. 'Three thousand years ago, a man with a halfhand and a white gold ring saved the Land from being completely destroyed by the Grey Slayer. Do you mean to tell me that's been forgotten? Nobody remembers the story?'

The Graveller shifted his weight uncomfortably. 'I have heard such a tale – perhaps I alone in Mithil Stonedown. Nassic my father spoke of such things. But he was mad – lost in his wits like Jous and Prassan before him. He would have been sacrificed to the need of the Stonedown, had Kalina his wife and I permitted it.'

Sunder's tone was a revelation to Covenant. It provided him a glimpse of the Graveller's self-conflict. Sunder was torn between what his father had taught him and what the Stonedown accepted as truth. Consciously, he believed what his people believed; but the convictions of his half-mad father worked on him below the surface, eroding his confidence. He was a man unreconciled to himself.

This insight softened Covenant's vexation. He sensed a range of possibilities in Sunder, intuitions of hope; but he handled them gingerly. 'All right,' he said. 'Let that pass. How is killing us going to help you?'

'I am the Graveller. With blood I am able to shape the Sunbane.' The muscles along his jaw clenched and relaxed without rhythm or purpose. 'Today we lie under the desert sun – today, and for perhaps as many as three days more. Before this day, the sun of rain was upon us, and it followed the sun of pestilence. Our herd needs forage, as we need crops. With your blood, I will be able to draw water from the hard earth. I will be able to raise an acre, perhaps two acres, of grass and grain. Life for the Stonedown, until the fertile sun comes again.'

This made no sense to Covenant. Fumbling for comprehension, he asked, 'Can't you get water out of the river?'

'There is no water in the river.'

Abruptly, Linden spoke. 'No water?' The words conveyed the depth of her incredulity. 'That's not possible. It *rained* yesterday.'

'I have said,' Sunder snapped like a man in pain, 'that we lie under the desert sun. Have you not beheld it?'

In his astonishment, Covenant turned to Linden. 'Is he telling the truth?'

Sunder's head jerked up. His eyes flicked back and forth between Covenant and Linden.

Through her teeth, she said, 'Yes. It's true.'

Covenant trusted her hearing. He swung back to the Graveller. 'So there's no water.' Steadiness rose in him – a mustering of his resources. 'Let that pass, too.' The throb in his head insisted on his helplessness; but he closed his ears to it. 'Tell me how you do it. How you shape the Sunbane.'

Sunder's eyes expressed his reluctance. But Covenant held the Graveller with his demand. Whatever strength of will Sunder possessed, he was too unsure of himself now to refuse. How many times had his father told him about the Unbeliever? After a moment, he acceded. 'I am the Graveller.' He reached a hand into his jerkin. 'I bear the Sunstone.'

Almost reverently, he drew out a piece of rock half the size of his fist. The stone was smooth, irregularly shaped. By some trick of its surface, it appeared transparent, but nothing showed through it. It was like a hole in his hand.

'Hellfire,' Covenant breathed. Keen relief ran through him. Here was one hard solid piece of hope. '*Orcrest.*'

The Graveller peered at him in surprise. 'Do you have knowledge of the Sunstone?'

'Sunder.' Covenant spoke stiffly to control his excitement and anxiety. 'If you try to kill us with that thing, people are going to get hurt.'

The Stonedownor shook his head. 'You will not resist. *Mirkfruit* will be broken in your faces – the same melon which made you captive. There will be no pain.'

'Oh, there will be pain,' growled Covenant. 'You'll be in pain.' Deliberately, he put pressure on the Graveller. 'You'll be the only one in this whole Stonedown who knows you're destroying the last hope of the Land. It's too bad your father died. He would have found some way to convince you.'

'Enough!' Sunder almost shouted at the laceration of his spirit. 'I have uttered the words I came to speak. In this at least I have shown you what courtesy I may. If there is aught else that you would say, then say it and have done. I must be about my work.'

Covenant did not relent. 'What about Marid?'

Sunder jerked to his feet, stood glowering down at Covenant. 'He is a slayer, unshriven by any benefit to the Stonedown – a violator of the Rede which all accept. He will be punished.'

'You're going to punish him?' Covenant's control faltered in agitation. 'What for?' He struggled erect, thrust his face at the Graveller. 'Didn't you hear what I told you? He's innocent. He was taken over by a Raver. It wasn't his fault.'

'Yes,' Sunder retorted. 'And he is my friend. But you say he is innocent, and your words have no meaning. We know nothing of any Raver. The Rede is the Rede. He will be punished.'

'Goddamn it!' snapped Covenant. 'Did you touch him?'

'Am I a fool? Yes, I put my hand upon him. The fire of his guilt is gone. He has awakened and is tormented with the memory of a noisome thing which came upon him out of the rain. Yet his act remains. He will be punished.'

Covenant wanted to take hold of the Graveller, shake him. But his efforts only made the bonds cut deeper into his wrists. Darkly, he asked, 'How?'

'He will be bound.' The soft violence of Sunder's tone sounded like self-flagellation. 'Borne out into the Plains during the night. The Sunbane will have no mercy for him.' In ire or regret, he evaded Covenant's glare.

With an effort, Covenant put aside the question of Marid's fate, postponed everything he did not understand about the Sunbane. Instead, he asked, 'Are you really going to kill Kalina?'

Sunder's hands twitched as if they wanted Covenant's throat. 'Should it ever come to pass that I am free to leave this room,' he rasped acidly, 'I will do my utmost to heal her. Her blood will not be shed until her death is written on her forehead for all to see. Do you seek to prevent me from her side?'

The Graveller's distress touched Covenant. His indignation fell away. He shook his head, then urged quietly, 'Untie Linden. Take her with you. She's a healer. Maybe she – '

Linden interrupted him. 'No.' Despite its flatness, her voice carried a timbre of despair. 'I don't even have my bag. She needs a hospital, not wishful thinking. Let him make his own decisions.'

Covenant wheeled towards her. Was this the same woman who had insisted with such passion, *I can help her!* Her face was half hidden by her hair. 'Isn't there anything you can do?'

'Third-degree burns – ' she articulated each word as if it were a mask for the contradictions of her heart – 'are hard enough to treat under the best circumstances. If he wants to commit euthanasia, that's his business. Don't be so goddamn judgemental.'

Without transition, she addressed Sunder. 'We need food.'

He regarded her suspiciously. 'Linden Avery, there are things that I would give you for your ease, but food is not among them. We do not waste food on any man, woman, or child who is under judgement. Kalina my mother will not be given food unless I am able to show that she can be healed.'

She did not deign to look at him. 'We also need water.'

Cursing sourly, Sunder turned on his heel, slapped the curtain out of his way. As he left, he snapped, 'You will have water.' Outside, he yelled at someone, 'The prisoners require water!' Then he passed beyond earshot.

Covenant watched the swaying of the curtain, and strove to still his confusion. He could feel his pulse beating like the rhythm of slow flame in the bones of his skull. What was wrong with Linden? Moving carefully, he went to her. She sat with her gaze lowered, her features shrouded by the dimness of the room. He sank to his knees to ask her what was the matter.

She faced him harshly, shook her hair. 'I must be hysterical. These people are planning to kill us. For some silly reason, that bothers me.'

He studied her for a moment, measuring her belligerence, then retreated to sit against the opposite wall. What else could he do? She was already foundering; he could not insist that she surrender her secrets to him. In her straits, during his first experience with the Land, he had lost himself so badly – He closed his eyes, groped for courage. Then he sighed, 'Don't worry about it. They're not going to kill us.'

'Naturally not.' Her tone was vicious. 'You're Thomas Covenant, Unbeliever and white gold wielder. They won't dare.'

Her scorn hurt him; but he made an effort to suppress his anger. 'We'll get out of here tonight.'

'How?' she demanded bluntly.

'Tonight – ' he could not silence his weariness – 'I'll try to show Sunder why he ought to let us go.'

A moment later, someone pushed two large stoneware bowls of water past the curtain. Linden reacted to them as if they were the only explicable things in the room. She shuttled towards them on her knees, lowered her head to drink deeply.

When Covenant joined her, she ordered him to use the bowl she had used. He obeyed to avoid an argument; but her reasons became clear when she told him to put his hands in the still-full bowl. The water might reduce their swelling, allow more blood past the bonds – perhaps even loosen the bonds themselves.

Apparently, his wrists were tied with leather; as he followed her instructions, the cool fluid palliated his discomfort; and a short while later he felt a tingle of recovery in his palms. He tried to thank her with a smile: but she did not respond. When he left the water, she took his place, soaked her own hands for a long time.

Gradually, Covenant's attention drifted away from her. The sun was beginning to slant towards afternoon; a bright hot sliver of light dissected by iron bars lay on the floor. He rested his head, and thought about the Sunstone.

Orcrest – a stone of power. The former masters of stone-lore had used *orcrest* to wield the Earthpower in a variety of ways – to shed light, break droughts, test truth. If Sunder's Sunstone were indeed *orcrest* –

But what if it were not? Covenant returned to the dread which had struck him in Nassic's hut. *The world is not what it was.* If there were no Earthpower –

Something broken. He could not deny his anguish. He needed *orcrest*, needed its power; he had to have a trigger. He had never been able to call up wild magic of his own volition. Even in the crisis of his final confrontation with the Despiser, he would have been lost utterly without the catalyst of the Illearth Stone. If the Sunstone were not truly *orcrest* –

He wished that he could feel his ring; but even if his hands had not been bound, his fingers would have been too numb. Leper, he muttered. Make it work. Make it. The sunlight became a white cynosure, growing until it throbbed like the pain in his head. Slowly, his mind filled with a brightness more fearsome and punishing than any night. He opposed it as if he were a fragment of the last kind dark which healed and renewed.

Then Linden was saying, 'Covenant. You've slept enough. It's dangerous if you have a concussion. Covenant.'

The dazzle in his brain blinded him momentarily; he had to squint to see that the room was dim. Sunset faintly coloured the air. The sky beyond the window lay in twilight.

He felt stiff and groggy, as if his life had congealed within him while he slept. His pain had burrowed into the bone; but it, too, seemed imprecise – stupefied by fatigue. At Linden's urging, he drank the remaining water. It cleared his throat, but could not unclog his mind.

For a long time, they sat without speaking. Night filled the valley like an exudation from the mountains; the air turned cool as the earth lost its warmth to the clear heavens. At first, the stars were as vivid as language – an articulation of themselves across the distance and the unfathomable night. But then the sky lost its depth as the moon rose.

'Covenant,' Linden breathed, 'talk to me.' Her voice was as fragile as ice. She was near the limit of her endurance.

He searched for something that would help them both, fortify her and focus him.

'I don't want to die like this,' she grated. 'Without even knowing why.'

He ached because he could not explain why, could not give her his sense of purpose. But he knew a story which might help her to understand what was at stake. Perhaps it was a story they both needed to hear. 'All right,' he said quietly. 'I'll tell you how this world came to be created.'

She did not answer. After a moment, he began.

Even to himself, his voice sounded bodiless, as if the dark were speaking for him. He was trying to reach out to her with words, though he could not see her, and had no very clear idea of who she was. His tale was a simple one; but for him its simplicity grew out of long distillation. It made even his dead nerves yearn as if he were moved by an eloquence he did not possess.

In the measureless heavens of the universe, he told her, where life and space were one, and the immortals strode through an ether without limitation, the Creator looked about him, and his heart swelled with the desire to make a new thing to gladden his bright children. Summoning his strength and subtlety, he set about the work which was his exaltation.

First he forged the Arch of Time, so that the world he wished to make would have a place to be. And then within the Arch he formed the Earth. Wielding the greatness of his love and vision as tools, he made the world in all its beauty, so that no eye could behold it without joy. And then upon the Earth he placed all the myriads of its inhabitants – beings to perceive and cherish the beauty which he made. Striving for perfection because it was the nature of creation to desire all things flawless, he made the inhabitants of the Earth capable of creation, and striving, and love for the world. Then he withdrew his hand, and beheld what he had done.

There to his great ire he saw that evil lay in the Earth: malice buried and abroad, banes and powers which had no part in his intent. For while he had laboured over his creation, he had closed his eyes, and had not seen the Despiser, the bitter son or brother of his heart, labouring beside him – casting dross into the forge, adding malignancy to his intent.

Then the Creator's wrath shook the heavens, and he grappled with the son or brother of his heart. He overthrew the Despiser and hurled him to the Earth, sealing him within the Arch of Time for his punishment. Thus it became for the inhabitants of the Earth as it was with the Creator; for in that act he harmed the thing he loved, and so all living hearts were taught the power of self-despite. The Despiser was abroad in the Earth, awakening ills, seeking to escape his prison. And the Creator could not hinder him, for the reach of any immortal hand through the Arch would topple Time, destroying the Earth and freeing the Despiser. This was the great grief of the Creator, and the unending flaw and sorrow of those who lived and strove upon the Earth.

Covenant fell silent. Telling this story, essentially as he had heard it ten years ago, brought back many things to him. He no longer felt blurred and ossified. Now he felt like the night, and his memories were stars: Mhoram, Foamfollower, Bannor, the Ranyhyn. While he still had blood in his veins, air in his lungs, he would not turn his back on the world which had given birth to such people.

Linden started to ask a question; but the rustling of the curtain interrupted her. Sunder entered the room carrying an oil lamp. He set it on the floor and seated himself cross-legged in front of it. Its dim, yellow light cast haggard shadows across his visage. When he spoke, his voice wore ashes, as if he had been bereaved.

'I, too, have heard that tale,' he said thickly. 'It was told to me by Nassic my father. But the tale told in the Rede of the na-Mhoram is another altogether.'

Covenant and Linden waited. After a moment, the Graveller went on. 'In the Rede it is told that the Earth was formed as a jail and tormenting-place for the Lord of wickedness – him whom we name a-Jeroth of the Seven Hells. And life was placed upon the Earth – men and women, and all other races – to wreak upon a-Jeroth his proper doom. But time and again, throughout the ages, the races of the Land failed their purpose. Rather than exacting pain from a-Jeroth, meting out upon him the Master's just retribution, they formed alliances with the Lord, spared him in his weakness and bowed to him in his strength. And always – ' Sunder shot a glance at Covenant, faltered momentarily – 'the most heinous of these betrayals have been wrought by men born in the image of the First Betrayer, Berek, father of cowardice. Halfhanded men.

'Therefore in his wrath the Master turned his face from the Land. He sent the Sunbane upon us, as chastisement for treachery, so that

117

we would remember our mortality, and become worthy again to serve his purpose. Only the intercession of the Clave enables us to endure.'

Protests thronged in Covenant. He knew from experience that this conception of the Land was false and cruel. But before he could try to reply, Linden climbed suddenly to her feet. Her eyes were feverish in the lamplight, afflicted by fear and outrage and waiting. Her lips trembled. 'A Master like that isn't worth believing in. But you probably have to do it anyway. How else can you justify killing people you don't even know?'

The Graveller surged erect, faced her extremely. The conflict in him made him grind his teeth. 'All the Land knows the truth which the Clave teaches. It is manifest at every rising of the sun. None deny it but Nassic my father, who died in mind before his body was slain, and you, who are ignorant!'

Covenant remained on the floor. While Linden and Sunder confronted each other, he drew all the strands of himself together, braided anger, empathy, determination, memory to make the cord on which all their lives depended. Part of him bled to think of the hurt he meant to inflict on Sunder, the choice he meant to extort; part raged at the brutality which had taught people like Sunder to think of their own lives as punishment for a crime they could not have committed; part quavered in fear at the idea of failure, at the poverty of his grasp on power. When Linden began to retort to the Graveller, he stopped her with a wrench of his head. I'll do it, he thought silently to her. If it has to be done. Shifting his gaze to Sunder, he asked, 'How's your mother?'

A spasm contorted the Graveller's face; his hands bunched into knots of pain and uselessness. 'Her death is plain.' His eyes were dull, wounded, articulating the frank torment of his heart. 'I must shed her blood with yours at the sun's rising.'

Covenant bowed his head for a moment in tacit acknowledgment. Then, deliberately, he created a space of clarity within himself, set his questions and fears aside. All right, he murmured. Leper. It has to be done.

Taking a deep breath, he rose to his feet, faced the Stonedownor.

'Sunder,' he said softly, 'do you have a knife?'

The Graveller nodded as if the question had no meaning.

'Take it out.'

Slowly, Sunder obeyed. He reached to his back, slipped a long iron poniard out of his belt. His fingers held it as if they had no idea how to use it.

'I want you to see that you're safe,' Covenant said. 'You have a knife. My hands are tied. I can't hurt you.'

Sunder stared back at Covenant, transfixed by incomprehension.

All right, Covenant breathed. Leper. Do it now. His heartbeat seemed to fill his chest, leaving no room for air. But he did not waver.

'Get out that piece of *orcrest*. The Sunstone.'

Again, Sunder obeyed. Covenant's will held him.

Covenant did not permit himself to glance down at the stone. He was marginally aware that Linden regarded him as if he were no longer sane. A shudder of apprehension threatened his clarity. He had to grit his teeth to keep his voice steady. 'Touch me with it.'

'Touch – ?' Sunder murmured blankly.

'Touch my forehead.'

Doubt pinched the corners of Sunder's eyes. His shoulders hunched as he tightened his grip on the knife, the Sunstone.

Do it.

The Graveller's hand seemed to move without volition. The *orcrest* passed Covenant's face, came to rest cool and possible against his tense brow.

His attention dropped through him to his ring, seeking for the link between *orcrest* and white gold. He remembered standing in sunlight and desperation on the slopes of Mount Thunder; he saw Bannor take his hand, place his ring in contact with the Staff of Law. A trigger. He felt the detonation of power.

You are the white gold.

The silence in the room vibrated. His lips stretched back from his teeth. He squeezed his eyes shut against the strain.

A trigger.

He did not want to die, did not want the Land to die. Lord Foul abhorred all life.

Fiercely, he brought the *orcrest* and the white gold together in his mind, chose power.

A burst of argent sprang off his forehead.

Linden let out a stricken gasp. Sunder snatched back the *orcrest*. A gust of force blew out the lamp.

Then Covenant's hands were free. Ignoring the sudden magma of renewed circulation, he raised his arms in front of him, opened his eyes.

His hands blazed the colour of the full moon. He could feel the passion of the fire, but it did him no harm.

The flames on his left swiftly faded, died. But his right hand grew brighter as the blaze focused on his ring, burning without a sound.

Linden stared at him whitely, wildly. Sunder's eyes echoed the argent fire like a revelation too acute to bear.

You are stubborn yet. Yes! Covenant panted. You don't begin to know how stubborn.

With a thought, he struck the bonds from Linden's wrists. Then he reached for the Sunstone.

As he took it from Sunder's stunned fingers, a piercing white light exploded from the stone. It shone like a sun in the small room. Linden ducked her head. Sunder covered his eyes with his free arm, waved his poniard uncertainly.

'Wild magic,' Covenant said. His voice felt like flame in his mouth. The return of blood to his arms raked his nerves like claws. 'Your knife means nothing. I have the wild magic. I'm not threatening you. I don't want to hurt anybody.' The night had become cold, yet sweat streamed down his face. 'That's not why I'm here. But I won't let you kill us.'

'Father!' Sunder cried in dismay. 'Was it true? Was every word that you spoke a word of truth?'

Covenant sagged. He felt that he had accomplished his purpose; and at once a wave of fatigue broke through him. 'Here.' His voice was hoarse with strain. 'Take it.'

'Take – ?'

'The Sunstone. It's yours.'

Torn by this vision of power as if it turned the world he had always known to chaos, Sunder stretched out his hand, touched the bright *orcrest*. When its light did not burn him, he closed his fingers on it as if it were an anchor.

With a groan, Covenant released the wild magic. Instantly, the fire went out as if he had severed it from his hand. The Sunstone was extinguished; the room plunged into midnight.

He leaned back against the wall, hugged his pounding arms across his chest. Flares danced along his sight, turning slowly from white to orange and red. He felt exhausted; but he could not rest. He had silenced his power so that the Graveller would have a chance to refuse him. Now he had to meet the cost of his risk. Roughly, he forced out words. 'I want to get away from here. Before anything else happens. Before that Raver tries something worse. But we need help. A guide. Somebody who knows the Sunbane. We can't survive alone. I want you.'

From out of the darkness, Sunder answered as if he were foundering, 'I am the Graveller of Mithil Stonedown. My people hold me in their faith. How shall I betray my home to aid you?'

'Sunder,' Covenant replied, striving to convey the extremity of his conviction, 'I want to help the Land. I want to save it all. Including Mithil Stonedown.'

For a long moment, the Graveller was silent. Covenant clinched his chest, did not allow himself to beg for Sunder's aid; but his heart beat over and over again, Please; I need you.

Abruptly, Linden spoke in a tone of startling passion. 'You shouldn't have to kill your own mother.'

Sunder took a deep quivering breath. 'I do not wish to shed her blood. Or yours. May my people forgive me.'

Covenant's head swam with relief. He hardly heard himself say, 'Then let's get started.'

7

MARID

For a moment, there was silence in the small room. Sunder remained still, as if he could not force his reluctant bones to act on his decision. Out of the darkness, he breathed thickly, 'Thomas Covenant, do not betray me.'

Before Covenant could try to reply, the Graveller turned, eased the curtain aside.

Through the entryway, Covenant saw moonlight in the open centre of the Stonedown. Quietly, he asked, 'What about guards?'

'There are none here.' Sunder's voice was a rigid whisper. 'Lives to be shed are left in the charge of the Graveller. It is fitting that one who will commit sacrifice should keep vigil with those whose blood will be shed. The Stonedown sleeps.'

Covenant clenched himself against his fatigue and the Graveller's tone. 'What about outside the village?'

'Those guards we must evade.'

Grimly, Sunder slipped out of the room.

Linden began to follow the Stonedownor. But at Covenant's side she stopped, said softly. 'Do you trust him? He already regrets this.'

'I know,' Covenant responded. In the back of his mind, he cursed the acuity of her hearing. 'I wouldn't trust anybody who didn't regret a decision like this.'

She hesitated for a moment. She said bitterly, 'I don't think regret is such a virtue.' Then she let herself out into the night.

He stood still, blinking wearily at the dark. He felt wan with hunger; and the thought of what lay ahead sapped the little strength remaining to him. Linden's severity hurt him. Where had she learned to deny herself the simple humanity of regret?

But he had no time for such things. His need to escape was absolute. Woodenly, he followed his companions out of the room.

After the blackness behind him, the moon seemed bright. Sunder and Linden were distinct and vulnerable against the pale walls of the houses, waiting for him. When he joined them, the Graveller turned northward immediately, began moving with barefoot silence between the dwellings. Linden shadowed him; and Covenant stayed within arm's reach of her back.

As they neared the outer houses, Sunder stopped. He signed for Covenant and Linden to remain where they were. When Covenant nodded, Sunder crept away back into the Stonedown.

Covenant tried to muffle his respiration. At his side, Linden stood with her fists clenched. Her lips moved soundlessly as if she were arguing with her fear. The night was chilly; Covenant's anxiety left a cold trail down the small of his back.

Shortly, Sunder returned, bearing a dark oblong the size of a papaya. '*Mirkfruit*,' he whispered. At once, he moved off again.

Like spectres, the three of them left Mithil Stonedown.

From the last houses, Sunder picked his way towards the valley bottom. He travelled in a half crouch, reducing his silhouette as much as possible. Linden followed his example; she seemed to flit through the moonlight as if she had been born sure-footed. But Covenant's toes were numb, and his legs were tired. He stumbled over the uneven ground.

Abruptly, Sunder braced his hands on a rock, vaulted down into the long hollow of the riverbed.

Linden jumped after him. Sand absorbed her landing. Swiftly, she joined Sunder in the shadow under the bank.

Covenant hesitated on the edge. Looking downward, he became suddenly queasy with vertigo. He turned his head away. The barren length of the watercourse stretched serpentine out of the mountains on his left towards the South Plains on his right.

Last night, the Mithil River had been full to overflowing.

'Come!' whispered Sunder. 'You will be seen.'

Covenant jumped. He landed crookedly, sprawled in the sand. In an instant, Sunder reached his side, urged him to his feet. He ignored the Graveller. He dug his hands into the sand, groping for moisture. But even below the surface, the sand was completely dry. His hands raised dust that made him gag to stifle a cough.

Impossible!

The riverbed was as desiccated as a desert. Had the Law itself become meaningless?

'Covenant!' Linden hissed.

Sunder tugged at his shoulders. Fighting down a rush of blind rage, Covenant pulled his legs under him, stumbled into the shadow of the bank. A moment passed before he regained himself enough to look outward, away from his dismay.

Sunder pointed downriver, towards the black arc of a bridge a few hundred feet away. 'One guard,' he breathed. 'The others can no longer descry us. But him we cannot pass unseen.'

'What are we going to do?' whispered Linden.

The Graveller motioned for silence. Hefting his *mirkfruit*, he crept away along the course, staying carefully under the shelter of the bank.

Linden and Covenant followed.

Their progress was slow. The river bottom was littered with rocks

122

and unexpected holes, especially near the banks; Covenant had to watch his footing. Yet his gaze was drawn towards the bridge – the ominous black span blocking their way like a gate. He had crossed that bridge with Lena. And with Atiaran. The memory made his heart squirm.

He caught no glimpse of the guard. The man must have been hiding behind the parapets of the span.

Then they drew near the bridge, made their way under it. Covenant held his breath as Sunder moved to the riverbank. The Graveller climbed with acute caution; he eased his way upward as if every pebble and handful of dirt were treacherous. Slowly, he disappeared around the base of the bridge.

Suspense shivered in the air as if the night were about to shatter. Covenant's lungs knotted, demanding relief. Linden huddled into herself.

They heard a soft thud – the impact of Sunder's *mirkfruit* – followed by a groan, and the sound of a body falling on the stone over their heads.

The Graveller dropped with alacrity back into the riverbed. 'Now we must make haste,' he warned, 'before another comes to ward in his place.' He sounded angry. Turning on his heel, he strode away as if what he had just done to someone he had known all his life were unsupportable.

He set a stiff pace. Covenant and Linden had to hurry to keep up with him.

Moonlight gave the night a crisp patina of old silver, as if the darkness itself were a work of fine-spun craft. Stars winked like instances of perfection above the rims of the mountains, which rose rugged into the unattainable heavens on either side. While his strength held, Covenant took pleasure in this opportunity to recover the tangible loveliness of the Land.

But as the moon declined towards setting, and the spur of mountains on his left began to shrink, his momentum faltered. He was too weak. His heart limped as if it could not keep up with him; his muscles felt like sand. And escape was not enough; there was something else he had to do as well. With a dry croak, he called Sunder to a halt. Then he dropped to the ground, stretched out on his back, and sucked air.

Linden stopped nearby, winded but still capable. And Sunder stood erect and impatient; he was tough as well as strong, inured to fatigue by a lifetime of difficult survival. The little he had seen and heard had taught Covenant that life in Mithil Stonedown was arduous and costly. Why else were these villagers willing to sacrifice their own parents – willing to condemn strangers and innocents to death? It was intolerable, that the bountiful Land he loved had come to this.

He was still hunting fortitude when Sunder said stiffly, 'Here we are safe enough until the sun's rising – at least while our absence remains undiscovered in the Stonedown. But it avails nothing merely to abide here, awaiting chance or doom. The Rider who approaches Mithil Stonedown may come upon us. He will surely pursue when he is told of our flight. You have asked me to guide you. Thomas Covenant, where will you go?'

Groaning, Covenant pried himself into a sitting position. 'First things first.' He had learned enough to be sure Sunder would not like the larger answer to that question. So he concentrated on his immediate purpose. 'First I want to find Marid.'

'Marid?' The Graveller gaped. 'Did I not tell you the judgement of the Stonedown? He is condemned by ancient Rede and custom to the mercy of the Sunbane. It has already been done.'

'I know,' Covenant muttered. 'You told me. And I told you. He's innocent.'

'Guilt or innocence,' retorted Sunder, 'it avails nothing. It has already been done! The men and women entrusted with his doom returned before I came to speak with you.'

Weariness eroded Covenant's self-mastery. He could hardly restrain his old rage. 'What exactly did they do to him?'

Sunder cast a look of exasperation at the stars. 'They bore him into the Plains, and left him bound to await his judgement.'

'Do you know where they left him?'

'Somewhat. They spoke of their intent before departing. I was not among them to behold the very spot.'

'That's good enough.' Covenant felt as weak as water; but he climbed to his feet and faced the Graveller. 'Take us there.'

'There is not time!' Sunder's visage was a tangle of darkness. 'The distance is too great. We must find protection, lest we also fall prey to the sun's rising.'

'But Marid is *innocent*.' Covenant sounded wild to himself, but did not care. 'The only reason that Raver used him was because of us. I'm not going to let him be punished. Goddamn it.' He grabbed roughly at Sunder's jerkin. 'Guide us! I've got too much blood on my hands already.'

In a low strained tone, as if he had just glimpsed some crucial and frightening truth, the Graveller said, 'You do not understand the Sunbane.'

'Then explain it. What are you so afraid of?'

'We will suffer Marid's doom!'

From behind Sunder, Linden said, 'He means it. He thinks something awful is going to happen when the sun comes up.'

With an effort, Covenant forced himself to release Sunder. He faced Linden, bit down on his voice to keep it quiet. 'What do you think?'

She was silent for a moment. Then she said harshly, 'I didn't believe you when you said Joan was possessed. But I saw that Raver myself. I saw Marid afterwards. The Raver was gone.' She carved each word distinctly in the night air. 'If you want to stay with Sunder, I'll go looking for Marid myself.'

'Heaven and Earth!' protested Sunder. 'Did I betray my home merely so that you may meet ruin for a man you cannot save? If you place one foot amiss, you will end in beseeching the stones themselves for death!'

Covenant gazed into the darkness where Linden stood, gathering strength from her. Softly, he replied to Sunder, 'He was your friend.'

'You are mad!' Sunder raged. 'Nassic my father was mad!' He snatched up a stone, hurled it against the riverbank. 'I am mad.' Then he whirled on Covenant. Anger hammered in his voice. 'Very well. I will guide you. But I will *not* – ' his fist hit at the night – 'suffer the destruction of the Sunbane for any man or woman, mad or sane.'

Wrenching himself into motion, he turned and scrambled up out of the riverbed.

Covenant remained looking towards Linden. He wanted to thank her for her support, her willingness to risk herself in the name of Marid's innocence. But she brushed past him after Sunder. 'Come on,' she said over her shoulder. 'We've got to hurry. Whatever it is he's afraid of, I don't think I'm going to like it.'

He watched her while she climbed the bank. *End in beseeching* – He rubbed his right hand across his chin, verified his ring against the stiff stubble of his beard. Then he marshalled his waning resources and struggled to follow his companions.

On level ground, he found himself in an entirely different landscape. Except for the ragged weal of the Mithil, the Plains were nearly featureless. They spread north and west as far as he could see, marked only by the faint undulations of the terrain – bare even of shrubs or piles of rock. The low moonlight gave them an appearance of ghostly sterility, as if they had been weathered barren by ages of implacable thirst.

Sunder headed slightly east of north at a canter, roughly paralleling the mountains which still lay to the east. But Covenant could not endure such a pace. And he did not understand his guide's compelling dread. He called for Sunder to slow down.

The Graveller spun on his heel. '*There is not time.*'

'Then there's no reason for us to wear ourselves out.'

Sunder spat a curse, started moving again. But in spite of his almost frantic anxiety, he went no faster than a brisk walk.

Some time later, the moon fell below the horizon. But the scant light of the stars sufficed. The terrain was not difficult, and Sunder

125

knew his way. Soon a vague wash of grey from the east began to macerate the night.

The paling of the horizon agitated Sunder. He searched the earth near him while he walked, made digressions from his path like spurts of fright to study irregularities in the ground. But he could not find what he wanted. Within half a league, dawn had become imminent. Urgently, he faced Covenant and Linden. 'We must find stone. Any hard rock free of soil. Before the sun's rising. Search, if you value a hale life and a clean death.'

Covenant halted woodenly. His surroundings seemed to sway as if they were about to fall apart. He felt stunned by weariness.

'There,' Linden said. She was pointing off to her right.

He peered in that direction. He could discern nothing. But he did not have her eyes.

Sunder gaped at her for a moment, then hastened to investigate. With his hands, he explored the surface.

'Stone!' he hissed. 'It may suffice.' At once, he jumped erect. 'We must stand here. The stone will ward us.'

Fatigue blurred Covenant's sight. He could not see the Graveller clearly. Sunder's apprehension made no sense to him. Sunrise was only moments away; luminescence cast the horizon into stark relief. Was he supposed to be afraid of the *sun*?

Linden asked Sunder the same question. 'Do you think the sun's going to hurt us? That's nonsense. We spent half the morning yesterday in that test of silence of yours, and the only thing we suffered from was prejudice.'

'With stone underfoot!' fumed the Graveller. 'It is the first touch which destroys! You did not meet the first touch of the Sunbane unwarded by stone!'

I don't have time for this, Covenant muttered to himself. The eyes of his mind saw Marid clearly enough. Left to die in the sun. Unsteadily, he lurched into motion again.

'Fool!' Sunder shouted. 'For you I betrayed my born people!'

A moment later, Linden joined Covenant.

'Find stone!' The Graveller's passion sounded like raw despair. 'You destroy me! Must I slay you also?'

Linden was silent for a few steps. Then she murmured, 'He believes it.'

An innominate pang rang through Covenant. Involuntarily, he stopped. He and Linden turned to face the east.

They squinted at the first fiery rim of the rising sun.

It flared red along the skyline; but the sun itself wore an aura of brown, as if it shone through cerements of dust. It touched his face with dry heat.

'Nothing,' Linden said tightly. 'I don't feel anything.'

He glanced back at Sunder. The Graveller stood on his stone. His

126

hands had covered his face, and his shoulders shook.

Because he did not know what else to do, Covenant turned away, went rigidly in search of Marid.

Linden stayed with him. Hunger had abused her face, giving her a sunken aspect; and she carried her head as if the injury behind her ear still hurt. But her jaw was set, emphasizing the firm lines of her chin, and her lips were pale with severity. She looked like a woman who did not know how to fail. He braced himself on her determination, and kept moving.

The rising of the sun had altered the ambience of the Plains. They had been silver and bearable; now they became a hot and lifeless ruin. Nothing grew or moved in the wide waste. The ground was packed and baked until it was as intractable as iron. Loose dirt turned to dust. The entire landscape shimmered with heat like the aftermath of destruction.

Striving against the stupefaction of his fatigue, Covenant asked Linden to tell him about the condition of the terrain.

'It's wrong.' She bit out words as if the sight were an obloquy directed at her personally. 'It shouldn't be like this. It's like a running sore. I keep expecting to see it bleed. It isn't supposed to be like this.'

Isn't supposed to be like this! he echoed. The Land had become like Joan. Something broken.

The heat haze stung his eyes. He could not see the ground except as a swath of pale ichor; he felt that he was treading pain. His numb feet stumbled helplessly.

She caught his arm, steadied him. Clenching his old sorrow, he drew himself upright. His voice shook. 'What's causing it?'

'I can't tell,' she said grimly. 'But it has something to do with that ring around the sun. The sun itself – ' her hands released him slowly – 'seems natural.'

'Bloody hell,' he breathed. 'What has that bastard done?'

But he did not expect an answer. In spite of her penetrating vision, Linden knew less than he did. Deliberately, he gave himself a VSE. Then he went on looking for Marid. In his rue and pain, the thought of a man lying bound at the mercy of the sun loomed as the one idea which made everything else abominable.

Wearily, doggedly, he and Linden trudged through the heat-leeched landscape. The dust coated his mouth with the taste of failure; the glare lanced through his eyeballs. As his weakness deepened, he drifted into a vague dizziness. Only the landmark of the mountains, now east and somewhat south of him, enabled him to keep his direction. The sun beat down as if on to an anvil, hammering moisture and strength out of him like a smith shaping futility. He did not know how he stayed on his feet. At times, he felt himself wandering over the colourless earth, through the haze, as if he were a fragment of the desolation.

He might have wandered past his goal; but Linden somehow retained more alertness. She tugged him to a stop, dragged his attention out of the slow eddying sopor of the heat. 'Look.'

His lips framed empty questions. For a moment, he could not understand why he was no longer moving.

'Look,' she repeated. Her voice was an arid croak.

They stood in a wide bowl of dust. Clouds billowed from every shuffle of their feet. Before them, two wooden stakes had been driven into the ground. The stakes were some distance apart, as if they had been set to secure the arms of a man lying outstretched. Tied to the stakes were loops of rope.

The loops were intact.

A body's length from the stakes were two holes in the ground — the kind of holes made by stakes pounded in and then pulled out.

Covenant swallowed drily. 'Marid.' The word abraded his throat.

'He got away,' Linden said hoarsely.

Covenant's legs folded. He sat down, coughing weakly at the dust he raised. Got away.

Linden squatted in front of him. The nearness of her face forced him to look at her. Her voice scraped as if it were full of sand. 'I don't know how he did it, but he's better off than we are. This heat's going to kill us.'

His tongue fumbled. 'I had to try. He was innocent.'

Awkwardly, she reached out, wiped beads of useless sweat from his forehead. 'You look awful.'

He peered at her through his exhaustion. Dirt caked her lips and cheeks, collected in the lines on either side of her mouth. Sweat-trails streaked her face. Her eyes were glazed.

'So do you.'

'Then we'd better do something about it.' A tremor eroded her effort to sound resolute. But she stood up, helped him to his feet. 'Let's go back. Maybe Sunder's looking for us.'

He nodded. He had forgotten the Graveller.

But when he and Linden turned to retrace their way, they saw a figure coming darkly through the shimmer.

He stopped, squinted. Mirage? Linden stood near him as if to prevent him from losing his balance. They waited.

The figure approached until they recognized Sunder.

He halted twenty paces from them.

In his right hand, he gripped his poniard. This time, he seemed perfectly familiar with its use.

Covenant watched the Graveller dumbly, as if the knife had made them strangers to each other. Linden's hand touched a warning to his arm.

'Thomas Covenant.' Sunder's face looked like hot stone. 'What is my name?'

What – ? Covenant frowned at the intervening heat.

'Speak my name!' the Graveller spat fiercely. 'Do not compel me to slay you.'

Slay? Covenant made an effort to reach through the confusion. 'Sunder,' he croaked. 'Graveller of Mithil Stonedown. Holder of the Sunstone.'

Incomprehension stretched Sunder's countenance. 'Linden Avery?' he asked falteringly. 'What is the name of my father?'

'Was,' she said in a flat tone. 'His name was Nassic son of Jous. He's dead.'

Sunder gaped as if Covenant and Linden were miraculous. Then he dropped his hands to his sides. 'Heaven and Earth! It is not possible. The Sunbane – Never have I beheld – ' He shook his head in astonishment. 'Ah, you are a mystery! How can such things be? Does one white ring alter the order of life?'

'Sometimes,' Covenant muttered. He was trying to follow a fractured sequence of memories. Everything he did was an unintentional assault on the Graveller's preconceptions. He wanted to ease Sunder with some kind of explanation. The heat haze seemed to blur the distinction between past and present. Something about his boots – ? He forced words past his parched lips. 'The first time I was here – ' Boots – yes, that was it. Drool Rockworm had been able to locate him through the alien touch of his boots on the ground. 'My boots. Her shoes. They don't come from the Land. Maybe that's what protected us.'

Sunder grabbed at the suggestion as if it were a benison. 'Yes. It must be so. Flesh is flesh, susceptible to the Sunbane. But your footwear – it is unlike any I have seen. Surely you were shielded at the sun's first touch, else you would have been altered beyond any power to know me.' Then his face darkened. 'But could you not have told me? I feared – ' The clenching of his jaws described eloquently the extremity of his fear.

'We didn't know.' Covenant wanted to lie down, close his eyes, forget. 'We were lucky.' A moment passed before he found the will to ask, 'Marid – ?'

At once, Sunder put everything else aside. He went to look at the stakes, the holes. A frown knotted his forehead. 'Fools,' he grated. 'I warned them to ware such things. None can foretell the Sunbane. Now there is evil upon the Plains.'

'You mean,' asked Linden, 'he didn't escape? He isn't safe?'

In response, the Graveller rasped, 'Did I not say there was not time? You have achieved nothing but your own prostration. It is enough,' he went on stiffly. 'I have followed you to this useless end. Now you will accompany me.'

Linden stared at Sunder. 'Where are we going?'

'To find shelter,' he said in a calmer tone. 'We cannot endure this sun.'

Covenant gestured eastward, towards a region with which he was familiar. 'The hills – '

Sunder shook his head. 'There is shelter in the hills. But to gain it we must pass within scope of Windshorn Stonedown. That is certain sacrifice – for any stranger, as for the Graveller of Mithil Stonedown. We go west, to the Mithil River.'

Covenant could not argue. Ignorance crippled his ability to make decisions. When Sunder took his arm and turned him away from the sun, he began to scuffle stiffly out of the bowl of dust.

Linden moved at his side. Her stride was unsteady; she seemed dangerously weak. Sunder was stronger; but his eyes were bleak, as if he could see disaster ahead. And Covenant could barely lift his feet. The sun, still climbing towards mid-morning, clung to his shoulders, hagriding him. Heat flushed back and forth across his skin – a vitiating fever which echoed the haze of the scorched earth. His eyes felt raw from the scraping of his eyelids. After a time, he began to stumble as if the ligatures of his knees were parting.

Then he was in the dirt, with no idea of how he had fallen. Sunder supported him so that he could sit up. The Graveller's face was grey with dust; he, too, had begun to suffer. 'Thomas Covenant,' he panted, 'this is fatal to you. You must have water. Will you not make use of your white ring?'

Covenant's respiration was shallow and ragged. He stared into the haze as if he had gone blind.

'The white ring,' Sunder pleaded. 'You must raise water, lest you die.'

Water. He pulled the shards of himself together around that thought. Impossible. He could not concentrate. Had never used wild magic for anything except contention. It was not a panacea.

Both Sunder and Linden were studying him as if he were responsible for their hopes. They were failing along with him. For their sakes, he would have been willing to make the attempt. But it was impossible for other reasons as well. Tortuously, as if he had been disjointed, he shifted forward, got his knees under him, then his feet.

'Ur-Lord!' protested the Graveller.

'I don't,' Covenant muttered, half coughing, 'don't know how.' He wanted to shout. 'I'm a leper. I can't see – can't feel – ' The Earth was closed to him; it lay blank and meaningless under his feet – a concatenation of haze, nothing more. 'I don't know how to reach it.' *We need Earthpower. And a Lord to wield it.*

There's no Earthpower. The Lords are gone. He had no words potent enough to convey his helplessness. 'I just can't.'

Sunder groaned. But he hesitated only momentarily. Then he sighed in resignation, 'Very well. Yet we must have water.' He took out his knife. 'My strength is greater than yours. Perhaps I am able to spare a little blood.' Grimly, he directed the blade towards the mapwork of scars on his left forearm.

Covenant lurched to try to stop him.

Linden was quicker. She seized Sunder's wrist. 'No!'

The Graveller twisted free of her, gritted acutely, '*We must have water.*'

'Not like that.' The cuts on Nassic's hand burned in Covenant's memory; he rejected such power instinctively.

'Do you wish to die?'

'No.' Covenant upheld himself by force of will. 'But I'm not that desperate. Not yet, anyway.'

'Your knife isn't even clean,' added Linden. 'If septicaemia set in, I'd have to burn it out.'

Sunder closed his eyes as if to shut out what they were saying. 'I will outlive you both under this sun.' His jaws chewed his voice into a barren whisper. 'Ah, my father, what have you done to me? Is this the outcome of all your mad devoir?'

'Suit yourself,' Covenant said brutally, trying to keep Sunder from despair or rebellion. 'But at least have the decency to wait until we're too weak to stop you.'

The Graveller's eyes burst open. He spat a curse. 'Decency, is it?' he grated. 'You are swift to cast shame upon people whose lives you do not comprehend. Well, let us hasten the moment when I may decently save you.' With a thrust of his arm, he pushed Covenant into motion, then caught him around the waist to keep him from falling, and began half dragging him westward.

In a moment, Linden came to Covenant's other side, shrugged his arm over her shoulders so that she could help support him. Braced in that fashion, he was able to travel.

But the sun was remorseless. Slowly, ineluctably, it beat him towards abjection. By mid-morning, he was hardly carrying a fraction of his own weight. To his burned eyes, the haze sang threnodies of prostration; motes of darkness began to flit across his vision. From time to time, he saw small clumps of night crouching on the pale ground just beyond clarity, as if they were waiting for him.

Then the earth seemed to rise up in front of him. Sunder came to a halt. Linden almost fell; but Covenant clung to her somehow. He fought to focus his eyes. After a moment, he saw that the rise was a shelf of rock jutting westward.

Sunder tugged him and Linden forward. They limped past another clump like a low bush, into the shadow of the rock.

The jut of the shelf formed an eroded lee large enough to shelter several people. In the shadow, the rock and dirt felt cool. Linden helped Sunder place Covenant sitting against the balm of the stone. Covenant tried to lie down; but the Graveller stopped him, and Linden panted, 'Don't. You might go to sleep. You've lost too much fluid.'

He nodded vaguely. The coolness was only relative, and he was febrile with thirst. No amount of shade could answer the unpity of the sun. But the shadow itself was bliss to him, and he was content. Linden sat down on one side of him; Sunder, on the other. He closed his eyes, let himself drift.

Some time later, he became conscious of voices. Linden and Sunder were talking. The hebetude of her tone betrayed the difficulty of staying alert. Sunder's responses were distant, as if he found her enquiries painful but could not think of any way to refuse them.

'Sunder,' she asked dimly, 'what is Mithil Stonedown going to do without you?'

'Linden Avery?' He seemed not to understand her question.

'Call me Linden. After today – ' Her voice trailed away.

He hesitated, then said, 'Linden.'

'You're the Graveller. What will they do without a Graveller?'

'Ah.' Now he caught her meaning. 'I signify little. The loss of the Sunstone is of more import, yet even that loss can be overcome. The Stonedown is chary of its lore. My prentice is adept in all the rites which must be performed in the absence of the Sunstone. Without doubt, he shed Kalina my mother at the sun's rising. The Stonedown will endure. How otherwise could I have done what I have done?'

After a pause, she asked, 'You're not married?'

'No.' His reply was like a wince.

Linden seemed to hear a wide range of implications in that one word. Quietly, she said, 'But you were.'

'Yes.'

'What happened?'

Sunder was silent at first. But then he replied, 'Among my people, only the Graveller is given the choice of his own mate. The survival of the Stonedown depends upon its children. Mating for children is not left to the hazard of affection or preference. But by long custom, the Graveller is given freedom. As recompense for the burden of his work.

'The choice of my heart fell upon Aimil daughter of Anest. Anest was sister to Kalina my mother. From childhood, Aimil and I were dear to each other. We were gladly wed, and gladly sought to vindicate our choosing with children.

'A son came to us, and was given the name Nelbrin, which is "heart's child".' His tone was as astringent as the terrain. 'He was a pale child, not greatly well. But he grew as a child should grow and was a treasure to us.

'For a score of turnings of the moon he grew. He was slow in learning to walk, and not steady upon his legs, but he came at last to walk with glee. Until – ' He swallowed convulsively. 'Until by mischance Aimil my wife injured him in our home. She turned from the hearth bearing a heavy pot, and Nelbrin our son had walked to stand behind her. The pot struck him upon the chest.

'From that day, he sickened towards death. A dark swelling grew in him, and his life faltered.'

'Haemophilia,' Linden breathed almost inaudibly. 'Poor kid.'

Sunder did not stop. 'When his death was written upon his face for all to see, the Stonedown invoked judgement. I was commanded to sacrifice him for the good of the people.'

A rot gnawed at Covenant's guts. He looked up at the Graveller. The dryness in his throat felt like slow strangulation. He seemed to hear the ground sizzling.

In protest, Linden asked, 'Your own son? What did you do?'

Sunder stared out into the Sunbane as if it were the story of his life. 'I could not halt his death. The desert sun and the sun of pestilence had left us sorely in need. I shed his life to raise water and food for the Stonedown.'

Oh, Sunder! Covenant groaned.

Tightly, Linden demanded, 'How did Aimil feel about that?'

'It maddened her. She fought to prevent me – and when she could not, she became wild in her mind. Despair afflicted her, and she – ' For a moment, Sunder could not summon the words he needed. Then he went on harshly, 'She committed a mortal harm against herself. So that her death would not be altogether meaningless, I shed her also.'

So that her – Hellfire! Covenant understood now why the thought of killing his mother had driven Sunder to abandon his home. How many loved ones could a man bear to kill?

Grimly, Linden said, 'It wasn't your fault. You did what you had to do.' Passion gathered in her tone. 'It's this Sunbane.'

The Graveller did not look at her. 'All men and women die. It signifies nothing to complain.' He sounded as sun-tormented as the Plains. 'What else do you desire to know of me? You need only ask. I have no secrets from you.'

Covenant ached to comfort Sunder; but he knew nothing about comfort. Anger and defiance were the only answers he understood. Because he could not ease the Stonedownor, he tried to distract him. 'Tell me about Nassic.' The words were rough in his mouth. 'How did he come to have a son?'

Linden glared at Covenant as if she were vexed by his insensitivity;

but Sunder relaxed visibly. He seemed relieved by the question – glad to escape the futility of his mourning. 'Nassic my father,' he said, with a weariness which served as calm, 'was like Jous his father, and like Prassan his father's father. He was a man of Mithil Stonedown.

'Jous his father lived in the place he named his temple, and from time to time Nassic visited Jous, out of respect for his father, and also to ascertain that no harm had befallen him. The Stonedown wed Nassic to Kalina, and they were together as any young man and woman. But then Jous fell towards his death. Nassic went to the temple to bear his father to Mithil Stonedown for sacrifice. He did not return. Dying, Jous placed his hands upon Nassic, and the madness or prophecy of the father passed into the son. Thus Nassic was lost to the Stonedown.

'This loss was sore to Kalina my mother. She was ill-content with just one son. Many a time, she went to the temple, to give her love to my father and to plead for his. Always she returned weeping and barren. I fear – ' He paused sadly. 'I fear she hurled herself at Marid hoping to die.'

Gradually, Covenant's attention drifted. He was too weak to concentrate. Dimly, he noted the shifting angle of the sun. Noon had come, laying sunlight within inches of his feet. By mid-afternoon, the shade would be gone. By mid-afternoon –

He could not survive much more of the sun's direct weight.

The dark clump which he had passed near the shelf was still there. Apparently, it was not a mirage. He blinked at it, trying to make out details. If not a mirage, then what? A bush? What kind of bush could endure this sun, when every other form of life had been burned away?

The question raised echoes in his memory, but he could not hear them clearly. Exhaustion and thirst deafened his mind.

'Die?'

He was hardly aware that he had spoken aloud. His voice felt like sand rubbing against stone. What kind – ? He strove to focus his eyes. 'That bush.' He nodded weakly towards the patch of darkness. 'What is it?'

Sunder squinted. 'It is *aliantha*. Such bushes may be found in any place, but they are most common near the River. In some way, they defy the Sunbane.' He dismissed the subject. 'They are a most deadly poison.'

'*Poison?*' Pain sliced Covenant's lips; the vehemence of his outcry split them. Blood began to run through the dust like a trail of fury cleaving his chin. Not *aliantha*!

The Graveller reached towards Covenant's face as if those dirty red drops were precious. Empowered by memories, Covenant struck Sunder's hand aside. 'Poison?' he croaked. In times past, the rare

134

aliment of *aliantha* had sustained him more often than he could recollect. If they had become poison – ! He was abruptly giddy with violence. If they had become poison, then the Land had not simply lost its Earthpower. The Earthpower had been corrupted! He wanted to batter Sunder with his fists. '*How do you know?*'

Linden caught at his shoulder. 'Covenant!'

'It is contained in the Rede of the na-Mhoram,' rasped Sunder. 'I am a Graveller – it is my work to make use of that knowledge. I know it to be true.'

No! Covenant grated. 'Have you tried it?'

Sunder gaped at him. 'No.'

'Do you know anyone who ever tried it?'

'It is poison! No man or woman willingly consumes poison.'

'Hell and blood.' Bracing himself on the stone, Covenant heaved to his feet. 'I don't believe it. He can't destroy the entire Law. If he did, the Land wouldn't exist any more.'

The Graveller sprang erect, gripped Covenant's arms, shook him fiercely. 'It is *poison.*'

Mustering all his passion, Covenant responded, '*No!*'

Sunder's visage knurled as if only the clench of his muscles kept him from exploding. With one wrench of his hands, he thrust Covenant to the ground. 'You are mad.' His voice was iron and bitterness. 'You seduced me from my home, asking my aid – but at every turn you defy me. You must seek for Marid. Madness! You must refuse all safety against the Sunbane. Madness! You must decline to raise water, nor permit me to raise it. Madness! Now nothing will content you but poison.' When Covenant tried to rise, Sunder shoved him back. 'It is enough. Make any further attempts towards the *aliantha*, and I will strike you senseless.'

Covenant's gaze raged up at the Graveller; but Sunder did not flinch. Desperation inured him to contradiction; he was trying to reclaim some control over his doom.

Holding Sunder's rigid stare, Covenant climbed to his feet, stood swaying before the Graveller. Linden was erect behind Sunder; but Covenant did not look at her. Softly, he said, 'I do not believe that *aliantha* is poisonous.' Then he turned, and began to shamble towards the bush.

A howl burst from Sunder. Covenant tried to dodge; but Sunder crashed into him headlong, carried him sprawling to the dirt. A blow on the back of his head sent lights across his vision like fragments of vertigo.

Then Sunder fell away. Covenant levered his legs under him, to see Linden standing over the Graveller. She held him in a thumblock which pressed him to the ground.

Covenant stumbled to the bush.

His head reeled. He fell to his knees. The bush was pale with dust and bore little resemblance to the dark green-and-viridian plant he remembered. But the leaves were holly-like and firm, though few. Three small fruit the size of blueberries clung to the branches in defiance of the Sunbane.

Trembling, he plucked one, wiped the dust away to see the berry's true colour.

At the edge of his sight, he saw Sunder knock Linden's feet away, break free of her.

Gritting his courage, Covenant put the berry in his mouth.

'Covenant!' Sunder cried.

The world spun wildly, then sprang straight. Cool juice filled Covenant's mouth with a sapor of peach made tangy by salt and lime. At once, new energy burst through him. Deliciousness cleansed his throat of dirt and thirst and blood. All his nerves thrilled to a sapor he had not tasted for ten long years: the quintessential nectar of the Land.

Sunder and Linden were on their feet, staring at him.

A sound like dry sobbing came from him. His sight was a blur of relief and gratitude. The seed dropped from his lips. 'Oh, dear God,' he murmured brokenly. 'There's Earthpower yet.'

A moment later, Linden reached him. She helped him to his feet, peered into his face. 'Are you – ?' she began, then stopped herself. 'No, you're all right. Better. I can already see the difference. How – ?'

He could not stop shaking. He wanted to hug her; but he only allowed himself to touch her cheek, lift a strand of hair from her mouth. Then, to answer her, thank her, he plucked another berry and gave it to her.

'Eat – '

She held it gently looking at it. Sudden tears overflowed her eyes. Her lower lip trembled as she whispered, 'It's the first healthy – ' Her voice caught.

'Eat it,' he urged thickly.

She raised it to her mouth. Her teeth closed on it.

Slowly, a look of wonder spread over her countenance. Her posture straightened; she began to smile like a cool dawn.

Covenant nodded to tell her that he understood. 'Spit out the seed. Maybe another one will grow.'

She took the seed in her hand, gazed at it for a moment as if it had been sanctified before she tossed it to the ground.

Sunder had not moved. He stood with his arms clamped across his chest. His eyes were dull with the horror of watching his life become false.

Carefully, Covenant picked the last berry. His stride was almost steady as he went to Sunder. His heart sang: Earthpower!

'Sunder,' he said, half insisting, half pleading, 'this is *aliantha*. They used to be called treasure-berries – the gift of the Earth to

136

anybody who suffered from hunger or need. This is what the Land was like.'

Sunder did not respond. The glazing of his gaze was complete.

'It's not poison,' Linden said clearly. 'It's immune to the Sunbane.'

'Eat it,' Covenant urged. 'This is why we're here. What we want to accomplish. Health. Earthpower. Eat it.'

With a painful effort, Sunder dredged up his answer. 'I do not wish to trust you.' His voice was a wilderland. 'You violate all my life. When I have learned that *aliantha* are not poison, you will seek to teach me that the Sunbane does not exist – that all the life of the Land through all the generations has had no meaning. That the shedding I have done is no less than murder.' He swallowed harshly. 'But I must. I must find some truth to take the place of the truth you destroy.'

Abruptly, he took the berry, put it in his mouth.

For a moment, his soul was naked in his face. His initial anticipation of harm became involuntary delight; his inner world struggled to alter itself. His hands quavered when he took the seed from his mouth. 'Heaven and Earth!' he breathed. His awe was as exquisite as anguish. 'Covenant – ' His jaw worked to form words. 'Is this truly the Land – the Land of which my father dreamed?'

'Yes.'

'Then he was mad.' One deep spasm of grief shook Sunder before he tugged back about him the tattered garment of his self-command. 'I must learn to be likewise mad.'

Turning away, he went back to the shelf of rock, seated himself in the shade, and covered his face with his hands.

To give Sunder's disorientation at least a degree of privacy, Covenant shifted his attention to Linden. The new lightness of her expression ameliorated her habitual severity, lifted some of her beauty out from under the streaked dust on her face. 'Thank you.' He began to say, For trying to save my life. Back there in the woods. But he did not want to remember that blow. Instead, he said, 'For getting Sunder off me.' I didn't know you trusted me that much. 'Where did you learn that thumb-hold?'

'Oh, that.' Her grin was half grimness, half amusement. 'The med school I went to was in a pretty rough neighbourhood. The security guards gave self-defence lessons.'

Covenant found himself wondering how long it had been since a woman had last smiled at him. Before he could reply, she glanced upward. 'We ought to get out of the sun. One treasure-berry apiece isn't going to keep us going very long.'

'True.' The *aliantha* had blunted his hunger, eased his body's yearning for water, restored a measure of life to his muscles. But it could not make him impervious to the sun. Around him, the Plains swam with heat as if the fabric of the ground were being bleached away fibre by fibre. He rubbed absent-mindedly at the blood on his chin, started towards Sunder.

Linden halted him. 'Covenant.'

He turned. She stood facing eastward, back over the shelf of rock. Both hands shaded her eyes.

'Something's coming.'

Sunder joined them; together, they squinted into the haze. 'What the hell – ?' Covenant muttered.

At first he saw nothing but heat and pale dirt. But then he glimpsed an erect figure, shimmering darkly in and out of sight.

The figure grew steadier as it approached. Slowly, it became solid, transubstantiating itself like an avatar of the Sunbane. It was a man. He wore the apparel of a Stonedownor.

'Who – ?'

'Oh, my God!' Linden gasped.

The man came closer.

Sunder spat, 'Marid!'

Marid? An abrupt weakness struck Covenant's knees.

The Sunbane will have no mercy –

The man had Marid's eyes, chancreous with self-loathing, mute supplication, lust. He still wore stakes tied to each of his ankles. His gait was a shambling of eagerness and dread.

He was a monster. Scales covered the lower half of his face; both mouth and nose were gone. And his arms were snakes. Thick scale-clad bodies writhed from his shoulders; serpent-heads gaped where his hands had been, brandishing fangs as white as bone. His chest heaved for air, and the snakes hissed.

Hellfire.

Linden stared at Marid. Nausea distorted her mouth. She was paralysed, hardly breathing. The sight of Marid's inflicted ill reft her of thought, courage, motion.

'Ah, Marid, my friend,' Sunder whispered miserably. 'This is the retribution of the Sunbane, which none can foretell. If you were innocent, as the ur-Lord insists – ' He groaned in grief. 'Forgive me.'

But an instant later his voice hardened. 'Avaunt, Marid!' he barked. 'Ware us! Your life is forfeit here!'

Marid's gaze flinched as if he understood; but he continued to advance, moving purposefully towards the shelf of rock.

'Marid!' Sunder snatched out his poniard. 'I have guilt enough in your doom. Do not thrust this upon me.'

Marid's eyes shouted a voiceless warning at the Graveller.

Covenant's throat felt like sand; his lungs laboured. In the back of his mind, a pulse of outrage beat like lifeblood.

Three steps to his side, Linden stood frozen and appalled.

Hissing voraciously, Marid flung himself into a run. He sprinted to the rock, up the shelf.

For one splinter of time, Covenant could not move. He saw Marid launch himself at Linden, saw fangs reaching towards her face, saw her standing as if her heart had stopped.

Her need snatched Covenant into motion. He took two desperate strides, crashed head and shoulders against her. They tumbled together across the hard dirt.

He disentangled himself, flipped to his feet.

Marid landed heavily, rolling to get his legs under him.

Wielding his knife, Sunder attempted to close with Marid. But a flurry of fangs drove him back.

At once, Marid rushed towards Linden again.

Covenant met the charge. He stopped one serpent head with his right forearm, caught the other scaly body in his left fist.

The free snake reared back to strike.

In that instant, Sunder reached into the struggle. Too swiftly for the snakes to react, he cut Marid's throat. Viscid fluid splashed the front of Covenant's clothes.

Sunder dropped his dead friend. Blood poured into the dirt. Covenant recoiled several steps. As she rose to her knees, Linden gagged as if she were being asphyxiated by the Sunbane.

The Graveller paid no heed to his companions. A frenetic haste possessed him. 'Blood,' he panted. 'Life.' He slapped his hands into the spreading pool, rubbed them together, smeared red on to his forehead and cheeks. 'At least your death will be of some avail. It is my guilt-gift.'

Covenant stared in dismay. He had not known that a human body could be so lavish of blood.

Snatching out the Sunstone, Sunder bent his head to Marid's neck, sucked blood directly from the cut. With the stone held in both palms, he spewed fluid on to it so that it lay cupped in Marid's life. Then he looked upward and began to chant in a language Covenant could not understand.

Around him, the air concentrated as if the heat took personal notice of his invocation. Energy blossomed from the *orcrest*.

A shaft of vermeil as strait as the line between life and death shot towards the sun. It crackled like a discharge of lightning; but it was steady and palpable, sustained by blood.

It consumed the blood in Sunder's hands, drank the blood from Marid's veins, leeched the blood from the earth. Soon every trace of red was gone. Marid's throat gaped like a dry grin.

Still chanting, Sunder set down the Sunstone near Marid's head. The shaft binding the *orcrest* to the sun did not falter.

Almost at once, water bubbled up around the stone. It gathered force until it was a small spring, as fresh and clear as if it arose from mountain rock rather than from barren dust.

As he watched, Covenant's head began to throb. He was flushed and sweating under the weight of the sun.

Still Sunder chanted; and beside the spring, a green shoot raised its head. It grew with staggering celerity; it became a vine, spread itself along the ground, put out leaves. In a moment, it produced several buds which swelled like melons.

The Graveller gestured Linden towards the spring. Her expression had changed from suffocation to astonishment. Moving as if she were entranced, she knelt beside the spring, put her lips into the water. She jerked back at once, surprised by the water's coldness. Then she was drinking deeply, greedily.

A maleficent fire bloomed in Covenant's right forearm. His breathing was ragged. Dust filled his mouth. He could feel his pulse beating in the base of his throat.

After a time, Linden pulled away from the spring, turned to him. 'It's good,' she said in dim wonder. 'It's good.'

He did not move, did not look at her. Dread spurted up in him like water from dry ground.

'Come on,' she urged. 'Drink.'

He could not stop staring at Marid. Without shifting his gaze, he extended his right arm towards her.

She glanced at it, then gave a sharp cry and leaped to him, took hold of his arm to look at it closely.

He was loath to see what she saw; but he forced himself to gaze downward.

His forearm was livid. A short way up from his wrist, two puncture marks glared bright red against the darkness of the swelling. 'Bastard bit me,' he coughed as if he were already dying.

8

THE CORRUPTION OF THE SUN

'Sunder!' Linden barked. 'Give me your knife.'

The Graveller had faltered when he saw the fang marks; and the spring had also faltered. But he recovered quickly, restored the cadence of his chant. The shaft of Sunbane-fire wavered, then grew stable once more. The melons continued to ripen.

Still chanting, he extended his poniard towards Linden. She strode

140

over to him, took the blade. She did not hesitate; all her actions were certain. Stooping to one of Marid's ankles, she cut a section of the rope which bound the stake.

The pain became a hammer in Covenant's forearm, beating as if it meant to crush the bones. Mutely, he gripped the elbow with his left hand, squeezed hard in an effort to restrict the spread of the venom. He did not want to die like this, with all his questions unanswered, and nothing accomplished.

A moment later, Linden returned. Her lips were set in lines of command. When she said, 'Sit down,' his knees folded as if she held the strings of his will.

She sat in front of him, straightened his arm between them. Deftly, she looped the rope just above his elbow, pulled it tight until he winced; then she knotted it.

'Now,' she said evenly, 'I'm going to have to cut you. Get out as much of the venom as I can.'

He nodded. He tried to swallow, but could not.

She set the point of the blade against the swelling, abruptly snatched it back. Her tone betrayed a glimpse of strain. 'Goddamn knife's too dirty.'

Frowning, she snapped, 'Don't move,' and jumped to her feet. Purposefully, she went to the hot red shaft of Sunder's power. He hissed a warning, but she ignored him. With a physician's care, she touched the poniard to the beam.

Sparks sprayed from the contact; fire licked along the knife. When she withdrew it, she nodded grimly to herself.

She rejoined Covenant, braced his arm. For a moment, she met his gaze. 'This is going to hurt,' she said straight into his eyes. 'But it'll be worse if I don't do it.'

He fought to clear his throat. 'Go ahead.'

Slowly, deliberately, she cut a deep cross between the fang marks. A scream tore his flesh. He went rigid, but did not permit himself to flinch. This was necessary; he had done such things himself. Pain was life; only the dead felt no pain. He remained still as she bent her head to suck at the incisions. With his free hand, he gripped his forehead, clutching the bones of his skull for courage.

Her hands squeezed the swelling, multiplying fire. Her lips hurt him like teeth as she drew blood and venom into her mouth.

The taste shattered her composure; she spat his blood fiercely at the ground. 'God!' she gasped. 'What kind – ?' At once, she attacked the wound again, sucked and spat with violent revulsion. Her hands shuddered as she gripped his arm.

What kind – ? Her words throbbed along the pressure in his head. What was she talking about?

A third time she sucked, spat. Her features strained whitely, like clenched knuckles. With unintended brutality, she dropped his arm;

a blaze shot up through his shoulder. Springing to her feet, she stamped on the spat blood, ground it into the dirt as if it were an outrage she wanted to eradicate from the world.

'Linden,' he panted wanly through his pain, 'what is it?'

'Venom!' she fulminated with repugnance. 'What kind of place is this?' Abruptly, she hastened to Sunder's spring, began rinsing her mouth. Her shoulders were knots of abhorrence.

When she returned to Covenant, her whole body was trembling, and her eyes were hollow. 'Poison.' She hugged herself as if she were suddenly cold. 'I don't have words for it. That wasn't just venom. It was something more – something worse. Like the Sunbane. Some kind of moral poison.' She pulled her hands through her hair, fighting for control. 'God, you're going to be sick – ! You need a hospital. Except there's no antivenin in the world for poison like that.'

Covenant whirled in pain, could not distinguish between it and fear. Moral poison? He did not understand her description, but it clarified other questions. It explained why the Raver in Marid had allowed itself to be exposed. So that Marid would be condemned to the Sunbane, would become a monster capable of inflicting such poison. But why? What would Lord Foul gain if Covenant died like this? And why had Marid aimed his attack at Linden? Because she was sensitive to the Land, could see things the Despiser did not want seen?

Covenant could not think. The reek of blood on his shirt filled his senses. Everything became dread; he wanted to wail. But Linden came to his aid. Somehow, she suppressed her own distress. Urging him upright, she supported him to the water so that he could drink. He was already palsied. But his body recognized its need for water; he swallowed thirstily at the spring.

When he was done, she helped him into the shade of the shelf. Then she sat beside him and held his livid arm with her hands, trying in that way to make him comfortable.

Blood dripped unremarked from his cuts. The swelling spread darkness up towards his elbow.

Sunder had been chanting continuously; but now he stopped. He had at last been able to make his invocation briefly self-sustaining. When he fell silent, the *orcrest*'s vermeil shaft flickered and went out, leaving the stone empty, like a hole in the ground; but the spring continued to flow for a few moments. He had time to drink deeply before the water sank back into the barren earth.

With his poniard, he cut the melons from their vine, then bore them into the shade, and sat down on Covenant's left. Unsteadily, he began slicing the melons into sections, scooping out the seeds. The seeds he put away in a pocket of his jerkin. Then he handed sections of melon across to Linden.

'This is *ussusimiel*,' he said in a fragile tone, as if he were exhausted and feared contradiction. 'At need it will sustain life with no other food.' Wearily, he began to eat.

Linden tasted the fruit. She nodded her approval, then started to devour the sections Sunder had given her. Dully, Covenant accepted a piece for himself. But he felt unable to eat. Pain excruciated the bones of his right arm; and that fire seemed to draw all other strength out of him, leaving him to drown in a wide slow whirl of lassitude. He was going to pass out — And there were so many things his companions did not understand.

One was more important than the others. He tried to focus his sight on the Graveller. But he could not keep his vision clear. He closed his eyes so that he would not have to watch the way the Stonedownor blurred and ran.

'Sunder.'

'Ur-Lord?'

Covenant sighed, dreading Sunder's reaction. 'Listen.' He concentrated the vestiges of his determination in his voice. 'We can't stay here. I haven't told you where we're going.'

'Let it pass,' said his guide quietly. 'You are harmed and hungry. You must eat. We will consider such questions later.'

'Listen.' Covenant could feel midnight creeping towards him. He strove to articulate his urgency. 'Take me to Revelstone.'

'Revelstone?' Sunder exploded in protest. 'You wander in your wits. Do you not know that Revelstone is the Keep of the na-Mhoram? Have I not spoken of the Rede concerning you? The Riders journey throughout the Land, commanding your destruction. Do you believe that they will welcome you courteously?'

'I don't care about that.' Covenant shook his head, then found that he could not stop. The muscles of his neck jerked back and forth like the onset of hysteria. 'That's where the answers are. I've got to find out how this happened.' He tried to gesture towards the barrenness; but all his horizons were dark, blinded by dust and dead air. 'What the Sunbane is. I can't fight it if I don't know what it is.'

'Ur-Lord, it is three hundred leagues.'

'I know. But I've got to go. I have to know what happened.' He insisted weakly, like a sick child. 'So I can fight it.'

'Heaven and Earth!' Sunder groaned. 'This is the greatest madness of all.' For a long moment, he remained still, scouring himself for endurance or wisdom. Please, Covenant breathed into the silence. Sunder. Please.

Abruptly, the Graveller muttered, 'Ah, well. I have no longer any other demand upon me. And you are not to be denied. In the name of Nassic my father — and of Marid my friend, whose life you strove to redeem at your cost — I will guide you where you wish to go. Now eat. Even prophets and madmen require sustenance.'

Covenant nodded dimly. Shutting his mind to the smell of blood, he took a bite of the *ussusimiel*.

It could not compare with *aliantha* for taste and potency; but it felt clean in his mouth, and seemed to relieve some of the congestion of his pain. As he ate, the darkness receded somewhat.

After he had consumed his share of the fruit, he settled himself to rest for a while. But Sunder stood up suddenly. 'Come,' he said to Linden. 'Let us be on our way.'

'He shouldn't be moved,' she replied flatly.

'There will be *aliantha* nigh the River. Perhaps they will have power to aid him.'

'Maybe. But he shouldn't be moved. It'll make the venom spread.'

'Linden Avery,' Sunder breathed. 'Marid was my friend. I cannot remain in this place.'

Covenant became conscious of a dim fetor in the air. It came from his arm. Or from Marid's corpse.

For a moment, Linden did not respond. Then she sighed, 'Give me the knife. He can't travel with his arm like that.'

Sunder handed her his poniard. She looked closely at Covenant's swelling. It had grown upward past his elbow. Its black pressure made the rope bite deeply into his arm.

He watched tabidly as she cut away the tourniquet.

Blood rushed at his wound. He cried out.

Then the darkness came over him for a time. He was on his feet, and his arms were hooked over the shoulders of his companions, and they were moving westward. The sun beat at them as if they were an affront to its suzerainty. The air was turgid with heat; it seemed to resist respiration. In all directions, the stone and soil of the Plains shimmered as if they were evaporating. Pain laughed garishly in his head at every step. If Linden or Sunder did not find some kind of febrifuge for him soon –

Linden was on his left now, so that her stumbling would not directly jar his sick arm. Oblivion came and went. When Covenant became aware of the voice, he could not be sure of it. It might have been the voice of a dream.

> 'And he who wields white wild magic gold
> is a paradox-
> for he is everything and nothing,
> hero and fool,
> potent, helpless –
> and with the one word of truth or treachery
> he will save or damn the Earth
> because he is mad and sane,
> cold and passionate,
> lost and found.'

144

Sunder fell silent. After a moment, Linden asked, 'What is that?' She panted the words raggedly.

'A song,' said the Graveller. 'Nassic my father sang it – whenever I became angry at his folly. But I have no understanding of it, though I have seen the white ring, and the wild magic shining with a terrible loveliness.'

Terrible, Covenant breathed as if he were dreaming.

Later, Linden said, 'Keep talking. It helps – Do you know any other songs?'

'What is life without singing?' Sunder responded. 'We have songs for sowing and for reaping – songs to console children during the sun of pestilence – songs to honour those whose blood is shed for the Stonedown. But I have set aside my right to sing them.' He made no effort to conceal his bitterness. 'I will sing for you one of the songs of a-Jeroth, as it is taught by the Riders of the Clave.'

He straightened his shoulders, harrowing Covenant's arm. When he began, his voice was hoarse with dust, short-winded with exertion; but it suited his song.

'"Oh, come, my love, and bed with me;
Your mate knows neither lust nor heart –
Forget him in this ecstasy.
I joy to play the treacher's part."
Acute with blandishments and spells,
Spoke a-Jeroth of the Seven Hells.

'Diassomer Mininderain,
The mate of might, and Master's wife,
All stars' and heavens' chatelaine,
With power over realm and strife,
Attended well, the story tells,
To a-Jeroth of the Seven Hells.

'With a-Jeroth the lady ran;
Diassomer with fear and dread
Fled from the Master's ruling span.
On Earth she hides her trembling head,
While all about her laughter wells
From a-Jeroth of the Seven Hells.

'"Forgive!" she cries with woe and pain;
Her treacher's laughter hurts her sore.
"His blandishments have been my bane.
I yearn my Master to adore."
For in her ears the spurning knells
Of a-Jeroth of the Seven Hells.

145

'Wrath is the Master — fire and rage.
Retribution fills his hands.
Attacking comes he, sword and gage,
'Gainst treachery in all the lands.
Then crippled are the cunning spells
Of a-Jeroth of the Seven Hells.

'Mininderain he treats with rue;
No heaven-home for broken trust,
But children given to pursue
All treachery to death and dust.
Thus Earth become a gallow-fells
For a-Jeroth of the Seven Hells.'

The Graveller sighed. 'Her children are the inhabitants of the Earth. It is said that elsewhere in the Earth — across the seas, beyond the mountains — live beings who have kept faith. But the Land is the home of the faithless, and on the descendants of betrayal the Sunbane wreaks the Master's wrath.'

Covenant expostulated mutely. He knew as vividly as leprosy that the Clave's view of history was a lie, that the people of the Land had been faithful against Lord Foul for millennia. But he could not understand how such a lie had come to be believed. Time alone did not account for this corruption.

He wanted to deny Sunder's tale. But his swelling had risen black and febrile halfway to his shoulder. When he tried to find words, the darkness returned.

After a time, he heard Linden say, 'You keep mentioning the Riders of the Clave.' Her voice was constricted, as if she suffered from several broken ribs. 'What do they ride?'

'Great beasts,' Sunder answered, 'which they name Coursers.'

'Horses?' she panted.

'Horses? I do not know this word.'

Do not — ? Covenant groaned as if the pain in his arm were speaking. Not know the Ranyhyn? He saw a sudden memory in the heat-haze: the great horses of Ra rearing. They had taught him a lesson he could hardly bear about the meaning of fidelity. Now they were gone? Dead? The desecration which Lord Foul had wrought upon the Land seemed to have no end.

'Beasts are few in the Land,' Sunder went on, 'for how can they endure the Sunbane? My people have herds — some goats, a few cattle — only because large effort is made to preserve their lives. The animals are penned in a cave near the mountains, brought out only when the Sunbane permits.

'But it is otherwise with the Coursers of the Clave. They are bred in Revelstone for the uses of the Riders — beasts of great swiftness

146

and size. It is said that those on their backs are warded from the Sunbane.' Grimly, he concluded, 'We must evade all such aid if we wish to live.'

No Ranyhyn? For a time, Covenant's grief became greater than his pain. But the sun was coquelicot malice in his face, blanching what was left of him. The sleeve of his T-shirt formed a noose around his black arm; and his arm itself on Sunder's shoulder seemed to be raised above him like a mad, involuntary salute to the Sunbane. Even sorrow was leprosy, numb corruption: meaningless and irrefragable. Venom slowly closed around his heart.

Sometime later the darkness bifurcated, so that it filled his head, and yet he could gaze out at it. He lay on his back, looking at the moon; the shadows of the riverbanks rose on either side. A breeze drifted over him, but it seemed only to fan his fever. The molten lead in his arm contradicted the taste of *aliantha* in his mouth.

His head rested in Linden's lap. Her head leaned against the slope of the watercourse; her eyes were closed; perhaps she slept. But he had lain with his head in a woman's lap once before, and knew the danger. *Of your own volition* – He bared his teeth at the moon. 'It's going to kill me.' The words threatened to strangle him. His body went rigid, straining against invisible poison. 'I'll never give you the ring. Never.'

Then he understood that he was delirious. He watched himself, helpless, while he faded in and out of nightmare, and the moon crested overhead.

Eventually, he heard Sunder rouse Linden. 'We must journey now for a time,' the Graveller said softly, 'if we wish to find new *aliantha*. We have consumed all that is here.'

She sighed as if the vigil she kept galled her soul.

'Does he hold?' asked Sunder.

She shifted so that she could get to her feet. 'It's the *aliantha*,' she murmured. 'If we keep feeding him – '

Ah, you are stubborn yet. Are stubborn yet stubborn yet.

Then Covenant was erect, crucified across the shoulders of his companions. At first, he suffered under unquiet dreams of Lord Foul, of Marid lying throat-cut beneath an angry sun. But later he grew still, drifted into visionary fields – dew-bedizened leas decked with eglantine and meadow rue. Linden walked among them. She was Lena and Atiaran: strong, and strongly hurt; capable of love; thwarted. And she was Elena, corrupted by a misbegotten hate – child of rape, who destroyed herself to break the Law of Death because she believed that the dead could bear the burdens of the living.

Yet she was none of these. She was herself, Linden Avery, and her touch cooled his forehead. His arm was full of ashes, and his sleeve no longer cut into the swelling. Noon held the watercourse in a vice of heat; but he could breathe, and see. His heart beat unself-consciously. When he looked up at her, the sun made her hair radiant about her head.

'Sunder.' Her tone sounded like tears. 'He's going to be all right.'

'A rare poison, this *aliantha*,' the Graveller replied grimly. 'For that lie, at least, the Clave must give an accounting.'

Covenant wanted to speak; but he was torpid in the heat, infant-weak. He shifted his hips in the sand, went back to sleep.

When he awakened again, there was sunset above him. He lay with his head on Linden's lap under the west bank of the river, and the sky was streaked with orange and pink, sunlight striking through dust-laden air. He felt brittle as an old bone; but he was lucid and alive. His beard itched. The swelling had receded past his elbow; his forearm had faded from blackness to the lavender of shadows. Even the bruises on his face seemed to have healed. His shirt was long dry now, sparing him the smell of blood.

Dimness obscured Linden's mien; but she was gazing down at him, and he gave her a wan smile. 'I dreamed about you.'

'Something good, I hope.' She sounded like the shadows.

'You were knocking at my door,' he said because his heart was full of relief. 'I opened it, and shouted, "Goddamn it, if I wanted visitors I'd post a sign!" You gave me a right cross that almost broke my jaw. It was love at first sight.'

At that, she turned her head away as if he had hurt her. His smile fell apart. Immediately, his relief became the old familiar ache of loneliness, isolation made more poignant by the fact that she was not afraid of him. 'Anyway,' he muttered with a crooked grimace like an apology, 'it made sense at the time.'

She did not respond. Her visage looked like a helm in the crepuscular air, fortified against any affection or kinship.

A faint distant pounding accentuated the twilight; but Covenant hardly heard it until Sunder leaped suddenly down the east bank into the watercourse. 'Rider!' he cried, rushing across the sand to crouch at Linden's side. 'Almost I was seen.'

Linden coiled under Covenant, poised herself to move. He clambered into a sitting position, fought his heart and head for balance. He was in no condition to flee.

Fright sharpened Linden's whisper. 'Is he coming this way?'

'No,' replied Sunder quickly. 'He goes to Mithil Stonedown.'

'Then we're safe?' Already the noise was almost gone.

'No. The Stonedown will tell him of our flight. He will not ignore the escape of the halfhand and the white ring.'

Her agitation increased. 'He'll come after us?'

'Beyond doubt. The Stonedown will not give pursuit. Though they have lost the Sunstone, they will fear to encounter Marid. But no such fear will restrain the Rider. At the sun's rising – if not before – he will be ahunt for us.' In a tone like a hard knot, he concluded, 'We must go.'

'Go?' Linden murmured in distraction. 'He's still too weak.' But an instant later she pulled herself erect. 'We'll have to.'

Covenant did not hesitate. He extended a hand to Sunder. When the Graveller raised him to his feet, he rested on Sunder's shoulder while frailty whirled in his head, and forced his mouth to shape words. 'How far have we come?'

'We are no more than six leagues by the River from Mithil Stonedown,' Sunder answered. 'See,' he said, pointing southward. 'It is not far.'

Rising there roseate in the sunset were mountain-heads – the west wall of the Mithil valley. They seemed dangerously near. Six! Covenant groaned to himself. In two days. Surely a Rider could cover that distance in one morning.

He turned back to his companions. Standing upright in the waterway, he had better light; he could see them clearly. Loss and self-doubt, knowledge of lies and fear of truth, had burrowed into Sunder's countenance. He had been bereft of everything which had enabled him to accept what he had done to his son, to his wife. In exchange, he had been given a weak driven man who defied him, and a hope no larger than a wedding band.

And Linden, too, was suffering. Her skin had been painfully sunburned. She was caught in a world she did not know and had not chosen, trapped in a struggle between forces she could not comprehend. Covenant was her only link to her own life; and she had almost lost him. Ordinary mortality was not made to meet such demands. And yet she met them and refused even to accept his gratitude. She stored up pain for herself as if no other being had the right to touch her, care about her.

Regret raked at Covenant's heart. He had too much experience with the way other people bore the cost of his actions.

But he accepted it. There was a promise in such pain. It gave him power. With power, he had once wrested meaning for all the blood lost in his name from Lord Foul's worst Despite.

For a moment while his companions waited, trying to contain their haste, he gave himself a VSE. Then he said tightly, 'Come on. I can walk,' and began to shamble northward, along the watercourse.

With the thought of a Rider pressing against his back, he kept his legs in motion for half a league. But the aftermath of the venom had left him tabid. Soon he was forced to ask for help. He turned to Sunder; but the Graveller told him to rest, then scrambled out of the riverbed.

Covenant folded unwillingly to the ground, sat trying to find an answer to the incapacity which clung to his bones. As the moon rose, Sunder returned with a double handful of *aliantha*.

Eating his share of the treasure-berries, Covenant felt new strength flow into him, new healing. He needed water, but his thirst was not acute. When he was done, he was able to regain his feet, walk again.

With the help of frequent rests, more *aliantha*, and support from his companions, he kept moving throughout the night. Darkness lay cool and soothing on the South Plains, as if all the fiery malison of the Sunbane had been swept away, absorbed by the gaps of midnight between the stars. And the sandy bottom of the Mithil made easy going. He drove himself. The Clave had commanded his death. Under the moon, he held his weakness upright; but after moonset, his movements became a long stagger of mortality, dependent and visionless.

They rested before dawn; but Sunder roused them as sunrise drew near. 'The doom of the Sunbane approaches,' he murmured. 'I have seen that your footwear spares you. Yet you will ease my heart if you join me.' He nodded towards a broad plane of rock nearby – clean stone large enough to protect a score of people.

Trembling with exhaustion, Covenant tottered to his feet. Together, the companions stood on the rock to meet the day.

When the sun broke the horizon, Sunder let out a cry of exultation. The brown was gone. In its place, the sun wore a coronal of chrysoprase. The light green touch on Covenant's face was balmy and pleasant, like a caress after the cruel pressure of the desert sun.

'A fertile sun!' Sunder crowed. 'This will hamper pursuit, even for a Rider.' Leaping off the rock as if he had been made young again, he hurried to find a clear patch of sand. With the haft of his poniard he ploughed two swift furrows across the sand; and in them he planted a handful of his *ussusimiel* seeds. 'First we will have food!' he called. 'Can water be far behind?'

Covenant turned towards Linden to ask her what she saw in the sun's green. Her face was slack and puffy, untouched by Sunder's excitement; she was pushing herself too hard, demanding too much of her worn spirit. And her eyes were dull, as if she were being blinded by the things she saw – essential things neither Covenant nor Sunder could discern.

He started to frame a question; but then the sunshine snatched his attention away. He gaped at the west bank.

The light had moved part way down the side of the watercourse. And wherever it touched soil, new-green sprouts and shoots thrust into view.

They grew with visible rapidity. Above the rim of the river, a few bushes raised their heads high enough to be seen. Green spread downward like a mantle, following the sunline cast by the east wall; plants seemed to scurry out of the dirt. More bush tops appeared beyond the bank. Here and there, young saplings reached towards the sky. Wherever the anademed sunlight fell, the wasteland of the past three days became smothered by verdure.

'The fertile sun,' Sunder breathed gladly. 'None can say when it will rise. But when it rises, it brings life to the Land.'

'Impossible,' Covenant whispered. He kept blinking his eyes, unconsciously trying to clear his sight, kept staring at the way grass and vines came teeming down the riverbank, at the straight new trees which were already showing themselves beyond the shrubs along the river's edge. The effect was eldritch, and frightening. It violated his instinctive sense of Law. 'Impossible.'

'Forsooth,' chuckled the Graveller. He seemed new-made by the sun. 'Do your eyes lack credence? Surely you must now acknowledge that there is truth in the Sunbane.'

'Truth – ?' Covenant hardly heard Sunder. He was absorbed in his own amazement. 'There's still Earthpower – that's obvious. But it was never like this.' He felt an intuitive chill of danger. 'What's wrong with the Law?' Was that it? Had Foul found some way to destroy the Law itself? The *Law*?

'Often,' Sunder said, 'Nassic my father sang of Law. But he did not know its import. What is Law?'

Covenant stared sightlessly at the Graveller. 'The Law of Earthpower.' Fearsome speculations clogged his throat; dread rotted his guts. 'The natural order. Seasons. Weather. Growth and decay. What happened to it? What has he done?'

Sunder frowned as if Covenant's attitude were a denial of his gladness. 'I know nothing of such matters. The Sunbane I know – and the Rede which the na-Mhoram has given us for our survival. But seasons – Law. These words have no meaning.'

No meaning, Covenant groaned. No, of course not. If there were no Law, if there had been no Law for centuries, the Stonedownor could not possibly understand. Impulsively, he turned to Linden. 'Tell him what you see.'

She appeared not to hear him. She stood at the side of the rock, wearing an aspect of defenceless hebetude.

'Linden!' he cried, driven by his mortal apprehension. 'Tell him what you *see*.'

Her mouth twisted as if his demand were an act of brutality. She pushed her hands through her hair, glanced up at the green-wreathed sun, then at the green-thick bank.

Shuddering, she permitted herself to see.

Her revulsion was all the answer Covenant needed. It struck him like an instant of shared vision, momentarily gifting or blighting his senses with the acuity they lacked. Suddenly, the long grass and

151

curling vines, the thick bushes, the saplings no longer seemed lush to him. Instead, they looked frenetic, hysterical. They did not spring with spontaneous luxuriance out of the soil; they were forced to grow by the unnatural scourge of the sun. The trees clawed towards the sky like drowners; the creepers writhed along the ground as if they lay on coals; the grass grew as raw and immediate as a shriek.

The moment passed, leaving him shaken.

'It's wrong.' Linden rubbed her arms as if what she saw made her skin itch like an infestation of lice. The redness of her sunburn aggravated all her features. 'Sick. Evil. It's not supposed to be like this. It's killing me.' Abruptly, she sat down, hid her face in her hands. Her shoulders clenched as if she did not dare to weep.

Covenant started to ask, Killing you? But Sunder was already shouting.

'Your words signify nothing! This is the fertile sun! It is not *wrong*. It simply *is*. Thus the Sunbane has been since the punishment began. Behold!'

He stabbed a gesture towards the sandy patch in which he had planted his seeds. The sun-line lay across one of his furrows. In the light, *ussusimiel* were sprouting.

'Because of this, we will have food! The fertile sun gives life to all the Land. In Mithil Stonedown – now, while you stand thus decrying wrong and ill – every man, woman, and child sings. All who have strength are at labour. While the fertile sun holds, they will labour until they fall from weariness. Searching first to discover places where the soil is of a kind to support crops, then striving to clear that ground so seeds may be planted. Thrice in this one day, crops will be planted and harvested, thrice each day of the fertile sun.

'And if people from another Stonedown come upon this place, seeking proper soil for themselves, then there will be killing until one Stonedown is left to tend the crops. And the people will *sing*! The fertile sun is life! It is fibre for rope and thread and cloth, wood for tools and vessels and fire, grain for food, and for the *metheglin* which heals weariness. Speak not to me of wrong!' he cried thickly. But then his passion sagged, leaving him stooped and sorrowful. His arms hung at his sides as if in betraying his home he had given up all solace. 'I cannot bear it.'

'Sunder.' Covenant's voice shook. How much longer could he endure being the cause of so much pain? 'That isn't what I meant.'

'Then enlighten me,' the Graveller muttered. 'Comfort the poverty of my comprehension.'

'I'm trying to understand your life. You endure so much – just being able to sing is a victory. But that isn't what I meant.' He gripped himself so that his anger would not misdirect itself at Sunder. 'This isn't a punishment. The people of the Land aren't criminals – betrayers. No!' *I have been preparing retribution.* 'Your lives aren't wrong. The Sunbane is wrong. It's an evil that's being done to the Land. I don't know how. But I know who's responsible. Lord Foul – you call him a-Jeroth. It's his doing.

'Sunder, he can be fought. Listen to me.' He appealed to the scowling Graveller. 'He can be fought.'

Sunder glared at Covenant, clinging to ideas, perceptions, he could understand. But after a moment he dropped his gaze. When he spoke, his words were a recognition. 'The fertile sun is also perilous, in its way. Remain upon the safety of the rock while you may.' With his knife, he went to clean away grass and weeds from around his vines.

Ah, Sunder, Covenant sighed. You're braver than I deserve.

He wanted to rest. Fatigue made the bones of his skull hurt. The swelling of his forearm was gone now; but the flesh was still deeply bruised, and the joints of his elbow and wrist ached. But he held himself upright, turned to face Linden's mute distress.

She sat staring emptily at nothing. Pain dragged her mouth into lines of failure, acutely personal and forlorn. Her hands gripped her elbows, hugging her knees, as if she strove to anchor herself on the stiff mortality of her bones.

Looking at her, he thought he recognized his own first ordeals in the Land. He made an effort to speak gently. 'It's all right. I understand.'

He meant to add, Don't let it overwhelm you. You're not alone. There are reasons for all this. But her reply stopped him. 'No, you don't.' She did not have even enough conviction for bitterness. 'You can't see.'

He had no answer. The flat truth of her words denied his empathy, left him groping within himself as if he had lost all his fingers. Defenceless against his incapacity, his responsibility for burdens he was unable to carry, he sank to the stone, stretched out his tiredness. She was here because she had tried to save his life. He yearned to give her something in return, some help, protection, ease. Some answer to her own severity. But there was nothing he could do. He could not even keep his eyes open.

When he looked up again, the growth on both sides of the watercourse, and down the west bank to the edge of the rock, had become alarmingly dense. Some of the grass was already knee-deep. He wondered how it would be possible to travel under such a sun. But he left that question to Sunder.

While melon buds ripened on his vines, the Graveller occupied himself by foraging for wild creepers. These he cut into strands. When he was satisfied with what he had gathered, he returned to the rock, and began knotting and weaving the vines to form a mesh sack.

By the time he had finished this chore, the first of the *ussusimiel* were ripe. He sectioned them, stored the seeds in his pocket, then meted out rations to his companions. Covenant accepted his share deliberately, knowing his body's need for aliment. But Sunder had to nudge Linden's shoulder to gain her attention. She frowned at the *ussusimiel* as if it were unconscionable, received it with a look of gall.

When they had eaten, Sunder picked the rest of the melons and put them in his sack. He appeared to be in a lighter mood; perhaps his ability to provide food had strengthened his sense of how much he was needed; or perhaps he was now less afraid of pursuit. Firmly, he announced, 'We must leave the riverbed. We will find no water here.' He nodded towards the east bank. 'At first it will be arduous. But as the trees mount, they will shade the ground, slowing the undergrowth. But mark me – I have said that the fertile sun is perilous. We must travel warily, lest we fall among plants which will not release us. While this sun holds, we will sojourn in daylight, sleeping only at night.'

Covenant rubbed lightly at the scabs on his forearm, eyed the rim of the bank. 'Did you say water?'

'As swiftly as strength and chance permit.'

Strength, Covenant muttered. Chance. He lacked one, and did not trust the other. But he did not hesitate. 'Let's go.'

Both men looked at Linden.

She rose slowly to her feet. She did not raise her eyes; but she nodded mutely.

Sunder glanced a question at Covenant; but Covenant had no answer. With a shrug, the Graveller lifted his sack to his shoulder and started down the river bottom. Covenant followed, with Linden behind him.

Sunder avoided the grass and weeds as much as possible until he reached a place where the sides were less steep. There he dug his feet into the dirt, and scrambled upward.

He had to burrow through the underbrush which lipped the slope to gain level ground. Covenant watched until the Graveller disappeared, then attempted the climb himself. Handholds on long dangling clumps of grass aided his ascent. After a moment of slippage, he crawled into Sunder's burrow.

Carefully, he moved along the tunnel of bracken and brush which Sunder had brunted clear. The teeming vegetation made progress difficult; he could not rise above his hands and knees. He felt enclosed by incondign verdancy, a savage ecstasy of growth more insidious than walls, and more stifling. He could not control the shudders of his muscles.

Crawling threatened to exhaust him; but after some distance, the tunnel ended. Sunder had found an area where the bracken was only waist-high, shaded by a crowded young copse of wattle. He was stamping down the brush to make a clearing when Covenant and then Linden caught up with him.

'We are fortunate,' Sunder murmured, nodding towards one of the nearest trees. It was a new mimosa nearly fifteen feet tall; but it would not grow any more; it was being strangled by a heavy creeper as thick as Covenant's thigh. This plant had a glossy green skin, and it bore a cluster of yellow-green fruit which vaguely resembled papaya. 'It is *mirkfruit*.'

Mirkfruit? Covenant wondered, remembering the narcoleptic pulp with which he and Linden had been captured by Mithil Stonedown. 'How is that fortunate?'

Sunder took out his knife. 'The fruit is one matter, the vine another.' Drawing Covenant with him, he stepped towards the creeper, gripped his poniard in both hands. 'Stand ready,' he warned. Then he leaped upwards and spiked his blade into the plant above the level of his head.

The knife cut the vine like flesh. When Sunder snatched back his blade, clear water gushed from the wound.

In his surprise, Covenant hesitated.

'Drink!' snapped Sunder. Brusquely, he thrust Covenant under the spout.

Then Covenant was gulping at water that splashed into his face and mouth. It was as fresh as night air.

When he had satisfied his body's taut thirst, Linden took his place, drank as if she were frantic for something, anything, which did not exacerbate the soreness of her nerves. Covenant feared the vine would run dry. But after she stepped aside, Sunder was able to drink his fill before the stream began to slacken.

While the water lasted, the companions used it to wash their hands and faces, sluice some of the dust from their clothes. Then the Graveller shouldered his sack. 'We must continue. Nothing motionless is free of hazard under this sun.' To demonstrate his point, he kicked his feet, showed how the grass tried to wind around his ankles. 'And the Rider will be abroad. We will journey as near the Mithil as soil and sun allow.'

He gestured northward. In that direction, beyond the shade of the copse, lay a broad swath of raw grey grass, chest-high and growing. But then the grass faded into a stand of trees, an incongruous aggregation of oak and sycamore, eucalyptus and jacaranda. 'There is great diversity in the soil,' Sunder explained, 'and the soil grows what is proper to it. I cannot foresee what we will encounter. But we will strive to stay among trees and shade.' Scanning the area as if he expected to see signs of the Rider, he began to breast his way through the thick grass.

Covenant followed unsteadily, with Linden at his back.

By the time they neared the trees, his arms were latticed with fine scratches from the rough blades; and the grass itself waved above his head.

But later, as Sunder had predicted, the shade of the trees held the undergrowth to more natural proportions. And these trees led to a woodland even more heavily shadowed by cypress, flowering mulberry, and a maple-like tree with yellow leaves which Covenant recognized poignantly as Gilden. The sight of these stately trees, which the people of the Land had once treasured so highly, now being grown like puppets by the Sunbane, made ire pound like vertigo in the bones of his forehead.

He turned to share his outrage with Linden. But she was consumed by her own needs, and did not notice him. Her gaze was haunted by misery; her eyes seemed to wince away from everything around her, as if she could not blind herself to the screaming of the trees. Neither she nor Covenant had any choice but to keep moving.

Shortly after noon, Sunder halted in a bower under a dense willow. There the companions ate a meal of *ussusimiel*. Then, half a league further on, they came across another *mirkfruit* creeper. These things sustained Covenant against his convalescent weakness. Nevertheless, he reached the end of his stamina by mid-afternoon. Finally, he dropped to the ground, allowed himself to lie still. All his muscles felt like mud; his head wore a vice of fatigue that constricted his sight and balance. 'That's enough,' he mumbled. 'I've got to rest.'

'You cannot,' the Graveller said. He sounded distant. 'Not until the sun's setting – or until we have found barren ground.'

'He has to,' panted Linden. 'He hasn't got his strength back. He still has that poison in him. He could relapse.'

After a moment, Sunder muttered, 'Very well. Remain with him – ward him. I will search for a place of safety.' Covenant heard the Graveller stalking away through the brush.

Impelled by Sunder's warning, Covenant crawled to the shade of a broad Gilden trunk, seated himself against the bark. For a short time, he closed his eyes, floated away along the wide rolling of his weariness.

Linden brought him back to himself. She must have been tired, but she could not rest. She paced back and forth in front of him, gripping her elbows with her hands, shaking her head as if she were arguing bitterly with herself. He watched for a moment, tried to squeeze the fatigue from his sight. Then he said carefully, 'Tell me what's the matter.'

'That's the worst.' His request triggered words out of her; but she replied to herself rather than to him. 'It's all terrible, but that's the worst. What kind of tree is that?' She indicated the trunk against which he sat.

'It's called a Gilden.' Spurred by memories, he added, 'The wood used to be considered very special.'

'It's the worst.' Her pacing tightened. 'Everything's hurt. In such pain – ' Tremors began to scale upward in her voice. 'But that's the worst. All the Gilden. They're on fire inside. Like an auto-da-fé.' Her hands sprang to cover the distress on her face. 'They ought to be put out of their misery.'

Put out of – ? The thought frightened him. Like Sunder's mother? 'Linden,' he said warily, 'tell me what's the matter.'

She spun on him in sudden rage. 'Are you deaf as well as blind? Can't you feel anything? I said they're in pain! They ought to be put out of their misery!'

'No.' He faced her fury without blinking. That's what Kevin did. The Land's need broke his heart. So he invoked the Ritual of Desecration, trying to extirpate evil by destroying what he loved. Covenant winced to remember how close he had come to walking that path himself. 'You can't fight Lord Foul that way. That's just what he wants.'

'Don't tell me that!' she spat at him. 'I don't want to hear it. You're a leper. Why should you care about pain? Let the whole world scream! It won't make any difference to you.' Abruptly, she flung herself to the ground, sat against a tree with her knees raised to her chest. 'I can't take any more.' Suppressed weeping knurled her face. She bowed her head, sat with her arms outstretched and rigid across her knees. Her hands curled into fists, clinging futilely to thin air. 'I can't.'

The sight of her wrung his heart. 'Please,' he breathed. 'Tell me why this hurts you so much.'

'I can't shut it out.' Hands, arms, shoulders – every part of her was clenched into a rictus of damned and demanding passion. 'It's all happening to me. I can see – feel – the trees. In me. It's too personal. I can't take it. It's killing me.'

Covenant wanted to touch her, but did not dare. She was too vulnerable. Perhaps she would be able to feel leprosy in the contact of his fingers. For a moment, he grappled with a desire to tell her about Kevin. But she might hear that story as a denial of her pain. Yet he had to offer her something.

'Linden,' he said, groaning inwardly at the arduousness of what he meant to say, 'when he summoned us here, Foul spoke to me. You didn't hear him. I'm going to tell you what he said.'

Her hands writhed; but she made no other reply. After a difficult moment, he began to repeat the Despiser's cold scorn.

Ah, you are stubborn yet.

He remembered every word of it, every drop of venom, every infliction of contempt. The memory came upon him like a *geas*, overwhelming his revulsion, numbing his heart. Yet he did not try to stop. He wanted her to hear it all. Since he could not ease her, he tried to share his sense of purpose.

You will be the instrument of my victory.

As the words fell on her, she coiled into herself – curled her arms around her knees, buried her face against them – shrank from what he was saying like a child in terror.

There is despair laid up for you here beyond anything your petty mortal heart can bear.

Yet throughout his recitation he felt that she hardly heard him, that her reaction was private, an implication of things he did not know about her. He half expected her to break out in keening. She seemed so bereft of the simple instinct for solace. She could have sustained herself with anger at the Despiser, as he did; but such an outlet seemed to have no bearing on her complex anguish. She sat folded trembling into herself, and made no sound.

Finally, he could no longer endure watching her. He crawled forward as if he was damning himself, and sat beside her. Firmly, he pried her right hand loose from its clinch, placed his halfhand in her grip so that she could not let go of his maimed humanity unless she released her hold on herself. 'Lepers aren't numb,' he said softly. 'Only the body gets numb. The rest compensates. I want to help you, and I don't know how.' Through the words, he breathed, Don't hurt yourself like this.

Somehow, the touch of his hand, or the empathy in his voice, reached her. As if by a supreme act of will, she began to relax her muscles, undo the knots of her distress. She drew a shuddering breath, let her shoulders sag. But still she clung to his hand, held the place of his lost fingers as if that amputation were the only part of him she could understand.

'I don't believe in evil.' Her voice seemed to scrape through her throat, come out smeared with blood. 'People aren't like that. This place is *sick*. Lord Foul is just something you made up. If you can blame sickness on somebody, instead of accepting it for what it is, then you can avoid being responsible for it. You don't have to try to end the pain.' Her words were an accusation; but her grip on his hand contradicted it. 'Even if this is a dream.'

Covenant could not answer. If she refused to admit the existence of her own inner Despiser, how could he persuade her? And how could he try to defend her against Lord Foul's manipulations? When she abruptly disengaged her hand, rose to her feet as if to escape the implications of his grasp, he gazed after her with an ache of loneliness indistinguishable from fear in his heart.

9

RIVER-RIDE

A short time later, Sunder returned. If he noticed Linden's tension as she stood there pale and absolute with her back to Covenant, he did not ask for any explanation. Quietly, he announced that he had found a place where they could rest safely until the next morning. Then he offered Covenant his hand.

Covenant accepted the help, let himself be pulled to his feet. His muscles felt like ashes in his limbs; but by leaning on Sunder's shoulder he was able to travel another half a league to reach a stretch of rock. It was hidden among high brush, which provided at least some protection against discovery. Reclining on the rough stone, Covenant went to sleep for the remainder of the afternoon. After a supper of *ussusimiel*, he surprised himself by sleeping throughout the night.

In spite of the hardness of his bed, he did not awaken until shortly after sunrise. By that time, Sunder had already cleared a patch of ground and planted a new crop of melons.

When Covenant arose, Linden joined him. Avoiding his gaze as if she could not tolerate the sight of his thoughts, his concern for her, his countervailing beliefs, she examined him mutely, then pronounced him free of fever, fit to travel. Something she saw disturbed her, but she did not say what it was, and he did not ask.

As soon as Sunder's new crop was ripe, he replenished his stock of seeds and refilled his sack of melons. Then he led Covenant and Linden away into the brush.

The Mithil River had turned towards the north-west, and they continued to follow its course as closely as the terrain permitted. Initially, their progress was slow; their way traversed a tangle of ground-ivy which threatened to baffle even the Graveller's strength. But beyond the ivy they entered a deep forest of banyan trees, and walking became easier.

The second day of the fertile sun raised the banyans to heights far beyond anything Covenant would have believed possible. Huge avenues and galleries lay between the trunks; the prodigious intergrown branches arched and stretched like the high groined ceiling and towering pillars of a place of reverence in Revelstone — or like the grand cavern of Earthroot under *Melenkurion* Skyweir. But the effect was ominous rather than grand. Every bough and trunk seemed to be suffering under its own weight.

Several times, Covenant thought he heard a rumble of hooves in the distance, though he saw nothing.

The next day, the companions met some of the consequences of the sun's necrotic fecundity. By mid-morning, they found themselves struggling through an area which, just the day before, had been a stand of cedars many hundreds of feet tall. But now it looked like the scene of a holocaust.

Some time during the night, the trees had started to topple; and each falling colossus had chopped down others. Now the entire region was a chaos of broken timber — trunks and branches titanically rent, splintered, crushed. The three companions spent the whole day wrestling with the ruins.

Near sunset, they won through to a low hillside of heather, seething in the breeze and twice their height. Sunder attacked the wrist-thick stems with his poniard, and eventually succeeded in clearing an area large enough for them to lie down. But even then he could not rest; he was taut with anxiety. While they ate, Covenant made no comment; and Linden, wrapped in her privacy, seemed unaware of the Graveller. But later Covenant asked him what troubled him.

Grimly, Sunder replied, 'I have found no stone. The moon wanes, and will not penetrate this heather sufficiently to aid my search. I know not how to avoid Marid's fate.'

Covenant considered for a moment, then said, 'I'll carry you. If I'm protected, you ought to be safe, too.'

The Graveller acceded with a stiff shrug. But still he did not relax. Covenant's suggestion violated a lifetime of ingrained caution. Quietly, Covenant said, 'I think you'll be all right. I was right about the *aliantha*, wasn't I?'

Sunder responded by settling himself for sleep. But when Covenant awakened briefly during the night and looked about him, he saw the Graveller staring up into the darkness of the heather like a man bidding farewell to the use of his eyes.

The companions rose in the early grey of dawn. Together, they moved through the heather until they found a thinning through which they could glimpse the eastern horizon. The breeze had become stronger and cooler since the previous evening. Covenant felt a low chill of apprehension. Perhaps he and Linden had not been protected by their footwear; perhaps they were naturally immune to the Sunbane. In that case —

They had no time to search for alternatives. Sunrise was imminent. Linden took the sack of melons. Covenant stooped to let Sunder mount his back. Then they faced the east. Covenant had to compel himself not to hold his breath.

The sun came up flaring azure, blue-clad in an aura of sapphire. It shone for only a moment. Then black clouds began to roll westward like the vanguard of an attack.

'The sun of rain.' With an effort, Sunder ungnarled his fingers from Covenant's shoulders and dropped to the ground. 'Now,' he rasped against the constriction of his chest, 'we will at last begin to travel with some swiftness. If we do not foil pursuit altogether, we will at least prolong our lives.'

At once, he turned towards the River, started plunging hurriedly through the heather as if he were racing the clouds.

Covenant faced Linden across the rising wind. 'Is he all right?'

'Yes,' she replied impatiently. 'Our shoes block the Sunbane.' When he nodded his relief, she hastened after Sunder.

The heather spread westward for some distance, then changed abruptly into a thicket of knaggy bushes as tall as trees along the riverbank. The clouds were overhead, and a few raindrops had begun to spatter out of the sky, as Sunder forged into the high brush. While he moved, he hacked or broke off stout branches nearly eight feet long, cut loose long sections of creeper. These he dragged with him through the thicket. When he had collected all he could manage, he gave the branches and vines to his companions, then gathered more wood of the same length.

By the time they came in sight of the riverbed, only a small strip of sky remained clear in the west.

Sunder pressed forward to the edge of the bank. There he prepared a space in which he could work. Obeying his terse orders, though they did not know what he had in mind, Covenant and Linden helped him strip his vines and branches of twigs and leaves. Then they put all the wood together lengthwise, and Sunder lashed it into a secure bundle with the vines. When he was done, he had a tight stack thicker than the reach of his arms.

Wind began to rip the top of the thicket. Heavy drops slapped against the leaves, producing a steady drizzle within the brush. But Sunder appeared to have forgotten his haste. He sat down and did what he could to make himself comfortable.

After a moment, Covenant asked, 'Now what?'

Sunder looked at him, at Linden. 'Are you able to swim?'

They both nodded.

'Then we will await the rising of the River.'

Covenant blinked the water out of his eyes. Damnation, he muttered. A raft.

The idea was a good one. The current of the Mithil would provide a faster pace than anything they could hope to match by travelling overland. And Sunder's raft would give them something to hold on to so that they did not exhaust themselves. The Graveller had been in such a hurry because the chore of making even this small raft would have been far more difficult under the full weight of the rain.

Covenant nodded to himself. Sunder was a more resourceful guide than he deserved.

Linden seated herself near the raft and folded her arms over her knees. In a flat voice, she said, 'It's going to be cold.'

That was true; the rain was already chilly. But Covenant ignored it, moved to look down into the river bottom.

The sight made him dubious. The bed was choked with growth almost to the level of the rim. He did not know how long the water would take to rise; but when it did, the trees and brush would make it extremely hazardous.

As Sunder handed out rations of *ussusimiel*, Covenant continued studying the watercourse. The downpour was hard and flat now, beating into the brush as steadily as a waterfall, and the air darkened gradually; but he could see well enough to make out the first muddy stirrings of the River. Initially, he feared that the water would rise too slowly. But the thicket had caused him to under-estimate the force of the storm. The torrents fell heavily – and more heavily moment by moment. The rain sounded like a great beast thrashing in the brush.

The water began to run more rapidly. Moiling like a current of snakes, the stream slipped between the trees, rushed slapping and gurgling through the shrubs. All this region of the South Plains drained into the watercourse. Covenant had barely finished his meal when a sudden change came over the flow. Without warning, the current seemed to leap upward, forward, like a pouncing predator; and some of the bushes shifted.

They were shallow-rooted. The stream tugged them free. They caught promptly in the limbs of the trees, hung there like desperation in the coils of the current. But the water built up against them. The trees themselves started to topple.

Soon uprooted trunks and branches thronged the River, beating irresistibly downstream. The water seethed with the force of an avalanche. Rain crashed into the Mithil, and it rose and ran avidly. Foot by foot, it swept itself clean.

The current was more than halfway up the banks when Sunder got to his feet. He spent a moment ensuring that his few possessions were secure, then stooped to the raft, lashed the sack of melons tightly to the wood.

A spasm of fear twisted Covenant's chest. 'It's too dangerous!' he shouted through the noise of the rain. 'We'll be battered to pieces!' I'm a leper!

'No!' Sunder returned. 'We will ride with the current – with the trees! If the hazard surpasses you, we must wait! The River will not run clear until the morrow!'

Covenant thought about the Rider, about beings he had encountered who could sense the presence of white gold. Before he could respond, Linden barked, 'I'll go crazy if I have to spend my time sitting here!'

Sunder picked up one end of the raft. 'Cling to the wood, lest we become lost to each other!'

At once, she bent to the other end of the bundle, locked her hands among the branches, lifted them.

Cursing silently, Covenant placed himself beside her and tried to grip the wet branches. The numbness of his fingers threatened to betray him; he could not be sure of his hold.

'We must move as one!' Sunder warned. 'Out into the centre!'

Covenant growled his understanding. He wanted to pause for a VSE. The watercourse looked like an abyss to his ready vertigo.

The next moment, Sunder yelled, 'Now!' and hurled himself towards the edge.

Hellfire! The raft yanked at Covenant as Sunder and Linden heaved it forward. He lurched into motion.

Sunder sprang for the water. The raft dived over the bank. Covenant's grip tore him headlong past the edge. With a shattering jolt, he smashed into the water.

The impact snatched his inadequate fingers from the raft. The Mithil swept him away and down. He whirled tumbling along the current, lost himself in turbulence and suffocation. An instant of panic made his brain as dark as the water. He flailed about him without knowing how to find the surface.

Then a bush still clinched to its roots struck his leg a stinging blow. It righted him. He clawed upward.

With a gasp that made no sound, he broke water.

Amid the tumult of the rain, he was deaf to everything except air and fear, the current shoving at his face, and the gelid fire of the water. The cold stunned his mind.

But a frantic voice was howling, 'Covenant!'

The urgency of Linden's cry reached him. Fighting the drag of his boots, he surged head and shoulders out of the racing boil, scanned the darkness.

Before he plunged underwater again, he caught a glimpse of the raft.

It was nearby, ten feet further downriver. As he regained the surface, he struck out along the current.

An arm groped for him. He kicked forward, grabbed at Linden's waist with his half-hand. His numb fingers could not hold. Water closed over his head.

Her hand clamped on to his forearm, heaved him towards the raft. He grappled for one of the branches and managed to fasten himself to the rough bark.

His weight upset Sunder's control of the raft. The bundle began to spin. Covenant had an impression of perilous speed. The riverbanks were only a vague looming; they seethed past him as he hurtled along the watercourse.

'Are you all right?' Linden shouted.

'Yes!'

Together, they battled the cold water, helped Sunder right the raft's plunging.

The rain deluged them, rendered them blind and mute. The current wrestled constantly for mastery of the raft. Repeatedly, they had to thrash their way out of vicious backwaters and fend off trees which came beating down the River like triremes. Only the width of the Mithil prevented logjams from developing at every bend.

And the water was cold. It seemed to suck at their muscles, draining their strength and warmth. Covenant felt as if his bones were being filled with ice. Soon he could hardly keep his head above water, hardly hold on to the wood.

But as the River rose, its surface gradually grew less turbulent. The current did not slow; but the increase of water blunted the moiling effect of the uneven bottom and banks. The raft became easier to manage. Then, at Sunder's instructions, the companions began to take turns riding prone on the raft while the other two steered, striving to delay the crisis of their exhaustion.

Later, the water became drinkable. It still left a layer of grit on Covenant's teeth; but rain and run-off slowly macerated the mud, clarifying the Mithil.

He began to hear an occasional dull booming like the sounds of battle. It was not thunder; no lightning accompanied it. Yet it broke through the loud water-sizzle of the rain.

Without warning, a sharp splintering rent the air. A monstrous shadow hove above him. At the last instant, the current rushed the raft out from under the fall of an immense tree. Too tall for its roots, overburdened by the weight of the storm, the tree had riven its moorings and toppled across the River.

Now Covenant heard the same rending everywhere, near and far. The Mithil traversed a region of megalithic trees; the clamour of their destruction broke and boomed incessantly.

He feared that one of them would strike the raft or dam the River. But that did not happen. The trees which landed in the Mithil occluded the current without blocking it. And then the noise of their ruin receded as the River left that region behind.

Rain continued to fall like the collapse of the sky. Covenant placed himself at one end of the raft and used the weight of his boots to steady its course. Half-paralysed with cold, he and his companions rode through a day that seemed to have no measure and no end. When the rain began to dwindle, that fact could not penetrate his dogged stupor. As the clouds rolled back from the east, uncovering the clear heavens of evening, he gaped at the open air as if it spoke a language which had become alien to him.

Together, the companions flopped like dying fish to the riverbank, crawled out of the water. Somehow, Sunder mustered the strength to secure the raft against the rising of the River. Then he joined Covenant and Linden in the wind-shelter of a copse of preternatural gorse, and slumped to the ground. The teeming black clouds slid away to the west; and the sun set, glorious with orange and red. The gloaming thickened towards night.

'Fire.' Linden's voice quivered; she was trembling from head to foot. 'We've got to have a fire.'

Covenant groaned his mind out of the mud on which he lay, raised his head. Long vibrations of cold ran through him; shivers knotted his muscles. The sun had not shone on the Plains all day, and the night was as clear as perfect ice.

'Yes,' Sunder said through locked teeth. 'We must have fire.'

Fire. Covenant winced to himself. He was too cold to feel anything except dread. But the need was absolute. And he could not bear to think of blood. To forestall the Graveller, he struggled to his hands and knees, though his bones seemed to clatter together. 'I'll do it.'

They faced each other. The silence between them was marked only by the chill breeze rubbing its way through the copse, and by the clenched shudder of breathing. Sunder's expression showed that he did not trust Covenant's strength, did not want to set aside his responsibility for his companions. But Covenant kept repeating inwardly, You're not going to cut yourself for me, and did not relent. After a moment, Sunder handed him the *orcrest*.

Covenant accepted it with his trembling halfhand, placed it in contact with his ring, glared at it weakly. But then he faltered. Even in ten years, he had not been able to unlearn his instinctive fear of power.

'Hurry,' Linden whispered.

Hurry? He covered his face with his left hand, striving to hide his ague. Bloody hell. He lacked the strength. The *orcrest* lay inert in his fist; he could not even concentrate on it. You don't know what you're asking.

But the need was indefensible. His anger slowly tightened. He became rigid, clenched against the chills. Ire indistinguishable from pain or exhaustion shaped itself to the circle of his ring. The Sunstone had no life; the white gold had no life. He gave them his life. There was no other answer.

Cursing silently, he hammered his fist at the mud.

White light burst in the *orcrest*: flame sprang from his ring as if the metal were a band of silver magma. In an instant, his whole hand was ablaze.

He raised his fist, brandished fire like a promise of retribution against the Sunbane. Then he dropped the Sunstone. It went out;

but his ring continued to spout flame. In a choking voice, he gasped, 'Sunder!'

At once, the Graveller gave him a dead gorse-branch. He grasped the wet bark in his halfhand: his arm shook as he squeezed white flame into the wood. When he set it down, it was afire.

Sunder supplied more wood, then knelt to tend the weak fire. Covenant set flame to the second branch, to a third and fourth. Sunder fed the burning with leaves and twigs, blew carefully on the flames. After a moment, he announced, 'It is enough.'

With a groan, Covenant let his mind fall blank, and the blaze of his ring plunged into darkness. Night closed over the copse, huddled around the faint yellow light and smoke of the fire.

Soon he began to feel heat on his face.

Sagging within himself, he tried to estimate the consequences of what he had done, measure the emotional umbrage of power.

Shortly, the Graveller recovered his sack of melons from the raft, and dealt out rations of *ussusimiel*. Covenant felt too empty to eat; but his body responded without his volition. He sat like an effigy, with wraiths of moisture curling upward from his clothes, and looked dumbly at the inanition of his soul.

When she finished her meal, Linden threw the rinds away. Staring into the flames, she said remotely, 'I don't think I can take another day of this.'

'Is there choice?' Fatigue dulled Sunder's eyes. He sat close to the heat, as if his bones were thirsty for warmth. 'The ur-Lord aims towards Revelstone. Very well. But the distance is great. Refusing the aid of the River, we must journey afoot. To gain the Keep of the na-Mhoram would require many turnings of the moon. But I fear we would not gain it. The Sunbane is too perilous. And there is the matter of pursuit.'

The set of Linden's shoulders showed her apprehension. After a moment, she asked tightly, 'How much longer?'

The Graveller sighed. 'None can foretell the Sunbane,' he said in a dim voice. 'It is said that in generations past each new sun shone for five and six, even as many as seven days. But a sun of four days is now uncommon. And with my own eyes I have beheld only one sun of less than three.'

'Two more days,' Linden muttered. 'Dear God.'

For a while, they were silent. Then, by tacit agreement, they both arose to gather wood for the fire. Scouring the copse, they collected a substantial pile of brush and branches. After that, Sunder stretched out on the ground. But Linden remained sitting beside the fire. Slowly, Covenant noticed through his numbness that she was studying him.

In a tone that seemed deliberately inflectionless, she asked, 'Why does it bother you to use your ring?'

166

His ague had abated, leaving only a vestigial chill along his bones. But his thoughts were echoes of anger. 'It's hard.'

'In what way?' In spite of its severity, her expression said that she wanted to understand. Perhaps she needed to understand. He read in her a long history of self-punishment. She was a physician who tormented herself in order to heal others, as if the connection between the two were essential and compulsory.

To the complexity of her question, he gave the simplest answer he knew. 'Morally.'

For a moment, they regarded each other, tried to define each other. Then, unexpectedly, the Graveller spoke. 'There at last, ur-Lord,' he murmured, 'you have uttered a word which lies within my comprehension.' His voice seemed to arise from the wet wood and the flames. 'You fear both strength and weakness, both power and lack of power. You fear to be in need – and to have your need answered. As do I.

'I am a Graveller – well acquainted with such fear. A Stonedown trusts the Graveller for its life. But in the name of that life, that trust, he must shed the blood of his people. Those who trust must be sacrificed to meet the trust. Thus trust becomes a matter of blood and death. Therefore I have fled my home – ' the simple timbre of lament in his tone relieved what he said of any accusation – 'to serve a man and a woman whom I cannot trust. I know not how to trust you, and so I am freed of the burden of trust. There is naught between us which would require me to shed your lives. Or to sacrifice my own.'

Listening to Sunder's voice and the fire, Covenant lost some of his fear. A sense of kinship came over him. This dour self-doubting Stonedownor had suffered so much, and yet had preserved so much of himself. After a long moment, Covenant chose to accept what Sunder was saying. He could not pay every price alone. 'All right,' he breathed like the night breeze in the copse. 'Tomorrow night you can start the fire.'

Quietly, Sunder replied, 'That is well.'

Covenant nodded. Soon he closed his eyes. His weariness lowered him to the ground beside the fire. He wanted to sleep.

But Linden held his attention. 'It isn't enough,' she said stiffly. 'You keep saying you want to fight the Sunbane, but you can hardly light a fire. You might as well be afraid of rubbing sticks together. I need a better answer than that.'

He understood her point. Surely the Sunbane – capable of torturing nature itself at its whim – could not be abrogated by anything as paltry as a white gold ring. He distrusted power because no power was ever enough to accomplish his heart's desires. To heal the world. Cure leprosy. Bridge the loneliness which thwarted his capacity for love. He made an effort not to sound harsh. 'Then find one. Nobody else can do it for you.'

She did not respond. His words seemed to drive her back into her isolation. But he was too tired to contend with her. Already he had begun to fade. As she settled herself for the night, he rode the susurration of the River into sleep.

He awoke cramped and chilled beside a pile of dead embers. The stars had been effaced; and in the dawn, the rapid Mithil looked dark and cold, as fatal as sleet. He did not believe he could survive another day in the water.

But, as Sunder had said, they had no choice. Shivering in dire anticipation, he awakened his companions. Linden looked pale and haggard, and her eyes avoided the River as if she could not bear to think about it. Together, they ate a scant breakfast, then stood on a boulder to face the dawn. As they had expected, the sun rose in a glow of blue, and menacing clouds began to pile out of the east. Sunder shrugged in resignation and went to re-tie his shrinking sack of melons to the raft.

The companions launched the bundle of wood. The sting of the water burned Covenant's breath out of his lungs; but he fought the cold and the current and the weight of his boots with his old leper's intransigence, and survived the first shock.

Then the rain commenced. During the night, the River had become less violent; it had washed itself free of floating brush and trees and had risen above the worst of its turbulence. But the rain was more severe, had more wind behind it. Gusts drove the raindrops until they hit like flurries of hail. Torrents lashed into the water with a hot, scorching sound.

The downpour rapidly became torment for the companions. They could not escape from the sodden and insidious cold. From time to time, Covenant glimpsed a burst of lightning in the distance, rupturing the dark; but the unremitting slash of rain into the Mithil drowned out any thunder. Soon his muscles grew so leaden, his nerves so numb, that he could no longer grip the raft. He jammed his hand in among the branches, hooked his elbow over one of the bindings, and survived.

Somehow, the day passed. At last, a line of clear sky broke open along the east. Gradually, the rain and wind eased. More by chance than intent, the companions gained a small cove of gravel and sand in the west bank. As they drew their raft out of the water, Covenant's legs failed, and he collapsed face-down on the pebbles as if he would never be able to move again.

Linden panted, 'Firewood.' He could hear the stumbling scrunch of her shoes. Sunder also seemed to be moving.

Her groan jerked up his head, heaved him to his hands and knees. Following her wounded stare, he saw what had dismayed her.

There was no firewood. The rain had washed the gravel clean. And the small patch of shore was impenetrably surrounded by a tangle of briar with long barbed thorns. Exhaustion and tears thickened her voice as she moaned, 'What are we going to do?'

Covenant tried to speak, but was too weak to make any sound.

The Graveller locked his weary knees, mustered a scant smile. 'The ur-Lord has granted permission. Be of good heart. Some little warmth will ease us greatly.'

Lurching to his feet, Covenant watched blankly as Sunder approached the thickest part of the briar.

The muscles of his jaw knotted and released irrhythmically, like a faltering heartbeat. But he did not hesitate. Reaching his left hand in among the thorns, he pressed his forearm against one of the barbs and tore a cut across his skin.

Covenant was too stunned by fatigue and cold and responsibility to react. Linden flinched, but did not move.

With a shudder, Sunder smeared the welling blood on to his hands and face, then took out his *orcrest*. Holding the Sunstone so that his cut dripped over it, he began to chant.

For a long moment, nothing happened. Covenant trembled in his bones, thinking that without sunlight Sunder would not be able to succeed. But suddenly a red glow awakened in the translucent stone. Power the colour of Sunder's blood shafted in the direction of the sun.

The sun had already set behind a line of hills, but the Sunstone was unaffected by the intervening terrain; Sunder's vermeil shaft struck towards the sun's hidden position. Some distance from the cove, the shaft disappeared into the dark base of the hills; but its straight, bright power was not hindered.

Still chanting, Sunder moved his hands so that the shaft encountered a thick briar stem. Almost at once, flame burst from the wood.

When the stem was well afire, he shifted his power to the nearest branches.

The briar was wet and alive; but his shaft lit new stems and twigs easily, and the tangle was so dense that the flames fed each other. Soon he had created a self-sustaining bonfire.

He fell silent; and the blood-beam vanished. Tottering weakly, he went to the River to wash himself and the Sunstone.

Covenant and Linden hunched close to the blaze. Twilight was deepening around them. At their backs, the Mithil sounded like the respiration of the sea. In the firelight, Covenant could see that her lips were blue with cold, her face drained of blood. Her eyes reflected the flames as if they were devoid of any other vision. Grimly, he hoped that she would find somewhere the desire or the resolution to endure.

Shortly, Sunder returned, carrying his sack of *ussusimiel*. Linden bestirred herself to tend his arm; but he declined quietly. 'I am a Graveller,' he murmured. 'Such work would not have fallen to me, were I slow of healing.' He raised his forearm, showed her that the bleeding had already stopped. Then he sat down near the flames, and began to prepare a ration of melons for supper.

The three of them ate in silence, settled themselves for the night in silence. Covenant was seeking within himself for the courage to face another day under the sun of rain. He guessed that his companions were doing the same. They wore their private needs like cerements, and slept in isolation.

The next day surpassed Covenant's worst expectations. As clouds sealed the Plains, the wind mounted to rabid proportions, whipping the River into froth and flailing rain like the barbs of a scourge. Lightning and thunder bludgeoned each other across the heavens. In flashes, the sky became as lurid as the crumbling of a firmament, as loud as an avalanche. The raft rode the current like dead wood, entirely at the mercy of the Mithil.

Covenant thrashed and clung in constant fear of the lightning, expecting it to strike the raft, to fry him and his companions. But that killing blow never fell. Late in the day, the lightning itself granted them an unexpected reprieve. Downriver from them, a blue-white bolt sizzled into a stand of prodigious eucalyptus. One of the trees burned like a torch.

Sunder yelled at his companions. Together, they heaved the raft towards the bank, then left the River and hastened to the trees. They could not approach the burning eucalyptus; but when a blazing branch fell nearby, they used other dead wood to drag the branch out from under the danger of the tree. Then they fed brush, broken tree limbs, eucalyptus leaves as big as scythes, to the flames until the blaze was hot enough to resist the rain.

The burning tree and the campfire shed heat like a benediction. The ground was thick with leaves which formed the softest bed Covenant and his companions had had for days. Sometime after sunset, the tree collapsed, but it fell away from them; after that they were able to rest without concern.

Early in the dawn, Sunder roused Covenant and Linden so that they would have time to break their fast before the sun rose. The Graveller was tense and distracted, anticipating a change in the Sunbane. When they had eaten, they went down to the riverbank and found a stretch of flat rock where they could stand to await the morning. Through the gaunt and blackened trees, they saw the sun cast its first glance over the horizon.

It appeared baleful, fiery and red; it wore coquelicot like a crown of thorns, and cast a humid heat entirely unlike the fierce intensity of the desert sun. Its corona seemed insidious and detrimental.

Linden's eyes flinched at the sight. And Sunder's face was strangely blanched. He made an instinctive warding gesture with both hands. 'Sun of pestilence,' he breathed; and his tone winced. 'Ah, we have been fortunate. Had this sun come upon us after the desert sun, or the fertile – ' The thought died in his throat. 'But now, after a sun of rain – ' He sighed. 'Fortunate, indeed.'

'How so?' asked Covenant. He did not understand the attitude of his companions. His bones yearned for the relief of one clear clean day. 'What does this sun do?'

'Do?' Sunder gritted. 'What harm does it not? It is the dread and torment of the Land. Still water becomes stagnant. Growing things rot and crumble. All who eat or drink of that which has not been shaded are afflicted with a disease which few survive and none cure. And the insects – !'

'He's right,' Linden whispered with her mouth full of dismay. 'Oh, my God.'

'It is the Mithil River which makes us fortunate, for it will not stagnate. Until another desert sun, it will continue to flow from its springs, and from the rain. And it will ward us in other ways also.' The reflected red in Sunder's eyes made him look like a cornered animal. 'Yet I cannot behold such a sun without faint-heartedness. My people hide in their homes at such a time and pray for a sun of two days. I ache to be hidden also. I am homeless and small against the wideness of the world, and in all the Land I fear a sun of pestilence more than any other thing.'

Sunder's frank apprehension affected Covenant like guilt. To answer it, he said, 'You're also the only reason we're still alive.'

'Yes,' the Graveller responded as if he were listening to his own thoughts rather than to Covenant.

'Yes!' Covenant snapped. 'And some day every Stonedown is going to know that this Sunbane is not the only way to live. When that day comes, you're going to be just about the only person in the Land who can teach them anything.'

Sunder was silent for a time. Then he asked distantly, 'What will I teach them?'

'To re-make the Land.' Deliberately, Covenant included Linden in his passion. 'It used to be a place of such health and loveliness – if you saw it, it would break your heart.' His voice gave off gleams of rage and love. 'That can be true again.' He glared at his companions, daring them to doubt him.

Linden covered her gaze; but Sunder turned and met Covenant's ire. 'Your words have no meaning. No man or woman can re-make the Land. It is in the hands of the Sunbane, for good or ill. Yet this I say to you,' he grated when Covenant began to protest. 'Make the attempt.' Abruptly, he lowered his eyes. 'I can no longer bear to believe that Nassic my father was a mere witless fool.' Retrieving his sack of melons, he went brusquely and tied it to the centre of the raft.

'I hear you,' Covenant muttered. He felt an unexpected desire for violence. 'I hear you.'

Linden touched his arm. 'Come on.' She did not meet his glance. 'It's going to be dangerous here.'

He followed mutely as she and Sunder launched the raft.

Soon they were out in the centre of the Mithil, riding the current under a red-wreathed sun and a cerulean sky. The warmer air made the water almost pleasant; and the pace of the River had slowed during the night, easing the management of the raft. Yet the sun's aurora nagged at Covenant. Even to his superficial sight, it looked like a secret threat, mendacious and bloodthirsty. Because of it, the warm sunlight and clear sky seemed like concealment for an ambush.

His companions shared his trepidation. Sunder swam with a dogged wariness, as if he expected an attack at any moment. And Linden's manner betrayed an innominate anxiety more acute than anything she had shown since the first day of the fertile sun.

But nothing occurred to justify this vague dread. The morning passed easily as the water lost its chill. The air filled with flies, gnats, midges, like motes of vehemence in the red-tinged light; but such things did not prevent the companions from stopping whenever they saw *aliantha*. Slowly, Covenant began to relax. Noon had passed before he noticed that the River was becoming rougher.

During the days of rain, the Mithil had turned directly northward; and now it grew unexpectedly broader, more troubled. Soon, he descried what was happening. The raft was moving rapidly towards the confluence of the Mithil and another river.

Their speed left the companions no time for choice. Sunder shouted 'Hold!' Linden thrust her hair away from her face, tightened her grip. Covenant jammed his numb fingers in among the branches of the raft. Then the Mithil swept them spinning and tumbling into the turbulent centre of the confluence.

The raft plunged end over end. Covenant felt himself yanked through the turmoil, and fought to hold his breath. But almost at once the current rushed the raft in another direction. Gasping for air, he shook water from his eyes and saw that now they were travelling north-eastward.

For more than a league, the raft seemed to hurtle down the watercourse. But finally the new stream eased somewhat between its banks. Covenant started to catch his breath.

'What was that?' Linden panted.

Covenant searched his memory. 'Must have been the Black River.' From Garroting Deep. And from *Melenkurion* Skyweir, where Elena had broken the Law of Death to summon Kevin Landwaster from his grave, and had died herself as a result. Covenant flinched at the recollection, and at the thought that perhaps none of the Land's ancient forests had survived the Sunbane. Gritting himself, he added, 'It separates the South and Centre Plains.'

'Yes,' said the Graveller. 'And now we must choose. Revelstone lies north of north-west from us. The Mithil no longer shortens our way.'

Covenant nodded. But the seine of his remembering brought up other things as well. 'That's all right. It won't increase the distance.' He knew vividly where the Mithil River would take him. 'Anyway, I don't want to walk under this sun.'

Andelain.

He shivered at the suddenness of his hope and anxiety. If *aliantha* could endure the Sunbane, could not Andelain also preserve itself? Or had the chief gem and glory of the Land already been brought to ruin?

That thought outweighed his urgency to reach Revelstone. He estimated that they were about eighty leagues from Mithil Stonedown. Surely they had outdistanced any immediate pursuit. They could afford this digression.

He noticed that Sunder regarded him strangely. But the Graveller's face showed no desire at all to brave the sun of pestilence afoot. And Linden seemed to have lost the will to care where the River carried them.

By turns, they began trying to get some rest after the strain of the confluence.

For a time, Covenant's awareness of his surroundings was etiolated by memories of Andelain. But then a flutter of colour almost struck his face, snatching his attention to the air over his head. The atmosphere thronged with bugs of all kinds. Butterflies the size of his open hand, with wings like flakes of chiaroscuro, winked and skimmed erratically over the water; huge horseflies whined past him; clusters of gnats swirled like mirages. They marked the air with constant hums and buzzings, like a rumour of distant violence. The sound made him uneasy. Itching skirled down his spine.

Sunder showed no specific anxiety. But Linden's agitation mounted. She seemed inexplicably cold; her teeth chattered until she locked her jaws to stop them. She searched the sky and the riverbanks apprehensively, looking –

The air became harder to breathe, humid and dangerous.

Covenant was momentarily deaf to the swelling hum. But then he heard it – a raw thick growling like the anger of bees.

Bees!

The noise augered through him. He gaped in dumb horror as a swarm dense enough to obscure the sun rose abruptly out of the brush along the River and came snarling towards the raft.

'Heaven and Earth!' Sunder gasped.

Linden thrashed the water, clutched at Covenant. 'Raver!' Her voice scaled into a shriek. 'Oh, my God!'

10

VALE OF CRYSTAL

The presence of the Raver, lurid and tangible, burned through Linden Avery's nerves like a discharge of lightning, stunning her. She could not move. Covenant thrust her behind him, turned to face the onslaught. Her cry drowned as water splashed over her.

Then the swarm hit. Black-yellow bodies as long as her thumb clawed the air, smacked into the River as if they had been driven mad. She felt the Raver all around her – a spirit of ravage and lust threshing viciously among the bees.

Impelled by fear, she dived.

The water under the raft was clear; she saw Sunder diving near her. He gripped his knife and the Sunstone as if he intended to fight the swarm by hand.

Covenant remained on the surface. His legs and body writhed; he must have been swatting wildly at the bees.

At once, her fear changed directions, became fear for him. She lunged towards him, grabbed one ankle, heaved him downwards as hard as she could. He sank suddenly in her grasp. Two bees still clung to his face. In a fury of revulsion, she slapped them away. Then she had to go up for air.

Sunder rose nearby. As he moved, he wielded his knife. Blood streamed from his left forearm.

She split the surface, gulped air, and dived again.

The Graveller did not. Through the distortion of the water, she watched red sunfire raging from the *orcrest*. The swarm concentrated darkly around Sunder. His legs scissored, lifting his shoulders. Power burst from him, igniting the swarm; bees flamed like hot spangles.

An instant later, the attack ended.

Linden broke water again, looked around rapidly. But the Raver was gone. Burnt bodies littered the face of the Mithil.

Sunder hugged the raft, gasping as if the exertion of so much force had ruptured something in his chest.

She ignored him. Her swift scan showed her that Covenant had not regained the surface.

Snatching air into her lungs, she went down for him.

She wrenched herself in circles, searching the water. At first, she could find nothing. Then she spotted him. He was some distance away across the current, struggling upward. His movements were desperate. In spite of the interference of the River, she could see that he was not simply desperate for air.

With all the strength of her limbs, she swam after him.

He reached the surface; but his body went on thrashing as if he were still assailed by bees.

She raised her head into the air near him, surged to his aid.

'Hellfire!' he spat like an ague of fear or agony. Water streamed through his hair and his ragged beard, as if he had been immersed in madness. His hands slapped at his face.

'Covenant!' Linden shouted.

He did not hear her. Wildly, he fought invisible bees, pounded his face. An inchoate cry tore through his throat.

'Sunder!' she panted. 'Help me!' Ducking around Covenant, she caught him across the chest, began to drag him towards the bank. The sensation of his convulsions sickened her; but she bit down her nausea, wrestled him through the River.

The Graveller came limping after her, dragging the raft. His mien was tight with pain. A thin smear of blood stained his lips.

Reaching the bank, she dredged Covenant out of the water. Spasms ran through all his muscles, resisting her involuntarily. But his need gave her strength; she stretched him out on the ground, knelt at his side to examine him.

For one horrific moment, her fear returned, threatening to swamp her. She did not want to see what was wrong with him. She had already seen too much; the wrong of the Sunbane had excruciated her nerves so long, so intimately, that she half-believed she had lost her mind. But she was a doctor; she had chosen this work for reasons which brooked no excuse of fear or repugnance or incapacity. Setting her self aside, she bent the new dimension of her senses towards Covenant.

Clenchings shook him like bursts of brain-fire. His face contorted around the two bee stings. The marks were bright red and swelling rapidly; but they were not serious. Or they were serious in an entirely different way.

Linden swallowed bile, and probed him more deeply.

His leprosy became obvious to her. It lay in his flesh like a malignant infestation, exigent and dire. But it was quiescent.

Something else raged in him. Baring her senses to it, she suddenly remembered what Sunder had said about the sun of pestilence – and what he had implied about insects. He stood over her. In spite of his pain, he swatted grimly at mosquitoes the size of dragonflies, keeping them off Covenant. She bit her lips in apprehension, looked down at Covenant's right forearm.

His skin around the pale scars left by Marid's fangs and Sunder's poniard was already bloated and dark, as if his arm had suffered a new infusion of venom. The swelling worsened as she gazed at it. It was tight and hot, as dangerous as a fresh snake-bite. Again, it gave her a vivid impression of moral wrong, as if the poison were as much spiritual as physical.

Marid's venom had never left Covenant's flesh. She had been disturbed by hints of this in days past, but had failed to grasp its significance. Repulsed by *aliantha*, the venom had remained latent in him, waiting – Both Marid and the bees had been formed by the Sunbane: both had been driven by Ravers. The bee-stings had triggered this reaction.

That must have been the reason for the swarm's attack, the reason why the Raver had chosen bees to work its will. To produce this relapse.

Covenant gaped back at her sightlessly. His convulsions began to fade as his muscles weakened. He was slipping into shock. For a moment, she glimpsed a structure of truth behind his apparent paranoia, his belief in an Enemy who sought to destroy him. All her instincts rebelled against such a conception. But now for an instant she seemed to see something deliberate in the Sunbane, something intentional and cunning in these attacks on Covenant.

The glimpse reft her of self-trust. She knelt beside him, unable to move or choose. The same dismay which had incapacitated her when she had first seen Joan came upon her.

But then the sounds of pain reached her – the moan of Sunder's racked breathing. She looked up at him, asking mutely for answers. He must have guessed intuitively the connection between venom and bees. That was why he defied his own hurt to prevent further insect bites. Meeting her sore gaze, he said, 'Something in me has torn.' He winced at every word. 'It is keen – but I think not perilous. Never have I drawn such power from the Sunstone.' She could feel his pain as a palpable emission; but he had clearly rent some of the ligatures between his ribs, not broken any of the ribs themselves, or damaged anything vital.

Yet his hurt, and his resolute self-expenditure on Covenant's behalf, restored her to herself. A measure of her familiar severity returned, steadying the labour of her heart. She climbed to her feet. 'Come on. Let's get him back in the water.'

Sunder nodded. Gently, they lifted Covenant down the bank. Propping his left arm over the raft so that his right arm could hang free in the cool water, they shoved out into the centre of the current. Then they let the River carry them downstream under the bale of red-ringed sun.

During the remainder of the afternoon, Linden struggled against her memory of Joan, her sense of failure. She could almost hear her mother whining for death. Covenant regained consciousness several times, lifted his head; but the poison always dragged him back before he could speak. Through the water, she watched the black tumescence creep avidly up his arm. It seemed much swifter than the previous time; Marid's poison had increased in virulence during its dormancy. The sight blurred her eyes. She could not silence the fears gnawing at her heart.

Then, before sunset, the River unbent among a clump of hills into a long straight line leading towards a wide ravine which opened on the Mithil. The sides of the ravine were as sheer as a barranca, and they reflected the low sunshine with a strange brilliance. The ravine was like a vale of diamonds; its walls were formed of faceted crystal which caught the light and returned it in delicate shades of white and pink. When the sun of pestilence dipped towards the horizon, washing the terrain in a bath of vermilion, the barranca became a place of rare glory.

People moved on the river-shore; but they gave no indication that they saw the raft. The River was already in shadow, and the brightness of the crystal was dazzling. Soon they left the bank and went up into the ravine.

Linden and Sunder shared a look, and began to steer towards the mouth of the barranca. In dusk macerated only by the last gleamings along the vale rim, they pulled their raft part way up the shore and carefully eased Covenant to dry ground. His arm was black and thick to the shoulder, cruelly pinched by both his ring and his shirt, and he moaned when they moved him.

She sat beside him, stroked his forehead; but her gaze was fixed on Sunder. 'I don't know what to do,' she said flatly. 'We're going to have to ask these people for help.'

The Graveller stood with his arms around his chest, cradling his pain. 'We cannot. Have you forgotten Mithil Stonedown? We are blood that these people may shed without cost to themselves. And the Rede denounces him. I redeemed you from Mithil Stonedown. Who will redeem us here?'

She gripped herself. 'Then why did we stop?'

He shrugged, winced. 'We must have food. Little *ussusimiel* remains to us.'

'How do you propose to get it?' She disliked the sarcasm in her tone, but could not stifle it.

'When they sleep — ' Sunder's eyes revealed his reluctance as clearly as words — 'I will attempt to steal what we must have.'

Linden frowned involuntarily. 'What about guards?'

'They will ward the hills, and the River from the hills. There is no other approach to this place. If they have not yet observed us, perhaps we are safe.'

177

She agreed. The thought of stealing was awkward to her; but she recognized that they had no alternative. 'I'll come with you.' Sunder began to protest; she stopped him with a brusque shake of her head. 'You're not exactly healthy. If nothing else, you'll need me to watch your back. And,' she sighed, 'I want to get some *mirkfruit*. He needs it.'

The Graveller's face was unreadable in the twilight. But he acquiesced mutely. Retrieving the last of his melons from the raft, he began to cut them open.

She ate her ration, then did what she could to feed Covenant. The task was difficult; she had trouble making him swallow the thin morsels she put in his mouth. Again, dread constricted her heart. But she suppressed it. Patiently, she fed slivers of melon to him, then stroked his throat to trigger his swallowing reflex, until he had consumed a scant meal.

When she finished, the night was deep around her, and a waning moon had just begun to crest the hills. She rested beside Covenant for a while, trying to gather up the unravelled ends of her competence. But she found herself listening to his respiration as if she expected every hoarse intake to be his last. She loathed her helplessness so keenly – A distinct fetor rode the breeze from across the River, the effect of the sun of pestilence on the vegetation. She could not rest.

Abruptly, Covenant began to flinch. A faint white light winked along his right side – burned and vanished in an instant.

She sat up, hissed, 'Sunder.'

The light came again – an evanescent stutter of power from the ring embedded deep in Covenant's swollen finger.

'Heaven and Earth!' whispered Sunder. 'It will be seen.'

'I thought – ' She watched stupidly as the Graveller slid Covenant's hand into the pocket of his pants. The movement made him bare his teeth in a grin of pain. His dry stare was fixed on the moon. 'I thought he needed the Sunstone. To trigger it.' His pocket muffled the intermittent gleaming, but did not conceal it entirely. 'Sunder.' Her clothing was still damp; she could not stop shivering. 'What's happening to him?'

'Ask me not,' Sunder breathed roughly. 'I lack your sight.' But a moment later he enquired, 'Can it be that this Raver of which he speaks – that this Raver is within him?'

'No!' she snapped, repudiating the idea so swiftly that she had no chance to control her vehemence. 'He isn't Marid.' Her senses were certain of this; Covenant was ill, not possessed. Nevertheless, Sunder's suggestion struck chords of anger which took her by surprise. She had not realized that she was investing so much of herself in Thomas Covenant. Back on Haven Farm, in the world she understood, she had chosen to support his embattled integrity, hoping to learn a lesson of strength. But she had had no conception of where that decision would carry her. She had already witnessed too much when she had watched him smile for Joan – smile, and forfeit his life. An inchoate part of her clung to this image of him; his self-sacrifice seemed so much cleaner than her own. Now, with a pang, she wondered how much more she had yet to comprehend about him. And about herself. Her voice shook. 'Whatever else he is, he isn't a Raver.'

Sunder shifted in the darkness as if he were trying to frame a question. But before he could articulate it, the dim flicker of Covenant's ring was effaced by a bright spangling from the walls of the barranca. Suddenly, the whole ravine seemed to be on fire.

Linden sprang erect, expecting to find scores of angry Stonedownors rushing towards her. But as her eyes adjusted, she saw that the source of the reflection was some distance away. The village must have lit an immense bonfire. Flames showed the profile of stone houses between her and the light; fire echoed off the crystal facets in all directions. She could hear nothing to indicate that she and her companions were in danger.

Sunder touched her shoulder. 'Come,' he whispered. 'Some high purpose gathers the Stonedown. All its people will attend. Perhaps we have been granted an opportunity to find food.'

She hesitated, bent to examine Covenant. A complex fear made her reluctant. 'Should we leave him?' His skin felt crisp with fever.

'Where will he go?' the Graveller responded simply.

She bowed her head. Sunder would probably need her. And Covenant seemed far too ill to move, to harm himself. Yet he looked so frail – But she had no choice. Pulling herself upright, she motioned for the Graveller to lead the way.

Without delay, Sunder crept up the ravine. Linden followed as stealthily as she could.

She felt exposed in the brightness of the vale; but no alarm was raised. And the light allowed them to approach the Stonedown easily. Soon they were among the houses.

Sunder stopped at every corner to be sure that the path was clear. But they saw no one. All the dwellings seemed to be empty. The Graveller chose a house. Motioning for Linden to guard the doorway, he eased himself past the curtain.

The sound of voices reached her. For an instant, she froze with a warning in her throat. But then her hearing clarified, located the sound. It came from the centre of the Stonedown. She gripped her relief and waited.

Moments later, Sunder returned. He had a bulging leather knapsack under his arm. In her ear, he breathed that he had found *mirkfruit* as well as food.

He started to leave. But she stopped him, gestured inward. For a moment, he considered the advantages of knowing what transpired in the village. Then he agreed.

Together, they sneaked forward until only one house stood between them and the centre. The voices became distinct; she could hear anger and uncertainty in them. When Sunder pointed at the roof, she nodded at once. He set his knapsack down, lifted her to the flat eaves. Carefully, she climbed on to the roof.

Sunder handed her the sack. She took it, then reached down to help him join her. The exertion tore a groan from his sore chest; but the sound was too soft to disturb the voices. Side by side, they slid forward until they were able to see and hear what was happening in the centre of the Stonedown.

The people were gathered in a tight ring around the open space. They were a substantially larger number than the population of Mithil Stonedown. In an elusive way, they seemed more prosperous, better-fed, than the folk of Sunder's home. But their faces were grim, anxious, fearful. They watched the centre of the circle with tense attention.

Beside the bonfire stood three figures – two men and a woman. The woman was poised between the men in an attitude of prayer, as if she were pleading with both of them. She wore a sturdy leather shift like the other Stonedownor women. Her pale delicate features were urgent, and the disarray of her raven hair gave her an appearance of fatality.

The man nearest to Linden and Sunder was also a Stonedownor, a tall square individual with a bristling black beard and eyes darkened by conflict. But the person opposite him was unlike anyone Linden had seen before. His raiment was a vivid red robe draped with a black chasuble. A hook shadowed his features. His hands held a short iron rod like a sceptre with an open triangle affixed to its end. Emanations of heiratic pride and vitriol flowed from him as if he were defying the entire Stonedown.

'A Rider!' Sunder whispered. 'A Rider of the Clave.'

The woman – she was hardly more than a girl – faced the tall Stonedownor. 'Croft!' she begged. Tears suffused her mien. 'You are the Graveller. You must forbid!'

'Aye, Hollian,' he replied with great bitterness. While he spoke, his hands toyed with a slim wooden wand. 'By right of blood and power, I am the Graveller. And you are an eh-Brand – a benison beyond price to the life of Crystal Stonedown. But he is Sivit na-Mhoram-wist. He claims you in the name of the Clave. How may I refuse?'

'You may refuse – ' began the Rider in a sepulchral tone.

'You must refuse!' the woman cried.

'But should you refuse,' Sivit continued remorselessly, 'should you think to deny me, I swear by the Sunbane that I will levy the

180

na-Mhoram's *Grim* upon you, and you will be ground under its might like chaff!'

At the word *Grim*, a moan ran through the Stonedown; and Sunder shivered.

But Hollian defied their fear. 'Croft!' she insisted, 'forbid! I care nothing for the na-Mhoram or his *Grim*. I am an eh-Brand. I foretell the Sunbane! No harm, no *Grim* or any curse, will find you unwary while I abide here. Croft! My people!' She appealed to the ring of Stonedownors. 'Am I nothing, that you cast me aside at the whim of Sivit na-Mhoram-wist?'

'Whim?' barked the Rider. 'I speak for the Clave. I do not utter whims. Harken to me, girl. I claim you by right of service. Without the mediation of the Clave – without the wisdom of the Rede and the sacrifice of the na-Mhoram – there would be no life left in any Stonedown or Woodhelven, despite your arrogance. And we must have life for our work. Do you think to deny me? Contemnible folly!'

'She is precious to us,' said the tall Graveller softly. 'Do not enforce your will upon us.'

'Is she?' Sivit raged, brandishing his sceptre. 'You are sick with her folly. She is not precious. She is an abomination! You think her an eh-Brand, a boon rare in the Land. I say to you, she is a Sun-Sage! Damned as a servant of a-Jeroth! She does not foretell the Sunbane. She causes it to be as she chooses. Against her and her foul kind the Clave strives, seeking to undo the harm such things wreak.'

The Rider continued to rant; but Linden turned away. To Sunder, she whispered, 'Why does he want her?'

'Have you learned nothing?' he replied tightly. 'The Clave has power over the Sunbane. For power, they must have blood.'

'Blood?'

He nodded. 'At all times, Riders journey the Land, visiting again and again every village. At each visit, they take one or two or three lives – ever young and strong lives – and bear them to Revelstone, where the na-Mhoram works his work.'

Linden clenched her outrage, kept her voice at a whisper. 'You mean they're going to kill her?'

'Yes!' he hissed.

At once, all her instincts rebelled. A shock of purpose ran through her, clarifying for the first time her maddening relationship to the Land. Some of Covenant's ready passion became suddenly explicable. 'Sunder,' she breathed, 'we've got to save her.'

'Save – ?' He almost lost control of his voice. 'We are two against a Stonedown. And the Rider is mighty.'

'We've got to!' She groped for a way to convince him. The murder of this woman could not be allowed. Why else had Covenant tried to save Joan? Why else had Linden herself risked her life to prevent his death? Urgently, she said, 'Covenant tried to save Marid.'

'Yes!' rasped Sunder. 'And behold the cost!'

'No.' For a moment, she could not find the answer she needed. Then it came to her. 'What's a Sun-Sage?'

He stared at her. 'Such a being cannot exist.'

'What,' she enunciated, 'is it?'

'The Rider has said,' he murmured. 'It is one who can cause the Sunbane.'

She fixed him with all her determination. 'Then we need her.'

His eyes seemed to bulge in their sockets. His hands grasped for something to hold on to. But he could not deny the force of her argument. 'Mad,' he exhaled through his teeth. 'All of us – mad.' Briefly, he searched the Stonedown as if he were looking for valour. Then he reached a decision. 'Remain here,' he whispered. 'I go to find the Rider's Courser. Perhaps it may be harmed, or driven off. Then he will be unable to bear her away. We will gain time to consider other action.'

'Good!' she responded eagerly. 'If they leave here, I'll try to see where they take her.'

He gave a curt nod. Muttering softly to himself, 'Mad. Mad,' he crept to the rear of the roof and dropped to the ground, taking his knapsack with him.

Linden returned her attention to Hollian's people. The young woman was on her knees, hiding her face in her hands. The Rider stood over her, denouncing her with his sceptre; but he shouted at the Stonedownors.

'Do you believe that you can endure the na-Mhoram's *Grim*? You are fey and anile. By the Three Corners of Truth! At one word from me, the Clave will unleash such devastation upon you that you will grovel to be permitted to deliver up this foul eh-Brand, and it will avail you nothing!'

Abruptly, the woman jerked upright, threw herself to confront the Graveller. 'Croft!' she panted in desperation, 'slay this Rider! Let him not carry word to the Clave. Then I will remain in Crystal Stonedown, and the Clave will know nothing of what we have done.' Her hands gripped his jerkin, urging him. 'Croft, hear me. Slay him!'

Sivit barked a contemptuous laugh. Then his voice dropped, became low and deadly. 'You have not the power.'

'He speaks truly,' Croft murmured to Hollian. Misery knurled his countenance. 'He requires no *Grim* to work our ruin. I must meet his claim, else we will not endure to rue our defiance.'

An inarticulate cry broke from her. For a moment, Linden feared that the young woman would collapse into hysteria. But out of Hollian's distress came an angry dignity. She raised her head, drew herself erect. 'You surrender me,' she said bitterly. 'I am without help or hope. Yet you must at least accord to me the courtesy of my worth. Restore to me the *lianar*.'

Croft looked down at the wand in his hands. The rictus of his shoulders revealed his shame and decision. 'No,' he said softly. 'With this wood you perform your foretelling. Sivit na-Mhoram-wist has no claim upon it – and for you it has no future. Crystal Stonedown will retain it. As a prayer for the birth of a new eh-Brand.'

Triumph shone from the Rider as if he were a torch of malice.

At the far side of the village, Linden glimpsed a sudden hot flaring of red. Sunder's power. He must have made use of his Sunstone. The beam cast vermeil through the crystal, then vanished. She held her breath, fearing that Sunder had given himself away. But the Stonedownors were intent on the conflict in their midst: the instant of force passed unnoticed.

Mute with despair, Hollian turned away from the Graveller, then stopped as if she had been slapped, staring past the corner of the house on which Linden lay. Muffled gasps spattered around the ring; everyone followed the eh-Brand's stare.

What – ?

Linden peered over the eaves in time to see Covenant come shambling into the centre of the village. He moved like a derelict. His right arm was hideously swollen. Poison blazed in his eyes. His ring spat erratic bursts of white fire.

No! she cried silently. Covenant!

He was so weak that any of the Stonedownors could have toppled him with one hand. But the rage of his fever commanded their restraint; the circle parted for him involuntarily, admitting him to the open space.

He lurched to a stop, stood glaring flames around him. 'Linden,' he croaked in a parched voice. 'Linden.'

Covenant!

Without hesitation, she dropped from the roof. Before they could realize what was happening, she thrust her way between the Stonedownors, hastened to Covenant.

'Linden?' He recognized her with difficulty; confusion and venom wrestled across his visage. 'You left me.'

'The Halfhand!' Sivit yelled. 'The white ring!'

The air was bright with peril; it sprang from the bonfire, leaped off the walls of the barranca. Scores of people trembled on the verge of violence. But Linden held everything else in abeyance, concentrated on Covenant. 'No. We didn't leave you. We came to find food. And to save her.' She pointed at Hollian.

The stare of his delirium did not shift. 'You left me.'

'I say it is the Halfhand!' shouted the Rider. 'He has come as the Clave foretold! Take him! Slay him!'

The Stonedownors flinched under Sivit's demand; but they made no move. Covenant's intensity held them back.

'No!' Linden averred to him urgently. 'Listen to me! That man is a Rider of the Clave. The *Clave*. He's going to kill her so that he can use her blood. We've got to save her!'

His gaze twisted towards Hollian, then returned to Linden. He blinked at her incomprehendingly. 'You left me.' The pain of finding himself alone had closed his mind to every other appeal.

'Fools!' Sivit raged. Suddenly, he flourished his sceptre. Blood covered his lean hands. Gouts of red fire spewed from the iron triangle. Swift as vengeance, he moved forward.

'She's going to be sacrificed!' Linden cried at Covenant's confusion. 'Like Joan! *Like Joan!*'

'Joan?' In an instant, all his uncertainty became anger and poison. He swung to face the Rider. 'Joan!'

Before Sivit could strike, white flame exploded around Covenant, enveloping him in conflagration. He burned with silver fury, coruscated the air. Linden recoiled, flung up her hands to ward her face. Wild magic began to erupt in all directions.

A rampage of force tore Sivit's sceptre from his hands. The iron fired black, red, white, then melted into slag on the ground. Argent lashed the bonfire; flaming brands scattered across the circle. Wild lightning sizzled into the heavens until the sky screamed and the crystal walls rang out celestial peals of power.

The very fabric of the dirt stretched under Linden's feet, as if it were about to tear. She staggered to her knees.

The Stonedownors fled. Shrieks of fear escaped among the houses. A moment later, only Croft, Hollian, and Sivit remained. Croft and Hollian were too stunned to move. Sivit huddled on the ground like a craven, with his arms over his head.

Abruptly, as if Covenant had closed a door in his mind, the wild magic subsided. He emerged from the flame; his ring flickered and went out. His legs started to fold.

Linden surged to her feet, caught him before he fell. Wrapping her arms around him, she held him upright.

Then Sunder appeared, carrying the knapsack. He ran forward, shouting, 'Flee! Swiftly, lest they regain their wits and pursue us!' Blood still marked a new cut on his left forearm. As he passed her, he snatched at Hollian's arm. She resisted; she was too numb with shock to understand what was happening. He spun on her, fumed into her face, '*Do you covet death?*'

His urgency pierced her stupor. She regained her alertness with a moan. 'No. I will come. But – but I must have my *lianar*.' She pointed at the wand in Croft's hands.

Sunder marched over to the tall Stonedownor. Croft's grasp tightened reflexively on the wood.

Wincing with pain, Sunder struck Croft a sharp blow in the

stomach. As the taller man doubled over, Sunder neatly plucked the *lianar* from him.

'Come!' Sunder shouted at Linden and Hollian. 'Now!'

A strange grim relief came over Linden. Her first assessments of Covenant had been vindicated; at last, he had shown himself capable of significant power. Bracing his left arm over her shoulders, she helped him out of the centre of the Stonedown.

Sunder took Hollian's wrist. He led the way among the houses as fast as Covenant could move.

The vale was dark now; only the crescent moon, and the reflection of dying embers along the walls, lit the ravine. The breeze carried a sickly odour of rot from across the Mithil, and the water looked black and viscid, like a Satanist's chrism. But no one hesitated. Hollian seemed to accept her rescue with mute incomprehension. She helped Linden ease Covenant into the water, secure him across the raft. Sunder urged them out into the River, and they went downstream clinging to the wood.

11

THE CORRUPTION OF BEAUTY

There was no pursuit. Covenant's power had stunned the people of Crystal Stonedown; the Rider had lost both sceptre and Courser; and the River was swift. Soon Linden stopped looking behind her, stopped listening for the sounds of chase. She gave her concern to Covenant.

He had no strength left, made no effort to grip the raft, did not even try to hold up his head. She could not hear his respiration over the lapping of the water, and his pulse seemed to have withdrawn to a place beyond her reach. His face looked ghastly in the pale moonlight. All her senses groaned to her that he suffered from a venom of the soul.

His condition galled her. She clung to him, searching among her ignorances and incapacities for some way to succour him. A voice in her insisted that if she could feel his distress so acutely she ought to be able to affect it somehow, that surely the current of perception which linked her to him could run both ways. But she shied away from the implications. She had no power, had nothing with which to oppose his illness except the private blood of her own life. Her fear of so much vulnerability foiled her, left her cursing because she lacked even the limited resources of her medical bag – lacked anything which could have spared her this intimate responsibility for his survival.

For a time, her companions rode the River in silence. But at last Hollian spoke. Linden was dimly cognizant of the young woman's plight. The eh-Brand had been surrendered to death by her own village, and had been impossibly rescued – Eventually, all the things she did not understand overcame her reluctance. She breathed clenched apprehension into the darkness. 'Speak to me. I do not know you.'

'Your pardon.' Sunder's tone expressed weariness and useless regret. 'We have neglected courtesy. I am Sunder son of Nassic, at one time – ' he became momentarily bitter – 'Graveller of Mithil Stonedown, four score leagues to the south. With me are Linden Avery the Chosen and ur-Lord Thomas Covenant, Unbeliever and white gold wielder. They are strangers to the Land.'

Strangers, Linden murmured. She saw herself as an unnatural visitant. The thought had sharp edges on all sides.

The eh-Brand answered like a girl remembering her manners with difficulty. 'I am Hollian Amith-daughter, eh-Brand of Crystal Stonedown. I am – ' She faltered, then said in a sore voice, 'I know not whether to give you thanks for redeeming my life – or curses for damning my home. The na-Mhoram's *Grim* will blacken Crystal Stonedown for ever.'

Sunder spoke roughly. 'Perhaps not.'

'How not?' she demanded in her grief. 'Surely Sivit na-Mhoram-wist will not forbear. He will ride forthwith to Revelstone, and the *Grim* will be spoken. Nothing can prevent it.'

'He will not ride to Revelstone. I have slain his Courser.' Half to himself, Sunder muttered, 'The Rede did not reveal to me that a Sunstone may wield such might.'

Hollian gave a low cry of relief. 'And the *rukh* with which he moulds the Sunbane is destroyed. Thus he cannot call down ill upon my people.' A recovery of hope silenced her. She relaxed in the water as if it were a balm for her fears.

Covenant's need was loud in Linden's ears. She tried to deafen herself to it. 'The Rider's sceptre – his *rukh*? Where did he get the blood to use it? I didn't see him cut himself.'

'The Riders of the Clave,' Sunder responded dourly, 'are not required to shed themselves. They are fortified by the young men and women of the Land. Each *rukh* is hollow, and contains the blood with which the Sunbane is wielded.'

Echoes of the outrage which had determined her to rescue Hollian awoke in Linden. She welcomed them, explored them, hunting for courage. The rites of the Sunbane were barbaric enough as Sunder practised them. To be able to achieve such power without personal

186

cost seemed to her execrable. She did not know how to reconcile her ire with what she had heard of the Clave's purpose, its reputation for resistance to the Sunbane. But she was deeply suspicious of that reputation. She had begun to share Covenant's desire to reach Revelstone.

But Covenant was dying.

Everything returned to Covenant and death.

After a while, Hollian spoke again. A different fear prompted her to ask, 'Is it wild magic? Wild magic in sooth?'

'Yes,' the Graveller said.

'Then why — ?' Linden could feel Hollian's disconcertion. 'How did it transpire that Mithil Stonedown did not slay him, as the Rede commands?'

'I did not permit it,' replied Sunder flatly. 'In his name, I turned from my people, so that he would not be shed.'

'You are a Graveller,' Hollian whispered in her surprise. 'A Stonedownor like myself. Such a deed — surely it was difficult for you. How were you brought to commit such transgression?'

'Daughter of Amith,' Sunder answered like a formal confession, 'I was brought to it by the truth of the Rede. The words of the ur-Lord were words of beauty rather than evil. He spoke as one who owns both will and power to give his words substance. And in my heart the truth of the Rede was unbearable.

'Also,' he went on grimly, 'I have been made to learn that the Rede itself contains falsehood.'

'Falsehood?' protested Hollian. 'No. The Rede is the life of the Land. Were it false, all who rely upon it would die.'

Sunder considered for a moment, then said, 'Eh-Brand, do you know the *aliantha*?'

She nodded. 'It is most deadly poison.'

'No.' His certitude touched Linden. In spite of all that had happened, he possessed an inner resilience she could not match. 'It is good beyond any other fruit. I speak from knowledge. For three suns, we have eaten *aliantha* at every chance.'

'Surely — ' Hollian groped for arguments — 'it is the cause of the ur-Lord's sickness?'

'No. This sickness has come upon him previously, and the *aliantha* gave him healing.'

At this, she paused, trying to absorb what she had heard. Her head turned from side to side, searching the night for guidance. When she spoke again, her voice came faintly over the wet sounds of the River. 'You have redeemed my life. I will not doubt you. I am homeless and without purpose, for I cannot return to Crystal Stonedown, and the world is perilous, and I do not comprehend my fate. I must not doubt you.

'Yet I would ask you of your goal. All is dark to me. You have

187

incurred the wrath of the Clave for me. You journey great distances under the Sunbane. Will you give me reason?'

Sunder said deliberately, 'Linden Avery?' passing the question to her. She understood; he was discomfited by the answer, and Hollian was not likely to take it calmly. Linden wanted to reject the difficulty, force Sunder and Hollian to fend for themselves. But, because her own weakness was intolerable to her, she responded squarely, 'We're going to Revelstone.'

Hollian reacted in horror. 'Revelstone? You betray me!' At once, she thrust away from the raft, flailing for an escape.

Sunder lunged after her. He tried to shout something, but his damaged chest changed it to a gasp of pain.

Linden ignored him. His lunge had rolled the raft, dropping Covenant into the water.

She grappled for Covenant, brought him back to the surface. His respiration was so shallow that he did not even cough at the water which streamed from his mouth. In spite of his weight, he conveyed a conviction of utter frailty.

Sunder fought to prevent Hollian's flight; but he was hampered by his hurt ribs. 'Are you mad?' he panted at her. 'If we sought your harm, Sivit's intent would have sufficed!'

Struggling to support Covenant, Linden snapped, 'Let her go!'

'Let − ?' the Graveller protested.

'Yes!' Ferocity burned through her. 'I need help. By God, if she wants to leave, that's her right!'

'Heaven and Earth!' retorted Sunder. 'Then why have we imperilled our lives for her?'

'Because she was going to be killed! I don't care if we need her or not. We don't have the right to hold her against her will. *I need help.*'

Sunder spat a curse. Abruptly, he abandoned Hollian, came limping through the water to take some of Covenant's weight. But he was livid with pain and indignation. Over his shoulder, he rasped at Hollian, 'Your suspicion is unjust!'

'Perhaps.' The eh-Brand trod water twenty feet away; her head was a piece of darkness among the shadows of the River. 'Assuredly, I have been unjust to Linden Avery.' After a moment, she demanded, 'What purpose drives you to Revelstone?'

'That's where the answers are.' As quickly as it had come, Linden's anger vanished, and a bone-deep dread took its place. She had been through too much. Without Sunder's aid, she could not have borne Covenant back to the raft. 'Covenant thinks he can fight the Sunbane. But he has to understand it first. That's why he wants to talk to the Clave.'

'Fight?' asked Hollian in disbelief. 'Do you speak of altering the Sunbane?'

'Why not?' Linden clung to the raft. Dismay clogged her limbs. 'Isn't that what you do?'

'I?'

'Aren't you a Sun-Sage?'

'No!' Hollian declared sharply. 'That is a lie, uttered by Sivit na-Mhoram-wist to strengthen his claim upon me. I am an eh-Brand. I see the sun. I do not shape it.'

To Linden, Sunder growled, 'Then we have no need of her.'

Dimly, Linden wondered why he felt threatened by Hollian. But she lacked the courage to ask him. 'We need all the help we can get,' she murmured. 'I want her with us. If she's willing.'

'Why?'

At the same time, Hollian asked, 'Of what use am I to you?'

Without warning, Linden's throat filled with weeping. She felt like a lorn child, confronted by extremities she could not meet. She had to muster all her severity in order to articulate, 'He's dying, I can feel it.' In a shudder of memory, she saw Marid's fangs. 'It's worse than it was before. I need help.' The help she needed was vivid and appalling to her; but she could not stop. 'One of you isn't enough. You'll just bleed to death. Or I will.' Impelled by her fear of losing Covenant, she wrenched her voice at Hollian. 'I need power. To heal him.'

She had not seen the eh-Brand approach; but now Hollian was swimming at her side. Softly, the young woman said, 'Perhaps such shedding is unnecessary. It may be that I can succour him. An eh-Brand has some knowledge of healing. But I do not wish to fall prey to the Clave a second time.'

Linden gritted her teeth until her jaw ached, containing her desperation. 'You've seen what he can do. Do you think he's going to walk into Revelstone and just let them sacrifice him?'

Hollian thought for a moment, touched Covenant's swelling gently. Then she said, 'I will attempt it. But I must await the sun's rising. And I must know how this harm came upon him.'

Linden's self-command did not reach so far. Sunrise would be too late. Covenant could not last until dawn. The Chosen! she rasped at herself. Dear God. She left the eh-Brand's questions for Sunder to answer. As he began a taut account of what had happened to Covenant, Linden's attention slipped away to the Unbeliever's racked and failing body.

She could feel the poison seeping past the useless constriction of his shirt sleeve. Death gnawed like leprosy at the sinews of his life. He absolutely could not last until dawn.

Her mother had begged to die; but he wanted to live. He had exchanged himself for Joan, had smiled as if the prospect were a benison; yet his every act showed that he wanted to live. Perhaps he *was* mad; perhaps his talk about a Despiser *was* paranoia rather than truth. But the conclusions he drew from it were ones she could not refute. She had learned in Crystal Stonedown that she shared them.

Now he was dying.

She had to help him. She was a doctor. Surely she could do something about his illness. Impossible that her strange acuity could not cut both ways. With an inward whimper, she abandoned resistance, bared her heart.

Slowly, she reached her awareness into him, inhabited his flesh with her private self. She felt his eviscerated respiration as her own, suffered the heat of his fever, clung to him more intimately than she had ever held to any man.

Then she was foundering in venom. She was powerless to repel it. Nausea filled her like the sick breath of the old man who had told her to *Be true*. No part of her knew how to give life in this way. But what she could do, she did. She fought for him with the same grim and secretly hopeless determination which compelled her to study medicine as if it were an act of rage against the ineffectuality of her parents – a man and woman who had understood nothing about life except death, and had coveted the thing they understood with the lust of lovers. They had taught her the importance of efficacy. She had pursued it without rest for fifteen years.

That pursuit had taken her to Haven Farm. And there her failure in the face of Joan's affliction had cast her whole life into doubt. Now that doubt wore the taste and corruption of Covenant's venom. She could not quench the poison. But she tried by force of will to shore up the last preterite barriers of his life. This sickness was a moral evil; it offended her just as Marid had offended her, as Nassic's murder and the hot knife had offended her; and she denied it with every beat of her heart. She squeezed air into his lungs, pressured his pulse to continue, opposed the gnawing and spread of the ill.

Alone, she kept him alive through the remainder of the night.

The bones of her forehead ached with shared fever when Sunder brought her back to herself. Dawn was in the air. He and Hollian had drawn the raft towards the riverbank. Linden looked about her tabidly. Her soul was full of ashes. A part of her panted over and over, No. Never again. The River ran through a lowland which should have been composed of broad leas; but instead, the area was a grey waste where mountains of preternatural grass had been beaten down by three days of torrential rain, then rotted by the sun of pestilence. As the approach of day stirred the air, currents of putrefaction shifted back and forth across the Mithil.

But she saw why Sunder and Hollian had chosen this place. Near the bank, a sandbar angled part way across the watercourse, forming a swath where Covenant could lie, away from the fetid grass.

The Stonedownors secured the raft, lifted Covenant to the sand, then raised him into Linden's arms. Hugging him erect, though she herself swayed with exahaustion, she watched as Sunder and Hollian hastened to the riverbank and began hunting for stone. Soon they were out of sight.

With the thin remnant of her strength, Linden confronted the sun.

It hove over the horizon wearing incarnadine like the sails of a plague ship. She welcomed its warmth – needed to be warm, yearned to be dry – but its corona made her moan with empty repugnance. She lowered Covenant to the sand, then sat beside him, studied him as if she were afraid to close her eyes. She did not know how soon the insects would begin to swarm.

But when Sunder and Hollian returned, they were excited. The tension between them had not relaxed; but they had found something important to them both. Together, they carried a large bush which they had uprooted as if it were a treasure.

'*Voure!*' Hollian called as she and Sunder brought the bush to the sandbar. Her pale skin was luminous in the sunlight. 'This is good fortune. *Voure* is greatly rare.' They set the bush down nearby, and at once began to strip its leaves.

'Rare, indeed,' muttered Sunder. 'Such names are spoken in the Rede, but I have never beheld *voure*.'

'Does it heal?' Linden asked faintly.

In response, the eh-Brand gave her a handful of leaves. They were as pulpy as sponges; clear sap dripped from their broken stems. Their pungent odour made her wince.

'Rub the sap upon your face and arms,' said Hollian. '*Voure* is a potent ward against insects.'

Linden stared until her senses finally registered the truth of the eh-Brand's words. Then she obeyed. When she had smeared sap over herself, she did the same to Covenant.

Sunder and Hollian were similarly busy. After they had finished, he stored the remaining leaves in his knapsack.

'Now,' the eh-Brand said promptly, 'I must do what lies within my capacity to restore the Halfhand.'

'His name is Covenant,' Linden protested dimly. To her, *Halfhand* was a Clave word: she did not like it.

Hollian blinked as if this were irrelevant, made no reply.

'Do you require my aid?' asked Sunder. His stiffness had returned. In some way that Linden could not fathom, Hollian annoyed or threatened him.

The eh-Brand's response was equally curt. 'I think not.'

'Then I will put this *voure* to the test.' He stood up. 'I will go in search of *aliantha*.' Moving brusquely, he went back to the riverbank, stalked away through the rotting grass.

Hollian wasted no time. From within her shift, she drew out a small iron dirk and her *lianar* wand. Kneeling at Covenant's right shoulder, she placed the *lianar* on his chest, took the dirk in her left hand.

The sun was above the horizon now, exerting its corruption. But the pungence of the *voure* seemed to form a buckler against putrefaction. And though large insects had begun to buzz and gust in all directions, they did not come near the sandbar. Linden ached to concentrate on such things. She did not want to watch the eh-Brand's bloody rites. Did not want to see them fail. Yet she attached her eyes to the knife, forced herself to follow it.

Like Sunder's left forearm, Hollian's right palm was laced with old scars. She drew the iron across her flesh. A runnel of dark rich blood started down her bare wrist.

Setting down her dirk, she took up the *lianar* in her bleeding hand. Her lips moved, but she made no sound.

The atmosphere focused around her wand. Abruptly, flames licked the wood. Fire the colour of the sun's aura skirled around her fingers. Her voice became an audible chant, but the words were alien to Linden. The fire grew stronger; it covered Hollian's hand, began to tongue the blood on her wrist.

As she chanted, her fire sent out long delicate shoots like tendrils of wisteria. They grew to the sound, stretched along the water like veins of blood in the current, went searching up the riverbank as if they sought a place to root.

Supported by a shimmering network of power tendrils, she tightened her chant, and lowered the *lianar* to Covenant's envenomed forearm. Linden flinched instinctively. She could taste the ill in the fire, feel the preternatural force of the Sunbane. Hollian drew on the same sources of power which Sunder tapped with his Sunstone. But after a moment Linden discerned that the fire's effect was not ill. Hollian fought poison with poison. When she lifted her wand from Covenant's arm, the tension of his swelling had already begun to recede.

Carefully, she shifted her power to his forehead, set flame to the fever in his skull.

At once, his body sprang rigid, head jerked back; a scream ripped his throat. From his ring, an instant white detonation blasted sand over the two women and the River.

Before Linden could react, he went completely limp.

The eh-Brand sagged at his side. The flame vanished from her *lianar*, leaving the wood pale, clean, and whole. In the space of a heartbeat, the fire-tendrils extinguished themselves; but they continued to echo across Linden's sight.

She rushed to examine Covenant. Apprehension choked her. But as she touched him, he inhaled deeply, began to breathe as if he were only asleep. She felt for his pulse; it was distinct and secure.

Relief flooded through her. The Mithil and the sun grew oddly dim. She was prone on the sand without realizing that she had reclined. Her left hand lay in the water. That cool touch seemed to be all that kept her from weeping.

In a weak voice, Hollian asked, 'Is he well?'

Linden did not answer because she had no words.

Shortly, Sunder returned, his hands laden with treasure-berries. He seemed to understand the exhaustion of his companions. Without speaking, he bent over Linden, slipped a berry between her lips.

Its deliciousness restored her. She sat up, estimated the amount of *aliantha* Sunder held, took her share. The berries fed a part of her which had been stretched past its limits by her efforts to keep Covenant alive.

Hollian watched in weariness and dismay as Sunder consumed his portion of the *aliantha*. But she could not bring herself to touch the berries he offered her.

As her strength returned, Linden propped Covenant into a half-sitting position, then pitted berries and fed them to him. Their effect was almost immediate; they steadied his respiration, firmed his muscle tone, cleansed the colour of his skin.

Deliberately, she looked at Hollian. The exertion of aiding Covenant had left the eh-Brand in need of aliment. And her searching gaze could find no other answer. With a shudder of resolution, she accepted a berry, put it in her mouth. After a moment, she bit down on it.

Her own pleasure startled her. Revelation glowed in her eyes, and her fear seemed to fall away like a discarded mantle.

With a private sigh, Linden lowered Covenant's head to the sand, and let herself rest.

The companions remained on the sandbar for a good part of the morning, recuperating. Then, when Covenant's swelling had turned from black to a mottled yellow-purple, and had declined from his shoulder, Linden judged that he was able to travel. They set off down the Mithil once more.

The *voure* continued to protect them from insects. Hollian said the sap would retain its potency for several days; and Linden began to believe this when she discovered that the odour still clung to her after more than half a day immersed in the water.

In the lurid red of sunset, they stopped on a broad slope of rock spreading northward out of the River. After the strain of the past days, Linden hardly noticed the discomfort of sleeping on stone. Yet part of her stayed in touch with Covenant, like a string tuned to resonate sympathetically at a certain pitch. In the middle of the night, she found herself staring at the acute sickle of the moon. Covenant was sitting beside her. He seemed unaware of her. Quietly, he moved to the water's edge for a drink.

She followed, anxious that he might be suffering from a relapse of delirium. But when he saw her, he recognized her with a nod, and drew her away to a place where they could at least whisper without disturbing their companions. The way he carried his arm showed that it was tender but utile. His expression was obscure in the vague light; but his voice sounded lucid.

'Who's the woman?'

She stood close to him, peered into the shadow of his countenance. 'You don't remember?'

'I remember bees.' He gave a quick shudder. 'That Raver. Nothing else.'

Her efforts to preserve his life had left her vulnerable to him. She had shared his extremity; and now he seemed to have a claim on her which she would never be able to refuse. Even her heartbeat belonged to him. 'You had a relapse.'

'A relapse – ?' He tried to flex his sore arm.

'You were stung, and went into shock. It was like another snakebite in the same place, only worse. I thought – ' She touched his shoulder involuntarily. 'I thought you weren't going to make it.'

'When was that?'

'A day and a half ago.'

'How did – ?' he began, then changed his mind. 'Then what?'

'Sunder and I couldn't do anything for you. We just went on.' She started to speak rapidly. 'That night, we came to another Stonedown.' She told him the story as if she were in a hurry to reach the end of it. But when she tried to describe the power of his ring, he stopped her. 'That's impossible,' he whispered.

'You don't remember at all?'

'No. But I tell you it's impossible. I've always – always had to have some kind of trigger. The proximity of some other power. Like the *orcrest*. It never happens by itself. Never.'

'Maybe it was the Rider.'

'Yes.' He grasped the suggestion gratefully. 'That must be it. That sceptre – his *rukh*.' He repeated the name she had told him as if he needed reassurance.

She nodded, then resumed her narration.

When she was done, he spoke his thoughts hesitantly. 'You say I was delirious. I must have been – I don't remember any of it. Then this Rider tried to attack. All of a sudden, I had power.' His tone conveyed the importance of the question. 'What set me off? I shouldn't have been able to defend myself, if I was that sick. Did you get hurt? Did Sunder – ?'

'No.' Suddenly, the darkness between them was full of significance. She had risked herself extravagantly to keep him alive – and for what? In his power and delirium he had believed nothing about her except that she had abandoned him. And even now he did not

194

know what he had cost her. No. She could hardly muffle her bitterness as she replied, 'We're all right. It wasn't that.'

Softly, he asked, 'Then what was it?'

'I made you think Joan was in danger.' He flinched; but she went on, struck at him with words. 'It was the only thing I could find. You weren't going to save yourself – weren't going to save me. You kept accusing me of deserting you. By God,' she grated, 'I've stood by you since the first time I saw Joan. No matter how crazy you are, I've stood by you. You'd be dead now if it weren't for me. But you kept accusing me, and I couldn't reach you. The only name that meant anything to you was *Joan*.'

She hurt him. His right hand made a gesture towards her, winced away. In the darkness, he seemed to have no eyes; his sockets gaped at her as if he had been blinded. She expected him to protest that he had often tried to help her, often striven to give her what support he could. But he stood there as he had stood when she had first confronted him on Haven Farm, upright under the weight of impossible burdens. When he spoke, his voice was edged with rage and exquisite grief.

'She was my wife. She divorced me because I had leprosy. Of all the things that happened to me, that was the worst. God knows I've committed crimes. I've raped – killed – betrayed – But those were things I *did*, and I did everything I could to make restitution. She treated me as if I were a crime. Just being who I was, just suffering from a physical affliction I couldn't have prevented or cured any more than I could have prevented or cured my own mortality, I terrified her. That was the *worst*. Because I believed it. I felt that way about leprosy myself.

'It gave her a claim on me. I spent eleven years living with it – I couldn't bear being the cause. I sold my soul to pay that debt, and it doesn't make any difference.' The muscles of his face contorted at the memory. 'I'm a leper. I'm never going to stop being a leper. I'm never going to be able to quit her claim on me. It goes deeper than any choice.' His words were the colour of blood.

'But, Linden,' he went on; and his direct appeal stung her heart. 'She's my *ex*-wife.' In spite of his efforts to control it, his voice carried fatality like a lament. 'If the past is any indication, I'm never going to see her again.'

She clung to him with her eyes. Uncertainties thronged in her. Why would he not see Joan again? How had he sold himself? How much had he withheld? But in her vulnerability one question mattered more than all the others. As steadily, noncommittally, as she could, she asked, 'Do you want to see her again?'

To her tense ears, the simplicity of his reply bore the weight of a declaration. 'No. I don't particularly like being a leper.'

She turned away so that he would not see the tears in her eyes.

She did not want to be so exposed to him. She was in danger of losing herself. And yet her relief was as poignant as love. Over her shoulder, she said flatly, 'Get some rest. You need it.' Then she went back to where Sunder and Hollian lay, stretched out on the rock, and spent a long time shivering as if she were caught in a winter of unshielded loneliness.

The sun had already risen, red and glowering, when she awoke. A pile of *aliantha* near Sunder's knapsack showed that the Stone-downors had foraged successfully for food. Covenant and the eh-Brand stood together, making each other's acquaintance. Sunder sat nearby as if he were grinding his teeth.

Linden climbed to her feet. Her body felt abused by the hardness of her bed, but she ignored it. Averting her eyes from Covenant as if in shame, she went to the river to wash her face.

When she returned, Sunder divided the treasure-berries. The travellers ate in silence: *aliantha* was a food which imposed stillness. Yet Linden could not deafen herself to the ambience of her companions. Covenant was as rigid as he had ever been on Haven Farm. Hollian's delicate features wore perplexity as if it were a kind of fear. And the darkness of the Graveller's mood had not lifted – resentment directed at the eh-Brand, or at himself.

They made Linden feel lost. She was responsible for their various discomforts – and inadequate to do anything about it. In sustaining Covenant, she had opened doors which she now could not close, though she swore she would close them. Muttering sourly to herself, she finished her *aliantha*, scattered the seeds beyond the rock, then went severely through the motions of preparing to enter the River.

But Hollian could not bear her own trouble in silence. After a moment, she addressed the Unbeliever. 'You say that I am to name you Covenant – though it is a name of ill omen, and sits unquietly in my mouth. Very well. Covenant. Have you considered where you go? The Graveller and Linden Avery say that you are destined for Revelstone. My heart shrinks from the thought – but if such is your goal, I will not gainsay it. Yet Revelstone lies there.' She pointed northwestward. 'Eleven score leagues distant. The Mithil no longer shares your way.'

'That is known to us, eh-Brand,' Sunder muttered.

She ignored him. 'It may be that we can journey afoot, with the aid of *voure*.' She hesitated, recognizing the difficulty of what she proposed. 'And great good fortune.' Her eyes did not leave Covenant's face.

'Maybe.' His tone betrayed that he had already made his decision. 'But I don't want to take the chance of getting stung again. We'll stay on the River for another day or two, anyway.'

'Covenant.' Hollian's gaze was poignant. 'Do you know what lies that way?'

'Yes.' He met her squarely. 'Andelain.'

Andelain? The concealed intensity with which he said that name brought Linden to alertness.

'Do you – ' Hollian wrestled against her apprehension. 'Do you *choose* to approach Andelain?'

'Yes.' Covenant's resolution was complete. But he studied the eh-Brand closely, as if her concern disturbed him. 'I want to see it. Before I go to Revelstone.'

His assertion appalled her. She recoiled. Gasping, she strove to shout, but could not find enough air in all the wide morning. 'You are mad. Or a servant of a-Jeroth, as the Rede proclaims.' She turned towards Linden, then Sunder, beseeching them to hear her. 'You must not permit it.' She snatched a raw breath, cried out, 'You must not!'

Covenant sprang at her, dug his fingers into her shoulders, shook her. '*What's wrong with Andelain?*'

Hollian's mouth worked; but she could find no words.

'Sunder!' Covenant barked.

Stiffly, the Graveller replied, 'I am four score leagues from my home. I know nothing of this Andelain.'

Hollian fought to master herself. 'Covenant,' she said in a livid tone, 'you may eat *aliantha*. You may defy the Clave. You may trample upon the Rede, and cast your challenge to the Sunbane itself. But you must not enter Andelain.'

Covenant lowered his voice, demanded dangerously, 'Why not?'

'It is a snare and a delusion!' she moaned. 'An abomination in the Land. It lies lovely and cruel before the eyes, and seduces all who look upon it to their destruction. It is impervious to the Sunbane!'

'Impossible!' snapped Sunder.

'No!' Hollian panted. 'I speak truly. Sun after sun, it remains unaltered, imitating paradise.' She thrust all her dismay at Covenant. 'Many people have been betrayed – The tale of them is often told in all this region. But I speak not only of tales. I have known four – four brave Stonedownors who succumbed to that lure. Distraught by their lives, they left Crystal Stonedown to test the tale of Andelain. Two entered, and did not return. Two made their way to Crystal Stonedown once more – and the madness in them raved like the na-Mhoram's *Grim*. No succour could anele their violence. Croft was driven to sacrifice them.

'Covenant,' she begged, 'do not journey there. You will meet a doom more terrible than any unshielded Sunbane.' Her every word vibrated with conviction, with honest fear. 'Andelain is a desecration of the soul.'

Roughly, Covenant thrust the eh-Brand away from him. He

whirled, strode down the slope to stand at the water's edge. His fists clenched and unclenched, trembling, at his sides.

Linden went to him at once, seeking a way to dissuade him. She believed Hollian. But when she touched his arm, the savagery in him struck her mute. 'Andelain.' His voice was taut with fatality and rage. Without warning, he turned on her. His eyes blazed through her. 'You say you've stood by me.' His whisper expressed more bloodshed than any shout. 'Do it now. Nothing else matters. Stand by me.'

Before she could try to respond, he spun towards Sunder and Hollian. They stared at him, dumbfounded by his passion. The sun limned his profile like a cynosure. 'Andelain used to be the heart of the Land.' He sounded as if he were strangling. 'I have to find out what happened to it.' The next moment, he was in the water, swimming downriver with all his strength.

Linden checked herself, did not follow him. He could not keep up that pace; she would be able to rejoin him. *Stand by me.* Her senses told her that Hollian spoke the truth. There was something heinous concealed in Andelain. But Covenant's appeal outweighed any conviction of peril. She had striven with the intimacy of a lover to save his life. The cost of that intimacy she could not endure; but she could do other things for him. She faced the Stonedownors. 'Sunder?'

The Graveller glanced away along the River, then over at Hollian, before he met Linden's demand. 'The eh-Brand is a Stonedownor,' he replied, 'like myself. I trust her fear. But my lot now lies with the ur-Lord. I will accompany him.'

With a simple nod, Linden accepted his decision. 'Hollian?'

The eh-Brand seemed unable to confront the choice she had to make. Her eyes wandered the stone, searching it for answers it did not contain. 'Does it come to this?' she murmured bitterly. 'That I have been rescued from peril into peril?' But slowly she summoned up the strength which had enabled her to face Croft and Sivit with dignity. 'It is stated in the Rede beyond any doubt that the Halfhand is a servant of a-Jeroth.'

Flatly, Linden said, 'The Rede is wrong.'

'That cannot be!' Hollian's fear was palpable in the air. 'If the Rede is false, how can it sustain life?'

Unexpectedly, Sunder interposed himself. 'Eh-Brand.' His voice knotted as if he had arrived without warning or preparation at a crisis. 'Linden Avery speaks of another wrong altogether. To her, all things are wrong which arise from the Sunbane.'

Hollian stared at him. And Linden, too, watched him narrowly. She chafed to be on her way; but the Graveller's efforts to resolve his own feelings kept her still.

'Eh-Brand,' he went on, gritting his teeth, 'I have held you in resentment. Your presence is a reproach to me. You are a Stonedownor. You comprehend what has come to pass when a Graveller betrays his home. Whether you choose or no, you accuse me. And your plight is enviable to me. You are innocent of where you stand. Whatever path you follow from this place, none can lay blame upon you. All my paths are paths of blame.

'My vindication has been that I am necessary to the ur-Lord, and to Linden Avery, and to their purpose. His vision touched my heart, and the survival of that vision has been in my hands. Lacking my aid, they would be long dead, and with them the one clear word of beauty I have been given to hear.

'Whether you choose or no, you deprive me of my necessity. Your knowledge of the Sunbane and of the perils before us surely excels mine. You give healing where I cannot. You have not shed life. In your presence, I have no answer to my guilt.'

'Sunder,' Hollian breathed. 'Graveller. This castigation avails nothing. The past is beyond change. Your vindication cannot be taken from you.'

'All things change,' he replied tightly. 'Ur-Lord Covenant alters the past at every turning. Therefore – ' he cut off her protest. 'I am without choice. I cannot bear that this alteration should be undone. But there is choice for you. And because you own choice, eh-Brand, I implore you. Give your service to the ur-Lord. He offers much – and is in such need. Your aid is greater than mine.'

Hollian's gaze scoured him as he spoke. But she did not find any answer to her fear. 'Ah,' she sighed bitterly, 'I do not see this choice. Death lies behind me and horror before. This is not choice. It is torment.'

'It is *choice*!' Sunder shouted, unable to restrain his vehemence. 'Neither death nor horror is compulsory for you. You may depart from us. Find a new people to be your home. They will distrust you for a time – but that will pass. No Stonedown would willingly sacrifice an eh-Brand.'

His words took both Hollian and Linden by surprise. Hollian had plainly given no thought to the idea he raised. And Linden could not guess why he used such an argument. 'Sunder,' she said carefully, 'what do you think you're doing?'

'I seek to persuade her.' He did not take his eyes from Hollian. 'A choice made freely is stronger than one compelled. We must have her strength – else I fear we will not gain Revelstone.'

Linden strove to understand him. 'Do you mean to tell me that now you *want* to go to Revelstone?'

'I must,' he responded; but his words were directed towards the eh-Brand. 'No other purpose remains to me. I must see the lies of the Rede answered. Throughout all the generations of the Sunbane, the Riders have taken blood in the name of the Rede. Now they must be required to speak the truth.'

Linden nodded, bent her attention on Hollian as the eh-Brand absorbed his argument, hunted for a reply. After a moment, she said slowly, holding his gaze, 'In the *aliantha* – if in no other way – I have been given cause to misdoubt the Rede. And Sivit na-Mhoram-wist sought my death, though it was plain for all to see that I was of great benefit to Crystal Stonedown. If you follow ur-Lord Covenant in the name of truth, I will accompany you.' At once, she turned to Linden. 'But I will not enter Andelain. That I will not do.'

Linden acknowledged this proviso. 'All right. Let's go.' She had been too long away from Covenant; her anxiety for him tightened all her muscles. But one last requirement held her back. 'Sunder,' she said deliberately. 'Thanks.'

Her gratitude seemed to startle him. But then he replied with a mute bow. In that gesture, they understood each other.

Leaving the knapsack and the raft to the Stonedownors, Linden dived into the water and went after Covenant.

She found him resting on a sand-spit beyond a bend in the River. He looked weary and abandoned, as if he had not expected her to come. But when she pulled herself out of the water near him, shook her eyes clear, she could see the relief which lay half-hidden behind his convalescence and his unkempt beard.

'Are you alone?'

'No. They're coming. Sunder talked her into it.'

He did not respond. Lowering his head to his knees, he hid his face as if he did not want to admit how intensely he felt that he had been reprieved.

Shortly, Sunder and Hollian swam into view; and soon the companions were on their way downriver again. Convenant rode the current in silence, with his gaze always fixed ahead. And Linden, too, remained still, trying to gather up the scattered pieces of her privacy. She felt acutely vulnerable, as if any casual word, any light touch, could drive her to the edges of her own secrets. She did not know how to recollect her old autonomy. Through the day, she could feel the sun of pestilence impending over her as she swam; and her life seemed to be composed of threats against which she had no protection.

Then, late in the afternoon, the River began to run straight into the east, and the terrain through which it flowed underwent a dramatic change. Steep hills lay ahead on both sides like poised antitheses. Those on the right were rocky and barren – a desolation unlike the wilderland of the desert sun. Linden saw at once that they were always dead, that no sun of fertility ever alleviated their detrition. Some ancient and concentrated ruin had blasted their capacity for life long ago, before the Sunbane ever came upon them.

But the hills on the left were a direct contradiction. The power with which they reached her senses sent a shock through all her nerves.

North of the Mithil lay a lush region untouched by stress or wrong. The stands of elm and Gilden which crowned the boundary were naturally tall and vividly healthy; no fertile sun had aggravated their growth, no sun of pestilence had corroded their strong wood and clean sap. The grass sweeping away in long greenswards from the riverbank was pristine with *aliantha* and amaryllis and buttercups. An analystic air blew from these hills, forever sapid and virginal.

The demarcation between this region and the surrounding terrain was as clear as a line drawn in the dirt; at that border, the Sunbane ended and loveliness began. On the riverbank, like a marker and ward to the hills, stood an old oak, gnarled and sombre, wearing long shrouds of bryony like a cloak of power – a hoary majesty untrammelled by desert or rot. It forbade and welcomed, according to the spirit of those who approached.

'Andelain,' Covenant whispered thickly, as if he wanted to sing, and could not unclose his throat. 'Oh, Andelain.'

But Hollian gazed on the Hills with unmitigated abhorrence. Sunder glowered at them as if they posed a danger he could not identify.

And Linden, too, could not share Covenant's gladness. Andelain touched her like the taste of *aliantha* embodied in the Land. It unveiled itself to her particular percipience with a visionary intensity. It was as hazardous as a drug which could kill or cure, according to the skill of the physician who used it.

Fear and desire tore at her. She had felt the Sunbane too personally, had exposed herself too much in Covenant. She wanted loveliness as if her soul were starving for it. But Hollian's dread was entirely convincing. Andelain's emanations felt as fatal as prophecy against Linden's face. She saw intuitively that the Hills could bereave her of herself as absolutely as any wrong. She had no ability to gauge or control the potency of this drug. Impossible that ordinary trees and grass could articulate so much might! She was already engaged in a running battle against madness. Hollian had said that Andelain drove people mad.

No, she repeated to herself. Not again. Please.

By mute consent, she and her companions stopped for the night among the ruins opposite the oak. A peculiar spell was on them, wrapping them within themselves. Covenant gazed, entranced, at the shimmer of health. But Hollian's revulsion did not waver. Sunder carried distrust in the set of his shoulders. And Linden could not shake her senses free of the deadness of the southern hills. The waste of this region was like a shadow cast by Andelain, a consequence of power. It affected her as if it demonstrated the legitimacy of fear.

201

Early in the evening, Hollian pricked her palm with the point of her dirk, and used the blood to call up a slight green flame from her *lianar*. When she was done, she announced that the morrow would bring a fertile sun. But Linden was locked within her own apprehensions, and hardly heard the eh-Brand.

When she arose in the first grey of dawn with her companions, she said to Covenant, 'I'm not going with you.'

The crepuscular air could not conceal his surprise. 'Not? Why?' When she did not answer immediately, he urged her. 'Linden, this is your chance to taste something besides sickness. You've been so hurt by the Sunbane. Andelain can heal you.'

'No.' She tried to sound certain, but memories of her mother, of the old man's breath, frayed her self-command. She had shared Covenant's illness, but he had never shared his strength. 'It only looks healthy. You heard Hollian. Somewhere in there, it's cancerous.' *I've already lost too much.*

'Cancerous?' he demanded. 'Are you losing your eyes? That is *Andelain.*'

She could not meet his dark stare. 'I don't know anything about Andelain. I can't tell. It's too powerful. I can't stand any more. I could lose my mind in there.'

'You could find it in there,' he returned intensely. 'I keep talking about fighting the Sunbane, and you don't know whether to believe me or not. The answer's in there. Andelain denies the Sunbane. Even I can see that. The Sunbane isn't omnipotent.

'Of course Andelain's powerful,' he went on in a rush of ire and persuasion. 'It has to be. But we need power. We've got to know how Andelain stays clear.

'I can understand Hollian. Even Sunder. The Sunbane made them what they are. It's cruel and terrible, but it makes sense. A world full of lepers can't automatically trust someone with good nerves. But *you*. You're a doctor. Fighting sickness is your business.'

'Linden.' His hands gripped her shoulders, forced her to look at him. His eyes were gaunt and grim, placing demands upon her as if he believed that anybody could do the things he did. As if he did not know that he owed her his life, that all his show of determination or bravery would already have come to nothing without her. 'Come with me.'

In spite of his presumption, she wanted to be equal to him. But her recollections of venom were too acute to be endured. She needed to recover herself. 'I can't. I'm afraid.'

The fury in his gaze looked like grief. She dropped her eyes. After a moment, he said distantly, 'I'll be back in two or three days. It's probably better this way. Numbness has its advantages. I probably won't be so vulnerable to whatever's in there. When I get back, we'll decide what to do.'

She nodded dumbly. He released her.

The sun was rising, clothed in a cymar of emerald. When she raised her head again, he was in the River, swimming towards Andelain as if he were capable of anything. Green-tinged light danced on the ripples of his passing. The venom was still in him.

PART II

Vision

12

THE ANDELAINIAN HILLS

As Thomas Covenant passed the venerable oak and began angling his way up into Andelain, he left a grieved and limping part of himself with Linden. He was still weak from the attack of the bees, and did not want to be alone. Unwillingly, almost unconsciously, he had come to depend on Linden's presence. He felt bound to her by many cords. Some of them he knew: her courage and support; her willingness to risk herself on his behalf. But others seemed to have no name. He felt almost physically linked to her without knowing why. Her refusal to accompany him made him afraid.

Part of his fear arose from the fear of his companions; he dreaded to learn that behind its beauty Andelain was secretly chancrous. But he had been a leper for too long, was too well acquainted with cunning disease; that kind of dread could only increase his determination. Most of his trepidation sprang from Linden's rejection, from what that decision might mean.

For most of his hopes revolved around her. Doubt eroded his previous victory in the Land. He could not shake the gnawing conviction that in choosing to buy Joan's safety he had sold himself to the Despiser, had given up the freedom on which efficacy against Despite depended; he had felt that knife strike his chest, and knew he might fail. *The wild magic is no longer potent against me. Of your own volition you will give the white gold into my hand.* But Linden was another question. She had been chosen by the old man who had once told him to *Be true.* In their summoning, Lord Foul had betrayed no knowledge of or desire for her presence. And since then she had showed herself capable of many things. Behind her self-severity, she was beautiful. How could he not place hope in such a woman?

But now her refusal of Andelain seemed to imply that his hope was based on quicksand, that her clenched will was an articulation of cowardice rather than courage.

He understood such things. He was a leper, and lepers were taught cowardice by every hurt in all the world. If anything, her decision increased his empathy for her. But he was alone; and he knew from long and brutal experience how little he could accomplish alone. Even the apotheosis of his former power against Lord Foul would have gone for nothing without the support and laughter of Saltheart Foamfollower.

So as he climbed into Andelain, he felt that he was walking into a bereavement, a loss of comradeship, of hope, perhaps of courage, from which he might never recover.

At the hillcrest, he paused to wave at his companions. But they did not reply; they were not looking at him. Their lack of response hurt him as if they had deliberately turned their backs.

But he was a man who had always been faithful to his griefs; and the Land had become a rending and immedicable sorrow to him. He went on into Andelain because he needed health, power, knowledge. So that he could try to restore what had been lost.

Soon, however, his mood changed. For this was Andelain, as precious to his memory as his dearest friendships in the Land. In this air – ether as crisp as sempiternal spring – he could not even see the sun's chrysoprastic aura; the sunshine contained nothing except an abundance of beauty. The grass unrolling under his feet was lush and beryl-green, freshly jewelled with dew. Woodlands extended north and east of him. Broad Gilden fondled the breeze with their wide gold leaves; stately elms fronted the azure of the sky like princes; willows as delicate as filigree beckoned to him, inviting him into their heart-healing shade. All about the hale trunks, flowers enriched the greensward: daisies and columbine and elegant forsythia in profusion. And over everything lay an atmosphere of pristine and vibrant loveliness, as if here and in no other place lived quintessential health, nature's pure gift to assuage the soul.

Munching *aliantha* as he passed, loping down long hillsides, bursting occasionally into wild leaps of pleasure, Thomas Covenant travelled swiftly into Andelain.

Gradually, he grew calmer, became more attuned to the taintless tranquillity of the Hills. Birds sang among the branches; small woodland animals darted through the trees. He did nothing to disturb them. And after he had walked for some distance, drinking in thirstily the roborant of Andelain, he returned his thoughts to his companions, to Hollian and Sunder. He felt sure now that the Hills were not cancerous, that they contained no secret and deadly ill. Such an idea had become inconceivable. But at the same time the intensity of what he saw and felt and loved increased his comprehension of the Stonedownors.

They were like lepers; all the people of the Land were like lepers. They were the victims of the Sunbane, victims of an ill for which there was no cure and no escape. Outcast from the beauty of the world. And under such conditions, the need to survive exacted harsh penalties. No thing under the sun was as perilous to a leper as his own yearning for the kind of life, companionship, hope, denied him by his disease. That susceptibility led to despair and self-contempt, to the conviction that the outcasting of the leper was just – condign punishment for an affliction which must have been deserved.

Seen in that way, Andelain was a living vindication of the Sunbane. The Land was not like Andelain because the people of the Land merited retribution rather than loveliness. What else could they believe, and still endure the penury of their lives? Like so many lepers, they were driven to approve their own destitution. Therefore Sunder could not trust anything which was not ruled by the Sunbane. And Hollian believed that Andelain would destroy her. They had no choice.

No choice at all. Until they learned to believe that the Sunbane was not the whole truth of their lives. Until Covenant found an answer which could set them free.

He was prepared to spend everything he possessed, everything he was, to open the way for Sunder, and Hollian, and Linden to walk Andelain unafraid.

Through the day, he journeyed without rest. He did not need rest. The *aliantha* healed the effects of the venom, and the water in the cleanly streams made him feel as fresh as a newborn; and each new vista was itself a form of sustenance, vivid and delicious. The sun set in splendour long before he was ready to stop. He could not stop. He went on, always north-eastward, until the gloaming became night, and the stars came smiling out of their celestial deeps to keep him company.

But the darkness was still young when he was halted by the sight of a faint yellow-orange light, flickering through the trees like a blade of fire. He did not seek to approach it; memories held him still. He stood hushed and reverent while the flame wandered towards him. And as it came, it made a fine clear tinkling sound, like the chime of delicate crystal.

Then it bobbed in the air before him, and he bowed low to it, for it was one of the Wraiths of Andelain – a flame no larger than his hand dancing upright as if the darkness were an invisible wick. Its movement matched his obeisance; and when it floated slowly away from him, he followed after it. Its lustre made his heart swell. Towards the Wraiths of Andelain he felt a keen grief which he would have given anything to relieve. At one time, scores of them had died because he had lacked the power to save them.

Soon this Wraith was joined by another – and then by still others – and then he was surrounded by dancing as he walked. The bright circle and high, light ringing of the flames guided him, so that he went on and on as if he knew his way until a slim sliver-moon rose above the eastern Hills.

Thus the Wraiths brought him to a tall knoll, bare of trees but opulently grassed. There the chiming faded into a stronger music. The very air became the song to which the stars measured out their gavotte, and every blade of grass was a note of the harmony. It was a stern song behind its quietude, and it held a long sorrow which he understood. The Wraiths remained at the base of the knoll, forming a long ring around it; but the music carried him upward, towards the crest.

And then the song took on words, so distinct that they could never be forgotten. They were sad and resolute, and he might have wept at them if he had been less entranced.

'Andelain I hold and mould within my fragile spell,
    While world's ruin ruins wood and wold.
Sap and bough are grief and grim to me, engrievement fell,
    And petals fall without relief.
    Astricken by my power's dearth,
I hold the glaive of Law against the Earth.

'Andelain I cherish dear within my mortal breast;
    And faithful I withhold Despiser's wish. .
But faithless is my ache for dreams and slumbering and rest,
    And burdens make my courage break.
    The Sunbane mocks my best reply.
And all about and in me beauties die.

'Andelain! I strive with need and loss, and ascertain
    That the Despiser's might can rend and rive.
Each falter of my ancient heart is all the evil's gain;
    And it appalls without relent.
    I cannot spread my power more,
Though teary visions come of wail and gore.

'Oh, Andelain! Forgive! for I am doomed to fail this war.
    I cannot bear to see you die — and live,
Foredoomed to bitterness and all the grey Despiser's lore.
    But while I can I heed the call
    Of green and tree; and for their worth,
I hold the glaive of Law against the Earth.'

Slowly through the music, Covenant beheld the singer.

The man was tall and strong, and robed all in whitest sendaline. In his hand, he held a gnarled tree limb as a staff. Melody crowned his head. Music flowed from the lines of his form in streams of phosphorescence. His song was the very stuff of power, and with it he cupped the night in the palm of his hand.

His face had neither eyes nor eye sockets. Though he had changed mightily in the ten years or thirty-five centuries since Covenant had last seen him, he did not appear to have aged at all.

An impulse to kneel swept through Covenant, but he refused it. He sensed that if he knelt now there would be no end to his need to prostrate himself. Instead, he stood quiet before the man's immense white music, and waited.

After a moment, the man hummed sternly, 'Thomas Covenant, do you know me?'

Covenant met his eyeless gaze. 'You're Hile Troy.'

'No.' The song was absolute. 'I am Caer-Caveral, the Forestal of Andelain. In all the Land I am the last of my kind.'

'Yes,' Covenant said. 'I remember. You saved my life at the Colossus of the Fall – after I came out of Morinmoss. I think you must have saved me in Morinmoss, too.'

'There is no Morinmoss.' Caer-Caveral's melody became bleakness and pain. 'The Colossus has fallen.'

No Morinmoss? No forests? Covenant clenched himself, held the tears down. 'What do you want from me? I'll do anything.'

The Forestal hummed for a moment without answering. Then he sang, 'Thomas Covenant, have you beheld Andelain?'

'Yes.' Clenching himself. 'I've seen it.'

'In all the Land, it is the last keep of the Law. With my strength, I hold its fabric unrent here. When I fail in the end – as fail I must, for I am yet Hile Troy withall, and the day comes when I must not refuse to sacrifice my power – there will be no restitution for the abysm of that loss. The Earth will pass into its last age, and nothing will redeem it.'

'I know.' With his jaws locked. 'I know.'

'Thomas Covenant,' the tall man sang, 'I require from you everything and nothing. I have not brought you here this night to ask, but to give. Behold!' A sweeping gesture of his staff scattered the grass with music; and there, through the melody like incarnations of song, Covenant saw them. Pale silver as if they were made of moonshine, though the moon had no such light, they stood before him. Caer-Caveral's streaming argence illumined them as if they had been created out of Forestal-fire.

Covenant's friends.

High Lord Mhoram, with the wise serenity of his eyes, and the crookedness of his smile.

Elena daughter of Lena and rape, herself a former High Lord, beautiful and passionate. Covenant's child; almost his lover.

Bannor of the Bloodguard, wearing poise and capability and the power of judgement which could never be wrested from him.

Saltheart Foamfollower, who towered over the others as he towered over all mortals in size, and humour, and purity of spirit.

Covenant stared at them through the music as if the sinews of his soul were fraying. A moan broke from his chest, and he went forward with his arms outstretched to embrace his friends.

'Hold!'

The Forestal's command froze Covenant before he could close the separation. Immobility filled all his muscles.

'You do not comprehend,' Caer-Caveral sang more kindly. 'You cannot touch them, for they have no flesh. They are the Dead. The Law of Death has been broken, and cannot be made whole again. Your presence here has called them from their sleep, for all who enter Andelain encounter their Dead here.'

Cannot − ? After all this time? Tears streamed down Covenant's cheeks; but when Caer-Caveral released him, he made no move towards the spectres. Almost choking on his loss, he said, 'You're killing me. What do you want?'

'Ah, beloved,' Elena replied quickly, in the clear irrefusable voice which he remembered with such anguish, 'this is not a time for grief. Our hearts are glad to behold you here. We have not come to cause you pain, but to bless you with our love. And to give you gifts, as the Law permits.'

'It is a word of truth,' added Mhoram. 'Feel joy for us, for none could deny the joy we feel in you.'

'Mhoram,' Covenant wept. 'Elena. Bannor. Oh, Foamfollower!'

The Forestal's voice took on a rumble like the threat of thunder. 'Thus it is that men and women find madness in Andelain. This must not be prolonged. Thomas Covenant, it is well that your companions did not accompany you. The man and woman of the Land would break at the sight of their Dead. And the woman of your world would raise grim shades here. We must give our gifts while mind and courage hold.'

'Gifts?' Covenant's voice shook with yearning. 'Why − ? How − ?' He was so full of needs that he could not name them all.

'Ah, my friend, forgive us,' Mhoram said. 'We may answer no questions. That is the Law.'

'As in the summoning of dead Kevin which broke the Law of Death,' interposed Elena, 'the answers of the Dead rebound upon the questioner. We will not harm you with our answers, beloved.'

'And you require no answers.' Foamfollower was laughing in his gladness. 'You are sufficient to every question.'

Foamfollower! Tears burned Covenant's face like blood. He was on his knees, though he could not remember kneeling.

'Enough,' the Forestal hummed. 'Even now he falters.' Graceful and stately, he moved to Covenant's side. 'Thomas Covenant, I will not name the thing you seek. But I will enable you to find it.' He touched Covenant's forehead with his staff. A white blaze of music ran through Covenant's mind. 'The knowledge is within you, though you cannot see it. But when the time has come, you will find the means to unlock my gift.' As the song receded, it left nothing in its wake but a vague sense of potential.

Caer-Caveral stepped aside; and High Lord Mhoram came sound-lessly forward. 'Ur-Lord and Unbeliever,' he said gently, 'my gift to you is counsel. When you have understood the Land's need, you must depart the Land, for the thing you seek is not within it. The one word of truth cannot be found otherwise. But I give you this caution: do not be deceived by the Land's need. The thing you seek is not what it appears to be. In the end, you must return to the Land.'

He withdrew before Covenant could ask him to say more.

Elena took the High Lord's place. 'Beloved,' she said with a smile of deep affection, 'it has befallen me to speak a hard thing to you. The truth is as you have feared it to be; the Land has lost its power to remedy your illness, for much great good has been undone by the Despiser. Therefore I rue that the woman your companion lacked heart to accompany you, for you have much to bear. But she must come to meet herself in her own time. Care for her, beloved, so that in the end she may heal us all.'

Then her voice grew sharper, carrying an echo of the feral hate which had led her to break the Law of Death. 'This one other thing I say to you also. When the time is upon you, and you must confront the Despiser, he is to be found in Mount Thunder – in Kiril Threndor, where he has taken up his abode.'

Elena, Covenant moaned. You still haven't forgiven me, and you don't even know it.

A moment later, Bannor stood before him. The Bloodguard's *Haruchai* face was impassive, implacable. 'Unbeliever, I have no gift for you,' he said without inflection. 'But I say to you, Redeem my people. Their plight is an abomination. And they will serve you well.'

Then Foamfollower came foward; and Covenant saw that the Giant was not alone. 'My dear friend,' said Foamfollower gaily, 'to me has fallen the giving of a gift beyond price. Behold!'

He indicated his companion; and Covenant could tell at once that this figure was not one of the Dead. He wore a short grey tunic, and under it all his skin from head to foot was as black as the gaps between the stars. His form was perfectly shaped and strong; but his hair was black, his teeth and gums were black, his pupilless eyes were pure midnight. He held himself as if he were oblivious to the Dead and the Forestal and Covenant. His eyes gazed emptily, regarding nothing.

'He is Vain,' said Foamfollower, 'the final spawn of the ur-viles.' Covenant flinched, remembering ur-viles. But the Giant went on, 'He crowns all their generations of breeding. As your friend, I implore you: take him to be your companion. He will not please you, for he does not speak, and serves no purpose but his own. But that purpose is mighty, and greatly to be desired. His makers have ever been lore-wise, though tormented, and when it comes upon him he, at least, will not fail.

'I say that he serves no purpose but his own. Yet in order that you may accept him, the ur-viles have formed him in such a way that he may be commanded once. Once only, but I pray it may suffice. When your need is upon you, and there is no other help, say to him, "*Nekhrimah*, Vain," and he will obey.

'Thomas Covenant. My dear friend.' Foamfollower bent close to him, pleading with him. 'In the name of Hotash Slay, where I was consumed and reborn, I beg you to accept this gift.'

Covenant could hardly refrain from throwing his arms around the Giant's neck. He had learned a deep dread of the ur-viles and all their works. But Foamfollower had been his friend, and had died for it. Thickly, he said, 'Yes. All right.'

'I thank you,' the Giant breathed, and withdrew.

For a moment, there was silence. Wraith-light rose dimly, and the Dead stood like icons of past might and pain. Caer-Caveral's song took on the cadence of a threnody. Crimson tinged the flow of his phosphorescence. Covenant felt suddenly that his friends were about to depart. At once, his heart began to labour, aching for the words to tell them that he loved them.

The Forestal approached again; but High Lord Mhoram stayed him. 'One word more,' Mhoram said to Covenant. 'This must be spoken, though I risk much in saying it. My friend, the peril upon the Land is not what it was. Lord Foul works in new ways, seeking ruin, and his evil cannot be answered by any combat. He has said to you that you are his Enemy. Remember that he seeks always to mislead you. It boots nothing to avoid his snares, for they are ever beset with other snares, and life and death are too intimately intergrown to be severed from each other. But it is necessary to comprehend them, so that they may be mastered. When – ' He hesitated momentarily. 'When you have come to the crux, and have no other recourse, remember the paradox of white gold. There is hope in contradiction.'

Hope? Covenant cried. Mhoram! Don't you know I'm going to fail?

The next moment, Caer-Caveral's song came down firmly on the back of his neck, and he was asleep in the thick grass.

13

DEMONDIM-SPAWN

When he awoke, his face itched as if the grass had grown into his beard, and his back was warm with mid-morning sun.

He raised his head. He was still atop the knoll where he had met Caer-Caveral and the Dead. Andelain lay around him, unfolded like a flower to the sun. But he observed the trees and sky abstractly; the Hills had temporarily lost their power over him. He was too full of ashes to be moved.

He remembered the previous night clearly. He remembered everything about it except the conviction of its reality.

But that lasted for only a moment. When he sat up, changed his range of sight, he saw Vain.

The Demondim-spawn made everything else certain.

He stood just as he had the night before, lightly poised and oblivious. Covenant was struck once again by Vain's physical perfection. His limbs were smooth and strong; his flesh bore no blemish; he might have been an idealized piece of statuary. He gave no sign that he was aware of Covenant's awakening, that he was cognizant of Covenant at all. His arms hung relaxed, with the elbows slightly crooked, as if he had been made for readiness but had not yet been brought to life. No respiration stirred his chest; his eyes neither blinked nor shifted.

Slowly, Covenant reviewed the other gifts he had been given. They were all obscure to him. But Vain's solidity conveyed a kind of reassurance. Covenant took his companion as a promise that the other gifts would prove to be equally substantial.

Seeking relief from his sense of loss, he rose to his feet, faced Vain. He considered the dark form briefly, then said, 'Foamfollower says you don't talk. Is that true?'

Vain did not react. An ambiguous smile hung on his lips, but no expression altered the fathomless ebony of his orbs. He might as well have been blind.

'All right,' Covenant muttered. 'You don't speak. I hope the other things he said are true, too. I don't want to test it. I'm going to put off commanding you as long as I can. If those ur-viles lied – ' He frowned, trying to penetrate the mystery of his companion; but no intuition came to his aid. 'Maybe Linden can tell me something about you.' Vain's black gaze did not shift. After a moment,

Covenant growled, 'I also hope I don't get in the habit of talking to you. This is ridiculous.'

Feeling vaguely foolish, he glanced at the sun to ascertain his directions, then started down the knoll to begin the journey back to his friends.

The Demondim-spawn followed a few paces behind him. Vain moved as if he had memorized his surroundings long ago, and no longer needed to take notice of them. In spite of his physical solidity, his steps made no sound, left no impression in the grass.

Covenant shrugged, and set off south-westward through the Hills of Andelain.

By noon, he had eaten enough *aliantha* to comprise a feast, and had begun to recover his joy. Andelain did far more for him than give comfort to his eyes and ears or provide solace for his loss. Lord Foul had deprived him of the most exquisite pleasure of his previous visit here – the ability to *feel* health like a palpable cynosure in every green and living thing about him. But the Hills seemed to understand his plight, and adjust their appeal to offer him what he could enjoy. The air was refulgent with gay birds. The grass cushioned his feet, so that his knees and thighs felt exuberant at every stride. *Aliantha* nourished him until all his muscles were suffused with vitality.

Thus Andelain transformed his grief, melded it into a granitic sense of purpose. He considered the hazards ahead of him without dread, and swore an implacable oath without fear or fury, an oath that Andelain would not fall while he still had breath or pulse to defend it.

In the middle of the afternoon, he came upon a stream running placidly over a bed of fine sand, and stopped to give himself a bath. He knew that he would not be able to rejoin his companions by nightfall, so he did not begrudge the time. Stripping off his clothes, he scrubbed himself from head to foot with sand until he began to feel clean for the first time in many days.

Vain stood beside the stream as if he had been rooted to that spot all his life. A mischievous impulse came over Covenant; without warning, he slapped a spray of water at the Demondim-spawn. Droplets gleamed on Vain's obsidian flesh and dripped away, but he betrayed no flicker of consciousness.

Hellfire, Covenant muttered. A touch of prescience darkened his mood. He began almost grimly to wash his clothes.

Soon he was on his way again, with Vain trailing behind him.

He had planned to continue walking until he reached the Mithil valley and his companions. But this night was the dark of the moon, and the stars did not give much light. As the last illumination of evening faded from the air, he decided to stop.

For a time, he had trouble sleeping. An innominate anxiety disturbed his rest. Vain held himself like an effigy of darkness, hinting at dangers. An ur-vile, Covenant growled. He could not trust an ur-vile. They, the Demondim-spawn, were one of the ancient races of the Land; and they had served Lord Foul for millennia. Covenant had been attacked time and again by the roynish creatures. Eyeless and bloodthirsty, they had devoured scores of Wraiths at a time when he had been empty of power. Now he could not believe that the ur-viles which had given Vain to Foamfollower had told the truth.

But the air and grass of Andelain were an elixir that answered his vague distress; and eventually he slept.

He was awake and travelling in the exultation of sunrise. Regret clouded his mood now; he did not want to leave Andelain. But he did not let that slow him. He was concerned for his companions. Well before noon, he crested the last line of hills above the Mithil River.

He had reached the valley too far east; the old oak at the corner of Andelain was half a league or more away to his right. He moved briskly towards it along the crests, watching intently for a glimpse of his friends.

But when he neared the majestic tree, he could see no sign of Linden, Sunder, or Hollian.

He stopped, scanned the barren region across the Mithil for some sign of his companions. It was larger than he had realized. In his eagerness to enter Andelain, he had paid little attention to the area. Now he saw that the wrecked rock and dead shale spread some distance south through the hills, and perhaps a league west into the Plains. Nothing grew anywhere in that blasted region; it lay opposite him like a corpse of stone. But its edges were choked by the teeming verdure of the fertile sun. Two periods of fertility without a desert interval between them to clear the ground made the area look like a dead island under green siege.

But of Linden and the two Stonedownors there was no trace.

Covenant pelted down the hillside. He hit the water in a shallow dive, clawed the surface of the Mithil to the south bank. In moments, he stood on the spot where he had said farewell to Linden.

He remembered the place exactly, all the details matched his recollection, it was here, here – ! 'Linden!' His shout sounded small against the desolation of the rocks, disappeared without echo into the surrounding jungle. *'Linden!'*

He could find no evidence that she had been here, that he had ever had any companions at all.

The sun wore its green carcanet like a smirk of disdain. His mind went blank against his stupefaction. His companions were gone. He had left them, and in his absence something had happened to them. Another Rider? Without him to defend them – ! What have I done?

Pounding his fists dumbly at each other, he found himself staring into Vain's unreachable eyes.

The sight jarred him. 'They were *here!*' he spat as if the Demondim-spawn had contradicted him. A shudder ran through him, became cold fury. He began to search the region. 'They didn't abandon me. Something chased them off. Or they were captured. They weren't killed – or badly hurt. There's no blood.'

He picked a tall pile of boulders and scrambled up it, regardless of his vertigo. Standing precariously atop the rocks, he looked across the River towards the Plains bordering Andelain. But the tangle of the monstrous vegetation was impenetrable; his companions could have been within hailing distance, and he would not have been able to see them. He turned, studied the wreckage south and west of him. That wilderland was rock-littered and chaotic enough to conceal a myriad perils.

'Linden!' he yelled. 'Sunder! Hollian!'

His voice fell stricken to the ground. There was no answer.

He did not hesitate. A *geas* was upon him. He descended from the boulders, returned to the place where he had last seen Linden. As he moved, he gathered small stones. With them, he made an arrow on the rock, pointing towards the interior of the wilderland, so that, if his companions returned for him, they would know where he had gone. Then he set off along the line of his arrow.

Vain followed him like an embodied shadow.

Covenant moved rapidly, urgently. His gaze hunted the terrain like a VSE. He wanted to locate or fall prey to whatever was responsible for the disappearance of his friends. When he knew the nature of the peril, he would know how to respond. So he made no attempt at stealth. He only kept his eyes alert, and went scuttling across the rocks and shale like a man bent on his own destruction.

He drove himself for a league through the ruins before he paused to reconsider his choice of directions. He was badly winded by his exertions; yet Vain stood nearby as if he had never stood anywhere else – indefatigable as stone. Cursing Vain's blankness or his own mortality, Covenant chose a leaning stone spire, and climbed it to gain a vantage on his surroundings.

From the spire, he saw the rims of a long canyon perhaps half a league due west of him. At once, he decided to turn towards it; it was the only prominent feature in the area.

He slid back down the spire too quickly. As he landed, he missed his balance and sprawled in front of Vain.

When he regained his feet, he and the Demondim-spawn were surrounded by four men.

They were taller than Stonedownors, slimmer. They wore rock-hued robes of a kind which Covenant had learned to associate with Woodhelvennin. But their raiment was ill-kempt. A fever of violence glazed their eyes. Three of them wielded long stone clubs; the fourth had a knife. They held their weapons menacingly, advanced together.

'Hellfire,' Covenant muttered. His hands made unconscious warding gestures. 'Hell and blood.'

Vain gazed past the men as if they were trivial.

Malice knotted their faces. Covenant groaned. Did every human being in the Land want to kill him? But he was too angry to retreat. Hoping to take the Woodhelvennin by surprise, he snapped abruptly, 'Where's Linden?'

The man nearest him gave a glint of recognition.

The next instant, one of them charged. Covenant flinched; but the others did not attack. The man sprang towards Vain. With his club, he levelled a smashing blow at Vain's skull.

The stone burst into slivers. The man cried out, backed away clutching his elbows.

Vain's head shifted as if he were nodding. He did not acknowledge the strike with so much as a blink of his black eyes. He was uninjured and oblivious.

Amazed uncertainty frightened the other men. A moment later, they started forward with the vehemence of fear.

Covenant had no time for astonishment. He had a purpose of his own, and did not intend to see it fail like this. Before the men had advanced two steps, he spread his arms and shouted, 'Stop!' with all the ferocity of his passion.

His cry made the air ring. The men halted.

'Listen!' he rasped. 'I'm not your enemy, and I don't intend to get beaten to death for my innocence!' The man with the knife waved it tentatively. Covenant jabbed a finger in his direction. 'I mean it! If you want us, here we are. But you don't have to kill us.' He was trembling; but the sharp authority in his voice leashed his attackers.

The man who had recognized Linden's name hesitated, then revealed himself as the leader. 'If you resist,' he said tautly, 'all Stonemight Woodhelven will arise to slay you.'

Covenant let bitterness into his tone. 'I wouldn't dream of resisting. You've got Linden. I want to go wherever she is.'

Angry and suspicious, the man tried to meet Covenant's glare, but could not. With his club, he pointed towards the canyon. 'There.'

'There,' Covenant muttered. 'Right.' Turning his back on the Woodhelvennin, he marched off in that direction.

The leader barked an order; and the man with the stunned arms hurried past Covenant. The man knew the rocks and ruins intimately; the path he chose was direct and well-worn. Sooner than he had expected, Covenant was led into a crevice which split the canyon-rim. The floor of the crevice descended steeply before it opened into its destination.

Covenant was surprised by the depth of the canyon. The place resembled a gullet; the rock of the upper edges looked like dark teeth silhouetted against the sky. Unforeseen dangers seemed to crouch, waiting, in the shadows of the walls. For a moment, he faltered. But his need to find his companions impelled him. As he was steered towards the dwellings of the Woodhelven, he studied everything he could see, searching for information, hope.

He was struck initially by the resemblance between the village and the men who had captured him. Stonemight Woodhelven was slovenly; its inhabitants were the first careless people he had met in the Land. The canyon floor around the houses was strewn with refuse; and the people wore their robes as if they had no interest in the appearance or even the wholeness of their apparel. Many of them looked dirty and ill-used, despite the fact that they were obviously well-fed. And the houses were in a similar condition. The wooden structures were fundamentally sound. Each stood on massive stilts for protection against the force of water which ran through the canyon during a sun of rain; and all had frames of logs as heavy as vigas. But the construction of the walls was sloppy, leaving gaps on all sides; and many of the door-ladders had broken rungs and twisted runners.

Covenant stared with surprise and growing trepidation as he moved through the disorganized cluster of huts. How – ? he wondered. How can people this careless survive the Sunbane?

Yet in other ways they did not appear careless. Their eyes smouldered with an odd combination of belligerence and fright as they regarded him. They reminded him strangely of Drool Rockworm, the Cavewight who had been ravaged almost to death by his lust for the Illearth Stone.

Covenant's captors took him to the largest and best-made of the houses. There, the leader called out, 'Graveller!' After a few moments, a woman emerged and came down the ladder to face Covenant and Vain. She was tall, and moved with a blend of authority and desperation. Her robe was a vivid emerald colour – the first bright raiment Covenant had seen – and it was whole; but she wore it untidily. Her hair lay in a frenzy of snarls. She had been weeping; her visage was dark and swollen, battered by tears.

He was vaguely confused to meet a Graveller in a Woodhelven. Formerly, the people of wood and stone had kept their lores separate. But he had already seen evidence that such distinctions of devotion no longer obtained. After Lord Foul's defeat, the villages must have had a long period of interaction and sharing. Therefore Crystal Stonedown had raised an eh-Brand who used wood, and Stonemight Woodhelven was led by a Graveller.

She addressed the leader of the captors. 'Brannil?'

The man poked Covenant's shoulder. 'Graveller,' he said in a tone of accusation, 'this one spoke the name of the stranger, companion to the Stonedownors.' Grimly, he continued, 'He is the Halfhand. He bears the white ring.'

She looked down at Covenant's hand. When her eyes returned to his face, they were savage. 'By the Stonemight!' she snarled. 'We will yet attain recompense.' Her head jerked a command. Turning away, she went towards her house.

Covenant was slow to respond. The woman's appearance – and the mention of his friends – had stunned him momentarily. But he shook himself alert, shouted after the Graveller, 'Wait!'

She paused. Over her shoulder, she barked, 'Brannil, has he shown power against you?'

'No, Graveller,' the man replied.

'Then he has none. If he resists you, strike him senseless.' Stiffly, she re-entered her dwelling and closed the door.

At once, hands grabbed Covenant's arms, dragged him towards another house, thrust him at the ladder. Unable to regain his balance, he fell against the rungs. Immediately, several men forced him up the ladder and through the doorway with such roughness that he had to catch himself on the far wall.

Vain followed him. No one had touched the Demondim-spawn. He climbed into the hut of his own accord, as if he were unwilling to be separated from Covenant.

The door slammed shut. It was tied with a length of vine.

Muttering, 'Damnation,' Covenant sank down the wall to sit on the woven-wood floor and tried to think.

The single room was no better than a hovel. He could see through chinks in the walls and the floor. Some of the wood looked rotten with age. Anybody with strength or a knife could have broken out. But freedom was not precisely what he wanted. He wanted Linden, wanted to find Sunder and Hollian. And he had no knife. His resources of strength did not impress him.

For a moment, he considered invoking his one command from Vain, then rejected the idea. He was not that desperate yet. For some time, he studied the village through the gaps in the walls, watched the afternoon shadows lengthen towards evening in the canyon. But he saw nothing that answered any of his questions. The hovel oppressed him. He felt more like a prisoner – more ineffectual and doomed – than he had in Mithil Stonedown. A sense of impending panic constricted his heart. He found himself clenching his fists, glaring at Vain as if the Demondim-spawn's passivity were an offence to him.

His anger determined him. He checked through the front wall to be sure the two guards were still there. Then he carefully selected a place in the centre of the door where the wood looked weak, measured his distance from it, and kicked.

221

The house trembled. The wood let out a dull splitting noise.

The guards sprang around, faced the door.

Covenant kicked the spot again. Three old branches snapped, leaving a hole the size of his hand.

'Ware, prisoner!' shouted a guard. 'You will be clubbed!'

Covenant answered with another kick. Splinters showed along one of the inner supports.

The guards hesitated, clearly reluctant to attempt opening the door while it was under assault.

Throwing his weight into the blow, Covenant hit again.

One guard poised himself at the foot of the ladder. The other sprinted towards the Graveller's dwelling.

Covenant grinned fiercely. He went on kicking at the door, but did not tire himself by expending much effort. When the Graveller arrived, he gave the wood one last blow and stopped.

At a command from the Graveller, a guard ascended the ladder. Watching Covenant warily through the hole, he untied the lashings, then sprang away to evade the door if Covenant kicked it again.

Covenant did not. He pushed the door aside with his hand and stood framed in the entryway to confront the Graveller. Before she could address him, he snapped, 'I want to talk to you.'

She drew herself up haughtily. 'Prisoner, I do not wish to speak with you.'

He overrode her. 'I don't give a good goddamn what you wish. If you think I don't have power, you're sadly mistaken. Why else does the Clave want me dead?' Bluffing grimly, he rasped, 'Ask your men what happened when they attacked my companion.'

The narrowing of her eyes revealed that she had already been apprised of Vain's apparent invulnerability.

'I'll make a deal with you,' he went on, denying her time to think. 'I'm not afraid of you. But I don't want to hurt you. I can wait until you decide to release me yourself. If you'll answer some questions, I'll stop breaking this house down.'

Her eyes wandered momentarily, returned to his face. 'You have no power.'

'Then what are you afraid of?'

She hesitated. He could see that she wanted to turn away; but his anger undermined her confidence. Apparently, her confidence had already taken heavy punishment from some other source. After a moment, she murmured thickly, 'Ask.'

At once, he said, 'You took three prisoners – a woman named Linden Avery and two Stonedownors. Where are they?'

The Graveller did not meet his gaze. Somehow, his question touched the cause of her distress. 'They are gone.'

'Gone?' A lurch of dread staggered his heart. 'What do you mean?' She did not reply. '*Did you kill them?*'

'No!' Her look was one of outraged hunger, the look of a predator robbed of its prey. 'It was our *right*! The Stonedownors were enemies! Their blood was forfeit by right of capture. They possessed Sunstone and *lianar*, also forfeit. And the blood of their companion was forfeit as well. The friend of enemies is also an enemy. It was our right.

'But we were reft of our right.' A corrupt whine wounded her voice. 'The three fell to us in the first day of the fertile sun. And that same night came Santonin na-Mhoram-in on his Courser.' Her malignant grief was louder than shouting. 'In the name of the Clave, we were riven of that which was ours. Your companions are nothing, Halfhand. I acceded them to the Rider without compunction. They are gone to Revelstone, and I pray that their blood may rot within them.'

Revelstone? Covenant groaned. Hellfire! The strength drained from his knees; he had to hold himself up on the door frame.

But the Graveller was entranced by her own suffering, and did not notice him. 'Yes, and rot the Clave as well,' she screamed. 'The Clave and all who serve the na-Mhoram. For by Santonin we were riven also of the power to live. The Stonemight − !' Her teeth gnashed. 'When I discover who betrayed our possession of the Stonemight to Santonin na-Mhoram-in, I will rend the beating heart from that body and crush it in my hands!'

Abruptly, she thrust her gaze, as violent as a lance, at Covenant. 'I pray your white ring is such a periapt as the Riders say. That will be our recompense. With your ring, I will bargain for the return of the Stonemight. Yes, and more as well. Therefore make ready to die, Halfhand. In the dawn I will spill your life. It will give me joy.'

Fear and loss whirled through Covenant, deafening him to the Graveller's threat, choking his protests in his throat. He could grasp nothing clearly except the peril of his friends. Because he had insisted on going into Andelain −

The Graveller turned on her heel, strode away: he had to struggle to gasp after her, 'When did they go?'

She did not reply. But one of the guards said warily, 'At the rising of the second fertile sun.'

Damnation! Almost two days − ! On a Courser! As the guards shoved him back into the hovel and re-tied the door, Covenant was thinking stupidly, I'll never catch up with them.

A sea of helplessness broke over him. He was imprisoned here while every degree of the sun, every heartbeat of time, carried his companions closer to death. Sunder had said that the Earth was a prison for a-Jeroth of the Seven Hells, but that was not true: it was a jail for him alone, Thomas Covenant the Incapable. If Stonemight Woodhelven had released him at this moment, he would not have been able to save his friends.

And the Woodhelven would not release him; that thought penetrated his dismay slowly. They intended to kill him. At dawn. To make use of his blood. He unclenched his fists, raised his head. Looking through the walls, he saw that the canyon had already fallen into shadow. Sunset was near; evening approached like a leper's fate. Mad anguish urged him to hurl himself against the weakened door; but the futility of that action restrained him. In his fever for escape, for the power to redeem what he had done to his companions, he turned to his wedding band.

Huddling there against the wall in the gathering dusk, he considered everything he knew about wild magic, remembered everything that had ever given rise to white fire. But he found no hope. He had told Linden the truth: in all his past experience, every exertion of wild magic had been triggered by the proximity of some other power. His final confrontation with Lord Foul would have ended in failure and Desecration if the Despiser's own weapon, the Illearth Stone, had not been so mighty, had not raised such a potent response from the white gold.

Yet Linden had told him that in his delirium at Crystal Stonedown his ring had emitted light even before the Rider had put forth power. He clung to that idea. High Lord Mhoram had once said to him, *You are the white gold*. Perhaps the need for a trigger arose in him, in his own unresolved reluctance, rather than in the wild magic itself. If that were true –

Covenant settled into a more comfortable position and composed his turmoil with an effort of will. Deliberately, he began to search his memory, his passions, his need, for the key which had unlocked wild magic in his battle with Lord Foul.

He remembered the completeness of his abjection, the extremity of his peril. He remembered vividly the cruelty with which the Despiser had racked him, striving to compel the surrender of his ring. He remembered the glee with which Lord Foul had envisioned the Land as a cesspit of leprosy.

And he remembered the awakening of his rage for lepers, for victims and destitution. That passion – clear and pure beyond any fury he had ever felt – had carried him into the eye of the paradox, the place of power between conflicting impossibilities: impossible to believe the Land real; impossible to refuse the Land's need. Anchored by the contradiction itself, made strong by rage, he had faced Lord Foul, and had prevailed.

He remembered it all, re-experienced it with an intensity that wrung his heart. And from his intensity he fashioned a command for the wild magic – a command of fire.

The ring remained inert on the second finger of his halfhand. It was barely visible in the dimness.

Despair twisted his guts; but he repressed it, clenched his purpose in both hands like a strangler. Trigger, he panted. Proximity. Bearing memory like an intaglio of flame in his mind, he rose to his feet and confronted the only external source of power available to him. Swinging his half-fist through a tight arc, he struck Vain in the stomach.

Pain shot through his hand; red bursts like exploding carbuncles staggered across his mind. But nothing happened. Vain did not even look at him. If the Demondim-spawn contained power, he held it at a depth Covenant could not reach.

'God damn it!' Covenant spat, clutching his damaged hand and shaking with useless ire. 'Don't you understand? They're going to kill me!'

Vain did not move. His black features had already disappeared in the darkness.

'Damnation.' With an effort that made him want to weep, Covenant fought down his pointless urge to smash his hands against Vain. 'Those ur-viles probably lied to Foamfollower. You're probably just going to stand there and watch them cut my throat.'

But sarcasm could not save him. His companions were in such peril because he had left them defenceless. And Foamfollower had been killed in the cataclysm of Covenant's struggle with the Illearth Stone. Foamfollower, who had done more to heal the Despiser's ill than any wild magic – killed because Covenant was too frail and extreme to find any other answer. He sank to the floor like a ruin overgrown with old guilt, and sat there dumbly repeating his last hope until exhaustion dragged him into slumber.

Twice he awakened, pulse hammering, heart aflame, from dreams of Linden wailing for him. After the second, he gave up sleep; he did not believe he could bear that nightmare a third time. Pacing around Vain, he kept vigil among his inadequacies until dawn.

Gradually, the eastern sky began to etiolate. The canyon walls detached themselves from the night, and were left behind like deposits of darkness. Covenant heard people moving outside the hut, and braced himself.

Feet came up the ladder; hands fumbled at the lashings.

When the vine dropped free, he slammed his shoulder against the door, knocking the guard off the ladder. At once, he sprang to the ground, tried to flee.

But he had misjudged the height of the stilts. He landed awkwardly, plunged headlong into a knot of men beyond the foot of the ladder. Something struck the back of his head, triggering vertigo. He lost control of his limbs.

The men yanked him to his feet by the arms and hair. 'You are fortunate the Graveller desires you wakeful,' one of them said. 'Else I would teach your skull the hardness of my club.' Dizziness numbed Covenant's legs: the canyon seemed to suffer from nystagmus. The

225

Woodhelvennin hauled him away like a collection of disarticulated bones.

They took him towards the north end of the canyon. Perhaps fifty or sixty paces beyond the last house, they stopped.

A vertical crack split the stone under his feet. Wedged into it was a heavy post, nearly twice his height.

He groaned sickly and tried to resist. But he was helpless.

The men turned him so that he faced the village, then bound his arms behind the post. He made a feeble effort to kick at them; they promptly lashed his ankles as well.

When they were done, they left without a word.

As the vertigo faded, and his muscles began to recover, he gagged on nausea; but his guts were too empty to release anything.

The houses were virtually invisible, lost in the gloaming of the canyon. But after a moment he realized that the post had been placed with great care. A deep gap marked the eastern wall above him; and through it came a slash of dawn. He would be the first thing in Stonemight Woodhelven to receive the sun.

Moments passed. Sunlight descended like the blade of an axe towards his head.

Though he was protected by his boots, dread ached in his bones. His pulse seemed to beat behind his eyeballs.

The light touched his hair, his forehead, his face. While the Woodhelven lay in twilight, he experienced the sunrise like an annunciation. The sun wore a corona of light brown haze. A breath of arid heat blew across him.

Damnation, he muttered. Bloody damnation.

As the glare covered his mien, blinding him to the Woodhelven, a rain of sharp pebbles began to fall on him. Scores of people threw small stones at him.

He squeezed his eyes shut, bore the pain as best he could.

When the pebbles stopped, he looked up again and saw the Graveller approaching out of the darkness.

She held a long, iron knife, single-edged and hiltless. The black metal appeared baleful in her grasp. Her visage had not lost its misery; but it also wore a corrupt exaltation which he could not distinguish from madness.

Twenty paces or more behind the Graveller stood Vain. The Woodhelvennin had wrapped him in heavy vines, trying to restrain him; but he seemed unaware of his bonds. He held himself beyond reach as if he had come simply to watch Covenant die.

But Covenant had no time to think about Vain. The Graveller demanded his attention. 'Now,' she rasped. 'Recompense. I will shed your life, and your blood will raise water for the Woodhelven.' She glanced down at the narrow crevice. 'And with your white ring we will buy back our Stonemight from the Clave.'

Clutching his dismally-rehearsed hope, Covenant asked, 'Where's your *orcrest?*'

'*Orcrest?*' she returned suspiciously.

'Your Sunstone.'

'Ah,' she breathed, 'Sunstone. The Rede speaks of such matters.' Bitterness twisted her face. 'Sunstone is permitted – yet we were reft of our Stonemight. It is not just!' She eyed Covenant as if she were anticipating the taste of his blood. 'I have no Sunstone, Halfhand.'

No Sunstone? Covenant gasped inwardly. He had hoped with that to ignite his ring. But the Graveller had no Sunstone. No Sunstone. The desert sun shone on him like the bright, hot flood which had borne him into the Land. Invisible vulture-wings beat about his head – heart strokes of insanity. He could barely thrust his voice through the noise. 'How can – ? I thought every Graveller needed a Sunstone.' He knew this was not true, but he wanted to make her talk, delay her. He had already been stabbed once: any similar blow would surely end him. 'How else can you work the Sunbane?'

'It is arduous,' she admitted, though the hunger in her gaze did not blink. 'I must make use of the Rede. The Rede!' Abruptly, she spat into the crack at her feet. 'For generations Stonemight Woodhelven has had no need of such knowledge. From Graveller to Graveller the Stonemight has been handed down, and with it we made *life!* Without it, we must grope for survival as we may.'

The sun sent sweat trickling through Covenant's beard, down the middle of his back. His bonds cut off the circulation in his arms, tugged pain into his shoulders. He had to swallow several times to clear his throat. 'What is it? The Stonemight?'

His question reached her. He saw at once that she could not refuse to talk about the Stonemight. A nausea of love or lust came into her face. She lowered her knife; her eyes lost their focus on him. 'Stonemight,' she breathed ardently. 'Ah, the Stonemight.' Her breasts tightened under her green robe as if she were remembering rapture. 'It is power and glory, wealth and comfort. A stone of dearest emerald, alight with possibility and cold beyond the touch of any stone. That such might is contained in so small and lovely a periapt! For the Stonemight is no larger than my palm. It is flat, and sharp of edge, like a flake stricken from a larger stone. And it is admirable beyond price.'

She went on, unable to rein the rush of her entrancement. But Covenant lost her words in a flash of intuitive horror. Suddenly he was certain that the talisman she described was a fragment of the Illearth Stone.

That conviction blazed through him like appalled lightning. It explained so many things: the ruined condition of this region; the easiness of the Woodhelven's life; the gratuitous violence of the people; the Graveller's obsession. For the Illearth Stone was the very

227

essence of corruption, a bane so malignant that he had been willing to sacrifice Foamfollower's life as well as his own in order to extirpate that evil from the Land. For a moment of dismay, he believed he had failed to destroy the Stone, that the Illearth Stone itself was the source of the Sunbane.

But then another explanation occurred to him. At one time, the Despiser had given each of his Ravers a piece of the Stone. One of these Ravers had marched to do battle against the Lords, and had been met here, at the south-west corner of Andelain – met and held for several days. Perhaps in that conflict a flake of the Raver's Stone had fallen undetected among the hills, and had remained there, exerting its spontaneous desecration, until some unhappy Woodhelvennin had stumbled across it.

But that did not matter now. A Rider had taken the Stonemight. To Revelstone. Suddenly, Covenant knew that he had to live, had to reach Revelstone. To complete the destruction of the Illearth Stone. So that his past pain and Foamfollower's death would not have been for nothing.

The Graveller was sobbing avidly, 'May they rot!' She clenched the haft of her knife like a spike. 'Be damned to interminable torment for bereaving me! I curse them from the depths of my heart and the abyss of my anguish!' She jerked the knife above her head. The blade glinted keen and evil in the desert sun. She had lost all awareness of Covenant; her gaze was bent inward on a savage vision of the Clave. 'I will slay you all!'

Covenant's shout tore his throat. In horror and desperation, he yelled, '*Nekhrimah*, Vain! Save me.'

The Graveller paid no heed. With the whole force of her body, she drove her knife at his chest.

But Vain moved. While the blade arced through its swing, he shrugged his arms free of the bindings.

He was too far away, too late –

From a distance of twenty paces, he closed his fist.

Her arms froze in mid-plunge. The knife tip strained at the centre of Covenant's shirt; but she could not complete the blow.

He watched wildly as Vain approached the Graveller. With the back of his hand, Vain struck her. She crumpled. Blood burst from her mouth. As it ran, she twitched once, then lay still.

Vain ignored her. He gestured at the post, and the wood sprang into splinters. Covenant fell; but Vain caught him, set him on his feet.

Covenant allowed himself no time to think. Shedding splinters and vines, he picked up the knife, thrust it into his belt. His arms felt ferocious with the return of circulation. His heart laboured acutely. But he forced himself forward. He knew that if he did not keep moving he would collapse in an outrage of reaction. He strode among the paralysed Woodhelvennin back into the village, and entered the first large house he reached.

His eyes took a moment to pierce the dimness. Then he made out the interior of the room. The things he sought hung on the walls: a woven-vine sack of bread, a leather pouch containing some kind of liquid. He had taken them before he noticed a woman sitting in one of the corners. She held herself small and still in an effort to protect the baby sucking at her breast.

He unstopped the pouch and swallowed deeply. The liquid had a cloying taste, but it washed some of the gall from his throat. Roughly, he addressed the woman. 'What is it?'

In a tiny voice, she answered, '*Metheglin*.'

'Good.' He went to the door, then halted to rasp at her, 'Listen to me. This world's going to change. Not just here – not just because you lost your bloody Stonemight. The whole Land is going to be different. You've got to learn to live like human beings. Without all this sick killing.'

As he left the house, the baby started crying.

14

PURSUIT

He moved brusquely among the stupefied Woodhelvennin. The baby's crying was like a spur in the air; the men and women began to shift, blink their eyes, glance around. In moments, they would recover enough to act. As he reached Vain, he muttered, 'Come on. Let's get out of here,' and strode away towards the north end of the canyon.

Vain followed.

The sunrise lit Covenant's path. The canyon lay crookedly beyond him, and its rims began to draw together, narrowing until it was little more than a deep sheer ravine. He marched there without a backward look, clinched by the old intransigent stricture of his illness. His friends were already two days ahead of him, and travelling swiftly.

Shouts started to echo along the walls: anger, fear, loss. But he did not falter. Borne on the back of a Courser, Linden and the two Stonedownors might easily reach Revelstone ten days before him. He could conceive of no way to catch up with them in time to do them any good. But leprosy was also a form of despair for which there was no earthly cure; and he had learned to endure it, to make a life for himself in spite of it, by stationing himself in the eye of the paradox, affirming the acceptable humanity of all the contradictions – and by locking his soul in the most rigid possible discipline. The same resources enabled him to face the futile pursuit of his friends.

And he had one scant reason for hope. The Clave had decreed *his* death, not Linden's, Sunder's, Hollian's. Perhaps his companions would be spared, held hostage, so that they could be used against him. Like Joan. He clung to that thought, and strode down the narrow canyon to the tight beat of his will.

The shouts rose to a crescendo, then stopped abruptly. In the frenzy of their loss, some of the Woodhelvennin set out after him. But he did not look back, did not alter his pace. The canyon was constricted enough now to prevent his pursuers from reaching him without first passing Vain. He trusted that the Demondim-spawn would prove too intimidating for the Woodhelvennin.

Moments later, he heard bare feet slapping stone, echoing. Apprehension knotted his shoulders. To ease himself, he attempted a bluff. 'Vain!' he shouted without turning his head. 'Kill the first one who tries to get past you!' His words danced between the walls like a threat of murder.

But the runners did not hesitate. They were like their Graveller, addicts of the Illearth Stone; violence was their only answer to loss. Their savage cries told Covenant that they were berserk.

The next instant, one of them screamed hideously. The others scrambled to a halt.

Covenant whirled.

Vain stood facing the Woodhelvennin – five of them, the nearest still ten paces away. That man knelt with his back arched and straining, black agony in his face. Vain clenched his fist towards the man. With a wrench, he burst the man's heart.

'Vain!' Covenant yelled. 'Don't – ! I didn't mean it!'

The next Woodhelvennin was fifteen paces away. Vain made a clawing gesture. The man's face, the whole front of his skull, tore open, spilling brains and gore across the stone.

'*Vain!*'

But Vain had not yet satisfied Covenant's command. Knees slightly bent, he confronted the three remaining men. Covenant howled at them to flee; but the berserkergang was on them, and they could not flee. Together, they hurled themselves at Vain.

He swept them into his embrace, and began to crush them with his arms.

Covenant leaped at Vain's back. 'Stop!' He strove to pry Vain's head back, force him to ease his grip. 'You don't have to do this!' But Vain was granite and unreachable. He squeezed until the men lost the power to scream, to breathe. Their ribs broke like wet twigs.

Covenant pounded his fury at the Demondim-spawn; but Vain did not release the men until they were dead.

Then in panic Covenant saw a crowd of Woodhelvennin surging towards him. 'No!' he cried. 'Get back!' and the echoes ran like terror down the canyon. But the people did not stop.

He could not think of anything else to do. He left Vain and fled. The only way he could prevent Vain from butchering more people was by saving himself, completing the command. Desperately, he dashed away, running like the virulence of his curses.

Soon the rims of the canyon closed above him, forming a tunnel. But the light behind him and the glow at the far end of the passage enabled him to keep up his pace. The loud reiteration of his boots deafened him to the sounds of pursuit.

When he cast a glance backward, he saw Vain there, matching his speed without effort.

After some distance, he reached sunlight in the dry riverbed of the Mithil. Panting raggedly, he halted, rested against the bank. As soon as he could muffle his respiration, he listened at the tunnel; but he heard nothing. Perhaps five corpses were enough to check the extremity of the Woodhelvennin. With rage fulminating in his heart, he swung on Vain.

'Listen to me,' he spat. 'I don't care how bad it gets. If you *ever* do something like that again, I swear to God I'll take you back where I found you, and you and your whole bloody purpose can just *rot*!'

But the Demondim-spawn looked as blank as stone. He stood with his elbows slightly bent, his eyes unfocused, and betrayed no awareness of Covenant's existence.

'Sonofabitch,' Covenant muttered. Deliberately, he turned away from Vain. Gritting his will, he forced his anger into another channel, translated it into strength for what he had to do. Then he went to climb the north bank of the Mithil.

The sack of bread and the pouch of *metheglin* hampered him, making the ascent difficult; but when he gained the edge and stopped, he did not stop because he was tired. He was halted by the effect of the desert sun on the monstrous vegetation.

The River was dry. He had noticed that fact without pausing to consider it. But he considered it now. As far as he could see, grass as high as houses, shrubs the size of hillocks, forests of bracken, trees that pierced the sky – all had already been reduced to a necrotic grey sludge lying thigh-deep over every contour of the terrain.

The brown-clad sun melted every form of plant fibre, desiccated every drop of sap or juice, sublimated everything that grew. Every wood and green and fertile thing simply ran down itself like spilth, making one turgid puddle which the Sunbane sucked away as if the air were inhaling sludge. When he stepped into the muck in order to find out whether or not he could travel under these conditions, he was able to see the level of the viscid slop declining. It left a dead grey stain on his pants.

The muck sickened him. Involuntarily, he delayed. To clear his throat, he drank some of the *metheglin*, then chewed slowly at half a loaf of unleavened bread as he watched the sludge evaporate. But the pressure in him would not let him wait long. As the slop sank to the middle of his shins, he took a final swig of *metheglin*, stopped the pouch, and began slogging north-westward towards Revelstone, eleven score leagues distant.

The heat was tremendous. By mid-morning, the ground was bare and turning arid; the horizons had begun to shimmer, collapsing in on Covenant as if the desert sun shrank the world. Now there was nothing to hinder his progress across the waste of the Centre Plains – nothing except light as eviscerating as fire, and air which seemed to wrench the moisture from his flesh, and giddy heatwaves, and Sunbane.

He locked his face towards Revelstone, marched as if neither sun nor wilderland had the power to daunt him. But dust and dryness clogged his throat. By noon, he had emptied half his leather pouch. His shirt was dark with sweat. His forehead felt blistered, flushed by chills. The haze affected his balance, so that he stumbled even while his legs were still strong enough to be steady. And his strength did not last; the sun leeched it from him, despite his improvident consumption of bread and *metheglin*.

For a time, indecision clouded his mind. His only hope of gaining on Linden lay in travelling day and night without let up. If he acted rationally, journeyed only at night while the desert sun lasted, then the Rider's Courser would increase the distance between them every day. But he could not endure this pace. The hammer of the Sunbane was beating his endurance thinner and thinner; at confused moments, he felt translucent already.

When his brain became so giddy that he found himself wondering if he could ask Vain to carry him, he acknowledged his limitations. In a flinch of lucidity, he saw himself clinging to Vain's shoulders while the Demondim-spawn stood motionless under the sun because Covenant was not moving. Bitterly, he turned north-east towards Andelain.

He knew that the marge of Andelain ran roughly parallel to his direct path towards Revelstone; so in the Hills he would be able to stay near the route the Rider must have taken. Yet Andelain was enough out of his way to gall him. From the Hills he might not be able to catch sight of Linden and her companions, even if by some piece of good fortune the Rider was delayed; and the rumpled terrain of Andelain might slow him. But the choice was not one of speed: not under this sun. In Andelain he might at least reach the Soulsease River alive.

And perhaps, he thought, trying to encourage himself, perhaps even a Rider of the Clave could not travel swiftly through the various avatars of the Sunbane. Clenching that idea in his sore throat, he angled in the direction of the Hills.

With Vain striding impassively behind him, he crossed into lushness shortly before dusk. In his bitterness, he did not rejoice to be back within the Land's last bastion of health and Law; but the spring of the turf and the vitality of the *aliantha* affected him like rejoicing. Strength flowed back into his veins; his sight cleared; his raw mouth and throat began to heal. Through the gold-orange emblazonry of the sunset, he stiffened his pace and headed grimly along the skirts of the Hills.

All that night, he did not stop for more than scant moments at a time. Sustained by Andelain, his body bore the merciless demand of his will. The moon was too new to give him aid; but few trees grew along the edges of the Hills and, under an open sky, star-glister sufficed to light his way. Drinking *metheglin* and chewing bread for energy, he stalked the hillsides and the vales. When his pouch was empty, he discarded it. And at all times his gaze was turned westward, searching the Plains for any sign of a fire which might indicate, beyond hope or chance, that the Rider and his prisoners were still within reach. By dawn, he was twenty leagues from Stonemight Woodhelven, and still marching, as if by sheer stubbornness he had abrogated his mortality.

But he could not make himself immune to exhaustion. In spite of *aliantha* and clear spring water, bounteous grass and air as vital as an elixir, his exertions eroded him like leprosy. He had passed his limits, and travelled now on borrowed endurance – stamina wrested by plain intransigence from the ruinous usury of time. Eventually, he came to believe that the end was near, waiting to ambush him at the crest of every rise, at the bottom of every slope. Then his heart rose up in him and, because he was Thomas Covenant the Unbeliever, responsible beyond any exculpation for the outcome of his life, he began to run.

Staggering, stumbling at every third stride, he lumbered north-west, always north-west, within the marge of Andelain, and did not count the cost. Only one concession did he make to his racked breathing and torn muscles: he ate treasure-berries from every *aliantha* he passed, and threw the seeds out into the wasteland. Throughout the day he ran, though by mid-afternoon his pace was no better than a walk; and throughout the day Vain followed, matching stride for stride with his own invulnerability the exhaustion which crumbled Covenant.

Shortly after dark, Covenant broke. He missed his footing, fell, and could not rise. His lungs shuddered for air, but he was not aware of them. Everything in his chest seemed numb, beyond help. He lay stunned until his pulse slowed to a limp and his lungs stopped shivering. Then he slept.

He was awakened near midnight by the touch of a cold hand on his soul. A chill that resembled regret more than fear ran through him. He jerked up his head.

Three silver forms like distilled moonlight stood before him. When he had squeezed the blur of prostration from his sight, he recognized them.

Lena, the woman he had raped.

Atiaran and Trell, her parents.

Trell – tall, bluff, mighty Trell – had been deeply hurt by the harm Covenant had done to Lena and by the damage Atiaran had inflicted on herself in her efforts to serve the Land by saving her daughter's rapist. But the crowning anguish of his life, the pain which had finally unbalanced his mind, had been dealt him by the love Elena Lena-daughter bore for Covenant.

Atiaran had sacrificed all her instincts, all her hard-won sense of rectitude, for Covenant's sake; she had believed him necessary to the Land's survival. But the implications of that self-injury had cost her her life in the end.

And Lena – ah, Lena! She had lived on for almost fifty years, serene in the mad belief that Covenant would return and marry her. And when he had returned – when she had learned that he was responsible for the death of Elena, that he was the cause of the immense torment of the Ranyhyn she adored – she had yet chosen to sacrifice herself in an attempt to save his life.

She did not appear before him in the loveliness of youth, but rather in the brittle caducity of age; and his worn heart cried out to her. He had paid every price he could find in an extravagant effort to rectify his wrongs; but he had never learned to shed the burden of remorse.

Trell, Atiaran, Lena. In each of their faces, he read a reproach as profound as human pain could make it. But when Lena spoke, she did not derogate him. 'Thomas Covenant, you have stressed yourself beyond the ability of your body. If you sleep further, it may be that Andelain will spare you from death, but you will not awaken until a day has been lost. Perhaps your spirit has no bounds. Still you are not wise to punish yourself so. Arise! You must eat and move about, lest your flesh fail you.'

'It is truth,' Atiaran added severely. 'You punish yourself for the plight of your companions. But such castigation is a doom which achieves itself. Appalling yourself thus, you ensure that you will fail to redeem your companions. And failure demonstrates your unworth. In punishing yourself, you come to merit punishment. This is Despite, Unbeliever. Arise and eat.'

Trell did not speak. But his mute stare was unarguable. Humbly, because of who they were, and because he recognized what they said, Covenant obeyed. His body wept in every joint and thew; but he could not refuse his Dead. Tears ran down his face as he understood that these three – people who in life had had more cause to hate him than anyone else – had come to him here in order to help him.

Lena's arm pointed silver towards a nearby *aliantha*. 'Eat every berry. If you falter, we will compel you.'

He obeyed, ate all the ripe fruit he could find in the darkness with his numb fingers. Then, tears cold on his cheeks, he set off once again in the direction of Revelstone with his Dead about him like a cortege.

At first, every step was a torment. But slowly he came to feel the wisdom of what his Dead required him to do. His heart grew gradually steadier; the ache of his breathing receded as his muscles loosened. None of the three spectres spoke again, and he had neither the temerity nor the stamina to address them. In silence, the meagre procession wound its argent, ghostly way along the border of Andelain. For a long time after his weeping stopped, Covenant went on shedding grief inwardly because his ills were irrevocable, and he could never redeem the misery he had given Trell, Atiaran, and Lena. Never.

Before dawn, they left him – turned abruptly away towards the centre of Andelain without allowing him an opportunity to thank them. This he understood; perhaps no gall would have been as bitter to them as the thanks of the Unbeliever. So he said nothing of his gratitude. He stood facing their departure like a salute, murmuring promises in his heart. When their silver had faded, he continued along the path of his purpose.

Dawn and a fresh, gay brook, which lay like music across his track, gave him new strength; he was able to amend his pace until it bore some resemblance to his earlier progress. With Vain always behind him like a detached shadow, he spent the third day of the desert sun travelling Andelain as swiftly as he could without risking another collapse.

That evening, he stopped soon after sunset, under the shelter of a hoary willow. He ate a few *aliantha*, finished the last of his bread, then spent some time seated with his back to the trunk. The tree stood high above the Plains, and he sat facing westward, studying the open expanse of the night without hope almost without volition, because the plight of his companions did not allow him to relax.

The first blink of fire snatched him instantly to his feet.

The flame vanished as suddenly as it had appeared. But a moment later it recurred. This time, it caught. After several tentative flickers, it became steady.

It was due west of him.

In the darkness, he could not estimate the distance. And he knew logically that it could not be a sign of Linden and the Stonedownors; surely a Rider could travel further than this on a Courser in five days. But he did not hesitate. Gesturing to Vain, he started down the hill.

The pressure within him mounted at every stride. As he crossed out of Andelain, he was moving at a lope. The fire promptly disappeared beyond a rise in the ground. But he had the direction firmly fixed in his mind. Across the Sunbane-ruined earth he went with alacrity and clenched breath, like a man eager to confront his doom.

He had covered half a league before he glimpsed the fire again. It lay beyond still another rise. But he was close enough now to see that it was large. As he ascended the second rise, he remembered caution and slowed his pace. Climbing the last way in a stealthy crouch, he carefully peered over the ridge.

There: the fire.

Holding his breath, he scanned the area around the blaze.

From the ridge, the ground sloped sharply, then swept away in a long shallow curve for several hundred feet before curling steeply upward to form a wide escarpment. In a place roughly opposite his position, the contour of the ground and the overhang of the escarpment combined to make a depression like a bowl half-buried on edge against the wall of the higher terrain.

The fire burned in this vertical concavity. The half bowl reflected much of the light, but the distance still obscured some details. He could barely see that the fire blazed in a long, narrow mound of wood. The mound lay aimed towards the heart of the bowl; and the fire had obviously been started at the end away from the escarpment, so that, as new wood caught flame, the blaze moved into the bowl. Half the length of the woodpile had already been consumed.

The surrounding area was deserted. Covenant descried no sign of whoever had contrived such a fire. Yet the arrangement was manifestly premeditated. Except for the hunger of the flames, an eerie silence lay over the Plains.

A figure snagged the corner of Covenant's vision. He turned, and saw Vain standing beside him. The Demondim-spawn made no attempt to conceal himself below the ridge.

'Idiot!' whispered Covenant fiercely. 'Get down!'

Vain paid no attention. He regarded the fire with the same blind, ambiguous smile that he had worn while travelling through Andelain. Or while killing the people of Stonemight Woodhelven. Covenant grabbed at his arm; but Vain was immovable.

Through his teeth, Covenant muttered, 'Damn you, anyway. Some day you're going to be the death of me.'

When he looked back towards the fire, it had moved noticeably towards the escarpment, and the bowl was brighter. With a sudden rush of dismay, he saw that the mound of wood ended in a pile around an upright stake as tall and heavy as a man.

Someone or something was tied to the stake. Tied alive. The indistinct figure was struggling.

Hell and blood! Covenant instinctively recognized a trap. For a moment, he was paralysed. He could not depart, leave that bound figure to burn. And he could not approach closer. An abominable purpose was at work here, malice designed to snare him – or someone else equally vulnerable. Someone else? That question had no answer. But as he gritted himself, trying to squeeze a decision out of his paralysis, he remembered Mhoram's words: *It boots nothing to avoid his snares* –

Abruptly, he rose to his feet. 'Stay here,' he breathed at Vain. 'No sense both of us getting into trouble.' Then he went down the slope and strode grimly towards the fire.

Vain followed as usual. Covenant could hardly keep from raging at the Demondim-spawn. But he did not stop.

As he neared the escarpment, the fire began to lick at the woodpile around the stake. He broke into a run. In moments, he was within the bowl and staring at the bait of the trap.

The creature bound to the stake was one of the Waynhim.

Like the ur-viles, the Waynhim were Demondim-spawn. Except for their grey skin and smaller stature, they resembled the ur-viles closely. Their hairless bodies had long trunks and short limbs, with the arms and legs matched in length so that the creatures could run on all fours as well as walk erect. Their pointed ears sat high on their bald skulls; their mouths were like slits. And they had no eyes; they used scent instead of vision. Wide nostrils gaped in the centres of their faces.

As products of the Demondim, the Waynhim were lorewise and cunning. But, unlike their black kindred, they had broken with Lord Foul after the Ritual of Desecration. Covenant had heard that the Waynhim as a race served the Land according to their private standards; but he had seen nothing more of them since his last stay at Revelstone, when a Waynhim had escaped from Foul's Creche to bring the Council word of Lord Foul's power.

The creature before Covenant now was in tremendous pain. Its skin was raw. Dark blood oozed from scores of lash-marks. One of its arms bent at an angle of agony, and its left ear had been ripped away. But it was conscious. Its head followed his approach, nostrils quivering. When he stopped to consider its situation, it strained towards him, begging for rescue.

'Hang on,' he rasped, though he did not know if the creature could understand him. 'I'll get you out.' Fuming in outrage, he began to scatter the wood, kicking dead boughs and brush out of his way as he reached towards the stake.

But then the creature seemed to become aware of a new scent. Perhaps it caught the smell of his wedding ring. He knew that Demondim-spawn were capable of such perceptions. It burst into a fit of agitation, began barking in its harsh, guttural tongue. Urgency filled its voice. Covenant grasped none of its language; but he heard one word which sent a chill of apprehension down his spine. Again and again, the Waynhim barked, '*Nekhrimah!*'

Bloody hell! The creature was trying to give Vain some kind of command.

Covenant did not stop. The creature's desperation became his. Heaving wood aside, he cleared a path to the stake. At once, he snatched the Graveller's knife from his belt and began to slash the vines binding the Waynhim.

In a moment, the creature was free. Covenant helped it limp out of the woodpile. Immediately, the creature turned on Vain, emitted a stream of language like a curse. Then it grabbed Covenant's arm and tugged him away from the fire.

Southward.

'No.' He detached his arm with difficulty. Though the Waynhim probably could not comprehend him, he tried to explain. 'I'm going north. I've got to get to Revelstone.'

The creature let out a muffled cry as if it knew the significance of that word *Revelstone*. With a swiftness which belied its injuries, it scuttled out of the bowl along the line of the escarpment. A moment later, it had vanished in the darkness.

Covenant's dread mounted. What had the Waynhim tried to tell him? It had infected him with a vivid sense of peril. But he did not intend to take even one step that increased the distance between him and Linden. His only alternative was to flee as quickly as possible. He turned back towards Vain.

The suddenness of the surprise froze him.

A man stood on the other side of the fire.

He had a ragged beard and frenzied eyes. In contrast, his lips wore a shy smile. 'Let it be,' he said, nodding after the Waynhim. 'We have no more need of it.' He moved slowly around the fire, drawing closer to Covenant and Vain. For all its surface nonchalance, his voice was edged with hysteria.

He reached Covenant's side of the blaze. A sharp intake of air hissed through Covenant's teeth.

The man was naked to the waist, and his torso was behung with salamanders. They grew out of him like excrescences. Their bodies twitched as he moved. Their eyes glinted redly in the firelight, and their jaws snapped.

A victim of the Sunbane!

Remembering Marid, Covenant brandished his knife. 'That's close enough,' he warned; but his voice shook, exposing his fear. 'I don't want to hurt you.'

'No,' the man replied, 'you do not wish to hurt me.' He grinned like a friendly gargoyle. 'And I have no wish to hurt you.' His hands were clasped together in front of him as if they contained something precious. 'I wish to give you a gift.'

Covenant groped for anger to master his fear. 'You hurt that Waynhim. You were going to kill it. What's the matter with you? There isn't enough murder in the world – you have to add more?'

The man was not listening. He gazed at his hands with an expression of mad delight. 'It is a wondrous gift.' He shuffled forward as if he did not know that he was moving. 'No man but you can know the wonder of it.'

Covenant willed himself to retreat; but his feet remained rooted to the ground. The man exerted a horrific fascination. Covenant found himself staring involuntarily at those hands as if they truly held something wonderful.

'Behold,' the man whispered with gentle hysteria. Slowly, carefully, like a man unveiling treasure, he opened his hands.

A small furry spider sat on his palm.

Before Covenant could flinch, recoil, do anything to defend himself, the spider jumped.

It landed on his neck.

As he slapped it away, he felt the tiny prick of its sting.

For an instant, a marvellous calm came over him. He watched unperturbed as the man moved forward as if he were swimming through the sudden thickness of the firelight. The sound of the blaze became woolly. Covenant hardly noticed when the man took away his knife. Vain gazed at him for no reason at all. With imponderable delicacy, the floor of the bowl began to tilt.

Then his heart gave a beat like the blow of a sledgehammer, and everything shattered. Flying shards of pain shredded his thoughts. His brain had time to form only two words: *venom relapse*. After that, his heart beat again; and he was conscious of nothing except one long raw howl.

For some time, he wandered lorn in a maze of anguish, gibbering for release. Pain was everywhere. He had no mind, only pain – no respiration that was not pain – no pulse which did not multiply pain. Agony swelled inside his right forearm. It hurt as if his limb were nothing but a bloody stump; but that harm was all of him, everything, his chest and bowels and head and on and on in an unbearably litany of pain. If he screamed, he did not hear it; he could not hear anything except pain and death.

Death was a dervish, vertigo, avalanche, sweeping him over the precipice of his futility. It was everything he had ever striven to redeem, every pointless anguish to which he had ever struggled to give meaning. It was unconsolable grief and ineradicable guilt and savage wrath; and it made a small clear space of lucidity in his head.

Clinging shipwrecked there, he opened his eyes.

Delirium befogged his sight; grey shapes gambolled incomprehensibly across his fever, threatening the last lucid piece of himself. But he repulsed the threat. Blinking as if the movement of his eyelids were an act of violence, he cleared his vision.

He was in the bowl, bound at the stake. Heaps of firewood lay around him. Flames danced at the edges of the pyre.

The bowl was full of figures dancing like flames. They capered around the space like ghouls. Cries of blood-lust sprang off the walls of the escarpment; voices shrill with cannibalism battered his ears. Men with chatoyant eyes and prehensile noses leered at him. Women with adder-breasts, fingers lined by fangs, flared past him like fragments of insanity, cackling for his life. Children with hideous facial deformities and tiger maws in their bellies puked frogs and obscenities.

Horror made him spin, tearing clarity from his grasp. His right arm blasted pain into his chest. Every nerve of that limb was etched in agony. For an instant, he almost drowned.

But then he caught sight of Vain.

The Demondim-spawn stood with his back to the Plains, regarding the fervid dancers as if they had been created for no other purpose than to amuse him. Slowly, his eyes shifted across the frenzy until they met Covenant's.

'Vain!' Covenant gasped as if he were choking on blood. 'Help me!'

In response, Vain bared his teeth in a black grin.

At the sight, Covenant snapped. A white shriek of fury exploded from his chest. And with his shriek came a deflagration that destroyed the night.

15

'BECAUSE YOU CAN *SEE*'

No. Never again.

After Covenant had passed beyond the hill crest in Andelain, Linden Avery sat down among the dead stones, and tried to recover her sense of who she was. A black mood was on her. She felt futile and bereft of life, as she had so often felt in recent years; all her efforts to rise above her parents had accomplished nothing. If Sunder or Hollian had spoken to her, she might have screamed, if she were able to summon the energy.

Now that she had made her decision, had struck a blow in defence of her difficult autonomy against Covenant's strange power to persuade her from herself, she was left with the consequences. She could not ignore them; the old and for ever unassuaged barrenness around her did not permit them to be ignored. These dead hills climbed south and west of her, contradicting Andelain as if she had chosen death when she had been offered life.

And she was isolated by her blackness. Sunder and Hollian had found companionship in their mutual rejection of the Hills. Their lives had been so fundamentally shaped by the Sunbane that they could not question the discomfiture Andelain gave them. Perhaps they could not perceive that those lush trees and greenswards were healthy. Or that health was beautiful.

But Linden accepted the attitude of the Stonedownors. It was explicable in the context of the Sunbane. Her separateness from them did not dismay her.

The loss of Covenant dismayed her. She had made her decision, and he had walked out of her life as if he were taking all her strength and conviction with him. The light of the fertile sun had danced on the Mithil as he passed, burning about him like a recognition of his efficacy against the Land's doom. She had shared the utmost privacy of his life, and yet he had left her for Andelain. And the venom was still in him.

She would not have been more alone if he had riven her of all her reasons for living.

But she had made her decision. She had experienced Covenant's illness as if it were her own, and knew she could not have chosen otherwise. She preferred this lifeless waste of stone over the loveliness of Andelain because she understood it better, could more effectively seal herself against it. After her efforts to save Covenant, she had vowed that she would never again expose herself so intimately to anything, never again permit the Land-born sensitivity of her senses to threaten her independent identity. That vow was easier to keep when the perceptions against which she closed her heart were perceptions of ruin, of dead rock like the detritus of a cataclysm, rather than of clean wood, aromatic grasses, bountiful *aliantha*. In her private way, she shared Hollian's distrust. Andelain was far more seductive than the stone around her. She knew absolutely that she could not afford to be seduced.

Lost in her old darkness, with her eyes and ears closed as if she had nailed up shutters, barred doors, she did not understand Sunder's warning shout until too late. Suddenly, men with clubs and knives boiled out of hiding. They grappled with Sunder as he fought to raise his poniard, his Sunstone. Linden heard a flat thud as they stunned him. Hollian's arms were pinioned before her dirk could make itself felt. Linden leaped into motion; but she had no chance. A heavy blow staggered her. While she retched for breath, her arms were lashed behind her.

A moment later, brutal hands dragged her and her companions away from the River.

For a time while she gasped and stumbled, she could not hold up her defences. Her senses tasted the violence of the men, experiencing their roughness as if it were a form of ingrained lust. She felt the contorted desecration of the terrain. Involuntarily, she knew that she was being taken towards the source of the deadness, that these people were creatures of the same force which had killed this region. She had to shut her eyes, tie her mind in dire knots, to stifle her unwilling awareness of her straits.

Then the companions were manhandled down a narrow crevice into the canyon of Stonemight Woodhelven.

Linden had never seen a Woodhelven before, and the sight of it revolted her. The carelessly made homes, the slovenly people, the blood-eagerness of the Graveller – these things debased the arduous rectitude she had learned to see in people like Sunder and Hollian. But everything else paled when she caught her first glimpse of the Graveller's steaming, baleful green stone. It flooded her eyes with ill, stung her nostrils like virulent acid; it dwarfed every other power she had encountered, outshone everything except the Sunbane itself. That emerald chip was the source of the surrounding ruin, the cause of the imminent and uncaring wildness of the Woodhelvennin. Tears blinded her. Spasms clenched her mind like a desire to vomit. Yet she could not deafen herself to the Graveller's glee when that woman announced her intention to slay her captives the next morning.

Then Linden and the Stonedownors were impelled into a rude hut on stilts, and left to face death as best they could. She could not resist. She had reached a crisis of self-protection. This close to the Stonemight, she was always aware of it. Its emanations leeched at her heart, sucked her towards dissolution. Rocking against the wall to remind herself that she still existed, still possessed a separate physical identity, she repeated, No, never again. She iterated the words as if they were a litany against evil, and fought for preservation.

She needed an answer to Joan, to venom and Ravers, to the innominate power of the Stonemight. But the only answer she found was to huddle within herself and close her mind as if she were one of her parents, helpless to meet life, avid for death.

Yet when dawn came, the door of the hut was flung open, not by the Graveller or any of the Woodhelvennin, but by a Rider of the

Clave. The fertile sun vivified his stark red robe, etched the outlines of his black *rukh*, made the stiff thrust of his beard look like a grave digger's spade. He was tall with authority and unshakably confident. 'Come,' he said as if disobedience were impossible. 'I am Santonin na-Mhoram-in. You are mine.' To Sunder's glower and Hollian's groan, he replied with a smile like the blade of a scimitar.

Outside, the Woodhelvennin stood moaning and pleading. The Graveller protested abjectly. But Santonin compelled her. Weeping, she surrendered her Stonemight. Another man delivered to him the Stonedownors' Sunstone, *lianar*, knives.

Watching the transaction, Linden was unable to think anything except that Covenant would return from Andelain soon, and his companions would be gone. For one mad instant, Santonin's smile almost drew her to confess Covenant's existence; she wanted to keep him from falling into the hands of Stonemight Woodhelven. But Sunder and Hollian were silent; and their silence reminded her that the Clave desired Covenant's death. With the remnants of her will, she swallowed everything which might betray him.

After that, her will was taken from her altogether. Under the green doom of the sun, Santonin na-Mhoram-in ignited his *rukh*. Coercion sprang from the blaze, seized possession of her soul. All choice left her. At his word, she mounted Santonin's Courser. The shred of her which remained watched Sunder and Hollian as they also obeyed. Then Santonin took them away from Stonemight Woodhelven. Away towards Revelstone.

His *geas* could not be broken. She contained nothing with which she might have resisted it. For days, she knew that she should attempt to escape, to fight. But she lacked the simple volition to lift her hands to her face or push her hair out of her eyes without Santonin's explicit instructions. Whenever he looked into her dumb gaze, he smiled as if her imposed docility pleased him. At times, he murmured names that meant nothing to her, as if he were mocking her: Windscour, Victuallin Tayne, Andelainscion. And yet he did not appear to be corrupt. Or she was not capable of perceiving his corruption.

Only once did his mastery fail. Shortly after sunrise on the first day of a desert sun, eight days after their departure from Stonemight Woodhelven, a silent shout unexpectedly thrilled the air, thrilled Linden's heart. Santonin's hold snapped like an overtight harpstring.

As if they had been straining at the leash for this moment, Sunder and Hollian grappled for the *rukh*. Linden clamped an arm-lock on Santonin, flung him to the ground, then broke away south-eastward in the direction of the shout.

But a moment later, she found herself wandering almost aimlessly back to Santonin's camp. Sunder and Hollian were packing the

Rider's supplies. Santonin wore a fierce grin. The triangle of his *rukh* shone like blood and emerald. Soon he took his captives on towards Revelstone, as if nothing had happened.

Nothing had happened. Linden knew nothing, understood nothing, chose nothing. The Rider could have abused her in any way he desired. She might have felt nothing if he had elected to exercise a desire. But he did not. He seemed to have a clear sense of his own purpose. Only the anticipation in his eyes showed that his purpose was not kind.

After days of emptiness, Linden would have been glad for any purpose which could restore her to herself. Any purpose at all. Thomas Covenant had ceased to exist in her thoughts. Perhaps he had ceased to exist entirely. Perhaps he had never existed. Nothing was certain except that she needed Santonin's instructions in order to put food in her mouth.

Even the sight of Revelstone itself, the Keep of the na-Mhoram rising from the high jungle of a second fertile sun like a great stone ship, could not rouse her spirit. She was only distantly aware of what she was seeing. The gates opened to admit the Rider, closed behind his Courser, and meant nothing.

Santonin na-Mhoram-in was met by three or four other figures like himself; but they greeted him with respect, as if he had stature among them. They spoke to him, words which Linden could not understand. Then he commanded his prisoners to dismount.

Linden, Sunder and Hollian obeyed in an immense, ill-lit hall. With Santonin striding before them, they walked the ways of the great Keep. Passages and chambers, stairs and junctions, passed unmarked, unremembered. Linden moved like a hollow vessel, unable to hold any impression of the ancient gut-rock. Santonin's path had no duration and no significance.

Yet his purpose remained. He brought his captives to a huge chamber like a pit in the floor of Revelstone. Its sloping sides were blurred and blunt, as if a former gallery or arena had been washed with lava. At its bottom stood a man in a deep ebony robe and a chasuble of crimson. He gripped a tall iron crozier topped with an open triangle. His hood was thrown back, exposing features which were also blurred and blunt in the torchlight.

His presence pierced Linden's remaining scrap of identity like a hot blade. Behind her passivity, she began to wail.

He was a Raver.

'Three fools,' he said in a voice like cold scoria. 'I had hoped for four.'

Santonin and the Raver spoke together in alien, empty words. Santonin produced the Stonemight and handed it to the Raver. Emerald reflected in the Raver's eyes; an eloquent smile shaped the flesh of his lips. He closed his fist on the green chip, so that it plumed lush ferns of force. Linden's wail died of starvation in the poverty of her being.

Then the Rider stepped to one side, and the Raver faced the captives. His visage was a smear of ill across Linden's sight. He gazed at her directly, searched out the vestiges of her self, measured them, scorned them. 'You I must not harm,' he said dully, almost regretfully. 'Unharmed, you will commit all harm I could desire.' His eyes left her as if she were too paltry to merit further notice. 'But these treachers are another matter.' He confronted Sunder and Hollian. 'It signifies nothing if they are broken before they are shed.'

He heid the Stonemight against his chest. Its steam curled up his face. Nostrils dilating, he breathed the steam as if it were a rare narcotic. 'Where is Thomas Covenant?'

The Stonedownors did not react, could not react. Linden stood where she had been left, like a disregarded puppet. But her heart contracted in sudden terror.

The Raver made a slight gesture. Santonin muttered softly over his *rukh*. Abruptly, the *geas* holding Sunder and Hollian ended. They stumbled as if they had forgotten how to manage their limbs and jerked trembling erect. Fear glazed Sunder's eyes, as if he were beholding the dreadful font and master of his existence. Hollian covered her face like a frightened child.

'Where is Thomas Covenant?'

Animated by an impulse more deeply inbred than choice or reason, the Stonedownors struggled into motion and tried to flee.

The Raver let Hollian go. But with the Stonemight he put out a hand of force which caught Sunder by the neck. Hot emerald gripped him like a garrotte, snatched him to his knees.

Reft of her companion, Hollian stopped and swung around to face the Raver. Her raven hair spread about her head like wings.

The Raver knotted green ill at Sunder's throat. 'Where is Thomas Covenant?'

Sunder's eyes were blind with fear and compulsion. They bulged in their sockets. But he did not answer. Locking his jaws, he held himself still.

The Raver's fingers tightened. 'Speak.'

The muscles of Sunder's jaw pulled together, clenched as if he were trying to break his teeth, grind his voice into silence for ever. As the force at his throat grew stronger, those muscles became distinct, rigid, etched against the darkness of his fear and strangulation. It seemed impossible that he could so grit his teeth without tearing the ligatures of his jaw. But he did not answer. Sweat seemed to burst from his pores like bone marrow squeezed through his skin. Yet his rictus held.

A frown of displeasure incused the Raver's forehead. 'You will speak to me,' he soughed. 'I will tear words from your soul, if need be.' His hand clinched the Stonemight as if he were covetous to use all its power. 'Where is Thomas Covenant?'

'Dead.' Whimpers contorted Hollian's voice. Linden felt the lie in the core of her helplessness. 'Lost.'

The Raver did not glance away from Sunder, did not release his garrotte. 'How so?'

'In Andelain,' the eh-Brand panted. 'He entered. We awaited him. He did not return.' To complete her lie, she moaned, 'Forgive me, Sunder.'

'And the white ring?'

'I know not. Lost. He did not return.'

Still the Raver gave no look or answer to Hollian. But he eased slightly his grasp on the Graveller. 'Your refusal,' he breathed, 'says to me that Thomas Covenant lives. If he is lost, why do you wish me to believe that he lives?'

Within the scraps of herself, Linden begged Sunder to support Hollian's lie, for his own sake as well as for Covenant's.

Slowly, the Graveller unlocked his jaw. Clarity moved behind the dullness of his eyes. Terribly, through his knotted throat, he grated, 'I wish you to fear.'

A faint smile like a promise of murder touched the Raver's lips. But, as with Santonin, the certainty of his purpose restrained him. To the Rider, he said, 'Convey them to the hold.' Linden could not see whether he believed Hollian's lie. She could descry nothing but the loud wrong of the Raver's purpose.

With a few words, Santonin returned the Stonedownors to Linden's condition. Walking like wooden articulations of his will, his captives followed him dumbly out of the stone pit.

Again, they traversed halls which had no meaning, crossed thresholds that seemed to appear only to be forgotten. Soon they entered a cavern lined into the distance on both sides with iron doors. Small barred windows in the doors exposed each cell, but Linden was incapable of looking for any glimpse of other prisoners. Santonin locked away first Sunder, then Hollian. Further down the row of doors, he sent Linden herself into a cell.

She stood, helpless and soul-naked, beside a rank straw pallet while he studied her as if he were considering the cost of his desires. Without warning, he quenched his *rukh*. His will vanished from her mind, leaving her too empty to hold herself upright. As she crumpled to the pallet, she heard him chuckling softly. Then the door clanged shut and bolts rasped into place. She was left alone in her cell as if it contained nothing except the louse-ridden pallet and the blank stone of the walls.

She huddled foetally on the straw, while time passed over her like the indifference of Revelstone's granite. She was a cracked gourd and could not refill herself. She was afraid to make the attempt,

246

afraid even to think of making any attempt. Horror had burrowed into her soul. She desired nothing but silence and darkness, the peace of oblivion. But she could not achieve it. Caught in the limbo between revulsion and death, she crouched among her emptiness, and waited for the contradictions of her dilemma to tear her apart.

Guards came and went, bringing her unsavoury food and stale water; but she could not muster enough of herself to notice them. She was deaf to the clashing of iron which marked the movements of the guards, the arrival or departure of prisoners. Iron meant nothing. There were no voices. She would have listened to voices. Her mind groped numbly for some image to preserve her sanity, some name or answer to reinvoke the identity she had lost. But she lost all names, all images. The cell held no answers.

Then there was a voice, a shout as if a prisoner had broken free. She heard it through her stupor, clung to it. Fighting the cramps of motionlessness, the rigidity of hunger and thirst, she crawled like a cripple towards the door.

Someone spoke in a flat tone. A voice unlike any she had heard before. She was so grateful for it that at first she hardly caught the words. She was clawing herself up towards the bars of her window when the words themselves penetrated her.

'Ur-Lord Thomas Covenant,' the voice was saying. 'Unbeliever and white gold wielder, I salute you. You are remembered among the *Haruchai*.' The speaker was inflexible, denying his own need. 'I am Brinn. Will you set us free?'

Covenant! She would have screamed the name, but her throat was too dry even to whisper.

The next instant, she heard the impact of iron on flesh. Covenant! A body slumped to the stone. Guards moved around it. Hauling herself to the window, she crushed her face against the bars and tried to see; but no one entered her range of vision. A moment later, feet made heavy by a burden moved out of the hold, leaving her lorn under a cairn of silence.

She wanted to sob; but even that was an improvement for her. She had been given a name to fill her emptiness. Covenant. Helplessness and hope. Covenant was still alive. He was here. He could save her. He did not know that she needed saving.

For a time which seemed long and full of anguish, she slumped against the door while her chest shook with dry sobs and her heart clung to the image of Thomas Covenant. He had smiled for Joan. He was vulnerable to everything, and yet he appeared indomitable. Surely the guards had not killed him?

Perhaps they had. Perhaps they had not. His name itself was hope to her. It gave her something to be, restored pieces of who she was. When exhaustion etiolated her sobbing, she crept to her water-bowl, drank it dry, then ate as much of the rancid food as she could stomach. Afterward, she slept for a while.

But the next iron clanging yanked her awake. The bolts of her door were thrown back. Her heart yammered as she rolled from the pallet and lurched desperately to her feet. Covenant – ?

Her door opened. The Raver entered her cell.

He seemed to have no features, no hands; wherever his robe bared his flesh, such potent emanations of ill lanced from him that she could not register his physical being. Wrong scorched the air between them, thrusting her back against the wall. He reeked of Marid, of the malice of bees. Of Joan. His breath filled the cell with gangrene and nausea. When he spoke, his voice seemed to rot in her ears.

'So it appears that your companions lied. I am astonished. I had thought all the people of the Land to be cravens and children. But no matter. The destruction of cravens and children is small pleasure. I prefer the folly of courage in my victims. Fortunately, the Unbeliever – ' he sneered the name – 'will not attempt your redemption. He is unwitting of your plight.'

She tried to squeeze herself into the stone, strove to escape through bluff granite. But her body, mortal and useless, trapped her in the Raver's stare. She could not shut her eyes to him. He burned along her nerves, etching himself into her, demeaning her soul with the intaglio of his ill.

'But he also,' continued the Raver in a tone like stagnant water, 'is no great matter. Only his ring signifies. He will have no choice but to surrender it. Already he has sold himself, and no power under the Arch of Time can prevent his despair.

'No, Linden Avery,' the Raver said without a pause. 'Abandon all hope of Thomas Covenant. The principal doom of the Land is upon your shoulders.'

No! She had no defence against so much corruption. Night crowded around her, more cruel than any darkness – night as old as the pain of children, parents who sought to die. Never!

'You have been especially chosen for this desecration. You are being forged as iron is forged to achieve the ruin of the Earth.' His voice violated all her flesh. 'You have been chosen, Linden Avery, because you can *see*. Because you are open to that which no other in the Land can discern, you are open to be forged. Through eyes and ears and touch, you are made to be what the Despiser requires. Descrying destruction, you will be driven to commit all destruction. I will relish that ruin.

'Therefore I have forewarned you. So that you will know your peril, and be unable to evade it. So that as you strive to evade it, the Despiser may laugh in scorn and triumph.'

No. It was not possible. She was a doctor; she could not be forced to destroy. No power, no cunning, no malevolence, could unmake who she chose to be. Never! A rush of words surged up in her, burst from her as if she were babbling.

'You're sick. This is all sickness. It's just disease. You have some disease that rots your mind. Physiological insanity. A chemical imbalance of the brain. You don't know what you're saying. I don't believe in *evil!*'

'No?' The Raver was mildly amused. 'Forsooth. That lie, at least, I must rectify.' He advanced on her like a tide of slaughter. 'You have committed murder. Are you not evil?'

He spread his arms as if he meant to embrace her. He had no face, no hands. A bright hallucination at the sleeve of his robe stretched towards her, caressed her cheek.

Terror bloomed from the touch like a nightshade of the soul. Gelid ill froze her face, spread ice across her senses like the concatenation and fulfilment of all her instinctive revulsion. It flamed through her and became truth. The truth of Despite. Wrong suppurated over her features, festering her severity and beauty, corrupting who she was. The Sunbane shone in her flesh: desert, pestilence, the screaming of trees. She would have howled, but she had no voice.

She fled. There was no other defence. Within herself, she ran away. She closed her eyes, her ears, her mouth, closed the nerves of her skin, sealed every entrance to her mind. *No.* Horror gave her the power of paralysis. *Never.* Striking herself blind and deaf and numb, she sank into the darkness as if it were death, the ineluctable legacy of her birth.

Never again.

16

THE WEIRD OF THE WAYNHIM

I won't!

Covenant fought to sit up, struggled against blankets that clogged his movements, hands that restrained him.

I'll never give it up!

Blindly, he wrestled for freedom. But a massive weakness fettered him where he lay. His right arm was pinned by a preterite memory of pain.

I don't care what you do to me!

And the grass under him was fragrant and soporific. The hands could not be refused. An uncertain blur of vision eased the darkness.

The face bending over him was gentle and human.

'Rest, ring-wielder,' the man said kindly. 'No harm will come upon you in this sanctuary. There will be time enough for urgency when you are somewhat better healed.'

The voice blunted his desperation. The analystic scent of the grass reassured and comforted him. His need to go after Linden mumbled past his lips, but he could no longer hear it.

The next time he awakened, he arrived at consciousness slowly, and all his senses came with him. When he opened his eyes, he was able to see. After blinking for a moment at the smooth dome of stone above him, he understood that he was underground. Though he lay on deep fresh grass, he could not mistake the fact that this spacious chamber had been carved out of the earth. The light came from braziers in the corners of the room.

The face he had seen earlier returned. The man smiled at him, helped him into a sitting position. 'Have care, ring-wielder. You have been mortally ill. The weakness will be slow to depart.' The man placed a bowl of dark fluid in Covenant's hands and gently pressed him to drink. The liquid had a musty, alien flavour, but it steadied him as it went down into his emptiness.

He began to look around more closely. His bed was in the centre of the chamber, raised above the floor like a catafalque of grass. The native stone of the walls and dome had been meticulously smoothed and shaped. The ceiling was not high, but he would be able to stand erect. Low entryways marked opposite walls of the room. The braziers were made of unadorned grey stone and supported by iron tripods. The thick, black fluid in them burned without smoke.

When he turned his head far enough, he found Vain near him.

The Demondim-spawn stood with his arms hanging slightly bent. His lips wore a faint, ambiguous smile, and his eyes, black without pupil or iris, looked like the orbs of a blind man.

A quiver of revulsion shook Covenant. 'Get – ' His voice scraped his throat like a rusty knife. 'Get him out of here.'

The man supported him with an arm around his back. 'Perhaps it could be done,' he said, smiling wryly. 'But great force would be required. Do you have cause to fear him?'

'He – ' Covenant winced at chancrous memories: Sunbane victims dancing; Vain's grin. He had difficulty forcing words past the blade in his throat. 'Refused to help me.' The thought of his own need made him tremble. 'Get rid of him.'

'Ah, ring-wielder,' the man said with a frown, 'such questions are not so blithely answered. There is much that I must tell you – and much I wish to be told.'

He faced Covenant; and Covenant observed him clearly for the first time. He had the dark hair and stocky frame of a Stonedownor, though he wore nothing but a wide piece of leather belted around his waist. The softness of his brown eyes suggested sympathy; but his cheeks had been deeply cut by old grief, and the twitching of his mouth gave the impression that he was too well acquainted with fear and incomprehension. His skin had the distinctive pallor of a man who had once been richly tanned. Covenant felt an immediate surge of empathy for him.

'I am Hamako,' the man said. 'My former name was one which the Waynhim could not utter, and I have foresworn it. The Waynhim name you ring-wielder in their tongue – and as ring-wielder you are well known to them. But I will gladly make use of any other name you desire.'

Covenant swallowed, took another drink from the bowl. 'Covenant,' he said hoarsely. 'I'm Thomas Covenant.'

The man accepted this with a nod. 'Covenant.' Then he returned to the question of Vain. 'For two days,' he said, 'while you have lain in fever, the Waynhim have striven with the riddle of this Demondim-spawn. They have found purpose in him, but not harm. This is an astonishment to them, for they perceive clearly the hands of the ur-viles which made him, and they have no trust for ur-viles. Yet he is an embodiment of lore which the Waynhim comprehend. Only one question disturbs them.' Hamako paused as if reluctant to remind Covenant of past horrors. 'When you freed *dhraga* Waynhim from fire, thus imperilling your own life, *dhraga* spoke the word of command to this Demondim-spawn, ordering him to preserve you. Why did he not obey?'

The dark fluid salved Covenant's throat, but he still sounded harsh. 'I already used the command. He killed six people.'

'Ah,' said Hamako. He turned from Covenant, and called down one of the entryways in a barking tongue. Almost immediately, a Waynhim entered the chamber. The creature sniffed enquiringly in Covenant's direction, then began a rapid conversation with Hamako. Their voices had a roynish sound that grated on Covenant's nerves – he had too many horrid memories of ur-viles – but he suppressed his discomfort, tried not to think balefully of Vain. Shortly, the Waynhim trotted away as if it carried important information. Hamako returned his attention to Covenant.

The man's gaze was full of questions as he said, 'Then you came not upon this Demondim-spawn by chance. He did not seek you out without your knowledge.'

Covenant shook his head.

'He was given to you,' Hamako continued, 'by those who know his purpose. You comprehend him.'

'No. I mean, yes, he was given to me. I was told how to command him. I was told to trust him.' He scowled at the idea of Vain's trustworthiness. 'But nothing else.'

Hamako searched for the right way to phrase his question. 'May I ask – who was the giver?'

Covenant felt reluctant to answer directly. He did not distrust Hamako; he simply did not want to discuss his experience with his Dead. So he replied gruffly, 'I was in Andelain.'

'Ah, Andelain,' Hamako breathed. 'The Dead.' He nodded in comprehension, but it did not relieve his awkwardness.

Abruptly, Covenant's intuition leaped. 'You know what his purpose is.' He had often heard that the lore of the Waynhim was wide and subtle. 'But you're not going to tell me.'

Hamako's mouth twitched painfully. 'Covenant,' he said, pleading to be understood, 'the Dead were your friends, were they not? Their concern for you is ancient and far-seeing. It is sooth – the Waynhim ken much, and guess more. Doubtless there are many questions to which they hold answers. But – '

Covenant interrupted him. 'You know how to fight the Sunbane, and you're not going to tell me that either.'

His tone made Hamako wince. 'Surely your Dead have given to you all which may be wisely told. Ah, Thomas Covenant! My heart yearns to share with you the lore of the Waynhim. But they have instructed me strictly to forbear. For many reasons.

'They are ever loath to impart knowledge where they cannot control the use to which their knowledge is placed. For the ring-wielder, perhaps they would waive such considerations. But they have not the vision of the Dead, and fear to transgress the strictures which have guided the gifts of the Dead. This is the paradox of lore, that it must be achieved rather than granted, else it misleads. This only I am permitted to say: were I to reveal the purpose of this Demondim-spawn, that revelation could well prevent the accomplishment of his purpose.' Hamako's face held a look of supplication. 'That purpose is greatly desirable.'

'At any rate, the ur-viles desire it greatly.' Frustration and weakness made Covenant sarcastic. 'Maybe these Waynhim aren't as different as you think.'

He emptied the bowl, then tried to get to his feet. But Hamako held him back. Covenant had touched anger in the man. Stiffly, Hamako said, 'I owe life and health and use to the succour of the Waynhim. Aye, and many things more. I will not betray their wishes to ease your mind, ring-wielder though you are.'

Covenant thrust against Hamako's grasp, but could not break free. After an effort like palsy, he collapsed back on the grass. 'You said two days,' he panted. Futility enfeebled him. Two more days! 'I've got to go. I'm already too far behind.'

'You have been deeply harmed,' Hamako replied. 'Your flesh will not yet bear you. What urgency drives you?'

Covenant repressed a querulous retort. He could not denigrate

Hamako's refusal to answer crucial questions; he had done such things himself. When he had mastered his gall, he said, 'Three friends of mine were kidnapped by a Rider. They're on their way to Revelstone. If I don't catch up with them in time, they'll be killed.'

Hamako absorbed this information, then called again for one of the Waynhim. Another rapid conversation took place. Hamako seemed to be stressing something, urging something; the responses of the Waynhim sounded thoughtful, unpersuaded. But the creature ended on a note which satisfied Hamako. As the Waynhim departed, he turned back to Covenant.

'*Durhisitar* will consult the Weird of the Waynhim,' the man said, 'but I doubt not that aid will be granted. No Waynhim will forget the redemption of *dhraga* – or the peril of the trap which ensnared you. Rest now, and fear not. This *rhysh* will accord you power to pursue your companions.'

'How? What can they do?'

'The Waynhim are capable of much,' returned Hamako, urging Covenant to lie back. 'Rest, I say. Hold only this much trust, and put care aside. It will be bitter to you if you are offered aid, and are too weak to avail yourself of it.'

Covenant could not resist. The grass exuded a somnolent air. His body was leaden with weariness; and the roborant he had drunk seemed to undermine his anxiety. He allowed Hamako to settle him upon the bed. But as the man prepared to leave, Covenant said distantly, 'At least tell me how I ended up here. The last thing I remember – ' he did not look at Vain – 'I was as good as dead. How did you save me?'

Hamako sat on the edge of the bed. Once again, his countenance wore an awkward sympathy. 'That I will relate,' he said. 'But I must tell you openly that we did not save you.'

Covenant jerked up his head. 'No?'

'Softly.' Hamako pushed him flat again. 'There is no need for this concern.'

Grabbing the man's arms with both hands, Covenant pulled their faces together. 'What the hell am I doing alive?'

'Covenant,' said Hamako with a dry smile, 'how may I tell the tale if you are so upwrought?'

Slowly, Covenant released him. 'All right.' Spectres crowded his head; but he forced himself to relax. 'Tell it.'

'It came to pass thus,' the man said. 'When *dhraga* Waynhim was set free by your hand, and learned that this Demondim-spawn would not obey the word of command, it desired you to share its flight. But it could not gain your comprehension. Therefore *dhraga* summoned all the haste which the harm to its body permitted, and sped to inform the *rhysh* of your plight. *Dhraga* had been made the bait of a snare. This snare – '

Covenant interrupted him. 'What's a *rhysh*?'

'Ah, pardon me. For a score of turnings of the moon, I have heard no human voice but those warped by the Sunbane. I forget that you do not speak the Waynhim tongue.

'In our speech, the word *rhysh* means stead. It gives reference to a community of Waynhim. In all the Land, there are many hundred score Waynhim, but all live in *rhysh* of one or two score. Each *rhysh* is private unto itself – though I am told that communication exists between them. In the great war of Revelstone, nigh two score centuries past, five *rhysh* fought together against the ur-viles of the Despiser. But such sharing is rare. Each *rhysh* holds to itself and interprets the Weird in its own way. Long has this *rhysh* lived here, serving its own vision.'

Covenant wanted to ask the meaning of the term *Weird*; but he already regretted having halted Hamako's tale.

'The *rhysh*,' Hamako resumed, 'was informed of your plight by *dhraga*. At once we set out to attempt your aid. But the distance was too great. When first *dhraga* was captured the decision was taken to make no rescue. It was bitter to all the *rhysh* to abandon one of its own. But we had cause to fear this snare. Long have we laboured all too near a strong number of those warped by the Sunbane.' Unexplained tears blurred his eyes. 'Long have the ill souls that captured you striven to undo us. Therefore we believed the snare to be for us. Having no wish to slay or be slain, we abandoned *dhraga* to its doom.'

Covenant was struck by the closeness with which Hamako identified himself with the *rhysh*, and by the man's evident grief over the Sunbane victims. But he did not interrupt again.

'Also,' Hamako went on, suppressing his emotion, 'for three days of desert sun prior to the setting of this snare, the Waynhim tasted Raver spoor.'

A Raver! Covenant groaned. Hellfire! That explained the trap. And the spider.

'Therefore we feared the snare deeply. But when we learned that the ring-wielder had fallen prey, we comprehended our error, and ran to succour you. But the distance,' he repeated, 'was too great. We arrived only in time to behold the manner in which you redeemed yourself with wild magic.'

Redeemed – ! An ache wrung Covenant's heart. No!

'Though your arm was terrible and black, your white ring spun a great fire. The bonds dropped from you. The wood was scattered. The Sunbane-warped were cast aside like chaff, and fled in terror. Rocks were riven from the escarpment. Only this Demondim-spawn stood scatheless amid the fire.

'The power ended as you fell. Perceiving your venom-ill, we bore you here, and the Waynhim tended you with all their cunning until your death receded from you. Here you are safe until your strength returns.'

Hamako fell silent. After studying Covenant for a moment, he rose to his feet and began to depart.

'The Raver?' Covenant gritted.

'All spoor of him is gone,' Hamako replied quietly. 'I fear his purpose was accomplished.'

Or else he's afraid of me, Covenant rasped inwardly. He did not see Hamako leave the chamber. He was consumed by his thoughts. Damnation! First Marid, then the bees, now this. Each attack worse than the one before. And a Raver involved each time. Hell and blood! Why? Bile rose in him. Why else? Lord Foul did not want him dead, not if his ring might fall to a Raver. The Despiser wanted something entirely different. He wanted surrender, voluntary abdication. Therefore the purpose of these attacks lay in their effect on him, in the way they drew power from his delirium, violence over which he had no control.

No control!

Was Foul trying to scare him into giving up his ring?

God bloody damn it to hell! He had always felt an almost overwhelming distrust of power. In the past, he had reconciled himself to the might with which he had defeated Lord Foul only because he had refrained from making full use of it; rather than attempting to crush the Despiser utterly, he had withheld the final blow, though in so doing he had ensured that Lord Foul would rise to threaten the Land again. Deliberately, he had made himself culpable for Lord Foul's future ill. And he had chosen that course because the alternative was so much worse.

For he believed that Lord Foul was part of himself, an embodiment of the moral peril lurking for the outcast in the complex rage against being outcast, a leper's doom of Despite for everything including himself. Restraint was the only possible escape from such a doom. If he had allowed his power to rise unchecked, committed himself completely to wild magic in his battle against Lord Foul, he would have accomplished nothing but the feeding of his own inner Despiser. The part of him which judged, believed, affirmed, was the part which refrained. Utter power, boundless and unscrupulous rage, would have corrupted him, and he would have changed in one stroke from victim to victimizer. He knew how easy it was for a man to become the thing he hated.

Therefore he profoundly feared his wild magic, his capacity for power and violence. And that was precisely the point of Foul's attack. The venom called up his might when he was beyond all restraint – called it up and increased it. In Mithil Stonedown, he had almost failed to light Sunder's *orcrest*; but two days ago he had apparently broken boulders. Without volition.

And still he did not know why. Perhaps in saving Joan, he *had* sold himself; perhaps he was no longer free. But no lack of freedom could force him to surrender. And every increase in his power improved his chances of besting the Despiser again.

His danger lay in the venom, the loss of restraint. But if he could avoid further relapses, learn control –

He was a leper. Control and discipline were the tools of his life. Let Lord Foul consider that before he counted his victory.

With such thoughts, Covenant grew grim and calm. Slowly, the effects of his illness came over him. The scent of the grass soothed him like an anodyne. After a time, he slept.

When Hamako nudged him awake again, he had the impression that he had slept for a long time. Nothing in the chamber had changed; yet his instincts were sure. Groaning at the way everything conspired to increase the peril of his friends, he groped into a sitting position. 'How many days have I lost now?'

Hamako placed a large bowl of the dark, musty liquid in Covenant's hands. 'You have been among us for three days of the sun of pestilence,' he answered. 'Dawn is not yet nigh, but I have awakened you because there is much I wish to show and say before you depart. Drink.'

Three days. Terrific! Dismally, Covenant took a deep swallow from the bowl.

But as the liquid passed into him, he recognized the improvement in his condition. He held the bowl steadily: his whole body felt stable. He looked up at Hamako. To satisfy his curiosity, he asked, 'What is this stuff?'

'It is *vitrim*.' Hamako was smiling: he seemed pleased by what he saw in Covenant. 'It resembles an essence of *aliantha*, but has been created by the lore of the Waynhim rather than drawn from the *aliantha* itself.'

In a long draught, Covenant drained the bowl, and felt immediately more substantial. He returned the bowl, and rose to his feet. 'When can I get started? I'm running out of excuses.'

'Soon after the sun's rising, you will renew your sojourn,' answered Hamako. 'I assure you that you will hold your days among us in scant regret.' He handed the bowl to a Waynhim standing nearby and accepted a leather pouch like a wineskin. This he gave to Covenant. '*Vitrim*,' he said. 'If you consume it prudently, you will require no other aliment for three days.'

Covenant acknowledged the gift with a nod and tied the pouch to his belt by its drawstring. As he did so, Hamako said, 'Thomas Covenant, it pains me that we have refused to answer your most urgent questions. Therefore I desire you to comprehend the Weird of the Waynhim ere you depart. Then perhaps you will grasp my conviction that their wisdom must be trusted. Are you willing?'

Covenant faced Hamako with a rueful grimace. 'Hamako, you saved my life. I may be a natural-born ingrate, but I can still appreciate the significance of not being dead. I'll try to understand anything you want to tell me.' Half involuntarily, he added, 'Just don't take too long. If I don't *do* something soon, I won't be able to live with myself.'

'Then come,' Hamako said, and strode out of the chamber.

Covenant paused to tuck in his shirt, then followed.

As he stooped to pass through the entryway, he noted sourly that Vain was right behind him.

He found himself in a corridor, scrupulously delved out of native rock, where he could barely walk erect. The passage was long, and lit at intervals by small censers set into the walls. In them, a dark fluid burned warmly, without smoke.

After some distance, the passage branched, became a network of tunnels. As Covenant and Hamako passed, they began to meet Waynhim. Some went by in silence; others exchanged a few comments with Hamako in their roynish tongue; but all of them bowed to the ring-wielder.

Abruptly, the tunnel opened into an immense cavern. It was brightly-lit by vats of burning liquid. It appeared to be more than a hundred feet high and three times that across. At least a score of Waynhim were busily at work around the area.

With a thrill of astonishment, Covenant saw that the whole cavern was a garden.

Thick grass covered the floor. Flowerbeds lay everywhere, hedged by many different varieties of bushes. Trees – pairs of Gilden, oak, peach, sycamore, elm, apple, jacaranda, spruce, and others – stretched their limbs towards the vaulted ceiling. Vines and creepers grew up the walls.

The Waynhim were tending the plants. From plot to tree they moved, barking chants and wielding short iron staves; and dark droplets of power sprang from the metal, nourishing flowers and shrubs and vines like a distilled admixture of loam and sunshine.

The effect was incomparably strange. On the surface of the Land, the Sunbane made everything unnatural; nothing grew without violating the Law of its own being, nothing died without ruin. Yet here, where there was no sunlight, no free air, no pollinating insects, no age-nurtured soil, the garden of the Waynhim blossomed lush and lovely, as natural as if these plants had been born to fructify under a stone sky.

Covenant gazed about with undisguised wonder; but when he started to ask a question, Hamako gestured him silent, and led him into the garden.

Slowly, they walked among the flowers and trees. The murmurous chanting of the Waynhim filled the air; but none of the creatures spoke to each other or to Hamako; they were rapt in the concentration of their work. And in their concentration, Covenant caught a glimpse of the prodigious difficulty of the task they had set for themselves. To keep such a garden healthy underground must have required miracles of devotion and lore.

But Hamako had more to show. He guided Covenant and Vain to the far end of the cavern, into a new series of corridors. These angled steadily upward; and as he ascended, Covenant became aware of a growing animal smell. He had already guessed what he was about to see when Hamako entered another large cave, not as high as the garden, but equally broad.

It was a zoo. The Waynhim here were feeding hundreds of different animals. In small pens cunningly devised to resemble their natural dens and habitats lived pairs of badgers, foxes, hounds, marmosets, moles, racoons, otters, rabbits, lynx, muskrats. And many of them had young.

The zoo was less successful than the garden. Animals without space to roam could not be healthy. But that problem paled beside the amazing fact that these creatures were alive at all. The Sunbane was fatal to animal life. The Waynhim preserved these species from complete extinction.

Once again, Hamako silenced Covenant's questions. They left the cave, and continued to work upward. They met no Waynhim in these tunnels. Soon their ascent became so pronounced that Covenant wondered just how deep in the Earth he had slept for three days. He felt a pang over the insensitivity of his senses; he missed the ability to gauge the rock weight above him, assess the nature of the *vitrim*, probe the spirits of his companions. That regret made him ache for Linden. She might have known whether or not he could trust Vain.

Then the passageway became a spiral stair which rose to a small round chamber. No egress was visible; but Hamako placed his hands against a section of the wall, barked several Waynhim words, and thrust outward. The stone divided along an unseen crack and opened.

Leaving the chamber, Covenant found himself under the stars. Along the eastern horizon, the heavens had begun to pale. Dawn was approaching. At the sight, he felt an unexpected reluctance to leave the safety and wonder of the Waynhim demesne. Grimly, he tightened his resolve. He did not look back when Hamako sealed the entrance behind him.

Vague in the darkness, Hamako led him through an impression of large, crouching shapes to a relatively open area. There he sat down, facing the east. As he joined Hamako, Covenant discovered that they were on a flat expanse of rock – protection against the first touch of the Sunbane.

Vain stood off to one side as if he neither knew nor cared about the need for such protection.

'Now I will speak,' Hamako said. His words went softly into the night. 'Have no fear of the Sunbane-warped who sought your life. Never again will they enter this place. That much at least of mind and fear they retain.' His tone suggested that he held the area sacred to some private and inextinguishable sorrow.

Covenant settled himself to listen; and after a deep pause Hamako began.

'A vast gulf,' he breathed, a darker shape amid the dark crouching of the night, 'lies between creatures that are born and those that are made. Born creatures, such as we are, do not suffer torment at the simple fact of physical form. Perhaps you desire keener sight, greater might of arm, but the embodiment of eyes and limbs is not anguish to you. You are born by Law to be as you are. Only a madman loathes the nature of his birth.

'It is far otherwise with the Waynhim. They were made – as the ur-viles were made – by deliberate act in the breeding dens of the Demondim. And the Demondim were themselves formed by lore rather than blood from the Viles who went before them. Thus the Waynhim are not creatures of Law. They are entirely alien in the world. And they are unnaturally long of life. Some among this *rhysh* remember the Lords and the ancient glory of Revelstone. Some tell the tale of the five *rhysh* which fought before the gates of Revelstone in the great siege – and of the blue Lord who rode to their aid in folly and valour. But let that pass.

'The numbers of the Waynhim are only replenished because the ur-viles continue the work of their Demondim makers. Much breeding is yet done in the deeps of the Earth, and some are ur-viles, some Waynhim – and some are altogether new, enfleshed visions of lore and power. Such a one is your companion. A conscious making to accomplish a chosen aim.'

In the east, the sky slowly blanched. The last stars were fading. The shapes around Covenant and Hamako grew more distinct, modulating towards revelation.

'That is the Weird of all Demondim-spawn. Each Waynhim and ur-vile beholds itself and sees that it need not have been what it is. It is the fruit of choices it did not make. From this fact both Waynhim and ur-viles draw their divergent spirits. It has inspired in the ur-viles a quenchless loathing for their own forms and an overweening lust for perfection, for the power to create what they are not. Their passion is extreme, careless of costs. Therefore they have given millennia of service to the Despiser, for Lord Foul repays them with both knowledge and material for their breedings. Thus comes your companion.

'And therefore the Waynhim have been greatly astonished to find no ill in him. He is an – an apotheosis. In him, it appears that the ur-viles have at last transcended their unscrupling violence and achieved perfection. He is the Weird of the ur-viles incarnate. More of him I may not say.

'But the spirit of the Waynhim is different entirely. They are not reckless of costs; from the great Desecration which Kevin Landwaster and Lord Foul conceived upon the Land, they learned a horror of such passions. They foresaw clearly the price the ur-viles paid, and will ever pay, for self-loathing, and they turned in another way. Sharing the Weird, they chose to meet it differently. To seek self-justification.'

Hamako shifted his position, turned more squarely towards the east.

'In the Waynhim tongue, Weird has several meanings. It is fate or destiny – but it is also choice, and is used to signify council or decision-making. It is a contradiction – fate and choice. A man may be fated to die, but no fate can determine whether he will die in courage or cowardice. The Waynhim choose the manner in which they meet their doom.

'In their loneness, they have chosen to serve the Law of which they do not partake. Each *rhysh* performs its own devoir. Thus the garden and the animals. In defiance of the Sunbane and all Lord Foul's ill, this *rhysh* seeks to preserve things which grow by Law from natural seed, in the form which they were born to hold. Should the end of Sunbane ever come, the Land's future will be assured of its natural life.'

Covenant listened with a tightness in his throat. He was moved by both the scantness and the nobility of what the Waynhim were doing. In the myriad square leagues which comprised the vast ruin of the Sunbane, one cavern of healthy plants was a paltry thing. And yet the cavern represented such commitment, such faith in the Land, that it became grandeur. He wanted to express his appreciation, but could find no adequate words. Nothing could ever be adequate except the repeal of the Sunbane, allowing the Waynhim to have the future they served. The fear that their self-consecration might prove futile in the end blurred his vision, made him cover his eyes with his hands.

When he looked up again, the sun was rising.

It came in pale brown across the Plains, a desert sun. Land features were lifted out of darkness as the night bled away. When he glanced about him, he saw that he was sitting in the centre of a wrecked Stonedown.

Houses lay in rubble; lone walls stood without ceilings to support;

architraves sprawled like corpses; slabs of stone containing windows canted against each other. At first, he guessed that the village had been hit by an earthquake. But as the light grew stronger, he saw more clearly.

Ragged holes the size of his palm riddled all the stone as if a hail of vitriol had fallen on the village, chewing through the ceilings until they collapsed, tearing the walls into broken chunks, burning divots out of the hard ground. The place where he sat was pocked with acid marks. Every piece of rock in the area which had ever stood upright had been sieved into ruin.

'Hellfire!' he murmured weakly. 'What happened here?'

Hamako had not moved; but his head was bowed. When he spoke, his tone said plainly that he was acutely familiar with the scene. 'This also I desire to tell,' he sighed. 'For this purpose I brought you here.'

Behind him, a hillock cracked and opened, revealing within it the chamber from which he and Covenant had left the underground corridors. Eight Waynhim filed into the sunrise, closing the entrance after them. But Hamako seemed unaware of them.

'This is During Stonedown, home of the Sunbane-warped who sought your life. They are my people.'

The Waynhim ranged themselves in a circle around Hamako and Covenant. After an initial glance, Covenant concentrated on Hamako. He wanted to hear what the man was saying.

'My people,' the former Stonedownor repeated. 'A proud people – all of us. A score of turnings of the moon ago, we were hale and bold. Proud. It was a matter of great pride to us that we had chosen to defy the Clave.

'Mayhap you have heard of the way in which the Clave acquires blood. All submit to this annexation, as did we for many generations. But it was gall and abhorrence to us, and at last we arose in refusal. Ah, pride. The Rider departed from us, and During Stonedown fell under the na-Mhoram's *Grim*.'

His voice shuddered. 'It may be that you have no knowledge of such abominations. A fertile sun was upon us, and we were abroad from our homes, planting and reaping our sustenance – recking little of our peril. Then of a sudden the green of the sun became black – blackest ill – and a fell cloud ran from Revelstone towards During Stonedown, crossing against the wind.'

He clenched his hand over his face, gripping his forehead in an effort to control the pain of memory.

'Those who remained in their homes – infants, mothers, the injured and the infirm – perished as During Stonedown perished, in agony. All the rest were rendered homeless.'

The events he described were vivid to him, but he did not permit himself to dwell on them. With an effort of will, he continued, 'Then despair came upon us. For a day and a night, we wandered the brokenness of our minds, heeding nothing. We had not the heart to heed. Thus the Sunbane took my people unprotected. They became as you have seen them.

'Yet I was spared. Stumbling alone in my loss – bemoaning the death of wife and daughter – I came by chance upon three of the Waynhim ere the sun rose. Seeing my plight, they compelled me to shelter.'

He raised his head, made an attempt to clear his throat of grief. 'From that time, I have lived and worked among the *rhysh*, learning the tongue and lore and Weird of the Waynhim. In heart and will, I have become one of them as much as a man may. But if that were the extent of my tale – ' he glanced painfully at Covenant – 'I would not have told it. I have another purpose.'

Abruptly, he stood and gazed around the gathered Waynhim. When Covenant joined him, he said, 'Thomas Covenant, I say to you that I have become of the Waynhim. And they have welcomed me as kindred. More. They have made my loss a part of their Weird. The Sunbane-warped live dire lives, committing all possible harm ere they die. In my name, this *rhysh* has taken upon itself the burden of my people. They are watched and warded – preserved from hurt, sustained in life – prevented from wreaking the damage of their wildness. For my sake, they are kept much as the animals are kept, both aided and controlled. Therefore they remain alive in such numbers. Therefore the *rhysh* was unwilling to redeem *dhraga*. And therefore – ' he looked squarely at Covenant – 'both *rhysh* and I are to blame for the harm you suffered.'

'No,' Covenant protested. 'It wasn't your fault. You can't blame yourself for things you can't foresee.'

Hamako brushed this objection aside. 'The Waynhim did not foresee their own creation. Yet the Weird remains.' But then, somehow, he managed a smile. 'Ah, Covenant,' he said, 'I do not speak for any love of blame. I desire only your comprehension.' He gestured around him. 'The Waynhim have come to offer their aid in pursuit of your companions. I wish you to know what lies behind this offer, so that you may accept it in the spirit of its giving, and forgive us for what we have withheld from you.'

A surge of respect and empathy blurred Covenant's responses again. Because he had no other way to express what he felt, he said formally, as Atiaran had taught him, 'I thank you. The giving of this gift honours me. Accepting it, I return honour to the givers.' Then he added, 'You've earned the right.'

Slowly, the strain faded from Hamako's smile. Without releasing Covenant's gaze, he spoke to the Waynhim; and they answered in a tone of readiness. One of them stepped forward, placed something in his hand. When Hamako raised his hand, Covenant saw that the object was a stone dirk.

He winced inwardly. But Hamako's smile was the smile of a friend. Seeing Covenant's uncertainty, the man said, 'There is no harm for you in this. May I have your hand?'

Consciously repressing a tremor, Covenant extended his right hand, palm downward.

Hamako grasped his wrist, looked for a moment at the scars left by Joan's nails, then abruptly drew a cut across the veins.

Covenant flinched; but Hamako held him, did not permit him to withdraw.

His anxiety turned to amazement as he saw that the cut did not bleed. Its edges opened, but no blood came from the wound.

Dhraga approached. Its broken arm hung in a splint, but its other wounds were healing.

It raised its uninjured hand. Carefully, Hamako made an incision in the exposed palm. At once, dark blood swarmed down *dhraga*'s forearm.

Without hesitation, the Waynhim reached out, placed its cut directly on Covenant's. Hot blood smeared the back of his hand.

At that instant, he became aware of the other Waynhim. They were chanting softly in the clear desert dawn.

Simultaneously, strength rushed up his arm, kicked his heart like a burst of elation. He felt suddenly taller, more muscular. His vision seemed to expand, encompassing more of the terrain. He could easily have wrested free of Hamako's grasp. But he had no need to do so.

Dhraga lifted its hand away.

The bleeding had stopped. Its blood was being sucked into his cut.

Dhraga withdrew. Hamako gave the dirk to *durhisitar*. While *durhisitar* cut its palm just as *dhraga*'s had been cut, Hamako said, 'Soon the power will come to appear unbearable, but I ask you to bear it. Remain quiet until all the Waynhim have shared this giving. If the ritual is completed, you will have the strength you require for a day – perhaps two.'

Durhisitar put its cut upon Covenant's. More might surged into him. He felt abruptly giddy with energy, capable of anything, everything. His incision absorbed *durhisitar*'s blood. When the creature stepped back, he could hardly hold himself still for the next Waynhim.

Only after the third infusion did he realize that he was receiving something more than power. *Dhraga* he had recognized by its injuries – but how had he known *durhisitar*? He had never looked closely at that particular Waynhim. Yet he had known it by name, just as he knew the third Waynhim, *dhubha*, and the fourth, *vraith*.

He felt ecstatic with knowledge.

Drhami was fifth; *ghohritsar*, sixth. He was dancing with uncontainable might. Hamako's knuckles whitened; but his grip had the weight of a feather. Covenant had to leash himself firmly to keep from exploding free and cavorting around the ruins like a wild man. The range of his hearing had become so wide that he could hardly distinguish words spoken nearby.

Hamako was saying,' – remember your companions. Waste not this power. While it remains, stop for neither night nor doom.'

Ghramin.

Covenant felt as colossal as Gravin Threndor, as mighty as Fire-Lions. He felt that he could crush boulders in his arms, destroy Ravers with his hands.

Dhurng: eighth and last.

Hamako snatched back his hand as if the power in Covenant burned him. 'Go now!' he cried. 'Go for Land and Law, and may no malison prevail against you!'

Covenant threw back his head, gave a shout that seemed to echo for leagues:

'Linden!'

Swinging around to the north-west, he released the flood-fire of his given strength and erupted, running towards Revelstone like a coruscation in the air.

17

BLOOD-SPEED

The sun ascended, brown-mantled and potent, sucking the moisture of life from the Land. Heat pressed down like the weight of all the sky. Bare ground was baked as hard as travertine. Loose dirt became dust and dust became powder until brown clogged the air and every surface gave off clouds like dead steam. Chimeras roamed the horizons, avatars of the Sunbane. The Centre Plains lay featureless and unaneled under the bale of that sun.

But Waynhim strength was glee in Covenant's veins. Running easily, swiftly, he could not have stopped, even by choice; his muscles thronged with power; gaiety exalted his heart; his speed was delicious to him. Without exertion, he ran like the Ranyhyn.

His progress he measured on a map in his mind – names of regions so dimly remembered that he could no longer identify when he had first heard them.

Across the wild wilderland of Windscour: eleven leagues. Through the ragged hills of Kurash Festillin: three leagues.

By noon he had settled into a long, fast stride, devouring distance as if his appetite for it were insatiable. Fortified by *vitrim* and power, he was immune to heat, dust, hallucination.

Yet Vain followed as if the Demondim-spawn had been made for such swiftness. He ran the leagues lightly, and the ground seemed to leap from under his feet.

Along the breadth of Victuallin Tayne, where in ancient centuries great crops had flourished: ten leagues. Up the long stone rise of Greshas Slant to higher ground: two leagues. Around the dry hollow of Lake Pelluce in the centre of Andelainscion, olden fruiterer to the Land: five leagues.

Covenant moved like a dream of strength. He had no sense of time, of strides measured by sweat and effort. The Waynhim had borne the cost of this power for him, and he was free to run and run. When evening came upon him, he feared he would have to slacken his pace; but he did not. Stars burnished the crisp desert night, and the moon rose half full, shedding silver over the waste. Without hesitation or hindrance, he told out the dark in names.

Across the Centerpith Barrens: fourteen leagues. Down the Fields of Richloam, Sunbane-ruined treasure of the Plains: six leagues. Up through the jagged ridges of Emacrimma's Maw: three leagues. Along Boulder Fash, strewn with confusion like the wreckage of a mountain: ten leagues.

The night unfurled like an oriflamme: it snapped open over the Plains, and snapped away; and he went on running through the dawn. Outdistancing moon and stars, he caught the sunrise in the dry watercourse of the Soulsease River, five score leagues and more from Stonemight Woodhelven. Speed was as precious to him as a heart-gift. With Vain always at his back, he sipped *vitrim* and left the Soulsease behind, left the Centre Plains behind to run and run, north-west towards Revelstone.

Over the open flat of Riversward: five leagues. Through the fens of Graywightswath, which the desert sun made traversable: nine leagues. Up the rocks of the Bandsoil Bounds: three leagues.

Now the sun was overhead, and at last he came to the end of his exaltation. His eldritch strength did not fail – not yet – but he began to see that it would fail. The knowledge gave him a pang of loss. Consciously, he increased his pace, trying to squeeze as many leagues as possible from the gift of Hamako's *rhysh*.

Across the rolling width of Riddenstretch: twelve leagues.

Gradually his mortality returned. He had to exert effort now to maintain his speed. His throat ached on the dust.

Among the gentle hills, smooth as a soft-rumpled mantle, of Consecear Redoin: seven leagues.

As the last rays of sunset spread from the Westron Mountains, he went running out of the hills, stumbled and gasped and the power was gone. He was mortal again. The air rasped his lungs as he heaved for breath.

For a while, he rested on the ground, lay panting until his respiration eased. Mutely, he searched Vain for some sign of fatigue; but the Demondim-spawn's black flesh was vague in the gloaming, and nothing could touch him. After a time, Covenant took two swallows from his dwindling *vitrim*, and started walking.

He did not know how much time he had gained; but it was enough to renew his hope. Were his companions two days ahead of him? Three? He could believe that the Clave might not harm them for two or three days. If he met no more delays –

He went briskly on his way, intending to walk through the night. He needed sleep; but his body felt less tired than it usually did after a hike of five leagues. Even his feet did not hurt. The power and the *vitrim* of the Waynhim had sustained him wondrously. With the sharpness of the air to keep him alert, he expected to cover some distance before he had to rest.

But within a league he caught sight of a fire burning off to the left ahead of him.

He could have bypassed it; he was far enough from it for that. But after a moment he shrugged grimly and started towards the fire. His involuntary hope that he had caught up with his friends demanded an answer. And if this light represented a menace, he did not want to put it behind him until he knew what it was.

Creeping over the hard uneven ground, he crouched forward until he could make out details.

The light came from a simple campfire. A few pieces of wood burned brightly. A bundle of faggots lay near three large sacks.

Across the fire sat a lone figure in a vivid red robe. The hood of the robe had been pushed back, revealing the lined face and grey-raddled hair of a middle-aged woman. Something black was draped around her neck.

She triggered an obscure memory in Covenant. He felt he had seen someone like her before, but he could not recollect where or when. Then she moved her hands, and he saw that she held a short iron sceptre with an open triangle affixed to its end. Curses crowded against his teeth. He identified her from Linden's description of the Rider at Crystal Stonedown.

Gritting to himself, he began to withdraw. This Rider was not the one he wanted. The Graveller of Stonemight Woodhelven had indicated that Linden's abductor, Santonin na-Mhoram-in, was a man. And Covenant had no intention of risking himself against any Rider until no other choice remained. With all the stealth he could muster, he edged away from the light.

Suddenly, he heard a low snarl. A huge shape loomed out of the darkness, catching him between it and the fire. Growling threats, the shape advanced like the wall of a house.

Then a voice cut the night.

'Din!'

The Rider. She stood facing Covenant and Vain and the snarl. 'Din!' she commanded. 'Bring them to me!'

The shape continued to approach, forcing Covenant towards the campfire. As he entered the range of light, he became gradually able to see the immense beast.

It had the face and fangs of a sabre-tooth, but its long body resembled that of a horse – a horse with shoulders as high as the top of his head, a back big enough to carry five or six people, and hair so shaggy that it hung to the creature's thighs. Its feet were hooved. From the back of each ankle grew a barbed spur as long as a swordthorn.

Its eyes were red with malice, and its snarl vibrated angrily. Covenant hastened to retreat as much as he could without moving too close to the Rider.

Vain followed calmly with his back to the beast.

'Halfhand!' the Rider barked in surprise. 'I was sent to await you, but had no thought to meet you so soon.' A moment later, she added, 'Have no fear of Din. It is true – the Coursers are creatures of the Sunbane. But therefore they have no need of meat. And they are whelped in obedience. Din will lift neither fang nor spur against you without my command.'

Covenant put the fire between him and the woman. She was a short, square individual, with a blunt nose and a determined chin. Her hair was bound carelessly at the back of her neck as if she had no interest in the details of her appearance. But her gaze had the directness of long commitment. The black cloth hanging around her neck ritualized the front of her robe like a chasuble.

He distrusted her completely. But he preferred to take his chances with her rather than with her Courser. 'Show me.' He cast a silent curse at the unsteadiness of his voice. 'Send it away.'

She regarded him over the flames. 'As you wish.' Without shifting her gaze, she said, 'Begone, Din! Watch and ward.'

The beast gave a growl of disappointment. But it turned away and trotted out into the night.

In an even tone, the Rider asked, 'Does this content you?'

Covenant answered with a jerk of his knotted shoulders. 'It takes orders from you.' He did not relax a jot of his wariness. 'How content do you expect me to get?'

She considered him as if she had reason to fear him, and did not intend to show it. 'You misdoubt me, Halfhand. Yet it appears to me that the right of misdoubt is mine.'

Harshly, he rasped, 'How do you figure that?'

'In Crystal Stonedown you reft Sivit na-Mhoram-wist of his rightful claim, and nigh slew him. But I give you warning.' Her tone involuntarily betrayed her apprehension. 'I am Memla na-Mhoram-in. If you seek my harm, I will not be so blithely dispatched.' Her hands gripped her *rukh*, though she did not raise it.

He suppressed an angry denial. 'Crystal Stonedown is just about a hundred and fifty leagues from here. How do you know what happened there?'

She hesitated momentarily, then decided to speak. 'With the destruction of his *rukh*, Sivit was made helpless. But the fate of every *rukh* is known in Revelstone. Another Rider who chanced to be in that region was sent at once to his aid. Then that Rider spoke with his *rukh* to Revelstone, and the story was told. I knew of it before I was sent to await you.'

'Sent?' Covenant demanded, thinking, Be careful. One thing at a time. 'Why? How did you know I was coming?'

'Where else but Revelstone would the Halfhand go with his white ring?' she replied steadily. 'You fled Mithil Stonedown in the south, and appeared again at Crystal Stonedown. Your aim was clear. As for why I was sent – I am not alone. Seven of the Clave are scattered throughout this region, so that you would not find the Keep unforewarned. We were sent to escort you if you come as friend. And to give warning if you come as foe.'

Deliberately, Covenant let his anger show. 'Don't lie to me. You were sent to kill me. Every village in the Land was told to kill me on sight. You people think I'm some kind of threat.'

She studied him over the jumping flames. 'Are you not?'

'That depends. Whose side are you on? The Land's – or Lord Foul's?'

'Lord Foul? That name is unknown to me.'

'Then call him a-Jeroth. A-Jeroth of the Seven Hells.'

She stiffened. 'Do you ask if I serve a-Jeroth? Have you come such a distance in the Land, and not learned that the Clave is dedicated entirely to the amelioration of the Sunbane? – To accuse – '

He interrupted her like a blade. 'Prove it.' He made a stabbing gesture at her *rukh*. 'Put that thing down. Don't tell them I'm coming.'

She stood still, trapped by indecision.

'If you really serve the Land,' he went on, 'you don't need to be afraid of me. But I've got no reason to trust you. Goddamn it, you've been trying to kill me! I don't care how much tougher you are than Sivit.' He brandished his ring, hoping she had no way of recognizing his incapacity. 'I'll take you apart. Unless you give me some reason not to.'

Slowly, the Rider's shoulders sagged. In a tight voice, she said, 'Very well.' Taking her sceptre by the triangle, she handed it past the fire to him.

He accepted it with his left hand to keep it away from his ring. A touch of relief eased some of his tension. He slipped the iron into his belt, then tugged at his beard to keep himself from becoming careless, and began to marshal his questions.

Before he could speak, Memla said, 'Now I am helpless before you. I have placed myself in your hands. But I desire you to understand the Clave before you choose my doom. For generations, the soothreaders have foretold the coming of the Halfhand and the white ring. They saw it as an omen of destruction for the Clave – a destruction which only your death could prevent.

'Halfhand, we are the last bastion of power in the Land. All else has been undone by the Sunbane. Only our might, constant and vigilant, preserves any life from Landsdrop to the Westron Mountains. How can our destruction be anything other than heinous to the Land? Therefore we sought your death.

'But Sivit's tale held meaning for Gibbon na-Mhoram. Your power was revealed to the Clave for the first time. The na-Mhoram took counsel for several days, and at last elected to dare his doom. Power such as yours, he declared, is rare and precious, and must be used rather than resisted. Better, he said, to strive for your aid, risking fulfilment of the soothreaders' word, than to lose the hope of your puissance. Therefore I do not seek your hurt, though Sivit did, to his cost.'

Covenant listened intently, yearning for the ability to hear whether or not she spoke the truth. Sunder and Hollian had taught him to fear the Clave. But he needed to reach Revelstone – and reach it in a way which would not increase the danger to his friends. He decided to attempt a truce with Memla.

'All right,' he said, moderating the harshness of his tone. 'I'll accept that – for now. But there's something I want *you* to understand. I didn't lift a finger against Sivit until he attacked me.' He had no memory of the situation; but he felt no need to be scrupulously candid. Bluffing for his safety, he added, 'He forced me. All I wanted was the eh-Brand.'

He expected her to ask why he wanted an eh-Brand. Her next sentence took him by surprise.

'Sivit reported that you appeared to be ill.'

A chill spattered down his spine. Careful, he warned himself. Be careful. 'Sunbane-fever,' he replied with complex dishonesty. 'I was just recovering.'

'Sivit reported,' she went on, 'that you were accompanied by a man and a woman. The man was a Stonedownor, but the woman appeared to be a stranger to the Land.'

Covenant clenched himself, decided to chance the truth. 'They were captured by a Rider. Santonin na-Mhoram-in. I've been chasing them for days.'

He hoped to surprise a revelation from her; but she responded with a frown. 'Santonin? He has been absent from Revelstone for many days – but I think he has taken no captives.'

'He's got three,' rasped Covenant. 'He can't be more than two days ahead of me.'

She considered for a moment, then shook her head. 'No. Had he taken your companions, he would have spoken of it through his *rukh* to the Readers. I am na-Mhoram-in. Such knowledge would not be withheld from me.'

Her words gave him a sick sense of being out of his depth – caught in a web of falsehood with no possibility of extrication. Who is lying? The Graveller of Stonemight Woodhelven? Memla? Or Santonin, so that he could keep a fragment of the Illearth Stone for himself? His inability to discern the truth hurt Covenant like vertigo. But he fought to keep his visage flat, free of nausea. 'Do you think I'm making this up?'

Memla was either a consummate prevaricator or a brave woman. She met his glare and said evenly, 'I think you have told me nothing concerning your true companion.' With a nod, she indicated Vain.

The Demondim-spawn had not moved a muscle since he had first come to a halt near the fire.

'He and I made a deal,' Covenant retorted. 'I don't talk about him, and he doesn't talk about me.'

Her eyes narrowed. Slowly, she said, 'You are a mystery, Halfhand. You enter Crystal Stonedown with two companions. You reave Sivit of an eh-Brand. You show power. You escape. When you appear once more, swift beyond belief, your three companions are gone, replaced by this black enigma. And you demand to be trusted. Is it power which gives you such arrogance?'

Arrogance, is it? Covenant grated. I'll show you arrogance. Defiantly, he pulled the *rukh* from his belt, tossed it to her. 'All right,' he snapped. 'Talk to Revelstone. Tell them I'm coming. Tell them anybody who hurts my friends is going to answer for it!'

Startlement made her hesitate. She looked at the iron and back at him, debating rapidly with herself. Then she reached her decision. Reluctantly, she put the *rukh* away within her robe. Straightening her black chasuble, she sighed, 'As you wish.' Her gaze hardened. 'If your companions have indeed been taken to Revelstone, I will answer for their safety.'

Her decision softened his distrust. But he was still not satisfied. 'Just one more thing,' he said in a quieter tone. 'If Santonin was on his way to Revelstone while you were coming here, could he get past you without your knowing it?'

'Clearly,' she responded with a tired lift of her shoulders. 'The Land is wide, and I am but one woman. Only the Readers know the place and state of every *rukh*. Though seven of us were sent to await you, a Rider could pass by unseen if he so chose. I rely on Din to watch and ward, but any Rider could command Din's silence, and I would be none the wiser. Thus if you desire to believe ill of Santonin, I cannot gainsay you.

'Please yourself,' she continued in a tone of fatigue. 'I am no longer young, and mistrust wearies me. I must rest.' Bending like an old woman, she seated herself near the fire. 'If you are wise, you will rest also. We are three score leagues from Revelstone – and a Courser is no palanquin.'

Covenant gazed about him, considering his situation. He felt too tight – and too trapped – to rest. But he intended to remain with Memla. He wanted the speed of her mount. She was either honest or she was not; but he would probably not learn the truth until he reached Revelstone. After a moment, he, too, sat down. Absent-mindedly, he unbound the pouch of *vitrim* from his belt, and took a small swallow.

'Do you require food or water?' she asked. 'I have both.' She gestured towards the sacks near her bundle of firewood.

He shook his head. 'I've got enough for one more day.'

'Mistrust.' Reaching into a sack, she took out a blanket and spread it on the ground. With her back to Covenant, she lay down, pulled the blanket over her shoulders like a protection against his suspicions, and settled herself for sleep.

Covenant watched her through the declining flames. He was cold with a chill which had nothing to do with the night air. Memla na-Mhoram-in challenged too many of his assumptions. He hardly cared that she cast doubt on his distrust of the Clave; he would know how to regard the Clave when he learned more about the Sunbane. But her attack on his preconceptions about Linden and Santonin left him sweating. Was Santonin some kind of rogue Rider? Was this a direct attempt by Lord Foul to lay hands on the ring? An attack similar to the possession of Joan? The lack of any answers made him groan.

If Linden were not at Revelstone, then he would need the Clave's help to locate Santonin. And he would have to pay for that help with co-operation and vulnerability.

Yanking at his beard as if he could pull wisdom from the skin of his face, he glared at Memla's back and groped for prescience. But he could not see past his fear that he might indeed be forced to surrender his ring.

No. Not that. Please. He gritted his teeth against his chill dread.

The future was a leper's question, and he had been taught again and again that the answer lay in single-minded dedication to the exigencies of the present. But he had never been taught how to achieve single-mindedness, how to suppress his own complex self-contradictions.

Finally, he dozed. His slumber was fitful. The night was protracted by fragmentary nightmares of suicide — glimpses of a leper's self-abandonment that terrified him because they came so close to the facts of his fate, to the manner in which he had given himself up for Joan. Waking repeatedly, he strove to elude his dreams; but whenever he faded back towards unconsciousness, they renewed their ubiquitous grasp.

Some time before dawn, Memla roused herself. Muttering at the stiffness in her bones, she used a few faggots to restore the fire, then set a stoneware bowl full of water in the flames to heat. While the water warmed, she put her forehead in the dirt towards Revelstone and mumbled orisons in a language Covenant could not understand.

Vain ignored her as if he had been turned to stone.

When the water was hot enough, she used some of it to lave her hands, face, and neck. The rest she offered to Covenant. He accepted. After the night he had just spent, he needed to comfort himself somehow. While he performed what ablutions he could, she took food for breakfast from one of her sacks.

He declined her viands. True, she had done nothing to threaten him. But she was a Rider of the Clave. While he still had *vitrim* left, he was unwilling to risk her food. And also, he admitted to himself, he wanted to remind her of his distrust. He owed her at least that much candour.

She took his refusal sourly. 'The night has not taught you grace,' she said. 'We are four days from Revelstone, Halfhand. Perhaps you mean to live on air and dust when the liquid in your pouch fails.'

'I mean,' he articulated, 'to trust you exactly as much as I have to, and no more.'

She scowled at his reply, but made no retort.

Soon dawn approached. Moving briskly now, Memla packed away her supplies. As soon as she had tied up her sacks, bound her bundles together by lengths of rope, she raised her head, and barked, 'Din!'

Covenant heard the sound of hooves. A moment later, Memla's Courser came trotting out of the dusk.

She treated it with the confidence of long familiarity. Obeying her brusque gesture, Din lowered itself to its belly. At once, she began to load the beast, heaving her burdens across the middle of its back so that they hung balanced in pairs. Then, knotting her fingers in its long hair, she pulled herself up to perch near its shoulders.

Covenant hesitated to follow. He had always been uncomfortable around horses, in part because of their strength, in part because of their distance from the ground; and the Courser was larger and more dangerous than any horse. But he had no choice. When Memla snapped at him irritably, he took his courage in both hands, and heaved himself up behind her.

Din pitched to its feet. Covenant grabbed at the hair urgently to keep himself from falling. A spasm of vertigo made everything reel as Memla turned Din to face the sunrise.

The sun broke the horizon in brown heat. Almost at once, haze began to ripple the distance, distorting all the terrain. His memories of the aid the Waynhim had given him conflicted with his vertigo and with his surprise at Memla's immunity.

Answering his unspoken question, she said, 'Din is a creature of the Sunbane. His body wards us as stone does.' Then she swung her beast in the direction of Revelstone.

Din's canter was unexpectedly smooth; and its hair gave Covenant a secure hold. He began to recover his poise. The ground still seemed fatally far away; but it no longer appeared to bristle with falling. Ahead of him, Memla sat crosslegged near the Courser's shoulders, trusting her hands to catch her whenever she was jostled off balance. After a while, he followed her example. Keeping both fists constantly clutched in Din's coat, he made himself as secure as he could.

Memla had not offered Vain a seat. She had apparently decided to treat him exactly as he treated her. But Vain did not need to be carried by any beast. He loped behind Din effortlessly and gave no sign that he was in any way aware of what he was doing.

Covenant rode through the morning in silence, clinging to the Courser's back and sipping *vitrim* whenever the heat made him dizzy. But when Memla resumed their journey after a brief rest at noon, he felt a desire to make her talk. He wanted information; the wilderness of his ignorance threatened him. Stiffly, he asked her to explain the Rede of the Clave.

'The Rede!' she ejaculated over her shoulder. 'Halfhand, the time before us is reckoned in days, not turnings of the moon.'

'Summarize,' he retorted. 'If you don't want me dead, then you want my help. I need to know what I'm dealing with.'

She was silent.

Deliberately, he rasped, 'In other words, you *have* been lying to me.'

Memla leaned abruptly forward, hawked and spat past Din's shoulder. But when she spoke, her tone was subdued, almost chastened. 'The Rede is of great length and complexity, comprising all the accumulated knowledge of the Clave in reference to life in the Land, and to survival under the Sunbane. It is the task of the Riders to share this knowledge throughout the Land, so that Stonedown and Woodhelven may endure.'

Right, Covenant muttered. And to kidnap people for their blood.

'But little of this knowledge would have worth to you,' she went on. 'You have sojourned scatheless under the Sunbane. What skills it to tell you of the Rede?

'Yet you desire comprehension. Halfhand, there is only one matter which the bearer of the white ring need understand. It is the triangle.' She took the *rukh* from her robe, showed it to him over her shoulder. 'The Three Corners of Truth. The foundation of all our service.'

To the rhythm of Din's strides, she began to sing:

> 'Three the days of Sunbane's bale:
> Three the Rede and sooth:
> Three the words na-Mhoram spake:
> Three the Corners of Truth.'

When she paused, he said, 'What do you mean – "three the days"? Isn't the Sunbane accelerating? Didn't each sun formerly last for four or five days, or even more?'

'Yes,' she replied impatiently, 'beyond doubt. But the soothreaders have ever foretold that the Clave would hold at three – that the generations-long increase of our power and the constant mounting of the Sunbane would meet and match at three days, producing balance. Thus we hope now that in some way we may contrive to tilt the balance to our side, sending the Sunbane towards decline. Therefore the na-Mhoram desires your aid.

'But I was speaking of the Three Corners of Truth,' she continued with asperity before Covenant could interrupt again. 'This knowledge at least you do require. On these three facts the Clave stands, and every village lives.

'First, there is no power in Land or life comparable to the Sunbane. In might and efficacy, the Sunbane surpasses all other puissance utterly.

'Second, there is no mortal who can endure the Sunbane. Without great knowledge and cunning, none can hope to endure from one sun to the next. And without opposition to the Sunbane, all life is doomed. Swift or slow, the Sunbane will wreak entire ruin.

'Third, there is no power sufficient to oppose the Land's doom, except power which is drawn from the Sunbane itself. Its might must be reflected against it. No other hope exists. Therefore does the Clave shed the blood of the Land, for blood is the key to the Sunbane. If we do not unlock that power, there will be no end to our perishing.

'Hear you, Halfhand?' Memla demanded. 'I doubt not that in your sojourn you have met much reviling of the Clave. Despite all our labour, Stonedown and Woodhelven must believe that we exact their blood for pleasure or self.' To Covenant's ears, her acidity was the gall of a woman who instinctively abhorred her conscious convictions. 'Be not misled! The cost is sore to us. But we do not flinch from it because it is our sole means to preserve the Land. If you must cast blame, cast it upon a-Jeroth, who incurred the just wrath of the Master – and upon the ancient betrayers, Berek and his ilk, who leagued with a-Jeroth.'

Covenant wanted to protest. As soon as she mentioned Berek as a betrayer, her speech lost its persuasiveness. He had never known Berek Halfhand; the Lord-Fatherer was already a legend when Covenant had entered the Land. But his knowledge of the effects of Berek's life was nearly two score centuries more recent than Memla's. Any set of beliefs which counted Berek a betrayer was founded on a lie; and so any conclusions drawn from that foundation were false. But he kept his protest silent because he could conceive of no way to demonstrate its accuracy. No way short of victory over the Sunbane.

To spare himself a pointless argument, he said, 'I'll reserve judgement on that for a while. In the meantime, satisfy my curiosity. I've got at least a dim notion of who a-Jeroth is. But what are the seven Hells?'

Memla was muttering sourly to herself. He suspected that she resented his distrust precisely because it was echoed by a distrust within herself. But she answered brusquely, 'They are rain, desert, pestilence, fertility, war, savagery, and darkness. But I believe that there is also an eighth. Blind hostility.'

After that, she rebuffed his efforts to engage her in any more talk.

When they halted for the night, he discarded his empty pouch and accepted food from her. And the next morning, he did what he could to help her prepare for the day's journey.

Sitting on Din, she faced the sunrise. It crested the horizon like a cynosure in green; and she shook her head. 'A fertile sun,' she murmured. 'A desert sun wreaks much ruin, and a sun of rain may be a thing of great difficulty. A sun of pestilence carries peril and abhorrence. But for those who must journey, no other sun is as arduous as the sun of fertility. Speak not to me under this sun, I adjure you. If my thoughts wander, our path will also wander.'

By the time they had covered half a league, new grass blanketed the ground. Young vines crawled visibly from place to place: bushes unfolded buds the colour of mint.

Memla raised her *rukh*. Uncapping the hollow sceptre, she decanted enough blood to smear her hands. Then she started chanting under her breath. A vermilion flame, pale and small in the sunlight, burned within the open triangle.

Under Din's hooves, the grass parted along a straight line stretching like a plumb towards Revelstone. Covenant watched the parting disappear into the distance. The line bared no ground; but everything nearby – grass, shrubs, incipient saplings – bent away from it as if an invisible serpent were sliding north-westward through the burgeoning vegetation.

Along the parting, Din cantered as if it were incapable of surprise.

Memla's chant became a low mumble. She rested the end of her *rukh* on Din's shoulders; but the triangle and the flame remained erect before her. At every change in the terrain, the verdure thickened, compressing whole seasons into fractions of the day. Yet her line remained open. Trees shunned it; copses parted as if they had been riven by an axe; bushes edging the line had no branches or leaves on that side.

When Covenant looked behind him, he saw no trace of the path; it closed the moment Memla's power passed. As a result, Vain had to fend for himself. But he did so with characteristic disinterest, slashing through grass and brush at a run, crashing thickets, tearing across briar patches which left no mark on his black skin. He could not have seemed less conscious of difficulty. Watching the Demon-dim-spawn, Covenant did not know which amazed him more: Memla's ability to create this path; or Vain's ability to travel at such speed without any path.

That night, Memla explained her line somewhat. Her *rukh*, she said, drew on the great Banefire in Revelstone, where the Clave did its work against the Sunbane, and the Readers tended the *master-rukh*. Only the power for the link to the *master-rukh* came from her; the rest she siphoned from the Banefire. So the making of her path demanded stern concentration, but did not exhaust her. And the nearer she drew to Revelstone, the easier her access to the Banefire became. Thus she was able to form her line again the next day, defying the resistance of huge trees, heather and bracken as high as Din's shoulders, grass like thickets and thickets like forests.

Yet Vain was able to match the Courser's pace. He met the sharper test of each new league as if no size or density of vegetation could ever estimate his limits. And the third day made no change. It intensified still more the extravagance of the verdure, but did not hamper the nonchalant ease with which he followed Din. Time and again, Covenant found himself craning his neck, watching Vain's progress and wondering at the sheer unconscious force it represented.

But as the afternoon passed, his thoughts turned from Vain, and he began to look ahead. The mammoth jungle concealed any landmarks the terrain might have offered, but he knew that Revelstone was near. All his anxiety, dread, and anticipation returned to him; and he fought to see through the thronging foliage as if only an early glimpse of the ancient Keep would forewarn him of the needs and hazards hidden there.

But he received no forewarning. Late in the afternoon, Memla's path started up a steep hillside. The vegetation suddenly ended on the rock of the foothills. Revelstone appeared before Covenant as if in that instant it had been unfurled from the storehouse of his most vivid memories.

The Courser had arrived athwart the great stone city, Giant-wrought millennia ago from the gut-rock of the plateau. Out of the furthest west, mountains came striding eastward, then, two leagues away on Covenant's left, dropped sheer to the upland plateau, still a thousand feet and more above the foothills. The plateau narrowed to form a wedged promontory half a league in length; and into this promontory the ancient Giants had delved the immense and intricate habitation of Revelstone.

The whole cliff face before Covenant was coigned and fortified, lined with abutments and balconies, punctuated by oriels, architraves, embrasures, from a level fifty or a hundred feet above the foothills to the rim of the plateau. On his left, Revelstone gradually faded into native rock; but on his right, it filled the promontory to the wedge-tip, where the watchtower guarded the massive gates of the Keep.

The tremendous and familiar size of the city made his heart ache with pride for the Giants he had loved – and with sharp grief, for those Giants had died in a body, slain by a Raver during the war against Lord Foul's Illearth Stone. He had once heard that there was a pattern graven into the walls of Revelstone, an organization of meaning too huge for un-Giantish minds to grasp; and now he would never have it explained to him.

But that was not all his grief. The sight of Revelstone recalled other people, friends and antagonists, whom he had hurt and lost: Trell Atiaran-mate; Hile Troy, who had sold his soul to a Forestal so that his army might survive; Saltheart Foamfollower; Elena. High Lord Mhoram. Then Covenant's sorrow turned to anger as he considered that Mhoram's name was being used by a Clave which willingly shed innocent blood.

His wrath tightened as he studied Revelstone itself. Memla's line ran to a point in the middle of the city; and from the plateau above that point sprang a prodigious vermeil beam, aimed towards the heart of the declining sun. It was like the Sunbane shaft of Sunder's *orcrest*; but its sheer size was staggering. Covenant gaped at it, unable to conceive the number of lives necessary to summon so much power. Revelstone had become a citadel of blood. He felt poignantly that it would never be clean again.

But then his gaze caught something in the west, a glitter of hope. There, halfway between Revelstone and the Westron Mountains, lay Furl Falls, where the overflow of Glimmermere came down the cliff to form the White River. And the Falls held water; tumbling spray caught the approaching sunset, and shone. The Land had been eighteen days without a sun of rain, and six of them had been desert; yet the springs of Glimmermere had not failed.

Gripping anger and hope between his teeth, Covenant set himself to face whatever lay ahead.

Memla gave a sigh of accomplishment, and lowered her *rukh*. Turning Din's head with a muttered command, she sent the beast trotting towards the gates under the south-east face of the tower.

The watchtower was barely half the height of the plateau, and its upper reaches stood independent of the main Keep, joined only by wooden crosswalks. Covenant remembered that a courtyard lay open to the sky within the granite walls which sealed the base of the tower to the Keep; and the megalithic stone gates under the watchtower were repeated beyond the courtyard, so that Revelstone possessed a double defence for its only entrance. But as he approached the tower, he was shocked to see that the outer gates lay in rubble. Sometime in the distant past, Revelstone had needed its inner defence.

The abutments over the ruined gates were deserted, as were the fortifications and embrasures above it; the whole tower seemed empty. Perhaps it was no longer defensible. Perhaps the Clave saw no need to fear the entry of strangers. Or perhaps this air of desertion was a trap to catch the unwary.

Memla headed directly into the tunnel, which led to the court-yard; but Covenant slipped off Din's back, lowering himself by handholds of hair. She stopped, looked back at him in surprise. 'Here is Revelstone,' she said. 'Do you not wish to enter?'

'First things first.' His shoulders were tight with apprehension. 'Send the na-Mhoram out here. I want him to tell me in person that I'll be safe.'

'He is the na-Mhoram!' she snapped indignantly. 'He does not come or go according to the whims of others.'

'Good for him.' He controlled his tension with sarcasm. 'The next time I have a whim, I'll keep that in mind.' She opened her mouth to retort. He cut her off. 'I've already been taken prisoner twice. It's not going to happen to me again. I'm not going in there until I talk to the na-Mhoram.' On the spur of a sudden intuition, he added, 'Tell him I understand the necessity of freedom as well as he does. He can't get what he wants by coercion. He's just going to have to co-operate.'

Memla glared at him for a moment, then muttered, 'As you wish.' With a gruff command, she sent Din into the tunnel, leaving Covenant alone with Vain.

Covenant took hold of his anxiety, and waited. Across the peaks, the sun was setting in green and lavender; the shadow of Revelstone spread out over the monstrous verdure like an aegis of darkness.

Watching the tower for signs of hostile intent, he observed that no pennons flew from its crown, none were needed: the hot red shaft of Sunbane-force marked Revelstone as the home of the Clave more surely than any oriflamme.

Unable to possess himself in patience, he growled to Vain, 'I'm damned if I know what you want here. But I've got too many other problems. You'll have to take care of yourself.'

Vain did not respond. He seemed incapable of hearing.

Then Covenant saw movement in the tunnel. A short man wearing a stark black robe and a red chasuble came out past the ruined gates. He carried an iron crozier as tall as himself, with an open triangle at one end. He did not use the hood of his robe; his round face, bald head, and beardless cheeks were exposed. His visage was irenic, formed in a mould of habitual beatitude or boredom, as if he knew from experience that nothing in life could ruffle his composure. Only his eyes contradicted the hebetude of his mien. They were a piercing red.

'Halfhand,' he said dully. 'Be welcome in Revelstone. I am Gibbon na-Mhoram.'

The simple blandness of the man's manner made Covenant uncomfortable. 'Memla tells me I'm safe here,' he said. 'How am I supposed to believe that, when you've been trying to kill me ever since I first set foot in the Land?'

'You represent great peril to us, Halfhand.' Gibbon spoke as if he were half asleep. 'But I have come to believe that you also represent great promise. In the name of that promise, I accept the risk of the peril. The Land has need of every power. I have come to you alone so that you may see the truth of what I say. You are as safe among us as your own purposes permit.'

Covenant wanted to challenge that assertion; but he was not ready to hazard a test. He changed his tack. 'Where's Santonin?'

Gibbon did not blink. 'Memla na-Mhoram-in spoke to me of your belief that your companions have fallen into the hands of a Rider. I know nothing of this. Santonin has been long from Revelstone. We feel concern for him. His *rukh* is silent. Perhaps – if what you say of him is true – your companions have mastered him, and taken his *rukh*. I have already commanded the Riders who were sent to meet you to begin a search. If your companions are found, I assure you that we shall value their safety.'

Covenant had no answer. He scowled at the na-Mhoram, and remained silent.

The man showed no uncertainty or confusion. He nodded towards Vain, and said, 'Now I must ask you concerning your companion. His power is evident, but we do not comprehend him.'

'You see him,' Covenant muttered. 'You know as much about him as I do.'

Gibbon permitted his gaze to widen. But he did not mention his incredulity. Instead, he said, 'My knowledge of him is nothing. Therefore I will not permit him to enter Revelstone.'

Covenant shrugged. 'Suit yourself. If you can keep him out, you're welcome.'

'That will be seen.' The na-Mhoram gestured towards the tunnel. 'Will you accompany me?'

For one more moment, Covenant hesitated. Then he said, 'I don't think I have much choice.'

Gibbon nodded ambiguously, acknowledging either Covenant's decision or his lack of options, and turned towards the tower.

Walking behind the na-Mhoram, Covenant entered the tunnel as if it were a gullet into peril. His shoulders hunched involuntarily against his fear that people might leap on him from the openings in the ceiling. But nothing attacked him. Amid the echoing of his footsteps, he passed through to the courtyard.

There he saw that the inner gates were intact. They were open only wide enough to admit the na-Mhoram. Members of the Clave stood guard on the fortifications over the entrance.

Motioning for Covenant to follow him, Gibbon slipped between the huge stone doors.

Hellfire, Covenant rasped, denying his trepidation. With Vain at his back, he moved forward.

The gates were poised like jaws. The instant he passed them, they closed with a hollow granite thud, sealing Vain outside.

There was no light. Revelstone crouched around Covenant, as dark as a prison.

18

REVELSTONE IN RAIN

'Gibbon!' Fear and ire lashed Covenant's voice.

'Ah, your pardon,' the na-Mhoram replied out of the darkness. 'You desire light. A moment.'

Robes rustled around Covenant. He flung his arms wide to ward them off; but they did not assail him. Then he heard a word of command. Red flame burst from the triangle of a *rukh*. Other lights followed. In moments, the high, wide entry hall of Revelstone was garishly incarnadine.

'Your pardon,' Gibbon repeated. 'Revelstone is a place of caution.

The Clave is unjustly despised by many, as your own mistrust demonstrates. Therefore we admit strangers warily.'

Groping to recover his inner balance, Covenant grated, 'Have you ever stopped to consider that maybe there's a reason why people don't like you?'

'Their mislike is natural,' said the na-Mhoram, unperturbed. 'Their lives are fear from dawn to dusk, and they do not behold the fruit of our labour. How should they believe us when we say that without us they would perish? We do not resent this. But we take caution against it.'

Gibbon's explanation sounded dangerously plausible. Yet Covenant distrusted the na-Mhoram's lack of passion. Because he could think of no apt retort, he simply nodded when Gibbon asked, 'Will you come?' At the na-Mhoram's side, he walked down the hall, flanked by members of the Clave carrying fires.

The hall was as large as a cavern: it had been formed by Giants to accommodate Giants. But Gibbon soon turned from it into a side passage, and began to ascend broad stairways towards the upper levels of the city. Revelstone was as complex as a maze because it had been laid out according to criteria known only to the long-dead Giants. However, it was familiar to Covenant; though he had not been here for ten of his years, he found that he knew his way. He took a grim satisfaction from the fact.

Loyal to the Keep he remembered, he followed Gibbon upward and away from the spine of Revelstone. Once the entry hall was well behind them, their way was lit by torches smoking in sconces along the walls. Before long, they entered a corridor marked at long intervals by granite doors with wooden handles. Opposite one of them stood a hooded figure wearing a red robe but no chasuble. When the na-Mhoram approached, the figure opened the door for him. Covenant took a moment to be sure the entrance had no hidden locks or bolts, then went in after Gibbon.

Beyond the door lay a suite of rooms: a central area containing stone chairs and a table; a bedroom to one side and a bathroom to the other; an outer balcony. On the table was a tray of food. Brands lit the suite, covering the air with a patina of smoke. Remembering the untrammelled fires of the Lords, Covenant began to marshal bitter questions for the na-Mhoram.

'You will have comfort here,' Gibbon said. 'But if you are displeased, we will provide any quarters you require. Revelstone is larger than the Clave, and much unused.' Beckoning for the hooded figure beyond the doorway, he continued, 'This is Akkasri na-Mhoram-cro. She will answer your wants. Speak to her of any lack or desire.' The hooded woman bowed without revealing her face or hands, and withdrew. 'Halfhand, are you content?'

Content? Covenant wanted to snarl. Oh, sure! Where the goddamn bloody hell is Linden? But he repressed that impulse. He did not wish to betray how much his companions mattered to him. Instead, he said, 'I'll be fine. As long as nobody tries to stick a knife into me – or lock my door – or poison my food.'

Gibbon's beatitude smothered every emotion. His eyes were as bland as their colour permitted. He regarded Covenant for a moment, then moved to the table. Slowly, he ate a bite from every dish on the tray – dried fruit, bread, stew – and washed them down with a swallow from the flask. Holding Covenant's gaze, he said, 'Halfhand, this mistrust does not become you. I am moved to ask why you are here, when you expect such ill at our hands.'

That question Covenant was prepared to answer honestly. 'Not counting what happened to my friends, I need information. I need to understand this Sunbane. So I need the Clave. The villagers I've met – ' They had been too busy trying to kill him to answer questions. 'They just survive. They don't understand. I want to know what causes the Sunbane. So I can fight it.'

Gibbon's red eyes glinted ambiguously. 'Very well,' he replied in a tone that expressed no interest in what he heard or said. 'As to fighting the Sunbane, I must ask you to wait until the morrow. The Clave rests at night. But the causes of the Sunbane are plain enough. It is the Master's wrath against the Land for the evil of past service to a-Jeroth.'

Covenant growled inwardly. That idea was either a lie or a cruel perversion. But he did not intend to argue metaphysics with Gibbon. 'That isn't what I mean. I need something more practical. How is it done? How did it happen? How does it work?'

Gibbon's gaze did not waver. 'Halfhand, if I possessed such knowledge, I would make use of it myself.'

Terrific. Covenant did not know whether to believe the na-Mhoram. A wave of emotional fatigue rolled over him. He began to see how hard it would be to glean the information he needed; and his courage quailed. He did not know the right questions. He simply nodded when Gibbon said, 'You are weary. Eat, now. Sleep. Perhaps the morrow will bring new insight.'

But as Gibbon moved to the door, Covenant felt compelled to try once more. 'Tell me. How come Glimmermere still has water?'

'We moderate the Sunbane,' the na-Mhoram answered with easy patience. 'Therefore the Earth retains some vitality.' A blink of hesitation touched his eyes, vanished. 'An old legend avers that a nameless periapt lies in the deeps of the lake, sustaining it against the Sunbane.'

Covenant nodded again. He knew of at least one thing, powerful or not, which lay at the bottom of Glimmermere.

Then Gibbon left the room, closing the door behind him, and Covenant was alone.

He remained still for a while, allowing his weakness to flow over him. Then he took a chair out on to the balcony, so that he could sit and think in the privacy of the night.

His balcony stood halfway up the south face of the Keep. A gibbous moon was rising, and he was able to descry the vast dark jumble of trees left by the fertile sun. Sitting with his feet braced against the rail of the balcony to appease his fear of heights, he ran his fingers through his tangled beard, and tried to come to grips with his dilemma.

He did not in fact anticipate a physical attempt upon his life. He had insisted on the necessity of freedom in order to remind the Clave that they would gain nothing by killing him; but the truth was that he accused the Clave of meditating murder primarily as a release for an entirely different dread.

He was afraid for Linden, poignantly afraid that his friends were in far more danger than he was. And this fear was aggravated by his helplessness. Where were they? Were Gibbon and Memla lying about Santonin? If so, how could he learn the truth? If not, what could he do? He felt crippled without Linden; he needed her perceptions. She would have been able to tell him whether or not Gibbon was honest.

Cursing the numbness of his leprosy, he asked the night why *he* of all people in the Land – Thomas Covenant, Unbeliever and white gold wielder, who had once mastered the Despiser in mortal combat – why he should feel so helpless. And the answer was that his self-knowledge, his fundamental confidence in what he was, was torn by doubt. His resources had become a contradiction. All the conscious extremity of his will was unable to call up one jot or tittle of power from his ring; yet when he was delirious, he exerted a feral might utterly beyond conscious control. Therefore he distrusted himself, and did not know what to do.

But to the question the night turned a deaf ear. Finally he abandoned the interrogation, and set about preparing for sleep.

In the bathroom, he stripped off his clothes, scrubbed both them and himself thoroughly, then draped them over chairbacks to dry. He felt vulnerable in his nakedness; but he accepted that risk by eating the food he had been given, drinking to the bottom the flask of *metheglin*. The mead added a physical drowsiness to his moral fatigue. When he investigated the bed, he found it comfortable and clean-smelling. Expecting nightmares, surprises, anguish, he crouched under the blankets, and slept.

He awoke to the sound of rain – torrents beating like the rush of a river against Revelstone's granite. The air of the bedroom felt moist; he had not closed off the balcony before going to bed. But for a time he did not move; he lay in the streaming susurration and let the sound carry him towards alertness.

When at last he rolled over on to his back and opened his eyes, he found Vain standing near the bed.

The Demondim-spawn bore himself as always — arms hanging slightly bent, stance relaxed, eyes focused on nothing.

'What the hell — ?' Covenant jerked out of bed and hurried into the next room. Rain came slashing from the balcony, drenching the floor. He braved the deluge, went outside to look for some indication of how Vain had reached him.

Through the downpour, he saw a huge tree bough leaning against the end of the balcony. The butt of the limb rested on another balcony thirty or forty feet below; apparently, Vain had climbed several hundred feet up the wall of Revelstone by scaling this bough to the lower abutments, then pulling it up behind him and using it to reach the next parapets, ascending by stages until he gained Covenant's room. How Vain had known the right room Covenant had no idea.

Scattering water, he rushed back into his suite and swung shut the balcony-door. Naked and dripping, he gaped at the Demondim-spawn, amazed by Vain's inexplicable capabilities. Then a grim grin twisted his mouth. 'Good for you,' he rasped. 'This will make them nervous.' Nervous people made mistakes.

Vain gazed vacuously past him like a deaf-mute. Covenant nodded sharply at his thoughts and started towards the bathroom to get a towel. But he was pulled to a halt by the sight of the livid raw patch running from the left side of Vain's head down his shoulder. He had been injured; his damaged skin oozed a black fluid as if he had been severely burned.

How — ? Over the past days, Covenant had become so convinced of Vain's invulnerability that now he could not think. The Demondim-spawn could be hurt? Surely — But the next instant his astonishment disappeared in a flaring of comprehension. Vain had been attacked by the Clave-Riders testing the mysterious figure outside their gates. They had burned him. Perhaps he had not even deigned to defend himself.

But his mien betrayed no knowledge of pain. After a moment, Covenant went cursing into the bathroom and began to towel himself dry. Bastards! I'll bet he didn't lift a finger. Swiftly, he donned his clothes, though they were still somewhat damp. Striding to the door of his suite, he pushed it open.

Akkasri na-Mhoram-cro stood in the passage with a fresh tray of food at her feet. Covenant beckoned roughly to her. She picked up the tray and carried it into his suite.

He stopped her inside the doorway, took the new tray and handed her the old one, then dismissed her. He wanted her to have a chance to report Vain's presence to the na-Mhoram. It was a small revenge, but he took it. Her hood concealed her face, so that he could not see her reaction. But she left with alacrity.

Muttering darkly, he sat down to breakfast.

Shortly after he finished, there was a knock at his door. He thrust the slab of stone open, and was disappointed to find Akkasri alone outside.

'Halfhand,' she said in a muffled tone, 'you have asked for knowledge concerning the Clave's resistance of the Sunbane. The na-Mhoram commands me to serve you. I will guide you to the place where our work is wrought and explain it as best I may.'

This was not what Covenant had expected. 'Where's Gibbon?'

'The na-Mhoram,' replied Akkasri, stressing Gibbon's title, 'has many duties. Though I am only na-Mhoram-cro, I can answer certain enquiries. Gibbon na-Mhoram will attend you, if I do not suffice to your need.'

Oh, hell, he growled. But he concealed his disconcertion. 'We'll see. I've got a lot of questions.' He stepped out into the hallway, held the door open for Vain. 'Let's go.'

At once, Akkasri moved off down the passage, ignoring Vain completely. This struck Covenant as unnatural; the Demondim-spawn was not easily discounted. Perhaps she had been told what to do? Then his revenge had not been wasted.

His nerves tightened. Striding at Akkasri's side, he began his search for comprehension by asking bluntly, 'What's a na-Mhoram-cro?'

'Halfhand,' the woman said without giving him a glimpse of her face, 'the na-Mhoram-cro are the novices of the Clave. We have been taught much, but have not yet mastered the *rukh* sufficiently to become Riders. When we have gained that skill, we will be na-Mhoram-wist. And with much experience and wisdom, some of us will advance to become the hands of the na-Mhoram himself, the na-Mhoram-in. Such is Memla, who bore you to Revelstone. She is greatly honoured for her courage and sagacity.'

'If you're a novice,' he demanded, 'how much can you explain?'

'Only Gibbon na-Mhoram holds all the knowledge of the Clave.' Akkasri's tone was tinged with indignation. 'But I am unskilled, not ignorant.'

'All right.' With Vain behind them, she led Covenant downward, tending generally towards the central depths of the Keep. 'Tell me this. Where did the Clave come from?'

'Halfhand?'

'It hasn't been here for ever. Other people used to live in Revelstone. What happened to them? How did the Clave get started? Who started it?'

'Ah.' She nodded. 'That is a matter of legend. It is said that many and many generations ago, when the Sunbane first appeared in the sky, the Land was governed by a Council. This Council was decadent, and made no effort to meet the peril. Therefore precious time was lost before the coming of the Mhoram.'

Covenant began to recognize where she was taking him; this was the way to the sacred enclosure. He was faintly surprised by the general emptiness of the halls and passages. But he reflected that Revelstone was huge. Several thousand people could live in it without crowding each other.

'It is his vision which guides us now,' the na-Mhoram-cro was saying. 'Seeing that the Council had fallen to the guile of a-Jeroth, he arose with those few who retained leal and foresight, and drove out the treachers. Then began the long struggle of our lives to preserve the Land. From the Mhoram and his few has the Clave descended, generation after generation, na-Mhoram to na-Mhoram, seeking ever to consummate his opposition to the Sunbane.

'It is a slow work. We have been slow to master the skill and gain the numbers which we need – and slow as well to muster blood.' She said the word *blood* with perfect impersonality, as if it cost nothing. 'But now we approach the fruition of our long dream. The Sunbane has reached a rhythm of three days – and we hold. We hold, Halfhand!' She claimed pride; but she spoke blandly, as if pride, too, were impersonal. As if she had been carefully groomed to answer Covenant's questions.

But he held his suspicion in abeyance. They walked one of the main hallways along the spine of the Keep; and ahead he could see the passage branching to circle left and right around the outer wall of the sacred enclosure, where the long-dead Lords had held their Vespers of self-consecration to the Land and to Peace.

As he drew closer, he observed that all the many doors, which were regularly spaced around the wall and large enough for Giants, were kept shut. The brief opening as a Rider came out of the enclosure revealed a glimpse of lurid red heat and muffled roaring inside.

The na-Mhoram-cro stopped before one of the doors, addressing Covenant. 'Speech is difficult within this space.' He wanted to behold her face; she sounded as if she had evasive eyes. But her hood concealed her visage. If he had not seen Memla and Gibbon, he might have suspected that all the Clave were hiding some kind of deformity. 'It is the hall of the Banefire and the *master-rukh*. When you have seen it, we will withdraw, and I will tell you concerning it.'

He nodded in spite of a sudden reluctance to see what the Clave had done to the sacred enclosure. When Akkasri opened the nearest door, he followed her into a flood of heat and noise.

The place blazed with garish fire. The enclosure was an immense cavity in the gut-rock of Revelstone, a cylinder on end, rising from below the level of the foothills more than halfway up the height of the Keep. From a dais on the floor, the Lords had spoken to the city. And in the walls were seven balconies circling the space, one directly above the next. There the people of Revelstone had stood to hear the Lords.

No more. Akkasri had brought Covenant to the fourth balcony; but even here, at least two hundred feet above the floor, he was painfully close to the fire.

It roared upwards from a hollow where the dais had been, sprang yowling and raging almost as high as the place where he stood. Red flame clawed the air as if the very roots of the Keep were afire. The blast of heat half-blinded him; the fire seemed to scorch his cheeks, crisp his hair. He had to blink away a blur of·tears before he could make out any details.

The first thing he saw was the *master-rukh*. It rested at three points on the rail of this balcony, a prodigious iron triangle. The centre of each arm glowed dull vermeil.

Two members of the Clave stood at each corner of the *master-rukh*. They seemed impervious to the·heat. Their hands gripped the iron, concentrated on it as if the Banefire were a script which they could read by touch. Their faces shone ruddy and fanatical above the flames.

Clearly, this was the place from which the red shaft of Sunbane power leaped to the sun.

The doors at the base of the cavity and around the highest balcony were open, providing ventilation. In the lurid brilliance, Covenant saw the domed ceiling for the first time. Somehow, the Giants had contrived to carve it ornately. Bold figures strode the stone, depicting scenes from the early history of the Giants in the Land: welcome, gratitude, trust. But the fire made the images appear strangely distorted and malefic.

Grinding his teeth, he cast his gaze downward. A movement at the base of the fire caught his attention. He saw now that several troughs had been cut into the floor, feeding the hollow. A figure apparelled like the na-Mhoram-cro approached one of the troughs, carrying two heavy pails which were emptied into the trough. Dark fluid ran like the ichor of Revelstone into the hollow. Almost at once, the Banefire took on a richer texture, deepening towards the ruby hue of blood.

Covenant was suffocating on heat and inchoate passion. His heart struggled in his chest. Brushing past Akkasri and Vain, he hastened towards the nearest corner of the *master-rukh*.

The people there did not notice him; the deep roar of the flame covered the sound of his boots, and their concentration was intent.

He jerked one of them by the shoulder, pulled the individual away from the iron. The person was taller than he – a figure of power and indignation.

Covenant yelled up at the hooded face, 'Where's Santonin?'

A man's voice answered, barely audible through the howl of the Banefire. 'I am a Reader, not a soothreader!'

Covenant gripped the man's robe. 'What happened to him?'

'He has lost his *rukh*!' the Reader shouted back. 'At the command of the na-Mhoram, we have searched for him diligently! If his *rukh* were destroyed – if he were slain with his *rukh* still in his hands – we would know of it. Every *rukh* answers to the *master-rukh*, unless it falls into ignorant hands. He would not choose to release his *rukh*. Therefore he has been overcome and bereft. Perhaps then he was slain. We cannot know!'

'Halfhand!' Akkasri clutched at Covenant's arm, urging him towards the door.

He let her draw him out of the sacred enclosure. He was dizzy with heat and blind wild hope. Maybe the Reader spoke the truth; maybe his friends had overpowered their captor; maybe they were safe! While the na-Mhoram-cro closed the door, he leaned against the outer wall and panted at the blessedly cool air.

Vain stood near him, as blank and attentive as ever.

Studying Covenant, Akkasri asked, 'Shall we return to your chamber? Do you wish to rest?'

He shook his head. He did not want to expose that much of his hope. With an effort, he righted his reeling thoughts. 'I'm fine.' His pulse contradicted him; but he trusted she could not perceive such things. 'Just explain it. I've seen the *master-rukh*. Now tell me how it works. How you fight the Sunbane.'

'By drawing its power from it,' she answered simply. 'If more water is taken from a lake than its springs provide, the lake will be emptied. Thus we resist the Sunbane.

'When the Mhoram first created the Banefire, it was a small thing, and accomplished little. But the Clave has increased it generation after generation, striving for the day when sufficient power would be consumed to halt the advance of the Sunbane.'

Covenant fumbled mentally, then asked, 'What do you do with all this power? It's got to go somewhere.'

'Indeed. We have much use for power, to strengthen the Clave and continue our work. As you have learned, much is drawn by the Riders, so that they may ride and labour in ways no lone man or woman could achieve without a ruinous expenditure of blood. With other power are the Coursers wrought, so that the Sunbane will have no mastery over them. And more is consumed by the living of Revelstone. Crops are grown on the upland plateau – kine and goats nourished – looms and forges driven. In early generations, the Clave was hampered by need and paucity. But now we flourish, Halfhand. Unless some grave disaster falls upon us,' Akkasri said in a pointed tone, 'we will not fail.'

'And you do it all by killing people,' he rasped. 'Where do you get that much blood.'

She turned her head away in distaste for his question. 'Doubtless you possess that knowledge,' she said stiffly. 'If you desire further enlightenment, consult the na-Mhoram.'

'I will,' he promised. The state of the sacred enclosure reminded him that the Clave saw as evil a whole host of things which he knew to be good; and actions which they called good made his guts heave. 'In the meantime, tell me what the na-Mhoram' — to irritate her, he used the title sardonically — 'has in mind for me. He wants my help. What does he want me to do?'

This was obviously a question for which she had come prepared. Without hesitation, she said, 'He desires to make of you a Reader.'

A Reader, he muttered to himself. Terrific.

'For several reasons,' she went on evenly. 'The distinction between Reading and soothreading is narrow, but severe. Perhaps with your white ring the gap may be bridged, giving the Clave knowledge to guide its future. Also with your power, perhaps still more of the Sunbane may be consumed. Perhaps you may exert a mastery over the region around Revelstone, freeing it from the Sunbane. This is our hope. As you wielded more power, the Sunbane would grow weaker, permitting the expansion of your mastery, spreading safety further out into the Land. Thus the work of generations might be compressed into one lifetime.

'It is a brave vision, Halfhand, worthy of any man or woman. A great saving of life and Land. For that reason Gibbon na-Mhoram rescinded the command of your death.'

But he was not persuaded. He only listened to her with half his mind. While she spoke, he became aware of an alteration in Vain. The Demondim-spawn no longer stood completely still. His head shifted from side to side, as if he heard a distant sound and sought to locate its source. His black orbs were focused. When Akkasri said, 'Will you answer, Halfhand?' Covenant ignored her. He felt suddenly sure that Vain was about to do something. An obscure excitement pulled him away from the wall, poised him for whatever might happen.

Abruptly, Vain started away along the curving hall.

'Your companion!' the na-Mhoram-cro barked in surprise and agitation. 'Where does he go?'

'Let's find out.' At once, Covenant strode after Vain.

The Demondim-spawn moved like a man with an impeccable knowledge of Revelstone. Paying no heed to Covenant and Akkasri, or to the people he passed, he traversed corridors and stairways, disused meeting halls and refectories; and at every opportunity he descended, working his way towards the roots of the Keep.

Akkasri's agitation increased at every descent. But, like Vain, Covenant had no attention to spare for her. Searching his memory, he tried to guess Vain's goal. He could not. Before long, Vain led him into passages he had never seen before. Torches became infrequent. At times, he could barely distinguish the black Demondim-spawn from the dimness.

Then, without warning, Vain arrived in a cul-de-sac lit only by light reflecting from some distance behind him. As Covenant and Akkasri caught up with him, he was staring at the end of the corridor as if the thing he desired were hidden beyond it.

'What is it?' Covenant did not expect Vain to reply; he spoke only to relieve his own tension. 'What are you after?'

'Halfhand,' snapped the na-Mhoram-cro, 'he is your companion.' She seemed afraid, unprepared for Vain's action. 'You must control him. He must stop here.'

'Why?' Covenant drawled, trying to vex her into a lapse of caution, a revelation. 'What's so special about this place?'

Her voice jumped. 'It is forbidden!'

Vain faced the blind stone as if he were thinking. Then he stepped forward and touched the wall. For a long moment, his hands probed the surface.

His movements struck a chord in Covenant's memory. There was something familiar about what Vain was doing.

Familiar?

The next instant, Vain reached up to a spot on the wall above his head. Immediately, lines of red tracery appeared in the stone. They spread as if he had ignited an intaglio: in moments, red limned a wide doorway.

The door swung open, revealing a torch-lit passage.

Yes! Covenant shouted to himself. When he and Foamfollower had tried to enter Foul's Creche, the Giant had found and opened a similar door just as Vain had found and opened this one.

But what was that kind of door doing in Revelstone? Neither the Giants nor the Lords had ever used such entrances.

In a sudden rush of trepidation, he saw Akkasri's movement a moment too late to stop her. Swift with urgency, she snatched a *rukh* from under her robe and decanted blood on to her hands. Now fire sprang from the triangle; she began shouting words he could not understand.

Vain had already disappeared into the passage. Before the door could close itself again, Covenant sprinted after the Demondim-spawn.

This hall doubled back parallel to the one he had just left. It was well-lit. He could see that this place had not been part of the original Giant-work. Walls, floor, ceiling, all were too roughly formed. The Giants had never delved stone so carelessly. Leaping intuitively ahead of himself, he guessed that this tunnel had not been cut until after the passing of the Council. It had been made by the Clave for their own secret purposes.

Beyond him, a side corridor branched off to the left. Vain took this turning. Covenant followed rapidly.

In ten strides, the Demondim-spawn reached a massive iron door. It had been sealed with heavy bolts sunk deep into the stone, as if the Clave intended it to remain shut for ever.

A faint pearly light marked the cracks around the metal.

Vain did not hesitate. He went to the door, found a place to wedge his fingers into the cracks. His back and shoulders tensed. Pressure squeezed new fluid from his burns.

Covenant heard running behind him, but did not turn away. His amazement tied him to Vain.

With a prodigious burst of strength, Vain tore the door from its moorings. Ringing like an anvil, it fell to the floor. In a wash of nacreous illumination, he stepped past the threshold.

Covenant followed like a man in a trance.

They entered a large chamber crammed with tables, walled to the ceiling with shelves. Hundreds of scrolls, caskets, pouches, periapts filled the shelves. The tables were piled high with staffs, swords, scores of talismans. The light came from three of the richest caskets, set high on the back wall, and from several objects on the tables. Dumb with astonishment, Covenant recognized the small chest which had once held the *krill* of Loric Vilesilencer. The chest was open and empty.

He gaped about him, unable to think, realize, understand.

A moment later, Akkasri and two people dressed like Riders raced into the chamber and leaped to a halt. They brandished flaming *rukhs*. 'Touch nothing!' one of them barked.

Vain ignored them as if he had already forgotten they had the power to harm him. He moved to one of the far tables. There he found what he sought: two wide bands of dull grey iron.

Covenant identified them more by instinct than any distinctive feature.

The heels of the Staff of Law.

The Staff of Law, greatest tool of the Council of Lords, formed by Berek Halfhand from a branch of the One Tree. It was destroyed by wild magic when Lord Foul had forced dead Elena to wield it against the Land. Bannor had borne the heels back to Revelstone after the Despiser's defeat.

Before anyone could react, Vain donned the bands.

291

One he slipped over his right hand. It should have been too small; but it went past his knuckles without effort, and fitted snugly to his wrist.

The other he pulled on to his left foot. The iron seemed elastic. He drew it over his arch and heel easily, settled it tight about his ankle.

A Rider gasped. Akkasri and another woman faced Covenant. 'Halfhand,' Akkasri's companion snapped, 'this is upon your head. The Aumbrie of the Clave is forbidden to all. We will not tolerate such violation.'

Her tone brought Covenant back to himself. Dangers bristled in the air. Thinking rapidly, he said, 'All the lore of the Lords — everything that used to belong to the Council. It's all here. It's all intact.'

'Much is intact,' Akkasri said rigidly. 'The Council was decadent. Some was lost.'

Covenant hardly heard her. 'The First and Second Wards.' He gestured towards the shining caskets. 'The Third Ward? Did they find the Third Ward?' Foreseeing the Ritual of Desecration, Kevin Landwaster had hidden all his knowledge in Seven Wards to preserve it for future Councils; but during High Lord Mhoram's time, only the first two and the last had been found.

'Evidently,' a Rider retorted. 'Little good it did them.'

'Then why' — Covenant put all his appalled amazement into his voice — 'don't you *use* it?'

'It is lore for that which no longer exists.' The reply had the force of an indictment. 'It has no value under the Sunbane.'

Oh, hell. Covenant could find no other words for his dismay. Hell and blood.

'Come!' The Rider's command cut like a lash. But it was not directed at Covenant. She and her companions had turned towards Vain. Their *rukhs* burned redly, summoning power.

Vain obeyed, moving as if he had remembered the source of his injury. Akkasri grabbed his arm, tried to pull the band from his wrist; but the metal was iron and inflexible.

Gesturing with their *rukhs*, she and the Riders escorted Vain from the Aumbrie as if Covenant were not present.

He followed them. To his surprise, they herded Vain away from the hidden doorway.

They went some distance down the rough corridor. Then the passage turned sharply, and debouched into a huge hall lit by many torches. The air was grey with smoke.

With a stab of shock, Covenant realized that the hall was a dungeon.

Scores of bolted iron doors seriated both walls. In each, heavy bars guarded a small window. Half a thousand people could have been imprisoned here, and no one who lacked Vain's instincts or knowledge could ever have found them.

As Covenant stared about him, the implications of the Riders' anger burned into clarity in his mind. Gibbon had not intended him to know of this place.

How many other secrets were there in Revelstone?

One of the Riders hurried to a door and shot back the bolts. Within lay a cell barely wide enough to contain a straw pallet.

With their *rukhs*, Akkasri and the other Rider forced Vain towards the door.

He turned under the architrave. His captors flourished threats of fire; but he made no move against them. He aimed one look at Covenant. His black face wore an expression of appeal.

Covenant glared back, uncomprehending. Vain?

A gift beyond price, Foamfollower had said. *No purpose but his own.*

Then it was too late. The door clanged shut on Vain. The Rider thrust home the bolts.

Uselessly Covenant protested, What do you want from me?

The next instant, a brown arm reached between the window bars of a nearby cell. Fingers clawed the air, desperate for freedom.

The gesture galvanized Covenant. It was something he understood. He dashed towards that door.

A Rider shouted at him, forbidding him. He paid no heed.

As he gained the door, the arm withdrew. A flat face pressed against the bars. Impassive eyes gazed out at him.

He almost lost his balance in horror. The prisoner was one of the *Haruchai* – one of Bannor's people, who made their home high in the fastnesses of the Westron Mountains. He could not mistake the stern characteristic mien of the race that had formed the Bloodguard, could not mistake the resemblance to Bannor, who had so often saved his life.

In Andelain, Bannor's shade had said, *Redeem my people. Their plight is an abomination.*

Suppressing the tonal lilt of his native tongue, the *Haruchai* said, 'Ur-Lord Thomas Covenant, Unbeliever and white gold wielder, I salute you. You are remembered among the *Haruchai*.' The implacable rigour of his personality seemed incapable of supplication. 'I am Brinn. Will you set us free?'

Then hot iron struck the back of Covenant's neck, and he stumbled like a cripple into darkness.

His unconsciousness was agony, and he could do nothing to assuage it. For a time as painful as frenzy, he lay deaf and blind. But gradually the darkness turned to rain. Torrents, muffled by granite, poured down walls, cascaded off eaves and parapets, rattled against oriels. The sound carried him back to himself. He became aware of the texture of blankets against his skin, aware of the deadness in his fingers and feet, the numbness of loss.

Remembering leprosy, he remembered everything, with an acuteness that made him press his face to the bed, knot his hands in the blanket under him. Vain. The *Haruchai*. The attack of the Riders.

That hidden door, which led to the Aumbrie, and the dungeon.

It was the same kind of door which the Despiser had formerly used in Foul's Creche. What was such a door doing in Revelstone?

A shudder ran through him. He rolled over, wincing at the movement. The back of his neck was stiff and sore. But the bones were intact, and the damage to his muscles did not seem permanent.

When he opened his eyes, he found Gibbon sitting beside his bed. The na-Mhoram's beatific face was tightened to express concern; but his red eyes held only peril.

A quick glance showed Covenant that he lay in the bedroom of his suite. He struggled to sit up. Sharp pains lanced through his back and shoulders; but the change of position enabled him to cast a glance at his right hand.

His ring was still there. Whatever else the Clave intended, they apparently did not intend to steal the white gold.

That steadied him. He looked at the na-Mhoram again, and made an intuitive decision not to raise the issue of the door. He had too many other dangers to consider.

'Doubtless,' Gibbon said with perfect blandness, 'your neck gives you pain. It will pass. Swarte employed excessive force. I have reprimanded her.'

'How – ?' The hurt seemed to cramp his voice. He could barely squeeze out a hoarse whisper. 'How long have I been out?'

'It is now midday of the second day of rain.'

Damnation, Covenant groaned. At least one whole day. He tried to estimate how many people the Clave had killed in that period of time, but could not. Perhaps they had killed Brinn – He thrust the idea away.

Akkasri,' he breathed, filling the name with accusation.

Gibbon nodded calmly. 'Akkasri na-Mhoram-in.'

'You lied to me.'

The na-Mhoram's hebetude seemed impervious to offence. 'Perhaps. My intent was not false. You came to Revelstone rife with hostility and suspicion. I sought means to allay your mistrust – and at the same time to ward against you if your purpose was evil. Therefore I informed you that Akkasri was of the na-Mhoram-cro. I desired to win your faith. In that I was not false. Guised as a na-Mhoram-cro, Akkasri could answer many questions without presenting to you the apparent threat of power. This I believed because of your treatment of Memla na-Mhoram-in. I regret that the outcome went amiss.'

This sounded plausible; but Covenant rejected it with a shake of his head. Immediately, a stab of soreness made him grimace. Muttering darkly to himself, he massaged his neck. Then he changed the subject, hoping to unsettle Gibbon. 'What the hell are you doing with one of the *Haruchai* in your goddamn prison?'

But the na-Mhoram appeared immune to discomfiture. Folding his arms, he said, 'I sought to withhold that knowledge from you. Already you believe that you have sufficient cause for mistrust. I desired that you should have no more such reasons until you learned to see the sovereign importance of our work.'

Abruptly, Gibbon went in another direction. 'Halfhand, did the *Haruchai* name you truly? Are you indeed ur-Lord Thomas Covenant, Unbeliever and white gold wielder?'

'What difference does that make?' growled Covenant.

'That name is mentioned often in the ancient legends. After the First Betrayer, Thomas Covenant was the greatest of all a-Jeroth's servants.'

'That's ridiculous.' This new distortion of the Land's history dismayed him. But he was determined to evade Gibbon's snare. 'How could I possibly be that Thomas Covenant? Where I come from, the name's common. So are white gold rings.'

Gibbon gazed redly at him; but Covenant did not blink. A lie for a lie, he rasped. Finally, the na-Mhoram admitted, 'You have not the look of such age.' Then he went on, 'But I was speaking of the *Haruchai.*

'Halfhand, we have not one *Haruchai* in our hold. We have three score and seven.'

Three — ! Covenant could not keep the horror off his face.

'There.' Gibbon gestured at him. 'I had cause to fear your response.'

'By God!' Covenant spat fiercely. 'You ought to fear the *Haruchai*! Don't you know what you're dealing with?'

'I respect them entirely.' The na-Mhoram's dull calm was complete. 'Their blood is potent and precious.'

They were my friends! Covenant could hardly refrain from shouting aloud. What in the name of all bloody hellfire and damnation do you think you're doing?

'Halfhand, you know that our work requires blood,' Gibbon continued reasonably. 'As the Sunbane grows, the Banefire must grow to resist it. We are long beyond the time when the people of the Land could meet all our need.

'Five generations past, when Offin na-Mhoram led the Clave, he was faced with the defeat of our dream. He had neared the limit of what the Land could supply, and it did not suffice. I will not dwell on his despair. It is enough to say that at that time – by chance or mercy – the *Haruchai* came to our aid.'

He shrugged. 'It is true that they did not intend the aid we found in them. Five came from the Westron Mountains in the name of their legends, seeking the Council. But Offin did not flinch his opportunity. He took the five captive.

'With the passage of time, five more came in search of their lost kindred. These also were captured. They were hardy and feral, but the power of the Banefire mastered them. And later more *Haruchai* came seeking the lost. First by five, then by ten, then by the score they came, with long lapses between. They are a stubborn people, and generation after generation they did not relent. Generation after generation, they were captured.' Covenant thought he saw a glint of amusement in Gibbon's red eyes. 'As their numbers increased, so grew the Banefire. Thus not a one of them prevailed or escaped.

'Their most recent foray comprised five score – a veritable army in their sight.' Gibbon's blandness sounded like the serenity of a pure heart. 'Three score and seven remain.'

An abomination. The na-Mhoram's tale made Covenant ache for violence. He could hardly muffle his vehemence as he asked, 'Is this supposed to convince me that you're my friend?'

'I do not seek your conviction here,' replied Gibbon. 'I seek only to explain, so that you will comprehend why I sought to withhold this knowledge – and why Swarte struck you when you beheld the *Haruchai.* You must perceive the extent of our consecration to our task. We count any one life – or any score of lives – or any myriad – as nothing against the life of the Land. The Sunbane is an immense ill, and we must spend immensely to combat it.

'Also I desire you to understand that *your* aid – the service of your white ring – promises the redemption of the Land, the saving of many times many lives. Does our shedding distress you? Then aid us, so that the need for blood may be brought to an end. You cannot serve the Land in any other way.'

Covenant held Gibbon with a glare. Through his teeth, he breathed, 'I knew the original Mhoram. The last time I was here, I made him choose between the hope of the Land and the life of one little girl. He chose the girl.' No words could articulate all the bile in his mouth. 'You're worse than the Sunbane.'

He expected the na-Mhoram to retort; but Gibbon only blinked, and said, 'Then it is sooth that you are the Unbeliever?'

'Yes!' Covenant snapped, casting subterfuge and safety aside. 'And I'm not going to let you commit genocide on the *Haruchai.*'

'Ah,' Gibbon sighed, rising to his feet, 'I feared that we would come to this.' He made a placating gesture. 'I do not seek your harm. But I see only one means by which we may win your aid. I will ready the Clave for a soothtell. It will reveal the truth you covet. Lies will be exposed, hearts laid bare.'

He moved to the doorway. 'Rest now, Halfhand. Eat – regain your strength. Walk where you wish. I ask only that you eschew the

Aumbrie and the hold until that which stands between us has been resolved. I will send for you when the soothtell has been prepared.' Without waiting for an answer, he left the suite.

Soothtell, Covenant snarled. His inner voice sounded like a croak. By God, yes!

Ignoring the pain in his neck, he threw off the blankets and went to the next room in search of food.

There was a fresh tray on the table. The room had been closed against the rain, and the air reeked of smoke. Strangely certain now that the Clave would not try to poison or drug him, he attacked the food, wolfing it down to appease his empty rage. But he did not touch the flask of *metheglin*; he did not want anything to dull his alertness, hamper his reflexes. He sensed that Gibbon's soothtell would be a crisis, and he meant to survive it.

He felt a compelling need to leave his suite and roam Revelstone, measuring his tension and resolve against the huge Keep. But he did not. Exerting a leper's discipline, he sat down in one of the chairs, stretched his legs to another, rested his sore neck on the chairback, and forced himself to be still. Muscle by muscle, he loosened his body, relaxed his forehead, softened his pulse, in an effort to achieve the concentration and poise he required in order to be ready.

Faces intruded on him: Linden, Sunder, Brinn. Brinn's visage was as absolute as Bannor's. Linden's features were strained, not by severity or choice, but by fear. He closed his mind to them, so that his own passion would not blind him. Instead, he thought about the hidden door Vain had discovered.

He could sense the answer in him, mumbling towards clarity. But it was still blocked by his preconceptions. Yet its very nearness drew beads of trepidation-sweat from his face. He was not prepared for the mendacity it represented.

Mendacity. He reached out for that idea, tried to take hold of its implications. But the hands of his mind were halfhands, inadequate.

The knock at his door jerked him erect. A pang stung his neck; droplets of sweat spattered the floor.

Before he could leave his chair, the door sprang open. Memla burst into the room.

A tangle of grey-streaked hair framed her pale visage. She clutched her *rukh* as if she meant to strike him with it. But it held no flame. Her eyes were full of broken honesty.

'False!' she gasped. 'They have been false to me!'

He lurched to confront her across the table.

She gasped momentarily for words, unable to compress the enormity of her indignation into mere speech. Then she broke out, 'They are here! Santonin – your companions! All here!'

Covenant gripped the table to keep himself from falling.

'Two Stonedownors and a stranger. In the hold.' Passion

obstructed her breathing. 'Santonin I saw, where he did not expect to be seen. The na-Mhoram uttered direct falsehood to me!

'I challenged Santonin. He revealed the truth – why I and others were sent to meet you. Smirking! Not to escort you, no. To ensure that you did not catch him. He gained Revelstone on the second day of the fertile sun. One day before us!'

One day? Something in Covenant began to howl. *One day?*

'Had I not halted you – had you walked through the night – you might have come upon him before dawn. He passed near me.'

With an inchoate snarl, Covenant swung his arm, swept the tray from the table. Stoneware broke; *metheglin* splashed the floor. But the act steadied him. 'Memla.' He had been unjust to her. He regained control of his limbs, his purpose; but he could not control his voice. 'Take me to Gibbon.'

She stared at him. His demand took her aback. 'You must flee. You are in peril.'

'Now.' He needed to move, begin, so that the trembling in his chest would not spread to his legs. 'Take me to him now.'

She hesitated, then gave a fierce nod. 'Yes. It is right.' Turning on her heel, she strode out of the room.

He surged after her in anguish and fury. Down towards the roots of Revelstone she guided him, along ways which he remembered. It was a long descent, but it seemed to pass swiftly. When she entered a familiar hall lit from its end by torches, he recognized the place where the Lords of the Council had had their private quarters.

The wide, round court beyond the hall both was and was not as he remembered it. The floor was burnished granite, as smooth as if it had been polished by ages of use and care. The ceiling rose far above the floor; and the walls were marked at intervals with coigns by which other levels of the Keep communicated with the dwellings spaced around the base of the cavity. These things accorded with his memory. But the light was altogether different. The Lords had not needed torches; the floor itself had shone with Earthpower. According to the old tales, the stone had been set aglow by Kevin Landwaster and the Staff of Law. But that illumination – so expressive of the warmth and fidelity of the Council – was gone now. The torches which replaced it seemed garish and unreliable by comparison.

But Covenant had neither time nor attention to spare for lost wonder. A score of the Clave stood around the centre of the floor. All held their *rukhs* ready; and the na-Mhoram's crozier dominated them. They had turned to the sound of Covenant's entrance. Their hoods concealed their faces.

Within their circle lay a stone slab like a catafalque. Heavy iron fetters chained a man to it.

One of the *Haruchai*.

When Covenant stalked ahead of Memla to approach the circle, he recognized Brinn.

'Halfhand,' the na-Mhoram said. For the first time, Covenant heard excitement in Gibbon's tone. 'The soothtell is prepared. All your questions will be answered now.'

19

SOOTHTELL

The vibration of augury in the na-Mhoram's voice stopped Covenant. The high dome of the space was dark, untouched by the light of the torches; the Riders stood on the dead floor as if it were the bottom of an abyss. Behind the concealment of their hoods, they might have been ur-viles; only the pale flesh of their hands revealed that they were human as they poised their *rukhs* for fire. Santonin was probably among them. Stonemight Woodhelven's fragment of the Illearth Stone was probably hidden somewhere in this circle. Gibbon's tone told Covenant that the Clave had not gathered here to do him any benefit.

He came to a halt. Echoes of his rage repeated within him like another voice iterating ridicule. Instinctively, he clenched his half-fist around his wedding-band. But he did not retreat. In a raw snarl, he demanded, 'What the bloody hell have you done with my friends?'

'The soothtell will answer.' Gibbon was eager, hungry. 'Do you choose to risk the truth?'

Brinn gazed at Covenant. His mien was impassive; but sweat sheened his forehead. Abruptly, he tensed against his fetters, straining with stubborn futility to break the chains.

Memla had not left the mouth of the hall. 'Ware, Halfhand!' she warned in a whisper. 'There is malice here.'

He felt the force of her warning. Brinn also was striving to warn him. For an instant, he hesitated. But the *Haruchai* had recognized him. Somehow, Brinn's people had preserved among them the tale of the Council and of the old wars against Corruption – the true tale, not a distorted version. And Covenant had met Bannor among his Dead in Andelain.

Gripping his self-control, he stepped into the circle, went to the catafalque. He rested a hand momentarily on Brinn's arm. Then he faced the na-Mhoram.

'Let him go.'

The na-Mhoram did not reply directly. Instead, he turned towards Memla. 'Memla na-Mhoram-in,' he said, 'you have no part in this soothtell. I desire you to depart.'

'No.' Her tone brandished outrage. 'You have been false to him. He knows not what he chooses.'

'Nevertheless,' Gibbon began quietly, then lost his hebetude in a strident yell, 'you will *depart*!'

For a moment, she refused. The air of the court was humid with conflicting intentions. Gibbon raised his crozier as if to strike at her. Finally, the combined repudiation of the circle was too strong for her. In deep bitterness, she said, 'I gave promise to the Halfhand for the safety of his companions. It is greatly wrong that the na-Mhoram holds the word of a na-Mhoram-in in such slight trust.' Turning on her heel, she strode away down the hall.

Gibbon dismissed her as if she had ceased to exist. Facing Covenant once again, he said, 'There is no power without blood.' He seemed unable to suppress the acuity of his excitement. 'And the soothtell requires power. Therefore this *Haruchai*. We will shed him to answer your questions.'

'No!' Covenant snapped. 'You've killed enough of them already.'

'We must have blood,' the na-Mhoram said.

'Then kill one of your bloody Riders!' Covenant was white with fury. 'I don't give a good goddamn what you do! Just leave the *Haruchai* alone!'

'As you wish,' Gibbon sounded triumphant.

'Ur-Lord!' Brinn shouted.

Covenant misread Brinn's warning. He sprang backward, away from the catafalque – into the hands of the Riders behind him. They grappled with him, caught his arms. Faster than he could defend himself, two knives flashed.

Blades slit both his wrists.

Two red lines slashed across his sight, across his soul. Blood spattered to the floor. The cuts were deep, deep enough to kill him slowly. Staring in horror, he sank to his knees. Pulsing rivulets marked his arms to the elbows. Blood dripped from his elbows, spreading his passion on the stone.

Around him, the Riders began to chant. Scarlet rose from their *rukhs*; the air became vermeil power.

He knelt helpless within the circle. The pain in his neck paralysed him. A spike of utter trepidation had been driven through his spine, nailing him where he crouched. The outcry of his blood fell silently.

Gibbon advanced, black and exalted. With the tip of his crozier, he touched the growing pool, began to draw meticulous red lines around Covenant.

Covenant watched like an icon of desolation as the na-Mhoram enclosed him in a triangle of his blood.

The chanting became words he could not prevent himself from understanding.

> 'Power and blood, and blood and flame:
> Soothtell visions without name:
> Truth as deep as Revelstone,
> Making time and passion known.
>
> 'Time begone, and space avaunt —
> Nothing may the seeing daunt.
> Blood uncovers every lie:
> We will know the truth, or die.'

When Gibbon had completed the triangle, he stepped back and raised his iron. Flame blossomed thetic and incarnadine from its end.

And Covenant exploded into vision.

He lost none of his self-awareness. The fires around him became more lurid and compelling; his arms felt as heavy as millstones; the chant laboured like the thudding of his heart. But behind the walls he saw and the stone he knew, other sights reeled, other knowledge gyred, tearing at his mind.

At first, the vision was chaos, impenetrable. Images ruptured past the catafalque, the Riders, burst in and out of view so feverishly that he comprehended none of them. But when in anguish he surrendered to them, let them sweep him into the eye of their vertigo, some of them sprang towards clarity.

Like three blows of a fist, he saw Linden, Sunder, Hollian. They were in the hold, in cells. Linden lay on her pallet in a stupor as pale as death.

The next instant, those images were erased. With a wrench that shook him to the marrow of his bones, the chaos gathered towards focus. The Staff of Law appeared before him. He saw places: Revelstone besieged by the armies of the Despiser; Foul's Creche crumbling into the Sea; Glimmermere opening its waters to accept the *krill* of Loric. He saw faces: dead Elena in ecstasy and horror; High Lord Mhoram wielding the *krill* to slay a Raver's body; Foamfollower laughing happily in the face of his own death. And behind it all he saw the Staff of Law. Through everything, implied by everything, the Staff. Destroyed by an involuntary deflagration of wild magic when dead Elena was forced to use it against the Land.

Kneeling there like a suicide in a triangle of blood, pinned to the stone by an iron pain, with his life oozing from his wrists, Covenant saw.

The Staff of Law. Destroyed.

The root of everything he needed to know.

For the Staff of Law had been formed by Berek Halfhand as a tool to serve and uphold the Law. He had fashioned the Staff from a limb of the One Tree as a way to wield Earthpower in defence of the health of the Land, in support of the natural order of life. And because Earthpower was the strength of mystery and spirit, the Staff became the thing it served. It was the Law; the Law was incarnate in the Staff. The tool and its purpose were one.

And the Staff had been destroyed.

That loss had weakened the very fibre of the Law. A crucial support was withdrawn, and the Law faltered.

From that seed grew both the Sunbane and the Clave.

They came into being together, gained mastery over the Land together, flourished together.

After the destruction of Foul's Creche, the Council of Lords had prospered in Revelstone for centuries. Led first by High Lord Mhoram, then by successors equally dedicated and idealistic, the Council had changed the thrust and tenor of its past service. Mhoram had learned that the Lore of the Seven Wards, the knowledge left behind by Kevin Landwaster, contained within it the capacity to be corrupted. Fearing a renewal of Desecration, he had turned his back on that Lore, thrown the *krill* into Glimmermere, and commenced a search for new ways to use and serve the Earthpower.

Guided by his decision, Councils for generations after him had used and served, performing wonders. Trothgard had been brought back to health. All the old forests – Grimmerdhore, Morinmoss, Garroting Deep, Giant Woods – had thrived to such an extent that Caerroil Wildwood, the Forestal of Garroting Deep, had believed his labour ended at last, and had passed away; and even the darkest trees had lost much of their enmity for the people of the Land. All the war-torn wastes along Landsdrop between Mount Thunder and the Colossus of the Fall had been restored to life. The perversity of Sarangrave Flat had been reduced; and much had been done to ease the ruin of the Spoiled Plains.

For a score of centuries, the Council served the Land's health in peace and fruitfulness. And at last the Lords began to believe that Lord Foul would never return, that Covenant had driven Despite utterly from the Earth. Paradise seemed to be within their grasp. Then in the confidence of peace, they looked back to High Lord Mhoram, and chose to change their names to mark the dawning of a new age. Their High Lord they christened the na-Mhoram; their Council they called the Clave. They saw no limit to the beauty they could achieve. They had no one to say to them that their accomplishments came far too easily.

For the Staff of Law had been destroyed. The Clave flourished in part because the old severity of the Law, the stringency which matched the price paid to the beauty of the thing purchased, had been weakened; and they did not know their peril.

Finding the Third Ward, they had looked no further for knowledge. Through the centuries, they had grown blind, and had lost the means to know that the man who had been named the na-Mhoram, who had transformed the Council in the Clave, was a Raver.

For when Covenant had defeated the Despiser, reduced him by wild magic and laughter to a poverty of spirit so complete that he could no longer remain corporeal, the Despiser had not died. Despite did not die. Fleeing the destruction of his Creche, he had hidden at the fringes of the one power potent enough to heal even him: the Earthpower itself.

And this was possible because the Staff had been destroyed. The Law which had limited him and resisted him since the creation of the Earth had been weakened; and he was able to endure it while he conceived new strength, new being. And while he endured, he also corrupted. As he gained stature, the Law sickened.

The first result of this decay was to make the work of the Council more easy; but every increment strengthened Lord Foul, and all his might went to increase the infection. Slowly, he warped the Law to his will.

His Ravers shared his recovery; and he did not act overtly against the Land until *samadhi* Sheol had contrived his way into the Council, had begun its perversion, until several generations of na-Mhorams, each cunningly mastered by *samadhi*, had brought the Clave under Lord Foul's sway.

Slowly, the Oath of Peace was abandoned; slowly, the ideals of the Clave were altered. Therefore when the Clave made a secret door to its new hold and Aumbrie, it made one such as the Ravers had known in Foul's Creche. Slowly, the legends of Lord Foul were transmogrified into the tales of a-Jeroth, both to explain the Sunbane and to conceal Lord Foul's hand in it.

Labouring always in secret, so that the Clave at all times had many uncorrupted members – people like Memla, who believed the Raver's lies, and were therefore sincere in their service – *samadhi* Sheol fashioned a tool for the Despiser, ill enough to preach the shedding of blood, pure enough to be persuasive. Only then did Lord Foul let his work be seen.

For the Staff of Law had been destroyed, and his hands were on the reins of nature. By degrees, mounting gradually over centuries, he inflicted his abhorrence upon the Land, corrupting the Earthpower with Sunbane. This he was able to do because the Clave had been made incapable of conceiving any true defence. The Banefire was not a defence, had never been a defence. Rather, it was *samadhi*'s means to commit further afflictions. The shedding of blood to invoke the Sunbane only made the Sunbane stronger. Thus Lord Foul caused the increase of the Sunbane without cost to himself.

And all this, Covenant saw as his blood deepened around his knees, had been done in preparation for one thing, the capstone and masterstroke of Lord Foul's mendacity: the summoning of white gold to the Land. Lord Foul desired possession of the wild magic; and he did to the Land what he had done to Joan, so that Covenant would have no final choice except surrender.

The loss of the Staff explained why Covenant's summoning had been so elaborate. In the past, such summons had always been an act of Law, performed by the holder of the Staff. Only when he had been close to death from starvation and rattlesnake venom, and the Law of Death had been broken, had summoning been possible without the Staff. Therefore this time the Despiser had been forced to go to great lengths to take hold of Covenant. A specific location had been required, specific pain, a triangle of blood, freedom of choice and death. Had any of these conditions failed, the summoning would have failed, and Lord Foul would have been left to harm the Land, the Earth, without hope of achieving his final goal – the destruction of the Arch of Time. Only by destroying the Arch could he escape the prison of Time. Only with wild magic could he gain freedom and power to wage his hatred of the Creator across the absolute heavens of the cosmos.

But the summoning had not failed, and Covenant was dying. He understood now why Gibbon had driven Memla from the court. If she had shared this vision of the truth, her outrage might have led her to instigate a revolt among the uncorrupted Riders; for Gibbon, too, was a Raver.

He understood what had happened to the Colossus of the Fall. It had been an avatar of the ancient forests, erected on Landsdrop to defend against Ravers; and the Sunbane had destroyed the forests, unbinding the will of wood which had upheld for millennia that stone monolith.

He understood how Caer-Caveral had been driven to Andelain by the erosion of Morinmoss – and why the last of the Forestals was doomed to fail. At its root, the power of the Forestal was an expression of Law, just as Andelain was the quintessence of Law; and the Sunbane was a corruption Caer-Caveral could resist but not defeat.

He understood what had become of the Ranyhyn, the great horses, and of the Ramen who served them. Perceiving the ill of the Sunbane in its earliest appearances, both Ranyhyn and Ramen had simply fled the Land, sojourning south along the marge of the Sunbirth Sea in search of safer grasslands.

These things came to him in glimpses, flares of vision across the central fact of his situation. But there were also things he could not see: a dark space where Caer-Caveral had touched his mind; a blur that might have explained Vain's purpose; a blankness which concealed the reason why Linden was chosen. Loss gripped him: the ruin of the Land he loved; all the fathomless ill of the Sunbane and the Clave was his fault, his doing.

He had no answer for the logic of his guilt. The Staff of Law had been destroyed – and he had destroyed it. Wild magic had burst from his ring to save his life; power beyond all choice or mastery had riven the Staff, so that nothing remained but its heels. For such an act, he deserved to die. The lassitude of blood-loss seemed condign and admirable. His pulse shrank towards failure. He was culpable beyond any redemption and had no heart to go on living.

But a voice spoke in his mind:

Ur-Lord.

It was a voice without sound, a reaching of thought to thought. It came from Brinn. He had never before heard the mind-speech of the *Haruchai;* but he recognized the speaker in the intensity of Brinn's gaze. The power of the soothtell made possible things which could not otherwise have occurred.

Unbeliever. Thomas Covenant.

Unbeliever, he answered to himself. Yes. It's my fault. My responsibility.

You must fight.

The images before him whirled towards chaos again.

Responsible. Yes. On my head. He could not fight. How could any man hope to resist the Desecration of a world?

But guilt was the voice of the Clave, the Riders and the Raver who had committed such atrocities. Brinn strained against his bonds as if he would rupture his thews rather than accept failure. Linden still lay in the hold, unconscious or dead. And the Land – Oh, the Land! That it should die undefended!

Fight!

Somewhere deep within him, he found the strength for curses. Are you nothing but a leper? Even lepers don't have to surrender.

Visions reeled through the air. The scarlet light faded as Gibbon brought the soothtell to an end.

Stop! He still needed answers: how to fight the Sunbane; how to restore the Law; to understand the venom in him; to cure it. He groped frantically among the images, fought to bring what he needed into clarity.

But he could not. He could see nothing now but the gaping cuts in his wrists, the ooze of his blood growing dangerously slower. The Riders took the soothtell away from him before he gained the most crucial knowledge. They were reducing their power – No, they were not reducing it, they were changing it, translating it into something else.

Into coercion.

He could feel them now, a score of wills impending on the back of his neck, commanding him to abandon resistance, take off his ring and surrender it before he died. Telic red burned at him from all sides; every *rukh* was aflame with compulsion. Release the ring. Set it aside. Before you die. This, he knew, was not part of Lord Foul's intent. It was Gibbon's greed; *samadhi* Sheol wanted the white gold for himself.

The ring!

Brinn's mind-voice was barely audible:

Unbeliever! They will slay us all!

All, he thought desperately. Three score and seven of the *Haruchai*. Vain, if they could. Sunder. Hollian. Linden.

The Land.

Release the *ring*!

No.

His denial was quiet and small, like the first ripple presaging a tsunami.

I will not permit this.

Extravagant fury and need gathered somewhere beyond the shores of his consciousness, piled upward like a mighty sea.

His mind was free now of everything except helplessness and determination. He knew he could not call up wild magic to save him. He required a trigger; but the Riders kept their power at his back, out of reach. At the same time, his need was absolute. Slashing his wrists was a slow way to kill him, but it would succeed unless he could stop the bleeding, defend himself.

He did not intend to die. Brinn had brought him back to himself. He was more than a leper. No abjections could force him to abide his doom. No. There were other answers to guilt. If he could not find them, he would create them out of the raw stuff of his being.

He was going to fight.

Now.

The tsunami broke. Wrath erupted in him like the madness of venom.

Fire and rage consumed all his pain. The triangle and the will of the Clave splintered and fell away.

A wind of passion blew through him. Wild argent exploded from his ring.

White blazed over his right fist. Acute incandescence covered his hand as if his flesh were power. Conflagration tore the red air.

Fear assailed the Clave. Riders cried out in confusion. Gibbon shouted commands.

For a moment, Covenant remained where he was. His ring flamed like one white torch among the vermeil *rukhs*. Deliberately, he drew power to his right wrist; shaping the fire with his will, he stopped the flow of blood, closed the knife wound. A flash of ire seared and sealed the cut. Then he turned the magic to his left wrist.

His concentration allowed Gibbon time to marshal a defence. Covenant could feel the Riders surging around him, mustering the Banefire to their *rukhs*. But he did not care. The venom in him counted no opposition, no cost. When his wrists were healed, he rose direly to his feet and stood erect like a man who had lost no blood and could not be touched.

His force staggered the atmosphere of the court. It blasted from his entire body as if his very bones were avid for fire.

Gibbon stood before him. The Raver wielded a crozier so fraught with heat and might that the iron screamed. A shaft of red malice howled at Covenant's heart.

Covenant quenched it with a shrug.

One of the Riders hurled a coruscating *rukh* at his back.

Wild magic evaporated the metal in mid-flight.

Then Covenant's wrath became ecstasy, savage beyond all restraint. In an instant of fury which shocked the very gut-rock of Revelstone, his wild magic detonated.

Riders screamed, fell. Doors in the coigns above the floor burst from their hinges. The air sizzled like frying flesh.

Gibbon shouted orders Covenant could not hear, threw an arc of emerald across the court, then disappeared.

Under a moil of force, the floor began to shine like silver magma.

Somewhere amid the wreckage of the soothtell, he heard Lord Foul laughing.

The sound only strung his passion tighter.

When he looked about him, bodies lay everywhere. Only one Rider was left standing. The man's hood had been blown back, revealing contorted features and frantic eyes.

Intuitively, Covenant guessed that this was Santonin.

In his hands, he grasped a flake of stone which steamed like green ice, held it so that it pressed against his *rukh*. Pure emerald virulence raged outward.

The Illearth Stone.

Covenant had no limits, no control. A rave of force hurled Santonin against the far wall, scorched his raiment to ashes, blackened his bones.

The Stone rolled free, lay pulsing like a diseased heart on the bright floor.

Reaching out with flames, Covenant drew the Stone to himself. He clenched it in his halfhand. Foamfollower had died so that the Illearth Stone could be destroyed.

Destroyed!

A silent blast stunned the cavity; a green shriek devoured by argent. The Stone-flake vanished in steam and fury.

With a tremendous splitting noise, the floor cracked from wall to wall.

'Unbeliever!'

He could barely hear Brinn.

'Ur-Lord!'

He turned and peered through fire at the *Haruchai*.

'The prisoners!' Brinn barked. 'The Clave holds your friends! Lives will be shed to strengthen the Banefire!'

The shout penetrated Covenant's mad rapture. He nodded. With a flick of his mind, he shattered Brinn's chains.

At once, Brinn sprang from the catafalque and dashed out of the cavity.

Covenant followed in flame.

At the end of the hall, the *Haruchai* launched himself against three Riders. Their *rukhs* burned. Covenant lashed argent at them, sent them sprawling, reduced their *rukhs* to scoria.

He and Brinn hastened away through the passages of Revelstone.

Brinn led; he knew how to find the hidden door to the hold. Shortly, he and Covenant reached the Raver-made entrance. Covenant summoned fire to break down the door; but before he could strike, Brinn slapped the proper spot in the invisible architrave. Limned in red tracery, the portal opened.

Five Riders waited within the tunnel. They were prepared to fight; but Brinn charged them with such abandon that their first blasts missed. In an instant, he had felled two of them. Covenant swept the other three aside, and followed Brinn, running towards the hold.

The dungeon had no other defenders: the Clave had not had time to organize more Riders. And if Gibbon were still alive, he might conceivably withdraw his forces rather than risk losses which would cripple the Clave. When Brinn and Covenant rushed into the hold and found it empty, Brinn immediately leaped to the nearest door and began to throw back the bolts.

But Covenant was rife with might, wild magic which demanded utterance. Thrusting Brinn aside, he unleashed an explosion that made the very granite of Revelstone stagger. With a shrill scream of metal, all the cell doors sprang from their moorings and clanged to the floor, ringing insanely.

At once, scores of *Haruchai* emerged, ready to fight. Ten of them raced to defend the entrance to the tunnel; the rest scattered towards other cells, searching for more prisoners.

Eight or nine people of the Land – Stonedownors and Woodhelvennin – appeared as if they were dazzled by the miracle of their reprieve.

Vain left his cell slowly. When he saw Covenant, saw Covenant's passionate fire, his face stretched into a black grin, the grin of a man who recognized what Covenant was doing. The grin of a fiend.

Two *Haruchai* supported Sunder. The Graveller had a raw weal around his neck, as if he had been rescued from a gibbet, and he looked weak. He gaped at Covenant.

Hollian came, wan and frightened, from her cell. Her eyes flinched from Covenant as if she feared to know him. When she saw Sunder, she hastened to him and wrapped herself in his arms.

Covenant remained still, aching for Linden. Vain grinned like the sound of Lord Foul's laughter.

Then Brinn and another *Haruchai* bore Linden out into the hall. She lay limp in their arms, dead or unconscious, in sopor more compulsory than any sleep.

When Covenant saw her, he let out a howl which tore chunks from the ceiling and pulverized them until the air was full of fine powder.

He could not stop himself until Brinn yelled to him that she was alive.

PART III

Purpose

20

THE QUEST

He left the hold, left his companions, because he could not bear to watch the impenetrable nightmares writhe across Linden's mien. She was not afraid of his leprosy. She had supported him at every crisis. This was the result. No one could rouse her. She lay in a stupor like catatonia, and dreamed anguish.

He went towards the upland plateau because he needed to recover some kind of hope.

Already, the frenzy of his power had begun to recoil against him. Vain's smile haunted him like an echo of horror and scorn. His rescue from Stonemight Woodhelven was no different than this. How many people had he killed? He had no control over his power. Power and venom controlled him.

Yet he did not release the wild magic. Revelstone was still full of Riders. He glimpsed them running past the ends of long halls, preparing themselves for defence or counterattack. He did not have enough blood in his veins to sustain himself without the fire of his ring: once he dropped his power, he would be beyond any self-protection. He would have to trust the *Haruchai* to save him, save his friends. And that thought also was bitter to him. Bannor's people had paid such severe prices in his name. How could he permit them to serve him again?

How many people had he killed?

Shedding flames like tears, he climbed up through the levels of Revelstone towards the plateau.

And Brinn strode at his side as if the *Haruchai* had already committed himself to this service. Somewhere he had found a cloak which he now draped across Covenant's shoulders. The Unbeliever shrugged it into place, hardly noticing. It helped to protect him against the shock of blood-loss.

Covenant needed hope. He had gained much from the soothtell; but those insights paled beside the shock of Linden's straits, paled beside the mounting self-abomination of what he had done with his power. He had not known he was so capable of slaughter. He could not face the demands of his new knowledge without some kind of hope.

He did not know where else to turn except to Glimmermere. To the Earthpower which remained still vital enough to provide Glimmermere with water, even when all the Land lay under a desert sun. To the blade which lay in the deeps of the lake.

Loric's *krill*.

He did not want it because it was a weapon. He wanted it because it was an alternative, a tool of power which might prove manageable enough to spare him any further reliance upon his ring.

And he wanted it because Vain's grin continued to knell through his head. In that grin, he had seen Vain's makers, the roynish and cruel beings he remembered. They had lied to Foamfollower. Vain's purpose was not greatly to be desired. It was the purpose of a fiend. Covenant had seen Vain kill, seen himself kill, and knew the truth.

And Loric, who was Kevin's father, had been called Vilesilencer. He had formed the *krill* to stem the harm of Vain's ancestors. Perhaps the *krill* would provide an answer to Vain.

That, too, was a form of hope. Covenant needed hope. When he reached the open plateau, the brightness of his power made the night seem as black and dire as Vain's obsidian flesh.

No one had been able to rouse Linden. She was caught in the toils of a heinous nightmare, and could not fight free. What evil had been practised upon her?

And how many people had he killed? He, who had sworn never to kill again, and had not kept that oath. How many?

His own fire blinded him; he could not see any stars. The heavens gaped over him like a leper's doom. How could any man who lacked simple human sensitivity hope to control wild magic? *The wild magic which destroys peace*. He felt numb, and full of venom, and could not help himself.

Wrapped in argent like a new incarnation of the Sunbane, he traversed the hills towards Glimmermere. The tarn was hidden by the terrain; but he knew his way.

Brinn walked beside him, and did not speak. The *Haruchai* seemed content to support whatever Covenant intended. In this same way, the Bloodguard had been content to serve the Lords. Their acceptance had cost them two thousand years without love or sleep or death. And it had cost them corruption; like Foamfollower, Bannor had been forced to watch his people become the thing they hated. Covenant did not know how to accept Brinn's tacit offer. How could he risk repeating the fate of the Bloodguard? But he was in need, and did not know how to refuse.

Then he saw it: Glimmermere lying nestled among the hills. Its immaculate surface reflected his silver against the black night, so that the water looked like a swath of wild magic surrounded, about to be smothered, by the dark vitriol of ur-viles. Avid white which only made Vain grin. But Covenant's power was failing; he had lost too much blood; the reaction to what he had done was too strong.

He lumbered stiff-kneed down to the water's edge, stood trembling at the rim of Glimmermere, and fought himself to remain alight just a little longer.

Fire and darkness sprang back at him from the water. He had bathed once in Glimmermere; but now he felt too tainted to touch this vestige of Earthpower. And he did not know the depth of the pool. High Lord Mhoram had thrown the *krill* here as an act of faith in the Land's future. Surely he had believed the blade to be beyond reach. Covenant would never be able to swim that far down. And he could not ask Brinn to do it. He felt dismayed by the implications of Brinn's companionship; he could not force himself to utter an active acceptance of Brinn's service. The *krill* seemed as distant as if it had never existed.

Perhaps none of this had ever existed. Perhaps he was merely demented, and Vain's grin was the leer of his insanity. Perhaps he was already dead with a knife in his chest, experiencing the hell his leprosy had created for him.

But when he peered past the flaming silver and midnight, he saw a faint echo from the depths. The *krill*. It replied to his power as it had replied when he had first awakened it. Its former arousal had led ineluctably to Elena's end and the breaking of the Law of Death. For a moment, he feared it, feared the keenness of its edges and the weight of culpability it implied. He had loved Elena – But the wild magic was worse. The venom was worse. He could not control them.

'How many – ?' His voice tore the silence clenched in his throat. 'How many of them did I kill?'

Brinn responded dispassionately out of the night, 'One score and one, ur-Lord.'

Twenty-one? Oh, God!

For an instant, he thought that the sinews of his soul would rend, must rend, that his joints would be ripped asunder. But then a great shout of power blasted through his chest, and white flame erupted towards the heavens.

Glimmermere repeated the concussion. Suddenly, the whole surface of the lake burst into fire. Flame mounted in a gyre; the water of the lake whirled. And from the centre of the whirl came a clear white beam in answer to his call.

The *krill* rose into view. It shone, bright and inviolate, in the heart of the lake – a long double-edged dagger with a translucent gem forged into the cross of its guards and haft. The light came from its gem, reiterating Covenant's fire, as if the jewel and his ring were brothers. The night was cast back by its radiance, and by his power, and by the high flames of Glimmermere.

Still the *krill* was beyond reach. But he did not hesitate now. The whirl of the water and the gyring flames spoke to him of things

315

which he understood: vertigo and paradox; the eye of stability in the core of the contradiction. Opening his arms to the fire, he stepped out into the lake.

Earthpower upheld him. Conflagration which replied to his conflagration spun around him and through him, and bore his weight. Floating like a flicker of shadow through the argence, he walked towards the centre of Glimmermere.

In his weakness, he felt that the fire would rush him out of himself, reduce him to motes of mortality and hurl him at the empty sky. The *krill* seemed more substantial than his flesh; the iron more full of meaning than his wan bones. But when he stooped to it and took hold of it, it lifted in his hands and arced upwards, leaving a slash of brilliance across the night.

He clutched it to his chest and turned back towards Brinn.

Now his fatigue closed over him. No longer could he keep his power alight. The fingers of his will unclawed their grip and failed. At once, the flames of Glimmermere began to subside.

But still the lake upheld him. The Earthpower gave him this gift as it had once gifted Berek Halfhand's despair on the slopes of Mount Thunder. It sustained him, and did not let him go until he stumbled to the shore in darkness.

Night lay about him and in him. His eyes descried nothing but the dark as if they had been burned out of his head. Even the shining of the gem seemed to shed no illumination. Shorn now of power, he could no longer grasp the *krill*. It became hot in his hands, hot enough to touch the nerves which still lived. He dropped it to the ground, where it shone like the last piece of light in the world. Mutely, he knelt beside it, with his back to Glimmermere as if he had been humbled. He felt alone in the Land, and incapable of himself.

But he was not alone. Brinn tore a strip from his tunic – a garment made from an ochre material which resembled vellum – and wrapped the krill so that it could be handled. For a moment, he placed a gentle touch on Covenant's shoulder. Then he said quietly, 'Ur-Lord, come. The Clave will attempt to strike against us. We must go.'

As the gleam of the *krill* was silenced, the darkness became complete. It was a balm to Covenant, solace for the aggrievement of power. He ached for it to go on assuaging him for ever. But he knew Brinn spoke the truth. Yes, he breathed. We must go. Help me.

When he raised his head, he could see the stars. They glittered as if only their own beauty could console them for their loneliness. The moon was rising. It was nearly full.

In silence and moonlight, Covenant climbed to his feet and began to carry his exhaustion back towards Revelstone.

After a few steps, he accepted the burden of the *krill* from Brinn and tucked it under his belt. Its warmth rested there like a comfort against the knotted self-loathing in his stomach.

Stumbling and weary, he moved without knowing how he could ever walk as far as Revelstone. But Brinn aided him, supported him when he needed help, let him carry himself when he could. After a time that passed, like the sequences of delirium, they gained the promontory and the mouth of the na-Mhoram's Keep.

One of the *Haruchai* awaited them outside the tunnel which led down into Revelstone. As Covenant lurched to a halt, the *Haruchai* bowed; and Brinn said, 'Ur-Lord, this is Ceer.'

'Ur-Lord,' Ceer said.

Covenant blinked at him, but could not respond. He seemed to have no words left.

Expressionlessly, Ceer extended a leather pouch towards him.

He accepted it. When he unstopped the pouch, he recognized the smell of *metheglin*. At once, he began to drink. His drained body was desperate for fluid. Desperate. He did not lower the pouch until it was empty.

'Ur-Lord,' Ceer said then, 'the Clave gathers about the Banefire. We harry them, and they make no forays – but there is great power in their hands. And four more of the *Haruchai* have been slain. We have guided all prisoners from Revelstone. We watch over them as we can. Yet they are not safe. The Clave holds coercion to sway our minds, if they but choose to exert it. We know this to our cost. We must flee.'

Yes, Covenant mumbled inwardly. Flee. I know. But when he spoke, the only word he could find was, 'Linden – ?'

Without inflection, Ceer replied, 'She has awakened.'

Covenant did not realize that he had fallen until he found himself suspended in Brinn's arms. For a long moment, he could not force his legs to straighten. But the *metheglin* helped him. Slowly, he took his own weight, stood upright again.

'How – ?'

'Ur-Lord, we strove to wake her.' Suppressing the lilt of his native tongue to speak Covenant's language made Ceer sound completely detached. 'But she lay as the dead, and would not be succoured. We bore her from the Keep, knowing not what else to do. Yet your black companion – ' He paused, asking for a name.

'Vain,' Covenant said, almost choking on the memory of that grin. 'He's an ur-vile.'

A slight contraction of his eyebrows expressed Ceer's surprise; but he did not utter his thoughts aloud. 'Vain,' he resumed, 'stood by unheeding for a time. But then of a sudden he approached Linden Avery the Chosen.' Dimly, Covenant reflected that the *Haruchai* must already have spoken to Sunder or Hollian. 'Knowing nothing of him, we strove to prevent him. But he cast us aside as if we were not who we are. He knelt to the Chosen, placed his hand upon her. She awakened.'

A gròan of incomprehension and dread twisted Covenant's throat; but Ceer went on. 'Awakening, she cried out and sought to flee. She did not know us. But the Stonedownors your companions comforted her. And still – ' a slight pause betrayed Ceer's uncertainty – 'Vain had not done. Ur-Lord, he bowed before her – he, who is heedless of the *Haruchai*, and deaf to all speech. He placed his forehead upon her feet.

'This was fear to her,' Ceer continued. 'She recoiled to the arms of the Stonedownors. They also do not know this Vain. But they stood to defend her if need be. He rose to his feet, and there he stands yet, still unheeding, as a man caught in the coercion of the Clave. He appears no longer conscious of the Chosen, or of any man or woman.'

Ceer did not need to speak his thought; Covenant could read it in his flat eyes.

We do not trust this Vain.

But Covenant set aside the question of Vain. The *krill* was warm against his belly; and he had no strength for distractions. His path was clear before him, had been clear ever since he had absorbed the meaning of the soothtell. And Linden was awake. She had been restored to him. Surely now he could hold himself together long enough to set his purpose in motion.

Yet he took the time for one more enquiry. 'How is she?'

Ceer shrugged fractionally. 'She has gazed upon the face of Corruption. Yet she speaks clearly to the Stonedownors.' He paused, then said, 'She is your companion. You have redeemed us from abomination. While we live, she and all your companions will suffer no further hurt.' He looked towards Brinn. 'But she has warned us of a Raver. Ur-Lord, surely we must flee.'

A Raver, thought Covenant. Gibbon. Yes.

What did he do to her? The nightmare on her face was still vivid to him. What did that bastard do to her?

Without a word, he locked himself erect, and started stiffly down the tunnel into Revelstone.

The way was long; but *metheglin* and darkness sustained him. Vain's grin sustained him. The Demondim-spawn had awakened her? Had knelt to her? The ur-viles must have lied to Foamfollower. Hamako's *rhysh* must have been mistaken or misled. Did Vain bow in acknowledgment of Gibbon's effect on her?

What did that bastard do to her?

If Covenant had doubted his purpose before, or had doubted himself, he was sure now. No Clave or distance or impossibility was going to stand in his way.

Down through the city he went, like a tight curse. Down past

Haruchai who scouted the city and watched the Riders. Down to the gates, and the passage under the watchtower. He had already killed twenty-one people; he felt that for himself he had nothing left to fear. His fear was for his companions; and his curse was for the Despiser. His purpose was clear.

As he moved through the tunnel, a score of *Haruchai* gathered around him like an honour-guard. They wore supplies which they had scoured from Revelstone for the flight of the prisoners.

With them, he passed the broken outer gates into the night.

Below him on the rocky slope of the foothill burned a large bonfire. Stark against the massed jungle beyond it, it flamed with a loud crepitation, fighting the rain-drenched green wood which the *Haruchai* fed to it. Its yellow light enclosed all the prisoners, defending them from darkness.

He could see a group of Stonedownors and Woodhelvennin huddling uncertainly near the fire. *Haruchai* moved around the area, preparing supplies, wresting more firewood from the jungle, standing watch. Vain stood motionless among them. Sunder, Hollian, and Linden sat close together as if to comfort each other.

He had eyes only for Linden. Her back was to him. He hardly noticed that all Brinn's people had turned towards him and dropped to one knee, as if he had been announced by silent trumpets. With the dark citadel rising behind him, he went woodenly towards Linden's back as if he meant to fall at her feet.

Sunder saw him, spoke quickly to Linden and Hollian. The Stonedownors jumped upright and faced Covenant as if he came bearing life and death. More slowly, Linden, too, climbed erect. He could read nothing but pain in the smudged outlines of her mien. But her eyes recognized him. A quiver like urgency ran through her. He could not stop himself. He surged to her, wrapped his arms around her, hid his face in her hair.

Around him, the *Haruchai* went back to their tasks.

For a moment, she returned his embrace as if she were grateful for it. Then, suddenly, she stiffened. Her slim, abused body became nausea in his arms. He tried to speak, but could not, could not sever the knots in his chest. When she tried to pull away from him, he let her go; and still he could not speak.

She did not meet his stare. Her gaze wandered his frame to the old cut in the centre of his shirt. 'You're sick.'

Sick? Momentarily, he failed to understand her. 'Linden – ?'

'Sick.' Her voice trailed like blood between her lips. 'Sick.' Moving as if she were stunned by abhorrence or grief, she turned her back on him. She sank to the ground, covered her face with her hands, began to rock back and forth. Faintly, he heard her murmuring, 'Sick. Sick.'

His leprosy.

The sight almost tore away his last strength. If he could have found his voice, he would have wailed. *What did that bastard do to you?* But he had come too far and had too many responsibilities. The pressure of the *krill* upheld him. Clenching himself as if he, too, could not be touched, he looked at Sunder and Hollian.

They seemed abashed by Linden's reaction. 'Ur-Lord,' Sunder began tentatively, then faltered into silence. The weal around his neck appeared painful; but he ignored it. Old frown-marks bifurcated his forehead as if he were caught between rage and fear, comradeship and awe, and wanted Covenant to clarify them for him. His jaws chewed words he did not know how to utter.

'Ur-Lord,' Hollian said for him, 'she has been sorely hurt in some way. I know not how, for Gibbon na-Mhoram said to her, "You I must not harm." Yet an anguish torments her.' Her pale features asked Covenant to forgive Linden.

Dumbly, he wondered where the eh-Brand found her courage. She was hardly more than a girl, and her perils often seemed to terrify her. Yet she had resources – She was a paradox of fright and valour; and she spoke when Sunder could not.

'You have bought back our lives from the na-Mhoram,' she went on, 'at what cost to yourself I cannot know. I know not how to behold such power as you wield. But I have tasted the coercion of the Riders, and the imprisonment of the Clave. I thank you from my heart. I pray I may be given opportunity to serve you.'

Serve – ? Covenant groaned. *How can I let you serve me? You don't know what I'm going to do.* Yet he could not refuse her. Somewhere in his own inchoate struggle of need and conviction, he had already accepted the service of the *Haruchai*, though their claim on his forbearance was almost forty centuries older than hers. Gripping himself rigid because he knew that if he bent he would break, he asked the only question he could articulate in the poverty of his courage. 'Are you all right?'

She glanced at Sunder, at his neck. When he nodded, she replied, 'It is nothing. A little hunger and fear. We are acquainted with such things. And,' she continued more strongly, 'we have been blessed with more than our lives. The *Haruchai* are capable of wonders.' With a gesture, she indicated three of Brinn's people who stood nearby. 'Ur-Lord, here are Cail, Stell, and Harn.' The three sketched bows towards Covenant.

'When we were guided from the hold, I was content with my life. But the *Haruchai* were not content.' Reaching into her robe, she brought out her dirk and *lianar*. 'They sought throughout Revelstone and recovered these for me. Likewise they recovered Sunder's Sunstone and blade.' Sunder agreed. Covenant wondered vaguely at the new intimacy which allowed Hollian to speak for Sunder. How much had they been through together? 'How does it come to pass,'

Hollian concluded, 'that the Land has so forgotten the *Haruchai*?'

'You know nothing of us,' the one named Harn responded. 'We know nothing of you. We would not have known to seek your belongings, had not Memla na-Mhoram-in revealed that they had been taken from you.'

Memla, Covenant thought. Yes. Another piece of his purpose became momentarily lucid. 'Brinn.' The night seemed to be gathering around him. Sunder and Hollian had drifted out of focus. 'Find her. Tell her what we need.'

'Her?' Brinn asked distantly. 'What is it that we need?'

Until he understood the question, Covenant did not perceive that he was losing consciousness. He had lost too much blood. The darkness on all sides was creeping towards vertigo. Though he yearned to let himself collapse, he lashed out with curses until he had brought his head up again, re-opened his eyes.

'Memla,' he said thickly. 'Tell her we need Coursers.'

'Yes, ur-Lord.' Brinn did not move. But two or three *Haruchai* left the fire and loped easily up towards the watchtower.

Someone placed a bowl of *metheglin* in Covenant's hands. He drank it, tried to squeeze a semblance of clarity into his vision, and found himself staring at Vain.

The Demondim-spawn stood with his arms slightly bent, as if he were ready to commit acts which could not be foreseen. His black eyes stared at nothing; the ghoul grin was gone from his black lips. But he still wore the heels of the Staff of Law, one on his right wrist, the other on his left ankle. The burns he had received two nights ago were almost healed.

As a man caught in the coercion – Was that it? Was the Clave responsible for Vain? Ur-viles serving the Clave? How far did the na-Mhoram's mendacity extend? Vain's blackness echoed the night. How had he roused Linden? And *why*? Covenant wanted to rage at the Demondim-spawn. But he himself had killed – without control or even reluctance. He lacked the rectitude to unravel Vain's intent. There was too much blood on his head.

And not enough in his veins. He was failing. The illumination cast by the bonfire seemed to shrink around him. He had so little time left –

Listen, he started to say. This is what we're going to do. But his voice made no sound.

His hand groped for Brinn's shoulder. Help me. I've got to hold on. A little longer.

'Covenant.'

Linden's voice tugged him back into focus. She stood before him. Somehow, she had pulled herself out of her inner rout. Her eyes searched him. 'I thought I saw – ' She regarded the wild tangle of his beard as if it had prevented her from identifying him earlier.

321

Then her gaze found the thick red scars on his wrists. A sharp gasp winced through her teeth.

At once, she grabbed his forearms, drew his wrists into the light. 'I was right. You've lost blood. A lot of it.' Her physician's training rose up in her. She studied him, gauging his condition with her eyes and hands. 'You need a transfusion.'

The next moment, she perceived the newness of the scars. Her gaze jumped to his face. 'What did they do to you?'

At first, he could not respond. The soothtell was too exigent; he felt unable to bear the answer she needed.

But she misunderstood his silence. Abomination stretched her visage. 'Did you – ?'

Her apprehension broke him out of his paralysis. 'No. Not that. They did it to me. I'll be all right.'

A sag of relief softened her expression. But her eyes did not leave his face. She struggled for words as if the conflict of her emotions blocked her throat. Finally, she said hoarsely, 'I heard you shout. We almost got free.' Her stare drifted out of focus, turned inward. 'For a while, I would have given my soul to hear you shout again.' But memories made her flee outward again. 'Tell me – ' she began, fighting for severity as if it were essential to her. 'Tell me what happened to you.'

He shook his head. 'I'm all right.' What else could he say? 'Gibbon wanted blood. I didn't have a chance to refuse.' He knew that he should explain, that all his companions needed to know what he had learned in the soothtell. But he had no strength.

As if to spare Covenant the necessity of speech, Brinn said flatly, 'The ur-Lord's life was forfeit in the soothtell. Yet with wild magic he healed himself.'

At that, Linden's orbs darkened. Her lips echoed soundlessly, Healed? Her gaze dropped to the old scar behind the cut in his shirt. The recovery of determination which had drawn her out of herself seemed to crumple. Losses which he could not begin to understand overflowed from her eyes. She turned away from him, turned her face towards the night. 'Then you don't need me.'

Hollian reached out to her. Like a child, Linden put her arms around Hollian's neck and buried her face in the eh-Brand's shoulder.

Covenant did not react. The pressure of his rage and grief was all that stood between him and darkness. He could not move without falling. *What did that bastard do to you?*

'Ur-Lord,' Brinn said, 'we must not delay. The na-Mhoram was not slain. Surely the Clave will soon strike against us.'

'I know.' Covenant's heart was crying uselessly, Linden! and hot streaks of self-reproach ran from his eyes; but his voice was adamantine. 'We'll go. As soon as Memla gets here.' He did not doubt that Memla would come. She had no choice; she had already betrayed the Clave for him. Too many people had already done too much for him.

'That is well,' Brinn replied. 'Where will we go?'

Covenant did not falter. He was sure of what he had to do. His Dead had prepared him for this. 'To find the One Tree. I'm going to make a new Staff of Law.'

His auditors fell abruptly silent. Incomprehension clouded Hollian's face. Sunder frowned as if he wanted to speak but could not find the right words. The knot of Stonedownors and Woodhelvennin held themselves still. Vain betrayed no flicker of interest. But the eyes of the *Haruchai* shone.

'The old tellers,' Brinn said slowly, 'relate that the Lords, even at the time of Kevin, had a legend of the One Tree, from which the Staff of Law was made. Ur-Lord Covenant, you conceive a bold undertaking. You will be accompanied. But how will you seek the One Tree? We have no knowledge of it.'

No knowledge, Covenant breathed wanly. He had guessed as much. South of the Land lay the lifeless Grey Desert. In the north, the long winter and the Northron Climbs was said to be impassable. And to the west, where the *Haruchai* lived, there was no knowledge of the One Tree. He accepted that. If Berek had gone west to find the One Tree, he would surely have encountered Brinn's people. With an effort, Covenant answered, 'Neither do I. But we'll go east. To the Sea.' Where the Giants had come from. 'To get away from the Clave. After that – I don't know.'

Brinn nodded. 'It is good. This the *Haruchai* will do. Cail, Stell, Ceer, Harn, Hergrom, and myself will share your quest, to ward you and your companions. Two score will return to our people, to give them the knowledge we have gained.' His voice sharpened slightly. 'And to consider our reply to the depredations of this Clave. Those who remain will see these Stonedownors and Woodhelvennin to their homes – if such aid is desired.'

The faces of the nine freed people of the Land expressed immediately their eagerness to accept Brinn's offer.

'The old tellers speak much of the Giants – of their fidelity and laughter, and of their dying,' Brinn concluded. 'Gladly will we look upon their home and upon the Sea which they loved.'

Now, Covenant said to himself. If ever he intended to refuse the *Haruchai*, escape his being dependent on and responsible for them again after four thousand years, now was the time. But he could not. He was no longer able to stand without Brinn's support. Isn't it bad enough, he groaned, that I'm the one who destroyed the Staff? Opened the door for the Sunbane? Do I have to carry this, too? But he needed the *Haruchai* and could not refuse.

For a moment, the night reeled; but then he felt hands touch his chest, and saw Sunder standing before him. The Graveller held his chin up, exposing his damaged neck as if with that injury he had earned answers. His eyes reflected the firelight like the echoing of his torn mind.

'Covenant,' he said in a clenched tone, using that name instead of the title ur-Lord, as if he sought to cut through awe and power and command to the man behind them. 'I have journeyed far in your name, and will journey further. But there is fear in me. The eh-Brand foretells a sun of pestilence – after but two days of rain. In freeing us, you have damaged the Clave. And now the Sunbane quickens. Perhaps you have done such harm that the Clave can no longer moderate the Sunbane. Perhaps you have wrought a great peril for the Land.'

Covenant heard the personal urgency of Sunder's question; but for a time he lacked the fortitude to reply. Sunder's doubt pained him, weakened him. His veins were empty of life, and his muscles could no longer support him. Even the warmth of the *krill* under his belt had faded into his general inurement. But Sunder was his friend. The Graveller had already sacrificed too much for him. Fumbling among his frailties, he gave the first answer he found.

'The na-Mhoram is a Raver. Like Marid.'

But that did not satisfy Sunder. 'So Linden Avery has said. Yet the Clave moderated the Sunbane for the sake of the Land, and now that moderation has been weakened.'

'No.' Somewhere within him, Covenant discovered a moment of strength. 'The Clave doesn't moderate the Sunbane. They've been using it to hurt the Land. Feeding it with blood. They've been serving Lord Foul for centuries.'

Sunder stared; incredulity seemed to hurt his face. Covenant's asseveration violated everything he had ever believed. 'Covenant.' Dismay scarred his voice. His hands made imploring gestures. 'How can it be true? It is too much. How can I know that it is true?'

'Because I say it's true.' The moment passed, leaving Covenant as weary as death. 'I paid for that soothtell with my blood. And I was here. Four thousand years ago. When the Land was healthy. What the Clave taught you is something they made up to justify all that bloodshed.' A distant part of him saw what he was doing, and protested. He was identifying himself with the truth, making himself responsible for it. Surely no man could keep such a promise. Hile Troy had tried – and had lost his soul to the Forestal of Garroting Deep as a consequence.

'Then – ' Sunder wrestled for comprehension. His features showed horror at the implications of what Covenant said – horror turning to rage. 'Then why do you not fight? Destroy the Clave – end this ill? If they are such an abomination?'

Covenant drooped against Brinn. 'I'm too weak.' He hardly heard himself. 'And I've already killed – ' A spasm of grief twisted his face. Twenty-one people! 'I swore I would never kill again.' But for Sunder's sake, he made one more effort to articulate what he believed. 'I don't want to fight them until I stop hating them.'

Slowly, the Graveller nodded. The bonfire became a roaring in Covenant's ears. For an instant of giddiness, he thought that Sunder was Nassic. Nassic with young, sane eyes. The Graveller, too, was capable of things which humbled Covenant.

There was movement around him. People were readying themselves for departure. They saluted him; but his numbness prevented him from responding. Escorted by nearly a score of *Haruchai*, they left the foothills. He did not watch them go. He hung on the verges of unconsciousness and fought to remain alive.

For a time, he drifted along the current of the bonfire. But then he felt himself turned in Brinn's arms, gently shaken erect. He pried his eyes wide, scraped his eyelids across the sabulous exhaustion in his gaze, and saw Memla.

She stood grimly before him. Her chasuble was gone, and her robe had been singed in places. Her age-stained hair straggled about her shoulders. Fire blisters marred her right cheek; her blunt features were battered. But her eyes were angry, and she faced Covenant with her *rukh* held ready.

At her back champed five of the Clave's huge Coursers.

Brinn nodded to her. 'Memla na-Mhoram-in,' he said flatly. 'The ur-Lord has awaited you.'

She gave Brinn a gesture of recognition without taking her eyes from Covenant. Her gruff voice both revealed and controlled her wrath. 'I cannot live with lies. I will accompany you.'

Covenant had no words for her. Mutely, he touched his right hand to his heart, then raised the palm towards her.

'I have brought Coursers,' she said. 'They were not well defended – but well enough to hamper me. Only five could I wrest from so many of the na-Mhoram-cro.' The beasts were laden with supplies. 'They are Din, Clang, Clangor, Annoy, and Clash.'

Covenant nodded. His head went on bobbing feebly, as if the muscles of his neck had fallen into caducity.

She gripped his gaze. 'But one matter must be open between us. With my *rukh*, I can wield the Banefire to aid our journey. This the Clave cannot prevent. But I in turn cannot prevent them from knowing where I am and what I do, through my *rukh*, Halfhand.' Her tone took on an inflection of appeal. 'I do not wish to set aside the sole power I possess.'

Her honesty and courage demanded an answer. With an effort that disfocused his eyes and made his head spin, he said, 'Keep it. I'll take the chance.'

His reply softened her features momentarily. 'When first we met,'

325

she said, 'your misdoubt was just, though I knew it not. Yet trust is preferable.' Then, abruptly, she stiffened again. 'But we must depart. Gibbon has gathered the Clave at the Banefire. While we delay, they raise the *Grim* against us.'

The *Grim*! Covenant could not block the surge of his dismay. It carried him over the edge, and he plunged like dead stone into darkness.

As he fell, he heard a cold wail from Revelstone – a cry like the keening of the great Keep, promising loss and blood. Or perhaps the wail was within himself.

21

SENDING

Sometime during the night, he wandered close to consciousness. He was being rocked on the back of a Courser. Arms reached around him from behind and knotted together over his heart. They supported him like bands of stone. *Haruchai* arms.

Someone said tensely, 'Are you not a healer? You must succour him.'

'No.' Linden's reply sounded small and wan, and complete. It made him moan deep in his throat.

Glints of *rukh*-fire hurt his eyes. When he shut out the sight, he faded away once more.

The next time he looked up, he saw the grey of dawn in fragments through the monstrous jungle. The lightening of the sky lay directly ahead of him. He was mounted on Din, with Memla before him and Brinn behind. Another Courser, carrying Ceer and Hergrom, led the way along the line Memla created with her *rukh*. The rest of the company followed Din.

As Covenant fumbled towards wakefulness, Memla's path ran into an area of relatively clear ground under the shade of a towering stand of rhododendron. There she halted. Over her shoulder, she called to the company, 'Remain mounted. The Coursers will spare us from the Sunbane.'

Behind him, Covenant heard Sunder mutter, 'Then it is true – '

But Hergrom dropped to the ground, began to accept supplies handed down by Ceer; and Brinn said, 'The *Haruchai* do not share this need to be warded.'

Immune? Covenant wondered dimly. Yes. How else had so many

of them been able to reach Revelstone unwarped?

Then the sun began to rise, sending spangles of crimson and misery through the vegetation. Once again, the eh-Brand had foretold the Sunbane accurately.

When the first touch of the sun was past, Memla ordered the Coursers to their knees, controlling them all with her command. The company began to dismount.

Covenant shrugged off Brinn's help and tried to stand alone. He found that he could. He felt as pale and weak as an invalid; but his muscles were at least able to hold his weight.

Unsteadily, he turned to look back westward through the retreating night for some sign of the na-Mhoram's *Grim*.

The horizon seemed clear.

Near him, Sunder and Stell had descended from one Courser, Hollian and Harn from another. Cail helped Linden down from the fifth beast. Covenant faced her with his frailty and concern; but she kept her gaze to herself, locked herself in her loneliness as if the very nerves of her eyes, the essential marrow of her bones, had been humiliated past bearing.

He left her alone. He did not know what to do, and felt too tenuous to do it.

While the *Haruchai* prepared food for the company — dried meat, bread, fruit, and *metheglin* — Memla produced from one of her sacks a large leather pouch of distilled *voure*, the pungent sap Covenant's friends had once used to ward off insects under the sun of pestilence. Carefully, she dabbed the concentrate on each of her companions, excluding only Vain. Covenant nodded at her omission. Perhaps *rukh*-fire could harm the Demondim-spawn. The Sunbane could not.

Covenant ate slowly and thoroughly, feeding his body's poverty. But all the time, a weight of apprehension impended towards him from the west. He had seen During Stonedown, had seen what the *Grim* could do. With an effort, he found his voice to ask Memla how long the raising of a *Grim* took.

She was clearly nervous. 'That is uncertain,' she muttered. 'The size of the *Grim*, and its range, must be considered.' Her gaze flicked to his face, leaving an almost palpable mark of anxiety across his cheek. 'I read them. Here.' Her hands tightened on her *rukh*. 'It will be very great.'

Very great, Covenant murmured. And he was so weak. He pressed his hands to the *krill*, and tried to remain calm.

A short time later, the company remounted. Memla drew on the Banefire to open a way for the huge Coursers. Again, Hergrom and Ceer — on Annoy, Memla said: the names of the beasts seemed important to her, as if she loved them in her blunt fashion — went first, followed by Covenant, Brinn, and the Rider on Din, then by

Cail and Linden on Clash, Sunder and Stell on Clang, Harn and Hollian on Clangor. Vain brought up the rear as if he were being sucked along without volition in the wake of the Coursers.

Covenant dozed repeatedly throughout the day. He had been too severely drained; he could not keep himself awake. Whenever the company paused for food, water, and rest, he consumed all the aliment he was given, striving to recover some semblance of strength. But between stops the rocking of Din's stride unmoored his awareness, so that he rode tides of dream and dread and insects, and could not anchor himself.

In periods of wakefulness, he knew from the rigidity of Memla's back that she wanted to flee and flee, and never stop. She, too, knew vividly what the *Grim* could do. But, towards evening, her endurance gave out. Under the shelter of a prodigious Gilden, she halted the quest for the night.

At first, while she started a fire, the air thronged with flying bugs of every description; and the boughs and leaves of the tree seethed with things which crawled and bored. But *voure* protected the company. And gradually, as dusk seeped into the jungle, macerating the effect of the Sunbane, the insects began to disappear. Their viscid stridulation faded as they retreated into gestation or sleep. Memla seated her weary bones beside the fire, dismissed the Coursers, and let the *Haruchai* care for her companions.

Sunder and Hollian seemed tired, as if they had not slept for days; but they were sturdy, with funds of stamina still untapped. Though they knew of the *Grim*, at least by rumour, their relief at escaping Revelstone outweighed their apprehension. They stood and moved together as if their imprisonment had made them intimate. Sunder seemed to draw ease from the eh-Brand, an anodyne for his old self-conflicts; her youth and her untormented sense of herself were a balm to the Graveller, who had shed his own wife and son and had chosen to betray his people for Covenant's sake. And she, in turn, found support and encouragement in his knotted resourcefulness, his determined struggle for conviction. They both had lost so much: Covenant was relieved to think that they could comfort each other. He could not have given them comfort.

But their companionship only emphasized Linden's isolation in his eyes. The Raver had done something to her. And Covenant, who had experience with such things, dreaded knowing what it was — and dreaded the consequences of not knowing.

As he finished his meal, he arrived at the end of his ability to support his ignorance. He was sitting near the fire. Memla rested, half-asleep, on one side of him. On the other sat Sunder and Hollian. Four of the *Haruchai* stood guard beyond the tree. Brinn and Cail moved silently around the fringes of the Gilden, alert for peril. Vain stood at the edge of the light like the essence of all black secrets. And among them, across the fire from Covenant, Linden huddled within herself, with her arms clasped around her knees and her eyes fixed on the blaze, as if she were a complete stranger.

He could not bear it. He had invested so much hope in her and knew so little about her; he had to know why she was so afraid. But he had no idea how to confront her. Her hidden wound made her untouchable. So for his own sake, as well as for the sake of his companions, he cleared his throat and began to tell his tale.

He left nothing out. From Andelain and the Dead to Stonemight Woodhelven, from Vain's violence to Hamako's *rhysh*, from his run across the Centre Plains to Memla's revelation of the Clave's mendacity, he told it all. And then he described the soothtell as fully as he could. His hands would not remain still as he spoke; so much of the memory made him writhe. He tugged at his beard, knitted his fingers together, clutched his left fist over his wedding band, and told his friends what he had witnessed.

He understood now why the Raver had been willing to let him see the truth of the Land's history. Lord Foul wanted him to perceive the fetters of action and consequence which bound him to his guilt, wanted him to blame himself for the destruction of the Staff, and for the Sunbane, and for every life the Clave sacrificed. So that he would founder in culpability, surrender his ring in despair and self-abhorrence. Lord Foul, who laughed at lepers. *At the last there will be but one choice for you.* In that context, the venom in him made sense. It gave him power he could not control. Power to kill people. Guilt. It was a prophecy of his doom – a self-fulfilling prophecy.

That, too, he explained, hoping Linden would raise her eyes, look at him, try to understand. But she did not. Her mouth stretched into severity; but she held to her isolation. Even when he detailed how the seeds planted by his Dead had led him to conceive a quest for the One Tree, intending to make a new Staff of Law so that thereby he could oppose Lord Foul and contest the Sunbane without self-abandonment, even then she did not respond. Finally, he fell silent, bereft of words.

For a time, the company remained still with him. No one asked any questions; they seemed unwilling to probe the pain he had undergone. But then Sunder spoke. To answer Covenant, he told what had happened to Linden, Hollian, and him after Covenant had entered Andelain.

He described Santonin and the Stonemight, described the Rider's coercion, described the way in which he and Hollian had striven to convince Gibbon that Covenant was lost or dead. But after that, he had not much to tell. He had been cast into a cell with little food and water, and less hope. Hollian's plight had been the same. Both had heard the clamour of Covenant's first entrance into the hold, and nothing more.

Then Covenant thought that surely Linden would speak. Surely she would complete her part of the tale. But she did not. She hid her face against her knees and sat huddled there as if she were bracing herself against a memory full of whips.

'Linden.' How could he leave her alone? He needed the truth from her. 'Now you know how Kevin must have felt.'

Kevin Landwaster, last of Berek's line. Linden had said, *I don't believe in evil.* Kevin also had tried not to believe in evil. He had unwittingly betrayed the Land by failing to perceive Lord Foul's true nature in time, and had thereby set the Despiser on the path to victory. Thus he had fallen into despair. Because of what he had done, he had challenged the Despiser to the Ritual of Desecration, hoping to destroy Lord Foul by reaving the Land. But in that, too, he had failed. He had succeeded at laying waste the Land he loved, and at losing the Staff of Law; but Lord Foul had endured.

All this Covenant told her. 'Don't you see?' he said, imploring her to hear him. 'Despair is no answer. It's what Foul lives on. Whatever happened to you, it doesn't have to be like this.' Linden, listen to me!

But she did not listen, gave no sign that she was able to hear him. If he had not seen the shadows of distress shifting behind her eyes, he might have believed that she had fallen back into the coma which Gibbon had levied upon her.

Sunder sat glowering as if he could not choose between his empathy for Linden and his understanding of Covenant. Hollian's dark eyes were blurred with tears. Brinn and Cail watched as if they were the models for Vain's impassivity. None of them offered Covenant any help.

He tried a different tack. 'Look at Vain.' *Linden!* 'Tell me what you see.'

She did not respond.

'I don't know whether or not I can trust him. I don't have your eyes. I need you to tell me what he is.'

She did not move. But her shoulders tautened as if she were screaming within herself.

'That old man.' His voice was choked by need and fear. 'On Haven Farm. You saved his life. He told you to *Be true.*'

She flinched. Jerking up her head, she gaped at him with eyes as injured as if they had been gouged into the clenched misery of her soul. Then she was on her feet, fuming like a magma of bitterness. '*You!*' she cried. 'You keep talking about desecration. This is your doing. Why did you have to sell yourself for Joan? Why did you have to get us into this? Don't you call *that* desecration?'

'Linden.' Her passion swept him upright; but he could not reach out to her. The fire lay between them as if she had lit it there in her fury.

'Of course you don't. You can't *see*. You don't *know*.' Her hands clawed the air over her breasts as if she wanted to tear her flesh. 'You think it will help if you go charging off on some crazy quest. Make a new Staff of Law.' She was savage with gall. 'You don't count, and you don't even *know it*!'

He repeated her name. Sunder and Hollian had risen to their feet. Memla held her *rukh* ready, and Cail stood poised nearby, as if both Rider and *Haruchai* felt violence in the air.

'What did he do to you?' *What did that bastard do to you?*

'He said you don't count!' Abruptly, she was spouting words, hurling them at him as if he were the cause of her distress. 'All they care about is your ring. The rest is me. He said, "You have been especially chosen for this desecration. You are being forged as iron is forged to achieve the ruin of the Earth."' Her voice thickened like blood around the memory. 'Because I can *see*. That's how they're going to make me do what they want. By torturing me with what I see, and feel, and hear. You're making me do exactly what they want!'

The next instant, her outburst sprang to a halt. Her hands leaped to her face, trying to block out visions. Her body went rigid, as if she were on the verge of convulsions; a moan tore its way between her teeth. Then she sagged.

In desolation, she whispered, 'He touched me.'

Touched — ?

'Covenant.' She dropped her hands, let him see the full anguish in her visage. 'You've got to get me out of here. Back to where I belong. Where my life means something. Before they make me kill you.'

'I know,' he said, because she had to have an answer. 'That's another reason why I want to find the One Tree.' But within himself he felt suddenly crippled. *You don't count*. He had placed so much hope in her, in the possibility that she was free of Lord Foul's manipulations; and now that hope lay in wreckage. 'The Lords used the Staff to call me here.' In one stroke, he had been reft of everything. 'A Staff is the only thing I know of that can send us back.'

Everything except the *krill*, and his old intransigence.

Especially chosen — Hell and blood! He wanted to cover his face; he could have wept like a child. But Linden's eyes clung to him desperately, trying to believe in him. Sunder and Hollian held each other against a fear they could not name. And Memla's countenance was blunt-moulded into a shape of sympathy, as if she knew what it meant to be discounted. Only the *Haruchai* appeared unmoved — the *Haruchai*, and Vain.

When Linden asked, 'Your ring?' he met her squarely.

'I can't control it.'

Abruptly, Memla's expression became a flinch of surprise, as if he had uttered something appalling.

He ignored her. While his heart raged for grief, as if tears were a debt which he owed to his mortality and could not pay, he stretched out his arms. There in front of all his companions he gave himself a VSE.

Ah, you are stubborn yet.

Yes. By God. Stubborn.

Acting with characteristic detached consideration, Brinn handed Covenant a pouch of *metheglin*. Covenant lifted it between himself and his friends, so that they could not see his face, and drank it dry. Then he walked away into the darkness around the Gilden, used the night to hide him. After a time, he lay down among the things he had lost, and closed his eyes.

Brinn roused him with the dawn, got him to his feet in time to meet the second rising of the sun of pestilence, protected by his boots. The rest of the quest was already awake. Sunder and Hollian had joined Memla on pieces of stone; the *Haruchai* were busy preparing food; Linden stood gazing at the approaching incarnadine. Her face was sealed against its own vulnerability; but when she noticed Covenant, her eyes acknowledged him sombrely. After the conflicts of the previous evening, her recognition touched him like a smile.

He found that he felt stronger. But with recovery came a renewal of fear. The na-Mhoram's *Grim* –

Memla bore herself as if throughout the night she had not forgotten that peril. Her ageing features were lined with apprehension, and her hands trembled on her *rukh*. To answer Covenant's look, she murmured, 'Still he raises it, and is not content. It will be a *Grim* to rend our souls.' For a moment, her eyes winced to his face as if she needed reassurance. But then she jerked away, began snapping at her companions to make them hurry.

Soon the company was on its way, moving at a hard canter down the path which Memla invoked from the Banefire. Her urgency and Covenant's tight dread infected the Stonedownors, marked even Linden. The quest rode in silence, as if they could feel the *Grim* poised like a blade at the backs of their necks.

The jungle under the sun of pestilence aggravated Covenant's sense of impending disaster. The insects thronged around him like incarnations of disease. Every malformed bough and bush was a-crawl with malformed bugs. Some of the trees were so heavily veined with termites that the wood looked leprous. And the smell of rot had become severe. Under the aegis of the Sunbane, his guts ached, half expecting the vegetation to break open and begin suppurating.

Time dragged. Weakness crept through his muscles again. When the company finally rode into the relief of sunset, his neck and shoulders throbbed from the strain of looking backward for some sign of the *Grim*. Shivers ran through the marrow of his bones. As soon as Memla picked a camping place under the shelter of a megalithic stand of eucalyptus, he dropped to the ground, hoping to steady himself on the Earth's underlying granite. But his hands and feet were too numb to feel anything.

Around him, his companions dismounted. Almost at once, Linden went over to Hollian. The flesh of Linden's face was pale and taut, stretched tight over her skull. She accosted the eh-Brand purposefully, but then had to fumble for words. 'The insects,' she murmured. 'The smell. It's worse. Worse than any other sun. I can't shut it all out.' Her eyes watched the way her hands clung together, as if only that knot held her in one piece. 'I can't – What's it going to be tomorrow?'

Sunder had moved to stand near Hollian. As Linden fell silent, he nodded grimly. 'Never in all my life have I faced a sun of pestilence and encountered so little harm.' His tone was hard. 'I had not known the Clave could journey so untouched by that which is fear and abhorrence to the people of the Land. And now ur-Lord Covenant teaches us that the Clave's immunity has been purchased by the increase rather than the decline of the Sunbane.' His voice darkened as if he were remembering all the people he had shed. 'I do not misdoubt him. But I, too, desire tidings of the morrow's sun.'

Memla indicated with a shrug that such tidings could not alter her anxiety. But Covenant joined Linden and Sunder. He felt suddenly sickened by the idea that perhaps the soothtell had been a lie designed by Gibbon-Raver to mislead him. If two days of rain were followed by only two days of pestilence – Gripping himself, he waited for Hollian's response.

She acceded easily. Her light smile reminded him that she was not like Sunder. With her *lianar* and her skill, she had always been able to touch the Sunbane for the benefit of others; she had never had to kill people to obtain blood. Therefore she did not loathe her own capabilities as Sunder did his.

She stepped a short distance away to give herself space, then took out her dirk and wand. Seating herself on the leaves which littered the ground, she summoned her concentration. Covenant, Linden, and Sunder watched intently as she placed the *lianar* on her lap, gripped her dirk in her left hand and directed the point against her right palm. The words of invocation soughed past her lips. They clasped the company like a liturgy of worship for something fatal. Even the *Haruchai* left their tasks to stand ready. The thought that she was about to cut herself made Covenant scowl; but he had long ago left behind the days when he could have protested what she was doing.

Slowly, she drew a small cut on her palm. As blood welled from the incision, she closed her fingers on the *lianar*. Dusk had deepened into night around the quest, concealing her from the watchers. Yet even Covenant's impercipient senses could feel her power thickening like motes of fire concatenating towards flame. For a bated moment, the air was still. Then she sharpened her chant, and the wand took light.

Red flames bloomed like Sunbane orchids. They spread up into the air and down her forearm to the ground. Crimson tendrils curled about her as if she were being overgrown. They seemed bright; but they cast no illumination; the night remained dark.

Intuitively, Covenant understood her fire. With chanting and blood and *lianar*, she reached out towards the morrow's sun; and the flames took their colour from what that sun would be. Her fire was the precise hue of the sun's pestilential aura.

A third sun of pestilence. He sighed his relief softly. Here, at least, he had no reason to believe that the soothtell had been false.

But before the eh-Brand could relax her concentration, release her foretelling, the fire abruptly changed.

A streak of blackness as absolute as Vain's skin shot from the wood, scarred the flames with ebony. At first, it was only a lash across the crimson. But it grew, expanded among the flames until it dominated them, obscured them.

Quenched them.

Instantly, night covered the companions, isolating them from each other. Covenant could perceive nothing except a faint tang of smoke in the air, as if Hollian's wand had been in danger of being consumed.

He swore hoarsely under his breath and swung out his arms until he touched Brinn on one side, Linden on the other. Then he heard feet spring through the leaves and heard Sunder cry, 'Hollian!'

The next moment, Memla also cried out in horror. 'Sending!' Fire raged from her *rukh*, cracked like a flail among the trees, making the night lurid. 'It comes!' Covenant saw Ceer standing behind the Rider as if to protect her from attack. The other *Haruchai* formed a defensive ring around the company.

'*Gibbon!*' Memla howled. 'Abomination!' Her fire savaged the air as if she were trying to strike at Revelstone from a distance of nearly two score leagues. 'By all the Seven Hells – !'

Covenant reacted instinctively. He surged into the range of Memla's fire and gripped her forearms to prevent her from striking at him. 'Memla!' he yelled into her face. '*Memla!* How much time have we got?'

His grin or his demand reached her. Her gaze came into focus on him. With a convulsive shudder, she dropped her fire, let darkness close over the quest. When she spoke, her voice came out of the

334

night like the whispering of condor wings.

'There is time. The *Grim* cannot instantly cross so many leagues. Perhaps as much as a day remains to us.

'But it is the na-Mhoram's *Grim*, and has been two days in the raising. Such a sending might break Revelstone itself.'

She took a breath which trembled. 'Ur-Lord, we cannot evade this *Grim*. It will follow my *rukh* and rend us utterly.' Her voice winced in her throat. 'I had believed that the wild magic would give us hope. But if it is beyond your control – '

At Covenant's back, a small flame jumped into life and caught wood. Sunder had lit a faggot. He held it up like a torch, lifting the company out of the dark.

Hollian was gasping through her teeth, fighting not to cry out. The violation of her foretelling had hurt her intimately.

'That's right,' Covenant gritted. 'I can't control it.' His hands manacled Memla's wrists, striving to keep her from hysteria. 'Hang on. Think. We've got to do something about this.' His eyes locked hers. 'Can you leave your *rukh* behind?'

'Covenant!' she wailed in immediate anguish. 'It is who I am! I am nothing to you without it.' He tightened his grasp. She flinched away from his gaze. Her voice became a dry moan. 'Without my *rukh*, I cannot part the trees. And I cannot command the Coursers. It is the power to which they have been bred. Losing it, my hold upon them will be lost. They will scatter from us. Perhaps they will turn against us.' Her mien appeared to be crumbling in the unsteady torchlight. 'This doom is upon my head,' she breathed. 'In ignorance and folly, I lured you to Revelstone.'

'Damnation!' Covenant rasped, cursing half to himself. He felt trapped; and yet he did not want Memla to blame herself. He had asked for her help. He wrestled down his dismay. 'All right,' he panted. 'Call the Coursers. Let's try to outrun it.'

She gaped at him. 'It is the *Grim*! It cannot be outrun.'

'Goddamn it, he's only one Raver!' His fear made him livid. 'The further he has to send it, the weaker it's going to be. Let's try!'

For one more moment, Memla could not recover her courage. But then the muscles of her face tightened, and a look of resolution or fatality came into her eyes. 'Yes, ur-Lord,' she gritted. 'It will be weakened somewhat. Let us make the attempt.'

As he released her, she began shouting for the Coursers.

They came out of the night like huge chunks of darkness. The *Haruchai* threw sacks of supplies and bundles of firewood on to the broad backs. Covenant wheeled to face his companions.

Sunder and Hollian stood behind Linden. She crouched among the leaves, with her hands clamped over her face. The Stonedownors made truncated gestures towards her but did not know how to reach her. Her voice came out as if it were being throttled.

335

'I can't – '

Covenant exploded. *'Move!'*

She flinched, recoiled to her feet. Sunder and Hollian jerked into motion as if they were breaking free of a trance. Cail abruptly swept Linden from the ground and boosted her lightly on to Clash. Scrambling forward, Covenant climbed up behind Memla. In a whirl, he saw Sunder and Hollian on their mounts, saw the *Haruchai* spring into position, saw Memla's *rukh* gutter, then burst alive like a scar across the dark.

At once, the Coursers launched themselves down the line of Memla's path.

The night on either side of her fire seemed to roil like thunderheads. Covenant could not see past her back; he feared that Din would career at any moment into a failure of the path, crash against boulders, plunge into lurking ravines or gullies. But more than that, he feared his ring, feared the demand of power which the *Grim* would put upon him.

Memla permitted no disaster. At unexpected moments, her line veered past sudden obstacles; yet with her fire and her will she kept the company safe and swift. She was running for her life, for Covenant's life, for the hope of the Land; and she took her Coursers through the ruinous jungle like bolts from a crossbow.

They ran while the moon rose – ran as it arced overhead – ran and still ran after it had set. The Coursers were creatures of the Sunbane, and did not tire. Just after dawn, Memla slapped them to a halt. When Covenant dismounted, his legs trembled. Linden moved as if her entire body had been beaten with clubs. Even Sunder and Hollian seemed to have lost their hardiness. But Memla's visage was set in lines of extremity; and she held her *rukh* as if she strove to tune her soul to the pitch of iron.

She allowed the company only a brief rest for a meal. But even that time was too long. Without warning, Stell pointed towards the sun. The mute intensity of his gesture snatched every eye eastwards.

The sun stood above the horizon, its sick red aura burning like a promise of infirmity. But the corona was no longer perfect. Its leading edge wore a stark black flaw.

The mark was wedge-shaped, like an attack of ur-viles, and aligned as if it were being hammered into the sun from Revelstone.

Linden's groan was more eloquent than any outcry.

Shouting a curse, Memla drove her companions back to the Coursers. In moments, the quest had remounted, and the beasts raced against black malice.

They could not win. Though Memla's path was strong and true – though the Coursers ran at the full stretch of their great legs – the blackness grew swiftly. By mid-morning, it had devoured half the sun's anadem.

Pressure mounted against Covenant's back. His thoughts took on the rhythm of Din's strides: I was not – Must not – Visions of killing came; ten years or four millennia ago, at the battle of Soaring Woodhelven, he had slain Cavewights. And later, he had driven a knife into the heart of the man who had murdered Lena. He could not think of power except in terms of killing.

He had no control over his ring.

Then the company burst out of thick jungle towards a savannah. There, nothing obstructed the terrain except the coarse grass, growing twice as tall as the Coursers, north, south, and east, and the isolated mounds of rock standing like prodigious cairns at great distances from each other. Covenant had an instant of overview before the company plunged down the last hillside into the savannah. The sky opened; and he could not understand how the heavens remained so untrammelled around such a sun. Then Memla's path sank into the depths of the grass.

The quest ran for another league before Hollian cried over the rumble of hooves, 'It comes!'

Covenant flung a look behind him.

A thunderhead as stark as the sun's wound boiled out of the west. Its seething was poised like a fist; and it moved with such swiftness that the Coursers seemed not to be racing at all.

'Run!' he gasped at Memla's back.

As if in contradiction, she wrenched Din to a halt. The Courser skidded, almost fell. Covenant nearly lost his seat. The other beasts veered away, crashing frenetically through the grass. 'Heaven and Earth!' Sunder barked. Controlling all the Coursers, Memla sent them wheeling and stamping around her, battering down the grass to clear a large circle.

As the vegetation east of him was crushed, Covenant saw why she had stopped.

Directly across her path marched a furious column of creatures.

For a moment, he thought that they were Cavewights – Cavewights running on all fours in a tight swath sixty feet wide, crowding shoulder to shoulder out of the south in a stream without beginning or end. They had the stocky frames, gangrel limbs, blunt heads of Cavewights. But if these were Cavewights they had been hideously altered by the Sunbane. Chitinous plating armoured their backs and appendages; their fingers and toes had become claws; their chins were split into horned jaws like mandibles. And they had no eyes, no features; their faces had been erased. Nothing marked their foreskulls except long antennae which hunted ahead of them, searching out their way.

They rushed as if they were running headlong towards prey. The line of their march had already been torn down to bare dirt by the leaders. In their haste, they sounded like the swarming of gargantuan ants – formication punctuated by the sharp clack of jaws.

'Hellfire!' Covenant panted. The blackness around the sun was nearly complete; the *Grim* was scant leagues away, and closing rapidly. And he could see no way past this river of pestilential creatures. If they were of Cavewightish stock – He shuddered at the thought. The Cavewights had been mighty earth delvers, tremendously strong. And these creatures were almost as large as horses. If anything interrupted their single-minded march, they would tear even Memla's beasts limb from limb.

Linden began to whimper, then bit herself into silence. Sunder stared at the creatures with dread-glazed eyes. Hollian's hair lay on her shoulders like raven wings, emphasizing her pale features as if she were marked for death. Memla sagged in front of Covenant like a woman with a broken spine.

Turning to Brinn, Covenant asked urgently, 'Will it pass?'

In answer, Brinn nodded towards Hergrom and Ceer. Ceer had risen to stand erect on Annoy's back. Hergrom promptly climbed on to Ceer's shoulders, balanced there to gain a view over the grass. A moment later, Brinn reported, 'We are far-sighted, but the end of this cannot be seen.'

Bloody hell! He was afraid of wild magic, power beyond control or choice. I must not – ! But he knew that he would use it if he had to. He could not simply let his companions die.

The thunderhead approached like the blow of an axe. Blackness garrotted the sun. The light began to dim.

A rush of protest went through him. Fear or no fear, this doom was intolerable. 'All right.' Ignoring the distance to the ground, he dropped from Din's back. 'We'll have to fight here.'

Brinn joined him. Sunder and Stell dismounted from Clang, Hollian and Harn from Clangor. Cail pulled Linden down from Clash and set her on her feet. Her hands twitched as if they were searching for courage; but she found none. Covenant tore his gaze away, so that her distress would not make him more dangerous. 'Sunder,' he rapped out, 'you've got your *orcrest*. Memla has her *rukh*. Is there some way you can work together? Can you hit that thing – ' he grimaced at the *Grim* – 'before it hits us?'

The cloud was almost overhead. It shed a preternatural twilight across the savannah, quenching the day.

'No.' Memla had not dismounted. She spoke as if her mouth were full of ashes. 'There is not time. It is too great.'

Her dismay hurt Covenant like a demand for wild magic. He wanted to shout, I can't control it! Don't you understand? I might kill you all! But she went on speaking as if his power or incapacity had become irrelevant. 'You must not die. That is certain.' Her quietness seemed suddenly terrible. 'When the way is clear, cross instantly. This march will seal the gap swiftly.' She straightened her shoulders and lifted her face to the sky. 'The *Grim* has found you because of me. Let it be upon my head.'

Before anyone could react, she turned Din and guided it towards the blind rushing creatures. As she moved, she brought up the fire of her *rukh*, holding it before her like a sabre.

Covenant and Sunder sprang after her. But Brinn and Stell interposed themselves. Cursing, the Graveller fought to break free; but Stell mastered him without effort. Furiously, Sunder shouted, 'Release me! Do you not see that she means to die?'

Covenant ignored Sunder: he locked himself to Brinn's flat eyes. Softly, dangerously, he breathed, 'Don't do this.'

Brinn shrugged. 'I have sworn to preserve your life.'

'Bannor took the same Vow.' Covenant did not struggle. But he glared straight at the *Haruchai*. People have died because of me. How much more do you think I can stand? 'That's how Elena got killed. I might have been able to save her.'

The *Grim* began to boil almost directly above the quest. But the Cavewightlike creatures were unaware of it. They marched on like blind doom, shredding the dirt of the plains.

'Bannor maintained his Vow,' Brinn said, as if it cost him no effort to refute Covenant. 'So the old tellers say, and their tale has descended from Bannor himself. It was First Mark Morin, sworn to the High Lord, who failed.' He nodded towards Ceer. In response, Ceer sprinted after Memla and vaulted lightly on to Din's back. 'We also,' Brinn concluded, 'will maintain the promise we have made, to the limit of our strength.'

But Memla reacted in rage too thick for shouting. 'By the Seven Hells!' she panted. 'I will not have this. You have sworn nothing to me.' Brandishing her *rukh*, she faced Ceer. 'If you do not dismount, I will burn you with my last breath, and all this company shall die for naught!'

Memla! Covenant tried to yell. But he could not. He had nothing to offer her; his fear of wild magic choked him. Helplessly, he watched as Ceer hesitated, glanced towards Brinn. The *Haruchai* consulted together in silence, weighing their commitments. Then Ceer sprang to the ground and stepped out of Din's way.

No! Covenant protested. She's going to get herself killed!

He had no time to think. Gloaming occluded the atmosphere. The ravening *Grim* poised itself above Memla, focused on her fire. The heavens around the cloud remained impossibly cerulean; but the cloud itself was pitch and midnight. It descended as it seethed, dropping towards its victims.

Under it, the air crackled as if it were being scorched.

The Coursers skittered. Sunder took out his *orcrest*, then seized Hollian's hand and pulled her to the far side of the circle, away from Memla. The *Haruchai* flowed into defensive positions among the companions and the milling beasts.

Amid the swirl of movement, Vain stood, black under black, as if he were inured to darkness.

Hergrom placed himself near Vain. But Memla was planning to die; Linden was foundering in ill; and Covenant felt outraged by the unanswerable *must/must not* of his ring. He yelled at Hergrom, 'Let him take care of himself!'

The next instant, he staggered to his knees. The air shattered with a heart-stopping concussion. The *Grim* broke into bits, became intense black flakes floating downwards like a fall of snow.

With fearsome slowness, they fell — crystals of sun-darkness, tangible night, force which not even stone could withstand.

Howling defiance, Memla launched fire at the sky.

Din bunched under her and charged out into the march of the creatures. A series of tremendous heaves carried beast and Rider towards the centre of the stream.

The flakes of the *Grim* drifted in her direction, following the lodestone of her *rukh*. Its dense centre, the nexus of its might, passed beyond the quest.

The creatures immediately mobbed her mount. Din let out a piercing scream at the tearing of claws and mandibles. Only the plunging of its hooves, the slash of its spurs, the thickness of its coat, protected it.

Then the *Grim* fell skirling around her head. Her fire blazed: she lashed out, trying to keep herself and Din from being touched. Every flake her flame struck burst in a glare of darkness, and was gone. But for every flake she destroyed, she was assailed by a hundred more.

Covenant watched her in an agony of helplessness, knowing that if he turned to his ring now he could not strike for her without striking her. The *Grim* was thickest around her; but its edges covered the march as well as the quest. The creatures were swept into confusion as killing bits as big as fists fell among them.

Vermeil shot from Sunder's *orcrest* towards the darkened sun. Covenant yelled in encouragement. By waving the Sunstone back and forth, the Graveller picked flakes out of the air with his shaft, consuming them before they could reach him or Hollian.

Around the company, the *Haruchai* dodged like dervishes. They used flails of pampas grass to strike down the flakes. Each flake destroyed the whip which touched it; but the *Haruchai* snatched up more blades and went on fighting.

Abruptly, Covenant was thrust from his feet. A piece of blackness missed his face. Brinn pitched him past it, then jerked him up again. Heaving Covenant from side to side, Brinn danced among the falling *Grim*. Several flakes hit where they had been standing. Obsidian flares set fire to the grass.

The grass began to burn in scores of places.

Yet Vain stood motionless, with a look of concentration on his face. Flakes struck his skin, his tunic. Instead of detonating, they melted on him and ran hissing down his raiment, his legs, like water on hot metal.

Covenant gaped at the Demondim-spawn, then lost sight of him as Brinn went dodging through the smoke.

He caught a glimpse of Memla. She fought extravagantly for her life, hurled fire with all the outrage of her betrayal by the na-Mhoram. But the focus of the *Grim* formed a mad swarm around her. And the moiling creatures had already torn Din to its knees. In patches, its hide had been bared to the bone.

Without warning, a flake struck the Courser's head. Din collapsed, tumbling the Rider headlong among the creatures.

Memla! Covenant struggled to take hold of his power. But Brinn's thrusting and dodging reft him of concentration. And already he was too late.

Yet Ceer leaped forward with the calm abandon of the *Haruchai*. Charging into the savagery, he fought towards Memla.

She regained her feet in a splash of fire. For an instant, she stood, gallant and tattered, hacking fury at the creatures. Ceer almost reached her.

Then Covenant lost her as Brinn tore him out from under a black flurry. Flames and *Haruchai* reeled about him; the flakes were everywhere. But he fought upright in time to see Memla fall with a scream of darkness in her chest.

As she died and dropped her *rukh*, the four remaining Coursers went berserk.

They erupted as if only her will had contained the madness of their fear. Yowling among the grass fires, two of them dashed out of the circle and fled across the savannah. Another ploughed into the breach the *Grim* had made in the march. As it passed, Ceer suddenly appeared at its side. Fighting free of the creatures, he grabbed the Courser's hair and used the beast to pull him away.

The fourth beast attacked the company. Its vehemence caught the *Haruchai* unprepared. Its eyes burned scarlet as it plunged against Hergrom, struck him down with its chest.

Hergrom had been helping Cail to protect Linden.

Instantly, the beast reared at her.

Cail tried to shove her aside. She stumbled, fell the wrong way.

Covenant saw her sprawl under the Courser's hooves. One of them clipped her head as the beast stamped, trying to crush her.

Again, the Courser reared.

Cail stood over her. Covenant could not strike without hitting the *Haruchai*. He fought to run forward.

As the Courser hammered down, Cail caught its legs. For one

impossible moment, he held the huge animal off her. Then it began to bend him.

Linden!

With a prodigious effort, Cail heaved the Courser to the side. Its hooves missed Linden as they landed.

Blood appeared. From shoulder to elbow, Cail's left arm had been ripped open by one of the beast's spurs.

It reared again.

Covenant's mind went instantly white with power. But before he could grasp it, use it, Brinn knocked him away from another cluster of flakes. The grass was giddy fire and death, whirling. He flipped to his feet and swung back towards Linden; but his heart had already frozen within him.

As his vision cleared, he saw Sunder hurl a blast of Sunbane-fire which struck the Courser's chest, knocking it to its knees. Lurching upright again, it pounded its pain away from the quest.

But Linden lay under the *Grim*, surrounded by growing fires, and did not move.

22

PLAIN OF FIRE

Fires leaped in front of him, obscuring her from his sight. The *Grim*-fall darkened the air. The thrashing and clatter of the creatures filled his ears. He could not see if Linden were still alive. Brinn kept heaving him from side to side, kept lashing handfuls of grass around his head.

Sunder's fire scored the atmosphere like straight red lightning. Now the corrosive flakes began to concentrate around him.

Covenant broke free of Brinn, went surging towards Linden.

Hergrom had lifted her from the ground. The *Haruchai* carried her in an elaborate dance of evasion. She hung limp in his arms. Blood seeping from the back of her head matted her hair.

An argent shout gathered in Covenant's chest.

But as he raised his head to howl power, he saw the blackness around the sun fraying. Pestilential red glistened through the ebony. The last *Grim*-flakes were drifting towards Sunder's head. The Graveller was able to consume them all.

At once, Covenant locked his throat, left the wild magic unspoken. In a rush, he reached Hergrom and Linden.

Cail stood nearby. He had torn a strip from his tunic; with Harn's help, he bound the cloth as a tourniquet about his arm. His ripped flesh bled heavily.

The other *Haruchai* were marked with smoke and fire, but had not been injured. And Sunder and Hollian were unharmed, though his exertions left the Graveller tottering. Hollian supported him.

Vain stood a short distance away as if nothing had happened. Flames licked about his feet like crushed serpents.

Covenant ignored them all. Linden's visage was lorn alabaster. Blood stained her wheaten tresses. Her lips wore an unconscious grimace of pain. He tried to take her from Hergrom's arms; but Hergrom would not release her.

'Ur-Lord.' Brinn's alien voice seemed incapable of urgency. 'We must go. Already the gap closes.'

Covenant pulled uselessly at Hergrom's grasp. It was intolerable that she might die! She was not meant to end like this. Or why had she been Chosen? He called out to her, but did not know how to reach her.

'Covenant!' Sunder's ragged breathing made his tone hoarse. 'It is as Brinn says. The na-Mhoram-in spent her life to provide this passage. We must go.'

Memla. That name pierced Covenant. She had given her life. Like Lena. And so many others. With a shudder, he turned from Hergrom. His hands groped for support. 'Yes.' He could hardly hear himself through the flames. 'Let's go.'

At once, the *Haruchai* sprang into motion. Harn and Stell led the way; Hergrom and Brinn followed with Covenant; Cail guarded Sunder and Hollian. They paid no attention to Vain. In a body, they dodged the grass fires towards the breach in the march.

The creatures milled insanely around the scorched and pitted ground where Memla had fallen. Their leaders had already marched out of sight, uncognizant of what had happened behind them. But more warped beings poured constantly from the south. They would have overrun the company immediately; but their own dead delayed them. The arriving creatures fell on the many slain and injured, tearing flesh apart with claws and mandibles, feeding ravenously. And the fires added fear to their hunger.

Into the confusion, the *Haruchai* guided Covenant and the Stonedownors.

The quest appeared small and fragile beside those large, blind creatures, vulnerable against those ferocious jaws, those plated limbs. But Brinn's people threaded the roil with uncanny stealth. And whenever a creature blundered towards them, Stell and Harn struck cunningly, breaking the antennae so that the creature could not locate its prey. Thus maimed, the beasts were swept into mortal combat with other creatures. Covenant, Sunder, and Hollian were impelled past gaping jaws, under rearing bellies, across moments of clear ground, as if their lives were preserved by the charm of *Haruchai* competence.

A few shreds of red cloth marked the place of Memla's death, unambergrised by any grave or chance for mourning.

Running as well as they could, the companions broke into the thick grass beyond the march. Creatures veered to follow. With all their strength, Stell and Harn attacked the grass, forcing a way through it. Only Vain did not make haste. He had no need for haste: every creature which touched him fell dead, and was devoured by the oncoming surge.

A short distance into the grass, Ceer joined the company. He did not speak; but the object he held explained what he had done.

Memla's *rukh*.

The sight of it halted Covenant. Possibilities reeled through his head. He grappled to take hold of them.

But he had no time. A sharp crepitation cut the grass like a scythe; thousands of creatures were chewing their way in pursuit.

Brinn thrust Covenant forward. The company ran.

Ceer, Stell, Brinn, and Harn dropped back to defend the rear. Now Cail led. In spite of his wounded arm and the abrasion of the raw, stiff grass, he forced a path with his body. Hergrom followed, carrying Linden; and Covenant crowded on Hergrom's heels, with Hollian and Sunder behind him.

The creatures gave chase as if they were prepared to reap the savannah in order to feast on human flesh. The noise of their charge hunted the company like fire.

Cail attacked the thick blades with all the ancient valour of the *Haruchai*; but he could not open a path swiftly enough to outdistance the pursuit. Covenant soon began to waver in exhaustion. He was still convalescing from the soothtell. Sunder and Hollian were in little better condition. Linden lay like defeat in Hergrom's arms. And Cail left smears of blood across the grass.

In the back of Covenant's desperation, a demand panted. Use your ring! But he could not, could not. He was so weak. He began to lose ground. Cail and Hergrom seemed to fade through the whipping backlash of the grass. If he let the venom rise in him, he did not know what he would kill. He heard himself yelling as if his exertions were a knife in his chest; but he could not silence the pain.

Suddenly, Brinn was at his side. Speaking only loud enough to be heard, the *Haruchai* reported, 'Cail has found a place which may be defended.'

Covenant staggered, fell thrashing among serrated grass-spears. A miasma of rot clogged his breathing. But Brinn heaved him back to his feet. Vertigo whirled through him. Clinging to Brinn's shoulder as if it were the only solid thing left in the world, he let the *Haruchai* half carry him forward.

Cail's path led to a pile of boulders rising incongruously out of the savannah, like a cairn left by Giants. It stood half again as high as the surrounding grass. Hergrom had already climbed to the crown, set Linden down in relative safety, and returned to help Sunder and Hollian ascend. Ignoring his pain, Cail joined Hergrom. Stell and Harn followed. They caught Covenant when Brinn and Ceer boosted him upward.

He scrambled to Linden's side, fought down his weakness, tried to examine her. Lifting her head, parting her hair as gently as he could with his numb fingers, he found that the wound in her scalp did not appear serious. The bleeding had almost ceased. Yet she remained unconscious. All her muscles were limp. Her face looked like the aftermath of a battle. His truncated senses could not measure her condition. He was useless to her.

Sunder and Hollian climbed up to him. Kneeling beside Linden, Sunder scrutinized her. Fatigue and trepidation dragged at his features. 'Ah, Linden Avery,' he breathed. 'This is a sore mischance.'

Covenant stifled a groan and sought to contradict the dismay in Sunder's tone. 'It doesn't look that serious.'

The Graveller avoided Covenant's stare. 'The injury itself – Perhaps even Cail's hurt does not threaten his life. But this is a sun of pestilence.' He faltered into silence.

'Ur-Lord,' Hollian said tightly, 'any wound is fatal under a sun of pestilence. There is no healing for the Sunbane sickness.'

'*None?*' The word was torn from Covenant.

'None,' Sunder rasped through his teeth. And Hollian said with pain in her gaze, 'None that is known to the people of the Land. If the Clave has knowledge of a cure – '

She did not need to complete her thought. Covenant understood her; Memla was dead. Because she was honest, she had turned against the na-Mhoram; because she was brave she had drawn the *Grim* on to herself; and because Covenant had not used his wild magic, she was dead. His fear had cost her her life.

He had cost the company even the bare possibility that she might have known how to treat Linden. And Cail.

Any wound is fatal.

And that was not all. The Coursers were gone. The quest had no supplies.

It was his fault, because he had been afraid. With power, he killed. Without power, he caused people to die.

Memla had given her life for him.

Eyes burning, he rose dangerously to his feet. The height of his perch threatened him; but he ignored it as if he were impervious to vertigo, or lost.

'Brinn!'

The *Haruchai* had ranged themselves defensively around the rocks at the level of the grass tops. Over his shoulder, Brinn said, 'Ur-Lord?'

'Why did you let Memla die?'

Brinn replied with a shrug. 'The choice was hers.' His confidence in his own rectitude seemed immaculate. 'Ceer made offer of his life. She refused.'

Covenant nodded. Memla had refused. Because he had told her he could not control his ring.

He was not satisfied with Brinn's answer. The Bloodguard had once made a similar decision about Kevin – and had never forgiven themselves for the outcome. But such questions did not matter now. Memla was dead. Linden and Cail were going to die. Blinking at the heat in his eyes, he looked around him.

The quest was poised on the mound of boulders – all except Vain, who remained below, as if he were comfortable among the grass and the stench. The jungle lay out of sight to the west. In all directions, the savannah stretched to the horizons, an island sea of grey-green, waving lightly in the breeze.

But it wore a scar of bare dirt running imponderably northward. And from this scar, a similar swath had veered towards the company's knoll. Already, the fires of the *Grim* had faded to smoke and smouldering. Freed from that peril, the creatures rushed in a straight line towards the boulders. The grass boiled as it was thrust aside, tramped down, eaten. Soon the knoll stood alone among a seethe of beasts.

Covenant could barely discern Vain. The Demondim-spawn held his ground with perfect nonchalance, and every creature which touched him died.

The *Haruchai* were ready when the attack began. As the creatures scrambled up the rocks, Brinn and his people used the advantage of elevation to break each assailant's antennae, then strove to dislodge the creature so that it fell back into the boil and was consumed.

They were surprisingly successful. Their strength, accuracy, and balance made them effective; and the fallen beasts slowed the rest of the attack.

But the knoll was too large; five *Haruchai* could not defend it completely. Gradually, they were driven backward.

Covenant did not hesitate. Cold fury filled his bones like power. Snarling at himself, he pulled the bundle from under his belt and unwrapped the *krill* of Loric Vilesilencer.

The brightness of its gem stopped him momentarily; he had forgotten the intensity of that white, pure light, the keenness of the edges, the heat of the metal. A leper's fear made him reluctant to touch the *krill* without the protection of cloth.

But then the company's need came over him like a *geas*. His fingers were already numb, irrelevant. No burn could alter the doom which defined him. He dropped the cloth, took the *krill* in his half-hand, and went to join the *Haruchai*.

Beings like misborn Cavewights came jerking upward on their long limbs. Their claws scored the stone; their jaws gaped and clacked. One gouge could disembowel him; one bite could sever an arm. Their feelers reached towards him.

Moving as if he were accursed, he began to slash at them.

The *krill* sliced their plating like bare flesh, cut through antennae, even mandibles, as if the blade were a broadsword with the weight and puissance of a Giant behind it. The *krill* was a tool of Law, and the creatures were the Lawless spawn of the Sunbane. A dull ache of fire spread up through Covenant's palm to his wrist, his arm; but he hacked and flailed urgently, and his every stroke sent a beast to the ungentle death of the mass below it.

Soon Sunder joined the defence. His poniard was not a good weapon for such work; but he was sturdy, and his blade could cripple feelers. He was unable to dislodge the beasts as the *Haruchai* did. But often that was unnecessary. With damaged antennae, the creatures became disoriented, turned aside, grappled with each other, toppled to the ground. And Stell or Ceer warded him.

The attack did not falter, hundreds of creatures replaced the scores which fell. But the company held. In time, all the ground around the knoll was denuded of grass; and a storm of mute rage covered the bare dirt, seeking to strike upward. But only a certain number of beasts could assail the boulders at any one moment. Against these limited numbers, the company held. Their ordeal dragged out like slow torture. Covenant's arms became leaden; he had to grip the *krill* in both hands. Sunder kept up a mutter of curses, lashing himself to continue the struggle long after he had exhausted his strength. But Hollian gave him periods of rest by taking his place, using his poniard because her dirk was too small for the task. And Vain's power helped, though he seemed unaware of what he did. The company held.

The afternoon wore on. Covenant became little more than a blank reflex. He grew numb to the passage of time, the progress of the assault. His joints were cramped with fire. Time and again, Brinn saved him from attacks he was too slow to meet.

He hardly noticed when the sun started to set, and the frenzy of the creatures began to abate. At the onset of twilight, the beasts seemed to lose purpose or direction. By ones and twos, then by scores, they scuttled away, wandering hurriedly into the grass. As dusk thickened over the savannah, the goad of the Sunbane faded. Soon all the creatures were fleeing.

Covenant stopped. His heart trembled like prostration in his chest.

He was gasping for breath. He dropped the *krill* among the rocks. The knoll tilted under him. On his hands and knees, he tried to crawl up to Linden. But he could not reach her. His dizziness became suddenly violent. It whirled him out into the blind night.

Sometime after the moon had passed its apex, he was awakened by Linden's knotted retching as she went into convulsions.

He lurched upright and groped through a blur of fatigue, hunger, thirst, to try to see what was happening.

The crown of the boulders was lit by the *krill*; it had been wedged among the stones so that it shed illumination over the company. Sunder and Hollian crouched beside Linden, watching her anxiously. Ceer and Hergrom restrained her so that she would not hurt herself, as long, mad clenchings shook her muscles.

On the lower boulders, the other *Haruchai* clustered as if they were fighting each other. With a quick glance, Covenant saw Brinn, Stell, and Harn struggling to quell Cail. Like Linden, the injured *Haruchai* lay in the grip of frenetic seizures.

Seeing Covenant, Sunder rasped grimly, 'The sun of pestilence has infected her wound. From this sickness none recover.'

Oh, God.

A rush of panic started up in him, then shattered as he realized that Linden was gagging, choking on her tongue.

He grabbed for her face and tried to pry her jaws open. But he could not break the locking of her teeth. Her whole body sprang rigid.

'She's swallowed her tongue! Get her mouth open!'

Instantly, Ceer clinched both her wrists in his left hand. With his right, he tried to wedge open her jaws. For one heartbeat, even his strength was not enough. Then he succeeded in forcing her teeth apart. She quivered under a lash of pain. Holding her mouth open with the width of his hand, he reached deftly down her throat, cleared her tongue.

She drew breath as if she wanted to scream; but convulsions blocked the wail in her chest.

With a feral spasm, Cail hurled Brinn from him. Twisting in the air, Brinn landed lightly on the ground, came bounding upward again as Stell and Harn grappled with their kinsman.

Linden's face was ghastly in the *krill*-light. Her breathing wept in and out of her excruciated lungs.

Cail sounded as if he were asphyxiating. An obscure part of Covenant thought, He's immune to the Sunbane. There must have been poison in the spur.

He concentrated on Linden as if he could keep her alive by sheer force of will. His hand shook as he stroked her forehead, wiped the sweat away; but he could feel nothing.

'Ur-Lord,' Hollian said in a stretched whisper, 'I must speak of this. It must be uttered.' He could not read her countenance: her face was averted from the *krill*. Out of the shadow, she breathed, 'I have consulted the *lianar*. The morrow will bring a desert sun.'

Covenant clung to Linden's torment, willing it to ease. 'I don't give a damn.'

'There is more.' Hollian's tone sharpened. She was an eh-Brand, accustomed to respect. 'There will be fire, as if the sun were a sun of flame. This will become a place of ill. We must flee.'

'Now?'

'At once. We must return to the west – to the soil where trees grow. The earth of this grassland will be death to us.'

'She's in no condition!' His sudden fury shocked the night, struck the company into a silence punctuated only by the hoarse breathing of the injured. With a wrench of his shoulders, he dismissed Hollian's warning. 'I'm not going to move her.'

She started to protest. Sunder interrupted her gruffly. 'He is the ur-Lord.'

'He is *wrong*. The truth must be met. These deaths cannot be prevented. To remain here will be death for us all.'

'He is the ur-Lord.' Sunder's roughness grew gentle. 'Every task to which he sets his hand is impossible – yet it is accomplished. Have courage, eh-Brand.'

Linden broke into another series of spasms. Watching the way her illness brutalized her, Covenant feared that every breath would be her last. But then, abruptly, her convulsions ended; she fell limp as if the puppet strings of her plight had been cut. Slowly, her respiration deepened as she sank into the sleep of exhaustion.

Cail's affliction was more advanced. The fits which racked him went on until moonset. Brinn's people had to fight incessantly to prevent him from battering himself to death on the rocks.

'Dawn is near,' Sunder murmured softly, as if he feared to disturb the stillness, feared that the sound of his voice might trigger Linden or Cail into frenzy again.

'We are too late.' Hollian could not suppress her bitterness. 'We must remain here. We cannot gain safety in time.'

Covenant ignored both of them. He sat with Linden in his embrace and sought to believe that she would live.

No one moved. They sat in the *krill*-light while the east paled towards sunrise. A dusty glow began to silhouette the earth. All the stars were washed away. The sky modulated as brown gathered around the imminence of the dawn. The atmosphere grew palpably drier, foretelling heat.

When the sun rose, it wore a cloak of desiccation. Its touch reminded Covenant that he had not had food or fluid since the previous morning. A giddy dispassion began to revolve in him, distancing him from his fate. Linden's flagrant slumber felt like an accomplished fact in his arms.

As the Sunbane coloured the savannah, the pampas grass began to melt. Its fibre turned to a dead grey sludge, and slumped to the ground like spilth. This, Covenant mused in a mood of canted detachment, was what had happened to Morinmoss. To Grimmerdhore and Garroting Deep. A desert sun had risen over them, and tens of thousands of years of sentient forest had simply dissolved into muck. *And the glory of the world becomes less than it was.* For a moment, he recovered enough passion to ache out, Damn you, Foul! It would be better if you just killed me.

In a voice like Covenant's inanition, but infintely steadier, Brinn addressed Hollian. 'Eh-Brand, you spoke of fire.'

'The *lianar* spoke of fire.' Both affronted dignity and nagging self-doubt marked her words. 'Never have I seen such a flame in my foretelling. Do not question me. I cannot answer.'

Covenant thought dimly that there was no reason for fire. The quest was without water under a desert sun. Nothing else was necessary.

The truth of Hollian's augury became clear when the sun rose high enough, and the grass sank low enough, for light to contact the bare ground around the knoll. And with the light came a faint shimmer which seemed to transmogrify the texture of the soil. The dirt began to glow.

Covenant believed that he was hallucinating.

Without warning, Vain ascended the boulders. Everyone stared at him; but his black eyes remained unfocused, private, as if he were unaware of his own intentions.

Brinn and Hergrom placed themselves to guard Covenant and Linden. But Vain stopped without acknowledging the *Haruchai* and stood gazing like a void into the blank air.

Slowly, the soil took on a reddish tinge enriched with yellow. The colour deepened, hardened.

Heat radiated from the ground.

Around the edges of the clearing, the sludge started to smoulder. Viscid smoke went up in wisps, then in billows which thickened steadily, clogging the atmosphere.

In moments, the muck was afire.

As it burned, smoke began to mount in other places across the savannah. Soon there were blazes everywhere.

And the bare dirt continued to darken.

The company watched tensely; even the *Haruchai* seemed to be holding their breath. Only Linden and Cail were oblivious. Vain was not. He studied Linden between the shoulders of Brinn and Hergrom, and his visage sharpened, as if vague purposes were being whetted towards clarity within him.

Numbly, Covenant studied the ground. That rich, half-orange light and heat brought up recollections. Gradually, the face of Lena's father, Trell, became vivid to him; he did not know why. He could see Trell standing like granite in Lena's home. The big Stonedownor's face was ruddy with light. Reflections gleamed in his beard – the precise colour of these emanations.

Then Covenant remembered.

Gravelling. Fire-stones.

Under the touch of the desert sun, this entire savannah was being transformed into a sea of gravelling.

Fire consumed the sludge; and under it lay clear gravelling which sent one long, silent shout of heat into the heavens.

Covenant and his companions might as well have been perched above a flow of lava.

He sat and stared as if his eyeballs had been scorched blind. He could feel death lying like a familiar in his arms.

Memla had sacrificed herself. Linden and Cail were going to die. Everyone was going to die.

Vain gave no hint of his intent. The suddenness of his movement took even the wary *Haruchai* by surprise. With a frightening swiftness, he thrust Brinn and Hergrom aside and stepped between them towards Covenant and Linden.

Hergrom caught himself on an outcropping of rock. Brinn was saved from a fall into the gravelling only by the celerity with which Ceer grabbed for him.

Effortlessly, Vain took Linden from Covenant's arms.

Stell surged forward, pounded Vain between the eyes. The Demondim-spawn did not react; he went about his purpose as if he had not been touched. Stell was knocked back against Harn.

Cradling Linden gently, Vain stepped to the eastern edge of the mound and leaped down into the fire-stones.

'*Vain!*'

Covenant was on his feet. His hearing roared as if the heat had become a gale. Venom pulsed in his veins. He wanted wild magic, wanted to strike – !

But if he hit Vain, hurt him, the Demondim-spawn might drop Linden into the gravelling.

Linden!

Vain paid no heed to the danger behind him. Firmly, surely, he strode away.

At that instant, Hergrom sprang pantherish from the boulders. At the furthest stretch of his leap, he impacted against Vain's shoulders.

The Demondim-spawn did not even stumble. He walked on across the gravelling with Linden held before him and Hergrom clinging to his back as if he were unconscious of them both.

Covenant's shouting died in his chest. He was hardly aware that

Brinn and Sunder were holding his arms as if to prevent him from pursuing Vain.

'He does not feel the fire,' Brinn remarked distantly. 'Perhaps he will save her. Perhaps he intends to save her.'

To save — ? Covenant sagged. Was it possible? The muscles of his face hurt, but he could not unclench his grimace. To save her so that she could serve Lord Foul? 'Then why — ' his voice knotted — 'didn't he help her before? During the *Grim*?'

Brinn shrugged. 'Perhaps he saw then that his aid was not needed. He acts now to save her because we are helpless.'

Vain? Covenant panted. No. He could not suppress the tremors in him. 'We're not helpless.' It was unbearable. Not even a leper could bear it. *We are not helpless.*

He cast one abrupt glance towards Vain. The Demondim-spawn was running, fading into the shimmer of the gravelling.

Covenant wrenched free of Brinn and Sunder. He confronted his companions. The effort to control his trembling made him savage. 'Ceer. Give me the *rukh*.'

Sunder scowled. Hollian's eyes widened as if she felt an intuitive hope or fear. But the *Haruchai* showed no surprise. Ceer took Memla's *rukh* from his tunic and handed it to Covenant.

With a jerk, Covenant thrust the iron towards Sunder. 'All right. You're the Graveller. Use it.'

Sunder's lips formed words without sound: Use it?

'Call the Coursers back. They're bred to the Sunbane. They can carry us out of here.'

The Graveller breathed a strangled protest. 'Covenant!'

Covenant jabbed the *rukh* against Sunder's chest. 'Do it. I can't. I don't know the Sunbane the way you do. I can't touch it. I'm a leper.'

'And I am not a Rider!'

'I don't care.' Covenant clinched ire around his dread. 'We're all going to die. Maybe I don't count. But you do. Hollian does. You know the truth about the Clave.' Again, he punched Sunder with the *rukh*. '*Use* it.'

The heat spread sweat across Sunder's face, made his features look like they were about to melt like the grass. Desperately, he turned an imploring gaze towards Hollian.

She touched his scarred forearm. The stature of her calling was upon her. 'Sunder,' she said quietly. 'Graveller. Perhaps it may be done. Surely the Sunstone empowers you to the attempt. And I will aid you as I can. Through the *lianar*, I am able to perceive the state of the Sunbane. It may be that I can guide you to mastery.'

For a moment, they held each other's eyes, measuring what they saw. Then Sunder swung back to Covenant. The Graveller's expression was rent by fear of failure, by instinctive loathing for anything which belonged to the Clave. But he accepted the *rukh*.

Grimly, he climbed to sit atop the highest boulder, near the white radiance of the *krill*.

Hollian stood on a lower rock so that her head was level with his. She watched gravely as he set his *orcrest* in his lap, then fumbled to uncap the hollow handle of the *rukh*.

Covenant's legs quavered as if they could no longer bear the weight of who he was. But he braced himself on the rocks, remained erect like a witness and a demand.

Sunder poured the last fluid from the *rukh* into his hand. Hollian placed her palm in his, let it rest there for a moment, sharing the blood like a gesture of comradeship. Then she wrapped her stained fingers around the *lianar*, and began to chant softly to herself. Sunder rubbed his hands together, dabbed red on to his forehead and cheeks, then picked up the Sunstone.

The rigid accents of his invocation formed a counterpoint to her lilting murmur. Together, they wove the silence into a skein of Sunbane power: bloodshed and fire.

Soon, his familiar vermeil shaft shot like a quarrel towards the sun. A crepitation like the discharge of slow lightning made the air squirm.

He lifted the *rukh* and held it so that the Sunstone's beam ran along the iron. His knuckles whitened, cording the backs of his hands.

Delicate flames opened like buds along the *lianar*. Hollian closed her eyes. Her fire turned slowly to the colour of the sun's brown aura, began to put out tendrils. One of them reached Sunder's hands. It wound around his grasp, then started to climb the *rukh* and the Sunstone shaft.

He blinked fiercely at the sweat in his eyes, glared as if the *rukh* were an adder he could neither hold nor release.

The poignance in Covenant's chest told him that he had forgotten to breathe. When he forced himself to inhale, he seemed to suck in vertigo from the air. Only his braced arms kept him from losing his balance.

None of the *Haruchai* were watching Sunder and Hollian. Cail had gone into convulsions. The others fought to keep him still.

Memories of Linden wrung Covenant's guts. He shut his eyes against the nausea.

He looked up again when the chanting ended. Sunder's shaft and Hollian's flame vanished. The Stonedownors clung to each other. The Graveller's shoulders shook.

Covenant knelt without knowing how he had lost his feet.

When Sunder spoke, his voice was muffled against Hollian's neck.

'After all, it is not greatly difficult to be a Rider. I am attuned to the *rukh*. The Coursers are distant. But they have heard. They will come.'

Eventually, Cail's seizure receded. For a while, he regained consciousness; but he spoke in the alien tongue of the *Haruchai*, and Covenant did not understand what he said.

The first of the great beasts returned shortly before noon. By then, thirst and hunger had reduced Covenant to stupefaction; he could not focus his eyes to see which of the Coursers it was, or whether the animal still bore any supplies. But Brinn reported, 'It is Clangor, the Courser which assailed Linden Avery. It limps. Its chest is burned. But it suffers no harm from the gravelling.' A moment later, he added, 'Its burdens are intact.'

Intact, Covenant thought dizzily. He peered through the haze as Ceer and Stell leaped down to the Courser, then returned carrying sacks of water and food. Oh dear God.

By the time he and the Stonedownors had satisfied the first desperation of their thirst and had begun to eat a meal, Annoy came galloping from the south. Like Clangor, it was unscathed by the gravelling; but it skittered uncomfortably around the knoll, champing to escape the fire-stones.

Clash and Clang also returned. Sunder frowned at them as if he did not like the pride he felt in what he had achieved; but Hollian's smile shone.

At once, the *Haruchai* began to prepare for departure.

Using the pieces of cloth he had discarded, Covenant rewrapped the *krill* and tucked it under his belt. Then he descended the boulders to the level of the Coursers' backs.

At close range, the heat of the gravelling felt severe enough to char his flesh. It triggered involuntary memories of Hotash Slay and Saltheart Foamfollower. The Giant had spent himself in lava and agony to help Covenant.

Distrusting the Coursers and himself, Covenant could not leap the small distance to a mount. No more, he yearned. Don't let any more friends die for me. He had to cling where he was, squinting against the radiance, until the *Haruchai* could help him.

In a moment, Ceer and Brinn joined him, carrying Cail. Sunder raised the *rukh*, uncertain of his mastery; but the Coursers obeyed, crowding close to the knoll. Leaving Cail, Ceer stepped to Annoy's back. Harn tossed the sacks to him. He placed them across Annoy's huge withers, then accepted Cail from Brinn.

Cail's arm was livid and suppurating badly. It made Covenant groan. Cail needed Linden. She was a doctor.

She was as sick as the *Haruchai*.

Practising his control, Sunder sent Annoy out of the way of the other Coursers. Then Harn and Hollian mounted Clangor. The Graveller joined Stell on Clang. Before Covenant could suppress his dread, Brinn lifted him on to Clash.

He dropped to the broad back, knotted his fists in Clash's hair. Heat blasted at him like slow roasting and suffocation. But he fought to raise his voice. 'Find Vain. Fast.'

With a gesture, Sunder launched the beasts eastward. They galloped away through air burnished orange by gravelling.

Clang bore Sunder and the *rukh* at a staggering pace; but the other mounts matched it. Even Clangor, oozing pain from its wound, did not fall behind; it ran like a storm-wind with frenzy in its red eyes. It had been formed by the power of the Banefire to obey any *rukh*. It could not refuse Sunder's authority.

Covenant could not gauge their speed; he could hardly keep his eyes open against the sharp heat, hardly breathe. He only knew that he was travelling swiftly. But he did not know how fast Vain could run. The Demondim-spawn's lead was as long as the morning.

Wind scorched his face. His clothes felt hot on his skin, as if the fabric had begun to smoulder. He wore warm sweat down the length of his body. His eyes bled tears against the shine and heat of the gravelling. But the Coursers ran as if they were being borne by the passion of the fire-stones. Hollian clung to Harn's back. Sunder hunched over Clang's neck. The *Haruchai* rode with magisterial detachment. And the Coursers ran.

The gravelling unfurled as if it would never end. Fire deepened the sky, coloured the heavens with molten grandeur. Through the haze, the sun's corona looked like an outer ring of incandescence. The entire savannah was a bed of coals: the Coursers were traversing an accentuated hell. But Sunder had mastered the *rukh*. While he lived, the beasts could not falter.

They did not. They ran as if they had been born in flames. Smoothly, indefatigably, they swept the leagues behind them like dead leaves in a furnace.

Covenant's breathing sobbed, not because he lacked air, but rather because his lungs were being seared. He began to have visions of Glimmermere, the cool tarn tinged with Earthpower. His bones throbbed to inhale water. And the Coursers ran.

When they broke out of the gravelling on to hard dirt, the suddenness of the change made the desert air feel like bliss. It snatched his head up. Relief slammed into his chest like a polar wind. In an instant, the Coursers were clattering across dead, sun-baked soil, raising pennons of dust. The haze retreated; abruptly, the terrain had features, texture, meaning.

As his sight cleared, he saw Vain ahead of him.

The Demondim-spawn stood, black and fatal, on the bank of a gully which twisted emptily across the company's way. The dull iron bands of the Staff of Law emphasized his midnight form. He watched the Coursers thunder towards him as if he had been waiting for them.

He was alone.

Alone?

Covenant tumbled from Clash's back as the beast pounded to a halt. He landed hard, sprawled across the dirt. Rolling his feet under him, he hurled himself at Vain.

'What have you done with her?'

Vain did not move: Covenant crashed into the Demondim-spawn, recoiled as if he had hit a wall of obsidian.

The next moment, Hergrom appeared out of the gully. He seemed uninjured, though his raiment had been singed by the gravelling. Without expression, as if he did not deign to judge Covenant's precipitation, he said, 'She is here. In the shade.'

Covenant surged past him, jumped down into the gully.

The dry watercourse was not deep. He landed in sand and whirled, searching for Linden.

She lay on her back under the shadow of the gully wall. Her skin seemed faintly red in the dimmer light; she had been so close to the gravelling. He could see her as clearly as if she were engraved on his mind: her raw colour, the streaks of sweat in her wheaten hair, the frown scar between her brows like an expostulation against the life she had lived.

She was in convulsions. Her heels drummed the sand; her fingers attacked the ground on either side; spasms racked her body, arched her back. A skull-grin clinched her face. Small gasps whimpered through her teeth like shreds of pain.

Covenant dived to her side, gripped her shoulders to restrain her arms. He could not make a sound, could not thrust words past his panic.

Sunder and Hollian joined him, followed by Harn and Hergrom. Brinn, Ceer, and Stell came a moment later, bearing Cail. He, too, was in the throes of another seizure.

Sunder rested a hand on Covenant's shoulder. 'It is the Sunbane sickness,' he said softly. 'I am sorry. She cannot endure.'

Her whimpering turned to a rasp in her throat like a death-rattle. She seemed to be groaning. 'Covenant.'

Linden! he moaned. I can't help you!

Abruptly, her eyes snapped open, staring wildly. They gaped over the rictus which bared her teeth.

'Cove – ' Her throat worked as the muscles knotted, released. Her jaws were locked together like the grip of a vice. Her eyes glared white delirium at him. 'Help – '

Her efforts to speak burned his heart. 'I don't – ' He was choking. 'Don't know how.'

Her lips stretched as if she wanted to sink her teeth into the skin of his cheek. Her neck cords stood out like bone. She had to force the word past her seizure by sheer savagery.

'*Voure.*'

'What?' He clung to her. '*Voure?*'

'Give – ' Her extremity cut him like a sword. '*Voure.*'

The sap that warded off insects? His orbs were as dry as fever. 'You're delirous.'

'*No.*' The intensity of her groan pierced the air. 'Mind – ' Her wild, white stare demanded, beseeched. With every scrap of her determination, she fought her throat. 'Clear.' The strain aggravated her convulsions. Her body kicked against his weight as if she were being buried alive. 'I – ' For an instant, she dissolved into whimpers. But she rallied, squeezed out, 'Feel.'

Feel? he panted. Feel what?

'*Voure.*'

For one more horrific moment, he hung on the verge of understanding her. Then he had it.

Feel!

'Brinn!' he barked over his shoulder. 'Get the *voure!*'

Feel! Linden could feel. She had the Land-born health sense; she could perceive the nature of her illness, understand it precisely. And the *voure* as well. She knew what she needed.

The angle of her stare warned him. With a jolt, he realized that no one had moved, that Brinn was not obeying him.

'Covenant,' Sunder murmured painfully. 'Ur-Lord. She – I beg you to hear me. She has the Sunbane sickness. She knows not what she says. She – '

'Brinn.' Covenant spoke softly, but his lucid passion sliced through Sunder's dissuasion. 'Her mind is clear. She knows exactly what she's saying. Get the *voure.*'

Still the *Haruchai* did not comply. 'Ur-Lord,' he said, 'the Graveller has knowledge of this sickness.'

Covenant had to release Linden's arms, clench his fists against his forehead to keep from screaming. 'The only reason – ' his voice juddered like a cable in a high wind – 'Kevin Landwaster was able to perform the Ritual of Desecration, destroy all the life of the Land for hundreds of years, was because the Bloodguard stood by and let him do it. He ordered them not to do anything, and he had knowledge, so they obeyed. For the rest of their lives, their Vow was corrupt, and they didn't know it. They didn't even know they were tainted until Lord Foul rubbed their noses in it. Until he proved he could make them serve him.' Foul had maimed three of them to make them resemble Covenant. 'Are you going to just stand there again and let more people die?' Abruptly, his control shattered. He hammered the sand with his fists. '*Get the VOURE!*'

Brinn glanced at Sunder, at Cail. For a moment, he seemed to hesitate. Then he sprang from the gully towards the Coursers.

He was back almost at once, carrying Memla's leather flask of *voure*. With an air of disinterest, as if he eschewed responsibility, he handed it to Covenant.

Trembling, Covenant unstopped the flask. He had to apply a crushing force of will to steady his hands so that he could pour just a few drops through Linden's teeth. Then he watched in a trance of dread and hope as she fought to swallow.

Her back arched, went slack as if she had broken her spine.

His gaze darkened. The world spun in his head. His mind became the swooping and plunge of condors. He could not see, could not think, until he heard her whisper, 'Now Cail.'

The *Haruchai* responded immediately. Her understanding of Cail's plight demonstrated her clarity of mind. Brinn took the flask, hurried to Cail's side. With Stell's help, he forced some of the *voure* between Cail's locked jaws.

Relaxation spread through Linden, muscle by muscle. Her breathing eased; the cords of her neck loosened. One by one, her fingers uncurled. Covenant lifted her hand, folded her broken nails in his clasp, as he watched the rigor slipping out of her. Her legs became limp along the sand. He held to her hand because he could not tell whether she were recovering or dying.

Then he knew. When Brinn came over to him and announced without inflection, 'The *voure* is efficacious. He will mend,' she gave a low sigh of relief.

23

SARANGRAVE FLAT

Covenant watched her while she slept, human and frail, until some time after sunset. Then, in the light of a campfire built by the *Haruchai* he roused her. She was too weak for solid food, so he fed her *metheglin* diluted with water.

She was recovering. Even his blunt sight could not be mistaken about it. When she went back to sleep, he stretched out on the sand near her, and fell almost instantly into dreams.

They were dreams in which wild magic raged, savage and irremediably destructive. Nothing could be stopped, and every flare of power was the Despiser's glee. Covenant himself became a waster of the world, became Kevin on a scale surpassing all conceivable Desecrations. The white fire came from the passions which made him who he was, and he could not – !

But the stirring of the company awakened him well before dawn. Sweating in the desert chill, he climbed to his feet and looked around. The embers of the fire revealed that Linden was sitting up, with her back against the gully wall. Hergrom attended her soundlessly, giving her food.

She met Covenant's gaze. He could not read her expression in the dim light, did not know where he stood with her. His sight seemed occluded by the after-images of nightmare. But the obscurity and importance of her face drew him to her. He squatted before her, studied her mien. After a moment, he murmured to explain himself, 'I thought you were finished.'

'I thought,' she replied in a restrained voice, 'I was never going to make you understand.'

'I know.' What else could he say? But the inadequacy of his responses shamed him. He felt so unable to reach her.

But while he fretted against his limitations, her hand came to him, touched the tangle of his beard. Her tone thickened. 'It makes you look older.'

One of the *Haruchai* began to rebuild the fire. A red gleam reflected from her wet eyes as if they were aggravated by coals, were bits of fire in her mind. She went on speaking, fighting the emotion in her throat.

'You wanted me to look at Vain.' She nodded towards the Demondim-spawn; he stood across the gully from her. 'I've tried. But I don't understand. He isn't alive. He's got so much power, and it's imperative. But it's – it's inanimate. Like your ring. He could be anything.'

Her hand covered her eyes. For a moment, she could not steady herself. 'Covenant, it hurts. It hurts to see him. It hurts to see anything.' Reflections formed orange-red beads below the shadow of her hand.

He wanted to put his arms around her; but he knew that was not the comfort she needed. A Raver had touched her, had impaled her soul. Gibbon had told her that her health sense would destroy her. Gruffly, he answered, 'It saved your life.'

Her shoulders clenched.

'It saved Cail's life.'

She shuddered, dropped her hand, let him see her eyes streaming in the new light of the fire. 'It saved *your* life.'

He gazed at her as squarely as he could, but said nothing, gave her all the time she required.

'After Crystal Stonedown.' The words came huskily past her lips. 'You were dying. I didn't know what to do.' A grimace embittered her mouth. 'Even if I'd had my bag – Take away hospitals, labs, equipment, and doctors aren't much good.' But a moment later she swallowed her insufficiency. 'I didn't know what else to do. So I went inside you. I felt your heart and your blood and your lungs and your nerves – Your sickness. I kept you alive. Until Hollian was able to help you.'

Her eyes left his, wandered the gully like guilt. 'It was horrible. To feel all that ill. *Taste* it. As if I were the one who was sick. It was like breathing gangrene.' Her forehead knotted in revulsion or grief; but she forced her gaze back to his visage. 'I swore I would never do anything like that again as long as I lived.'

Pain made him bow his head. He glared into the shadows between them. A long moment passed before he could say without anger, 'My leprosy is that disgusting to you.'

'No.' Her denial jerked his eyes up again. 'It wasn't leprosy. It was venom.'

Before he could absorb her asseveration, she continued, 'It's still in you. It's growing. That's why it's so hard to look at you.' Fighting not to weep, she said hoarsely, 'I can't keep it out. Any of it. The Sunbane gets inside me. I can't keep it out. You talk about desecration. Everything desecrates *me*.'

What can I do? he groaned. Why did you follow me? Why did you try to save my life? Why doesn't my leprosy disgust you? But aloud he tried to give her answers, rather than questions. 'That's how Foul works. He tries to turn hope into despair. Strength into weakness. He attacks things that are precious, and tries to make them evil.' The Despiser had used Kevin's love of the Land, used the Bloodguard's service, the Giants' fidelity, used Elena's passion, to corrupt them all. And Linden had looked at Vain because he, Covenant, had asked it of her. 'But that knife cuts both ways. Every time he tries to hurt us is an opportunity to fight him. We have to find the strength of our weakness. Make hope out of despair.

'Linden.' He reached out with his halfhand, took one of her hands, gripped it. 'It doesn't do any good to try to hide from him.' *It boots nothing to avoid his snares*. 'If you close your eyes, you'll just get weaker. We have to accept who we are. And deny him.' But his fingers were numb; he could not tell whether or not she answered his clasp.

Her head had fallen forward. Her hair hid her face.

'Linden, it saved your *life*.'

'No.' Her voice seemed to be muffled by the pre-dawn dusk and the shadows. 'You saved my life. I don't have any power. All I can do is see.' She pulled her hand away. 'Leave me alone,' she breathed. 'It's too much. I'll try.'

He wanted to protest. But her appeal moved him. Aching stiffly in all his joints, he stood up and went to the fire for warmth.

Looking vaguely around the gully, he noticed the Stonedownors. The sight of them stopped him.

They sat a short distance away. Sunder held the *rukh*. Faint red flames licked the triangle. Hollian supported him as she had when he had first attuned himself to the *rukh*.

Covenant could not guess what they were doing. He had not paid any attention to them for too long, had no idea what they were thinking.

Shortly, they dropped their fires. For a moment, they sat gazing at each other, holding hands as if they needed courage.

'It cannot be regretted.' Her whisper wafted up the gully like a voice of starlight. 'We must bear what comes as we can.'

'Yes,' Sunder muttered. 'As we can.' Then his tone softened. 'I can bear much – with you.' As they rose to their feet, he drew her to him, kissed her forehead.

Covenant looked away, feeling like an intruder. But the Stonedownors came straight to him; and Sunder addressed him with an air of grim purpose. 'Ur-Lord, this must be told. From the moment of your request – ' he stressed the word ironically – 'that I take up this *rukh*, there has been a fear in me. While Memla held her *rukh*, the Clave knew her. Therefore the *Grim* came upon us. I feared that in gaining mastery of her *rukh* I, too, would become known to the Clave.

'Covenant – ' He faltered for only an instant. 'My fear is true. We have ascertained it. I lack the skill to read the purpose of the Clave – but I have felt their touch, and know that I am exposed to them.'

'Ur-Lord,' asked Hollian quietly, 'what must we do?'

'Just what we've been doing.' Covenant hardly heard her, hardly heard his answer. 'Run. Fight, if we have to.' He was remembering Linden's face in convulsions, her rigid mouth, the sweat streaks in her hair. And wild magic. 'Live.'

Fearing that he was about to lose control, he turned away.

Who was he, to talk to others about living and striving, when he could not even handle the frightening growth of his own power? The venom! It was part of him now. As the wild magic became more possible to him, everything else seemed more and more impossible. He was so capable of destruction. And incapable of anything else.

He picked up a jug of *metheglin* and drank deeply to keep himself from groaning aloud.

He was thinking, Power corrupts. Because it is unsure. It is not enough. Or it is too much. It teaches doubt. Doubt makes violence.

The pressure for power was growing in him. Parts of him were hungry for the rage of wild fire.

For a time, he was so afraid of himself, of the consequences of his own passions, that he could not eat. He drank the thick mead and stared into the flames, trying to believe that he would be able to contain himself.

He had killed twenty-one people. They were vivid to him now in the approaching dawn. Twenty-one! Men and women whose only crime had been that their lives had been deformed by a Raver.

When he raised his head, he found Linden standing near him.

She was insecure on her feet, still extremely weak; but she was able to hold herself upright. She gazed at him soberly. As he dropped his eyes, she said with an echo of her old severity, 'You should eat something.'

He could not refuse her. He picked up a piece of dried meat. She nodded, then moved woodenly away to examine Cail. Covenant chewed abstractedly while he watched her.

Cail appeared to be both well and ill. He seemed to have recovered from the Sunbane sickness, regained his native solidity and composure. But his injury was still hotly infected; *voure* had no efficacy against the poison of the Courser's spur.

Linden glared at the wound as if it wrung her nerves, then demanded fire and boiling water. Hergrom and Ceer obeyed without comment. While the water heated, she borrowed Hollian's dirk, burned it clean in the flames, then used it to lance Cail's infection. He bore the pain stoically; only a slight tension between his brows betrayed what he felt. Blood and yellow fluid splashed a stain on to the sand. Her hands were precise in spite of her weakness. She knew exactly where and how deeply to cut.

When the water was ready, she obtained a blanket from Brinn. Slashing the material into strips, she used some of them to wash out the wound; with others, she made a crude bandage. Fine beads of sweat mirrored the firelight from Cail's forehead; but he did not wince. He did not appear to be breathing.

'You'll be all right as soon as we stop the infection.' Her voice sounded impersonal, as if she were reading from some medical tome. 'You're healthy enough for any five people.' Then her severity frayed. 'This is going to hurt. If I could think of any way to kill the pain, I'd do it. But I can't. I left everything in my bag.'

'Have no concern, Linden Avery,' Cail replied evenly. 'I am well. I will serve you.'

'Serve yourself!' she grated at once. 'Take care of that arm.' As she spoke, she made sure that his bandage was secure. Then she poured boiling water over the fabric.

Cail made no sound. She stumbled to her feet, moved away from him and sat down against the gully wall, as if she could not bear the sight of his courage.

A moment later, Vain caught Covenant's attention. The first light of the sun touched Vain's head, etched it out of the gloaming – a cynosure of blackness and secrets. Sunder and Hollian went quickly to find rock. Covenant helped Linden erect. The *Haruchai* stood. All the company faced the dawn.

The sun broached the rim of the gully, wearing brown like the cerements of the world. Thirst and hallucination, bleached bones, fever-blisters. But Linden gasped involuntarily, 'It's weaker!'

Then, before Covenant could grasp what she meant, she groaned in disappointment. 'No. I must be losing my mind. It hasn't changed.'

Changed? Her bitterness left him in a whirl of anxiety as the quest broke camp, mounted the Coursers, and set off eastward. Was she so badly stressed by fear that she could no longer trust her eyes? In her convulsions, sweat had darkened her hair like streaks of damp anguish. But she seemed to be recovering. Her wound had been relatively minor. The company rode the sun-trammelled wasteland of the North Plains as if they were traversing an anvil. Why did he know so little about her?

But the next morning she was steadier, surer. She carried her head as if it had ceased to pain her. When she faced the dawn and saw the third desert sun rise, her whole body tensed. 'I was right,' she gritted. 'It *is* weaker.' A moment later, she cried, 'There!' Her arm accused the horizon. 'Did you see it? Right there, it changed! It was weaker and then it became as strong as ever. As if it crossed a boundary.'

No one spoke. Sunder and Hollian watched Linden as if they feared that the Sunbane sickness had affected her mind. The *Haruchai* gazed at her without expression.

'I saw it.' Her voice stiffened. 'I'm not crazy.'

Covenant winced. 'We don't have your eyes.'

She glared at him for an instant, then turned on her heel and strode away towards the waiting Coursers.

Now she rode as if she were angry. In spite of the dry brutality of the sun and the strain of clinging to Clash's back, her strength was returning. And with it came ire. Her ability to see had already cost her so much; and now her companions appeared to doubt what she saw. Covenant himself half disbelieved her. Any weakening of the Sunbane was a sign of hope. Surely therefore it was false? After what she had been through?

When the company stopped for the night, she ate a meal, tended Cail's arm, and set herself to sleep. But long before dawn, she was pacing the dead shale as if she were telling the moments until a revelation. Her tension articulated clearly how much she needed to be right, how sorely her exacerbated soul needed relief.

That morning, the sun rose in red pestilence. It tinged the stark outlines of the wilderness crimson, making the desert roseate, lovely, and strange, like a gilded burial ground; but though he strained his sight until his brain danced with images of fire, Covenant could not descry any lessening of the Sunbane. Yet Linden gave a fierce nod as if she had been vindicated. And after a moment, Brinn said impassively, 'The Chosen is far-sighted.' He used her title like a recognition of power. 'The corruption about the sun has lessened.'

'I am surpassed,' Sunder muttered in frustration. 'I do not see this lessening.'

'You will,' Linden replied. 'We're getting closer.'

Covenant was suddenly dizzy with hope. 'Closer to what?' Was the Sunbane failing?

'Enquire of the Chosen.' Brinn's shrug disavowed all responsibility for what he saw. 'We know nothing of this.'

Covenant turned to her.

'I'll tell you.' She did not meet his gaze. 'When I'm sure.'

He swallowed a curse, gritted himself still. *It's too much*, she had said. *I'll try*. He understood. She was trying. She wanted to trust what she saw and feared to be misled, to be hurt again. With difficulty, he left her alone.

She continued to stare eastward while the *Haruchai* distributed food, water, and *voure*. She ate heedlessly, ignoring Brinn's people as they readied the Coursers. But then, just as Sunder brought the beasts forward, her arm stabbed out, and she barked, 'There!'

Brinn glanced at the sun. 'Yes. The corruption regains its strength.'

Covenant groaned to himself. No wonder she did not wish to explain what she saw. How could she bear it?

Morosely, he mounted Clash behind Linden and Brinn. The quest moved out across the ragged wasteland.

Under this sun, the desert became a place of silence and scorpions. Only the rattle of the Coursers' hooves punctuated the windless air; and soon that noise became part of the silence as well. Insects scuttled over the rocks, or waded the sand, and made no sound. The sky was as empty of life as a tomb. Slowly, Covenant's mood became red and fatal. The Plains seemed eerie with all the blood he had shed. Involuntarily, he toyed with his ring, turning it around his finger as if his bones itched for fire. Yet he loathed killing, loathed himself. And he was afraid.

We have to accept who we are. Where had he learned the arrogance of at least the insensitivity to say such things?

That night, his memories and dreams made his skin burn as if he were eager for immolation, for a chance to anneal his old guilt in flame. Lena filled his sight as if she had been chiselled on the backs of his eyes. A child, in spite of her body's new maturity. He had struck her, knotted his hands in her shift and rent — The memory of her scream was distilled nightmare to him. *A moral leper.*

You are mine.

He was a creature of wild magic and doubt; and the long night, like the whole Land stretched helpless under the Sunbane, was also a desert.

But the next morning, when the sun rose in its crimson infestation, he, too, could see that its aurora was weaker. It seemed pale, almost uncertain. Sunder and Hollian could see it as well.

And this time the weakness did not vanish until mid-morning. Ascending from the first quarter of the sky, the aura crossed a threshold; and the Sunbane closed over the Plains like a lid. Intuitions tried to clarify themselves in Covenant's head; he felt that he should have been able to name them. But he could not. Lacking Linden's eyes, he seemed also to lack the ability to interpret what he saw. A strange blindness —

That evening, the company reached Landsdrop.

Now Covenant knew where he was. Landsdrop was the precipice which separated the Upper Land in the west from the Lower Land in the east. It stretched roughly north-north-west from deep in the Southron Range far towards the unexplored Northern Climbs. Many leagues south of him, Mount Thunder, ancient Gravin Threndor, crouched against the cliff, kneeling with its knees on the Lower Land and its elbows on the Upper. Deep in its dark roots lay the place where the Illearth Stone had been found. And deep in its dark heart was the secret chamber of Kiril Threndor, where Lord Foul the Despiser now made his home.

The sun was setting as the quest halted. The shadow of Landsdrop, three or four thousand feet high in this region, obscured all the east. But Covenant knew what lay ahead. The deadly marsh of Sarangrave Flat.

In past ages, the Sarangrave had become what it was — a world of intricate waterways, exotic life, and cunning peril — through the effects of the river called the Defiles Course. This water emerged between the knees of Mount Thunder from the catacombs in the bowels of the mountain, where it had run through Wightwarrens and Demondim breeding dens, through charnals and offal pits, laboratories and forges, until it was polluted by the most irrefragable filth. As sewage spread throughout the Flat from the river, it corrupted a once-fair region, changed a marsh home for egrets and orchids into a wild haven for the misborn. During the last wars, Lord Foul had found much of the raw material for his armies in Sarangrave Flat.

Covenant knew about the Flat because at one time he had seen it for himself, from Landsdrop to the south of Mount Thunder. He had seen with Land-sharpened eyes, vision he no longer possessed. But he had other knowledge of the region as well. He had heard some things during his visits to Revelstone. And he had learned more from Runnik of the Bloodguard. At one time, Runnik had accompanied Korik and two Lords, Hyrim and Shetra, on a mission to

Seareach, to ask the aid of the Giants against Lord Foul. Lord Shetra had been slain in the Sarangrave, and Runnik had barely survived to bring back the tale.

Covenant's guts squirmed at the thought of the Sarangrave under a sun of pestilence. Beyond doubt, he was going to have to tell Runnik's tale to his companions.

The *Haruchai* set camp a stone's throw from the great cliff because Covenant refused to go any closer in the dark; he already felt too susceptible to the lure of precipices. After he had eaten, fortified himself with *metheglin*, he huddled near the jumping allusions of the campfire, wrapped his memories around him, and asked the quest to listen.

Linden sat down opposite him. He wanted to feel that she was nearby; but the intervening fire distanced her. Sunder and Hollian were vague at the edges of his sight. His attention narrowed to the crackling wood and the recollection of Runnik's tale.

Fist and faith, the Bloodguard had said. *We will not fail*. But they had failed. Covenant knew that now. They had failed, and fallen into Corruption, and died. The Vow had been broken. And the Giants had been slain.

But such things were not part of what he had to tell. To control the old ache of remembrance, he envisioned Runnik's face before him. The Bloodguard had stood, with a pang in his eyes, before High Lord Elena, Lord Mhoram, Hile Troy, and the Unbeliever. A bonfire had made the night poignant. Covenant could recall Runnik's exact words. *The attacks of the lurker. The fall of Lord Shetra*. Bloody hell.

In a dull tone, he told the essential tale. When he had first seen the Sarangrave, it had been a place of fervid luxuriance and subtle death: alive with shy water-bred animals and malicious trees; adorned with pools of clear poison; waylaid with quicksand; spangled with flowers of loveliness and insanity. A place where nature had become vastly treacherous, polluted and hungry. But not evil. It was blameless in the same way that storms and predators were blameless. The Giants, who knew how to be wary, had always been able to travel the Flat.

But forty years later, when Korik's mission had looked out from Landsdrop, the Sarangrave had changed. Slumbering ill had been stirred to wakefulness. And this ill, which Runnik had called *the lurker of the Sarangrave*, had snatched Lord Shetra to her death, despite the fact that she had been under the protection of fifteen Bloodguard. Fifteen – The lurker had been alert to strength, attracted to power. First the Ranyhyn, then the Bloodguard themselves, had unwittingly brought peril down on Korik's mission. And of the messengers Korik had sent to carry the tale back to the High Lord, only Runnik had survived.

After Covenant fell silent, his companions remained still for a moment. Then Hollian asked unsurely, 'May we not ride around this place of risk?'

Covenant did not raise his head. 'That used to be a hundred leagues out of the way. I don't know what it is now.' Had Sarangrave Flat grown or dwindled under the Sunbane?

'We have not such time,' Sunder said immediately. 'Do you desire to confront a second *Grim*? The Clave reads us as we speak of such matters. When I place my hand upon the iron, I feel the eyes of the Banefire fixed in my heart. They hold no benison.'

'The Clave can't – ' Linden began, then stopped herself.

'The Clave,' Covenant responded, 'kills people every day. To keep the bloody Banefire going. How many lives do you think a hundred leagues are going to cost?'

Hollian squirmed. 'Mayhap this lurker no longer lives? The Sunbane alters all else. Will not Sarangrave Flat be altered also?'

'No,' Linden said. But when Covenant and the Stonedownors looked at her sharply, she muttered, 'I'll tell you about it in the morning.' Wrapping blankets around her as if they were a buckler against being touched, she turned away.

For a while after Sunder and Hollian had gone to their rest, Covenant sat and watched the fire die, striving with himself, trying to resist the way Landsdrop plucked at the bottom of his mind, to guess what Linden had learned about the Sunbane, to find the courage he needed for the Sarangrave.

You are mine.

He awoke, haggard and power-haunted, shortly before dawn and found that Linden and the Stonedownors, with Cail, Harn, and Stell, had already left their beds to stand on the edge of Landsdrop. The air was cold; and his face felt stiff and dirty, as if his beard were the grip of his dreams, clutching his visage with unclean fingers. Shivering, he arose, slapping his arms to warm them, then accepted a drink of *metheglin* from Brinn.

As Covenant drank, Brinn said, 'Ur-Lord.'

His manner caught Covenant's attention like a hand on his shoulder. Brinn looked as inscrutable as stone in the crepuscular air; yet his very posture gave an impression of importance.

'We do not trust these Coursers.'

Covenant frowned. Brinn had taken him by surprise.

'The old tellers,' Brinn explained, 'know the tale which Runnik of the Bloodguard told to High Lord Elena. We have heard that the mission to the Giants of Seareach was betrayed to the lurker of the Sarangrave by Earthpower. The Earthpower of the Ranyhyn was plain to all who rode them. And the Vow of the Bloodguard was a thing of Earthpower.

'But we have sworn no life-shaping Vow. The wild magic need

not be used. The Graveller and the eh-Brand need not employ their lore. The lurker need not be aware of us.'

Covenant nodded as he caught Brinn's meaning. 'The Coursers,' he muttered. 'Creatures of the Sunbane. You're afraid they'll give us away.'

'Yes, ur-Lord.'

Covenant winced, then shrugged. 'We don't have any choice. We'll lose too much time on foot.'

Brinn acquiesced with a slight bow. For an instant, the *Haruchai* seemed so much like Bannor that Covenant almost groaned. Bannor, too, would have voiced his doubt – and then would have accepted Covenant's decision without question. Suddenly, Covenant felt that his Dead were coming back to life, that Bannor was present in Brinn, impassive and unfrangibly faithful; that Elena was reborn in Linden. The thought wrenched his heart.

But then a shout snatched him towards Landsdrop.

The sun was rising.

Gritting himself against incipient vertigo, he hurried to join his companions on the lip of the cliff.

Across the east, the sun came up in pale red, as if it had just begun to ooze blood. Light washed the top of the precipice, but left all the Lower Land dark, like a vast region where night was slowly sucked into the ground. But though he could see nothing of the Flat, the sun itself was vivid to him.

Its aura was weaker.

Weaker than it had been the previous morning.

Linden stared intently at it for a moment, then whirled and sent her gaze arcing up and down the length of Landsdrop. Covenant could hear insects burring as if they had been resurrected from the dead ground.

'By God.' She was exultant. 'I was *right*.'

He held himself still, hardly daring to exhale.

'This is the line.' She spoke in bursts of excitement, comprehension. 'Landsdrop. It's like a border.' Her hands traced consequences in the air. 'You'll see. When the sun passes over the cliff – at noon – the Sunbane will be as strong as ever.'

Covenant swallowed thickly. 'Why?'

'Because the atmosphere is different. It doesn't have anything to do with the sun. That corona is an illusion. We see it because we're looking at the sun through the atmosphere. The Sunbane is in the air. The sun doesn't change. But the *air* – '

He did not interrupt. But in the back of his mind he sifted what she said. Some of it made sense: the power required literally to change the sun was inconceivable.

'The Sunbane is like a filter. A way of warping the normal energy of the sun. Corrupting it.' She aimed her words at him as if she were trying to drive insight through his blindness. 'And it's all west from here. The Upper Land. What you see out there – ' she jerked her head eastward – 'is just spillover. That's why it looks weak. The Clave won't be able to reach us any more. And the Sarangrave might be just as you remember it.'

All – ? Covenant thought. But how? Winds shift – storms –

Linden seemed to see his question in his face. 'It's in the air,' she insisted. 'But it's like an emanation. From the ground. It must have something to do with the Earthpower you keep talking about. It's a corruption of the Earthpower.'

A corruption of the Earthpower! At those words, his head reeled, and his own vague intuitions came into focus. She was right. Absolutely. He should have been able to figure it out for himself. The Staff of Law had been destroyed –

And Lord Foul had made his new home in Mount Thunder, which crouched on the edge of Landsdrop, facing west. Naturally, the Despiser would concentrate his Sunbane on the Upper Land. Most of the east already lay under his power. It was all so clear. Only a blind man could fail to see such things.

For a long moment, other facets of the revelation consumed him. Lord Foul had turned the Earthpower itself against his Land. The Sunbane was limited in its reach. But if it became intense enough, deep enough –

But then he seemed to hear for the first time something else Linden had said. *The Sarangrave might be* –

Bloody hell! He forced himself into motion, drove his reluctant bones towards Landsdrop so that he could look over the edge.

The shadow of the horizon had already descended halfway down the cliff. Faint, pink light began to reflect off the waters of the Sarangrave. Pale jewels, rosy and tenuous, spread across the bottom of the shadow, winking together to form reticular lines, intaglios, like a map of the vanishing night. Or a snare. As the sun rose, the gems yellowed and grew more intricate. In links and interstices, they articulated the venous life of the Flat – explication, trap, and anatomy in one. Then all the waterways burned white, and the sun itself shone into Sarangrave Flat.

After five days in the wasted plains, Covenant felt that the lush green and water below him were exquisite, lovely and fascinating, as only adders and belladonna could be. But Linden stood beside him, staring white-eyed at the marsh. Her lips said over and over again, Oh, my God. But the words made no sound.

Covenant's heart turned over in fear. 'What do you see?'

'Do you want to go down there?' Horror strangled her voice. 'Are you crazy?'

'Linden!' he snapped, as if her dread were an accusation he could not tolerate. The backs of his hands burned venomously, lusting of their own volition to strike her. Was she blind to the pressures building in him? Deaf to the victims of the Clave? 'I can't see what you see.'

'I'm a doctor,' she panted as if she were bleeding internally. 'Or I was. I can't bear all this *evil*.'

No! His anger vanished at the sight of her distress. Don't say that. You'll damn us both. 'I understand. Better than anybody. Tell me what it is.'

She did not raise her eyes, would not look at him. 'It's alive.' Her voice was a whisper of anguish. 'The whole thing's alive.' Gibbon had promised her that she would destroy the Land. 'It's hungry.' Covenant knew nothing about her. 'It's like a Raver.'

A Raver? He wanted to shout, What kind of person are you? Why did Foul choose you? But he crushed himself to quietness. '*Is* it a Raver?'

She shook her head. She went on shaking her head, as if she could not reach the end of all the things she wanted to deny. 'Ravers are more – ' She had to search herself for an adequate description – 'more specific. Self-conscious. But it's still *possession*.' She said that word as if it sickened her. Her hands fumbled towards her mouth. 'Help me.'

'No.' He did not mean to refuse her; his arms ached to hold her. But that was not what she needed. 'You can stand it. That old man chose you for a reason.' Groping for ways to succour her, he said, 'Concentrate on it. Use what you see to help yourself. Know what you're up against. Can that thing see us? Is it that specific? If we try to cross – will it know we're there?'

She closed her eyes, covered them to shut out the sight. But then she forced herself to look again. Struggling against revulsion, she jerked out, 'I don't know. It's so big. If it doesn't notice us – If we don't attract its attention – '

If, he finished for her, we don't show the kind of power it feeds on. Yes. But a sudden vision of wild magic stunned him. He did not know how long he could contain the pressure. With a wrench, he made himself move, turned to Brinn, then winced at the way his voice spattered emotion. 'Get the Coursers ready. Find a way down there. As soon as we eat, we're going through.'

Swinging away from the *Haruchai*, he almost collided with Sunder and Hollian. They were leaning against each other as if for support. The knots at the corners of Sunder's jaw bulged; a frown of apprehension or dismay incused his forehead. The young eh-Brand's features were pale with anxiety.

The sight was momentarily more than Covenant could bear. Why was he for ever so doomed to give pain? With unwanted harshness, he rasped, 'You don't have to go.'

Sunder stiffened. Hollian blinked at Covenant as if he had just slapped her face. But before he could master himself enough to apologize, she reached out and placed her hand on his arm. 'Ur-Lord, you miscomprehend us.' Her voice was like the simple gesture of her touch. 'We have long and long ago given up all thought of refusing you.'

With an effort, Sunder loosened the clenching of his teeth. 'That is sooth. Do you not understand this of us? The peril is nothing. We have sojourned so far beyond our knowledge that all perils are become equal. And Linden Avery has said that soon we will be free of the threat of the Clave.'

Covenant stared at the Graveller, at the eh-Brand.

'No, Covenant,' Sunder went on. 'Our concern is otherwise. We journey where the Sunbane does not obtain. We do not love the Sunbane. We are not mad. But without it – ' He hesitated, then said, 'What purpose do we serve? What is our value to you? We have not forgotten Andelain. The Sunbane has made us to be who we are. Perhaps under another sun we will merely burden you.'

The frankness of their uncertainty touched Covenant. He was a leper; he understood perfectly what they were saying. But he believed that the Sunbane could be altered, had to believe that it was not the whole truth of their lives. How else could he go on? Against the sudden thickness in his throat, he said, 'You're my friends. Let's try it and see.'

Fumbling for self-control, he went to get something to eat.

His companions joined him. In silence, they ate as if they were chewing the gristle of their apprehensions.

Shortly, Ceer brought word of a path down the cliff. Hergrom and Cail began to load the Coursers. Long before Covenant had found any courage, the quest was mounted and moving.

Ceer, Hergrom, and Cail led the way on Annoy. With Linden's care and the native health of the *Haruchai*, Cail had essentially recovered from his wound. Brinn, Linden, and Covenant followed on Clash. Then came Harn and Hollian on Clangor, Stell and Sunder on Clang. Vain brought up the rear.

They went northward for half a league to a wide trail cut into the face of Landsdrop. This was a vestige of one of the ancient Giant-ways, by which the Unhomed had travelled between Seareach and Revelstone. Covenant locked his hands in Clash's hair, and fought his vertigo as the company began to descend.

The sheer drop to the Lower Land pulled at him constantly. But the trail had been made by Giants; though it angled and doubled steeply, it was wide enough for the huge Coursers. Still, the swing of Clash's back made him feel that he was about to be pitched over the edge. Even during a brief rest, when Brinn halted the company to refill the waterskins from a rill trickling out of the cliff face, the Flat seemed to reel upward at him like a green storm. He spun, sweating, down the last slope and lurched out into the humid air of the foothills with a pain in his chest, as if he had forgotten how to breathe.

The foothills were clear for some distance before they rolled down into the peril of the Sarangrave. Brinn took the Coursers forward at a clattering run, as if he meant to plunge straight into the verdant sea. But he stopped on the verge of the thick marshgrass which lapped the hills. For a moment, he surveyed the quest, studying Vain briefly, as if he wondered what to expect from the Demondim-spawn. Then he addressed Linden.

'Chosen,' he said with flat formality, 'the old tellers say that the Bloodguard had eyes such as yours. That is not true of us. We understand caution. But we also understand that your sight surpasses ours. You must watch with me, lest we fall to the snares of the Sarangrave.'

Linden swallowed. Her posture was taut, keyed beyond speech by dread. But she answered with a stiff nod.

Now Clash led. Covenant glared out past Linden and Brinn, past Clash's massive head, towards the Sarangrave. The hillside descended into a breeze-ruffled lake of marshgrass, and beyond the grass stood the first gnarled brush of the Flat. Dark shrubs piled towards trees which concealed the horizon. The green of their leaves seemed vaguely poisonous under the pale red sun. In the distance, a bird cried, then fell silent. The Sarangrave was still, as if it waited with bated breath. Covenant could hardly force himself to say, 'Let's go.'

Brinn nudged Clash forward. Bunched together like a fist, the company entered Sarangrave Flat.

Clash stepped into the marshgrass, and immediately sank to its knees in hidden mire.

'Chosen,' Brinn murmured in reproof as the Courser lumbered backwards to extricate itself.

Linden winced. 'Sorry. I'm not – ' She took a deep breath, straightened her back. 'Solid ground to the left.'

Clash veered in that direction. This time, the footing held. Soon, the beast was breasting its way through chest-high grass.

An animal the size of a crocodile suddenly thrashed out from under Clash's hooves – a predator with no taste for such large prey. Clash shied; but the *rukh* steadied it quickly. Clinging to his seat, Covenant forced his gaze ahead and tried not to believe that he was riding into a morass from which there was no outlet and no escape.

Guided by Linden's senses, Brinn led the company towards the trees. In spite of past suns, the growth here was of normal size; yet even to Covenant's blunt perceptions, the atmosphere felt brooding and chancrous, like an exhalation of disease, the palpable leprosy of pollution.

As they reached the trees, the quest passed under thickening blotches of shade. At first, clear ground lay between the trunks, wind-riffled swaths of bland grass concealed things at which Covenant could not guess. But as the riders moved inward, the trees intensified. The grass gave way to shallow puddles, stretches of mud which sucked like hunger at the hooves of the Coursers. Branches and vines variegated the sky. At the edges of hearing came the sounds of water, almost subliminal, as if wary behemoths were drinking from a nearby pool. The ambience of the Sarangrave settled in Covenant's chest like a miasma.

Abruptly, an iridescent bird blundered, squalling, skyward out of the brush. His guts lurched. Sweating, he gaped about him. The jungle was complete; he could not see more than fifty feet in any direction. The Coursers followed a path which wandered out of sight between squat grey trees with cracked bark and swollen trunks. But when he looked behind him, he could see no sign of the way he had come. The Sarangrave sealed itself after the company. Somewhere not far away, he could hear water dripping, like the last blood from Marid's throat.

His companions' nerves were raw. Sunder's eyes seemed to flinch from place to place. Hollian's mien wore a look of unconscious fright, as if she were a child expecting to be terrified. Linden sat hunched forward, gripping Brinn's shoulders. Whenever she spoke, her voice was thin and tense, etiolated by her vulnerability to the ill on all sides. Yet Vain looked as careless as the accursed, untouched even by the possibility of wrong.

Covenant felt that his lungs were filling up with moisture.

The Coursers seemed to share his difficulty. He could hear them snuffling stertorously. They grew restive by degrees, choppy of gait, alternately headstrong and timorous. What do they – ? he began. But the question daunted him, and he did not finish it.

At noon, Brinn halted the company on a hillock covered with pimpernels, and defended on two sides by a pool of viscid sludge which smelled like tar. In it, pale flagellant creatures swam. They broke the surface, spread sluggish ripples about them, then disappeared. They looked like corpses, wan and necrotic, against the darkness of the fluid.

Then Linden pointed through the branches towards the sun. When Covenant peered at the faint aura, he saw it change, just as she had predicted. The full power of the Sunbane returned, restoring pestilence to the Sarangrave.

At the sight, a nameless chill clutched his viscera. The Sarangrave under a sun of pestilence –

Hollian's gasp yanked the company towards her. She was gaping at the pool, with her knuckles jammed between her teeth.

At every spot where sunlight touched the dark surface, pale creatures rose. They thrust blind heads into the light, seemed to yearn upward. A slight wind ruffled the trees, shifting pieces of sunshine back and forth. The creatures flailed to follow the spots of light.

When any creature had kept its head in the light for several moments, it began to expand. It swelled like ripening fruit, then split open, scattering green droplets around the pool. The droplets which fell in shadow quickly turned black and faded. But the ones which fell in the light became bright —

Covenant closed his eyes; but he could not shut out the sight. Green flecks danced against red behind his eyelids. He looked again. The droplets were luminescent and baleful, like liquid emeralds. They grew as they swam, feeding on sludge and pestilence.

'Good God!' Horror compacted Linden's whisper. 'We've got to get out of here!'

Her tone carried complete conviction. The *Haruchai* sprang into motion. Sunder called the Coursers forward. Cail boosted first Linden, then Covenant, upward, so that Clash would not have to kneel. Stell and Harn did the same for the Stonedownors.

Skirting the pool, Brinn guided the beasts eastward as swiftly as he dared, deeper into the toils of Sarangrave Flat.

Fortunately, the Sunbane seemed to steady the Coursers, enforcing the hold of Sunder's *rukh*. Their ponderous skittishness eased. When malformed animals scuttled out from under their hooves, or shrieking birds flapped past their heads, they remained manageable. After half a league, the riders were able to eat a meal without dismounting.

As they ate, Covenant looked for a way to question Linden. But she forestalled him. 'Don't ask.' Spectres haunted the backs of her eyes. 'It hurt. I just knew we were in danger. I don't want to know what it was.'

He nodded. The plight of the company required her to accept visions which wrung her soul. She was so exposed. And he had no way to help her.

The *Haruchai* passed around a pouch of *voure*. As he dabbed the pungent sap on his face and arms, Covenant became aware that the air was alive with butterflies.

Fluttering red and blue, yellow like clean sunshine, gleams of purple and peacock-green, they clouded the spaces between the trees like particoloured snow, alert and lovely. The dance of the Sarangrave — Sarangrave Flat under a sun of pestilence. The insects made him feel strangely bemused and violent. They were beautiful. And they were born of the Sunbane. The venom in him answered their entrancement as if, despite himself, he yearned to fry every lambent wing in sight. He hardly noticed when the company began moving again through the clutches of the marsh. At one time, he had watched helplessly while Wraiths died. Now every memory increased the pressure in him, urged him towards power. But in this place power was suicide.

Piloted by Brinn's caution and Linden's sight, the questors worked eastward. For a time, they travelled the edges of a water channel clogged with lilies. But then the channel cut towards the north, and they were forced to a decision. Linden said that the water was safe. Brinn feared that the lily-stems might fatally tangle the legs of the Coursers.

The choice was taken out of their hands. Hergrom directed their attention north-westward. For a moment, Covenant could see nothing through the obscure jungle. Then he caught a glimpse.

Fragments of livid green. The same green he had watched aborning in the pool of tar.

They were moving. Advancing –

Linden swore urgently. 'Come on.' She clinched Brinn's shoulders. 'Cross. We've got to stay away from those things.'

Without hesitation, Brinn sent Clash into the water.

At once, the Courser's legs were toiled in the stems. But the channel was shallow enough to give the beast a purchase on its bottom. Clash fought forward in a series of violent heaves, thrashing spray in all directions.

The other mounts followed to the east bank. Cascading water from their thick coats, they began to move as swiftly as Sarangrave Flat allowed.

Through stretches of jungle so dense that the trees seemed to claw at the quest, and the creepers dangled like garrottes. Across waving greenswards, intricately beset with quagmires. Along the edges of black bogs which reeked like carrion eaters, pools which fulminated trenchantly. Into clear streams, slime-covered brooks, avenues of mud. Everywhere the riders went, animals fled from them; birds betrayed them in raucous fear or outrage; insects hove and swarmed, warded away only by the smell of *voure*.

And behind them came glimpses of green, elusive spangles, barely seen, as if the company were being stalked by emeralds.

Throughout the afternoon, they wrestled with the Flat; but, as far as Covenant could see, they gained nothing except a sense of panic. They could not outdistance those iridescent green blinks. He felt threats crawling between his shoulder blades. From time to time, his hands twitched as if they ached to fight, as if he knew no other answer to fear except violence.

In the gloaming of sunset, Brinn halted the company for supper. But no one suggested that they should make camp. The pursuit was more clearly visible now.

Green shapes the size of small children, burning inwardly like swamp lights, crept furtively through the brush – creatures of emerald stealth and purpose. Scores of them. They advanced slowly, like a malison that had no need for haste.

A thin rain began to fall, as if the ambience of the Sarangrave were sweating in eagerness.

One of the Coursers snorted. Annoy stamped its feet, tossed its head. Covenant groaned. Shetra had been one of the most potent Lords of Elena's Council, adept at power. Fifteen Bloodguard and Lord Hyrim had been unable to save her.

He clutched at his mount and yearned forward as Brinn and Linden picked their way through the drizzle.

Water slowly soaked his hair and trickled into his eyes. The susurrus of the rain filled the air like a sigh. Everything else had fallen still. The advance of the lambent green creatures was as silent as gravestones. Sunder began to mutter at the Coursers, warning them to obedience.

'Quicksand,' Linden gritted. 'To the right.'

Through his knees, Covenant could feel Clash trembling.

For a moment, the quicksand made a sucking noise. Then the sound of the rain intensified. It became an exhalation of wet lust. Behind the drizzle, Sarangrave Flat waited.

The creatures were within a stone's throw of the company and drawing closer.

A gasp stiffened Linden. Covenant jerked his gaze ahead, searched the night.

In the distance lay a line of green lights.

It cut the quest off from the east.

The line arced to the north, spreading out to join the pursuit.

Hellfire!

The company had ridden into a snare. Flickering through the trees and brush and rain, the fires began to contract around the riders like a noose. They were being herded southward.

Clangor stumbled to its knees, then lurched upright again, blowing fearfully.

Linden panted curses under her breath. Covenant heard them as if they were the voice of the rain. She was desperate, dangerously close to hysteria. Opening her senses in this place must have violated her like submitting to a rape.

A stream he could not see gave an undertone to the rain, then faded. For a time, the beasts slapped through shallow water between knurled old cypresses. The drizzle fell like chrism, anointing the company for sacrifice. He did not want to die like this, unshriven and without meaning. His halfhand clenched and loosened around his ring like an unconscious prophecy.

Linden continued instructing Brinn, barking what she saw into his ear as if that were her only defence against the mad night; but Covenant no longer heard her. He twisted in his seat, trying to gauge the pursuit. The rain sounded like the sizzling of water against hot gems. If he fell from Clash's back, the creatures would be on him in moments.

Out of the darkness, Sunder croaked, 'Heaven and Earth!' A noise like a whimper broke from Hollian.

Covenant turned and saw that the south, too, was lined with green fires. They pent the company on all sides.

The terrain had opened; nothing obscured the encirclement. To one side, streaks of green reflected off a small pond. The water seemed to be leering. The creatures advanced like leprosy. The night held no sound except the sighing of the rain.

Clang danced like a nervous colt. Annoy snorted heavily, winced from side to side. But Sunder kept the Coursers under control. He urged them forward until they stood in the centre of the green circle. There he stopped.

In a flat voice, Brinn said, 'Withhold your power. The lurker must not be made to notice us.'

Linden panted as if she could hardly breathe.

The creatures came seething noiselessly through the dark. The ones beyond the water stopped at its edge; the others continued to approach. They were featureless and telic, like lambent gangrene. They looked horribly like children.

Hergrom dismounted, became a shadow moving to meet the line. For a moment, he was limned by slime fire. Rain stippled his silhouette.

Then Linden coughed, 'No! Don't touch them!'

'Chosen.' Brinn's voice was stone. 'We must breach this snare. Hergrom will make trial, that we may learn how to fight.'

'No.' Her urgency suffocated her. 'They're acid. They're made out of acid.'

Hergrom stopped.

Pieces of darkness whirled at him from Ceer's direction. He caught them, two brands from the quest's store of firewood.

Hefting them by their ends, he confronted the creatures.

Stark against the green, he swung one of the faggots like a club, striking the nearest child-form.

It burst like a wineskin, spilling emerald vitriol over the ground. His brand broke into flame.

The creatures on either side appeared not to care that one of them had fallen. But they promptly shifted to close the gap.

He struck with the other brand, ruptured another shape. Then he returned, bearing the faggots like torches.

In the firelight, Covenant saw that the company stood in an incongruously open stretch of grass. Beyond the advancing children, black trees crouched like craven ghouls. The pool on his left was larger than he had guessed it to be. Scant inches below its surface lay thick, dark mud. A quagmire.

The green creatures sought to herd the quest into it.

As if he could read Covenant's thoughts, Brinn said warningly, 'Ur-Lord. Withhold.'

Covenant tried to reply, could not. His lungs were full of moisture. His chest tugged at the air. He seemed to be asphyxiating on rain. Water ran down his face like blood sweat.

No, it was not the rain. It was the air itself, strangling him.

Gradually, the drizzle changed pitch. It began to sound like a cry. From deep in the night, a wail rose towards the sky.

It was in Covenant's lungs. The very air was howling. He could hear Sunder gasp, feel Linden's muscles jerking to breathe, taste his own acrid fear.

The lurker.

Damnation!

The cry scaled upward in pitch and passion, became a throttling scream. It clawed the depths of his chest, sucked at his courage like quicksand.

Panic.

The company stood like sacrificial cattle, trembling and dumb, while the acid-creatures advanced.

An instant later, Clash's distress became a convulsion. Bucking savagely, the Courser scattered Linden and Covenant to the grass, then sprang insanely against Clang. With Brinn clinging to its neck, Clash knocked Sunder and Stell from Clang's back. At once, the rampaging Courser tried to leap over Clang.

Covenant regained his feet in time to see Clangor go mad. Ignoring Hollian's cries and Harn's commands, the beast plunged against Clash and Clang and drove them to their knees.

Suddenly, all four mounts were possessed by a mad frenzy to attack Sunder and Stell. Annoy crashed squealing into the roil of Coursers. Ceer and Cail dived free. Stell and Harn snatched Hollian out from under Clangor's hooves.

Vain stood near the edge of the pool, watched the confusion as if it pleased him.

Covenant could not understand why the acid-creatures did not charge. They continued to approach incrementally, but did not take the opportunity to attack.

Brinn still clung to Clash's neck, fending off the teeth of the other Coursers with his free hand. The *Haruchai* appeared insignificant, helpless, amid the madness of the beasts.

Darkness gathered in Covenant like venom. It leaped instinctively towards his ring. White gold. Power.

He wanted to shout, but could not get enough air. The howl of the lurker made the rain ring, choked his chest, covered his skin with formication.

He cocked his arm. But Linden, catching his halfhand in both her fists, gasped at him like hysteria, 'No!'

The force of her desperation struck him still and cold. A gelid wind blew in his mind. Use it! Pressure threatened to burst him. His ring. Don't! But the lurker –

The lurker was already aware. It was –

Why was it aware? What had alerted it?

Diving forward, Ceer joined Brinn among the Coursers. Together, the two of them began casting down sacks of supplies and bundles of firewood.

Before they could finish, the tangle abruptly clarified itself. Clangor surged to its feet, followed by Annoy. Clash and Clang heaved upright.

Driven mad by the rain and the piercing shriek of the lurker, they assailed Sunder.

The Graveller ducked under Clangor, dodged Annoy, so that the beasts collided with each other. But the grass was slick under his feet. As he tried to spin out of the way, he went down. A chaos of hooves exploded around him.

Linden clinched Covenant's arm as if he had tried to break free. But he had not, could not have moved to save his life. The acid-children – The howl – Coursers whirling. Rain swarming against his skin.

What had alerted – ?

Stell appeared somehow among the beasts, stood over Sunder, and fought to protect him; he heaved legs aside, punched at heads, forced animals against each other.

Brinn and Ceer sought to distract the Coursers. But their insane fury at Sunder consumed them. He rolled from side to side, avoiding blows. But their savagery was too great.

The Coursers! Covenant gagged. His eyes bulged under the pressure of asphyxiation, vertigo. Creatures of the Sunbane. Corrupted Earthpower.

The lurker was alert to such power.

Then this attack was directed against the Coursers. And they knew it. They were mad with fear.

Why didn't they flee?

Because they were held!

Hellfire!

Covenant sprang into motion with a wrench that knocked Linden to the ground. His eyes locked on to Sunder. He could not breathe, had to breathe. The howl filled his lungs, strangling him. But he could not let Sunder die. With a convulsion of will, he ripped words out of himself.

'The *rukh*! Throw it away!'

Sunder could not have heard him. The screaming of the lurker drowned every other sound. The Graveller jerked over on to his chest as if he had been pounded by a hoof, then jerked back again.

With the *rukh* in his hands.

Stell snatched it from him, hurled it. Arcing over the Coursers, it splashed into the centre of the quagmire.

Instantly, the beasts wheeled. They charged after the iron as if it were the lure of their doom. In their terror, they strove to destroy the thing which prevented them from flight.

One of them smashed into Vain.

He made no effort to evade the impact. In his habitual pose, he stood as if no power on Earth could touch him. But the beast was a creature of the Sunbane, made feral and tremendous by fear. Its momentum knocked him backward.

He toppled into the pool.

The Coursers crashed after him, drove him down with their hooves. Then they, too, were caught in the quagmire.

At once, the water began to boil. Turbulence writhed across the surface, wringing screams from the Coursers; upheavals squirmed as if the quag were about to erupt. One by one, the beasts were wrenched downward, disappearing in dark froth like blood. Sucking noises came from the pool as if it were a gullet.

Moments later, the turmoil ended. The water relaxed with a sigh of satiation.

When the heaving subsided, Vain stood alone in the centre of the pool.

He was sinking steadily. But the unfocus of his eyes was as blind as ever in the light of the torches. The water reached his chest. He did not struggle or cry out.

'Brinn!' Covenant panted. But the *Haruchai* were already moving. Harn pulled a coil of rope from one of the rescued sacks and threw it to Brinn. Promptly, but without haste, Brinn unwound one end of the rope and tossed it towards Vain.

The rope landed across Vain's shoulder.

He did not blink, gave no sign that he had seen it. His arms remained at his sides. The diffusion of his gaze was as complete as the quagmire.

'Vain!' Linden's protest sounded like a sob. The Demondim-spawn did not acknowledge it.

Brinn snatched back the rope, swiftly made a loop with a slip-knot. The water lapped at Vain's neck as the *Haruchai* prepared to throw again.

With a flick, Brinn sent the rope snaking outward. The loop settled around Vain's head. Carefully, Brinn tugged it taut, then braced himself to haul on the rope. Ceer and Harn joined him.

Abruptly, Vain sank out of sight.

When the *Haruchai* pulled, the rope came back empty. The loop was intact.

Until he heard himself swearing, Covenant did not realize that he could breathe.

The howling of the lurker was gone. The acid-creatures were gone. They had vanished into the night.

There was nothing left except the rain.

24

THE SEARCH

Covenant hugged his chest in an effort to steady his quivering heart. His lungs seized air as if even the rain of the Sarangrave were sweet.

Through the stillness, he heard Hollian moan Sunder's name. As Sunder groaned, she gasped, 'You are hurt.'

Covenant squeezed water out of his eyes, peered through the torchlight at the Graveller.

Pain gnarled Sunder's face. Together, Hollian and Linden were removing his jerkin. As they bared his ribs, they exposed a livid bruise where one of the Coursers had kicked him.

'Hold still,' Linden ordered. Her voice shook raggedly, as if she wanted to scream. But her hands were steady. Sunder winced instinctively at her touch, then relaxed as her fingers probed his skin without hurting him. 'A couple broken,' she breathed. 'Three cracked.' She placed her right palm over his lung. 'Inhale. Until it hurts.'

He drew breath; a spasm knotted his visage. But she gave a nod of reassurance. 'You're lucky. The lung isn't punctured.' She demanded a blanket from one of the *Haruchai*, then addressed Sunder again. 'I'm going to strap your chest – immobilize those ribs as much as possible. It's going to hurt. But you'll be able to move without damaging yourself.' Stell handed her a blanket, which she promptly tore into wide strips. Caring for Sunder seemed to calm her. Her voice lost its raw edge.

Covenant left her to her work and moved towards the fire Hergrom and Ceer were building. Then a wave of reaction flooded him, and he had to squat on the wet grass, hunch inward with his arms wrapped around his stomach to keep himself from whimpering. He could hear Sunder hissing thickly through his teeth as Linden bound his chest; but the sound was like the sound of the rain, and Covenant was already soaked. He concentrated instead on the way his heart flinched from beat to beat, and fought for control.

When the attack passed, he climbed to his feet, and went in search of *metheglin*.

Brinn and Ceer had been able to save only half the supplies; but Covenant drank freely of the mead which remained. The future would have to fend for itself. He was balanced precariously on the outer edge of himself and did not want to fall.

He had come within instants of calling up the wild magic – of declaring to the lurker that the Coursers were not the only available prey. If Linden had not stopped him – The drizzle felt like mortification against his skin. If she had not stopped him, he and his companions might already have met Lord Shetra's doom. His friends – he was a snare for them, a walking deathwatch. How many of them were going to die before Lord Foul's plans fructified?

He drank *metheglin* as if he were trying to drown a fire, the fire in which he was fated to burn, the fire of himself. Leper outcast unclean. Power and doubt. He seemed to feel the venom gnawing hungrily at the verges of his mind.

Vaguely, he watched the *Haruchai* fashion scant shelters out of the remaining blankets, so that the people they guarded would not have to lie in rain. When Linden ordered Sunder and Hollian to rest, he joined them.

He awoke, muzzy-headed, in the dawn. The two women were still asleep – Linden lay like a battered wife with her hair sticking damply to her face – but Sunder was up before him. The rain had stopped. Sunder paced the grass slowly, carrying his damaged ribs with care. Concentration or pain accentuated his forehead.

Covenant lurched out of his sodden bed and shambled to the supplies for a drink of water. Then, because he needed companionship, he went to stand with the Graveller.

Sunder nodded in welcome. The lines above his nose seemed to complicate his vision. Covenant expected him to say something about the *rukh* or the Coursers; but he did not. Instead, he muttered tightly, 'Covenant, I do not like this Sarangrave. Is all life thus, in the absence of the Sunbane?'

Covenant winced at the idea. It made him think of Andelain. The Land was like the Dead; it lived only in Andelain, where for a while yet the Sunbane could not stain or ravish. He remembered Caer-Caveral's song:

> But while I can I heed the call
> Of green and tree; and for their worth,
> I hold the glaive of Law against the Earth.

The mourning of that music brought back grief and old rage. Was he not Thomas Covenant, who had beaten the Despiser and cast Foul's

Creche into the Sea? 'If it is,' he answered to the tone of dirges, poisons, 'I'm going to tear that bastard's heart out.'

Distantly, the Graveller asked, 'Is hate such a good thing? Should we not then have remained at Revelstone, and given battle to the Clave?'

Covenant's tongue groped for a reply; but it was blocked by recollections. Unexpectedly, he saw *turiya* Raver in the body of Triock, a Stonedownor who had loved Lena. The Raver was saying, *Only those who hate are immortal.* His ire hesitated. Hate? With an effort, he took hold of himself. 'No. Whatever else happens, I've already got too much innocent blood on my hands.'

'I hear you,' Sunder breathed. His wife and son were in his eyes; he had reason to understand Covenant's denial.

Sunlight had begun to angle into the clearing through the trees, painting streaks across the damp air. A sunrise free of the Sunbane. Covenant stared at it for a moment, but it was indecipherable to him.

The sun roused Linden and Hollian. Soon the company began to prepare for travel. No one spoke Vain's name, but the loss of him cast a pall over the camp. Covenant had been trying not to think about it. The Demondim-spawn was unscrupulous and lethal. He smiled at unreined power. But he was also a gift from Saltheart Foamfollower. And Covenant felt irrationally shamed by the thought that he had let a companion, any companion, sink into that quagmire, even though Linden had said that Vain was not alive.

A short time later, the *Haruchai* shouldered the supplies, and the quest set off. Now no one spoke at all. They were afoot in Sarangrave Flat, surrounded by hazards and by the ears of the lurker. Betrayals seemed to wait for them behind every tree, in every stream. None of them had the heart to speak.

Brinn and Cail led the way, with Linden between them. Turning slightly north of east, they crossed the clearing, and made their way back into the jungle.

For a while, the morning was white and luminous with sun-gilt mist. It shrouded the trees in evanescence. The company seemed to be alone in the Flat, as if every other form of life had fled. But as the mist frayed into wisps of humidity and faded, the marsh began to stir. Birds rose in brown flocks or individual blurs of colour; secretive beasts scurried away from the travellers. At one point, the quest encountered a group of large grey monkeys, feeding at a thicket of berries as scarlet as poison. The monkeys had canine faces and snarled menacingly. But Brinn walked straight towards them with no expression in his flat eyes. The monkeys broke for the trees, barking like hyenas.

For most of the morning, the company edged through a stretch of jungle with solid ground underfoot. But during the afternoon, they had to creep across a wide bog, where hillocks of sodden and mangy grass were interspersed with obscure pools and splotches of quicksand. Some of the pools were clear; others, gravid and mephitic. At sudden intervals, one or another of them was disturbed, as if something vile lay on its bottom. Linden and the *Haruchai* were hard pressed to find a path through the region.

In the distance behind them, the sun passed over Landsdrop and took on the blue aura of rain. But the sky over Sarangrave Flat stayed deep cerulean, untainted and unscathed.

By sunset, they had travelled little more than five leagues.

It would have been better, Covenant thought as he chewed his disconsolate supper, if we'd ridden around. But he knew that such regrets had no meaning. It would have been better if he had never harmed Lena or Elena – never lost Joan – never contracted leprosy. The past was as indefeasible as an amputation. But he could have borne his slow progress more lightly if so many lives, so much of the Land, had not been at stake.

That night came rain. It filled the dark, drenched the dawn, and did not lift until the company had been slogging through mud for half the morning.

In the afternoon, they had to wade a wetland of weeds and bulrushes. The water covered Covenant's thighs; the rushes grew higher than his head. A preterite fear of hidden pits and predators scraped at his nerves. But the company had no choice; this swamp blocked their way as far as the *Haruchai* could see.

The density of the rushes forced them to move in single file. Brinn led, followed immediately by Linden and Cail; then went Harn, Hollian, Stell, Sunder, Covenant, Ceer, and Hergrom. The water was dark and oily; Covenant's legs vanished as if they had been cut off at the waterline. The air was clouded with mosquitoes; and the marsh stank faintly, as if its bottom were littered with carcasses. The sack perched high on Stell's shoulders blocked Covenant's view ahead; he did not know how far he would have to go like this. Instinctively, he tried to hurry, but his boots could not keep their footing in the mud, and the water was as heavy as blood.

The mirk dragged at his legs, stained his clothes. His hands clutched the reeds involuntarily, though they could not have saved him if he fell. His mind cursed at thoughts of Vain. The Demondim-spawn had not even looked at the people who were trying to rescue him. Covenant's pulse laboured in his temples.

Without warning, the rushes beside him thrashed. The water seethed. A coil as thick as his thigh broke the surface.

Instantly, Sunder was snatched out of sight.

Twenty feet away, he heaved up again, with a massive serpent body locked around his hips and neck. Gleaming scales covered strength enough to snap his back like a dry stick.

All the celerity of the *Haruchai* seemed insignificant to Covenant. He saw Stell release his sack, crouch, start a long dive forward, as if each piece of the action were discrete, time-consuming. Ceer carried no sack; he was one fraction of a heartbeat ahead of Stell. Hollian's mouth stretched towards a scream. Every one of the reeds was distinct and terrible. The water had the texture of filthy wool. Covenant saw it all: wet scales; coils knotted to kill; Ceer and Stell in the first reach of their dives; Hollian's mouth –

Marid! A man with no mouth, agony in his eyes, snakes for arms. Fangs agape for Linden's face. Sunder. Marid. Fangs fixed like nails of crucifixion in Covenant's right forearm.

Venom.

In that instant, he became a blaze of fury.

Before Ceer and Stell covered half the distance. Covenant fried the coils straining Sunder's back. Wild magic burned the flesh transparent. Lit spine, ribs, entrails with incandescence.

Linden let out a cry of dismay.

The serpent's death throes wrenched Sunder underwater.

Ceer and Stell dived into the convulsions. They disappeared, then regained their feet, with the Graveller held, gasping, between them. Dead coils thudded against their backs as they bore Sunder out of danger.

All Covenant's power was gone, snuffed by Linden's outcry. Cold gripped the marrow of his bones. Vision of green children and suffocating. Bloody hell.

His companions gaped at him. Linden's hands squeezed the sides of her head, fighting to contain her fear. Covenant expected her to shout abuse at him. But she did not. 'It's my fault.' Her voice was a low rasp. 'I should have seen that thing.'

'No.' Stell spoke as if he were immune to contradiction. 'It came when you had passed. The fault is mine. The Graveller was in my care.'

Hellfire, Covenant groaned uselessly. Hell and damnation.

With an effort, Linden jerked down her hands and forced herself to the Graveller's side. He breathed in short gasps over the pain in his chest. She examined him for a moment, scowling at what she perceived. Then she muttered, 'You'll live.' Outrage and helplessness made her voice as bitter as bile.

The *Haruchai* began to move. Stell retrieved his sack. Brinn reformed the line of the company. Holding herself rigid, Linden took her place. They went on through the swamp.

They tried to hurry. But the water became deeper, holding them back. Its cold rank touch shamed Covenant's skin. Hollian could not keep her feet; she had to cling to Harn's sack and let him pull her. Sunder's injury made him wheeze as if he were expiring.

But finally the reeds gave way to an open channel; and a short distance beyond it lay a sloping bank of marshgrass. The bottom dropped away. The company had to swim.

When they gained solid ground, they saw that all their apparel was covered with a slick brown slime. It stank in Covenant's nostrils. Linden could not keep the nausea off her mien.

With characteristic dispassion, the *Haruchai* ignored their uncleanliness. Brinn stood on the bank, studying the west. Hergrom moved away until he reached a tree he could climb. When he returned, he reported flatly that none of the green acid-creatures were in sight.

Still the company hurried. Beyond the slope, they dropped into a chaos of stunted copses and small poisonous creeks which appeared to run everywhere without moving. Twilight came upon them while they were still winding through the area, obeying Linden's strident command to let no drop of the water touch them.

In the dusk, they saw the first sign of pursuit. Far behind them among the copses was a glimpse of emerald. It disappeared at once. But no one doubted its meaning.

'Jesus God,' Linden moaned. 'I can't stand it.'

Covenant cast an intent look at her. But the gloaming obscured his face. The darkness seemed to gnaw at her features.

In silence, the quest ate a meal and tried to prepare to flee throughout the night.

Dark tensed about them as the sunset was cut off by Landsdrop. But then, strangely, the streams began to emit light. A nacreous glow, ghostly and febrile, shone out of the waters like diseased phosphorescence. And this light, haunting the copses with lines of pearly filigree, seemed to flow, though the water had appeared stagnant. The glow ran through the region, commingling and then separating again like a web of moonlight, but tending always toward the north-east.

In that direction, some distance away, Sarangrave Flat shone brightly. Eldritch light marked the presence of a wide radiance.

Covenant touched Brinn's arm, nodding towards the fire. Brinn organized the company, then carefully led the way forward.

Darkness made the distance deceptive; the light was further away than it appeared to be. Before the questers covered half the intervening ground, tiny emerald fires began to gather behind them. Shifting in and out of sight as they passed among the copses, the acid-creatures stole after the company.

Covenant closed his mind to the pursuit, locked his gaze on the silver ahead. He could not endure to think about the coming attack – the attack which he had made inevitable.

Tracking the glow lines of the streams as if they were a map, Brinn guided the quest forward as swiftly as his caution permitted.

Abruptly, he stopped.

Pearl-limned, he pointed ahead. For a moment, Covenant saw

nothing. Then he caught his breath between his teeth to keep himself still.

Stealthy, dark shapes were silhouetted between the company and the light. At least two of them, as large as saplings.

Firmly, Hergrom pressed Covenant down into a crouch. His companions hid against the ground. Covenant saw Brinn gliding away, a shadow in the ghost-shine. Then the *Haruchai* was absorbed by the copses and the dark.

Covenant lost sight of the moving shapes. He stared towards where he had last seen them. How long would Brinn take to investigate and return?

He heard a sound like a violent expulsion of breath.

Instinctively, he tried to jump to his feet. Hergrom restrained him. Something heavy fell through underbrush. Blows were struck. The distance muffled them; but he could hear their strength.

He struggled against Hergrom. An instant later, the *Haruchai* released him. The company rose from hiding. Cail and Ceer moved forward. Stell and Harn followed with the Stonedownors.

Covenant took Linden's hand and pulled her with him after Sunder.

They crossed two streams diagonally, and then all the glowing rills lay on their right. The flow of silver gathered into three channels, which ran crookedly towards the main light. But the quest had come to firm ground. The brush between the trees was heavy. Only the *Haruchai* were able to move silently.

Near the bank of the closest stream, they found Brinn. He stood with his fists on his hips. Nacre reflected out of his flat eyes like joy.

He confronted a figure twice as tall as himself. A figure like a reincarnation in the eldritch glow. A dream come to life. Or one of the Dead.

A Giant!

'The old tellers spoke truly,' Brinn said. 'I am gladdened.'

The Giant folded his thick arms over his chest, which was as deep and solid as the trunk of an oak. He wore a sark of mail, formed of interlocking granite discs, and heavy leather leggings. Across his back, he bore a huge bundle of supplies. He had a beard like a fist. His eyes shone warily from under massive brows. The blunt distrust of his stance showed that he and Brinn had exchanged blows – and that he did not share Brinn's gladness.

'Then you have knowledge which I lack.' His voice rumbled like stones in a subterranean vault. 'You and your companions.' He glanced over the company. 'And your gladness – ' he touched the side of his jaw with one hand – 'is a weighty matter.'

Suddenly, Covenant's eyes were full of tears. They blinded him; he could not blink away visions of Saltheart Foamfollower – Foamfollower, whose laughter and pure heart had done more to defeat

Lord Foul and heal the Land than any other power, despite the fact that his people had been butchered to the last child by a Giant-Raver wielding a fragment of the Illearth Stone, thus fulfilling the unconscious prophecy of their home in Seareach, which they had named *Coercri*, The Grieve.

All killed, all the Unhomed. They sprang from a sea-faring race, and in their wandering they had lost their way back to their people. Therefore they had made a new place for themselves in Seareach where they had lived for centuries, until three of their proud sons had been made into Giant-Ravers, servants of the Despiser. Then they had let themselves be slain, rather than perpetuate a people who could become the thing they hated.

Covenant wept for them, for the loss of so much love and fealty. He wept for Foamfollower, whose death had been gallant beyond any hope of emulation. He wept because the Giant standing before him now could not be one of the Unhomed, not one of the people he had learned to treasure.

And because, in spite of everything, there were still Giants in the world.

He did not know that he had cried aloud until Hollian touched him. 'Ur-Lord. What pains you?'

'Giant!' he cried. 'Don't you know me?' Stumbling, he went past Linden to the towering figure. 'I'm Thomas Covenant.'

'Thomas Covenant.' The Giant spoke like the murmuring of a mountain. With gentle courtesy, as if he were moved by the sight of Covenant's tears, he bowed. 'The giving of your name honours me. I take you as a friend, though it is strange to meet friends in this fell place. I am Grimmand Honninscrave.' His eyes searched Covenant. 'But I am disturbed at your knowledge. It appears that you have known Giants, Giants who did not return to give their tale to their people.'

'No,' Covenant groaned, fighting his tears. Did not return? Could not. They lost their way, and were butchered. 'I've got so much to tell you.'

'At another time,' rumbled Honninscrave, 'I would welcome a long tale, be it however grievous. The Search has been scarce of story. But peril gathers about us. Surely you have beheld the *skest*? By mischance, we have placed our necks in a garrotte. The time is one for battle or cunning rather than tales.'

'*Skest?*' Sunder asked stiffly over the pain of his ribs. 'Do you speak of the acid-creatures, which are like children of burning emerald?'

'Grimmand Honninscrave.' Brinn spoke as if Sunder were not present. 'The tale of which the ur-Lord speaks is known among us also. I am Brinn of the *Haruchai*. Of my people, here also are Cail, Stell, Harn, Ceer, and Hergrom. I give you our names in the name of a proud memory.' He met Honninscrave's gaze. 'Giant,' he concluded softly, 'you are not alone.'

Covenant ignored both Brinn and Sunder. Involuntarily, only half conscious of what he was doing, he reached up to touch the Giant's hand, verify that Honninscrave was not a figment of silvershine and grief. But his hands were numb, dead for ever. He had to clench himself to choke down his sorrow.

The Giant gazed at him sympathetically. 'Surely,' he breathed, 'the tale you desire to tell is one of great rue. I will hear it – when the time allows.' Abruptly, he turned away. 'Brinn of the *Haruchai*, your name and the names of your people honour me. Proper and formal sharing of names and tales is a joy for which we also lack time. In truth, I am not alone.

'Come!' he cried over his shoulder.

At his word, three more Giants detached themselves from the darkness of the trees and came striding forward.

The first to reach his side was a woman. She was starkly beautiful, with hair like fine-spun iron, and stern purpose on her visage. Though she was slimmer than he, and slightly shorter, she was fully caparisoned as a warrior. She wore a corselet and leggings of mail, with greaves on her arms; a helm hung from her belt, a round iron shield from her shoulders. In a scabbard at her side, she bore a broadsword nearly as tall as Covenant.

Honninscrave greeted her deferentially. He told her the names which the company had given him, then said to them, 'She is the First of the Search. It is she whom I serve.'

The next Giant had no beard. An old scar like a sword cut lay under both his eyes across the bridge of his nose. But in countenance and apparel he resembled Honninscrave closely. His name was Cable Seadreamer. Like Honninscrave, he was unarmed and carried a large load of supplies.

The fourth figure stood no more than an arm's reach taller than Covenant. He looked like a cripple. In the middle of his back, his torso folded forward on itself, as if his spine had crumbled, leaving him incapable of upright posture. His limbs were grotesquely muscled, like tree boughs being choked by heavy vines. And his mien, too, was grotesque – eyes and nose misshapen, mouth crookedly placed. The short hair atop his beardless head stood erect as if in shock. But he was grinning, and his gaze seemed quaintly gay and gentle; his ugliness formed a face of immense good cheer.

Honninscrave spoke the deformed Giant's name: 'Pitchwife.'

Pitchwife? Covenant's old empathy for the destitute and the crippled made him wonder. Doesn't he even rate two names.

'Pitchwife, in good sooth,' the short Giant replied as if he could read Covenant's heart. His chuckle sounded like the running of a clear spring. 'Other names have I been offered in plenty, but none pleased me half so well.' His eyes sparkled with secret mirth. 'Think on it, and you will comprehend.'

'We comprehend.' The First of the Search spoke like annealed iron. 'Our need now is for flight or defence.'

Covenant brimmed with questions. He wanted to know where these Giants had come from, why they were here. But the First's tone brought him back to his peril. In the distance, he caught glimpses of green, a line forming like a noose.

'Flight is doubtful,' Brinn said dispassionately. 'The creatures of this pursuit are a great many.'

'The *skest*, yes,' rumbled Honninscrave. 'They seek to herd us like cattle.'

'Then,' the First said, 'we must prepare to make defence.'

'Wait a minute.' Covenant grasped at his reeling thoughts. 'These *skest*. You know them. What do you know about them?'

Honninscrave glanced at the First, then shrugged. 'Knowledge is a tenuous matter. We know nothing of this place or of its life. We have heard the speech of these beings. They name themselves *skest*. It is their purpose to gather sacrifices for another being, which they worship. This being they do not name.'

'To us – ' Brinn's tone hinted at repugnance – 'it is known as the lurker of the Sarangrave.'

'It *is* the Sarangrave.' Linden sounded raw, over-wrought. Days of intimate vulnerability had left her febrile and defenceless. 'This whole place is alive somehow.'

'But how do you even know that much?' Covenant demanded of Honninscrave. 'How can you understand their language?'

'That also,' the Giant responded, 'is not knowledge. We possess a gift of tongues, for which we bargained most acutely with the *Elohim*. But what we have heard offers us no present aid.'

Elohim. Covenant recognized that name. He had first heard it from Foamfollower. But such memories only exacerbated his sense of danger. He had hoped that Honninscrave's knowledge would provide an escape; but that hope had failed. With a wrench, he pulled himself into focus.

'Defence isn't going to do you any good either.' He tried to put force into his gaze. 'You've got to escape.' *Foamfollower died because of me.* 'If you break through the lines, they'll ignore you. I'm the one they want.' His hands made urging gestures he could not restrain. 'Take my friends with you.'

'Covenant!' Linden protested, as if he had announced an intention to commit suicide.

'It appears,' Pitchwife chuckled, 'that Thomas Covenant's knowledge of Giants is not so great as he believes.'

Brinn did not move; his voice held no inflection. 'The ur-Lord knows that his life is in the care of the *Haruchai*. We will not leave him. The Giants of old also would not depart a companion in peril.

But there is no bond upon you. It would sadden us to see harm come upon you. You must flee.'

'Yes!' Covenant insisted.

Frowning, Honninscrave asked Brinn, 'Why does the ur-Lord believe that the *skest* gather against him?'

Briefly, Brinn explained that the company knew about the lurker of the Sarangrave.

At once, the First said, 'It is decided.' Deftly, she unbound her helm from her belt, settled it on her head. 'This the Search must witness. We will find a place to make defence.'

Brinn nodded towards the light in the north-east. The First glanced in that direction. 'It is good.' At once, she turned on her heel and strode away.

The *Haruchai* promptly tugged Covenant, Linden, and the Stonedownors into motion. Flanked by Honninscrave and Seadreamer, with Pitchwife at their backs, the company followed the First.

Covenant could not resist. He was paralysed with dread. The lurker knew of him, wanted him; he was doomed to fight or die. But his companions – the Giants – Foamfollower had walked into the agony of Hotash Slay for his sake. They must not – !

If he hurt any of his friends, he felt sure he would go quickly insane.

The *skest* came in pursuit. They thronged out of the depths of the Flat, forming an unbroken wall against escape. The lines on either side tightened steadily. Honninscrave had described it accurately: the questers were being herded towards the light.

Oh, hell!

It blazed up in front of them now, chasing the night with nacre, the colour of his ring. He guessed that the water glowed as it did precisely because his ring was present. They were nearing the confluence of the streams. On the left, the jungle retreated up a long hillside, leaving the ground tilted and clear as far ahead as he could see; but the footing was complicated by tangled ground creepers and protruding roots. On the right, the waters formed a lake the length of the hillside. Silver hung like a preternatural vapour above the surface. Thus concentrated, the light gave the surrounding darkness a ghoul-begotten timbre, as if such glowing were the peculiar dirge and lamentation of the accursed. It was altogether lovely and heinous.

A short way along the hillside, the company was blocked by a barrier of *skest*. Viscid green fire ran in close-packed child forms from the water's edge up the hillside to curve around behind the quest.

The First stopped and scanned the area. 'We must cross this water.'

'No!' Linden yelped at once. 'We'll be killed.'

The First cocked a stern eyebrow. 'Then it would appear,' she said after a moment of consideration, 'that the place of our defence has been chosen for us.'

A deformed silence replied. Pitchwife's breathing whistled faintly in and out of his cramped lungs. Sunder hugged Hollian against the pain in his chest. The faces of the *Haruchai* looked like death masks. Linden was unravelling visibly towards panic.

Softly, invidiously, the atmosphere began to sweat under the ululation of the lurker.

It mounted like water in Covenant's throat, scaled slowly upwards in volume and pitch. The *skest* poured interminably through the thick scream. Perspiration crawled his skin like formication. Venom beat in him like a fever.

Cable Seadreamer clamped his hands over his ears, then dropped them when he found he could not shut out the howl. A mute snarl bared his teeth.

Calmly, as if they felt no need for haste, the *Haruchai* unpacked their few remaining bundles of firewood. They meted out several brands apiece among themselves, offering the rest to the Giants. Seadreamer glared at the wood incomprehendingly; but Pitchwife took several faggots and handed the rest to Honninscrave. The wood looked like mere twigs in the Giants' hands.

Linden's mouth moved as if she were whimpering; but the yammer and shriek of the lurker smothered every other cry.

The *skest* advanced, as green as corruption.

Defying the sheen of suffocation on his face, Brinn said, 'Must we abide this? Let us attempt these *skest*.'

The First looked at him, then looked around her. Without warning, her broadsword leaped into her hands, seemed to ring against the howl as she whirled it about her head. 'Stone and Sea!' she coughed – a strangled battle cry.

And Covenant, who had known Giants, responded:

> 'Stone and Sea are deep in life,
> two unalterable symbols of the world.'

He forced the words through his anoxia and vertigo as he had learned them from Foamfollower.

> 'Permanence at rest, and permanence in motion;
> participants in the Power that remains.'

Though the effort threatened to burst his eyeballs, he spoke so that the First would hear him and understand.

Her eyes searched him narrowly. 'You have known Giants indeed,' she rasped. The howling thickened in her throat. 'I name you Giantfriend. We are comrades, for good or ill.'

392

Giantfriend. Covenant almost gagged on the name. The Seareach Giants had given that title to Damelon father of Loric. To Damelon, who had foretold their destruction. But he had no time to protest. The *skest* were coming. He broke into a fit of coughing. Emeralds dizzied him as he struggled for breath. The howl tore at the marrow of his bones. His mind spun. Giantfriend, Damelon, Kevin; names in gyres. Linden Marid venom.

Venomvenomvenom.

Holding brands ready, Brinn and Ceer went out along the edge of the lake to meet the *skest*.

The other *Haruchai* moved the company in that direction. Sweat running into Pitchwife's eyes made him wink and squint like a madman. The First gripped her sword in both fists.

Reft by vertigo, Covenant followed only because Hergrom impelled him.

Marid. Fangs.

Leper outcast unclean.

They were near the burning children now. Too near.

Suddenly, Seadreamer leaped past Brinn like a berserker to charge the *skest*.

Brinn croaked, 'Giant!' and followed.

With one massive foot, Seadreamer stamped down on a creature. It ruptured, squirting acid and flame.

Seadreamer staggered as agony screamed up his leg. His jaws stretched, but no sound came from his throat. In an inchoate flash of perception, Covenant realized that the Giant was mute. Hideously, Seadreamer toppled towards the *skest*.

The lurker's voice bubbled and frothed like the lust of quicksand.

Brinn dropped his brands, caught Seadreamer's wrist. Planting his strength against the Giant's weight, he pivoted Seadreamer away from the creatures.

The next instant, Pitchwife reached them. With prodigious ease, the cripple swept his injured comrade on to his shoulders. Pain glared across Seadreamer's face; but he clung to Pitchwife's shoulders and let Pitchwife carry him away from the *skest*.

At the same time, Ceer began to strike. He splattered one of the acid-children with a back-handed blow of a brand. Conflagration tore half the wood to splinters. He hurled the remains at the next creature. As this *skest* burst, he was already snatching up another faggot, already striking again.

Stell and Brinn joined him. Roaring, Honninscrave slashed at the line with a double handful of wood, scattering five *skest* before the brands became fire and kindling in his grasp.

Together, they opened a gap in the lurker's noose.

The howl tightened in fury, raked the lungs of the company like claws.

Hergrom picked up Covenant and dashed through the breach. Cail followed, carrying Linden. Brinn and Ceer kept the gap open with the last of the firewood while Honninscrave and the First strode past the flames, relying on their Giantish immunity to fire. Pitchwife waded after them, with Seadreamer on his back.

Then the *Haruchai* had no more wood. *Skest* surged to close the breach, driven by the lurker's unfaltering shriek.

Stell leaped the gap. Harn threw Hollian bodily to Stell, then did the same with Sunder.

As one, Brinn, Ceer, and Harn dived over the creatures.

Already, the *skest* had turned in pursuit. The lurker gibbered with rage.

'Come!' shouted the First, almost retching to drive her voice through the howl. The Giants raced along the lake shore, Pitchwife bearing Seadreamer with the agility of a *Haruchai*.

The company fled. Sunder and Hollian sprinted together, flanked by Harn and Stell. Covenant stumbled over the roots and vines between Brinn and Hergrom.

Linden did not move. Her face was alabaster with suffocation and horror. Covenant wrenched his gaze towards her to see the same look which had stunned her mien when she had first seen Joan. The look of paralysis.

Cail and Ceer took her arms and started to drag her forward.

She fought; her mouth opened to scream.

Urgently, the First gasped, 'Ware!'

A wail ripped Hollian's throat.

Brinn and Hergrom leaped to a stop, whirled towards the lake.

Covenant staggered at the sight and would have fallen if the *Haruchai* had not upheld him.

The surface of the lake was rising. The water became an arm like a concatenation of ghost-shine – a tentacle with scores of fingers. It mounted and grew, reaching into the air like the howling of the lurker incarnate.

Uncoiling like a serpent, it struck at the company, at the people who were nearest.

At Linden.

Her mouth formed helpless mewling shapes. She struggled to escape. Cail and Ceer pulled at her. Unconsciously, she fought them.

As vividly as nightmare, Covenant saw her left foot catch in the fork of a root. The *Haruchai* hauled at her. In a spasm of pain, her ankle shattered. It seemed to make no sound through the rage of the lurker.

The arm lashed phosphorescence at her. Cail met the blow, tried to block it. The arm swatted him out of the way. He tumbled headlong towards the advancing *skest*.

They came slowly, rising forward like a tide.

Linden fought to scream, and could not.

The arm swung back again, slamming Ceer aside.

Then Honninscrave passed Covenant, charging towards Linden.

Covenant strove with all his strength to follow the Giant. But Brinn and Hergrom did not release him.

Instantly, he was livid with fury. A flush of venom pounded through him. Wild magic burned.

His power hurled the *Haruchai* away as if they had been kicked aside by an explosion.

The arm of the lurker struck. Honninscrave dived against it, deflected it. His weight bore it to the ground in a chiaroscuro of white sparks. But he could not master it. It coiled about him, heaved him into the air. The pain of its clutch seemed to shatter his face. Viciously, the arm hammered him down. He hit the hard dirt, bounced, and lay still.

The arm was already reaching towards Linden.

Blazing like a torch, Covenant covered half the distance to her. But his mind was a chaos of visions and vertigo. He saw Brinn and Hergrom blasted, perhaps hurt, perhaps killed. He saw fangs crucifying his forearm, felt venom committing murders he could not control.

The shining arm sprang on its fingers at Linden.

For one lurching beat of his heart, horror overcame him. All his dreads became the dread of venom, of wild magic he could not master, of himself. If he struck at the arm now, he would hit Linden. The power ran out of him like a doused flame.

The lurker's fingers knotted in her hair. They yanked her towards the lake. Her broken ankle remained caught in the root fork. The arm pulled, excruciating her bones. Then her foot twisted free.

Linden!

Covenant surged forward again. The howling had broken his lungs. He could not breathe.

As he ran, he snatched out Loric's *krill*, cast aside the cloth, and locked his fingers around the haft. Bounding to the attack, he drove the blade like a spike of white fire into the arm.

The air became a detonation of pain. The arm released Linden, wrenched itself backwards, almost tore the *krill* out of his grasp. Argent poured from the wound like moon flame, casting arcs of anguish across the dark sky.

In hurt and fury, the arm coiled about him, whipping him from the ground. For an instant, he was held aloft in a crushing grip; the lurker clenched him savagely at the heavens. Then it punched him into the water.

It drove him down as if the lake had no bottom and no end. Cold burned his skin, plugged his mouth; pressure erupted in his ears like nails pounding into his skull; darkness drowned his mind. The lurker was tearing him in half.

But the gem of the *krill* shone bright and potent before him. Loric's *krill*, forged as a weapon against ill. A weapon.

With both hands, Covenant slammed the blade into the coil across his chest.

A convulsion loosened the grip. Lurker blood scoured his face.

He was still being dragged downward, for ever deeper into the abysm of the lurker's demesne. The need for air shredded his vitals. Water and cold threatened to burst his bones. Pressure spots marked his eyes like scars of mortality and failure, failure, the Sunbane, Lord Foul laughing in absolute triumph.

No!

Linden in her agony.

No!

He twisted around before the lurker's grasp could tighten again, faced in the direction of the arm. Downward for ever. The *krill* blazed indomitably against his sight.

With all the passion of his screaming heart – with everything he knew of the *krill*, wild magic, rage, venom – he slashed at the lurker's arm.

His hot blade severed the flesh, passed through the appendage like water.

Instantly, all the deep burned. Water flashed and flared; white coruscations flamed like screams throughout the lake. The lurker became tinder in the blaze. Suddenly, its arm was gone, its presence was gone.

Though he still held the *krill*, Covenant could see nothing. The lurker's pain had blinded him. He floated alone in depths so dark that they could never have held any light.

He was dying for air.

25

'IN THE NAME OF THE PURE ONE'

Miserably, stubbornly, he locked his teeth against the water and began to struggle upwards. He felt power-seared and impotent, could not seem to move through the rank depths. His limbs were dead for lack of air. Nothing remained to him except the last convulsion of his chest which would rip his mouth open — nothing except death, and the memory of Linden with her ankle shattered, fighting to scream.

In mute refusal, he went on jerking his arms, his legs, like a prayer for the surface.

Then out of the darkness, a hand snagged him, turned him. Hard palms took hold of his face. A mouth clamped over his. The hands forced his jaws open; the mouth expelled breath into him. That scant taste of air kept him alive.

The hands drew him upwards.

He broke the surface and exploded into gasping. The arms upheld him while he sobbed for air. Time blurred as he was pounded in and out of consciousness by his intransigent heart.

In the distance, a voice — Hollian's? — called out fearfully, 'Brinn? Brinn?'

Brinn answered behind Covenant's head. 'The ur-Lord lives.'

Another voice said, 'Praise to the *Haruchai*.' It sounded like the First of the Search. 'Surely that name was one of great honour among the Giants your people have known.'

Then Covenant heard Linden say as if she were speaking from the bottom of a well of pain, 'That's why the water looked so deadly.' She spoke in ragged bursts through her teeth, fighting to master her hurt with words. 'The lurker was there. Now it's gone.' In the silence behind her voice, she was screaming.

Gone. Slowly, the burn of air starvation cleared from Covenant's mind. The lurker was gone, withdrawn though certainly not dead; no, that was impossible; he could not have slain a creature as vast as the Sarangrave. The lake was lightless. The fires started by the spilling of *skest* acid had gone out for lack of fuel. Night covered the Flat. But somehow he had retained his grip on the *krill*. Its shining enabled him to see.

Beyond question, the lurker was still alive. When Brinn swam him to the shore and helped him out on to dry ground, he found that the atmosphere was too thick for comfort. Far away, he heard the creature keening over its pain; faint sobs seemed to bubble in the air like the self-pity of demons.

On either hand, *skest* gleamed dimly. They had retreated; but they had not abandoned the lurker's prey.

He had only injured the creature. Now it would not be satisfied with mere food. Now it would want retribution.

A torch was lit. In the unexpected flame, he saw Hergrom and Ceer standing near Honninscrave with loads of wood which they had apparently foraged from the trees along the hill crest. Honninscrave held a large stone firepot, from which Ceer lit torches, one after another. As Hergrom passed brands to the other *Haruchai*, light slowly spread over the company.

Dazedly, Covenant looked at the *krill*.

Its gem shone purely, as if it were inviolable. But its light brought back to him the burst of fury with which he had first awakened the blade, when Elena was High Lord. Whatever else Loric had made the *krill* to be, Covenant had made it a thing of savagery and fire. Its cleanliness hurt his eyes.

In silent consideration, Brinn reached out with the cloth Covenant had discarded. He took the *krill* and wrapped its heat into a neat bundle, as if thereby he could make the truth bearable for Covenant. But Covenant went on staring at his hands.

They were unharmed; free even of heat-damage. He had been protected by his own power; even his flesh had become so accustomed to wild magic that he guarded himself instinctively, without expense to any part of himself except his soul. And if that were true –

He groaned.

If that were true, then he was already damned.

For what did damnation mean, if it did not mean freedom from the mortal price of power? Was that not what made Lord Foul what he was? The damned purchased might with their souls; the innocent paid for it with their lives. Therein lay Sunder's true innocence, though he had slain his own wife and son – and Covenant's true guilt. Even in Foul's Creche, he had avoided paying the whole price. At that time, only his restraint had saved him, his refusal to attempt Lord Foul's total extirpation. Without restraint, he would have been another Kevin Landwaster.

But where was his restraint now? His hands were undamaged. Numb with leprosy, blunt and awkward, incapable, yes; yet they had held power without scathe.

And Brinn offered the bundle of the *krill* to him as if it were his future and his doom.

He accepted it. What else could he do? He was a leper; he could not deny who he was. Why else had he been chosen to carry the burden of the Land's need? He took the bundle and tucked it back under his belt, as if in that way he could at least spare his friends from sharing his damnation. Then, with an effort like an acknowledgement of fatality, he forced himself to look at the company.

In spite of his bruises, Honninscrave appeared essentially whole. Seadreamer was able to stand on his acid-burned foot; and Pitchwife moved as if his own fire walk were already forgotten. They reminded Covenant of the *caamora*, the ancient Giantish ritual fire of grief. He remembered Foamfollower burying his bloody hands among the coals of a bonfire to castigate and cleanse them. Foamfollower had been horrified by the lust with which he had slaughtered Cavewights and he had treated his dismay with fire. The flames had hurt him, but not damaged him; when he had withdrawn his hands, they had been hale and clean.

Clean, Covenant murmured. He ached for the purification of fire. But he compelled his eyes to focus beyond the Giants.

Gazing directly at Brinn, he almost cried out. Both Brinn and Hergrom had been scorched by the lash of wild magic; eyebrows and hair were singed, apparel darkened in patches. He had come so close to doing them real harm –

Like Honninscrave, Cail and Ceer were battered but intact. They held torches over Linden.

She lay on the ground with her head on Hollian's lap. Sunder knelt beside her, holding her leg still. His knuckles were white with strain; and he glowered as if he feared that he would have to sacrifice her for her blood.

The First stood nearby with her arms folded over her mail like an angry monolith, glaring at the distant *skest*.

Linden had not stopped talking: the pieces of her voice formed a ragged counterpoint to the moaning of the lurker. She kept insisting that the water was safe now, the lurker had withdrawn, it could be anywhere, it was the Sarangrave, but it was primarily a creature of water, the greatest danger came from water. She kept talking so that she would not sob.

Her left foot rested at an impossible angle. Bone splinters pierced the skin of her ankle, and blood oozed from the wounds in spite of the pressure of Sunder's grip.

Covenant's guts turned at the sight. Without conscious transition, he was kneeling at her side. His kneecaps hurt as if he had fallen. Her hands closed and unclosed at her sides, urgent to find something that would enable her to bear the pain.

Abruptly, the First left her study of the *skest*. 'Giantfriend,' she said, 'her hurt is sore. We have *diamondraught*. For one who is not of Giantish stature, it will bring swift surcease.' Covenant did not lift his eyes from Linden's embattled visage. He was familiar with *diamondraught*; it was a liquor fit for Giants. 'Also, it is greatly healing,' the First continued, 'distilled for our restitution.' Covenant heard glints of compassion along her iron tone. 'But no healing known to us will repair the harm. Her bones will knit as they now lie. She – '

She will be crippled.

No. Anger mounted in him, resentment of his helplessness, rage for her pain. The exhaustion of his spirit became irrelevant. 'Linden.' He hunched forward to make her meet his gaze. Her eyes were disfocused. 'We've got to do something about your ankle.' Her fingers dug into the ground. 'You're the doctor. Tell me what to do.' Her countenance looked like a mask, waxen and aggrieved. '*Linden*.'

Her lips were as white as bone. Her muscles strained against Sunder's weight. Surely she could not bear any more.

But she breathed hoarsely, 'Immobilize the leg.' Wails rose in her throat; she forced them down. 'Above the knee.'

At once, Sunder shifted to obey. But the First gestured him aside. 'The strength of a Giant is needed.' She wrapped Linden's leg in her huge hands, holding it like a vice of stone.

'Don't let me move.'

The company answered her commands. Her pain was irrefusable. Ceer grasped her shoulders. Harn anchored one of her arms; Sunder pinned the other. Brinn leaned along her uninjured leg.

'Give me something to bite.'

Hollian tore a strip from the fringe of her robe, folded it several times, and offered it to Linden's mouth.

'Take hold of the foot.' Dry dread filled her eyes. 'Pull it straight away from the break. Hard. Keep pulling until all the splinters slip back under the skin. Then turn it into line with the leg. Hold the foot so the bones don't shift. When I feel everything's right – ' She panted feverishly; but her doctor's training controlled her. ' – I'll nod. Let go of the foot slowly. Put a splint on it. Up past the knee. Splint the whole leg.'

Immediately, she squeezed her eyes shut, opened her mouth to accept Hollian's cloth.

A nausea of fear twisted in Covenant's bowels; but he ignored it. 'Right,' he grated. 'I'll do it.' Her courage appalled him. He moved to her foot.

Cail brushed him away.

Curses jumped through Covenant's teeth; but Cail responded without inflection, 'This I will do for her.'

Covenant's vitals trembled. His hands had held power enough to maim the lurker and had suffered no harm. 'I said *I'll* do it.'

'No.' Cail's denial was absolute. 'You have not the strength of the *Haruchai*. And the blame for this injury is mine.'

'Don't you understand?' Covenant could not find sufficient force for his remonstration. 'Everything I touch turns to blood. All I do is kill.' His words seemed to drop to the ground, vitiated by the distant self-pity of the lurker. 'She's here because she tried to save my life. I need to help her.'

Unexpectedly, Cail looked up and met Covenant's wounded gaze. 'Ur-Lord,' he said as if he had judged the Unbeliever to the marrow of his bones, 'you have not the strength.'

You don't understand! Covenant tried to shout. But no sound came past the knot of self-loathing in his throat. Cail was right; with his halfhand, he would not be able to grip Linden's foot properly; he could never help her, had not the strength. And yet his hands were unharmed. He could not resist when Pitchwife took hold of him, drawing him away from the group around Linden.

Without speaking, the malformed Giant led him to the campfire Honninscrave was building. Seadreamer sat there, resting his acid-burned foot. He gazed at Covenant with eloquent, voiceless eyes. Honninscrave gave Covenant a sharp glance, then picked up a stone cup from one of his bundles and handed it to Covenant. Covenant knew from the smell that the cup contained *diamondraught*, potent as oblivion. If he drank from that cup, he might not regain consciousness until the next day. Or the day after that.

Unconsciousness bore no burdens, felt no blame.

He did not drink. He stared into the flames without seeing them, without feeling the clench of grief on his features. He did nothing but listen to the sounds of the night: the lurker bubbling pain softly to itself; Pitchwife's faint stertorous breathing; Linden's gagged scream as Cail started to pull at her foot. Her bones made a noise like a breaking of sodden sticks as they shifted against each other.

Then the First said tightly, 'It is done.'

The fire cast streaks of orange and yellow through Covenant's tears. He did not want ever to be able to see again, wished himself for ever deaf and numb. But he turned to Pitchwife and lifted the stone cup towards the Giant. 'Here. She needs this.'

Pitchwife carried the cup to Linden. Covenant followed like a dry leaf in his wake.

Before Covenant reached her, he was met by Brinn and Cail. They blocked his way; but they spoke deferentially. 'Ur-Lord.' Brinn's alien inflection expressed the difficulty of apologizing. 'It was necessary to deny you. No disservice was intended.'

Covenant fought the tightness of his throat. 'I met Bannor in Andelain. He said, "Redeem my people. Their plight is an abomination. And they will serve you well."'

But no words were adequate to articulate what he meant. He fumbled past the *Haruchai*, went to kneel at Linden's side.

She was just emptying the cup which the First held for her. The skin of her face looked as bloodless as marble; a patina of pain clouded her gaze. But her respiration was growing steadier, and the clench of her muscles had begun to loosen. With numb fingers, he rubbed the tears from his eyes, trying to see her clearly, trying to believe that she would be all right.

The First looked at him. Quietly, she said, 'Trust the *diamondraught*. She will be healed.'

He groped for his voice. 'She needs bandages. A splint. That wound should be cleaned.'

'It will be done.' The quaver of stress in Hollian's tone told him that she needed to help. 'Sunder and I —'

He nodded mutely, remaining at Linden's side while the Stone-downors went to heat water and prepare bandages and splints. She seemed untouchable in her weakness. He knelt with his arms braced on the ground and watched the *diamondraught* carry her to sleep.

He also watched the care with which Hollian, Sunder, and Stell washed and bandaged Linden's ankle, then splinted her leg securely. But at the same time, a curious bifurcation came over him – a split like the widening gulf between his uselessness and his power. He was sure now – though he feared to admit it to himself – that he had healed himself with wild magic when he had been summoned to Kevin's Watch with the knife-wound still pouring blood from his chest. He remembered his revulsion at Lord Foul's refrain, *You are mine*, remembered heat and white flame –

Then why could he not do the same for Linden, knit her bones just as he had sealed his own flesh? For the same reason that he could not draw water from the Earth or oppose the Sunbane. Because his senses were too numb for the work, unattuned to the spirit within the physical needs around him. Clearly, this was deliberate, a crucial part of the Despiser's intent. Clearly, Lord Foul sought at every turn to increase both Covenant's might and his helplessness, stretch him on the rack of self-contradiction and doubt. But why? What purpose did it serve?

He had no answer. He had invested too much hope in Linden, in her capacity for healing. And Lord Foul had chosen her on precisely the same grounds. It was too much. Covenant could not think. He felt weak and abject of soul. For a moment, he listened to the misery of the lurker. Then, numbly, he left Linden's side and returned to the campfire, seeking warmth for his chilled bones.

Sunder and Hollian joined him. They held each other as if they, too, felt the cold of his plight. After a few moments, Harn and Hergrom brought food and water. Covenant and the Stonedownors ate like the survivors of a shipwreck.

Covenant's dullness grew in spite of the meal. His head felt as heavy as prostration; his heart lay under a great weight. He hardly noticed that the First of the Search had come to speak with Honninscrave. He stood, leaning towards the flames like a man contemplating his own dissolution. When Honninscrave addressed him, veils of fatigue obscured the Giant's words.

'The First has spoken,' Honninscrave said. 'We must depart. The lurker yet lives. And the *skest* do not retreat. We must depart while they are thus thinly scattered and may be combated. Should the lurker renew its assault now, all your power – and all the Chosen's pain – will have gained us naught.'

Depart, Covenant mumbled. Now. The importance of the words was hidden. His brain felt like a tombstone.

'You speak truly,' Brinn replied for Covenant. 'It would be a gladness to travel with Giants, as the old tellers say *Haruchai* and Giants travelled together in the ancient days. But perhaps our paths do not lie with each other. Where do you go?'

The First and Honninscrave looked at Seadreamer. Seadreamer closed his eyes as if to ignore them; but with one long arm he pointed towards the west.

Brinn spoke as if he were immune to disappointment. 'Then we must part. Our way is eastward, and it is urgent.'

Part? A pang penetrated Covenant's stupor. He wanted the company of the Giants. He had a world of things to tell them. And they were important to him in another way as well, a way he could not seem to articulate. He shook his head. 'No.'

Honninscrave cocked an eyebrow. The First frowned at Covenant.

'We just met,' Covenant murmured. But that was not what he had to say. He groped for clarity. 'Why west?' Those words disentangled some of his illucidity. 'Why are you here?'

'Giantfriend,' the First responded with a hint of iron, 'that tale is long, and the time is perilous. This lurker is a jeopardy too vast to be disdained.'

Covenant knotted his fists and tried to insist. 'Tell me.'

'Thomas Covenant – ' Honninscrave began in a tone of gentle dissuasion.

'I beat that thing once,' Covenant croaked. 'I'll beat it again if I have to.' Don't you understand? All your people were killed. 'Tell me why you're here.'

The First considered her companions. Honninscrave shrugged. Seadreamer kept his eyes closed, communing with a private pain. Pitchwife hid his face behind a cup of *diamondraught*.

Stiffly, she said, 'Speak briefly, Grimmand Honninscrave.'

Honninscrave bowed, recognizing her right to command him. Then he turned to Covenant. His body took on a formal stance, as if even his muscles and sinews believed that tales were things which should be treated with respect. His resemblance to Foamfollower struck Covenant acutely.

'Hear, then, Thomas Covenant,' Honninscrave said with a cadence in his deep voice, 'that we are the leaders of the Search – the Search of the Giants, so called for the purpose which has brought us thus far across the world from our Home. To our people, from time to time among the generations, there is born one possessed of a gift which we name the Earth-Sight – a gift of vision such as only the *Elohim* comprehend. This gift is strange surpassingly, and may be neither foretold nor bound, but only obeyed. Many are the stories I would wish to tell, so that you might grasp the import of what I say. But I must content myself with this one word: the Earth-Sight has become a command to all Giants, which none would willingly shirk or defy. Therefore we are here.

'Among our generation, a Giant was born, brother of my bone and blood, and the Earth-Sight was in him. He is Cable Seadreamer, named for the vision which binds him, and he is voiceless, scalded mute by the extravagance and horror of what the Earth-Sight has seen. With the eyes of the gift, he beheld a wound upon the Earth, sore and terrible – a wound like a great nest of maggots, feeding upon the flesh of the world's heart. And he perceived that this wound, if left uncleansed, unhealed, would grow to consume all life and time, devouring the foundation and corner-stone of the Earth, unbinding Stone and Sea from themselves, birthing chaos.

'Therefore a Giantclave was held, and the Search given its duty. We are commanded to seek out this wound and oppose it, in defence of the Earth. For that reason, we set sail from our Home in the proudest *dromond* of all Giantships, Starfare's Gem. For that reason, we have followed Seadreamer's gaze across the wide oceans of the world – we, and two score of our people, who tend the Gem. And for that reason, we are here. The wound lies in this land, in the west. We seek to behold it, discover its nature, so that we may summon the Search to resist or cleanse it.'

Honninscrave stopped and stood waiting for Covenant's reply. The other Giants studied the Unbeliever as if he held the key to a mystery, the First grimly, Seadreamer as intensely as an oracle, Pitchwife with a gaze like a chuckle of laughter or loss. Possibilities widened the faces of the Stonedownors as they began to understand why Covenant had insisted on hearing the explanation of the Giants. But Covenant was silent. He saw the possibilities, too; Honninscrave's narration had opened a small clear space in his mind, and in that space lay answers. But he was preoccupied with an old grief. Foamfollower's people had died because they were unable to find their way Home.

'Ur-Lord,' Brinn said. 'Time demands us. We must depart.'

Depart. Covenant nodded. 'Yes.' *Give me strength.* He swallowed, asked thickly, 'Where's your ship?'

'The *dromond* Starfare's Gem,' Honninscrave replied as if he desired Covenant to use the ship's title, 'stands anchored off the delta of a great swamp which lies in the east. A distance of perhaps seven score leagues.'

Covenant closed his eyes. 'Take me there. I need your ship.'

The First's breath hissed through her teeth. Pitchwife gaped at the ur-Lord's audacity. After a moment, Honninscrave began hesitantly, 'The First has named you Giantfriend. We desire to aid you. But we cannot – '

'Thomas Covenant,' the First said in a voice like a broadsword, 'what is your purpose?'

'Oh, forsooth!' Pitchwife laughed. 'Let this lurker await our good readiness. We will not be hastened.' His words could have been sarcastic; but he spoke them in a tone of clean glee. 'Are we not Giants? Are not tales more precious to us than life?'

Quietly, almost gently, the First said, 'Peace, Pitchwife.'

At her command, Pitchwife stopped; but his grin went on contradicting the grief of the lurker.

In the core of his numbness, Covenant held to the few things he understood, kept his eyes shut so that he would not be distracted. Distanced from himself by darkness and concentration, he hardly heard what he was saying.

'I know that wound. I know what it is. I think I know what to do about it. That's why we're here. I need you – your ship, your knowledge – your help.'

The thing you seek is not within the Land.

The Staff of Law. The One Tree.

Yet Mhoram had also said, *Do not be deceived by the Land's need. The thing you seek is not what it appears to be.*

Carefully, Honninscrave said, 'Cable Seadreamer asks that you speak more plainly.'

More plainly? For an instant, Covenant's grasp on clarity faltered. Do I have to tell you that it's my fault? That I'm the one who opened the door? But he steadied himself in the eye of all the things he did not understand and began to speak.

There in the night, with his eyes closed against the firelight and the immaculate stars, he described the Sunbane and the purpose for which Lord Foul had created the Sunbane. He outlined its origin in the destruction of the Staff of Law, then told of his own role in the destruction, so that the Giants would understand why the restitution of the Staff was his responsibility. And he talked about what he had learned in Andelain. All these things ran together in his mind; he did not know whether the words he spoke aloud made any sense.

When he finished, he fell silent and waited.

After a time, the First said thoughtfully, 'You ask the use of Starfare's Gem so that you may seek across the world for this One Tree. You ask our aid and our knowledge of the Earth, to aid your seeking.'

Covenant opened his eyes then, let his mortal weariness speak for him. Yes. Look at me. How else can any of this be healed?

'Stone and Sea!' she muttered, 'this is a hard matter. If you speak truly, then the path of the Search lies with you.'

'The ur-Lord,' Brinn said without inflection, 'speaks truly.'

She rejected his assertion with a brusque shrug. 'I doubt not that he speaks truly concerning his own belief. But is his belief a sure knowledge? He asks us to place all the Search into his hands – without any secure vision of what we do. Granted, he is mighty, and has known the friendship of Giants. But might and surety are not children of the same parent.'

'Do you – ' Covenant could feel himself failing into stupidity again, becoming desperate – 'know where the One Tree is?'

'No,' she replied stiffly. She hesitated for only a moment. 'But we know where such knowledge may be gained.'

'Then take me there.' His voice was husky with supplication. 'The Sunbane's getting worse. People are killed every day to feed it. The Land is dying.' I swore I'd never kill again – swore it in the name of Foamfollower's *caamora*. But I can't stop. 'Please.'

Indecision held the First. She glared at the dilemma he had given her. Honninscrave knelt by the fire, tending it as if he needed something to do with his hands. Seadreamer's face wore pain as if he were maimed by his muteness. Near him, Sunder and Hollian waited in suspense.

Whistling thinly through his teeth, Pitchwife began to repack the Giants' bundles. His features expressed a complete confidence that the First would make the right choice.

Without warning, a bolt of white shot through the depths of the lake. It flickered, disappeared. Fired again.

Instantly, the whole lake caught silver. Ghost-shine sprang into the night. The water came to life.

In the distance, the lurker's sobbing mounted towards rage. At once, the air seemed to congeal like fear.

Sunder spat a hoarse curse. Harn and Hergrom dived towards the quest's supplies. Pitchwife tossed a bundle to Honninscrave. Honninscrave caught it, slipped his shoulders into the bindings. The First had already kicked the campfire apart. She and Honninscrave picked up brands to use as torches. Pitchwife threw the other bundle to Seadreamer, then snatched up a torch himself.

Ceer and Cail had lifted Linden. But the splint made her awkward for them. Covenant saw dazedly that they would not be able to carry her, run with her, without hurting her ankle.

He did not know what to do. His lungs ached. The lurker's rising howl tore open the scars of past attacks. Sweat burst from the bones of his skull. The *skest* were moving, tightening their fire around the company. There was nothing he could do.

Then Seadreamer reached Cail and Ceer. The Giant took Linden from them; his huge arms supported her as securely as a litter.

The sight unlocked Covenant's paralysis. He trusted the Giant instinctively. The company began to climb the hillside northward. He left them, turned to confront the water.

Just try it! His fists jerked threats at the fell lustre and the howl. Come on! Try to hurt us again!

Brinn yanked him away from the lake shore and dragged him stumbling up the hill.

Reeling with exertion and anoxia, he fought to keep his feet. Dark trees leaped across his vision like aghast dancers in the nacreous light. He tripped repeatedly. But Brinn upheld him.

The lurker's cry whetted itself on pain and frustration, shrilled into his ears. At the fringes of his sight, he could see the *skest*. They moved in pursuit, as if the lurker's fury were a scourge at their backs.

Then Brinn impelled him over the crest of the hill.

At once, the ghost-light was cut off. Torches bounded into the jungle ahead of him. He struggled after them as if he were chasing swamp-fires. Only Brinn's support saved him from slamming into trunks, thick brush, vines as heavy as hawsers.

The howling scaled towards a shriek, then dropped to a lower, more cunning pitch. But the sound continued to impale Covenant like a swordthorn. He retched for air; the night became vertigo. He did not know where he was going.

A lurid, green blur appeared beyond the torches. The *skest* angled closer on the left, forcing the company to veer to the right.

More *skest*.

The flight of the torches swung further to the right.

Lacking air, strength, courage, Covenant could hardly bear his own weight. His limbs yearned to fall, his chest ached for oblivion. But Hergrom gripped his other arm. Stumbling between *Haruchai*, he followed his companions.

For long moments, they splashed down the length of a cold stream which ran like an aisle between advancing hordes of *skest*. But then the stream faded into quicksand. The company lost time hunting for solid ground around the quagmire.

They gained a reach of clear dirt, soil so dead that even marshgrass could not grow there. They began to sprint. Brinn and Hergrom drew Covenant along more swiftly than he could move.

Suddenly, the whole group crashed to a halt, as if they had blundered against an invisible wall.

The First hissed an oath like a sword-cut. Sunder and Hollian sobbed for air. Pitchwife hugged his crippled chest. Honninscrave swung in circles, scanning the night. Seadreamer stood like a tree with Linden asleep in his arms and stared into the darkness as if he had lost his sight.

With his own breath rending like an internal wound, Covenant jerked forward to see why the company had stopped.

Herded! Bloody hell.

The dead ground stretched like a peninsula out into a region of mud: mire blocked the way for more than a stone's throw on three sides. The muck stank like a charnel, seething faintly, as if corpses writhed in its depths. It looked thick enough to swallow even Giants without a trace.

Already, *skest* had begun to mass at the head of the peninsula, sealing the company in the lurker's trap. Hundreds of *skest*, scores of hundreds. They made the whole night green, pulsing like worship. Even armed with a mountain of wood, no Giant or *Haruchai* could have fought through that throng; and the company had no wood left except the torches.

Covenant's respiration became febrile with cursing.

He looked at his companions. Emerald etched them out of the darkness, as distinct as the accursed. Linden lay panting in Seadreamer's arms as if her sleep were troubled by nightmares. Hollian's face was bloodless under her black hair, pale as prophecy. Sunder's whole visage clenched around the grinding of his teeth. Their vulnerability wrung Covenant's heart. The *Haruchai* and the Giants could at least give some account of themselves before they fell. What could Linden, Sunder, and Hollian do except die?

'Ur-Lord.' Brinn's singed hair and dispassion looked ghastly in the green light. 'The white ring. May these *skest* be driven back?'

Thousands of them? Covenant wanted to demand. I don't have the strength. But his chest could not force out words.

One of Honninscrave's torches burned down to his hand. With a grimace, he tossed the sputtering wood into the mire.

Instantly, the surface of the mud lake caught fire.

Flames capered across the mire like souls in torment. Heat like a foretaste of hell blasted against the company, drove them into a tight cluster in the centre of the peninsula.

The First discarded her torches, whipped out her sword, and tried to shout something. The lurker drowned her voice. But the Giants understood. They placed themselves around their companions, using their bodies as shields against the heat. The First, Honninscrave, and Pitchwife faced outward; Seadreamer put his back to the fire, protecting Linden.

The next instant, a concussion shook the ground. Pitchwife stumbled. Hollian, Sunder, and Covenant fell.

As Covenant climbed back to his feet, he saw a tremendous spout of flame mounting out of the mud.

It rose like a fire-storm and whirled towards the heavens. Its fury tore a gale through the night. Towering over the peninsula, it leaned to hammer the company. The howl of the lurker became a gyre of conflagration.

No!

Covenant eluded Brinn's grasp, wrenched past Honninscrave. He forged out into the heat to meet the firespout.

Baring the *krill*, he raised it so that its gem shone clear. Purest argent pierced the orange mudfire, defying it as hotly as lightning.

In the silence of his clogged lungs, Covenant raged words he did not understand. Words of power.

Melenkurion abatha! Duroc minas mill khakaal!

Immediately, the firespout ruptured. In broken gouts and fear, it crashed backwards as if he had cut off another arm of the lurker. Flames skirted like frustrated ire across the mud. Abruptly, the air was free. Wind empty of howling fed the fire. Covenant's companions coughed and gasped as if they had been rescued from the hands of a strangler.

He knelt on the dead ground. Peals of light rang in his head, tintinnabulating victory or defeat; either one, there was no difference; triumph and desecration were the same thing. He was foundering –

But hands came to succour him. They were steady and gentle. They draped cloth over the *krill*, took it from his power-cramped fingers. Relative darkness poured through his eye-sockets as if they were empty pits, gaping for night. The dark spoke in Brinn's voice. 'The lurker has been pained. It fears to be pained again.'

'Sooth,' the First muttered starkly. 'Therefore it has given our deaths into the hands of its acolytes.'

Brinn helped Covenant to his feet. Blinking at numberless *krill* echoes, he fought to see. But the afterflares were too bright. He was still watching them turn to emerald when he heard Hollian's gasp. The Giants and *Haruchai* went rigid. Brinn's fingers dug reflexively into Covenant's arm.

By degrees, the white spots became orange and green – mudfire and *skest*. The acid-creatures thronged at the head of the peninsula, shimmering like religious ecstasy. They oozed forward slowly, not as if they were frightened, but rather as if they sought to prolong the anticipation of their advance.

Covenant's companions stared in the direction of the *skest*. But not at the *skest*.

Untouched amid the green forms, as if he were impervious to every conceivable vitriol, stood Vain.

His posture was one of relaxation and poise; his arms hung, slightly bent, at his sides. But at intervals he took a step, two steps, drew gradually closer to the leading edge of the *skest*. They broke against his legs and had no effect.

His gaze was unmistakably fixed on Linden.

In a flash of memory, Covenant saw Vain snatch Linden into his arms, leap down into a sea of gravelling. The Demondim-spawn had returned from quicksand and loss to rescue her.

'Who – ?' the First began.

'He is Vain,' Brinn replied, 'given to ur-Lord Thomas Covenant by the Giant Saltheart Foamfollower among the Dead in Andelain.'

She cleared her throat, searching for a question which would produce a more useful answer. But before she could speak, Covenant heard a soft popping noise like the bursting of a bubble of mud.

At once, Vain came to a halt. His gaze flicked past the company, then faded into disfocus.

Covenant turned in time to see a short figure detach itself from the burning mud, step queasily on to the hard ground.

The figure was scarcely taller than the *skest*, and shaped like them, a misborn child without eyes or any other features. But it was made of mud. Flames flickered over it as it climbed from the fire, then died away, leaving a dull brown creature like a sculpture poorly wrought in clay. Reddish pockets embedded in its form glowed dully.

Paralysed by recognition, Covenant watched as a second clay form emerged like a damp sponge from the mud. It looked like a crocodile fashioned by a blind man.

The two halted on the bank and faced the company. From somewhere within themselves, they produced modulated squishing noises which sounded eerily like language. Mud talking.

The First and Pitchwife stared, she sternly, he with a light like hilarity in his eyes. But Honninscrave stepped forward and bowed formally. With his lips, he made sounds which approximated those of the clay forms.

In a whisper. Pitchwife informed his companions, 'They name themselves the *sur-jheherrin*. They ask if we desire aid against the *skest*. Honninscrave replies that our need is absolute.' The clay creatures spoke again. A look of puzzlement crossed Pitchwife's face. 'The *sur-jheherrin* say that we will be redeemed. "In the name of the Pure One,"' he added, then shrugged. 'I do not comprehend it.'

The *jheherrin*. Covenant staggered inwardly as memories struck him like blows. Oh dear God.

The soft ones. They had lived in the caves and mud pits skirting Foul's Creche. They had been the Despiser's failures, the rejected mischances of his breeding dens. He had let them live because the torment of their craven lives amused him.

But he had misjudged them. In spite of their ingrown terror, they had rescued Covenant and Foamfollower from Lord Foul's minions, had taught Covenant and Foamfollower the secrets of Foul's Creche, enabling them to reach the thronehall and confront the Despiser. In the name of the Pure One —

The *sur-jheherrin* were clearly descendants of the soft ones. They had been freed from thrall, as their old legend had foretold. But not by Covenant, though he had wielded the power. His mind burned with remembrance; he could hear himself saying, because he had had no choice, *Look at me, I'm not pure. I'm corrupt.* The word *jheherrin* meant 'the corrupt'. His reply had stricken the clay creatures with despair. And still they had aided him.

But Foamfollower — The Pure One. Burned clean by the *caamora* of Hotash Slay, he had cast down the Despiser, broken the doom of the *jheherrin*.

And now their inheritors lived in the mud and mire of Sarangrave Flat. Covenant clung to the *sur-jheherrin* with his eyes as if they were an act of grace, the fruit of Foamfollower's great clean heart, which they still treasured across centuries that had corroded all human memories of the Land.

The acid-creatures continued to advance, oblivious to Vain and the *sur-jheherrin*. The first *skest* were no more than five paces away, radiating dire emerald. Hergrom, Ceer, and Harn stood poised to sacrifice themselves as expensively as possible, though they must have known that even *Haruchai* were futile against so much green vitriol. Their expressionlessness appeared demonic in that light.

The two *sur-jheherrin* speaking with Honninscrave did not move. Yet they fulfilled their offer of aid. Without warning, the muck edging the peninsula began to seethe. Mud rose like a wave leaping shorewards, then resolved into separate forms. *Sur-jheherrin* like stunted apes, misrecollected reptiles, inept dogs. Scores of them came wetly forward, trailing fires which quickly died on their backs. They surged with surprising speed past the *Haruchai*. And more of them followed. Out of mud lit garishly by the lurker's fire, they arose to defend the company.

The forces met, vitriol and clay pouring bluntly into contact. There was no fighting, no impact of strength or skill. *Skest* and *sur-jheherrin* pitted their essential natures against each other. The *skest* were created to spill green flame over whatever opposed them. But the clay forms absorbed acid and fire. Each *sur-jheherrin* embraced one of the *skest*, drew the acid-creature into itself. For an instant, emerald glazed the mud. Then the green was quenched, and the *sur-jheherrin* moved to another *skest*.

Covenant watched the contest distantly. To his conflicted passions, the battle seemed to have no meaning apart from the *sur-jheherrin* themselves. While his eyes followed the struggle, his ears clinched every word of the dialogue between Honninscrave and the first mud-forms. Honninscrave went on questioning them as if he feared that the outcome of the combat was uncertain, and the survival of the Search might come to depend on what he could learn.

'Honninscrave asks – ' Pitchwife continued to translate across the mute conflict – 'if so many *skest* may be defeated. The *sur-jheherrin* reply that they are greatly outnumbered. But in the name of the Pure One, they undertake to clear our way from this trap and to aid our flight from the Sarangrave.'

More clay forms climbed from the mud to join the struggle. They were needed. The *sur-jheherrin* were not able to absorb *skest* without cost. As each creature took in more acid, the green burning within it became stronger, and its clay began to lose shape. Already, the leaders were melting like heated wax. With the last of their solidity, they oozed out of the combat and ran down the sides of the peninsula back into the mud.

411

'Honninscrave asks if the *sur-jheherrin* who depart are mortally harmed. They reply that their suffering is not fatal. As the acid dissipates, their people will be restored.'

Each of the clay forms, consumed several of the *skest* before being forced to retreat. Slowly, the assault was eaten back, clearing the ground. And more *sur-jheherrin* continued to rise from the mud, replacing those which fled.

Another part of Covenant knew that his arms were clamped over his stomach, that he was rocking himself from side to side, like a sore child. Everything was too vivid. Past and present collided in him: Foamfollower's agony in Hotash Slay; the despair of the soft ones; innocent men and women slaughtered; Linden helpless in Seadreamer's arms; fragments of insanity.

Yet he could hear Pitchwife's murmur as distinctly as a bare nerve. 'Honninscrave asks how the *sur-jheherrin* are able to survive so intimately with the lurker. They reply that they are creatures of mire, at home in quicksand and bog and claybank, and the lurker cannot see them.'

Absorbing their way forward, the *sur-jheherrin* reached Vain, shoved past his thighs. The Demondim-spawn did not glance at them. He remained still, as if time meant nothing to him. The clay forms were halfway to the head of the pininsula.

'Honninscrave asks if the *sur-jheherrin* know this man whom you name Vain. He asks if they were brought to our aid by Vain. They reply that they do not know him. He entered their clay pits to the west, and began journeying at once in this direction, traversing their demesne as if he knew all its ways. Therefore they followed him, seeking an answer to his mystery.' Again, Pitchwife seemed puzzled. 'Thus he brought them by apparent chance to an awareness that the people of the Pure One were present in Sarangrave Flat – and imperilled. At once, they discarded the question of this Vain and set themselves to answer their ancient debt.'

Back-lit by emeralds, orange mudfire in his face, Vain gazed enigmatically through the company revealing nothing.

Behind him, the *skest* began to falter. Some sense of peril seemed to penetrate their dim minds; instead of oozing continuously towards absorption, they started to retreat. The *sur-jheherrin* advanced more quickly.

Honninscrave made noises with his lips. Pitchwife murmured, 'Honninscrave asks the *sur-jheherrin* to speak to him of this Pure One, whom he does not know.'

'No,' the First commanded over her shoulder. 'Enquire into such matters at another time. Our way clears before us. The *sur-jheherrin* have offered to aid us from this place. We must choose our path.' She faced Covenant dourly, as if he had given her a dilemma she did not like. 'It is my word that the duty of the Search lies westward. What is your reply?'

Seadreamer stood at her side, bearing Linden lightly. His countenance wore a suspense more personal than any mere question of west or east.

Covenant hugged his chest, unable to stop rocking. 'No.' His mind was a jumble of shards like a broken stoneware pot, each as sharp-edged and vivid as blame. 'You're wrong.' The Stonedownors stared at him; but he could not read their faces. He hardly knew who he was. 'You need to know about the Pure One.'

The First's eyes sharpened. 'Thomas Covenant,' she rasped, 'do not taunt me. The survival and purpose of the Search are in my hands. I must choose swiftly.'

'Then choose.' Suddenly, Covenant's hands became fists, jerking blows at the invulnerable air. 'Choose, and be ignorant.' His weakness hurt his throat. 'I'm talking about a Giant.'

The First winced, as if he had unexpectedly struck her to the heart. She hesitated, glancing past the company to gauge the progress of the *sur-jheherrin*. The head of the peninsula would be clear in moments. To Covenant, she said sternly, 'Very well, Giant-friend. Speak to me of this Pure One.'

Giantfriend! Covenant ached. He wanted to hide his face in grief; but the passion of his memories could not be silenced.

'Saltheart Foamfollower. A Giant. The last of the Giants who lived in the Land. They'd lost their way Home.' Foamfollower's visage shone in front of him. It was Honninscrave's face. All his Dead were coming back to him. 'Every other hope was gone. Foul had the Land in his hands, to crush it. There was nothing left. Except me. And Foamfollower.

'He helped me. He took me to Foul's Creche, so that I could at least fight, at least make that much restitution, die if I had to. He was burned – ' Shuddering, he fought to keep his tale in order. 'Before we got there, Foul trapped us. We would have been killed. But the *jheherrin* – the ancestors – They rescued us. In the name of the Pure One.

'That was their legend – the hope that kept them sane. They believed that some day somebody pure – somebody who didn't have Foul's hands clenched in his soul – would come and free them. If they were worthy. Worthy! They were so tormented. There wasn't enough weeping in all the world to describe their worth. And I couldn't – ' He choked on his old rage for victims, the preterite and the dispossessed. 'I had power, but I wasn't pure. I was so full of disease and violence – ' His hands groped the air, came back empty. 'And they still helped us. They thought they had nothing to live for, and they helped – '

His vision of their courage held him silent for a moment. But his friends were waiting; the First was waiting. The *sur-jheherrin* had begun to move off the peninsula, absorbing *skest*. He drove himself to continue.

'But they couldn't tell us how to get across Hotash Slay. It was lava. We didn't have any way to get across. Foamfollower – ' The Giant had shouted, *I am the last of the Giants. I will give my life as I choose.* Covenant's memory of that cry would never be healed. 'Foam-follower carried me. He just walked the lava until it sucked him down. Then he threw me to the other side.' His grief resounded in him like a threat of wild magic, unaneled power. 'I thought he was dead.'

His eyes burned with recollections of magma. 'But he wasn't dead. He came back. I couldn't do it alone, couldn't even get into Foul's Creche, never mind find the thronehall, save the Land. He came back to help me. Purified. All his hurts seared, all his hate and lust for killing and contempt for himself gone. He gave me what I needed when I didn't have anything left, gave me joy and laughter and courage. So that I could finish what I had to do without committing another Desecration. Even though it killed him.'

Oh, Foamfollower!

'He was the Pure One. The one who freed the *jheherrin*. Freed the Land. By laughing. A Giant.'

He glared at the company. In the isolation of what he remembered, he was prepared to fight them all for the respect Foamfollower deserved. But his unquenched passion had nowhere to go. Tears reflected orange and green from Honninscrave's cheeks. Pitchwife's mien was a clench of sorrow. The First swallowed thickly, fighting for sternness. When she spoke, her words were stiff with the strain of self-mastery.

'I must hear more of the Giants you have known. Thomas Covenant, we will accompany you from this place.'

A spasm of personal misery knotted Seadreamer's face. The scar under his eyes ached like a protest; but he had no voice.

In silence, Brinn took Covenant's arm and drew him away towards the end of the peninsula. The company followed. Ahead, the *sur-jheherrin* had consumed a passage through the *skest*. Brinn moved swiftly, pulling Covenant at a half-run towards the free night.

When they had passed the *skest*, the *Haruchai* turned eastwards.

As the company fled, a screech of rage shivered the darkness, rang savagely across the Sarangrave. But in front of Covenant and Brinn, *sur-jheherrin* appeared, glowing orange and red.

Guided by clay forms, the company began to run.

26

COERCRI

Five days later, they reached the verge of Sarangrave Flat and broke out of jungle and wetland into the late afternoon of a cloudless sky. The *sur-jheherrin* were unexpectedly swift, and their knowledge of the Flat was intimate; they set a pace Covenant could not have matched. And Sunder and Hollian were in little better condition. Left to their own strength, they would have moved more slowly. Perhaps they would have died.

So for a large portion of each day, the Giants carried them. Seadreamer still bore Linden supine in his arms to protect her leg; but Sunder sat against the First's back, using her shield as a sling; Hollian straddled Pitchwife's hunched shoulders; and Covenant rode in the crook of Honninscrave's elbow. No one protested this arrangement. Covenant was too weary to feel any shame at his need for help. And peril prevented every other form of pride.

At intervals throughout those five days, the air became turgid screams, afflicting the company with an atavistic dread for which there was no anodyne except flight. Four times, they were threatened. Twice, hordes of *skest* appeared out of dark streams and tarpits; twice, the lurker itself attacked. But, aided by the *sur-jheherrin* and by plentiful supplies of green wood, the *Haruchai* and the Giants were able to repulse the *skest*. And Covenant opposed the lurker with the light of the *krill*, lashing white fire from the unveiled gem until the lurker quailed and fled, yowling insanely.

When he had the chance, during times of rest or less frenetic travel, Honninscrave asked the *sur-jheherrin* more questions, gleaning knowledge of them. Their story was a terse one, but it delineated clearly enough the outlines of the past.

For a time which must have been measured in centuries after the fall of Foul's Creche, the *jheherrin* had huddled fearfully in their homes, not daring to trust their redemption, trust that they had been found worthy. But at last they had received proof strong enough for their timorous hearts. Freed from the Despiser's power and from the corruptive might of the Illearth Stone, the *jheherrin* had regained the capacity to bring forth children. That was redemption, indeed. Their children they named the *sur-jheherrin*, to mark their new freedom. In the age which followed, the soft ones began the long migration which took them from the place of their former horror.

From cave to mud pit, quagmire to swamp, underground spring to riverbed, they moved northward across the years, seeking terrain in which they could flourish. And they found what they needed in the Sarangrave. For them, it was a place of safety: their clay flesh and mobility, their ability to live in the bottoms of quicksands and streams, suited them perfectly to the Flat. And in safety they healed their old terror, became creatures who could face pain and risk, if need arose.

Thus their gratitude towards the Pure One grew rather than diminished through the generations. When they saw Giants in peril, their decision of aid was made without hesitation for all the *sur-jheherrin* throughout the Sarangrave.

And with that aid, the company finally reached the narrow strip of open heath which lay between the time-swollen Sarangrave and the boundary hills of Seareach. The quest was in grim flight from the most desperate assault of the *skest*. But suddenly the trees parted, unfurling the cerulean sky like a reprieve overhead. The smell of bracken replaced the dank stenches and fears of the Flat. Ahead, the grass-mantled hills rose like the battlements of a protected place.

The Giants ran a short distance across the heath like Ranyhyn tasting freedom, then wheeled to look behind them.

The *skest* had vanished. The air was still, unappalled by lust or rage, empty of any sound except bird calls and breeze. Even the solidity of the ground underfoot was a surcease from trepidation.

The *sur-jheherrin*, too, melted back into the Flat as if to avoid thanks. At once, Covenant shrugged himself from Honninscrave's arm and returned to the edges of the jungle, trying to find the words he wanted. But his heart had become a wilderland where few words grew. He could do nothing except stare dumbly through the trees with the sun in his face, thinking like an ache, Foamfollower would be proud.

The First joined him and gazed into the Sarangrave with an unwanted softness in her eyes. Brinn joined him; all his companions joined him, standing like a salute to the unquestionable worth of the *sur-jheherrin*.

Later, the *Haruchai* unpacked their supplies and prepared a meal. There between the Sarangrave and Seareach, the company fed and tried to measure the implications of their situation.

Linden sat, alert and awkward, with her back braced against Seadreamer's shin; she needed the support because of the rigid splint on her left leg. She had awakened a day and a half after her injury and had taken pains to assure her companions that her ankle was knitting properly. *Diamondraught* was a potent healer. But since then, Covenant had had no chance to talk to her. Though Seadreamer carried a constant unhappiness on his face, he tended Linden as if she were a child.

Covenant sorely wanted to speak with her. But for the present, sitting in the bracken with the afternoon sun slanting towards evening across his shoulders, he was preoccupied by other questions. The Giants had brought him this far; but they had not been persuaded to give him the help he needed. And he had promised them the tale of the Unhomed. He could not imagine having enough courage to tell it.

Yet he had to say something. Sunder and Hollian had moved away into the dark, seeking a private relief. Covenant understood. After all their other losses, they now had before them a world for which they were not equipped – a world without the Sunbane that made them valuable to their companions. But the Giants sat expectantly around the flames, waiting to hear him argue for their aid. Something he must say. Yet it was not in him.

At last, the First broke the silence. 'Giantfriend.' She used the title she had given him gently. 'You have known Giants – the people of your friend, Saltheart Foamfollower. We deeply desire to hear their story. We have seen in you that it is not a glad tale. But the Giants say that joy is in the ears that hear, not in the mouth that speaks. We will know how to hear you with joy, though the telling pains you.'

'Joy.' Covenant swallowed the breaking of his voice. Her words seemed to leech away what little fortitude he had left. He knew what the Giants would do when they heard his story. 'No. Not yet. I'm not ready.'

From his position behind Covenant, Brinn said, 'That tale is known among the old tellers of the *Haruchai*.' He moved closer to the fire, met the sudden dismay in Covenant's face. 'I will tell it, though I have not been taught the skill of stories.' In spite of its dispassion, his gaze showed that he was offering a gift, offering to carry one of Covenant's burdens for him.

But Covenant knew the story too well. The fate of the Bloodguard and their Vow was inextricably bound up with the doom of the Seareach Giants. In his *Haruchai* honesty, Brinn would certainly reveal parts of the story which Covenant, would never choose to tell. Brinn would disclose that Korik's mission to the Unhomed had reached *Coercri* with Lord Hyrim during the slaughter of the Giants by a Giant-Raver. Three of the Bloodguard had survived, had succeeded in killing the Giant-Raver, had captured a fragment of the Illearth Stone. But the Stone had corrupted them, turning them to the service of Lord Foul. And this corruption had so appalled the Bloodguard that they had broken their Vow, had abandoned the Lords during the Land's gravest peril. Surely Brinn would describe such things as if they were not a great grief to his people, not the reason why group after group of *Haruchai* had returned to the Land, falling prey to the butchery of the Clave. This Covenant could not bear. The Bloodguard had always judged themselves by standards which no mortal could meet.

'No,' Covenant almost moaned. He faced Brinn, gave the only answer he had. You don't have to do that. It's past. It wasn't their fault. ' "Corruption wears many faces." ' He was quoting Bannor. ' "Blame is a more enticing face than others, but it is none the less a mask for the Despiser." ' Do you know that Foul maimed those three Bloodguard? Made them into halfhands? 'I'll tell it.' It's on my head. 'When I'm ready.' A pang of augury told him that *Haruchai* were going to die because of him.

Brinn studied him for a moment. Then the *Haruchai* shrugged fractionally, withdrew to his place guarding Covenant's back. Covenant was left with nothing between him and the intent eyes of the Giants.

'Giantfriend,' the First said slowly, 'such tales must be shared to be borne. An untold tale withers the heart. But I do not ask that you ease your heart. I ask for myself. Your tale concerns my kindred. And I am the First of the Search. You have spoken of the Sunbane which so appalls the Earth. My duty lies there. In the west. Seadreamer's Earth-Sight is clear. We must seek out this evil and oppose it. Yet you desire our aid. You ask for our proud *dromond* Starfare's Gem. You assert that your path is the true path of the Search. And you refuse to speak to us concerning our people.

'Thomas Covenant, I ask for your tale because I must choose. Only in stories may the truth to guide me be found. Lacking the knowledge which moves your heart, I lack means to judge your path and your desires. You must speak.'

Must? In his emotional poverty, he wanted to cry out. You don't know what you're doing! But the Giants regarded him with eyes which asked and probed. Honninscrave wore his resemblance to Foamfollower as if that oblique ancestry became him. Seadreamer's stare seemed rife with Earth-Sight. Empathy complicated Pitchwife's smile. Covenant groaned inwardly.

'These hills — ' He gestured eastward, moving his halfhand like a man plucking the only words he could find. 'They're the boundary of Seareach. Where the Giants I knew used to live. They had a city on the Sea. *Coercri*: The Grieve. I want to go there.'

The First did not reply, did not blink.

He clenched his fist and strove to keep himself intact. 'That's where they were murdered.'

Honninscrave's eyes flared. Pitchwife drew a hissing breath through his teeth. 'In their homes?'

'Yes.'

The First of the Search glared at Covenant. He met her look, saw dismay, doubt, judgement, seethe like sea shadows behind her eyes. In spite of his fear, he felt strangely sure that her anger would give him what he wanted.

In a tone of quiet iron, she said, 'Honninscrave will return to Starfare's Gem. He will bring the Giantship northward. We will meet at this *Coercri*. Thus I prepare to answer your desires – if I am persuaded by your tale. And the others of the Search will wish to behold a city of Giants in this lost land.

'Thomas Covenant, I will wait. We will accompany you to the coast of Seareach. But – ' her voice warned him like a sword in her hands – 'I will hear this tale of murder.'

Covenant nodded. He folded his arms over his knees, buried his face between his elbows; he needed to be alone with his useless rue. You'll hear it. Have mercy on me.

Without a word, Honninscrave began to pack the supplies he would need. Soon he was gone, striding briskly towards the Sea as if his Giantish bones could do without rest for ever.

The sound of Honninscrave's departure seemed to stretch out Covenant's exhaustion until it covered everything. He settled himself for sleep as if he hoped that he would never awaken.

But he came out of dreams under the full light of the moon. In the last flames of the campfire, he could see the Giants and the Stonedownors slumbering. Dimly, he made out the poised, dark shapes of the *Haruchai*. Vain stood at the edge of the light, staring at nothing like an entranced prophet.

A glimpse of orange-red reflecting from Linden's eyes revealed that she also was awake. Covenant left his blankets. His desire for the escape of sleep was strong, but his need to talk to her was stronger. Moving quietly, he went to her side.

She acknowledged him with a nod, but did not speak. As he sat beside her, she went on staring into the embers.

He did not know how to approach her; he was ignorant of any names which might unlock her. Tentatively, he asked, 'How's your leg?'

Her whisper came out of the dark, like a voice from another world. 'Now I know how Lena must have felt.'

Lena? Surprise and shame held him mute. He had told her about that crime when she had not wanted to hear. What did it mean to her now?

'You raped her. But she believed in you and she let you go. It's like that for me.'

She fell silent. He waited for a long moment, then said in a stiff murmur, 'Tell me.'

'Almost everything I see is a rape.' She spoke so softly that he had to strain to hear her. 'The Sunbane. The Sarangrave. When that Raver touched me, I felt as if I had the Sunbane inside me. I don't

419

know how you live with that venom. Sometimes I can't even stand to look at you. That touch denied everything about me. I've spent half my life fighting to be a doctor. But when I saw Joan, I was so horrified – I couldn't bear it. It made me into a lie. That's why I followed you.

'That Raver – It was like with Joan, but a thousand times worse. Before that, I could at least survive what I was seeing – the Sunbane, what it did to the Land – because I thought it was a disease. But when he touched me, he made everything evil. My whole life. Lena must have felt like that.'

Covenant locked his hands together and waited. After a while, she went on. 'But my ankle is healing. I can feel it. When it was broken, I could see inside it, see everything that needed to be done, how to get the bones back into place. I knew when they were set right. And now I can feel them healing. They're fusing just the way they should. The tissues, the blood-vessels and nerves – ' She paused as if she could not contain all her emotion in a whisper. 'And that *diamondraught* speeds up the process. I'll be able to walk in a few days.'

She turned to face him squarely. 'Lena must have felt like that, too. Or she couldn't have let you get away with it.

'Covenant.' Her tone pleaded for his understanding. 'I need to heal things. I need it. That's why I became a doctor, and why I can't stand all this evil. It isn't something I can heal. I can't cure souls. I can't cure myself.'

He wanted to understand, yearned to comprehend her. Her eyes reflected the embers of the fire like echoes of supplication. But he had so little knowledge of who she was, how she had come to be such a person. Yet the surface of her need was plain enough. With an effort, he swallowed his uncertainty, his fear. 'The One Tree,' he breathed. 'We'll find it. The Giants know whom to ask to find out where it is. We'll make a Staff of Law. You'll be able to go home. Somehow.'

She looked away, as if this were not the answer she desired. But when she spoke, she asked, 'Do you think they're going to help us? Seadreamer doesn't want to. I can see it. His Earth-Sight is like what I feel. But it's with him all the time. Distance doesn't make any difference. The Sunbane eats at him all the time. He wants to face it. Fight it. End what's happening to him. And the First trusts him. Do you think you can convince her?'

'Yes.' What else could he offer her? He made promises he did not know how to keep because he had nothing else to give. 'She isn't going to like it. But I'll find a way.'

She nodded as if to herself. For a while she was still, musing privately over the coals like a woman who needed courage and only knew how to look for it alone. Then she said, 'I can't go back to the

Sunbane.' Her whisper was barely audible. 'I can't.'

Hearing her, Covenant wanted to say, You won't have to. But that was a promise he feared to make. In Andelain, Mhoram had said, *The thing you seek is not what it appears to be. In the end, you must return to the Land.* Not what it appears – ? Not the One Tree? The Staff of Law?

That thought took him from Linden's side; he could not face it. He went like a craven back to his blankets and lay there hugging his apprehension until his weariness pulled him back to sleep.

The next morning, while the sunrise was still hidden, lambent and alluring behind the hills, the company climbed into Seareach.

They ascended the slope briskly, in spite of Covenant's grogginess, and stood gazing out into the dawn and the wide region which had once been Saltheart Foamfollower's home. The crisp breeze chilled their faces; and in the taintless light, they saw that autumn had come to the fair land of Seareach. Below them, woods nestled within the curve of the hills: oak, maple, and sycamore anademed in fall-change; Gilden gloriously bedecked. And beyond the woods lay rolling grasslands as luxuriously green as the last glow of summer.

Seeing Seareach for the first time – seeing health and beauty for the first time since he had left Andelain – Covenant felt strangely dry and detached. Essential parts of him were becoming numb. His ring hung heavily on his halfhand, as if, when his two fingers had been amputated, he had also lost his answer to self-doubt. Back at Revelstone, innocent men and women were being slain to feed the Sunbane. While that crime continued, no health in all the world could make a difference to him.

Yet he was vaguely surprised that Sunder and Hollian did not appear pleased by what they saw. They gazed at the autumn as if it were Andelain – a siren-song, seductive and false, concealing madness. They had been taught to feel threatened by the natural loveliness of the Earth. They did not know who they were in such a place. With the Sunbane, Lord Foul had accomplished more than the corruption of nature. He had dispossessed people like the Stonedownors from the simple human capacity to be moved by beauty. Once again, Covenant was forced to think of them as lepers.

But the others were keenly gladdened by the view. Appreciation softened the First's stern countenance; Pitchwife chuckled gently under his breath, as if he could not contain his happiness; Seadreamer's misery melted somewhat, allowing him to smile. The *Haruchai* stiffened slightly, as if in their thoughts they stood to attention out of respect for the fealty and sorrow which had once inhabited Seareach. And Linden gazed into the sunrise as if the autumn offered her palliation for her personal distress. Only Vain showed no reaction. The Demondim-spawn seemed to care for nothing under any sun.

At last, the First broke the silence. 'Let us be on our way. My heart has conceived a desire to behold this city which Giants have named The Grieve.'

Pitchwife let out a laugh like the cry of a kestrel, strangely lorn and glad. With a lumbering stride, he set off into the morning. Ceer and Hergrom followed. The First also followed. Seadreamer moved like the shifting of a colossus, stiff and stony in his private pain. Sunder scowled apprehensively; Hollian gnawed at her lower lip. Together, they started after the Giants, flanked by Stell and Harn. And Covenant went with them like a man whose spirit had lost all its resilience.

Descending towards the trees, Pitchwife began to sing. His voice was hoarse, as if he had spent too much of his life singing threnodies; yet his song was as heart-lifting as trumpets. His melody was full of wind and waves, of salt and strain, and of triumph over pain. As clearly as the new day, he sang:

> 'Let breakers crash against the shore –
> let rocks be rimed with sea and weed,
> cliffs carven by the storm –
> let calm becalm the deeps,
> or wind appal the waves, and sting –
> and sting –
> nothing overweighs the poise of Sea and Stone.
> The rocks and water-battery of Home endure.
> We are the Giants,
> born to live,
> and bold for going where the dreaming goes.
>
> 'Let world be wide beyond belief,
> the ocean be as vast as time –
> let journeys end or fail,
> seaquests fall in ice or blast,
> and wandering be for ever. Roam –
> and roam –
> nothing tarnishes the poise of Sea and Stone.
> The hearth and harbourage of Home endure.
> We are the Giants,
> born to sail,
> and bold to go wherever dreaming goes.'

On his song went, on through the trees and the fall-fire of the leaves, on into poignancy and yearning and the eagerness to hear any tale the world told. It carried the quest forward, lightened Seadreamer's gaze; it eased the discomfort of the Stonedownors like an affirmation against the unknown, gave a spring to the dispassionate strides of the *Haruchai*. Echoing in Covenant's mind like the thronged glory of the trees, it solaced his unambergrised heart for a time, so that he could walk the land which had been Foamfollower's home without faltering.

He had been too long under the Sunbane, too long away from the Land he remembered. His eyes drank at the trees and the grasslands, the scapes and vistas, as if such things ended a basic drought, restored to him the reasons for his quest. Beyond the hills, Seareach became a lush profusion of grapes, like a vineyard gone wild for centuries; and in it birds flocked, beasts made their homes. If he had not lacked Linden's vision, he could have spent days simply renewing his sense of health.

But he was condemned to the surface of what he beheld. As the leagues stretched ahead of him, three score or more to the coast, his urgency returned. At his back, people were dying to pay for every day of his journey. Yet he could not walk any faster. A crisis was brewing within him. Power; venom; rage. Impossible to live with wild magic. Impossible to live without it. Impossible to keep all the promises he had made. He had no answer. He was as mortal as any leper. His tension was futile. Seeking to delay the time of impact, when the storm born of venom and doubt would hit, he cast around for ways to occupy his mind.

Linden was wrapped up in her efforts to recover from the damage the Sunbane and Sarangrave Flat had done to her. Sunder and Hollian shared an air of discomfiture, as if they no longer knew what they were doing. So Covenant turned to the Giants, to Pitchwife, who was as loquacious as the First was stern.

His misshapen features worked grotesquely as he talked; but his appearance was contradicted by his lucid gaze and irrepressible humour. At the touch of a question, he spoke about the ancient Home of the Giants, about the wide seas of the world, about the wonders and mysteries of roaming. When he became excited, his breathing wheezed in his cramped lungs; but for him, even that difficult sound was a form of communication, an effort to convey something quintessential about himself. His talk was long and full of digressions, Giantish apostrophes to the eternal grandeur of rock and ocean; but gradually he came to speak of the Search, and of the Giants who led it.

Cable Seadreamer's role needed no explanation; his Earth-Sight guided the Search. And his muteness, the extravagant horror which had bereft him of voice, as if the attempt to put what he saw into speech had sealed his throat, only made his claim on the Search more absolute.

But being Seadreamer's brother was not the reason for Grimmand Honninscrave's presence. The Giantclave had selected him primarily for his skill as pilot and captain; he was the Master of the *dromond*

Starfare's Gem, and proud in the pride of his ship.

As for the First, she was a Swordmain, one of the few Swordmain-nir among the current generation of the Giants, who had maintained for millennia a cadre of such fighters to aid their neighbours and friends at need. She had been chosen because she was known to be as resolute as Stone, as crafty as Sea – and because she had bested every other Swordmain to win a place at the head of the Search.

'But why?' asked Covenant. 'Why did she want the job?'

'Why?' Pitchwife grinned. 'In good sooth, why should she not? She is a Swordmain, trained for battle. She knows, as do we all, that this wound will grow to consume the Earth unless it is opposed. And she believes that its ill is already felt, even across the land of Home, giving birth to evil seas and blighted crops. And cripples.' His eyes glinted merrily, defying Covenant to pity his deformity.

'All right.' Covenant swallowed the indignation he usually felt whenever he encountered someone whose happiness seemed to be divorced from the hard fact of pain. 'Tell me about yourself. Why were you chosen?'

'Ah, that is no great mystery. Every ship, however proud, must have a pitchwife, and I am an adept, cunning to mend both hawser and shipstone. Also, my lesser stature enables me for work in places where other Giants lack space. And for another reason, better than all others.' He lowered his voice and spoke privately to Covenant. 'I am husband to the First of the Search.'

Involuntarily, Covenant gaped. For an instant, he believed that Pitchwife was jesting ironically. But the Giant's humour was personal. 'To me,' he whispered, so that the First could not hear him, 'she is named Gossamer Glowlimn. I could not bear that she should sail on such a Search without me.'

Covenant remained silent, unable to think of any adequate response. *I am husband* – Echoes of Joan ran through him; but when he tried to call up her face, he could find nothing except images of Linden.

During the evening of the quest's third day in Seareach, Linden borrowed Hollian's dirk to cut the splint away from her leg. Her companions watched as she tentatively flexed her knee, then her ankle. Light twinges of pain touched her face, but she ignored them, concentrating on the inner state of her bones and tissues. After a moment, her features relaxed. 'It's just stiff. I'll try walking on it tomorrow.'

A sigh rustled through the company. 'That is good,' the First said kindly. Sunder nodded gruff agreement. Hollian stooped to Linden, hugged her. Linden accepted their gladness; but her gaze reached towards Covenant, and her eyes were full of tears for which he had no answer. He could not teach her to distinguish between the good and ill of her health sense.

The next morning, she put weight on her foot, and the bones held. She was not ready to do much walking; so Seadreamer continued to carry her. But the following day she began working to redevelop the strength of her legs, and the day after that she was able to walk at intervals for nearly half the company's march.

By that time, Covenant knew they were nearing the Sea. The terrain had been sloping slowly for days, losing elevation along rumpled hills and wide, wild, hay leas, down fields like terraces cut for Giants. Throngs of grave old woods leaned slightly, as if they were listening to the Sea; and now the crispness of the air had been replaced by moisture and weight, so that every breeze felt like the sighing of the ocean. He could not smell salt yet; but he did not have much time left.

That night, his dreams were troubled by the hurling of breakers. The tumult turned his sleep into a nightmare of butchery, horror made all the more unbearable by vagueness, for he did not know who was being butchered or why, could not perceive any detail except blood, blood everywhere, the blood of innocence and self-judgement, permitting murder. He awoke on the verge of screams, and found that he was drenched by a thunderstorm. He was cold, and could not stop shivering.

After a time, the blue lash and clap of the storm passed, riding a stiff wind out of the east; but the rain continued. Dawn came, shrouded in torrents which soaked the quest until Covenant's bones felt sodden, and even the Giants moved as if they were carrying too much weight. Shouting over the noise, Pitchwife suggested that they find or make shelter to wait out the storm. But Covenant could not wait. Every day of his journey cost the lives of people whose only hope arose from their belief in the Clave; and the Clave was false. He drove his friends into movement with a rage which made the nerves of his right arm ache as if his fingers could feel the hot burden of his ring. The companions went forward like lonely derelicts, separated from each other by the downpour.

And when at last the storm broke, opening a rift of clear sky across the east, there against the horizon stood the lorn stump of *Coercri*'s lighthouse. Upraised like a stonework forearm from which the fist had been cut away, it defied weather and desuetude as if it were the last gravestone of the Unhomed.

Giants who had loved laughter and children and fidelity, and had been slaughtered in their dwellings because they had not chosen to defend themselves.

As the rain hissed away into the west, Covenant could hear waves pounding the base of The Grieve. A line of grey ocean lay beyond the rim of the cliff; and above it, a few hardy terns had already taken flight after the storm, crying like the damned.

He advanced until he could see the dead city.

Its back was towards him; *Coercri* faced the Sea. The Unhomed had honeycombed the sheer cliff above the breakers so that their city confronted the east and hope. Only three entrances marked the rear of The Grieve, three tunnels opening the rock like gullets, for ever gaping in granite sorrow over the blow which had reft them of habitation and meaning.

'Thomas Covenant.' The First was at his side, with Pitchwife and Seadreamer behind her. 'Giantfriend.' She held her voice like a broadsword at rest, unthreatening, but ready for combat. 'You have spoken of Giants and *jheherrin*; and in our haste, we did not question that which we did not understand. And we have waited in patience for the other tale of which you gave promise. But now we must ask. This place is clearly Giant-wrought – clearly the handiwork of our people. Such craft is the blood and bone of Home to us. About it we could not be mistaken.'

Her tone tightened. 'But this place which you name The Grieve has been empty for many centuries. And the *jheherrin* of which you spoke are also a tale many centuries old. Yet you are human – more short-lived than any other people of the Earth. How is it possible that you have known Giants?'

Covenant grimaced; he had no room in his heart for that question. 'Where I come from,' he muttered, 'time moves differently. I've never been here before. But I knew Saltheart Foamfollower. Maybe better than I knew myself. Three and a half thousand years ago.' Then abruptly the wrench of pain in his chest made him gasp. Three and a half – ! It was too much – a gulf so deep it might have no bottom. How could he hope to make restitution across so many years?

Clenching himself to keep from panting, he started down the slope towards the central tunnel, the main entrance to *Coercri*.

The clouds had withdrawn westward, uncovering the sun. It shone almost directly into the stone passage, showed him his way to the cliff face. He strode the tunnel as if he meant to hurl himself from the edge when he reached it. But Brinn and Hergrom flanked him, knowing what he knew. His companions followed him in silence, hushed as if he were leading them into a graveyard hallowed by old blood. Formally, they entered The Grieve.

At its end, the tunnel gave on to a rampart cut into the east-most part of the cliff. To the north and south, *Coercri* curved away, as if from the blunt prow of the city. From that vantage, Covenant was able to see all The Grieve outstretched on either hand. It was built vertically, level after level of ramparts down the precipice; and the tiers projected or receded to match the contours of the rock. As a result, the city front for nearly a thousand feet from cliff edge to base had a knuckled aspect, like hands knotted against the weather and the eroding Sea.

This appearance was emphasized by the salt deposits of the centuries. The guardwalls of the lower ramparts wore grey-white knurs as massive as travertine; and even the highest levels were marked like the mottling of caducity, the accumulated habit of grief.

Behind the ramparts, level after level, were doorways into private quarters and public halls, workshops and kitchens, places for songs and stories and Giantclaves. And at the foot of the cliff, several heavy stone piers stood out from the flat base which girdled the city. Most of these had been chewed to ruins; but, near the centre of *Coercri*, two piers and the levee between them had endured. Combers rolling in the aftermath of the storm beat up the levee like frustration and obstinance, determined to break the piers, breach the rock, assail *Coercri*, even if the siege took the whole life of the Earth to succeed.

Considering the city, the First spoke as if she did not wish to show that she was moved. 'Here is a habitation, in good sooth – a dwelling fit for Giants. Such work our people do not lightly undertake or inconsiderately perform. Perhaps the Giants of this place knew that they were lost to Home. But they were not lost to themselves. They have given pride to all their people.' Her voice held a faint shimmer like the glow of hot iron.

And Pitchwife lifted up his head as if he could not contain his wildness, and sang like a cry of recognition across the ages:

'We are the Giants,
born to sail,
and bold to go wherever dreaming goes.'

Covenant could not bear to listen. Not lost to themselves. No. Not until the end, until it killed them. He, too, could remember songs. *Now we are Unhomed, bereft of root and kith and kin*. Gripping his passions with both hands to control them, restrain them for a little while yet, he moved away along the rampart.

On the way, he forced himself to look into some of the rooms and halls, like a gesture of duty to the dead.

All the stone of the chambers – chairs, utensils, tables – was intact, though every form of wood or fibre had long since fallen away. But the surfaces were scarred with salt: whorls and swirls across the floors; streaks down the walls; encrustations over the bedframes; spontaneous slow patterns as lovely as frost-work and as corrosive as guilt. Dust or cobwebs could not have articulated more eloquently the emptiness of The Grieve.

Impelled by his private urgency, Covenant returned to the centre of the city. With his companions trailing behind him, he took a crooked stairway which descended back into the cliff, then towards the Sea again. The stairs were made for Giants; he had to half-leap down them awkwardly, and every landing jolted his heart. But the daylight had begun to fade, and he was in a hurry. He went down three levels before he looked into more rooms.

The first doorway led to a wide hall large enough for scores of Giants. But the second, some distance further along the face of the city, was shut. It had been closed for ages; all the cracks and joints around the architrave were sealed by salt. His instincts ran ahead of his mind. For reasons he could not have named, he barked to Brinn, 'Get this open. I want to see what's inside.'

Brinn moved to obey; but the salt prevented him from obtaining a grip.

At once, Seadreamer joined him and began scraping the crust away like a man who could not stand closed doors, secrets. Soon, he and Brinn were able to gain a purchase for their fingers along the edge of the stone. With an abrupt wrench, they swung the door outwards.

Air, which had been tombed for so long that it no longer held any taint of must or corruption, spilled through the opening.

Within was a private living chamber. For a moment, dimness obscured it. But as Covenant's eyes adjusted, he made out a dark form sitting upright and rigid in a chair beside the hearth.

Mummified by dead air and time and subtle salt, a Giant.

His hands crushed the arms of the chair, perpetuating for ever his final agony. Splinters of old stone still jutted between his fingers.

His forehead above his vacant eyesockets was gone. The top of his head was gone. His skull was empty, as if his brain had exploded, tearing away half his cranium.

Hellfire!

'It was as the old tellers have said.' Brinn sounded like the dead air. 'Thus they were slain by the Giant-Raver. Unresisting in their homes.'

Hell and blood!

Trembling, Seadreamer moved forward. 'Seadreamer,' the First said softly from the doorway, warning him. He did not stop. He touched the dead Giant's hand, tried to unclose those rigid fingers. But the ancient flesh became dust in his grasp and sifted like silence to the floor.

A spasm convulsed his face. For an instant, his eyes glared madly. His fists bunched at the sides of his head, as if he were trying to fight back against the Earth-Sight. Then he whirled and surged towards Covenant as if he meant to wrest the tale of the Unhomed from Covenant by force.

'Giant!'

The First's command struck Seadreamer. He veered aside, lurched

428

to press himself against the wall, struggling for self-mastery.

Shouts that Covenant could not still went on in his head: curses that had no meaning. He forced his way from the room, hastened to continue his descent towards the base of *Coercri*.

He reached the flat headrock of the piers as the terns were settling to roost for the night and the last pink of sunset was fading from the Sea. The waves gathered darkly as they climbed the levee, then broke into froth and phosphorescence against the stone. *Coercri* loomed above him; with the sun behind it, it seemed to impend towards the Sea as if it were about to fall.

He could barely discern the features of his companions. Linden, the Giants, Sunder and Hollian, the *Haruchai*, even Vain – they were night and judgement to him, a faceless jury assembled to witness the crisis of his struggle with the past, with memory and power, and to pronounce doom. He knew what would happen as if he had foreseen it with his guts, though his mind was too lost in passion to recognize anything except his own need. He had made promises – He seemed to hear the First saying before she spoke, 'Now, Thomas Covenant. The time has come. At your behest, we have beheld The Grieve. Now we must have the story of our lost kinfolk. There can be neither joy nor decision for us until we have heard the tale.'

The water tumbled its rhythm against the levee, echoing her salt pain. He answered without listening to himself, 'Start a fire. A big one.' He knew what the Giants would do when they heard what they wanted. He knew what he would do.

The *Haruchai* obeyed. With brands they had garnered from Seareach, and Seadreamer's firepot, they started a blaze near the base of the piers, then brought driftwood to stoke the flames. Soon the fire was as tall as Giants, and shadows danced like memories across the ramparts.

Now Covenant could see. Sunder and Hollian held back their apprehension sternly. Linden watched him as if she feared he had fallen over the edge of sanity. The faces of the Giants were suffused with firelight and waiting, with hunger for any anodyne. Reflecting flames, the flat countenances of the *Haruchai* looked inviolate and ready, as pure as the high mountains where they made their homes. And Vain – Vain stood black against the surrounding night, and revealed nothing.

But none of that mattered to Covenant. The uselessness of his own cursing did not matter. Only the fire held any meaning; only *Coercri*, and the lorn reiteration of the waves. He could see Foamfollower in the flames. Words which he had suppressed for long days of dread and uncertainty came over him like a creed, and he began to speak.

He told what he had learned about the Unhomed, striving to heal their slaughter by relating their story.

Joy is in the ears that hear.

Foamfollower! Did you let your people die because you knew I was going to need you?

The night completed itself about him as he spoke, spared only by stars from being as black as The Grieve. Firelight could not ease the dark of the city or the dark of his heart. Nothing but the surge of the Sea – rise and fall, dirge and mourning – touched him as he offered their story to the Dead.

Fully, formally, omitting nothing, he described how the Giants had come to Seareach through their broken wandering. He told how Damelon had welcomed the Unhomed to the Land and had foretold that their bereavement would end when three sons were born to them, brothers of one birth. And he spoke about the fealty and friendship which had bloomed between the Giants and the Council, giving comfort and succour to both; about the high Giantish gratitude and skill which had formed great Revelstone for the Lords; about the concern which had led Kevin to provide for the safety of the Giants before he kept his mad tryst with Lord Foul and invoked the Ritual of Desecration; about the loyalty which brought the Giants back to the Land after the Desecration, bearing with them the First Ward of Kevin's Lore so that the new Lords could learn the Earthpower anew. These things Covenant detailed as they had been told to him.

But then Saltheart Foamfollower entered his story, riding against the current of the Soulsease towards Revelstone to tell the Lords about the birth of three sons. That had been a time of hope for the Unhomed, a time for the building of new ships and the sharing of gladness. After giving his aid to the Quest for the Staff of Law, Foamfollower had returned to Seareach; and the Giants had begun to prepare for the journey Home.

At first, all had gone well. But forty years later a silence fell over Seareach. The Lords were confronted with the army of the Despiser and the power of the Illearth Stone. Their need was sore, and they did not know what had happened to the Giants. Therefore Korik's mission was sent to *Coercri* with the Lords Hyrim and Shetra, to give and ask whatever aid was possible.

The few Bloodguard who survived brought back the same tale which Foamfollower later told Covenant.

And he related it now as if it were the unassuageable threnody of the Sea. His eyes were full of firelight, blind to his companions. He heard nothing except the breakers in the levee and his own voice. Deep within himself, he waited for the crisis, knowing it would come, not knowing what form it would take.

For doom had befallen the three brothers: a fate more terrible to the Giants than any mere death or loss of Home. The three had been captured by Lord Foul, imprisoned by the might of the Illearth

430

Stone, mastered by Ravers. They became the mightiest servants of the Despiser. And one of them came to The Grieve.

Foamfollower's words echoed in Covenant. He used them without knowing what they would call forth. 'Fidelity,' the Giant had said. 'Fidelity was our only reply to our extinction. We could not have borne our decline if we had not taken pride.

'So my people were filled with horror when they saw their pride riven – torn from them like rotten sails in the wind. They saw the portent of their hope of Home – the three brothers – changed from fidelity to the most potent ill by one small stroke of the Despiser's evil. Who in the Land could hope to stand against a Giant-Raver? Thus the Unhomed became the means to destroy that to which they had held themselves true. And in horror at the naught of their fidelity, their folly practised through long centuries of pride, they were transfixed. Their revulsion left no room in them for thought or resistance or choice. Rather than behold the cost of their failure – rather than risk the chance that more of them would be made Soulcrusher's servants – they elected to be slain.'

Foamfollower's voice went on in Covenant's mind, giving him words. 'They put away their tools.'

But a change had come over the night. The air grew taut. The sound of the waves was muffled by the concentration of the atmosphere. Strange forces roused themselves within the city.

'And banked their fires.'

The ramparts teemed with shadows, and the shadows began to take form. Light as eldritch and elusive as sea phosphorescence cast rumours of movement up and down the ways of *Coercri*.

'And made ready their homes.'

Glimpses which resembled something Covenant had seen before flickered in the rooms and solidified, shedding a pale glow like warm pearls. Tall ghosts of nacre and dismay began to flow along the passages.

'As if in preparation for departure.'

The Dead of The Grieve had come to haunt the night.

For one mute moment, he did not comprehend. His companions stood across the fire from him, watching the spectres; and their shadows denounced him from the face of *Coercri*. Was it true after all that Foamfollower had deserted his people for Covenant's sake? That Lord Foul's sole reason for destroying the Unhomed was to drive him, Thomas Covenant, into despair?

Then his crisis broke over him at last, and he understood. The Dead had taken on definition as if it were the flesh of life, had drifted like a masque of distress to the places which had been their homes. And there, high on the southmost rampart of The Grieve, came the Giant-Raver to appal them.

He shone a lurid green, and his right fist clenched a steaming image of emerald, dead echo of the Illearth Stone. With a deliberate hunger which belied his swiftness, he approached the nearest Giant. She made no effort to escape or resist. The Raver's fist and Stone passed into her skull, into her mind; and both were torn away with a flash of power.

In silence and rapine, the Giant-Raver moved to his next victim.

The Dead of The Grieve were re-enacting their butchery. The flow of their movements, the Giant-Raver's progress from victim to victim, was as stately as a gavotte; and the flash of each reiterated death glared across the waves without noise or end, punctuating heinously the ghost dance of the Unhomed. Damned by the way they had abandoned the meaning of their lives, they could do nothing in the city which was their one great grave except repeat their doom, utter it again and again across the ages whenever *Coercri* held any eyes to behold their misery.

From room to room the Giant-Raver went, meting out his ancient crime. Soon, a string of emeralds covered the highest rampart as each new blast pierced Covenant's eyes, impaled his vision and his mind like the nails of crucifixion.

And as the masque went on; multiplying its atrocity, the living Giants broke, as he had known they would. His anguish had foreseen it all. *Joy is in the ears that hear.* Yes, but some tales could not be redeemed by the simple courage of the listener, by the willingness of an open heart. Death such as this, death piled cruelly upon death, century after century, required another kind of answer. In their desperation, the living Giants accepted the reply Covenant had provided for them.

Pitchwife led the way. With a sharp wail of aggrievement, he rushed to the bonfire and plunged his arms to the shoulders in among the blazing firewood. Flames slapped his face, bent his head back in a mute howl against the angle of his crippled chest.

Linden cried out. But the *Haruchai* understood, and did not move.

The First joined Pitchwife. Kneeling on the stone, she clamped her hands around a raging log and held it.

Seadreamer did not stop at the edge of the flames. Surging as if the Earth-Sight had deprived him of all restraint, he hurled his whole body into the fire, stood there with the blaze writhing about him like the utterance of his agony.

Caamora: the ritual fire of grief. Only in such savage physical hurt could the Giants find release and relief for the hurting of their souls.

Covenant had been waiting for this, anticipating and dreading it. *Caamora.* Fire. Foamfollower had walked selflessly into the magma of Hotash Slay and had emerged as the Pure One.

The prospect terrified him. But he had no other solution to the venom in his veins, to the power he could not master, had no other answer to the long blame of the past. The Dead repeated their doom in The Grieve above him, damned to die that way for ever unless he could find some grace for them. Foamfollower had given his life gladly so that Covenant and the Land could live. Covenant began moving, advancing towards the fire.

Brinn and Hergrom opposed him. But then they saw the hope and ruin in his eyes. They stepped aside.

'Covenant!'

Linden came running towards him. But Cail caught her, held her back.

Heat shouted against Covenant's face like the voice of his destiny; but he did not stop. He could not stop. Entranced and compelled, he rode the mourning of the Sea forward.

Into the fire.

At once, he became wild magic and grief, burning with an intense white flame that no other blaze could touch. Shining like the gem of the *krill*, he strode among the logs and embers to Seadreamer's side. The Giant did not see him, was too far gone in agony to see him. Remembering Foamfollower's pain, Covenant thrust at Seadreamer. Wild magic blasted the Giant from the fire, sent him sprawling across the cold stone.

Slowly, Covenant looked around at his companions. They were distorted by the flames, gazing at him as if he were a ghoul. Linden's appalled stare hurt him. Because he could not reply to her in any other way, he turned to his purpose.

He took hold of the wild magic, shaped it according to his will, so that it became his own ritual, an articulation of compassion and rage for all torment, all loss.

Burning, he opened himself to the surrounding flames.

They rushed to incinerate him; but he was ready. He mastered the bonfire with argence, bent it to his command. Flame and power were projected outward together, so that the blaze lashed tremendously into the night.

He spread his arms to the city, stretched himself as if he yearned to embrace the whole of The Grieve.

In wild magic, white puissance without sound, he shouted:

Come! This is the *caamora*! Come and be healed!

And they came. His might and his will interrupted the masque, broke the *geas* which locked the Dead in their weird damnation. Hearing him, they turned as if they had been waiting through all the long ages of their anguish for his call. In throngs and eagerness, they began flowing down the passages of *Coercri*.

Like a river, they swept out on to the headrock of the piers.

Towards the fire.

The Giant-Raver tried to pursue them. But the breaking of their eternal round seemed to break also his hold over them, break the spell of his maleficent glee. His form frayed as he moved, blurred until he was only a tingling green smear of memory across The Grieve – until he faded into the night, and was lost.

And the Dead continued towards the fire.

The *Haruchai* drew back, taking Linden and the Stonedownors with them. Pitchwife and the First went with aching bones to tend Seadreamer.

Vain did not move. He stood in the path of the Dead and watched Covenant's immolation with gaiety in his eyes.

But the Dead passed around him, streamed forward. Need and hope shone through their pearl faces.

Reaching out to them as if they were all one, as if they were only Foamfollower in multiform guise, Covenant took them into his embrace, and wept white fire.

The wild magic struck pain into them, seared them the way a physical conflagration would have seared their bodies. Their forms went rigid, jaws stretched, eyes stared – spectres screaming in soul-anguish. But the screaming was also laughter.

And the laughter prevailed.

Covenant could not hold them. They came into his arms, but they had no bodies that he could hug. Nothing filled his embrace; no contact or benison restored him to himself. He might have been alone in the fire.

Yet the laughter stayed with him. It was glad mirth, joy and restitution which Foamfollower would have known how to share. It ran in his ears like the Sea and sustained him until everything else was gone – until his power was spent against the heavens, and the night closed over him like all the waters of the world.

27

GIANTFRIEND

The next morning, the *dromond* Starfare's Gem arrived in a gleam of white sails, as if it had been newly created from the sun's reflection on the blue Sea. It hove into sight like a stone castle riding gallantly before the wind, beautifully both swift and massive, matching the grace and strength of the Giants.

Covenant watched its approach from the cliff above *Coercri*. He sat far enough back from the edge to appease his fear of heights, but close enough to have a good view. Linden, Sunder, and Hollian were with him, though he had only asked for the company of the two

Stonedownors. Brinn and Cail, Stell and Harn were there also. And Vain had followed Covenant or Linden up through The Grieve, though his blackness offered no explanation of why he had done so. Only Hergrom and Ceer remained below with the Giants.

Earlier, Sunder had told Covenant how he had been saved when his power failed. Linden had watched him amid the blaze, reading his wild magic, gauging the limits of his endurance. One moment before the white flame had guttered and gone out, she had shouted a warning. Seadreamer had dashed into the bonfire and had emerged on the far side with Covenant in his arms, unharmed. Even Covenant's clothing had not been singed.

In the dawn, he had awakened as if from the first irenic sleep of his life. Sunrise had lain across the headrock of the city, lighting the faces of Linden and the First as they sat regarding him. The First had worn her iron beauty as if behind it lay a deep gentleness. But Linden's gaze was ambiguous, undecided.

In a severe tone, she asked, 'Why didn't you tell me what you were going to do?'

'I didn't dare,' he replied, giving her the truth. 'I was too afraid of it. I couldn't even admit it to myself.'

She shifted her position, drawing somewhat away from him. 'I thought you'd gone crazy.'

He sighed, allowed himself to express at least that much of his loneliness. 'Maybe I did. Sometimes it's hard to tell the difference.'

She frowned and fell silent, looking away towards the Sunbirth Sea. After a moment, the First roused herself to speak.

'Thomas Covenant,' she said, 'I know not whether in truth the path of the Search lies with you. I have not seen with my own eyes the Sunbane, nor met in my own person the malice of him whom you name the Despiser, nor felt in my own heart the nature of what must be done. But Pitchwife urges that I trust you. Cable Seadreamer has beheld a vision of healing, when he had learned to believe that no healing remained in all the world. And for myself – ' She swallowed thickly. 'I would gladly follow a man who can so give peace to the damned.

'Giantfriend,' she said, containing her emotion with formality, 'the Search will bear you to the land of the *Elohim*. There we believe that knowledge of the One Tree may be gained. If it lies within our doing, we will accompany you to the Tree, hoping for an answer to the peril of the Earth. This we will do in the name of our people, who have been redeemed from their doom.'

She passed a hand over her tears and moved away, leaving him eased, as if it were the outcome of his dreams.

But he arose, because there were still things he had to do, needs to be met, responsibilities to be considered. He spoke to the Stonedownors, led them to the upper rim of *Coercri* with Linden, the

Haruchai, and Vain behind him, sat facing the morning and the Sea and the unknown Earth.

Now he would have liked to be alone with the aftermath of his *caamora*. But he could see the time of his departure from the Land arriving. It sailed the same salt wind which ruffled his hair and beard, and he knew he had no choice. Every day, more lives were shed to feed the Sunbane. The Land's need was a burden he could not carry alone.

For a time, he sat exchanging silence with his companions. But at last he found the will to speak. 'Sunder. Hollian.' They sat attentively, as if he had become a figure of awe. He felt like a butcher as he said, 'I don't want you to come with me.'

The eh-Brand's eyes widened as if he had slapped her without warning or cause. Surprise and pain made Sunder snap, 'Ur-Lord?'

Covenant winced, fumbled to apologize. 'I'm sorry. This is hard to say. I didn't mean it the way it sounded.' He took hold of himself. 'There's something else I want you to do.'

Hollian frowned at him, echoing Sunder's uncertainty.

'It's the Sunbane,' he began. 'I'm going to leave the Land – try to find the One Tree. So I can replace the Staff of Law. I don't know what else to do. But the Clave – ' He swallowed at the anger rising in his throat. 'I don't know how long I'm going to be gone, and every day they kill more people. Somebody has to stop them. I want you to do it.'

He stared out to Sea, went on speaking as if he feared the reaction of his friends. 'I want you to go back to the Upper Land. To the villages – to every Stonedown or Woodhelven you can find. Tell them the truth about the Clave. Convince them. Make them stop surrendering to the Riders. So the Sunbane won't destroy everything before I get back.'

'Thomas Covenant.' Sunder's fists were clenched as if to hold off outrage. 'Have you forgotten Mithil Stonedown? Have you forgotten Stonemight Woodhelven? The people of the Land shed strangers to answer their own need for blood. We will convince no one. We will be slain by the first Stonedown we dare to enter.'

'No.' Covenant shook his head flatly. He knew what he meant to do, and felt sure of it. 'You'll have something that will make them listen to you. And you can use it to defend yourselves if you have to.' With both hands, he removed the cloth-wrapped *krill* from under his belt, and extended it towards Sunder.

'Covenant?' The Graveller looked his astonishment at Linden, at Hollian, then back towards Covenant. Linden sat with her eyes downcast, watching the way her fingers touched the stone. But Hollian's face brightened as if in recognition. 'The *krill* is yours,' Sunder murmured, asking for comprehension. 'I am a Graveller – nothing more. Of what use is such a periapt to me?'

Deliberately, Covenant held out his hope. 'I think you can attune yourself to it. The way you did to Memla's *rukh*. I think you can use the *krill* the way you use the Sunstone. And if you put the two together, you won't need to shed blood to have power. You can use the *krill* to rouse the *orcrest*. You'll be able to raise water, grow plants, do it all. Without blood. Any village will listen to that. They won't try to kill you. They'll try to keep you.

'And that's not all. This is *power*. Proof that the Sunbane isn't the whole truth. It proves that they have a choice. They don't have to obey the Clave, don't have to let themselves be slaughtered.'

With a twitch of his hands, he flung off part of the cloth so that the *krill* shone into the faces of his companions. 'Sunder,' he implored. 'Hollian. Take it. Convince them. We're all responsible — all of us who know the na-Mhoram is a Raver. Don't let the Clave go on killing them.' The light of the *krill* filled his orbs; he could not see how his friends responded. 'Give me a chance to save them.'

For a moment, he feared the Stonedownors would refuse the burden he offered them. But then the *krill* was taken from him. Sunder flipped cloth back over the gem. Carefully, he re-wrapped the blade, tucked it away under his leather jerkin. His eyes gleamed like echoes of white fire.

'Thomas Covenant,' he said, 'ur-Lord and Unbeliever, white gold wielder, I thank you. It is sooth that my heart did not relish this quest across unknown seas and lands. I have no knowledge of such matters and little strength for them. You have Giants with you, and *Haruchai*, and the power of the white ring. I am of no use to you.

'I have learned that the Sunbane is a great evil. But it is an evil which I comprehend and can confront.' Hollian's countenance supported his words. Her relief was a glow of gratitude. 'I desire to strive somewhat for my people — and to strive against this Clave, which so maligns our lives.'

Covenant blinked at the repetitions of silver arcing across his sight. He was too proud of Sunder and Hollian to speak.

They rose to their feet. 'Ur-Lord,' the Graveller said, 'we will do as you ask. If any blow may be struck against Clave and Sunbane by mortals such as we are, we will strike it. You have restored to me the faith of Nassic my father. Be certain of us while we live.'

'And be swift,' added Hollian, 'for we are but two, and the Sunbane is as vast as all the Land.'

Covenant had not noticed Stell and Harn unobtrusively leave the cliff; but they returned now, carrying supplies on their backs. Before Covenant or the Stonedownors could speak, Brinn said, 'The Sunbane is indeed vast, but you will not meet it alone. The *Haruchai* will not surrender their service. And I say to you that my people also will not suffer the Clave unopposed. Look for aid wherever you go, especially when your way leads within reach of Revelstone.'

Sunder swallowed thickly, unable to master his voice. Hollian's eyes reflected the sunshine wetly.

The sight of them standing there in their courage and peril made Covenant's fragile calm ache. 'Get going,' he said huskily. 'We'll be back. Count on it.'

In a rush of emotion, Hollian came to him, stooped to grip her arms around his neck and kiss his face. Then she went to Linden. Linden returned her embrace stiffly.

A moment later, the Stonedownors turned away. They left the cliff with Stell and Harn beside them.

Covenant watched them go. The two *Haruchai* moved as if nothing could ever change who they were. But Sunder and Hollian walked like people who had been given the gift of meaning for their lives. They were just ordinary people, pitifully small in comparison to the task they had undertaken; and yet their valour was poignant to behold. As they passed over the ridge where the ruined lighthouse stood, they had their arms around each other.

After a moment, Linden broke the silence. 'You did the right thing.' Her voice wore severity like a mask. 'They've been uncomfortable ever since we left Landsdrop – the Sunbane is the only world they understand. And they've lost everything else. They need to do something personal and important. But you – ' She stared at him as if in her eyes he had become an object of fear and desire. 'I don't know you. I don't know if you're the strongest man I've ever met, or the sickest. With all that venom in you, you still – I don't know what I'm doing here.' Without a pause, as if she were still asking the same question, she said, 'Why did you give them the *krill*? I thought you needed it. A weapon against Vain.'

Yes, Covenant breathed. And an alternative to wild magic. That's what I thought. But by accepting the *krill*, Sunder and Hollian had made it once more into a tool of hope. 'I don't want any more weapons,' he murmured to Linden. 'I'm already too dangerous.'

She held his gaze. The sudden clarity of her expression told him that, of all the things he had ever said to her, this, at least, was one she could comprehend.

Then a shout echoed up the face of *Coercri*. 'Giantfriend!' It was Pitchwife's voice. 'Come! Starfare's Gem approaches!'

The echoes went on in Covenant's mind after the shout had faded. Giantfriend. He was who he was, a man half crippled by loneliness and responsibility and regret. But he had finally earned the title the First had given him.

The *dromond* came drifting slowly, neatly, towards the piers. Its rigging was full of Giants furling the sails.

Carefully, like a man who did not want to die, Covenant got to his feet. With Linden, Brinn, and Cail, he left the cliff.

They went down to meet the ship.

THE ONE
TREE

'You are mine'

PART I

Risk

1

STARFARE'S GEM

Linden Avery walked beside Covenant down through the ways of *Coercri*. Below them, the stone Giantship, Starfare's Gem, came gliding towards the sole intact levee at the foot of the ancient city; but she paid no heed to it. Earlier, she had witnessed the way the *dromond* rode the wind like a boon – at once massive and delicate, full-sailed and precise – a vessel of hope for Covenant's quest, and for her own. As she and the Unbeliever, with Brinn, Cail, and then Vain behind them, descended towards the headrock and piers of The Grieve, she would have studied that craft with pleasure. Its vitality offered gladness to her senses.

But Covenant had just sent the two Stonedownors, Sunder and Hollian, back towards the Upper Land in the hope that they would be able to muster resistance among the villages against the depredations of the Clave. And that hope was founded on the fact that he had given them Loric's *krill* to use against the Sunbane. Covenant needed that blade, both as a weapon to take the place of the wild magic which destroyed peace and as a defence against the mystery of Vain, the Demondim-spawn. Yet this morning he had given the *krill* away. When Linden had asked him for an explanation, he had replied, *I'm already too dangerous.*

Dangerous. The word resonated for her. In ways which none but she could perceive, he was sick with power. His native illness, his leprosy, was quiescent, even though he had lost or surrendered most of the self-protective disciplines which kept it slumberous. But in its place grew venom that a Raver and the Sunbane had afflicted upon him. That moral poison was latent at present, but it crouched in him like a predator, awaiting its time to spring. To her sight, it underlay the hue of his skin as if it had blackened the marrow of his bones. With his venom and his white ring, he was the most dangerous man she had known.

She desired that danger in him. It defined for her the quality of strength which had originally attracted her to him on Haven Farm. He had smiled for Joan when he had sold his life for hers; and that smile had revealed more of his strange potency, his capacity to outwrestle fate itself, than any threat or violence could have. The *caamora* of release he had given to the Dead of The Grieve had shown the lengths to which he was able to go in the name of his complex guilts and passions. He was a paradox, and Linden ached to emulate him.

For all his leprosy and venom, his self-judgment and rage, he was an affirmation – an assertion of life and a commitment to the Land, a statement of himself in opposition to anything the Despiser could do. And what was she? What had she done with her whole life except flee from her past? All her severity, all her drive towards medical effectiveness against death, had been negative from the start – a rejection of her own mortal heritage rather than an approval of the beliefs she nominally served. She was like the Land under the tyranny of the Clave and the Sunbane – a place ruled by fear and bloodshed rather than love.

Covenant's example had taught her this about herself. Even when she had not understood why he was so attractive to her, she had followed him instinctively. And now she knew she wanted to be like him. She wanted to be a danger to the forces which impelled people to their deaths.

She studied him as they walked trying to imprint the gaunt, prophetic lines of his visage, the strictness of his mouth and the wild tangle of his beard, upon her own resolve. He emanated a strait anticipation that she shared.

Like him, she looked forward to the prospect of a voyage of hope in the company of Giants. Although she had spent only a few days with Grimmand Honninscrave, Cable Seadreamer, Pitchwife, and the First of the Search, she already comprehended the pang of love which entered Covenant's voice whenever he spoke of the Giants he had known. But she also possessed a private eagerness, an anticipation of her own.

Almost from the moment when her health-sense had awakened, it had been a source of pain and dismay for her. Her first acute perception had been of the ill of Nassic's murder. And that sight had launched a seemingly endless sequence of Ravers and Sunbane which had driven her to the very edge of survival. The continuous onslaught of palpable evil – moral and physical disease which she would never be able to cure – had filled her with ineffectuality, demonstrating her unworth at every touch and glance. And then she had fallen into the hands of the Clave, into the power of Gibbon-Raver. The prophecy which he had uttered against her, the sabulous atrocity which he had radiated into her, had crammed every corner of her soul with a loathing and rejection indistinguishable from self-abhorrence. She had sworn that she would never again open the doors of her senses to any outward appeal.

But she had not kept that vow. The obverse of her sharp vulnerability was a peculiar and necessary usefulness. The same percipience which so exposed her to dismay had also enabled her to provide for her own recovery from Courser-poison and broken bones. That capacity had touched her medical instincts deeply, giving a validation to her identity which she had thought lost when she had been translated out of the world she understood. In addition, she had been able to serve her companions by helping them against the murderous ill of the lurker of the Sarangrave.

And then the company had escaped Sarangrave Flat into Seareach, where the Sunbane did not reign. Surrounded by natural health, by fall weather and colour as pristine as the beginning of life, and accompanied by Giants, especially by Pitchwife, whose irrepressible humour seemed a balm for every darkness, she had felt her ankle heal under the eldritch influence of *diamondraught*. She had tasted the tangible loveliness of the world, had experienced keenly the gift Covenant had given to the Dead of The Grieve. She had begun to know in the most visceral way that her health-sense was accessible to good as well as evil – and that perhaps she could exercise some choice over the doom which Gibbon had foretold for her.

That was her hope. Perhaps in that way if in no other she would be able to transform her life.

The old man whose life she had saved on Haven Farm had said, *Be true. There is also love in the world.* For the first time, those words did not fill her with dread.

She hardly looked away from Covenant as they descended the Giant-wrought stairs. He appeared equal to anything. But she was also aware of other things. The clear morning. The long salt-rimed emptiness of *Coercri*. The intransigent black peril of Vain. And at her back, the *Haruchai*. The way they paced the stone belied their characteristic dispassion. They seemed almost avid to explore the unknown Earth in the company of Covenant and Giants. Linden concentrated on these details as if they formed the texture of the new life she desired.

However, as the companions moved out into the direct sunlight on the base of the city, where the First, Seadreamer, and Pitchwife waited with Ceer and Hergrom, Linden's gaze leaped outward as if it were drawn by a lodestone; and she saw Starfare's Gem easing its way into the levee.

The Giantship was a craft to amaze her heart. It rose above her, dominating the sky as her sight rushed to take it in. While its Master, Grimmand Honninscrave, shouted orders from the wheeldeck which stood high over the vessel's heel, and Giants swarmed its rigging to furl the canvas and secure the lines, it coasted into its berth with deft accuracy. The skill of its crew and the cunning of its construction defied the massive tan-and-moire granite of which it was made. Seen from nearby, the sheer weight of the *dromond*'s seamless sides and masts disguised the swiftness of its shape, the long sweep of the decks, the jaunty angle of the prow, the just balance of the spars. But when her perceptions adjusted to the scale of the ship, she could see that it was apt for Giants. Their size attained a proper dimension among the shrouds. And the moire of the stone sides rose from the water like flames of granite eagerness.

That stone surprised Linden. Instinctively, she had questioned the nature of the Giantship, believing that granite would be too brittle to withstand the stress of the seas. But as her vision sprang into the ship, she saw her error. This granite had the slight but necessary flexibility of bone. Its vitality went beyond the limitations of stone.

And that vitality shone through the *dromond*'s crew. They were Giants; but on their ship they were more than that. They were the articulation and service of a brave and breathing organism, the hands and laughter of a life which exalted them. Together, the stone and the Giants gave Starfare's Gem the look of a vessel which contended against the powerful seas simply because no other test could match its native exultation.

Its three masts, each rising high enough to carry three sails, aspired like cedars over the wheeldeck, where Honninscrave stood. He lolled slightly with the faint unevenness of the Sea as if he had been born with combers underfoot, salt in his beard, mastery in every glance of his cavernous eyes. His shout in answer to Pitchwife's hail echoed off the face of *Coercri*, making The Grieve resound with welcome for the first time in many centuries. Then the sunlight and the ship blurred before Linden as sudden tears filled her eyes as if she had never seen joy before.

After a moment, she blinked her sight clear and looked again at Covenant. Tautness had twisted his face into a grin like a contortion; but the spirit behind that grimace was clear to her. He was looking at his means to achieve his quest for the One Tree, for the survival of the Land. And more than that: he was looking at Giants, the kindred of Saltheart Foamfollower, whom he had loved. She did not need him to explain the desire and fear which caused his grin to look so much like a snarl. His former victory over Lord Foul had been cleansed of Despite by the personal anodyne of Foamfollower's laughter. And the cost of that victory had been the Giant's life. Covenant now regarded the Giants of Starfare's Gem with yearning and memory: he feared he would bring them to Foamfollower's fate.

That also Linden understood. Like his obduracy, her own stubbornness had been born in loss and guilt. She knew what it meant to distrust the consequences of her desires.

But the arrival of the Giantship demanded her attention. Noise bubbled out of the vessel like a froth of gaiety. Hawsers were thrown to Pitchwife and Seadreamer, who snubbed them taut to the long-unused belaying-posts of the pier. Starfare's Gem rubbed its shoulders against the sides of the levee, settled itself at rest. And as soon as the *dromond* had been secured, the Master and his crew of two score Giants swung down ropes and ladders, bounding to the piers.

There they saluted the First with affection, hugged Seadreamer, shouted their pleasure at Pitchwife. The First returned their respects gravely: with her iron hair and her broadsword, she held their familiarity at a distance. But Pitchwife expressed enough mirth to compensate for Seadreamer's mute resignation; and shortly the Giants began to roil forward to look at the city of the Unhomed, their ancient lost kindred.

Linden found herself surrounded by weathered, brawny men and women twice her height – sailors built like oaks, and yet as full of movement and wonder as saplings. All of them were plainly dressed in the habiliments of their work – in sarks of mail formed of interlocking stone discs and heavy leather leggings – but nothing else about them was drab. They were colourful in language and exuberance and salt humour. With a swirl of activity, they restored life to The Grieve.

Their impulse to explore the city, investigate the handiwork of their long-dead people, was palpable to Linden. And Covenant's eyes shone in response – a recollection of the *caamora* by which he had redeemed *Coercri* from anguish, earning the title the First had given him, *Giantfriend*. But through the tumult, monolithic jests and laughter to which Pitchwife riposted gleefully, questions that the *Haruchai* answered with characteristic tersity, salutations which dazzled Linden and made Covenant straighten his back as if he sought to be taller, the First addressed Honninscrave sternly, telling him of her decision to aid Covenant's quest. And she spoke of urgency, of the growing chancre of the Sunbane and of the difficulty of locating the One Tree, creating a new Staff of Law in time to prevent the Sunbane from tearing the heart out of the Earth. The Master's excitement sobered rapidly. When she asked about the state of the Giantship's supplies, he replied that the Anchormaster, his second-in command, had reprovisioned the *dromond* while waiting off the littoral of the Great Swamp. Then he began calling his crew back to the ship.

Several of the Giants protested good-naturedly, asking for the story of The Grieve. But Covenant was nodding to himself as if he were thinking of the way the Clave fed the Banefire and the Sunbane with blood. Honninscrave did not hesitate. 'Patience, sluggards!' he responded. 'Are you Giants, that a little patience eludes you? Let stories await their turn, to ease the labour of the seas. The First requires haste!'

His command gave Linden a pang of regret. The ebullience of these Giants was the happiest thing she had seen in a long time. And she thought that perhaps Covenant might want a chance to savour what he had achieved here. But she understood him well enough to know that he would not accept honour for himself without persuasion. Moving closer to him, she thrust her voice through the clamour. 'Berek found the One Tree, and he didn't have any Giants to help him. How far away can it be?'

He did not look at her. The *dromond* held his gaze. Under his beard, he chewed a mood which was half excitement, half trepidation.

'Sunder and Hollian will do everything they can,' she went on. 'And those *Haruchai* you freed aren't going to sit on their hands. The Clave is already in trouble. We can afford a little time.'

His eyes did not shift. But she felt his attention turn toward her. 'Tell me,' he murmured, barely audible through the interchanges of the Giants. They and the *Haruchai* had ranged themselves expectantly along the pier. 'Do you think I should have tried to destroy the Clave? While I had the chance?'

The question struck a nerve in her. It resembled too closely another question he would have asked if he had known enough about her. 'Some infections have to be cut out,' she replied severely. 'If you don't kill the disease somehow, you lose the patient. Do you think those fingers of yours were cut off out of spite?'

His brow flinched. He regarded her as if she had startled him out of his personal concerns, made him aware of her in a way which would not allow peace between them. The muscles of his throat were tight as he asked, 'Is that what you would have done?'

She could not keep from wincing. Gibbon had said to her, *You have committed murder. Are you not evil?* Suddenly, she felt sure that Covenant would have agreed with Raver. Fighting to conceal her self-betrayal, she answered, 'Yes. Why else do you have all that power?' She already knew too well how much she wanted power.

'Not for that.' Around them, the Giants had fallen silent, waiting for his decision. In the unanticipated quiet, the vehemence rang out like a promise over the lapping of the Sea. But he ignored his audience. Facing Linden squarely, he articulated, 'I've already killed twenty-one of them. I'm going to find some other answer.'

She thought he would go on. But a moment later he seemed to see and recognize her abashment, though he could not have known its cause. At once, he turned to the First. Softly, he said, 'I'd feel better if we got started.'

She nodded, but did not move. Instead, she drew her falchion, gripped it in both hands like a salute.

'Giantfriend.' As she spoke, there was a shout in her words, though her voice was quiet. 'To all our people you have given a gift which we will repay. This I say in the name of the Search, and of the Earth-Sight' – she glanced at Seadreamer – 'which guides us still, though I have chosen another path to the same goal.' Seadreamer's face knotted around the white scar running under his eyes across the bridge of his nose; but he permitted himself to show no protest. The First concluded, 'Covenant Giantfriend, we are yours while your purpose holds.'

Covenant remained silent, a man tangled in gratitude and self-doubt. But he bowed his head to the leader of the Search.

The gesture touched Linden. It became him, as if he had found in himself the grace, or perhaps the sense of worth, to accept help. But at the same time she was relieved to escape the hidden conflicts which had surfaced in his questions. When the First said firmly, 'Let us sail,' Linden followed the Giants without hesitation towards Starfare's Gem.

The side of the Giantship leaned hugely over her; and when she set her hands and feet to the heavy thews of the rope-ladder which the crew held for her, the ascent seemed to carry her surprisingly high, as if the vessel were even larger than it appeared to be. But Cail climbed protectively behind her, and Giants surged upward on all sides. As she stooped through the railing on to the foredeck, she forgot her discomfiture. The *dromond* reached out to her like an entrancement. Unaccustomed to such stone, she could not extend her percipience very far around her; but all the granite within her range felt as vital as living wood. She half expected to taste sap flowing beneath the surfaces of the Giantship. And that sensation intensified as her companions boarded the craft. Because of his vertigo and his halfhand, Covenant had difficulty climbing; but Brinn soon helped him past the rail. Following either Covenant or Linden, Vain smoothly ascended the ladder, then stopped like a statue at the edge of the foredeck, smiling his black, ambiguous smile. Ceer and Hergrom appeared to flow up the ropes. And as every set of feet took hold of the stone, Starfare's Gem radiated more bustling energy to Linden's nerves. Even through her shoes, the granite felt too buoyant to be overborne by any Sea.

Sunlight covered the piers, spangled the gently heaving strip of water along the shipside, shone into the face of *Coercri* as if this day marked the first true dawn since the destruction of the Unhomed. Responding to Honninscrave's commands, some of the Giants positioned themselves to release the moorings. Others leaped into the rigging, climbing the heavy cables as lightly as children. Still others went below, where Linden could feel them tending the inner life of the ship until they passed beyond her inexperienced perceptions. In moments, the lower sails began to ripple in the breeze; and Starfare's Gem eased out to Sea.

2

BLACK MOOD

Linden tried to watch everything as the *dromond* slipped backwards from the levee, then turned towards open water. Shifting from side to side, she saw the Giants unfurling canvas as if the labour were done by incantation rather than effort. Under her feet, the deck began to roll; but the seas were light, and the Giantship's great weight made it stable. She felt no discomfort. Her gaze repeatedly intersected Covenant's, and his excitement heightened hers. His expression was free of darkness; even his beard seemed to bristle with possibilities. After a moment, she became aware that he was breathing words along the breeze:

> 'Stone and Sea are deep in life,
> two unalterable symbols of the world:
> permanence at rest, and permanence in motion;
> participants in the Power that remains.'

They resonated in her memory like an act of homage.

When she changed positions to look back towards *Coercri*, the breeze caught her hair, fluttering it across her face. She ran her fingers into her wheaten tresses, held them in place; and that simple gesture gave her more pleasure in herself than she had felt for a long time. Salt tanged the air, sharpening the very sunlight so that The Grieve looked like a place of rebirth as it receded. She began to think that perhaps more things had been reborn there than she would have dared to hope.

Then Pitchwife began to sing. He stood some distance away, but his voice carried like light across the *dromond*, rising strongly from his deformed chest over the slapping of the waves and the snap of the canvas. His tune was a plainsong spiced with accents and suggestions of harmony; and the other Giants joined him:

> 'Come sea and wave —
> broad footpath of those who roam
> and gateway to the world!
> All ways lead the way to Home.

'Come wind and speed —
sky-breath and the life of sail!
Lines and sheets unfurled,
our hearts covet every gale.

'Come travel and quest!
Discovery of the Earth:
mysteries unknurled:
roaming without stint or dearth:

'Risk and journey save
the heart of life from loss and need.
We are the ocean's guest,
and we love the vasty world!'

The Giants were joyful singers, and their voices formed a counterpoint to the rocking of the masts, a song punctuated by a rising staccato as the breeze knocked the canvas. Starfare's Gem appeared to ride music as well as wind.

And as the wind stiffened, *Coercri* slid towards the horizon with surprising clerity while the sun rose into midday. Honninscrave and his crew exchanged comments and jests as if they were all negligent; but his eyes under the bulwark of his brows missed nothing. At his orders, the rest of the sails had been raised; and Starfare's Gem strode into the Sunbirth Sea with a fleetness that fulfilled the prophecy of its moire-marked sides. Linden could feel vibrancy running like a thrill through the stone. In the hands of the Giants, even granite became a thing of swiftness and graceful poise.

Before long, her sensations became so sapid that she could no longer remain still. Instinctively, she moved away to begin exploring the ship.

At once, Cail was at her shoulder. As she crossed the foredeck, he surprised her by asking if she wanted to see her quarters.

She stopped to stare at him. The impassive wall of his mien gave no hint of how he had come by enough knowledge of the *dromond* to make such an offer. His short tunic left his brown limbs always free and ready; but his question made him appear not only prepared but also prescient. However, he answered her mute inquiry by explaining that Ceer and Hergrom had already spoken to the Storesmaster and had obtained from her at least a skeletal understanding of the ship.

For a moment, Linden paused to consider the continuing providence of the *Haruchai*. But then she realized that Cail had offered her exactly what she did want — a place of her own; privacy in which to accustom herself to the sensations of the Giantship; a change to clarify the new things that were happening to her. And perhaps the hospitality of the Giants would extend as far as bath-water? *Hot* bathwater? Images of luxuriance filled her head. How long had it been since she had last taken a hot bath? Since she had felt genuinely clean? She nodded to Cail, and followed him toward the stern of the *dromond*.

Amidship stood a flat-roofed structure that separated the fore- and afterdecks, completely spanning the vessel from side to side. When Cail led her into the housing through a seadoor with a storm-sill as high as her knees, she found herself in a long eating-hall with a galley on one side and a warren of storage-lockers on the other. The structure had no windows, but lanterns made it bright and cheery. Their light gleamed on the stone of the midmast as it passed straight through the hall like a rooftree. The shaft was carved like a hatchment with patterns at which she was tempted to look more closely. But Cail moved through the hall as if he already knew all its secrets; and she went with him out to the afterdeck.

Together, they crossed to the Giantship's stern. She acknowledged Honninscrave's salute from the wheeldeck, then followed Cail through another seadoor to starboard below the Master's position. That entrance gave access to a smooth stone ladder leading down-ward. The ladder had been formed for Giants, but she was able to use it. And she only had to descend one level. There, in a passageway lit by more lanterns, she found a series of doors — rooms, Cail explained, which had been set aside for her, Vain, Ceer, and himself. Covenant, Brinn, and Hergrom were to be similarly housed on the port side of the vessel.

When she entered her cabin, she discovered that it was a chamber which would have been small for a Giant but seemed almost wastefully large for her. A long hammock hung near one wall; two massive chairs and a table occupied most of the floor. These furnishings outsized her: the chair-seats reached to her waist; and she would have to stand on the table to gain the hammock. But for the present those difficulties did not bother her. The chamber was bright with sunshine reflecting through an open port, and it offered privacy. She was glad to have it.

But moments after Cail left in search of the food and bathwater she requested of him, a tension which had been nagging at her underneath her excitement demanded her notice. The withdrawal of Cail's hard *Haruchai* presence pulled aside a veil within her. A hand of darkness hidden somewhere inside the depths of the *dromond* reached out one dire finger towards her heart. At its touch, all her relief and anticipation and newness eroded and fell down like a sea-doused castle of sand. An old and half forgotten black mood began to seep back into her.

It stank of her parents and Gibbon.

After all, what had truly changed for her? What right or reason did she have to be where she was? She was still the same – a woman driven by the need to flee death rather than to pursue life. She did not know how to change. And the na-Mhoram had explicitly denied her hope. He said, *You are being forged as iron is forged to achieve the ruin of the Earth. Because you are open to that which no other in the Land can discern, you are open to be forged.* She would never be free of his eager cruelty, of the gelid ill with which he had desecrated her private flesh – or of the way she had responded. The message of his doom came back to her now, rising as if it grew from the keel of the Starfare's Gem – as if the health of the *dromond* contained a cankerspot which fed on the Giants and their ship.

The blackness had contorted much of her life. It was her parents, her father and mother. And it was here. It was within her, and yet she inhaled it as if the air were full of it as well. A fate she could neither name nor endure seemed to lurk in ambush for her, so that her cabin felt more like a cell in the hold of Revelstone than a sunwashed chamber in the company of Giants.

For several long moments, she fought the oppression, struggled to define the strange way it appeared to spring from outside her. But her past was too strong; it blinded her percipience. Long before Cail could return, she fled her cabin, rushed back up to the open air. Clinging to the starboard rail with hands that trembled, she swallowed repeatedly, heavily, at the old dread rising in her throat like a recognition of Gibbon's touch.

But gradually the darkness lessened. She could think of no reason why this should be true; but she felt instinctively that she had put some distance between herself and the source of the mood. Seeking to increase that distance, she turned towards the nearest stairway to the wheeldeck.

Ceer had appeared at her side to ward her while Cail was away. She could hardly refrain from leaning against him, bracing her frailty on his rectitude. But she hated that weakness. Striving to ignore it, deny it, she impelled herself up the stairs alone.

On the wheeldeck, she found Honninscrave, the First, Covenant, Brinn, and another Giant who held the great wheel which guided the ship. This wheel was formed of stone and stood half again as tall as Linden; but the steerswoman turned its spokes as lightly as if it had been carved of balsa wood. Honninscrave greeted the Chosen, and the First gave her a nod of welcome; yet Linden felt immediately that she had interrupted a discussion. Covenant looked towards her as if he meant to ask her opinion. But then he closed his mouth and gazed at her more intently. Before she could speak, he said, 'Linden, what's the matter?'

She frowned back at him, vexed and shamed by the transparency of her emotions. Clearly, she had not changed in any way that

453

mattered. She still could not tell him the truth – not here, under an open sky and the eyes of the Giants. She tried to dismiss his question with a shrug, smooth out the lines of her face. But his attention did not lose its acuity. In a careful voice, she said, 'I was thinking about Gibbon.' With her eyes, she asked him to let the matter pass. 'I'd rather think about something else.'

At that, his stare softened. He looked like a man who was willing to do almost anything for her. Clearing his throat, he said, 'We were talking about Vain. He hasn't moved since he came aboard. And he's in the way. Interferes with some of the rigging. The crew asked him to move – but you know how much good that did.'

She knew. Time and again, she had seen the Demondim-spawn in his familiar relaxed stance, arms slightly bent, eyes focused on nothing – as motionless as an obelisk.

'So they tried to shift him. Three of them. He didn't budge.' Covenant shook his head at the idea that anyone could be heavy or strong enough to defeat three Giants. Then he concluded, 'We were trying to decide what to do about it. Honninscrave wants to use a block-and-tackle.'

Linden gave an inward sigh of relief. The darkness retreated another step, pushed back by this chance to be of use. 'It won't do any good,' she replied. Vain's purposes were a mystery to her; but she had seen deeply enough into him to know that he could become denser and less tractable than the granite of the ship. 'If he doesn't want to move, he won't move.'

Covenant nodded as if she had confirmed his expectations. The First muttered sourly to herself. With a shrug, Honninscrave ordered his crew to work around the Demondim-spawn.

Linden was glad of their company. Her sense of oppression was definitely weaker now. The huge health of the Giants seemed to shield her. And Covenant's considerateness eased her. She could breathe as if her lungs were not clogged with memories of death. Moving to the taffrail, she sat down against one of the posts and tried to tune herself to the Giantship.

Shortly, Cail came to take Ceer's place. His features betrayed no reproach for the wasted errand on which she had sent him. For that forbearance also she was grateful. She sensed the presence of a fierce capacity for judgment behind the impassivity of the *Haruchai*. She did not want it turned against her.

Almost without volition, her gaze returned to Covenant. But his attention was elsewhere. Starfare's Gem and its crew had taken hold of him again. He was so entranced by the *dromond*, so moved by the companionship of the Giants, that everything else receded. He asked Honninscrave and the First questions to start them talking, then listened to their responses with the hunger of a man who had found no other answer to his loneliness.

Following his example, Linden also listened and watched.

Honninscrave talked at glad length about the life and workings of his craft. The crew was divided into three watches under the command of the Master, the Anchormaster, and the ship's third-in-command, the Storesmaster. However, like their officers, the Giants did not appear to rest when they were off duty. Their affection would not permit them to leave Starfare's Gem alone, and they spent their time doing odd jobs around the vessel. But when Honninscrave began to describe these tasks, and the purposes they served, Linden lost her way. The crew had Giantish names for every line and sheet, every part of the ship, every implement; and she could not absorb the barrage of unfamiliar words. Some stayed with her: Dawngreeter, the highest sail on the foremast; Horizonscan, the lookout atop the midmast; Shipsheartthew, the great wheel which turned the rudder. But she did not know enough about ships and sailing to retain the rest.

This problem was aggravated by the fact that Honninscrave rarely phrased his instructions to his watch as direct orders. More often, he shouted a comment about the state of the sails, or the wind, or the seas, and left the choice of appropriate action to any Giant who happened to be near the right place. As a result, the tacking of the ship seemed to happen almost spontaneously – a reaction to the shifting air rather than to Honninscrave's mastery, or perhaps a theurgy enacted by the vivid and complex vibrations of the rigging. This beguiled Linden, but did not greatly enhance her grasp of the plethora of names the Master used.

Later, she was vaguely surprised to see Ceer and Hergrom in the shrouds of the aftermast. They moved deftly among the lines, learning from and aiding the Giants with an easy alacrity which seemed almost gay. When she asked Cail what his people were doing, he replied that they were fulfilling an old dream of the *Haruchai*. During all the centuries that the Unhomed and the Bloodguard had known each other before and after the Ritual of Desecration, no *Haruchai* had ever set foot on a Giantship. Ceer and Hergrom were answering a desire which had panged their ancestors more than three thousand years ago.

Cail's terse account touched her obscurely, like a glimpse of an unsuspected and occult beauty. The steadfastness of his people transcended all bounds. During Covenant's previous visits to the Land, the Bloodguard had already been warding the Council of Lords without sleep or death for nearly two thousand years, so extravagant had been their Vow of service. And now, millennia later, Cail and his people still preserved the memories and commitments of those Bloodguard.

But the implications of such constancy eventually cast Linden back upon herself; and as the afternoon waned, her gloom returned.

Her senses were growing steadily more attuned to the Giantship. She could read the movements and mirth of the Giants passing through the decks below her; with effort, she could estimate the number of people in Foodfendhall, the midship housing. This should have eased her. Everything she consciously felt was redolent with clean strength and good humour. And yet her darkness thickened along the slow expansion of her range.

Again, she was troubled by the sensation that her mood grew from an external source, from some fatal flaw or ill in the Giantship. Yet she could not disentangle that sensation from her personal response. She had spent too much of her life in this oppression to think seriously that it could be blamed on anything outside herself. Gibbon had not created her blackness: he had only given her a glimpse of its meaning. But familiarity did not make it more bearable.

When the call for supper came, she resisted her depression to answer it. Covenant did not hesitate; and she meant to follow him to the ends of the Earth if necessary to learn the kind of courage which made him forever active against his doom. Beneath his surface, leprosy slept and Lord Foul's venom awaited the opportunity to work its intended desecration. Yet he seemed equal to his plight, more than equal to it. He did not suffer from the particular fear which had paralysed her in the face of Joan's possession, Marid's monstrous ill, Gibbon-Raver's horror. But for that very reason she was determined to accompany him until she had found his answer. Hastening to his side, she went with him towards Foodfendhall.

However, as night gathered over the decks, her uneasiness mounted. The setting of the sun left her exposed to a stalking peril. In the eating-hall, she was crowded among Giants whose appetites radiated vitality; but she could barely force food past the thickness of defeat in her throat, although she had not had a meal since that morning. Steaming stew, cakes full of honey, dried fruit; her black mood made such things vaguely nauseating.

Soon afterward, Honninscrave ordered the sails shortened for the night; and the time came for tales. The Giants responded eagerly, gathering on the afterdeck and in the shrouds of the aftermast so that the First and Covenant could speak to them from the wheeldeck. Their love of tales was plain in them – a love which made them appear child-like, and yet also gave them a precious and encompassing courage. And Covenant went aft to meet them as though this, too, were something he already knew how to bear. But Linden had reached the limit of her endurance. Above the masts, the stars appeared disconsolate in their immense isolation. The noises of the ship – the creak of the rigging, the uncertainty of the sails whenever the wind shifted, the protest of the waves as the *dromond* shouldered through them – sounded like pre-echoes of anger or grief. And she had already heard many stories – the tales of the Earth's creation, of Kevin Landwaster's despair, of Covenant's victory. She was not ready for any more.

Instead, she forced herself to go back to her cabin. Down into the darkness rather than away from it.

She found that in her absence the old furniture had been replaced with chairs and a table more to her size; and a stepladder had been provided to give her easier access to the hammock. But this courtesy did not relieve her. Still the oppression seeped into her from the stone of the *dromond*. Even after she threw open the port, letting in the wind and the sounds of the Sea under the ship's heel, the chamber's ambience remained viscid, comfortless. When she mustered the courage to extinguish her lantern, the dark concentrated inward on her, hinting at malice.

I'm going crazy. Despite its special texture, the granite around her began to feel like the walls of Revelstone, careless and unyielding. Memories of her parents gnawed at the edges of her brain. *Have committed murder.* Going crazy. The blood on her hands was as intimate as any Covenant had ever shed.

She could hear the Giants singing overhead, though the noise of the Sea obscured their words. But she fought her impulse to flee the cabin, run back to the misleading security of the assemblage. Instead, she followed the faint scent of *diamondraught* until she found a flask of the potent Giantish liquor on her table. Then she hesitated. *Diamondraught* was an effective healer and roborant, as she knew from personal experience; but it was also strongly soporific. She hesitated because she was afraid of sleep, afraid that slumber represented another flight from something she needed desperately to confront and master. But she had faced these moods often enough in the past, endured them until she had wanted to wail like a lost child – and what had she ever accomplished by it? Estimating the effect of the *diamondraught*, she took two small swallows. Then she climbed into the hammock, pulled a blanket over herself to help her nerves feel less exposed, and tried to relax. Before she was able to unknot her muscles, the sea-sway of the *dromond* lifted her into slumber.

For a time, the world of her unconsciousness was blissfully empty. She rode long slow combers of sleep on a journey from nowhere into nowhere and suffered no harm. But gradually the night became the night of the woods behind Haven Farm, and ahead of her burned the fire of invocation to Lord Foul. Joan lay there, possessed by a cruelty so acute that it stunned Linden to the soul. Then Covenant took Joan's place, and Linden broke free, began running down the hillside to save him, forever running down the hillside to save him and never able to reach him, never able to stop the astonishing violence which drove the knife into his chest. It pierced him whitely, like an evil and tremendous fang. When she reached him, blood was gushing from the wound – more blood than she had ever seen in her life. Impossible that one body held so much blood! It welled out of him as if any number of people had been slain with that one blow.

She could not stop it. Her hands were too small to cover the wound. She had left her medical bag in her car. Feverishly, she tore off her shirt to try to staunch the flow, leaving herself naked and defenceless; but the flannel was instantly soaked with blood, useless. Blood slicked her breasts and thighs as she strove to save his life and could not. Despite every exigency of her training and self-mortification, she could not stop that red stream. The firelight mocked her. The wound was growing.

In moments, it became as wide as his chest. Its violence ate at his tissues like venom. Her hands still clutched the futile sop of her shirt, still madly trying to exert pressure to plug the well; but it went on expanding until her arms were lost in him to the elbows. Blood poured over her thighs like the ichor of the world. She was hanging from the edge by her chest, with her arms extended into the red maw as if she were diving to her death. And the wound continued to widen. Soon it was larger than the stone on which Covenant had fallen, larger than the hollow in the woods.

Then with a shock of recognition she saw that the wound was more than a knife-thrust in his chest: it was a stab to the very heart of the Land. The hole had become a pit before her, and its edge was a sodden hillside, and the blood spewing over her was the life of the Earth. The Land was bleeding to death. Before she could even cry out, she was swept away across the murdered body of the ground. She had no way to save herself from drowning.

The turbulence began to buffet her methodically. The hot fluid made her throat raw, burned her voice out of her. She was helpless and lost. Her mere flesh could not endure or oppose such an atrocity. Better if she had never tried to help Covenant, never tried to staunch his wound. This would never have happened if she had accepted her paralysis and simply let him die.

But the shaking of her shoulders and the light slapping across her face insisted that she had no choice. The rhythm became more personal; by degrees, it dragged her from her *diamondraught*-sopor. When she wrenched her eyes open, the moonlight from the open port limned Cail's visage. He stood on the stepladder so that he could reach her to awaken her. Her throat was sore, and the cabin still echoed her screaming.

'Cail!' she gasped. Oh my God!

'Your sleep was troubled.' His voice was as flat as his mien. 'The Giants say their *diamondraught* does not act thus.'

'No.' She struggled to sit up, fought for self-possession. Images of nightmare flared across her mind; but behind them the mood in

458

which she had gone to sleep had taken on a new significance. 'Get Covenant.'

'The ur-Lord rests,' he replied inflectionlessly.

Impelled by urgency, Linden flung herself over the edge of the hammock, forced Cail to catch her and lower her to the floor. 'Get him.' Before the *Haruchai* could respond, she rushed to the door.

In the lantern-lit companionway, she almost collided with Sea-dreamer. The mute Giant was approaching her cabin as if he had heard her cries. For an instant, she was stopped by the similarity between her nightmare and the vision which had reft him of his voice — a vision so powerful that it had compelled his people to launch a Search for the wound which threatened the Earth. But she had no time. The ship was in danger! Sprinting past him, she leaped for the ladder.

When she reached open air, she was in the shadow of the wheeldeck as the moon sank towards setting. Several Giants were silhouetted above her. Heaving herself up the high stairs, she confronted the Storesmaster, a Giant holding Shipsheartthew, and two or three companions. Her chest strained to control her fear as she demanded, 'Get the First.'

The Storesmaster, a woman named Heft Galewrath, had a bulky frame tending towards fat which gave her an appearance of stolidity; but she wasted no time on questions or hesitancy. With a nod to one of her companions, she said simply, 'Summon the First. And the Master.' The crewmember obeyed at once.

As Linden regained her breath, she became aware that Cail was beside her. She did not ask him if he had called Covenant. The pale scar which marked his left arm from shoulder to elbow had been given him by a Courser-spur aimed at her; it seemed to refute any doubt of him.

Then Covenant came up the stairs with Brinn at his back. He looked dishevelled and groggy in the moonlight; but his voice was tight as he began, 'Linden – ?' She gestured him silent, knotting her fists to retain her fragile grip on herself. He turned to Cail; but before Covenant could phrase a question, Honninscrave arrived with his beard thrust forward like a challenge to any danger threatening his vessel. The First was close behind him.

Linden faced them all, forestalled anything they might ask. Her voice shook.

'There's a Raver on this ship.'

Her words stunned the night. Everything was stricken into silence. Then Covenant asked, 'Are you sure?' His question appeared to make no sound.

The First overrode him. 'What is this "Raver"?' The mettle of her tone was like an upraised sword.

One of the sails retorted dully in its gear as the wind changed slightly. The deck tilted. The Storesmaster called softly aloft for adjustments to be made in the canvas. Starfare's Gem righted its tack. Linden braced her legs against the ship's movement, and hugged the distress in her stomach, concentrating on Covenant.

'Of course I'm sure.' She could not suppress her trembling. 'I can feel it.' The message in her nerves was as vivid as lightning. 'At first I didn't know what it was. I've felt like this before. Before we came here.' She was dismayed by the implications of what she was saying – by the similarity between her old black moods and the taste of a Raver. But she compelled herself to go on. 'But I was looking for the wrong thing. It's on this ship. Hiding. That's why I didn't understand sooner.' As her throat tightened, her voice rose towards shrillness. 'On this ship.'

Covenant came forward, gripped her shoulders as if to prevent her from hysteria. 'Where is it?'

Honninscrave cut off Covenant's question. '*What* is it? I am the Master of Starfare's Gem. I must know the peril.'

Linden ignored Honninscrave. She was focused on Covenant, clinching him for strength. 'I can't tell.' And to defend him. Gibbon-Raver had said to her, *You are being forged.* She, not Covenant. But every attack on her had proved to be a feint. 'Somewhere below.'

At once, he swung away from her, started towards the stairs. Over his shoulder, he called, 'Come on. Help me find it.'

'*Are you crazy?*' Surprise and distress wrung the cry from her. 'Why do you think it's *here*?'

He stopped, faced her again. But his visage was obscure in the moonlight. She could see only the waves of vehemence radiating from his bones. He had accepted his power and meant to use it.

'Linden Avery,' said the First grimly. 'We know nothing of this Raver. You must tell us what it is.'

Linden's voice reached out to Covenant in supplication, asking him not to expose himself to this danger. 'Didn't you tell them about The Grieve? About the Giant-Raver who killed all those – ?' Her throat knotted, silencing her involuntarily.

'No.' Covenant returned to stand near her, and a gentler emanation came from him in answer to her fear. 'Pitchwife told that story. In *Coercri* I talked about the Giant-Raver. But I never described what it was.'

He turned to the First and Honninscrave. 'I told you about Lord Foul. The Despiser. But I didn't know I needed to tell you about the Ravers. They're his three highest servants. They don't have bodies of their own, so they work by taking over other beings. Possessing them.' The blood in his tone smelled of Joan – and of other people Linden did not know.

'The old Lords used to say that no Giant or *Haruchai* could be mastered by a Raver. But *turiya* Herem had a fragment of the Illearth

Stone. That gave it the power to possess a Giant. It was the one we saw in *Coercri*. Butchering the Unhomed.'

'Very well.' The First nodded. 'So much at least is known to us, then. But why has this evil come among us? Does it seek to prevent our quest? How can it hold that hope, when so many of us are Giants and *Haruchai*?' Her voice sharpened. 'Does it mean to possess you? Or the Chosen?'

Before Linden could utter her fears, Covenant grated, 'Something like that.' Then he faced her once more. 'You're right. I won't go looking for it. But it's got to be found. We've got to get rid of it somehow.' The force of his will was focused on her. 'You're the only one who can find it. Where is it?'

Her reply was muffled by her efforts to stop trembling. 'Somewhere below,' she repeated.

The First looked at Honninscrave. He protested carefully, 'Chosen, the underdecks are manifold and cunning. Much time will be required for a true search. And we have not your eyes. If this Raver holds no flesh, how will we discover it?'

Linden wanted to cry out. Gibbon had touched her. She carried his evil engraved in every part of her body, would never be clean of it again. How could she bear a repetition of that touch?

But Honninscrave's question was just; and an answering anger enabled her to meet him. The ship was threatened; Covenant was threatened. And here at least she had a chance to show that she could be a danger to Lord Foul and his machinations, not only to her friends. Her failures with Joan, with Marid, with Gibbon had taught her to doubt herself. But she had not come this far, only to repeat the surrender of her parents. Tightly, she replied, 'I won't go down there. But I'll try to locate where it is.'

Covenant released his pent breath as if her decision were a victory.

The First and Honninscrave did not hesitate. Leaving the wheel-deck to the Stóresmaster, they went down the stairs; and he sent a Giant hastening ahead of him to rouse the rest of the crew. Linden and Covenant followed more slowly. Brinn and Cail, Ceer and Hergrom formed a protective cordon around them as they moved forward to meet the Giants who came springing out of the hatchways from their hammocks in Saltroamrest below the foredeck. Shortly, every crewmember who could be spared from the care of the *dromond* was present and ready.

Pitchwife and Seadreamer were there as well. But the First's demeanour checked Pitchwife's natural loquacity; and Seadreamer bore himself with an air of resignation.

In a tone of constricted brevity, forcibly restraining his Giantish outrage at the slayer of the Unhomed, Honninscrave detailed the situation to his crew, described what had to be done. When he finished, the First added sternly, 'It appears that this peril is directed

461

towards Covenant Giantfriend and the Chosen. They must be preserved at any hazard. Forget not that he is the redeemer of our lost kindred and holds a power which must not fall to this Raver. And she is a physician of great skill and insight, whose purpose in this quest is yet to be revealed. Preserve them and rid the Search of this ill.'

She might have said more. She was a Swordmain; her desire to strike blows in the name of the Unhomed was plain in her voice. But Pitchwife interposed lightly, 'It is enough. Are we not Giants? We require no urging to defend our comrades.'

'Then make haste,' she responded. 'The scouring of Starfare's Gem is no small matter.'

Honninscrave promptly organized the Giants into groups of two and sent them below. Then he turned to Linden. 'Now, Chosen.' The command came from him firmly, as if he were bred for emergencies. 'Guide us.'

She had been groping for a way to find the Raver, but had conceived no other method than to pace the ship, trying to track down the intruder's presence. As severely as she could, she said, 'Forget everything under the wheeldeck. My cabin's down there. If it were that close, I would've known sooner.'

Through one of the open hatches, the Anchormaster relayed this information to the search parties below.

As the moon set behind Starfare's Gem, Linden Avery began to walk the afterdeck.

Working her way between the railings, she moved deliberately forward. At every step, she fought to overcome her instinctive resistance, struggled to open herself to the Raver's ambience. Even through her shoes, her senses were alive to the stone of the *dromond*. The granite mapped itself under her: she could feel the Giants hunting below her until they descended beyond her range. But the evil remained hidden, vague and fatal.

Soon the muscles along the backs of her legs began to cramp. Her nerves winced at each step. Gibbon had taught every inch of her body to dread Ravers. But she did not stop.

Dawn came not long after moonset, though the time felt long to her; and the sun caught her halfway up the afterdeck, nearly level with the midmast. She was shivering with strain and could not be certain that she had not already passed over the Raver's covert. When Ceer offered her a drink of water, she paused to accept it. But then she went on, knurling her concentration in both fists so that she would not falter.

Covenant had seated himself in a coil of hawser as large as a bed on one side of Foodfendhall. Brinn and Hergrom stood poised near him. He was watching her with a heavy scowl, radiating his frustration and helplessness, his anger at the blindness of his senses.

In fear that she would weaken, fail again, *again*, Linden increased her pace.

Before she reached the housing, a sudden spasm in her legs knocked her to the deck.

At once, Cail and Ceer caught her arms, lifted her erect.

'Here,' she panted. A fire of revulsion burned through her knees into her hips. She could not straighten her legs. 'Under here. Somewhere.'

The Anchormaster shouted word down to the search parties.

Honninscrave studied her with perplexity. 'That seems a strange hiding,' he muttered. 'From deck to keel below you lie only grainholds, foodlockers, watercests. And all are full. Sevinhand' – he referred to the Anchormaster – 'found pure water, wild maize, and much good fruit on the verges of the Great Swamp.'

Linden could not look at him. She was thinking absurdly, The verges of the Great Swamp. Where all the pollution of Sarangrave Flat drained into the Sea.

Gritting her teeth, she felt the darkness gather under her like a thunderhead. For a time, it lay fragmented in the depths of the ship – pieces of malice. Then it stirred. Thrumming like an assault through the granite, it began to swarm. The sunlight filled her eyes with recollections of bees, forcing her to duck her head, huddle into herself. Somewhere above her head, untended sails flapped limply, Starfare's Gem had become still, braced for the onslaught of the Raver.

It began to rise.

Abruptly, shouts of anger and surprise echoed from the under-decks. Fighting for breath, she gasped, 'It's coming!'

The next instant, a dark grey tumult came flooding over the storm-sill out of Foodfendhall.

Rats.

Huge rats: rodents with sick yellow fangs and vicious eyes, hundreds of them. The Raver was in them. Their savagery filled the air with teeth.

They poured straight towards Covenant.

He staggered upright. At the same time, Brinn and Hergrom threw themselves between him and the attack. Ceer sped to their assistance.

Leaping like cats, the rodents sprang for the *Haruchai*. Covenant's defenders seemed to vanish under the grey wave.

At once, Honninscrave and Seadreamer charged into the assault. Their feet drummed the deck as they kicked and stamped about them. Blood spattered in all directions.

More Giants surged out of the housing in pursuit, pounded into the fray. Brinn and Ceer appeared amid the slashing moil, followed by Hergrom. With hands and feet, they chopped and kicked, crushing rats faster than Linden's eyes could follow.

Without warning, she felt a concatenation of intensity as Covenant's power took fire within him. But his defenders were too close to him. He could not unleash the wild magic.

Yet for a moment she thought he would be preserved. The *Haruchai* were dervish-wild, flinging rats away on all sides; the Giants trampled slaughter through the pack. The air became a scream which only she could hear – the fury of the Raver. In her fear for Covenant, she thought that she was rushing to his defence. But she had not moved, could not move. The simple proximity of the Raver overwhelmed her. It violated her volition, affirmed everything she had ever striven to deny about herself; and the contradiction held her. Only her vision swept forward as Covenant stumbled and fell, grappling frantically at his right leg.

Then he rolled back to his feet, snapped erect with a rat writhing clenched in both hands. White fire gutted the beast before he pitched it overboard. Revulsion twisted his face.

He seemed unaware of the blood which stained the shin of his pants.

In the confusion of the struggle, no one noticed that all the winds had died.

3

RELAPSE

The Giantship went dark around Linden. The blood on Covenant's pants became the blood of his knife-wound, the blood of her nightmare: it blotted out the world. She could taste the venom she had sucked from his forearm after Marid had bitten him. A moral poison. Not just sick: evil. It tasted like the nauseous breath of the strange figure on Haven Farm who had told her to *Be true*.

In spite of that man's putrid halitosis, she had saved his life when his heart had stopped. But she could not save Covenant. The darkness was complete, and she could not move.

But then the Raver disappeared. Its presence burst like an invisible bubble, sunlight and vision rushed back over the ship. Covenant stood motionless near the rail, as distinct in her sight as if he wore a penumbra of fire. All the rats that could still move were scrabbling in his direction. But now they were driven by their fears, not by the

Raver. Instead of trying to harm him, they ran headlong into the Sea.

Linden had taken two steps towards him before her knees failed. The relief of the Raver's flight turned her muscles to water. If Cail had not caught her, she would have fallen.

As Linden started forward again, Covenant looked down at his leg, saw the blood.

Everyone else was silent. The Giantship lay still as if it had been nailed to the water. The atmosphere seemed to sweat as realization whitened his features. His eyes widened, his lips fumbled denials, his hands pleaded at the empty air.

Then she reached him. He stumbled backwards, sat down on the coiled hawser. At once, she stooped to his leg, pulled his pants up to the knee.

The rat-bite had torn a hunk out of his shin between the bones. It was not a large wound, though it bled copiously. For anyone else, the chief danger would have arisen from infection. Even without her bag, she could have treated that.

But before she could act, Covenant's whole frame sprang rigid. The force of the convulsion tore a curse from his corded throat. His legs scissored, the involuntary violence of his muscles knocked her away. Only Brinn's celerity kept him from cracking his head open as he tumbled off the coil.

Impossible that any venom could work so swiftly!

Blood suffused his face as he struggled to breathe. Spasms threatened to rend the ligatures of his chest and abdomen. His heels hammered the deck. His beard seemed to bristle like an excrudescence of pain.

Already, his right forearm had begun to darken as if an artery were haemorrhaging.

This was the way the venom affected him. Whether it was triggered by bee stings or spider bites, it focused on his forearm, where Marid's fangs had first pierced his flesh. And every relapse multiplied the danger horrendously.

'Hellfire!' His desperation sounded like fury. 'Get back!'

She felt the pressure rising in him, poison mounting towards power, but she did not obey. Around her, the Giants retreated instinctively, mystified by what they were seeing. But Brinn and Hergrom held Covenant's shoulders and ankles, trying to restrain him. Cail touched Linden's arm in warning. She ignored him.

Frantically, she threw her senses into Covenant, scrambled to catch up with the venom so that she might attempt to block it. Once before, she had striven to help him and had learned that the new dimension of her sensitivity worked both ways: it made her so vulnerable that she experienced his illness as if it were her own, as if she were personally diseased by the Sunbane; but it also enabled her to succour him, shore up his life with her own. Now she raced to enter him, fighting to dam the virulence of the poison. His sickness flooded coruscations of malice through her; but she permitted the violation. The venom pounding along his veins was on its way to his brain.

She had to stop it. Without him, there would be no Staff of Law — no meaning for the quest; no hope for the Land; no escape for her from this mad world. His ill hurt her like a repetition of Gibbon-Raver's defilement; but she did not halt, did not —

She was already too late. Even with years of training in the use of her health-sense, she would have been no match for this poison. She lacked that power. Covenant tried to shout again. Then the wild magic went beyond all restraint.

A blast of white fire sprang from his right fist. It shot crookedly into the sky like a howl of pain and rage and protest, rove the air as if he were hurling his extremity at the sun.

The concussion flung Linden away like a bundle of rags. It knocked Brinn back against the railing. Several of the Giants staggered. Before the blast ended, it tore chunks from the roof of Foodfendhall and burned through two of the sails from bottom to top.

It also caught Cail. But he contrived to land in a way which absorbed Linden's fall. She was unhurt. Yet for a moment the sheer force of the detonation — the violence severing her from Covenant — stunned her. White fire and disease recoiled through her, blinding her senses. The entire Giantship seemed to whirl around her. She could not recover her balance, could not stifle the nausea flaming in her.

But then her sight veered back into focus, and she found herself staring at Vain. Sometime during the confusion, the Demondim-spawn had left his position on the foredeck, come aft to watch. Now he stood gazing at Covenant with a ghoulish grin on his teeth, as if he were near the heart of his secret purpose. The iron bands on his right wrist and left ankle — the heels of the Staff of Law — gleamed dully against his black skin.

Cail lifted Linden to her feet. He was saying, 'You are acquainted with this ill. What must be done?'

Her nerves were raw with power-burn, shrill with anguish. Flame flushed across her skin. She wrenched free of Cail's grasp. Another spasm shook Covenant. His muscles tautened almost to the ripping point. His forearm was already black and swollen, fever-hot. Fire flickered on and off his ring. And every flicker struck at her exacerbated heart.

She did not know what to do.

No, that was not true. She knew. In the past, he had been brought

466

back from this death by *aliantha*, by Hollian's succour, by the roborant of the Waynhim. Perhaps *diamondraught* would also serve. But he was already in the grip of delirium. How could he be induced to drink the liquor?

Brinn tried to approach Covenant. A white blast tore half the rigging from the midmast, compelling Brinn to retreat. Its force heated Linden's cheeks like shame.

All the *Haruchai* were looking at her. The Giants were looking at her. The First held her silence like a sword. They were waiting for her to tell them what to do.

She knew the answer. But she could not bear it. To *possess* him? Try to take over his mind, force him to hold back his power, accept *diamondraught*? After what she had seen in Joan?

His blast still wailed in her. Gritting her teeth against that cry, she rasped, 'I can't do it.'

Without conscious decision, she started to leave, to flee.

The First stopped her. 'Chosen.' The Swordmain's tone was hard. 'We have no knowledge of this illness. That such harm should come from the bite of one rat is beyond our ken. Yet he must be aided. Were he merely a man, he would require aid. But I have named him Giantfriend. I have given the Search into his hands. He must be given succour.'

'No.' Linden was full of fear and revulsion. The horror was too intimate: Gibbon had taught her to understand it too well. That she was powerless − that all her life had been a lie! Her eyes bled tears involuntarily. In desperation, she retorted, 'He can take care of himself.'

The First's stare glinted dangerously; and Honninscrave started to expostulate. Linden denied them.

'He can do it. When we first showed up here, he had a knife stuck in his chest, and he healed that. The Clave slit his wrists, and he healed that. He can do it.' As she articulated them, the words turned to falsehood in her mouth. But the alternative was heinous to her beyond bearing.

In shame, she thrust her way past the First towards Foodfendhall. The combined incomprehension and anger of so many brave, valuable people pressed against her back. To *possess* him? His power had come close to burning through her as virulently as Gibbon's touch. Was this how Lord Foul meant to forge her for desecration? Pressure and protest sent her half running through the hall to the empty foredeck.

Afterimages of Covenant's blast continued to dismay her senses for a long time. She had been hugging one of the cross-supports of the rail near the prow for half the morning before she realized that the ship was not moving.

Its motionlessness was not due to the damage Covenant had done. The gear of the midmast hung in shambles still. Erratic bursts of wild magic had thwarted every attempt at repair. But even with whole canvas on all three masts, Starfare's Gem would have lain dead in the water. There was no wind. No movement in the Sea at all. The ocean had become a blank echo of the sky – deep azure and flat, as empty of life as a mirror. The *dromond* might have been fused to the surface of the water. Its sails hung like cerements from the inanimate yards: lines and shrouds which had seemed alive in the wind now dangled like stricken things, shorn of meaning. And the heat – The sun was all that moved across the Sea. Shimmerings rose from the decks as though Starfare's Gem were losing substance, evaporating off the face of the deep.

Heat made the dull trudge of Linden's thoughts giddy. She half believed that the Raver had taken away the wind, that this calm was part of Lord Foul's design. Trap the ship where it lay, impale the quest until Covenant's venom gnawed through the cords of his life. And then what? Perhaps in his delirium he would sink the *dromond* before he died. Or perhaps he would be able to withhold that blow. Then the ring and the quest would be left to someone else.

To her?

Dear God! she protested vainly. I can't!

But she could not refute that logic. Why else had Marid feinted towards her before attacking Covenant – why else had Gibbon spared her, spoken to her, touched her – if not to confirm her in her paralysing fear, the lesson of her own ill? And why else had the old man on Haven Farm told her to *Be true*? Why indeed, if both he and the Despiser had not known that she would eventually inherit Covenant's ring?

What kind of person had she become?

At painful intervals, blasts of wild magic sent tremors of apprehension through the stone. Repeatedly Covenant cried out, 'Never! Never give it to him!' hurling his refusal at the blind sky. He had become a man she could not touch. After all her years of evasion, she had finally received the legacy of her parents. She had no choice but to possess him or to let him die.

When Cail came to speak with her, she did not turn her head, did not let him see her forlornness, until he demanded, 'Linden Avery, you must.'

At that, she rounded on him. He was sweating faintly. Even his *Haruchai* flesh was not immune to this heat. But his manner denied any discomfort. He seemed so secure in his rectitude that she could not hold herself from snapping at him, 'No. *You* swore to protect him. *I* didn't.'

'Chosen.' He used her title with a tinge of asperity. 'We have done what lies within our reach. But none can approach him. His fire lashes out at all who draw near. Brinn has been burned – but that is nothing. *Diamondraught* will speed his healing. Consider instead the Giants. Though they can withstand fire, they cannot bear the force of his white ring. When the First sought to near him, she was nigh thrown from the deck. And the Anchormaster, Sevinhand, also assayed the task. When he regained consciousness, he named himself fortunate that he had suffered no more than a broken arm.'

Burned, Linden thought dumbly. Broken. Her hands writhed against each other. She was a doctor, she should already have gone to treat Brinn and Sevinhand. But even at this distance Covenant's illness assaulted her sanity. She had made no decision. Her legs would not take one step in that direction. She could not help him without violating him. She had no other power. That was what she had become.

When she did not speak, Cail went on, 'It is a clean break, which the Storesmaster is able to tend. I do not speak of that. I desire you to understand only that we are surpassed. We cannot approach him. Thus it falls to you. You must succour him.

'We believe that he will not strike at you. You are his nearest companion – a woman of his world. Surely even in his madness he will know you and withhold his fire. We have seen that he holds you in his heart.'

In his heart? Linden almost cried out. But still Cail addressed her as if he had been charged with a speech and meant to deliver it in the name of his duty.

'Yet perhaps in that we are misled. Perhaps he would strike at you also. Yet you must make the attempt. You are possessed of a sight which no *Haruchai* or Giant can share or comprehend. When the Sunbane-sickness came upon you, you perceived that *voure* would restore you. When your ankle was broken beyond all other aid, you guided its setting.' The demand in his expressionless mien was as plain as a fist. 'Chosen, you must gaze upon him. You must find the means to succour him.'

'Must?' she returned huskily. Cail's flat insistence made her wild. 'You don't know what you're saying. The only way I can help him is go into him and take over. Like the Sunbane. Or a Raver. It would be bad enough if I were as innocent as a baby. But what do you think I'll turn into if I get that much power?'

She might have gone on, might have cried at him, And he'll hate me for it! He'll never trust me again! Or himself. But the simple uselessness of shouting at Cail stopped her. Her intensity seemed to have no purpose. His uncompromising visage leeched it away from her. Instead of protesting further, she murmured dimly, 'I'm already too much like Gibbon.'

Cail's gaze did not waver from her face. 'Then he will die.'

I know. God help me. She turned from the *Haruchai*, hung her arms over the cross-supports of the rail to keep herself from sagging to her knees. *Possess* him?

After a moment, she felt Cail withdrawing towards the afterdeck. Her hands twisted against each other as if their futility threatened to drive them mad. She had spent so many years training them, teaching them to heal, trusting them. Now they were good for nothing. She could not so much as touch Covenant.

Starfare's Gem remained becalmed throughout the day. The heat baked down until Linden thought that her bones would melt; but she could not resolve the contradictions in her. Around the ship, the Giants were strangely silent. They seemed to wait with bated breath for Covenant's eruptions of fire, his ranting shouts. No hint of wind stirred the sails. At times, she wanted to fall overboard – not to immerse herself in the Sea's coolness, though anything cool would have been bliss to her aching nerves, but simply to break the unrelieved stillness of the water. Through the stone, she could feel Covenant's delirium worsening.

At noon and again at eventide, Cail brought her food. He performed this task as if no conflict between them could alter his duty; but she did not eat. Though she had not taken one step towards Covenant, she shared his ordeal. The same rack of venom and madness on which he was stretched tortured her as well. That was her punishment for failure – to participate in the anguish she feared to confront.

The old man on Haven Farm had said, *You will not fail, however he may assail you. There is also love in the world.* Not fail? She ached to herself. Good God! As for love, she had already denied it. She did not know how to turn her life around.

So the day ended, and later the waxing moon began to ascend over the lifeless Sea, and still she stood at the railing on the long foredeck, staring sightlessly into the blank distance. Her hands knotted together and unknotted like a nest of snakes. Sweat darkened the hair at her temples, drew faint lines down through the erosions which marked her face; but she paid no heed. The black water lay unmoving and benighted, as empty of life as the air. The moon shone as if it were engrossed in its own thoughts; but its reflection sprawled on the flat surface like a stillborn. High above her, the sails hung limp among their shrouds, untouched by any rumour or foretaste of wind. Again and again, Covenant's voice rose ranting into the hot night. Occasional white lightning paled the stars. Yet she did not respond, though she knew he could not heal himself. The Despiser's venom was a moral poison, and he had no health-sense to guide his fire. Even if his power had been hers to wield as she willed, she might not have been able to burn out that ill without tearing up his life by the roots.

Then Pitchwife came towards her. She heard his determination to speak in the rhythm of his stride. But when she turned her head to him, the sight of her flagrant visage silenced him. After a moment, he retreated with a damp sheen of moonlight or tears in his misshapen eyes.

She thought then that she would be left alone. But soon she felt another Giant looming nearby. Without looking at him, she recognized Seadreamer by his knotted aura. He had come to share his muteness with her. He was the only Giant who suffered anything comparable to her vision, and the pervading sadness of his mood held no recrimination. Yet after a time his silence seemed to pull at her, asking for answers.

'Because I'm afraid.' His muteness enabled her to speak. 'It terrifies me.

'I can understand what Covenant's doing. His love for the Land – ' She envied Covenant his passion, his accessible heart. She had nothing like it. 'I'd do anything to help him. But I don't have that kind of power.'

Then she could not stop; she had to try to explain herself. Her voice slipped out into the night without touching the air or the Sea. But her companion's gentle presence encouraged her.

'It's all possession. Lord Foul possessed Joan to make Covenant come to the Land.' Joan's face had worn a contortion of predatory malice which still haunted Linden. She could not forget the woman's thirst for Covenant's blood. 'A Raver possessed Marid to get that venom into him. A Raver possessed the na-Mhoram of the Clave so that the Clave would serve the Sunbane. And the Sunbane itself! Foul is trying to possess the Law. He wants to make himself the natural order of the Earth. Once you start believing in evil, the greatest evil there is is *possession*. It's a denial of life – of humanity. Whatever you possess loses everything. Just because you think you're doing it for reasons like pity or help doesn't change what it *is*. I'm a doctor, not a Raver.'

She tried to give her insistence the force of affirmation, but it was not true enough for that.

'He needs me to go into him. Take over. Control him so he can drink some *diamondraught*, stop fighting the people who want to help him. But that's evil. Even if I'm trying to save him.' Struggling to put the truth into words, she said, 'To do it, I'd have to take his power away from him.'

She was pleading for Seadreamer's comprehension. 'When I was in Revelstone, Gibbon touched me. I learned something about myself then.' The na-Mhoram had told her she was evil. That was the truth. 'There's a part of me that wants to do it. Take over him. Take his power. I don't have any of my own, and I want it.' *Want* it. All her life, she had striven for power, for effectiveness against death. For

471

the means to transcend her heritage – and to make restitution. If she had possessed Covenant's power, she would have gladly torn Gibbon soul from body in the name of her own crime. That's what paralyses me. I've spent my life trying to deny evil. When it shows up, I can't escape it.' She did not know how to escape the contradiction between her commitment to life and her yearning for the dark might of death. Her father's suicide had taught her a hunger she had satisfied once and dreaded to face again. The conflict of her desires had no answer. In its own way, Gibbon-Raver's touch had been no more horrible than her father's death; and the black force of her memories made her shiver on the verge of crying.

'Yet you must aid him.'

The hard voice pierced Linden. She turned sharply, found herself facing the First of the Search. She had been so caught up in what she was saying to Seadreamer, so locked into herself, that she had not felt the First's approach.

The First glared at her sternly. 'I grant that the burden is terrible for you. That is plain.' She bore herself like a woman who had made a fierce decision of her own. 'But the Search has been given into his hands. It must not fail.'

With a brusque movement, she drew her broadsword, held it before her as though she meant to enforce Linden's compliance with keen iron. Linden pressed her back against the rail in apprehension; but the First bent down, placed her glaive on the deck between them. Then she drew herself erect, fixed Linden with the demand of her stare. 'Have you the strength to wield my blade?'

Involuntarily, Linden looked down at the broadsword. Gleaming densely in the moonlight, it appeared impossibly heavy.

'Have you the strength to lift it from where it lies?'

Linden wrenched her eyes back to the First in dumb protest.

The Swordmain nodded as if Linden had given her the reply she sought. 'Nor have I the insight to act against the Giantfriend's illness. You are Linden Avery the Chosen. I am the First of the Search. We cannot bear each other's burdens.'

Her gaze shed midnight into Linden's upturned face. 'Yet if you do not shoulder the lot which has befallen you, then I swear by my glaive that I will perform whatever act lies within my strength. He will not accept any approach. Therefore I will risk my people, and Starfare's Gem itself, to distract him. And while he strikes at them, with this sword I will sever the envenomed arm from his body. I know no other way to rid him of that ill – and us of the peril of his power. If fortune smiles upon us, we will be able to staunch the wound ere his life is lost.'

Sever? Sudden weakness flooded through Linden. If the First succeeded – ! In a flash of vision, she saw that great blade hacking like an execution at Covenant's shoulder. And blood. Dark under the waxing moon, it would gush out almost directly from his heart. If it were not stopped in an instant, nothing could save him. She was a world away from the equipment she would need to give him transfusions, suture the wound, keep his heart beating until his blood pressure was restored. That blow could be as fatal as the knifethrust which had once impaled his chest.

The back of her head struck the cross-support of the railing as she sank to the deck; and for a moment pain laboured in the bones of her skull. *Sever*? He had already lost two fingers to surgeons who knew no other answer to his illness. If he lived – She groaned. Ah, if he lived, how could she ever meet his gaze to tell him that she had done nothing – that she had stood by in her cowardice and allowed his arm to be cut away?

'No.' Her hands covered her face. Her craven flesh yearned to deny what she was saying. He would have reason to hate her if she permitted the First's attempt. And to hate her forever if she saved his life at the cost of his independent integrity. Was she truly this hungry for power? 'I'll try.'

Then Cail was at her side. He helped her to her feet. As she leaned on his shoulder, he thrust a flask into her hands. The faint smell of diluted *diamondraught* reached her. Fumbling weakly, she pulled the flask to her mouth and drank.

Almost at once, she felt the liquor exerting its analystic potency. Her pulse carried life back into her muscles. The pain in her head withdrew to a dull throbbing at the base of her neck. The moonlight seemed to grow firmer as her vision cleared.

She emptied the flask, striving to suck strength from it – any kind of strength, anything which might help her withstand the virulence of the venom. Then she forced herself into motion towards the afterdeck.

Beyond Foodfendhall, she came into the light of lanterns. They had been placed along the roof of the housing and around the open deck so that the Giants and *Haruchai* could watch Covenant from a relatively safe distance. They shed a yellow illumination which should have comforted the stark night. But their light reached upward to the wreckage of sails and rigging. And within the pool they cast, all the blood and bodies of the rats had been burned away. Scars of wild magic marked the stone like lines of accusation pointing towards Covenant's rigid anguish.

The sight of him was almost too much for Linden. From head to foot, he looked force-battered, as if he had been beaten with truncheons. His eyes were wide and staring; but she could see no relict of awareness or sanity in them. His lips had been torn by the convulsive gnashing of his teeth. His forehead glistened with extreme sweat. In his illness, the beard which had formerly given him a heuristic aspect, an air of prophecy, now looked like a reification of his leprosy. And his right arm –

Hideously black, horrendously swollen, it twitched and grasped beside him, threatening his friends and himself with every wince. The dull silver of his wedding band constricted his second finger like blind cruelty biting into his defenceless flesh. And at his shoulder, the arm of his T-shirt was stretched to the tearing point. Fever radiated from the swelling as if his bones had become faggots for the venom.

That emanation burned against Linden's face even though she stood no closer to him than the verge of the lantern-light. He might already have died if he had not been able to vent the pressure of the poison through his ring. That release was all that kept his illness within bounds his flesh could bear.

Unsteadily, she gestured for Cail to retreat. Her hands shook like wounded birds. He hesitated; but Brinn spoke, and Cail obeyed. The Giants held themselves back, locking their breath behind their teeth. Linden stood alone in the margin of the light as if it were the littoral of a cast danger.

She stared at Covenant. The scars on the deck demonstrated beyond any argument that she would never get near enough to touch him. But that signified nothing. No laying on of hands could anele his torment. She needed to reach him with her soul. Take hold of him, silence his defences long enough to allow some *diamondraught* to be poured down his throat. Possess him.

Either that or tear his power from him. If she was strong enough. Her health-sense made such an attempt feasible. But he was potent and delirious; and nothing in her life had prepared her to believe that she could wrestle with him directly for control of his ring. If she failed, he might kill her in the struggle. And if she succeeded –

She decided to aim herself against his mind. That seemed to be the lesser evil.

Trembling, she fought her visceral paresis, compelled her frightened legs to take two steps into the light. Three. There she stopped. Sinking to the stone, she sat with her knees hugged protectively against her chest. The becalmed air felt dead in her lungs. A waifish voice in the back of her brain pleaded for mercy or flight.

But she did not permit herself to waver. She had made her decision. Defying her mortality, her fear of evil and possession and failure, she opened her senses to him.

She began at his feet, hoping to insinuate herself into his flesh, sneak past his defences. But her first penetration almost made her flee. His sickness leaped the gap to her nerves like ghoul-fire, threatening her self-mastery. For a moment, she remained frozen in fear.

Then her old stubbornness came back to her. It had made her who she was. She had dedicated her life to healing. If she could not use medicine and scalpel, she would use whatever other tools were available. Squeezing her eyes shut to block out the distraction of his torment, she let her perceptions flow up Covenant's legs towards his heart.

His fever grew in her as her awareness advanced. Her pulse laboured; paraesthesia flushed across her skin; the ice of deadened nerves burned in her toes, sent cramps groping through her arches into her calves. She was being sucked towards the abyss of his venom. Blackness crowded the night, dimming the lanterns around her. Power – she wanted power. Her lungs shared his shuddering. She felt in her own chest the corrosion which gnawed at his heart, making the muscle flaccid, the beat limp. Her temples began to ache.

He was already a wasteland, and his illness and power ravaged her. She could hardly hold back the horror pounding at the back of her thoughts, hardly ignore the self-protective impetus to abandon this mad doom. Yet she went on creeping through him, studying the venom for a chance to spring at his mind.

Suddenly, a convulsion knotted him. Her shared reactions knocked her to the deck. Amid the roil of his delirium, she felt him surging towards power. She was so open to him that any blast would sear through her like a firestorm.

Desperation galvanized her resolve. Discarding stealth, she hurled her senses at his head, tried to dive into his brain.

For an instant, she was caught in the throes of wild magic as he thrashed towards an explosion. Images whirled insanely into her: the destruction of the Staff of Law; men and women being bled like cattle to feed the Banefire; Lena and rape; the two-fisted knife-blow with which he had slain a man she did not know; the slashing of his wrists. And power – white fire which crashed through the Clave, turned Santonin and the Stonemight to tinder, went reaving among the Riders to garner a harvest of blood. *Power*. She could not control him. He shredded her efforts as if her entire being and will were made of brittle old leaves. In his madness, he reacted to her presence as if she were a Raver.

She cried out to him. But the outrage of his ring blew her away.

For a time, she lay buffeted by gusts of midnight. They echoed in her – men and women shed like cattle, guilt and delirium, wild magic made black by venom. Her whole body burned with the force of his blast. She wanted to scream, but could not master the spasms which convulsed her lungs.

But gradually the violence receded until it was contained within her head; and the dark began to take shape around her. She was sitting half upright, supported by Cail's arms. Vaguely, she saw the First, Honninscrave, and Pitchwife crouched before her. A lantern revealed the tight concern in their faces.

When she fought her gaze into focus on the Giants, Honninscrave breathed in relief, 'Stone and Sea!' Pitchwife chortled. 'By the Power that remains, Chosen! You are hardy. A lesser blast broke Sevinhand Anchormaster's arm in two places.'

He knew it was me, Linden answered, unaware of her silence. He didn't let it kill me.

'The fault is mine,' said the First grimly. 'I compelled you to this risk. Take no blame upon yourself. Now nothing lies within our power to aid him.'

Linden's mouth groped to form words. 'Blame – ?'

'He has put himself beyond our reach. For life or death, we are helpless now.'

Put – ? Linden grappled with the surrounding night to look towards Covenant. The First nodded at Honninscrave. He moved aside, unblocking Linden's view.

When she saw Covenant, she almost wailed aloud.

He lay clenched and rigid, as though he would never move again, with his arms locked at his sides and need like a rictus on his lips. But he was barely visible through the sheath of wild magic which encased him. Shimmering argent covered him as completely as a caul.

Within his cocoon, his chest still struggled for breath, heart still beat weakly. The venom went on swelling his right arm, went on gnawing at his life. But she did not need any other eyes to tell her that nothing known on Starfare's Gem could breach this new defence. His caul was as indefeasible as leprosy.

This was his delirious response to her attempted possession. Because she had tried to take hold of his mind, he had put himself beyond all succour. He would not have been less accessible if he had withdrawn to another world altogether.

4

THE *NICOR* OF THE DEEP

Helplessly, Linden watched herself go numb with shock. The residue of Covenant's leprosy seemed to well up in her, deadening her. She had done *that* to him? Brinn went stubbornly about the task of proving to himself that no strength or tool he could wield was capable of penetrating Covenant's sheath; but she hardly noticed the *Haruchai*. It was her doing.

Because she had tried to possess him. And because he had spared

476

her the full consequences of his power.

Then Brinn blurred and faded as tears disfocused her vision. She could no longer see Covenant, except as a pool of hot argent in the streaked lambency of the lanterns. Was this why Lord Foul had chosen her? So that she would cause Covenant's death? Yes. She had done such things before.

She retreated into the numbness as if she needed it, deserved it. But the hands which grasped her shoulders were gentle and demanding. Softly, they insisted on her attention, urged her out of her inner morass. They were kind and refused to be denied. When she blinked her gaze clear, she found herself looking into Pitchwife's pellucid eyes.

He sat in front of her, holding her by the shoulders. The deformation of his spine brought his misshapen face down almost to her level. His lips smiled crookedly.

'It is enough, Chosen,' he breathed in a tone of compassion. 'This grief skills nothing. It is as the First has said. The fault is not yours.'

For a moment, he turned his head away. 'And also not yours, my wife,' he said to the shadow of the First. 'You could not have foreknown this pass.'

Then his attention returned to Linden. 'He lives yet, Chosen. He lives. And while he lives, there must be hope. Fix your mind upon that. While we live, it is the meaning of our lives to hope.'

I – She wanted to speak, wanted to bare her dismay to Pitchwife's empathy. But the words were too terrible to be uttered.

His hands tightened slightly, pulling her posture more upright. 'We do not comprehend this caul which he has woven about him. We lack your sight. You must guide us now.' His gentleness tugged at the edges of her heart. 'Is this power something to be feared? Has he not perchance brought it into being to preserve his life?'

His words seemed to cast her gaze towards Covenant. She could barely see him through his shield. But she could see Vain. The Demondim-spawn stood near Covenant, and all suggestion of grinning was gone from his black mien. He bore himself as he always did, his hidden purpose untouched by any other morality. He was not even alive in any normal sense. But he concentrated on Covenant's racked form as if together they were being put to the question of a cruel doom.

'No.' Linden's voice husked roughly out of her emptiness. 'He still has that venom. He's dying in there.'

'Then' – Pitchwife's tone brought her back to his probing – 'we must find the means to unweave this power, so that he may be succoured.'

At that, her stomach turned over in protest. She wanted to cry out, Weren't you watching? I tried to *possess* him. This is my doing. But her ire was useless; and the Giant's empathy sloughed it away.

Her remaining bitterness compressed itself into one word: 'How?'

'Ah, Chosen.' Pitchwife smiled like a shrug. 'That you must tell me.'

She flinched, closed her eyes. Unconsciously, her hands covered her face. Had she not done enough harm? Did he want her to actually hold the knife that killed Covenant?

But Pitchwife did not relent. 'We lack your sight,' he repeated in quiet suasion. 'You must guide us. Think on hope. Clearly, we cannot pierce this caul. Very well. Then we must answer it with understanding. What manner of power is it? What has transpired in his mind, that he is driven to such defence? What need is occulted within him? Chosen.' Again his hands tightened, half lifting her to her feet. 'How may we appeal to him, so that he will permit our aid?'

'Appeal – ?' The suggestion drew a gasp of bile from her. Her arms dropped, uncovering her indignation. 'He's dying! He's deaf and blind with venom and delirium! Do you think I can just go over there and ask him to please stop defending himself?'

Pitchwife cocked an eyebrow at her anger; but he did not flinch. A smile softened his features. 'It is good,' he said through his twisted grin. 'If you are capable of wrath, then you are also capable of hope.'

She started to spit at him, *Hope*? but he overrode her firmly. 'Very well. You see no means of appeal. But there are other questions to which you might reply, if you chose.'

'What do you want from me?' she burned into his face. 'Do you want me to convince you that it's my fault? Well, it *is*. He must've thought I was a Raver or something. He was delirious – in terrible pain. The last thing he knew before he relapsed, he was being attacked by those rats. How was he supposed to know I was trying to help him? He didn't know it was me. Until too late.

'It's like – ' She fumbled momentarily for a description. 'Like hysterical paralysis. He's so afraid of his ring – and so afraid Foul's going to get it. And he's a leper. His numbness makes him think he can't control the power. He hasn't got the nerves to control it. Even without the venom, he's afraid all the time. He never knows when he's going to kill somebody else.'

Words poured from her. In the back of her mind, she relived what she had learned before Covenant hurled her away. As she spoke, those inchoate images took shape for her.

'And he knew what was happening to him. He's had relapses before. When the venom came over him, probably the only conscious thing he had left was fear. He knew he was defenceless. Not against us – against himself. Against Foul. He was already full of power when I tried to take over. What else could he do? He struck back. And then – '

478

For an instant, she faltered in pain. But she could not halt the momentum of the words.

'Then he saw it was me. For all he knew, he might've killed me. Exactly the kind of thing that terrified him most.' She gritted herself to keep from shivering in dismay. 'So he closed all the doors. Shut himself off. Not to keep us out. To keep himself in.'

Deliberately, she fixed Pitchwife with her glare. 'There is no way to appeal to him. You can stand there and shout at him until it breaks your heart, and he won't hear you. He's trying to protect you.' But then she ran out of ire, and her voice trailed away as she conceded lornly, 'Us.' Me.

Around her, silence spread out into the stagnant night. Starfare's Gem lay still as if the loss of wind had slain it. The Giants remained motionless, becalmed, as if their vitality were leaking out of them into the dead Sea. Her speech seemed to hang like futility in the air, denying hope. She could not find any end to the harm she had inflicted on her companions.

But when Pitchwife spoke again, his resilience astonished her. 'Linden Avery, I hear you.' No hue or timbre of despair marred his voice. He talked as though his lifetime as a cripple had taught him to overcome anything. 'But this despond ill becomes us. By my heart, I flounder to think that so many Giants may be rendered mirthless! If words have such power, then we are behooved to consider them again. Come, Chosen. You have said that Covenant Giantfriend seeks to preserve us, and that he will not hear us if we speak. Very well. What will he hear. What language will touch him?'

Linden winced. His insistence simply reaffirmed her failure.

'What does he desire?' the Giant went on steadily. 'What need or yearning lies uppermost in him? Mayhap if we provide an answer to his heart, he will perceive that we are not harmed — that his protection is needless — and he will let his power go.'

She gaped at him. His question took her by surprise; and her response came automatically, without forethought. 'The One Tree. The quest.' Covenant's images were still in her. Pitchwife's calm drew them out of her. 'He doesn't know what else to do. He needs a new Staff of Law. And we're not moving — '

At that, Pitchwife grinned.

An inchoate prescience shocked her. She surged at him, grabbed for the front of his sark. 'The One Tree? He's dying! You don't know where it is!'

Pitchwife's eyes gleamed in response. From somewhere nearby, the Storesmaster's blunt voice said, 'It may be done. I have taken soundings. The Sea is apt for *Nicor*.'

At once, the First said harshly, 'Then we will make the attempt.'

A chuckle widened Pitchwife's grin. His hale aura stroked Linden's

479

senses with a steady confidence she could not comprehend. 'There, Chosen,' he said. 'Hope. We cannot bespeak Covenant Giantfriend, to say that we are well. But we can move Starfare's Gem. Mayhap he will feel that movement and be consoled.'

Move − ? Linden's lips formed words she could not utter. You're kidding?

Heft Galewrath addressed her stolidly. 'I can make no beginning until dawn. We must have light. And then the answer − if I am answered − may be slow in coming. Will the Giantfriend endure so long?'

'He − ' Linden fought the extremity which closed her throat. Her brain kept repeating, Move Starfare's Gem? Without wind? 'I don't know. He has the power. Maybe − maybe what he's doing will slow down the venom. He's shut his mind to everything else. Maybe he's stopped the venom too. If he has − ' She struggled to achieve a coherent assessment. 'He'll live until the venom eats through his heart. Or until he starves to death.'

Move Starfare's Gem?

Abruptly, Honninscrave started shouting orders. Around him, Giants sprang into motion as if they had been brought back to life by a sense of purpose. Their feet spread new energy through the stone as they hastened to their tasks. Several of them went below towards the storage-lockers; but many more swung up into the rigging, began to furl the sails. They worked on all three masts at once, repairing the damage which behung the midmast while they clewed up and lashed the canvas fore and aft.

Linden watched them as if the confusion in her head had become an external madness. They meant to move the ship. Therefore they furled the sails? Pitchwife had already followed the First and Galewrath forward; Honninscrave had positioned himself on the wheeldeck. And Seadreamer, who stood nearby with a private smoulder in his eyes, could not speak. She felt like a lost child as she turned to Cail.

Instead of replying, he offered her a bowl of food and another flask of macerated *diamondraught*.

She accepted them because she did not know what else to do.

Deliberately, she moved back into the lanternlight around Covenant, sat down with her back to Foodfendhall as close to him as her nerves could bear. Her viscera still trembled at the taste of his illness, but she forced herself to remain near enough to monitor his shield − near enough to act promptly if the shield failed. And near enough to keep watch on Vain. The Demondim-spawn's strange attentiveness had not wavered; but his obsidian flesh gave no hint of his intent. With a sigh, she leaned against the stone and compelled herself to eat.

What else could she do? She did not believe that his shield would fail. It looked as absolute as his torment. And Vain went on gazing at that caul as though he expected the Unbeliever to drop through the bottom of the world at any moment.

Later, she slept.

She awoke in the first muggy gloaming of the becalmed dawn. Without their sails, the masts above her looked skeletal against the paling sky, like boughs shorn of leaves, of life. Starfare's Gem was little more than a floating rock under her – a slab of stone crucified between water and sky by the death of all winds. And Covenant, too, was dying: his respiration had become perceptibly shallower, more ragged. He wore his power intimately, like a winding-sheet.

The afterdeck was empty of Giants; and only two remained on the wheeldeck, Sevinhand Anchormaster and a steerswoman. No one was in the rigging, though Linden thought she glimpsed a figure sitting high overhead in Horizonscan, the lookout. Except for herself, Covenant, and Vain, Brinn, Cail, Hergrom, and Ceer, everyone had gone forward. She felt their activity through the stone.

For a while, she could not decide what to do. Her desire to learn what the Giants were about tugged at her. At the same time, she knew she belonged beside Covenant. Yet she obviously could not help him, and her uselessness wore at her. His power, like his mind, was beyond her reach. Soon she became too tense to remain where she was. As a compromise, she went and ascended to the wheeldeck to examine Sevinhand's broken arm.

The Anchormaster was lean for a Giant, and his old face was engraved with an unGiantlike melancholy. In him, the characteristic cheer of his people had been eroded by a habitual grief. The lines on his cheeks looked like galls. But his mien lightened as Linden approached, and the smile with which he answered her desire to inspect his arm was plainly genuine.

He carried his limb in a sling. When she slipped back the cloth, she saw that the forearm had been properly splinted. Probing his skin with her fingers, she discerned that Cail had reported the injury accurately: the breaks were clean – and cleanly set. Already the bones had begun to knit.

She nodded her satisfaction, turned to go back to Covenant. But Sevinhand stopped her.

She looked at him inquiringly. His melancholy had returned. He remained silent for a moment while he considered her. Then he said, 'Heft Galewrath will attempt a calling of *Nicor*. That is perilous.' The flinch of his eyes showed that he was personally acquainted with the danger. 'Mayhap there will be sore and instant need for a healer. It is Galewrath who tends the healing of Starfare's Gem – yet the gravest peril will befall her. Will you not offer your aid?' He nodded forward. 'Surely the *Haruchai* will summon you with all speed, should you be required by Covenant Giantfriend.'

His earnest gaze moved her. The Giants had already shown their concern and support for her in many ways. Seadreamer had carried her out of Sarangrave Flat after the breaking of her ankle. And Pitchwife had tried several times to demonstrate that there were other smiles in the world than the fatal one Covenant had given Joan. She welcomed a chance to offer some kind of service in return. And she was clearly valueless to Covenant as matters stood. Vain did not appear to pose any threat.

Turning to Cail, she said, 'I'm counting on you.' His slight bow of acceptance reassured her. The flatness of his visage seemed to promise that his people could be trusted beyond any possibility of dereliction or inadequacy.

As she left the wheeldeck, she felt Sevinhand's relief smiling wanly at her back.

Hastening across the long afterdeck, she passed through Foodfendhall towards the prow of the ship. There she joined a milling press of Giants. Most were busy at tasks she did not understand; but Pitchwife noticed her arrival and moved to her side. 'You are well come, Chosen,' he said lightly. 'Perchance we will have need of you.'

'That's what Sevinhand said.'

His gaze flicked aft like a wince, then returned to Linden. 'He speaks from knowledge.' His misformed eyes cast a clear echo of the Anchormaster's sorrow. 'At one time – perhaps several brief human lives past – Sevinhand Mastered another Giantship, and Seatheme his wife served as Storesmaster. Ah, that is a tale worth the telling. But I will curtail it. The time is not apt for that story. And you will have other inquiries.

'To speak shortly – ' Abruptly, he grimaced in vexation. 'Stone and Sea, Chosen! It irks my heart to utter such a tale without its full measure. I am surpassed to credit that any people who speak briefly are in good sooth alive at all.' But then his eyes widened as if he were startled by his own intensity, and his expression cleared. 'Nevertheless, I bow to the time.' He saluted Linden as if he were laughing at himself. 'Shortly, then. Sevinhand and his Giantship sailed a sea which we name the Soulbiter, for it is ever fell and predictless, and no craft passes it without cost. There a calm such as we now suffer came upon them. Many and many a day the vessel lay stricken, and no life stirred the sails. Water and food became dire. Therefore the choice was taken to attempt a calling of *Nicor*.

'As Storesmaster, the task fell chiefly to Seatheme, for such was her training and skill. She was a Giant to warm the heart, and – ' Again, he stopped. Ducking his head, he passed a hand over his eyes, muttered, 'Ah, Pitchwife. Shortly.' When he looked up once more, he was smiling crookedly through his tears. 'Chosen, she mistimed the catch. And rare is the Giant who returns from the jaws of the *Nicor*.'

Linden met his gaze with an awkwardness in her throat. She wanted to say something, but did not know how to offer comfort to a Giant. She could not match his smile.

Beyond the foremast, the crew had completed the construction of three large objects under Galewrath's direction. They were coracles – boats made of leather stretched over wooden frames, each big enough to hold two Giants. But their sides rose and curved so that each vessel was three-quarters of a sphere. A complex of hawsers and iron rings connected the coracles to each other; they had to be lifted and moved together. At Galewrath's orders, the boats were borne forward and pitched over the prow.

Guiding Linden with a touch on her shoulder, Pitchwife took her to a vantage from which she had a clear view of the coracles. They floated lightly on the flat Sea.

A moment later, the Storesmaster's blunt voice carried over the foredeck. 'The calling of *Nicor* is hazardous, and none may be commanded to share it. If I am answered by one alone, mayhap it will be a rogue, and we will be assailed. If I am answered by many, this Sea will become a discomfortable swimming-place. And if I am not answered – ' She shrugged brusquely. 'For good or ill, the attempt must be made. The First has spoken. I require the aid of three.'

Without hesitation, several Giants stepped forward. Seadreamer moved to join them; but the first halted him, saying, 'I will not risk the Earth-Sight.' Quickly, Galewrath chose three crewmembers. The rest went to uncoil a rope as thick as Linden's thigh from its cablewell near the foremast. This hawser they fed down towards the coracles.

The Storesmaster looked to Honninscrave and the First for parting words. But the First said simply, 'Have care, Heft Galewrath. I must not lose you.'

Together, Galewrath and her three companions dove overboard.

Swimming with accustomed ease, they moved to the coracles, towing behind them the free hawser. When they reached the tackle connecting the boats, they threaded their line through a central iron ring. Then they pulled it towards the foremost coracle.

This craft formed the apex of a triangle pointing eastward. With a prodigious heave of her legs, Galewrath rose up in the water and flipped herself over the edge into the coracle. It rocked under her weight, but continued to float. She braced it as another Giant joined her. Then they accepted the hawser from the remaining swimmers.

The two separated, one to each of the outer coracles, as Galewrath and her partner tugged a length of cable from Starfare's Gem through the ring into their craft. When she was satisfied with the amount of line she had available, she began to knot a large loop into the end of the hawser.

As soon as the other Giants had boarded their coracles, they announced that they were ready. They sounded tense; but one was grinning fiercely, and the other could not resist her temptation to cast a mock bow towards Starfare's Gem, rocking her coracle as she clowned.

Heft Galewrath responded with a nod. Shifting her weight, she tilted the edge of her craft down almost to the waterline. From that position, she placed an object that looked like a one-sided drumhead in the water. Her partner helped her balance the coracle so that it remained canted without shipping water.

Pitchwife tightened expectantly; but Galewrath's stolid mien gave no sign that she had undertaken anything out of the ordinary. From her belt, she drew out two leather-wrapped sticks and at once began on the drum, sending an intricate, cross-grained rhythm into the Sea.

Faintly through the stone, Linden felt that beat carrying past the keel, spreading outward like a summons.

'Pitchwife.' She was still conscious of Covenant, though the intervening Giants muffled her perception of him. He was like a bruise between her shoulder-blades. But Galewrath held her attention. Anticipation of danger made her nervous. She needed to hear voices, explanations. 'What the hell is going on?'

The deformed Giant glanced at her as if to gauge the implications of her acerbic tone. After a moment, he breathed softly, 'A calling of *Nicor*. The *Nicor* of the Deep.'

That told her nothing. But Pitchwife seemed to understand her need. Before she could ask for a better answer, he went on, 'Such calling is rarely greeted swiftly. Belike we confront a wait of some durance. I will tell you the tale.'

Behind her, most of the crew had left the prow. Only the First, Honninscrave, Seadreamer, and one or two others remained; the rest ascended the ratlines. Together, they kept watch on all the horizons.

'Chosen,' Pitchwife murmured, 'have you heard the name of the Worm of the World's End?' She shook her head. 'Well, no matter.' A gleam of quickening interest ran along his tone – a love for stories.

Galewrath's rhythm continued, complex and unvarying. As it thudded flatly into the dead air and the rising heat and the Sea, it took on a plaintive cast, like a keening of loneliness, a call for companionship. Her arms rose and fell tirelessly.

'It is said among the *Elohim*, whose knowledge is wondrous, and difficult of contradiction' – Pitchwife conveyed a chortle of personal amusement – 'that in the ancient and eternal youth of the cosmos, long ere the Earth came to occupy its place, the stars were as thick as sand throughout all the heavens. Where now we see multitudes of bright beings were formerly multitudes of multitudes, so that the cosmos was an ocean of stars from shore to shore, and the great depth of their present solitude was unknown to them – a sorrow which they could not have comprehended. They were the living peoples of the heavens, as unlike to us as gods. Grand and warm in their bright loveliness, they danced to music of their own making and were content.'

A rustle went through the Giants watching from the foremast, then subsided. Their keen sight had picked out something in the distance; but it had vanished.

'But far away across the heavens lived a being of another kind. The Worm. For ages it slumbered in peace – but when it awakened, as it awakens at the dawn of each new eon, it was afflicted with a ravenous hunger. Every creation contains destruction, as life contains death, and the Worm was destruction. Driven by its immense lust, it began to devour the stars.

'Perhaps this Worm was not large among the stars, but its emptiness was large beyond measure, and it roamed the heavens, consuming whole seas of brightness, cutting great swaths of loneliness across the firmament. Writhing along the ages, avid and insatiable, it fed on all that lay within its reach, until the heavens became sparsely peopled as a desert.'

As Linden listened, she tasted some of the reasons behind the Gaints' love of stories. Pitchwife's soft narration wove a thread of meaning into the becalmed sky and the Sea. Such tales made the world comprehensible. The mood of his telling was sad; but its sadness did no harm.

'Yet the devoured stars were beings as unlike to us as gods, and no Worm or doom could consume their power without cost. Having fed hugely, the Worm became listless and gravid. Though it could not sleep, for the eon's end of its slumber had not come, it felt a whelming desire for rest. Therefore it curled its tail about itself and sank into quiescence.

'And while the Worm rested, the power of the stars wrought within it. From its skin grew excrescences of stone and soil, water and air, and these growths multiplied upon themselves and multiplied until the very Earth beneath our feet took form. Still the power of the stars wrought, but now it gave shape to the surface of the Earth, forging the seas and the land. And then was brought forth life upon the Earth. Thus were born all the peoples of the Earth, the beasts of the land, the creatures of the deep – all the forests and greenswards from pole to pole. And thus from destruction came forth creation, as death gives rise to life.

'Therefore, Chosen,' said Pitchwife firmly, 'we live, and strive, and seek to define the sense of our being. And it is good for though we compose a scant blink across the eyes of eternity, yet while the blink lasts we choose what we will, create what we may, and share ourselves with each other as the stars did ere they were bereaved. But it must pass. The Worm does not slumber. It merely rests. And the time must come when it is roused, or rouses itself. Then it will slough off this skin of rock and water to pursue its hunger across the cosmos until eon's end and slumber. For that reason, it is named the Worm of the World's End.'

There Pitchwife fell silent. Linden glanced at him, saw his gaze fixed on Galewrath as though he feared the limitations of her strength. But the Storesmaster did not falter. While her partner balanced the coracle, she went on articulating her rhythm steadfastly, reaching out into the deeps for an answer. Ripples danced around the edges of the drum and were swallowed by the flat calm of the Sea.

Slowly, Pitchwife turned his eyes to Linden; but he seemed not to see her. His mind still wandered the paths of his tale. Gradually, however, he came back to himself. When his sight focused, he smiled in bemusement.

'Chosen,' he said lightly, as if to soften the import of his words, 'it is said that the *Nicor* are offspring of the Worm.'

That announcement brought back her anxiety. It gave her her first hint of what the Giants were doing, how they meant to move the ship. Perhaps his tale was nothing more than a myth; but it accounted for the purpose which had galvanized the *dromond*. Implications of peril pulled her attention outward, sent her senses hunting over the inert Sea. She could hardly believe what she was thinking. Do they mean to capture – ?

Before she could ask Pitchwife if she had understood him correctly, a distant thrumming like a sensation of speed touched her feet through the stone of Starfare's Gem. An instant later, a shout cracked across the masts.

'*Nicor!*'

The cry snatched her around. Searching the shrouds, she saw a Giant pointing southward.

Other shouts verified the first. Linden's gaze reached for the starboard horizon. But she could descry nothing. She held her breath, as if in that way she could force her vision into focus.

More with her feet than her ears, she heard Galewrath's rhythm change.

And the change was answered. Thudding beats echoed against the keel of the *dromond*. Something had heard Galewrath's call – and was replying.

Abruptly, the horizon broke as a surge of water like a bowwave rose out of the calm. The Sea piled upward as though a tremendous head were rushing forward just below the surface. The surge was still a great distance away, but it came towards the ship at a staggering rate. The wave slashed out to either side, climbing higher and higher until it looked large enough to swamp the Giantship.

Galewrath's rhythm took on a febrile edge, like pleading. But the answer did not vary, gave no sign that it understood. Yet it cast suggestions of power which made Linden's knees tremble.

Now through the water she could see a dark shape. It writhed like a serpent, and every heave of its form bespoke prodigious strength. As the *Nicor* came within jerrid-range of the vessel, its head-wave reached the height of the rails.

With the clarity of panic, Linden thought, It's going to ram us.

Then the Storesmaster hit her drum a resounding blow which split it; and the creature sounded.

Its long body flashed ahead of the wave as the *Nicor* angled into the depths. A moment later, the surge hit with a force which rocked the *dromond*. Linden staggered against Cail, rebounded from the railing. Starfare's Gem bobbed like a toy on the Sea.

Gripping Cail for balance as the Giantship resettled itself, Linden threw a glance downward and saw the colossal length of the *Nicor* still passing the keel. The creature was several times as long as Starfare's Gem.

The coracles lurched in the waves which recoiled from the sides of the *dromond*. But the four Giants kept their poise, held themselves ready. Galewrath had abandoned her riven drum. She stood now with the loop of the hawser in both hands; and her eyes watched the Sea.

Another shout. Some distance off to port, the *Nicor* broke water. For an instant, its head was visible, its snout like a prow, foam streaming from its gargantuan jaws. Then the creature arced back underwater and ploughed away in a long curve westward.

Starfare's Gem fell still. Linden could feel nothing except the pervasive ache of Covenant's need and the rapid beating of the *Nicor*'s talk. She lost sight of the wave as it passed behind Foodfend-hall towards the stern of the vessel. Every eye in the rigging followed the creature's path; but no one made a sound.

Her fingers dug into Cail's shoulder until she thought the joints would part. The thrumming of the creature became louder to her nerves than Covenant's plight.

'Ward!'

The suddenness of the cry stung Linden's hearing.

'It comes!'

Instantly, Giants scrambled out of the rigging. Honninscrave and the Anchormaster yelled orders. The crew gained the deck, braced themselves for a collision. Half a score of them slapped holding-blocks around the hawser near the cablewell.

The Storesmaster's strident shout rang over the vessel.

'How does it come?'

A Giant sprang into the prow, responded, 'It comes truly!'

Linden had no time to do anything except cling to Cail. In that instant, the heel of the Giantship began to rise. Starfare's Gem tilted forward as the *Nicor*'s head-wave struck the stern. The creature was passing along the ship's keel.

At the same moment, Galewrath dove into the Sea. Hauling the hawser behind her, she plunged to meet the *Nicor*.

Linden saw the Storesmaster kicking strongly downward. For one suspended heartbeat, Galewrath was alone in the water. Then the head of the *Nicor* flashed out from under the ship. The creature drove straight towards Galewrath.

As the two forms came together, a flurry of movement confused the sight. Linden clutched Cail's hard flesh, ground her grip towards bone. The *Nicor* seemed to shout at her through the Sea and the stone. She heard its brute hunger, its incomprehension of what had called out to it. At her side, Pitchwife's hands wrestled the railing as if it were alive.

All at once, the hawser sprang outward. It leaped past the coracles, rushed hissing like fire into the water.

'Now!' cried the First.

Immediately, Galewrath's helpers abandoned their craft. As they did so, they overturned the coracles. With the openings downward and air trapped inside, the coracles floated like buoys, supporting between them the tackle and the iron ring through which the hawser sped.

Beneath the swimmers, the long dark body of the *Nicor* went writhing eastward. Lines were thrown down to them; but they did not respond. Their attention was focused on the place where Galewrath had disappeared.

When she broke water some distance past the coracles, a great shout went up from the Giantship. She waved her arms brusquely to signal that she was unharmed. Then she began to swim towards the *dromond*.

Short moments later, she and her companions stood dripping before the First. 'It is done,' she panted, unable to conceal her pride. 'I have looped the snout of the *Nicor*.'

The First returned an iron grin. But at once she swung towards the Giants poised on either side of the hawser near the cablewell. The cable was running headlong through the holding-blocks. 'Our line is not endless,' she said firmly. 'Let us begin.'

Ten Giants answered her with grins, nods, muttered promises. They planted their legs, braced their backs. At Honninscrave's command, they began to put pressure on the holding-blocks.

A scream of tortured cable shrilled across the deck. Smoke leaped from the blocks. The Giants were jerked forward a step, two steps, as they tried to halt the unreeling of the hawser.

The prow dipped under them like a nod; and Starfare's Gem started forward.

The screaming mounted. Honninscrave called for help. Ten more Giants slapped holding-blocks on to the hawser and threw their weight against it. Muscles knotted, thews stood out like bone, gasps burst along the line. Linden felt the strain in them and feared that not even Giants could bear such pressure. But by degrees the shrilling faded as the hawser slowed. The *dromond* gained speed. When the cable stopped, Starfare's Gem was knifing through the Sea as fast as the *Nicor* could tow it.

'Well done!' Honninscrave's eyes glinted under his massive brows. 'Now let us regain what line we may, ere this *Nicor* conceives a desire to sound.'

Grunting with exertion, the Giants heaved on the hawser. Their feet seemed to clinch the granite of the deck, fusing ship and crew into a single taut organism. One arm's-length at a time, they drew in the cable. More of the crew came to their aid. The *dromond* began to gain on the *Nicor*.

Slowly, Linden uncramped her grip from Cail's shoulder. When she glanced at him, he appeared unconscious of her. Behind the flatness of his visage, he was watching the Giants with an acuity like joy, as if he almost shared her astonishment.

From the prow, crewmembers kept watch on the hawser. The buoys held the line's guide-ring above water; by observing the cable's movement in the ring, the Giants were able to see any change of direction made by the *Nicor*. This information they relayed to the steerswoman, so that she could keep Starfare's Gem on the creature's course.

But the buoys served another, more important purpose as well: they provided forewarning in case the *Nicor* should sound. If the creature dove suddenly and strongly enough, the prow of the Giantship might be pulled down before the hawser could be released. Perhaps some of the crew might be rent overboard when the others dropped the line. The buoys would give the Giants advance warning so that they could let go of the cable together safely.

For a few moments, Linden was too full of amazement to think about anything else. But then a pang of recollection reminded her of Covenant.

Immediately, urgently, she sent her senses scrambling towards the afterdeck. At first, she could not feel her way past the immense straining of the Giants. They were a cynosure of effort, blocking her percipience. But then her grasp on the ambience of the *dromond* clarified, and she felt Covenant lying as she had left him − locked rigid within his argent caul, rendered by his own act untouchable and doomed. An ache of dismay sucked at her when she thought

489

that perhaps the ploy of the Giants had already failed. She protested, but could not seal herself against the fear. They did not deserve to fail.

The next moment, the *Nicor* thrashed through a violent change of direction. Starfare's Gem canted as if it had been stricken below the waterline. Swiftly, the steerswoman spun Shipsheartthew. The *dromond* began to straighten.

The *Nicor* wrenched itself the other way. Hooked by its prow, the Giantship pitched to that side. Water leaped towards the railing and Linden like a hammer blow.

The Sea curled away scant feet from her face. Then Honninscrave shouted, 'Ease the line!'

The Giants obeyed; and the hawser leaped to a squeal through the holding-blocks, shot with a loud yammer past the prow. As the steerswoman fought the wheel, Starfare's Gem righted itself.

'Once more!' the Master ordered. 'Hold!'

At his signal, blocks bit back into the cable, brought it squalling to a halt.

Linden found that she had forgotten to breathe. Her chest burned with the strain.

Before she could recover her balance, the *dromond* sagged back on its stern. Then the deck was nearly ripped from under her. The *Nicor* had surged to a stop, coiled its strength, and leaped forward again with redoubled ferocity.

In the instant that the pressure was released, all the Giants staggered backward. Some of them fell. Then the hawser tore at their arms as the *Nicor* began to run.

They were off-balance, could not hold. Honninscrave barked urgently, 'Release!' They struggled to obey.

But they could not all unclose their holding-blocks at the same instant. One of them was late by a fraction of a heartbeat.

With the whole force of the *Nicor*, he was snatched forward. His grip appeared to be tangled on the hawser. Before he could let go, he crashed head and body against the rail of the prow.

The impact tore him free of the line. He tumbled backward, lay there crushed and still.

Shouts echoed unheard around Linden as Honninscrave mustered his crew to grip the hawser again. Her whole attention was fixed on the broken Giant. His pain cried out to her. Thrusting away from Cail, she jumped the hissing cable as if she were inured to peril, dashed to the sprawled form. All her instincts became lucid and precise.

She saw his shattered bones as if they were limned in light, felt his shredded tissues and internal bleeding as though the damage were incused on her own flesh. He was severely mangled. But he was still alive. His heart still limped; air still gurgled wetly from his pierced lungs. Perhaps he could be saved.

No. The harm was too great. He needed everything a modern hospital could have provided – transfusions, surgery, traction. She had nothing to offer except her health-sense.

Behind her, the ululation of the hawser fell silent as the Giants regained their hold. At once, they strove to win back the line they had lost. Starfare's Gem swept forward.

And yet his heart still beat. He still breathed. There was a chance. It was worth the attempt.

Without hesitation, she knelt at his side, cleared her mind of everything else. Reaching into him with her senses, she committed herself to the support of his faltering life.

With her own pulse, she steadied his, then bent her attention to the worst of his internal injuries. His pain flooded through her, but she refused to be mastered by it. His need outweighed pain. And it enabled her to trace his wounds as if they were laid bare before her. First she confronted his lungs. Broken ribs had punctured them in several places. Firmly, she nudged his tissues closed around the bones so that his lungs would not fill with blood. Then she followed the damage elsewhere. His bowels had been lacerated, but that was not the most immediate danger. Other organs were bleeding profusely. She poured herself towards them, fought to –

'Chosen.' Cail's voice cut through her concentration. 'Brinn calls. The ur-Lord rouses himself.'

The words pierced her like cold death. Involuntarily, her awareness sprang in the direction of the afterdeck.

Cail was right. Covenant's sheath had begun to flash back and forth, flickering towards disaster. Within it, he twisted as though he were on the verge of the last rigor.

But the Giant – ! His life was seeping out of him. She could feel it flow as if it formed a palpable pool around her knees. Like the wound in her nightmare.

No!

As it flashed, Covenant's power gathered for one more blast. The import of that accumulation was written in the distress of his aura. He was preparing to release his white fire, let go of it entirely. Then the last barrier between him and the venom would be gone. She knew without seeing him that his whole right side from hand to shoulder, waist to neck, was grotesquely swollen with poison.

One or the other, Covenant or the Giant.

While she sat there, stunned with indecision, they might both die. *No*!

She could not endure it. Intolerable that either of them should be lost!

Her voice broke as she cried out, 'Galewrath!' But she did not listen to the way her call cracked across the foredeck, did not wait for an answer. Cail tugged at her shoulder; she ignored him. Panting urgently, frenetically, *Covenant!* she plunged back into the stricken Giant.

The injuries which would kill him most quickly were *there* and *there* – two hurts bleeding too heavily to be survived. His lungs might go on working, but his heart could not continue. It had already begun to falter under the weight of so much blood-loss. With cold accuracy she saw what she would have to do. To keep him alive. Occupying his abdomen with her percipience, she twisted his nerves and muscles until the deeper of the two bleedings slowed to a trickle.

Then Heft Galewrath arrived, knelt opposite her. Covenant was going to die. His power gathered. Still Linden did not permit herself to flinch. Without shifting her attention, she grabbed Galewrath's hand, directed the thumb to press deeply into the Giant's stomach at a certain point. *There.* That pressure constricted the flow of the second fatal hurt.

'Chosen.' Cail's tone was as keen as a whip.

'Keep pressing there.' Linden sounded wild with hysteria, but she did not care. 'Breathe into him. So he doesn't drown on blood.' She prayed that the experience of the seas had taught Galewrath something akin to artificial respiration.

In a frenzy of haste, she scrambled towards Covenant.

The foredeck appeared interminable. The Giants straining at the hawser dropped behind her one by one as if their knotted muscles and arched backs, the prices they were willing to pay in Covenant's name, measured out the tale of the belatedness. The sun shone into their faces. Beyond Foodfendhall, the flickering of Covenant's power grew slower as it approached its crisis.

Hergrom seemed to materialize in front of her, holding open the door to the housing. She hurdled the storm-sill, pounded through the hall. Ceer flung open the far door.

With a wrench of nausea, she felt white fire collecting in Covenant's right side. Gathering against the venom. In his delirium, blind instinct guided him to direct the power inward, at himself, as if he could eradicate the poison by fire. As if such a blast would not also tear his life to shreds.

She had no time to try for any control over him. Springing out on to the afterdeck, she dove headlong towards him, skidded across the stone past Vain's feet to collide with Covenant so that any fire he unleashed would strike her as well. And as she hurled herself into danger, she drove her senses as far into him as she could reach.

Covenant! Don't!

She had never made such an attempt before, never tried to thrust a message through the link of her percipience. But now, impelled by desperation and hazard, she touched him. Far below his surface extremity, the struggling vestiges of his consciousness heard her. Barriers fell as he abandoned himself to her. A spring of fire broke open from his right hand, releasing the pressure. Flame gushed out of him and flowed away, harming nothing.

A wave of giddiness lifted her out of herself. She tottered to her feet, staggered against Cail. Her lips formed words she could hardly hear.

'Give him *diamondraught*. As much as you can.'

Dimly, she watched Brinn obey. She wanted to return to the foredeck. But her limbs were so full of palsy and relief that she could not move. Around her, the deck started to spin. She had to summon more strength than she knew she owned before she was able to tell Cail to take her back to Galewrath and the injured Giant.

At sunset, Starfare's Gem passed out of the zone of calm. Waves began to rock the vessel and wind kicked at the shrouds, drawing a cheer from the weary crew. By that time, they had recaptured half the line connecting them to the *Nicor*. Honninscrave spoke to the First. With a flourish, she drew her broadsword, severed the hawser at one stroke.

Other Giants climbed into the rigging and began to unfurl the sails. Soon Starfare's Gem was striding briskly before a stiff wind into the eastern night.

By that time, Linden had done everything she could for the wounded Giant. She felt certain he would live. When he regained consciousness enough to gaze up into her exhausted visage, he smiled.

That was enough. She left him in Galewrath's charge. Pulling together what remained of her spent courage, she stumbled back down the long foredeck to care for Covenant.

5

FATHER'S CHILD

During the night, squalls came up like a reaction against the earlier calm. They gusted and drove the *dromond* until it seemed to breast its way ponderously eastward like a worn-out grampus. But that impression was misleading. The masts were alive with lines and canvas and Giants, and Starfare's Gem raced through the cross-hacked waves like a riptide.

For four days, a succession of small storms battered the region, permitted the ship's crew little rest. But Linden hardly noticed the altercation of wind and rain and quiet.

She grew unconsciously accustomed to the background song of the rigging, the rhythm of the prow in the Sea, to the pitching of the stone and the variable swaying of the lanterns and hammocks. At unexpected intervals, the Giants greeted her with spontaneous celebrations, honouring her for what she had done; and their warmth brought tears to her eyes. But her attention was elsewhere. The little strength she gained from troubled snatches of sleep and nibbled meals, she spent watching over Thomas Covenant.

She knew now that he would live. Though he had shown no hint of consciousness, the *diamondraught* was vivid in him – antivenin, febrifuge, and roborant in one. Within the first day, the swelling had receded from his right side and arm, leaving behind a deep mottled black-and-yellow bruise but no sign of any permanent damage. Yet he did not awaken. And she did not try to reach into him, either to gain information or to nudge him towards consciousness. She feared that perhaps the sickness still gnawed at his mind, exacting its toll from his bare sanity; but she was loath to ascertain the truth. If his mind were healing as well as his body, then she had no reason or excuse to violate his privacy. And if he were being corroded towards madness, she would need more strength than she now possessed to survive the ordeal.

The venom was still in him. Because of her, he had been driven right to the edge of self-extirpation. And even then she had risked him further for another's sake. But she had also called him back from that edge. Somehow through his delirium and looming death he had recognized her – and trusted her. That was enough. Whenever the continuing vulnerability of his sopor became more than she could bear, she went to tend the injured Giant.

His name was Mistweave, and his hardiness was vaguely astounding her. Her own restless exhaustion, the inner clench of her tension, the burning of her red-rimmed eyes on the salt air, made him seem healthier than she was. By the second day of the squalls, his condition had stabilized to such an extent that she was able to attempt the setting of his fractured ribs. Guiding Galewrath and Seadreamer as they applied traction to Mistweave's torso, she bent those bones away from his lungs back into their proper alignment so that they could heal without crippling him. He bore the pain with a fierce grin and a flask of *diamondraught*; and when at last he lapsed into unconsciousness Linden could hear the new ease of his breathing.

The Storesmaster complimented the success of the manipulation with a blunt nod, as if she had expected nothing else from the Chosen. But Cable Seadreamer lifted her from her feet and gave her a tight hug that felt like envy. The flexing of his oaken muscles told her how severely the Master's brother ached for healing – for the Earth, and for his own misery. The scar under his eyes gleamed pale and aggrieved.

In recognition and empathy, she returned his clasp. Then she left Saltroamrest, where Mistweave lay, and went back to Covenant.

Late at night after the third day of squalls, he began to rouse himself.

He was too weak to raise his head or speak. He seemed too weak to comprehend where he was, who she was, what had happened to him. But behind the dullness of his gaze he was free of fever. The venom had returned to latency.

Propping up his head, she fed him as much as he could eat of the food and drink which Cail had brought for her earlier. Immediately afterward, he slipped away into a more natural sleep.

For the first time in long days, Linden went to her own chamber. She had stayed away from it as if it were still full of nightmares; but now she knew that that darkness had receded at least temporarily. Stretching out her exhaustion in the hammock, she let herself rest.

Throughout the next day, Covenant awakened at intervals without fully regaining consciousness. Each time he opened his eyes, tried to lift his head, she fed him; and each time he drifted almost at once back into his dreams. But she did not need her health-sense to see that he was growing stronger as his flesh drank in sleep and aliment. And that gave her a strange easement. She felt that she was linked to him symbiotically, that the doors of perception and vulnerability which she had opened to him could not be closed again. His recuperation comforted her in more ways than she could name.

This baffled her lifelong desire for independence, frustrated her severe determination to live at no behest but her own. If she had ever permitted herself to be thus accessible to someone else's needs and passions, how could she have survived the legacy of her parents? Yet she could not wish herself free of this paradoxically conflicted and certain man. The knots within her softened to see him healing.

Early the next morning, she fed him again. When he went back to sleep, she ascended to the afterdeck and found that the squalls had blown away. A steady wind carried Starfare's Gem lightly through the seas. Overhead, the sails curved like wings against the untrammelled azure of the sky.

Honninscrave hailed her like a shout of praise from the wheeldeck, then asked about Covenant. She replied briefly, almost dourly, not because the question troubled her, but because she did not know how to handle the unwonted susceptibility of her answer. Something within her wanted to laugh in pleasure at the breeze, and the clean sunshine, and the dancing of the waves. The *dromond* sang under her. And yet, unexpectedly, she felt that she was on the verge of tears. Her innominate contradictions confused her. She was no longer certain of who she was.

Scanning the afterdeck, she saw Pitchwife near the place where Covenant had lain in his cocoon. Vain still stood in the vicinity – he had not moved at all since Covenant's rescue – and Pitchwife ignored him. The deformed Giant bore a rude slab of rock over one shoulder. In the opposite hand, he carried a stone cauldron. Impelled partly by curiosity, partly by a rising pressure of words, Linden went to see what he was doing. He seemed to have a special empathy for confusion.

'Ah, Chosen,' he said in greeting as she approached; but his gaze was distracted, and concentration furrowed his brows. 'You behold me about my craft.' In spite of his preoccupation, he gave her a smile. 'Doubtless you have observed the workings of Starfare's Gem and seen that each Giant serves the needs of the ship. And doubtless also you have noted that the exception is myself. Pitchwife rides no rigging, bears no duty at Shipsheartthew. He labours not in the galley, neither does he tend either sail or line. What purpose then does he serve among this brave company?'

His tone hinted at humour; but most of his attention was elsewhere. Setting down his rock and cauldron, he examined first the wild magic scars in the deck, then the damage done to the roof of the housing. To reach the roof, he ascended a ladder which he must have positioned earlier for that purpose.

'Well,' he went on as he studied the harmed granite, 'it is plain for all to see that I am inaptly formed for such labour. My frame ill fits the exertion of Shipsheartthew. I move without celerity, whether on deck or aloft. In the galley' – he laughed outright – 'my stature poorly suits the height of stoves and tables. A Giant such as I am was not foreseen by the makers of Starfare's Gem. And as to the tending of sail and line – ' with a nod of satisfaction at the condition of the roof, or at his thoughts, he returned to the cauldron. 'That is not my craft.'

Reaching into the stone pot, he stirred the contents with one hand, then brought out a rank brown mass which looked like partially-hardened tar. 'Chosen,' he said as he worked the mass with both hands. 'I am condignly named Pitchwife. This is my "pitch", which few Giants and no others may grasp with impunity, for without Giant-flesh and Giant-craft any hand may be turned to stone. And the task for which I mould such pitch is "wiving".

'Witness!' he exclaimed as if his work made him gay. Climbing the ladder, he began to mould his pitch like clay into the broken wall at the edge of the roof. Deftly, he shaped the pitch until it filled the breach, matching the lines of the wall exactly. Then he descended, returned to his slab of rock. His mighty fingers snapped a chip the size of his palm off the slab. His eyes gleamed. Chortling cheerfully, he went back to the roof.

With a flourish, as if to entertain a large audience, he embedded his chip in the pitch. At once, he snatched back his hand.

To Linden's amazement, the chip seemed to crystallize the pitch. Almost instantly, the mass was transformed to stone. In the space between two heartbeats, the pitch fused itself into the breach. The wall was restored to wholeness as if it had never been harmed. She could find no mark or flaw to distinguish the new stone from the old.

The expression on her face drew a spout of glee from Pitchwife. 'Witness, and be instructed,' he laughed happily. 'This bent and misbegotten form is an ill guide to the spirit within.' With precarious bravado, he thrust out his arms. 'I am Pitchwife the Valorous!' he shouted. 'Gaze upon me and suffer awe!'

His mirth was answered by the Giants nearby. They shared his delight, relished his comic posturing. But then the First's voice carried through the jests and ripostes. 'Surely you are valorous,' she said; and for an instant Linden misread her tone. She appeared to be reprimanding Pitchwife's levity. But a quick glance corrected this impression. The First's eyes sparkled with an admixture of fond pleasure and dark memory. 'And if you descend not from that perch,' she went on, 'you will become Pitchwife the Fallen.'

Another shout of laughter rose from the crew. Feigning imbalance, Pitchwife tottered down the ladder; but his mien shone as if he could hardly refrain from dancing.

Shortly, the Giants returned to their tasks; the First moved away; and Pitchwife contented himself with continuing his work more soberly. He repaired the roof in small sections so that his pitch would not sag before he could set it; and when he finished, the roof was as whole as the wall. Then he turned his attention to the fire-scars along the deck. These he mended by filling them with pitch, smoothing them to match the deck, then setting each with a chip of stone. Though he worked swiftly, he seemed as precise as a surgeon.

Sitting against the wall of the housing, Linden watched him. At first, his accomplishments fascinated her; but gradually her mood turned. The Giant was like Covenant – gifted with power; strangely capable of healing. And Covenant was the question to which she had found no answer.

In an almost perverse way, that question appeared to be the same one which so bedevilled her in another form. Why was she here? Why had Gibbon said to her, *You are being forged as iron is forged to achieve the ruin of the Earth*, and then afflicted her with such torment to convince her that he spoke the truth?

She felt that she had spent her life with that question and still could not reply to it.

'Ah, Chosen.' Pitchwife had finished his work. He stood facing her with arms akimbo and echoes of her uncertainty in his eyes. 'Since first I beheld you in the dire mirk of the Sarangrave, I have witnessed no lightening of your spirit. From dark to dark it runs, and no dawn comes. Are you not content with the redemption of Covenant Giantfriend and Mistweave – a saving which none other could have performed?' He shook his head, frowning to himself. Then, abruptly, he moved forward, seated himself against the wall near her. 'My people have an apothegm – as who does not in this wise and contemplative world?' He regarded her seriously, though the corners of his mouth quirked. 'It is said among us, "A sealed door admits no light." Will you not speak to me? No hand may open that door but your own.'

She sighed. His offer touched her; but she was so full of things she did not know how to say that she could hardly choose among them. After a moment, she said, 'Tell me there's a reason.'

'A reason?' he asked quietly.

'Sometimes – ' She groped for a way to articulate her need. 'He's why I'm here. Either I got dragged along behind him by accident. Or I'm supposed to do something to him. For him,' she added, remembering the old man on Haven Farm. 'I don't know. It doesn't make sense to me. But sometimes when I'm sitting down there watching him, the chance he might die terrifies me. He's got so many things I need. Without him, I don't have any *reasons* here. I never knew I would feel' – she passed a hand over her face, then dropped it, deliberately letting Pitchwife see as much of her as he could – 'feel so maimed without him.

'But it's more than that.' Her throat closed at what she was thinking. I just don't want him to die! 'I don't know how to help him. Not really. He's right about Lord Foul – and the danger to the Land. Somebody has got to do what he's doing. So the whole world won't turn into a playground for Ravers. I understand that. But what can I do about it? I don't know this world the way he does. I've never even *seen* the things that made him fall in love with the Land in the first place. I've never seen the Land *healthy*.

'I have tried,' she articulated against the old ache of futility, 'to help. God preserve me, I've even tried to accept the things I can see when nobody else sees them and for all I know I'm just going crazy. But I don't know how to share his commitment. I don't have the power to *do* anything.' Power, yes. All her life, she had wanted power. But her desire for it had been born in darkness – and wedded there more intimately than any marriage of heart and will. 'Except try to keep him alive and hope he doesn't get tired of dragging me around after him. I don't think I've ever done anything with my life except *deny*. I didn't become a doctor because I wanted people to live. I did it because I hate death.'

She might have gone on, then. There in the sunlight, with the stone warm under her, the breeze in her hair, Pitchwife's gentleness at her side, she might have risked her secrets. But when she paused, the Giant spoke into the silence.

'Chosen, I hear you. There is doubt in you, and fear, and also concern. But these things pass as well by another name, which you do not speak.'

He shifted his posture, straightened himself as much as the contortion of his back allowed. 'I am a Giant. I desire to tell you a story.'

She did not answer. She was thinking that no one had ever spoken to her with the kind of empathy she heard from Pitchwife.

After a moment, he commenced by saying, 'Perchance it has come to your ears that I am husband to the First of the Search, whom I name Gossamer Glowlimn.' Mutely, she nodded. 'That is a tale worthy of telling.

'Chosen,' he began, 'you must first understand that the Giants are a scant-seeded people. It is rare among us for any family to have as many as three children. Therefore our children are precious to us — aye, a very treasure to all the Giants, even such a one as myself, born sickly and malformed like an augury of Earth-Sight to come. But we are also a long-lived people. Our children are children yet when they have attained such age as yours. Therefore our families may hope for lives together in spans more easily measured by decades than years. Thus the bond between parent and child, generation after generation, is both close and enduring — as vital among us as any marriage.

'This you must grasp in order to comprehend that my Glowlimn has been twice bereaved.'

He placed his words carefully into the sunshine as if they were delicate and valuable. 'The first loss was a sore one. The life of Spray Frothsurge her mother failed in childbed — which in itself is a thing of sad wonder, for though our people are scant-seeded we are hardy, and such a loss is rare. Therefore from the first my Glowlimn had not the love of her mother, which all cherish. Thus she clung with the greater strength — a strength which some have named urgency — to Brow Gnarlfist her father.

'Now Brow Gnarlfist was the Master of a roaming Giantship proudly named Wavedancer, and his salt yearning took him often from his child, who grew to be so lissome and sweet that any heart which beheld her ached. And also she was the memory of Frothsurge his wife. Therefore he bore young Glowlimn with him on all his sailings, and she grew into her girlhood with the deck lifting beneath her feet and the salt in her hair like gems.

'At that time' — Pitchwife cast Linden a brief glance, then returned his gaze to the depths of the sky and his story — 'I served my craft upon Wavedancer. Thus Glowlimn became known to me until her face was the light in my eyes and her smile was the laughter in my throat. Yet of me she kenned little. Was she not a child? What meaning should a cripple of no great age have to her? She lived in the joy of her father, and the love of the ship, and knew me only as one Giant among many others more clearly akin to Gnarlfist her father. With that I was content. It was my lot. A woman – and more so a girl – looks upon a cripple with pity and kindness, perhaps, and with friendship, but not desire.

'Yet the time came – as mayhap it must come to all ships in the end – when Wavedancer ran by happenstance into the Soulbiter.

'I say happenstance, Linden Avery, for so I believe it was. The Soulbiter is a perilous and imprecise Sea, and no chart has ever told its tale surely. But Brow Gnarlfist took a harsher view. He faulted his navigation, and as the hazard into which we had blundered grew, so grew his self-wrath.

'For it was the season of gales in the Soulbiter, and the water was woven with cross-winds, buffeting Wavedancer in all ways at once. No sail could serve, and so the *dromond* was driven prow after keel southward, towards the place of reefs and peril known as Soulbiter's Teeth.

'Towards the Teeth we were compelled without help or hope. As we neared that region, Gnarlfist in desperation forced up canvas. But only three sails could be set – and only Dawngreeter held. The others fled in scraps from the spars. Yet Dawngreeter saved us, though Gnarlfist would not have credited it, for he was enmeshed in his doom and saw no outcome to all his choices but disaster.

'Torn from wind to wind among the gales, we stumbled into Soulbiter's Teeth.'

Pitchwife's narration carried Linden with him: she seemed to feel a storm rising behind the sunlight, gathering just out of sight like an unforeseen dismay.

'We were fortunate in our way. Fortunate that Dawngreeter held. And fortunate that we were not driven into the heart of the Teeth. In that place, with reefs ragged and fatal on all sides, Wavedancer would surely have been battered to rubble. But we struck upon the outermost reef – struck, and stuck, and heeled over to our doom with all the Soulbiter's wrath piling against us.

'At that moment, Dawngreeter caught a counterposing gale. Its force lifted us from the reef, hurling us away along a backlash of the current before the sail tore. In that way were we borne from the imminent peril of the Teeth.

'Yet the harm was done. We knew from the listing of the *dromond* that the reef had breached our hull. A craft of stone is not apt for buoyancy with such a wound. Pumps we had, but they made no headway.

'Gnarlfist cried his commands to me, but I scarce heard them, and so caught no hint of his intent. What need had I of commands at such a time? Wavedancer's stone had been breached, and the restoration of stone was my craft. Pausing only to gather pitch and setrock, I went below.'

His tone was focused and vivid now, implying rather than detailing the urgency of his story. 'To the breach I went, but could not approach it. Though the wound was no larger than my chest, the force of the water surpassed me, thrust as it was by the *dromond*'s weight and the Soulbiter's fury. I could not stand before the hole. Still less could I set my pitch. Already the sea within Wavedancer had risen to my waist. I did not relish such a death belowdecks, on the verge of Soulbiter's Teeth, with nothing gained for my life at all.

'But as I strove beyond reason or hope to confront the breach, I learned the import of Gnarlfist's commands. To my uttermost astonishment, the gush of water was halted. And in its place, I beheld the chest of Brow Gnarlfist covering the hole. Driven by the extremity of his self-wrath or his courage, he had leaped into the water, fought his way to the breach. With his own flesh, he granted me opportunity for my work.

'That opportunity I took. With terrible haste, I wrought pitch and setrock into place, thinking in desperation and folly to heal the wound ere Gnarlfist's breath gave way. Were I only swift enough, he might regain air in time.'

The knotting of his voice drew Linden's gaze towards him. Deep within himself, he relived his story. His fists were clenched. 'Fool!' he spat at himself.

But a moment later he took a long breath, leaned back against the wall of the housing. 'Yet though I was a fool, I did what required to be done, for the sake of the *dromond* and all my companions. With pitch and setrock, I sealed the breach. And in so doing I sealed Gnarlfist to the side of Wavedancer. My pitch took his chest in a grip of stone and held him.'

Pitchwife sighed. 'Giants dove for him. But they could not wrest him from the granite. He died in their hands. And when at last Wavedancer won free to clear weather, allowing our divers to work at less hazard, the fish of the deep had taken all of him but the bound bones.'

With an effort, he turned to Linden, let her see the distress lingering in his gaze. 'I will not conceal from you that I felt great blame at the death of Brow Gnarlfist. You surpass me, for you saved Mistweave and yet did not lose the Giantfriend. For a time which endured beyond the end of that voyage, I could not bear to meet the loss in Glowlimn's countenance.' But gradually his expression lightened. 'And yet a strange fruit grew from the seed of her father's end, and of my hand in that loss. After her bereavement, I gained a place in her eyes – for had not her father and I saved a great many Giants whom she loved? She saw me, not as I beheld myself – not as a cripple to be blamed – but rather as the man who had given her father's death meaning. And in her eyes I learned to put aside my blame.

'In losing her father, she had also lost his salt yearning. Therefore she turned from the Sea. But there was yearning in her still, born of the heart-deep reaving she had suffered. When the spirit is not altogether slain, great loss teaches men and women to desire greatly, both for themselves and for others. And her spirit was not slain, though surely it was darkened and tempered so that she stands among our people as iron stands among stone.' He was watching Linden intently now, as if he were unsure of her ability to hear what he was saying. 'Her yearning she turned to the work of the Swordmainnir.' His tone was serious, but did not disguise the smile in his eyes. 'And to me.'

Linden found that she could not meet his complex attention. Perhaps in truth she did not hear him, did not grasp the reasons why he had told her this story. But what she did hear struck her deeply. Gnarlfist's suicide contrasted painfully with her own experience. And it shed a hard light on the differences between her and the First – two daughters who had inherited death in such divergent ways.

In addition, Pitchwife's willingness to look honestly and openly at his past put the subterfuge of Linden's own history to shame. Like him, she had memories of desperation and folly. But he relived his and came out of them whole, with more grace than she could conceive. Hers still had so much power –

He was waiting for her to speak. But she could not. It was too much. All the things she needed drew her to her feet, sent her moving almost involuntarily towards Covenant's cabin.

She had no clear idea of what she meant to do. But Covenant had saved Joan from Lord Foul. He had saved Linden herself from Marid. From Sivit na-Mhoram-wist. From Gibbon-Raver. From Sunbane-fever and the lurker of the Sarangrave. And yet he seemed helpless to save himself. She needed some explanation from him. An account which might make sense of her distress.

And perhaps a chance to account for herself. Her failures had nearly killed him. She needed him to understand her.

Woodenly, she descended to the first underdeck, moved towards Covenant's cabin. But before she reached it, the door opened, and Brinn came out. He nodded to her flatly. The side of his neck showed the healing vestiges of the burn he had received from Covenant. When he said, 'The ur-Lord desires speech with you,' he spoke as if his native rectitude and her twisted uncertainty were entirely alien to each other.

So that he would not see her falter, she went straight into the cabin. But there she stopped, abashed by the bared nerves of her need. Covenant lay high in his hammock; his weakness was written in the pallor of his forehead, in his limp recumbency. But she could see at a glance that the tone of his skin had improved. His pulse and respiration were stable. Sunlight from the open port reflected lucidly out of his orbs. He was recuperating well. In a day or two, he would be ready to get out of bed.

The grey in his tousled hair seemed more pronounced, made him appear older. But the wild growth of his beard could not conceal the chiselled lines of his mouth or the tension in his gaunt cheeks.

For a moment, they stared at each other. Then the flush of his dismay impelled her to look away. She wanted to move to the hammock – take his pulse, examine his arm and shin, estimate his temperature – touch him as a physician if she could not reach out to him in any other way. Yet her abashment held her still.

Abruptly, he said, 'I've been talking to Brinn.' His voice was husky with frailty; but it conveyed a complex range of anger, desire, and doubt. 'The *Haruchai* aren't very good at telling stories. But I got everything I could out of him.'

At once, she felt herself grow rigid as if to withstand an attack. 'Did he tell you that I almost let you die?'

She read his reply in the pinched lines around his eyes. She wanted to stop there, but the pressure rising in her was too strong. What had Brinn taught him to think of her? She did not know how to save herself from what was coming. Severely, she went on, 'Did he tell you that I might have been able to help you when you were first bitten? Before the venom really took over? But I didn't.'

He tried to interrupt; she overrode him. 'Did he tell you that the only reason I changed my mind was because the First was going to cut off your arm? Did he tell you' – her voice gathered harshness – 'that I tried to *possess* you? And that was what forced you to defend yourself so we couldn't reach you? And that was why they had to call the *Nicor*?' Unexpected rage rasped in her throat. 'If I hadn't done that, Mistweave wouldn't have been hurt at all. Did he tell you that?'

Covenant's face was twisted into a grimace of ire or empathy. When she jerked to a stop, he had to swallow roughly before he could say, 'Of course he told me. He didn't approve. The *Haruchai* don't have much sympathy for ordinary·human emotions like fear and doubt. He thinks everything else should be sacrificed for me.' For a moment, his eyes shifted away as if he were in pain. 'Bannor used to make me want to scream. He was so absolute about everything.' But then he looked back at her. 'I'm glad you helped Mistweave. I don't want more people dying for me.'

At that, her anger turned against him. His reply was so close to what she wanted, but his constant assumption of responsibility and blame for everything around him infuriated her. He seemed to deny her the simple right to judge her own acts. The *Haruchai* at least she could understand.

But she had not come here to shout at him. In a sense, it was his sheer importance to her that made her angry. She wanted to assail him because he meant so much to her. And that frightened her.

But Covenant seemed scarcely aware that she had not left the cabin. His gaze was fixed on the stone above him, and he was wrestling with his own conception of what had happened to him. When he spoke, his voice ached with trouble.

'It's getting worse.'

His arms were hugged over his chest as if to protect the scar of his old knife-wound.

'Foul is doing everything he can to teach me power. That's what this venom is all about. The physical consequences are secondary. The main thing is spiritual. Every time I become delirious, that venom eats away my restraint. The part of me that resists being so dangerous. That's why – why everything. Why that Raver got us into trouble in Mithil Stonedown. Why we've been attacked over and over again. Why Gibbon risked showing me the truth in that soothtell. Part of the truth.'

Abruptly, he shifted in the hammock, raised his right hand. 'Look.' When he clenched his fist, white fire burst from his knuckles. He brought it to a brightness that almost dazzled Linden, then let it drop. Panting, he relaxed in the hammock.

'I don't need a reason anymore.' He was trembling. 'I can do that more easily than getting out of bed. I'm a timebomb. He's making me more dangerous than he is. When I explode – ' His visage contorted in dismay. 'I'll probably kill everybody who has any chance of fighting him. I almost did it this time. Next time – or the time after that.'

His exigency was vivid in him; but still he did not look at her. He seemed to fear that if he looked at her the peril would reach out to doom her as well. 'It's happening to me. The same thing that ruined Kevin. Broke the Bloodguard Vow. Butchered the Unhomed. I'm becoming what I hate. If I keep going like this, I'll kill you all. But I can't stop it. Don't you understand? I don't have your eyes. I can't *see* what I need to fight the venom. Something physical – my wrists – or my chest – that's different. My nerves are still alive enough for that. But I don't have the health-sense.

'That's probably the real point of the Sunbane. To cripple the Earthpower so I won't be healed, won't become able to see what ⁀ˢ see. Everyone here has already lost it. You have it because you ⁀ᵒᵐ outside. You weren't shaped by the Sunbane. And I ⁀ᵗ If I weren't – '

He snatched back what he had been about to say. But his tension poured from him like anguish, and he could not refrain from turning his distress towards her. His gaze was stark, bloodridden, haunted; his eyes were wounds of understanding. And the depth of his self-dread caught at her throat, so that she could not have spoken, even if she had known how to comfort him.

'That's why I've got to get to the One Tree. *Got* to. Before I become too deadly to go on living. A Staff of Law is my only hope.' Fatality stalked through his tone. He had his own nightmares – dreams as heinous and immedicable as hers. 'If we don't do it in time, this venom will take over everything, and there won't be any of us left to even care what happens to the Land, much less *fight*.'

She gaped at him, at the implications of what he was saying. In the past, he had always spoken of needing a Staff for the Land – or for her, to return her to her own life. She had not grasped the true extent of his personal exigency. Behind all his other commitments, he was wrestling for a way to save himself. That was why the movement of the ship when the Giants snared the *Nicor* had been able to reach him. It had restored his most fundamental hope: the One Tree. Restitution for the harm he had wrought when he had destroyed the old Staff. And escape from the logic of his venom. No wonder he looked so ravaged. She did not know how he endured it.

But he must have misunderstood her silence. He returned his gaze to the ceiling. When he spoke again, his voice was flat with bitterness.

'That's why you're here.'

She winced as if he had struck her. But he did not see her.

'That old man – the one you met on Haven Farm. You said you saved his life.' That was true. And he had spoken to her. But she had never told Covenant all the old man had said. 'He chose you for your eyes. And because you're a doctor. You're the only one in this whole mess who can even grasp what's happening to me, never mind do anything about it.

'And Foul – ' he continued dismally. 'If Gibbon was telling the truth. Not just trying to scare you. Foul chose you because he thinks he can make you fail. He thinks you can be intimidated. That's why Gibbon touched you. Why Marid jumped at you first. To set you up for failure. So that you won't help me. Or won't do the right thing when you try. He knows how vulnerable I am. How long I've needed – '

Without warning, his voice sharpened in pure protest. 'Because you're not afraid of me! If you were afraid, you wouldn't be here. None of this would've happened to you. It would all be different.

'Hell and blood, Linden!' Suddenly, he was shouting with all the scant strength of his convalescence. 'You're the only woman in the world who doesn't look at me like I'm some kind of reified crime!

Damn it, I've paid *blood* to try to spare you everything I can. I killed twenty-one people to rescue you from Revelstone! But I can't reach you. What in the hell do you – '

His passion broke her out of her silence. She interrupted him as if she were furious at him; but her ire was running in a different direction.

'I don't want to be *spared*. I want *reasons*. You tell me why I'm here, and it doesn't mean anything. It doesn't have anything to do with me. So I'm a doctor from outside the Land. So what? So is Berenford, but this didn't happen to him. I need a better reason than that. *Why me?*'

For an instant, he glared reflections of sunlight at her. But her words seemed to penetrate him by degrees, forcing him backward muscle by muscle until he was lying limp in the hammock again. He appeared exhausted. She feared that he would not be able to find the strength to tell her to get out of his cabin. But then he surprised her as he had so often surprised her in the past. After all this time, she still could not estimate the workings of his mind.

'Of course you're right,' he murmured, half musing to himself. 'Nobody can ever spare anybody else. I've got so much power – I keep forgetting it isn't good for what I want. It's never enough. Just a more complicated form of helplessness. I should know better. I've been on this kind of journey before.

'I can't tell you why you.' He appeared too weary or defeated to raise his head. 'I know something about the needs that drive people into situations like this. But I don't know your needs. I don't know *you*. You were chosen for this because of who you are, but from the beginning you haven't told me a thing. My life depends on you, and I don't really have any idea what it is I'm depending on.

'Linden.' He appealed to her without looking at her, as if he feared that his gaze would send her away. 'Please. Stop defending yourself. You don't have to fight me. You could make me understand.' Deliberately, he closed his eyes against the risk he was taking. 'If you chose to.'

Again she wanted to refuse him. The habit of flight ran deep in her. But this was why she had come to him. Her need was too clear to be denied.

Yet the question was so intimate that she could not approach it directly. Perhaps if she had not heard Pitchwife's tale she would not have been able to approach it at all. But his example had galvanized her to this hazard. He had the courage to relive his own past. And his story itself, the story of the First's father.

'Sometimes,' she said, though she was hardly ready to begin, 'I have these black moods.' There was a chair near her; but she remained standing rigidly. 'I've had them ever since I was a girl. Since my father died. When I was eight. They feel like – I don't know how to describe them. Like I'm drowning and there's nothing I can do to save myself. Like I could scream forever and nobody would hear me.' Powerless. 'Like the only thing I can do to help myself is just die and get it over with.

'That's what I started feeling after we left *Coercri*. It piled up the way it always does, and I never know why it comes when it does or why it goes away again. But this time was different. It felt the same to me – but it was different. Or maybe what you said is true – when we were on Kevin's Watch. That here the things inside us are externalized, so we meet them as if they were somebody else. What I was feeling was that Raver.

'So maybe there is a reason why I'm here.' She could not stop now, though an invidious trembling cramped her chest. 'Maybe there's a connection between who I am and what Foul wants.' She almost gagged on the memory of Gibbon's touch; but she knotted her throat to keep the nausea down. 'Maybe that's why I freeze. Why I get so scared. I've spent my whole life trying to prove it isn't true. But it goes too deep.

'My father – ' There she nearly faltered. She had never exposed this much of herself to anyone. But now for the first time her craving to be healed outweighed her old revulsion. 'He was about your age when he died. He even looked a bit like you.' And like the old man whose life she had saved on Haven Farm. 'Without the beard. But he wasn't like you. He was *pathetic*.'

The sudden vitriol of her ejaculation stopped her momentarily. This was what she had always wanted to believe so that she could reject it. But it was not even true. Despite his abject life, her father had been potent enough to warp her being. In his hammock, Covenant seemed to be resisting a temptation to watch her; but he spared her the self-consciousness of his gaze.

Impacted emotion hardened her tone as she went on, 'We lived a mile outside a dead little town like the one where you live. In one of those tottering square frame houses. It hadn't been painted since my parents moved in, and it was starting to slump.

'My father raised goats. God knows where he even got the money to *buy* goats so he could raise them. Every job he had was worse than the last one. His idea of being proud and independent was selling vacuum cleaners door-to-door. When that failed, he tried encyclopedias. Then water-purifiers. Water-purifiers! Everybody in thirty miles had their own well, and the water was already good. And every time a new career failed he just seemed to get shorter. Collapsing in on himself. He thought he was being a rugged individualist. Make his own way. Bow to no man. Good Christ! He probably went down on his knees to get the money to start raising those goats.

'He had ideas about milk and cheese. Breeding stock. Meat. So of

507

course he had no more conception of how to raise goats than I did. He just put them on leashes and let them graze around the house. Soon we were living in dust for a hundred yards in all directions.

'My mother's reaction was to eat everything she could get her hands on, to go to church three times a week and punish me whenever I got my clothes dirty.

'By the time I was eight, the goats had finished off our property and started on land that belonged to somebody else. Naturally my father didn't see anything wrong with that. But the owner did. The day my father was supposed to appear in court to defend himself – I found this out later – he still hadn't told my mother we were in trouble. So she took the car to go to church, and he didn't have any way to get to the county seat – unless he walked, which didn't really make sense because it was twenty miles away.

'It was summer, so I wasn't in school. I was out playing, and as usual I got my clothes dirty, and then I got nervous. My mother wasn't due home for hours yet, but at that age I didn't have much sense of time. I wanted to be someplace where I could feel safe, so I went up to the attic. On the way, I played a game I'd been playing for a long time, which was to get up the stairs without making them squeak. That was part of what made the attic feel safe. No one could hear me go up there.'

The scene was as vivid to her as if it had been etched in acid. But she watched it like a spectator, with the severity she had spent so many years nurturing. She did not want to be that little girl, to feel those emotions. Her orbs were hot marbles in their sockets. Her voice had grown clipped and precise, like a dissecting instrument. Even the strain rising through her knotted back did not make her move. She stood as still as she could, instinctively denying herself.

'When I opened the door, my father was there. He was sitting in a half-broken rocker, and there was red stuff on the floor around him. I didn't even understand that it was blood until I saw it coming from the gashes in his wrists. The smell made me want to puke.'

Covenant's gaze was fixed on her now, his eyes wide with dismay; but she disregarded him. Her attention was focused on her efforts to survive what she was saying.

'He looked at me. For a minute, he didn't seem to know who I was. Or maybe he hadn't figured out that I mattered. But then he hauled himself out of the chair and started to swear at me. I couldn't understand him. But I worked it out later. He was afraid I was going to stop him. Go to the phone. Get help somehow. Even though I was only eight. So he slammed the door, locked me in with him. Then he threw the key out the window.

'Until then, I hadn't even realized there *was* a key. It must've been in the lock all the time, but I'd never noticed it. If I had, I would've locked myself in any number of times, just so I could feel safer.

'Anyway, I was there watching him die. What was happening took a while to filter through to me. But when I finally understood, I got frantic.' Frantic, indeed. That was a mild word for her distress. Behind Linden's rigid self-command huddled a little girl whose heart had been torn in shreds. 'I did a lot of screaming and crying, but that didn't help. My mother was still at church, and we didn't have any neighbours close enough to hear me. And it just made my father madder. He was doing it out of spite to begin with. My crying made him worse. If there was ever a chance he might change his mind, I lost it. Maybe that was really what got him so mad. At one point, he mustered enough strength to stand up again so he could hit me. Got blood all over me.

'So then I tried pleading with him. Be his little girl. Beg him not to leave me. I told him he should let me die instead of him. I even meant it. Eight year olds have a lot of imagination. But that didn't work either. After all, I was just another burden dragging him down. If he hadn't had a wife and daughter to worry about, he wouldn't have failed all those times.' Her sarcasm was as harsh as a rasp. For years, she had striven to deny that her emotions had such force. 'But his eyes were glazing. I was just desperate. I tried being angry at him. Worked myself in a fit telling him I wouldn't love him anymore if he died. Somehow that reached him. The last thing I heard him say was, "You never loved me anyway."' And then the blow had fallen, the stroke which had nailed her forever to her horror. There was no language in the world to describe it.

From out of the cracked floorboards and the untended walls had come pouring a flood of darkness. It was not there: she was still able to see everything. But it rose into her mind as if it had been invoked by her father's self-pity – as if while he sprawled there dying he had transcended himself, had raised himself by sheer abjection to the stature of power, and had summoned the black malice of nightmares to attend upon his passing. She was foundering in the viscid midnight of his condemnation, and no rescue could reach her.

And while she sank, his face had changed before her eyes. His mouth had stretched into what should have been a cry; but it was not – it was laughter. The triumphant glee of spite, soundless and entire. His mouth had held her gaze, transfixed her. It was the dire cavern and plunge from which the darkness issued, hosting forth to appal her. *You never loved me anyway. Never loved me. Never loved.* A darkness indistinguishable now from the vicious malevolence of Gibbon-Raver's touch. Perhaps it had all taken place in her mind – a product of her young, vulnerable despair. That made no difference. It had taught her her powerlessness, and she would never be free of it.

Unwillingly, she saw Covenant's face, grown aghast for her. She did not want that from him. It weakened her defences. Her mouth was full of the iron taste of rage. She could no longer keep her voice from shivering. But she was unable to stop.

'A long time after that, he died. And a long time after *that*, my mother came home. By then I was too far gone to know anything. Hours passed before she missed us enough to find out the attic was locked. Then she had to call the neighbours to help her get the door open. I was conscious the whole time – I remember every minute of it – but there was nothing I could do. I just lay there on the floor until they broke down the door and took me to the hospital.

'I was there for two weeks. It was the only time I can remember ever feeling safe.'

Then abruptly the quivering of her joints became so strong that she could no longer stand. Covenant's open stare was a mute cry of empathy. She fumbled to the chair, sat down. Her hands would not stop flinching. She gripped them between her knees as she concluded the story.

'My mother blamed me for the whole thing. She had to sell the goats and the house to the man who was suing my father so she could pay the funeral costs and hospital bills. When she was having one of her pathos orgies, she even accused me of killing her dear husband. But most of the time she just blamed me for causing the whole situation. She had to go on welfare – God knows she couldn't get a job, that might interfere with church – and we had to live in a grubby little apartment in town. Somehow it was my fault. Compared to her, an eight year old in shock was an effective adult.'

The long gall of her life might have continued to pour from her, releasing some of her pent outrage; but Covenant stopped her. In a voice congested with pain and care, he said, 'And you've never forgiven her. You've never forgiven either of them.'

His words stunned her. Was that *all* he had garnered from her difficult story – from the fact that she had chosen to tell it? At once, she was on her feet beside the hammock, raging up at him, 'You're goddam *right* I never forgave them! They raised me to be another bloody suicide! to be a servant of the Despiser. I've spent my whole life trying to prove they were *wrong*!'

The muscles around his eyes pinched; his gaze bled at her. But he did not waver. The chiselled lines of his mouth, the gauntness of his cheeks, reminded her that he was familiar with the attractions of suicide. And he was a father who had been bereft of his son and wife for no other fault than an illness he could not have prevented. Yet he lived. He fought for life. Time and again, she had seen him turn his back on actions and attitudes that were dictated by hate. And he did not compromise with her, in spite of all that she had told him.

'Is that why you think people shouldn't tell each other their secrets? Why you didn't want me to tell you about Lena? Because

510

you're afraid I'll say something you don't want to hear?'

Then she wanted to howl at him like a maddened child; but she could not. Once again, she was foiled by her health-sense. She could not blind herself to the quality of his regard. No man had ever looked at her in that way before.

Shaken, she retreated to the chair, sagged against its stone support.

'Linden,' he began as gently as his worn hoarseness allowed. But she cut him off.

'No.' She felt suddenly defeated. He was never going to understand. Or he understood too well. 'That's not why. I haven't forgiven them, and I don't care who knows it. It's kept me alive when I didn't have anything else. I just don't trust these confessions.' Her mouth twisted. 'Knowing about Lena doesn't mean anything to me. You were different then. You paid for what you did. She doesn't change anything for me. But she does for you. Every time you accuse yourself of rape, you make it true. You bring it into the present. You make yourself guilty all over again.

'The same thing happens to me. When I talk about my parents. Even though I was only eight then and I've spent twenty-two years trying to make myself into somebody else.'

In response, Covenant gripped the edge of the hammock, pulled his weakness that much closer to her. Aiming himself at her like a quarrel, he replied, 'You've got it backward. You're doing it to yourself. Punishing yourself for something you didn't have the power to change. You can't forgive yourself, so you refuse to forgive anybody else.'

Her eyes leaped to his; protest and recognition tangled each other so that she could not retort.

'Aren't you doing the same thing Kevin did? Blaming yourself because you aren't equal to every burden in the world? Killing your father in your mind because you can't bear the pain of being helpless? Destroying what you love because you can't save it?'

'No.' Yes. I don't know. His words pierced her too deeply. Even though he had no health-sense, he was still able to reach into her, wrench her heart. The roots of the screaming she had done for her father seemed to grow all through her; and Covenant made them writhe. 'I don't love him. I can't. If I did, I wouldn't be able to keep on living.'

She wanted to flee then, go in search of some way to protect her loneliness. But she did not. She had already done too much fleeing. Glaring up at him because she had no answer to his complex empathy, she took a flask of *diamondraught* from the table, handed it to him, and required him to drink until he had consumed enough to make him sleep.

After that, she covered her face with her hands and huddled into herself. Slumber softened the rigor of his face, increasing his resemblance to her father. He was right, she could not forgive herself. But she had failed to tell him why. The darkness was still in her, and she had not confessed what she had done with it.

6

THE *QUESTSIMOON*

She did not want to sleep. Afterimages of her father glared across the back of her thoughts from time to time, as if she had looked at that story too closely and had burned the nerves of her sight. She had not exorcised the memory. Rather, she had stripped away the defensive repression which had swaddled it. Now her own eight-year-old cries were more vivid to her than they had been for years. She tried to fend off sleep because she feared the hunger of her nightmares.

But what she had done in speaking to Covenant also gave her a curious half-relief, a partial release of tension. It was not enough, but it was something – an act for which she had never before been able to find the courage. That steadied her. Perhaps restitution was more possible than she had believed. At last she returned to her cabin, rolled over the edge into her hammock. Then the motion of Starfare's Gem lifted her out of herself along the waves until she was immersed in the width and depth of the Sea.

The next day, she felt stronger. She went to check on Covenant with some trepidation, wondering what he would make of the things which had passed between them. But he greeted her, spoke to her, accepted her ministrations in a way clearly intended to show that his challenges and demands had not been meant as recrimination. In a strange way, his demeanour suggested that he felt a kind of kinship towards her, a leper's attraction towards the wounded and belorn. This surprised her, but she was glad of it. When she left him, her forehead was lightened by the lifting of an unconscious frown.

The following morning, he came out on deck. Blinking against the unaccustomed sunlight, he stepped through the port seadoor under the wheeldeck, moved towards her. His gait was tentative, weakened by incomplete recuperation; his skin was pallid with frailty. But she could see that he was mending well.

The unexpected fact that his beard was gone startled her. His bare cheeks and neck seemed to gleam vulnerably in the light.

His gaze was uncertain, abashed. She had become so used to his beard that he seemed almost young without it. But she did not understand his evident embarrassment until he said in a conflicted tone, 'I burned it off. With my ring.'

'*Good.*' Her own intensity took her aback. But she approved of his dangerous power. 'I never liked it.'

Awkwardly, he touched his cheek, trying with numb fingers to estimate the exposure of his skin. Then he grimaced ruefully. 'Neither did I.' He glanced downward as if to begin a VSE, then returned his attention to her face. 'But I'm worried about it. What scares me is being able to do something like this so easily.' The muscles of his face bunched in reference to the strictures which had formerly limited the wild magic, permitting it to arise only in desperation and contact with other, triggering powers. 'I did it because I'm trying to teach myself control. The venom — I'm so tangled up. I've got to learn to handle it.'

While he spoke, his eyes slid away to the open Sea. It lay choppy and cerulean to the horizons, as complex as himself. 'But it isn't good enough. I can make that fire do anything I want — if I hold it down to a trickle. But I can feel the rest of it inside me, ready to boil. It's like being crazy and sane at the same time. I can't seem to have one without the other.'

Studying his troubled tension, Linden remembered the way he had said, *That's why I've got to get to the One Tree. Before I become too deadly to go on living.* He was tormented by the same peril that made him irrefusable to her. For an instant, she wanted to put her arms around him, hug him in answer to the ache of her desire.

She refrained because she was too conscious of her own inadequate honesty. She had told him enough to make him think that she had told him everything. But she had not told him about her mother. About the brutal and irreducible fact which kept her from becoming the person she wanted to be. Worthy of him.

Since the day after the squalls had ended, Grimmand Honninscrave had been wrestling Starfare's Gem through a confusion of winds, tacking incessantly to find a way eastward across the ragged seas. The Giants laboured cheerfully, as though their pleasure in their skill and the vessel outweighed almost any amount of fatigue. And Ceer and Hergrom gave regular assistance in the shrouds, compensating with swift strength for their lesser bulk and reach. But still the *dromond*'s progress was relatively slow. Day by day, that fact deepened the First's frown. It darkened the knurled frustration which lay like a shadow behind the surface of Seadreamer's mien. And as Covenant's health slowly returned, his own inner knots squirmed tighter. Goaded by his fear of venom and failure, by the numberless people who were dying to feed the Sunbane, he began to pace the decks as if he were trying to will the Giantship forward.

But after three more days of tortuous movement, tack after tack through the intricate maze of the winds, the air shifted into a steady blow out of the south-west. Honninscrave greeted the change with a loud holla. Giants swarmed to adjust the canvas. Starfare's Gem heeled slightly to port, dipped its prow like an eager animal freed of its leash, and began surging swiftly into the east. Spray leaped from its sides like an utterance of the moire-marked granite — stone shaped and patterned to exult in the speed of the Sea. In a short time, the Giantship was racing gleefully across the waves.

To the Storesmaster, who was standing near him, Covenant said, 'How long will this keep up?'

Galewrath folded her arms over her heavy breasts, fixed her gaze on the sails. 'In this region of the Earth,' she returned, 'such freakish winds as we have fled are rare. This blow we name the *Questsimoon*. The Roveheartswind. We will sight Bareisle ere it falters.' Though her tone was stolid, her eyes glistened at the white thrust of the canvas and the humming of the sheets.

And she was right. The wind held, rising so steadfastly out of the south-west that at night Honninscrave felt no need to shorten sail. Though the full of the moon had passed some nights ago, and the stars gave scant light by which to manage the *dromond*, he answered the implicit needs of the Search by maintaining his vessel in its tireless run. The wind in the rigging and the canted roll of the deck, the constant slap and susurrus of water like an exhalation along the sides, made Starfare's Gem thrill under Linden's feet. Constantly now she felt the *dromond* breathing through the swells, a witchery of stone and skill — as vibrant as the timbre of life. And the straight thrust of the *Questsimoon* accorded the crew a rest from their earlier exertions.

Their pace gave the First a look of stern satisfaction, eased Honninscrave's work until at times he responded to Pitchwife's jests and clowning like a playful behemoth. Grins took even Sevinhand Anchormaster's old sorrow by surprise, and the healing of his arm gave him a clear pleasure.

But no speed or Giantish gaiety etiolated Covenant's mounting tension. He appeared to enjoy the good humour around him, the spray from the *dromond*'s prow, the firm vitality of the wind. At times, he looked like a man who had spent years yearning for the company of Giants. But such pleasures no longer sustained him. He was in a hurry. Time and again, he carried his anxiety across the listing deck towards wherever Linden happened to be standing and awkwardly engaged her in conversation, as if he did not want to face his thoughts alone. Yet he seldom spoke of the memories and needs which lay uppermost in his mind, so near the surface that they were almost legible through the bones of his forehead. Instead, he picked up more distant threads, questions, doubts and worried at them, trying to weave himself into readiness for his future.

During one of their colloquies, he said abruptly, 'Maybe I did sell myself for Joan.' He had spoken about such things before. 'Freedom doesn't mean you get to choose what happens to you. But you do get to choose how you react to it. And that's what the whole struggle against Foul hinges on. In order to be effective against him – or *for* him – we have to make our own decisions. That's why he doesn't just possess us. Take the ring by force. He has to take the risk we might choose against him. And so does the Creator. That's the paradox of the Arch of Time. And white gold. Power depends on choice. The necessity of freedom. If Foul just conquers us, if we're under his control, the ring won't give him the power to break out. But if the Creator tries to control us through the Arch, *he'll* break it.' He was not looking at her; his eyes searched the rumpled waves like a VSE. 'Maybe when I took Joan's place I gave up my freedom.'

Linden had no answer for him and did not like to see him in such doubt. But she was secretly pleased that he was healthy enough to wrestle with his questions. And she needed his reassurance that she might be able to make choices that mattered.

At another time, he turned her attention to Vain. The Demondim-spawn stood on the afterdeck near Foodfendhall exactly as he had since the moment when Covenant had fallen there. His black arms hung slightly crooked at his sides as if they had been arrested in the act of taking on life; and the midnight of his eyes gazed emptily before him like an assertion that everything which took place on the Giantship was evanescent and nugatory.

'Why – ?' Covenant mused slowly. 'Why do you suppose he wasn't hurt by that bloody *Grim*? It just rolled off him. But the Riders were able to burn him with their *rukhs*. He actually obeyed them when they forced him into the hold.'

Linden shrugged. Vain was an enigma. The way he had reacted towards her – first bowing to her outside Revelstone, then carrying her away from her companions when she was helpless with Sun-bane-fever – disturbed her. 'Maybe the *Grim* wasn't directed at him personally,' she offered. 'Maybe the' – she groped for the name – 'the ur-viles? Maybe they could make him immune to anything that happened around him – like the Sunbane, or the *Grim*. But not to something aimed *at* him.' Covenant listened intently, so she went on guessing. 'Maybe they didn't want to give him the power to actually defend himself. If he could do that, would you trust him?'

'I don't trust him anyway,' muttered Covenant. 'He was going to let Stonemight Woodhelven kill me. Not to mention those Sunbane-victims around During Stonedown. And he butchered – ' His hands fisted as he remembered the blood Vain had shed.

'Then maybe,' she said with a dull twist of apprehension, 'Gibbon knows more about him than you do.'

But the only time his questions drew a wince from her was when he raised the subject of Kevin's Watch. Why, he asked, had Lord Foul not spoken to her when they had first appeared in the Land? The Despiser had given him a vitriolic message of doom for himself and the Land. She still remembered that pronouncement exactly as Covenant had relayed it to her: *There is despair laid up for you here beyond anything your petty mortal heart can bear.* But Lord Foul had said nothing to her. On Kevin's Watch, he had let her pass untouched.

'He didn't need to,' she replied bitterly. 'He already knew everything he needed about me.' Gibbon-Raver had revealed the precision of the Despiser's knowledge.

He regarded her with a troubled aspect; and she saw that he had already considered that possibility. 'Maybe not,' he returned in denial. 'Maybe he didn't talk to you because he hadn't planned for you to be there. Maybe when you tried to rescue me you took him by surprise and just got swept along. If that's true, then you weren't part of his original plan. And everything Gibbon said to you is a lie. A way to defuse the danger you represent. Make you think you don't have a chance. When the truth is that you're the biggest threat to him there is.'

'How?' she demanded. His interpretation did not comfort her. She would never be able to forget the implications of Gibbon's touch. 'I don't have any *power*.'

He grimaced crookedly. 'You've got the health-sense. Maybe you can keep me alive.'

Alive, she rasped to herself. She had expressed the same idea to Pitchwife, and it had not eased her. But how else could she hope to alter the course of her life? She had an acute memory of the venom in Covenant, the accumulating extremity of his need. Perhaps by dedicating herself to that one task – a responsibility fit for a doctor – she would be able to appease her hunger and hold the darkness back.

The Roveheartswind blew as steadily as stone for five days. Since the sails required so little care, the crew busied itself with the manifold other tasks of the ship; cleaning away every hint of encrusted salt; replacing worn ratlines and gear; oiling unused cable and canvas to preserve them against the weather. These smaller chores the Giants performed with the same abiding enthusiasm that they gave to the more strenuous work of the *dromond*. Yet Honninscrave watched them and the ship, scanned the Sea, consulted his astrolabe, studied his parchment charts as if he expected danger at any moment. Or, Linden thought when she looked at him closely, as if he needed to keep himself busy.

She rarely saw him leave the wheeldeck, though surely neither Sevinhand nor Galewrath would have warded Starfare's Gem less vigilantly than he did. At times when his gaze passed, unseeing, through her, she read a clinch of hope or dread in his cavernous orbs. It left her with the impression that he was caught up in an idea which had not yet occurred to anyone else.

For five days, the Roveheartswind blew; and as the fifth day relaxed into late afternoon, a shout from Horizonscan snatched every eye on deck towards the east: 'Bareisle!' And there off the port bow stood the black burned rock of the island.

From a distance, it appeared to be no more than a dark eyot amid the sun-burnished blue of the Sea. But as the wind swept Starfare's Gem forward on south, Bareisle's true size became manifest. With its towering igneous peaks and sheer valleys, its barren stone scarcely fringed by the stubborn clutch of vegetation, the island looked like a tremendous cairn or marker, erected towards the sky in warning. Birds cycled above it as if it were a dead thing. As she studied the craggy rock, Linden felt a quiver of foreboding.

At the same time, Honninscrave lifted his voice over the Giantship. 'Hear me!' he cried – a shout of yearning and trepidation, as lorn and resonant as the wind. 'Here we pass from the safe Sea into the demesne and ken of the *Elohim*. Be warned! They are lovely and perilous, and none can foretell them. If they so desire, the very Sea will rise against us.' Then he barked his commands, turning Starfare's Gem so that it passed around Bareisle with its stern braced on the wind, running now straight into the north-east.

Linden's foreboding tightened. The *Elohim*, she murmured. What kind of people marked the verge of their territory with so much black stone? As her view of the island changed from south to east, Bareisle came between her and the sunset and was silhouetted in red glory. Then the rock appeared to take on life, so that it looked like the stark straining fist of a drowner, upraised against the fatal Sea. But as the sun slipped past the horizon, Bareisle was lost in dusk.

That night, the *Questsimoon* faded into a succession of crosswinds which kept each watch in turn almost constantly aloft, fighting the sails from tack to tack. But the next day the breezes clarified, allowing Starfare's Gem to make steady progress. And the following dawn, when Linden hurried from her cabin to learn why the *dromond* was rising at rest, she found that the Giants had dropped anchor off a jutting coast of mountains.

The ship stood with its prow aimed squarely towards a channel which lay like a fjord between rugged peaks. Bifurcated only by the inlet, these mountains spread away to the north and south as far as Linden could see, forming an impassable coast. In the distance on both sides, the littoral curved as if it were receding from the Sea. As a result, the cliffs directly facing the *dromond* appeared to be out-thrust like jaws to grab whatever approached their gullet.

The dawn was crisp; behind the salt breeze and the sunlight glittering along the channel, the air tasted like late fall. But the mountains looked too cold for autumn. Their dour cols and tors were cloaked with evergreens which seemed to take a grey hue from the granite around them, as if this land passed without transition and almost without change from summer into winter. Yet only the highest peaks cast any hints of snow.

The Giants had begun to gather near the wheeldeck. Linden went to join them. Honninscrave's words, *Lovely and perilous*, were still with her. And she had heard other hints of strangeness concerning the *Elohim*.

Covenant and Brinn, Pitchwife and the First had preceded her, and Seadreamer followed her up to the wheeldeck almost on Cail's heels. On the afterdeck, Sevinhand and the Storesmaster stood with the other Giants and *Haruchai*, all waiting to hear what would be said. Only Vain seemed oblivious to the imminence in the air. He remained motionless near Foodfendhall, with his back to the coast as if it meant nothing to him.

Linden expected the First to speak, but it was Honninscrave who addressed the gathering. 'My friends,' he said with a wide gesture, 'behold the land of the *Elohim*. Before us lies our path. This inlet is named the *Raw*. It arises from the River Callowwail, and the River Callowwail in turn arises from the place which the *Elohim* name their *clachan* – from the spring and fountainhead of *Elemesnedene* itself. These mountains are the Rawedge Rim, warding *Elemesnedene* from intrusion. Thus are the *Elohim* preserved in their peace, for no way lies inward except the way of the *Raw*. And from the *Raw* no being or vessel returns without the goodwill of those who hold the *Raw* and the Callowwail and Woodenwold in their mastery.

'I have spoken of the *Elohim*. They are gay and subtle, warm and cunning. If they are at all limited in lore or power, that limit is unknown. None who have emerged from the *Raw* have gained such knowledge. And of those who have not emerged, no tale remains. They have passed out of life, leaving no trace.'

Honninscrave paused. Into the silence, Covenant protested, 'That's not the way Foamfollower talked about them.' His tone was sharp with memory. 'He called them "the sylvan faery *Elohim*. A laughing people." Before the Unhomed got to Seareach, a hundred of them decided to stay and live with the *Elohim*. How perilous can they be? Or have they changed too – ?' His voice trailed off into uncertainty.

The Master faced Covenant squarely. 'The *Elohim* are what they are. They do not alter. And Saltheart Foamfollower bespoke them truly.

'Those of our people whom you have named the Unhomed were

known to us as the Lost. In their proud ships they ventured the Earth and did not return. In the generations which followed, search was made for them. The Lost we did not find, but signs of their sojourn were found. Among the *Bhrathair* still lived a handful of our people, descendants of those few Giants who remained to give aid against the Sandgorgons of the Great Desert. And among the *Elohim* were found tales of those five score Lost who chose to take their rest in *Elemesnedene*.

'But Saltheart Foamfollower spoke as one descended from those who emerged from the *Raw*, permitted by the goodwill of the *Elohim*. What of the five score who remained? Covenant Giantfriend, they were more surely Lost than any of the Unhomed, for they were Lost to themselves. Twice a hundred years later, naught remained of them but their tale in the mouths of the *Elohim*. In such a span, five score Giants would not have died of age – yet these were gone. And behind them they left no children. None, though our people love children and the making of children as dearly as life.

'No.' The Master straightened his shoulders, confronted the channel of the *Raw*. 'I have said that the *Elohim* are perilous. I have not said that they desire hurt to any life, or to the Earth. But in their own tales they are portrayed as the bastion of the last truth, and that truth they preserve in ways which baffle all who behold them. On Starfare's Gem, I alone have once entered the *Raw* and emerged. As a youth on another *dromond*, I came to this place with my companions. We returned scatheless, having won no boon from the *Elohim* by all our gifts and bargaining but the benison of their goodwill. I speak from knowledge.

'I do not anticipate harm. In the name of the white ring – of the Earth-Sight' – he glanced intently at Seadreamer, betraying a glimpse of the pressure which had been driving him – 'and of our need for the One Tree – I trust we will be well received. But such surpassing power is ever perilous. And this power is both squandered and withheld for purposes which the *Elohim* do not deign to reveal. They are occult beyond the grasp of any mortal.

'From time to time, their power is given in gift. Such is the gift of tongues, won for our people in a time many and many generations past, yet still unwaning and untainted. And such a gift we now seek. But the *Elohim* grant no gifts unpurchased. Even their goodwill must be won in barter – and in this bartering we are blind, for the quality which gives a thing or a tale value in their sight is concealed. For precious stone and metal they have no need. Of knowledge they have no dearth. Many tales hold scant interest for them. Yet it was with a tale that the gift of tongues was won – the tale, much loved by Giants, of Bahgoon the Unbearable and Thelma Twofist who tamed him. And the goodwill of the *Elohim* for me and my companions was won by the teaching of a simple knot – a thing so common among us that we scarcely thought to offer it, yet it was deemed of worth to the *Elohim*.

'Therefore we emerged from *Elemesnedene* in wonder and bafflement. And in conviction of peril, for a people of power who find such delight in a knot for which they have no use are surely perilous. If we give them offence, the *Raw* will never yield up our bones.'

As he spoke, tension mounted in Linden. Some of it grew from Covenant; his aggravated aura was palpable to her. Perplexity and fear emphasized the gauntness of his eyes, compressed the strictness which lined his face. He had based his urgent hope on what Foamfollower had told him about the *Elohim*. Now he was asking himself how he could possibly barter with them for the knowledge he needed. What did he have that they might want?

But beyond the pressure she read in him, she had conceived a tightness of her own. She had thought of a gift herself, a restitution for which she wanted to ask. If the *Elohim* could give the entire race of Giants the gift of tongues, they could answer other needs as well. Like Covenant – and Honninscrave – she did not know what to offer in exchange.

Then the First said, 'It is enough.' Though she made no move to touch her sword, or the round shield at her back, or the battle-helm attached to her belt, she conveyed the impression that she was girding herself for combat. Her corselet, leggings, and greaves gleamed like readiness in the early light. 'We are forewarned. Do you counsel that Starfare's Gem be left at anchor here? Surely a longboat will bear us up this *Raw* if need be.'

Her question forced the Master to examine himself. When he replied, his voice was wary. 'It boots nothing for the Search if Starfare's Gem is saved while you and Covenant Giantfriend and the Earth-Sight are lost.' And I do not wish to be left behind, his eyes added.

The First nodded decisively. Her gaze was fixed on the Rawedge Rim; and Linden suddenly realized that the Swordmain was uncognisant of the yearning in Honninscrave. 'Let us sail.'

For a moment, the Master appeared to hesitate. Conflicting emotions held him: the risk to his ship was tangled up in his other needs. But then he threw back his head as if he were baring his face to a wind of excitement; and commands like laughter sprang from his throat.

At once, the crew responded. The anchors were raised; the loosened sails were sheeted tight. As the wheel came to life, the prow dipped like a nod. Starfare's Gem began to gather headway towards the open mouth of the *Raw*.

Assigning Shipshearthew to the Anchormaster, Honninscrave went forward so that he could keep watch over the *dromond*'s safety from the foredeck. Impelled by his own tension, Covenant followed.

Brinn, Hergrom, and Ceer joined him, accompanied by all the Giants who were not at work.

Instead of going after them, Linden turned to the First. Her health-sense was a special form of sight, and she felt responsible for what she saw. The Swordmain stood gazing into the *Raw* as if she were testing the iron of her decision against those cliffs. Without preamble, Linden said, 'Honninscrave has something he wants to ask the *Elohim*.'

The statement took a moment to penetrate the First. But then her eyes shifted towards Linden. Sternly, she asked, 'Have you knowledge of it?'

Linden shrugged with a tinge of asperity. She could not descry the content of Honninscrave's thoughts without violating his personal integrity. 'I can see it in him. But I don't know what it is. I thought maybe you would.'

The First shook her head as she strove to assess the importance of Linden's words. 'It is not my place to question the privacy of his heart.' Then she added, 'Yet I thank you for this word. Whatever his desire, he must not barter himself to purchase it.'

Linden nodded and left the matter to the First. Hurrying down to the afterdeck, she went forward.

As she reached the foredeck, she saw the Rawedge Rim vaulting into the sky on either side. Starfare's Gem rode swiftly before the wind, though it carried no more than half its sails; and the cliffs seemed to surge closer as if they were reaching out to engulf the *dromond*. Finding herself a place near the prow, she scanned the *Raw* as far ahead as she could see, looking for some hint of rocks or shoals; but the water appeared deep and clear until it disappeared beyond a bend. Since its rising, the sun had angled to the south over the range, leaving the channel in shadow. As a result, the water looked as grey and hard as the winter-bourne of the mountains. The surface mirrored the granite cliffs rather than the high cerulean sky. It gave her the impression that Starfare's Gem was sailing into an abyss.

Steadily, the *dromond* slipped ahead. Honninscrave called for the sails to be shortened more. Still the vessel glided with a strange celerity, as if it were being inhaled by the *Raw*. Now Starfare's Gem was committed. With this wind behind it, it would never be able to turn and retreat. The Giantship went riding into shadow until only the highest sails and Horizonscan held the light. Then they, too, were extinguished, and the *dromond* seemed to go down into darkness.

As Linden's eyes adjusted to the gloom, she saw the grey walls more clearly. The granite looked wounded and unforgiving, as if it had been unnaturally reft to provide this channel and was now waiting in rigid impatience for any upheaval which would allow it to close back over the water, sealing its dire heart from further intrusion. Studying them with her percipience, she knew that these mountains were angry. Affronted. Only the ancient slowness of their life prevented their umbrage from taking palpable form.

And still the *dromond* moved with eerie quickness. The cliffs gathered the wind at the Giantship's back, and as the *Raw* narrowed the force of the blow grew. Honninscrave responded by steadily loosening and shortening the canvas. Yet when Linden looked back towards the open Sea, she saw the maw of the channel shrink into the distance. Soon it disappeared altogether as Starfare's Gem passed a bend in the *Raw*. But in spite of the bends and narrowing of the channel, Honninscrave and Sevinhand were able to keep their vessel in the centre, where the water was deepest.

Apart from the giving of commands – shouts which resounded off the walls and chased in the wake of the *dromond* like bitter warnings, helpless wrath – the Giants were hushed. Even Pitchwife's native volubility was rapt in the concentration of the ship. Linden's legs and back grew stiff with tension. The cliffs had risen a thousand feet above her head, and as the channel narrowed they loomed over the Giantship as if they were listening for one sound which would release them from their ancient paresis, bring them crashing down in fury and vindication.

A league passed as if Starfare's Gem were being drawn inward involuntarily by the dark water. The only light came from the sun's reflection on the northern peaks. For a few moments, the wet, grey silence acquired an undertone as Covenant muttered abstract curses to himself, venting his trepidation. But soon he lapsed as if he were humbled by the way the granite listened to him. The walls continued to crowd ponderously together.

In another league, the channel had become so strait that Starfare's Gem could not have turned to retreat even if the wind had changed. Linden felt that she was having trouble breathing in the gloom. It raised echoes of the other darkness, hints of crisis. The omen of Bareisle came back to her. Powerless, she was being borne with or without volition into a place of power.

Then, unexpectedly, the *dromond* navigated another bend; and the *Raw* opened into a wide lagoon like a natural harbour among the mountains. Beyond the lagoon, the Rawedge Rim tried to close, but did not, leaving a wedge of low ground between the cliffs. From the mouth of this valley came a brisk river which fed the lagoon: the Callowwail. Its banks were thickly grown with trees. And on the trees beyond the mouth of the valley, the sun shone.

Yet the lagoon itself was strangely still. All ardour was absorbed into the black depths of the mountain-roots, imposing mansuetude on the confluence of the waters.

And the air, too, seemed peaceful now. Linden found herself

breathing the pellucid and crackling scents of autumn as if her lungs were eager for the odd way in which the atmosphere here tasted telic, deliberate – wrested from the dour Rim and the *Raw* by powers she could not begin to comprehend.

At a shout from Honninscrave, Sevinhand spun the wheel, turning Starfare's Gem so that its prow faced the channel again, ready to retreat if the wind shifted. Then all the anchors were lowered. Promptly, several Giants moved to detach one of the longboats from its mooring below the rail of the wheeldeck. Like the *dromond*, the longboat was formed of stone, moire-marked and lithe. After readying its oars, the Giants set the craft into the water.

With a cumulative sigh like a release of shared suspense, the rest of the crew began to move as if they had awakened into a trance. The irenic air seemed to amaze and relieve them. Linden felt vaguely spellbound as she followed Covenant aft. Tasting the atmosphere, she knew that the woods beyond the mouth of the valley were rife with colour. After the passage of the *Raw*, she wanted to see those trees.

The First scented the air keenly. Pitchwife was on the verge of laughing aloud. Seadreamer's visage had cleared as if the cloud of Earth-Sight had been temporarily blown from his soul. Even Covenant appeared to have forgotten peril: his eyes burned like fanned coals of hope. Only the *Haruchai* betrayed no reaction to the ambience. They bore themselves as if they could not be touched. Or as if they saw the effect of the air on their companions – and did not trust it.

Honninscrave faced the valley with his hands knotted. 'Have I not said it?' he breathed softly. 'Lovely and perilous.' Then, with an effort, he turned to the First. 'Let us not delay. It ill becomes us to relate our purpose in this place.'

'Speak of yourself, Master,' Pitchwife replied like a gleam, 'I am very well become to stand and savour such air as this.'

The First nodded as if she were agreeing with her husband. But then she addressed Honninscrave. 'It is as you have said. We four, with Covenant Giantfriend, the Chosen, and their *Haruchai*, will go in search of these *Elohim*. Caution Sevinhand Anchormaster to give no offence to any being who may chance upon him here.'

The Master bowed in acknowledgment, started towards the wheeldeck. But the First stopped him with a hand on his arm.

'You also I will caution,' she said quietly. 'We must be wary of what we attempt to buy and sell with these folk. I will have no offers made, or gifts asked, without my consent.'

At once, Honninscrave's mien hardened. Linden thought that he would refuse to understand. But he chose a different denial. 'This life is mine. I will barter with it as I desire.'

Covenant looked at the Giants with guesses leaping in his gaze. In a tone of studied nonchalance, he said, 'Hile Troy felt the same way. So far, it's cost him more than three thousand years.'

'No.' The First ignored Covenant, met Honninscrave squarely. 'It is not yours. You are the Master of Starfare's Gem, sworn and dedicated to the Search. I will not lose you.'

Rebellions tautened Honninscrave's forehead, emphasizing the way his brows buttressed his eyes. But after a moment he acceded, 'I hear you.' His voice was roughed by conflict. Turning, he went to give his commands to Sevinhand.

The First studied his back as he departed. When he was gone, she spoke to Linden. 'Observe him well, Chosen. Inform me of what you see. I must not lose him.'

Not lose him, Linden echoed. Her answering nod had no meaning. If Honninscrave was in danger, then so was she.

While the Master conferred with Sevinhand, a rope-ladder was secured above the longboat. As soon as Honninscrave was ready, Ceer and Hergrom swarmed down to the craft to hold the ladder for the rest of the company. Seadreamer joined them, seated himself at the first set of oars. The First's blunt nod sent Pitchwife after Seadreamer. Then she turned to Covenant and Linden, waiting for them.

Linden felt a sharp emanation of abashment from Covenant. 'I'm no good at ladders,' he muttered awkwardly. The fumbling of his hands indicated both their numbness and his old vertigo. But then he shrugged. 'So what? Brinn can always catch me.' With his shoulders clenched, he moved to the railing.

Brinn went protectively ahead of the Unbeliever. Bracing his arms on either side of Covenant, he kept the ur-Lord as safe as a hammock. Vaguely, Linden wondered if there were any danger the *Haruchai* could not match. That they judged her for her weaknesses should have been no surprise.

When her turn came, she followed Cail downward. Pitchwife steadied her as she dropped into the bottom of the slightly rocking boat. Carefully, she seated herself opposite Covenant.

The next moment, a shout of surprise and warning echoed off the *dromond*. Vain came lightly over the side, descending the ladder as easily as a born sailor. Yet as soon as he was aboard the longboat he lapsed back into immobility.

The First and Honninscrave followed at once, anticipating trouble. But Vain did not react to them. She looked at Covenant: he answered with a shrug of disavowal. She frowned as if she wanted to heave Vain overboard; but instead she sat down dourly in the stern of the longboat.

Honninscrave took the other set of oars. Stroking together, the two brothers sent the craft skimming towards the shore near the mouth of the Callowwail.

As they rowed, Linden tried to do something to ease or distract Covenant's knotted rigidity. Because she could think of nothing new to say about Vain, she commented instead, 'You've talked about Hile Troy before. The Forestal of Andelain. But you never told me what happened to him.'

Covenant seemed unable to take his eyes away from the Rim. 'I wasn't there.' Or perhaps he did not want to acknowledge the point of her question. 'The story is that he and Mhoram tried to bargain with Caerroil Wildwood, the Forestal of Garroting Deep. Troy's army was caught between one of Foul's Giant-Ravers and Garroting Deep. In those days, the Forestal killed anyone who had the gall to set foot in his forest. Troy wanted to save his army by luring the Giant-Raver into the Deep. He and Mhoram were trying to bargain for a safe-conduct.

'Caerroil Wildwood said there was a price for his help. Troy didn't ask any questions. He just said he'd pay it.'

With a grimace, Covenant looked at Linden. He was glaring, but his ire was not directed towards her. 'The price was Troy's life. He was transformed into some sort of apprentice Forestal. Ever since, he's been living the life Caerroil Wildwood chose for him.' Covenant's hot stare reminded her that he was a man who had already paid extravagant prices. He meant to pay them again, if he had to.

Shortly, the longboat ground into the shingle which edged the lagoon. Ceer and Hergrom sprang out, to hold the craft as the others disembarked. While Honninscrave and Seadreamer secured the longboat, Linden climbed to the first fringe of the grass which led away into the trees. The air felt stronger here – a crisp and tranquil exudation from the valley ahead. Her nose thrilled to the piquant scents of fall. A backward glance showed her the Giantship. It appeared small against the dark uprise of the Rawedge Rim. With its sails furled, its masts and spars stark in the half-light, it looked like a toy on the still surface of the lagoon.

Covenant stood near her. His stiff frown could not conceal the moiling within him: venom, power; people dying in the Land; doubt. They were a volatile mixture, crowding close to deflagration. She wondered if he were truly prepared to sell himself to gain access to the One Tree. Yes, she could see that he was. But if the *Elohim* were not to be trusted – ?

Honninscrave interrupted her thoughts. With Pitchwife, the First, and Seadreamer, he came up the shingle in long Giantish strides. Then he gestured towards the trees. 'Yonder lies Woodenwold,' he said in a tight voice. 'Our way is there, along the Callowwail. I adjure you to touch nothing. Harm nothing! In this place, appearances deceive. Mayhap Woodenwold is another thorp of the *Elohim*, like unto *Elemesnedene* itself.'

Covenant scowled in that direction. 'How much farther? When

are we going to meet these *Elohim*?'

The Master's reply was sharp. 'We will not meet them. Perchance they will elect to meet us. If we give them no offence.'

Covenant met Honninscrave's hard gaze. After a moment, the Unbeliever nodded, swallowing the bile of his thoughts.

No one stirred. The air seemed to hold them back, urging them to accept this gentleness and be content. But then Ceer and Hergrom started forward; and the stasis of the company was broken. The First and Honninscrave went after the two *Haruchai*, followed by Linden and Covenant, Cail and Brinn, Seadreamer and Pitchwife. And behind them came Vain, walking as if he were blind and deaf. In this formation, they approached the River Callowwail and the marge of Woodenwold.

As they neared the trees, Hergrom and Ceer found a natural way along the riverbank. Soon the quest was among the woods, moving towards sunlight. Woodenwold was dense with oak and sycamore, ash and maple punctuated by willow, old cottonwood, and young mimosa. In the shadow of the Rim, they shared the mood of the dour stone: their browns and greens were underscored by grey and ire. But when the sun touched them, they sprang instantly into vibrant autumn blazonry. Crossing the shadowline, the companions passed from grey into glory. Woodenwold was an ignition of colour – flaming red and orange, sparkling yellow, russet and warm brown. And leaves danced about their feet as they walked, wreathing their legs in gay anadems so that they seemed to trail fire and loveliness at every step. Among them, Linden walked as if each stride carried her farther from her mortality.

The distance passed without effort as the mountains retreated on either hand to make room for the valley. The River Callowwail chuckled like the glee of leaves beside the company. It was not a wide river, but its depths were full of life and sun-spangles. Its waters shone like a new birth. The light of midday gleamed, clinquant and refulgent, on every treebough and swath of grass.

Around her, Linden thought she heard the sound of bells. They rang delicately in the distance, enhancing the woods with music. But none of her companions appeared to notice the chiming; and she could not stop to question it. It felt like the language of the trees, tanging and changing until it formed words she almost understood, though the meaning slipped away into music whenever she tried to grasp it. The bells were as lovely as the leaves; and yet in a vague way they disquieted her. She was troubled by an intuitive sense that she needed to comprehend them.

Ahead of her, Woodenwold was thinning, opening. The trees spread north and south around the foothills of the Rim; but along the Callowwail, Woodenwold faded into a sun-yellow lea which filled the whole bottom of the valley. Between the company and the mountains, purple with distance, which closed the east lay one wide bowl of golden grass, marked only by the line of the Callowwail as it curved slowly northeastward towards its source.

Honninscrave halted among the last trees. Indicating the lea, he said, 'This the *Elohim* name the *maidan* of *Elemesnedene*. At its centre lies the *clachan* itself, the spring and fountain of the Callowwail. But the *clachan* we will never find without the guidance of the *Elohim*. If they do not choose to meet us, we will wander the *maidan* as it were a maze, and there we will leave our bones to nourish the grass.'

The First studied him narrowly. 'What then is your counsel?'

'This,' he said, 'that we remain here, awaiting the goodwill of these folk. This is their land, and we are in their hands. Here, at least, if we are not welcomed we may return unmazed to Starfare's Gem and cast about us for some other hope.'

The First made some reply; but Linden did not hear her. The sound of bells became abruptly louder, filling her ears. Again, the chiming reminded her of language. Do you — ? she asked her companions. Do you hear bells? For the space of several heartbeats, she was unaware that she had not spoken aloud. The music seemed to enter her mind without touching her ears.

Then the company was no longer alone. With an eldritch concatenation like the slow magic of dreams, the belling swirled around the trunk of a nearby ash; and a figure flowed out of the wood. It did not detach itself from the tree, was not hidden against the bark: from within the ash, it stepped forward as if it were modulating into a new form. Features emerged as the figure shaped itself: eyes like chrysoprase, delicate brows, a fine nose and soft mouth. Wattle-slim and straight, deft and proud, with a grave smile on her lips and a luminous welcome in her gaze, the woman came forward like an incarnation of the soul of the ash in which she had been contained; and her departure left no mark of her presence or absence in the wood. A cymar draped her limbs like the finest sendaline.

Linden stared. Her companions started in surprise. The *Haruchai* were poised on the balls of their feet. Covenant's mouth opened and closed involuntarily.

But Honninscrave faced the approaching woman and bowed as if she were worthy of worship.

She stopped before them. Her smile radiated power of such depth and purity that Linden could hardly bear to look at it. The woman was a being who transcended any health-sense. Softly, she said, 'I am pleased that you so desire our goodwill.' Her voice also was music; but it did not explicate the ringing in Linden's mind. 'I am Daphin.' Then she nodded to Honninscrave's bow. 'You are Giants. We have known Giants.'

Still the bells confused Linden, so that she was not sure of what she was hearing.

Daphin turned to Brinn. 'You we do not know. Perhaps the tale of your people will interest us.'

The chiming grew louder. Daphin was gazing directly at Linden. Linden had no control over the sound in her head. But she almost gasped in shock when Daphin said, 'You are the Sun-Sage.'

Before Linden could react or respond, the woman had turned to Covenant. He was staring at her as if his astonishment were a wound. At once, her smile fell. The bells clamoured like surprise or fear. Distinctly, she said, 'You are not.'

As the questers gaped at her, she suddenly melted down in the grass and was gone, leaving no trace of her passage on the wide lea.

7

ELEMESNEDENE

Linden clamped her hands over her ears, and the chiming faded — not because of her hands, but because the gesture helped her focus her efforts to block or at least filter the sound. She was sweating in the humid sunlight. The Sun-Sage? Hints of panic flushed across her face. The *Sun-Sage*?

Covenant swore repeatedly under his breath. His tone was as white as clenched knuckles. When she looked at him, she saw him glaring at the grass where Daphin had vanished as if he meant to blight it with fire.

The *Haruchai* had not moved. Honninscrave's head had jerked back in astonishment or pain. Seadreamer gazed intently at Linden in search of understanding. Pitchwife stood beside the First as if he were leaning on her. Her eyes knifed warily back and forth between Linden and Covenant.

Vain's black mien wore an aspect of suppressed excitement.

'Sun-Sage?' the First asked rigidly. 'What is this "Sun-Sage"?'

Linden took a step towards Covenant. He appeared to be cursing at her. She could not bear it. 'I'm *not*.' Her voice sounded naked in the sunshine, devoid of any music which would have given it beauty. 'You know I'm not.'

His visage flamed at her. 'Damnation! Of course you are. Haven't you learned anything yet?'

His tone made her flinch. Daphin's *You are not* formed a knot of ire in him that Linden could see as clearly as if it had been outlined on his forehead. He would not be able to alter the Sunbane. And because of him, the *Elohim* had withdrawn her welcome.

With hard patience, the First again demanded, 'What is this "Sun-Sage"?'

Covenant replied like a snarl, 'Somebody who can control the Sunbane.' His features were acute with self-disgust.

'They will not welcome us.' Loss stretched Honninscrave's voice thin. 'Oh, *Elohim*!'

Linden struggled for a way to answer Covenant without berating him. *I don't have the power.* Sweat ran into her eyes, blurring her vision. The tension of the company felt unnatural to her. This anger and grief seemed to violate the wide mansuetude of Woodenwold and the *maidan*. But then her senses reached farther, and she thought, *No. That's not it.* In some way, the valley's tranquillity appeared to be the cause of this intensity. The air was like a balm which was too potent to give anything except pain.

But the opening of her percipience exposed her to the bells again. Or they were drawing closer. Chiming took over her mind. Pitchwife's voice was artificially muffled in her ears as he said, 'Mayhap their welcome is not yet forfeit. Behold!'

She blinked her sight clear in time to see two figures come flowing up out of the ground in front of her. Smoothly, they transformed themselves from grass and soil into human shapes.

One was Daphin. Her smile was gone; in its place was a sober calm that resembled regret. But her companion wore a grin like a smirk.

He was a man with eyes as blue as jacinths, the same colour as his mantle. Like Daphin's cymar, his robe was not a garment he had donned, but rather an adornment he had created within himself. With self-conscious elegance, he adjusted the folds of the cloth. The gleam in his eyes might have been pleasure or mockery. The distinction was confused by the obbligato of the bells.

'I am Chant,' he said lightly. 'I have come for truth.'

Both he and Daphin gazed directly at Linden.

The pressure of their regard seemed to expose every fibre of her nature. By contrast, her health-sense was humble and crude. They surpassed all her conceptions.

She reacted in instinctive denial. With a wrench of determination, she thrust the ringing into the background. The *Elohim* searched her as Gibbon had once searched her. *Are you not evil?* No. Not as long as the darkness had no power. 'I'm not the Sun-Sage.'

Chant cocked an eyebrow in disbelief.

'If anybody is, it's him.' She pointed at Covenant, trying to turn the eyes of the *Elohim* away. 'He has the ring.'

They did not waver. Daphin's mien remained pellucid; but Chant's smile hinted at fierceness. 'We have no taste for untruth' – His tone was satin – 'and your words are manifestly untrue. Deny not that you are what you are. It does not please us. Explain, rather, why this man holds possession of your white ring.'

At once, Covenant snapped, 'It's not her ring. It's mine. It's always been mine.' Beside the *Elohim*, he sounded petulant and diminished.

Chant's smile deepened, gripping Linden in its peril. 'That also is untrue. You are not the Sun-Sage.'

Covenant tensed for a retort. But Daphin forestalled him. Calmly, she said, 'No. The ring is his. Its mark lies deeply within him.'

At that, Chant looked towards his companion; and Linden sagged in relief. The shifting of his gaze gave her a palpable release.

Chant frowned as if Daphin's contradiction broke an unspoken agreement. But she went on addressing Linden. 'Yet here is a mystery. All our vision has seen the same truth – that the Sun-Sage and the ring-wielder who would come among us in quest are one being. Thereon hinge matters of grave import. And our vision does not lie. Rawedge Rim and Woodenwold do not lie. How may this be explained, Sun-Sage?'

Linden felt Covenant clench as if he were on the verge of fire. 'What do you want me to do?' he grated. 'Give it up?'

Chant did not deign to glance at him. 'Such power ill becomes you. Silence would be more seemly. You stand among those who surpass you. Permit the Sun-Sage to speak.' Notes of anger ran through the music of the bells.

Covenant growled a curse. Sensing his ire, Linden twisted herself out of the grip of the *Elohim* to face him. His visage was dark with venom. Again, his vehemence appeared unnatural – a reaction to the air rather than to his situation or the *Elohim*. That impression sparked an inchoate urgency in her. Something here outweighed her personal denials. Intuitively, she pitched her voice so that Covenant must hear her.

'I wouldn't be here without him.'

Then she began to tremble at the responsibility she had implicitly accepted.

The next moment, Pitchwife was speaking. 'Peace, my friends,' he said. His misshapen face was sharp with uncharacteristic apprehension. 'We have journeyed far to gain the boon of these *Elohim*. Far more than our lives hang in jeopardy.' His voice beseeched them softly. 'Give no offence.'

Covenant peered at Linden as if he were trying to determine the nature of her support and recognition. Suddenly, she wanted to ask him, Do you hear bells? If he did, he gave no sign. But what he saw in her both tightened and steadied him. Deliberately, he shrugged down his power. Without lifting his scrutiny from Linden, he said to the *Elohim*, 'Forgive me. The reason we're here. It's urgent. I don't carry the strain very well.'

The *Elohim* ignored him, continued watching Linden. But the timbre of anger drifted away along the music. 'Perhaps our vision has been incomplete,' said Daphin. Her voice lilted like birdsong. 'Perhaps there is a merging to come. Or a death.'

Merging? Linden thought quickly. Death? She felt the same questions leaping in Covenant. She started to ask, What do you mean?

But Chant had resumed his dangerous smile. Still addressing Linden as though she outranked all her companions, he said abruptly, 'It is known that your quest is exigent. We are not a hasty people, but neither do we desire your delay.' Turning, he gestured gracefully along the Callowwail. 'Will you accompany us to *Elemesnedene*?'

Linden needed a moment to muster her response. Too much was happening. She had been following Covenant's lead since she had first met him. She was not prepared to make decisions for him or anyone else.

But she had no choice. At her back crowded the emotions of her companions: Honninscrave's tension, the First's difficult silence, Pitchwife's suspense, Covenant's hot doubt. They all withheld themselves, waited for her. And she had her own reasons for being here. With a grimace, she accepted the role she had been given.

'Thank you,' she said formally. 'That's what we came for.'

Chant bowed as if she had shown graciousness; but she could not shake the impression that he was laughing at her secretly. Then the two *Elohim* moved away. Walking as buoyantly as if they shared the analystic clarity of the air, they went out into the yellow grass towards the heart of the *maidan*. Linden followed them with Cail at her side; and her companions joined her.

She wanted to talk to them, ask them for guidance. But she felt too exposed to speak. Treading behind Chant and Daphin at a slight distance, she tried to steady herself on the tough confidence of the *Haruchai*.

As she walked, she studied the surrounding *maidan*, hoping to descry something which would enable her to identify an *Elohim* who was not wearing human form. But she had not perceived any hint of Daphin or Chant before they had accosted the company; and now she was able to discern nothing except the strong autumn grass, the underlying loam, and the Callowwail's purity. Yet her sense of exposure increased. After a while, she discovered that she had been unconsciously clenching her fists.

With an effort, she ungarnled her fingers, looked at them. She could hardly believe that they had ever held a scalpel or hypodermic. When she dropped them, they dangled at her wrists like strangers.

She did not know how to handle the importance the *Elohim* had ascribed to her. She could not read the faint clear significance of the bells. Following Chant and Daphin, she felt that she was walking into a quagmire.

An odd thought crossed her mind. The *Elohim* had given no word of recognition to Vain. The Demondim-spawn trailed the company like a shadow; yet Chant and Daphin had not reacted to him at all. She wondered about that, but found no explanation.

Sooner than she had expected, the fountainhead of the Callowwail became visible – a cloud of mist set in the centre of the *maidan* like an ornament. As she neared it, it stood out more clearly through its spray.

It arose like a geyser from within a high mound of travertine. Its waters arched in clouds and rainbows to fall around the base of the mound, where they collected to form the River. The water looked as edifying as crystal, as clinquant as faery promises; but the travertine it had formed and dampened appeared obdurate, uncompromising. The mound seemed to huddle into itself as if it could not be moved by any appeal. The whorled and skirling shapes on its sides – cut and deposited by ages of spray, the old scrollwork of the water – gave it an elusive eloquence, but did not alter its essential purity.

Beckoning for the company to follow, Daphin and Chant stepped lightly through the stream and climbed as easily as air up the side of the wet rock.

There without warning they vanished as if they had melded themselves into travertine.

Linden stopped, stared. Her senses caught no trace of the *Elohim*. The bells were barely audible.

Behind her, Honninscrave cleared his throat. '*Elemesnedene*,' he said huskily. 'The *clachan* of the *Elohim*. I had not thought that I would live to see such sights again.'

Covenant scowled at the Master. 'What do we do now?'

For the first time since Starfare's Gem had dropped anchor outside the *Raw*, Honninscrave laughed. 'As our welcomers have done. Enter.'

Linden started to ask him how, then changed her mind. Now that the silence had been broken, another question was more important to her. 'Do you hear bells?'

The First looked at her sharply. 'Bells?'

Pitchwife's expression mirrored the First's ignorance. Seadreamer shook his head. Brinn gave a slight negative shrug.

Slowly, Honninscrave said, 'The *Elohim* are not a musical folk. I have heard no bells or any song here. And all the tales which the Giants tell of *Elemesnedene* make no mention of bells.'

Linden groaned to herself. Once again, she was alone in what she perceived. Without hope, she turned to Covenant.

He was not looking at her. He was staring like a thunderhead at the fountain. His left hand twisted his ring around the last finger of his halfhand.

'Covenant?' she asked.

He did not answer her question. Instead, he muttered between his teeth, 'They think I'm going to fail. I don't need that. I didn't come all this way to hear that.' He hated the thought of failure in every line of his gaunt stubborn form. But then his purpose stiffened. 'Let's get going. You're the Sun-Sage.' His tone was full of sharp edges and gall. For the sake of his quest, he fought to accept the roles the *Elohim* had assigned. 'You should go first.'

She started to deny once again that she was any kind of Sun-Sage. That might comfort him – or at least limit the violence coiling inside him. But again her sense of exposure warned her to silence. Instead of speaking, she faced the stream and the mound, took a deep breath, held it. Moving half a step ahead of Cail, she walked into the water.

At once, a hot tingling shot through her calves, soaked down into her feet. For one heartbeat, she almost winced away. But then her nerves told her that the sensation was not harmful. It bristled across the surface of her skin like formication, but did no damage. Biting down on her courage, she strode through the stream, and clambered out on to the old intaglio of the travertine. With Cail at her side, she began to ascend the mound.

Suddenly, power seemed to flash around her as if she had been dropped like a coal into a tinder box. Bells clanged in her head – chimes ringing in cotillion on all sides. Bubbles of glauconite and carbuncle burst into her blood; the air burned like a thurible; the world reeled.

The next instant, she staggered into a wonderland.

Stunned and gaping, she panted for breath. She had been translated by water and travertine to another place altogether – a place of eldritch astonishment.

An opalescent sky stretched over her, undefined by any sun or moon, or by any clear horizons, and yet brightly luminous and warm. The light seemed to combine moonglow and sunshine. It had the suggestive evanescence of night and the specificity of day. And under its magic, wonders thronged in corybantic succession.

Nearby grew a silver sapling. Though not tall, it was as stately as a prince; and its leaves danced about its limbs without touching them. Like flakes of precious metal, the leaves formed a chiaroscuro around the tree, casting glints and spangles as they whirled.

On the other side, a fountain spewed globes of colour and light. Bobbing upward, they broke into silent rain and were inhaled again by the fountain.

A furry shape like a jarcol went gambolling past, and appeared to trip. Sprawling, it became a profuse scatter of flowers. Blooms that resembled peony and amaryllis sprayed open across the glistening greensward.

Birds flew overhead, warbling incarnate. Cavorting in circles, they swept against each other, merged to form an abrupt pillar of fire in the air. A moment later, the fire leaped into sparks, and the sparks became gems – ruby and morganite, sapphire and porphyry, like a trail of stars – and the gems wafted away, turning to butterflies as they floated.

A hillock slowly pirouetted to itself, taking arcane shapes one after another as it turned.

And these were only the nearest entrancements. Other sights abounded; grand statues of water; a pool with its surface woven like an arras; shrubs which flowed through a myriad elegant forms; catenulate sequences of marble, draped from nowhere to nowhere; animals that leaped into the air as birds and drifted down again as snow; swept-wing shapes of malachite flying in gracile curves; sunflowers the size of Giants, with imbricated ophite petals.

And everywhere rang the music of bells – cymbals in carillon, chimes wefted into tapestries of tinkling, tones scattered on all sides – the metal-and-crystal language of *Elemesnedene*.

Linden could not take it all in; it dazzled her senses, left her gasping. When the silver sapling near her poured itself into human form and became Chant, she recoiled. She could hardly grasp the truth of what she saw.

These – ?

Oh my God.

As if in confirmation, a tumble of starlings swept to the ground and transformed themselves into Daphin.

Then Covenant's voice breathed softly behind her, 'Hellfire and bloody damnation,' and she became aware of her companions.

Turning, she saw them all – the Giants, the *Haruchai*, even Vain. But of the way they had come there was no sign. The fountainhead of the Callowwail, the mound of travertine, even the *maidan*, did not exist in this place. The company stood on a low knoll surrounded by astonishments.

For a moment, she remained dumbfounded. But then Covenant clutched her forearm with his halfhand, clung to her. 'What – ?' he groped to ask, not looking at her. His grip gave her an anchor on which to steady herself.

'The *Elohim*,' she answered. 'They're the *Elohim*.'

Honninscrave nodded as if he were speechless with memory and hope.

Pitchwife was laughing soundlessly. His eyes feasted on *Elemesnedene*. But the First's mien was grim – tensely aware that the company had no line of retreat and could not afford to give any offence. And

Seadreamer's orbs above the old scar were smudged with contradictions, as if his Giantish accessibility to exaltation were in conflict with the Earth-Sight.

'Be welcome in our *clachan*,' said Chant. He took pleasure in the amazement of the company. 'Set all care aside. You have no need of it here. However urgent your purpose, *Elemesnedene* is not a place which any mortal may regret to behold.'

'Nor will we regret it,' the First replied carefully. 'We are Giants and know the value of wonder. Yet our urgency is a burden we dare not shirk. May we speak of the need which has brought us among you?'

A slight frown creased Chant's forehead. 'Your haste gives scant worth to our welcome. We are not Giants or other children, to be so questioned in what we do.

'Also,' he went on, fixing Linden with his jacinth-eyes, 'none are admitted to the *Elohimfest*, in which counsel and gifts are bespoken and considered, until they have submitted themselves to our examination. We behold the truth in you. But the spirit in which you bear that truth must be laid bare. Will you accept to be examined?'

Examined? Linden queried herself. She did not know how to meet the demand of Chant's gaze. Uncertainly, she turned to Honninscrave.

He answered her mute question with a smile. 'It is as I have remembered it. There is no need of fear.'

Covenant started to speak, then stopped. The hunching of his shoulders said plainly that he could think of reasons to fear any examination.

'The Giant remembers truly.' Daphin's voice was irenic and reassuring. 'It is said among us that the heart cherishes secrets not worth the telling. We intend no intrusion. We desire only to have private speech with you, so that in the rise and fall of your words we may judge the spirit within you. Come.' Smiling like a sunrise, she stepped forward, took Linden's arm. 'Will you not accompany me?'

When Linden hesitated, the *Elohim* added, 'Have no concern for your comrades. In your name they are as safe among us as their separate needs permit.'

Events were moving too quickly, Linden did not know how to respond. She could not absorb all the sights and entrancements around her, could barely hold back the bells so that they did not deafen her mind. She was not prepared for such decisions.

But she had spent her life learning to make choices and face the consequences. And her experiences in the Land had retaught her the importance of movement. Keep going. Take things as they come. Find out what happens. Abruptly, she acquiesced to Daphin's slight pressure on her arm. 'I'll come. You can ask me anything you want.'

'Ah, Sun-Sage,' the *Elohim* rejoined with a light laugh, 'I will ask you nothing. You will ask me.'

Nothing. Linden did not understand. And Covenant's glare burned against the back of her neck as if she were participating in the way the *Elohim* demeaned him. He had travelled an arduous road to his power and did not deserve such treatment. But she would not retreat. She had risked his life for Mistweave's. Now she risked his pride, though the angry confusion he emitted hurt her. Accepting Daphin's touch, she started away down the knoll.

At the same time, other shapes in the area resolved themselves into human form – more *Elohim* coming to examine the rest of the company. Though she was now braced for the sight, she was still dazed to see trees, fountains, dancing aggregations of gems melt so unexpectedly into more familiar beings. As Cail placed himself protectively at her side opposite Daphin, she found a keen comfort in his presence. He was as reliable as stone. Amid the wild modulations of the *clachan*, she needed his stability.

They had not reached the bottom of the slope when Chant said sharply, 'No.'

At once, Daphin stopped. Deftly, she turned Linden to face the company.

Chant was looking at Linden. His gaze had the biting force of an augur. 'Sun-Sage.' He sounded distant through the warning clatter of the bells. 'You must accompany Daphin alone. Each of your companions must be examined alone.'

Alone? she protested. It was too much. How could such a stricture include Cail? He was one of the *Haruchai*. And she needed him. The sudden acuity of her need for him took her by surprise. She was already so alone.

She gathered herself to remonstrate. But Cail preceded her. 'The Chosen is in my care,' he said in a voice as flat as a wall. 'I will accompany her.'

His intransigence drew Chant's attention. The *Elohim*'s easy elegance tightened towards hauteur. 'No,' he repeated. 'I care nothing for such care. It is not binding here. Like the Sun-Sage, you will go alone to be examined.'

Covenant moved. The First made a warning gesture, urging forbearance. He ignored her. Softly, he grated, 'Or else?'

'Or else,' Chant mimicked in subtle mockery, 'he will be banished to the place of shades, from whence none return.'

'By hell!' Covenant rasped, 'over my dead – '

Before he could finish, the four *Haruchai* burst into motion. On the spur of a shared impulse, they hurled themselves forward in attack. Brinn launched a flying kick at Chant's chest, Ceer and Hergrom threw body-blows towards other *Elohim*, Cail slashed at

Daphin's legs, aiming to cut her feet from under her.

None of their blows had any effect.

Chant misted as Brinn struck. The *Haruchai* plunged straight through him, touching nothing. Then Chant became a tangle of vines that caught and immobilized Brinn. Daphin sprouted wings and rose lightly above Cail's blow. Before he could recover, she poured down on him like viscid spilth, clogging his movements until he was paralysed. And the *Elohim* assailed by Ceer and Hergrom slumped effortlessly into quicksand, snaring them at once.

The Giants watched. Honninscrave stared in dismay, unready for the violence which boiled so easily past the smooth surface of *Elemesnedene*. Seadreamer tried to charge to the aid of the *Haruchai*; but the First and Pitchwife held him back.

'No.' Among the Giants, Covenant stood like imminent fire, facing the *Elohim* with wild magic poised in every muscle. His passion dominated the knoll. In a low voice, as dangerous as a viper, he articulated, 'You can discount me. That's been done before. But the *Haruchai* are my friends. You will not harm them.'

'That choice is not yours to make!' Chant retorted. But now it was he who sounded petulant and diminished.

'Chant.' Daphin's voice came quietly from the sludge imprisoning Cail. 'Bethink you. It is enough. No further purpose is served.'

For a moment, Chant did not respond. But the bells took on a coercive note; and abruptly he shrugged himself back into human shape. At the same time, Daphin flowed away from Cail, and the other two *Elohim* arose from the quicksand as men. The *Haruchai* were free.

'Sun-Sage,' said Chant, nailing Linden with his gaze, 'these beings stand under the shelter of your name. They will suffer no harm. But this offence surpasses all endurance. *Elemesnedene* will not permit it. What is your will?'

Linden almost choked on the raw edges of the retort she wished to make. She wanted words which would scathe Chant, shame all the *Elohim*. She needed Cail with her. And the extravagance of his outrage was vivid behind the flatness of his face. The service of the *Haruchai* deserved more respect than this. But she clung to forbearance. The company had too much to lose. None of them could afford an open break with the *Elohim*. In spite of the secret perils of the *clachan*, she made her decision.

'Put them back on the *maidan*. Near the fountain. Let them wait for us. Safely.'

Covenant's visage flamed protest at her, then fell into a grimace of resignation. But it made no difference. Chant had already nodded.

At once, the four *Haruchai* began to float away from the knoll. They were not moving themselves. The ground under their feet swept them backward, as if they were receding along a tide. And as they went, they faded like vapour.

But before they were dispelled, Linden caught one piercing glance from Cail, a look of reproach as if he had been betrayed. His voice lingered in her after he was gone.

'We do not trust these *Elohim*.'

Chant snorted. 'Let him speak of trust when he has become less a fool. These matters are too high for him, and so he thinks in his arrogance to scorn them. He must count himself fortunate that he has not paid the price of our displeasure.'

'Your displeasure.' Linden controlled herself with difficulty. 'You're just looking for excuses to be displeased.' Cail's last look panged her deeply. And the magnitude of what she had just done made her tremble. 'We came here in good faith. And the *Haruchai* are good faith. They don't deserve to be dismissed. I'll be lucky if they ever forgive me. They're never going to forgive *you*.'

The First made a cautioning gesture. But when Linden looked stiffly in that direction, she saw a grim satisfaction in the First's eyes. Honninscrave appeared distressed; but Seadreamer was nodding, and Covenant's features were keen with indignation and approval.

'Your pardon.' In an instant, Chant donned an urbane calm like a second mantle. 'My welcoming has been unseemly. Though you know it not, my intent has been to serve the purpose which impels you. Let me make amends. Ring-wielder, will you accompany me?'

The invitation startled Covenant. But then he gritted, 'Try to stop me.'

Riding the effect of his approval, Linden turned to Daphin. 'I'm ready when you are.'

Daphin's countenance betrayed neither conflict nor disdain. 'You are gracious. I am pleased.' Taking Linden's arm once again, she led her away from the company.

When Linden glanced backward, she saw that all her companions were moving in different directions, each accompanied by an *Elohim*. A dim sense of incompleteness, of something missing, afflicted her momentarily; but she attributed it to the absence of the *Haruchai* and let Daphin guide her away among the wonders of *Elemesnedene*.

But she detached her arm from the *Elohim*'s touch. She did not want Daphin to feel her reactions. For all its amazements, the *clachan* suddenly seemed a cold and joyless place, where beings of inbred life and convoluted intent mimed an exuberance they were unable to share.

And yet on every hand *Elemesnedene* contradicted her. Sportive and gratuitous incarnations were everywhere as far as she could see – pools casting rainbows of iridescent fish; mists composed of myriad ice-crystals; flowers whose every leaf and petal burned like a cruse. And each of them was an *Elohim*, enacting transformations for reasons which eluded her. The whole of the *clachan* appeared to be one luxurious entertainment.

But who was meant to be entertained by it? Daphin moved as if she were bemused by her own thoughts, unaware of what transpired around her. And each performance appeared hermetic and self-complete. In no discernible way did they co-operate with or observe each other. Was this entire display performed for no other reason than the simple joy of wonder and play?

Her inability to answer such questions disturbed Linden. Like the language of the bells, the *Elohim* surpassed her. She had been learning to rely on the Land-born penetration of her senses; but here that ability did not suffice. When she looked at a fountain of feathers or a glode of ophite, she only knew it was one of the *Elohim* because she had already witnessed similar incarnations. She could not see a sentient being in the gavotte of butterflies or the budding of liquid saplings, just as she had not seen Chant and Daphin in the earth near her feet. And she could not pierce Daphin's blank beauty to whatever lay within. The spirit of what she saw and heard was beyond her reach. All she could descry clearly was power – an essential puissance that seemed to transcend every structure or law of existence. Whatever the *Elohim* were, they were too much for her.

Then she began to wonder if that were the purpose of her examination – to learn how much of the truth she could discern, how much she was worthy of the role the *Elohim* had seen in her. If so, the test was one she had already failed.

But she refused to be daunted. Covenant would not have surrendered his resolve. She could see him limned in danger and old refusal, prepared to battle doom itself in order to wrest out survival for the Land he loved. Very well. She would do no less.

Girding herself in severity, she turned her mind to her examination.

Daphin had said, *I will ask you nothing. You will ask me.* That made more sense to her now. She might reveal much in her questions. But she accepted the risk and looked for ways to gain information while exposing as little as possible.

She took a moment to formulate her words clearly against the incessant background of the bells, then asked in her flat professional voice, 'Where are we going?'

'Going?' replied Daphin lightly. 'We are not "going" at all. We merely walk.' When Linden stared at her, she continued, 'This is *Elemesnedene* itself. Here there is no other "where" to which we might go.'

Deliberately, Linden exaggerated her surface incomprehension. 'There has to be. We're moving. My friends are going somewhere else. How will we get back to them? How will we find that *Elohimfest* Chant mentioned?'

'Ah, Sun-Sage,' Daphin chuckled. Her laugh sounded like a moonrise in this place which had neither moon nor sun. 'In *Elemesnedene* all ways are one. We will meet with your companions when that meeting has ripened. And there will be no need to seek the place of the *Elohimfest*. It will be held at the centre, and in *Elemesnedene* all places are the centre. We walk from the centre to the centre, and where we now walk is also the centre.'

Is that what happened to those Giants who decided to stay here? Linden barely stopped herself from speaking aloud. Did they just start walking and never find each other again until they died?

But she kept the thought to herself. It revealed too much of her apprehension and distrust. Instead, she chose an entirely different reaction. In a level tone, as if she were simply reporting symptoms, she said, 'Well, I've been walking all day, and I'm tired. I need some rest.'

This was not true. Though she had not eaten or rested since the quest had left Starfare's Gem, she felt as fresh as if she had just arisen from a good sleep and a satisfying meal. Somehow, the atmosphere of the *clachan* had met all her physical needs. She made her assertion simply to see how Daphin would respond.

The *Elohim* appeared to perceive the lie; yet she delicately refrained from challenging it. 'There is no weariness in *Elemesnedene*,' she said, 'and all walking is pleasant. Yet it is also pleasant to sit or to recline. Here is a soothing place.' She indicated the slope of a low grassy hill nearby. On the hillcrest stood a large willow leaved entirely in butterfly-wings; and at the foot of the slope lay a still vlei with colours floating across its surface like a lacustrine portrait of the *clachan* itself. Daphin moved on to the hillside and sat down, disposing her cymar gracefully about her.

Linden followed. When she had found a comfortable position upon the lush grass, she framed her next question.

Pointing towards the vlei, she asked, 'Is that a man or a woman?' Her words sounded crude beside Daphin's beauty; but she made no attempt to soften them. She did not like exposing her impercipience; but she guessed that her past actions had already made the *Elohim* aware of this limitation.

'Morninglight?' replied Daphin, gazing at the colour-swept water. 'You would name him a man.'

'What's he doing?'

Daphin returned her apple-green eyes to Linden. 'Sun-Sage, what question is this? Are we not in *Elemesnedene*? In the sense of your word, there is no "doing" here. This is not an act with a purpose such as you name purpose. Morninglight performs self-contempla-tion. He enacts the truth of his being as he beholds it, and thus he explores the truth, beholding and enacting new truth. We are the *Elohim*. For certain visions we look elsewhere. The "doing" of which

540

you speak is more easily read on the surface of the Earth than in its heart. But all truths are within us, and for these truths we seek into ourselves.'

'Then,' Linden asked, reacting to a curious detachment in Daphin's tone, 'you don't watch him? You don't pay attention to each other? This' – she indicated Morninglight's water-show – 'Isn't intended to communicate something?'

The question seemed to give Daphin a gentle surprise. 'What is the need? I also am the heart of the Earth, as he is. Wherefore should I desire his truth, when I may freely seek my own?'

This answer appeared consistent to Linden; and yet its self-sufficiency baffled her. How could any being be so complete? Daphin sat there in her loveliness and her inward repose as if she had never asked herself a question for which she did not already know the answer. Her personal radiance shone like hints of sunlight, and when she spoke her voice was full of moonbeams. Linden did not trust her. But now she comprehended the wonder and excitement, the awe bordering on adoration, which Honninscrave had learned to feel towards these people.

Still she could not shake off her tremorous inner disquiet. The bells would not leave her alone. They came so close to meaning, but she could not decipher their message. Her nerves tightened involuntarily.

'That's not what Chant thinks. He thinks his truth is the only one there is.'

Daphin's limpid gaze did not waver. 'Perhaps that is true. Where is the harm? He is but one *Elohim* among many. And yet,' she went on after a moment's consideration, 'he was not always so. He has found within himself a place of shadow which he must explore. All who live contain some darkness, and much lies hidden there. Surely it is perilous, as any shadow which encroaches upon the light is perilous. But in us it has not been a matter of exigency – for are we not equal to all things? Yet for Chant that shadow has become exigent. Risking much, as he does, he grows impatient with those who have not yet beheld or entered the shadows cast by their own truths. And others tread this path with him.'

'Sun-Sage.' Now a new intentness shone from Daphin – the light of clear desire. 'This you must comprehend. We are the *Elohim*, the heart of the Earth. We stand at the centre of all that lives and moves and is. We live in peace because there are none who can do us hurt, and if it were our choice to sit within *Elemesnedene* and watch the Earth age until the end of Time, there would be none to gainsay us. No other being or need may judge us, just as the hand may not judge the heart which gives it life.

'But because we *are* the heart, we do not shirk the burden of the truth within us. We have said that our vision foreknew the coming

541

of Sun-Sage and ring-wielder. It is cause for concern that they are separate. There is great need that Sun-Sage and ring-wielder should be one. Nevertheless the coming itself was known. In the mountains which cradle our *clachan*, we see the peril of this Sunbane which requires you to your quest. And in the trees of Woodenwold we have read your arrival.

'Yet had such knowing comprised the limit of our knowledge, you would have been welcomed here merely as other visitors are welcomed, in simple kindness and curiosity. But our knowledge is not so small. We have found within ourselves this shadow upon the heart of the Earth, and it has altered our thoughts. It has taught us to conceive of the Sunbane in new ways – and to reply to the Earth's peril in a manner other than our wont.

'You have doubted us. And your doubts will remain. Perhaps it will grow until it resembles loathing. Yet I say to you, Sun-Sage, that you judge us falsely. That you should presume to judge us at all is incondign and displeasing. We are the heart of the Earth and not to be judged.'

Daphin spoke strongly; but she did not appear vexed. Rather, she asked for understanding in the way a parent might ask a child for good behaviour. Her tone abashed Linden. But she also rebelled. Daphin was asking her to give up her responsibility for discernment and action; and she would not. That responsibility was her reason for being here, and she had earned it.

Then the bells seemed to rise up in her like the disapproval of *Elemesnedene*. 'What *are* you?' she inquired in a constrained voice. 'The heart of the Earth. The centre. The truth. What does all that mean?'

'Sun-Sage,' replied Daphin, 'we are the Würd of the Earth.'

She spoke clearly, but her tone was confusing. Her Würd sounded like *Wyrd* or *Word*.

Wyrd? Linden thought. Destiny – doom? Or Word?'

Or both.

Into the silence, Daphin placed her story. It was an account of the creation of the Earth; and Linden soon realized that it was the same tale Pitchwife had told her during the calling of the *Nicor*. Yet it contained one baffling difference. Daphin did not speak of a *Worm*. Rather, she used that blurred sound, *Würd*, which seemed to signify both *Wyrd* and *Word*.

This *Würd* had awakened at the dawning of the eon and begun to consume the stars as if it intended to devour the cosmos whole. After a time, it had grown satiated and had curled around itself to rest, thus forming the Earth. And thus the Earth would remain until the Würd roused to resume its feeding.

It was precisely the same story as Pitchwife had told. Had the Giants who first brought that tale out of *Elemesnedene* misheard it?

Or had the *Elohim* pronounced it differently to other visitors?

As if in answer, Daphin concluded, 'Sun-Sage, we are the Würd – the direct offspring of the creation of the Earth. From it we arose, and in it we have our being. Thus we are the heart, and the centre, and the truth, and therefore we are what we are. We are all answers, just as we are every question. For that reason, you must not judge the reply which we will give to your need.'

Linden hardly heard the *Elohim*. Her mind was awhirl with implications. Intuitions rang against the limits of her understanding like the clamour of bells. *We are the Würd*. Morninglight swirling with colour like a portrait of the *clachan* in metaphor. A willow leaved in butterflies. Self-contemplation.

Power.

8

THE *ELOHIMFEST*

What the hell?

Linden could not move. The lucidity with which the sounding bells had spoken staggered her. She gaped at Daphin's outstretched hand. It made no impression on her. Feverishly, she grappled for the meaning of the music.

We must hasten –

Had she heard that – or invented it in her confusion?

Hear us too acutely.

Her Land-born percipience had stumbled on to something she had not been intended to receive. The speakers of the bells did not want her to know what they were saying.

She fought to concentrate. But she could not take hold of that language. Though it hushed itself as she groped towards it, it did not fall altogether silent. It continued to run in the background of her awareness like a conversation of fine crystal. And yet it eluded her. The more she struggled to comprehend it, the more it sounded like mere bells and nothing else.

Daphin and Morninglight were gazing at her as if they could read the rush of her thoughts. She needed to be left alone, needed time to think. But the eyes of the *Elohim* did not waver. Her trepidation tightened, and she recognized another need – to keep both the extent and the limitation of her hearing secret. If she were not intended to discern these bells, then in order to benefit from them she must conceal what she heard.

She had to glean every secret she could. Behind Daphin's apparent candour, the *Elohim* were keeping their true purposes hidden. And Covenant and the rest of her companions were dependent on her, whether they knew it or not. They did not have her ears.

The music had not been silenced. Therefore she had not entirely given herself away. Yet. Trying to cover her confusion, she blinked at Daphin and asked incredulously, 'Is that all? You're done examining me? You don't know anything about me.'

Daphin laughed lightly. 'Sun-Sage, this "examining" is like the "doing" of which you speak so inflexibly. For us, the word has another meaning. I have considered myself and garnered all the truth of you that I require. Now come.' She repeated the outreach of her hand. 'Have I not said that the *Elohimfest* awaits you? There the coming of Infelice will offer another insight. And also we will perform the asking and answering for which you have quested over such distances. Is it not your desire to attend that congregation?'

'Yes,' replied Linden, suppressing her discomfiture. 'That's what I want.' She had forgotten her hopes amid the disquieting implications of the bells. But her friends would have to be warned. She would have to find a way to warn them against the danger they could not hear. Stiffly, she accepted Daphin's hand, let the *Elohim* lift her to her feet.

With Daphin on one side and Morninglight on the other like guards, she left the hillside.

She had no sense of direction in this place; but she did not question Daphin's lead. Instead, she concentrated on concealing her thoughts behind a mask of severity.

On all sides were the wonders of *Elemesnedene*. Bedizened trees and flaming shrubs, fountains imbued with the colour of ichor, animals emblazoned like tapestries. Everywhere the *Elohim* enacted astonishment as if it were merely gratuitous – the spilth or detritus of their self-contemplations. But now each of these nonchalant theurgies appeared ominous to Linden, suggestive of peril and surquedry. The bells chimed in her head. Though she fought to hold them, they meant nothing.

For one blade-sharp moment, she felt as she had felt when she had first entered Revelstone: trapped in the coercion of Santonin's power, riven of every reason which had ever given shape or will to her life. Here the compulsion was more subtle; but it was as cloying as attar, and it covered everything with its pall. If the *Elohim* did not choose to release her, she would never leave *Elemesnedene*.

Yet surely this was not Revelstone, and the *Elohim* had nothing in common with Ravers, for Daphin's smile conveyed no hint of underlying mendacity, and her eyes were the colour of new leaves in springtime. And as she passed, the wonderments put aside their self-absorption to join her and the Sun-Sage. Melting, swirling, condensing into human form, they arrayed themselves behind her and moved in silence and chiming towards the conclave of the *Elohimfest*. Apparelled in cymars and mantles, in sendaline and jaconet and organdy like the cortege of a celebration, they followed Linden as if to do her honour. Once again, she felt the enchantment of the *clachan* exercising itself upon her, wooing her from her distrust.

But as the *Elohim* advanced with her, the land behind them lost all its features, became a vaguely undulating emptiness under a moonstone sky. In its own way, *Elemesnedene* without the activity of the *Elohim* was as barren and sterile as a desert.

Ahead lay the only landmark Linden had seen in the whole of the *clachan* – a broad ring of dead elms. They stood fingering the opalescent air with their boughs like stricken sentinels, encompassing a place which had slain them eons ago. Her senses were able to discern the natural texture of their wood, the sapless desiccation in their hearts, the black and immemorial death of their upraised limbs. But she did not understand why natural trees could not endure in the habitation of *Elohim*.

As she neared them, escorted by Daphin and Morninglight and a bright procession of *Elohim*, she saw that they ringed a broad low bare hill which shone with accentuated light like an eftmound. Somehow, the hill appeared to be the source of all the illumination in *Elemesnedene*. Or perhaps this effect was caused by the way the sky lowered over the eftmound so that the hill and the sky formed a hub around which the dead elms stood in frozen revolution. Passing between the trees, Linden felt that she was entering the core of the epiphany.

More *Elohim* were arriving from all sides. They flowed forward in their lambency like images of everything that made the Earth lovely; and for a moment Linden's throat tightened at the sight. She could not reconcile the conflicts these folk aroused in her, did not know where the truth lay. But for that moment she felt sure she would never again meet any people so capable of beauty.

Then her attention shifted as her companions began to ascend the eftmound from various directions around the ring. Honninscrave strode there with his head high and his face aglow as if he had revisited one of his most precious memories. And from the other side came Pitchwife. When he saw the First approaching near him, he greeted her with a shout of love that brought tears to Linden's eyes, making everything pure for an instant.

Blinking away the blur, she espied Seadreamer's tall form rising beyond the crest of the hill. Like the First, he did not appear to share Honninscrave's joy. Her countenance was dour and self-contained, as if in her examination she had won a stern victory. But his visage wore a look of active pain like a recognition of peril which his muteness would not permit him to explain.

Alarmed by the implications in his eyes, Linden quickly scanned the eftmound, hunting for a glimpse of Covenant. For a moment, he was nowhere to be seen. But then he came around the hill towards her.

He moved as if all his muscles were taut and fraying: his emanations were shrill with tension. In some way, his examination had proved costly to him. Yet the sight of him, white-knuckled and rigid though he was, gave Linden an infusion of relief. Now she was no longer alone.

He approached her stiffly. His eyes were as sharp and affronted as shards of mica. Chant was a few paces behind him, smirking like a toad. As Covenant brought his raw emotions close to her, her relief changed to dismay and ire. She wanted to shout at Chant, What have you done to him?

Covenant stopped in front of her. His shoulders hunched. In a tight voice, he asked, 'You all right?'

She shrugged away the surface of his question. What did Chant do to you? She ached to put her arms around him, but did not know how. She never knew how to help him. Grimly, she gripped herself, searched for a way to warn him of what she had learned. She could not put together any words that sounded innocent enough, so she assumed a tone of deliberate nonchalance and took the risk of saying, 'I wish I could talk to you about it. Cail had a good point.'

'I got that impression.' His voice was harsh. Since their first meeting with the *Elohim*, he had been on the verge of violence. Now he sounded rife with potential eruptions. 'Chant here tried to talk me into giving him my ring.'

Linden gaped. Her encounter with Daphin had not prepared her for the possibility that her companions might be examined more roughly.

'He had a lot to say on the subject,' Covenant went on. Behind his asperity, he was savage with distress. 'These *Elohim* consider themselves the centre of the Earth. According to him, everything important happens here. The rest of the world is like a shadow cast by *Elemesnedene*. Foul and the Sunbane are just symptoms. The real disease is something else – he didn't bother to say exactly what. Something about a darkness threatening the heart of the Earth. He wants my ring. He wants the wild magic. So he can attack the disease.'

Linden started to protest. He doesn't need it. He's *Earthpower*. But she was unsure of what she could afford to reveal.

'When I said no, he told me it doesn't matter.' Chant's mein wore an imperious confirmation. 'According to him, I don't count. I'm

546

already defeated.' Covenant bit out the words, chewing their fundamental gall. 'Anything that happens to me is all right.'

Linden winced for him. Trying to tell him that she understood,
she said, 'Now you know how I feel every day.'

But her attempt misfired. His brows knotted. His eyes were as
poignant as splinters. 'I don't need to be reminded.' The Giants had
gathered at his back. They stood listening with incomprehension in
their faces. But he was caught up in bitterness and seemed unaware
of the hurt he flung at Linden. 'Why do you think you're here?
Everybody expects me to fail.'

'I don't!' she snapped back at him, suddenly uncaring that she
might hurt him in return. 'That isn't what I meant.'

Her vehemence stopped him. He faced her, gaunt with memory
and fear. When he spoke again, he had regained some measure of
self-command. 'I'm sorry. I'm not doing very well here. I don't like
being this dangerous.'

She accepted his apology with a wooden nod. What else could she
do? Behind it, his purpose had hardened to the texture of adamantine. But she did not know what that purpose was. How far did he
intend to go?

Holding himself like stone, he turned from her to the Giants.
Brusquely, he acknowledged them. The First could not conceal the
worry in her eyes. Pitchwife emitted a bright empathy that told
nothing of his own examination; but Honninscrave appeared perplexed, unable to reconcile Covenant's report and Linden's attitude
with his own experiences. Once again, Linden wondered what kind
of bargain it was he so clearly hoped to make.

More *Elohim* continued to arrive, so many now that they filled the
inner curve of the elm-ring and spread halfway up the slopes of the
eftmound. Their movements made a murmurous rustling, but they
passed among each other without speaking. They were as composed
and contained here as they had been in their rites of self-contempla-
tion. Only the bells conveyed any sense of communication. Frowning, she strove once more to catch the gist of the chiming. But it
remained alien and unreachable, like a foreign tongue that was
familiar in sound but not in meaning.

Then her attention was arrested by the approach of another
Elohim. When he first entered the ring, she did not notice him.
Neither his clean white flesh nor his creamy robe distinguished him
from the gracile throng. But as he drew nearer – walking with an aim-
less aspect around the hill – he attracted her eyes like a lodestone.
The sight of him sent a shiver down her spine. He was the first
Elohim she had seen who chose to wear an appearance of misery.

He had taken a form which looked like it had been worn and
whetted by hardship. His limbs were lean, exposing the interplay of
the muscles; his skin had the pale tautness of scar-tissue; his hair

hung to his shoulders in a sweep of unkempt silver. His brows, his cheeks, the corners of his eyes, all were cut with the toolwork of difficulty and trepidation. Around the vague yellow of his eyes, his sockets were as dark as old rue. And he moved with the stiffness of a man who had just been cudgelled.

He did not accost the company, but rather went on his way among the *Elohim*, as heedless of them as they were of him. Staring after him, Linden abruptly risked another question.

'Who was *that*?' she asked Daphin.

Without a glance at either the man or Linden, Daphin replied, 'He is Findail the Appointed.'

'Appointed,' Linden pursued. 'What does that mean?'

Her companions listened intently. Though they lacked her sight, they had not failed to notice Findail. Among so many elegant *Elohim*, he wore his pains like the marks of torment.

'Sun-Sage,' said Daphin lightly, 'he bears a grievous burden. He has been Appointed to meet the cost of our wisdom.

'We are a people united by our vision. I have spoken of this. The truths which Morninglight finds within himself, I also contain. In this way we are made strong and sure. But in such strength and surety there is also hazard. A truth which one sees may perchance pass unseen by others. We do not blithely acknowledge such failure, for how may one among us say to another, "My truth is greater than yours"? And there are none in all the world to gainsay us. But it is our wisdom to be cautious.

'Therefore whensoever there is a need upon the Earth which requires us, one is Appointed to be our wisdom. According to the need, his purpose varies. In one age, the Appointed may deny our unity, challenging us to seek more deeply for the truth. In another, he may be named to fulfil that unity.' For an instant, her tone took on a more ominous colour. 'In all ages, he pays the price of doubt. Findail will hazard his life against the Earth's doom.'

Doom? The idea gave Linden a pang. How? Was Findail like Covenant, then – accepting the cost for an entire people? What cost? What had the *Elohim* seen for which they felt responsible – and yet were unwilling to explain?

What did they know of the Despiser? Was he Chant's shadow?

Her gaze continued to follow Findail. But while she grappled with her confusion, a change came over the eftmound. All the *Elohim* stopped moving; and Daphin gave a smile of anticipation. 'Ah, Sun-Sage,' she breathed. 'Infelice comes. Now begins the *Elohimfest*.'

Infelice? Linden asked mutely. But the bells gave no answer.

The *Elohim* had turned towards her left. When she looked in that direction, she saw a figure of light approaching from beyond the elms. It cast the tree limbs into black relief. With the grave and stately stride of a thurifer, the figure entered the ring, passed among the people to the crest of the hill. There she halted and faced the company of the quest.

She was a tall woman, and her loveliness was as lucent as gemfire. Her hair shone. Her supple form shed gleams like a sea in moonlight. Her raiment was woven of diamonds, adorned with rubies. A penumbra of glory outlined her against the trees and the sky. She was Infelice, and she stood atop the eftmound like the crown of every wonder in *Elemesnedene*.

Her sovereign eyes passed over the company, came to Linden, met and held her stare. Under that gaze, Linden's knees grew weak. She felt a yearning to abase herself before this regal figure. Surely humility was the only just response to such a woman. Honninscrave was already on his knees, and the other Giants were following his example.

But Covenant remained upright, an icon graven of hard bone and intransigence. And none of the *Elohim* had given Infelice any obeisance except their rapt silence. Only the music of the bells sounded like worship. Linden locked her joints and strove to hold her own against the grandeur of that woman's gaze.

Then Infelice looked away; and Linden almost sagged with relief. Raising her arms, Infelice addressed her people in a voice like the ringing of light crystal. 'I am come. Let us begin.'

Without warning or preparation, the *Elohimfest* commenced.

The sky darkened as if an inexplicable nightfall had come to *Elemesnedene*, exposing a firmament empty of stars. But the *Elohim* took light from Infelice. In the new dusk, they were wrapped around the eftmound like a mantle, multi-coloured and alive. And their gleaming aspired to the outreach of Infelice's arms. Viridian and crimson lights, emerald and essential white intensified like a spray of coruscation, mounting towards conflagration. A rainbow of fires rose up the hill. And as they grew stronger, the wind began to blow.

It tugged at Linden's shirt, ran through her hair like the chill fingers of a ghost. She clutched at Covenant for support; but somehow she lost him. She was alone in the emblazoned gloaming and the wind. It piled against her until she staggered. The darkness increased as the lights grew brighter. She could not locate the Giants, could not touch any of the *Elohim*. All the material substance of *Elemesnedene* had become wind, and the wind cycled around the eftmound as if Infelice had invoked it, giving it birth by the simple words of her summoning.

Linden staggered again, fell; but the ground was blown out from under her. Above her, globes of *Elohim*-fire had taken to the air. They were gyring upward like the sparks of a blaze in the heart of the Earth, wind-borne into the heavens. The starless sky became a bourne of bedizenings. And Linden went with them, tumbling helplessly along the wind.

But as she rose, her awkward unfiery flesh began to soar. Below her, the hill lay like a pit of midnight at the bottom of the incandescent gyre. She left it behind, sailed up the bright spin of the sparks. Fires rang on all sides of her like transmuted bells. And still she was larked skyward by the whirlwind.

Then suddenly the night seemed to become true night, and the wind lifted her towards a heaven bedecked with stars. In the light of the fires, she saw herself and the *Elohim* spring like a waterspout from the travertine fountain and cycle upward. The *maidan* spread out below her in the dark, then faded as she went higher. Woodenwold closed around the lea; the mountains encircled Woodenwold. Still she rose in the gyre, rushing impossibly towards the stars.

She was not breathing, could not remember breath. She had been torn out of herself by awe – a piece of darkness flying in the company of dazzles. The horizons of the unlit Earth shrank as she arced forever towards the stars. An umbilicus of conflagration ascended from the absolute centre of the globe like the ongoing gyre of eternity.

And then there was nothing left of herself to which she could cling. She was an unenlightened mote among perfect jewels, and the jewels were stars, and the abyss around her and within her was fathomless and incomprehensible – a void cold as dying, empty as death. She did not exist amid the magnificence of the heavens. Their lonely and stunning beauty exalted and numbed her soul. She felt ecstasy and destruction as if they were the last thoughts she would ever have; and when she lost her balance, stumbled to fall face down on the earth of the eftmound, she was weeping with a grief that had no name.

But slowly the hard fact of the ground penetrated her, and her outcry turned to quiet tears of loss and relief and awe.

Covenant groaned nearby. She saw him through a smear of weakness. He was on his hands and knees, clenched rigid against the heavens. His eyes were haunted by a doom of stars.

'Bastards,' he panted. 'Are you trying to break my heart?'

Linden tried to reach out to him. But she could not move.

The bells were speaking in her mind. As the *Elohim* slowly returned to human form around the eftmound, restoring light to the sky, their silent language attained a moment of clarity.

One string of bells said:

– Does he truly conceive that such is our intent?

Another answered:

– Is it not?

Then they relapsed into the metal and crystal and wood of their distinctive tones – implying everything, denoting nothing.

She shook her head, fought to recapture that tongue. But when she had blinked the confusion out of her eyes, she found Findail the

Appointed standing in front of her.

Stiffly, he bent to her, helped her to her feet. His visage was a hatchment of rue and strain. 'Sun-Sage.' His voice sounded dull with disuse. 'It is our intent to serve the life of the Earth as best we may. That life is also ours.'

But she was still fumbling inwardly. His words seemed to have no content; and her thoughts frayed away from them, went in another direction. His bruised yellow eyes were the first orbs she had seen in *Elemesnedene* that appeared honest. Her throat was sore with the grief of stars. She could not speak above a raw whisper. 'Why do you want to hurt him?'

His gaze did not waver. But his hands were trembling. He said faintly, so that no one else could hear him, 'We desire no hurt to him. We desire only to prevent the hurt which he will otherwise commit.' Then he turned away as if he could not endure the other things he wanted to say.

The four Giants were climbing to their feet near Linden. They wore stunned expressions, buffeted by vision. Seadreamer helped Covenant erect. The *Elohim* were gathering again about the slopes. She had understood the bells once more.

That such is our intent? She needed to talk to Covenant and the Giants, needed their reaction to what she had heard. *Is it not?* What harm did the *Elohim* think they could prevent by demeaning or wounding Covenant? And why were they divided about it? What made the difference between Daphin and Chant?

But Infelice stood waiting atop the eftmound. She wore her gleamings like a cocoon of chiaroscuro from which she might emerge at any moment to astonish the guests of the *Elohimfest* – a figure not to be denied. Firmly, she caught Linden's gaze and did not release it.

'Sun-Sage.' Infelice spoke like the light of her raiment. 'The *Elohimfest* has begun. What has transpired is an utterance of our being. You will be wise to hold it in your heart and seek to comprehend it. But it is past, and before us stand the purposes which have brought you among us. Come.' She beckoned gracefully. 'Let us speak of these matters.'

Linden obeyed as if Infelice's gesture had bereft her of volition. But she was immediately relieved to see that her companions did not mean to leave her alone. Covenant placed himself at her side. The Giants shifted forward behind her. Together, they passed among the *Elohim* and ascended the slope.

Near the crown of the eftmound, they stopped. Infelice's height, and the extra elevation of her position, placed her eyes on a level with Honninscrave's and Seadreamer's; but she kept her attention chiefly on Linden. Linden felt naked under that eldritch gaze; but she clung to her resolve and remained erect.

'Sun-Sage,' began Infelice, 'the Giant Grimmand Honninscrave has surely shared with you his knowledge of *Elemesnedene*. Thus it is known to you that the bestowal of our gifts is not done freely. We possess much which is greatly perilous, not to be given without care. And knowledge or power which is not truly purchased swiftly tarnishes. If it does not turn against the hand that holds it, it loses all value whatsoever. And lastly we have little cause to relish intrusion from the outskirts of the Earth. Here we have no need of them. Therefore it is our wont to exact a price for that which is besought from us – and to refuse the seeking if the seeker can meet no price which pleases us.

'But you are the Sun-Sage,' she went on, 'and the urgency of your quest is plain. Therefore from you and your companions I will require no feoffment. If your needs lie within our reach, we will meet them without price.'

Without – ? Linden stared up at Infelice. The belling intensified in her mind, tangling her thoughts. All the *Elohim* seemed to be concentrating towards her and Infelice.

'You may speak.' Infelice's tone conveyed only the barest suggestion of impatience.

Linden groaned to herself. Dear Christ. She turned to her companions, groping for inspiration. She should have known what to say, should have been prepared for this. But she had been braced for threats, not gifts. Infelice's offer and the bells confused everything.

The eagerness in Honninscrave's face stopped her. All his doubt had vanished. At once, she seized the opportunity. She needed a little time to take hold of herself. Without looking at Infelice, she said as flatly as she could, 'I'm a stranger here. Let Honninscrave speak first.'

Like the passing of a great weight, she felt Infelice's gaze shift to the Master. 'Speak, then, Grimmand Honninscrave,' the *Elohim* said in a timbre of graciousness.

At his side, the First stiffened as if she were unable to believe that he was truly in no danger. But she could not refuse him her nod of permission. Pitchwife watched the Master with anticipation. Seadreamer's eyes were shrouded, as if some inward vision muffled his perception of his brother.

Hope echoed like stars from under Honninscrave's massive brows as he stepped forward. 'You honour me,' he said, and his voice was husky. 'My desire is not for myself. It is for Cable Seadreamer my brother.'

At that, Seadreamer's attention leaped outward.

'Surely his plight is plain to you,' Honninscrave went on. 'The Earth-Sight torments him, and that anguish has riven him of his voice. Yet it is the Earth-Sight which pilots our Search, to oppose a great evil in the Earth. The gift I ask is the gift of his voice, so that

552

he may better guide us – and so that some easement may be accorded to his pain.'

Abruptly, he stopped, visibly restraining himself from supplication. His pulse laboured in the clenched muscles of his neck as he forced his Giantish passion to silence while Infelice looked toward Seadreamer.

Seadreamer replied with an expression of helpless and unexpected yearning. His oaken form was poignant with the acuteness of his desire for words, for some way to relieve the extravagant aggrievement of the Earth-Sight – or of the examination he had been given. He looked like a man who had glimpsed a saving light in the pall of his doom.

But Infelice took only a moment to consider him. Then she addressed Honninscrave again. She sounded faintly uninterested as she said, 'Surely the voice of your brother may be restored. But you know not what you ask. His muteness arises from this Earth-Sight as day arises from the sun. To grant the gift you ask, we must perforce blind the eyes of his vision. That we will not do. We would not slay him at your request. Neither will we do him this wrong.'

Honninscrave's eyes flinched wide. Protests gathered in him, desire and dismay fighting for utterance. But Infelice said, 'I have spoken,' with such finality that he staggered.

The brief light turned to ashes in Seadreamer's face. He caught at his brother's shoulder for support. But Honninscrave did not respond. He was a Giant. He seemed unable to comprehend how a hope he had been nurturing with such determination could be denied in so few words. He made no effort to conceal the grief which knuckled his features.

At the sight, Linden trembled in sudden anger. Apparently the graciousness of the *Elohim* masked an unpity like arrogance. She did not believe Infelice. These people were Earthpower incarnate. How could they be unable – ? No. They were not unable. They were unwilling.

Now she did not hesitate to face Infelice. Covenant tried to say something to her. She ignored him. Glaring upward, she spat out the gift she had meant to request.

'If that's true, then you're probably going to tell me you can't do anything about Covenant's venom.'

At her back, she felt her companions freeze in surprise and apprehension – taken aback by her unexpected demand, disturbed by her frank ire. But she ignored that as well, focused her shivering against Infelice's gaze.

'I don't ask you to do anything about his leprosy. That has too many implications. But the venom! It's killing him. It's making him dangerous to himself and everyone around him. It's probably the worst thing Foul has ever done to him. Are you going to tell me you can't do anything about *that*?'

The bells rang as if they were offended or concerned. One of them said:

– She transgresses incondignly upon our welcome.

Another replied:

– With good reason. Our welcome has not been kindly.

But a third said:

– Our path is too straight for kindness. He must not be permitted to destroy the Earth.

But Linden did not listen to them. All her wrath was fixed on Infelice, waiting for the tall woman to meet or deny her implicit accusation.

'Sun-Sage.' Infelice's tone had hardened like a warning. 'I see this venom of which you speak. It is plain in him – as is the wrong which you name leprosy. But we have no unction for this hurt. It is power-apt for good or ill – and too deeply entwined in his being for any disentanglement. Would you have us rip out the roots of his life? Power is life, and for him its roots are venom and leprosy. The price of such aid would be the loss of all power forever.'

Linden confronted Infelice. Rage set all her old abhorrence of futility afire. She could not endure to be rendered so useless. Behind her, Covenant was repeating her name, trying to distract her, warn or restrain her. But she had had enough of subterfuge and defalcation. The ready violence which lurked beneath the surface of *Elemesnedene* coursed through her.

'All right?' she flamed, daring Infelice to respond in kind, though she knew the *Elohim* had the might to snuff her like a candle. 'Forget it. You can't do anything about the venom.' A sneer twisted her mouth. 'You can't give Seadreamer back his voice. All right. If you say so. Here's something you goddamn well *can* do.'

'Chosen!' cautioned the First. But Linden did not stop.

'You can fight the Despiser for us.'

Her demand stunned the Giants into silence. Covenant swore softly as if he had never conceived of such a request. But her moiling passion would not let her halt.

Infelice had not moved. She, too, seemed taken aback.

'You sit here in your *clachan*,' Linden went on, choosing words like items of accusation, 'letting time go by as if no evil or danger in all the world has any claim on your hieratic self-contemplation, when you could be *doing* something! You're Earthpower! You're all *made* out of Earthpower. You could stop the Sunbane – restore the Law – defeat Lord Foul – just by making the *effort*!

'Look at you!' she insisted. 'You stand up there so you can be sure of looking down on us. And maybe you've got the right. Maybe Earthpower incarnate is so powerful we just naturally seem puny and pointless to you. But we're trying!' Honninscrave and Seadreamer had been hurt. Covenant had been denied. The whole quest was being betrayed. She flung out her sentences like jerrids, trying to strike some point of vulnerability or conscience in Infelice. 'Foul is trying to destroy the Land. And if he succeeds, he won't stop there. He wants the whole Earth. Right now, his only enemies are puny, pointless mortals like us. In the name of simple *shame* if nothing else, you should be willing to stop him!'

As she ran out of words, lurched into silence, voices rose around the eftmound – expostulations of anger, concern, displeasure. Among them, Chant's shout stood out stridently. 'Infelice, this is intolerable!'

'No!' Infelice shot back. Her denial stopped the protest of the *Elohim*. 'She is the Sun-Sage, and I will tolerate her!'

This unexpected response cut the ground from under Linden. She wavered inwardly; surprise daunted her ire. The constant adumbration of the bells weakened her. She was barely able to hold Infelice's gaze as the tall *Elohim* spoke.

'Sun-Sage,' she said with a note like sorrow or regret in her voice, 'this thing which you name Earthpower is our Würd.' Like Daphin, she blurred the sound so that it could have been either *Wyrd* or *Word*. 'You believe it to be a thing of suzerain might. In sooth, your belief is just. But have you come so far across the Earth without comprehending the helplessness of power? We are what we are – and what we are not, we can never become. He whom you name the Despiser is a being of another kind entirely. We are effectless against him. That is our Würd.

'And also,' she added as an afterthought, '*Elemesnedene* is our centre, as it is the centre of the Earth. Beyond its bounds we do not care to go.'

Linden wanted to cry out, You're lying! The protest was hot in her, burning to be shouted. But Covenant had come to her side. His halfhand gripped her shoulder like talons, digging inward as if to control her physically.

'She's telling the truth.' He spoke to her; but he was facing Infelice as if at last he had found the path of his purpose. Linden felt from him an anger to match her own – an anger that made him as rigid as bone. 'Earthpower is not the answer to Despite. Or Kevin would never have been driven to the Ritual of Desecration. He was a master of Law and Earthpower, but it wasn't what he needed. He couldn't save the Land that way.

'That's why the Land needs us. Because of the wild magic. It comes from outside the Arch of Time. Like Foul. It can do things Earthpower can't.'

'Then it comes to this.' Honninscrave lifted his voice over Covenant's. The frank loss in his tone gave him a dignity to equal his stature; and he spoke as if he were passing judgment on all the *Elohim*. 'In all parts of the Earth are told the legends of *Elemesnedene*. The *Elohim* are bespoken as a people of sovereign faery puissance and wonder, the highest and most treasurable of all wonders. Among the Giants these tales are told gladly and often, and those who have been granted the fortune of a welcome here account themselves blessed.

'But we have not been given the welcome of which the world speaks with such yearning. Nor have we been granted the gifts which the world needs for its endurance. Rather, we have been reft of the *Haruchai* our companions and demeaned in ourselves. And we have been misled in our asking of gifts. You offer giving with no feoffment, but it is no boon, for it places refusal beyond appeal. *Elemesnedene* is sadly altered, and I have no wish to carry this tale to the world.'

Linden listened to him urgently. Covenant's attitude appalled her. Did he think that Chant's desire for his ring was gratuitous? Was he deaf to the bells?

One of them was saying:

– He speaks truly. We are altered from what we were.

A darker answer knelled:

– No. It is only that these mortals are more arrogant than any other.

But the first replied:

– No. It is we who are more arrogant. In time past, would we not have taken this cost upon ourselves? Yet now we require the price of him, that we will be spared it.

At once, a third chime interposed:

– You forget that he himself is the peril. We have chosen the only path which offers hope to him as well as to the Earth. The price may yet befall the Appointed.

But still the *Elohimfest* went on as if there were no bells. Stiffly, Infelice said, 'Grimmand Honninscrave, you have spoken freely. Now be silent.' However, his dignity was beyond the reach of her reproof. Directing her gaze at Linden, she asked, 'Are you content?'

'*Content?*' Linden began. 'Are you out of – ?'

Covenant's grip stopped her. His fingers gouged her shoulder, demanding restraint. Before she could fight free of him, shout his folly into his face, he said to Infelice, 'No. All this is secondary. It's not why we're here.' He sounded like he had found another way to sacrifice himself.

'Continue, ring-wielder,' said Infelice evenly. The light in her hair and apparel seemed ready for anything he might say.

'It's true that Earthpower is not the answer to Despite.' He spoke as incisively as ice. 'But the Sunbane is another matter. That's a

556

question of Earthpower. If it isn't stopped, it's going to eat the heart out of the Earth.'

He paused. Calmly, Infelice waited for him.

And Linden also waited. Her distrust of the *Elohim* converged with an innominate dread. She was intuitively afraid of Covenant's intent.

'I want to make a new Staff of Law.' His voice was fraught with risks. 'A way to fight back. That's why we're here. We need to find the One Tree.' Slowly, he unclenched Linden's shoulder, released her and stepped aside as if to detach his peril from her. 'I want you to tell us where it is.'

At once, the bells rang insistently. One of them struck out:

— Infelice, do not. Our hope will be lost.

The crystal answer came clearly from her:

— It is understood and agreed. I will not.

But her eyes gave no hint of her other conversations. They met Covenant squarely, almost with relish. 'Ring-wielder,' she said carefully, 'you have no need of that knowledge. It has already been placed in your mind.'

With matching care, matching readiness, he replied, 'That's true. Caer-Caveral gave it to me. He said, "The knowledge is within you, though you cannot see it. But when the time has come, you will find the means to unlock my gift." But I don't know how to get at it.'

The chiming grew hushed, like bated breath. But Linden had caught the import of the bells. This was the moment for which they had been waiting.

In a rush of comprehension, she tried to fling herself at Covenant. Words too swift for utterance cried through her: They already know where the Tree is, this is what they want, don't you understand, *Foul got here ahead of us*! But her movements were too slow, clogged by mortality. Her heart seemed frozen between beats; no breath expanded her lungs. She had barely turned towards him when he spoke as if he knew he was committing himself to disaster.

'I want you to unlock the knowledge for me. I want you to open my mind.'

At the top of the eftmound, Infelice smiled.

9

THE GIFT OF THE FORESTAL

The next moment, Linden reached Covenant so hard that he staggered several steps down the slope. Catching hold of his shirt, she jerked at him with all her strength, 'Don't do it!'

He fought to regain his balance. His eyes burned like precursers of wild magic. 'What's the matter with you?' he barked. 'We have to know where it is.'

'Not that way!' She did not have enough strength, could not find enough force for her voice or her muscles. She wanted to coerce him physically; but even her passion was not enough. 'You don't have to do that! They can just *tell* you! They already know where it is.'

Roughly, he took hold of her wrists, wrenched himself out of her grip. The rising of venom and power in him made his grasp irrefusable. He held her wrists together near the cut in his shirt, and she could not break free. 'I believe you.' His glare was extreme. 'These people probably know everything. But they aren't going to tell us. What do you want me to do? Beg until they change their minds?'

'Covenant.' She raged and pleaded simultaneously. 'I can hear what they're saying to each other.' The words tumbled out of her. 'They've got some secret purpose. Foul got here ahead of us. Don't let them possess you!'

That pierced him. He did not release her wrists; but his grip loosened as he jerked up his head to look at Infelice.

'Is this true?'

Infelice did not appear to be offended. Repeatedly, she tolerated Linden. 'The Sun-Sage suggests that the Despiser has come upon us and bent us to his own ends. That is untrue. But that we have also our own purpose in this matter – that is true.'

'Then,' he gritted, 'tell me where the One Tree is.'

'It is not our custom to grant unnecessary gifts.' Her tone refused all contradiction, all suasion. 'For reasons which appear good to us, we have made our choice. We are the *Elohim* and our choices lie beyond your judgment. You have asked me to unlock the knowledge occulted within you. That gift I am willing to give – that and no other. You may accept or decline, according to the dictates of your doubt.

'If you desire another answer, seek it elsewhere. Inquire of the Sun-Sage why she does not enter your mind to gain this knowledge. The way is open to her.'

Linden recoiled. Enter – ? Memories of Covenant's last relapse flared through her. Suppressed dark hunger leaped up in her. Surely to save him from what the *Elohim* intended – ! But she had nearly cost him his life. Peril came crowding around her. It flushed like shame across her skin. The contradiction threatened to trap her. This was why she had been chosen, why Gibbon had touched her. Twisting out of Covenant's slackened grasp, she confronted Infelice and spat out the only answer she had – the only reply which enabled her to hold back the hunger.

'Possession is evil.'

Was it true after all that the *Elohim* were evil?

Infelice cocked an eyebrow in disdain, but did not reply.

'Linden.' Covenant's voice was gripped like a bit between his teeth. His hands reached out to her, turned her to face him again. 'I don't care whether we can trust them or not. We have *got* to know where the One Tree is. If they have something else in mind – ' He grimaced acidly. 'They think I don't count. How much of that do you think I can stand? After what I've been through?' His tone said clearly that he could not stand it at all. 'I saved the Land once, and I'll do it again. They are not going to take that away from me.'

As she recognized his emotions, she went numb inside. Too much of his anger was directed at her – at the idea that she was the Sun-Sage, that he was to be blamed for affirming himself. The bells were within her range now, but she hardly listened to them. It was happening again, everything was happening again, there was nothing she could do, it would always happen. She was as useless to him as she had been to either of her parents. And she was going to lose him. She could not even say to him, I don't have the power. Don't you understand that the reason I won't go into you is to protect *you*? Instead, she let the frozen place in her heart speak.

'You're just doing this because you feel insulted. It's like your leprosy. You think you can get even by sacrificing yourself. The universal victim.' *You never loved me anyway.* 'It's the only way you know how to live.'

She saw that she had hurt him – and that the pain made no difference. The more she reviled him, the more adamant he became. The hot mute glare with which he answered her rendered him untouchable. In his own terms, he had no choice. How could he rise above his plight, except by meeting it squarely and risking himself against it? When he turned his back on her to accept Infelice's offer, she did not try to stop him. Her numbness might as well have been grief.

'Covenant Giantfriend,' the First demanded. 'Be wary of what you do. I have given the Search into your hands. It must not be lost.'

He ignored her. Facing Infelice, he muttered in a brittle voice, 'I'm ready. Let's get on with it.'

A bell rang across the eftmound – a clamour of appeal or protest. Now Linden was able to identify its source. It came from Findail.

– Infelice, consider! It is *my* life you hazard. If this path fails, I must bear the cost. Is there no other way?

And once again Infelice surprised Linden. 'Sun-Sage,' the *Elohim* said as if she were denying herself, 'what is your word? In your name, I will refuse him if you wish it.' Covenant hissed like a curse; but Infelice was not done discounting him. She went on inflexibly, 'However, the onus will be upon your head. You must make promise that you will take his ring from him ere he brings the Earth to ruin – that you will make ring-wielder and Sun-Sage one in yourself.' Covenant radiated a desperate outrage which Infelice did not deign to notice. 'If you will not bind yourself to that promise, I must meet his request.'

Stiffly, Findail chimed;

– Infelice, I thank you.

But Linden had no way of knowing what Findail meant. She was reeling inwardly at the import of Infelice's proposal. This was a more insidious temptation than possession: it offered her power without exposing her to the threat of darkness. To accept responsibility for him? No, more than that: to accept responsibility for the whole quest, for the survival of the Earth and the defeat of Lord Foul. Here was her chance to protect Covenant from himself – to spare him in the same way he had so often striven to spare her.

But then she saw the hidden snare. If she accepted, the quest would have no way to find the One Tree. Unless she did what she had just refused to do – unless she violated him to pry out Caer-Caveral's secret knowledge. Everything came back to that. The strength of her buried yearning for that kind of power made her feel sick. But she had already rejected it, had spent her life rejecting it.

She shook her head. Dully, she said, 'I can't tell him what to do' – and tried to believe that she was affirming something, asserting herself and him against temptation. But every word she spoke sounded like another denial. The thought of his peril wrung her heart. 'Let him make his own decisions.'

Then she had to wrap her arms around her chest to protect herself against the force of Covenant's relief, Findail's clanging dismay, the apprehension of her friends – and against Infelice's eager radiance.

'Come,' the diamond-clad *Elohim* said at once. 'Let us begin.'

And her inner voice added:

– Let him be taken by the silence, as we have proposed.

Involuntarily, Linden turned, saw Covenant and Infelice focused on each other as if they were transfixed. She wore her gleaming like the outward sign of a cunning victory. And he stood with his shoulders squared and his head raised, braced on the crux of his circinate doom. If he had paused to smile, Linden would have screamed.

With a slow flourish of her raiment like a billowing of jewels, Infelice descended from the hillcrest. Her power became her as if she had been born for it. Flowing like the grateful breeze of evening, she moved to stand before Covenant.

When she placed her hand on his forehead, the silent air of the eftmound was shredded with anguish.

A shriek as shrill as fangs clawed through his chest. He plunged to his knees. Every muscle in his face and neck knotted. His hands leaped at his temples as if his skull were being torn apart. Convulsions made him pummel the sides of his head helplessly.

Almost as one, Linden and the Giants surged towards him.

Before they could reach him, his outcry became a scream of wild magic. White flame blasted in all directions. Infelice recoiled. The rock of the eftmound reeled. Linden and Pitchwife fell. Scores of the *Elohim* took other shapes to protect themselves. The First snatched out her glaive as if her balance depended on it. She was shouting furiously at Infelice; but amid the roar of Covenant's power her voice made no sound.

Struggling to her hands and knees, Linden saw a sight that seemed to freeze the blood in her veins.

This conflagration was like no other she had ever witnessed. It did not come from his ring, from his halffist pounding at his temple. It sprang straight from his forehead as if his brain had erupted in argence.

At first, the blaze spewed and flailed on every hand, scourging mad pain across the hill. But then the air became a tumult of bells, ringing in invocation, shaping the purpose of the *Elohim*; and the fire began to change. Slowly, it altered to a hot shining, as hard white as all agony fused together.

Instinctively, Linden shielded her eyes. Such brilliance should have blinded her. But it did not. Though it beat against her face as if she were staring into the furnace of the sun, it remained bearable.

And within its clear core, visions were born.

One after another, they emerged through the radiance.

A young girl, a child in a blue dress, perhaps four or five years old, stood with her back pressed against the black trunk of a tree. Though she made no sound, she was wailing in unmasked terror at a timber-rattler near her bare legs.

Then the snake was gone, leaving two fatal red marks on the pale flesh of the child's shin.

Covenant staggered into the vision. He looked battered and abused from head to foot. Blood ran from an untended cut on his lips, from his forehead. He took the girl into his arms, tried to comfort her. They spoke to each other, but the vision was mute. Fumbling, he produced a penknife, opened it. With the lace of one of his boots, he made a tourniquet. Then he steadied the girl in his embrace, poised his knife over her violated shin.

With the movement of the knife, the vision changed. First one, then the other, blades slashed his wrists, drawing lines of death. Blood ran. He knelt in a pool of passion while Riders swung their *rukhs* and drove him helpless and vermeil into the soothtell.

A chaos of images followed. Linden saw the Land sprawling broken under the Sunbane. From the deluge of the sun of rain, the stricken ground merged into a desert, then the desert was leeched into the red suppuration of the sun of pestilence. At the same time, all these things were happening to Joan's flesh as she lay possessed and bound on her bed in Covenant's house. She was racked through every form of disease until Linden nearly went mad at the sight.

The vision quivered with rage and revulsion, and wild magic appeared. Acute incandescence flamed like one white torch among the blood-lit *rukhs*. It bent itself to his slashed wrists, staunching the flow, sealing the wounds. Then he rose to his feet, borne erect by fury and conflagration, and his power went reaving among the Riders, slaying them like sheaves.

But as the white flame mounted towards concussion, the essence of its light changed, softened. Covenant stood on the surface of a lake, and its waters burned in a gyre before him, lifting the *krill* into his hands. The lake upheld him like a benison, changing his savagery to the light of hope; for there was Earthpower yet within the Land, and this one lake if no other still sustained itself against the Sunbane.

Again the fire changed. Now it streamed away in rills of phosphorescence from the tall figure of a man. He was robed all in whitest sendaline. In his hand, he held a gnarled tree-limb as a staff. He bore himself with dignity and strength; but behind its grave devotion, his face had neither eyes nor eyesockets.

As he addressed Covenant, other figures appeared. A blue-robed man with a crooked smile and serene eyes. A woman similarly clad, whose passionate features conveyed hints of love and hate. A man like Cail and Brinn, as poised and capable as judgment. And a Giant, who must have been Saltheart Foamfollower.

Covenant's Dead.

With them stood Vain, wearing his black perfection like a cloak to conceal his heart.

The figures spoke to Covenant through the mute vision. The blessing and curse of their affection bore him to his knees. Then the eyeless man, the Forestal, approached. Carefully, he stretched out his staff to touch Covenant's forehead.

Instantly, a blaze like a melody of flame sang out over the eftmound; and at once all *Elemesnedene* fell into darkness. Night arched within the vision – a night made explicit and familiar by stars. Slowly, the mapwork of the stars began to turn.

'See you, Honninscrave?' cried the First hoarsely.

'Yes!' he responded. 'This path I can follow to the ends of the Earth.'

For a time, the stars articulated the way to the One Tree. Then, in the place they had defined, the vision dropped towards the sea. Amid the waves, an isle appeared. It was small and barren, standing like a cairn against the battery of the Sea, marking nothing. No sign of any life relieved the desolation of its rocky sides. Yet the intent of the vision was clear: this was the location of the One Tree.

Over the ocean rose a lorn wail. Covenant cried out as if he had caught a glimpse of his doom.

The sound tore through Linden. She struggled to her feet, tried to thrust her scant strength forward. Covenant knelt with the power blazing from his forehead as if he were being crucified by nails of brain-fire.

For a moment, she could not advance against the light: it held her back like a palpable current pouring from him. But then the bells rang out in unison:

– It is accomplished!

Some of them were savage with victory. Others expressed a deep rue.

At the same time, the vision began to fade from its consummation on the sea-bitten isle. The brilliance macerated by degrees, restoring the natural illumination of *Elemesnedene*, allowing Linden to advance. Step after step, she strove her way to Covenant. Vestiges of vision seemed to burn across her skin, crackle like lightning in her hair; but she fought through them. As the power frayed away to its end, leaving the atmosphere as stunned and still as a wasteland, she dropped to the ground in front of the Unbeliever.

He knelt in a slack posture, resting back on his heels with his arms unconsciously braced on his knees. He seemed unaware of anything. His gaze stared through her like a blind man's. His mouth hung open as if he had been bereft of every word or wail. His breathing shook slightly, painfully. The muscles of his chest ached in Linden's sight as if they had been torn on the rack of Infelice's opening.

But when she reached out her hand to him, he croaked like a parched and damaged raven, 'Don't touch me.'

The words were clear. They echoed the old warning of his leprosy for all the *Elohim* to hear. But in his eyes the light of his mind had gone out.

PART II

Betrayal

10

ESCAPE FROM *ELOHIM*

The bells were clear to Linden now; but she no longer cared what they were saying. She was locked to Covenant's vacant eyes, his slack, staring face. If he could see her at all, the sight had no meaning to him. He did not react when she took hold of his head, thrust her horrified gaze at him.

The Giants were clamouring to know what had happened to him. She ignored them. Desperately marshalling her percipience, she tried to penetrate the flat emptiness of his orbs, reach his mind. But she failed: within his head, her vision vanished into darkness. He was like a snuffed candle, and the only smoke curling up from the extinguished wick was his old clenched stricture:

'Don't touch me.'

She began to founder in that dark. Something of him must have remained sentient, otherwise he could not have continued to articulate his self-despite. But that relict of his consciousness was beyond her grasp. The darkness seemed to leech away her own light. She was falling into an emptiness as eternal and hungry as the cold void between the stars.

Savagely, she tore herself out of him.

Honninscrave and Seadreamer stood with the First at Covenant's back. Pitchwife knelt beside Linden, his huge hands cupping her shoulders in appeal. 'Chosen.' His whisper ached among the trailing wisps of dark. 'Linden Avery. Speak to us.'

She was panting in rough heaves. She could not find enough air. The featureless light of *Elemesnedene* suffocated her. The *Elohim* loomed claustrophobically around her, as unscrupulous as ur-viles. 'You planned this,' she grated between gasps. 'This is what you wanted all along.' She was giddy with extremity. 'To destroy him.'

The First drew a sharp breath. Pitchwife's hands tightened involuntarily. Wincing to his feet as if he needed to meet his surprise upright, he lifted Linden erect. Honninscrave gaped at her. Seadreamer stood with his arms rigid at his sides, restraining himself from vision.

'Enough,' responded Infelice. Her tone was peremptory ice. 'I will submit no longer to the affront of such false judgment. The *Elohimfest* has ended.' She turned away.

'Stop!' Without Pitchwife's support, Linden would have fallen like pleading to the bare ground. All her remaining strength went into her voice. 'You've got to restore him! Goddamn it, you can't leave him like this!'

Infelice paused, but did not look back. 'We are the *Elohim*. Our choices lie beyond your questioning. Be content.' Gracefully, she continued down the hillside.

Seadreamer broke into motion, hurled himself after her. The First and Honninscrave shouted, but could not halt him. Bereft of his wan, brief hope, he had no other outlet for his pain.

But Infelice heard or sensed his approach. Before he reached her, she snapped, 'Hold, Giant!'

He rebounded as if he had struck an invisible wall at her back. The force of her command sent him sprawling.

With stately indignation, she faced him. He lay grovelling on his chest; but his lips were violent across his teeth, and his eyes screamed at her.

'Assail me not with your mistrust,' she articulated slowly, 'lest I teach you that your voiceless Earth-Sight is honey and benison beside the ire of *Elemesnedene*.'

'*No.*' By degrees, life was returning to Linden's limbs; but still she needed Pitchwife's support. 'If you want to threaten somebody, threaten me. I'm the one who accuses you.'

Infelice looked at her without speaking.

'You planned all this,' Linden went on. 'You demeaned him, dismissed him, insulted him – to make him angry enough so that he would let you into him and dare you to hurt him. And then you wiped out his mind. Now' – she gathered every shred of her vehemence – '*restore it!*'

'Sun-Sage,' Infelice said in a tone of glacial scorn, 'you mock yourself and are blind to it.' Moving disdainfully, she left the eftmound and passed through the ring of dead trees.

On all sides, the other *Elohim* also turned away, dispersing as if Linden and her companions held no more interest for them.

With an inchoate cry, Linden swung towards Covenant. For one wild instant, she intended to grab his ring, use it to coerce the *Elohim*.

The sight of him stopped her. The First had raised him to his feet. He stared through Linden as though she and everything about her had ceased to exist for him; but his empty refrain sounded like an unintentional appeal.

'Don't touch me.'

Oh, Covenant! Of course she could not take his ring. She could not do that to him, if for no other reason than because it was what the *Elohim* wanted. Or part of what they wanted. She ached in protest, but her resolve had frayed away into uselessness again. A surge of weeping rose up in her, she barely held it back. *What have they done to you?*

'It is sooth?' the First whispered to the ambiguous sky. 'Have we gained this knowledge at such a cost to him?'

Linden nodded dumbly. Her hands made fumbling gestures. She had trained them to be physician's hands, and now she could hardly contain the yearning to strangle. Covenant had been taken from her as surely as if he had been slain – murdered like Nassic by a blade still hot with cruelty. She felt that if she did not move, act, stand up for herself somehow, she would go mad.

Around her, the Giants remained still as if they had been immobilized by her dismay. Or by the loss of Covenant, of his determination. No one else could restore the purpose of the quest.

That responsibility gave Linden what she needed. Animated by preterite stubbornness, she lurched down the hillside to find if Seadreamer had been harmed.

He was struggling to his feet. His eyes were wide and stunned, confused by Earth-Sight. He reeled as if he had lost all sense of balance. When Honninscrave hastened to his side, he clung to the Master's shoulder as if it were the only stable point in a breaking world. But Linden's percipience found no evidence of serious physical hurt.

Yet the emotional damage was severe. Something in him had been torn from its moorings by the combined force of his examination, the loss of the hope his brother had conceived for him, and Covenant's plight. He was caught in straits for which all relief had been denied; and he bore his Earth-Sight as if he knew that it would kill him.

This also was something Linden could not cure. She could only witness it and mutter curses that had no efficacy.

Most of the bells had receded into the background, but two remained nearby. They were arguing together, satisfaction against rue. Their content was accessible now, but Linden no longer had any wish to make out the words. She had had enough of Chant and Daphin.

Yet the two *Elohim* came together up the eftmound towards her, and she could not ignore them. They were her last chance. When they faced her, she aimed her bitterness straight into Daphin's immaculate green gaze.

'You didn't have to do that. You could've told us where the One Tree is. You didn't have to possess him. And then leave him like *that.*'

Chant's hard eyes held a gleam of insouciance. His inner voice sparkled with relish.

But Daphin's mind had a sad and liquid tone as she returned

Linden's glare. 'Sun-Sage, you do not comprehend our Würd. There is a word in your tongue which bears a somewhat similar meaning. 'It is "ethic".'

Jesus God! Linden rasped in sabulous denial. But she kept herself still.

'In our power,' Daphin went on, 'many paths are open to us which no mortal may judge or follow. Some are attractive – others, distasteful. Our present path was chosen because it offers a balance of hope and harm. Had we considered only ourselves, we would have selected a path of greater hope, for its severity would have fallen not upon us but upon you. But we have determined to share with you the cost. We risk our hope. And also that which is more precious to us – life, and the meaning of life. We risk trust.

'Therefore some among us' – she did not need to refer openly to Chant – 'urged another road. For who are you, that we should hazard trust and life upon you? Yet our Würd remains. Never have we sought the harm of any life. Finding no path of hope which was not also a path of harm we chose the way of balance and shared cost. Do not presume to judge us, when you conceive so little the import of your own acts. The fault is not ours that Sun-Sage and ring-wielder came among us as separate beings.'

Oh, hell, Linden muttered. She had no heart left to ask Daphin what price the *Elohim* were paying for Covenant's emptiness. She could think of no commensurate expense. And the timbre of the bells told her that Daphin would give no explicit answer. She did not care to waste any more of her scant strength on arguments or expostulations. She wanted nothing except to turn her back on the *Elohim*, get Covenant out of this place.

As if in reply, Chant said, 'In good sooth, it is past time. Were the choice in my hands, your expulsion from *Elemesnedene* would long since have silenced your ignorant tongue.' His tone was nonchalant; but his eyes shone with suppressed glee and cunning. 'Does it please your pride to depart now, or do you wish to utter more folly ere you go?'

Clearly, Daphin chimed:

– Chant, this does not become you.

But he replied:

– I am permitted. They can not now prevent us.

Linden's shoulders hunched, unconsciously tensing in an effort to strangle the intrusion in her mind. But at that moment, the First stepped forward. One of her hands rested on the hilt of her broadsword. She had leashed herself throughout the *Elohimfest*; but she was a trained Swordmain, and her face now wore an iron frown of danger and battle. '*Elohim*, there remains one question which must be answered.'

Linden stared dumbly at the First. She felt that nothing remained to the company except questions; but she had no idea which one the First meant.

The First spoke as if she were testing her blade against an unfamiliar opponent. 'Perhaps you will deign to reveal what has become of Vain?'

Vain?

For an instant, Linden quailed. Too much had happened. She could not bear to think about another perfidy. But there was no choice. She would crack if she did not keep moving, keep accepting the responsibility as it came.

She cast a glance around the eftmound; but she already knew that she would see no sign of the Demondim-spawn. In a whirl of recollection, she realized that Vain had never come to the *Elohimfest*. She had not seen him since the company had separated to be examined. No: she had not seen him since the expulsion of the *Haruchai*. At the time, his absence had troubled her unconsciously; but she had not been able to put a name to her vague sense of incompleteness.

Trembling suddenly, she faced Chant. He had said as clearly as music, *They can not now prevent us*. She had assumed that he referred to Covenant; but now his veiled glee took on other implications.

'*That's* what you were doing.' Comprehension burned through her. 'That's why you provoked Cail – why you kept trying to pick fights with us. To distract us from Vain.' And Vain had walked into the snare with his habitual undiscriminating blankness. Then she thought again, No. That's not right. Vain had approached the *clachan* with an air of excitement, as if the prospect of it pleased him. And the *Elohim* had ignored him from the beginning, concealing their intent against him.

'What in hell do you want with him?'

Chant's pleasure was plain. 'He was a peril to us. His dark makers spawned him for our harm. He was an offence to our Würd, directed with great skill and malice to coerce us from our path. This we will never endure, just as we have not endured your anile desires. We have imprisoned him.

'We wrought covertly,' he went on like laughter, 'to avoid the mad ire of your ring-wielder. But now that peril has been foiled. Your Vain we have imprisoned, and no foolish beseechment or petty mortal indignation will effect his release.' His eyes shone. 'Thus the umbrage you have sought to cast upon us is recompensed. Consider the justice of your loss and be still.'

Linden could not bear it. Masking her face with severity so that she would not betray herself, she sprang at him.

He stopped her with a negligent gesture, sent her reeling backward. She collided with Covenant; and he sprawled to the hard ground, making no effort to soften the impact. His face pressed the dirt.

The Giants had not moved. They had been frozen by Chant's gesture. The First fought to draw her falchion. Seadreamer and Honninscrave tried to attack. But they were held motionless.

Linden scrambled to Covenant's side, heaved him upright. 'Please.' She pleaded with him uselessly, as if Chant's power had riven her of her wits. 'I'm sorry. Wake up. They've got Vain.'

But he might as well have been deaf and senseless. He made no effort to clean away the dirt clinging to his slack lips. Emptily, he responded to impulses utterly divorced from her and the Giants and the *Elohim*:

'Don't touch me.'

Cradling him, she turned to appeal one last time to Daphin's compassion. Tears streaked her face.

But Chant forestalled her. 'It is enough,' he said sternly. 'Now begone.' At that moment, he took on the stature of his people. His stance was grave and immitigable. She receded from him; but as the distance between them increased, he grew in her sight, confusing her senses so that she seemed to fall backward into the heavens. For an instant, he shone like the sun, burning away her protests. Then he was the sun, and she caught a glimpse of blue sky before the waters of the fountain covered her like weeping.

She nearly lost her balance on the steep facets of the travertine. Covenant's weight dragged her towards a fall. But at once Cail and Brinn came leaping through the spray to her aid. The water in their hair sparkled under the midday sun as if they – or she – were still in the process of transformation between *Elemesnedene* and the outer *maidan*.

The suddenness of the change dizzied her. She could not find her balance behind the sunlight as the *Haruchai* helped her and Covenant down the slope, through the gathering waters to dry ground. They did not speak, expressed no surprise; but their mute tension shouted at her from the contact of their hard hands. She had sent them away.

The sun seemed preternaturally bright. Her eyes had grown accustomed to the featureless lumination of *Elemesnedene*. Fiercely, she scrubbed at her face, trying to clear away the water and the glare as if she wanted to eradicate every suggestion of tears or weeping from her visage.

But Brinn caught hold of her wrists. He stood before her like an accusation. Ceer and Hergrom braced Covenant between them.

The four Giants had emerged from the trough around the fountain. They stood half-dazed in the tall yellow grass of the *maidan* as if they had just wandered out of a dream which should not have been a nightmare. The First clutched her broadsword in both fists, but it was of no use to her. Pitchwife's deformity appeared to have been accentuated. Seadreamer and Honninscrave moved woodenly together, linked by their pain.

But Brinn did not permit Linden to turn away. Inflectionlessly, he demanded, 'What harm has been wrought upon the ur-Lord?'

She had no answer to the accusation in his stare. She felt that her sanity had become uncertain. To herself, she sounded like a mad-woman as she responded irrelevantly, 'How long were we in there?'

Brinn rejected the importance of her question with a slight shake of his head. 'Moments only. We had hardly ceased our attempts to re-enter the *clachan* when you returned.' His fingers manacled her. 'What harm has been wrought upon the ur-Lord?'

Oh my God, she groaned. Covenant so sorely damaged. Vain lost. Gifts refused. Moments only? It was true: the sun had scarcely moved at all since her last glimpse of it before entering *Elemesnedene*. That so much pain could have been committed in such a little time! 'Let me go.' The plaint of a lorn and frightened child. 'I've got to think.'

For a moment, Brinn did not relent. But then Pitchwife came to her side. His misshapen eyes yearned on her behalf. In a hobbled tone, he said, 'Release her. I will answer as best I may.'

Slowly, Brinn unlocked his fingers; and Linden slumped into the grass.

She huddled there with her face hidden against her knees. Old, familiar screams echoed in her, cries which no one had been able to hear until long after her father had bled to death. Tears squeezed from her eyes like involuntary self-recrimination.

The voices of her companions passed back and forth over her head. Pitchwife began to recount the events in *Elemesnedene*; but shortly the demand for brevity dismayed his Giantish instincts, and he trailed off into directionless protests. The First took the task from him. Tersely, she detailed what she knew of Covenant's examin-ation, then described the *Elohimfest*. Her account was succinct and stark. Her tone said plainly that she, like Pitchwife, ached for a full and formal telling. But this *maidan* – with the *Elohim* so near at hand – was no place for such a tale; and she withheld it sternly. She related how the location of the One Tree had been revealed and what price Covenant had paid for that vision. Then she stiffened herself to her conclusion.

'Vain the *Elohim* have imprisoned. It is their word that he is perilous to them – a threat directed against them across the seas by those who made him. They will not suffer his release. Mayhap they have already taken his life.'

There she fell silent; and Linden knew that nothing else remained to be said. She could not hope for any inspiration to rescue her from her burdens. As if she knew what they were thinking, she watched while Ceer and Hergrom splashed back to the travertine slopes of the fountain, attempting once again to enter *Elemesnedene*. But the way was closed to them. It had been closed to all the company, and there was nothing else left to be done. Yet when the two *Haruchai* retreated to the *maidan*, the water seemed to gleam on the surface of their stubbornness; and she saw with a groan of recognition that she would have to fight them as well. They had not forgiven her for sending them out of *Elemesnedene*.

She tried to rise to her feet; but for a while she could not. The weight of decision held her down. Who was she, that she should try to take Covenant's place at the head of the quest? Gibbon-Raver had promised her an outcome of anguish and ruin.

But her companions were asking themselves how they could force or trick their way back into the *clachan*. Though she felt that she was going crazy, she seemed to be the only sane one among them. And she had already accepted her role. If she could not at least stand loyal to herself, to the decisions she had made and the people she cared about, then everything she had already been and borne came to nothing. Clinching her long intransigence, she interrupted the company by climbing upright. Then she muttered, 'There's nothing more we can do here. Let's get going.'

They were struck silent as if she had shocked them. They glanced among themselves, wondering at her – at her willingness to abandon Vain, or at her attempt to command them. The First had sheathed her blade, but she showed her desire for battle in every muscle. Honninscrave and Seadreamer had found their way past pain into anger. Even Pitchwife had become enthusiastic for combat. And the *Haruchai* stood poised as if they were looking for a place to hurl violence.

'Don't touch me,' Covenant answered. The abysm behind his eyes made him look like a blind man. His reiterated warning was the only evidence that he retained any vestige of mind at all.

'I mean it.' Linden's tongue was thick with despair; but she knew that if she recanted now she would never be able to stop fleeing. 'There's nothing we can do for Vain. Let's get back to the ship.'

'Chosen.' The First's voice was as keen as iron. 'We are Giants. Whatever his purpose, this Vain is our companion. We do not blithely turn from the succour of any companion.' Linden started to object; but the Swordmain cut her off. 'Also, we have been told that he was given to Covenant Giantfriend by the Dead of Andelain. By a Giant of the Lost – by Saltheart Foamfollower, the Pure One of the *sur-jheherrin*. Him we have beheld in the opening of Covenant's mind.

'We will not see such a gift lost. Though we do not comprehend him, we conceive that the gifts given to Covenant by his Dead are

- vital and necessary. Vain must be recovered.'

Linden understood. The *Elohim* had planted a seed of possibility, and its fruit was apparent in the gazes of her companions. That she should take Covenant's ring and use it.

She shook her head. That would be a violation as fundamental as any rape. His ring was his peril and his hope, and she would not take it from him. Its power meant too much to her.

And she had other reasons to deny the idea. Covenant's plight could wait, at least until the company was safely away from this place; but Vain's could not. What the Demondim-spawn needed from her was not what it appeared to be.

To the First, she said flatly, 'No.' In this, at least, she knew who she was. 'It isn't up to you.'

'I am the First — ' began the Swordmain.

'It would've been Covenant's decision,' Linden went on severely, clamping herself rigid with all her will, 'but he's in no condition. That leaves me.'

She could not explain herself for fear the *Elohim* would hear her and take action. They were surely able to hear anything they desired, uncover any purpose they chose. So she invented reasons as if she knew what she was talking about.

'You can't do it. He's so important because he comes from outside. Like the white gold. You don't. We wouldn't be here at all if the job could be done by anybody else. You can't take his place,' she insisted. 'I'm going to, whether I can or not.

'And I say we're going to leave. Let Vain take care of himself. We don't even know why he was given to Covenant. Maybe this *is* the reason. To get him into *Elemesnedene*, so he can do whatever he was created for. I don't know, and I don't care. We have what we came to get. And I don't want to keep Covenant here. They're after his ring. I'll be damned if we're going to stand around and let them hurt him again.'

The First replied with a perplexed frown, as though Linden's stability had become a matter of open doubt. But Brinn showed no doubt. In a voice like stone, he said, 'We know nothing of these questions. Our ignorance was thrust upon us when we sought to serve the promise we have given the ur-Lord.' His accusation was implicit. 'We know only that he has been harmed when he should have been in our care. And Vain is his, given to him in aid of his quest. For that reason alone, we must stand by the Demondim-spawn.

'Also,' he continued inflexibly, 'you have become a question in our sight. Vain made obeisance to you when you were redeemed from Revelstone. And he it was who strove to bear you from the peril of the gravelling and the Sunbane-sickness. Perchance it was he who brought the *sur-jheherrin* to our aid against the lurker, in your name.

Do you lack all wish to serve those who have served you?'

Linden wanted to cry out at his words. He rubbed them like salt into her failures. But she clung to her purpose until the knuckles of her will whitened. 'I understand what you're saying.' Her voice quivered, deserted by the flat dispassion which she had tried for so long to drill into herself. 'But you can't get in there. They've closed us out. And we don't have any way to make them change their minds. Covenant is the only one they were ever afraid of, and now they don't have that to worry about.' If Covenant had chosen that moment to utter his blank refrain, her control might have snapped. But he was mercifully silent, lost in the absence of his thoughts. 'Every minute we stay here, we're taking the chance they might decide to do something worse.'

The challenge of Brinn's gaze did not waver. When she finished, he replied as though her protest were gratuitous, 'Then heal him. Restore to him his mind, so that he may make his own choosing on Vain's behalf.'

At that, Linden thought she would surely break. She had already endured too much. In Brinn's eyes, she saw her flight from Covenant during his venom-relapse returning to impugn her. And Brinn also knew that she had declined to protect Covenant from Infelice's machinations. The First had not omitted that fact from her tale. For a moment, Linden could not speak through the culpability which clogged her throat.

But the past was unalterable; and for the present no one had the right to judge her. Brinn could not see Covenant deeply enough to judge her. Covenant's plight was hers to assess – and to meet as she saw fit. Gritting her control so hard that it ached in the bones of her skull, she said, 'Not here. Not now. What's happened to him is like amnesia. There's a chance it will heal itself. But even if it doesn't – even if I have to do something about it – I'm not going to take the risk. Where the *Elohim* can tamper with anything.' And Vain might be running out of time. 'If I'm not completely careful – ' She faltered as she remembered the darkness behind his eyes. 'I might extinguish what's left.'

Brinn did not blink. His stare said flatly that this argument was just another refusal, as unworthy of Covenant as all the others. Despairingly, Linden turned back to the First.

'I know what I'm doing. Maybe I've already failed too often. Maybe none of you can trust me. But I'm not losing my mind.' In her ears, her insistence sounded like the frail pleading of a child. 'We've got to get out of here. Go back to the ship. Leave.' With all her determination, she refrained from shouting, Don't you understand? That's the only way we can help Vain! 'We've got to do it now.'

The First debated within herself. Both Honninscrave and Seadrea-

576

mer looked studiously elsewhere, unwilling to take sides in this conflict. But Pitchwife watched Linden as if he were remembering Mistweave. And when the First spoke, he smiled like the lighting of a candle in a dark room.

Dourly, she said, 'Very well. I accept your command in this. Though I can fathom little concerning you, you are the Chosen. And I have seen evidence of strange strength in you, when strength was least looked for. We will return to Starfare's Gem.'

Abruptly, she addressed the *Haruchai*. 'I make no claim upon your choosing. But I ask you to accompany us. Vain lies beyond your reach. And the Giantfriend and the Chosen require every aid.'

Brinn cocked his head slightly as if he were listening to a silent consultation. Then he said, 'Our service was given to the ur-Lord – and to Linden Avery in the ur-Lord's name. Though we mislike that Vain should be abandoned, we will not gainsay you.'

That Vain should be abandoned. Linden groaned. Every word the *Haruchai* uttered laid another crime to her charge. More blood on her hands, though she had taken an oath to save every life she could. Maybe Brinn was right. Maybe her decision was just another denial. Or worse. *Are you not evil?*

But she was suddenly too weak to say anything else. The sunlight blurred her sight like sweat. When Cail offered her his arm she accepted it because she had no choice. She felt unable to support herself. As she joined her companions moving along the River Callowwail towards Woodenwold and the anchorage of Starfare's Gem, she was half-blind with sunlight and frailty, and with the extremity of her need to be right.

The *maidan* seemed to stretch out forever ahead of her. Only the cumulative rush of the River marked the expanse, promising that the grass was not like *Elemesnedene*, not featureless and unending. Cail's assistance was bitter and necessary to her. She could not comprehend the gentleness of his aid. Perhaps it was this quality of the *Haruchai* which had driven Kevin Landwaster to the Ritual of Desecration; for how could he have sustained his self-respect when he had such beings as the Bloodguard to serve him?

The Callowwail reflected blue in turbulent pieces back at the sky. She clung to her own self-respect by considering images of Vain, seeking to remember everything he had done. He had remained passive when the demented Coursers had driven him into a quagmire in Sarangrave Flat. And yet he had found a way to rejoin the company. And surely he had chosen to hazard *Elemesnedene* for his own secret reasons?

Slowly, her sight cleared. Now she could see the splendid autumn of Woodenwold rising before her. Soon she and her companions would be among the trees. Soon –

The sudden fierce clanging of the bells staggered her. Except for

Cail's grasp, she would have fallen. The *Elohim* had been silent since her expulsion from the *clachan*; but now the bells were outraged and desperate in her mind, clamouring woe and fury.

Pitchwife came to her, helped Cail uphold her. 'Chosen?' he asked softly, urgently. 'What harms you?' His tone reflected the stricken pallor of her countenance.

'It's Vain,' she panted through the silent clangour. Her voice sounded too thin and detached to have come from her. 'He's trying to escape.'

The next instant, a concussion like a thunderclap buffeted the company. The cloudless sky darkened, powers blasting against each other dimmed the sun. A long tremor like the opening howl of an earthquake ran through the ground.

Giants yelled. Fighting to keep their balance, the *Haruchai* circled defensively around Linden and Covenant.

As she looked back towards the fountainhead of the Callowwail, Linden saw that the water was on fire.

Burning and blazing, a hot surge of power spread flames down the current. Its leading edge spat out fury like the open door of a furnace. On either side of the swift fire, the *maidan* rippled and flowed as though it were evaporating.

In the heart of the heat, Linden descried a dark figure swimming. Vain!

He struggled down the Callowwail as if he were beset by acid. His strokes were frantic – and growing weaker every moment. The flames tore at his flesh, rent his black essence. He appeared to be dissolving in the fiery current.

'Help him!' Vain's need snatched Linden to a shout. 'They're killing him!'

The *Haruchai* reacted without hesitation. Their doubt of her did not hamper their gift for action. Springing forward, Ceer and Hergrom dove straight into the River and the crux of the flames.

For an instant, she feared that they would be consumed. But the fire did not touch them. It burned to the pitch of Vain's ebon being and left their flesh unharmed.

As the *Haruchai* reached him, he threw his arms around their necks; and at once the erosion of his strength seemed to pause as if he drew sustenance from them. Gathering himself suddenly, he thrust them beneath the surface. With a concentrated effort, he cocked himself, braced his feet on their shoulders. From that base, he leaped out of the Callowwail.

The flames tried to follow; but now they ran off his sleek skin like water, fraying in the sunlight. He had escaped their direct grasp. And the sun poured its light into him like an aliment. Over all the *maidan*, the air was dim with preternatural twilight; but on Vain the sun shed its full strength, reversing the dissolution which the *Elohim* had wrought against him. Spreading his arms, he turned his black eyes upward and let the light restore him to himself.

The bells rang out keen loss, wild threats, but did no more damage.

In the River, the power faded towards failure. Ceer and Hergrom broke the surface together, unscathed, and climbed the bank to stand with the rest of the company, watching Vain.

Slowly, the Demondim-spawn lowered his arms; and as he did so, midday returned to the *maidan*. In a moment, he stood as he had always stood, balanced between relaxation and readiness, with a faint, undirected smile on his lips. He seemed as uncognizant as ever of the company, blind to assistance or rescue.

'Your pardon,' said the First to Linden in quiet wonder. 'I had given too little thought to the compulsion which drives him to follow you.'

Linden remained still, held by vindication and relief. She did not know whether Vain followed herself or Covenant – and did not care. For once, she had been right.

But the company could not stay where it was. Many of the bells had faded back into silence, receding with the flames. However, others were too angry to retreat; and the threat they conveyed impelled her to say, 'Come on. Some of them want to try again. They might not let us leave.'

Honninscrave looked at her sharply. 'Not?' His glad memories of the *Elohim* had already suffered too much diminution. But he was a Giant and knew how to fight. 'Stone and Sea!' he swore, 'they will not prevent us. If we must, we will swim from the *Raw*, towing Starfare's Gem after us.'

The First gave him a nod of approval, then said, 'Still the Chosen speaks truly. We must depart.' At once, she swept Covenant into her arms and set off at a lope towards Woodenwold.

Before Linden could try to follow, Seadreamer picked her up, carried her away along the verge of the Callowwail. Cail and Ceer ran at his side. Brinn and Hergrom dashed ahead to join the First. Eager for his ship, Honninscrave sped past them. Pitchwife's deformed back hindered him, but he was able to match the pace the First set.

Behind them, Vain trotted lightly, like a man who had been running all his life.

Into Woodenwold they went as if, like Linden, they could hear bells hallooing on their heels. But the threats did not materialize into action. Perhaps *Elohim* like Daphin were able to dissuade those who shared Chant's way of thinking. And the distance passed swiftly. The companions devoured the stretch of trees between them and their ship as if they were hungry for hope.

Then they crossed into the shadow of the Rawedge Rim, and Woodenwold became abruptly grey and ire-bitten about them. The dire mountains appeared to reave the trees of autumn and calm. But Linden held up her courage, for she knew the lagoon was near. When Seadreamer bore her between the looming walls of the valley, she saw Starfare's Gem still at rest on the flat surface of the water, with its stone spars raised like defiance against the twilight and the mountains. The longboat remained where the company had left it.

Honninscrave began shouting orders at Sevinhand before he and Seadreamer had rowed the company halfway to the *dromond*. His commands rebounded from the high cliffs; and the echoes seemed to lift Giants into the rigging. By the time Linden had scrambled up the moire-marked side of the Giantship, gained the afterdeck, the unfurled canvas was stirring. A wind ran westward among the mountains.

Giants hurried to raise the longboat, hoist the anchors. Honninscrave sprang to the wheeldeck, barking instructions as he moved. Swiftly, Starfare's Gem awakened. With a bustle of activity and a lift of its prow, the *dromond* caught the wind, settled against its sails, and began sliding lightly down the gauntlet of the *Raw*.

11

A WARNING OF SERPENTS

Before Starfare's Gem had passed halfway to the open Sea, the wind became a stiff blow like a shout from the Rawedge Rim. It drove the *dromond* as if the *Elohim* in their wrath were determined to expel the quest for all time from their demesne. But Honninscrave did not let the wind have his vessel. The cliffs and turns of the *Raw* became darker, more bitter and hazardous, as the afternoon waned. Therefore he shortened sail, held the Giantship to a careful pace. The company did not reach the end of the gullet until nearly sunset.

There Starfare's Gem stumbled into a long fight to keep itself off the rocks of the coast. The exhalation of the *Raw* conflicted with the prevailing wind along the littoral; and they pulled the *dromond* into a maze of turbulence. Tacking in flurries, struggling to run one guess ahead of the next shift, Honninscrave and his crew laboured back and forth against the southern promontory of the *Raw*.

Twilight quickly darkened into night, turning the rocky verge to a blackness marked only by the Sea's phosphorescence and the wan light of the stars; for there was no moon. To Linden, who had lost track of the days, the absence of the moon felt ominous and chilling.

She could have believed that the *Elohim* had stricken it from the heavens in retribution. In the dark, she saw no way for the quest to win free of the moiling winds. Every shift seemed sharper than the one before, and every other tack carried the *dromond* closer to the ragged and fatal bluffs.

But Honninscrave was a cunning reader of aircurrents, and at last he found the path which ran towards the safety of the open Sea. Slipping free of the last toils of the *Elohim*, Starfare's Gem went south.

For the rest of the night, the littoral loomed against the port horizon. But the next morning, Honninscrave angled a few points farther west of south, and the headland began to sink into the Sea. During the afternoon, another promontory briefly raised its head. But after that nothing remained to be seen in any direction except the sunlight rolling in brocade across the long green ocean.

While they had fled through and away from the *Raw*, the Giants had held themselves clenched against the winds and the unknown purposes of the *Elohim*, tending the ship, springing to the Master's commands, with a tense and unwonted silence. But now their mood eased as Honninscrave allowed himself to relax and the ship sailed confidently into a perfect evening. At dusk, they gathered to hear the tale of *Elemesnedene*, which Pitchwife told with the full flourish and passion which the Giants loved. And Honninscrave described in detail what he had learned about the location of the One Tree. With the exact map of the stars to guide the quest, any possibility of failure appeared to fade. Slowly, Starfare's Gem regained much of its familiar good cheer.

Linden was glad for that easement. The Giants had earned it, and she watched it with a physician's unselfish approval. But she did not share it. Covenant's condition outweighed the instinct for hope which she absorbed empathically from the Giants.

The *Haruchai* had to care for him at every moment. He stayed wherever, and in whatever position, he was left. Standing or sitting, in motion or at rest, he remained caught in his blankness, devoid of will or intent or desire. Nothing lived in him except his most preterite instincts. When he was deprived of support, he retained his balance against the slow stone rolling of the ship; when food was placed in his mouth, he chewed, swallowed. But nothing assuaged the fathomless plunge which lay behind his gaze. At unmotivated intervals, he spoke as distinctly as if he were reading the fate written on his forehead. Yet he did not react when he was touched.

At last, Linden was driven to ask Brinn to take Covenant to his cabin. The pathos of his plight rested squarely on her shoulders, and she was unready to bear it. She had learned to believe that *possession* was evil – and she could think of no way to attempt his aid without possessing him.

She clung to the hope that rest and peace would cure him. But she saw no amelioration. Well, she had promised herself that she would not shirk his healing, regardless of the price. She had not chosen this burden, just as she had not chosen the role of the Sun-Sage; but she did not mean to flee it. Yet she felt bitterly worn in the aftermath of *Elemesnedene*. And she could not clear her mind of rage at the way Covenant had been harmed. Intuitively, she sensed that the mood in which she attempted to penetrate his blankness would be crucial. If she went into him with anger, she might be answered with anger; and his ire would have the power to send Starfare's Gem to the bottom of the Sea in pieces. Therefore for the present she stayed away from him and strove to compose herself.

But when Covenant was not before her to demand her attention, she found that her sore nerves simply shifted their worry to another – to Cable Seadreamer. His pain-bitten visage unconsciously wielded its ache over the entire Giantship. He wore a look of recognition, as if he had gained an insight which he would have feared to utter even if he had not already been bereft of his voice. Moving among his people, he stopped their talk, silenced their laughter like a loneliness that had no anodyne.

And he was conscious of the hurt his mute woe gave. After a time, he could no longer endure it. He tried to leave his comrades, spare them the discomfort of his presence. But Pitchwife would not let him go. The deformed Giant hugged his friend as if he meant to coerce Seadreamer into accepting the care of his people. And Honninscrave and Sevinhand crowded around; urging upon him their support.

Their response brought tears to Seadreamer's eyes, but not relief.

Softly, painfully, the First asked Linden, 'What has harmed him? His distress has grown beyond all bounds.'

Linden had no answer. Without violating him, she could see nothing in Seadreamer except the extremity of his struggle for courage.

She would have given anything to see such a struggle take place in Covenant.

For three days while the *dromond* ran steadily west of south at a slight angle to the wind, she stayed away from him. The *Haruchai* tended him in his cabin, and she did not go there. She told herself that she was allowing time for a spontaneous recovery. But she knew the truth: she was procrastinating because she feared and loathed what she would have to do if he did not heal himself. In her imagination, she saw him sitting in his chamber exactly as he sat within his mind, uttering the litany of his bereavement in that abandoned voice.

For those three days, Starfare's Gem returned to its normal

routine. The general thrust of the wind remained constant; but it varied enough to keep the Giants busy aloft. And the other members of the Search occupied themselves in their own ways. The First spent considerable time cleaning her battlegear and sharpening her broadsword, as if she could see combat mustering beyond the horizon. And on several occasions she and Pitchwife went below together to seek a little privacy.

Honninscrave seemed half feverish, unable to rest. When he was not actively commanding the *dromond*, he engaged in long deliberations with the Anchormaster and Galewrath, planning the ship's course. However, Linden read him well enough to be sure that it was not the path of the quest which obsessed him, but rather Seadreamer's plight.

She seldom saw Brinn, he did not leave his watch over Covenant. But Ceer and Hergrom busied themselves about the Giantship as they had formerly; and Cail shadowed her like a sentry. Whatever the *Haruchai* felt towards her did not show in their faces, in Cail's ready attendance. Yet she sensed that she was watched over, not out of concern for her, but to prevent her from harming the people around her.

At times, she thought that Vain was the only member of the Search who had not been changed by *Elemesnedene*. He stood near the rail of the afterdeck on the precise spot where he had climbed aboard. The Giants had to work around him, he did not deign to notice that he was in their way. His black features revealed nothing.

Again, Linden wondered what conceivable threat to themselves the *Elohim* had discerned in the Demondim-spawn, when his sole apparent purpose was to follow her and Covenant. But she could make nothing of it.

While Starfare's Gem travelled the open Sea, she grew to feel progressively more lost among things she did not comprehend. She had taken the burden of decision upon herself; but she lacked the experience and conviction – and the power – which enabled Covenant to bear it. He ached constantly at the back of her mind, an untreated wound. Only her stubborn loyalty to herself kept her from retreating to the loneliness of her cabin, hiding there like a little girl with a dirty dress so that the responsibility would fall to somebody else.

On the morning of the fifth day after Starfare's Gem's escape from the *Raw*, she awakened in a mood of aggravated discomfiture, as if her sleep had been troubled by nightmares she could not remember. A vague apprehension nagged at the very limit of her senses, too far away to be grasped or understood. Fearing what she might learn, she asked Cail about Covenant. But the *Haruchai* reported no change. Anxiously she left her cabin, went up to the afterdeck.

As she scanned the deck, her inchoate sense of trouble increased.

The sun shone in the east with an especial brightness, as if it were intent on its own clarity; but still the air seemed as chill as a premonition. Yet nothing appeared amiss. Galewrath commanded the wheeldeck with gruff confidence. And the crewmembers were busy about the vessel, warping it against the vagaries of the wind.

The First, Honninscrave, and Seadreamer were nowhere to be seen. However, Pitchwife was at work near the aftermast, stirring the contents of a large stone vat. He looked up as Linden drew near him and winced at what he saw. 'Chosen,' he said with an effort of good humour which was only partially successful, 'were I less certain of our viands, I would believe that you have eaten badly and been made unwell. It is said that Sea and sun conduce to health and appetite – yet you wear the wan aspect of the sickbed. Are you ailed?'

She shook her head imprecisely. 'Something – I can't figure it out. I feel a disaster coming. But I don't know – ' Groping for a way to distract herself, she peered into the vat. 'Is that more of your pitch? How do you make it?'

At that, he laughed, and his mirth came more easily. 'Yes, Chosen. In all good sooth, this is my pitch. The vat is formed of dolomite, that it may not be fused as would the stone of Starfare's Gem. But as to the making of pitch – ah, that it skills nothing for me to relate. You are neither Giant nor wiver. And the power of pitch arises as does any other, from the essence of the adept who wields it. All power is an articulation of its wielder. There is no other source than life – and the desire of that life to express itself. But there must also be a means of articulation. I can say little but that this pitch is my chosen means. Having said that, I have left you scarce wiser than before.'

Linden shrugged away his disclaimer. 'Then what you're saying,' she murmured slowly, 'is that the power of wild magic comes from Covenant himself? The ring is just his – his means of articulation?'

He nodded. 'I believe that to be sooth. But the means controls intimately the nature of what may be expressed. By my pitch I may accomplish nothing for the knitting of broken limbs, just as no theurgy of the flesh may seal stone as I do.'

Musing half to herself, she replied, 'That fits. At least with what Covenant says about the Staff of Law. Before it was destroyed. It supported the Law by its very nature. Only certain kinds of things could be done with it.'

The malformed Giant nodded again; but she was already thinking something else. Turning to face him more directly, she demanded, 'But what about the *Elohim*? They don't need any means. They *are* power. They can express anything they want, any way they want. Everything they said to us – all that stuff about Seadreamer's voice and Covenant's venom and how Earthpower isn't the answer to Despite. It was all a lie.'

Her rage came back to her in a rush. She was trembling and white-knuckled before she could stop herself.

Pitchwife considered her closely. 'Be not so hasty in your appraisal of these *Elohim*.' His twisted features seemed to bear Seadreamer's pain and Covenant's loss as if they had been inflicted on him personally; yet he rejected their implications, refused to be what he appeared. 'They are who they are – a high and curious people – and their might is matched and conflicted and saddened by their limitations.'

She started to argue; but he stopped her with a gesture that asked her to sit beside him against the base of the aftermast. Lowering himself carefully, he leaned his crippled back to the stone. When she joined him, her shoulderblades felt the sails thrumming through the mast. The vibrations tasted obscurely troubled and foreboding. They sent rumours along her nerves like precursors of something unpredictable. Starfare's Gem rolled with a discomforting irrhythm.

'Chosen,' Pitchwife said, 'I have not spoken to you concerning my examination by the *Elohim*.'

She looked at him in surprise. The tale he had told during the first night out from the *Raw* had glossed over his personal encounters in the *clachan* as mere digressions. But now she saw that he had his own reasons for having withheld the story then – and for telling it now.

'At the parting of our company in *Elemesnedene*,' he said quietly, as if he did not wish to be overheard, 'I was accorded the guidance of one who named himself Starkin. He was an *Elohim* of neither more nor less wonder than any other, and so I followed him willingly. Among the lovely and manifold mazements of his people, I felt I had been transported to the truest faery heart of all the legends which have arisen from that place. The Giants have held these *Elohim* in awe bordering on sanctity, and that awe I learned to taste in my own mouth. Like Grimmand Honninscrave before me, I came to believe that any giving or restitution was feasible in that eldritch realm.'

The grotesque lines of his face were acute with memory as he spoke; yet his tone was one of calm surety, belying the suggestion that he had suffered any dismay.

'But then,' he went on, 'Starkin turned momentarily from me, and my examination began. For when again he approached, he had altered his shape. He stood before me as another being altogether. He had put aside his robe and his lithe limbs and his features – had transformed even his stature – and now he wore the form and habiliments of a Giant.' Pitchwife sighed softly. 'In every aspect he

585

had recreated himself flawlessly.

'He was myself.

'Yet not myself as you behold me, but rather myself as I might be in dreams. A Pitchwife of untainted birth and perfect growth. Withal that the image was mine beyond mistaking, he stood straight and tall above me, in all ways immaculately made, and beautiful with the beauty of Giants. He was myself as even Gossamer Glowlimn my love might desire me in her pity. For who would not have loved such a Giant, or desired him?

'Chosen' – he met Linden with his clear gaze – 'there was woe in that sight. In my life I have been taught many things, but until that moment I had not been taught to look upon myself and descry that I was ugly. At my birth, a jest had been wrought upon me – a jest the cruelty of which Starkin displayed before me.'

Pain for him surged up in her. Only the simple peace of his tone and eyes enabled her to hold back her outrage. How had he borne it?

He answered squarely, 'This was an examination which searched me to the depths of my heart. But at last its truth became plain to me. Though I stood before myself in all the beauty for which I might have lusted, it was not I who stood there, but Starkin. This Giant was manifestly other than myself, for he could not alter his eyes – eyes of gold that shed light, but gave no warmth to what they beheld. And my eyes remained my own. He could not see himself with my sight. Thus I passed unharmed through the testing he had devised for me.'

Studying him with an ache of empathy, Linden saw that he was telling the truth. His examination had given him pain, but no hurt. And his unscathed aspect steadied her, enabling her to see past her anger to the point of his story. He was trying to explain his perception that the *Elohim* could only be who they were and nothing else – that any might was defined and limited by its very nature. No power could transcend the strictures which made its existence possible.

Her ire faded as she followed Pitchwife's thinking. No power? she wanted to ask. Not even wild magic? Covenant seemed capable of anything. What conceivable stricture could bind his white fire? Was there in truth some way that Foul could render him helpless in the end?

The necessity of freedom, she thought. If he's already sold himself –

But as she tried to frame her question, her sense of disquiet returned. It intruded on her pulse; blood began to throb suddenly in her temples. Something had happened. Tension cramped her chest as she fumbled for perception.

Pitchwife was saying wryly, 'Your pardon, Chosen. I see that I have not given you ease.'

She shook her head. 'That's not it.' The words left her mouth before she realized what she was saying. 'What happened to Vain?'

The Demondim-spawn was gone. His place near the railing was empty.

'Naught I know of,' Pitchwife replied, surprised by her reaction. 'A short while after the sun's rising, he strode forward as though his purpose had awakened in him. To the foremast he fared, and it he greeted with such a bow and smile as I mislike to remember. But then he lapsed to his former somnolence. There he stands yet. Had he moved, those who watch him would surely have informed us.'

'It is true,' Cail said flatly. 'Ceer guards him.'

Under her breath, Linden muttered, 'You've got to be kidding,' and climbed to her feet. 'This I've got to see.' When Pitchwife joined her, she stalked away towards Foodfendhall and the foredeck.

There she saw Vain as he had been described, facing the curved surface of the mast from an arm's length away. His posture was the same as always: elbows slightly crooked at his sides; knees flexing just enough to maintain his balance against the choppy gait of the *dromond*; back straight. Yet to her gaze he wore a telic air. He confronted the mast as if they were old comrades, frozen on the verge of greeting one another.

To herself, she murmured, 'What the hell – ?'

'Forsooth,' responded Pitchwife with a light chuckle. 'Had this Demondim-spawn not been gifted to the ur-Lord by a Giant, I would fear that he means to ravish the maidenhood of our foremast.'

At that, laughter spouted from the nearby crewmembers, then spread like a kinship of humour through the rigging as his jest was repeated to those who had not heard it.

But Linden was not listening to him. Her ears had caught another sound – a muffled shout from somewhere belowdecks. As she focused her hearing, she identified Honninscrave's stertorous tones.

He was calling Seadreamer's name. Not in anger or pain, but in surprise. And trepidation.

The next moment, Seadreamer erupted from one of the hatchways and charged forward as if he meant to hurl himself at Vain. Honninscrave followed him; but Linden's attention was locked on the mute Giant. He looked wild and visionary, like a prophet or a madman; and the scar across his visage stood out stark and pale, underlining his eyes with intensity. Cries he could not utter strained the muscles of his neck.

Mistaking the Giant's intent, Ceer stepped between him and Vain, balanced himself to defend the Demondim-spawn. But an instant later, Seadreamer struck, not at Vain, but at the foremast. With his full weight and momentum, he dove against the mast. The impact sent a palpable quiver through the stone.

The shock knocked him to the deck. At once, he rebounded to his feet, attacked again. Slapping his arms around the mast like a wrestler, he heaved at it as if he wanted to tear it from its moorings. His passion was so vivid that for a moment Linden feared he might succeed.

Honninscrave leaped at Seadreamer's back, tried to pull him away. But he could not break the hold of Seadreamer's ferocity. Ceer and Hergrom moved to help the Master.

A worn sad voice stopped them. 'Enough.' It seemed to sough from the air. 'I have no desire to cause such distress.'

Seadreamer fell back. Vain stiffened.

Out of the stone of the mast, a figure began to flow. Leaving its hiding place, it translated itself into human form.

One of the *Elohim*.

He wore a creamy and graceful robe, but it did not conceal the etched leanness of his limbs, the scar-pallor of his skin. Under the unkempt silver sweep of his hair, his face was cut and marked with onerous perceptions. Around his yellow eyes, his sockets were as dark as old blood.

Gasping inwardly, Linden recognized Findail the Appointed.

As he took shape, he faced Seadreamer. 'Your pardon,' he said in a voice like habitual grief. 'Miscomprehending the depth of your Earth-Sight, I sought to conceal myself from you. It was not my purpose to inspire such distrust. Yet my sojourn through the seas to accompany you was slow and sorely painful to one who has been sent from his home in *Elemesnedene*. In seeking concealment, I judged poorly – as the swiftness with which you have descried me witnesses. Please accept that I intended no harm.'

Everyone on the foredeck stared at him; but not one replied. Linden was stricken dumb. Pitchwife she could not see – he was behind her. But Honninscrave's features reflected what she felt. And Seadreamer sat huddled on the deck with his hands clamped over his face as if he had just beheld the countenance of his death. Only the *Haruchai* betrayed no reaction.

Findail appeared to expect no response. He shifted his attention to Vain. His tone tightened. 'To you I say, No.' He pointed rigidly at the centre of Vain's chest, and the muscles of his arm stood out like whipcord. 'Whatever else you may do, or think to do, *that* I will not suffer. I am Appointed to this task, but in the name of no duty will I bear that doom.'

In answer, Vain grinned like a ghoul.

A grimace deepened the erosion of Findail's mien. Turning his back on the Demondim-spawn, he moved swiftly forward to stand at the prow of the Giantship, gazing outward like a figurehead.

Linden gaped after him for a moment, looked around at her companions. Honninscrave and Pitchwife were crouched beside Seadreamer; the other Giants appeared too stunned to act. The *Haruchai* watched Findail, but did not move. With a convulsion of will, she wrenched herself into motion. To the nearest crewmember, she rasped, 'Call the First.' Then she went after the *Elohim*.

When she reached him, he glanced at her, gave her a perfunctory acknowledgment; but her presence made no impression on the old rue he had chosen to wear. She received the sudden impression that she was the cause of his distress – and that he meant to hide the fact from her at any cost. For no clear reason, she remembered that his people had expected the Sun-Sage and wielder to be the same person. At first, she could not find the words with which to accost him.

But one memory brought back others, and with them came the rage of helplessness and betrayal she felt towards the *Elohim*. Findail had faced back towards the open sea. She caught hold of his shoulder, demanded his notice. Through her teeth, she grated, 'What in hell are you doing here?'

He hardly seemed to hear her. His yellow eyes were vague with loss, as if in leaving *Elemesnedene* he had been torn out of himself by the roots. But he replied, 'Sun-Sage, I have been Appointed to this task by my people – to procure if I can the survival of the Earth. In the *clachan* you were given no better answer, and I may not answer more clearly now. Be content with the knowledge that I intend no hurt.'

'No *hurt*?' she spat back at him. 'You people have done nothing *but* hurt. You – ' She stopped herself, nearly choking on visions of Covenant and Vain and Seadreamer. 'By God, if you don't come up with a better answer than that, I'll have you thrown overboard.'

'Sun-Sage.' He spoke gently, but made no effort to placate her. 'I regret the necessity of the ring-wielder's plight. For me it is a middle way, balancing hazard and safety. I would prefer to be spared entirely. But it boots nothing to rail against me. I have been Appointed to stand among you, and no power accessible to you may drive me forth. Only he whom you name Vain has it within him to expel me. I would give much that he should do so.'

He surprised her. She believed him instinctively – and did not know what to do about it. 'Vain?' she demanded. *Vain?* But she received no reply. Beyond the prow, the rough waves appeared strangely brittle in the odd raw brilliance of the sunlight. Spray smacked up from the sides of the Giantship and was torn apart by the contradictory winds. They winced back and forth across the deck, troubling her hair like gusts of prescience. Yet she made one more attempt to pierce the *Elohim*. Softly, vehemently, she breathed, 'For the last time, I'm not the goddamn Sun-Sage! You've been wrong about that from the beginning. Everything you're doing is wrong.'

His yellow gaze did not flinch. 'For that reason among many others I am here.'

With an inward snarl she swung away from him – and nearly collided with the hard, mail-clad form of the First. The Swordmain stood there with iron and apprehension in her eyes. In a voice like a quiet blade, she asked, 'Does he speak truly? Do we lack all power against him?'

Linden nodded. But her thoughts were already racing in another direction, already struggling for the self-command she required. She might prove Findail wrong. But she needed to master herself. Searching for a focal point, an anchorage against which to brace her resolve, she lifted her face to the First.

'Tell me about your examination. In *Elemesnedene*. What did they do to you?'

The First was taken aback by the unexpectedness, the apparent irrelevance, of the question. But Linden held up her demand; and after a moment the First drew herself into a formal stance. 'Pitchwife has spoken to you,' she said flatly.

'Yes.'

'Then perhaps you will comprehend that which befell me.' With one hand, she gripped the hilt of her falchion. The other she held straight at her side as if to restrain it from impatience or protest.

'In my testing,' she said, 'one of the *Elohim* came before me in the semblance of a Giant. By some art, he contrived to wear the lineaments and countenance of Pitchwife. But not my husband as I have known him. Rather, he was Pitchwife as he might have grown from a perfect birth – flawless of limb, tall and proud of stance, hale in every way which becomes a Giant.' Memory suffused her gaze; but her tone held its cutting edge. 'He stood thus before me as Pitchwife should have been born and grown, so that the outward seeming well became the spirit I have learned to love.'

Pitchwife stood near her, listening with a crooked smile. But he did not try to express the things which shone in his orbs.

The First did not waver. 'At first I wept. But then I laughed. For all his cunning, that *Elohim* could not equal the joy which enlightens Pitchwife my husband.'

A glint of hard humour touched her tone. 'The *Elohim* misliked my laughter. But he could not answer it, and so my examination was brought to a displeasurable ending for him.'

Pitchwife's whole face chortled, though he made no sound.

A long shiver of recollection ran through Linden. Speaking half to the First, half to the discomfited Sea and the acute sky, she said, 'The only thing Daphin did to me was answer questions.' Then she stepped past the Giants, left their incomprehension behind as she made her way towards Foodfendhall and the underdecks. Towards Covenant's cabin.

The uncertainty of the *dromond*'s footing affected her balance. Starfare's Gem moved with a tight slewing pace, veering and shaking its head at the unexpected force of the swells. But Linden caught herself against walls when she had to, or against Cail, and kept going. Maybe she had not power to extort the truth from Findail. But Covenant did. If she could somehow pierce the veil which covered his consciousness like a winding-sheet. She was suddenly eager to make the attempt.

She told herself that she was eager for his restitution. She wanted his companionship, his conviction. But she was thin-lipped and stiff with anger, and within her there was darkness stirring.

At the door of Covenant's cabin, she met Brinn. He had come out to meet her. Stolidly, he barred her way. His distrust was tangible in the air of the companionway. Before *Elemesnedene*, he had never questioned her right of access to Covenant; but now he said bluntly, 'Chosen, what is your purpose here?'

She bit back a curse. Breathing deeply in an effort to steady herself, she said, 'We've got an *Elohim* aboard, in case you haven't heard. It's Findail. They sent him here for something, and there doesn't seem to be anything we can do about it. The only one of us who has that kind of power is Covenant. I'm going to try to reach him.'

Brinn glanced towards Cail as if he were asking Cail to vouch for her. Then he gave her a slight bow of acquiescence and opened the door.

Glaring, she moved into the cabin, then watched him until he closed the door after her, leaving her alone with Covenant.

There for a moment she hesitated, trying to muster her courage. But Covenant's featureless presence gripped her like a hand on the back of her neck; it compelled her to face him.

He sat in a stone chair beside the small round table as if he had been deliberately positioned there. His legs were straight, formally placed; he did not slouch; his forearms lay on his thighs, with his hands open and the palms laid bare. A tray on the table contained the remains of a meal. Apparently, Brinn had been feeding the Unbeliever. But Covenant was unaware of such things. His slack face confronted the empty air as if it were just another avatar of the emptiness within him.

Linden groaned. The first time she had ever seen him, he had thrown open the door of his house like a hurling of vituperation, the fire and fever of his eyes barely restrained; his mouth had been as strict as a commandment. In spite of his exhaustion, he had been living the life he had chosen, and he had appeared to her strangely indomitable and pure.

But now the definition of his features was obscured by the scruffy helplessness of his beard and the grey which raddled the hair over his forehead gave him an appearance of caducity. The flesh of his face sagged as if he had lost all hope. His eyes were dry – lustreless as death.

He looked like her father had looked when his last blood had fallen to the warped old floorboards of the attic.

But Covenant still had pulse and respiration. Food and fluids sustained his life. When he uttered his refrain, as distinct as an augur, he seemed beneath all his loss to be aware of her – and terrified of what she meant to do to him.

She would have to possess him. Like a Raver. The thought filled her mouth with acid revulsion. But she did not hesitate. She could feel paralysis crouching around her. The fear which had so often bereft her of will was imminent in every wrench of her heart. The fear of what she would become. Trembling, she pulled the other chair close to Covenant's knees, sat down, placed her hands in his flaccid grasp as if even now he might preserve them from failure. Then she tried to open herself to his dead gaze.

Again, his darkness flooded into her, pouring through the conduit of her senses.

There she saw the danger. Inspired by his passive slackness, his resemblance to futility, her old hunger rose up in her gorge.

Instinctively, she fought it, held herself in the outer twilight of his night, poised between consciousness and abandonment. But she could not look away from the fathomless well of his emptiness. Already she was able to perceive facets of his condition which were hidden from the outside. She saw to her surprise that the power which had silenced his mind had also stilled the venom in him. It was quiescent, he had sunk beyond its reach.

Also she saw the qualities which had made him pervious to the *Elohim*. They would not have been able to bereave him so deeply if he had not already been exposed to them by his native impulse to take all harm upon himself. From that source arose both his power and his defencelessness. It gave him a dignity which she did not know how to emulate.

But her will had fallen into its familiar trap. There could be no right or valid way to enter him like this, to desecrate his integrity with her uninvited exigencies – and no right or bearable way to leave him in his plight, to let his need pass without succour. And because she could not resolve the contradiction she had no answer to the dark, angry thing in the pit of her heart which came leaping up at the chance for power. Covenant's power: the chance to be a true arbiter of life and death.

Fierce with hunger, she sprang down into him.

Then the night bore her away.

For a time, it covered all the world. It seemed to stagger every firmament like a gale; yet it was nothing like a gale. Winds had direction and timbre; they were soft or strong, warm or chill. But his darkness was empty of anything which would have named it, given it definition. It was as lorn as the abysm between stars, yet it held no stars to chart its purpose. It filled her like Gibbon's touch, and she was helpless against it, helpless – her father had thrown the key out the window and she possessed no strength or passion that could call him back from death.

The dark swept her around and down like a maelstrom without movement or any other sensation except loss; and from its pit images began to emerge. A figure like an incarnation of the void came towards her across the desert. It was obscured by heatwaves and hallucinations. She could not see who it was. Then she could.

Covenant.

He struggled to scream, but had no mouth. Scales covered half his face. His eyes were febrile with self-loathing. His forehead was pale with the excruciation of his lust and abhorrence. Eagerness and dread complicated his gait; he moved like a cripple as he approached her, aimed himself at her heart.

His arms had become snakes. They writhed and hissed from his shoulders, gaping to breathe and bite. The serpent-heads which had been his hands brandished fangs as white as bone.

She was caught. She knew that she should raise her hands, try to defend herself; but they hung at her sides like mortality, too heavy to lift against the doom of those fangs.

Surging forward, Covenant rose in front of her like all the failures and crimes and loves of her life. When his serpents struck, they knocked her away into another darkness altogether.

Later, she felt that she was being strangled in massive coils. She squirmed and whimpered for release, unable to break free. Her failed hands were knotted in the blanket Cail had spread over her. The hammock constricted her movements. She wanted to scream and could not. Fatal waters filled her throat. The dimness of her cabin seemed as ruinous as Covenant's mind.

But then with a wrench the fact of her surroundings penetrated her. This was her hammock, her cabin. The air was obscured with the dusk of dawn or evening, not the dark void into which she had fallen. The faintly remembered taste of *diamondraught* in her mouth was not the taste of death.

The cabin appeared to lie canted around her, like a house which had been broken from its foundations by some upheaval. When she felt the *dromond's* pitching, she realized that Starfare's Gem was listing heavily, causing her hammock to hang at an angle to the walls. She sensed the vibration of winds and seas through the hull of the Giantship. The dimness did not come from dawn or evening. It was the cloud-locked twilight of a storm.

The storm was bad and becoming monstrous.

Her mind was full of snakes. She could not wrestle free of them. But then a movement near the table took her attention. Peering through the gloom, she made out Cail. He sat in one of the chairs, watching her as if no inadequacy or even betrayal on her part could alter his duty towards her. Yet in the obscurity of the cabin he looked as absolute as a figure of judgment, come to hold every count of her futility against her.

'How long — ?' she croaked. The desert was still in her throat, defying the memory of *diamondraught*. She felt that time had passed. Too much time — enough for everything to have recoiled against her. 'Have I been out?'

Cail rose to his feet. 'A day and a night.'

In spite of his inflexibility, she clung to his dim visage so that she would not slip back among the serpents. 'Covenant?'

The *Haruchai* shrugged fractionally. 'The ur-Lord's plight is unaltered.' He might as well have said, *You have failed. If it was ever your purpose to succeed.*

Clumsily, she left the hammock. She did not want to lie before him like a sacrifice. He offered to assist her; but she rejected his aid, lowered herself alone to the stepladder, then to the floor, so that she could try to face him as an equal.

'Of course I wanted to succeed.' Fleeing from images of Covenant's mind, she went farther than she intended. 'Do you blame me for *everything*?'

His mien remained blank. 'Those are your words.' His tone was as strict as a reproof. 'No *Haruchai* has spoken them.'

'You don't have to,' she retorted as if Covenant's plight had broken something in her chest. 'You wear them on your face.'

Again, Cail shrugged. 'We are who we are. This protest skills nothing.'

She knew that he was right. She had no cause to inflict her self-anger on him as if it were his fault. But she had swallowed too much loathing. And she had failed in paralysis. She had to spit out some of the bile before it sickened her. *We are who we are.* Pitchwife had said the same thing about the *Elohim*.

'Naturally not,' she muttered. 'God forbid that you might do or even think much less *be* anything wrong. Well, let me tell you something. Maybe I've done a lot of things wrong. Maybe I've done everything wrong.' She would never be able to answer the accusation of her failures. 'But when I had you sent out of *Elemesnedene* — when I let the *Elohim* do what they did to Covenant — I was at least *trying* to do something right.'

Cail gazed flatly at her as if he did not mean to reply. But then he spoke, and his voice held a concealed edge. 'That we do not question. Does not Corruption believe altogether in its own rightness?'

At that, Linden went cold with shock. Until now, she had not perceived how deeply the *Haruchai* resented her decisions in *Elemesnedene*. Behind Cail's stolid visage, she sensed the presence of something fatal – something which must have been true of the Bloodguard as well. None of them knew how to forgive.

Gripping herself tightly, she said, 'You don't trust me at all.'

Cail's answer was like a shrug. 'We are sworn to the ur-Lord. He has trusted you.' He did not need to point out that Covenant might feel differently if he ever recovered his mind. That thought had already occurred to her.

In her bitterness, she muttered, 'He tried to. I don't think he succeeded.' Then she could not stand any more. What reason did any of them have to trust her! The floor was still canted under her, and through the stone she felt the way Starfare's Gem was battered by the waves. She needed to escape the confinement of her cabin, the pressure of Cail's masked hostility. Thrusting past him, she flung open the door and left the chamber.

Impeded by the lurch of the Giantship's stride, she stumbled to the stairs, climbed them unsteadily to the afterdeck.

When she stepped over the storm-sill, she was nearly blown from her feet. A predatory wind struck at the decks, clawed at the sails. Angry clouds frothed like breakers at the tips of the yards. As she struggled to a handhold on one of the ascents to the wheeldeck, spray lashed her face, springing like sharp rain from the passion of a dark and viscid Sea.

12

SEA-HARM

There was no rain, just wind as heavy as torrents, and clouds which sealed the Sea in a glower of twilight from horizon to horizon, and keen spray boiling off the crests of the waves like steam to sting like hail. The blast struck the Giantship at an angle, canting it to one side.

Linden gasped for breath. As she fought her vision clear of spume, she was astonished to see Giants in the rigging.

She did not know how they could hold. Impossible that they should be working up there, in the full blow of the storm!

Yet they were working. Starfare's Gem needed enough sail to give it headway. But if the spars carried too much canvas, any sudden shift or increase in the wind might topple the *dromond* or simply drive it under. The crewmembers were furling the upper sails. They looked small and inconceivable against the hard dark might of the storm. But slowly, tortuously, they fought the writhing canvas under control.

High up on the foremast, a Giant lost his hold, had to release the clew-lines in order to save himself. Dawngreeter was instantly torn away. Flapping wildly, like a stricken albatross, it fluttered along the wind and out of sight.

The other Giants had better success. By degrees, Starfare's Gem improved its stance.

But towering seas still heaved at the vessel. Plunging across the trough of a wave, it crashed sideward up the next ragged and vicious slope, then dived again as if it meant to bury its prow in the bottom. Linden clutched the stairs to keep herself from being kicked overboard.

She could not remain there. She feared that Starfare's Gem was in danger for its life — that any increase in the storm might break the ship apart. And the storm was going to increase. She felt its fury concatenating in the distance. The *dromond* rode the fringes of the blast; its heart was drawing closer. This course would carry the Giantship into the worst of the violence.

She had to warn Honninscrave.

She tried to creep up on to the stairs; but the wind flung her hair against her face like a flail, sucked the air from her lungs, threatened to rend her away. An instant of panic flamed through her.

Cail's arm caught her waist like a band of stone. His mouth came to her ear. 'Seek shelter!' The wind ripped the words to pieces, making his shout barely audible.

She shook her head urgently, tried to drive her voice through the blow. 'Take me to the wheeldeck!'

He hesitated for a moment while he cast a look about him, estimating the dangers. Then he swung her up the stairs.

She felt like a ragdoll in his grasp. If he had been any ordinary man, they would both have been slashed overboard. But he was a *Haruchai*. Surging across the weight of the wind, he bore her to the wheeldeck.

Only three Giants were there: Honninscrave, Galewrath, and the First. The Storesmaster stood at the great wheel, embracing it with both arms. Her muscles were knotted under the strain; her feet were widely planted to brace herself. She looked like a granite monolith, capable of standing there and mastering Shipsheartthew until the sea and time broke Starfare's Gem into rubble.

Anchored by her weight and strength, the First remained still. The

Search was out of her hands. Under these conditions, it belonged to the storm – and to Starfare's Gem. And the *dromond* belonged to Honninscrave.

He stood near Galewrath; but all his attention was focused forward like a beacon, burning for the safety of his ship. The bony mass of his brows seemed to protect his sight. He bore himself as if he could see everything. His trenchant bellow pierced the wind. And the Giants responded like a manifestation of his will. Step by arduous step they fought sheets and shrouds and canvas, tuned Starfare's Gem to endure the peril.

Linden tried to shout; but the wind struck her in the teeth, stuffed her voice back down her throat. With a fervid gesture, she directed Cail towards the Master.

'Honninscrave!' She had to scream to make herself heard. 'Change course! We're running right into the storm!'

The import of her words snatched at his attention. Bending over her, he shouted, 'That cannot be! This storm rises from the south! Riding as we do, we shall remain on its verge and be driven only scantly from our path!'

The *south*? She gaped at him, disbelieving that he could be wrong about such a thing. When she forced her vision in that direction, she saw he was not wrong. Her senses plainly discerned a cusp of violence there, though it was several leagues distant. Honninscrave's present course would carry Starfare's Gem around the fierce core of that storm.

But a look towards the north-west verified what she had seen earlier. A hurricane crouched there, titanic and monstrous. The two storms were crowding together, with Starfare's Gem between them. Every heave and crash of the *dromond*'s keel angled it closer to the savagery of the stronger blast.

With a cry that seemed to tear her throat, she told Honninscrave what she saw.

Her news staggered him. He had never had a chance to see the hurricane. The first storm had taken hold of the Giantship before it entered the range of the second. Disaster loomed along the heading he had chosen. But he recovered swiftly. He was the Master of Starfare's Gem in every nerve and sinew. He sounded ready for any peril or mischance as he shouted, 'What is your counsel?'

Gritting herself, she tried to think – gauge the intersecting paths of the storm, estimate the effect they would have on each other. She was not adept at such visualizations. She was trained to map the insidious cunning of diseases, not the candid fury of gales. But she read them as best she could.

'If we keep on this way!' Her chest ached at the strain of yelling. 'We might be able to pass the one in the south! Or the worst of it! Before we get too far into the other one!'

Honninscrave nodded his approval. The abutment of his forehead seemed proof against any storm.

'But the other one!' She concluded as if she were screaming. 'It's terrible! If you have to choose, go south!'

'I hear you!' His shout was flayed into spray and tatters. He had already turned to hurl his orders across the wind.

His commands sounded as mad as the gale. Linden felt the hurricane ravening closer, always closer. Surely no vessel – especially one as heavy as the *dromond* – could withstand that kind of fury. The wind was a shriek in the ratlines. She could see the masts swaying. The yards appeared to waver like outstretched arms groping for balance. The deck kicked and lurched. If Galewrath did not weaken, the rudder might snap, leaving Starfare's Gem at the mercy of the hungry seas. While Linden hesitated, the last sail left on the aftermast sprang suddenly into shreds and was gone, torn thread from thread. Its gear lashed the air. Instinctively, she ducked her head, pressed herself against Cail's support.

Yelling like ecstasy, Honninscrave sent Giants to replace the lost canvas.

Linden pulled her face to the side of Cail's head, shouted, 'Take me forward! I've got an idea!'

He nodded his understanding and at once began to haul her towards a stairway, choosing the windward side rather than the lee to keep as much of the tilted deck as possible between her and the seething rush of the Sea.

As they reached the stairs, she saw several Giants – Pitchwife and others – hastening across the afterdeck, accompanied by Ceer and Hergrom. They were stringing lifelines. When she and Cail gained the foot of the stairs, Pitchwife and Ceer came slogging to join them. Blinking the spray from his eyes, Pitchwife gave her a grin. With a gesture towards the wheeldeck, he shouted like a laugh, 'Our Honninscrave is in his element, think you not?' Then he ascended the stairs to join his wife and the Master.

Linden's clothes were soaked. Her shirt stuck to her skin. Every gobbet of water the seas hurled at her seemed to slap into her bones. She had already begun to shiver. But the cold felt detached, impersonal, as if she were no longer fully inhabiting her body; and she ignored it.

Then rain gushed out of the clouds. It filled the air as if every wavecap had become foam, boiling up to put teeth into the wind. The ocean appeared to shrink around Starfare's Gem, blinding all the horizons. Linden could barely see as far as Foodfendhall. She spat curses, but the loud rain deafened her to her own voice. With so little visibility, how would Honninscrave know when to turn from the approaching hurricane?

She struggled to the nearest lifeline, locked her fingers around it, then started to pull her way forward.

She had an idea. But it might have been sane or mad. The gale rent away all distinctions.

The afterdeck seemed as long as a battlefield. Spray and rain sent sheets of water pouring against her ankles, nearly sweeping her down the deck. At every plunge of the Giantship, she shivered like an echo of the tremors which ran along the *dromond*'s keel. The lifeline felt raw with cold, abrading her palms. Yet she strove forward. She had failed at everything else. She could not bear to think that this simple task might prove beyond her strength.

Ceer went ahead to open the door of the housing. Riding an eddy of the storm, she pitched over the sill, stumbled to the floor. The two *Haruchai* slammed the door; and at once the air tensed as if pressure were building towards and explosion in Foodfendhall, aggravated by the yammer and crash outside. For a moment of panic, she thought she heard pieces of the ship breaking away. But as she regained her breath, she realized that she was hearing the protestations of the midmast.

In the lantern-light, the shaft of the mast was plain before her, marked by engravings she had never studied. Perhaps they revealed the story of the Starfare's Gem's making, or of its journeys. She did not know. As she worked forward, the groans and creaks rose into a sharp keening. The spars high above her had begun to sing.

She nearly fell again when Ceer opened the door, letting the howl strike at her like a condor. But Cail braced her, helped her back out into the blast. At once, the rain crashed down like thunder. She chose a lifeline anchored to the foremast. With the cable clamped under one arm so that it upheld her, she lowered her head and went on against the wind.

A Giant loomed ahead of her, following the lifeline aft. As they reached each other, she recognized Sevinhand. He paused to let her pass, then shouted like an act of comradeship, 'Such a storm! Were I less certain of our charting, I would believe that we have blundered unwitting into the Soulbiter!'

She had no time to reply. Her hands burned with friction and cold. The cable wore at her side like a gall. She had to reach Findail. He alone on Starfare's Gem had the power to avert the disaster of the advancing hurricane.

At the foremast she rested briefly, standing so that the wind pressed her to the stone. In that position, the torment of the mast thrummed acutely into her. The granite's vitality was being stressed mercilessly. For a moment, the sensation filled her with dread. But when she thrust her percipience into the mast, she was reassured. Like Honninscrave, the *dromond* was equal to this need. Starfare's Gem might tilt and keen, but it was not about to break.

Yet the heart of the hurricane was towering towards her like a mountain come to life, a dire colossus striding to stamp the Giantship down to its doom. Clinching a cable which ran in the direction of the prow, she went on.

As she squinted through sheets of water as binding as cerements, she caught sight of Vain. The Demondim-spawn stood midway between the foremast and the prow, facing forward as if to keep watch on Findail. And he was as rigid as if the heaving surface under him were a stationary platform. Even the wind had no effect upon him. He might have been rooted to the stone.

Findail became visible for a moment, then disappeared as the Giantship crashed into the trough of the seas and slammed its prow against the next wave. A deluge cut Linden's legs from under her. She barely kept her grip on the lifeline. Now she could only advance between waves. When Starfare's Gem lifted its head, she wrestled forward a few steps. When the prow hit the next wave as if the *dromond* were being snatched into the deeps, she clung where she was and prayed that her grip and the cable would hold.

But she moved by stages and at last reached the railing. From there, she had only a short way to go.

The last part was the hardest. She was already quivering with cold and exhaustion; and the Giantship's giddy motion, throwing her towards and then yanking her away from the Sea, left her hoarse with involuntary curses. At every downward crash, the force of the vessel's struggle hit her. The sheer effort of holding her breath for each inundation threatened to finish her. Several times, she was only saved by the support of Cail's shoulder.

Then she gained Findail's side. He glanced at her between plunges; and the sight of him stunned her. He was not even wet. The wind did not ruffle his hair; the rain did not touch him. He emerged from every smash into the waves with dry raiment and clear eyes, as if he had tuned his flesh to a pitch beyond the reach of any violence of weather or Sea.

But his unscathed aspect confirmed her determination. He was a being of pure Earthpower, capable of sparing himself the merest contact with wind and spray. And what was any storm, if not Earthpower in another form – unbridled and savage, but still acting in accordance with the Law of its nature?

At the impact of the next wave, she ducked her head. The water pounded her, covered her face with her hair. When the *dromond* lifted again, she loosed one hand from the rail to thrust the sodden strands aside. Then she drove her voice at Findail.

'Do something! Save us!'

His pain-lined expression did not alter. He made no attempt to shout; but his words reached her as clearly as if the storm had been stricken dumb.

'The *Elohim* do not tamper with the life of the Earth. There is no life without structure. We respect the workings of that structure in every guise.'

Structure, Linden thought. Law. *They are who they are. Their might is matched by their limitations.* Starfare's Gem dived. She clung to the rail for her life. Chaos was death. Energy could not exist without constriction. If the Lawless power of the Sunbane grew too strong, it might unbind the very foundations of the Earth.

As the deluge swept past her, she tried again.

'Then tell Honninscrave what to do! Guide him!'

The *Elohim* seemed faintly surprised. 'Guide him?' But then he shrugged. 'Had he inquired, the question would have searched me. In such a case, where would my ethic lie? But it boots nothing now.' The Giantship plunged again; yet Linden could hear him through the tumult of the water and the shrill wind. 'The time for such questions is lost.'

When the prow surfaced, she fought her sight clear and saw what he meant.

From out of the heart of the hurricane came rushing a wall of water as high as the first spars of the Giantship.

It was driven by wind – a wind so savage and tremendous that it dwarfed everything else; a wind which turned every upreaching Sea to steam, sheared off the crest of every wave, so that the ocean under it mounted and ran like a flow of dark magma.

Starfare's Gem lay almost directly athwart the wall.

Linden stared at it in a seizure of dread. In the last pause before the onslaught, she heard Honninscrave roaring faintly, 'Ward!' Then his shout was effaced by the wild stentorian rage of the wind, howling like the combined anguish and ferocity of all the damned.

As the wall hit, she lunged at Findail, trying to gain his help – or take him with her, she did not know which. The impact of the great wave ended all differences. But her hands seemed to pass through him. She got one last clear look at his face. His eyes were yellow with grief.

Then the starboard side of the Giantship rose like an orogenic upthrust, and she fell towards the sea.

She thought that surely she would strike the port rail. She flailed her arms to catch hold of it. But she was pitched past it into the water.

The Sea slammed at her with such force that she did not feel the blow, did not feel the waters close over her.

At the same moment, something hard snagged her wrist, wrenched her back to the surface. She was already ten or fifteen feet from the ship. Its port edge was submerged; the entire foredeck loomed over her. It stood almost vertically in the water, poised to fall on her, crush her between stone and Sea.

But it did not fall. Somehow, Starfare's Gem remained balanced on its side, with nearly half of its port decks underwater. And Cail did not let her go.

His right hand held her wrist at the farthest stretch of his arm. His ankles were grasped by Ceer, also fully outstretched.

Vain anchored the *Haruchai*. He still stood as if he were rooted to the deck, with his body at right angles to the stone, nearly parallel to the Sea. But he had moved down the deck, positioned himself almost at the waterline. At the end of his reach, he held Ceer's ankles.

He did not trouble to raise his head to find out if Linden were safe.

Heaving against the rush of water, Ceer hauled Cail closer to the deck; and Cail dragged Linden after him. Together, the *Haruchai* contracted their chain until Cail could grip Vain's wrist with his free hand. The Demondim-spawn did nothing to ease their task; but when both Cail and Ceer were clinched to him, holding Linden between them, he released Ceer's ankles. Then the *Haruchai* bore her up Vain's back to the deck.

Braced against his rigid ankles, they gave her a chance to draw breath.

She had swallowed too much water; she was gagging on salt. A spasm of coughing knotted her guts. But when it loosened, she found that she could breathe more easily than before the great wave struck. Lying on its side, Starfare's Gem formed a lee against the wind. The turbulence of the blast's passage pounded the Sea beyond the ship, so that the surface frothed and danced frenetically; but the decks themselves lay in a weird calm.

As she caught her breath, the *dromond*'s plight struck her like a hand of the gale.

On every level of her senses, the granite vessel burned with strain. It radiated pain like a racked animal caught in the unanswerable snare of the blast. From stem to stern, mast-top to keel, all the stone was shrill with stress, tortured by pressures which its makers could not have conceived. Starfare's Gem had fallen so far on to its side that the tips of its spars nearly touched the water. It lay squarely across the wind; and the wild storm swept it over the ocean with terrifying speed.

If there had been any waves, the *dromond* would certainly have foundered; but in that, at least, the vessel was fortunate, for the titanic gale crushed everything into one long flat and seething rush. Yet the Giantship hung only inches from capsizing. Had the great weight of its masts and yards not been counterbalanced by its enormous keel, it would already have plunged to its death.

In a way, the sheer force of the wind had saved the ship. It had instantly stripped the remaining canvas to ribbons, thus weakening the thrust of its turbulence against the masts. But still the vessel's poised survival was as fragile as an old bone. Any shift of the *dromond*'s position in the wind, any rise of the gale or surge of the Sea, would be enough to snap that balance. And every increase in the amount of water Starfare's Gem shipped threatened to drag it down.

Giants must have been at the pumps; but Linden did not know how they could possibly keep pace with the torrents that poured in through the hatches and ports, the broken doors of Foodfendhall. The wind's fury howled at the hull as if it meant to chew through the stone to get at her. And that sound, the incisive ululation and shriek of air blasting past the moire-granite, ripped across the grain of her mind like her own teeth until the pain began to feel like a wedge driven between the bones of her skull.

For a terrible moment, the ship's peril blanked everything else out of her mind. But then her heart seemed to come alive with a wrench, and implications of panic shot through her. Grabbing at Cail, she cried over the ferocious background of the wind, 'Covenant!' His cabin was to port below the wheeldeck. It must be underwater. He would not be able to save himself from the Sea as it rushed in through riven hatches, ruptured portholes, doors burst from their moorings. He would sit there, helpless and empty, while he drowned.

But Cail replied, 'Brinn was forewarned! The ur-Lord is safe!'

Safe! Good Christ! Clinging to that hope, she shouted, 'Take me to him!'

Ceer turned, called a hail up the deck. A moment later, a Giant near the foremast threw down the end of a rope. The two *Haruchai* caught it, knotted it around Linden's waist, then gripped it themselves as the Giant drew them all up the steep stone.

Vain remained where he was as if he were content to watch the Sea speeding within arm's reach of his face. For the present, at least, he had satisfied his purpose. The black rigor of his back said plainly that he cared for nothing else.

When the Giant had pulled Linden and the *Haruchai* up to him, he snatched her into a fervid hug. He was Mistweave; and the fear he had felt for her trembled in his thews. Over her shoulder, he shouted praise and thanks to the *Haruchai*.

His Giantish embrace tasted impossibly secure in the gale. But she could not bear to be delayed. The *dromond* hung on the verge of destruction. 'Where's Covenant?' she yelled.

Carefully, Mistweave set her down, then pointed away aft. 'The Master gathers the crew above the aftermast! Covenant Giantfriend is there! I go to assist at the pumps!'

The *Haruchai* nodded their comprehension. Mistweave tore himself away, scrambled to a hatch which gave access to the underdecks, and disappeared.

Holding Linden between them, Cail and Ceer began to move towards Foodfendhall.

Cautiously navigating the lifelines, they brought her to the upper door. Within the housing, they found that the Giants had strung more cables, enabling them to cross the wreckage to the afterdeck. One lantern still hung at a crazy angle from the midmast, and its wan light revealed the broken litter of tables and benches which lay half-submerged in the lower part of the hall. The destruction seemed like a blow struck at the very heart of the Giants – at their love of communal gathering.

But the *Haruchai* did not delay to grieve over the damage. Firmly, they bore Linden out to the afterdeck.

Most of her other shipmates were there, perched in various attitudes along the starboard rail above the mast. Through the clenched twilight, she could see more than a score of Giants, including Pitchwife, the First, Seadreamer, and Honninscrave. Pitchwife shouted a relieved welcome to her; but she hardly heard him. She was hunting for a glimpse of Covenant.

After a moment, she located the Unbeliever. He was partially hidden by Seadreamer's protective bulk. Brinn and Hergrom were braced on either side of him; and he hung slack between them as if all his bones had been broken.

Ceer and Cail took Linden up a lifeline to one of the cables which ran the length of the afterdeck eight or ten paces below the railing, lashed there to permit movement back and forth, and to catch anyone who might fall. In the arrangement of the lines, she recognized Honninscrave's meticulous concern for his crew, the life of his ship. He was busy directing the placement of more cables so that his people would be enclosed in a network of supports.

As she was brought near Covenant, his presence gave her a false energy. She took hold of the arm Seadreamer extended towards her, moved like braciation from him to Brinn and the railing. Then she huddled beside Covenant and at once began to explore him for injuries or deterioration.

He was nearly as wet as she, and automatic shivers ran through him like an ague in the marrow of his bones. But in other ways he was as well as the *Elohim* had left him. His eyes stared as if they had lost the capability of focus; his mouth hung open; water bedraggled his beard. When she examined him, he repeated his warning almost inaudibly against the background of the wind. But the words meant nothing to him.

Weakened by relief and pain, she sagged at his side.

The First and Pitchwife were nearby, watching for her verdict on Covenant's state. Linden shook her head; and Pitchwife winced. But the First said nothing. She held herself as if the absence of any bearable foe cramped her muscles. She was a trained warrior; but the Giantship's survival depended on sea-craft, not swords. Linden met the First's gaze and nodded. She knew how the Swordmain felt.

Looking around the *dromond*, she was appalled to see that Galewrath still stood at Shipsheartthew. Locked between the stone spokes of the wheel and the deck, the Storesmaster held her place with the stolid intransigence of a statue. At first, Linden did not understand why Galewrath stayed in a place of such exposure and strain – or why the Master allowed anyone to remain there. But then her thinking clarified. The *dromond* still needed its rudder to maintain its precarious balance. In addition, if the wind shifted forward Galewrath might be able to turn Starfare's Gem perpendicular to the blast again; for the Giantship would surely sink if any change sent its prow even slightly into the wind. And if the gale shifted aft, she might have a chance to turn away. With the storm at its back Starfare's Gem might be able to rise and run.

Linden did not know how even a Giant's thews could stand the strain Galewrath endured. But the blunt woman clung like hard hope to her task and did not let go.

At last, Honninscrave finished setting his lifelines. Swarming from cable to cable, he climbed to join the First and Pitchwife near Linden. As he moved, he shouted encouragements and jests to the hunched shapes of his crew. Pitchwife had described him accurately: he was in his element. His oaken shoulders bore the *dromond*'s plight as if the burden were light to him.

Reaching Linden's proximity, he called, 'Be not daunted, Chosen! Starfare's Gem will yet redeem us from this storm!'

She was no match for him. His fortitude only underscored her apprehension. Her voice nearly broke as she returned, 'How many have we lost?'

'Lost?' His reply pierced the blind ferocity of the hurricane. 'None! Your forewarning prepared us! All are here! Those you see not I have sent to the pumps!' As he spoke, Linden became aware that bursts of water were slashing away from the side of the ship above her, boiling into mist and darkness as the wind tore them from the pumpholes. 'Those to port we cannot employ. But those to starboard we have linked across the holds. Sevinhand, who commands below, reports that his crew keeps pace. We endure, Chosen! We will survive!'

She groped for a share of his faith and could not find it. 'Maybe we should abandon ship!'

He gaped at her. She heard the folly of her words before he responded, 'Do you wish to chance this Sea in a longboat?'

Helplessly, she asked, 'What're you going to do?'

'Naught!' he returned in a shout like a challenge. 'While this gale holds, we are too precarious. But when the change comes, as come it must – Then perhaps you will see that the Giants are sailors – and

Starfare's Gem, a ship – to make the heart proud!

'Until that time, hold faith! Stone and Sea, do you not comprehend that we are alive?' But she was no longer listening to him. The imponderable screech and yowl of the blast seemed to strike straight at Covenant. He was shivering with cold. His need was poignant to her; but she did not know how to touch him. Her hands were useless, so deeply chilled that she could hardly curl them into fists. Slow blood oozed from several abrasions on her palms, formed in viscid drops between her fingers. She paid no attention to it.

Later, large bowls of *diamondraught* were passed among the companions. The Giantish liquor reduced her weakness somewhat, enabling her to go on clinging for her life. But still she did not raise her head. She could not think why Vain had saved her. The force of the storm felt like an act of malice. Surely if the Demondim-spawn had not saved her the blast would have been appeased.

Her health-sense insisted that the hurricane was a natural one, not a manifestation of deliberate evil. But she was so badly battered by the wind's violence and the cold, so eroded by her fear, that she no longer knew the difference.

They were all going to die, and she had not yet found a way to give Covenant back his mind.

Later still, night effaced the last illumination. The gale did not abate; it appeared to have blown out the stars. Nothing but a few weak lanterns – one near Galewrath, the rest scattered along the upper edge of the afterdeck – reduced the blackness. The wind went on reaping across the Sea with a sound as shrill as a scythe. Through the stone came the groaning of the masts as they protested against their moorings, the repetitive thud and pound of the pumps. All the crewmembers took turns below, but their best efforts were barely enough to keep pace with the water. They could not reduce the great salt weight which held Starfare's Gem on its side. More *diamondraught* was passed around. The day had seemed interminable. Linden did not know how she could face the night and stay sane.

By degrees, her companions sank into themselves as she did. Dismay covered them like the night, soaked into them like the cold. If the wind shifted now, Galewrath would have no forewarning. In the distant light of her lantern, she looked as immobile as stone, no longer capable of the reactions upon which the *dromond* might depend. Yet Honninscrave sent no one to relieve her: any brief uncertainty while Shipsheartthew changed hands might cause the vessel to founder. And so the Giants who were not at the pumps had no other way to fight for their lives except to cling and shiver. Eventually, even the Master's chaffering could not rouse them to hope or spirit. They crouched against the rail, with the black Sea running almost directly below them, and waited like men and women who had been sentenced to death.

But Honninscrave did not leave them alone. When his guyings and jollyings became ineffective, he shouted unexpectedly, 'Ho, Pitchwife! The somnolence of these Giants abashes me! In days to come, they will hang their heads to hear such a tale told of them! Grant us a song to lift our hearts, that we may remember who we are!'

From a place near her, Linden heard the First mutter mordantly, 'Aye, Pitchwife. Grant them a song. When those who are whole falter, those who are halt must bear them up.'

But Pitchwife did not appear to hear her. 'Master!' he replied to Honninscrave with a frantic laugh, 'I have been meditating such a song! It may not be kept silent, for it swells in my heart, becoming too great for any breast to contain! Behold!' With a lugubrious stagger, he let himself fall down the deck. When he hit the first lifeline, it thrummed under his weight, but held. Half-reclining against the line, he faced upward. 'It will boon me to sing this song for you!'

Shadows cast by the lanterns made his misshapen face into a grimace. But his grin was unmistakable; and as he continued his humour became less forced.

'I will sing the song which Bahgoon sang, in the aftermath of his taming by his spouse and harridan, that many-legended odalisque Thelma Twofist!'

The power of his personal mirth drew a scattering of wan cheers and ripostes from the despondent Giants.

Striking a pose of exaggerated melancholy, he began. He did not actually sing; he could not make a singing voice audible. But he delivered his verses in a pitched rhythmic shout which affected his listeners like music.

> 'My love has eyes which do not glow
>   Her loveliness is somewhat formed askew,
>   With blemishes which number not a few,
> And pouting lips o'er teeth not in a row.

> 'Her limbs are doughtier than mine,
>   And what I do not please to give she takes.
>   Her hair were better kempt with hoes and rakes.
> Her kiss tastes less of *diamondraught* than brine.

> 'Her odorescence gives me ill
>   Her converse is by wit or grace unlit
>   Her raiment would become her if it fit.
> So think of me with rue: I love her still.'

It was a lengthy song; but after a moment Linden was distracted from it. Faintly, she heard the First murmuring to herself, clearly unaware that anyone could hear her.

'Therefore do I love you, Pitchwife,' she said into the wind and the night. 'In sooth, this is a gift to lift the heart. Husband, it shames me that I do not equal your grace.'

In a beneficial way, the deformed Giant seemed to shame all the crew. To answer his example, they stirred from their disconsolation, responded to each other as if they were coming back to life. Some of them were laughing; others straightened their backs, tightened their grips on the railing, as if by so doing they could better hear the song.

Instinctively, Linden roused herself with them. Their quickening emanations urged her to shrug off some of her numbness.

But when she did so, her percipience began to shout at her. Behind the restoration of the Giants rose a sense of peril. Something was approaching the Giantship – something malefic and fatal.

It had nothing to do with the storm. The storm was not evil. This was.

'Chosen?' Cail asked.

Distinctly, Covenant said, 'Don't touch me.'

She tried to rise to her feet. Only Cail's swift intervention kept her from tumbling towards Pitchwife.

'Jesus!' She hardly heard herself. The darkness and the gale deafened her. 'It's going to attack us here!'

The First swung towards her. 'Attack us?'

As Linden cried out, 'That Raver!' the assault began.

Scores of long dark shapes seethed out of the water below the aftermast. They broke through the reflections of the lanterns, started to wriggle up the steep stone.

As they squirmed upward, they took light. The air seemed to ignite them in fiery red.

Burning with crimson internal heat like fireserpents, they attacked the deck, swarming towards Covenant and Linden.

Eels!

Immense numbers of them.

They were not on fire, shed no flame. Rather, they radiated a hot red malice from their snakelike forms. Driven by the lust of the Raver in them, they shone like incandescent blood as they climbed. They were as large as Linden's arm. Their gaping teeth flashed light as incisive as razors.

The First yelled a warning that fled without echo into the wind.

The leading eels reached the level of the mast; but Linden could not move. The sheer force of the Raver's presence held her. Memories of Gibbon and Marid burned in her guts; and a black yearning answered, jumping within her like wild glee. Power! The part of her that desired possession and Ravers, lusted for the sovereign strength of death, lashed against her conscious loathing, her vulnerable and deliberate rejection of evil; and the contradiction locked her into immobility. She had been like this in the woods behind Haven Farm, when Lord Foul had looked out of the fire at her and she had let Covenant go down alone to his doom.

Yet that threat to him had finally broken her fear, sent her running to his rescue. And the eels were coming for him now, while he was entirely unable to defend himself. Stung by his peril, her mind seemed to step back, fleeing from panic into her old professional detachment.

Why had Foul chosen to attack now, when the *Elohim* had already done Covenant such harm? Had the *Elohim* acted for reasons of their own, without the Despiser's knowledge or prompting? Had she been wrong in her judgment of them? If Lord Foul did not know about Covenant's condition –

Hergrom, Ceer, and the First had already started downward to meet the attack; but Pitchwife was closer to it than anyone else. Quickly, he slipped below his lifeline to the next cable. Bracing himself there, he bent and scooped up an eel to crush it.

As his hand closed, a discharge of red power shot through him. The blast etched him, distinct and crimson, against the dark Sea. With a scream in his chest, he tumbled down the deck, struck heavily against the base of the mast. Sprawled precariously there, he lay motionless, barely breathing.

More eels crawled over his legs. But since he was still, they did not unleash their fire into him.

Hergrom slid in a long dive down to the stricken Giant. At once, he kicked three eels away from Pitchwife's legs. The creatures fell writhing back into the Sea; but their power detonated on Hergrom's foot, sent him into convulsions. Only the brevity of the blast saved his life. He retained scarcely enough control over his muscles to knot one fist in the back of Pitchwife's sark, the other on a cleat of the mast. Twitching and jerking like a wildman, he still contrived to keep himself and Pitchwife from sliding farther.

Every spasm threatened to bring either him or the Giant into contact with more of the creatures.

Then the First reached the level of the assault. With her feet planted on the deck, a lifeline across her belly, she poised her broadsword in both fists. Her back and shoulders bunched like a shout of fear and rage for Pitchwife.

The First's jeopardy snatched Linden back from her detachment. Desperately, she howled, 'No!'

She was too late. The First scythed her blade at the eels closest to her feet.

Power shot along the iron, erupted from her hands into her chest.

Fire formed a corona around her. Red static sprang from her hair. Her sword fell. Plunging in a shower of sparks, it struck the water with a sharp hiss and disappeared.

She made no effort to catch it. Her stunned body toppled over the lifeline. Below her, the water seethed with malice as more eels squirmed up the deck into air and fire.

Ceer barely caught her. Reading the situation with celerity bordering on prescience, he had taken an instant to knot a rope around his waist. As the First fell, he threw the rope to the nearest crewmember and sprang after her.

He snagged her by the shoulder. Then the Giant pulled on the rope, halting Ceer and the First just above the waterline. 'Don't move them!' Linden shouted instantly. 'She can't take any more!'

The First lay still. Ceer held himself motionless. The eels crawled over them as if they were a part of the deck.

With a fierce effort, Hergrom fought himself under command. He steadied his limbs, stopped jerking Pitchwife, a heartbeat before more eels began slithering over the two of them.

Linden could hardly think. Her friends were in danger. Memories of Revelstone and Gibbon pounded at her. The presence of the Raver hurt her senses, appalled every inch of her flesh. In Revelstone, the conflict of her reactions to that ill power had driven her deep into a catatonia of horror. But now she let the taste of evil pour through her and fought to concentrate on the creatures themselves. She needed a way to combat them.

Seadreamer's reflexes were swifter. Tearing Covenant from Brinn's grasp, he leaped down to the first cable, then began hauling himself towards Foodfendhall.

Brinn went after him as if to retrieve the ur-Lord from a Giant who had gone mad.

But almost immediately Seadreamer's purpose became clear. As the Giant conveyed Covenant forward, the eels turned in that direction, writhing to catch up with their prey. The whole thrust of the attack shifted forward.

Soon Ceer and the First were left behind. And a moment later Pitchwife and Hergrom were out of danger.

At once, the Giant holding Ceer's rope heaved the *Haruchai* and the First upward. Honninscrave skidded under the lifelines to the mast, took Pitchwife from Hergrom's damaged grasp.

But the eels still came, Raver-driven to hurl themselves at Covenant. Shortly, Seadreamer had transversed the cable to its mooring near the rail at the edge of Foodfendhall. There he hesitated, looked back at the pursuit. But he had no choice. He had committed himself, was cornered now between the housing and the rail. The nearest creatures were scant moments from his feet.

As Brinn caught up with him, Seadreamer grabbed the *Haruchai* by the arm, pulled him off his feet in a deft arc up to the canted roof. He landed just within the ship's lee below the mad gale. Almost in the same motion, Seadreamer planted one foot atop the railing and leaped after Brinn.

For an instant, the wind caught him, tried to hurl him out to sea. But his weight and momentum bore him back down to the roof. Beyond the edge of Foodfendhall, he dropped out of Linden's view. Then he appeared again as he stretched out along the midmast. He held Covenant draped over his shoulder.

In spite of the fearsome risks he took, Linden's courage lifted. Perhaps the wall of the housing would block the eels.

But the creatures had not been daunted by the steep slope of the deck; and now they began to squirm up the side of Foodfendhall, clinging to the flat stone with their bellies. As their fire rose, it came between her and the darkness at the mast, effacing Seadreamer and Covenant from her sight.

At Honninscrave's command, several Giants moved to engage the eels. They fought by using lengths of hawser as whips – and had some success. Discharges of power expended themselves by incinerating the ropes, did not reach the hands of the Giants. Many eels were killed by the force of the blows.

But the creatures were too numerous; and the Giants were slowed by their constant need for more rope. They could not clear their way to the wall, could not prevent scores of fireserpents from scaling upward. And more eels came surging incessantly out of the Sea. Soon Seadreamer would be trapped. Already, the creatures were wriggling on to the roof.

Urgency and instinct impelled Linden into motion. In a flash of memory, she saw Covenant standing, valiant and desirable, within the *caamora* he had created for the Dead of The Grieve – protected from the bonfire by wild magic. Fire against fire. Bracing herself on Cail, she snatched at the lantern hanging from the rail above her head. Though she was weak with cold and off-balance, she turned, hurled the lantern towards Foodfendhall.

It fell short of the red-bright wall. But when it hit the deck, it broke; and oil spattered over the nearest eels. Instantly, they burst into flame. Their own power became a conflagration which consumed them. Convulsed in their death throes, they fell back to the water and hissed their dying away into the dark.

Linden tried to shout; but Honninscrave was quicker. 'Oil!' he roared. 'Bring more oil!'

In response, Ceer and two of the Giants hurtled towards a nearby hatchway.

Other crewmembers grabbed for the remaining lanterns. Honninscrave stopped them. 'We will need the light!'

Seadreamer, Covenant, and Brinn were visible now in the advancing glare of the eels. Seadreamer stood on the mast, with Covenant on his shoulder. As the eels hastened towards him, he retreated up the mast. It was a treacherous place to walk – curved, festooned with cables, marked with belaying-cleats. But he picked his way up the slope, his eyes fixed on the eels. His gaze echoed mad determination to their fire. In the garish illumination, he looked heavy and fatal, as if his weight alone would be enough to topple Starfare's Gem.

Between him and the attack stood Brinn. The *Haruchai* followed Seadreamer, facing the danger like the last guardian of Covenant's life. Linden could not read his face at that distance; but he must have known that the first blow he struck would also be the last. Yet he did not falter.

Ceer and the two Giants had not returned. Measuring the time by her ragged breathing, Linden believed that they were already too late. Too many eels had gained the roof. And still more continued to rise out of the Sea as if their numbers were as endless as the malevolence which drove them.

Abruptly, Seadreamer stumbled into the turbulence beyond the lee of the ship. The gale buffeted him from his feet, almost knocked him off the mast. But he dropped down to straddle the stone with his legs, and his massive thighs held him against the blast. Light reflected from the scar under his eyes as if his visage were afire. Covenant dangled limp and insensate from his shoulder. The creatures were halfway up the mast to him. Between him and death stood one weaponless *Haruchai*.

Raging with urgency, Honninscrave shouted at his brother.

Seadreamer heard, understood. He shifted the Unbeliever so that Covenant lay cradled in his thighs. Then he began to unbind the shrouds around him.

When he could not reach the knots, or not untie them swiftly enough, he snapped the lines like string. And as he worked or broke them free, he passed the pieces to Brinn.

Thus armed, the *Haruchai* advanced to meet the eels.

Impossibly poised between caution and extravagance, he struck at the creatures, flailing them with his rough-made quirts. Some of the pieces were too short to completely spare him from hot harm; but somehow he retained his control and fought on. When he had exhausted his supply of weapons, he bounded back to Seadreamer to take the ones the Giant had ready for him.

From Linden's distance, Covenant's defenders looked heroic and doomed. The mast's surface limited the number of eels which could approach simultaneously. But Brinn's supply of quirts was also limited by the amount of line within Seadreamer's reach. That resource was dwindling rapidly. And no help could reach them.

Frantically, Linden gathered herself to shout at Honninscrave, tell him to throw more rope to Seadreamer. But at that moment, Ceer returned. Gripping a large pouch like a wineskin under his arm, he dashed out from under the wheeldeck, sprang to the nearest lifeline. With all his *Haruchai* alacrity, he sped forward.

Behind him came the two Giants. They moved more slowly because they each carried two pouches, but they made all the haste they could.

Honninscrave sent his crew scrambling out of Ceer's path. As he rushed forward past the aftermast, Ceer unstopped his pouch. Squeezing it under his arm, he spouted a dark stream of oil to the stone below him. Oil slicked the deck, spread its sheen downward.

When the oil met the eels, the deck became a sheet of flame.

Fire spread, burning so rapidly that it followed Ceer's spout like hunger. It ignited the eels, cast them on to each other to multiply the ignition. In moments, all the decks below him blazed. The Raver's creatures were wiped away by their own conflagration.

But hundreds of them had already gained the wall and roof of the housing; and now the crew's access to Foodfendhall was blocked. Fire alone would not have stopped the Giants. But the oil made the deck too slippery to be traversed. Until it burned away, no help could try to reach Seadreamer and Brinn except along the cable Ceer used.

They had only scant moments left. No more line lay within Seadreamer's reach. He tried to slide himself towards the first spar, where the shrouds were plentiful; but the effort took him farther into the direct turbulence of the gale. Before he had covered half the distance the blast became too strong for him. He had to hunch over Covenant, cling to the stone with all his limbs, in order to keep the two of them from being torn away into the night.

Ceer's pouch was emptied before he gained Foodfendhall. He was forced to stop. No one could reach the housing.

Honninscrave barked commands. At once, the nearer oil-laden Giant stopped, secured her footing, then threw her pouches forward, one after the other. The first flew to the Master as he positioned himself immediately behind Ceer. The second arced over them to hit and burst against the edge of the roof. Oil splashed down the wall. Flames cleared away the eels. Rapidly, the surviving remnant of the attack was erased from the afterdeck.

Honninscrave snapped instructions at Ceer. Ceer ducked around behind the Giant, climbed his back like a tree while Honninscrave crossed the last distance to the wall. From the Master's shoulders, Ceer leaped to the roof, then turned to catch the pouch Honninscrave tossed upward.

Flames leaped as Ceer began spewing oil at the eels.

With a lunge, Honninscrave caught at the edge of the roof. In spite of the oil, his fingers held, defying failure as he flipped himself over the eaves. Giants threw the last two pouches up to him.

Clutching one by the throat in each hand, he crouched under the gale and followed Ceer.

Linden could not see what was happening. Foodfendhall blocked the base of the mast from her view. But the red flaring across Brinn's flat visage as he retreated was the crimson of eel-light, not the orange-and-yellow of flames.

A moment later, his retreat carried him into the grasp of the wind.

He tottered. With all his strength and balance, he resisted; but the hurricane had him, and its savagery was heightened by the way it came boiling past the lee of the roof. He could not save himself from falling.

He lashed out at the eels as he dropped. Simultaneously, he pitched himself back towards Seadreamer. His blow struck an attacker away. Its power outlined him against the night like a lightning-burst of pain.

Then a pouch flashed into view, cast from Ceer or Honninscrave to Seadreamer. Fighting the wind, Seadreamer managed to raise his arms, catch the oilskin. Pumping the pouch under his elbow, he squeezed a gush of oil down the mast.

The eel-light turned to fire. Flames immersed the mast, fell in burning gouts of oil and blazing creatures towards the Sea.

Linden heard a scream that made no sound. Yowling in frustration, the Raver fled. Its malefic presence burst and vanished, freeing her like an escape from suffocation.

The illumination of eels and oil revealed Brinn. He hung from one of Seadreamer's ankles, twitching and capering helplessly. But in spite of seizures and wind which tossed him from side to side like a puppet, his grip held.

The oil burned away rapidly. Already, the afterdeck had relapsed into the darkness of the storm – night assuaged only by a few faint lanterns. Ceer and Honninscrave were soon able to ascend the mast.

Moored by a rope to Honninscrave, Ceer hung below the mast and swung himself outward until he could reach Brinn. Hugging his kinsman, he let Honninscrave haul the two of them back to relative safety. Then the Master went to aid his brother.

With Covenant supported between them, a link more intimate and binding than birth, Honninscrave and Seadreamer crept down out of the wind.

Linden could hardly believe that they had survived, that the Raver had been defeated. She felt at once weak with relief and exhaustion, fervid to have Covenant near her again, to see if he had been harmed.

He and his rescuers were out of sight beyond the edge of Foodfendhall. She could not bear to wait. But she had to wait. Struggling for self-possession, she went to examine Pitchwife, the First and Hergrom.

They were recovering well. The two stricken Giants appeared to have suffered no lingering damage. The First was already strong enough to curse the loss of her sword; and Pitchwife was muttering as if he were bemused by the foolhardiness with which he had charged the eels. Their Giantish immunity to burns had protected them.

Beside them, Hergrom seemed both less and more severely hurt. He had not lost consciousness; his mind had remained clear. But the twitching of his muscles was slow to depart. Apparently, his resistance to the eel-blast had prolonged its effect upon him. His limbs were steady for the most part, but the corners of his face continued to wince and tick like an exaggerated display of trepidation.

Perhaps, Linden thought as if his grimacing were an augury, perhaps the Raver had not been defeated. Perhaps it had simply learned enough about the condition of Covenant and the quest and had gone to inform Lord Foul.

Then she turned to meet the return of Ceer and Brinn, Honninscrave and Seadreamer. With the Unbeliever.

They came carefully along the lifelines. Like Hergrom, Brinn suffered from erratic muscular spasms. But they were receding. Seadreamer was sorely weary after his struggles; but his solid form showed no other hurt.

Honninscrave carried Covenant. At the sight, Linden's eyes filled with tears. She had never been able to control the way her orbs misted and ran at any provocation; and now she did not try. Covenant was unchanged – as empty of mind or will as an abandoned crypt. But he was safe. Safe. When the Master set him down, she went to him at once. Though she was unacquainted with such gestures, perhaps had no right to them, she put her arms around him and did not care who saw the fervour of her embrace.

But the night was long and cold, and the storm still raved like all fury incarnated. Starfare's Gem skidded in a mad rush along the seas, tenuously poised between life and death. There was nothing anybody could do except clinch survival and hope. In the bone-deep shivers which racked her, the weariness which enervated her limbs so thoroughly that even *diamondraught* scarcely palliated it, Linden was surprised to find that she was as capable of hope as the Giants. Their spirit seemed to express its essence in Honninscrave, who bore the command of the ship as if Starfare's Gem itself were indomitable. At Shipsheartthew, Galewrath no longer appeared too frozen by duty to meet the strain. Rather, her great arms gripped the spokes as if she were more indefeasible than the very storm. Brinn and Hergrom had recovered their characteristic imperviousness. The *dromond* lived. Hope was possible.

Yet when dawn came at last, Linden had fallen so far into bare knotted endurance that the sun took her by surprise. Stupefied by exhaustion, she did not know which astonished her more – the simple return of day, unlooked-for after the interminable battery of that night, or the fact that the sky was free of clouds.

She could hardly credit her eyes. Covered by the vessel's lee, she had not noticed that the rain had stopped sometime during the night. Now the heavens macerated from purple to blue as the sun appeared almost directly behind the Giantship's stern. The clouds were gone as if they had been worn away by the incessant tearing of the wind. And yet the gale continued to blow, unabated and unappeased.

Blinking weakly, she scanned her companions. They looked unnaturally distinct in the clear air, like men and women who had been whetted by stress to a keener edge, a sharper existence. Their apparel was rimed and crusted with salt: it marked their faces like the desiccated masks of their mortality, drifted in powder from the opening and closing of hands, the bending of arms, the shifting of positions. Yet they moved. They spoke hoarsely to each other, flexed the cramps out of their muscles, cast raw and gauging glances at the Sea. They were alive.

Linden took an inventory of the survivors to assure herself that no one had been lost. The stubborn thudding of the pumps gave her an estimate of the Giants who were below; and that number completed her count. Swallowing at the bitter salt in her throat, she asked Cail if anyone had seen Vain or Findail.

He replied that Hergrom had gone forward some time ago to see if the Demondim-spawn and the *Elohim* were still safe. He had found them as she had last seen them: Findail riding the prow like a figurehead; Vain standing with his face to the deep as if he could read the secrets of the Earth in that dark rush.

Linden nodded. She had not expected anything else. Vain and Findail deserved each other; they were both as secretive and unpredictable as Sea, as unreachable as stone. When Cail offered her a bowl of *diamondraught*, she took a sparing sip, then passed it to the Giant nearest her. Squinting against the unfamiliar light, she turned to study the flat seethe of the ocean.

But the Sea was no longer flat. Faint undulations ran along the wind. She felt no lessening of the gale; but it must have declined somewhat. Its force no longer completely effaced the waves.

With a sting of apprehension, she snatched her gaze to the waterline below her.

That line dipped and rose slightly. And every rise took hold of another slight fraction of the deck as the waves lifted more water into the Giantship. The creaking of the masts had become louder. The pumps laboured to a febrile pitch.

By slow degrees, Starfare's Gem was falling into its last crisis.

Linden searched the deck for Honninscrave, shouted his name. But when he turned to answer her hail, she stopped. His eyes were dark with recognition and grief.

'I have seen, Chosen.' His voice carried a note of bereavement. 'We are fortunate in this light. Had gloom still shrouded us – ' He trailed into a sad silence.

'Honninscrave.' The First spoke sharply, as though his rue angered her. 'It must be done.'

'Aye,' he echoed in a wan tone. 'It must be done.'

She did not relent. 'It must be done now.'

'Aye,' he sighed again. 'Now.' Misery twisted his visage. But a moment later he recaptured his strength of decision, and his back straightened. 'Since it must be done, I will do it.'

Abruptly, he indicated four of his crewmembers, beckoned for them to follow him, and turned aft. Over his shoulder, he said, 'Sevinhand I will send to this command.'

The First called after him like an acknowledgment or apology, 'Which will you select?'

Without turning, he replied with the Giantish name for the midmast, uttering the word grimly, like the appellation of a lost love. 'Starfare's Gem must not be unbalanced to fore or aft.'

With his four Giants behind him, he went below.

Linden groped her way in trepidation to the First's side. 'What's he going to do?'

The First swung a gaze as hard as a slap on Linden. 'Chosen,' she said dourly, 'you have done much – and will do more. Let this matter rest with the Master.'

Linden winced at the rebuff, started to retort. But then her hearing clarified, and she caught herself. The First's tone had been one of grief and frustration, not affront. She shared Honninscrave's emotions. And she was helpless. The *dromond*'s survival was in his hands, not hers. In addition, the loss of her sword seemed to take some vital confidence out of her, making her bitter with uncertainty.

Linden understood. But she had no comfort to offer. Returning to Covenant, she took hold of his arm as if even that one-sided contact were a reassurance and focused her attention on the waterline.

The faint dip and rise of the waves had increased, multiplying by increments the Sea's hold on the Giantship. She was sure now that the angle of the deck had become steeper. The tips of the spars hung fatally close to the undulating water. Her senses throbbed to the strain of the ship's balance. She perceived as vividly as vision that if those tips touched the Sea Starfare's Gem would be dragged down.

Moments later, Sevinhand came hurrying from the underdecks. His lean old face was taut with determination. Though he had spent the whole night and most of the previous day commanding the pumps, sweating at them himself, he moved as if Starfare's Gem's need transcended everything which might have made him weak. As he went forward he called several Giants after him. When they responded, he led them into Foodfendhall and out of sight.

Linden dug her fingers into Covenant's arm and fought to keep from trembling. Every dip of the waves consumed more of the Giantship, drew it another fraction farther on to its side.

Then Honninscrave's bellow of inquiry echoed from the underdecks. It seemed to come from the vicinity of the holds under the midmast.

In a raw shout, Sevinhand answered that he was ready.

At once, a fierce pounding vibrated through the stone. It dwarfed the exertion of the pumps, pierced the long howl of the wind. For a mad instant, Linden thought that Honninscrave and his crew must be attacking the underdecks with sledgehammers, trying to wreck the *dromond* from within, as if in that way they could make it valueless to the storm, not worth sinking. But the Giants around her tensed expectantly; and the First barked, 'Hold ready! We must be prepared to labour for our lives!'

The intensity of the pounding – fury desperate as bereavement – led Linden's attention to the midmast. The stone had begun to scream like a tortured man. The yards trembled at every blow. Then she understood. Honninscrave was attacking the butt of the mast. He wanted to break it free, drop it overboard, in order to shift the balance of the *dromond*. Every blow strove to break the moorings which held the mast.

Linden bruised Covenant's arm with her apprehension. The Master could not succeed. He did not have enough time. Under her, the Giantship leaned palpably towards its death. That fall was only heartbeats away.

But Honninscrave and his Giants struck and struck as if they were repudiating an unbearable doom. Another shriek sprang from the stone – a cry of protest louder than the gale.

With a hideous screech of rent and splintered granite, the mast started to topple.

It sounded like the death throes of a mountain as it rove its moorings. Below it, the roof of the housing crumpled. The falling mast crashed through the side of the Giantship. Shatterings staggered the *dromond* to its keel, sent massive tremors kicking through the vessel from prow to stern. Shared agony yammered in Linden's bones. She thought that she was screaming, but could not hear herself.

Then the cacophony of breakage dropped below the level of the wind. The mast struck the Sea like a pantomime of ruin, and the splash wet all the decks and the watchers soundlessly, as if they were deaf with sorrow.

From the shattered depths of the *dromond*, Honninscrave's outcry rose over the water that poured thunderously through the breach left by the mast.

And like his cry Starfare's Gem lifted.

The immense weight of the keel pulled against the inrushing Sea. Slowly, ponderously, the Giantship began to right itself.

Even then, it might have died. It had shipped far more water than the pumps could handle; and the gap in its side gaped like an open wound, admitting more water at every moment.

But Sevinhand and Galewrath were ready. The Anchormaster instantly sent his Giants up the foremast to unfurl the lowest sail. And as the wind clawed at the canvas, tried to tear it away or use it to thrust the vessel down again, Galewrath spun Shipsheartthew, digging the rudder into the furious Sea.

The Starfare's Gem was saved. That one sail and the rudder were enough: they turned the *dromond*'s stern to the wind. Running before the blast, the Giantship was able to stand upright, lifting its breached side out of the water.

For a time, the vessel was barely manageable, too heavily freighted with water. At every moment, its one sail was in danger of being shredded. But Sevinhand protected that sail with all the cunning of his sea-craft, all the valour of his crew. And the Giants at the pumps worked like titans. Their efforts kept the ship afloat until Honninscrave had cleared access to the port pumps. Then their progress improved. As the *dromond* was lightened, the strain on its canvas eased; and Sevinhand was able to raise another sail. Alive in spite of its wounds, Starfare's Gem limped before the gale into the clear south.

13

BHRATHAIRAIN HARBOUR

The gale diminished slowly. It did not fray out to the level of normal winds for two more days. During that time, Starfare's Gem had no choice but to run straight before the blast. It could not turn even slightly westward without listing to port; and that would have lowered the breach into the water. The Giants already had more than enough work to do without also being required to pump for their lives. Whenever the seas became heavy enough to slosh into the gap, Honninscrave was forced to shift his course a few points eastward so that Starfare's Gem leaned to starboard, protecting its injury.

He did not try to raise more canvas. Those two lone sails in that exigent wind required the constant attention of several Giants. More would have kept too many of the crew from the manifold other tasks which demanded their time.

The rigging needed a great deal of attention; but that was the least of the *dromond*'s problems. The havoc of the underdecks presented a much larger difficulty. The felling of the midmast had left chaos in its wake. And the day which Starfare's Gem had spent on its side had had other consequences as well. The contents of the holds were tumbled and confused or broken. Huge quantities of stores had been ruined by salt water. Also, the Sea had done severe damage to parts of the ship – the port cabins and supply-lockers, for example – which had not been designed to be submerged or overturned. Though the Giants worked hugely, they were not able to make the galley utile again until late afternoon; and the night was half gone before any of the port cabins had been rendered habitable.

But hot food gave some ease to Linden's abraded nerves; and Brinn was at last able to take Covenant down to his own chamber. Finally, she allowed herself to think of rest. Since her cabin lay to starboard, it had suffered only slight harm. With Cail's unasked aid, she soon set the table, chairs, and stepladder to rights. Then she climbed into her hammock and let the frustrated whine of the gale sweep her away from consciousness.

While the wind lasted, she did little but recuperate. She left her cabin periodically to check on Covenant, or to help Heft Galewrath tend the crew's injuries. And once she went forward with the idea of confronting Findail: she wanted to demand an explanation for his refusal to aid her or the Giantship. But when she saw him standing alone in the prow as if his people had Appointed him to be a pariah, she found that she lacked the will to contest him for answers. She was weary in every muscle and ligature. Any information she might conceivably wrest from him could wait. Dumbly, she returned to her cabin as if it were full of sleep.

She was sensitive to the restless labour of the crew; but she had neither the strength nor the skill to share their tasks. Still their exertions touched her more and more as she recovered from the strain of the storm. And eventually she felt the end of the gale approaching across the deeps. No longer able to sleep, she began to look for some chore with which she could occupy her mind, restore the meaning of her hands.

Seeing her tension, Seadreamer mutely took her and Cail below to one of the grainholds which was still clogged with a thick slush of seawater and ruined maize. She spent most of the day working there with him in a companionable silence. He with a shovel, she and Cail with dippers from the galley, they scooped the slush into a large vat which he took away at intervals to empty. The Giantish dipper was as large as a bucket in her hands, and somewhat unwieldy; but she welcomed the job and the effort. Once on Haven Farm she had laboured at a similar task to steady the clenched unease of her spirit.

From time to time, she bent her observation on Seadreamer. He seemed to appreciate her company, as if his Earth-Sight found a kind of companionship in her health-sense. And in other ways he appeared to have reached a point of calm. He conveyed the impression that his distress had been reduced to bearable dimensions, not by any change in his vision, but by the simple fact that Starfare's Gem was not travelling towards the One Tree. She did not have the heart to trouble him with questions he could not answer without an arduous and chancy effort of communication. But still he looked to her like a man who had seen his doom at the site of the One Tree.

Clearly something had changed for him in *Elemesnedene*, either in his examination or in the loss of the brief hope Honninscrave had given him. Perhaps his vision had shifted from the Sunbane to a new or different danger. And perhaps – The thought tightened her stomach. Perhaps he had seen beyond the Sunbane into Lord Foul's deeper intent. A purpose which would be fulfilled in the quest for the One Tree.

But she did not know how to tackle such issues. They were too personal. As she worked, a pang of yearning for Covenant went through her. She met it by turning her thoughts once again to the nature of his plight. In memory, she re-explored the unaneled cerements which enclosed his mind, sought the knot which would unbind them. But the only conclusion she reached was that her last attempt to enter him had been wrong in more ways than one – wrong because it had violated him, and wrong because of the rage and hunger which had impelled her. That dilemma surpassed her, for she knew she would not have made the attempt at all if she had not been so angry – and so vulnerable to darkness. In one way, at least, she was like Seadreamer: the voice in her which should have spoken to Covenant was mute.

Then, late in the afternoon, the last of the gale fell apart and wandered away like an assailant that had lost its wits; and Starfare's Gem relaxed like a sigh into more gentle seas. Through the stone, Linden felt the crew cheering. Seadreamer dropped his shovel to bow his head and stand motionless for a long moment, communing with his kindred in an act of gratitude or contrition. The Giantship had won free of immediate danger.

A short time later, Cail announced that the Master was calling for the Chosen. Seadreamer indicated with a shrug and a wry grimace that he would finish cleaning the grainhold. Thanking the mute Giant for more things than she could name – above all, for saving Covenant from the eels – Linden followed Cail towards Honninscrave's cabin.

When she arrived, she found the First, Pitchwife, and Galewrath already in the Master's austere quarters. The occasional shouts which echoed from the wheeldeck told her that Sevinhand was tending the ship.

Honninscrave stood at the end of a long table, facing his comrades. When Linden entered the cabin, he gave her a nod of welcome, then returned his attention to the table. Its top was level with her eyes and covered with rolls of parchment and vellum which made small crinkling noises when he opened or closed them.

'Chosen,' he said, 'we are gathered to take counsel. We must choose our way from this place. Here is the matter before us.' He unrolled a chart; then, realizing she could not see it, closed it again. 'We have been driven nigh twenty score leagues on a path which does not lead to the One Tree. Perhaps we are not greatly farther from our goal than we were ere the storm took us – but assuredly we are no nearer. And our quest is urgent. That was acute to us when first the Search was born in Cable Seadreamer's Earth-Sight.' A wince passed over his features. 'We see it more than plainly in his visage now.

'Yet,' he went on, setting aside his concern for his brother, 'Starfare's Gem has been grievously harmed. All seas are perilous to us now. And the loss of the stores – '

He looked at Galewrath. Bluntly, she said, 'If we eat and drink unrestrained, we will come to the end of our meat in five days. The watercests we will empty in eight. Mayhap the unspoiled grains and dried staples will endure for ten. Only *diamondraught* do we have in plenty.'

Honninscrave glanced at Linden. She nodded. Starfare's Gem was in dire need of supplies.

'Therefore,' the Master said, 'our choice is this. To pursue our Search, trusting our lives to the strictness of our restraint and the mercy of the Sea. Or to seek either landfall or port where we may hope for repairs and replenishment.' Reopening his chart, he held it over the edge of the table so that she could see it. 'By the chance of the storm, we now approach the littoral of *Bhrathairealm*, where dwell the *Bhrathair* in the Sandhold against the Great Desert.' He indicated a spot on the chart; but she ignored it to watch his face, trying to read the decision he wanted from her. With a shrug, he tossed the parchment back on to the table. 'In *Bhrathairain* Harbour,' he concluded, 'we may meet our needs, and those of Starfare's Gem. Winds permitting, we may perhaps gain that Harbour in two days.'

Linden nodded again. As she looked around at the Giants, she saw that each of them wanted to take the latter course, turn the *dromond* towards *Bhrathairain* Harbour. But there were misgivings in their eyes. Perhaps the right of command which she had wrested from them outside *Elemesnedene* had eroded their confidence in themselves. Or perhaps the quest itself made them distrust their own desires for a safe anchorage. Covenant had certainly spoken often enough about the need for haste.

Or perhaps, Linden thought with a sudden inward flinch, it's me they don't trust.

At once, she compressed her mouth into its old lines of severity. She was determined not to cede one jot of the responsibility she had taken upon herself. She had come too far for that. Speaking in her flat professional voice, like a physician probing symptoms, she asked Pitchwife, 'Is there any reason why you can't fix the ship at Sea?'

The deformed Giant met her soberly, almost painfully. 'Chosen, I am able to work my wiving wherever the seas permit. Grant that the waves and winds are kind, and I lack naught else for the immediate need. The wreckage belowdecks will provide ample stone to mend the *dromond*'s side — yes, and also to seal the decks themselves. But the walls, and Foodfendhall — ' He jerked a shrug. 'To mend Starfare's Gem entirely, I must have access to a quarry. And only the shipwrights of Home can restore the mast which was lost. It may be possible,' he concluded simply, 'for the Search to continue in the lack of such luxuries.'

'Do the *Bhrathair* have a quarry?'

At that, humour glinted from Pitchwife's eyes. 'In good sooth, the *Bhrathair* have little else but stone and sand. Therefore their Harbour has become a place of much trade and shipping, for they must have commerce to meet other needs.'

Linden turned to Galewrath. 'If you make the rations as small as possible, can we get to the One Tree and back to the Land with what we have?'

The Storemaster answered stolidly, 'No.' She folded her brawny forearms over her chest as if her word were beyond refute.

But Linden continued, 'You got supplies when you were off the coast of the Land. Couldn't we do the same thing? Without spending all the time to go to this Habour?'

Galewrath glanced at the Master, then said in a less assertive tone, 'It may be. At times land will lie nigh our course. But much of what is marked on these charts is obscure, explored neither by Giants nor by those who have told tales to Giants.'

Linden held Galewrath's doubt in abeyance. 'Honninscrave.' She could not shake her impression that the Giants had qualms about *Bhrathairealm*. 'Is there any reason why we shouldn't go to this Harbour?'

Honninscrave reacted as if the question made him uncomfortable.

'In times long past,' he said without meeting her gaze, 'the *Bhrathair* have been friends to the Giants, welcoming our ships as occasion came. And we have given them no cause to alter towards us.' His face was grey with the memory of the *Elohim*, whom he had trusted. 'But no Giant has sojourned to *Bhrathairealm* for three of our generations – ten and more of theirs. And the tales which have since come to us suggest that the *Bhrathair* are not what they were. They were ever a brusque and unhesitating people, for good or ill – made so by the long trial of their war for survival against the Sandgorgons of the Great Desert. The story told of them is that they have become gaudy.'

Gaudy? Linden wondered. She did not know what Honninscrave meant. But she had caught the salient point: he was unsure of the welcome Starfare's Gem would receive in *Bhrathairain* Harbour. Severely, she faced the First.

'If Covenant and I weren't here – if you were on this quest without us – what would you do?'

The gaze the First returned held none of Honninscrave's vague apprehension. It was as straight and grim as a blade.

'Chosen, I have lost my broadsword. I am a Swordmain, and my glaive was accorded to me as a trust and symbol at the rites of my achievement. Its name is known to none but me, and to those who bestowed it upon me, and that name may never be revealed while I hold faith among the Swordmainnir. I have lost it by my own misjudgment. I am greatly shamed.

'Yet some weapon I must have. In this lack, I am less than a Swordmain – less than the First of the Search.

'For all implements of battle, the *Bhrathair* are of far renown.'

Her look did not waver. 'In my own name I would not delay the Search. My place as the First I would give to another, and myself I would content with such service as lay within my grasp.' Pitchwife had covered his eyes with one hand, hurt by what he was hearing; but he did not interrupt. Now Linden understood the unwonted tenor of his reply to her earlier question: he knew what a decision to bypass *Bhrathairain* Harbour would mean to his wife. 'But the need of Starfare's Gem is clear,' the First went on. 'Given that need, and the proximity of *Bhrathairealm*, I would not scruple to sail there, for the *dromond*'s hope as well as for my own. The choice between delay and death is easily made.'

She continued to hold Linden's gaze straightly; and at last Linden dropped her eyes. She was moved by the First's frank avowal, her stubborn integrity. All the Giants seemed to overtop Linden in more than mere physical stature. Abruptly, her insistence on making decisions in such company appeared insolent to her. Covenant had earned his place among the Giants – and among the *Haruchai* as well. But she had no right to it. She required the responsibility, the

624

power to choose, for no other reason than to hold back her hunger for other kinds of power. Yet that exigency outweighed her unworth.

Striving to emulate Covenant, she said, 'All right. I hear you.' With an effort of will, she raised her head, suppressing her conflicted heart so that she could meet the eyes of the Giants. 'I think we're too vulnerable the way we are. We won't do the Land any good if we drown ourselves or starve to death. Let's take our chances with this Harbour.'

For a moment, Honninscrave and the others stared at her as if they had expected a different response. Then, softly, Pitchwife began to chuckle. A twitch of joy started at the corners of his mouth, quickly spread over his face. 'Witness me, Giants,' he said. 'Have I not avowed that she is well Chosen?'

With a flourish, he caught hold of the First's hand, kissed it hugely. Then he flung himself like glee out of the cabin.

An unfamiliar dampness filled the First's eyes. She placed a brief touch of recognition or thanks on Linden's shoulder. But she spoke to Honninscrave. In a husky tone, she said, 'I desire to hear the song which is now in Pitchwife's heart.' Turning brusquely to contain her emotion, she left the chamber.

Galewrath's face showed a blunt glower of satisfaction. She seemed almost glad as she picked up one of the charts and went to take the *dromond*'s new course to Sevinhand.

Linden was left alone with the Master.

'Linden Avery. Chosen.' He appeared uncertain of how to address her. A smile of relief had momentarily set aside his misgivings. But almost at once his gravity returned. 'There is much in the matter of this Search, and of the Earth's peril, which I do not comprehend. The mystery of my brother's vision appalls my heart. The alteration of the *Elohim* – and Findail's presence amongst us – ' He shrugged, lifting his hands as if they were full of uncomfortable ignorances. 'But Covenant Giantfriend had made plain to all that he bears a great burden of blood for those whose lives are shed in the Land. And in his plight, you have accepted to support his burdens.

'Accepted and more,' he digressed wryly. 'You have averred them as your own. In sooth, I had not known you to be formed of such stone.'

But then he returned to his point. 'Chosen, I thank you that you are willing for this delay. I thank you in the name of Starfare's Gem, that I love as dearly as life and yearn to see restored to wholeness.' An involuntary tremor knotted his hands as he remembered the blows he had struck against the midmast. 'And I thank you also in the name of Cable Seadreamer my brother. I am eased that he will be granted some respite. Though I dread that his wound will never be healed, yet I covet any act or delay which may accord him rest.'

'Honninscrave – ' Linden did not know what to say to him. She had not earned his thanks. And she had no answer for the vicarious suffering which linked him to his brother. As she looked at him, she thought that perhaps his misgivings had less to do with the unknown attitude of the *Bhrathair* than with the possible implications of any delay for the Search – for Seadreamer. He appeared to doubt the dictates of his concern for his ship, as if that instinct had been deprived of its purity by his apprehension for Seadreamer.

His inner disquiet silenced anything she might have said in support of her decision or in recognition of his thanks. Instead, she gave him the little knowledge she possessed.

'He's afraid of the One Tree. He thinks something terrible is going to happen there. I don't know why.'

Honninscrave nodded slowly. He was no longer looking at her. He stared past her as though he were blinded by his lack of prescience. Quietly, he murmured, 'He is not mute because he has lost the capacity of voice. He is mute because the Earth-Sight cannot be given words. He is able to convey that there is peril. But for him that peril has no utterable name.'

Linden saw no way to ease him. Gently she let herself out of the cabin, leaving him his privacy because she had nothing else to offer.

Troubled by uncertain winds, Starfare's Gem required two full days to come within sight of land; and the *dromond* did not near the mouth of *Bhrathairain* Harbour until the following morning.

During that time, the quest left behind the last hints of the northern autumn and passed into a hot dry clime unsoftened by any suggestion of approaching winter. The direct sun seemed to parch Linden's skin, leaving her always thirsty; and the normally cool stone of the decks radiated heat through her shoes. The weather-worn sails looked grey and tarnished against the acute sunlight and the brilliant Sea. Occasional suspirations of humidity breathed past her cheek; but they came from virga scudding overhead – isolated clouds shedding rain which evaporated before it could reach the Sea or the ship – and did not relieve the heat.

Her first view of the coast some leagues east of *Bhrathairealm* was a vision of rocks and bare dirt. The stony littoral had been bleached and battered by so many arid millennia that the boulders appeared sun-stricken and somnolent, as if they were only prevented from vanishing into haze by the quality of their stupefaction. All life had been squeezed or beaten out of the pale soil long ago. Sunset stained the shore with ochre and pink, transfiguring the desolation, but could not bring back what had been lost.

That night, as the *dromond* tacked slowly along the coast, the terrain modulated into a region of low cliffs which fronted the Sea like a frown of perpetual vexation. When dawn came, Starfare's Gem was moving past buttes the height of its yards. Standing beside

Pitchwife at the port rail of the afterdeck, Linden saw a gap in the cliffs some distance ahead like the opening of a narrow canyon or the mouth of a river. But along the edges of the gap stood walls which appeared to be thirty or forty feet high. The walls were formed of the same pale stone which composed the bluffs. At their ends – at the two points of the gap – they arose into watchtowers. These fortifications tapered so that they looked like fangs against the dusty horizon.

'Is that the Harbour?' Linden asked uncertainly. The space between the cliffs appeared too narrow to accommodate any kind of anchorage.

'*Bhrathairain* Harbour,' replied Pitchwife in a musing tone. 'Yes. There begins the Sandwall which seals all the habitation of *Bhrathairealm* – both *Bhrathairain* itself and the mighty Sandhold behind it – against the Great Desert. Surely in all this region there is no ship that does not know the Spikes which identify and guard the entrance to *Bhrathairain* Harbour.'

Drifting forward in the slight breeze, the Giantship moved slowly abreast of the two towers which Pitchwife had named the Spikes. There Honninscrave turned the *dromond* to pass between them. The passage was barely wide enough to admit Starfare's Gem safely; but, beyond it, Linden saw that the channel opened into a huge cove a league or more broad. Protected from the vagaries of the Sea, squadrons of ships could have staged manoeuvres in that body of water. In the distance, she descried sails and masts clustered against the far curve of the Harbour.

Past the berths where those vessels rose, a dense town ascended a slope rising just west of south from the water. It ended at the Sandwall which enclosed the entire town and Harbour. And beyond that wall stood the massive stone pile of the Sandhold.

Erected above *Bhrathairain* in five stages, it dominated the vista like a brooding titan. Its fifth level was a straight high tower like a stone finger brandished in warning.

As Starfare's Gem passed between the Spikes, Linden was conscious that the Harbour formed a cul-de-sac from which any escape might be extremely difficult. *Bhrathairealm* was well protected. Studying what she could see of the town and the Sandwall, she realized that if the occupants of the Sandhold chose to lock their gates the *Bhrathair* would have no egress from their own defences.

The size of the Harbour, the immense clenched shape of the Sandhold, made her tense with wonder and apprehension. Quietly, she murmured to Pitchwife, 'Tell me about these people.' After her meeting with the *Elohim*, she felt she did not know what to expect from any strangers.

He responded as if he had been chewing over that tale himself. 'They are a curious folk – much misused by this ungiving land, and by the chance of fate which pitted them in mortal combat against the most fearsome denizens of the Great Desert. Their history has made them hardy, stubborn, and mettlesome. Mayhap, it has also made them somewhat blithe of scruple. But that is uncertain. The tales which we have heard vary greatly, according to the spirit of the telling.

'It is clear from the words of Covenant Giantfriend, as well as from the later voyagings of our people, that the Unhomed sojourned for a time in *Bhrathairealm*, giving what aid they could against the Sandgorgons. For that reason, Giants have been well greeted here. But we have had scant need of the commerce and warlike implements which the *Bhrathair* offer, and the visits of our people to *Bhrathairain* have been infrequent. Therefore my knowledge lacks the fullness which Giants love.'

He paused for a moment to collect the pieces of his story, then continued, 'There is an adage among the *Bhrathair*: "He who waits for the sword to fall upon his neck will surely lose his head." This is undisputed sooth.' Grim humour twisted his mouth. 'Yet the manner in which a truth is phrased reveals much. Many generations of striving against the Sandgorgons have made of the *Bhrathair* a people who seek to strike before they are stricken.

'The Sandgorgons — so it is said — are beasts birthed by the immense violence of the storms which anguish the Great Desert. They are somewhat manlike in form and also in cunning. But the chief aspect of their nature is that they are horrendously savage and mighty beyond the strength of stone or iron. No aid of Giants could have saved the *Bhrathair* from loss of the land they deem their home — and perhaps from extinction as well — had the Sandgorgons been beasts of concerted action. But their savagery was random, like the storms which gave them life. Therefore the *Bhrathair* were able to fight, to endure. Betimes they appeared to prevail, or were reduced to a remnant, as the violence of the Sandgorgons swelled and waned across the depths of the waste. But no peace was secured. During one era of lesser peril, the Sandwall was built. As you see' — he gestured around him — 'it is a doughty work. Yet it was not proof against the Sandgorgons. Often has it been rebuilt, and often have one or several of these creatures chanced upon it and torn spans of it to rubble.

'Such the lives of the *Bhrathair* might have remained until the day of World's End. But at last — in a time several of our generations past — a man came from across the seas and presented himself to the *gaddhi*, the ruler of *Bhrathairealm*. Naming himself a thaumaturge of great prowess, he asked to be given the place of Kemper — the foremost counsellor, and, under the *gaddhi*, suzerain of this land. To earn this place, he proposed to end the peril of the Sandgorgons.

'This he did — I know not how. Mayhap he alone knows. Yet the accomplishment remains. By his arts, he wove the storms of the Great Desert into a prodigious gyre so mighty that it destroys and remakes the ground at every turn. And into this storm – now named Sandgorgons Doom – he bound the beasts. There they travail yet, their violence cycled and mastered by greater violence. It is said that from the abutments of the Sandhold Sandgorgons Doom may be seen blasting its puissance forever without motion from its place of binding and without let. It is said that slowly across the centuries the Sandgorgons die, driven one by one into despair by the loss of freedom and open sand. And it is said also' – Pitchwife spoke softly – 'that upon occasion the Kemper releases one or another of them to do his dark bidding.

'For the *gaddhi*'s Kemper, Kasreyn of the Gyre, remains in *Bhrathairealm*, prolonged in years far beyond even a Giant's span, though he is said to be as mortal as any man. The *Bhrathair* are no longer-lived than people of your kind, Chosen. Of *gaddhi*s they have had many since Kasreyn's coming, for their rulership does not pass quietly from generation to generation. Yet Kasreyn of the Gyre remains. He it was who caused the building of the Sandhold. And because of his power, and his length of years, it is commonly said that he holds each *gaddhi* in turn as a puppet, ruling through the ruler that his hand may be concealed.

'The truth of this I do not know. But I give you witness.' With one long arm, he indicated the Sandhold. As Starfare's Gem advanced down the Harbour, the edifice became more clear and dominant against the desert sky. 'There stands his handiwork in its five levels, each far-famed as a perfect circle resting to one side within others. The Sandwall conceals the First Circinate, which provides a pediment to the Second. Then arises the Tier of Riches, and above it, The Majesty. There sits the *gaddhi* on his Auspice. But the fifth and highest part is the spire which you see, and it is named Kemper's Pitch, for within it resides Kasreyn of the Gyre in all his arts. From that eminence I doubt not that he wields his will over the whole of *Bhrathairealm* – aye, and over the Great Desert itself.'

His tone was a blend of respect and misgiving; and he aroused mixed emotions in Linden. She admired the Sandhold – and distrusted what she heard about Kasreyn. A man with the power to bind the Sandgorgons also had the power to be an unconstrained tyrant. In addition, the plight of the Sandgorgons themselves disquieted her. In her world, dangerous animals were frequently exterminated; and the world was not improved thereby.

But Pitchwife was still speaking. He drew her attention back to the Harbour. The morning sun burned along the water.

'Yet the *Bhrathair* have flourished mightily. They lack much which is needful for a prosperous life, for it is said that in all *Bhrathairealm* are only five springs of fresh water and two plots of arable ground.

629

But also they possess much which other peoples covet. Under Kasreyn's peace, trade has abounded. And the *Bhrathair* have become prolific shipwrights, that they may reach out to their distant neighbours. The tales which we have heard of *Bhrathairain* and the Sandhold convey echoes of mistrust – and yet, behold. This is clearly not a place of mistrust.'

Linden saw what he meant. As Starfare's Gem approached the piers and levees at the foot of the town, she discerned more clearly the scores of ships there, the bustling activity of the docks. In the Harbour – some at the piers, some at berths around the Sandwall – were a variety of warships: huge pentaconters; triremes with iron prows for ramming; galleasses armed with catapults. But their presence seemed to have no effect on the plethora of other vessels which crowded the place. Brigantines, windjammers, sloops, merchantmen of every description teemed at the piers, creating a forest of masts and spars against the busy background of the town. Any distrust which afflicted *Bhrathairealm* had no influence upon the vitality of its commerce.

And the air was full of birds. Gulls, crows, and cormorants wheeled and squalled over the masts, amongst the spars, perching on the roofs of *Bhrathairain*, feeding on the spillage and detritus of the ships. Hawks and kites circled watchfully over both town and Harbour. *Bhrathairealm* must have been thriving indeed, if it could feast so many loud scavengers.

Linden was glad to see them. Perhaps they were neither clean nor gay; but they were alive. And they lent support to the Harbour's reputation as a welcoming port.

When the *dromond* drew close enough to hear the hubbub of the docks, a skiff came shooting out into the open water. Four swarthy men stroked the boat swiftly towards the Giantship; a fifth stood in the stern. Before the skiff was within clear hail, this individual began gesticulating purposefully at Starfare's Gem.

Linden's perplexity must have shown on her face, for Pitchwife replied with a low chuckle, 'Doubtless he seeks to guide us to a berth which may accommodate a ship of our draught.'

She soon saw that her companion was right. When Honninscrave obeyed the *Bhrathair*'s gestures, the skiff swung ahead of the Giantship and pulled back towards the docks. By following, Honninscrave shortly brought Starfare's Gem to a deep levee between jutting piers.

Dockworkers waited there to help the ship to its berth. However, they quickly learned that they could do little for the *dromond*. The hawsers which were thrown to the piers were too massive for them to handle effectively. As Giants disembarked to secure their vessel, the *Bhrathair* moved back in astonishment and observed the great stone craft from the head of the levee. Shortly a crowd gathered around them – other dockworkers, sailors from nearby ships, merchants and townspeople who had never seen a Giantship.

Linden studied them with interest while they watched the *dromond*. Most of their exclamations were in tongues she did not know. They were people of every hue and form; and their apparel ranged from habiliments as plain as those which Sunder and Hollian had worn to exotic regalia, woven of silk and taffeta in bright colours, which would have suited a sultan. An occasional sailor – perhaps the captain of a vessel, or its owner – was luxuriously caparisoned. But primarily the bravado of raiment belonged to the *Bhrathair* themselves. They were unquestionably prosperous. And prosperity had given them a taste for ostentation.

Then a stirring passed through the crowd as a man breasted his way out on to the pier. He was as swarthy as the men who had rowed the skiff, but his clothing indicated higher rank. He wore a tunic and trousers of a rich black material which shone like satin; his belt had been woven of a vivid silvery metal; and at his right shoulder was pinned a silver cockade like a badge of office. He strode forward as if to show the throng that a ship the size of Starfare's Gem could not daunt him, then stopped below the afterdeck and waited with a glower of impatience for the invitation and the means to come aboard.

At Honninscrave's order, a ladder was set for the black-clad personage. With Pitchwife, Linden moved closer to the ladder. The First and Seadreamer had joined the Master there, and Brinn had brought Covenant up from his cabin. Cail stood behind Linden's left shoulder; Ceer and Hergrom were nearby. Only Vain and Findail chose to ignore the arrival of the *Bhrathair*.

A moment later, the man climbed through the railing to stand before the assembled company. 'I am the Harbour Captain,' he said without preamble. He had a guttural voice which was exaggerated in Linden's ears by the fact that he was not speaking his native language. 'You must have my grant in order to berth or do trade here. Give me first your names and the name of your ship.'

Honninscrave glanced at the First; but she did not step forward. To the Harbour Captain, he said evenly, 'This vessel is the *dromond* Starfare's Gem. I am its Master, Grimmand Honninscrave.'

The official made a note on a wax tablet he carried. 'And these others?'

Honninscrave stiffened at the man's tone. 'They are Giants, and the friends of Giants.' Then he added, 'In times past, the Giants were deemed allies amongst the *Bhrathair*.'

'In times past,' the Harbour Captain retorted with a direct glare, 'the world was not what it is. My duty cares nothing for dead alliances. If you do not deal openly with me, my judgment will be weighed against you.'

The First's eyes gnashed with ready anger; but her hand gripped an empty scabbard, and she held herself still. Swallowing his vexation with an effort, Honninscrave named his companions.

The *Bhrathair* wrote officiously on his tablet. 'Very well,' he said as he finished. 'What is your cargo?'

'Cargo?' echoed Honninscrave darkly. 'We have no cargo.'

'None?' the Harbour Captain snapped in sudden indignation. 'Have you not come to do trade with us?'

The Master folded his arms across his massive chest. 'No.'

'Then you are mad. What is your purpose?'

'Your eyes will tell you our purpose.' The Giant's voice grated like boulders rubbing together. 'We have suffered severe harm in a great storm. We come seeking stone with which to work repairs and replenishment for our stores.'

'Paugh!' spat the *Bhrathair*. 'You are ignorant, Giant – or a fool.' He spoke like the heat, as if his temper had been formed by the constant oppression of the desert sun. 'We are the *Bhrathair*, not some peasant folk you may intimidate with your bulk. We live on the verge of the Great Desert, and our lives are exigent. What comfort we possess, we gain from trade. I grant nothing when I am offered nothing in return. If you have no cargo, you must purchase what you desire by some other coin. If you lack such coin, you must depart. That is my word.'

Honninscrave held himself still; but he looked ready for any peril. 'And if we do not choose to depart? Should you seek combat from us, you will learn to your cost that two score Giants are not blithely beaten.'

The Harbour Captain did not hesitate; his confidence in his office was complete. 'If you choose neither payment nor departure, your ship will be destroyed before nightfall. No man or woman here will lift hand against you. You will be free to go ashore, thieve all you desire. And while you do so, five galleasses with catapults will batter your ship with such stones and exploding fires that it will fall to rubble where it sits.'

For a moment, the Master of Starfare's Gem did not respond. Linden feared that he had no response, that she had made a fatal mistake in choosing to come here. No one moved or spoke.

Overhead, a few birds flitted downward to investigate the *dromond*, then scaled away again.

Quietly, Honninscrave said, 'Sevinhand.' His voice carried to the Anchormaster on the wheeldeck. 'Secure the *dromond* for assault. Prepare to forage supplies and depart. Galewrath.' The Storesmaster stood nearby. 'Take this Harbour Captain.' At once, she stepped forward, clamped one huge fist around the *Bhrathair*'s neck. 'He is swift to call down harm upon the needy. Let him share whatever harm we suffer.'

'Fools!' The official tried to rage, but the indignity of Galewrath's grasp made him look apoplectic and wild. 'There is no wind! You are trapped until the evening breeze!'

'Then you are likewise snared,' replied Honninscrave evenly. 'For the while, we will content ourselves by teaching your Harbour to comprehend the wrath of Giants. Our friendship was not lightly given in the need of the *Bhrathair* against the Sandgorgons. You will learn that our enmity may not be lightly borne.'

Commotion broke out amongst the onlookers around the levee. Instinctively, Linden swung around to see if they meant to attack the *dromond*.

In a moment, she perceived that their activity was not a threat. Rather, the throng was being roughly parted by five men on horseback.

Riding destriers as black as midnight, the five forced their way forward. They were clearly soldiers. Over their black shirts and leggings, they wore breastplates and greaves of a silverine metal; and they had quivers and crossbows at their backs, short swords at their sides, shields on their arms. As they broke out of the crowd, they stretched their mounts into a gallop down the pier, then reined sharply to a halt at the *dromond*'s ladder.

Four of them remained astride their horses; the fifth, who wore an emblem like a black sun in the centre of his breastplate, dismounted swiftly and leaped at the ladder. Quickly, he gained the afterdeck. Ceer, Hergrom, and the Giants poised themselves; but the soldier did not challenge them. He cast a glance of appraisal around the deck, then turned on the official half dangling in Galewrath's grip and began to shout at him.

The soldier spoke a brackish language which Linden did not understand – the native tongue of the *Bhrathair*. The Harbour Captain's replies were somewhat choked by Galewrath's fist; but he seemed to be defending himself. At the same time, Pitchwife gave Linden's shoulder a gentle nudge. When she looked at him, he winked deliberately. With a start, she remembered the Giantish gift of tongues – and remembered to keep it secret. The rest of the Giants remained expressionless.

After a yell which made the Harbour Captain appear especially crestfallen, the soldier faced Honninscrave and the First. 'Your pardon,' he said. 'The Harbour Captain's duty is clear, but he comprehends it narrowly' – the venom of his tone was directed at the official – 'and understands little else at all. I am Rire Grist, Caitiffin of the *gaddhi*'s Horse. The coming of your ship was seen in the Sandhold, and I was sent to give welcome. Alas, I was delayed in the crowded streets and did not arrive in time to prevent misapprehension.'

Before Honninscrave could speak, the Caitiffin went on, 'You may release this duty-proud man. He understands now that you must be given every aid in his grant, for the sake of old friendship of the Giants, and also in the name of the *gaddhi*'s will. I am certain that all your wants will be answered promptly – and courteously,' he added over his shoulder to the Harbour Captain. 'Will you not free him?'

'In a moment,' Honninscrave rumbled. 'It would please me to hear you speak further concerning the *gaddhi*'s will towards us.'

'Assuredly,' replied Rire Grist with a bow. 'Rant Absolain, *gaddhi* of *Bhrathairealm*, wishes you well. He desires that you be granted the fullest welcome of your need. And he asks those amongst you who may be spared from the labour of your ship to be his guests in the Sandhold. Neither he nor his Kemper, Kasreyn of the Gyre, have known Giants, and both are anxious to rectify their lack.'

'You speak hospitably.' Honninscrave's tone was noncommittal. 'But you will understand that our confidence has been somewhat daunted. Grant a moment for consultation with my friends.'

'Your vessel is your own,' responded the Caitiffin easily. He seemed adept at smoothing the path of the *gaddhi*'s will. 'I do not presume to hasten you.'

'That is well.' A hard humour had returned to Honninscrave's eyes. 'The Giants are not a hasty people.' With a bow like an ironic mimesis of courtesy, he moved away towards the wheeldeck.

Linden followed Honninscrave with the First, Seadreamer, and Pitchwife. Cail accompanied her; Brinn brought Covenant. Ascending to the wheeldeck, they gathered around Shipsheartthew, where they were safely beyond earshot of Rire Grist.

At once, Honninscrave dropped the role he had taken in front of the *Bhrathair*, resumed his accustomed deference to the First. In a soft voice, he asked her, 'What think you?'

'I mislike it,' she growled. 'This welcome is altogether too propitious. A people who must have the *gaddhi*'s express command ere they will grant aid to the simple fact of sea-harm are somewhat unscrupling for my taste.'

'Yet have we choice in the matter?' inquired Pitchwife. 'A welcome so strangely given may also be strangely rescinded. It is manifest that we require this *gaddhi*'s goodwill. Surely we will forfeit that goodwill, should we refuse his proffer.'

'Aye,' the First retorted. 'And we will forfeit it also if we set one foot or word amiss in that donjon, the Sandhold. There our freedom will be as frail as the courtesy of *Bhrathairealm*.'

She and Honninscrave looked at Seadreamer, asking him for the advice of the Earth-Sight. But he shook his head; he had no guidance to offer them.

Then all their attention was focused on Linden. She had not spoken since the arrival of the Harbour Captain. The hot sunlight seemed to cast a haze like an omen of incapacity over her thoughts.

The Sandhold loomed over *Bhrathairain* – an image in stone of the gyring power which had created Sandgorgons Doom. Intuitions for which she had no name told her that the *gaddhi* and his Kemper represented both hazard and opportunity. She had to struggle against a growing inner confusion in order to meet the eyes of the Giants.

With an effort, she asked, 'What did that Caitiffin say to the Harbour Captain?'

Slowly Honninscrave replied, 'Its purport was no other than the words he addressed to us – a strong reproof for trespass upon the *gaddhi*'s will to welcome us. Yet his vehemence itself suggests another intent. In some way, this welcome is not merely eager. It is urgent. I suspect that Rire Grist has been commanded not to fail.'

Linden looked away. She had been hoping for some clearer revelation. Dully she murmured, 'We've already made this decision – when we chose to come here in the first place.' Her attention kept slipping away towards the Sandhold. Immense powers lay hidden within those blank walls. And powers were answers.

The Giants regarded each other again. When the First nodded grimly, Honninscrave straightened his shoulders and turned to Sevinhand. 'Anchormaster,' he said quietly, 'I leave Starfare's Gem in your hands. Ward it well. Our first requirement is the safety of the Giantship. Our second, stone for Pitchwife's wiving. Our third, replenishment of our stores. And you must contrive means to send warning of any peril. If you judge it needful, you must flee this Harbour. Do not scruple to abandon us. We will essay to rejoin you beyond the Spikes.'

Sevinhand accepted the command. His lean and weathered face showed no hesitance. Risk and decision were congenial to him because they distracted him from his old melancholy.

'I will remain with Starfare's Gem,' Pitchwife said. He looked uncomfortable at the idea. He did not like to leave the First's side. 'I must begin my wiving. And at need Sevinhand will spare me to convey messages to the Sandhold.'

Again the First nodded. Honninscrave gave Pitchwife's shoulder a quick slap of comradeship, then faced towards the afterdeck. In a clear voice, he said, 'Storesmaster, you may release the Harbour Captain. We will accept the *gaddhi*'s gracious hospitality.'

Above the ships, the crows and gulls went on calling as if they were ravenous.

14

THE SANDHOLD

Linden followed Honninscrave, the First, and Seadreamer down
from the wheeldeck to rejoin Caitiffin. She was trying to decide
whether or not she should make an effort to prevent Brinn from
taking Covenant to the Sandhold. She was instinctively leery of that
place. But the haze on her thoughts blurred her thinking. And she
did not want to be parted from him. He looked so vulnerable in his
slack emptiness that she yearned to stand between him and any
danger. Also, she was better able than anyone else to keep watch
over his condition.

The Harbour Captain had already escaped over the side of the
dromond, his dignity in disarray. Rire Grist delivered himself of
several graceful assurances concerning the *gaddhi* Rant Absolain's
pleasure at the company's acceptance of his welcome; and Honninscrave responded with his own grave politesse. But Linden did not
listen to either of them. She was watching Vain and Findail.

They approached the gathering together as if they were intimately
familiar with each other. However, Vain's ambiguous blackness
formed an acute contrast to Findail's pale flesh, his creamy raiment
and expression of habitual misery. The erosion of his face seemed to
have worsened since Linden had last looked at him; and his yellow
eyes conveyed a constant wince, as though Vain's presence were a
nagging pain to him.

Clearly, they both intended to accompany her and Covenant to
the Sandhold.

But if Rire Grist felt any surprise at the strangeness of these two
beings, he did not show it. Including them in his courtesies, he
started back down to the pier. The Giants made ready to follow him.
The First gave Pitchwife a brief intent farewell, then swung over the
side after the Caitiffin. Honninscrave and Seadreamer went next.

Supporting Covenant between them, Brinn and Hergrom paused
at the railing as if to give Linden a chance to speak. But she had
nothing to say. The lucidity oozed from her thoughts like the sweat
darkening the hair at her temples. Brinn shrugged slightly; and the
Haruchai lowered Covenant past the rail into Seadreamer's waiting
grasp.

For a moment longer she hesitated, trying to recover some clarity.
Her percipience read something covert in Rire Grist: his aura tasted

of subtle ambition and purposive misdirection. Yet he did not appear evil. His emanations lacked the acid scent of malice. Then why was she so uneasy?

She had expected Vain and Findail to follow Covenant at once; but instead they were waiting for her. Vain's orbs revealed nothing, perhaps saw nothing. And Findail did not look at her; he seemed reluctant to confront her penetration.

Their silent attendance impelled her into motion. Walking awkwardly to the rail, she set her feet on the rungs of the ladder and let her weight pull her down to the pier.

When she joined the company, the other four soldiers dismounted, and the Caitiffin offered their destriers to her and her immediate companions. At once, Brinn swung up behind one of the saddles. Then Hergrom lifted Covenant to sit between Brinn's arms. Ceer and Hergrom each took a mount, leaving one for Linden and Cail. Now she did not let herself hesitate. These beasts were far smaller and less threatening than the Coursers of the Clave. Though she had no experience as a horsewoman, she put a foot in the near stirrup, grasped the pommel with both hands, and climbed into the seat. In an instant, Cail was sitting behind her.

While Rire Grist mounted his own beast, his cohorts took the reins of their destriers. Honninscrave and the First positioned themselves on either side of the Caitiffin; Seadreamer moved between the horses which bore Covenant and Linden. Ceer and Hergrom followed, with Vain and Findail behind them. In this formation, they left the pier and entered the town of *Bhrathairain* like a cortege.

The crew shouted no farewells after them. The risk the company was taking invoked a silent respect from Starfare's Gem.

At Rire Grist's command, the throng on the docks parted. A babble of curious voices rose around Linden in tongues she did not know. Foremost among them were the brackish accents of the *Bhrathair*. Only a few onlookers chose to express their wonder in the common language of the port – the language Linden understood. But those few seemed to convey the general tenor of the talk. They claimed to their neighbours that they had seen sights as unusual as Giants before, that the *Haruchai* and Findail were not especially remarkable. But Linden and Covenant – she in checked flannel shirt and tough pants, he in his old T-shirt and jeans – were considered to be queerly dressed; and Vain, as odd a being as any in this part of the world. Linden listened keenly to the exclamations and conversation, but heard nothing more ominous than surprise.

For some distance, the Caitiffin led the way along the docks, between the piers and an area of busy shops which catered to the immediate needs of the ships – canvas, caulking, timber, ropes, food. But when he turned to ascend along narrow cobbled streets towards the Sandhold, the character of the warerooms and merchantries

637

changed. Dealers in luxury-goods and weapons began to predominate; taverns appeared at every corner. Most of the buildings were of stone, with tiled roofs; and even the smallest businesses seemed to swarm with trade, as if *Bhrathairain* lay in a glut of wealth. People crowded every entryway and alley, every street, swarthy and begauded *Bhrathair* commingling with equal numbers of sailors, traders, and buyers from every land and nation in this region of the world. The smells of dense habitation thickened the air – exotic spices and perfumes, forges and metalworks, sweat, haggling, profit, and inadequate sewers.

And all the time, the heat weighed against the town like a millstone, squeezing odours and noise out of the very cobbles under the horses' hooves. The pressure blunted Linden's senses, restricting their range; but though she caught flashes of every degree of avarice and concupiscence, she still felt no hostility or machination, no evidence of malice. *Bhrathairain* might try to trick strangers into poverty, but would not attack them.

At intervals, Honninscrave interrupted his observation of the town to ask questions of the Caitiffin. One in particular caught Linden's attention. With perfect nonchalance, the Master inquired if perhaps the welcome accorded Starfare's Gem had come from the *gaddhi*'s Kemper rather than from Rant Absolain himself.

The Caitiffin's reply was as easy as Honninscrave's question. 'Assuredly the *gaddhi* desires both your acquaintance and your comfort. Yet it is true that his duties, and his diversions also, consume his notice. Thus some matters must perforce be delayed for the sake of others. Anticipating his will, the *gaddhi*'s Kemper, Kasreyn of the Gyre, bade me bid you welcome. For such anticipation, the Kemper is dearly beloved by his *gaddhi*, and indeed by all who hold the *gaddhi* in their hearts. I must say,' he added with a touch of the same irony which lay behind Honninscrave's courtesy, 'that those who do not so hold him are few. Prosperity teaches a great love of sovereigns.'

Linden stiffened at that statement. To her hearing, it said plainly that Rire Grist's allegiance lay with Kasreyn rather than the *gaddhi*. In that case, the purpose behind the Caitiffin's invitation might indeed be other than it appeared.

But Honninscrave remained carefully bland. 'Then Kasreyn of the Gyre yet lives among you, after so many centuries of service. In good sooth, that is a thing of wonder. Was it not this same Kasreyn who bound the Sandgorgons to their doom?'

'As you say,' Rire Grist responded. 'The Kemper of the *gaddhi* Rant Absolain is that same man.'

'Why is he so named?' pursued Honninscrave. 'He is far-famed throughout the Earth – yet I have heard no account of his name.'

'That is easily answered.' The Caitiffin seemed proof against any probing. '"Kasreyn" is the name he has borne since first he came to *Bhrathairealm*. And his epithet has been accorded him for the nature of his arts. He is a great thaumaturge, and his magicks for the most part manifest themselves in circles, tending upward as they enclose. Thus Sandgorgon's Doom is a circle of wings holding the beasts within its heart. And so also is the Sandhold itself of circular formation, ascending as it rounds. Other arts the Kemper has, but his chief works are ever cast in the mould of the whirlwind and the gyre.'

After that, the Master's questions drifted to less important topics; and Linden's attention wandered back into the crowded streets and scents and heat of *Bhrathairain*.

As the company ascended the winding ways towards the Sandwall, the buildings slowly changed in character. The merchantries became fewer and more sumptuous, catering to a more munificent trade than the general run of sailors and townspeople. And dwellings of all kinds began to replace most of the taverns and shops. At this time of day – the sun stood shortly past noon – the streets here were not as busy as those lower down. There was no breeze to carry away the cloying scents; and the dry heat piled on to everything. Whenever a momentary gap appeared among the people, clearing a section of a street, the cobbles shimmered whitely.

But soon Linden stopped noticing such things. The Sandwall rose up in front of her, as blank and sure as a cliff, and she did not look at anything else.

Rire Grist was leading the company towards the central of the three immense gates which provided egress from *Bhrathairain* and access to the Sandhold. The gates were stone slabs bound with great knurls and studs of iron, as if they were designed to defend the Sandhold against the rest of *Bhrathairealm*. But they stood open; and at first Linden could see no evidence that they were guarded. Only when her mount neared the passage between them did she glimpse the dark shapes moving watchfully behind the slitted embrasures on either side of the gates.

The Caitiffin rode through with Honninscrave and the First beside him. Following them while her heart laboured unsteadily in her chest, Linden found the Sandwall to be at least a hundred feet thick. Reaching the sunlight beyond the gate, she looked up behind her and saw that this side of the wall was lined with banquettes. But they were deserted, as if *Bhrathairealm*'s prosperity had deprived them of their function.

That gate brought the company to the smooth convex surface of another wall. The Sandhold was enclosed within its own perfect circle; and that wall was joined to the defences of *Bhrathairain* by an additional arm of the Sandwall on each side. These arms formed two roughly triangular open courts, one on either hand. And in the centre of each court arose one of *Bhrathairealm*'s five springs. They had been fashioned into fountains by ornate stonework, so that they looked especially lush and vital against the pale walls. Their waters gathered in pools which were kept immaculately clean and from there flowed into underground channels, one leading towards *Bhrathairain*, the other towards the Sandhold.

In the arm of the Sandwall which enclosed each court, a gate stood open to the outer terrain. These provided the *Bhrathair* with their only road to their scant fields and three other springs.

Two more gates facing the fountains gave admittance to the fortifications of the Sandhold. Rire Grist led the company towards the gate in the eastern court; and the fountain made the atmosphere momentarily humid. Confident that they were in no danger, crows hopped negligently away from the hooves of the horses.

As her mount traversed the distance, Linden studied the inner Sandwall. Like the defences of *Bhrathairain*, it was as uncompromising as the Kemper's arts could make it; but over the gate its upper edge rose in two distinct sweeps to form immense gargoyles. Shaped like basilisks, they crouched above the entrance with their mouths agape in silent fury.

The portals here were similar to those of the town. But the guards were not hidden. A squat muscular figure stood on either side, holding erect a long razor-tipped spear. They were caparisoned in the same manner as Rire Grist and his cohorts; yet Linden perceived with a visceral shock that they were scarcely human. Their faces were bestial, with tigerlike fangs, apish hair, porcine snouts and eyes. Their fingers ended in claws rather than nails. They looked strong enough to contend with Giants.

She could not be mistaken. They were not natural beings, but rather the offspring of some severe and involuntary miscegenation.

As the company approached, they blocked the gate, crossed their spears. Their eyes shone balefully in the sunlight. Speaking together as if they had no independent will, they said, 'Name and purpose.' Their voices grumbled like the growling of old predators.

Rire Grist halted before them. To the company, he said, 'These are *hustin* of the *gaddhi*'s Guard. Like the Harbour Captain they conceive their duty straitly. However,' he went on wryly, 'they are somewhat less accessible to persuasion. It will be necessary to answer them. I assure you that their intent is caution, not discourtesy.'

Addressing the *hustin*, he announced himself formally, then described the purpose of the company. The two Guards listened as stolidly as if they were deaf. When he finished, they replied in unison, 'You may pass. They must tell their names.'

The Caitiffin shrugged a bemused apology to Honninscrave.

Warnings knotted in Linden's throat. She was still shaken by her perception of the *hustin*. They were only tools, fashioned deliberately to be tools; yet the power or person that required such slaves!

But the company was too far from Starfare's Gem. And Starfare's Gem was too vulnerable. If she spoke, she might spring the trap. In this place, she and her companions could only hope for safety and escape by playing the game devised for them by the *gaddhi* or his Kemper. Gritting her teeth, she remained silent.

Honninscrave did not hesitate; his decisions had already been made. He stepped up to the *hustin* and gave his answer. His voice was calm; but his heavy brows lowered as if he wished to teach the Guards more politeness.

'You may pass,' they replied without expression and parted their spears. Rire Grist rode between them into the dim passage of the gate, stopped there to wait. Honninscrave followed him.

Before the First could pass, the Guards blocked the way again.

Her jaws chewed iron. One hand flexed in frustration at the place where the hilt of her broadsword should have been. Precisely, dangerously, she said, 'I am the First of the Search.'

The *ustin* stared primitive malice at her. 'That is not a name. It is a title.'

'Nevertheless' – her tone made Linden's muscles tighten in preparation for trouble or flight – 'it will suffice for you.'

For one heartbeat, the Guards closed their eyes as if they were consulting an invisible authority. Then they looked back at the First and raised their spears.

Glowering, she stalked between them to Honninscrave's side.

As Seadreamer stepped forward, the Master said with half-unintended roughness, 'He is Cable Seadreamer my brother. He has no voice with which to speak his name.'

The Guards appeared to understand; they did not bar Seadreamer's way.

A moment later, the soldier leading Linden's horse approached the gates and spoke his name, then paused for her to do the same. Her pulse was racing with intimations of danger. The *hustin* dismayed her senses. She felt intuitively certain that the Sandhold would be as hard to leave as a prison – that this was her last chance to flee a secret and premeditated peril. But she had already done too much fleeing. Although she strove to match Honninscrave's steadiness, a faint tremor sharpened her voice as she said, 'I'm Linden Avery the Chosen.'

Over her shoulder, Cail uttered his name dispassionately. The *hustin* admitted them to the gate.

Ceer and Hergrom were brought forward. They went through the same ritual and were allowed to enter.

Then came the soldier with Covenant and Brinn. After the soldier had given his name, Brinn said flatly, 'I am Brinn of the *Haruchai*. With me is ur-Lord Thomas Covenant, Giantfriend and white gold wielder.' His tone defied the *hustin* to challenge him.

Blankly, they lifted their spears.

Vain and Findail came last. They approached the gate and halted. Vain held himself as if he neither knew nor cared that he was no longer moving. But Findail gazed at the Guards with frank loathing. After a moment, he said grimly, 'I do not give my name to such as these. They are an abomination, and he who made them is a wreaker of great ill.'

A shiver of tension went through the air. Reacting as one, the *hustin* dropped back a step, braced themselves for combat with their spears levelled.

At once, the Caitiffin barked, 'Hold, you fools! They are the *gaddhi*'s guests!' His voice echoed darkly along the passage.

Linden turned against the support of Cail's arms. Ceer and Hergrom had already leaped from their mounts, poised themselves behind the *hustin*.

The Guards did not attack. But they also did not lower their weapons. Their porcine eyes were locked on Findail and Vain. Balanced on thick, widely-splayed legs, they looked mighty enough to drive their spears through solid ironwood.

Linden did not fear for Vain or Findail. Both were impenetrable to ordinary harm. But they might trigger a struggle which would damn the entire company. She could see disdain translating itself into ire and action on Findail's eroded mien.

But the next instant a silent whisper of power rustled through the passage, touching her ears on a level too subtle for normal hearing. At once, the *hustin* withdrew their threat. Lifting their spears, they stepped out of the way, returned to their posts as if nothing had happened.

To no one in particular, Findail remarked sardonically, 'This Kasreyn has ears.' Then he passed into the gloom of the gate with Vain at his side like a shadow.

Linden let a sigh of relief leak through her teeth. It was repeated softly by the First.

Promptly, Rire Grist began apologizing. 'Your pardon, I beg you.' His words were contrite, but he spoke them too easily to convey much regret. 'Again you have fallen foul of a duty which was not directed at you. Should the *gaddhi* hear of this, he will be sorely displeased. Will you not put the unwise roughness of these *hustin* from your hearts, and accompany me?' He made a gesture which was barely visible in the dimness.

'Caitiffin.' The First's tone was deliberate and hard. 'We are Giants and love all amity. But we do not shirk combat when it is thrust upon us. Be warned. We have endured much travail, and our appetite for affront has grown somewhat short.'

Rire Grist bowed to her. 'First of the Search, be assured that no affront was intended and no more will be given. The Sandhold and the *gaddhi*'s welcome await you. Will you come?'

She did not relent. 'Perhaps not. What will be your word should we choose to return to our Giantship?'

At that, a hint of apprehension entered the Caitiffin's voice. 'Do not do so,' he requested. 'I tell you plainly that Rant Absolain is little accustomed to such spurning. It is not in the nature of rulers to smile upon any refusal of their goodwill.'

Out of the gloom, the First asked, 'Chosen, how do you bespeak this matter?'

A tremor still gripped Linden's heart. After the sun's heat, the stone of the Sandwall felt preternaturally cold. Carefully she said, 'I think I want to meet the man who's responsible for those *hustin*.'

'Very well,' the First replied to Rire Grist. 'We will accompany you.'

'I thank you,' he responded with enough underlying sincerity to convince Linden that he had indeed been apprehensive. Turning his mount, he led the company on through the gate.

When she reached the end of the passage, Linden blinked the sun out of her eyes and found herself facing the sheer wall of the First Circinate.

A space bare, open and perhaps fifty feet wide lay between the Sandwall and the Sandhold. The inner curve of the wall here was also lined with banquettes; but these were not deserted. *Hustin* stood along them at precise intervals. Frequent entryways from the banquettes gave admittance to the interior wall. And opposite them the abutments of the First Circinate rose like the outward face of a donjon from which people did not return. Its parapets were so high that Linden could not see past them to any other part of the Sandhold.

Only one entrance was apparent – another massive stone gate which stood in line with the central gate of the outer Sandwall. She expected Rire Grist to ride in that direction; but instead he dismounted and stood waiting for her and Covenant to do the same. Cail promptly dropped to the sand, helped her down; Hergrom accepted Covenant from Brinn's grasp, lowering the ur-Lord as Brinn jumped lightly off his horse's back.

The Caitiffin's soldiers took the five mounts away to the left; but Rire Grist beckoned the company towards the gate. The heat of the sand rose through Linden's shoes; sweat stuck her shirt to her back. *Bhrathairealm* sprawled under a sempiternal desert sun like a distant image of the Sunbane. She felt ungainly and ineffectual as she trudged the yielding surface behind Honninscrave and the First. She had had nothing to eat or drink since dawn; and the wall before her raised strange tenebrous recollections of Revelstone, of Gibbon-Raver's hands. The sky overhead was the dusty hue of deserts. She had glanced up at it several times before she realized that it was empty of birds. None of the gulls and cormorants which flocked over *Bhrathairain* transgressed on the Sandhold.

Then an unexpected yearning for Pitchwife panged her; his insuppressible spirit might have buoyed her against her forebodings. Covenant had never looked as vulnerable and lost to her as he did in the sunlight which fell between these walls. Yet the *hustin* had done her one favour: they had reminded her of ill and anger. She did not permit herself to quail.

The gates of the Sandhold were closed; but at a shout from Rire Grist they opened outward, operated by forces or Guards within the walls. Honninscrave and the First entered with the Caitiffin. Clenching her fists, Linden followed.

As her eyes adjusted to the dimmer light, Rire Grist began speaking. 'As you perhaps heard, this is the First Circinate of the *gaddhi*'s Sandhold.' They were in a forecourt or mustering-hall large enough for several hundred people. The ceiling was lost in shadow far above the floor, as if this whole space had been formed for the explicit purpose of humbling anyone admitted to the Sandhold. In the light which streaked the air from huge embrasures high above the gates, Linden saw two wide stairways opposite each other at the far end of the forecourt. 'Here are housed the Guards and those like myself who are of the *gaddhi*'s Horse.' At least a score of the *hustin* stood on duty around the walls; but they did not acknowledge either the Caitiffin or the company. 'And here also are our kitchens, refectories, laving-rooms, training-halls. We number four score hundred Guards and fifteen score Horse.' Apparently, he sought to reassure the company by giving out information freely. 'Our mounts themselves are stabled within the Sandwall. Such was the Kemper's foresight that we do not yet fill this place, though our numbers grow with every passing year.'

Linden wanted to ask him why the *gaddhi* – or the *gaddhi*'s Kemper – required such an army. Or, for that matter, why *Bhrathairealm* needed all the warships she had seen in the Harbour. But she set those questions aside for another time and concentrated instead on understanding as much as possible of the Sandhold.

While he spoke, Rire Grist walked towards the stairway on the right. Honninscrave asked him a few seemingly disinterested questions about foodstores, water-supplies, and the like; and the Caitiffin's replies took the company as far as the stairs.

These led in a long sweep to the Second Circinate, which proved to be a smaller and more luxuriously appointed version of the First. Here, according to Rire Grist, lived all the people who comprised the *gaddhi*'s Chatelaine – his attendants, courtiers, advisers, and guests. There were no Guards in evidence; and the forecourt into which the stairways opened was bedecked and tapestried like a ballroom. Light came from many windows as well as from flaming cruses as big as cauldrons. The inner walls held balconies for spectators and musicians; sculpted stone tables stood ready to bear refreshments. But at the moment the hall was empty; and in spite of its light and accoutrements, it felt strangely cheerless.

Again, two wide stairways arced upward from the far end. Strolling in that direction, the Caitiffin explained that the company would be given chambers here, granted time for rest and sustenance in privacy, once they had been presented to Rant Absolain.

Honninscrave continued to ply their guide with easy inquiries and comments. But the First wore a glower as if she shared Linden's apprehension that the Sandhold would be difficult to leave. She carried her shield on her back like an assertion that she would not cheaply be made captive. But the swing of her arms, the flexing of her fingers, were as imprecise as a cripple's, betraying her bereavement of her broadsword.

No other voice intruded on the hollow air. Covenant shambled forward in Brinn's grasp like a negative image of Seadreamer's muteness. The *Haruchai* bore themselves in poised silence. And Linden was at once too daunted by, and too busy studying, the Sandhold to speak. With all the frayed attention she could muster, she searched the *gaddhi*'s donjon for signs of evil.

Then the company ascended from the Second Circinate and found themselves in the Tier of Riches.

That place was aptly named. Unlike the lower levels, it was structured in a warren of rooms the size of galleries. And each room was resplendent with treasure.

Here, Rire Grist explained, the *gaddhi* kept the finest works of the artists and artisans of *Bhrathairealm*, the most valuable weaving, artifacts, and jewels gained by the *Bhrathair* in trade, the most precious gifts given to the Sanhold's sovereign by the rulers of other lands. Hall after hall was dedicated to displays of weaponry: rank upon rank of sabres, falchions, longswords; rows of jerrids, spears, crossbows, and innumerable other tools for hurling death; intricate engines of war, such as siege-towers, catapults, battering-rams, housed in magnificent chambers. Other rooms contained gemwork of every conceivable description. Dozens of walls were covered with arras like acts of homage, recognition, or flattery. Several chambers showed finely wrought goblets, plate, and other table service. And each was brightly lit by a chandelier of lambent crystal.

As Rire Grist guided the company through the nearest rooms, Linden was amazed by the extent of the *gaddhi*'s wealth. If these were the fruits of Kasreyn's stewardship, then she was not surprised that no *gaddhi* had ever deposed the Kemper. How could any monarch resent the servant who made the Tier of Riches possible? Kasreyn's hold upon his position did not arise only from great age and thaumaturgy. It also arose from cunning.

The First's eyes gleamed at the display of swords, some of which were large and puissant enough to replace her lost blade; and even Honninscrave was struck silent by all he saw. Seadreamer appeared to be dazzled by splendour. Apart from Vain and Findail, only the *Haruchai* remained untouched. If anything, Brinn and his people became more watchful and ready than ever, tightening their protection around Linden and Covenant as if they felt they were nearing the source of the threat.

In the Tier, the company met for the first time men and women who were not soldiers or Guards. These were members of the *gaddhi*'s Chatelaine. As a group, they appeared uniquely handsome and desirable. Linden saw not one plain face or figure among them. And they were resplendently dressed in velvet gowns encrusted with gems, doublets and robes that shone like peacock-feathers, gauzy cymars which draped their limbs like the attire of seduction. They saluted Rire Grist in the tongue of the *Bhrathair*, gazed at the company with diversely startled or brazen curiosity. Yet their faces wore brightness and charm as vizards; and Linden noted that although they moved around the Tier like appreciative admirers, they did not give their attention to the displayed wealth. From each of them she felt a vibration of tension, as if they were waiting with concealed trepidation for an event which might prove hazardous — and against which they had no defence except their grace and attire.

However they were adept at concealment. Like the Caitiffin, they betrayed no disquiet which would have been apparent to any senses but hers. But her percipience told her plainly that the Sandhold was a place ruled by fear.

One of the men gave her a smile as superficially frank as a leer. Servants moved noiselessly through the rooms, offering goblets of wine and other courtesies. The First could hardly draw herself away from a particular glaive which hung at an angle in its mounts as if it were leaning towards her. With an inward shiver, Linden realized that the Tier of Riches had been designed for more than the *gaddhi*'s gratification. It also acted as bait. Its very luxuriance was dangerous to people who had reason to be wary.

Then a tremor passed through the air, pulling her to a halt. A moment passed before she understood that no one else had felt it. It was not a sound, but rather a presence that altered the ambience of the Tier in a way only she was able to perceive. And it was moving towards the company. As it drew closer, the susurrus of voices rustling from chamber to chamber fell still.

Before she could warn her companions, a man entered the gallery. She knew who he was before Rire Grist's bow and salutation had announced him as the *gaddhi*'s Kemper. The power which poured from him was as tangible as a pronouncement. He could not have been anyone other than a thaumaturge.

The aura he radiated was one of hunger.

He was a tall man, stood head and shoulders above her; but his frame was so lean that he appeared emaciated. His skin had the translucence of great age, exposing the blue mapwork of his veins. Yet his features were not ancient, and he moved as if his limbs were confident of their vitality. In spite of his reputed longevity, he might have been no more than seventy years of age. A slight rheum clouded his eyes, obscuring their colour but not the impact of their gaze.

In a flash of intuition, Linden perceived that the hunger shining from him was a hunger for *time* – that his desire for life, and more life, surpassed the satiation of centuries.

He was dressed in a gold-coloured robe which swept the floor as he approached. Suspended by a yellow ribbon, a golden circle like an ocular hung from his neck; but it held no lens.

A leather strap enclosed each shoulder as if he were carrying a rucksack. Linden did not see until he turned to answer the Caitiffin's greeting that the burden he bore was an infant swaddled in yellow samite.

After a brief word with Rire Grist, the Kemper stepped towards the company.

'I am pleased to greet you.' His voice revealed a faint quaver of age; but his tone was confident and familiar. 'Permit me to say that such guests are rare in *Bhrathairealm* – thus doubly welcome. Therefore have I desired to make your acquaintance ere you are summoned before the Auspice to receive the *gaddhi*'s benison. But we need no introduction. This worthy Caitiffin has already spoken my name. And in my turn I know you.

'Grimmand Honninscrave,' he went on promptly as if to set the company at ease with his knowledge, 'you have brought your vessel a great distance – and at some cost, I fear.'

He gave the First a slight bow. 'You are the First of the Search – and very welcome among us.' To Seadreamer, he said, 'Be at peace. Your muteness will not lessen the pleasure of your presence for either the *gaddhi* or his Chatelaine.'

Then he stood before Linden and Covenant. 'Thomas Covenant,' he said with an avid tinge in his voice. 'Linden Avery. How you gladden me. Among such unexpected companions' – a flick of one hand referred to the *Haruchai*, Vain, and Findail – 'you are the most unexpected of all, and the most pleasurable to behold. If the word of the *gaddhi*'s Kemper bears any weight, you will not lack comfort or service while you sojourn among us.'

Distinctly, as if on cue, Covenant said, 'Don't touch me.'

The Kemper raised an age-white eyebrow in surprise. After a quick scrutiny of Covenant, his eyes turned towards Linden as if to ask for an explanation.

She resisted his intense aura, trying to find a suitable response. But her mind refused to clear. He disturbed her. Yet the most unsettling aspect of him was not the man himself, not the insatiety he projected. Rather, it was the child on his back. It hung in its wrappings as if it were fast and innocently asleep; but the way its plump cheek rested against the top of his spine gave her the inexplicable impression that it fed on him like a succubus.

This impression was only aggravated by the fact that she could not confirm it. Though the infant was as plainly visible as the Kemper, it did not impinge at all on the other dimension of her senses. If she closed her eyes, she still felt Kasreyn's presence like a yearning pressure against her face; but the infant disappeared as if it ceased to exist when she stopped gazing at it. It might have been a hallucination.

Her stare was too obvious to escape Kasreyn's notice. A look of calculation crossed his mien, then changed to fondness. 'Ah, my son,' he said. 'I bear him so constantly that upon occasion I forget a stranger might wonder at him. Linden Avery, I am uxorious, and my wife is sadly ill. Therefore I care for our child. My duties permit no other recourse than this. But you need have no concern of him. He is a quiet boy and will not trouble us.'

'Forgive me,' Linden said awkwardly, trying to emulate Honninscrave's detached politeness. 'I didn't mean to be rude.' She felt acutely threatened by that child. But the Kemper's welcome might become something else entirely if she showed that she knew he was lying.

'Give no thought to the matter.' His tone was gently condescending. 'How can it offend me that you have taken notice of my son?' Then he returned his attention to the Giants.

'My friends, much time has passed since your people have had dealing with *Bhrathair*. I doubt not you have remained mighty roamers and adventurers, and your history has surely been rich in interest and edification. I hope you will consent to share with me some of the tales for which the Giants have gained such renown. But that must come later, as my service to the *gaddhi* permits.' Abruptly, he raised a long, bony finger; and at the same instant a chime rang in the Tier of Riches. 'At present, we are summoned before the Auspice. Rire Grist will conduct you to The Majesty.' Without farewell, he turned and strode vigorously from the room, bearing his son nestled against his back.

Linden was left with a sense of relief, as if a faintly nauseating scent had been withdrawn. A moment passed before she realized how deftly Kasreyn had prevented her companions from asking him any questions. And he had not voiced any inquiry about Covenant's condition. Was he that incurious? – or was he capable of discerning the answer himself?

Rire Grist beckoned the company in another direction. But Honninscrave said firmly, 'One moment, Caitiffin.' His posture showed that he also had doubts about Kasreyn. 'A question, if you will. I ask pardon if I am somewhat forward – yet I cannot but think that the *gaddhi*'s Kemper is more than a little advanced in years to be the father of such an infant.'

The Caitiffin stiffened. In an instant, his countenance became the visage of a soldier rather than of a diplomat. 'Giant,' he said coldly, 'there is no man or woman, Chatelaine or Guard, in all *Bhrathairealm* who will speak to you concerning the Kemper's son.' Then he stalked out of the room as if he were daring the company not to follow him.

Honninscrave looked at Linden and the First. Linden felt neither ready nor safe enough to do anything more than shrug; and the First said grimly, 'Let us attend this *gaddhi*. All other reasons aside, it rends my heart to behold so many brave blades I may not touch.'

The Master's discomfort at the role he played showed itself in the tightness of his shoulders, the weight of his brows. But he led the company after Rire Grist.

They caught up with the Caitiffin two galleries later. By then, he had recovered his courtly politeness. But he offered no apology for his change of manner. Instead, he simply ushered the company onward through the Tier of Riches.

The chime must have included all the Chatelaine in its call. The sumptuously clad men and women were now moving in the same direction Rire Grist took. Their ornaments glittered in accompaniment to their personal comeliness; but they walked in silence, as if they were bracing themselves for what lay ahead.

Linden was briefly confused by the complexity of the Tier, uncertain of where she was headed. But soon the chambers debouched into a hall that took the thickening stream of people towards a richly gilt and engraved stairway which spiralled upward to pierce the ceiling.

Surrounded by the courtiers, she was more sure than ever that she saw shadows of trepidation behind their deliberate gaiety. Apparently, attendance upon the *gaddhi* represented a crisis for them as well as for the company. But their knurled cheeriness did not reveal the nature of what they feared.

The treads climbed dizzily upward. Hunger, and the fatigue of her legs, sent low tremblings through Linden's thighs. She felt too unsteady to trust herself. But she drew a mental support from Cail's hardness at her shoulder and trudged on behind the Giants and Rire Grist.

Then the stairs opened into The Majesty, and she forgot her weariness.

The hall into which she stepped seemed almost large and grand enough to fill the entire level. At this end, the air was only dimly lit by reflected light, and the gloom made the place appear immense and cavernous. The ceiling was lost in shadow. The *hustin* that lined the long, curving wall nearby looked as vague as icons. And the wall itself was deeply carved with huge and tormented shapes – demons in basrelief which appeared to be animated by the dimness, tugging at the edges of Linden's sight as if they writhed in a gavotte of pain.

The floor was formed of stone slabs cut into perfect circles. But the gaps between the circles were wide, deep, and dark. Any misstep might easily break an ankle. As a result, the company had to advance with care in order to approach the light.

The rest of the hall was also designed to be daunting. All the light was concentrated around the Auspice: skylights, flaming vats of oil with polished reflectors, vivid candelabra on tall poles cast their illumination towards the *gaddhi*'s seat. And the Auspice itself was as impressive as art and wealth could make it. Rising from the tiered plinth of stairs, it became a monolith which reached for the ceiling like an outstretched forearm and hand. Its arm was crusted with precious stones and metals, and the hand was an aurora of concentric circles behind the seat.

The Auspice appeared to be enormous, dominating the hall. But after a moment Linden realized that this was a consequence of the light, enhancing the Auspice with an illusion of more size than it truly possessed. Spangled with lumination and jewel-work, the seat drew every eye as a cynosure. Linden had trouble forcing herself to watch where she put her feet; and her apprehension tightened another turn. As she strove to walk forward without stumbling into the gaps which marked the floor all the way to the Auspice, she learned to understand the Majesty. It was intended to make everyone who came here feel subservient and vulnerable.

She resisted instinctively. Glowering as if she had come to hurl revolt at the sovereign of *Bhrathairealm*, she followed the Giants, took her place among them when Rire Grist stopped a short distance from the plinth of the Auspice. Around them, the Chatelaine spread out to form a silent arc before the *gaddhi*'s seat. Looking at her companions, she saw that the Giants were not immune to the power of the Majesty; and even the *Haruchai* seemed to experience some of the awe which had led their ancestors to Vow fealty to Kevin Landwaster. Vain's blankness and Findail's unimpressed mien gave her no comfort. But she found a positive reassurance in the uncowed distinctness with which Covenant uttered his empty refrain:

'Don't touch me.'

She feared that she might be cunningly and dangerously touched in this place.

A moment later, another chime sounded. Immediately, the light grew brighter, as if even the sun had been called to attend the *gaddhi*'s arrival. The *hustin* snapped into still greater rigidity, raising their spears in salute. For an instant, no one appeared. Then several figures came out of the shadow of the Auspice as if they had been rendered material by the intensity of the illumination.

A man led the way up on to the plinth. To each of his arms a woman clung, at once deferential and possessive. Behind them came six more women. And at the rear of the party walked Kasreyn of the Gyre, with his son on his back.

Every courtier dropped to one knee and bowed deeply.

The Caitiffin also made a profound obeisance, though he remained standing. In a careful whisper, he breathed, 'The *gaddhi* Rant Absolain. With him are his Favoured, the Lady Alif and the Lady Benj. Also others who have recently been, or perhaps will be, Favoured. And the *gaddhi*'s Kemper, whom you know.'

Linden stared at the *gaddhi*. In spite of the opulence around him, he was plainly arrayed in a short satin tunic, as if he wished to suggest that he was unmoved by his own riches. But he had chosen a tunic which displayed his form proudly; and his movements hinted at narcissism and petulance. He accepted the adoring gazes of his women smugly. Linden saw that his hair and face had been treated with oils and paints to conceal his years behind an aspect of youthful virility.

He did not look like a sovereign.

The women with him – both the Favoured and the others – were all pretty, would have been lovely if their expressions of adoration had not been so mindless. And they were attired as odalisques. Their scant and transparent raiment was a candid appeal to desire: their perfumes, coifs, movements spoke of nothing except bedworthiness. They had found their own answer to the trepidation which beset the Chatelaine, and meant to pursue it with every allure at their command.

Smirking intimately, the *gaddhi* left his Favoured on the plinth with Kasreyn and ascended to his seat. There he was an effective figure. The design of the throne made him appear genuinely regal and commanding. But no artifice could conceal the self-satisfaction in his eyes. His gaze was that of a spoiled child – surquedry unjustified by any achievement, any true power.

For a long moment, he sat looking out over the obeisance of his Chatelaine, enjoying the way so many men and women humbled themselves before him. Perhaps the brightness dazzled him; he seemed unaware that Linden and her companions were still on their feet. But gradually he leaned forward to peer through the light; and vexation creased his face, betraying the lines which oil and paint had concealed.

'Kemper!' he snapped irritably. 'Who are these mad folk who do not take to their knees before Rant Absolain, *gaddhi* of *Bhrathairealm* and the Great Desert?'

'O *gaddhi*.' Kasreyn's reply was practised – and faintly sardonic. 'They are the Giants and voyagers of whom we spoke just now. Though they are ignorant of the greeting which should properly be accorded the *gaddhi* Rant Absolain, they have come to accept the welcome which you have so graciously proffered them, and to express their profound thanks, for you have redeemed them from severe distress.'

As he delivered this speech, his eyes were fixed purposefully on the company.

Honninscrave responded promptly. Moving like a man in a charade, he dropped to one knee. 'O *gaddhi*,' he said clearly, 'your Kemper speaks good sooth. We have come in glad thanks for your most hospitable and needful welcome. Forgive us that we are ill-schooled in the homage which is your due. We are rude folk and have little acquaintance with such regality.'

At the same time, Rire Grist made a covert gesture to the rest of the company, urging them to follow Honninscrave's example.

The First growled softly in her throat; but she acknowledged the necessity of the masque by lowering herself to one knee. Her shoulders were rigid with the knowledge that the company was surrounded by at least three hundred Guards.

Linden and Seadreamer also bowed. Her breathing was cramped with anxiety. She could think of no appeal or power which would induce the *Haruchai*, Vain, or Findail to make obeisance. And Covenant was altogether deaf to the need for this imitation of respect.

But the *gaddhi* did not press the issue. Instead, he muttered an impatient phrase in the brackish language of the *Bhrathair*; and at once the Chatelaine rose to their feet. The company did the same, the First stiffly, Honninscrave diffidently. Linden felt a moment of relief.

The *gaddhi* was now looking down at Kasreyn. His expression had fallen into a pout. 'Kemper, why was I called from the pleasure of my Favoured for this foolish assemblage?' He spoke the common tongue of the Harbour in an oddly defiant tone, like a rebellious adolescent.

But the Kemper's reply was unruffled. 'O *gaddhi*, it is to your great honour that you have ever been munificent to those whom you deign to welcome. Therefore is your name grateful to all who dwell within the blessing of your demesne, and the Chatelaine are exalted by the mere thought of attendance upon you. Now it is seemly that these your new guests should come before you to utter their thanks. And it is also seemly' – his voice sharpened slightly – 'that you should grant them your hearing. They have come in need, with requests in their hearts which only such a monarch as the *gaddhi* of *Bhrathairealm* may hope to satisfy, and the answer which you accord them will carry the fame of your grace across all the wide Earth.'

At this, Rant Absolain settled back in his seat with an air of cunning. His mood was plain to Linden's senses. He was engaged in a contest of wills with his Kemper. Glancing out over the company, he smiled nastily. 'It is as my servant' – he stressed that word – 'the Kemper has said. I delight to give pleasure to my guests. What do you desire of me?'

The company hesitated. Honninscrave looked to the First for guidance. Linden tightened her grip on herself. Here any request might prove dangerous by playing into the hands of either the *gaddhi* or his Kemper.

But after a momentary pause the First said, 'O *gaddhi*, the needs of our Giantship are even now being met at your decree. For this our thanks are unbounded.' Her tone held no more gratitude than an iron bar. 'But your graciousness inspires me to ask a further boon. You see that my scabbard is empty.' With one hand, she held the sheath before her. 'The *Bhrathair* are renowned for their weaponwork. And I have seen many apt blades in the Tier of Riches. O *gaddhi*, grant me the gift of a broadsword to replace that which I have lost.'

Rant Absolain's face broke into a grin of satisfaction. He sounded triumphant and petty as he replied, 'No.'

A frown interrupted Kasreyn's confidence. He opened his mouth to speak; but the *gaddhi* was already saying, 'Though you are my guest, I must refuse. You know not what you ask. I am the *gaddhi* of *Bhrathairealm* – the servant of my people. That which you have seen belongs not to me but to the *Bhrathair*. I hold it but in stewardship. For myself I possess nothing, and thus I have no sword or other riches in my gift.' He uttered the words vindictively, but his malice was directed at the Kemper rather than the First; as if he had found unassailable grounds on which he could spite Kasreyn. 'If you require a sword,' he went on, 'you may purchase it in *Bhrathairain*.' He made an effort to preserve his air of victory by not looking at Kasreyn; but he was frightened by his own bravado and unable to resist.

The Kemper met that glance with a shrug of dismissal which made Rant Absolain wince. But the First did not let the matter end. 'O *gaddhi*,' she said through her teeth. 'I have no means to make such a purchase.'

The *gaddhi* reacted in sudden fury. 'Then do without!' His fists

653

pounded the arms of his seat. 'Am I to blame for your penury? Insult me further, and I will send you to the Sandgorgons!'

Kasreyn shot a look towards the Caitiffin. Immediately, Rire Grist stepped forward, made a low bow. 'O *gaddhi*,' he said, 'they are strangers, unfamiliar with the selfless nature of your stewardship. Permit me to implore pardon for them. I am certain that no offence was intended.'

Rant Absolain sagged. He seemed incapable of sustaining any emotion which might contradict the Kemper's will. 'Oh, assuredly,' he muttered. 'I take no offence.' Clearly, he meant the opposite. 'I am above all offence.' To himself, he began growling words like curses in the tongue of the *Bhrathair*.

'That is well known,' said the Kemper evenly, 'and it adds much to your honour. Yet it will sadden you to turn guests away with no sign of your welcome in their hands. Perhaps another request lies within their hearts – a supplication which may be granted without aspersion to your stewardship.'

With a nameless pang, Linden saw Kasreyn take hold of his golden ocular, raise it to his left eye. A stiffening like a ghost of fear ran through the Chatelaine. Rant Absolain squeezed farther back in his throne. But the Kemper's gesture appeared so natural and inevitable that she could not take her eyes away from it, could not defend herself.

Then he met her gaze through his ocular; and without warning all her turmoil became calm. She realized at once that she had no cause for anxiety, no reason to distrust him. His left eye held the answer to everything. Her last, most visceral protests faded into relief as the *geas* of his will came over her, lifted the words he wanted out of her.

'O *gaddhi*, I ask if there is aught your Kemper can do to heal my comrade, Thomas Covenant.'

Rant Absolain showed immediate relief that the eyepiece had not been turned towards him. In an over-loud voice, he said, 'I am certain Kasreyn will do all in his power to aid you.' Sweat made streaks through the paint on his face.

'O *gaddhi*, I serve you gladly.' The Kemper's gaze left Linden; but its effect lingered in her, leaving her relaxed despite the raw hunger with which he regarded Covenant. Honninscrave and the First stared at her in alarm. Seadreamer's shoulders knotted. But the calm of the Kemper's *geas* remained on her.

'Come, Thomas Covenant,' said Kasreyn sharply. 'We will attempt your succour at once.'

Brinn looked a question at Linden. She nodded; she could do nothing but nod. She was deeply relieved that the Kemper had lifted the burden of Covenant's need from her.

The *Haruchai* frowned slightly. His eyes asked the same question of the Giants; but they did not contradict Linden. They were unable to perceive what had happened to her.

With a shrug, Brinn walked Covenant towards the Kemper.

Kasreyn studied the Unbeliever avidly. A faint shiver touched his voice as he said, 'I thank you, Brinn of the *Haruchai*. You may leave him safely in my hands.'

Brinn did not hesitate. 'No.'

His refusal drew a gasp from the Chatelaine, instantly stifled. Rant Absolain leaned forward in his seat, bit his lip as if he could not believe his senses.

The Giants rocked subtly on to the balls of their feet.

Explicitly, as if he were supporting Brinn, Covenant said, 'Don't touch me.'

Kasreyn held his golden circle to his eye, said in a tone of tacit command, 'Brinn of the *Haruchai*, my arts admit of no spectation. If I am to aid this man, I must have him alone.'

Brinn met that ocular gaze without blinking. His words were as resolute as granite. 'Nevertheless he is in my care. I will not part from him.'

The Kemper went pale with fury and amazement. Clearly, he was not accustomed to defiance – or to the failure of his *geas*.

A vague uneasiness grew in Linden. Distress began to rise against the calm, nagging her towards self-awareness. A shout struggled to form itself in her throat.

Kasreyn turned back to her, fixed her with his will again. 'Linden Avery, command this *Haruchai* to give Thomas Covenant into my care.'

At once, the calm returned. It said through her mouth, 'Brinn, I command you to give Thomas Covenant into his care.'

Brinn looked at her. His eyes glinted with memories of *Elemesnedene*. Flatly he iterated, 'I will not.'

The Chatelaine recoiled. Their group frayed as some of them retreated towards the stairs. The *gaddhi*'s women crouched on the plinth and whimpered for his protection.

Kasreyn gave them cause for fear. Rage flushed his mien. His fists jerked threats through the air. 'Fool!' he spat at Brinn. 'If you do not instantly depart, I will command the Guards to slay you where you stand!'

Before the words had left his mouth, the Giants, Hergrom, and Ceer were moving towards Covenant.

But Brinn did not heed their aid. Too swiftly for Kasreyn to counter, he put himself between Covenant and the Kemper. His reply cut through Kasreyn's ire. 'Should you give such a command, you will die ere the first spear is raised.'

Rant Absolain stared in apoplectic horror. The rest of the Chatelaine began scuttling from the hall.

Brinn did not waver. Three Giants and two *Haruchai* came to his support. The six of them appeared more absolutely ready for battle than all the *hustin*.

For a moment, Kasreyn's face flamed as if he were prepared to take any risk in order to gain possession of Covenant. But then the wisdom or cunning which had guided him to his present power and longevity came back to him. He recanted a step, summoned his self-command.

'You miscomprehend me.' His voice shook, but grew steadier at every word. 'I have not merited your mistrust. This hostility ill becomes you – ill becomes any man or woman who has been granted the *gaddhi*'s welcome. Yet I accede to it. My desire remains to work you well. For the present, I will crave your pardon for my unseemly ire. Mayhap when you have tasted the *gaddhi*'s goodwill you will learn also to taste the cleanliness of my intent. If you then wish it, I will offer my aid again.'

He spoke coolly; but his eyes did not lose their heat. Without waiting for a reply, he sketched a bow towards the Auspice, murmured, 'With your permission, O *gaddhi*.' Then he turned on his heel, strode away into the shadow behind the throne.

For a moment, Rant Absolain watched the Kemper's discomfited departure with glee. But abruptly he appeared to realize that he was now alone with people who had outfaced Kasreyn of the Gyre – that he was protected only by his women and the Guards. Squirming down from the Auspice, he thrust his way between his Favoured and hurried after the Kemper as if he had been routed. His women followed behind him in dismay.

The company was left with Rire Grist and fifteen score *hustin*.

The Caitiffin was visibly shaken; but he strove to regain his diplomacy. 'Ah, my friends,' he said thickly, 'I pray that you will pardon this unsatisfactory welcome. As you have seen, the *gaddhi* is of a perverse temper – doubtless vexed by the pressure of his duties – and thus his Kemper is doubly stressed, both by his own labours and by his sovereign. Calm will be restored – and recompense made – I assure you.' He fumbled to a halt as if he were stunned by the inadequacy of his words. Then he grasped the first idea which occurred to him. 'Will you accompany me to your guesting-rooms? Food and rest await you there.'

At that moment, Linden came out of her imposed passivity with a wrench of realization which nearly made her scream.

15

'DONT TOUCH ME.'

Thomas Covenant saw everything. He heard everything. From the moment when the *Elohim* had opened the gift of Caer-Caveral, the location of the One Tree, all his senses had functioned normally. Yet he remained as blank as a stone tablet from which every commandment had been effaced. What he saw and heard and felt simply had no meaning to him. In him, the link between action and impact, perception and interpretation, had been severed or blocked. Nothing could touch him.

The strange self-contradictions of the *Elohim* had not moved him. The storm which had nearly wrecked Starfare's Gem had conveyed nothing to him. The dangers of his own life — and the efforts of people like Brinn, Seadreamer, and Linden to preserve him — had passed by him like babblings in an alien tongue. He had seen it all. Perhaps on some level he had understood it, for he lacked even the exigency of incomprehension. Nothing which impinged upon him was defined by the barest possibility of meaning. He breathed when breath was necessary. He swallowed food which was placed in his mouth. At times, he blinked to moisten his eyes. But these reflexes also were devoid of import. Occasionally an uneasiness as vague as mist rose up in him; but when he uttered his refrain, it went away.

Those three words were all that remained of his soul.

So he watched Kasreyn's attempt to gain possession of him with a detachment as complete as if he were made of stone. The hungry *geas* which burned from the Kemper's ocular had no effect. He was not formed of any flesh which could be persuaded. And likewise the way his companions defended him sank into his emptiness and vanished without a trace. When Kasreyn, Rant Absolain, and the Chatelaine made their separate ways out of The Majesty, Covenant was left unchanged.

Yet he saw everything. He heard everything. His senses functioned normally. He observed the appraising glance which Findail cast at him as if the Appointed were measuring this *Elohim*-wrought blankness against the Kemper's hunger. And he witnessed the flush of shame and dismay which rushed into Linden's face as Kasreyn's will lost its hold over her. Her neck corded at the effort she made to stifle her instinctive outcry. She feared possession more than any other thing — and she had fallen under Kasreyn's command as easily as if she lacked all volition. Through her teeth, she gasped, 'Jesus God!' But her frightened and furious glare was fixed on Rire Grist, and she did not answer the consternation of her companions. Her taut self-containment said plainly that she did not trust the Caitiffin.

The sight of her in such distress evoked Covenant's miasmic discomfort, but he articulated his three words, and they carried all trouble away from him.

He heard the raw restraint in the First's tone as she replied to the Caitiffin, 'We will accompany you. Our need for rest and peace is great. Also we must give thought to what has transpired.'

Rire Grist acknowledged the justice of her tone with a grimace. But he made no effort to placate the company. Instead, he led the *gaddhi*'s guests towards the stairs which descended to the Tier of Riches.

Covenant followed because Brinn's grasp on his arm compelled him to place one foot in front of the other reflexively, as if he were capable of choosing to commit such an act.

Rire Grist took them down to the Second Circinate. In the depths of that level behind the immense forecourt or ballroom, he guided them along complex and gaily lit passages, among bright halls and chambers – sculleries and kitchens, music rooms, ateliers, and galleries – where the company encountered many of the Chatelaine who now contrived to mask their fear. At last he brought the questers to a long corridor marked at intervals by doors which opened into a series of comfortable bedrooms. One room had been set aside for each member of the company. Across the hall was a larger chamber richly furnished with settees and cushions. There the companions were invited to a repast displayed on tables intricately formed of bronze and mahogany.

But at the doorway of each bedroom stood one of the *hustin*, armed with its spear and broadsword; and two more waited near the tables of food like attendants or assassins. Rire Grist himself made no move to leave. This was insignificant to Covenant. Like the piquant aromas of the food, the unwashed musk of the Guards, it was a fact devoid of content. But it tightened the muscles of Honninscrave's arms, called a glint of ready ire from the First's eyes, compressed Linden's mouth into a white line. After a moment, the Chosen addressed Rire Grist with a scowl.

'Is this another sample of the *gaddhi*'s welcome? Guards all over the place?'

'Chosen, you miscomprehend.' The Caitiffin had recovered his equilibrium. 'The *hustin* are creatures of duty, and these have been given the duty of serving you. If you desire them to depart, they will do so. But they will remain within command, so that they may answer to your wants.'

Linden confronted the two Guards in the chamber. 'Get out of here.'

Their bestial faces betrayed no reaction; but together they marched out into the hall.

She followed them. To all the *hustin*, she shouted, 'Go away! Leave us alone!'

Their compliance appeased some of her hostility. When she returned, her weariness was apparent. Again, the emotion she aroused made Covenant speak. But his companions had become accustomed to his litany and gave it no heed.

'I also will depart,' the Caitiffin said, making a virtue of necessity. 'As occasion requires, I will bring you word of the *gaddhi*'s will, or his Kemper's. Should you have any need of me, summon the Guard and speak my name. I will welcome any opportunity to serve you.'

Linden dismissed him with a tired shrug; but the First said, 'Hold yet a moment, Caitiffin.' The expression in her eyes caused his mien to tense warily. 'We have seen much which we do not comprehend, and thereby we are disquieted. Ease me with one answer.' Her tone suggested that he would be wise to comply. 'You have spoken of four score hundred Guards – of fifteen score Horse. Battleremes we have seen aplenty. Yet the Sandgorgons are gone to their Doom. And the Kemper's arts are surely proof against any insurgence. What need has Rant Absolain for such might or arms?'

At that, Rire Grist permitted himself a slight relaxation, as if the question were a safe one. 'First of the Search,' he replied, 'the answer lies in the wealth of *Bhrathairealm*. No small part of that wealth has been gained in payment from other rulers or people for the service of our arms and ships. Our puissance earns much revenue and treasure. But it is a precarious holding, for our wealth teaches other lands and monarchs to view us jealously. Therefore our strength serves also to preserve what we have garnered since the formation of Sandgorgons Doom.'

The First appeared to accept the plausibility of this response. When no one else spoke, the Caitiffin bowed his farewell and departed. At once, Honninscrave closed the door; and the room was filled with terse, hushed voices.

The First and Honninscrave expressed their misgivings. Linden described the power of the Kemper's ocular, the unnatural birth of the *hustin*. Brinn urged that the company return immediately to Starfare's Gem. But Honninscrave countered that such an act might cause the *gaddhi* to rescind his welcome before the *dromond* was sufficiently supplied or repaired. Linden cautioned her companions that they must not trust Rire Grist. Vain and Findail stood aloof together.

With signs and gestures, Seadreamer made Honninscrave understand what he wanted to know; and the Master asked Brinn how the *Haruchai* had withstood Kasreyn's *geas*. Brinn discounted that power in a flat tone. 'He spoke to me with his gaze. I heard, but did not choose to listen.' For a moment, he gave Linden a look as straight as an accusation. She bit her lower lip as if she were ashamed of her vulnerability. Covenant witnessed it all. It passed by him as if he were insensate.

The company decided to remain in the Sandhold as long as they could, so that Pitchwife and Sevinhand would have as much time as possible to complete their work. Then the Giants turned to the food. When Linden had examined it, pronounced it safe, the questers ate. Covenant ate when Brinn put food in his mouth; but behind his emptiness he continued to watch and listen. Dangerous spots of colour accentuated Linden's cheeks, and her eyes were full of potential panic, as if she knew that she was being cornered. Covenant had to articulate his warning several times to keep the trouble at bay.

After that, the time wore away slowly, eroded in small increments by the tension of the company; but it made no impression on Covenant. He might have forgotten that time existed. The toll of days held no more meaning for him than a string of beads – although perhaps it was a preterite memory of bloodshed, rising like blame from the distance of the Land, which caused his vague uneasinesses; rising thicker every day as people he should have been able to save were butchered. Certainly, he had no more need for the One Tree. He was safe as he was.

His companions alternately rested, waited, stirred restlessly, spoke or argued quietly with each other. Linden could not dissuade Brinn from sending Ceer or Hergrom out to explore the Sandhold. The *Haruchai* no longer heeded her. But when the First supported Linden, they acceded, approving her insistence that the company should stay together.

Vain was as detached as Covenant. But the long pain did not leave Findail's face; and he studied Covenant as if he foresaw some crucial test for the Unbeliever.

Later, Rire Grist returned, bearing an invitation for the company to attend the Chatelaine in banquet. Linden did not respond. The attitude of the *Haruchai* had drained some essential determination out of her. But the First accepted; and the company followed the Caitiffin to a high bright dining-hall where bedizened ladies and smirking gallants talked and riposted, vied and feasted, to the accompaniment of soft music. The plain attire of the questers contrasted with the self-conscious display around them; but the Chatelaine reacted as though the company were thereby made more sapid and attractive – or as though the *gaddhi*'s court feared to behave otherwise.

Men surrounded Linden with opportunities for dalliance, blind to the possible hysteria in her mien. Women plied the impassive *Haruchai* determinedly. The Giants were treated to brittle roulades of wit.

Neither the *gaddhi* nor his Kemper appeared; but *hustin* stood against the walls like listening-posts, and even Honninscrave's most subtle questions gleaned no useful information. The foods were savoury; the wines, copious. As the evening progressed, the interchanges of the Chatelaine became more burlesque and corybantic. Seadreamer stared about him with glazed eyes, and the First's visage was a thunderhead. At intervals, Covenant spoke his ritual repudiation.

His companions bore the situation as long as they could, then asked Rire Grist to return them to their quarters. He complied with diplomatic ease. When he had departed, the company confronted the necessity for sleep.

Bedrooms had been provided for them all; and each contained only a single bed. But the questers made their own arrangements. Honninscrave and Seadreamer took one room together; the First and Ceer shared another. Linden cast one last searching look at Covenant, then went to her rest with Cail to watch over her. Brinn drew Covenant into the next chamber and put him to bed, leaving Hergrom on guard in the hall with Vain and Findail. When Brinn doused the light, Covenant reflexively closed his eyes.

The light returned, and he opened his eyes. But it was not the same light. It came from a small gilt cruse in the hand of a woman. She wore filmy draperies as suggestive as mist; her lush yellow hair spilled about her shoulders. The light spread hints of welcome around her figure.

She was the Lady Alif, one of the *gaddhi*'s Favoured.

Raising a playful finger to her lips, she spoke softly to Brinn. 'You need not summon your companions. Kasreyn of the Gyre desires speech with Thomas Covenant. Your accompaniment is welcome. Indeed, all your companions are welcome, should you think it meet to rouse them. The Kemper has repented of his earlier haste. But wherefore should they be deprived of rest? Surely you suffice to ward Thomas Covenant's safety.'

Brinn's countenance betrayed no reaction. He measured the risk and the opportunity of this new ploy impassively.

While he considered, the Lady Alif stepped to his side. Her movements were too soft and unwily to be dangerous. Tiny silver bells tinkled around her ankles. Then her free hand opened, exposing a small mound of fulvous powder. With a sudden breath, she blew the powder into Brinn's face.

One involuntary inhalation of surprise undid him. His knees folded, and he sank in a slow circle to the floor.

At once, the Lady swept towards Covenant, smiling with desire. When she pulled him by the arm, he rose automatically from the bed. 'Don't touch me,' he said; but she only smiled and smiled, and drew him towards the door.

In the corridor, he saw that Hergrom lay on the stone like Brinn. Vain faced Linden's chamber, observing nothing. But Findail watched the Lady Alif and Covenant with an assaying look.

The *gaddhi*'s Favoured took Covenant away from the bedrooms.

As they moved, he heard a door open, heard bare feet running almost silently as one of the *Haruchai* came in pursuit. Ceer or Cail must have sensed the sopor of Brinn and Hergrom and realized that something was wrong.

But beyond the last door, the stone of the walls altered, became mirrors. The Lady led Covenant between the mirrors. In an instant, their images were exactly reflected against them from both sides. Image and image and flesh met, fused. Before the *Haruchai* could catch them, Covenant and his guide were translated to an altogether different part of the Sandhold.

Stepping between two mirrors poised near the walls, they entered a large round chamber. It was comfortably lit by three or four braziers, seductively appointed like a disporting-place. The fathomless blue rugs asked for the pressure of bare feet; the velvet and satin cushions and couches urged abandon. A patina of incense thickened the air. Tapestries hung from the walls, depicting scenes like echoes of lust. Only the two armed *hustin*, standing opposite each other against the walls, marred the ambience. But they made no impression on Covenant. They were like the spiralling ironwork stairway which rose from the centre of the chamber. He looked at them and thought nothing.

'Now at last,' said the Lady with a sigh like a shiver of relish, 'at last we are alone.' She turned to face him. The tip of her tongue moistened her lips. 'Thomas Covenant, my heart is mad with desire for you.' Her eyes were as vivid as kohl could make them. 'I have brought you here, not for the Kemper's purpose, but for my own. This night will be beyond all forgetting for you. Every dream of your life I will awaken and fulfil.'

She studied him for some response. When none came, she hesitated momentarily. A flicker of distaste crossed her face. But then she replaced it with passion and spun away. Crying softly, 'Behold!' as if every line of her form were an ache of need, she began to dance.

Swaying and whirling to the rhythm of her anklets, she performed her body before him with all the art of a proud odalisque. Portraying the self-loss of hunger for him, she danced closer to him, and away, and closer again; and her hands caressed her thighs, her belly, her breasts as if she were summoning the fire in her flesh. At wily intervals, pieces of her raiment wafted in perfume and gauze to settle like an appeal among the cushions. Her skin had the texture of silk. The nipples of her breasts were painted and hardened like announcements of desire, the muscles within her thighs were smooth and flowing invitations.

But when she flung her arms around Covenant, pressed her body to his, kissed his mouth, his lips remained slack. He did not need to utter his refrain. He saw her as if she did not exist.

His lack of reply startled her; and the surprise allowed a pure fear to show in her eyes. 'Do you not desire me?' She bit her lips, groping for some recourse. 'You must desire me!'

She tried to conceal her desperation with brazenness; but every new attempt to arouse him only exposed her dread of failure more plainly. She did everything which experience or training could suggest. She stopped at no prostration or appeal which might conceivably have attracted a man. But she could not penetrate his *Elohim*-wrought emptiness. He was as impervious as if their purpose had been to defend rather than harm him.

Abruptly, she wailed in panic. Her fingers made small creeping movements against her face like spiders. Her loveliness had betrayed her. 'Ah, Kemper,' she moaned. 'Have mercy! He is no man. How could a man refuse what I have done?'

The effort of articulation pulled Covenant's countenance together for a moment. 'Don't touch me.'

At that, humiliation gave her the strength of anger. 'Fool!' she retorted. 'You destroy me, and it will avail you nothing. The Kemper will reduce me to beggary among the public houses of *Bhrathairain* for this failure, but he will not therefore spare you. You he will rend limb from limb to gain his ends. Were you man enough to answer me, then at least would you have lived. And I would have given you pleasure.' She struck out at him blindly, lashing her hand across his bearded cheek. '*Pleasure.*'

'Enough, Alif.' The Kemper's voice froze her where she stood. He was watching her and Covenant from the stairs, had already come halfway down them. 'It is not for you to harm him.' From that elevation, he appeared as tall as a Giant; yet his arms looked frail with leanness and age. The child cradled at his back did not stir. 'Return to the *gaddhi*.' His tone held no anger, but it cast glints of malice into the room. 'I have done with you. From this time forth, you will prosper or wane according to his whim. Please him if you can.'

His words condemned her; but this doom was less than the one she had feared, and she did not quail. With a last gauging look at Covenant, she drew herself erect and moved to the stairs, leaving her apparel behind with a disdain which bordered on dignity.

When she was gone, Kasreyn told one of the Guards to bring Covenant. Then he returned upward.

The *husta* closed a clawed hand around Covenant's upper arm. A prescient tremor forced him to repeat his litany several times before he found ease. The stairs rose like the gyre of Sandgorgons Doom, bearing him high into the seclusion of Kemper's Pitch. When they ended, he was in the lucubrium where Kasreyn practised his arts.

Long tables held theurgical apparatus of every kind. Periapts and vials of arcane powders lined the walls. Contrivances of mirrors made candles appear incandescent. Kasreyn moved among them, preparing implements. His hands clenched and unclosed repeatedly to vent his eagerness. His rheum-clouded eyes flicked from place to place. But at his back, his putative son slept. His golden robe rustled along the floor like a scurry of small animals. When he spoke, his voice was calm, faintly tinged with a weariness which hinted at the burden of his years.

'In truth, I did not expect her to succeed.' He addressed Covenant as if he knew that the Unbeliever could not reply. 'Better for you if she had – but you are clearly beyond her. Yet for her failure I should perhaps have punished her as men have ever punished women. She is a tasty wench withal, and knowledgeable. But that is no longer in me.' His tone suggested a sigh. 'In time past, it was otherwise. Then the *gaddhi* drew his Favoured from those who had first sated me. But latterly that pleasure comes to me solely through observation of the depraved ruttings of others in the chamber below. Therefore almost I hoped that you would succumb. For the unction it would have given me.'

A chair covered with bindings and apparatus stood to one side of the lucubrium. While Kasreyn spoke, the *husta* guided Covenant to the chair, seated him there. The Kemper set his implements on the nearest table, then began immobilizing Covenant's arms and legs with straps.

'But that is a juiceless pleasure,' he went on after a brief pause, 'and does not content me. *Age* does not content me. Therefore you are here.' He lashed Covenant's chest securely to the back of the chair. With a neck-strap he ensured that the Unbeliever would sit upright. Covenant could still have moved his head from side to side if he had been capable of conceiving a desire to do so; but Kasreyn appeared confident that Covenant had lost all such desires. A faint sense of trouble floated up out of the emptiness, but Covenant dispelled it with his refrain.

Next Kasreyn began to attach his implements to the apparatus of the chair. These resembled lenses of great variety and complexity. The apparatus held them ready near Covenant's face.

'You have seen,' the Kemper continued as he worked, 'that I possess an ocular of gold. Purest gold – a rare and puissant metal in such hands as mine. With such aids, my arts work great wonders, of which Sandgorgons Doom is not the greatest. But my arts are also pure, as a circle is pure, and in a flawed world purity cannot endure. Thus within each of my works I must perforce place one small flaw, else there would be no work at all.' He stepped back for a moment to survey his preparations. Then he leaned his face close to Covenant's as if he wished the Unbeliever to understand him. 'Even within the work of my longevity there lies a flaw, and through that flaw my life leaks from me drop by drop. Knowing perfection – possessing perfect implements – I have of necessity wrought imperfection upon myself.

'Thomas Covenant, I am going to die.' Once again, he withdrew, muttering half to himself. 'That is intolerable.'

He was gone for several moments. When he returned, he set a stool before the chair and sat on it. His eyes were level with Covenant's. With one skeletal finger, he tapped Covenant's half-hand.

'But you possess white gold.' Behind their rheum, his orbs seemed to have no colour. 'It is an imperfect metal – an unnatural alliance of metals – and in all the Earth it exists nowhere but in the ring you bear. My arts have spoken to me of such a periapt, but never did I dream that the white gold itself would fall to me. The white gold! Thomas Covenant, you reck little what you wield. Its imperfection is the very paradox of which the Earth is made, and with it a Master may form perfect works and fear nothing.

'Therefore' – with one hand, he moved a lens so that it covered Covenant's eyes, distorting everything – 'I mean to have that ring. As you know – or have known – I may not frankly sever it from you. It will be valueless to me unless you choose to give it. And in your present strait you are incapable of choice. Thus I must first pierce this veil which blinds your will. Then, while you remain within my grasp, I must wrest the choice I require from you.' A smile uncovered the old cruelty of his teeth. 'Indeed, it would have been better for you if you had succumbed to the Lady Alif.'

Covenant began his warning. But before he could complete it, Kasreyn lifted his ocular, focused his left eye through it and the lens. As that gaze struck Covenant's, his life exploded in pain.

Spikes drove into his joints; knives laid bare all his muscles; daggers dug down the length of every nerve. Tortures tore at his head as if the skin of his skull were being flayed away. Involuntary spasms made him writhe like a madman in his bonds. He saw Kasreyn's eye boring into him, heard the seizing of his own respiration, felt violence hacking every portion of his flesh to pieces. All his senses functioned normally.

But the pain meant nothing. It fell into his emptiness and vanished – a sensation without content or consequence. Even the writhings of his body did not inspire him to turn his head away.

Abruptly, the attack ended. The Kemper sat back, began whistling softly, tunelessly, through his teeth while he considered his next approach. After a moment, he made his decision. He added two more lenses to the distortion of Covenant's vision. Then he applied his eye to the ocular again.

Instantly, fire swept into Covenant as if every drop of his blood and tissue of his flesh were oil and tinder. It howled through him like the wailings of a banshee. It burst his heart, blazed in his lungs, cindered all his vitals. The marrow of his bones burned and ran like scoria. Savagery flamed into his void as if no power in all the world could prevent it from setting fire to the hidden relicts of his soul.

All his senses functioned normally. He should have been driven irremediably mad in that agony. But the void was more fathomless than any fire. From this, too, the *Elohim* had defended him.

With a snarl of frustration, Kasreyn looked away again. For a moment, he seemed at a loss.

But then new determination straightened his back. Briskly, he removed one of the lenses he had already used, replaced it with several others. Now Covenant could see nothing except an eye-watering smear. In the centre of the blur appeared Kasreyn's golden ocular as the Kemper once again bent his will inward.

For one heartbeat to two, nothing happened. Then the smear expanded, and the lucubrium began to turn. Slowly at first, then with vertiginous speed, the chamber spun. As it wheeled, the walls dissolved. The chair rose, though Kasreyn's compelling orb did not waver. Covenant went gyring into night.

But it was a night unlike any he had known before. It was empty of every star, every implication. Its world-spanning blackness was only a reflection of the inward void into which he fell. Kasreyn was driving him into himself.

He dropped like a stone, spinning faster and faster as the plunge lengthened. He passed through a fire which seared him – traversed tortures of knives until he fell beyond them. Still he sped down the gullet of the whirling, the nausea of his old vertigo. It impelled him as if it meant to hurl him against the blank wall of his doom.

Yet he saw everything, heard everything. Kasreyn's eye remained before him, impaling the smear of the lenses. In the distance, the Kemper's voice said sharply, 'Slay him.' But the command was directed elsewhere, did not touch Covenant.

Then up from the bottom of the gyre arose images which Covenant feared to recognize. Kasreyn's gaze coerced them from the pit. They flew and yowled about Covenant's head as he fell.

The destruction of the Staff of Law.

Blood pouring in streams to feed the Banefire.

Memla and Linden falling under the na-Mhoram's *Grim* because he could not save them.

His friends trapped and doomed in the Sandhold. The quest

defeated. The Land lying helpless under the Sunbane. All the Earth at Lord Foul's mercy.

Because he could not save them.

The *Elohim* had deprived him of everything which might have made a difference. They had rendered him helpless to touch or aid the people and the Land he loved.

Wrapped in his leprosy, isolated by his venom, he had become nothing more than a victim. A victim absolutely. The perceptions which poured into him from Kasreyn's orb seemed to tell the whole truth about him. The gyre swept him downward like an avalanche. It flung him like a spear, a bringer of death, into the pith of the void.

Then he might have broken. The wall defending him might have been pierced, leaving him as vulnerable as the Land to Kasreyn's eye. But at that moment, he heard a series of thuds. The sounds of combat: blows exchanged, gasp and grunt of impact. Two powerful figures were fighting nearby.

Automatically, reflexively, he turned his head to see what was happening.

With that movement, he broke Kasreyn's hold.

Freed from the distortion of the lenses, his vision reeled back into the lucubrium. He sat in the chair where the Kemper had bound him. The tables and equipment of the chamber were unchanged.

But the Guard lay on the floor, coughing up the last of its life. Over the *husta* stood Hergrom. He was poised to spring. Flatly, he said, 'Kemper, if you have harmed him you will answer for it with blood.'

Covenant saw everything. He heard everything.

Emptily, he said, 'Don't touch me.'

16

THE *GADDHI*'S PUNISHMENT

For a long time, Linden Avery could not sleep. The stone of the Sandhold surrounded her, limiting her percipience. The very walls seemed to glare back at her as if they strove to protect a secret cunning. And at the edges of her range moved the *hustin* like motes of ill. The miscreated Guards were everywhere, jailers for the Chatelaine as well as for the company. She had watched the courtiers at their banquet and had discerned that their gaiety was a performance upon which they believed their safety depended. But there could be no safety in the donjon which the Kemper had created for himself and his petulant *gaddhi*.

Her troubled mind longed for the surcease of unconsciousness. But underneath the wariness and alarm which the Sandhold inspired lay a deeper and more acute distress. The memory of the Kemper's *geas* squirmed in the pit of her heart. Kasreyn had simply looked at her through his ocular, and instantly she had become his tool, a mere adjunct of his intent. She had not struggled, had not even understood the need to struggle. His will had possessed her as easily as if she had been waiting for it all her life. The *Haruchai* had been able to resist. But she had been helpless. Her percipient openness had left her no defence. She was unable to completely close the doors the Land had opened in her.

As a result, she had betrayed Thomas Covenant. He was bound to her by yearnings more intimate than anything she had ever allowed herself to feel for any man; and she had sold him as if he had no value to her. No, not sold, she had been offered nothing in return. She had simply given him away. Only Brinn's determination had saved him.

That hurt surpassed the peril of the Sandhold. It was the cusp of all her failures. She felt like a rock which had been struck too hard or too often. She remained superficially intact; but within her fault lines spread at every blow. She no longer knew how to trust herself.

In her bedchamber after the banquet, she mimicked sleep because Cail was with her. But his presence also served to keep her awake. When she turned her face to the wall, she felt his hard aura like a pressure against her spine, denying what little courage she had left. He, too, did not trust her.

Yet the day had been long and arduous; and at last weariness overcame her tension. She sank into dreams of stone – the irrefragable gut-rock of Revelstone. In the hold of the Clave, she had tried to force herself bodily into the granite to escape Gibbon-Raver. But the stone had refused her. According to Covenant, the former inhabitants of the Land had found life and beauty in stone; but this rock had been deaf to every appeal. She still heard the Raver saying, *The principal doom of the Land is upon your shoulders. Are you not evil?* And she had cried out in answer, had been crying ever since in self-abomination, *No! Never!*

Then the voice said something else. It said, 'Chosen, arise. The ur-Lord has been taken.'

Sweating nightmares, she flung away from the wall. Cail placed a hand on her shoulder, the wail which Gibbon had spawned sprang into her throat. But the door stood open, admitting light to the bedchamber. Cail's mien held no ill glee. Instinctively, she bit down her unuttered cry. Her voice bled as she gasped, 'Taken?' The word conveyed nothing except inchoate tremors of alarm.

'The ur-Lord has been taken,' Cail repeated inflexibly. 'The Lady Alif came for him in the Kemper's name. She has taken him.'

She stared at him, groped through the confusion of her dreams. 'Why?'

Shadows accentuated Cail's shrug. 'She said, "Kasreyn of the Gyre desires speech with Thomas Covenant."'

Taken him. A knife-tip of apprehension trailed down her spine. 'Is Brinn with him?'

The *Haruchai* did not falter. 'No.'

At that, her eyes widened. 'You mean you *let* – ?' She was on her feet. Her hands grabbed at his shoulders. 'Are you crazy? Why didn't you call me?'

She was fractionally taller than he; but his flat gaze outsized her. He did not need words to repudiate her.

'Oh goddamn it!' She tried to thrust him away, but the effort only shoved her backward. Spinning, she flung towards the door. Over her shoulder, she snapped, 'You should've called me.' But she already knew his answer.

In the corridor, she found the Giants. Honninscrave and Seadreamer were straightening their sarks, dressing hurriedly. But the First stood ready, with her shield on her arm, as if she had slept that way. Ceer was also there. Vain and Findail had not moved. But Brinn and Hergrom were nowhere to be seen.

The First answered Linden's hot visage sternly.

'It appears that we have miscounted the Kemper's cunning. The tale I have from Ceer. While we slept, the Lady Alif approached Hergrom where he stood with Vain and this *Elohim*. Speaking words of courtesy and blandishment, she drew nigh and into his face cast a powder which caused him slumber. Neither Vain nor Findail' – a keen edge ran through her tone – 'saw fit to take action in this matter, and she turned from them as if their unconcern were a thing to be trusted. She then approached Brinn and the Giantfriend. Brinn also fell prey to her powder of slumber, and she bore Covenant away.

'Sensing the unwonted somnolence of his comrades, Ceer left me. In this passage, he saw the Lady Alif with Covenant, retreating.' She pointed down the corridor. 'He went in pursuit. Yet ere he could gain them, they vanished.'

Linden gaped at the First.

'The slumber of Brinn and Hergrom was brief,' the Swordmain concluded. 'They have gone in search of the Giantfriend – or of the Kemper. It is my thought that we must follow.'

The labour of Linden's heart cramped her breathing. What could Kasreyn possibly want from Covenant, that he was willing to risk so much coercion and stealth to gain it?

What else but the white ring?

A surge of hysteria rose up in her. She fought for self-command. Fear galvanized her. She turned on Ceer, demanded, 'How could they have vanished?'

'I know not.' His countenance remained impassive. 'At a certain place beyond these doors' – he searched momentarily for a word – 'an acuteness came upon them. Then they were before me no longer. The means of their vanishment I could not discover.'

Damn it to hell! With a wrench, Linden dismissed that unanswerable *how*. To the First, she gritted, 'Kemper's Pitch.'

'Aye.' In spite of her empty scabbard the Swordmain was whetted for action. 'Kemper's Pitch.' With a jerk of her head, she sent Honninscrave and Seadreamer down the corridor.

They broke into a trot as Ceer joined them. At once, the First followed; then Linden and Cail ran after them, too concerned for Covenant to think about the consequences of what they were doing.

At the first corner, she glanced back, saw Vain and Findail following without apparent haste or effort.

Almost at once, the company encountered the Guards that had been stationed outside their rooms earlier. The faces of the *hustin* registered brutish surprise, uncertainty. Some of them stepped forward; but when the Giants swept defiantly past them, the *hustin* did not react. Mordantly, Linden thought that Kasreyn's attention must be concentrated elsewhere.

Like the *Haruchai*, the Giants had obviously learned more about the layout of the Second Circinate than she had been able to absorb. They threaded their way unerringly through the halls and passages, corridors and chambers. In a short time, they reached the forecourt near the stairways to the Tier of Riches. Upward they went without hesitation.

The Tier was as brightly lit as ever; but at this time of night it was deserted. Honninscrave promptly chose an intricate route through the galleries. When he arrived in the resting-place of the longsword at which the First had gazed with such desire, he stopped. Looking intently at her, he asked in a soft voice, 'Will you not arm yourself?'

'Tempt me not.' Her features were cold. 'Should we appear before the *gaddhi* or his Kemper bearing a gift which was denied us, we will forfeit all choice but that of battle. Let us not rashly put our feet to that path.'

Linden felt dark shapes rising from the Second Circinate. 'Guards,' she panted. 'Somebody told them what to do.'

The First gave Honninscrave a nod of command. He swung away towards the stairs to The Majesty.

Linden ran dizzily after the Giants up the spiralling ascent. Her breathing was hard and sharp, the dry air cut at her lungs. She feared the *hustin* in The Majesty. If they, too, had been given orders, what could the company do against so many of them?

As she sprang out of the stairwell on to the treacherous floor of the Auspice-hall, she saw that her fears were justified. Scores of squat, powerful *hustin* formed an arc across the company's way. They bristled with spears. In the faint light reflecting from the vicinity of the Auspice, they looked as intractable as old darkness.

The pursuing Guards had reached the bottom of the stairs.

'Stone and Sea!' hissed the First through her teeth. 'Here is a gay pass.' Seadreamer took an impulsive step forward. 'Hold, Giant,' she ordered softly. 'Would you have us slain like cattle?' In the same tone, she addressed Linden over her shoulder. 'Chosen, if any thought comes to you, be not shy to utter it. I mislike this peril.'

Linden did not respond. The posture of the Guards described the nature of Kasreyn's intentions against Covenant eloquently. And Covenant was as defenceless as an infant. The *Elohim* had reft him of everything which might have protected him. She chewed silent curses in an effort to hold back panic.

The *hustin* advanced on the company.

The next moment, a high shout echoed across The Majesty:

'Halt!'

The Guards stopped. The ones on the stairs climbed a few more steps, then obeyed.

Someone began to thrust forward among the *hustin*. Linden saw a vehement head bobbing past their ears, accompanied by a thick flurry of yellow hair. The Guards parted involuntarily. Soon a woman stood before the company.

She was naked, as if she had just come from the *gaddhi's* bed.

The Lady Alif.

She cast a look at the questers, daring them to take notice of her nudity. Then she turned to the Guards. Her voice imitated anger; but beneath the surface it quivered with temerity.

'Why do you accost the guests of the *gaddhi*?'

The porcine eyes of the *hustin* shifted uncomfortably towards her, back to the company. Their thoughts worked tortuously. After a pause, several of them answered, 'These are not permitted to pass.'

'Not?' she demanded sharply. 'I command you to admit them.'

Again the *hustin* were silent while they wrestled with the imprecision of their orders. Others repeated, 'These are not permitted to pass.'

The Lady cocked her arms on her hips. Her tone softened dangerously. 'Guards, do you know me?'

Hustin blinked at her. A few licked their lips as if they were torn between hunger and confusion. At last, a handful replied, 'Lady Alif, Favoured of the *gaddhi*.'

'Forsooth,' she snapped sarcastically. 'I am the Lady Alif, Favoured of the *gaddhi* Rant Absolain. Has Kasreyn granted you to refuse the commands of the *gaddhi* or his Favoured?'

The Guards were silent. Her question was too complex for them.

Slowly, clearly, she said, 'I command you in the name of Rant Absolain, *gaddhi* of *Bhrathairealm* and the Great Desert, to permit his guests passage.'

Linden held her breath while the *hustin* struggled to sort out their priorities. Apparently, this situation had not been covered by their instructions; and no new orders came to their aid. Confronted by the Lady Alif's insistence, they did not know what else to do. With a rustling movement like a sigh, they parted, opening a path towards the Auspice.

At once, the Favoured faced the company. Her eyes shone with a hazardous revenge. 'Now make haste,' she said quickly, 'while Kasreyn is consumed by his intent against your Thomas Covenant. I have no cause to wish your companion well, but I will teach the Kemper that he is unwise to scorn those who labour in his service. Mayhap his pawns will someday gain the courage to defy him.' An instant later, she stamped her foot, sending out a tinkle of silver. 'Go, I say! At any moment, he may recollect himself and countermand me.'

The First did not hesitate. Striding from circle to circle, she moved swiftly among the *Hustin*. Ceer joined her. Honninscrave and Seadreamer followed, warding her back. Linden wanted to take a moment to question the Lady; but she had no time. Cail caught her arm, swung her after the Giants.

Behind the company, the Guards turned, reformed their ranks. Moving stiffly over the stone slabs, they followed Vain and Findail towards the Auspice.

When the Giants entered the brighter illumination around the throne, Brinn suddenly appeared out of the shadows. He did not pause to explain how he had come to be there. Flatly, he said, 'Hergrom has discovered the ur-Lord. Come.' Turning, he sped back into the darkness behind the *gaddhi*'s seat.

Linden glanced at the *hustin*. They were moving grimly, resolutely, but made no effort to catch up with the interlopers. Perhaps they had now been commanded to block any retreat.

She could not worry about retreat. Covenant was in the Kemper's hands. She ran after the First and Ceer into the shadow of the Auspice.

Here, too, the wall was deeply carved with tormented shapes like a writhe of ghouls. Even in clear light, the doorway would have been difficult to find, for it was cunningly hidden among the bas-reliefs. But Brinn had learned the way. He went directly to the door.

It swung inward under the pressure of his hand, admitting the company to a narrow stair which gyred upward through the stone. Brinn led, with Honninscrave, Seadreamer, and then Ceer at his back. Linden followed the First. Urgency pulled at her heart, denying the shortness of her breath, the scant strength of her legs. She wanted to cry out Covenant's name.

The stair seemed impossibly long; but at last it reached a door that opened into a large round chamber. The place was furnished and appointed like a seduction room. Braziers shed light over its intense blue rugs, its lush cushions and couches, the tapestries bedecking the walls depicting a variety of lurid scenes. Almost instantly, the incense in the air began to fill Linden's lungs with giddiness.

Ahead of her, the Giants and *Haruchai* came to a halt. A *husta* stood there with its spear levelled at the questers, guarding the ironwork stair which rose from the centre of the chamber.

This *husta* had no doubt of its duty. One cheek was discoloured with bruises, and Linden saw other signs that the Guard had been in a fight. If Hergrom had indeed found Covenant, he must have passed through this chamber to do so. But the *husta* was impervious to its pains. It confronted the company fearlessly.

Brinn bounded forward. He feinted at the Guard, then dodged the spear and leaped for the railing of the stair.

The *husta* tracked him with the point of its spear to strike him in the back. But Seadreamer was already moving. With momentum, weight, and oaken strength, he delivered a blow which stretched the Guard out among the cushions like a sated lover.

As a precaution, Honninscrave jumped after the *husta*, caught hold of its spear and snapped the shaft.

The rest of the company rushed after Brinn.

The stairs took them even higher into the seclusion of Kemper's Pitch.

Gripping the rail, Linden hauled herself from tread to tread, forced her leaden legs to carry her. The incense and the spiralling affected her like nightmare. She did not know how much farther she could ascend. When she reached the next level, she might be too weak to do anything except struggle for breath.

But her will held, carried her panting and dizzy into the lucubrium of the *gaddhi*'s Kemper.

Her eyes searched the place frenetically. This was clearly Kasreyn's laboratory, where he wrought his arts. But she could not bring anything she saw into focus. Long tables covered with equipment, crowded shelves, strange contrivances seemed to reel around her.

Then her vision cleared. Beyond the spot where the Giants and Brinn had stopped lay a Guard. It was dead, sprawled in a congealing pool of its own rank blood. Hergrom stood over it like a defiance. Deliberately, he nodded towards one side of the lucubrium.

Kasreyn was there.

In his own demesne, surrounded by his possessions and powers, he appeared unnaturally tall. His lean arms were folded like wrath over his chest; but he remained as still as Hergrom, as if he and the *Haruchai* were poised in an impasse. His golden ocular dangled from its ribbon around his neck. His son slept like a tumour on his back.

He was standing in front of a chair which bristled with bindings and apparatus.

Within the bindings sat Covenant.

He was looking at his companions; but his eyes were empty, as if he had no soul.

With her panting clenched between her teeth, Linden slipped past the Giants, hastened forward. For an instant, she glared at Kasreyn, let him see the rage naked in her face. Then she turned her back on him and approached Covenant.

Her hands shook as she tried to undo the bonds. They were too tight for her. When Brinn joined her, she left that task to him and instead concentrated on examining Covenant.

She found no damage. His flesh was unmarked. Behind the slackness of his mouth and the confusion of his beard, nothing had changed. She probed into his body, inspected his bones and organs with her percipience; but internally also he had suffered no harm.

His ring still hung like a fetter on the last finger of his halfhand.

Relief stunned her. For a moment, she became lightheaded with incomprehension, had to steady herself on Brinn's shoulder as he released the ur-Lord. Had Hergrom stopped Kasreyn in time? Or had the Kemper simply failed? Had the silence of the *Elohim* surpassed even his arts?

Had it in fact defended Covenant from hurt?

'As you see,' Kasreyn said, 'he is uninjured.' A slight tremble of age and ire afflicted his voice. 'Despite your thought of me, I have sought only his succour. Had this *Haruchai* not foiled me with his presence and needless bloodshed, your Thomas Covenant would have been restored to you whole and well. But no trustworthiness can withstand your suspicion. Your doubt fulfils itself, for it prevents me from accomplishing that which would teach you the honesty of my intent.'

Linden spun on him. Her relief recoiled into fury. 'You bastard. If you're so goddamn trustworthy, why did you do all this?'

'Chosen.' Indignation shone through the rheum of his eyes. 'Do any means exist by which I could have persuaded you to concede Thomas Covenant to me alone?'

With all the strength of his personality, he projected an image of offended virtue. But Linden was not daunted. The discrepancy between his stance and his hunger was palpable to her. She was angry enough to tell him what she saw, expose the range of her sight. But she had no time. Heavy feet rang on the iron stair. Behind the reek of death in the air, she felt the *hustin* surging upward. As

Brinn drew Covenant from the chair, she turned to warn her companions.

They did not need the warning. The Giants and *Haruchai* had already poised themselves in defensive positions around the room.

But the first individual who appeared from the stairwell was not one of the *hustin*. It was Rant Absolain.

The Lady Alif was at his back. She had taken the time to cover herself with a translucent robe.

Behind them came the guards.

When she saw the fallen *husta*, the Lady Alif's face betrayed an instant of consternation. She had not expected this. Reading her, Linden guessed that the Favoured had roused the *gaddhi* in an effort to further frustrate Kasreyn's plans. But the dead Guard changed everything. Before the Lady mastered her expression, it gave away her realization that she had made a mistake.

With a sting of apprehension, Linden saw what the mistake was.

The *gaddhi* did not glance at Kasreyn. He did not notice his guests. His attention was locked to the dead Guard. He moved forward a step, two steps, stumbled to his knees in the dark blood. It splattered thickly, staining his linen. His hands fluttered at the *husta*'s face. Then he tried to turn the Guard over on to its back; but it was too heavy for him. His hands came away covered with blood. He stared at them, gazed blindly up at the crowd around him. His mouth trembled. 'My Guard.' He sounded like a bereaved child. 'Who has slain my Guard?'

For a moment, the lucubrium was intense with silence. Then Hergrom stepped forward. Linden felt peril thronging in the air. She tried to call him back. But she was too late. Hergrom acknowledged his responsibility to spare his companions from the *gaddhi*'s wrath.

Hustin continued to arrive. The Giants and *Haruchai* held themselves ready; but they were weaponless and outnumbered.

Slowly, Rant Absolain's expression focused on Hergrom. He arose from his knees, dripping gouts of blood. For a moment, he stared at Hergrom as if he were appalled by the depth of the *Haruchai*'s crime. Then he said, 'Kemper.' His voice was a snarl of passion in the back of his throat. Grief and outrage gave him the stature he had lacked earlier. 'Punish him.'

Kasreyn moved among the Guards and questers, went to stand near Rant Absolain. 'O *gaddhi*, blame him not.' The Kemper's self-command made him sound stelic rather than contrite. 'The fault is mine. I have made many misjudgments.'

At that, the *gaddhi* broke like an over-stretched rope.

'I want him *punished*!' With both fists, he hammered at Kasreyn's chest, pounding smears of blood into the yellow robe. The Kemper recoiled a step; and Rant Absolain turned to hurl his passion at

Hergrom. 'That Guard is mine! *Mine!*' Then he faced Kasreyn again. 'In all *Bhrathairealm*, I possess nothing! I am the *gaddhi*, and the *gaddhi* is only a servant!' Rage and self-pity writhed in him. 'The Sandhold is not mine. The Riches are not mine! The Chatelaine attends me only at your whim!' He stooped to the dead *husta* and scooped up handfuls of the congealing fluid, flung them at Kasreyn, at Hergrom. A gobbet trickled and fell from Kasreyn's chin, but he ignored it. 'Even my Favoured come to me from you! After you have used them!' Rant Absolain's fists jerked blows through the air. 'But the Guard is *mine*! They alone obey me without looking first to learn your will!' With a shout, he concluded, '*I want him punished!*'

Rigid as madness, he faced the Kemper. After a moment, Kasreyn said, 'O *gaddhi*, your will is my will.' His tone was suffused with regret. But as he stepped slowly, ruefully, towards Hergrom, the tension concealed within his robe conveyed a threat. 'Hergrom – ' Linden began. Then her throat locked on the warning. She did not know what the threat was.

Her companions braced themselves to leap to Hergrom's aid. But they, too, could not define the threat.

The Kemper stopped before Hergrom, studied him briefly. Then Kasreyn lifted his ocular to his left eye. Linden tried to relax. The *Haruchai* had already proven themselves impervious to the Kemper's *geas*. Hergrom's flat orbs showed no fear.

Gazing through his eyepiece, Kasreyn reached out with careful unmenace and touched his index finger to the centre of Hergrom's forehead.

Hergrom's only reaction was a slight widening of his eyes.

The Kemper dropped both hands, sagged as if in weariness or sorrow. Without a word, he turned away. The Guards parted for him as he went to the chair where Covenant had been bound. There he seated himself, though he could not lean back because of the child he carried. With his fingers, he hid his face as if he were mourning.

But to Linden the emotion he concealed felt like glee.

She was unsure of her perception. The Kemper was adept at disguising the truth about himself. But Rant Absolain's reaction was unmistakable. He was grinning in fierce triumph.

His mouth moved as if he wanted to say something that would crush the company, demonstrate his own superiority; but no words came to him. Yet his passion for the Guards sustained him. He might indeed have been a monarch as he moved away. Commanding the *hustin* to follow him, he took the Lady Alif by the hand and left the lucubrium.

As she started downward, the Lady cast one swift look like a pang of regret towards Linden. Then she was gone, and the Guards were thumping down the iron stairs behind her. Two of them bore their dead fellow away.

None of the questers shifted while the *hustin* filed from the chamber. Vain's bland ambiguous smile was a reverse image of Findail's alert pain. The First stood with her arms folded over her chest, glaring like a hawk. Honninscrave and Seadreamer remained poised nearby. Brinn had placed Covenant at Linden's side, where the four *Haruchai* formed a cordon around the people they had sworn to protect.

Linden held herself rigid, pretending severity. But her sense of peril did not abate.

The Guards were leaving. Hergrom had suffered no discernible harm. In a moment, Kasreyn would be alone with the questers. He would be in their hands. Surely he could not defend himself against so many of them. Then why did she feel that the survival of the company had become so precarious?

Brinn gazed at her intently. His hard eyes strove to convey a message without words. Intuitively, she understood him.

The last *husta* was on the stairs. The time had almost come. Her knees were trembling. She flexed them slightly, sought to balance herself on the balls of her feet.

The Kemper had not moved. From within the covert of his hands, he said in a tone of rue, or cleverly mimicked rue, 'You may return to your rooms. Doubtless the *gaddhi* will later summon you. I must caution you to obey him. Yet I would you could credit that I regret all which has transpired here.'

The moment had come. Linden framed the words in her mind. Time and again, she had dreamed of slaying Gibbon-Raver. She had even berated Covenant for his restraint in Revelstone. She had said, *Some infections have to be cut out.* She had believed that. What was power for, if not to extirpate evil? Why else had she become who she was?

But now the decision was upon her – and she could not speak. Her heart leapt with fury at everything Kasreyn had done, and still she could not speak. She was a doctor, not a killer. She could not give Brinn the permission he wanted.

His mien wore an inflectionless contempt as he turned his back on her. Mutely, he referred his desires to the leadership of the First.

The Swordmain did not respond. If she were aware of her opportunity, she elected to ignore it. Without a word to the Kemper or her companions, she strode to the stairs.

Linden gave a dumb groan of relief or regret, she did not know which.

A faint frown creased Brinn's forehead. But he did not hesitate. When Honninscrave had followed the First, Brinn and Hergrom took Covenant downward. At once, Cail and Ceer steered Linden towards the stairs. Seadreamer placed himself like a bulwark behind the *Haruchai*. Leaving Vain and Findail to follow at their own pace, the company descended from Kemper's Pitch. Clenched in a silence like a fist, they returned to their quarters in the Second Circinate.

Along the way, they encountered no Guards. Even The Majesty was empty of *hustin*.

The First entered the larger chamber across the hall from the bedrooms. While Linden and the others joined the Swordmain, Ceer remained in the passage to ward the door.

Brinn carefully placed Covenant on one of the settees. Then he confronted the First and Linden together. His impassive voice conveyed a timbre of accusation to Linden's hearing.

'Why did we not slay the Kemper? There lay our path to safety.'

The First regarded him as if she were chewing her tongue for self-command. A hard moment passed between them before she replied, 'The *hustin* number four score hundred. The Horse, fifteen score. We cannot win our way with bloodshed.'

Linden felt like a cripple. Once again, she had been too paralysed to act, contradictions rendered her useless. She could not even spare herself the burden of supporting Brinn.

'They don't mean anything. I don't know about the Horse. But the Guards haven't got any minds of their own. They're helpless without Kasreyn to tell them what to do.'

Honninscrave looked at her in surprise. 'But the *gaddhi* said – '

'He's mistaken.' The cries she had been stifling tore at the edges of her voice. 'Kasreyn keeps him like a pet.'

'Then is it also your word,' asked the First darkly, 'that we should have slain this Kemper?'

Linden failed to meet the First's stare. She wanted to shout, Yes! And, *No*. Did she not have enough blood on her hands?

'We are Giants,' the Swordmain said to Linden's muteness. 'We do not murder.' Then she turned her back on the matter.

But she was a trained fighter. The rictus of her shoulders said as clearly as an expostulation that the effort of restraint in the face of so much peril and mendacity was tearing her apart.

A blur filled Linden's sight. Every judgment found her wanting. Even Covenant's emptiness was an accusation for which she had no answer.

What had Kasreyn done to Hergrom?

The light and dark of the world were invisible within the Sandhold. But eventually servants came to the chamber, announcing sunrise with trays of food. Linden's thoughts were dulled by fatigue and strain; yet she roused herself to inspect the viands. She expected treachery in everything. However, a moment's examination showed her that the food was clean. Deliberately, she and her companions ate their fill, trying to prepare themselves for the unknown.

With worn and red-rimmed eyes, she studied Hergrom. From the brown skin of his face to the vital marrow of his bones, he showed no evidence of harm, no sign that he had ever been touched. But the unforgiving austerity of his visage prevented her from asking him any questions. The *Haruchai* did not trust her. In refusing to call for Kasreyn's death, she had rejected what might prove the only chance to save Hergrom.

Some time later, Rire Grist arrived. He was accompanied by another man, a soldier with an atrabilious mien whom the Caitiffin introduced as his aide. He greeted the questers as if he had heard nothing concerning the night's activities. Then he said easily, 'My friends, the *gaddhi* chooses to pleasure himself this morning with a walk upon the Sandwall. He asks for your attendance. The sun shines with wondrous clarity, granting a view of the Great Desert which may interest you. Will you come?'

He appeared calm and confident. But Linden read in the tightness around his eyes that the peril had not been averted.

The bitterness of the First's thoughts was plain upon her countenance. Have we choice in the matter? But Linden had nothing to say. She had lost the power of decision. Her fears beat about her head like dark wings, making everything impossible. They're going to kill Hergrom!

Yet the company truly had no choice. They could not fight all the *gaddhi*'s Guards and Horse. And if they did not mean to fight, they had no recourse but to continue acting out their role as Rant Absolain's guests. Linden's gaze wandered the blind stone of the floor, avoiding the eyes which searched her, until the First said to Rire Grist, 'We are ready.' Then in stiff distress she followed her companions out of the room.

The Caitiffin led them down to the Sandhold's massive gates. In the forecourt of the First Circinate, perhaps as many as forty soldiers were training their mounts, prancing and curvetting the destriers around the immense, dim hall. The horses were all dark or black, and their shod hooves struck sparks into the shadows like the crepitation of a still-distant prescience. Rire Grist hailed the leader of the riders in a tone of familiar command. He was sure of himself among them. But he took the company on across the hall without pausing.

When they reached the band of open ground which girdled the donjon, the desert sun hit them a tangible blow of brightness and heat. Linden had to turn away to clear her sight. Blinking, she looked up at the dust-tinged sky between the ramparts, seeking some relief for her senses from the massy oppression of the Sandhold. But she found no relief. There were no birds. And the banquettes within the upper curve of the wall were marked at specific intervals with *hustin*.

Cail took her arm, drew her after her companions eastwards into the shadow of the wall. Her eyes were grateful for the dimness; but it did not ease the way the arid air scraped at her lungs. The sand shifted under her feet at every step, leeching the strength from her legs. When the company passed the eastern gate of the Sandwall, she felt an impossible yearning to turn and run.

Talking politely about the design and construction of the wall, Rire Grist led the company around the First Circinate towards a wide stair built into the side of the Sandwall. He was telling the First and Honninscrave that there were two such stairs, one opposite the other beyond the Sandhold – and that there were also other ways to reach the wall from the donjon, through underground passages. His tone was bland, but his spirit was not.

A shiver like a touch of fever ran through Linden as he started up the stairs. Nevertheless she followed as if she had surrendered her independent volition to the exigency which impelled the First.

The stairs were broad enough for eight or ten people at once. But they were steep, and the effort of climbing them in that heat drew a flush across Linden's face, stuck her shirt to her back with sweat. By the time she reached the top, she was breathing as if the dry air were full of needles.

Within its parapets, the ridge of the Sandwall was as wide as a road and smooth enough for horses or wains to travel easily. From this vantage, Linden was level with the rim of the First Circinate and could see each immense circle of the Sandhold rising dramatically to culminate in the dire shaft of Kemper's Pitch.

On the other side of the wall lay the Great Desert.

As Rire Grist had said, the atmosphere was clear and sharp to the horizons. Linden felt that her gaze spanned a score of leagues to the east and south. In the south, a few virga cast purple shadows across the middle distance; but they did not affect the etched acuity of the sunlight.

Under that light, the desert was a wilderness of sand – as white as salt and bleached bones, and drier than all the world's thirst. It caught the sun, sent it back diffused and multiplied. The sands were like a sea immobilized by the lack of any tide heavy enough to move it. Dunes serried and challenged each other towards the sky as if at one time the ground itself had been lashed to life by the fury of a cataclysm. But that orogeny had been so long ago that only the skeleton of the terrain and the shape of the dunes remembered it. No other life remained to the Great Desert now except the life of wind – intense desiccating blasts out of the deep south which could lift the sand like spume and recarve the face of the land at whim. And this day there was no wind. The air felt like a reflection of the sand, and everything Linden saw in all directions was dead.

But to the south-west there was wind. As the company walked along the top of the Sandwall, she became aware that in the distance, beyond the virga and the discernible dunes, violence was brewing. No, not brewing: it had already attained full rage. A prodigious storm galed around itself against the horizon as if it had a cyclone for a heart. Its clouds were as black as thunder, and at intervals it sent out lurid glarings like shrieks.

Until the Giants stopped to look at the storm, she did not realize what it was.

Sandgorgons Doom.

Abruptly, she was touched by a tremor of augury, as if even at this range the storm had the power to reach out and rend –

The *gaddhi* and his women stood on the south-west curve of the Sandwall, where they had a crystal view of the Doom. Nearly a score of *hustin* guarded the vicinity.

They were directly under the purview of Kemper's Pitch.

Rant Absolain hailed the questers as they approached. A secret excitement sharpened his welcome. He spoke the common tongue with a heartiness that rang false. On behalf of the company, Rire Grist gave appropriate replies. Before he could make obeisance, the *gaddhi* summoned him closer, drawing the company among the Guards. Quickly, Linden scanned the gathering, and discovered that Kasreyn was not present.

Free of his Kemper, Rant Absolain was determined to play the part of a warm host. 'Welcome, welcome,' he said fulsomely. He wore a long ecru robe designed to make him appear stately. His Favoured stood near him, attired like the priestesses of a love-god. Other young women were there also; but they had not been granted the honour of sharing the *gaddhi*'s style of dress. They were decked out in raiment exquisitely inappropriate to the sun and the heat. But the *gaddhi* paid no attention to their obvious beauty, he concentrated on his guests. In one hand, he held an ebony chain from which dangled a large medallion shaped to represent a black sun. He used it to emphasize the munificence of his gestures as he performed.

'Behold the Great Desert!' He faced the waste as if it were his to display. 'Is it not a sight? Under such a sun the true tint is revealed – a hue stretching as far as the *Bhrathair* have ever journeyed, though the tale is told that in the far south the desert becomes a wonderland of every colour the eye may conceive.' His arm flipped the medallion in arcs about him. 'No people but the *Bhrathair* have ever wrested bare life from such a grand and ungiving land. But we have done more.

'The Sandhold you have seen. Our wealth exceeds that of monarchs who rule lush demesnes. But now for the first time' – his voice tightened in expectation – 'you behold Sandgorgons Doom. Not elsewhere in all the Earth is such theurgy manifested.' In spite of herself, Linden looked where the *gaddhi* directed her gaze. The hot sand made the bones of her forehead ache as if the danger were just beginning; but that distant violence held her. 'And no other people have so triumphed over such fell foes.' Her companions seemed transfixed by the roiling thunder. Even the *Haruchai* stared at it as if they sought to estimate themselves against it.

'The Sandgorgons.' Rant Absolain's excitement mounted. 'You do not know them – but I tell you this. Granted time and freedom, one such creature might tear the Sandhold stone from stone. One! They are more fearsome than madness or nightmare. Yet there they are bound. Their lives they spend railing against the gyre of their Doom, while we thrive. Only at rare events does one of them gain release – and then but briefly.' The tension in his voice grew keener, whetted by every word. Linden wanted to turn away from the Doom, drag her companions back from the parapet. But she had no name for what dismayed her.

'For centuries, the *Bhrathair* lived only because the Sandgorgons did not slay them all. But now I am the *gaddhi* of *Bhrathairealm* and all the Great Desert, and they are mine!'

He ended his speech with a gesture of florid pride; and suddenly the ebony chain slipped from his fingers.

Sailing black across the sunlight and the pale sand, the chain and medallion arced over the parapet and fell near the base of the Sandwall. Sand puffed at the impact, settled again. The dark sun of the medallion lay like a stain on the clean earth.

The *gaddhi*'s women gasped, surged to the edge to look downward. The Giants peered over the parapet.

Rant Absolain did not move. He hugged his arms around his chest to contain a secret emotion.

Reacting like a good courtier, Rire Grist said quickly, 'Fear nothing, O *gaddhi*. It will shortly be restored to you. I will send my aide to retrieve it.'

The soldier with him started back towards the stairs, clearly intending to reach one of the outer gates and return along the base of the Sandwall to pick up the medallion.

But the *gaddhi* did not look at the Caitiffin. 'I want it now,' he snapped with petulant authority. 'Fetch rope.'

At once, two Guards left the top of the wall, descended to the banquette, then entered the wall through the nearest opening. Tautly, Linden searched for some clue to the peril. It thickened in the air at every moment. But the *gaddhi*'s attitude was not explicit enough to betray his intent. Rire Grist's careful poise showed that he was playing his part in a charade – but she had already been convinced of that. Of the women, only the two Favoured exposed

682

any knowledge of the secret. The Lady Benj's mien was hard with concealment. And the Lady Alif flicked covert glances of warning towards the company.

Then the *hustin* returned, bearing a heavy coil of rope. Without delay, they lashed one end to the parapet and threw the other snaking down the outer face of the Sandwall. It was just long enough to reach the sand.

For a moment, no one moved. The *gaddhi* was still. Honninscrave and Seadreamer were balanced beside the First. Vain appeared characteristically immune to the danger crouching on the wall; but Findail's eyes shifted as if he saw too much. The *Haruchai* had taken the best defensive positions available among the Guards.

For no apparent reason, Covenant said, 'Don't touch me.'

Abruptly, Rant Absolain swung towards the company. Heat intensified his gaze.

'*You.*' His voice stretched and cracked under the strain. His right arm jerked outward, stabbing his rigid index finger straight at Hergrom. 'I require my emblem.'

The gathering clenched. Some of the women bit their lips. The Lady Alif's hands opened, closed, opened again. Hergrom's face betrayed no reaction; but the eyes of all the *Haruchai* scanned the group, watching everything.

Linden struggled to speak. The pressure knotted her chest, but she winced out, 'Hergrom, you don't have to do that.'

The First's fingers were claws at her sides. 'The *Haruchai* are our comrades. We will not permit it.'

The *gaddhi* snapped something in the brackish tongue of the *Bhrathair*. Instantly, the *hustin* brought their spears to bear. In such close quarters, even the swiftness of the *Haruchai* could not have protected their comrades from injury or death.

'It is my *right*!' Rant Absolain spat up at the First. 'I am the *gaddhi* of *Bhrathairealm*! The punishment of offence is my duty and my right!'

'No!' Linden sensed razor-sharp iron less than a foot from the centre of her back. But in her fear for Hergrom she ignored it. 'It was Kasreyn's fault. Hergrom was just trying to save Covenant's life.' She aimed her urgency at the *Haruchai*. 'You don't have to do this.'

The dispassion of Hergrom's visage was complete. His detachment as he measured the Guards defined the company's peril more eloquently than any outcry. For a moment, he and Brinn shared a look. Then he turned to Linden.

'Chosen, we desire to meet this punishment, that we may see it ended.' His tone expressed nothing except an entire belief in his own competence – the same self-trust which had led the Bloodguard to defy death and time in the service of the Lords.

The sight clogged Linden's throat. Before she could swallow her dismay, her culpability, try to argue with him, Hergrom leaped up on to the parapet. Three strides took him to the rope.

Without a word to his companions, he gripped the line and dropped over the edge.

The First's eyes glazed at the extremity of her restraint. But three spears were levelled at her; and Honninscrave and Seadreamer were similarly caught.

Brinn nodded fractionally. Too swiftly for the reflexes of the Guards, Ceer slipped through the crowd, sprang to the parapet. In an instant, he had followed Hergrom down the rope.

Rant Absolain barked a curse and hastened forward to watch the *Haruchai* descend. For a moment, his fists beat anger against the stone. But then he recollected himself, and his indignation faded.

The spears did not let Linden or her companions move.

The *gaddhi* issued another command. It drew a flare of fury from the Swordmain's eyes, drove Honninscrave and Seadreamer to the fringes of their self-control.

In response, a Guard unmoored the rope. It fell heavily on to the shoulders of Hergrom and Ceer.

Rant Absolain threw a fierce grin at the company, then turned his attention back to the *Haruchai* on the ground.

'Now, slayer!' he cried in a shrill shout, 'I require you to speak!'

Linden did not know what he meant. But her nerves yammered at the cruelty he emanated. With a wrench, she ducked under the spear at her back, surged towards the parapet. As her head passed the edge, her vision reeled into focus on Hergrom and Ceer. They stood in the sand with the rope sprawled around them. The *gaddhi's* medallion lay between their feet. They were looking upward.

'Run!' she cried. 'The gates! Get to the gates!'

She heard a muffled blow behind her. A spearpoint pricked the back of her neck, pinning her against the stone.

Covenant was repeating his litany as if he could not get anyone to listen to him.

'Speak, slayer!' the *gaddhi* insisted, as avid as lust.

Hergrom's impassivity did not flicker. 'No.'

'You refuse? Defy me? Crime upon crime! I am the *gaddhi* of *Bhrathairealm*! Refusal is treachery!'

Hergrom gazed his disdain upward and said nothing.

But the *gaddhi* was prepared for this also. He barked another brackish command. Several of his women shrieked.

Forcing her head to the side, Linden saw a Guard dangling a woman over the edge of the parapet by one ankle.

The Lady Alif, who had tried to help the company earlier.

She squirmed in the air, battering her fear against the Sandwall.

But Rant Absolain took no notice of her. Her robe fell about her head, muffling her face and cries. Her silver anklets glinted incongruously in the white sunshine.

'If you do not speak the name,' the *gaddhi* yelled down at Hergrom, 'this Lady will fall to her death! And then if you do not speak the name' — he lashed a glance at Linden — 'she whom you title the Chosen will be slain! I repay blood with blood!'

Linden prayed that Hergrom would refuse. He gazed up at her, at Rant Absolain and the Lady, and his face revealed nothing. But then Ceer nodded to him. He turned away. Placing his back to the Sandwall as if he had known all along what would happen, he faced the Great Desert and Sandgorgons Doom, straightened his shoulders in readiness.

Linden wanted to rage, No! But suddenly her strength was gone. Hergrom understood his plight. And still chose to accept it. There was nothing she could do.

Deliberately, he stepped on the *gaddhi*'s emblem, crushing it with his foot. Then across the clenched hush of the crowd and the wide silence of the desert, he articulated one word:

'Nom.'

The *gaddhi* let out a cry of triumph.

The next moment, the spear was withdrawn from Linden's neck. All the spears were withdrawn. The *husta* lifted the Lady Alif back to the safety of the Sandwall, set her on her feet. At once, she fled the gathering. Smiling a secretive victory, the Lady Benj watched her go.

Turning from the parapet, Linden found that the Guards had stepped back from her companions.

All of them except Covenant, Vain, and Findail were glaring ire and protest at Kasreyn of the Gyre.

In her concentration on Hergrom, Linden had not felt or heard the Kemper arrive. But he stood now at the edge of the assembly and addressed the company.

'I desire you to observe that I have played no part in this chicane. I must serve my *gaddhi* as he commands.' His rheumy gaze ignored Rant Absolain. 'But I do not participate in such acts.'

Linden nearly hurled herself at him. *'What have you done?'*

'I have done nothing,' he replied stiffly. 'You are witness.' But then his shoulders sagged as if the infant on his back wearied him. 'Yet in my way I have earned your blame. What now transpires would not without me.'

Stepping to the parapet, he sketched a gesture towards the distant blackness. He sounded old as he said, 'The power of any art depends upon its flaw. Perfection cannot endure in an imperfect world. Thus when I bound the Sandgorgons to their Doom, I was compelled to place a flaw within my theurgy.' He regarded the storm as if he found it draining and lovely. He could not conceal that he admired what he had done.

'The flaw I chose,' he soughed, 'is this, that any Sandgorgon will be released if its name is spoken. It will be free while it discovers the one who spoke its name. Then it must slay the speaker and return to its Doom.'

Slay? Linden could not think. Slay?

Slowly, Kasreyn faced the company again. 'Therefore I must share blame. For it was I who wrought Sandgorgons Doom. And it was I who placed the name your companion has spoken in his mind.'

At that, giddy realizations wheeled through Linden. She saw the Kemper's mendacity mapped before her in white sunlight. She turned as if she were reeling, lurched back to the parapet. Run! she cried. Hergrom! But her voice made no sound.

Because she had chosen to let Kasreyn live. It was intolerable. With a gasp, she opened her throat. 'The gates!' Her shout was frail and hoarse, parched into effectlessness by the desert. 'Run! We'll help you fight!'

Hergrom and Ceer did not move.

'They will not,' the Kemper said, mimicking sadness. 'They know their plight. They will not bring a Sandgorgon among you, nor among the innocents of the Sandhold. And,' he went on, trying to disguise his pride, 'there is not time. The Sandgorgons answer their release swiftly. Distance has no meaning to such power. Behold!' His voice sharpened. 'Though the Doom lies more than a score of leagues hence, already the answer draws nigh.'

On the other side of the company, the *gaddhi* began to giggle.

And out from under the virga came a plume of sand among the dunes, arrowing towards the Sandhold. It varied as the terrain varied, raising a long serpentine cloud; but its direction was unmistakable. It was aimed at the spot where Ceer and Hergrom stood against the Sandwall.

Even from that distance, Linden felt the radiations of raw and hostile power.

She pressed her uselessness against the parapet. Her companions stood aching behind her; but she did not turn to look at them, could not. Rant Absolain studied the approaching Sandgorgon and trembled in an ague of eagerness. The sun leaned down on the Sandhold like a reproach.

Then the beast itself appeared. Bleached to an albino whiteness by ages of sun, it was difficult to see against the pale desert. But it ran forward with staggering speed and became clear.

It was larger than the *Haruchai* awaiting it, but it hardly had size enough to contain so much might. For an instant, Linden was struck by the strangeness of its gait. Its knees were back-bent like a bird's, and its feet were wide pads, giving it the ability to traverse sand with immense celerity and force. Then the Sandgorgon was almost upon Hergrom and Ceer; and she perceived other details.

It had arms, but no hands. Its forearms ended in flat flexible stumps like prehensile battering rams — arms formed to contend with sand, to break stone.

And it had no face. Its head was featureless except for the faint ridges of its skull beneath its hide and two covered slits like gills on either side.

It appeared as violent and absolute as a force of nature. Watching it, Linden was no longer conscious of breathing. Her heart might have stopped. Even Covenant with all his wild magic could not have equalled this feral beast.

Together, Hergrom and Ceer stepped out from the Sandwall, then separated so that the Sandgorgon could not attack them both at once.

The creature shifted its impetus slightly. In a flash of white hide and fury, it charged straight at Hergrom.

At the last instant, he spun out of its way. Unable to stop, the Sandgorgon crashed headlong into the wall.

Linden felt the impact as if the entire Sandhold had shifted. Cracks leaped through the stone, chunks recoiled outward and thudded to the ground.

Simultaneously, Ceer and Hergrom sprang for the creature's back. Striking with all their skill and strength, they hammered at its neck.

It took the blows as if they were handfuls of sand. Spinning sharply, it slashed at them with its arms.

Ceer ducked, evaded the strike. But one arm caught Hergrom across the chest, flung him away like a doll.

None of them made a sound. Only their blows, their movements on the sand, articulated the combat.

Surging forward, Ceer butted the beast's chin with such force that the Sandgorgon rebounded a step. Immediately, he followed, raining blows. But they had no effect. The beast caught its balance. Its back-bent knees flexed, preparing to spring.

Ceer met that thrust with a perfectly timed hit at the creature's throat.

Again the Sandgorgon staggered. But this time one of its arms came down on the *Haruchai*'s shoulder. Dumbly, Linden's senses registered the breaking of bones. Ceer nearly fell.

Too swiftly for any defence, the Sandgorgon raised one footpad and stamped at Ceer's leg.

He sprawled helplessly, with splinters protruding from the wreckage of his thigh and knee. Blood spattered the sand around him.

Seadreamer was at the edge of the parapet, straining to leap downward as if he believed he would survive the fall. Honninscrave and the First fought to restrain him.

The *gaddhi*'s giggling bubbled like the glee of a demon.

Cail's fingers gripped Linden's arm as if he were holding her responsible.

As Ceer fell, Hergrom returned to the combat. Running as hard as he could over the yielding surface, he leaped into the air, launched a flying kick at the Sandgorgon's head.

The beast retreated a step to absorb the blow, then turned, tried to sweep Hergrom into its embrace. He dodged. Wheeling behind the Sandgorgon, he sprang on to its back. Instantly, he clasped his legs to its torso, locked his arms around its neck and squeezed. Straining every muscle, he clamped his forearm into the beast's throat, fought to throttle the creature.

It flailed its arms, unable to reach him.

Rant Absolain stopped giggling. Disbelief radiated from him like a cry.

Linden forced herself against the corner of the parapet, clung to that pain. A soundless shout of encouragement stretched her mouth.

But behind the beast's ferocity lay a wild cunning. Suddenly, it stopped trying to strike at Hergrom. Its knees bent as if it were crouching to the ground.

Savagely, it hurled itself backward at the Sandwall.

There was nothing Hergrom could do. He was caught between the Sandgorgon and the hard stone. Tremors like hints of earthquake shuddered through the wall.

The beast stepped out of Hergrom's grasp, and he slumped to the ground. His chest had been crushed. For a moment, he continued to breathe in a wheeze of blood and pain, torturing his ruptured lungs, his pierced heart. As white and featureless as fate, the Sandgorgon regarded him as if wondering where to place the next blow.

Then a spasm brought dark red fluid gushing from his mouth. Linden saw the thews of his life snap. He lay still.

The Sandgorgon briefly confronted the wall as if wishing for the freedom to attack it. But the beast's release had ended. Turning away, it moved at a coerced run back towards its Doom. Shortly, it disappeared into the sand-trail it raised behind it.

Linden's eyes bled tears. She felt that something inside her had perished. Her companions were stunned into silence; but she did not look at them. Her heart limped to the rhythm of Hergrom's name, iterating that sound as though there must have been something she could have done.

When she blinked her sight clear, she saw that Rant Absolain had started to move away, taking his women and Guards with him. His chortling faded into the sunlight and the dry white heat.

Kasreyn was nowhere on the Sandwall.

17

CHARADE'S END

For a time that seemed as unanswerable as paralysis, Linden remained still. Kasreyn's absence – the fact that he had not stayed to watch the contest of the Sandgorgon – felt more terrible to her than the *gaddhi*'s mirth. She knew that there were needs to be met, decisions to be made; but she was unable to recognize them. Hergrom's name ran along her pulse, numbing her to everything else.

She nearly cried out when Covenant said like an augur, 'Don't touch me.'

Cail had released her; but the marks his fingers had left on her upper arm throbbed, echoing her heartbeat. He had dug his sternness into her flesh, engraved it on her bones.

Then the First moved. She confronted Rire Grist. The suffusion of her gaze made her appear purblind. She spoke in a raw whisper, as if she could not contain her passion in any other way.

'Bring us rope.'

The Caitiffin's face wore a look of nausea. He appeared to feel a genuine dismay at Hergrom's fate. Perhaps he had never seen a Sandgorgon at work before. Or perhaps he understood that he might some day displease his masters and have a name of terror placed in his mind as punishment. There was sweat on his brows, and in his voice, as he muttered a command to one of the *hustin*.

The Guard obeyed slowly. He snapped at it like a sudden cry, and it hastened away. In a short time, it came back carrying a second coil of heavy rope.

At once, Honninscrave and Seadreamer took the line. With the practised celerity of sailors, they secured it to the parapet, cast it outward. Though it seemed small in their hands, it was strong enough to support a Giant. First the Master, then Seadreamer slid down to the bloodied sand and to Ceer.

Cail's touch impelled Linden forward. Numbly, she moved to the rope. She had no idea what she was doing. Wrapping her arms and legs around the line, she let her weight pull her after Honninscrave and Seadreamer.

When she reached the ground, her feet fumbled in the sand. Hergrom's body slumped against the wall, accusing her. She could hardly force her futile legs to carry her towards Ceer.

Cail followed her downward. Then came Brinn with Covenant slung over his shoulder. In a rush of iron grace, the First swarmed down the rope.

Vain gazed over the parapet as if he were considering the situation. Then he, too, descended the line. At the same time, Findail melted out of the base of the Sandwall and reformed himself among the questers.

Linden paid no heed to them. Stumbling to her knees at Ceer's side, she hunched over him and tried not to see the extremity of his pain.

He said nothing. His visage held no expression. But perspiration ran from his forehead like droplets of agony.

Perceptions seemed to fly at her face. Assailed by arid heat and vision, her eyes felt like ashes in their sockets. His shoulder was not too badly damaged. Only the clavicle was broken – a clean break. But his leg –

Jesus Christ.

Shards of bone mangled the flesh of his thigh and knees. He was losing blood copiously through the many wounds. She could not believe that he would ever walk again. Even if she had had access to a good hospital, x-rays, trained help, she might not have been able to save his leg. But those things belonged to the world she had lost – the only world she understood. She possessed nothing except the vulnerability which made her feel every fraction of his pain as if it were mapped explicitly in her own flesh.

Groaning inwardly, she closed her eyes, sparing herself the sight of his hurt, his valour. He appalled her – and needed her. He needed her. And she had nothing to offer him except her acute and outraged percipience. How could she deny him? She had denied Brinn, and this was the result. She felt that she was in danger of losing everything as she murmured into the clenched silence of her companions. 'I need a tourniquet. And a splint.'

She heard a ripping noise. Brinn or Cail placed a long strip of cloth in her hands. At the same time, the First shouted up at Rire Grist, 'We require a spear!'

Working by touch, Linden knotted the cloth around Ceer's thigh above the damage. She pulled the tough material as tight as she could. Then she shifted back to his shoulder because that injury was so much less heinous and called for Cail to help her.

Her hands guided his to the points of pressure and stress she required. While she monitored Ceer's collarbone with her fingers, Cail moved and thrust according to her instructions. Together, they manipulated the clavicle into a position where it could heal safely.

She felt the Giants watching her intently, grimly. But she lacked the courage to open her eyes. She had to lock her jaw to keep from weeping in shared pain. Her nerves were being flayed by Ceer's hurt. Yet his need consumed every other consideration. With Cail and then Brinn beside her, she confronted his thigh again.

As her hands explored the wreckage, she feared that the mute screams in his leg would become her screams, reaving her of all resolve. She squeezed her eyelids shut until the pressure made her head throb. But she was professionally familiar with shattered bones. The ruin of Ceer's knee was explicable to her. She knew what needed to be done.

'I'm going to hurt you.' She could not silence the ache of her empathy. 'Forgive me.'

Guided by her percipience, she told Brinn and Cail what to do, then helped them do it.

Brinn anchored Ceer's upper leg. Cail grasped Ceer's ankle. At Linden's word, Cail pulled, opening the knee. Then he twisted it to realign the splinters of bone.

Ceer's breathing gasped through his teeth. Hard pieces of bone ground against each other. Sharp fragments tore new wounds around the joint. Linden felt everything in her own vitals and wanted to shriek. But she did not. She guided Cail's manipulations, pressed recalcitrant splinters back into place, staunched the oozing of blood. Her senses explored the ravaged territory of the wound, gauging what needed to be done next.

Then she had done everything she could. Chips of bone still blocked the joint, and the menisci had been badly torn; but she could not reach those things — or the torn blood vessels, the mutilated nerves — without surgery. Given Ceer's native toughness and a sharp knife, surgery was theoretically possible. But it could not be done here, on the unclean sand. She let Cail release Ceer's ankle and demanded a splint.

One of the Giants placed two smooth shafts of wood into her hands. Involuntarily, she looked at them and saw that they were sections of spear. And Seadreamer had already unbraided a long piece of rope, thereby obtaining strands with which to bind the wood.

For a moment longer, Linden held herself together. With Cail's help, she applied the splint. Then she removed the tourniquet.

But after that her visceral distress became too strong for suppression. Stiffly, she crawled away from Ceer's pain. Sitting with her back against the Sandwall, she clasped her arms around her knees, hid her face, and tried to rock herself back under control. Her exacerbated nerves wailed at her like lost children; and she did not know how to bear it.

Mistweave's plight had not hurt her like this. But she had not been to blame for it, though the fault for Covenant's condition had been hers then as it was now. And then she had not been so committed to what she was doing, to the quest and her own role in it – to the precise abandonment and exposure which Gibbon-Raver had told her would destroy both her and the world.

Ceer's pain showed her just how much of herself she had lost.

Yet as she bled for him she realized that she did not wish that loss undone. She was still a doctor, still dedicated to the one thing which had preserved her from the inbred darkness of her heritage. And now at least she was not fleeing, not denying. The pain was only pain, after all; and it slowly ebbed from her joints. Better this than paralysis. Or the unresolved hunger that was worse than paralysis.

So when the First knelt before her, placed gentle hands on her shoulders, she met the Giant's gaze. One of the First's hands accidentally brushed the bruises which Cail had left on her arm. Shuddering, she opened herself to the First's concern.

For a moment, her fearsome vulnerability and the First's arduous restraint acknowledged each other. Then the Swordmain stood, drawing Linden to her feet. Gruffly, like a refusal of tears, the First said to the company, 'We must go.'

Brinn and Cail nodded. They looked at Seadreamer; and he answered by stooping to Ceer, lifting the injured *Haruchai* carefully in his arms.

They were all ready to begin the walk to the gate.

Linden stared at them. Thickly, she asked, 'What about Hergrom?'

Brinn gazed at her as if he did not understand her question.

'We can't just leave him here.' Hergrom had spent his life to save the company. His body slumped against the wall like a sacrifice to the Great Desert. His blood formed a dark stain around him.

Brinn's flat eyes did not waver. 'He failed.'

The force of his absolute gaze stung her. His judgment was too severe; it was inhuman. Because she did not know any other way to repudiate it, she strode over the sand to strike at Brinn's detached countenance with all the weight of her arm.

He caught the blow deftly, gripped her wrist for a moment with the same stone strength which had ground Cail's fingers into her flesh. Then he thrust down her hand, released her. Taking Covenant by the arm, he turned away from her.

Abruptly, Honninscrave bent to pick up the ornament which Rant Absolain had dropped. The black sun of the medallion had been broken in half by Hergrom's foot. Honninscrave's eyes were rimmed with rue and anger as he handed the pieces to the First.

She took them and crumbled them in one fist. The chain she snapped in two places. Then she hurled all the fragments out into the Great Desert, turned and started eastward around the curve of the Sandwall.

Seadreamer and Honninscrave followed her. Brinn and Covenant followed them.

After a moment, Linden, too, thrust herself into motion. Her wrist and upper arm ached. She was beginning to make new promises to herself.

Cail behind her, and Vain and Findail behind Cail, she joined her companions, leaving Hergrom bereft of the dignity of care or burial by the simple fact that he had proven himself mortal.

The outer face of the wall was long; and the sun beat down as if it rode the immobile tide of the dunes to pound against the company. The sand made every stride strenuous. But Linden had recoiled from Ceer's pain into decision. Hergrom was dead. Ceer needed her. She would have to perform a miracle of surgery to preserve the use of his leg. And Covenant moved a few paces ahead of her, muttering his ritual at blind intervals as if the only thing he could remember was leprosy. She had endured enough.

At last, the Sandwall stopped curving. It became straight as its outer arm reached to join the wall which girdled *Bhrathairain* and the Harbour. In the middle of that section stood the gate the company sought. It admitted them to the open courtyard, where one of *Bhrathairealm*'s fountains glistened in the sunlight.

There the questers halted. To the right stood the gate which opened on the town; to the left, the entrance towards the Sandhold. The way back to Starfare's Gem seemed unguarded. But Rire Grist and his aide were waiting at the inner gate.

Here, again, there were birds – here, and everywhere around *Bhrathairain*, but not in the proximity of the Sandhold. Perhaps the donjon had never fed them. Or perhaps they shied from the Kemper's arts.

Unexpectedly, the Appointed spoke. His yellow eyes were hooded, concealing his desires. 'Will you not now return to your *dromond*? This place contains naught but peril for you.'

Linden and the Giants stared at him. His words appeared to strike a chord in the First. She turned to Linden, asking Findail's question mutely.

'Do you think they'll let us leave?' Linden rasped. She trusted the *Elohim* as much as she did Kasreyn. 'Did you see the Guards inside the wall when we came in? Grist is probably just waiting to give the order.' The First's eyes narrowed in acknowledgment; but still her desire to do something, anything, which might relieve her sense of helplessness was plain. Linden gripped herself more tightly. 'There's a lot I need to do for Ceer's leg. If I don't get the bonechips out of that joint, it'll never move again. But that can wait a while. Right now I need hot water and bandages. He's still bleeding. And this heat makes infection spread fast.' Her vision was precise and certain. She saw mortification already gnawing the edges of Ceer's wounds. 'That can't wait. If I don't help him soon, he'll lose the whole leg.' The *Haruchai* watched her as if they were fundamentally uncertain of her. But she clung to the promises she had made, forced herself to ignore their doubt. 'If we go on pretending we're the *gaddhi*'s guests, Grist can't very well refuse to give us what we need.'

For a moment, the company was silent. Linden heard nothing except the cool splashing of the fountain. Then Brinn said flatly, 'The *Elohim* speaks truly.'

At that, the First stiffened. 'Aye,' she growled, 'the *Elohim* speaks truly. And Hergrom expended his life for us though you deem it failure. I am prepared to hazard somewhat in the name of Ceer's hurt.' Without waiting for a response, she swung towards the Caitiffin, calling as she moved. 'Ho, Rire Grist! Our companion is sorely injured. We must have medicaments.'

'Instantly,' he replied. He could not conceal the relief in his tone. He spoke rapidly to his aide, sent the man running towards the Sandhold. Then he said to the First, 'All you require will await you in your chambers.'

Honninscrave and Seadreamer followed the First; and Linden went with them, giving Brinn and Cail no choice but to do the same. Vain and Findail brought up the rear.

The two Guards stepped aside. Either they were now able to identify the *gaddhi*'s guests, or they had been given new orders. Together, the company passed through the Sandwall, hastened as best they could over the sand towards the entrance to the Sandhold. Linden clinched herself against the moment when she might break and forced herself to match the First's pace.

Within the high forecourt of the First Circinate, the old gloom lurked, momentarily concealing everything beyond the direct light from the gates. Before her eyes adjusted, Linden received a confusing impression of Guards and people – and of another presence which surprised her.

For a fleeting moment, she was aware of the people. They were servants, but not the comely and graceful servitors who had waited on the Chatelaine the day before. Rather, they were the menials of the Sandhold, men and women who were too aged or unbecoming to please the eye of the *gaddhi* – of the Kemper. And the wealth of *Bhrathairealm* clearly did not extend to them. Dressed in the tattered habiliments of their impoverishment, they were on their hands and knees, cleaning up after the horses which had been exercised here earlier. Linden wondered how many of them had once been courtiers or Favoured.

But then her senses cleared, and she forgot the servants as her heart bounded towards Pitchwife.

Several *hustin* stood around him, holding him where he was but not threatening him. Apparently, they had been instructed to make him wait here for his friends.

At the sight of the First and her companions, relief stretched his misshapen features. But Linden read the nature of his tidings in the hunching of his shoulders and the unwonted darkness of his gaze.

The sudden softening of the First's features revealed how keenly she had been yearning for her husband. Pitchwife started towards her as if he could not wait to embrace her.

His mien brought back the company's peril to Linden. Deliberately, she keyed her voice to a pitch and timbre which compelled the attention of the Giants. 'Don't say anything. Kasreyn hears everything the Guards hear.'

Indirectly, she watched the Caitiffin. His face flushed as if he were suppressing apoplexy. In the privacy of her mind, she permitted herself a severe grin. She wanted the Kemper to know that she knew at least this much about him.

With one hand, Cail brushed her arm like a reminder of the marks he had left in her flesh. But she ignored him. She knew the risk she had taken.

Pitchwife's face clenched as he bit back his native volubility. The First tensed in recognition of Linden's ploy, shot a glance at Honninscrave. The Master dropped a shutter of blandness over his visage as he resumed his role as spokesman for the company; but the knotting of his jaw made his beard jut like belligerence. Smoothly, he introduced Pitchwife and Rire Grist to each other. Then he urged the Caitiffin to make haste for the sake of Ceer's leg.

Rire Grist appeared glad to comply, unintentionally eager for haste, as if he felt a personal need to finish this duty so that he would be free to consult with his master, ask for new instructions. Without delay, he led the company up out of the First Circinate, through the back ways of the Second to the guesting-rooms. Then he stood as if his kneecaps were quivering while he waited for the company to let him go.

In the sitting-room across from the bedchambers, the questers found Rire Grist's aide and an assortment of medical supplies: a large brass urn of boiling water; various dippers and cutting-implements; bolts of clean linen for bandages; an array of balms and unguents in small stoneware pots. While Linden inspected what he had brought, the aide asked her if she required the services of one of the Sandhold's chirurgeons. She refused – would have refused even if she had wanted such help. She and her companions needed a chance to talk freely, unheard by any ears.

When she nodded to the Giants, Honninscrave dismissed the Caitiffin and his aide. Linden took a grim satisfaction from the promptitude of their departure.

Cail placed himself on guard outside the door, which Brinn left open as a precaution against the kind of subterfuge the Lady Alif had practised earlier. Seadreamer had laid Ceer gently down among a pile of cushions. While Linden bent to the task of Ceer's knee, Pitchwife and the First confronted each other.

'Stone and Sea!' he began, 'I am gladdened by the sight of you – though it wrings my heart to discover you in such straits. What has become of Hergrom? How has such harm befallen Ceer? Surely this tale – '

The First interrupted him softly. The edges of her tone frayed as if she would have wept if she had been alone with him. 'What word do you bring from Starfare's Gem?'

All the feigned politesse was gone from Honninscrave's face. His eyes lanced at Pitchwife. But Seadreamer had turned away from them. He knelt opposite Linden to assist her if he could. His old scar was vivid with apprehension.

Carefully, Linden bathed Ceer's mangled leg. Her hands were deft and certain. But another part of her mind was focused on Pitchwife and the First.

The malformed Giant winced. But he shouldered the burden of his tidings. His voice wheezed faintly in his cramped chest.

'An attempt has been made upon the Giantship.'

Honninscrave hissed a sharp breath. Seadreamer knotted his hands in a pillow; but it was too insubstantial to steady him. With an effort, the First held herself as still as the *Haruchai*.

'After your departure' – his tale made Pitchwife awkward – 'the Harbour Captain complied with Rire Grist's commands. Stores were opened to us – food, water, and stone in abundance. Ere sundown, our holds were replenished, and with my pitch I had wived the side of Starfare's Gem, restoring it to seaworthiness – though much labour awaits me to repair the other damages.' He had to struggle against his instinctive desire to describe his work in detail. But he coerced himself to relate the pith of his tidings, nothing more. 'No harm or suggestion of harm was offered to us, and even the Harbour Captain swallowed some measure of his affronted pride.

'But it is well for us that Sevinhand Anchormaster holds caution in such esteem. At day's end, watches were set at all points, both within and upon the *dromond*. In my folly, I felt secure, for the moon rose nigh to fullness above *Bhrathairain*, and I conceived that no hurt could accost us unseen. But moonlight also cast a sheen upon the waters, concealing their depths. And while the moon crested above us, the watch which Sevinhand had set within Starfare's Gem heard unwonted sounds through the hull.'

Removing Ceer's splint, Linden finished cleaning his wounds. Then she turned her penetration to the medicaments Rire Grist's aide had provided. Clearly, the *Bhrathair* had a wide-ranging medical knowledge – the fruit of their violent history. She found cleansing salves, febrifuges, narcotic balms: drugs which promised effectiveness against a variety of battlehurts. They appeared to have been produced from the various sands and soils of the Great Desert itself. She chose an unguent for antisepsis and a balm for numbness, and began applying them to Ceer's leg.

But she did not miss a word of Pitchwife's tale.

'At once,' he said, 'Sevinhand asked for divers. Galewrath and Mistweave replied. Quietly entering the waters, they swam to the place the watch indicated, and there with their hands they discovered a large object clinging among the barnacles. Together they wrested it from the hull, bearing it with them to the surface. But Sevinhand instantly commanded them to discard it. Therefore they cast it to the pier, where it became an exploding fire which wrought great damage – though not to Starfare's Gem.'

In grim irony, he continued, 'To my mind, it is somewhat odd that no man or woman from all *Bhrathairain* came to consider the cause of that blast.' Then he shrugged. 'Nonetheless, Sevinhand's caution was not appeased. At his word, Galewrath Storesmaster and others explored all the outward faces of the Giantship with their hands, seeking further perils. None were found.

'In the dawn,' he concluded, 'I came in search of you. Without hindrance I was admitted to the First Circinate. But there I was given to understand' – he grimaced wryly – 'that I must await you.' His eyes softened as he regarded the First. 'The wait was long to me.'

Honninscrave could not contain himself. He stepped forward, required the First to look at him. 'We must return to Starfare's Gem.' He was urgent for his ship. 'We must flee this Harbour. It is intolerable that my *dromond* should fall prey to these *Bhrathair* – and I here helpless.'

The First replied darkly, 'Yes.' But she retained her command over him. 'Yet the Chosen is not yet done. Grimmand Honninscrave, relate to Pitchwife what has transpired among us here.'

For a moment, the Master's visage knotted as if her order were cruel. But it was not: it gave him a way to contain his apprehension. He scowled like a fist, and his beard bristled with ire; but he obeyed. In words like the pieces of the *gaddhi*'s medallion, he told Pitchwife what had happened.

Linden listened to him as she had to Pitchwife and clasped her promises within her. While Seadreamer supported Ceer's leg, she spread medicaments over his thigh and knee. Then she cut the linen into strips for bandages. Her hands did not hesitate. When she had wrapped his leg from midthigh to calf in firm layers of cloth, she reset the splints.

After that, she had Seadreamer lift Ceer into a sitting position while she strapped his shoulder to stabilize it. The *Haruchai*'s eyes were glazed with pain; but his mien remained as stolid as ever. When she was done with his shoulder, she lifted a flagon of diluted wine to his mouth and did not lower it until he had replaced a good measure of the fluid he had lost.

And all the time Honninscrave's words reached her ears starkly, adumbrating Hergrom's death until she seemed to relive it while she tended Ceer. The stubborn extravagance or gallantry of the *Haruchai* left her overtaut and certain. When the Master finished, she was ready.

Pitchwife was groping to take in everything he had heard. 'This *gaddhi*,' he murmured in fragments. 'As you have described him. Is he capable of enacting such a chicane?'

Linden rose to her feet. Though his question had not been directed at her, she answered, 'No.'

He looked at her, strove for comprehension. 'Then – '

'It was Kasreyn from the beginning.' She bit out the words. 'He controls everything, even when Rant Absolain doesn't realize it. He must have told the *gaddhi* exactly what to do. To get Hergrom killed. And he doesn't want us to know it,' she went on. 'He wants us to be afraid of Rant Absolain instead of him. He failed with Covenant once. He's trying to get another chance. Maybe he thinks we'll ask him to save us from the *gaddhi*.'

'We must flee this place,' Honninscrave insisted.

Linden did not look at him. She faced the First. 'I've got a better idea. Let's go to Rant Absolain. Ask his permission to leave.'

The First gauged Linden with her iron gaze. 'Will he grant us that?'

Linden shrugged. 'It's worth a try.' She was prepared for that eventuality as well.

With an inward leap, the First made her decision. Pitchwife's presence, and the prospect of action, seemed to restore her to herself. Striding out into the corridor, she shouted to the Guards that waited within earshot, 'Summon the Caitiffin Rire Grist! We must speak with him!'

Linden could not relax the over-tension of her nerves. The bruises Cail had left on her upper arm throbbed like a demand.

When she met the First's gaze again, they understood each other.

The Caitiffin returned shortly. Behind the desert-tan of his face lay a suggestion of pallor, as if he had not had time to consult with his master – or perhaps had been refused a hearing. His manner had ragged edges, betraying glimpses of strain.

But the First had recovered her certainty, and she met him with steady composure. 'Rire Grist,' she said as if he had nothing to fear from her, 'We desire an audience with the *gaddhi*.'

At that, his cheeks blanched unmistakably. Words tumbled out of him. 'My friends, let me dissuade you. Assuredly the loss of one comrade and the injury of another are sore to you – but you are unwise to hazard further offence to the *gaddhi*. He is sovereign here, and jealous. You must not task him for what he has done. Having obtained the punishment he sought, he is now perhaps inclined to be magnanimous. But if you dare his ill-favour, he will take umbrage swiftly, to your cost.'

He began to repeat himself, then jerked to a halt. Clearly, Kasreyn had not prepared him for this dilemma. Sweat spread around his eyes as he forced himself to meet the First's scrutiny.

She was unruffled. 'Caitiffin, we have taken decision among ourselves to respect the *gaddhi*'s right of punishment.' Linden felt the lie under the flat surface of the words, but she saw that Rire Grist did not. 'We are grieved for our companions, but we will not presume to judge your sovereign.' The First permitted herself a subtle inflection of contempt. 'Be assured that we will offer the *gaddhi* no offence. We desire merely to ask a frank boon of him — one easily within his grant and plainly honourable to him.'

For a moment, the Caitiffin's eyes shifted back and forth searching for a way to inquire what the boon was. But then he grasped that she did not mean to tell him. As he wiped a discomfited hand across his forehead he looked like a man for whom a lifetime of ambition had begun to crumble. Yet he remained tough enough to act. Striving to contain his uncertainty, he answered, 'It is rare for the *gaddhi* to grant audience at such a time. But for his guests he may perhaps make exception. Will you accompany me?'

When the First nodded, he turned as if he wanted to flee and left the chamber.

Quickly, she looked at her companions. None of them hesitated. Seadreamer lifted Ceer from the cushions. Brinn took hold of Covenant's arm. Honninscrave moved forward tightly, holding his emotions in both fists.

Vain remained as blank as ever; and Findail seemed to be entranced by his own distress. But neither of them lingered behind the company.

Linden led them after Rire Grist.

She followed him closely, with Cail and then the others behind her. She wanted to ensure that the Caitiffin had as little opportunity as possible to prepare surprises. She could not prevent the brackish shout he directed at the first *hustin* he met, sending two of them at a run ahead of him; but she saw no cunning in the set of his back, heard no duplicity in the tone of his voice. When he informed her over his shoulder that he had told the Guards to bear the company's request to Rant Absolain, she was able to believe him. Whatever hopes he had left did not require him to betray the quest now.

He led the company directly upward through the Tier of Riches to The Majesty. As Linden ascended into the audience-hall, she found everything arranged as it had been during the company's initial presentation to the *gaddhi*: scores of Guards were stationed around the wall; and all the light was focused towards the high Auspice. Only the Chatelaine were missing. Their absence made her realize that she had not seen any of them since the previous day. She grew tighter. Were they simply staying out of harm's way? – or had they been commanded into seclusion so that they would not interfere with Kasreyn's machinations?

The Caitiffin spoke to one of the *hustin* and received an answer which relieved him. He faced the company with a smile. 'The *gaddhi* elects to grant you audience.'

Linden and the First shared a moment of preparation. Then they followed Rire Grist across the circles of the floor towards the Auspice.

In the zone of light, they stopped beside him. The Auspice lifted its magnificence into the lumination as if it were more truly the suzerain of *Bhrathairealm* than Rant Absolain himself.

The *gaddhi* was not there.

But after only a moment's delay he emerged from the shadows behind his seat. He was alone, unaccompanied by either his women or the Kemper. And he was nervous. Linden sensed the trembling of his knees as he ascended the throne.

Rire Grist dropped to one knee. Linden and the Giants mimicked his obeisance. Her tension made her want to shout at Brinn and Cail, at Vain and Findail, to do the same; but she kept herself still. As Rant Absolain climbed through the brightness to take his seat, she studied him. He had put off his formal robe and now wore a light tunic which appeared to be a form of bed-attire. But underneath his raiment, his inner state was clouded. It was clear that he had been drinking heavily. The wine obscured his emanations.

When he took his seat, she and the First arose without waiting for his permission. The other Giants and Rire Grist also stood. Seadreamer held Ceer into the light like an accusation.

Rant Absolain peered out at the company, but did not speak. His tongue worked the inside of his mouth as if he were dry with thirst. A patina of wine blurred his vision, made him squint until aches squeezed his temples.

The First gave him a moment of silence like an act of forbearance towards his weakness. Then she took a step forward, bowed formally, and began to speak.

'O *gaddhi*, you honour us with this hearing. We are your guests and desire to ask a boon of you.' The edge of her voice was masked in velvet. 'Word has come to us that our vessel is now replenished and repaired, according to your grace. O *gaddhi*, the quest which drives us across the seas is urgent and consuming. We ask your grant to depart, that we may pursue our purpose, bearing the honour of your name with us as we go.'

She spoke in a reassuring tone; but her words brought down consternation on Rant Absolain. He shrank against the Auspice. His hands gripped the arms of the seat for an answer it did not provide. While he wrestled for a response, his lips mumbled, No. No.

Linden felt a touch of pity for him; but it was not enough to ease the pressure which stretched her to her resolve.

At last, he rasped against the desert in his throat, 'Depart?' His voice cracked helplessly. 'I cannot permit it. You have suffered in *Bhrathairealm*.' Somehow, he found the strength to insist defensively, 'Through no fault of mine. Blood was shed. I am required to exact justice.' But then he became timorous again, painfully aware of his isolation. 'But you must not bear such tidings of me to the world. You are guests, and the *gaddhi* is not harsh to his guests. I will make restitution.' His eyes winced as his brain scrambled in search of inspiration. 'Do you desire a sword? Take what you wish in the name of my goodwill and be content. You may not depart.' His gaze beseeched the First not to press him further.

But she did not relent. Her voice hardened. 'O *gaddhi*, I have heard it spoken that the *hustin* are yours, answering to your will absolutely.'

She surprised him; but he did not perceive the nature of her attack. The thought of the *hustin* restored to him a measure of confidence. 'That is true. The Guard is mine.'

'It is untrue.' The First slipped her intent like a dirk through his defences. 'If you command them to permit our departure, they will refuse.'

The *gaddhi* sprang to his feet. 'You lie!'

She overrode his protest. 'Kasreyn of the Gyre commands them. He made them, and they are his.' Sharply, she drove the deepest wedge she could find between Rant Absolain and the Kemper. 'They answer you only at his whim.'

'Lies!' he shouted at her. 'Lies!' Magenta anger or fear suffused his visage. 'They are mine!'

At once Linden responded. 'Then try it! Tell them to let us go. Give us permission to leave. You're the *gaddhi*. What have you got to lose?'

At her demand, all the colour drained from his face, leaving him as pallid as panic in the focus of the light. His mouth gaped, but no words came. His mind appeared to flee inward, reaving him of self-consciousness or choice. Dumbly, he turned, descended from the Auspice, came down to the level of the company. He trembled as he moved — as frail as if the moments were years and all the stone of the Sandhold had turned against him. Staring vaguely before him he shuffled towards Linden, brought his fear to her. He swallowed several times; his gaze slowly clarified. In a hoarse whisper like an internal wound, he said, 'I dare not.'

She had no reply. He was telling the truth — the whole truth of his life.

For a moment longer, he faced her, appealing to her with his dread. Then he turned away as if he understood that she had refused him. Stumbling over the gaps in the floor, he made his vulnerable way into the shadow of the Auspice and was gone.

The First looked at Linden.

'That does it.' Linden felt that she was near her breaking-point. 'Let's get the hell out of here.'

With a deft movement, the First unbound her helm from her belt, settled it upon her head. Her shield she unslung from her back. Lashing her left forearm into the straps of the shield, she strode towards the stairs.

Rire Grist started after her, spouting expostulations. But Honninscrave caught hold of him. A precise blow stretched the Caitiffin senseless on the floor.

None of the Guards reacted. They gripped their spears at rest and stood where they were, waiting for some voice they recognized to tell them what to do.

Linden hurried after the First; but she did not let herself run. The time for running had not yet come. Her senses were alert and sharp, etching out perceptions. Her companions were behind her in formation, poised for violence. But here nothing threatened them. Below them the Tier of Riches remained empty. Beyond that her percipience did not reach.

In silence marked only by the sounds of their feet the questers spiralled down to the Tier. There the First did not hesitate. With a warrior's stride, she passed among the galleries until she reached the one which displayed the blade she coveted.

'Heard my ears aright?' she murmured in stern irony as she lifted the longsword from its mounts, hefted it to ascertain its balance. 'Did the *gaddhi* not grant me this glaive?' The falchion's edges were as keen as the light in her eyes. Her mouth tasted names for this blade.

Chortling to himself, Pitchwife went with Honninscrave to find other weapons.

They rejoined the company at the stairs to the Second Circinate. Pitchwife bore a spiked cudgel as gnarled and massive as his own arms. And over one shoulder Honninscrave carried a huge iron-bound timber which must have been part of some large siege-engine. The thrust of his beard threatened peril to anyone who dared oppose him.

At the sight, Brinn's gaze brightened; and a look like a smile passed over Ceer's pain-disdaining visage.

Together, the companions started downward.

But when they reached the Second Circinate, Linden halted them. Her tension was scaling towards hysteria. 'Down there.' All her senses rang like hammered metal. Opposition too dense to be enumerated crowded the forecourt of the First Circinate. 'He's waiting for us.' Kasreyn's presence was as unmistakable as his hunger.

'That is well.' The First stroked her new sword. Her certainty was iron and beauty in her countenance. 'His life in *Bhrathairealm* will no longer be what it was. If he is required to declare his tyranny, many things will be altered – not least among them the prosperity of this land.' Her voice was acutely eager.

The company arrayed itself for battle. Knotting her fear in her throat, Linden took Covenant from Brinn, freeing the *Haruchai* to fight. The First and Honninscrave, Pitchwife and the two *Haruchai*, positioned themselves around Seadreamer, Ceer, Covenant, and Linden. Ignoring the Demondim-spawn and Findail, who needed no protection, the company walked defiantly down the stairs to the First Circinate.

There Kasreyn of the Gyre awaited them with four- or five-score *hustin* and at least that many unmounted soldiers.

He stood with his back to the gates. The gates were closed.

The only illumination came from the sunlight striking in shafts through the unattainable windows.

'Hold!' The Kemper's shout was clear and commanding. 'Return to your chambers! The *gaddhi* denies your departure.'

Fired by the mad peril of her promises, Linden retorted, 'He'd let us go if he dared!'

The company did not stop.

Kasreyn barked an order. The Guards levelled their spears. In a sharp hiss of metal, the soldiers drew their swords.

Stride by stride, the forces converged. The company looked as insignificant as a handful of sand thrown against the Sea. Without Covenant's power, they had no chance. Unless they could do what Brinn had wanted to do earlier – unless they could get to Kasreyn and kill him.

Then the First called like a tantara, 'Stone and Sea!' and Honninscrave attacked. Heaving his timber broadside against the *hustin*, he broke their ranks halfway to Kasreyn's position. At once, he sprang into the confusion, began felling Guards on every side with his great fists.

The First and Pitchwife went with him, passed him. Pitchwife had neither the First's grace nor the Master's strength; but his arms were as sturdy as oaks, and with his cudgel he bashed assailants away from the First's back while she slashed her way forward.

She went for Kasreyn as if she meant to reap blood right to the wellspring of his heart. She was the First; and he had manipulated and slain her comrades while she had been weaponless. Her sword flashed like lightning among the sunshafts, first iron and then red as she flailed bloodshed about her.

The spears of the Guards were awkward for such in-fighting. No soldier could reach the Giants with an ordinary sword. The three seafarers fought through the throng towards Kasreyn and were impossibly successful.

Seadreamer, carrying Ceer, herded Covenant and Linden forward. On either side, Brinn and Cail seemed to blur as they fought. Whirling and striking in all directions, they dealt out blows and swift death. For long moments of inchoate attack and precise rebuff, the company moved down the length of the forecourt.

But the task remained impossible. The questers were grievously outnumbered; and more *hustin* arrived constantly. Dodging the thrust of a spear, Seadreamer stumbled against Linden. She slipped in a swath of blood and fell. Warm fluid smeared her clothes, her arms. Covenant stopped moving. His empty eyes witnessed the movements around him; but he did not react to the clangour of combat, the cries of the wounded.

Scrambling to her feet, Linden looked back at Vain and Findail for help. Soldiers hacked wildly at the *Elohim*, but their blades passed through him without effect. Before their astonished eyes, he melted away into the floor.

Vain stood motionless, offering his aimless smile to his attackers. Speartips and swords shredded his raiment, but left his flesh unmarked. Blows rang against him and broke into splinters of pain for those who struck. He appeared capable of mastering all the *hustin* alone, if he but chose to act.

An assault rushed at Covenant, was barely beaten back. 'Vain!' Linden raged. 'Do something!' He had saved her life more than once. They all needed his help now.

But the Demondim-spawn remained deaf to her.

Then she saw the wide golden hoop which came shimmering through the air. Honninscrave roared a warning. Too late. The hoop settled towards Covenant's head before anyone could save him.

Desperately, Seadreamer released one arm from Ceer, tried to slap the lambent circle away. But it was formed of mist and light, and his hand passed through it, leaving no mark.

As the hoop dropped around Covenant, his knees folded.

Another was already in the air. It came from Kasreyn.

Towards Seadreamer.

Suddenly, Linden realized that the Guards and soldiers had fallen back, forming a thick cordon around the company.

In a fury of frustration, the First gave up her attack. With Pitchwife and Honninscrave, she retreated to defend her comrades.

Linden rushed to Covenant's side, swept his head into her arms, thrust her vision into him. Her stained hands smudged red into his shirt.

He was asleep. A slight frown marred his forehead like the implications of nightmare.

Seadreamer sprang away from the shimmering gold. But the *hustin* were ready, holding their spears to impale him if he fled. Brinn and the First charged the cordon. Spears splintered and broke; *hustin* fell. But there was not enough time.

Though the mute Giant struggled to evade it, the hoop encircled his head, wafted downward to cover Ceer. Seadreamer fell. The unconscious *Haruchai* sprawled across the floor.

Kasreyn waved his ocular, barking incantations. A third circle of gold light lifted from the metal, expanding as it floated forward. Pitchwife beat at it with his club; but his blows meant nothing to such theurgy.

With Covenant in her arms, Linden could not move. Gently, the hoop settled over her and carried her down into darkness.

18

SURRENDER

She awoke in dank dark, tugged step after step towards consciousness by the dull rhythmic repetition of a grunt of strain, a clash of metal.

Her upper arms ached like the folly of all promises.

She could see nothing. She was in a place as benighted as a sepulchre. But as her mind limped into wakefulness, her senses slowly began to function, giving names to what they perceived.

She did not want to be roused. She had failed at everything. Even her deliberate efforts to make Kasreyn unsure of himself — to aggravate the implicit distrust between the *gaddhi* and his Kemper — had come to ruin. It was enough. Within her lay death and peace, and she yearned for them because her life was as futile as everything she had ever striven to deny.

But the stubborn grunt and clash would not let her go. That even iteration rose from somewhere beyond her, repudiating her desire for sleep, demanding that she take it into account. Gradually, she began to listen to the messages of her nerves.

She was hanging upright: all her weight was suspended from her upper arms. Her biceps were clasped in tight iron circlets. When she found her footing, straightened her legs, the pressure of the fetters

705

eased; and spears of renewed circulation thrust pain down her arms to her swollen hands.

The movement made her aware of her ankles. They, too, were locked in iron. But those bonds were attached to chains and could be shifted slightly.

The fetters held her against a wall of stone. She was in a lightless rectangular chamber. Finished rock surrounded her, then faded into an immense impending weight. She was underground somewhere beneath the Sandhold. The walls and the air were chill. She had never expected anything in *Bhrathairealm* to be so chill.

The faint sick smell of dead blood touched her nostrils – the blood of *hustin* and soldiers, soaked into her clothes.

The sounds went on: grunt of effort, clash of resistance.

Within the dark, another darkness stood before her. The nerves of her cheeks recognized Vain. The Demondim-spawn was perhaps ten feet from her. He was harder than any granite, more rigid than any annealed metal. The purpose he obeyed seemed more sure of itself than the very bones of the Earth. But he had proven himself inaccessible to appeal. If she cried out, the walls would be more likely to answer her than he.

After all, he was no more to be trusted than Findail, who had fled rather than give the company aid.

The sounds of effort went on, articulating themselves across the blackness. Every exertion produced a dull ringing like the noise of a chain leaping taut.

With an inchoate throb of ire or anguish, Linden turned away from Vain and identified Honninscrave.

The Master stood upright no great distance from her. The chamber was not particularly large. His aura was a knurling of anger and resolve. At slow, rhythmic intervals, he bunched his great muscles, hurled all his strength and weight against his chains. But their clashing gave no hint of fatigue or failure. She felt raw pain growing where the fetters held his wrists. His breathing rasped as if the dank air hurt his chest.

From another part of the wall, the First said hoarsely, 'Honninscrave. In the name of pity.'

But the *Bhrathair* had tried to sink Starfare's Gem, and he did not stop.

The First's tone revealed no serious physical harm. Linden's senses began to move more swiftly. Her ears picked out the various respirations in the chamber. Her nerves explored the space. Somewhere between the First and Honninscrave, she located Pitchwife. The specific wheeze with which his crippled chest took and released air told her that he was unconscious. The pain he emitted showed that he had been dealt a heavy blow; but she felt no evidence of bleeding from him.

706

Beside her, she found Cail. He held himself still, breathed quietly; but his *Haruchai* flesh was unmistakable. He seemed no less judgmental and unyielding than the stone to which he was chained.

Brinn was bound against another wall, opposite the First. His abstract rigidity suggested to Linden that he had made the same attempt Honninscrave was making – and had judged it to be folly. Yet his native extravagance responded to what the Master was doing.

Seadreamer stood near Brinn, yearning out into the dark towards his brother. His muteness was as poignant as a wail. Deep within himself, he was a knot of Earth-Sight and despair.

For a moment, his intensity deafened Linden to Ceer. But then she became aware of the injured *Haruchai*. He also was chained to the wall across from the First, Pitchwife, and Honninscrave. His posture and respiration were as implacable as Brinn's or Cail's; but she caught the taste of pain-sweat from him. The emanations of his shoulder were sharp: his bonds held him in a position which accentuated his broken clavicle. But that hurt paled beside the shrill protest of his crushed knee.

Instinctive empathy struck at her legs, taking them out from under her. She could not stand upright again, bear her own weight, until the misery in her upper arms brought her back to herself. Ceer was so hurt, and held the damage in such disdain – all her training and her long labour cried out against what had happened to him. Groaning, she wrestled with the memory of Kasreyn's defalcation, tried to think of something she might have done to alter the outcome.

But there was nothing – nothing except submission. Give Covenant to the Kemper. Help Kasreyn work his will on Covenant's irreducible vulnerability. Betray every impulse which bound her to the Unbeliever. No. That she could not have done – not even to save Ceer from agony, Hergrom from death. Thomas Covenant was more to her than –

Covenant!

In the unaneled midnight of the dungeon, he was nowhere to be found.

Her senses clawed the dark in all directions, searching manically. But she discovered no glimmer of pulse or tremor of breath which might have been the Unbeliever. Vain was there. Cail was beside her. The First, Honninscrave in his exertions, Ceer bleeding: she identified them all. Opposite her, beyond Vain, she thought she perceived the flat iron of a door. But of Covenant there was no sign, nothing.

Oh dear God.

Her moan must have been audible; some of her companions

707

turned towards her. 'Linden Avery,' the First said tightly. 'Chosen. Are you harmed?'

The blackness became giddy and desperate, beating about her head. The smell of blood was everywhere. Only the hard accusation of the bonds kept her from slumping to the floor. She had brought the company to this. Covenant's name bled through her lips, and the dark took it away.

'Chosen,' the First insisted.

Linden's soul cried for an end, for any blankness or violence which would put a stop to it. But in return came echoes of the way her mother had begged for death, mocking her. Iron and stone scorned her desire for flight, for surcease. And she had to answer the concern of her friends. Somehow, she said, 'He's not here. I lost him.'

The First released a taut sigh. Covenant gone. The end of the quest. Yet she had been tempered to meet extremities; and her tone acknowledged no defeat. 'Nonetheless it was a good ploy. Our hope lay in setting the *gaddhi* and his Kemper at each other. We could not have done otherwise.'

But Linden had no heart for such cold comfort. 'Kasreyn has him.' The chill of the air sharpened her gall. 'We played right into his hands. He's got everything he wants.'

'Has he?' The First sounded like a woman who could stand upright under any doom. Near her, Honninscrave strained against his fetters with unceasing ferocity. 'Then why do we yet live?'

Linden started to retort, Maybe he just wants to play with us. But then the true import of the First's words penetrated her. Maybe Kasreyn did want to wreak cruelty on the questers, in punishment or sport. And maybe *maybe* he still needed them for something. He had already had one chance at the white gold and had not succeeded. Maybe now he intended to use the company against Covenant in some way.

If that were true, she might get one more chance. One last opportunity to make herself and her promises mean something.

Then passion burned like a fever through her chilled skin. The dark made a distant roaring in her ears, and her pulse laboured as if it had been goaded.

Sweet Christ. Give me one more chance.

But the First was speaking again. The need in her voice caught and held Linden's attention. 'Chosen, you have eyes which I lack. What has befallen Pitchwife my husband? I hear his breath at my side, yet he gives no response.'

Linden felt the First's suppressed emotion as if it were a link between them. 'He's unconscious.' She had become as lucid as perfect ice. 'Somebody hit him pretty hard. But I think he's going to be all right. I don't hear any sign of concussion or coma. Nothing broken. He should come out of it soon.'

The ferocity of Honninscrave's exertions covered the First's initial relief. But then she lifted up her voice to say clearly, 'Chosen, I thank you.' The intervening dark could not prevent Linden from tasting the First's silent tears.

Linden gripped her cold sharp lucidity and waited to make use of it.

Later, Pitchwife roused himself. Groaning and muttering, he slowly mastered his dismay. The First answered his questions simply, making no effort to muffle the ache in her voice.

But after a few moments, Linden stopped listening to them. From somewhere in the distance, she seemed to hear the sounds of feet. Gradually, she became sure of them.

Three or four sets of feet. *Hustin* – and someone else?

The iron clatter of the door silenced the company. Light sprang into the cell from a brightly lit corridor, revealing that the door was several high steps above the level of the floor. Two Guards bearing torches thudded heavily down the stairs.

Behind them came Rant Absolain.

Linden identified the *gaddhi* with her nerves. Blinded by the sudden illumination, she could not see him. Ducking her head, she blinked and squinted to drive the blur from her vision.

In the light on the floor between her and Vain lay Thomas Covenant.

All his muscles were limp; but his arms were flat against his sides and his legs were straight, betraying that he had been consciously arrayed in that position. His eyes stared sightlessly at the ceiling as if he were no more than the husk of a living man. Only the faint rise and fall of his chest showed that he was not dead. Smudges of blackened blood marked his shirt like the handprints of Linden's culpability.

The cell seemed to become abruptly colder. For a moment like the onset of hysteria, Linden could not grasp what she was seeing. Here was Covenant, plainly visible – yet he was completely invisible to the other dimension of her senses. When she squeezed her eyes shut in wonder and fear, he appeared to vanish. Her percipience found no evidence of him at all. Yet he was *there*, materializing for her the instant she reopened her eyes.

With an inward quaver, she remembered where she had sensed such a phenomenon before. The Kemper's son. Covenant had become like the infant Kasreyn bore constantly on his back.

Then she noticed the golden band clasped around Covenant's neck.

She was unable to read it, did not understand it. But at once she was intuitively certain that it explained what had happened to him.

It was Kasreyn's hold on him; and it blocked her senses as if it had been specifically designed for that purpose. To prevent her from reaching into him?

Oh, Kasreyn, you bastard!

But she had no time to think. The Guards had set their torches on either side of the door, and Rant Absolain advanced between them to confront the quest.

With a fierce effort, Linden forced her attention away from Covenant. When she looked at the *gaddhi*, she saw he was feverishly drunk. Purple splashes sotted his raiment; his orbs were raw with inebriation and dread.

He was staring at Honninscrave. The Giant's relentless fury for escape appalled him. Slowly, rhythmically, Honninscrave knotted his muscles, hurled himself against the chains, and did not stop. From manacle to elbow, his arms were lined with thin trails of blood.

Quickly, Linden took advantage of Rant Absolain's transfixion to scan her companions.

In spite of his impassivity, Ceer's pallor revealed the extent of his pain. His bandages were soaked with the red of a reopened wound. Pitchwife's injury was less serious; but it left a livid swelling on his right temple.

Then Linden found herself gaping at the First. She had lost both shield and helm; but in her scabbard hung her new falchion. Its grip was just beyond the reach of her chained hands. It must have been restored to her to taunt her helplessness. Or to mock Rant Absolain? Did Kasreyn mean to task the *gaddhi* for that ill-considered gift?

But the First bore herself as if she were impervious to such malice. While Rant Absolain stared his alarm at Honninscrave, she said distinctly, 'O *gaddhi*, it is not wise to speak in the presence of these *hustin*. Their ears are Kasreyn's ears, and he will learn the purpose of your coming.'

Her words pierced his stupefied apprehension. He looked away, staggered for balance, then shouted a dismissal in the *Bhrathair* tongue. The two Guards obeyed, leaving the door open as they departed.

Honninscrave fixed his gaze on that egress as he fought to break his fetters.

As soon as the Guards were gone, Rant Absolain fumbled forward as if the light were dim. For a moment, he tried to peer up at the First; but her height threatened his stability. He swung towards Linden, advanced on her until he was so close that she could not avoid breathing the miasma of his besottedness.

Squinting into her face, he hissed urgently, secretively, 'Free me from this Kemper.'

Linden fought down her revulsion and pity, held her voice level. 'Get rid of him yourself. He's your Kemper. All you have to do is exile him.'

He winced. His hands plucked at her shoulders as if he wanted to plead with her – or needed her help to keep from falling. 'No,' he whispered. 'It is impossible. I am only the *gaddhi*. He is Kasreyn of the Gyre. The power is his. The Guards are his. And the Sandgorgons – ' He was shivering. 'All *Bhrathairealm* knows – ' He faltered, then resumed, 'Prosperity and wealth are his to give. Not mine. My people care nothing for me'. He became momentarily lugubrious. But then his purpose returned to him. 'Slay him for me.' When she did not reply at once, he panted, 'You must.'

An odd pang for his folly and weakness touched her heart. But she did not let herself waver. 'Free us,' she said, as severely as she could. 'We'll find a way to get rid of him.'

'Free?' He gaped at her. 'I dare not. He will know. If you fail – ' His eyes were full of beggary. 'You must free yourselves. And slay him. Then I will be safe.' His lips twisted on the verge of sobs. 'I must be safe.'

At that moment, with her companions watching her, Linden heard footsteps in the corridor and knew that she had a chance to drive another nail into his coffin. Perhaps it would have been the final nail. She did not doubt who was coming. But she had mercy on him. Probably he could never have been other than he was.

Raising her voice, she said distinctly, 'We're your prisoners. It's cruel to mock us like this.'

Then Kasreyn stood in the doorway. From that elevation, he appeared commanding and indefeasible, certain of his mastery. His voice caressed the air like the soft stroke of a whip, playful and threatening. 'She speaks truly, O *gaddhi*. You demean yourself here. They have slain your Guards, giving offence to you and all *Bhrathairealm*. Do not cheapen the honour of your countenance with them. Depart, I bid you.'

Rant Absolain staggered. His face stretched as if he were about to wail. But behind his drunkenness some instinct for self-preservation still functioned. With an exaggerated lurch, he turned towards the Kemper. Slurring his words, he said, 'I desired to vent my wrath. It is my right.' Then he shambled to the stairs and worked his way up them, leaving the cell without a glance at either Kasreyn or the questers. In that way, he preserved the illusion which was his sole hope for survival.

Linden watched him go and clinched herself. Towards Kasreyn of the Gyre she felt no mercy at all.

The Kemper bowed unkindly to his *gaddhi*, then stepped into the cell, closed the iron door. As he came down the stairs, the intensity of his visage was focused on Linden; and the yellowness of his robe and his teeth seemed to concentrate towards her like a presage of his *geas*.

She made a resolute effort of self-command, looked to verify what she had seen earlier. It was true: like Covenant, the Kemper's infant was visible to her superficial sight but not to her deeper perceptions.

'My friends,' Kasreyn said, addressing all the company but gazing only at Linden, 'I will not delay. I am eager.' Rheum glazed his eyes like cataracts. 'Aye, eager.' He stepped over Covenant to stand before her. 'You have foiled me as you were able, but now you are ended.' Spittle reflected a globe of light at one corner of his mouth. 'Now I will have the white gold.'

She stared back at him direly. Her companions stood still, studying her and the Kemper – all except Honninscrave, who did not interrupt his exertions even for Kasreyn of the Gyre.

'I do not maze you.' His tongue quickly licked his lips. 'Well, it may not be denied that to some degree I have slighted your true measure. But no more.' He retreated slightly to her left. 'Linden Avery, you will grant the white gold to me.'

Clenching herself rigid – awaiting her opportunity – Linden rasped mordantly, 'You're crazy.'

He cocked an eyebrow like a gesture of scorn. 'Am I, indeed? Harken – and consider. I desire this Thomas Covenant to submit his ring into my hand. Such submission must be a matter of choice, and there is a veil in his mind which inures him to all choice. Therefore this veil must be pierced, that I may wrest the choice I desire from him.' Abruptly, he stabbed a bony finger at Linden. 'You will pierce it for me.'

At that, her heart leaped. But she strove to conceal her tension, did not let her angry glare waver. Articulating each word precisely, she uttered an obscene refusal.

His eyes softened like an anticipation of lust. Quietly, he asked, 'Do you deny me?'

She remained silent as if she did not deign to reply. Only the regular gasp and clatter of Honninscrave's efforts defined the stillness. She almost hoped that Kasreyn would use his ocular on her. She felt certain that she would be unable to enter Covenant at all if she were in the grip of the Kemper's *geas*.

But he appeared to understand the folly of coercing her with theurgy. Without warning, he whirled, lashed a vicious kick at Ceer's bloody knee.

The unexpected blow wrung pain through Ceer's teeth. For a moment, his ambience faded as if he were about to faint.

The First sprang against her manacles. Seadreamer tried to swipe at Kasreyn, but could not reach him.

The Kemper faced Linden again. His voice was softer than before. 'Do you deny me?'

Tremors built towards shuddering in her. She let them rise, let herself ache so that she might convince him. 'If I let you persuade me like that, Brinn and Cail will kill me.'

Deep within herself, she begged him to believe her. Another such blow would break her. How could she go on spending Ceer's agony to prevent the Kemper from guessing her intent?

'They will not live to lift finger against you!' barked Kasreyn in sudden anger. But a moment later he recollected himself. 'Yet no matter,' he went on with renewed gentleness. 'I have other suasions.' As he spoke, he moved past Vain until he was standing near Covenant's feet. Only the Demondim-spawn was able to ignore him. He held the company in a grasp of horror.

He relished their abomination. Slowly, he raised his right arm.

As he did so, Covenant rose from the floor, jerking erect as if he had been pulled upright by the band around his throat.

Kasreyn moved his hand in a circular gesture from the end of his thin wrist. Covenant turned. His eyes saw nothing. Controlled by the golden neckpiece, he was as blank as his aura. His shirt was stained with death. He went on turning until Kasreyn motioned for him to stop.

The sight nearly snapped Linden's resolve. That Covenant should be so malleable in the Kemper's hands! Whatever harms he had committed, he did not deserve this indignity. And he had made restitution! No man could have striven harder to make restitution. In *Coercri* he had redeemed the Unhomed Dead. He had once defeated Lord Foul. And he had done everything conceivable for Linden herself. There was no justice in his plight. It was evil.

Evil.

Tears coursed hotly down her cheeks like the acid of her mortality. With a flick of his wrist, Kasreyn sent Covenant towards her.

Fighting her manacles, she tried to fend him away. But he forced himself past her hands, thrust forward to plant a cold dead kiss on her groaning mouth. Then he retreated a step. With his halfhand, he struck her a blow that made her whole face burn.

The Kemper recalled him. He obeyed, as lifeless as a marionette. Kasreyn was still gazing at Linden. Malice bared his old teeth. In a voice of hunger, he said, 'Do you see that my command upon him is complete?'

She nodded. She could not help herself. Soon Kasreyn would be able to instruct her as easily as he used Covenant.

'Then witness.' The Kemper made complex gestures; and Covenant raised his hands, turned his fingers inward like claws. They dug into the flesh around his eyes.

713

'If you do not satisfy me' – Kasreyn's voice jumped avidly – 'I will command him to blind himself.'

That was enough. She could not bear any more. Long quivers of fury ran through all her muscles. She was ready now.

Before she could acquiesce, a prodigious effort tore a howl from Honninscrave's chest. With impossible strength, he ripped the chain binding his left arm from its bracket; and the chain cracked outward like a flail. Driven by all the force of his immense exertion, it struck Kasreyn in the throat.

The blow pitched the Kemper backward. He fell heavily on the steps, tumbled to the floor. There he lay still. So much iron and strength must have shattered every bone in his neck. Linden's vision leaped towards him, saw that he was dead. The fact stunned her. For an instant, she hardly realized that he was not bleeding.

The First let out a savage cry. 'Stone and Sea, Honninscrave! Bravely done!'

But a moment later Kasreyn twitched. His limbs shifted. Slowly, stiffly, he climbed to his hands and knees, then to his feet. An instant ago, he had had no pulse: now his heart beat with renewed vigour. Strength flowed back into him. He turned to face the company. He was grinning like a promise of murder.

Linden gaped at him, horrified. The First swore weakly.

The infant on his back was smiling sweetly in its sleep.

He looked at Honninscrave. The Giant sagged against the wall in near exhaustion. But his intent glare warned plainly that with one hand free he would soon be free altogether.

'My friend,' the Kemper said tightly, 'your death will be one to surpass your most heinous fears.'

Honninscrave responded with a gasping snarl. But Kasreyn remained beyond reach of the Master's chain.

Slowly, the Kemper shifted his attention away from Honninscrave. Facing Linden, he repeated, 'If you do not satisfy me.' Only the tautness of his voice betrayed that anything had happened to him. 'I will command him to blind himself.'

Covenant had not moved. He still stood with his fingers poised to gouge out his eyes.

Linden cast one last long look at his terrible defencelessness. Then she let herself sag. How could she fight a man who was able to rise from the dead? 'You'll have to take that band off his neck. It blocks me.'

Cail surged against his chains. 'Chosen!' the First cried in protest. Pitchwife gaped dismay at her.

Linden ignored them. She was watching Kasreyn. Grinning fiercely, he approached Covenant. With one hand, he touched the yellow band. It came away in his grasp.

At once, Covenant slumped back into his familiar emptiness. His eyes were void. For no reason, he said, 'Don't touch me.'

Before Linden could reach out to him in yearning or rage, try to keep her promises, the floor near Vain's feet began to swirl and melt. With surprising celerity, Findail flowed out of the granite into human form.

Immediately, he confronted Linden. 'Are you a fool?' The habitual misery of his features shouted at her. 'This is ruin!' She had never heard such anguish from any *Elohim*. 'Do you not comprehend that the Earth is at peril? Therefore did I urge you to your ship while the way was open, that these straits might be evaded. Sun-Sage, hear me!' When she did not respond, his apprehension mounted. 'I am the Appointed. The doom of the Earth is upon my head. I beg of you – do not do this thing!'

But she was not listening to him. Kasreyn stood grinning behind Covenant as if he knew he had nothing to fear from Findail. His hand held the golden band, the threat which compelled her. Yet she ignored the Kemper also. She paid no heed to the consternation of her companions. She had been preparing herself for this since the moment when the First had said, *Why do we yet live?* She had striven for it with every fibre of her will, fought for this chance to create her own answer. The removal of that neck-band. The opportunity to make good on at least one promise.

All of her was focused on Covenant. While her companions sought to distract her, dissuade her, she opened her senses to him. In a rush like an outpouring of ecstasy or loss, rage or grief, she surrendered herself to his emptiness.

Now she took no account of the passion with which she entered him. And she offered no resistance as she was swept into the long gulf. She saw that her former failures had been caused by her attempts to bend him to her own will, her own use; but now she wanted nothing for herself, withheld nothing. Abandoning herself entirely, she fell like a dying star into the blankness behind which the *Elohim* had hidden his soul.

Yet she did not forget Kasreyn. He was watching avidly, poised for the reawakening of Covenant's will. At that moment, Covenant would be absolutely vulnerable; for surely he would not regain full possession of his consciousness and his power instantly, and until he did he would have no defence against the Kemper's *geas*. Linden felt no mercy towards Kasreyn, contained nothing at all which might have resembled mercy towards him. As she fell and fell like death into Covenant's emptiness, she shouted voiceless instructions which echoed through the uninhabitation of his mind.

Now no visions came out of his depths to appal her. She had surrendered so completely that nothing remained to cause her dismay. Instead, she felt the layers of her independent self being stripped away. Severity and training and medical school were gone,

715

leaving her fifteen and loss-ridden, unable at that time to conceive of any answer to her mother's death. Grief and guilt and her mother were gone, so that she seemed to contain nothing except the cold unexpungeable horror and accusation of her father's suicide. Then even suicide was gone, and she stood under a clean sun in fields and flowers, full of a child's capacity for happiness, joy, love. She could have fallen that way forever.

The sunlight spread its wings about her, and the wind ruffled her hair like a hand of affection. She shouted in pleasure. And her shout was answered. A boy came towards her across the fields. He was older than she – he seemed much older, though he was still only a boy, and the Covenant he would become was nothing more than an implication in the lines of his face, the fire of his eyes. He approached her with a shy half-smile. His hands were open and whole and accessible. Caught in a whirl of instinctive exaltation, she ran towards him with her arms wide, yearning for the embrace which would transform her.

But when she touched him, the gap was bridged, and his emptiness flooded into her. At once, she could see everything, hear everything. All her senses functioned normally. Her companions had fallen silent: they were staring at her in despair. Kasreyn stood near Covenant with his ocular held ready, his hands trembling as if they could no longer suppress their caducity. But behind what she saw and heard, she wailed like a foretaste of her coming life. She was a child in a field of flowers, and the older boy she adored had left her. The love had gone out of the sunlight, leaving the day bereft as if all joy were dead.

Yet she saw him – saw the boy in the man, Thomas Covenant – as life and will spread back into his limbs. She saw him take hold of himself, lift his head. All her senses functioned normally. She could do nothing but wail as he turned towards Kasreyn, exposed himself to the Kemper's *geas*. He was still too far away from himself to make any defence.

But before the Kemper was able to use his ocular, the instructions she had left in Covenant reached him. He looked straight at Kasreyn and obeyed her.

Distinctly, he articulated one clear word:

'Nom.'

PART III

Loss

19

THE THAUMATURGE

That name seemed to stun the air, appalling the very stone of the Sandhold.

From a great and lonely distance, Covenant watched Kasreyn of the Gyre recoil. The Kemper dropped his eyepiece. Dismay and rage crumpled his old face. But he could not call back the word Covenant had spoken. An anguish of indecision gripped him for a moment, paralysing him. Then the old fear rose up in him, and he fled to preserve his life.

He flung the iron door shut behind him, thrust the bolts into place. But those metallic sounds meant nothing to Covenant. He was perfectly aware of his situation. All his senses had been functioning normally: he recognized his peril, understood the plight of his companions, knew what had to be done. Yet he was scarcely sentient. The gap between action and impact, perception and consequence, was slow to close. Consciousness welled up in him from the contact which Linden had forged; but the distance was great and could not be filled instantly.

At first, the recovery seemed swift. The bonds connecting him to his adolescence, then his young manhood, healed themselves in a surge of memory which felt like fire – annealment and cautery in one. And that fire rapidly became the numinous intensity with which he had given himself to writing and marriage. But then his progress slowed. With Joan on Haven Farm, before the publication of his novel and the birth of their son, he had felt that his luminescence was the most profound energy of life. But it had proven itself hollow at the core. His bestseller had been little more than an inane piece of self-congratulation. And his marriage had been destroyed by the blameless crime of leprosy.

After that, the things he recollected made him writhe.

His violent and involuntary isolation, his imposed self-loathing, had driven him deep into the special madness of lepers. He had stumbled into the Land as if it were the final summation and crisis of his life. Almost at once, he had raped the first person who befriended him. He had tormented and dismayed people who helped him. Unwittingly, he had walked the path Lord Foul marked out for him – had not turned aside from that doom until the consequences of his own actions came back to appal him. And then he might have achieved ruin instead of restitution, had he not been supported at every turn by people whose comprehension of love and valour far surpassed his own. Even now, years later, his heart cried out against the harm he had done to the Land, to the people of the Land — against the paucity with which he had finally served them.

His voice echoed in the dank constriction of the cell. His companions strained towards him as he knelt like abjection on the cold stone. But he had no attention to spare for them.

And he was not abject. He was wounded, yes; guilty beyond question; crowded with remorse. But his leprosy had given him strength as well as weakness. In the thronehall of Foul's Creche, confronting the Despiser and the Illearth Stone, he had found the eye of his paradox. Balanced between the contradictions of self-abhorrence and affirmation, of Unbelief and love — acknowledging and refusing the truth of the Despiser — he had come into his power. He felt it within him now, poised like the moment of clarity which lay at the heart of every vertigo. As the gap closed he resumed himself.

He tried to blink his eyes free of tears. Once again, Linden had saved him. The only woman he had met in more than eleven years who was not afraid of his illness. For his sake, she had insisted time after time on committing herself to risks, situations, demands she could neither measure nor control. The stone under his hands and knees felt unsteady; but he meant to climb to his feet. He owed her that. He could not imagine the price she must have paid to restore him.

When he tried to stand, the whole cell lurched. The air was full of distant boomings like the destruction of granite. A fine powder sifted through the torchlight, hinting at cracks in the ceiling. Again, the floor shifted. The cell door rang with stress.

A voice said flatly, 'The Sandgorgon comes.' Covenant recognized Brinn's characteristic dispassion.

'Thomas Covenant.' No amount of iron self-command could conceal the First's dismay. 'Giantfriend! Has the Chosen slain you? Has she slain us all? The Sandgorgon comes!'

He was unable to answer her with words. Words had not come back to him yet. Instead, he replied by planting his feet widely, lifting himself erect against the visceral trembling of the stone. Then he turned to face the door.

His ring hung inert on his halfhand. The venom which triggered his wild magic had been quiescent for long days; and he was too recently returned to himself. He could not take hold of his power. Yet he was ready. Linden had provided for this necessity by the same stroke with which she had driven Kasreyn away.

Findail sprang to Covenant's side. The *Elohim*'s distress was as loud as a yell, though he did not shout. 'Do not do this.' Urgency

720

etched his words across the trembling. 'Will you destroy the Earth?' His limbs strained with suppressed need. 'The Sun-Sage lusts for death. Be not such a fool. Give the ring to me.'

At that, the first embers of Covenant's old rage warmed towards fire.

The distant boomings went on as if parts of the Sandhold had begun to collapse; but the peril was much closer. He heard heavy feet slapping the length of the outer corridor at a run.

Instinctively, he flexed his knees for balance and battle.

The feet reached the door, paused.

Like a groan through his teeth, Pitchwife said, 'Gossamer Glowlimn, I love you.'

Then the cell door crumpled like a sheet of parchment as Nom hammered down and through it with two stumped arms as mighty as battering rams.

While metallic screaming echoed in the dungeon, the Sandgorgon stood hunched under the architrave. From the elevation of the doorway, the beast appeared puissant enough to tear the entire Sandhold stone from stone. Its head had no face, no features, betrayed nothing of its feral passion. Yet its attention was centred remorselessly on Covenant.

Leaping like a roar down into the chamber, the beast charged as if it meant to drive him through the back wall.

No mortal flesh and bone could have withstood that onslaught. But the Despiser's venom had only been rendered quiescent by the *Elohim*. It had not been purged or weakened. And the Sandgorgon itself was a creature of power.

In the instant before Nom struck, Thomas Covenant became an eruption of white flame.

Wild magic; keystone of the Arch of Time; power that was not limited or subdued by any Law except the inherent strictures of its wielder. High Lord Mhoram had said like a prophecy of fire, *You are the white gold*, and Covenant fulfilled those words. Incandescence came upon him. Argent burst from him as if from the heart of a silver furnace.

At his side, Findail cried in protest, '*No!*'

The Sandgorgon crashed into Covenant. Impact and momentum knocked him against the wall. But he hardly felt the attack. He was preserved from pain or damage by white fire, as if that flame had become the outward manifestation of his leprosy, numbing him to the limitations of his mortality. A man with living nerves might have felt the power too acutely to let it mount so high: Covenant had no such restraint. The venom was avid in him. The fang-scars on his forearm shone like the eyes of the Despiser. Almost without thought or volition, he buffered himself against Nom's assault.

The Sandgorgon staggered backward.

Like upright magma, he flowed after it. Nom dealt out blows that would have pulverized monoliths. Native savagery mutiplied by centuries of bitter imprisonment hammered at Covenant. But he responded with blasts like the fury of a bayamo. Chunks of granite fell from the ceiling and burst into dust. Cracks webbed the floor. The architrave of the door collapsed, leaving a gap like a wound to the outer corridor. Findail's protests sounded like the wailing of rocks.

Covenant continued to advance. The beast refused to retreat farther. He and Nom wrapped arms around each other and embraced like brothers of the same doom.

The Sandgorgon's strength was tremendous. It should have been able to crush him like a bundle of rotten twigs. But he was an avatar of flame, and every flare lifted him higher into the ecstasy of venom and rage. He had already become so bright that his companions were blinded. Argence melted and evaporated falling stone, enlarging the dungeon with every hot beat of his heart. He had been so helpless! Now he was savage with the desire to strike back. This Sandgorgon had slain Hergrom, crippled Ceer. And Kasreyn had set that harm in motion. Kasreyn! He had tortured Covenant when Covenant had been utterly unable to defend himself; and only Hergrom's intervention had saved him from death – or from a possession which would have been worse than death. Fury keened in him; his outrage burned like the wrath of the sun.

But Nom was not to blame. The beast was cunning, hungry for violence; but it lived and acted only at the whim of Kasreyn's power. Kasreyn, and again Kasreyn. Images of atrocity whirled through Covenant. Passion made him as unanswerable as a volcano.

He felt Nom weakening in his arms. Instinctively, he lessened his own force. The poison in him was newly awakened, and he could still restrain it. He did not want to kill.

At once, the Sandgorgon put out a new surge of strength that almost tore him in half.

But Covenant was too far gone in power to fail. With wild magic, he gripped the beast, bound it in fetters of flame and will. It struggled titanically, but without success. Clenching it, he extricated himself from its arms and stepped back.

For a long moment, Nom writhed, pouring all the ancient ferocity of its nature into an effort for freedom. But it could not break him.

Slowly, it appeared to understand that it had finally met a man able to destroy it. It stopped fighting. Its arms sank to its side. Long quiverings ran through its muscles like anticipations of death.

By degrees, Covenant relaxed his power, though he kept a handful of fire blazing from his ring. Soon the beast stood free of flame. Pitchwife began to chuckle like a man who had been brought back from the edge of hysteria. Findail gazed at Covenant as if he were uncertain of what he was seeing. But Covenant had no time yet for anything except the Sandgorgon. With tentative movements, Nom tested its release. Surprise aggravated its quivering. Its head jerked from side to side, implying disbelief. Carefully, as if it feared what it was doing, it raised one arm to aim a blow at Covenant's head.

Covenant clenched his fist, sending a spew of fire into the cavern he had created above him. But he did not strike. Instead, he fought his rusty voice into use.

'If you don't kill me, you won't have to go back to the Doom.'

Nom froze as if it understood him. Trembling in every muscle, it lowered its arm.

A moment later, the beast surprised him by sinking to the floor. Its quivering grew stronger, then began to subside. Deliberately, the Sandgorgon touched its forehead to the stone near Covenant's feet like an offer of service.

Before Covenant could react, Nom rose erect again. Its blank face revealed nothing. Turning with animal dignity, it climbed up to the broken doorway, picked its way without hesitation through the rubble of the architrave, and disappeared down the passage.

In the distance, the sounds of collapsing stone had receded; but at intervals an occasional dull thud reached the cell, as if a section of wall or ceiling had fallen. Nom must have done serious damage on the way inward.

Abruptly, Covenant became aware of the brightness of his fire. It pained his sight as if his orbs had relapsed into normalcy. He reduced his power until it was only a small flame on his ring. But he did not release it entirely. All of *Bhrathairealm* lay between the company and Starfare's Gem; and he did not mean to remain a prisoner any longer. Memories of Revelstone came back to him – helplessness and venom in revulsion. In the aftermath of the soothtell, he had killed twenty-one members of the na-Mhoram's Clave. The fang-marks on his forearm continued to gleam at him. He became suddenly urgent as he turned to look at his companions.

Vain stood nearby: the iconography of the ur-viles in human form. His lips wore a black grin of relish. But Covenant had no time to spend on the Demondim-spawn. How quickly would Kasreyn be able to rally the defences of the Sandhold? He thrust past Vain towards his friends.

The First murmured his name in a limping voice. She appeared hardly able to support the weight of her reprieve. At her side, Pitchwife shed tears unabashedly and faded in and out of laughter. The severe bruise at his temple seemed to damage his emotional balance. Honninscrave stood with a broken chain dangling from his free arm and blood dripping from his wrists; but his face was clenched around the new hope Covenant had given him.

From the other walls, *Haruchai* eyes reflected the white gold like pride. They looked as extravagant as the Vow which had bound the Bloodguard to the Lords beyond death and sleep. Even Ceer's orbs shone, though behind the reflections lay a pain so acute that even Covenant's superficial sight could read it. Red fluid oozed from the bandages around his knee.

Seadreamer seemed unaware of Covenant. The mute Giant's gaze was glazed and inward. His manacled hands strained towards his head as if he ached to cover his face. But at least he showed no physical hurt.

Then Covenant saw Linden.

She staggered him. She hung from her rigid fetters as if both her arms had been broken. Her head had slumped forward; her wheaten hair veiled her face and chest. Covenant could not tell if she were breathing, if he had hurt or killed her in his struggle with Nom.

Findail had been murmuring almost continuously. 'Praise the Würd that he has desisted.' The words came in snatches of apprehension. 'Yet the outcome of the Earth lies in the hands of a madman. She has opened the path of ruin. Was I not Appointed to prevent her? My life is now forfeit. It is insufferable.'

Covenant feared to approach her, dreaded to see that she had been wounded or worse. He flung his panic at Findail. His fists knotted the *Elohim*'s creamy mantle. His power gathered to blare through Findail's lean flesh.

'What happened to her?'

For an instant, Findail's yellow eyes seemed to consider the wisdom of simply melting out of Covenant's grasp. But instead he said, 'Withhold your fire, ring-wielder. You do not know the peril. The fate of the Earth is fragile in your ungentle hands.' Covenant sent out a flare of rage. At once, Findail added, 'I will answer.'

Covenant did not release him. Wild magic roiled in him like a nest of snakes. His heart beat on the verge of an outcry.

'She has been silenced,' Findail said carefully, studying Covenant as he spoke, 'as you were silenced at the *Elohimfest*. Entering you, she took the stillness which warded you into herself.' He spoke as if he were trying to make Covenant hear another message, an implied justification for what the *Elohim* had done. But Covenant had no ears for such things. Only the clench of his fists kept him from exploding.

'But for her it will not endure,' Findail went on. 'It is yours, formed for you, and will not hold her. She will return to herself in her own time. Therefore,' he continued more urgently, 'there is no call for this wild magic. You must quell it. Do you not hear me? The Earth rests upon your silence.'

Covenant was no longer listening. He thrust Findail away. Fire flashed from the opening of his hands like an instant of tinder. Turning to Linden, he struck the bonds from her arms, the chains from her ankles, then reached out to catch her. But she did not fall: her body reflexively found its balance as if her most primitive instincts prompted her to avoid the necessity of his embrace. Slowly, her head came up. In the yellow-and-white light of torches and wild magic, he saw that her eyes were empty.

Oh, Linden! He could not stop himself. He put his arms around her, hugged and rocked her as if she were a child. He had been like this himself. And she had done it to herself for him. His embrace spread a penumbra of argence over her. The flow of his power covered her as if he would never be able to let her go. He did not know whether to weep because she was alive or to cry out because she was so destitute. She had done it to herself. For him.

Brinn spoke firmly, without fear or any other inflection. 'Ur-Lord, this Kemper will not wish to permit our departure. We must hasten.'

'Aye, Giantfriend,' said the First. Every passing moment restored more of her combative steadiness. 'Starfare's Gem remains at risk, and we are far from it. I doubt neither Sevinhand's resource nor his valiance, but I am eager to quit this place and set my feet once again upon the *dromond*.'

Those were words that Covenant understood – not vague threats such as Findail uttered, but a concrete call to action. The *Elohim* had said, The outcome of the Earth lies in the hands of a madman. He had asked for the ring. And Covenant had killed so many people, despite his own revulsion for bloodshed. He distrusted all power. Yet the wild magic ran through him like a pulse of rapture, avid for use, and consuming. The First's urging restored to him the importance of his quest, the need for survival and flight.

She brought back images of Kasreyn, who had forced Linden to this extremity.

Carefully, he released Linden, stepped back from her. For a long moment, he studied her, fixing her blank and desirable face in his mind like a focus for all his emotions. Then he turned to his companions.

With a mental gesture, he struck the bonds from their wrists and ankles, beginning with Seadreamer and then Ceer so that the mute Giant could tend the injured *Haruchai*. Ceer's hurt gave him a renewed pang which made flame spill from his arms as if he were nothing more than firewood for the wild magic. More than once, he had healed himself, preserved himself from harm. Yet his numbness rendered him incapable of doing the same for his friends. He had to exert a fierce restraint to hold his frustration back from another explosion.

In a moment, the rest of the company was free. Pitchwife was uncertain on his feet, still suffering the effects of the blow he had received. But Brinn moved forward as if he were prepared to attempt anything in Covenant's service. Cail took charge of Linden. The First drew her new longsword, gripped it in both fists; and her eyes were as keen as the edges of the iron. Honninscrave flexed the chain he had broken, testing its usefulness as a weapon.

They spent a short moment savouring the taste of their release. Then the First sprang up the stairs out of the cell, and the company followed her.

The outer corridor disappeared around corners to left and right; but the First immediately chose the direction the departing Sandgorgon had taken. Covenant went down that passage behind her with Brinn and Honninscrave beside him and his other companions at his back. The Giants had to stoop because the corridor was too low-ceilinged for them. But beyond the first corner was a larger hallway marked by many cell doors. The *hustin* that had guarded the place were dead now, lying broken where Nom had left them. Covenant did not take the time to look into the cells; but he snapped all the door-bolts as he passed.

That hall gave into a warren of passages. The First was forced to halt, uncertain of her way. A moment passed before Brinn spotted a stair ascending from the end of one corridor. At once, the company started in that direction.

Ahead of them, a slim woman came down the stairs, began running towards them. When she saw them, she stumbled to a stop in surprise, then hurried forward again.

She was hardly recognizable as the Lady Alif. Her robe had been torn and blackened. Her hair hung about her in straggles; her scalp was mottled with sore bare patches. Four long red weals disfigured her right cheek.

Facing the First and Covenant, she panted, 'The Sandgorgon — How is it that you — ?' But an instant later, she registered Covenant's fire, the alert heat in his eyes. She sagged momentarily. 'Ah, I feared for you. You were my hope, and when the Sandgorgon — I came to look upon you, thinking to see my own death.' Her features winced around her wounds. But her thoughts came together quickly, and she cried out, 'You must flee! Kasreyn will levy all the might of the Sandhold against you.'

The First shot a glance at Covenant; but he was not Linden, and could not tell whether to trust this woman. Memories of the Lady filled him with unease. Would she be here now if he had been able to succumb to her?

Sternly, the First said, 'Lady, you have been harmed.'

She raised one hand to her cheek — a gesture of distress. She had been one of the Favoured; her position had depended on her beauty. But a moment later she dropped her hand, drew her dignity about her, and met the First's scrutiny squarely.

'The Lady Benj is not gentle in triumph. As she is the *gaddhi's* Favoured, I was not permitted to make defence.'

At that, the First gave a nod like a promise of violence. 'Will you guide us from this place?'

The Lady did not hesitate. 'Yes. There is no life for me here.'

The First started towards the stairs: the battered woman stopped her. 'That way leads to the First Circinate. From thence there is no path outward but that which lies through the gates – the strength of the Sandhold. I will show another way.'

Covenant approved. But he had other plans. His form shed flickers of power at every heartbeat. 'Tell me where you're going.'

Rapidly, she replied, 'The Sandgorgon has made a great breach in the Sandhold. Following the beast's path, we will gain the open sand within the Sandwall. Then the surest path to the Harbour lies atop the Sandwall itself. It will be warded, but mayhap the Kemper's mind will be bent otherwhere – towards the gates.'

'And we will be less easily assailed upon the wall,' said the First grimly, 'than within the gates, or in the streets of *Bhrathairain*. It is good. Let us go.'

But Covenant was already saying, 'All right. I'll find you on the wall. Somewhere. If I don't show up before then, wait for me at the Spikes.'

The First swung towards him, burned a stare at him. 'Where do you go?'

He was acute with venom and power. 'It won't do us any good to fight our way through the Guards. Kasreyn is the real danger. He can probably sink the ship without setting foot outside Kemper's Pitch.' Memories swirled in him – flaring recollections of the way he had once faced Foamfollower, Triock, and Lena after the defence of Mithil Stonedown and had made promises. Promises he had kept. 'I'm going to bring this bloody rock down around his ears.'

In those days, he had had little or no understanding of wild magic. He had made promises because he lacked any other name for his passion. But now Linden was silenced, had gone blank and blind for his sake; and he was limned in white fire. When the First gave him a nod, he left the company, went at a run towards the stairs.

Brinn was instantly at his side. Covenant cast a glance at the *Haruchai*. They would be two lone men against the entire Sandhold. But they would be enough. At one time, he and Brinn had faced all Revelstone alone – and had prevailed.

But as he started up the stairs, a flash of creamy white snagged his attention, and he saw Findail running after him.

He hesitated on the steps. The *Elohim* ran as easily as Vain. When he reached Covenant, Findail said intently, 'Do not do this. I implore you. Are you deaf as well as mad?'

For an instant, Covenant wanted to challenge Findail. His palms itched with power; flames skirled up and down his arms. But he held himself back. He might soon have a better chance to obtain the answers he wanted. Swinging away from the *Elohim*, he climbed the stairs as swiftly as the fire in his legs.

The stairs were long; and when they ended, they left him in the maze of halls and passages at the rear of the First Circinate. The place seemed empty. Apparently, the forces of the Sandhold had already been summoned elsewhere. He did not know which way to go. But Brinn was certain. He took the lead; and Covenant followed him at a run.

The breaking of rocks had stopped. The stones no longer trembled. But from a distance came the sound of sirens – raw and prolonged cries like the screaming of gargoyles. They wailed as if they were mustering all *Bhrathairealm* for war.

Chewing the knowledge that no flight from the Sandhold or *Bhrathairain* Harbour could hope to succeed while Kasreyn of the Gyre lived, Covenant increased his pace.

Sooner than he expected, he left the complex backways and poured like a flow of silver into the immense forecourt of the First Circinate, between the broad stairways which matched each other upward.

The forecourt was heavily guarded by *hustin* and soldiers.

A shout sprang at the ceiling. The forces of the Sandhold were ranked near the gates to fend off an attempted escape. They looked vast and dim, for night had fallen and the forecourt was lit only by torches held among the Guards. At the shout, assailants surged forward.

Brinn ignored them. He sped lightly to the nearest stairs, started upward. Covenant followed on the strength of wild magic. Findail moved as if the air about him were his wings.

Answering the shout, a cadre of *hustin* came clattering from the Second Circinate. Scores of Guards must have been waiting there, intending to catch the company in a pincer. Shadows flickered like disconcertion across their bestial faces as they saw the three men rising to meet them instead of fleeing.

Brinn tripped one of them, staggered a second, wrested the spear from a third. Then Covenant swept all the *hustin* from the stair with a sheet of flame and raced on.

Pausing only to hurl that spear at the pursuit, Brinn dashed back into the lead.

The Second Circinate was darker than the First. The squadrons poised there did not betray their presence with torches. But Covenant's power shone like a cynosure, exposing the danger. At every step, he seemed to ascend towards exaltation. Venom and fire conveyed him forward as if he were no longer making his own choices. Since the *hustin* and soldiers were too many for Brinn to attack effectively, Covenant called the *Haruchai* to his side, then raised a conflagration around the two of them and used it like the armour of a battlewain as he continued on his way. His blaze scored a trail across the floor. The attackers could not reach him through it. Spears were thrown at him, but wild magic struck them into splinters.

Outside the Sandhold, the sirens mounted in pitch, began to pulse like the ululation of the damned. Covenant paid no attention to them. Defended by fire, he moved to the next stairs and went up into the Tier of Riches.

The lights of that place had been extinguished; but it was empty of foes. Perhaps the Kemper had not expected his enemies to gain this level; or perhaps he did not wish to risk damage to centuries of accumulated treasure. At the top of the stairs, Covenant paused, gathered his armour of flame into one hot mass and hurled it downward to slow the pursuit. Then again he ran after Brinn, dodging through the galleries with his rage at Kasreyn fixed squarely before him.

Up the wide rich stairway from the Tier they spiralled like a gyre and burst into The Majesty.

Here the lights were undimmed. Huge cruses and vivid candelabra still focused their lumination towards the Auspice as if the dominion of the *gaddhi*'s seat were not a lie. But all the Guards had been withdrawn to serve Kasreyn elsewhere. Nothing interfered with Covenant's advance as he swept forward, borne along by wild magic and sirens. With Findail trailing behind them like an expostulation, Brinn and the Unbeliever moved straight to the hidden door which gave access to Kemper's Pitch, sprang upward towards Kasreyn's private demesne.

Covenant mounted like a blaze into a night sky. The climb was long, should have been arduous; but wild magic inured him to exertion. He breathed air like fire and did not weaken. The sirens cast glaring echoes about his head; and behind that sound he heard *hustin* pounding heavily after them as rapidly as the constriction of the stairway permitted. But he was condor-swift and puissant, outrunning any pursuit. In passion like the leading edge of an apotheosis, he felt he could have entered Sandgorgons Doom itself and been untouched.

Yet under the wild magic and the exultation, his mind remained clear. Kasreyn was a mighty thaumaturge. He had reigned over this region of the Earth for centuries. And if Covenant did not contrive a defence against the pursuing Guards, he would be forced to slay them all. That prospect struck cold through him. When this transport ended, how would he bear the weight of so much bloodshed?

As he entered the large chamber where the Lady Alif had attempted his seduction, he fought down his power, reduced it to a guttering suggestion around his ring. The effort made his head spin like vertigo; but he ground his teeth until the pressure was contained. It laboured in him; he feared he would not be able to hold it for long. Harshly, he called Brinn back from the ironwork ascent to Kasreyn's lucubrium.

The *Haruchai* looked at him with an inflection of surprise. In response, Covenant jerked a nod upward. 'That's my job.' His voice was stretched taut by restraint. Already, the lid he had placed over the pressure seemed to bulge and crack. 'You can't help me there. I won't risk you. And I need you here.' The sounds of pursuit rose clearly through the open doorway. 'Keep those Guards off my back.'

Brinn measured Covenant with a stare, then nodded. The stairway was narrow. Alone, he might be able to hold this chamber against any number of *hustin*. The task appeared to please him, as if it were condign work for an *Haruchai*. He gave the ur-Lord a formal bow. Covenant moved towards the stairs.

Still Findail remained at his back. The *Elohim* was speaking again, adjuring Covenant to withhold. Covenant did not listen to the words; but he used Findail's voice to help him steady himself. In his own fashion, Findail represented a deeper danger than Kasreyn of the Gyre. And Covenant had conceived a way to confront the two of them together.

If he could retain control long enough.

Without the wild magic, he had to ascend on the ordinary strength of his legs. The desert night was chilly; but sweat stood on his brow as if it were being squeezed from his skull by the wailing of the sirens. His restraint affected him like fear. His heart thudded, breathing rasped, as he climbed the final stairs and came face to face with the Kemper.

Kasreyn stood near one wall of the lucubrium, behind a long table. The table held several urns, flasks, retorts, as well as a large iron bowl which steamed faintly. He was in the process of preparing his arts.

A few steps to one side was the chair in which he had once put Covenant to question. But the chair's apparatus had been altered. Now golden circles like enlarged versions of his ocular sprouted from it in all directions on thin stalks like wands.

Covenant braced himself, expecting an immediate attack. Fire heaved at the leash of his will. But the Kemper cast a rheumy glance at him, a look of old disdain, then returned his attention to his bowl. His son slept like a dead thing in the harness on his back. 'So you have mastered a Sandgorgon.' His voice rustled like the folds of his robe. For centuries, he had demonstrated that nothing could harm him. Honninscrave's blow had left no mark. 'That is a mighty deed. It is said among the *Bhrathair* that any man who slays a Sandgorgon will live forever.'

Covenant struggled for control. Venom and power raged to be released. He felt that he was suffocating on his own restraint. The blood in his veins was afire with reasons for this man's death. But standing there now, facing the *gaddhi*'s Kemper, he found he could not self-consciously choose to kill. No reasons were enough. He had already killed too many people.

He answered hoarsely, like a rasp of bereavement, 'I didn't.'

That caught Kasreyn's attention. '*Not?*' Suddenly, he was angry. 'Are you mad? Without death, no power can recompel that beast to its imprisonment. Alone, it may bring down upon us the former darkness. You are mighty, in good sooth,' he snapped. 'A mighty cause of ruin for all *Bhrathairealm.*'

His ire sounded sincere; but a moment later he seemed to forget it. Other concerns preoccupied him. He looked back into his bowl as if he were waiting for something. 'But no matter,' he murmured. 'I will attend to that in my time. And you will not escape me. Already, I have commanded the destruction of your much vaunted Giantship. Its flames brighten *Bhrathairain* Harbour even as you stand thus affronting me.'

Covenant flinched involuntarily. Starfare's Gem in flames! Strands of wild magic slipped their fetters, reached for the Kemper. The effort of calling them back hurt Covenant's chest like a rupture. His skull throbbed with strain as he articulated thickly, 'Kasreyn, I can kill you.' White fire outlined each word. 'You know I can kill you. Stop what you're doing. Stop that attack on the ship. Let my friends go.' Power blurred his sight like the frightful imprecision of nightmare. 'I'll burn every bone in your body to cinders.'

'Will you, forsooth?' The Kemper laughed – a barking sound without humour. His gaze was as raw and pitiless as the sirens. 'You forget that I am Kasreyn of the Gyre. By my arts was Sandgorgons Doom formed and this Sandhold raised, and I hold all *Bhrathairealm* in my hands. You are mighty in your way and possess that which I desire. But you are yet petty and incapable withal, and you offend me.'

He spoke sternly; but still he did not attack. With one hand, he made a slow, unthreatening gesture towards his chair. 'Have you observed my preparation?' His manner was firm. 'Such gold is rare in the Earth. Mayhap it may be found no otherwhere than here. Therefore came I hither, taking the mastery of *Bhrathairealm* upon myself. And therefore also do I strive to extend my sway over other realms, other regions, seeking more gold. With gold I perform my arts.' He watched Covenant steadily. 'With gold I will destroy you.'

As he uttered those words, his hands jumped forward, tipped and hurled his iron bowl.

A black liquid as viscid as blood poured over the table, setting it afire – splashed to the floor, chewed holes in the stone – gusted and spattered towards Covenant.

Acid vitriol as potent as the dark fluid of ur-viles. Instinctively,

Covenant flung up his arms, throwing white flame in all directions. Then, a fraction of a heartbeat later, he rallied. Focusing his power, he swept the black liquid away.

During that splinter of time, the Kemper moved. As Covenant's eyes cleared, Kasreyn no longer stood behind his table. He was sitting in his chair, surrounded by small golden hoops.

Covenant could not hold back. The wild magic required utterance. Too swiftly for restraint or consideration, he flung silver-white at the Kemper – a blast feral enough to incinerate any mortal flesh.

He barely heard Findail's anguished shout: '*No!*'

But his fire did not reach Kasreyn. It was sucked into the many circles around the chair. Then it recoiled, crashing throughout the lucubrium with doubled, tripled ferocity.

Tables shattered; shelves burst from the walls; shards scored the air with shrill pain. A rampage of debris and fire assailed Covenant from every side at once. Only his reflexive shout of wild magic saved him.

The concussion knocked him to the floor. The stone seemed to quiver under him like wounded flesh. Echoes of argent reeled across his vision.

The echoes did not dissipate. Kasreyn had taken hold of Covenant's defensive conflagration. It burned wildly back and forth within the gold circles, mounting flare after flare. Its increase scalded the air.

Findail crouched in front of Covenant. 'Withhold, you fool!' His fists pounded at Covenant's shoulders. 'Do you not hear me? You will havoc the Earth! You must withhold!'

Caught in a dazzling confusion of flares and pressure, Covenant could hardly think. But a hard grim part of him remained clear, wrestled for choice. He panted, 'I've got to stop him. If I don't he'll destroy the quest.' Kill Linden. The Giants. The *Haruchai*. 'There won't be anybody left to defend the Earth.'

'Madman!' Findail retorted. 'It is you who imperil the Earth, *you*! Are you blind to the purpose of the Despiser's venom?'

At that, Covenant reeled; but he did not break. Holding himself in a grip of ire and fear, he demanded, 'Then you stop him!'

The Appointed flinched. 'I am *Elohim*. The *Elohim* do not take life.'

'One or the other.' Flame rose in Covenant's voice. 'Stop him. Or answer my questions. All of them. Why you're here. What you're afraid of. Why you want me to hold back.' Findail did not move. Kasreyn's power mounted towards cataclysm moment by moment. '*Make up your mind.*'

The *Elohim* drew a breath like a sob. For an instant, his yellow eyes were damp with pain.

Then his form frayed, melted. He lifted into the air in the shape of a bird.

Fire coruscated around him. He flitted scatheless through it, a swift darting of Earthpower. Elongating and flattening himself as he flew, he swooped like a manta towards the Kemper.

Before Kasreyn could react, Findail flashed past his face, pounced on to his son.

At once, the *Elohim* became a hood over the infant's head. He sealed himself under the small chin, behind the downy-haired skull, clung there like a second skin.

Suffocating the child.

A scream ripped from Kasreyn's chest. He sprang upright, staggered out of the protection of his chair. His hands groped behind him, clawed at Findail; but he could not rake the *Elohim* loose. His limbs went rigid. Asphyxiation mottled his face with splotches of madness and terror.

Again he screamed – a cry of horror from the roots of his being:

'*My life!*'

The shriek seemed to break his soul. He toppled to the floor like a shattered tower.

Slowly, the theurgy blazing about his chair began to fade.

Covenant was on his feet as if he had intended to rush to Kasreyn's aid. Pressure for power and abomination of death shone from him like the onset of an involuntary ecstasy.

Lifting back into human shape, Findail stepped away from the Kemper's body. His visage was engraved with grief. Softly, he said, 'That which he bore was no son of his flesh. It was of the *croyel* – beings of hunger and sustenance which demnify the dark places of the Earth. Those who bargain thus for life or might with the *croyel* are damned beyond redemption.' His voice sounded like mist and tears. 'Ring-wielder, are you content?'

Covenant could not respond. He hung on the verge of eruption, had no choice but to flee the damage he was about to do. Fumbling for mastery, he went to the stairs. They seemed interminable. Yet somehow he withheld himself – a nerve-tearing effort he made more for Brinn's sake than his own. So that Brinn would not die in the outcome.

In the chamber below, he found the *Haruchai*. Brinn had choked the stair so effectively with fallen *hustin* that he had nothing to do except wait until the Guards farther down were able to clear their way.

He looked a question at Covenant; but Covenant had no answer for him either. Trembling in every muscle, the Unbeliever unreined only enough wild magic to open the long dead gyre of the stairway. Then he went downward with Brinn and Findail behind him.

Before he reached The Majesty, he lost control. Flame tore him out of himself. He became a blaze of destruction. The stairs lurched. Cracks leaped through the stone.

Far above him, the top of Kemper's Pitch began to crumble.

20

FIRE IN *BHRATHAIREALM*

Linden Avery could see and hear normally. Cail was steering her along a subterranean passage lit only at distant intervals by torches. The First and Honninscrave were ahead of her, following a woman who appeared to be the Lady Alif. Pitchwife and Seadreamer were nearby. Seadreamer cradled Ceer across his massive forearms. Vain moved like a shadow at the rear of the company. But Covenant was gone. Brinn and Findail were nowhere to be seen. Linden observed these facts as clearly as the light permitted. In a sense, she understood them. Her upper arms throbbed, especially where Cail had bruised her.

But the reportage of her senses conveyed so little meaning that it might have been in an alien language. Covenant was gone. Behind what she saw and heard, behind her physical sensations, she was a child who had just lost a new friend; and nothing around her offered any solace for her grief.

Because Cail drew her forward by the sore part of her arm, she went with him. But she was preoccupied with images like anticipations of bereavement, and that pain did not touch her.

Later, the company arrived at a scene of destruction. A long chamber which had apparently been a Guard-room lay under the foundations of a section of the Sandhold's outer wall. Now both were a jumbled slope of fallen wreckage leading towards the open night. Covenant was gone. The corpses of *hustin* sprawled or protruded at spots from the chaos the Sandgorgon had made. Stark against the stars, the rim of the Sandwall was visible through the breach.

Without hesitation, the Lady Alif tried to climb the slope. But the ragged chunks of rock were too large for her. The First lifted the Lady on to her own strong back. Then she bounded upward.

Honninscrave did the same with Linden. One of his huge hands locked her wrists together under his beard. His shoulders hurt her arms. She began remembering her father.

In spite of his deformed chest and damaged head, Pitchwife ascended without difficulty. He was a Giant, familiar with stone and climbing. Cail's strength and balance compensated for his human stature. Vain was capable of anything. Only Seadreamer had trouble: holding Ceer, he did not have the assistance of his hands. But Pitchwife helped him. As rapidly as possible, the company went up into the night.

When they reached the open sand within the Sandwall, the First set the Lady Alif down. Honninscrave lowered Linden to the ground. Now she saw that the hole in the First Circinate was matched by a breach in the Sandwall. Given time and freedom, the Sandgorgon could almost certainly have brought down the entire Sandhold. But apparently the thoughts of those beasts did not run to sustained destruction. Perhaps they had no thought of destruction at all, but simply broke down obstacles which stood between them and their obscure desires.

In the distance rose the wail of sirens. Raw and shrill, like the crying of stone, the Sandhold's outrage cut through the moonlight and the dark.

But other cries were in Linden's ears – her own screams as she begged at her dying father. Night had flooded her soul then, though her father had died in daylight. He had sat in a half-broken rocker in the attic with blood pouring like despair from his gashed wrists. She could smell the sweet reek of blood, feel her former nausea more explicitly than Cail's grasp on her arm. Her father had thrown the key out of the window, enforcing his self-pity on her, denying her the power to save him. Darkness had risen at her out of the floorboards and the walls, out of his mouth – his mouth stretched black in fathomless abjection and triumph, the insatiable hunger for darkness. He had spattered blood like Hergrom's on her. The attic which she had thought of as her personal haven had become horrible.

The Lady Alif led the company westward, hastening towards the nearest stairs to the top of the Sandwall. She was too badly battered to sustain any pace faster than a quick walk. The First strode beside her. The chain Honninscrave carried clanked faintly over the scrunch and shuffle of feet. Repeatedly, he surged ahead in his urgency for his ship. Cail drew Linden forward. Her steps were awkward on the sand, but the emptiness which had come upon her for Covenant made her helpless to resist. She was helpless to save her father. She had tried – tried everything her young mind had been able to conceive. In her last desperation, she had told him that she would not love him if he died. He had replied, *You never loved me anyway.* Then he had bled to death as if to demonstrate that his words were true: a lesson of darkness which had paralysed her body for days afterward, while it sank down into the roots of her being.

Darkness. The light of a moon only one day from its full and already descending towards the west. Sirens. And then, in the shadow of the Sandwall, stairs.

They were wide. The questers ascended them in a scant cordon around Linden and Cail, Seadreamer and Ceer. Linden's exhausted flesh was not equal to the climb, this pace. But her past-locked mind made no effort to hang back against Cail's insistence. Covenant was gone. Of all her companions, only Pitchwife seemed vulnerable to fatigue. The distortion of his chest cramped his lungs, exacerbated his movements, so that his respiration wheezed and his strides appeared to stagger. He might have been the only mortal friend Linden had.

As she was drawn back into the moonlight, she stumbled involuntarily. Cail snatched her upright again like the shout which jerked across the Sandwall, piercing the ululation of the sirens anharmonically. 'We are seen!' the Lady Alif panted. 'Your pardon. I fear I have led you amiss.' Though she was struggling for breath, she bore herself bravely. 'From the moment when I conceived the desire to exact from Kasreyn the price of my humiliation, all my choices have gone awry. We are discovered too soon.'

'Covenant Giantfriend will obtain the payment you desire,' growled the First. She was staring towards the south. In answer to the shout, squat dark shapes had begun to appear there as *hustin* emerged from the inner passages of the Sandwall. 'For the rest, have no fear.' Her fists anchored her courage to her new sword. 'We are free in the night, with our way plain before us. We will live or die as we may, and no blame to you.'

Like a glare of iron in the moonlight, she started towards the outer arm of the wall which led to *Bhrathairain* and the Harbour. The rest of the company followed as if she had become as certain as the long surge of the Sea.

Dozens and then scores of the Guards came in pursuit, brandishing spears. They looked black and fatal against the pale stone. But they had been formed for strength rather than swiftness; and the company was able to remain ahead of them. For a short time, the child in Linden recovered a semblance of normalcy as her life settled into new patterns after her father's death. Masked by the resilience of youth, she had lived as if the very bones of her personality had not been bent and reshaped by what had happened. Yet her mother's continually reiterated self-pity and blame had eroded her as rocks were worn away by water. Pretending that she did not care, she had laid the foundation for all her later pretences, all her denials. Even her commitment to the medical burden of life and death had taken the form of denial rather than affirmation.

Covenant was gone. Her senses functioned normally, but she did not know she was returning to herself slowly from the void where she had been left and lost by her efforts to save him. The company was nearing the arm of the Sandwall which formed the western courtyard between *Bhrathairain* and the Sandhold. And from that direction came pouring *hustin* like a flood along the top of the wall. Already the junction of the inner and outer walls was blocked.

For a few strides, the First continued forward, narrowing the gap between her and the path she wished to take towards *Bhrathairain* Harbour. Then she halted so that the company would have a moment in which to prepare for battle.

The Guards began closing rapidly. They made no sound except the clatter of their feet. They were creations of the Kemper's will, lacking even the capacity for independent blood-lust or triumph. The Sandwall stood level with the rim of the First Circinate; but the Sandhold towered towards the stars for four more levels, dominating all that side of the firmament. There, Kemper's Pitch affronted the heavens. It seemed high beyond comprehension and as ineluctable as any doom. No flight could escape the purview of that eminence. Kasreyn's lust for eternity was written where any eye might read it.

Through the stone of the Pitch, Linden's senses caught hints of white fire. They affected her like glimpses of her mother's cancer. The sirens cried out like her mother's terror.

In a flat voice, Ceer demanded to be set down so that he would not hamper Seadreamer in the coming fight. At a nod from the First, Seadreamer lowered the injured *Haruchai* gently on his good leg.

Around Linden, the Lady Alif, and Ceer, the four Giants and Cail placed themselves in a protective formation, at the points of a pentacle of combat.

Linden saw what they were doing. But she understood only that they had turned their backs. The doctors had turned their backs on her mother. Not on her mother's melanoma, which they fought with unremitting tenacity, careless of the battleground on which their struggle was waged. But to the older woman's abjection they had been deaf and unheeding, as if they were unable to grasp the fact that she did not fear death as much as pain or slow suffocation. Her lungs were filling with a fluid which no postural drainage could relieve. She was afraid not of dying but of what dying cost, just as she had always been afraid of the cost of life.

And there had been no one to listen to her except Linden herself. A girl of fifteen, with a black hunger where her soul should have been. *Please, God, let me die.* She had been alone in her mother's room day after day because there had been no one else. Even the nurses had stopped coming, except as required by the doctor's orders. The Lady Alif placed her back to Linden's. Linden could not see any faces except Ceer's and Vain's. The Demondim-spawn was as blank as death. Sweat left trails of discounted pain down the sides of Ceer's visage. Covenant was gone. In the moonlight the *hustin* lost their human aspect, became beasts.

The only sounds were the haste of heavy feet, the raw threat of the sirens, the First's defiance. Then the massed Guards struck at both sides of the company at once.

Their movements were sluggish and vague. Kasreyn's mind was elsewhere, and they lacked precise instructions. Perhaps they could have destroyed the company immediately if they had simply stood back and thrown their spears. But they did not. Instead, they charged forward, seeking combat hand-to-hand.

The First's blade shed faint lightning under the gleam of the moon. Honninscrave's chains smashed about him like a bludgeon. Pitchwife rent a spear from the first *hustin* to assail him, then jabbed the razor-tip in the faces of his attackers. Seadreamer slapped weapons aside, stepped within range of the spears to fell Guards with both fists.

Lacking the sheer bulk of the Giants, Cail could not match their blunt feats. But his swift precision surpassed the *hustin*. He broke the shafts in their hands, blinded their eyes, impelled them into collision with each other.

Yet the top of the Sandwall thronged with Guards, and their numbers were irresistible. The First dealt out death around her, wielded her blade as suddenly as fire; but she could not prevent the gushing corpses from being thrust against her, could not keep the blood from making slick swaths under her feet. Honninscrave's chain frequently tangled itself among the spears, and while he tore it free he was forced to retreat. Pitchwife held his position, but slew few *hustin*. And neither Seadreamer nor Cail could completely seal their sides of the defence. Guards threatened to break into the zone behind them.

Kemper's Pitch stood over the company as if Kasreyn's attention were bent in that direction, slowly squeezing the questers in the fist of his malice. For an instant, abrupt wild magic made the high stone appear translucent; but it had no effect upon the *hustin*. The sirens screamed like the glee of ghouls.

And a Guard slipped into the centre of the defence.

Charging massively forward, it aimed its spear at Linden.

She did not move. She was snared by the old seduction of death – the preterite and immedicable conviction that any violence directed at her was condign, that she deserved the punishment she had always denied. *Let me die*. She had inherited that cry, and nothing would ever silence it. She deserved it. Her bereft gaze followed the advancing iron as if it were welcome.

But then Ceer hopped in front of her. Half immobilized by the splints on his leg, the bindings around his shoulder, he could not defend her in any other way. Diving forward, he accepted the spear-tip in his belly.

The blow drove him against her. They fell together to the stone.

Savagely, Seadreamer wheeled, broke the Guard's back.

Ceer sprawled across Linden's legs. The weight of his life pinned her there. Blood tried to pour from his guts, but he jammed his fist into the wound. Around her, her companions fought at the edges of their lives, survived for moments longer because they were too stubborn to acknowledge defeat. Impressions of horror shone out of Kemper's Pitch. But Linden was unable to lift her eyes from Ceer. The torn agony within him etched itself across her nerves. His features were empty of import; but his pain was as vivid as memory in her.

His gaze focused on her face. It was acute with need. Moonlight burned like fever in his orbs. When he spoke, his voice was a whisper of blood panting between his lips.

'Help me rise. I must fight.'

She heard him – and did not hear him. *Let me die.* She had heard that appeal before, heard it until it had taken command of her. It had become the voice of her private darkness, her intimate hunger. The stone around her was littered with fallen spears, some whole, some broken. Unconsciously, her hands found an iron-tipped section of wood as long as her forearm. When Gibbon-Raver had touched her, part of her had leaped up in recognition and lust: her benighted powerlessness had responded to power. And now that response came welling back from its fountainhead of violence. *You never loved me anyway.* Silence bereft her of the severe resolve which had kept that black greed under control. Power.

Gripping the wood like a spike, she copied the decision which had shaped her life. Ceer lifted the fist from his belly too slowly to stop her. She raised both arms and tried to drive the spear point down his throat.

Cail kicked out at her. His foot caught the upper part of her right arm, where the bruises were deepest, made her miss her thrust and flop backward like a dismembered doll. The stone stunned her. For a moment, she could not breathe. Like her mother. Her head reeled as if she had been thrown into the sky. Her arm went numb from shoulder to fingertip.

Sobbing filled her mind. But to her outer hearing that grief sounded like the sharp dismay of animals. The *hustin* were wailing together – one loss in many throats. The fighting had stopped.

Panting hugely, the First gasped, 'Has she – ?'

Some of the Guards flung themselves from the parapet towards the Sandhold. Others shambled like cripples towards the nearest descents from the Sandwall. None of them remembered the company at all.

'No,' replied Cail inflexibly. 'Her intent failed. It is the wound which reaves him of life.' His voice held no possibility of forgiveness.

Linden felt Ceer's superficial weight being lifted from her legs. She did not know what she was saying. She possessed only a distant consciousness that there were words in her mouth.

'You never loved me anyway.'

Cail dragged her to her feet. His visage was adamantine in the moonlight. His hands vised her right arm; but she felt nothing there.

The Giants were not looking at her. They stared up at Kemper's Pitch as if they were entranced.

High against the heavens, worms of white fire crawled through the stone, gnawing it inexorably to rubble. Already the top of the spire had begun to collapse. And moment by moment more of the Pitch crumbled, falling ponderously towards ruin. Wild magic glared against the dark dome of the sky. Havoc veined the base of Kasreyn's tower like serpents.

Through her teeth, the First breathed, 'Thus have the *hustin* lost their master.'

Faintly underfoot Linden sensed the plunge of the spire. And those vibrations were followed by other shocks as megalithic shards of stone crashed on to The Majesty.

'Now,' Pitchwife coughed, 'let us praise the name of Covenant Giantfriend – and pray that he may endure the destruction he has wrought. Surely The Majesty also will fall – and perhaps the Tier of Riches as well. Much will be lost, both lives and wealth.' His tone faded into an ache. 'I will grieve for the Chatelaine, whom Kasreyn held in cruel thrall.'

'Aye,' Honninscrave affirmed softly. 'And I will grieve for the Sandhold itself. Kasreyn of the Gyre wrought ill in many things, but in stone he wrought well.'

Seadreamer remained locked in his muteness, hugged his arms like bonds over his heart. But his eyes reflected the feral argent emblazoning the heavens. And Vain stood as straight as a statue, facing the site of Covenant's power with a grin like the ancient ferocity of the ur-viles.

Around them, the air shivered to the timbre of wreckage.

Then the Lady Alif spoke across the incessant squalling of the sirens. 'We must go.' Her features were stretched taut by what she saw, by the ruin of the life she recognized – and yet elevated also, gifted with a new vision to replace the old. 'Kasreyn is ended – and his Guards with him. Yet our peril remains. None now in the Sandhold can call back the commands he has given. And I fear as well that there will be war this night, to determine who will hold power in *Bhrathairain*. You must flee if you wish to live.'

The First nodded. She bent quickly to look at Ceer. He was dead – had bled to death like Linden's father, though the two men could not have been more dissimilar. The First touched his cheek in benediction, sent a dark glance at Linden. But she did not speak.

Honninscrave was still urgent for his ship. Picking her way among the dead and dying *hustin*, she set off along the top of the Sandwall at a swinging stride.

Honninscrave joined her. Pitchwife scrambled to follow. Moaning inarticulately deep in his throat, Seadreamer left Ceer. And Cail, who had not eased one jot of his grip on Linden's lifeless arm, impelled her roughly after the Giants.

She had no sensation from the shoulder to the hand of her right arm. It hung strengthless and empty in spite of the way her heart laboured. Cail's kick must have crushed a nerve. There was blood on her head, responsibility which she had never acknowledged to anyone. Her pants were thickly soaked with blood. They stuck to her legs like skin. The void was closing more rapidly now, afflicting her with pangs of self-awareness. How could she walk with Ceer's life so intimately drenched about her? It was the same potent *Haruchai* blood with which the Clave had fed the Banefire for generations: and she was only one ineffectual woman, numbed of arm and soul. She would never escape the sweet cloying stain and adhesion of blame.

The sounds of breakage from the heights of the Sandhold went on, a granite counterpoint to the sirens; but the wild light of power began to fade. Darkness slowly regained its hold over *Bhrathairealm*. Moonlight covered the huge bulk of the Sandhold and the wide ridge of the Sandwall with a suggestion of evanescence, lay across the duned waste of the Great Desert like the caress of a lover. In that illusive light, the pulsing screech of the alarms sounded fanatic and belorn.

The company was drawing closer to their source. As the questers hastened out on to the arm which stretched towards the Harbour, crossed above the western courtyard, the screaming seemed to change pitch. It arose from the gargoyles which crouched like basilisks over the inner gates.

Instinctively, the companions quickened pace. The gates themselves appeared deserted. The *hustin* had left their posts, and the *gaddhi*'s Horse was surely occupied elsewhere. But the sirens still compelled apprehension and flight. Kasreyn was dead; the peril he had set in motion was not. As swiftly as Linden and the Lady Alif could move, the company hurried northward.

From the juncture beyond the courtyard, the wall sloped downward as the terrain declined towards the sea. In moments, stone came between the questers and the sirens, blunting the wail. And the companions were able to see out over *Bhrathairain*.

Laid bare under the moon, the town swept towards the Harbour in a complex network of fixed and moving lights. The lamps of aroused homes and defended merchantries stood against roving

741

brands held by looters, or soldiers, or fleeing sailors. *Bhrathairain* looked like a writhe of sparks, as if the whole town were gathering towards flame.

In the Harbour, the fire had already begun.

The Giants sprang to the parapet, stared fervidly towards the berth where they had left Starfare's Gem. Honninscrave chewed curses as if he could hardly prevent himself from leaping over the wall.

Linden was not as far-eyed as either the Giants or the *Haruchai*. But she was nearly restored to herself. The void still muffled all her thoughts and movements as if her brain were swaddled in cotton; but it did not keep her from tasting the urgency of her companions. She followed them to the parapet, tried to see what they saw.

In the area where the *dromond* had been docked, all the ships were ablaze.

The shock brought her back into her body. The weight of her numb arm, and Cail's grip on it, became suddenly too heavy to be borne. She stumbled forward. At once, the *Haruchai* hauled her back. The force of his jerk swung her to face him.

She confronted his flat face, the fires reflecting in his eyes. 'I can't — ' Her voice seemed as inutile as her arm. There were so many things she should say to him, would have to say to him. But not now. She swallowed thickly. 'Can't see. That far. What happened to the ship?'

Cail's gaze narrowed as he gauged the change in her. Slowly, he unclawed his fingers from her arm. His expression did not relent. But he lifted one hand to point towards the Harbour.

Pitchwife had heard her. He placed a hand on her shoulder as if he were accepting her from Cail — or perhaps interposing himself between them — and steered her to a view of the bay. As he did so, he spoke carefully, like a man whose lungs had been damaged by his exertions.

'This is the Anchormaster's doing. It was his intent to contrive a means that we might be warned, should the *Bhrathair* once again attempt to harm Starfare's Gem. Now it appears that such an attempt was indeed made. Therefore he has set this fire, hoping that some word of it might tell us of his peril.'

'But where — ?' Her thoughts limped after him. She saw nothing along the wharves but one huge blaze. 'Where's the ship?'

'There.' He directed her gaze some distance out from the piers. Still she could not see the *dromond*. 'Sevinhand has done bravely.' Pitchwife's voice was tight in his throat. 'But now Starfare's Gem must strive for its life.'

Then she saw it.

Small in the distance, a fireball arced silently over the black face of the water, casting a lurid light and wide reflections. It came from an armoured galleass with a catapult braced on its decks.

The fireball carried towards the unmistakable stone spars of Starfare's Gem.

Sevinhand had raised every span of canvas which the Gaintship's two remaining masts could hold. Vivid in the moment of light, the gap between them gaped like a fatal wound; and the sails themselves seemed to reach out for the fireball.

Other ships were there as well: two penteconters nearly as large as Starfare's Gem; two triremes, both massively iron-powered for ramming; another catapult-armed galleass. They were hounding the *dromond*, seeking a way to bring it down.

But it was already turning. The fireball carried over its stern, crashed into the oily heaving of the Sea. At once, the ball detonated, spreading sheets of flame across the water. Gouts and blazes struck the Giantship's sides; but they fell back from the moire-stone, did no damage.

Before the flames guttered out, Linden saw one of the triremes curving inward, racing to sink its prow athwart the *dromond*. Ranks of oars frothed the Sea. Then the light was gone. In spite of the moon, the ships disappeared.

Through his teeth, Honninscrave snarled instructions Sevinhand could not hear. The Master was desperate for his vessel.

Linden held her breath involuntarily.

No sound reached them. The tumult in *Bhrathairain*, the battle in the Harbour, were inaudible through the sirens. But then a new fireball kicked upward from the second galleass. It had been hastily-launched, poorly aimed. It accomplished nothing except illumination.

In the glare, Linden saw Starfare's Gem veering through the wreckage of the trireme. The back of the attacker had been broken. Its remains went down under the *dromond*'s keel. For a moment, the flames were full of tiny writhing shapes. Then the darkness returned, effacing Starfare's Gem as it moved to engage the nearest penteconter.

Honninscrave and Seadreamer were unable to look away from the combat. But the Lady Alif pulled at the First's arm. With an effort, the First wrenched her attention back from the Harbour.

'You must hasten to the Spikes,' the Lady was saying. 'Be wary — they are warded. But only there may you hope to rejoin your vessel. And the way is long.'

'Do you not accompany us?' the First asked in quick concern.

'There is a stair nigh,' came the reply. 'I will return to my people.'

'Lady.' The First's voice was soft with protest. 'What life do you hope here? After this night, *Bhrathairealm* will not be what it was. You have risked much for us. Let us in return bear you from this place. Our way will neither be easy nor unjeopardous, but it will spare you the whims of tyrants.'

But the Lady Alif had found strengths in herself which appeared to surprise her. 'You speak truly,' she said as if in wonder at her own audacity. '*Bhrathairealm* will not be what it was. And I have forgotten the trick of taking joy in the whims of tyrants. But now there will be work for any who no longer love the *gaddhi*. And I possess some of the secrets of the Sandhold. That knowledge may be of service to those who do not wish to replace one Rant Absolain with another.' She stood erect in her tattered robes, a woman who had at last come into her heart's estate. 'I thank you for what you have offered – and for what you have wrought this night. But I will depart now. The Spikes are warded. Be wary.'

'Lady!' the First called after her; but she had already retreated into the dark, and the shadows along the parapet had swallowed her. Gently, the First sighed, 'Go well. There is hope and beauty for any folk who give birth to such as you.' But no one heard her except Linden and Pitchwife.

Shivering to herself, Linden turned back towards the Harbour in time to see Dawngreeter burning like a torch.

Faintly, she descried Giants in the rigging. They cut loose the sail, sent it fluttering like a wounded bird into the Sea. Before the light ended, they were busy clewing another sail to the yards.

The *dromond* had left more damage in its wake. One of the penteconters and a galleass had collided side-to-side. Many of the penteconter's oars were shattered; and that wreckage made a shambles of the galleass's decks, crippling the catapult. While the three remaining vessels scrambled to renew their attack, Starfare's Gem rode the night breeze towards open water.

'Now!' the First snapped, breaking the fixed attention of her comrades. 'We must make speed towards the Spikes. The Giantship will gain them with fire and pursuit at its back. It must not be asked to delay there for our coming.'

Shadows of fear and wrath obscured Honninscrave's face; but he did not pause. Though he could not keep his gaze from the Harbour, he swung northward, broke into a trot.

Assuming that she would be obeyed, the First followed him.

But Linden hesitated. She was already exhausted. Ceer's death was slowly encrusting her pants; and she did not know what had become of Covenant. The things she had done left a metallic taste of horror in her mouth. First Hergrom and now Ceer. Like her mother. The doctors had refused to accept responsibility for her mother's death, and now she was a doctor, and she had tried to kill Ceer. Covenant was gone.

While the First fled, Linden turned back towards the Sandhold, hunting for any sign of power which would indicate that Covenant was still alive.

There was nothing. The donjon hunched against the night sky like a ruin. Behind its pale walls, it was full of a darkness which the moon could not assuage. The only discernible life was the life of the sirens. They squalled as if their rage would never be appeased.

Her right arm hung at her side as if she had taken Covenant's leprosy upon herself. Stiffly, she started towards the Sandhold.

Cail caught her by the arm, swung her around as if he meant to strike her. But Pitchwife and Seadreamer had not left her. Pitchwife's eyes burned as he slapped Cail's grasp away from her. A distant part of her wondered if she were going to lose her arm. With a gesture, Pitchwife summoned Seadreamer. At once, the mute Giant lifted her into his embrace. Carrying her as he had carried her through Sarangrave Flat, he went in pursuit of Honninscrave and the First.

Gradually, the sirens faded into the distance. The company was moving faster than Covenant would ever be able to follow. If he were still able to follow at all. The rims of her right shoulder ached dimly, like the shock after an amputation. When she looked up, she saw nothing but the long scar like a slash of old moonlight under Seadreamer's eyes. The position in which he held her blocked Starfare's Gem's progress from view. She had been reduced to this and lacked even the strength for protest.

She was taken by surprise when Seadreamer abruptly wheeled back to the south and halted. The other Giants had also stopped. Cail stood poised on the balls of his feet. They all peered into the vague light towards Vain — or something beyond Vain.

Then she heard it: hooves beating the stone of the Sandwall. Iron-shod hooves, many of them. Twisting in Seadreamer's grasp, she saw a massed cluster of shadows pour forward. They appeared to surge and seethe as they galloped.

'Honninscrave,' the First said like iron, 'you and Seadreamer must continue to the Spikes. Bear the Chosen and Cail *Haruchai* with you. Pitchwife and I will do what we may to ward you.'

Neither brother protested. No Giant of the Search could have refused her when she used that tone. Slowly, Honninscrave and Seadreamer withdrew. After only a fraction of hesitation, Cail also retreated. Vain moved to stay with Linden. Together, the First and Pitchwife stood to meet the *gaddhi*'s Horse.

But soon both Honninscrave and Seadreamer stopped. Linden felt Seadreamer's muscles yearning towards the First. Honninscrave clenched himself as if he did not know how to abandon a comrade. Caught between conflicting needs, they watched the mounted soldiers pound forward.

The First held her falchion in her hands and waited. Pitchwife hunched forward with his hands braced on his knees, gathering breath and strength for battle. In the immanent silver of the light, they looked like colossal icons, numinously silent and puissant.

Then a command was barked in the *Bhrathair* tongue. The horses bunched to a halt. Sparks squealed between iron and stone.

While the others stopped, one of the mounts came dancing with froth on its lips to confront the Giants. A familiar voice said, 'First of the Search, I salute you. Who would have believed you capable of so casting *Bhrathairealm* into chaos?'

The First made a warding sign with the tip of her sword. 'Rire Grist,' she said in a voice of quiet danger. 'Return whence you have come. I do not desire to shed more blood.'

The Caitiffin's mount fought its bit; he controlled the frightened animal roughly. 'You mistake me.' His urbane diplomacy was gone. He sounded now like a soldier, and his tone held a note of eagerness. 'Had I possessed the wisdom to take your true measure, I would have aided you earlier.' A note of ambition. 'Kasreyn is dead. The *gaddhi* is little better than a madman. I have come to escort you to the Spikes, that at least you may hope for your vessel in safety.'

The First's blade did not waver. Softly, she asked, 'Will you rule *Bhrathairealm*, Caitiffin?'

'If I do not, another will.'

'Perhaps,' she pursued. 'Yet why do you seek to aid us?'

He had his answer ready. 'I wish the goodwill of the tale you will bear to other lands. And I wish also that you should begone swiftly, that I may set about my work free of powers I can neither comprehend nor master.'

He paused, then added with a palpable sincerity, 'Moreover, I am grateful. Had you failed, I would not have endured long in Kasreyn's favour. Perhaps I would have been given to the Sandgorgons.' A shudder tinged his voice. 'Gratitude has meaning to me.'

The First considered him for a moment. Then she demanded, 'If you speak sooth, call back the warships which harry our *dromond*.'

His horse flinched. He wrestled with it momentarily before he answered. 'That I cannot do.' He was taut with strain. 'They obey the sirens, which I know not how to silence. I have no means to make myself heard at such a distance.'

As if involuntarily, the First looked out into the Harbour. There, the swift trireme had forced Starfare's Gem to turn. The Giantship sailed broadside to the galleass, exposed for attack. The penteconter was closing rapidly.

'Then I require evidence of your good faith.' For an instant, her voice quivered; but she quickly smothered her concern with sternness. 'You must send your command back to the Sandhold in search of Thomas Covenant. Those who oppose him must be stopped. He must have a mount, that he may overtake us with all haste. And you must accompany us alone. You will provide for our safety at the Spikes. And from that vantage you will seek means to be heard by these warships.' Her threat was as plain as her blade.

For a moment, the Caitiffin hesitated. He let his horse curvet as if its prancing could help him to a decision. But he had come too far to turn back. Wheeling towards his soldiers, he dismounted. One of them took the reins of his destrier while he barked a string of commands. At once, his squad turned, sprang into a gallop back up the long slope of the Sandwall.

When they were gone, Rire Grist bowed to the First. She acknowledged his decision with a nod. In silence, she put out her hand to Pitchwife's shoulder. Together, they started again towards the Spikes. If she recognized the disobedience of her companions, she did not reprove it.

With Cail at his side like a warder, Rire Grist hurried to keep pace with the Giants as they strode northward.

Another fireball revealed that Sevinhand had somehow eluded the snare of the warships. The *dromond* was once again cutting straight for the Spikes.

In the glare as the fireball burst across the water, the Spikes themselves were clearly visible. They rose ominously against the horizon, and the gap between them seemed too small for any escape.

Every tack and turn the Giantship was forced to make delayed its progress. The company was well in advance of the *dromond* as they approached the western tower. There the Caitiffin ran ahead with Cail beside him, shouted commands up at the embrasures. In moments, he was answered. The particular timbre of Seadreamer's muscles told Linden that he understood what the *Bhrathair* said — and that Rire Grist was not betraying the company.

But his fidelity made no impression on her. She felt empty of everything except her arm's numbness and Starfare's Gem's peril and Covenant's absence. She did not listen to the *Bhrathair*. Her hearing was directed back along the Sandwall towards the sirens and the hope of hoof beats.

Soldiers came out of the Spike, saluted Rire Grist. He spoke to them rapidly. They trotted back into the tower, accompanied by the Caitiffin. The First sent Honninscrave in Cail's place to ensure that Rire Grist did not change his mind. Shortly, commands echoed in the narrows as the Caitiffin shouted across to the eastern Spike.

Together, the Giants moved to the corner of the tower so that they could watch both the Harbour and the Sandwall. There they waited. In Seadreamer's arms Linden also waited. But she felt that she shared nothing with them except their silence. Her eyes did not reach as far as theirs. Perhaps her hearing also did not reach as far. And the *dromond*'s granite dance of survival across the water frayed her concentration. She did not know how to believe that either Covenant or the Giantship would endure.

After a long moment, Pitchwife breathed, 'If he comes belatedly — If Starfare's Gem must await him within these narrows — '

'Aye,' growled the First. 'No catapult will fail at such a target.

Then Rire Grist's good faith will count for nothing.'

Cail did not speak. He stood with his arms folded on his chest as if his rectitude were full of violence and had to be restrained.

Softly, Pitchwife muttered, 'Now, Sevinhand.' His fists beat lightly on the parapet. 'Now.'

After a time which contained no sound except the distant and forlorn rage of the alarms and the faint wet soughing of water against the base of the Spike, the Sandwall suddenly echoed with the clamour of oars. Tricked by one of Sevinhand's manoeuvres, the trireme and the penteconter fought to avoid disabling each other. A fireball broke on the rocks directly below the company, sending tremors of detonation through the stone.

The blast absorbed Linden's senses. White blotches burned towards red across her vision. She did not hear him coming.

Abruptly, the Giants turned to face the crooked length of the Sandwall. Seadreamer set her on her feet. Her balance failed her; she nearly fell. Cail took three steps forward, then stopped like an act of homage.

A horse appeared to condense out of the moonlight at a run. As the thud and splash of the oars regained rhythm, hooves came staccato through the noise. Almost without transition, the horse neared the company. It stumbled to a halt, stood with its legs splayed on the edge of exhaustion. Brinn sat in the saddle.

He saluted the Giants. Lifting one leg over the saddlehorn, he dismounted. Only then did Covenant become visible. He had been crouching against the *Haruchai*'s back as if he feared for his life – dismayed by the speed and height of the horse. Brinn had to help him down.

'Well come, Giantfriend,' the First murmured. Her tone expressed more gladness than a shout. 'Well come indeed.'

From out of the dark, wings rustled. A shadow flitted up the roadway towards Covenant. For a moment, an owl poised itself in the air above him as if it meant to land on his shoulder. But then the bird and its shadow dissolved, poured together on the stone as Findail reshaped his human form. In the vague light, he looked like a man who had been horrified, and could see no end to it.

Covenant stood where Brinn had set him as if all the courage had run out of him. He seemed benighted and beyond hope. He might have fallen back under the power of the *Elohim*. Linden started towards him without thinking. Her good arm reached out to him like an appeal.

His power-ravaged gaze turned towards her. He stared at her as if the sight surpassed everything he had suffered. 'Linden – ' His voice broke on her name. His arms hung at his sides as if they were weighed down with pity and need. His tone rasped with the effort he made to speak. 'Are you all right?'

She dismissed the question. It had no importance compared to the anguish reflecting from his face. His dismay at all the killing he had done was palpable to her. Urgently, she said, 'You had to do it. There was no other way. We'd already be dead if you hadn't. Covenant, please! Don't blame yourself for saving our lives.'

But her words brought back his pain, as if until now only his concern for her and the company had protected him from what he had done. 'Hundreds of them,' he groaned; and his face crumpled like Kemper's Pitch. 'They didn't have a chance.' His features seemed to break into tears, repeating the fires of the Harbour and the Spike in fragments of grief or sweat. 'Findail says I'm the one who's going to destroy the Earth.'

Oh, Covenant! Linden wanted to embrace him, but her numb arm dangled from her shoulder as if it were withering.

'Giantfriend,' the First interposed, driven by exigency. 'We must go down to Starfare's Gem.'

He bore himself like a cripple. Yet somewhere he found the strength to hear the First, understand her. Or perhaps it was guilt rather than strength. He moved past Linden towards the Spike as if he could not face his need for her. He was still trying to refuse her.

Unable to comprehend his abnegation, she had no choice but to follow him. Her pants had become stiff and necessary as death after Ceer's last wound. Her arm would not move. After all, Covenant was right to refuse her. Sooner or later, the *Haruchai* would tell him about Ceer. Then she would never be able to touch him. When Pitchwife took the place Cail had repudiated at her side, she let him steer her into the tower.

There Honninscrave rejoined the company. Guided by information Rire Grist had given him, he led the way down a series of stairs which ended on a broad shelf of rock no more than the height of a Giant above the Sea. Starfare's Gem had already thrust its prow between the Spikes.

Here at last the sirens became inaudible, drowned by the echoing surge of water. But Honninscrave made himself heard over the noise, caught the *dromond*'s attention. Moments later, as Starfare's Gem drew abreast of the rock, lines were thrown outward. In a flurry of activity, the companions were hauled up to the decks of the Giantship.

The huge penteconter came beating into the gap hardly a spear's cast behind the *dromond*. But as Starfare's Gem fled, Rire Grist kept his word. He and his soldiers launched a volley of fire-arrows across the bows of the penteconter, signalling unmistakably his intent to prevent any pursuit of the Giantship. Like the Lady Alif, he had found his own conception of honour in the collapse of Kasreyn's rule.

The warship could not have been aware of that collapse. But Rire

Grist was known as the Kemper's emissary. Accustomed to the authority and caprice of tyrants, the crew of the penteconter began to back oars furiously.

Lifting its sails to the wind, Starfare's Gem ran scatheless out into the open Sea and the setting of the moon.

21

MOTHER'S CHILD

Finally Linden's arm began to hurt. Her blood became acid, a slow dripping of corrosion from her shoulder down along the nerves above her elbow. Her forearm and hand still remained as numb and heavy as dead meat; but now she knew that they would eventually be restored as well. Every sensate inch of her upper arm burned and throbbed with aggrievement.

That pain demanded attention, awareness, like a scourge. Repeatedly her old black mood rolled in like a fog to obscure the landscape of her mind; and repeatedly the hurt whipped it back. *You never loved me anyway.* When she looked out from her cabin at the grey morning lying fragmented on the choppy seas, her eyes misted and ran as if she were dazzled by sheer frustration. Her right hand lay in her lap. She kneaded it fiercely, constantly, with her left, trying to force some meaning into the inert digits. Ceer! she moaned to herself. The thought of what she had done made her writhe.

She was sitting in her cabin as she had sat ever since Pitchwife had brought her below. His concern had expressed itself in murmurings and weak jests, tentative offers of consolation; but he had not known what to do with her, and so he had left her to herself. Shortly after dawn – a pale dawn, obscured by clouds – he had returned with a tray of food. But she had not spoken to him. She had been too conscious of who it was that served her. Pitchwife, not Cail. The judgment of the *Haruchai* hung over her as if her crimes were inexpiable.

She understood Cail. He did not know how to forgive. And that was just. She also did not know.

The burning spread down into her biceps. Perhaps she should have taken off her clothes and washed them. But Ceer's blood suited her. She deserved it. She could no more have shed that blame than Covenant could have removed his leprosy. Suffering on the rack of his guilt and despair, he had held himself back from her as if he did

750

not merit her concern; and she had missed her chance to touch him. One touch might have been enough. The image of him that she had met when she had opened herself to him, rescued him from the affliction of the *Elohim*, was an internal ache for which she had no medicine and no anodyne – an image as dear and anguished as love. But surely by now Cail had told him about Ceer. And anything he might have felt towards her would be curdled to hate. She did not know how to bear it.

Yet it had to be borne. She had spent too much of her life fleeing. Her ache seemed to expand until it filled the cabin. She would never forget the blood that squeezed rhythmically, fatally, past the pressure of Ceer's fist. She rose to her feet. Her pants scraped her thighs, had already rubbed the skin raw. Her numb hand and elbow dangled from her shoulder as if they had earned extirpation. Stiffly, she moved to the door, opened it, and went out to face her ordeal.

The ascent to the afterdeck was hard for her. She had been more than a day without food. The exertions of the previous night had exhausted her. And Starfare's Gem was not riding steadily. The swells were rough, and the *dromond* bucked its way through them as if the loss of its midmast had made it erratic. But behind the sounds of wind and Sea, she could hear voices slapping against each other in contention. That conflict pulled her towards it like a moth towards flame.

Gusts of wind roiled about her as she stepped out over the storm-sill to the afterdeck. The sun was barely discernible beyond the grey wrack which covered the Sea, presaging rain somewhere but not here, not this close to the coast of *Bhrathairealm* and the Great Desert.

The coast itself was no longer visible. The Giantship was running at an angle northwestward across the froth and chop of the waves; and the canvas gave out muffled retorts, fighting the unreliable winds. Looking around the deck, Linden saw that Pitchwife had indeed been able to repair the side of the vessel and the hole where Foodfendhall had been, making the *dromond* seaworthy again. He had even contrived to build the starboard remains of the hall into a housing for the galley. Distressed though she was, she felt a pang of untainted gratitude towards the deformed Giant. In his own way, he was a healer.

But no restoration in his power healed the faint unwieldiness of the way Starfare's Gem moved without its midmast. That Sevinhand had been able to outmanoeuvre the warships of the *Bhrathair* was astonishing. The Giantship had become like Covenant's right hand, incomplete and imprecise.

Yet Covenant stood angrily near the centre of the afterdeck as if he belonged there, as if he had the right. On one side were the First and Pitchwife; on the other, Brinn and Cail. They had fallen silent as Linden came on deck. Their faces were turned towards her, and she saw in their expressions that she was the subject of their contention.

Covenant's shirt still bore the black hand-smears of *hustin* blood with which she had stained him in the forecourt of the First Circinate.

Behind her, Honninscrave's voice arose at intervals from the wheeldeck, commanding the Giantship. Because Foodfendhall no longer blocked her view forward, she was able to see that Findail had resumed his place in the prow. But Vain remained standing where his feet had first touched the deck when he had climbed aboard.

Seadreamer was nowhere to be seen. Linden found that she missed him. He might have been willing to take her part.

Stiffly, she advanced. Her face was set and hard because she feared that she was going to weep. The wind fluttered her long-unwashed hair against her cheeks. Under other circumstances, she would have loathed that dirt. She had a doctor's instinct for cleanliness; and a part of her had always taken pride in the sheen of her hair. But now she accepted her grimy appearance in the same spirit that she displayed the dark stains on her thighs. It, too, was just.

Abruptly, Pitchwife began to speak. 'Chosen,' he said as if he were feverish, 'Covenant Giantfriend has described to us his encounter with Kasreyn of the Gyre. That tale comes well caparisoned with questions, which the Appointed might answer if he chose — or if he were potently persuaded. He perceives some unhermeneuticable peril in — '

Brinn interrupted the Giant flatly. His voice held no inflection, but he wielded it with the efficacy of a whip. 'And Cail has spoken to the ur-Lord concerning the death of Ceer. He has related the manner in which you sought Ceer's end.'

An involuntary flush burned Linden's face. Her arm twitched as if she were about to make some request. But her hand hung lifeless at the end of her dead forearm.

'Chosen.' The First's throat was clenched as if words were weapons which she gripped sternly. 'There is no need that you should bear witness to our discord. It is plain to all that you are sorely burdened and weary. Will you not return to your cabin for aliment and slumber?'

Brinn remained still while she spoke. But when she finished, he contradicted her squarely. 'There is need. She is the hand of Corruption among us, and she sought Ceer's death when he had taken a mortal wound which should have befallen her.' The dispassion of his tone was as trenchant as sarcasm. 'Let her make answer — if she is able.'

'Paugh!' Pitchwife spat. His grotesque features held more ire than

Linden had ever seen in him. 'You judge in great haste, *Haruchai*. You heard as all did the words of the *Elohim*. To Covenant Giant-friend he said, "She has been silenced as you were silenced at the *Elohimfest*." And in taking that affliction upon herself she purchased our lives from the depths of the Sandhold. How then is she blameworthy for her act?'

Covenant was staring at Linden as if he were deaf to the inter-changes around him. But the muscles at the corners of his eyes and mouth reacted to every word, wincing almost imperceptibly. His beard and his hot gaze gave him a strange resemblance to the old man who had once told her to *Be true*. But his skin had the hue of venom; and beneath the surface lay his leprosy like a definitive conviction or madness, indefeasible and compulsory. He was sure of those things – and of nothing else, either in himself or in her.

Are you not evil?

In a rush of weakness, she wanted to plead with him, beg him to call back those terrible words, although he was not the one who had uttered them. But Brinn was casting accusations at her, and she could not ignore him.

'No, Giant,' the *Haruchai* replied to Pitchwife. 'The haste is yours. Bethink you. While the silence of the *Elohim* was upon him, ur-Lord Thomas Covenant performed no act. He betrayed neither knowledge nor awareness. Yet was she not capable of action?'

Pitchwife started to retort. Brinn stopped him. 'And have we not been told the words which Gibbon-Raver spoke to her? Did he not say, "You have been especially chosen for this desecration"? And since that saying, have not all her acts wrought ill upon us?' Again, Pitchwife tried to protest; but the *Haruchai* overrode him. 'When the ur-Lord fell to the Raver, her hesitance' – he stressed that word mordantly – 'imperilled both him and Starfare's Gem. When the *Elohim* sought to bereave him of our protection, she commanded our dismissal, thus betraying him to the ill intent of those folk. Though she was granted the right of intervention, she refused to wield her sight to spare him from his doom.

'Then, Giant,' Brinn went on, iterating his litany of blame, 'she did not choose to succour the ur-Lord's silence. She refused us to assail Kasreyn in Hergrom's defence, when the Kemper was alone in our hands. She compelled us to re-enter the Sandhold when even the Appointed urged flight. Her aid she did not exercise until Hergrom had been slain and Ceer injured – until all were imprisoned in the Kemper's dungeon, and no other help remained.

'Hear me.' His words were directed at the First now – words as hard as chips of flint. 'Among our people, the old tellers speak often of the Bloodguard who served the former Lords of the Land – and of Kevin Landwaster, who wrought the Ritual of Desecration. In that mad act, the old Lords met their end, for they were undone by the

Desecration. And so also should the Bloodguard have ended. Had they not taken their Vow to preserve the Lords or die? Yet they endured, for Kevin Landwaster had sent them from him ere he undertook the Ritual. They had obeyed, not knowing what lay in his heart.

'From that obedience came doubt among the Bloodguard, and with doubt the door to Corruption was opened. The failure of the Bloodguard was that they did not judge Kevin Landwaster – or did not judge him rightly. Therefore Corruption had its way with the old Lords and with the Bloodguard. And the new Lords would have likewise fallen, had not the ur-Lord accepted upon himself the burden of the Land.

'Now I say to you, we will not err in that way again. The purity of any service lies in those who serve, not in that which they serve, and we will not corrupt ourselves by trust of that which is false.

'Hear you, Giant?' he concluded flatly. 'We will not again fail of judgment where judgment is needed. And we have judged this Linden Avery. She is false – false to the ur-Lord, false to us, false to the Land. She sought to slay Ceer in his last need. She is the hand of Corruption among us. There must be retribution.'

At that, Covenant flinched visibly. The First glowered at Brinn. Pitchwife gaped aghast. But Linden concentrated on Covenant alone. She was not surprised by Brinn's demand. Outside the Sandwall, his apparent callousness towards Hergrom's death had covered a passion as extravagant as his commitment. But Covenant's silence struck her as a final refusal. He was not looking at her now. From the beginning, he had doubted her. She wanted to go to him, pound at him with her fists until he gave some kind of response. Is that what you think of me? But she could barely lift her arm from the shoulder, still could not flex her elbow.

A stutter of canvas underscored the silence. Gusts beat Linden's shirt against her. The First's expression was hooded, inward. She appeared to credit the picture Brinn had painted. Linden felt herself foundering. All of these people were pushing her towards the darkness that lurked like a Raver in the bottom of her heart.

After a moment, the First said, 'The command of the Search is mine. Though you are not Giants – not bound to me – you have accepted our comradeship, and you will accept my word in this matter.' Her assertion was not a threat. It was a statement as plain as the iron of her broadsword. 'What retribution do you desire?'

Without hesitation, Brinn replied, 'Let her speak the name of a Sandgorgon.'

Then for an instant the air seemed to fall completely still, as if the very winds of the world were horrified by the extremity of Brinn's judgment. The deck appeared to cant under Linden's feet; her head reeled. Speak – ?

Is that what you think of me?

Slowly, words penetrated her dismay. The First was speaking in a voice thick with suppressed anguish.

'Chosen, will you not make answer?'

Linden fought to take hold of herself. Covenant said not one word in her defence. He stood there and waited for her, as the Giants and *Haruchai* waited. Her numb hand slapped softly against the side of her leg, but the effort was futile. She still had no feeling there.

Thickly, she said, 'No.'

The First started to expostulate. Pitchwife's face worked as if he wanted to cry out. Linden made them both fall silent.

'They don't have the right.'

Brinn's mouth moved. She cracked at him in denial, 'You don't have the *right*.'

Then every voice around the afterdeck was stilled. The Giants in the rigging watched her, listening through the ragged run of the seas, the wind-twisted plaint of the shrouds. Brinn's visage was closed against her. Deliberately, she forced herself to face the raw distress in Covenant's eyes.

'Did you ever ask yourself why Kevin Landwaster chose the Ritual of Desecration?' She was shivering in the marrow of her bones. 'He must've been an admirable man – or at least powerful' – she uttered that word as if it nauseated her – 'if the Bloodguard were willing to give up death and even sleep to serve him. So what happened to him?'

She saw that Covenant might try to answer. She did not let him. 'I'll tell you. The goddamn *Bloodguard* happened to him. It wasn't bad enough that he was failing – that he couldn't save the Land himself. He had to put up with *them* as well. Standing there like God Almighty and *serving* him while he lost everything he loved.' Her voice snarled like sarcasm; but it was not sarcasm. It was her last supplication against the dark place towards which she was being impelled. *You never loved me anyway.* 'Jesus Christ! No wonder he went crazy with despair. How could he keep any shred of self-respect, with people like them around? He must've thought he didn't have any choice except to destroy everything that wasn't *worthy* of them.'

She saw shock in Covenant's expression, refusal in Brinn's. Quivering, she went on, 'Now you're doing the same thing.' She aimed her fierce pleading straight at Covenant's heart. 'You've got all the power in the world, and you're so *pure* about it. Everything you do is so dedicated.' Dedicated in a way that made all her own commitments look like just so much cowardice and denial. 'You drive everyone around you to such extremes. And I don't have the power to match you. It's not my – '

But there she stopped herself. In spite of her misery, she was not willing to blame him for what she had done. He would take that charge seriously – and he did not deserve it. Bitter with pain at the contrast between his deserts and hers, she concluded stiffly, 'You don't have the right.'

Covenant did not respond. He was no longer looking at her. His gaze searched the stone at her feet like shame or pleading.

But Brinn did not remain silent. 'Linden Avery.' The detachment of his tone was as flat as the face of doom. 'Is it truly your claim that the Bloodguard gave cause to Kevin Landwaster's despair?'

She made no reply. She was fixed on Covenant and had no room for anyone else.

Abruptly, something in him snapped. He jerked his fists through the air like a cry; and wild magic left an arc of argent across the silence. Almost at once, the flame vanished. But his fists did not unclose. 'Linden.' His voice choked in his throat – at once harsh and gentle. 'What happened to your arm?'

He took her by surprise. The Giants stared at him. Cail's brows tensed into a suggestion of a scowl. But that brief flare of power took hold of the gathering. In an instant, the conflict changed. It was no longer a contest of *Haruchai* against Linden. Now it lay between Covenant and her, between him and anyone who sought to gainsay him. And she found that she had to answer him. She had lost any defence she might have had against his passion.

Yet her sheer loathing for what she had done made the words acid. 'Cail kicked me. To stop me from killing Ceer.'

At that stark statement, his breath hissed through his teeth like a flinch of pain.

Brinn nodded. If he had taken any hurt from Linden's accusation, he did not show it.

For a moment, Covenant grasped after comprehension. Then he muttered, 'All right. That's enough.'

The *Haruchai* did not retreat. 'Ur-Lord, there must be retribution.'

'No,' Covenant responded as if he had heard a different reply. 'She's a doctor. She saves lives. Do you think she isn't already suffering?'

'I know nothing of that,' retorted Brinn. 'I know only that she attempted Ceer's life.'

Without warning, Covenant broke into a shout. 'I don't care!' He spat vehemence at Brinn as if it were being physically torn out of him. 'She saved me! She saved all of us! Do you think that was easy? I'm not going to turn my back on her, just because she did something I don't understand!'

'Ur-Lord – ' Brinn began.

'No!' Covenant's passion carried so many implications of power that it shocked the deck under Linden's feet. 'You've gone too far already!' His chest heaved with the effort he made to control himself.

'In Andelain – with the Dead – Elena talked about her. She said, "Care for her, beloved, so that in the end she may heal us all." *Elena*,' he insisted. 'The High Lord. She loved me, and it killed her. But never mind that. I won't have her treated this way.' His voice shredded under the strain of self-containment. 'Maybe you don't trust her.' His half-fist jabbed possibilities of fire around him. 'Maybe you don't trust me.' He could not keep himself from yelling. 'But you are *by God* going to leave her *alone!*'

Brinn did not reply. His flat eyes blinked as if he were questioning Covenant's sanity.

Instantly, light on the verge of flame licked from every line of the Unbeliever's frame. The marks on his forearm gleamed like fangs. His shout was a concussion of force which staggered the atmosphere.

'*Do you hear me?*'

Brinn and Cail retreated a step as if Covenant's might awed them. Then, together, they bowed to him as scores of the *Haruchai* had bowed when he had returned from Glimmermere with Loric's *krill* and their freedom in his hands. 'Ur-Lord,' Brinn said in recognition. 'We hear you.'

Panting through his teeth, Covenant wrestled down the fire.

The next moment, Findail appeared at his side. The Appointed's mien was lined with anxiety and exasperation; and he spoke as if he had been trying to get Covenant's attention for some time.

'Ring-wielder, they hear you. All who inhabit the Earth hear you. You alone have no ears. Have I not said and said that you must not raise this wild magic? You are a peril to all you deem dear.'

Covenant swung on the *Elohim*. With the index finger of his half-hand, he stabbed at Findail as if to mark the spot where he meant to strike.

'If you're not going to answer questions,' he snarled, 'don't talk to me at all. If you people had any goddamn scruples, none of this would've happened.'

For a moment, Findail met Covenant's ire with his yellow gaze. Then, softly, he asked, 'Did we not preserve your soul?'

He did not wait for a reply. Turning with the dignity of old pain, he went back to his chosen station in the prow.

At once Covenant faced Linden again. The pressure in him burned as hotly as ever; and it forced her to see him more clearly. It had nothing to do with Findail – or with the *Haruchai*. In surprise, she perceived now that he had never intended to permit any retribution against her. He was raw with grief over Ceer and Hergrom – nearly mad with venom and power – appalled by what she had done. But he had never considered the idea of punishment.

He gave her no time to think. 'Come with me.' His command was as absolute as the *Haruchai*. Pivoting sharply, he stalked to the new junction of the fore- and afterdecks. He seemed to choose that place so that he would not be overheard. Or so that he would not be a hazard to the masts and sails.

Pitchwife's misshapen features expressed relief and apprehension on different parts of his face. The First raised a hand to the sweat of distress on her forehead, and her gaze avoided Linden as if to eschew comment on anything the Giantfriend did or wanted. Linden feared to follow him. She knew instinctively that this was her last chance to refuse – her last chance to preserve the denials on which she had founded her life. Yet his stress reached out to her across the grey unsunlit expanse of the afterdeck. Stiffly, abrading her thighs at every step, she went towards him.

For a moment, he did not look at her. He kept his back to her as if he could not bear the sight of what she had become. But then his shoulders bunched, bringing his hands together in a knot like the grasp of a strangler, and he turned to confront her. His voice spattered acid as he said, 'Now you're going to tell me why you did it.'

She did not want to answer. The answer was in her. It lay at the root of her black mood, felt like the excruciation which clawed the nerves of her elbow. But it dismayed her completely. She had never admitted that crime to anyone, never given anyone else the right to judge her. What he already knew about her was bad enough. If she could have used her right hand, she would have covered her face to block the harsh penetration and augury of his gaze. In an effort to fend him off, she gritted severely, 'I'm a doctor. I don't like watching people die. If I can't save them – '

'No.' Threats of wild magic thickened his tone. 'Don't give me any cheap rationalizations. This is too important.'

She did not want to answer. But she did. All the issues and needs of the past night came together in his question and demanded to be met. Ceer's blood violated her pants like the external articulation of other stains, other deaths. Her hands had been scarred with blood for so long now that the taint had sunk into her soul. Her father had marked her for death. And she had proved him right.

At first, the words came slowly. But they gathered force like a possession. Soon their hold over her was complete. They rose up in her one after another until they became gasping. She needed to utter them. And all the time Covenant watched her with nausea on his visage as if everything he had ever felt for her were slowly sickening within him.

'It was the silence,' she began – words like the faint, almost pointless hammerstrokes which could eventually break granite. 'The distance.' The *Elohim* had driven it into him like a wedge, breaking the necessary linkage of sensation and consciousness, action and import. 'It was in me. I knew what I was doing. I knew what was happening around me. But I didn't seem to have any choice. I didn't know how or even why I was still breathing.'

She avoided his gaze. The previous night came back to her, darkening the day so that she stood lightless and alone in the wasteland she had made of her life.

'We were trying to escape from the Sandhold, and I was trying to climb out of the silence. I had to start right at the bottom. I had to remember what it was like – living in that old house with the attic, the fields and sunshine, and my parents already looking for a way to die. Then my father cut his wrists. After that, there didn't seem to be any distinction between what we were doing and what I remembered. Being on the Sandwall was exactly the same thing as being with my father.'

And her mother's gall had soured the very blood in her veins. In losing her husband, being so selfishly abandoned by him, the older woman had apparently lost her capacity for endurance. She had been forced by her husband's financial wreckage – and by Linden's hospital bills – to sell her house; and that had affected her like a fundamental defeat. She had not abrogated her fervour for her church. Rather, she had transferred much of her dependency there. Though her welfare cheques might have been sufficient, she had wheedled an apartment from one member of the church, imposed on others for housework jobs which she performed with tremendous self-pity. The services and prayer-meetings and socials she used as opportunities to demand every conceivable solace and support. But her bitterness had already become unassuageable.

By a process almost as miraculous as resurrection, she had transformed her husband into a gentle saint driven to his death by the cruel and inexplicable burden of a daughter who demanded love but did not give it. This allowed her to portray herself as a saint as well, and to perceive as virtue the emotional umbrage she levied against her child. And still it was not enough. Nothing was enough. Virtually every penny she received, she spent on food. She ate as if sheer physical hunger were the symbol and demonstration of her spiritual aggrievement, her soul's innurturance. At times, Linden would not have been adequately clothed without the charity of the church she had learned to abhor – thus vindicating further her mother's grievance against her. Both chidden and affirmed by the fact that her daughter wore nothing but cast-offs, and yet could not be cajoled or threatened into any form of gratitude, the mother raised her own sour ineffectuality to the stature of sanctification.

The story was hot in Linden's mouth – an acrid blackness which seemed to well up from the very pit of her heart. Her eyes had already begun to burn with the foretaste of tears. But she was determined now to pay the whole price. It was justified.

'I suppose I deserved it. I wasn't exactly easy to get along with. When I got out of the hospital, I was different inside. It was like I wanted to show the world that my father was right – that I never did love him. Or anybody else. For one thing, I started hating that church. The reason I told myself was that if my mother hadn't been such a religion addict she would've been home the day my father killed himself. She could've helped him. Could've helped *me*. But the real reason was, that church took her away from me and I was just a kid and I *needed* her.

'So I acted like I didn't need anybody. Certainly not her or God. She probably needed me as badly as I needed her, but my father had killed himself as if he wanted to punish me personally, and I couldn't see anything about her needs. I think I was afraid that if I let myself love her – or at least act like I loved her – she would kill herself too.

'I must've driven her crazy. Nobody should've been surprised when she got cancer.'

Linden wanted to hug herself, comfort somehow the visceral anguish of recollection; but her right hand and forearm failed her. Memories of disease crept through her flesh. She strove for the detached severity with which she had told Covenant about her father; but the sickness was too vivid for repression. Suffocation seemed to gather in the bottom of her lungs. Covenant emitted a prescient dismay.

'It could have been treated. Extirpated surgically. If she had been treated in time. But the doctor didn't take her seriously. She was just a fat whiner. Widow's syndrome. By the time he changed his mind – by the time he got her into the hospital and operated – the melanoma had metastasized. There wasn't anything left for her to do except lie there until she died.'

She panted involuntarily as she remembered that last month, re-enacting the way her mother gasped on the thick fluids which had filled her with slow strangulation. She had sprawled on the hospital bed as if the only parts of her which remained alive were her respiration and her voice. Heavy folds and bulges of flesh sagged against the mattress as if they had been severed from her bones. Her limbs lay passive and futile. But every breath was a tortuous sibilant invocation of death. And her voice went on and on berating her daughter's sins. She was not trying to win her daughter to the church. She had come to need that denial, to depend upon it. Her protest against it was her only answer to terror. How else could she be sure she had a claim on God's love?

'It was summer then.' Memory possessed Linden. She was hardly aware of the Giantship, of the cloud-locked sky lowering like a bereavement. 'I didn't have school. There wasn't anywhere else for me to go. And she was my mother.' The words could not convey a fifteen-year-old girl's grief. 'She was all I had left. The people of the church took care of me at night. But during the day I didn't have anything else to do. I spent a month with her. Listening to her sob

760

and moan as if it were my fault.

'The doctors and nurses didn't care. They gave her medication and oxygen, and twice a day they cleaned her up. But after that they didn't know what to do about her. They didn't let themselves care. I was just alone with her. Listening to her blame me. That was her way of begging. The nurses must've thought I wanted to help. Or else they couldn't stand it themselves. They gave me a job. They gave me boxes and boxes of tissue and told me to wipe her when she needed it. The sweat. And the mucus that dribbled out of her mouth even when she didn't have enough strength to cough. I had to sit right beside her. Under all that weight, she was just a skeleton. And her breath – the fluid was rotting in her lungs. It got so bad it made me sick.' A stench like the gangrenous reek of the old man whose life she had saved on Haven Farm. 'The nurses gave me food, but I flushed it down the toilet.'

Be true.

'She wouldn't look at me. I couldn't make her look at me. When I tried, she squeezed her eyes shut and went on begging.'

Please, God, let me die.

And after a month, the girl had taken that frail life into her own hands. Grief and affront and culpability had covered her more entirely than all Ceer's blood, stained her more intimately, outraged her more fundamentally. She had needed the power to take some kind of action, create some kind of defence; and because her conscious mind lacked the strength, the dark hunger she had inherited from her father's death had raised its head in her. *You never loved me anyway.* Swarming up from the floorboards of the attic, spewing like a hatred of all life from his stretched and gleeful mouth. His mouth, which should have been open in pain or love. Facing her mother, the blackness had leaped up like a visage of nightmare, had appeared full-formed, precise, and unquestionable not in her mind but rather in her hands, so that her body knew what she meant to do while her brain could only watch and wail, not prevent, control, or even choose. She had been weeping violently, but without sound, had not dared to let one sob through her teeth to be heard by the nurses, betray her. She had hardly seen what she was doing as she unhooked the tubes of oxygen from her mother's nostrils. The darkness in her had begun to gibber. It laughed like lust at the prospect of nourishment. Death was power. *Power.* The strength to stuff accusations back down the throats of those who accused her. *Are you not evil?* Shedding the tears which had dogged her all her life and would never stop, never be forgiven, she began thrusting sheets of tissue one by one into her mother's mouth.

'At least that made her look at me.' Covenant was a blur across her sight; but she felt him aching at her as if he were broken by her words. 'She tried to stop me. But she didn't have the strength. She couldn't lift her own weight enough to stop me.

'Then it was over. I didn't have to breathe that stench any more.' She was no longer trembling. Something inside her had parted. 'When I was sure, I went on as if I'd already planned exactly what I was going to do. I took the tissues out of her mouth — flushed them down the toilet. I put the oxygen tubes back in her nose. Then I went and told the nurses I thought my mother had stopped breathing.'

The deck canted under her feet; she almost fell. But then Starfare's Gem righted itself, righted her. Her eyes felt as livid as the fire which spilled from her right shoulder, etching the nerves until it vanished into the numbness beyond her elbow. Now Covenant's emanations were so poignant that she could not be blind to them. He regarded her in stricken recognition, as if he and the Giantship were cripples together. Through her tears, she saw that even his leprosy and venom were precious to her. They were the flaws, the needs, that made him honest and desirable. He wanted to cry out to her — or against her, she did not know which. But she was not finished.

'I gave her what she wanted. God Himself couldn't do anything except let her suffer, but I gave her what she wanted.

'It was evil.'

He started to protest as if he felt more grief than she had ever allowed herself. She cut him off.

'That's why I didn't want to believe in evil. I didn't want to have to look at myself that way. And I didn't want to know your secrets because I didn't want to tell you mine.

'But it's true. I took away her life. I took away the chance that she might find her own answer. The chance that a miracle might happen. I took away her humanity.' She would never be finished with it. There was no expiation in all the world for what she had done. 'Because of me, the last thing she felt in her life was terror.'

'No.' Covenant had been trying to stop her. 'Linden. Don't. Don't blame yourself like this.' He was gaunt with dismay. Every line of his form was an appeal to her across the stone of the deck. 'You were just a kid. You didn't know what else to do. You're not the only one. We all have Lord Foul inside us.' He radiated a leper's yearning for the wounded and the bereft. 'And you saved me. You saved us all.'

She shook her head. 'I possessed you. You saved yourself.' He had let the *Elohim* bereave him of mind and will until all that remained was the abject and unsupportable litany of his illness. He had accepted even that burden in the name of his commitment to the Land, his determination to battle the Despiser. And she had surrendered herself entirely, braved the worst horrors of her past, to bring him back. But she saw no virtue in that. She had done as much as anyone to drive him into his plight. And she had helped create the conditions which had forced her to violate him. 'All my life' – her hands flinched – 'I've had the darkness under control. One way or another. But I had to give that up, so I could get far enough inside you. I didn't have any left for Ceer.' Severely, she concluded, 'You should've let Brinn punish me.'

'*No*.' His contradiction was a hot whisper that seemed to jump the gap between them like a burst of power. Her head jerked back. She saw him clearly, facing her as if her honesty meant more to him than any act of bloodshed. From the depths of his own familiarity with self-judgment, he averred, 'I don't care about your mother. I don't care if you possessed me. You had good reason. And it isn't the whole story. You saved the quest. You're the only woman I know who isn't afraid of me.' His arms made a wincing movement like an embrace maimed from its inception by need and shame. 'Don't you understand that I love you?'

Love? Her mouth tried to shape the word and could not. With that avowal, he changed everything. In an instant, her world seemed to become different from what it was. Stumbling forward, she confronted him. He was pallid with exhaustion, damaged by the pressure of his doom. The old knife-cut marked the centre of his stained shirt like the stroke of fatality. But his passion resonated against that added dimension of her hearing; and she was suddenly alive and trembling. He had not intended to refuse her. The efforts he made to withhold himself were not directed at her. It was himself that he struggled to reject. He was rife with venom and leprosy; but she recognized those things, accepted them. Before he could retreat, she caught her left arm around him, raised her right as high as she could to hold him. For a moment longer, he strove against himself, stood rigid and unyielding in her clasp. But then he surrendered. His arms closed around her, and his mouth came down on hers as if he were falling.

22

'ALSO LOVE IN THE WORLD'

Late the next morning, after the long night of the full moon, she awakened in her hammock. She felt deeply comfortable, assuaged by sleep. Her right arm was warm and drowsy to the tips of the fingers, like a revenant of her former self, the child unacquainted with death – aneled with numbness as if her blood had become chrism. She was reluctant to open her eyes. Though the cabin beyond her eyelids was refulgent with sunshine, she did not want the day to begin, did not want the night to end.

Yet the whole length of her body – freshly scrubbed the night before and alert to caresses – remembered the pressure of Covenant's presence, knew that he was gone. Somehow, he had contrived to leave the hammock without rousing her. She started to murmur a sleepy protest. But then the nerves of her cheek felt a faint tingle of wild magic. He was still in the cabin with her. She smiled softly to herself as she raised her head, looked over the edge of the hammock towards him.

He stood barefoot and vivid in the sunlight on the floor below her. His clothes, and hers, hung on chairbacks, where they had been left to dry after being washed by the *Haruchai* – a task which Brinn and Cail had undertaken the previous afternoon at the behest of their particular sense of duty. But he made no move to get dressed. His hands covered his face like an unconscious mimicry of sorrow. With the small flame of his ring, he was cleaning the beard from his cheeks and neck.

In silence so that she would not interrupt his concentration, she watched him intently, striving to memorize him before he became aware of her scrutiny, became self-conscious. He was lean to the point of gauntness, all excess burned away by his incessant heat. But the specific efficiency of his form pleased her. She had not known that she was capable of taking such an unprofessional interest in someone else's body. Then his beard was gone, and he dropped his fire. Turning, he saw that she was studying him. A momentary embarrassment concealed the other things in his eyes. He made a vague gesture like an apology. 'I keep thinking I ought to be able to control it. I keep trying to learn.' He grimaced wryly. 'Besides which, I don't like the itch.' Then his mouth became sombre. 'If it's small enough – and if I don't let myself get angry – I can handle it. But as soon as I try to do anything that matters – '

She went on smiling until he noticed her expression. Then he dismissed the question of power with a shrug. Half smiling himself, he touched his pale clean chin. 'Did I get it all? I can't tell – my hands are too numb.'

She answered with a nod. But his tone made her aware of the complexity in his gaze. He was looking at her with more than just his memories of the past night. He was disturbed about something. She did not want to give up her rare and tender easement; but she did not hesitate. Gently, she asked, 'What's the matter?'

His eyes retreated from her, then returned with a tangible effort. 'Too many things.' He faced her as if he did not know how to accept her care. 'Wild magic. Questions. The sheer selfishness of taking your love when – ' He swallowed thickly. 'When I love you so much, and I'm so dangerous, and maybe I'm not even going to live through it.' His mouth was a grimace of difficult honesty. 'Maybe we're not going to get back in time for you to do anything about that knife in my chest. I want out. I don't want to be responsible any more. Too many people have already been killed, and it just gets worse.'

She heard him, understood him. He was a hungry man who had at last tasted the aliment for which his soul craved. She was no different. But the possibility he dreaded — the knife-wound in his chest — was not real to her. The old scar was barely visible. It had faded into the pallor of his skin. She could not imagine that healing undone, abrogated as if it had never occurred.

Yet that was only part of what she felt. In her own way, she was content to be where she was — with him on Starfare's Gem, seeking the One Tree accompanied by Giants and *Haruchai*, Findail and Vain. She was willing to confront the future Lord Foul prepared for them. As clearly as possible, she gave that to Covenant.

'I don't care. You can be as dangerous or selfish as you want.' The danger in him had been attractive to her from the beginning. And his selfishness was indistinguishable from love. 'I'm not afraid.'

At that, his gaze clouded. He blinked at her as if she were brighter than sunlight. She thought that he would ascend the stepladder, return to her arms; but he did not. His countenance was open and vulnerable, childlike in apprehension. His throat knotted, released, as he repeated, 'Findail says I'm going to destroy the Earth.'

Then she saw that he needed more from her than an avowal. He needed to share his distress. He had been alone too long. He could not open one door to her without opening others as well. In response, she climbed out of her comfort, sat up to face him more squarely. Findail, she thought. Recollections sharpened her mood. The *Elohim* had tried to prevent her from entering Covenant. He had cried at her, *Are you a fool? This is ruin! The doom of the Earth is upon my head.* Her voice took on severity as she asked, 'What did he mean — "Did we not preserve your soul"? When he talked to you yesterday?'

Covenant's mouth twisted. 'That's one of the things that scares me.' His eyes left her to focus on what had happened to him. 'He's right. In a way. They saved me. When I was alone with Kasreyn — before Hergrom rescued me.' His voice was lined with bitterness. 'I was helpless. He should have been able to do anything he wanted. But he couldn't get past that silence. I heard every word he said, but I wasn't able to do anything about it, and he wasn't able to make me try. If I hadn't been that way, he probably would've got my ring.

'But that doesn't tell me why?' He looked up at her again, his features acute with questions. 'Why did they do it to me in the first place? Why is Findail so afraid of me?'

765

She watched him closely, trying to gauge the complexity of what he knew and remembered and needed. He had the face of a single-minded man – a mouth as strict as a commandment, eyes capable of fire. Yet within him nothing was simple, everything was a contradiction. Parts of him lay beyond the reach of her senses, perhaps even of her comprehension. She answered him as firmly as she could.

'You're afraid of yourself.'

For a moment, he frowned as if he were on the edge of retorting, You mean if I were arrogant or inexperienced or maybe just stupid enough, there wouldn't be anything to be afraid of? But then his shoulders sagged. 'I know,' he murmured. 'The more power I get, the more helpless I feel. It's never enough. Or it's the wrong kind. Or it can't be controlled. It terrifies me.'

'Covenant.' She did not want to say harsh things to him, as questions which hurt. But she had never seen him evade anything which might prove harsh or painful; and she wanted to match him, show herself a fit companion for him. 'Tell me about the necessity of freedom.'

He stiffened slightly, raised his eyebrows at the unexpected direction of her thoughts. But he did not object. 'We've talked about this before,' he said slowly. 'It's hard to explain. I guess the question is, are you a person – with volition and maybe some stubbornness and at least the capacity if not the actual determination to do something surprising – or are you a tool? A tool just serves it user. It's only as good as the skill of its user, and it's not good for anything else. So if you want to accomplish something special – something more than you can do for yourself – you can't use a tool. You have to use a person and hope the surprises will work in your favour. You have to use something that's free to not be what you had in mind.

'That's what it comes down to on both sides. The Creator wants to stop Foul. Foul wants to break the Arch of Time. But neither of them can use a tool, because a tool is just an extension of who they are, and if they could get what they wanted that way they wouldn't need anything else. So they're both trying to use us. The only difference I can see is that the Creator doesn't manipulate. He just chooses and then takes his chances. But Foul is something else. How free are we?'

'No.' Linden did her best to face him without flinching. 'Not we.' She did not want to hurt him; but she knew it would be false love if she tried to spare him. 'You're the one with the ring. How free are you? When you took Joan's place – ' Then she stopped. She did not have the heart to finish that sentence.

He understood her. Her unspoken words echoed the pang of his own fear. 'I'm not sure.' Once again, his gaze left her, not to avoid her, but to follow the catenations of his memories.

But she was not done, and what remained to be said was too

difficult to wait. 'After the *Elohimfest*. When I tried to get inside you.' She spoke in pieces, feeling unable to pick up all the fragments at once. With a shudder of recollection, she strove for clarity. 'It was the same day Findail showed up. I was waiting – hoping you would recover spontaneously. But then I couldn't wait any longer. If nothing else, I thought you would be able to get answers out of him.'

She closed her eyes, shutting out the way he looked at her. 'But I only got so far.' Dark and hungry for power, she had tried to take mastery of him. And now the virulence of the result came back to her. She began rocking unconsciously against the faint sway of the hammock, seeking to comfort herself, persuade her memories into language. 'Then I was thrown out. Or I threw myself out. To escape what I saw.' Aching, she described her vision of him as a Sunbane-victim, as monstrous and abominable as Marid.

At once, she sought his face as if it were an image to dispel dismay. He was watching her sharply, ire and dread conflicted in his gaze. With a harshness she did not intend and could not suppress, she rasped, 'Can you really tell me you aren't already sold? You aren't already a tool of the Despiser?'

'Maybe I'm not.' The lines of his face became implacable, as if she had driven him beyond reach, compelled him to retreat to the granite foundation of his pain and isolation. His voice sounded as cold as leprosy. 'Maybe the *Elohim* just think I am. Maybe what you saw is just their image of me.' Then his features clenched. He shook his head in self-coercion. 'No. That's just one more cheap answer.' Slowly, his grimace softened like a chosen vulnerability, exposing himself to her. 'Maybe Findail's right. I ought to give him my ring. Or give it to you. Before it's too late. But I'll be goddamned if I'm going to surrender like that. Not while I still have hopes left.'

Hopes? she mouthed silently. But he was already replying.

'You're one. That old man on Haven Farm chose you. He told you *Be True*. You're still here, and you're willing, and that's one. What you just told me is another. If what you saw is the truth – if I really am Foul's tool or victim – then I can't stop him. But he won't be able to use me to get what he wants.'

Roughly, he jerked himself to a stop, paused to give her a chance to consider the implications of what he was saying. That Lord Foul's purposes did in fact revolve around her. That the onus of the Earth's survival rested on her in ways which she could not begin to envision. That she was being manipulated *To achieve the ruin of the Earth*.

For a moment, the conception froze her, brought back fear to the sunlit cabin. But then Covenant was speaking again, answering her apprehension.

'And there's one more. One more hope.' His tone was softer now, almost tender – suffused with sorrow and recognition. 'I told you I've been to the Land three times before. In a way, it was four, not three. The first three times, I didn't have any choice. I was summoned whether I wanted to go or not. After the first time, I didn't want to.

'But the third was the worst. I was in the woods behind the Farm, and there was this little girl who was about to get bitten by a timber-rattler. I went to try to save her. But I fell. The next thing I knew, I was halfway into Revelstone, and Mhoram was doing his damnedest to finish summoning me.

'I refused. That girl was in the real world, and the snake was going to kill her. That was more important to me than anything else, no matter what happened to the Land.

'When I told Mhoram about her' – his voice was a clench of loss – 'he let me go.' The tension of his arms and shoulders seemed to echo, *Mhoram.*

Yet he forced himself to continue. 'I got back too late to stop the snake. But the girl was still there. I managed to suck out some of the venom, and then somehow I got her back to her parents. By that time, the fourth summoning had already started. And I accepted it. I went by choice. There wasn't anything else I wanted except one last chance to fight Foul.'

He was gazing up at Linden squarely now, letting her see his unresolved contradictions, his difficult and ambiguous answers. 'Did I sell myself to Foul by refusing Mhoram? Or to the Creator by accepting that last summons? I don't know. But I think that no human being can be made into a tool involuntarily. Manipulated into destruction, maybe. Misled or broken. But if I do what Foul wants, it'll be because I failed somehow – misunderstood something, surrendered to my own inner Despiser, lost courage, fell in love with power or destruction, *something.*' He articulated each word like an affirmation. 'Not because I'm anybody's tool.'

'Covenant.' She yearned towards him past the gentle ship-roll swaying of the hammock. She saw him now as the man she had first met, the figure of strength and purpose who had persuaded her against her will to accept his incomprehensible vision of Joan and possession, and then had drawn her like a lover in his wake when he had gone to meet the crisis of Joan's redemption – as the upright image of power and grief who had broken open the hold of the Clave to rescue her, and later had raised a mere bonfire in The Grieve to the stature of a *caamora* for the long-dead Unhomed. She said his name as if to ascertain its taste in her mouth. Then she gave him her last secret, the last piece of information she had consciously withheld from him.

'I haven't told you everything that old man said to me. On Haven Farm. He told me *Be True.* But that wasn't all.' After the passage of so much time, she still knew the words as if they had been incused on her brain. 'He said, "Ah my daughter, do not fear. You will not fail, however he may assail you."' Meeting Covenant's gaze, she tried to give her eyes the clarity her voice lacked. '"There is also love in the world."'

For a moment, he remained motionless, absorbing the revelation. Then he lifted his halfhand towards her. His flesh gleamed in the sunshine which angled into the cabin from the open port. The wry lift at the corners of his mouth counterpoised the dark heat of his orbs as he said, 'Can you believe it? I used to be impotent. Back when I thought leprosy was the whole story.'

In reply, she rolled over the edge of the hammock, dropped her feet to the stepladder. Then she took his hand, and he drew her down into the light.

Later, they went out on deck together. They did not wear their own clothes, but rather donned short robes of grey, flocked wool which one of the Giants had sewn for them – left behind their old apparel as if they had sloughed off at least one layer of their former selves. The bulk of the robes was modest and comfortable; but still his awareness of her was plain in his gaze. Barefoot on the stone as if they had made their peace with the Giantship, they left her cabin, ascended to the afterdeck.

Then for a time Linden felt that she was blushing like a girl. She strove to remain detached; but she could not stifle the blood which betrayed her face. Every Giant they met seemed to look at her and Covenant with knowledge, laughter, and open approval. Pitchwife grinned so hugely that his pleasure dominated the disformation of his features. Honninscrave's eyes shone from under his fortified brows, and his beard bristled with appreciation. Sevinhand Anchormaster's habitual melancholy lifted into a smile which was both rue-trammelled and genuine – the smile of a man who had lost his own love so long ago that envy no longer hindered his empathy. Even Galewrath's stolid face crinkled at what she saw. And a rare softness entered the First's demeanour, giving a glimpse of her Giantish capacity for glee.

Finally their attentions became so explicit that Linden wanted to turn away. Embarrassment might have made her sound angry if she had spoken. But Covenant faced them all with his arms cocked mock-seriously on his hips and growled, 'Does *everybody* on this bloody rock know what we do with our privacy?'

At that, Pitchwife burst into laughter; and in a moment all the Giants within earshot were chortling. Covenant tried to scowl, but could not. His features kept twitching into involuntary humour. Linden found herself laughing as if she had never done such a thing before.

Overhead the sails were taut and brave with wind, bellying firmly under the flawless sky. She felt the vitality of the stone and the crew like a tingling in the soles of her feet. Starfare's Gem strode the bright Sea as though it had been restored to wholeness. Or perhaps it was Linden herself who had been restored.

She and Covenant spent the afternoon moving indolently about the *dromond*, talking with the Giants, resting in shared silence on the sun-warmed deck. She noted obliquely that Vain had not left his position at the railing: he stood like a piece of obsidian statuary, immaculate and beautiful, the blackness of his form contrasted or defined only by his tattered tunic and the dull iron bands on his right wrist and left ankle. He might have been created to be the exact opposite of Findail who remained in the vessel's prow with his creamy raiment ruffling in the wind as if the fabric were as fluid as he, capable of dissolving into any form or nature he desired. It seemed impossible that the Appointed and the Demondim-spawn had anything to do with each other. For a while, Linden and Covenant discussed that mystery; but they had no new insights to give each other.

Brinn and Cail held themselves constantly available, but at a distance, as if they did not wish to intrude – or were uncomfortable in Linden's proximity. Their thoughts lay hidden behind a magisterial impassivity; but she had learned that their expressionlessness was like a shadow cast by the extremity of their passions. She seemed to feel something unresolved in them. Covenant had demanded and won their forbearance. Apparently, their trust or mistrust was not so readily swayed.

Their impenetrable regard discomfited her. But she was soothed by Covenant's nearness and accessibility. At intervals, she brushed his scarred forearm with her fingertips as if to verify him. Beyond this, she let herself relax.

As they sprawled in a wide coil of hawser, Pitchwife came to join them. After some desultory conversation, she commented that she had not seen Seadreamer. She felt bound to the mute Giant by a particular kinship and was concerned about him.

'Ah, Seadreamer,' Pitchwife sighed. 'Honninscrave comprehends him better than I – and yet comprehends him not at all. We are now replenished and restored. While this wind holds, we are arrow-swift towards our aim. Thus cause for hope need not be widely sought or dearly purchased. Yet a darkness he cannot name gathers in him. He confronts the site of the One Tree as a spawning-ground of dread.' For a moment, Pitchwife's voice rose. 'Would that he could speak! The heart of a Giant is not formed to bear such tales in silence and solitude.' Then he grew quiet again. 'He remains in his cabin. I conceive that he seeks to spare us the visions he cannot utter.'

Or maybe, Linden mused, he simply can't stand having people watch him suffer. He deserves at least that much dignity. Of all the people on Starfare's Gem, she alone was able to experience something comparable to what he felt. Yet her percipience was not Earth-Sight and she could not bridge the gap between them. For the present, she set the question of Seadreamer aside and let her mood drift back into the jocund ambience of the Giants.

So the day passed; and in the evening Honninscrave shortened sail, freeing as much of the crew as possible for a communal gathering. Soon after supper, nearly two score Giants came together around the foremast, leaving only Sevinhand at Shipsheartthew and three or four crewmembers in the shrouds. Linden and Covenant joined them as if drawn there by laughter and badinage and the promise of stories. The foredeck was dark except for an occasional lantern; but the dark was warm with camaraderie and anticipation, comfortable with the clear-eyed comfort of Giants. High above the slow dance of the masts, stars elucidated the heavens. When the singing began, Linden settled herself gladly against the foremast and let the oaken health of the crew carry her away.

The song had a pulse like the unalterable dirge of the Sea; but the melody rose above it in arcs of eagerness and laughter, relish for all joy or sorrow, abundance or travail. The words were not always glad, but the spirit behind them was glad and vital, combining melancholy and mirth until the two became articulations of the same soul – irrepressibly alive, committed to life.

And when the song was done, Honninscrave stepped forward to address the gathering. In a general way, the story he told was the tale of *Bhrathairealm*; but he concentrated specifically on the *Haruchai* so that all the Giants would know how Hergrom had lived and died. This he did as a homage to the dead and a condolence for the living. Ceer's valour he did not neglect; and his people remained silent around him in a stillness which Brinn and Cail could not have failed to recognize as respect.

Then other tales followed. With a finely mimicked lugubriousness, Heft Galewrath narrated the story of two preternaturally atrabilious and solitary Giants who thrashed each other into a love which they persistently mistook for mortal opposition. Pitchwife offered an old sea-rimmed ballad to the memory of the Unhomed. And Covenant rose from Linden's side to tell the gathering about Berek Halfhand, the ancient hero of the Land who had perceived the Earthpower in the awakening of the Fire-Lions of Mount Thunder, fashioned the Staff of Law to wield and support that puissance, and founded the Council of Lords to serve it. Covenant told the story quietly, as if he were speaking primarily to himself, trying to clarify his sense of purpose; but the tale was one which the Giants knew how to appreciate, and when he finished several of them bowed to him, acknowledging the tenebrous and exigent link between him and the Land's age-long-dead rescuer.

After a moment, Pitchwife said, 'Would that I knew more of this rare Land. The lives of such as Berek make proud hearing.'

'Yes,' murmured Covenant. Softly, he quoted, 'And the glory of the world becomes less than it was.' But he did not explain himself or offer a second tale.

A pause came over the Giants while they waited for a new story or song to commence. Then the dimness in front of Linden and Covenant swirled, and Findail appeared like a translation of the lamplight. His arrival sparked a few startled exclamations; but quiet was restored almost at once. His strangeness commanded the attention of the gathering. When the stillness was complete beyond the faint movements of the sheets and the wet stone-on-Sea soughing of the *dromond*, he said in a low voice, 'I will tell a tale, if I may.'

With a stiff nod, the First granted him permission. She appeared uncertain of him, but not reluctant to hear whatever he might say. Perhaps he would give some insight into the nature or motives of his people. Linden tensed, focused all her senses on the Appointed. At her side, Covenant drew his back straight as if in preparation for a hostile act.

But Findail did not begin his tale at once. Instead, he lifted his eroded visage to the stars, spread his arms as if to bare his heart, and raised a song into the night.

His singing was unlike anything Linden had heard before. It was melodic in an eldritch way which tugged at her emotions. And it was self-harmonized on several levels at once, as if he were more than one singer. Just as he occasionally became stone or wind or water, he now became song; and his music arose, not from the human form he had elected to wear, but from his essential being. It was so weird and wonderful that Linden was surprised to find she could understand the words.

> 'Let those who sail the Sea bow down;
> Let those who walk bow low;
> For there is neither peace nor dream
> Where the Appointed go.

> 'Let those who sail the Sea bow down,
> For they have never seen
> The Earth-Wrack rise against the stars
> And ruin blowing keen.

> 'Mortality has mortal eyes.
> Let those who walk bow low,
> For they are chaff before the blast
> Of what they do not know.

The price of sight is risk and dare
Or loss of life and all,
For there is neither peace nor dream
When earth begins to fall.

'And therefore let the others bow
Who neither see nor know;
For they are spared from voyaging
Where the Appointed go.'

The song arose from him without effort, and when it was gone it left conviction like an entrancement behind it. In spite of her instinctive distrust, her reasons for anger, Linden found herself thinking that perhaps the *Elohim* were indeed honest. They were beyond her judgment. How could she understand – much less evaluate – the ethos of a people who partook of everything around them, sharing the fundamental substance of the Earth?

Yet she resisted. She had too many causes for doubt. One song was not answer enough. Holding herself detached, she waited for the Appointed's tale.

Quietly over the stilled suspirations of the Giants, he began. For his tale he resumed his human voice, accepted the stricture of a mortal throat with deliberate forbearance, as if he did not want his hearers to be swayed for the wrong reasons. Or, Linden thought, as if his story were poignant to him, and he needed to keep his distance from it.

'The *Elohim* are unlike the other peoples of the Earth,' he said into the lantern-light and the dark. 'We are of the Earth, and the Earth is of us, more quintessentially and absolutely than any other manifestation of life. We are its Würd. There is no other apposite or defining name for us. And therefore have we become a solitary people, withholding ourselves from the outer world, exercising care in the encroachments we permit the outer world to have upon us. How should we do otherwise? We have scant cause to desire intercourse with lives other than ours. And it is often true that those who seek us derive scant benefit from what they find.

'Yet is was not always so among us. In a time which we do not deem distant, but which has been long forgotten among your most enduring memories, we did not so hold to ourselves. From the home and centre of *Elemesnedene*, we sojourned all the wide Earth, seeking that which we have now learned to seek within ourselves. In the way of the Earth, we do not age. But in our own way, we were younger than we are. And in our youngness we roamed many places and many times, participating perhaps not always wisely in that which we encountered.

'But of that I do not speak. Rather, I speak of the Appointed. Of

773

those who have gone before me, passing out of name and choice and time for the sake of the frangible Earth. The fruit of sight and knowledge, they have borne the burdens upon which much or all of the Earth has depended.

'Yet in all their work youth has played its part. In past ages upon occasion we accepted – I will not say smaller – but less vital hazards. Perceiving a need which touched our hearts, we met together and Appointed one to answer that need. I will name one such, that you may comprehend the manner of need of which I speak. In the nigh-unremembered past of the place which you deem the Land, the life was not the life of men and women, but of trees. One wide forest of sentience and passion filled all the region – one mind and heart alive in every leaf and bough of every tree among the many myriad throngs and glory of the woods. And that life the *Elohim* loved.

'But, hate rose against the forest, seeking its destruction. And this was dire, for a tree may know love and feel pain and cry out, but has few means of defence. The knowledge was lacking. Therefore we met, and from among us Appointed one to give her life to that forest. This she did by merging among the trees until they gained the knowledge they required.

'Their knowledge they employed to bind her in stone, exercising her name and being to form and interdict against that hate. Thus was she lost to herself and to her people – but the interdict remained while the will of the forest remained to hold it.'

'The Colossus,' Covenant breathed. 'The Colossus of the Fall.'

'Yes,' Findail said.

'And when people started coming to the Land, started cutting down the trees as if they were just so much timber and difficulty, the forest used what it'd learned to create the Forestals in self-defence. Only it took too long, and there were too many people, and the Forestals weren't enough, they couldn't be everywhere at once, couldn't stop the many blind or cruel or simply unscrupulous axes and fires. They were lucky to keep the mind of the forest awake as long as they did.'

'Yes,' Findail said again.

'Hellfire!' Covenant rasped. 'Why didn't you do something?'

'Ring-wielder,' replied the *Elohim*, 'we had become less young. And the burden of being Appointed is loathly to us, who are not made for death. Therefore we grew less willing to accept exigencies not our own. Now we roam less, not that we will know less – for what the Earth knows we will know wherever we are – but that we will be less taken by the love which leads to death.

'But,' he went on without pause, 'I have not yet told my tale. I desire to speak of Kastenessen, who alone of those who have been Appointed sought to refuse the burden.

774

'In the youth of the *Elohim*, he was more youthful than others – a youth such as Chant is now, headstrong and abrupt, but of another temperament altogether. Among those who sojourned, he roved farther and more often. At the time of his election, he was not present in *Elemesnedene*.

'Rather, he inhabited a land to the east, where the *Elohim* are neither known nor guessed. And there he did that which no *Elohim* has ever done. He gave himself in love to a mortal woman. He walked among her folk as a man of their own kind. But in her private home he was an *Elohim* to ravish every conception of which flesh that dies is capable.

'That was an act which we repudiated, and would repudiate again, though we do not name it evil. In it lay a price for the woman which she could neither comprehend nor refuse. Gifted or in sooth blighted by all Earth and love and possibility in one man-form, her soul was lost to her in the manner of madness or possession rather than of mortal love. Loving her, he wrought her ruin and knew it not. He did not choose to know it.

'Therefore was he Appointed, to halt the harm. For at that time was a peril upon the Earth to which we could not close our eyes. In the farthest north of the world, where winter has its roots of ice and cold, a fire had been born among the foundations of the firmament. I do not speak of the cause of that fire, but only of its jeopardy to the Earth. Such was its site and virulence that it threatened to rive the shell of the world. And when the *Elohim* gathered to consider who should be Appointed, Kastenessen was not among us. Yet had he been present to bespeak his own defence, still would he have been Appointed, for he had brought harm to a woman who could not have harmed him, and he had called it love.

'But such was the strength of the thing which he named love that when the knowledge of his election came to him, he took the woman his lover by the hand and fled, seeking to foil the burden.

'So it fell to me, and to others with me, to give pursuit. He acted as one who had wandered into madness, for surely it was known to him that in all the Earth there was no hiding-place from us. And were it possible that he might pass beyond our reach, immerse himself in that from which we would be unable to extricate him, he could not have done so with the woman for companion. Her mortal flesh forbade. Yet he would not part from her, and so we came upon him and took him.

'Her we gave what care we could, though the harm or love within her lay beyond our solace. And him we bore to the fire which burned in the north. To us he remained *Elohim*, not to be freed from his burden. But to him he was no longer of us, or of the Earth, but only of the woman he had lost. He became a madness among us. He would not accept that he had been Appointed, or that the need of

775

the Earth was not one which might be eschewed. He railed against us, and against the heavens, and against the Würd. To me especially he gave curses, promising a doom which would surpass all his dismay – for I had been nearer to him among the *Elohim* than any other, and I would not hear him. Because of his despair, we were compelled to bind him to his place, reaving him of name and choice and time to get him as a keystone for the threatened foundation of the north. Thus was the fire capped, and the Earth preserved, and Kastenessen lost.'

Findail stopped. For a moment, he remained still amid the stillness of the Giants; and all his hearers were voiceless before him, lost like Kastenessen in the story of the Appointed. But then he turned to Linden and Covenant, faced them as if everything he had said was intended to answer their unresolved distrust; and a vibration of earnestness ran through his voice.

'Had we held any other means to combat the fire, we would not have Appointed Kastenessen as we did. He was not chosen in punishment or malice, but in extremity.' His yellow eyes appeared to collect the lantern-light, shining out of the dark with a preternatural brightness. 'The price of sight is risk and dare. I desire to be understood.'

Then his form frayed, and he flowed out of the gathering, leaving behind him silence like an inchoate and irrefragable loneliness.

When Linden looked up at the stars, they no longer made sense to her. Findail might as well have said, *This is ruin*.

For three more days the weather held, bearing Starfare's Gem with brisk accuracy at a slight angle along the wind. But on the fifth day out from *Bhrathairealm*, the air seemed to thicken suddenly, condensing until the breeze itself became sluggish, vaguely stupefied. The sky broke into squalls as if it were crumbling under its own weight. Abrupt gusts and downpours thrashed the Giantship in all directions. At unpredictable intervals, other sounds were muffled by the staccato battery of canvas, the hot hissing of rain. Warm, capricious, and temperamental, the squalls volleyed back and forth between the horizons. They were no threat to the *dromond*; but they slowed its progress to little more than a walk, made it stagger as it tacked from side to side. Hampered by the loss of its midmast, Starfare's Gem limped stubbornly on towards its goal, but was unable to win free of the playground of the storms.

After a day of that irregular lurch and stumble, Linden thought she was going to be seasick. The waves confused the stability she had learned to expect from the stone under her bare feet. She felt the protracted frustration of the crew vibrating through the moiregranite, felt the *dromond*'s prow catch the seas every way but squarely. And Covenant fretted at her side; his mood gave a pitch of urgency to the Giantship's pace. Beneath the surface of their companionship, he was febrile for his goal. She could not stifle her nausea until Pitchwife gave her a gentle mixture of *diamondraught* and water to quiet her stomach.

That night she and Covenant put together a pallet on the floor of her cabin so that they would not have to endure the aggravated motion of the hammock. But the next day the squalls became still more sportive. After sunset, when a gap in the clouds enabled him to take his bearings from the stars, Honninscrave announced that the quest had covered little more than a score of leagues since the previous morning. 'Such is our haste,' he muttered through his beard, 'that the Isle of the One Tree may sink altogether into the Sea ere we draw nigh to it.'

Pitchwife chuckled. 'Is it a Giant who speaks thus? Master, I had not known you to be an admirer of haste.'

Honninscrave did not respond. His eyes held reminders of Seadreamer, and his gaze was fixed on Covenant.

After a moment, Covenant said, 'A few centuries after the Ritual of Desecration, a Cavewight named Drool Rockworm found the Staff of Law. One of the things he used it for was to play with the weather.'

Linden looked at him sharply. She started to ask, do you think someone is causing – ? But he went on, 'I blundered into one of his little storms once. With Atiaran.' The memory roughened his tone. 'I broke it. Before I believed there even was such a thing as wild magic.'

Now everyone in the vicinity was staring at him. Unspoken questions marked the silence. Carefully, the First asked, 'Giantfriend, do you mean to attempt a breaking of this weather?'

For a time, he did not reply. Linden saw in the set of his shoulders, the curling of his fingers, that he wanted to take some kind of action. Even when he slept, his bones were rigid with the remembered urgency. The answer to his self-distrust lay at the One Tree. But when he spoke, he said, 'No.' He tried to smile. The effort made him grimace. 'With my luck, I'd knock another hole in the ship.'

That night, he lay facedown on the pallet like an inverted cenotaph of himself, and Linden had to knead his back for a long time before he was able to turn and look at her.

And still the storms did not lessen. The third day made them more numerous and turbid. Linden spent most of her time on deck, peering through wind and rain for some sign that the weather might change. Covenant's tension soaked into her through her senses. The One Tree. Hope for him. For the Land. And for her? The question disturbed her. He had said that a Staff of Law could be used to send her back to her own life.

During a period of clear sky between squalls in the middle of the afternoon, they were standing at the rail halfway up the starboard foredeck, watching clouds as black as disaster drag purple and slashing rain across the water like sea-anchors, when a shout sprang from the foremast. A shout of warning. Honninscrave replied from the wheeldeck. An alarm spread through the stone. Heavy feet pounded the decks. The First and Pitchwife came trotting towards Linden and Covenant.

'What – ?' Covenant began.

The Swordmain reached the rail beside Linden, pointed outward. Her gaze was as acute as a hawk's.

Pitchwife positioned himself directly behind the Unbeliever.

Suddenly, Seadreamer also appeared. For an instant, Linden leaped to the impossible conclusion that the Isle of the One Tree was near. But Seadreamer's stare lacked the precise dread which characterized his Earth-Sight. He looked like a man who saw a perilous wonder bearing down on him.

Her heart pounding, she swung to face the Sea.

The First's pointing arm focused Linden's senses. With a shock of percipience, she felt an eldritch power floating towards the Giantship.

The nerves of her face tasted the weird theurgy before her eyes descried it. But then an intervening squall abruptly frayed and fell apart, dissipated as if its energy had encountered an apt and hungry lightning rod. She saw an area of calm advancing across the face of the Sea.

It was wider than the length of the *dromond* and its periphery was not calm. Around the rim, waterspouts kicked into the air like geysers. They burst straight upward as if no wind could touch them, reached as high as the Giantship's spars, then fanned into spray and rainbows, tumbled sun-bedizened back into the Sea. In turn, irrhythmically, now here, now at the farther edge, the spouts stretched towards the sky like celebrants, defining the zone of calm with their innominate gavotte. But within their circle the Sea lay flat, motionless, and reflective – a sopor upon the heart of the deep.

The waterspouts and the calm were moving with slow, bright delicacy towards Starfare's Gem.

Covenant tried again. 'What – ?' His tone was clenched and sweating, as if he felt the approaching power as vividly as Linden did.

Stiffly, the First replied, '*Merewives.*' And Pitchwife added in a soft whisper, 'The Dancers of the Sea.'

Linden started to ask, What *are* they? But Pitchwife had already begun to answer. Standing at Covenant's back, he breathed, 'They are a widely told tale. I had not thought to be vouchsafed such a sight.'

The waterspouts were drawing near. Linden tasted their strength like a spray against her cheeks, though the sensation had no flavour except that of the strength itself – and of the faint poignance which seemed to arise like longing from the upward reach of the waters. But Honninscrave and Starfare's Gem made no attempt to evade the approach. All the Giants were entranced by wonder and trepidation.

'Some say,' Pitchwife went on, 'that they are the female soul of the Sea, seeking forever among the oceans for some male heart hardy enough to consummate them. Others say that they are the lost mates of a race which once lived within the deeps, and that their search is for their husbands, who have been slain or mazed or concealed. The truth I know not. But all tales agree that they are perilous. Their song is one which no man may gainsay or deny. Chosen, do you hear their song?' Linden did not speak. He took her response for granted. 'I also do not hear it. Perhaps the *merewives* have no desire for Giants, as they have none for women. Our people have never suffered scathe from these folk.' His voice sharpened involuntarily as the first spouts wet the sides of the Giantship. 'Yet for other men – !'

Linden recoiled instinctively. But the spray was only salt-water. The strength of the *merewives* did not touch her. She heard no song, although she sensed some kind of passion moving around her, intensifying the air like a distant crepitation. Then the first spouts had passed the *dromond*, and Starfare's Gem sat inside the zone of calm, resting motionless within a girdle of rainbows and sun-diamonds and dancing. The sails hung in their lines, deprived of life. Slowly, the Giantship began to revolve as if the calm had become the eye of the whirlpool.

'If they are not answered,' Pitchwife concluded, nearly shouting, 'they will pass.'

Linden heard the strain in his voice, the taut silence beside her. With a jerk, she looked towards Covenant.

He was bucking and twisting against Pitchwife's rigid grasp on his shoulders.

23

WITHDRAWAL FROM SERVICE

The call of the *merewives* went through Covenant like an awl, so bright and piercing that he would not have known it for music if his heart had not leaped up in response. He did not feel himself plunging

779

against Pitchwife's hold, did not know that he was gaping and gasping as if he could no longer breathe air, were desperate to inhale water. The song consumed him. Its pointed loveliness and desire entered him to the marrow. Vistas of grandeur and surcease opened beyond the railing as if the music had words –

Come to us for heart-heal and soul-assuage, for consummation of every flesh

– as if the sun-glistered and gracile dance of the waterspouts were an utterance in a language he understood. Only Pitchwife's hands prevented him from diving into the deep Sea in reply.

Linden's face appeared in front of him, as vivid as panic. She was shouting, but he did not hear her through the song. Only those hands prevented him from sweeping her aside on his way to the Sea. His heart had stopped beating – or perhaps no time had passed. Only those hands – !

In a flash, his fire gathered. Wild magic burned through his bones to blast Pitchwife away from him.

But power and venom turned the music of the *merewives* to screaming in his mind. Revulsion flooded through him – the Dancers' or his, he could not tell the difference. They did not want a man like him – and Pitchwife was his friend, he did not wish to hurt his friend, not again, he had already hurt more friends than he could endure. In spite of Pitchwife's Giantish capacity to sustain fire, his grip had been broken. *Not again!*

Free of the song, Covenant stumbled forward, collided with Linden.

She grappled for him as if he were still trying to hurl himself into the Sea. He wrestled to break loose. The passing of the music left incandescent trails of comprehension through him. The *merewives* did not want the danger he represented. But they desired men – potent and vital men, men to sustain them. Linden fought to hold him, using the same skills she had once used against Sunder. He tried to shout, Let me go! It isn't me they want! But his throat was clogged with memories of music. *Consummation of every flesh*. He twisted one arm free, pointed wildly.

Too late.

Brinn and Cail were already sprinting towards the rail.

Everyone had been watching Covenant. Seadreamer and the First had moved towards him to catch him if Linden failed. And they had all learned to rely on the invulnerability of the *Haruchai*. None of them could react in time.

Together, Brinn and Cail bounded on to the railing. For a fractional instant, they were poised in the sunlight, crouched to leap forward like headlong joy. Then they dived for the Sea as if it had become the essence of all their hearts' desires.

For a moment like the pause of an astonished heart, no one moved. The masts stood straight and still, as if they had been nailed to the clenched air. The sails dangled like amazement in their shrouds. Yet the *dromond* went on turning. As soon as the calm gathered enough momentum, the vessel would be sucked down. The *Haruchai* had left no splash or ripple behind to mark their existence.

Covenant's mouth stretched into a lost shout. He was panting to himself, Brinn, *Brinn*. He had placed so much faith in the *Haruchai*, needed them so much. Were their hearts mortal and frangible after all? Bannor had commanded him, *Redeem my people*. He had failed again.

With an effort like a convulsion, he flung Linden aside. As she staggered away, he let out a cry of flame.

His eruption broke the onlookers out of their trance. The First and Honninscrave yelled orders. Giants leaped into action.

Linden tried to take hold of Covenant again. Her fear for him mottled her face. But his blaze kept her back. He moved towards the railing like a wash of fire.

Seadreamer and Pitchwife were there ahead of him. They fought like foemen, Seadreamer trying to reach the Sea, Pitchwife restraining him. As he struggled, Pitchwife gasped out, 'Are you not male? Should they turn their song against you, how will you refuse it?'

Covenant put out an arm of flame, yanked Seadreamer back on to the foredeck. Then he was at the rail himself. Fire poured down his arms as if he were summoning a cataclysm against the Dancers.

People shouted at him – Linden, Findail, the First. He did not know what he would do if the *merewives* directed their song at him again – and did not care. He was rapt with fury for Brinn and Cail. The *Haruchai* had served him steadfastly when his need had been so great that he could not even ask for help.

Abruptly, a hand struck his shoulder, turned him to the side. The First, confronted him, her arm raised for another blow. 'Giantfriend, hear me!' she shouted. 'Withhold your might, lest they find means to bend it against you!'

'They're my friends!' His voice was a blare of vehemence.

'And mine!' she responded, matching his ire with iron. 'If they may be reached by any rescue, I will do it!'

He did not want to stop. The venom in his veins was alight with glee. For an instant, he was on the verge of simply brushing her aside, a mere annoyance to his power.

But then Linden joined the First, imploring him with her eyes, her open hands. Trepidation aggrieved her face, made her suddenly poignant to him. Her hair shone about her shoulders like yearning. He remembered who he was – a leper with good reason to fear wild magic. 'They're my *friends*,' he repeated hoarsely. But if he heard the song of the Dancers again he would not be able to refuse it. He had no way to rescue Brinn and Cail except with a violence so immense that it might destroy Starfare's Gem as well.

He turned from the railing, raised his face to the cerulean stasis of the sky as if he meant to shock it with expostulation. But he did not. Sagging, he let the fire fray away from his bones. His ring seemed to manacle the second finger of his halfhand.

He heard Findail's tight sigh of relief. But he ignored the *Elohim*. He was gazing at Seadreamer. He might have injured the mute Giant –

But Seadreamer was like his kindred, immune to fire if not to pain. He had mastered himself and met Covenant's look as if they shared reasons for abashment.

Covenant winced voicelessly. When Linden came to him, put her hands on his arm like a gesture of consolation, he closed his numb fingers over hers and turned towards the preparations of the Giants.

The First had been joined by Galewrath. Crewmembers hastened between them and the nearest hatchway. With grim celerity, the First unbelted her sword, removed her mail. Her eyes were fixed on the flat water as if it had become a place of concealment for something fatal. In moments, the Giants brought up two long canvas tubes like hoses from the underdecks. They reached in long coils across the foredeck and out of sight through the hatch. Then a shout echoed from below; and the tubes began to writhe and hiss like serpents as air was forced through them.

They were taking too long. Covenant's grip whitened Linden's hand, but he could not relax it. He could not judge how long Cail and Brinn had been gone. Surely they were dying for lack of air. Heat rose in him again. The effort of self-restraint made his head spin as if the *dromond*'s movement had accelerated.

To the Giants near her, the First muttered, 'Forewarn the Master. It is said that the *merewives* know little kindness when they are reft of their prey. If we do not fail, there will be need of his sea-craft.'

One of the crew dashed away to convey her message. For an instant, she looked at Covenant, at Linden. 'Hold hope,' she said tautly. 'I do not mean to fail.'

Go, he wanted to bark at her. Go!

Linden pulled away from him, took a step towards the First. Her lips were compressed with severity; the lines of her mien were as acute as Brinn's accusations. Covenant was learning to read her with an intimacy that almost matched her percipience. He heard the desire for vindication in her voice as she said, 'Take me with you. I can help.'

The First did not hesitate. 'Chosen, in this need we are swifter and more able than you.'

Without delay, she and Galewrath took hold of the tubes, climbed over the railing and jumped for the water.

Pitchwife watched them as if he were afraid. Covenant followed Linden to the hunched Giant's side, drawn there by the rush of the hoses. Like the *Haruchai*, the First and the Storesmaster appeared to vanish without marking the static water. But the tubes ran into the depths swiftly, and bubbles trailed back to the surface.

The waterspouts did not lessen. Rather, they seemed to grow more eager, as if they were tasting an answer to their long insatiation. Beyond them, the squalls continued to batter each other back and forth. The afternoon thickened towards evening. Yet the bubbles rose like implications of hope. Belowdecks, Giants laboured at the pumps, forcing air down the tubes.

The suspense clawed at Covenant's restraint, urging fire. His fists closed and unclosed helplessly. Abruptly, he shoved himself from the railing. 'I've got to do *some*thing.' Rigid with suppression, he stalked towards the prow of the *dromond*.

Linden accompanied him as if she still feared he might succumb to madness or *merewives* at any moment. But her presence steadied him. When he reached the prow, he was able to confront the Appointed without shouting his desperation.

Findail's yellow eyes squinted in potential anguish. Covenant measured him with a glare. Then, roughly, he said, 'You want to be trusted. No, not trusted. You're *Elohim*. You don't need anything as mortal and fallible as trust. You want to be understood. This is your chance. Help my friends. They've done everything flesh and blood can do to keep me alive. And not just me. Linden. The Sun-Sage. That has got to count for something.' His arms were locked at his sides; his hands, knurled into fists. Flame bled between his fingers, too potent and necessary to be quenched. The scars on his forearm ached with the memory of fangs. 'By hell, you've got to do something to help my friends.'

'And if I do not?' Findail's tone held no hauteur. Difficulty and apprehension seamed his voice. 'Will you compel me? Will you rend the Earth from its foundations to compel me?'

Covenant's shoulders were trembling. He could not still them. Word by word, he articulated, 'I am asking you.' Danger bled in his throat. 'Help my friends.'

Implicit recognitions filled Findail's gaze. But he did not relent. Slowly, he said, 'It is sooth that there are many tales told of these *merewives*, the Dancers of the Sea. One such is the tale that they are the descendants and inheritors of the woman whom Kastenessen loved – that she took with her the power and knowledge which she gained from him, and also the daughters of all men-betrayed women, and set herself and them to seek restitution from all men who abandon their homes in the name of the Sea. The *Haruchai*

783

have gone to meet a jeopardy which arises only from the quenchless extravagance of their own hearts for the *merewives* did naught except sing — but the *Haruchai* answered. I will not offend further against that which was born of Kastenessen's mad love.'

Deliberately, he turned his back as if he were daring Covenant to smite him.

Passion ran down Covenant's arm, itching for violence. Findail refused every gesture which might have palliated the harm his people had done. Covenant had to grit his teeth to hold back protests which would have written themselves in fire across the Giantship. But Linden was with him. Her touch felt cool on his hot forearm. 'It wouldn't do any good.' His voice choked between his teeth. 'Even if I tore his heart out with my bare hands.' But he believed in restraint. Blood-willingness appalled him, his own more than any other. Why else had he let Lord Foul live?

Her soft eyes regarded him as if she were about to say, How else can you fight? Bitter with vulnerability, she had once said, *Some infections have to be cut out*. That pain was still apparent in the marks of death and severity around her mouth; but now it took a different form, surprising him. Arduously, she said, 'After Hergrom rescued you — killed that Guard — For a while, we were alone with Kasreyn. Brinn wanted to kill him then. And I wanted him to do it. But I couldn't — Couldn't let him. Even though I knew something terrible was going to happen to Hergrom. I couldn't be responsible for more killing.' Her mother was vivid in her eyes. 'Maybe Brinn's right. Maybe that makes me responsible for what happened. But it wouldn't have made any difference. We couldn't have killed him anyway.'

She stopped. She did not need to go on. Covenant understood her. He could not have killed Lord Foul. Despite was not something which could be made to die.

Yet she was wrong about one thing: it would have made a difference. The same difference that killing her mother had made to her.

He wanted to tell her that he was glad she had not unleashed Brinn at Kasreyn. But he was too crowded with other needs. He remained still for a moment in recognition of her. Then he jerked into motion back towards the knot of Giants who paid out the hoses over the edge of the *dromond*.

Pressing himself against the rail, he stared at the bubbles. The cross-support was like a bar across his chest. Terrible amounts of time had passed. How could Brinn and Cail still be alive? The bubbles rose in bursts, as if the two Giants had reached a depth where the pressure threatened their lungs. The tubes throbbed and wheezed stertorously, articulating the labour of the pumps. He found himself breathing to the same rhythm.

He wrenched his gaze from the Sea. The imponderable dance of the waterspouts went on, slowly invoking Starfare's Gem to its grave. The First's longsword lay in its scabbard on the deck like an abandoned thing, bereft of use and name. Linden was peering distractedly around the zone of calm, registering unspecified perceptions. Unconsciously, her lips spelled out the high geyser and spray of an alien tongue.

Abruptly, the hoses stopped moving.

At once, the enclosed atmosphere shivered as if it had been shocked. For an instant, a sound burned Covenant's brain like the song of the *merewives* violated into outrage. The squalls seemed to loom forward like fists of wrath, clenched for retribution.

Reacting to some felt signal, the Giants began to haul the tubes upward, pulling hand-over-hand with swift strength.

Covenant tried to turn towards them. But the sight of Linden held him. She had gone as pale as panic. Her hands covered her mouth; her eyes gaped whitely into the distance.

He grabbed at her arms, dug his numb fingers into her flesh. Her gaze stared past him, through him. 'Linden!' he snapped, acid with fear and truncated sight. 'What is it?'

'The squalls.' She spoke to herself, hardly seemed aware she was speaking aloud. 'They're part of the Dance. The *merewives* raise them to catch ships. I should've seen it before.'

As suddenly as a flash of intuition, her eyes sprang into focus. She thrashed against him. 'The squalls!' she panted urgently. 'I've got to warn Honninscrave! They're going to *attack!*'

In bare comprehension, he released her. She staggered backward, caught her balance, flung herself into a run towards the wheeldeck.

He almost went after her. Her tense, fleet form drew him powerfully. But the First and Galewrath were being lifted towards the surface. With Brinn and Cail? Why else did the Dancers want to attack?

Giants heaved at the hoses. White-knuckled with anticipation, Pitchwife's hands clenched one of the rails. Seadreamer stood ready to dive if the First or Galewrath needed aid. The scar under his eyes was avid for anything which was not Earth-Sight.

The atmosphere concentrated towards a detonation.

Voices rose from the direction of the wheeldeck – first Linden's, then Honninscrave's. The Master was bellowing commands across the Giantship. Every crewmember who was not needed at the hoses leaped for the rigging.

Peering far over the side in spite of his vertigo, Covenant saw vague shapes rise. Pitchwife called unnecessarily for ropes; they were already at hand. As heads broke water, the lines were cast downward.

The First snatched a look upward, caught one of the ropes with her free hand. Galewrath did the same. Immediately, they were pulled out of the Sea.

The First clutched Brinn to her chest with one arm. Galewrath had Cail draped over her shoulder.

Both the *Haruchai* hung as limp as sleep.

Pitchwife and Seadreamer stretched out their hands to help the divers aboard. Covenant tried to squeeze past them to get a closer look at Brinn and Cail, but could not.

As the Swordmain and Galewrath gained the foredeck, the entire sky shattered.

The waterspouts and the stillness vanished in one fractured instant. From every direction, squalls sprang at the Giantship with the fury of gales. Rain hammered the decks; ire blotted out the horizons. In the midst of its spin, Starfare's Gem staggered into a vicious concussion of waters. The stone quivered from mast to keel.

Covenant stumbled against Seadreamer, clung to the mute Giant for support. If Honninscrave had not been forewarned, the *dromond* might have lost its yards in the twisting savagery of the blasts. The masts themselves might have been torn from their moorings. But the crew had started to slacken sail before the violence hit. The *dromond* lurched and bucked, kicked wildly from side to side. Sheets leaped into snarls and chaos; canvas retorted in the conflict of winds. But Starfare's Gem was not hurt.

Then all the squalls became one, and the confusion resolved into a blast like the howling of a riven heart. It caught the Giantship broadside, heeled it far over on to its side. Covenant might have tumbled overboard if Seadreamer had not held him. Rain scythed against his face. The Master was no longer audible through the roar and slash of the storm.

Yet the Giants knew what had to be done. Somehow, they tautened a sail on the foremast. Canvas bit into the blast: Starfare's Gem surged upright as it turned. For an instant, the vessel trembled from stem to stern, straining against the leash of its own immense weight. Then more sail took hold, and the *dromond* began to run along the wind.

Covenant reeled from Seadreamer to the First. He clutched at Brinn, imploring the *Haruchai* for some sign of life. But Brinn dangled with his face open to the rain and did not move. Perhaps he was not breathing. Covenant could not tell. He tried to shout up at the First, but no words came. Two more deaths on his head – two men who had served him with a fidelity as great as any Vow. Despite his power, he was helpless to succour them.

Torrents gnashed at the decks. 'Saltroamrest!' the First barked. At once, she strode towards the nearest hatchway.

Covenant followed as if no mere storm, no simple battering of wind and rain, no plunge and roll of footing, could keep him from her.

A deluge pursued him through the hatch, tried to tear him from the ladder as he struggled downward. Then it was cut off as Seadreamer heaved the hatch shut. Instantly, the sounds of the storm were muffled by granite. Yet the companionway pitched as the *dromond* crashed through the seas. The lanterns hanging from the walls swung wildly. Starfare's Gem's peril felt more personal in the constriction of the underdecks – unavoidable, not to be escaped. Covenant hurried after the First and Galewrath, but did not catch up with them until they reached the huge bunkhold of Saltroamrest.

The space appeared as large as a cavern – a hall where nearly two score Giants slung their hammocks without intruding on each other. Lamps hung from all the pillars which supported the hammocks, making Saltroamrest bright. It was virtually empty. The crew was busy fighting for the *dromond*, either at the pumps or aloft. In the centre of the hall, a longtable had been formed into the floor. The First and the Storesmaster hastened to this table, laid Brinn and Cail carefully atop it.

Covenant went to the edge of the longtable. It was as high as the middle of his chest. While he blinked at the water dripping from his hair, the prone *Haruchai* retained their semblance of death. Their brown limbs lay perfect and devoid of life.

But then he saw that they were breathing. Their chests rose and fell gently. Their nostrils flared slightly at each inhalation.

A different salt stung Covenant's eyes. 'Brinn,' he said. 'Cail.' Oh dear God.

They lay as if they were wrapped in the sleep of the damned and did not move.

From the emotional distance, he heard the First say, 'Bring *diamondraught*.' Pitchwife went to obey. 'Storesmaster,' she continued, 'can you waken them?'

Galewrath approached the longtable. She studied the *Haruchai* bluntly, raised their eyelids, chaffed their wrists. After a moment spent listening to their respirations, she announced that their lungs were free of water. With the First's permission, she slapped Cail's face gently, then harder and harder until his head lolled suddenly from side to side. But no flicker of consciousness touched his visage. He and Brinn were twinned in sopor.

She stepped back with a frown knotted between her brows. '*Merewives*,' the First muttered. 'How could we have believed that comrades as staunch as these *Haruchai* would fall prey?'

Pitchwife returned at a swift, awkward gait, carrying a pouch in one hand. The First took it from him. While Galewrath propped Brinn into a sitting position, the First raised the leather mouth to his lips. The smell of *diamondraught* filled the air. Brinn swallowed reflexively. But he did not awaken. Cail also swallowed the liquor which was poured into his mouth. Nothing changed.

Covenant was beating his fists lightly against his thighs, trying to contain his urgency. He did not know what to do. The Giants scowled their ignorance at each other. 'Linden,' he said as if they had spoken to him. 'We need Linden.'

As if in answer to his need, a door at the aft end of Saltroamrest opened. The Chosen entered the hall, lurching against the pitch of the *dromond*'s pace. Mistweave came with her, shadowing her in Cail's place. She was drenched and storm-battered – hair bedraggled, robe scattering water about her legs. But she came purposefully forward.

Covenant did not trust himself to speak. He remained silent and desperate as she approached the longtable.

After a moment, the First found her voice. 'Stone and Sea, Chosen,' she muttered harshly, 'you are not come too soon. We know not how to rouse them. *Diamondraught* they have been given, but it avails nothing. We have no lore for such somnolence.'

Linden stopped, stared at the First. Roughly, the Swordmain continued, 'It is our fear that the hand of the *merewives* yet holds them – and that their peril is also the peril of Starfare's Gem. Mayhap we will not escape the wrath of the Dancers while they remain thus bound to the *Haruchai*. How else to regain what they desire, but to break the *dromond* with their storm?'

At that, Linden flinched. Her eyes flashed splinters of the unsteady lantern-light. 'And you want me to go into them.' Covenant saw a vein in her temple throbbing like a small labour of fear. 'Break the hold. Is that it?' Her glare demanded, Again? How much more do you think I can stand?

Covenant felt her protest acutely. At times in the past, he had experienced the health-sense which dismayed her, though he had never possessed it as keenly as she did. And the *Haruchai* had inflicted so much distrust upon her. But he was more helpless here than she. Blinded by the truncation of his nerves, he could not use his white fire for anything except destruction. Brinn and Cail lay as if they were less alive than Vain. He held Linden's hot gaze, made a broken gesture towards the *Haruchai*. Thickly, he replied, 'Please.'

For a moment longer, she did not move. Pitchwife and the First held themselves still. Then Linden shrugged like a wince, as if her shoulders were sore. 'It can't be any worse than what I've already done.' Deliberately, she stepped to the edge of the longtable.

Covenant watched her hungrily as she explored Brinn and Cail with her hands and eyes. As soon as she accepted the risk, apprehension for her rose up in him. Her every movement was distinct and hazardous. He had felt the power of the *merewives*, knew what it could do. And he remembered how she had looked in the dungeon of the Sandhold, after she had rescued him from the silence of the *Elohim*. Behind her rigid mouth and tormented past, behind her fear and grimness, she had a capacity for self-expenditure that shamed him.

But as she studied the *Haruchai* her manner softened. Her expression eased. The surety of the *Haruchai* seemed to flow into her through her hands. Softly, she said to herself, 'At least those *merewives* know health when they see it.' Then she stepped back.

She did not look at her companions. In a tone of abrupt command, she told Pitchwife to take hold of Brinn's left arm, anchor the *Haruchai* to the table.

Pitchwife complied, mystification in his eyes. The First said nothing. Galewrath frowned noncommittally. Seadreamer's gaze shifted back and forth between Linden and Brinn as if he were trying to guess her intentions.

She did not hesitate. Grasping Brinn's right limb, she pulled it over the edge of the table, leaned her weight on it to stretch it against its socket. When she was sure of her position, she put her mouth close to his ear. Slowly, explicitly, she articulated, 'Now I'm going to break your arm.'

The instant violence of Brinn's reaction took Pitchwife by surprise, broke his hold. He failed to stop the hard arc of Brinn's fist as the *Haruchai* flipped towards Linden, struck at her face.

His blow caught her on the forehead. She reeled backward, crashed against one of the pillars. Holding her ears as if the lanterns were caterwauling like banshees, she slumped to the floor.

For an instant, Covenant's life stopped. Cursing, the First strode towards Linden. Brinn dropped from the table, landed lightly on his feet. Galewrath planted herself in front of him, cocked her massive fist to keep him away from Linden. Cail sat up as if he meant to go to Brinn's aid. Together, Pitchwife and Seadreamer grappled for his arms.

Linden knotted her knees to her chest, clamped her head in both hands, rolled herself weakly from side to side as if she were beset by all the Dancers at once.

From a great distance, Covenant heard a voice snarling, 'Damn you, Brinn! If she's hurt, I'll break your bloody arm myself!' It must have been his voice, but he ignored it. He was swarming towards Linden. Somehow, he shouldered the First aside. Crouching beside Linden, he pulled her into his lap, wrapped his arms around her. She writhed in his embrace as if she were going mad.

A shout gathered in his mind, pounded towards utterance:

Let her go!

The puissance in him seemed to reach her. She dragged her hands down from her head, flung her face towards him. Her mouth shaped

789

a word that might have been, No!

He held himself still as her eyes struggled into focus on his face. One by one, her muscles unclenched. She looked as pale as fever; her breathing rattled in her throat. But she raised a whisper out of her stunned chest. 'I think I'm all right.'

Around Covenant, the lights capered to the tune of the storm's ire. He closed his eyes so that he would not lose control.

When he opened them again, the First and Pitchwife were squatting on either side, watching Linden's fragile recovery. Brinn and Cail stood a short distance away. Behind them Seadreamer loomed as if he were prepared to break both their necks. Galewrath waited to help him. But the *Haruchai* ignored the Giants. They looked like men who had made up their minds.

'There is no need to damn us,' said Brinn flatly. Neither he nor Cail met Covenant's glower. 'We have already gazed upon the visage of our doom. Yet we seek pardon. It was not my intent to do harm.'

He appeared to have no interest in his own apology. 'We withdraw our accusation against the Chosen. She has adjudged us rightly. Mayhap she is in sooth the hand of Corruption among us. But there are other Corruptions which we hold in greater abhorrence.

'We speak neither for our people among their mountains nor for those *Haruchai* who may seek to wage themselves against the depredations of the Clave. But we will no longer serve you.'

At that, a pang of astonishment went through Covenant. *No longer serve* – ? He hardly understood the words. Distress closed his throat. Linden tensed in his arms. *What are you talking about?*

What did they do to you?

Then the First was on her feet. With her stern, iron beauty, her arms folded like bonds across her chest, she towered over the *Haruchai*. 'There is delusion upon you.' She spoke like the riposte of a blade. 'The song of the *merewives* has wrought madness into your hearts. You speak of doom, but that which the Dancers offer is only death, nothing more. Are you blind to the peril from which you were retrieved? Almost Galewrath and I failed of your rescue, for we found you at a depth nigh to our limits. There you lay like men bemused by folly. I know not what dream of joy or transport you found in that song – and I care not. Recumbent like the dead, you lay in no other arms than the limbs of coral which had by chance preserved you from a still deeper plunge. Whatever visions filled your unseeing eyes were the fruit of entrancement and brine. *That* is truth. Is it your intent to return to these *merewives* in the name of delusion?' Her arms corded with anger. 'Stone and Sea, I will not – !'

Brinn interrupted her without looking at her. 'That is not our intent. We do not seek death. We will not again answer the song of the Dancers. But we will no longer serve either the ur-Lord or the

Chosen.' His tone did not relent. He spoke as if he were determined to show himself no mercy. 'We cannot.'

'Can't?' Covenant's expostulation was muffled by alarm.

But Brinn went on as if he were speaking to the First or to no one. 'We doubt not what you have said. You are Giants, long-storied among the old tellers of the *Haruchai*. You have said that the song of the *merewives* is delusion. We acknowledge that you speak truth. But such delusion – '

Then his voice softened in a way that Covenant had never heard before. 'Ur-Lord, will you not rise to confront us? We will not stoop to you. But it is unseemly that we should thus stand above you.'

Covenant looked at Linden. Her features were tense with the effort she made to recollect some semblance of stability; but she nodded, made a groping gesture towards Pitchwife. At once, the Giant lifted her out of Covenant's arms, leaving him free to face the *Haruchai*.

Stiffly, he climbed to his feet. He felt wooden with emotions he was afraid to admit. Was he going to lose the *Haruchai*? The *Haruchai* who had been as faithful as Ranyhyn from the beginning?

What did they do *to you?*

But then Brinn met his gaze for the first time; and the passion in those dispassionate orbs made him tremble. Starfare's Gem heaved among the angry seas as if at any moment the granite might break. He started to spit out every word that came into his head. He did not want to hear what Brinn would say.

'You made a promise.' His chest rose and fell with the rough force of his knowledge that he had no right to accuse the *Haruchai* of anything. 'I didn't want to accept it. I didn't want to be responsible for any more service like the kind Bannor insisted on giving me. But I had no choice.' He had been more than half crippled by loss of blood, might have died of sheer remorse and futility on the upland plateau above Revelstone if Brinn had not aided him. 'What in hell are you talking about?'

'Ur-Lord.' Brinn did not swerve from the path he had chosen. 'Did you not hear the song of the *merewives*?'

'What has that got to do with it?' Covenant's belligerence was hollow, but he could not set it aside. It was his only defence. 'The only reason they took you is because they didn't want anybody as flawed or at least destructive as I am.'

Brinn shook his head. 'Also,' he went on, 'is it not truly said of the Unbeliever that at one time in his distress he vowed the Land to be a dream – a thing of falseness and seduction, not to be permitted?'

That struck Covenant voiceless. Everything he might have said seemed to curdle in him, sickened by anticipation. He had told Linden on Kevin's Watch, *We're sharing a dream* – a belief he had once needed and later outgrew. It had become irrelevant. Until this moment, he had considered it to be irrelevant.

Are you going to blame me for *that* too?

Deliberately, the *Haruchai* continued, 'The First has said that the song of the Dancers is delusion. Perhaps in our hearts we knew it for delusion as we harkened to it. But we are *Haruchai*, and we gave it answer.

'Mayhap you know too little of us. The lives of our people upon the mountains are strict and costly, for peaks and snows are no gentle bourne. Therefore we are prolific in our seed, that we may endure from generation to generation. The bond joining man to women is a fire in us, and deep. Did not Bannor speak to you of this? For those who became Bloodguard, the loss of sleep and death was a little thing, lightly borne. But the loss of wives – It was that which caused them to end their Vow when Corruption placed his hand upon them. Any man may fail or die. But how may one of the *Haruchai* who has left his wife in the name of a chosen fidelity endure to know that even his fidelity may be riven from him? Better the Vow had never been uttered, no service given.

'Ur-Lord.' Brinn did not look away. He hardly blinked. Yet the unwonted implication of softness in his tone was unmistakable. 'In the song of the *merewives* we heard the fire of our yearning for that which we have left behind. Assuredly we were deluded – but the delusion was sweet. Mountains sprang about us. The air became the keen breath which the peaks exhale from their snows. And upon the slopes moved the women who call to us in their longing for fire and seed and offspring.' For a moment, he broke into the tonal tongue of the *Haruchai*; and that language seemed to transform his visage, giving him an aspect of poetry. 'Therefore did we leap to answer, disregarding all service and safety. The limbs of our women are brown from sun and birth. But there is also a whiteness as acute as the ice which bleeds from the rock of mountains, and it burns as the purest snow burns in the most high tor, the most wind-flogged col. For that whiteness, we gave ourselves to the Dancers of the Sea.'

Covenant could no longer meet Brinn's gaze. Bannor had hinted at these things – things which made the *Haruchai* explicable. Their rigid and judgmental stance against the world came from this, that every breath they took was an inhalation of desire and loss.

He looked to his companions for help; but none of them had any to offer. Linden's eyes were misted with pain or recognition. Empathy twisted Pitchwife's mien. And the First, who understood extravagance, stood beside Brinn and Cail as if she approved.

Inflexibly, Brinn went on, 'Thus we demonstrated ourselves false. Our given fidelity we betrayed at the behest of a delusion. Our promise to you we were unable to keep. We are unworthy. Therefore we will no longer serve you. Our folly must end now, ere greater promises than ours become false in consequence.'

'Brinn,' Covenant protested as if he were choking. 'Cail.' His distress demanded utterance. 'You don't need to do that. Nobody blames you.' His voice was harsh, as if he meant to be brutal. Linden reached a hand weakly towards him like a plea for pity. Her eyes streamed with comprehension of the plight of the *Haruchai*. But he ignored her. The hard clench of his passion prevented him from speaking in any other way.

'Bannor did the same thing. Just what you're doing. We were standing on Landsdrop – with Foamfollower. He refused to come with us, when I needed – ' He swallowed convulsively. 'I asked him what he was ashamed of. He said, "I am not shamed. But I am saddened that so many centuries were required to teach us the limits of our worth. We went too far, in pride and folly. Mortal men should not give up wives and sleep and death for any service – lest the face of failure become too abhorrent to be endured." The same thing you're saying now. But don't you understand? It's not that simple. Anybody can fail. But the Bloodguard didn't just fail. They lost faith. Or why do you think Bannor had to meet me in Andelain? If you're right, why didn't he let you just go on paying the price of your unworth?'

Covenant wanted to beat his frustration at Brinn. Grimly, he restrained himself, strove instead to make his words felt through the *Haruchai*'s intransigence.

'I'll tell you why. Maybe no Vow or promise is the answer to Despite – but neither is abdication. He didn't give me any promises, any gifts. He just said, "Redeem my people. Their plight is an abomination. And they will serve you well."'

Then he stopped. He could not go on; he understood too well the extremity of the man he faced. For a moment, Saltroamrest was silent except for the labour of the *dromond*'s pumps, the creaking of the masts, the muffled fury of the seas and wind. The lanterns continued to sway vulnerably. Seadreamer's eyes burned at the *Haruchai* as if he sensed a strange hope in their intractable self-judgment.

At last, Brinn spoke. He sounded almost gentle. 'Ur-Lord, have we not served you well?'

Covenant's features contorted in bereavement. But he made a fierce effort, forced himself to reply, 'You know you have.'

Brinn did not flinch or hesitate. 'Then let it end.'

Covenant turned to Linden. His hands groped for contact with her. But his fingers were numb. He found no other answer in her.

Later that night, in the privacy of her cabin, while the storm thrashed and clawed at the Giantship, he rubbed the sore muscles of her neck and back. His fingers worked at her as if they were desperate with loss. Gradually, the *diamondraught* she had consumed to speed her recovery put her to sleep; but he did not stop massaging her until his hands were too tired to continue. He did not know what else to do with his despair. The defection of the *Haruchai* seemed to presage the collapse of all his hopes.

Later still, Starfare's Gem lifted its sails into the grey dawn and ran beyond the grief of the *merewives*. The rain ended like tears which had fallen too long; the wind frayed away towards other parts of the Sea. Honninscrave needed only a slight adjustment of course to head the *dromond* directly for its goal.

But the *Haruchai* did not relent.

24

THE ISLE

The sky remained beclouded and blustery for two days, echoing the grey moil of the Sea like indignation, as if Starfare's Gem were an intrusion which vexed the region. But then the wind rose in dismissal, and the *dromond* was swept into a period of clear days and crystal nights. Under the sun, the Sea joined the heavens without seam or taint; and at night the specific glitter of the stars marked out the path of the quest for any experienced gaze to read.

Grimmand Honninscrave grew more eager every day. And the immaculate wind seemed to fan both the First and Pitchwife into a heat of anticipation. At unguarded moments, his misborn grotesquerie and her iron beauty looked oddly similar, as if their progress towards the One Tree were deepening their intimacy. The three of them studied the distance constantly, searching the horizon for validation of the choices which had taken them away from the Land in spite of Seadreamer's plain Earth-Sight.

Their keenness spread out across the Giantship, affecting all the crew. Even Heft Galewrath's blunt features took on a whetted aspect. And Sevinhand's old sadness passed through periods of sunshine like hope.

Linden Avery watched them as she watched the ship itself and Covenant, trying to find her place among them. She understood the Giants, knew that much of their eagerness arose on Seadreamer's behalf. His dumb misery was vivid to everyone. His people champed to accomplish their purpose and head back towards the Land, where he might be able to seek relief in the crisis of the Sunbane, the apotheosis of his vision. But she did not share that particular longing.

794

She feared that the Giants did not recognize the true nature of his vision.

And Covenant's mood only aggravated her apprehension. He seemed avid for the One Tree to the point of fever. Emotionally if not physically, he had drawn away from her. The rejection of the *Haruchai* had driven him into a state of rigid defensiveness. When he talked, his voice had a ragged edge which he could not blunt; and his eyes sent out reflections of bloodshed. She saw in his face that he was remembering the Clave, people butchered to feed the Banefire, self-distrust; remembering power and venom over which he had no control. At times, his gaze was hollow with recollections of silence. Even his lovemaking became strangely vehement as if despite their embraces he believed he had already lost her.

She could not forget that he intended to send her back to her former life. He was fervid for the One Tree for his own reasons, hoping that it would enable him to fight Lord Foul with something other than white fire and destruction. But he also wanted it because of her. To send her back.

She dreaded that, dreaded the One Tree. Seadreamer's mute and untouchable trepidation ached in her like an open wound. Whenever he came within range of her senses, she felt his ambience bleeding. At times, she could barely rein herself from urging Covenant, the First, anyone who would listen to abandon the quest — forget the One Tree, return to the Land, fight the Sunbane with whatever weapons were available and accept the outcome. She believed that Seadreamer knew exactly what Lord Foul was doing. And she did not want to be sent back.

Late one night, when Covenant had at last fallen into a sleep free of nightmares, she left his side, went up to the decks. She wore her woollen robe. Though the air had become noticeably cooler during the past few days, she shied away from her old clothes as if they represented exigencies and failures she did not wish to reconsider. On the afterdeck, she found Starfare's Gem riding unerringly before the wind under a moon already in its last quarter. Soon nothing would stand between the *dromond* and darkness except the ambiguous stars and a few lanterns. But for this night, at least, a crescent of light remained acute in the heavens.

Sevinhand greeted her quietly from the wheeldeck; but she did not go to him. Beyond the wind, the long stone sea-running of the *dromond*, the slumber of the Giants who were not on watch, she sensed Seadreamer's presence like a hand of pain cupped against her cheek. Huddling into her robe, she went forward.

She found the mute Giant sitting with his back to the foremast, facing the prow and Findail's silhouette. The small muscles around his eyes winced and tightened as he stared at Findail — and through Findail towards the One Tree — as if he were begging the Appointed to say the things which he, Seadreamer, could not. But Findail seemed immune to the Giant's appeal. Or perhaps such supplications were a part of the burden which he had been Appointed to bear. He also faced the prospect of the One Tree as if he feared to take his eyes from it.

In silence, Linden seated herself beside Seadreamer. He sat cross-legged, with his hands in his lap. At intervals, he turned the palms upward as if he were trying to open himself to the night, accept his doom. But repeatedly his fists clenched, shoulders knotted, transforming him to a figure of protest.

After a moment, she breathed, 'Try.' The frail sickle-moon lit none of his visage except the pale scar which underlined his gaze; the rest remained dark. 'There's got to be some way.'

With a violence that made her flinch, his hands leaped upward. Their heels thudded bitterly against his forehead. But an instant later he snatched air in through his teeth, and his hands began sketching shapes across the night.

At first, she was unable to follow his gestures: the outline he attempted to form eluded her. But he tried again, strove to grasp an image out of the blank air. This time, she understood him.

'The One Tree.'

He nodded rigidly. His arms made an arc around him.

'The ship,' she whispered. 'Starfare's Gem.'

Again, he nodded. He repeated the movement of his arms, then pointed forward past the prow. His hands redelineated the tree-shape.

'The ship's going to the One Tree.'

Seadreamer shook his head.

'When the ship gets to the One Tree.'

This time, his nod was stiff with grief. With one finger, he tapped his chest, pointing at his heart. Then his hands came together, twisted each other – a wrench as violent as a rupture. Trails of silver gleamed across his scar.

When Linden could no longer bear the sight, she looked away – and found Findail there, come to witness the Giant's pantomime. The moon lay beyond his right shoulder, all his face and form were dark.

'Help him,' she demanded softly. Help me. 'Can't you see what he's going through?'

For a long moment, the *Elohim* did not move or reply. Then he stepped close to the Giant, reached out one hand to Seadreamer's forehead. His fingertips pressed gentleness on to the fate written there. Almost at once, Seadreamer slumped. Muscle by muscle, the pressure ran out of him as if it were being absorbed by Findail's touch. His chin sagged to his breast. He was asleep.

796

In silence, Findail turned back to the station he had chosen in the *dromond*'s prow.

Carefully, so that she would not disturb the Giant's rest, Linden rose to her feet, returned like mute rue to lie at Covenant's side and stare at the ceiling of her cabin until she slept.

The next morning, she brought up the question of Seadreamer in front of the First, Pitchwife, Honninscrave, and Covenant. But the Master had no new insight to give her. And Pitchwife reiterated his hope that Seadreamer would gain some relief when their quest for the One Tree had been accomplished.

Linden knew better. Severely, she described her encounter with the mute Giant the previous night.

Pitchwife made no effort to conceal his dismay. Cocking her fists on her hips, the First gazed away past the prow and muttered long Giantish curses under her breath. Honninscrave's features knotted like the stiff tangle of his beard.

Covenant stood among them as if he were alone; but he spoke for them all. His gaze wandered over the stone, avoiding Linden as he rasped, 'Do you think we should turn back?'

She wanted to answer, Yes! But she could not. He had invested all his hope in the One Tree.

For a time, Honninscrave's commands to the crew were tinged with uncertainty, as if within a voice of denial cried out that the *dromond* should be turned at once, sent with all possible speed away from its fatal destination. But he kept his fear to himself. The Giantship's path across the seas did not waver.

That clear wind blew for five days. It became gradually but steadily cooler as the vessel angled into the north; but it remained dry, firm, and insistent. And for three of those days, the quest arrowed swiftly along the waters without incident, meeting no danger, sighting no landfall.

But on the fourth day, a cry of astonishment and alarm rang down from the lookout. The stone under Linden's feet began to vibrate as if the Sea were full of tremors. Honninscrave shortened sail, readied his ship for emergency. In another league, Starfare's Gem found itself gliding through a region crowded with *Nicor*.

Their immense shapes each broke water in several places; together, they marked the Sea like a multitude. Their underwater talk thrummed against Linden's senses. Remembering the one *Nicor* she had seen previously, she feared for the safety of the *dromond*. But these creatures appeared oblivious to Starfare's Gem. Their voices conveyed no timbre of peril to her percipience. They moved without haste or hunger, lolling vaguely as if they were immersed in lethargy, boredom, or contentment. Occasionally, one of them lifted a massive snout, then subsided with a distant soughing of water like a sigh of indifference. Honninscrave was able to steer his vessel among them without attracting their attention.

'Stone and Sea!' Pitchwife breathed softly to Linden, 'I had not thought that all the seas of the Earth together contained so many such creatures. The stories of them are so scanty that one *Nicor* alone might account for them all. What manner of ocean is it that we have entered with such blithe ignorance?'

The First was standing beside him. He looked up at her as he concluded, 'Yet this will be a tale to delight any child.' She did not meet his gaze; but the smile which softened her eyes was as private as the affection in his tone.

Honninscrave's care took the Giantship slowly among the *Nicor*; but by midafternoon the creatures had been left behind, and Starfare's Gem resumed its flying pace. And that night, a mood of over-stretched gaiety came upon the Giants. They roistered and sang under the implacable stars like feverish children, insensate to the quest's purpose or Seadreamer's pain; and Pitchwife led them in one long caper of enforced mirth, as if he were closer to hysteria than any of them. But Linden heard the truth of their emotion. They were affirming themselves against their own apprehensions, venting their suspense in communal frolic. And Pitchwife's wild effort heightened the mood to catastasis, finally giving rise to a humour that was less desperate and more solacing – warm, purified, and indomitable. If Covenant had sought to join them, Linden would have gone with him.

But he did not. He stood apart as if the recanting of the *Haruchai* had shaken him to the core of his strength, rendering him inaccessible to consolation. Or perhaps he held back because he had forgotten how to be alone, how to confront his doom without loathing his loneliness. When he and Linden went below to her cabin, he huddled on the pallet as if he could hardly endure the bare comfort of her flesh. The One Tree was near. With the muffled uproar of the Giants in her ears, she hung on the verge of urging him, Don't send me back. But her inbred fears paralysed her, and she did not take the risk.

All night, she felt that she was redreaming familiar nightmares. But when she awakened, they were gone from her memory.

Covenant stood beside the hammock with his back to her. He held his old clothes as if he meant to don them. She watched him with an ache in her eyes, begging him mutely not to return to what he had been, what they had been towards each other.

He seemed to feel her gaze on him: he turned to her, met her look. His face wore a grimace of bile. But he did not retreat from what he saw. Though his anticipation of the One Tree felt more like

798

dread than eagerness, he was strong yet, as dangerous as she remembered him. After a moment, he threw his garments deliberately into the corner. Then he knelt to her, took her in his arms.

When they went on deck later, he wore the woollen robe he had been given as if his leprosy inured him to the late autumn coolness of the air. His choice relieved her; and yet he appeared curiously ill-prepared in that robe, as if his love for her had robbed him of more defences than she knew how to estimate or compensate for.

They paced out the day across the decks, waiting. They were all waiting, she and Covenant and the Giants with them. Time and again, she saw crewmembers pause in their tasks to peer past the ship's prow. But throughout the morning they saw nothing except the expanse of the Sea, stretching to the edges of the world. After their noon meal, they went on waiting and still saw nothing.

But in the middle of the afternoon, the call came at last – a shout of annunciation which nevertheless struck Linden's tension like a wail. Giants sprang for the rigging to see what the lookout had seen. Seadreamer appeared from belowdecks, climbed grimly upward. Covenant pressed his chest against the foredeck rail for a moment, as if in that way he might force himself to see farther. Then he muttered to Linden, 'Come on,' and set off towards the vantage of the wheeldeck. Like him, she could hardly keep from running.

The First and Pitchwife were there with Honninscrave and a Giant tending Shipsheartthew. Sevinhand and Galewrath arrived shortly. Together, the companions stared ahead for some glimpse of the Isle of the One Tree.

For a league or more, the horizon remained immaculate and unexplained. Then Honninscrave's arm leaped to point almost directly over the prow. Linden was not as far-eyed as the Giants; but after another league she also spotted the Isle. Tiny in the distance, it stood like a point of fatality at the juncture of Sea and sky – the pivot around which the Earth turned. As the wind carried Starfare's Gem swiftly forward, the Isle grew as if it would fulfil all the quest's expectations.

She looked at Covenant; but he did not meet her gaze. His attention was fixed ahead: his stance was as keen as if he were on the verge of fire. Though he did not speak, the strict, gaunt lines of his visage said as clearly as words that his life or death would be decided here.

By slow degrees, the island revealed itself to the approaching vessel. It stood like a cairn of old rock piled on the surface of the Sea. Weather had softened and rimed the grey, jumbled stones, with the result that they seemed almost pure white where the sun touched them, nearly black where they lay in shadow. It was an eyot of day and night – rugged, hoary, and irrefragable. Its crown stood high above the Giantship; but the shade of its upper rims suggested that the island had once been a volcano, or that it was now hollow.

Later, the *dromond* drew close enough to discern that the Isle sat within a ragged circle of reefs. These jutted into the air like teeth, with many gaps between them; but none of the openings were large enough to admit Starfare's Gem.

As the sun declined, Honninscrave set the Giantship on a curving course to pass around the cairn so that he could look for a passage while his companions searched for some sign of the One Tree. Linden's eyes clung to the island: she studied every variation of its light-and-dark from crown to shore with every dimension of her sight. But she found nothing. The Isle was composed of nothing but blind stone, immune to every form of vitality but its own. Even among the rocks where the waves surged and fell, there lived no weeds or other sea-growths.

The rocks themselves were vivid to her, as massive and consequential as compressed granite – an outcropping of the essential skeleton of the Earth. But perhaps for that very reason they played host to none of the more transient manifestations of life. As she studied them, she realized that they did not even provide a roost for birds. Perhaps the water within the reefs did not hold fish.

'Where is it?' Covenant muttered, speaking to everyone and no one. 'Where is it?'

After a moment, Pitchwife replied, 'Upon the crest. Is that not a natural bourne for the thing we seek?'

Linden kept her doubts to herself. As the sun began to set, casting orange and gold in an unreadable chiaroscuro across the slopes, Starfare's Gem completed its circuit of the Isle; and she had seen nothing to indicate that the One Tree was here – or that it had ever existed.

At a nod from the First, Honninscrave ordered the furling of the sails, the anchoring of the *dromond* beyond the northern reefs. For a few moments, no one on the wheeldeck spoke; the emblazoned visage of the Isle held them. In this light, they could see that they were facing a place of power. The sun withdrew as if it were bidding farewell to the Earth. Behind the murmurous labour of the Giants, the complaining of lines and pulleys, the wet embrace of the waves upon the reefs, everything was silent. Not one kestrel raised its cry to ameliorate the starkness of the Isle. The eyot stood within its protective teeth as if it had stood that way forever and would never be appeased.

Then the First said quietly, 'Giantfriend, will you not await the new day, ere you attempt this place?'

A shudder like a sudden chill ran through him. In a rough voice, he replied, 'No.'

The First sighed. But she did not demur. She spoke to Sevinhand; and he went to supervise the launching of a longboat.

Then she addressed Covenant again. 'We have come a great way to this Isle. Because of your might – and of that which you wrought in The Grieve of our lost kindred – we have not questioned you concerning your purpose. But now I ask.' In the west, the sun seemed to be dying behind the long curve of the Sea. Covenant's gaze was an echo of fire. 'Have you given thought to the how of this Staff of Law you desire to conceive?'

Linden answered for him, claiming her place in the company because she did not know any other way to dissuade him from his intent for her. 'That's why I'm here.'

He looked at her sharply; but she kept her eyes on the First. 'My senses,' she said, awkward with self-consciousness. 'The things I see and feel. Health. Rightness. Honesty. What else can it mean? I'm sensitive to Law. I can tell when things fit – and when they don't. I can guide him.'

Yet as soon as she made her claim, she knew that it was not enough. His emanations were precise. He had been counting on her help. But he did not change his mind. Instead, he regarded her as if she had expressed a desire to leave him. Hope and grief were indistinguishable in him.

Uncognizant of Covenant's self-contradiction, the First accepted Linden's answer. With Pitchwife and Honninscrave, she left the wheeldeck, went to the railing where the longboat was being lowered.

Galewrath assumed command of Starfare's Gem. When she had satisfied herself that the *dromond* was being given proper care, she said to Covenant and Linden, 'Go well.'

Covenant made no reply. He stared at the Isle as if he could read his doom in the fading glory of the sun.

Linden stepped close to him, placed her hand upon his shoulder. He turned stiffly, letting her see the conflicts in his face. He was a figure of illumination and darkness, like the Isle.

She tried again to make him understand her. 'Seadreamer is afraid. I think he knows what Lord Foul is doing.'

His features knotted once, then released as if he were about to afflict her with a smile like the one he had once given Joan. 'That doesn't matter.' Slowly, his expression grew more gentle. 'When I was in Andelain, Mhoram said, "It boots nothing to avoid his snares, for they are ever beset with other snares, and life and death are too intimately intergrown to be severed from each other. But it is necessary to comprehend them, so that they may be mastered."' Then he stiffened again. 'Come on. Let's go find out what kind of trouble we're in.'

She did not want to let him go. She wanted to fling her arms around him, hug and hold him, make him stop what he was doing. But she did not. Was this not why she loved him – because he did not shy from his own pain? Gritting her courage, she followed him down the stairs as if he were leading her into night.

Sunset still held the masts, but the afterdeck had fallen into gloaming. She needed a moment to adjust her sight before she was able to descry Seadreamer standing at the rail with Honninscrave, the First, and Pitchwife. Vain was there also, as black as the coming dark. Findail had moved aft as well; his robe formed a pale blur beside Vain's ebony. And Brinn and Cail had come. Linden was surprised to see them. Covenant's stride faltered as he neared them. But they did not speak, and he went abruptly past them. Reaching the First, he asked, 'Are we ready?'

'As ready as may be,' she replied, 'with our fate unknown before us.'

He answered like the darkness thickening around the *dromond*, 'Then let's get started.'

At once, Findail interposed in a tone of warning and supplication, 'Ring-wielder, will you not bethink you? Surrender this mad purpose while choice yet remains to you. I tell you plainly that you are the plaything of powers which will destroy you – and the Earth with you. This attempt upon the One Tree must not be made.'

Mutely, Seadreamer nodded as if he had no choice.

Covenant jerked around to face the Appointed. Speaking softly, almost to himself, he breathed, 'I should've known that's what you're afraid of. The One Tree. The Staff of Law. You're afraid I might actually succeed. Or why did you try to capture Vain? Why have you tried so hard to keep us from trusting ourselves? You are going to lose something if we succeed. I don't know what it is, but you're terrified about it.

'Well, take a look,' he went on grimly. 'Vain's still with us. He's still got the heels of the old Staff.' He spoke as if his doubt of the Demondim-spawn no longer mattered. 'I'm still here. I've still got my ring. Linden's still here.' Suddenly, his voice dropped to a whisper like a suspiration of anguish. 'By hell, if you want me to surrender, you have got to give me a *reason*.'

The Appointed returned Covenant's demand in silence. Clearly, he did not intend to answer.

After a moment, Covenant swung back to the rest of the company, glaring as if he expected them to argue with him. But Honninscrave was tense with empathy. There was no hesitation in the First's stern resolve or Pitchwife's anticipation of wonder. And Seadreamer made no attempt to dissuade the Unbeliever.

Driven by the demons of his personal exigency, Covenant moved to the railing, set his feet to the rope-ladder leading down to the longboat.

Linden followed him at once, unwilling to let even one Giant take her place at his side.

Cail and Brinn were right behind her.

All of the Isle had now fallen into shadow except its crown, which held the fading sunset like an oriflamme that was about to be swallowed by the long night of the Earth. But while the light lasted, it made the crest look like a place where the One Tree might indeed be found. As she turned her back on the sight in order to descend the ladder, Linden remembered that this night would be the dark of the moon. Instinctively, she shivered. Her robe seemed suddenly scanty against the chill dark which appeared to rise out of the water like an exhalation. The rocking of the waves forced a splash up between the *dromond* and the longboat just as she was reaching one leg towards the smaller craft; and the water stung her bare flesh as if its salt were as potent as acid. But she muffled her involuntary gasp, lowered herself into the bottom of the boat, then moved to take a seat with Covenant in the prow. The water tightened the skin of her legs as it dried, sending a tingle through her nerves.

The *Haruchai* were followed by Honninscrave. While his bulk came downward, the sun lost its grasp on the Isle's crown, fell entirely beyond the horizon. Now the Isle was visible only as a shadow on the deep, silhouetted by the slowly emerging stars. Linden could not discern the lines of the reef at all. But as Honninscrave and Seadreamer seated themselves at the oars, their oaken shoulders expressed no doubt of their ability to find their way. The Master was speaking to his brother, but the chatter and splash of water covered the words.

Pitchwife and the First descended to the longboat in silence. From out of the night, a shadow floated into the bottom of the craft at Seadreamer's back, where it solidified and became Findail. Vain placed himself in the other half of the boat with Brinn and Cail, near the stern where the First and Pitchwife sat.

Linden reached out, took Covenant's hand. His fingers felt icy; his numbness had become a palpable cold.

The First waved a salute to the Giants of Starfare's Gem. If Sevinhand or Galewrath returned an answer, it was inaudible over the chill chuckling of the waters. Deftly, Honninscrave unmoored the longboat, thrust it away from the *dromond* with his oar. Surrounded only by lapping waves, the company moved out into the night.

For several moments, no one spoke. Covenant sat with his face turned to the dark, clenching Linden's hand as if it were an anchor. She watched the Isle gradually clarify itself as the stars behind it became more explicit; but still she could not make out the reefs. The blackness rising from the water seemed impenetrable. Yet the oars beat steadily, slipping in and out of the unquiet seas; and the boat moved forward as if it were being impelled at great speed, headlong towards its unknown end. The Isle loomed massively out of the night, as dangerous to approach as the entryway of hell.

Linden became suddenly and irrationally alarmed that the boat would strike one of the reefs and sink. But then the First said softly, 'Somewhat to starboard.' The longboat changed direction slightly. A few heartbeats later, jagged coral shapes leaped up on either hand. Their unexpected appearance made Linden start. But the longboat passed safely between them into calmer water.

From this vantage – so close to the Sea, with the night complete from horizon to horizon – the Isle seemed much farther away than it had from Starfare's Gem. But for a while the company made good progress. Guided by vision, Seadreamer hauled heavily against his oars, knocking them in their locks at every stroke; and Honninscrave matched the rhythm if not the urgency of his brother's pull. As a result, the Isle grew slowly taller and more implacable, reaching towards the sky as if it were the base upon which the firmament of the stars stood. Linden began to think that the slopes would be unscalable in the dark – that perhaps they could not be climbed at all, especially if Covenant could not master his vertigo. His hand in hers felt as chill as if his very bones were cold.

But a short time later she forgot that anxiety, forgot even to grip Covenant's fingers. She was staring at the change which came over the Isle.

The First and Pitchwife stood. The boat glided to a stop in the water. Honninscrave and Seadreamer had lifted their oars so that they might look past the prow towards their destination.

Plumes and streamers of mist had begun to flow down off the sides of the island. The mist seemed to arise like steam from unseen cracks among the rocks. Some of it curled upward, frayed away into the sharp night. But most of it poured towards the Sea, gathering and thickening as the streams commingled.

The mist was alight. It did not appear to shine of its own accord. Rather, it looked like ordinary fog under a full moon. But there was no moon. And the illumination was cast only upon the mist. Stately banners and rills of air came downward like condensations of moonglow, revealing nothing but themselves.

When its nimbus spread like a vapour of frost around the shores of the eyot, the mist began to pile out over the Sea. Gradually all the Isle except the crown disappeared. Silver and ghostly, the glowing fog expanded towards the longboat as if it meant to fill the entire zone of the reefs.

Linden had to suppress a desire for flight. She felt viscerally certain that she did not want that eldritch and inexplicable air to touch her. But the quest's path lay forward. With an oddly stern and gentle command, the First returned Honninscrave and Seadreamer to their oars. 'I am done with waiting,' she said. 'If this is our future, let us at least meet it by our own choice.'

Thrust and sweep, the oars measured out the quest's progress towards the advancing mist. The stars overhead glittered as if in warning; but the longboat went on straight at the heart of the wet vapour. The mist continued to pile on to the Sea. Already, it had become so thick that the sides of the eyot could no longer be seen, had accumulated so high that the rocky crown was almost obscured. Its illumination made it look gnashed and lambent with moonlight. Its outward flow accentuated the speed of the longboat; the craft seemed to rush madly across the dark face of the water.

Then the First murmured a command. Honninscrave and Seadreamer raised their oars. The boat glided in silence and poised apprehension into the mist.

At once, the sky disappeared. Linden felt the touch of moist light on her face and flinched, expecting danger or harm. But then her senses told her that the mist's power was too elusive, too much like moonshine, to cause damage – or to convey comprehension. Her companions were clearly visible; but the Sea itself had vanished under a dense silver carpet, and the ends of the oars passed out of sight as if they had been gnawed off.

With a new twist of anxiety, she wondered how the quest would be able to find its way. But when the First spoke again, sending Honninscrave and Seadreamer back to their labour, her voice held an iron certainty; and she suggested small corrections of course as if her sense of direction were immune to confusion.

The movement of the longboat made the mist float against Linden's face. Beads of evanescent light condensed in Covenant's hair like the nacre sweat of his need and might. After a few moments, the mist swirled and folded, opening a glimpse of the crest of the Isle. Before the gap closed, Linden saw that the First's aim was accurate.

Pitchwife began speaking. His voice seemed to rise with difficulty, as if his cramped lungs were filling with mist and moisture. He complimented Honninscrave and Seadreamer on their rowing, wryly praised Vain's inscrutability, described other mists he had encountered in his voyages. The words themselves had no significance: only the act of uttering them mattered. For the sake of his companions – and of himself – he sought to humanize the entrancement of the mist. But an odd echo paced his speech, as if the vapour were a cavern. The First finally whispered tightly to him. He desisted.

In silence punctuated only by the splashing of the oars, the longboat went forward.

By degrees, the mist came to feel like a dream in which long spans of time passed with indefeasible haste. The obscure light exerted a hypnotic fascination. Drops of water like tiny globes fell from the line of Covenant's jaw, leaving faint spatters of illumination on his robe. Linden's raiment was bedizened with dying gems. Her hair hung wet and dark against the sides of her face.

When the mist unwound itself enough to permit another momentary view of the Isle she hardly noticed that the rocks were no closer than before.

Honninscrave and Seadreamer continued rowing; but their breath slowly stiffened in their lungs, and their backs and shoulders cast emanations of strain. They made Linden aware of the passage of time. The trancelike vapour seemed to have consumed half the night. She tried to throw off her numbness, rub the damp stupefaction from her cheeks. At the next opening of the mist, she saw the Isle clearly.

The longboat had not advanced at all.

'Hellfire,' Covenant rasped. 'Hell and blood.'

'Now am I mazed in good sooth,' began Pitchwife. 'This atmosphere – ' But he lost the words he needed.

Findail stood facing the Isle. His mien and hair were dry, untouched by the mist. He held his arms folded across his chest as if the Sea were gripped motionless in the crooks of his elbows. The focus of his eyes was as intent as an act of will.

'Findail – ' Linden began. 'What in God's name are you doing to us?'

But then violence broke out behind the Appointed.

Brinn attempted to leap past Honninscrave and Seadreamer. Seadreamer grappled for him, held him back. Thrashing together, they fell into the bottom of the boat. Honninscrave shipped his oars, then caught hold of Seadreamer's as they slipped from the locks. At once, Pitchwife came forward, to take the oars.

Honninscrave swung around and began trying to extricate Brinn and Seadreamer from each other.

Cail moved towards the fray. Rising to her feet, the First caught hold of him, jerked him unceremoniously behind her. Then her sword was in her hands.

'Enough!'

Honninscrave shifted out of her way. Seadreamer stopped fighting. Before Brinn could evade her, she had her blade at his throat.

Cail tried to go to Brinn's aid. Honninscrave blocked him.

'Now,' the First said, 'you will tell me the meaning of this.'

Brinn did not reply to her. He directed his voice at Covenant. 'Ur-Lord, permit me to speak with you.'

At once, Seadreamer shook his head vehemently.

Covenant started to respond. Linden stopped him. 'Just a minute.' She was panting as if the mist were hard to breathe. Quickly, she crossed the thwarts to Seadreamer. He huddled in the bottom of the longboat. His eyes met hers like a plea.

'You've seen something,' she said. 'You know what's going on here.'

His visage was wet with condensed mistglow. The moisture made his scar look like an outcry.

'You don't want Brinn to talk to Covenant.'

Seadreamer's eyes winced. She had guessed wrongly.

She tried again. 'You don't want him to do what he has in mind. You don't want him to persuade Covenant to let him do it.'

At that, the mute Giant nodded with fierce urgency.

Her intuitions outran her. Seadreamer's intensity conveyed a personal dismay which transcended logic. 'If Brinn does it – what he wants to do – then all the terrible things you've been seeing are going to happen. We won't be able to stop them.' Then the sight of his distress closed her throat. *This is your only chance to save yourself.*

Fighting to regain her voice, she confronted Covenant across the forepart of the boat. 'Don't – ' She was trembling. 'Don't let him do it. The consequences – '

Covenant was not looking at her. He watched Brinn with an aghast nausea which forced Linden to wheel in that direction.

The *Haruchai* had gripped the First's blade in one hand. Against her great strength, he strove to thrust the iron away from his throat. Blood coursed down his forearm as the longsword bit his flesh; but his determination did not waver. In a moment, he would sever his fingers if the First did not relent.

'Brinn!' Linden protested.

The *Haruchai* showed no sign that he heard her.

Cursing under her breath, the First withdrew her sword. 'You are mad.' She was hoarse with emotion. 'I will not accept the burden of your maiming or death in this way.'

Without a glance at her, Brinn climbed to his feet, moved towards Covenant. His hand continued to bleed, but he ignored it – only clenched his fingers around the wound and let it run. He seemed to carry his fist cocked as if he meant to attack the Unbeliever.

But near Covenant he stopped. 'Ur-Lord, I ask you to hear me.'

Covenant stared at the *Haruchai*. His nod appeared oddly fragile; the acuity of his passion made him brittle. Around them, the mist flowed and seethed as if it would never let them go.

'There is a tale among the *Haruchai*,' Brinn began without inflection, 'a legend preserved by the old tellers from the farthest distance of our past, long ages before our people ever encountered Kevin Landwaster and the Lords of the Land. It is said that upon the edge of the Earth at the end of time stands a lone man who holds the meaning of the *Haruchai* – a man whom we name *ak-Haru Kenaustin Ardenol*. It is said that he has mastered all skill and prowess that we desire, all restraint and calm, and has become perfection – passion and mastery like unto the poised grandeur of mountains. And it is said, should ever one of the *Haruchai* seek out *ak-Haru Kenaustin Ardenol* and contest with him, we will learn the measure of our worth, in defeat or triumph. Therefore are the *Haruchai* a seeking people. In each heart among us beats a yearning for this test and the knowledge it offers.

'Yet the path which leads to *ak-Haru Kenaustin Ardenol* is unknown, has never been known. It is said that this path must not be known – that it may only be found by one who knows without knowledge and has not come seeking the thing he seeks.' In spite of its flatness, Brinn's voice expressed a mounting excitement. 'I am that one. To this place I have come in your name rather than my own, seeking that which I have not sought.

'Ur-Lord, we have withdrawn from your service. I do not seek to serve you now. But you wield the white ring. You hold power to prevent my desire. Should you take this burden upon yourself, it will be lost to me – perhaps to all *Haruchai* forever. I ask that you permit me. Of Cable Seadreamer's Earth-Sight I comprehend nothing. It is clear to me that I will only succeed or fail. If I fail, the matter will fall to you. And if I succeed – ' His voice dropped as if in no other way could he contain the strength of his yearning. 'Ur-Lord.' Clenched as if it were squeezing blood out of itself, his fist rose like an appeal. 'Do not prevent me from discovering the meaning of our lives.'

Linden had no idea what Brinn was talking about. His speech seemed as unmotivated as an oration in a nightmare. Only Seadreamer and Findail showed any understanding. Seadreamer sat with his hands closed over his face as if he could not bear what he was hearing. And Findail stood alone like a man who knew all the answers and loathed them.

Roughly, Covenant scrubbed the mist-sweat from his forehead. His mouth fumbled several different responses before he rasped, 'What in hell are you talking about?'

Brinn did not speak. But he lifted his arm, pointed in the direction of the Isle.

His gesture was so certain that it drew every eye with it.

Somewhere beyond the prow of the craft, a window opened in the mist, revealing a stark ledge of rock. It stood at a slight elevation above the Sea. The elusive pearl vapour made distances difficult to estimate; but the damp, dark rock appeared to be much closer than the Isle had been only a short time ago. In fact, the ledge might not have been a part of the Isle at all. It seemed to exist only within the context of the mist.

Cross-legged on the shelf sat an ancient man in a tattered colourless robe.

His head was half bowed in an attitude of meditation. But his eyes were open. The milky hue of cataracts or blindness filled his orbs.

Faint wisps of hair marked the top of his head; a grey stubble emphasized the hollowness of his cheeks. His skin was seamed with age, and his limbs had been starved to the point of emaciation. Yet he radiated an eerie and unfathomable strength.

Brinn or Cail might have looked like that if the intensity of their lives had permitted them to reach extreme old age.

Almost at once, the mist closed again, swirling back upon itself in ghostly silence.

'Yes,' Findail said as if he did not expect anyone to hear him. 'The Guardian of the One Tree. He must be passed.'

Covenant stared at the Appointed. But Findail did not answer his gaze. With a wrench, the Unbeliever aimed himself at Brinn. The mist lit his face like the lambency of dismay.

'Is that what you want to do?' His voice croaked in the nacre stillness. 'Confront the Guardian? *Fight* him?'

Softly, Brinn replied, 'The *Elohim* has said that you must pass him to attain the One Tree. And I conceive him to be *ak-Haru Kenaustin Ardenol*. If I succeed, we will both be served.'

'And if you *fail?*' Covenant lashed the word at Brinn's dispassion. 'You already believe you're unworthy. How much more do you think you can stand?'

Brinn's visage remained inflexible. 'I will know the truth. Any being who cannot bear the truth is indeed unworthy.'

Covenant winced. His bruised gaze came to Linden for help.

She saw his conflict clearly. He feared to hazard himself – his capacity for destruction – against the Guardian. But he had never learned how to let anyone take his place when he was afraid: his fear was more compulsory than courage. And he did not want to deny Seadreamer. The mute Giant still hid his face as if he had passed the limits of his soul's endurance.

Linden wavered, caught by her own contradictions. She instinctively trusted Seadreamer; but the need which had driven Brinn to thrust aside the First's sword moved her also. She understood the severity of the *Haruchai*, yearned to make her peace with it. Yet she could not forget Seadreamer's rending efforts to communicate his vision to her.

The First and Pitchwife were standing together, watching her. Honninscrave's fingers kneaded Seadreamer's shoulders; but his eyes also studied her. Covenant's gaze bled at her. Only Brinn was not waiting for her response. His attention was locked to the Unbeliever.

Unable to say yes or no, she tried to find another way out of the dilemma. 'We've been rowing half the night' – she directed her words at Brinn, fought to force the tremors out of them – 'and we aren't getting any closer. How do you think you can reach that man to fight him?'

Then she cried out; but she was too late. Brinn had taken her question as a form of permission. Or had decided to forego Covenant's approval. Too swiftly to be stopped, he leaped into the prow of the longboat and dived towards the Isle.

The mist swallowed him. Linden heard the splash as he hit the water, but did not see the wake of his passage.

She surged forward with Covenant and Honninscrave. But the *Haruchai* was beyond reach. Even his swimming made no sound.

'Damn you!' Covenant shouted. His voice echoed and then fell dead in the cavernous fog. 'Don't fail!'

For a moment like a pall, no one spoke. Then the First said, 'Honninscrave.' Her voice was iron. 'Seadreamer. Now you will row as you have not rowed before. If it lies within the strength of Giants, we will gain that Isle.'

Honninscrave flung himself back to his oar-seat. But Seadreamer was slower to respond. Linden feared that he would not respond, that he had fallen too far into horror. She gathered herself to protest at the First's demand. But she had underestimated him. His hands came down from his face into fists. Lurching, he returned to his seat, recovered his oars. Gripping their handles as if he meant to crush them, he attacked the water.

Linden staggered at the suddenness of the thrust, then caught herself on a thwart and turned to face forward at Covenant's side.

For a moment, Honninscrave flailed to match his brother's frenetic rhythm. Then they were stroking like twins.

The mist opened again. A glimpse of stars and night beyond the crest of the Isle demonstrated that the longboat was still making no progress.

A heartbeat later, the vapour moiled, and the shelf of rock became visible once more.

It appeared far closer than the island. And it was empty. The old man had left it.

But this time the mist did not reclose immediately.

From behind it, Brinn stepped up on to one end of the ledge. He bowed formally to the blank air as if he were facing an honoured opponent. Smoothly, he placed himself in a stylized combatant's stance. Then he recoiled as if he had been struck by fists too swift to be evaded.

As he fell, the mist swirled and shut.

Linden hardly noticed that the Giants had stopped rowing. Twisting in their seats, Honninscrave and Seadreamer stared forward intensely. There were no sounds in the longboat except Pitchwife's muttering and Covenant's bitten curses.

Shortly, the mist parted again. This time, it exposed a cluster of boulders at a higher elevation than the shelf.

Brinn was there, leaping and spinning from rock to rock in a

810

death-battle with the empty atmosphere. His cut hand was covered with blood; blood pulsed from a wound on his temple. But he moved as if he disdained the damage. With fists and feet he dealt out flurries of blows which appeared to impact against the air – and have effect. Yet he was being struck in turn by a rapid vehemence that surpassed his defences. Cuts appeared below one eye, at the corner of his mouth; rents jerked through his tunic, revealing bruises on his torso and thighs. He was beaten backward and out of sight as the mist thickened anew.

Covenant crouched feverishly in the prow of the craft. He was marked with beads of illumination like implications of wild magic. But no power rose in him. Linden was certain of that. The chill sheen on his skin seemed to render him inert, numbing his instinct for fire. His bones appeared precise and frail to her percipience. He had stopped cursing as if even rage and protest were futile.

Cail had come forward and now stood staring into the mist. Every line of his face was sharp with passion; moisture beaded on his forehead like sweat. For the first time, Linden saw one of the *Haruchai* breathing heavily.

After a prolonged pause, another vista appeared through the mist. It was higher than the others, but no farther away. Immense stones had crushed each other there, forming a battleground of shards and splinters as keen as knives. They lacerated Brinn's feet as he fought from place to place, launching and countering attacks with the wild extravagance of a man who had utterly abandoned himself. His apparel fluttered about him in shreds. No part of his body was free of blood or battery.

But now the Guardian was faintly visible. Flitting from blow to blow like a shadow of himself, the old man feinted and wheeled among the shards as if he could not be touched. Yet many of Brinn's efforts appeared to strike him, and each contact made him more solid. With every hit, Brinn created his opponent out of nothingness.

But the Guardian showed no sign of injury; and Brinn was receiving punishment beyond measure. Even as Linden thought that surely he could not endure much more, the *Haruchai* went down under a complex series of blows. He had to hurl himself bodily over the stones, tearing his skin to pieces, in order to evade the old man's attempt to break his back.

He could not flee quickly enough. The Guardian pounced after him while the mist blew across the scene, obscuring them with its damp radiance.

'I've got – ' Covenant beat his fists unconsciously against the stone prow. Blood seeped from the cracked skin of his knuckles. 'Got to help him.' But every angle of his arms and shoulders said plainly that he did not know how.

Linden clung to herself and fought to suppress her instinctive tears. Brinn would not survive much longer. He was already so badly injured that he might bleed to death. How could he go on fighting, with the strength running from his veins moment by moment?

When the mist opened for the last time, it revealed an eminence high above the Sea. She had to crane her neck to descry the slight downward slope which led to the sharp precipice. And beyond the precipice lay nothing except an avid fall from a tremendous height.

After a moment, Brinn appeared. He was being beaten backward down the slope, towards the cliff – reeling as if the life had gone out of his legs. All his clothing had been shredded away; he wore nothing but thick smears and streams of blood. He was hardly able to raise his arms to fend off the blows which impelled him to retreat.

The Guardian was fully substantial now. His milky eyes gleamed in the mist-light as he kicked and punched Brinn towards the precipice. His attacks struck with a sodden silence more vivid than any noise of battered flesh. His robe flowed about his limbs as if its lack of colour were the essence of his strength. No hint or flicker of expression ruffled his detachment as he drove Brinn towards death.

But he seemed to become more adept and irresistible as he grew more solid. Almost at once, he brushed aside Brinn's counter-attack. Lashing out like lightning of flesh and bone, he coerced Brinn to the precipice again. A cunning feint towards Brinn's abdomen lowered his arms defensively. At once, the old man followed with a hammer-blow to Brinn's forehead.

Brinn swayed on the rim, tottered. Began to fall.

Covenant's shout tore through the mist like despair.

'Brinn!'

In the fractional pause as his balance failed, Brinn glanced towards the aghast spectators. Then he shifted his feet in a way that ensured his fall. But as he dropped, his hands reached out. His fingers knotted into the old man's robe.

Surrendering himself to the precipice, he took the Guardian with him.

Linden crouched against the thwarts. She did not hear Seadreamer's inchoate groan, Pitchwife's astonished pain, Cail's shout of praise. Brinn's fall burned across her senses, blinding her to everything else. That plunge repeated in her like the labour of her heart. He had chosen –

Then rock scraped the side of the longboat; its prow thudded into a gap between boulders. Water sloshed along the impact. Linden and Covenant pitched against each other. Grappling together automatically, they stumbled into the bottom of the craft.

When they regained their feet, everything had changed around them. The mist was gone and with it most of the stars; for the sun had begun to rise, and its nascent light already greyed the heavens. Starfare's Gem could be seen vaguely in the distance, riding at anchor beyond the barrier of the reefs. And above the craft, the Isle of the One Tree towered like a mound of homage to all the Earth's brave dead.

Honninscrave stepped past Linden and Covenant, climbed on to the boulder-strewn shore to secure the longboat in the place where it had wedged itself. Then he stooped and offered to help Linden and Covenant out of the boat. His face was blank with unexpected loss. He might have been a figure in a dream.

Cail approached Linden like triumph, put his hands on her waist and boosted her up to Honninscrave. The Master set her on the rocks behind him. Stiffly, she ascended over several boulders, then stopped and stared about her as if she had lost her sight. Covenant struggled towards her. Dawn set light to the crown of the Isle. The absence of the *dromond*'s midmast was painfully obvious. Seadreamer fumbled at the rocks as if his exertions or Earth-Sight had made him old. The First, Pitchwife, and Honninscrave climbed behind him like a cortege. Vain and Findail followed the Giants like mourners. But it was all superficial. Beneath everything lay the stark instant of Brinn's fall. Haunted by what they had witnessed, the companions did not look at each other as they gathered a short distance above the longboat.

Only Cail showed no distress. Though his expression remained as dispassionate as ever, his eyes gleamed like an inward grin. If she could have found her voice, Linden would have railed at him. But she had no words in her, or no strength to utter them. Brinn had met Covenant's cry with recognition – and had fallen. No words were enough. No strength was enough.

Pitchwife moved to Covenant's side, placed a gentle hand on his shoulder. The First put her arms around Seadreamer as if to lift him up out of himself. Vain stared at nothing with his ambiguous smile. Findail betrayed no reaction. Yet Cail's gaze danced in the rising sunlight, bright with exaltation. After a moment, he said, 'Have no fear. He did not fail.'

And Brinn appeared as if he had been invoked by Cail's words. Moving easily over the rocks, he came down towards the company. His strides were light and uninjured; the swing of his arms expressed no pain. Not until he stood directly before her was Linden able to see that he had indeed been severely wounded. But all his hurts were healed. His face and limbs wore an intaglio of pale new scars; but his muscles bunched and slid under his skin as if they were full of joy.

In the place of his lost apparel, he wore the colourless robe of the Guardian.

Linden gaped at him. Covenant's mouth formed his name over and over again, but made no sound. Honninscrave and the First were stunned. A slow grin spread across Pitchwife's face, echoing the gleam in Cail's eyes. Seadreamer stood upright in the dawn and nodded like a recognition of doom. But none of them were able to speak.

Brinn bowed to Covenant. 'Ur-Lord,' he said firmly, 'the approach to the One Tree lies before you.' He gestured towards the sun-burnished crown of the Isle. His tone carried a barely discernible timbre of triumph. 'I have opened it to you.'

Covenant's face twisted as if he did not know whether to laugh or weep.

Linden knew. Her eyes burned like the birth of the morning.

The mute Giant went on nodding as if Brinn's victory had bereft him of every other answer.

Covenant was going to send her back.

25

THE ARRIVAL OF THE QUEST

Covenant stared at Brinn and felt ruin crowding around him. The whole island was a ruin, a place of death. Why were there no mouldering corpses, no bleached bones? Not death, then, but eradication. All hope simply swept out of the world. The sunrise lay as rosy as a lie on the hard rocks.

I'm losing my mind.

He did not know what to do. Every path to this Isle was littered with gravestones. The Isle itself loomed above the company like a massif, rugged and arduous. The boulders of the slopes swarmed with implications of vertigo. And yet he had already made his decision, in spite of the fact that he hated it – and feared it was wrong, dreaded to learn that it was wrong, that after all he had endured and still meant to endure the only thing he could really do for the Land was die. That the logic of the old knife-scar over his heart could not be broken.

His voice sounded distant and small to him, insanely detached. He was as mad as the *Haruchai*. Impossible to talk about such things as if they were not appalling. Why did he not sound appalled? *The approach to the One Tree lies before you.* So the Tree was here after all, in this place of piled death. Not one bird trammelled the immense sky with its paltry life, not one weed or patch of lichen marked the rocks. It was insane to stand here and talk as if such things could be borne.

He was saying, 'You're not Brinn.' Lunatic with distance and detachment. 'Are you?' His throat would not accept that other name.

Brinn's expression did not waver. Perhaps there was a smile in his eyes; it was difficult to see in the early light. 'I am who I am,' he said evenly. '*Ak-Haru Kenaustin Ardenol*. The Guardian of the One Tree. Brinn of the *Haruchai*. And many other names. Thus am I renewed from age to age, until the end.'

Vain did not move; but Findail bowed as if Brinn had become a figure whom even the *Elohim* were required to respect.

'No,' Covenant said. He could not help himself. Brinn. 'No.' The First, Pitchwife, and Honninscrave were staring at the *Haruchai* with dumbfounded eyes. Seadreamer went on nodding like a puppet with a broken neck. Somehow, Brinn's victory had sealed Seadreamer's plight. By opening the way to the One Tree? *Brinn*.

Brinn's gaze was knowing and absolute. 'Be not dismayed, ur-Lord.' His tone reconciled passion and self-control. 'Though I may no longer sojourn in your service, I am not dead to life and use. Good will come of it, when there is need.'

'Don't tell me that!' The protest broke from Covenant involuntarily. I'm going to die. Or break my heart. 'Do you think I can stand to lose you?'

'You will endure it,' that composed voice replied. 'Are you not Thomas Covenant, ur-Lord and Unbeliever? That is the grace which has been given to you, to bear what must be borne.' Then Brinn's visage altered slightly, as if even he were not immune to loss. 'Cail will accept my place at your side until Revelstone has fallen – until the word of the Bloodguard Bannor has been carried to its end. Then he will follow his heart.' Cail's face caught the light ambiguously. 'Ur-Lord, do not delay,' Brinn concluded, gesturing towards the sun-limned crest. 'The way of hope and doom lies open to you.'

Covenant swore to himself. He did not seem to have the strength to curse aloud. The cold numb mist of the night clung to his bones, defying the sun's warmth. He wanted to storm and rave, expostulate like a madman. It would be condign. He had done such things before – especially to Bannor. But he could not. Brinn's mien held the completeness towards which Bannor had only aspired. Abruptly, Covenant sat down, thudded his back against a boulder and fought to keep his grief apart from the quick tinder of his venom.

A shape squatted in front of him. For an instant, he feared that it was Linden and nearly lost his grip. He would not have been able to sustain an offer of comfort from her. He was going to lose her no matter what he did, if he sent her back or if he failed, either way. But she still stood with her back to the sun and her face covered as if she did not want the morning to see her weep. With an effort, he forced himself to meet Pitchwife's anxious gaze.

The deformed Giant was holding a leather flask of *diamondraught*. Mutely, he offered it to Covenant.

For a moment like an instance of insanity, Covenant saw Foamfollower there, as vivid as Pitchwife. Foamfollower was commenting wryly, *Some old seers say that privation refines the soul – but I say that it is soon enough to refine the soul when the body has no other choice.* At that, the knot in Covenant loosened a bit. With a raw sigh, he accepted the flask and drank a few swallows of the analystic liquor.

The way of hope and doom, he thought mordantly. Hellfire.

But the *diamondraught* was a blessing to his abraded nerves, his taut and weary muscles. The ascent of the Isle promised vertigo; but he had faced vertigo before. *To bear what must be borne.* Ah, God.

Handing the flask back to Pitchwife, he rose to his feet. Then he approached Linden.

When he touched her shoulder, she flinched as if she feared him – feared the purpose which she could surely perceive in him as clearly as if it were written on his forehead. But she did not pull away. After a moment, he began, 'I've got – ' He wanted to say, I've got to do it. Don't you understand? But he knew she did not understand. And he had no one to blame but himself. He had never found the courage to explain to her why he had to send her back, why his life depended on her return to their former world. Instead, he said, 'I've got to go up there.'

At once, she turned as if she meant to attack him with protests, imprecations, pleas. But her eyes were distracted and elsewhere, like Elena's. Words came out of her as if she were forcing herself to have pity on him.

'It's not as bad as it looks. It isn't really dead.' Her hands indicated the Isle with a jerk. 'Not like all that ruin around Stonemight Woodhelven. It's powerful – too powerful for anything mortal to live here. But not dead. It's more like sleep. Not exactly. Something this' – she groped momentarily – 'this eternal doesn't sleep. Resting, maybe. Resting deeply. Whatever it is, it isn't likely to notice us.'

Covenant's throat closed. She was trying to comfort him after all – offering him her percipience because she had nothing else to give. Or maybe she still wanted to go back, wanted her old life more than him –

He had to swallow a great weight of grief before he could face the company again and say, 'Let's go.'

They looked at him with plain apprehension and hope. Seadreamer's face was knotted around his stark scar. The First contained herself with sternness; but Pitchwife made no effort to conceal his mixed rue and excitement. Honninscrave's great muscles bunched and released as if he were prepared to fight anything which threatened his brother. They were all poised on the culmination of their quest, the satisfaction or denial of the needs which had brought them so far across the seas of the world.

All except Vain. If the Demondim-spawn wore the heels of the Staff of Law for any conceivable reason, he did not betray it. His black visage remained as impenetrable as the minds of the ur-viles that had made him.

Covenant turned from them. It was on his head. Every one of them was here in his name – driven through risk and betrayal to this place by his self-distrust, his sovereign need for any weapon which would not destroy what he loved. *Hope and doom.* Vehemently, he forced himself to the ascent.

At once, Pitchwife and the First sprang ahead of him. They were Giants, adept at stone, and better equipped than he to find a bearable path. Brinn came to his side; but Covenant refused the Guardian's tacit offer of aid, and he stayed a few steps away. Cail supported Linden as she scrambled upward. Then came Honninscrave and Seadreamer, moving shoulder-to-shoulder. Vain and Findail brought up the rear like the shadows of each other's secrets.

From certain angles, certain positions, the crest looked unattainable. The Isle's ragged sides offered no paths; and neither Covenant nor Linden was able to scale sheer rock-fronts. Covenant only controlled the dizziness that tugged at his mind by locking his attention to the boulders in front of him. But the First and Pitchwife seemed to understand the way the stones would fit together, know what any given formation implied about the terrain above it. Their climb described a circuit which the company had no serious trouble following around the roughly conical cairn.

Yet Covenant was soon panting as if the air were too pure for him. His life aboard Starfare's Gem had not hardened him for such exertions. Each new upward step became more difficult than the last. The sun baked the complex light-and-dark of the rocks until every shadow was as distinct as a knife-edge and every exposed surface shimmered. By degrees, his robe began to weigh on him as if in leaving behind his old clothes he had assumed something heavier than he could carry. Only the numbness of his bare feet spared him from limping as Linden did at the small bruises and nicks of the stones. Perhaps he should have been more careful with himself. But he had no more room in his heart for leprosy or self-protection. He followed the First and Pitchwife as he had followed his summoner into the woods behind Haven Farm, towards Joan and fire.

The ascent took half the morning. By tortuous increments, the company rose higher and higher above the immaculate expanse of the Sea. From the north, Starfare's Gem was easily visible. A pennon hung from the aftermast, indicating that all was well. Occasional sun-flashes off the ocean caught Covenant's eyes brilliantly, like reminders of the white flame which had borne him up through the

Sandhold to confront Kasreyn. But he had come here to escape the necessity for that power.

Then the crown of the Isle was in sight. The sun burned in the cloudless sky. Sweat streamed down his face, air rasped hoarsely in his chest, as he trudged up the last slope.

The One Tree was not there. His trembling muscles had hoped that the eyot's top would hold a patch of soil in which a tree could grow. But it did not.

From the rim of the crest, a black gulf sank into the centre of the Isle.

Covenant groaned at it as Linden and Cail came up behind him. A moment later, Honninscrave and Seadreamer arrived. Together, the companions gaped into the lightless depths.

The gulf was nearly a stone's throw across; and the walls were sheer, almost smooth. They descended like the sides of a well far beyond the range of Covenant's sight. The air rising from the hole was as black and cold as an exhalation of night. It carried a tang that stung his nostrils. When he looked to Linden for her reaction, he saw her eyes brimming as if the air were so sharp with power that it hurt her.

'Down there?' His voice was a croak. He had to take hold of Brinn's shoulder to defend himself from the sick giddy yawning of the pit.

'Aye,' muttered Pitchwife warily. 'No otherwhere remains. We have encountered this Isle with sufficient intimacy to ascertain that the One Tree does not lie behind us.'

Quietly, Brinn confirmed, 'This is the way.' He was unruffled by the climb, unwearied by his night of battle. Beside him, even Cail appeared frangible and limited.

Covenant bared his teeth. He had to fight for breath against the dark air of the gulf. 'How? Do you expect me to jump?'

'I will guide you.' Brinn pointed to the side of the hole a short distance away. Peering in that direction, Covenant saw a ledge which angled into the pit, spiralling steeply around the walls like a rude stairway. He stared at it, and his guts twisted.

'But I must say again,' Brinn went on, 'that I may no longer serve you. I am *ak-Haru Kenaustin Ardenol*, the Guardian of the One Tree. I will not interfere.'

'Terrific,' Covenant snarled. Dismay made him bitter. When he let his anger show, a flicker of fire ran through him like a glimpse of distant lightning. In spite of everything that frightened or grieved or restrained him, his nerves were primed for wild magic. He wanted to demand, Interfere with *what*? But Brinn was too complete to be questioned.

For a moment, Covenant searched the area like a cornered animal.

His hands fumbled at the sash of his robe. Fighting the uncertainty of his numb fingers, his halfhand, he jerked the sash tight as if it were a lifeline.

Linden was looking at him now. She could not blink the dampness out of her eyes. Her face was pale with alarm. Her features looked too delicate to suffer the air of that hole much longer.

With a wrench, he tore himself into motion towards the ledge.

She caught at his arm as if he had started to fall. 'Covenant – ' When his glare jumped to her face, she faltered. But she did not let herself duck his gaze. In a difficult voice, as if she were trying to convey something that defied utterance, she said, 'You look like you did on Kevin's Watch. When you had to go down the stairs. You were the only thing I had, and you wouldn't let me help you.'

He pulled his arm away. If she tried to make him change his mind now, she would break his heart. 'It's only vertigo,' he said harshly. 'I know the answer. I just need a little while to find it again.'

Her expression pierced him like a cry. For one terrible moment, he feared that she was going to shout at him, No! It's not vertigo. You're so afraid of sharing anything, of letting anybody else help you – you think you're so destructive to everything you love – that you're going to *send me back*! He nearly cringed as he waited for the words to come. Echoes of his passion burned across the background of her orbs. But she did not rail against him. Her severity made her appear old and care-carved as she said, 'You can't make the Staff without me.'

Even that was more than he could stand. She might as well have said, You can't save the Land without me. The implications nearly tore away what little courage he had left. Was it true? Was he really so far gone in selfishness that he intended to sell the Land so that he could live?

No. It was not true. He did not want the life he would be forced to live without her. But he had to live anyway, *had* to, or he would have no chance to fight Lord Foul. One man's sole human love was not too high a price.

Yet the mere sight of her was enough to tie his face into a grimace of desire and loss. He had to excoriate himself with curses in order to summon the grace to respond, 'I know. I'm counting on you.'

Then he turned to the rest of the company. 'What're we waiting for? Let's get it over with.'

The Giants passed a glance among themselves. Seadreamer's eyes were as red-rimmed as lacerations; but he nodded to the First's mute question. Pitchwife did not hesitate. Honninscrave made a gesture that exposed the emptiness of his hands.

The First's mouth tightened grimly. Drawing her longsword, she held it before her like the linchpin of her resolve.

Linden stared darkly down into the gulf as if it were the empty void into which she had thrown herself in order to rescue Covenant and the quest from Kasreyn.

Moving as surely as if he had spent all his life here, Brinn approached the ledge. In spite of its crude edges and dangerous slope, the ledge was wide enough for a Giant. The First followed Brinn with Pitchwife immediately behind her.

Bracing his numb hands against Pitchwife's crippled back, Covenant went next. A rearward glance which threatened to unseat his balance told him that Cail was right behind him, poised between Linden and him to protect them both. Vain and Findail came after Linden. Then the pull of the gulf became too strong, plucked too perilously at his mind. Clinging to Pitchwife's sark with his futile fingers, he strove for the still point of clarity at the heart of his vertigo.

But when he had gone partway around the first curve, Linden called his name softly, directing his attention backward. Over his shoulder, he saw that Honninscrave and Seadreamer had not begun to descend. They faced each other on the rim in silence like an argument of life and death. Seadreamer was shaking his head now, refusing what he saw in Honninscrave's visage. After a moment, the Master slumped. Stepping aside, he let Seadreamer precede him down the ledge.

In that formation, the company slowly spiralled into darkness.

Two turns within the wall left the sunlight behind. Its reach lengthened as the sun rose towards midday; but the quest's descent was swifter. Covenant's eyes refused to adjust; the shadow baffled his vision. He wanted to look upward, see something clearly – and was sure he would fall if he did. The dark accumulated around him and was sucked into the depths, trying to sweep him along. Those depths were giddy and certain, as requisite as vertigo or despair. They gnawed at his heart like the acid of his sins. Somewhere down there was the eye of the spin, the still point of strength between contradictions on which he had once stood to defeat Lord Foul, but he would never reach it.

This ledge was the path of all the Despiser's manipulations. *Seadreamer is afraid. I think he knows what Lord Foul is doing.* A misstep took him as close as panic to the lip of the fall. He flung himself against Pitchwife's back, hung there with his heart knocking. Even to his blunt senses, the air reeked of power.

As if the venom were not enough, here was another force driving him towards destruction. The atmosphere chilled his skin, made his sweat scald down his cheeks and ribs like trails of wild magic.

Cail reached out to steady him from behind. Pitchwife murmured reassurances over his shoulder. After a while, Covenant was able to move again. They went on downward.

He needed the thickness of his robe to keep him from shivering. He seemed to be entering a demesne which had never been touched by the sun – a place of such dark and somnolent force that even the direct radiance of the sun would not be able to soften its ancient cold. Perhaps no fire would ever be strong enough to etiolate the midnight gaping beyond his feet. Perhaps none of the questers except Brinn had any right to be here. At every step, he became smaller. The dark isolated him. Beyond Pitchwife and Cail, he only recognized his friends by the sounds of their feet. The faint slap and thrust of their soles rose murmurously in the well, like the soughing of bat wings.

He had no way to measure time in that night, could not count the number of rounds he had made. For a mad instant, he looked up at the small oriel of the sky. Then he had to let Cail uphold him while his balance reeled.

The air of the gulf became colder, more crowded with faint susurrations, less endurable. For some reason, he believed that the pit became wider as it sank into the bowels of the Isle. In spite of his numbness, every emanation of the walls was as palpable as a fist – and as secret as an unmarked grave. He was suffocating on power which had no source and no form. He heard Linden behind him. Her respiration shuddered like imminent hysteria. The air made him feel veined with insane fire. It must have been flaying her nerves exquisitely.

Yet he wanted to cry out because he did not feel what she was feeling, had no way to estimate his plight or the consequences of his own acts. His numbness had become too deadly – a peril to the world as well as to his friends and to Linden.

And still he did not stop. *It boots nothing to avoid his snares* – He went on as if he were trudging down into Vain's black heart.

When the end came, he had no warning of it. Abruptly, the First said, 'We are here,' and her voice sent echoes upward like a flurry of frightened birds. The position of Pitchwife's back changed. Covenant's next step struck level stone.

He began to tremble violently with reaction and cold. But he heard Linden half sobbing far back in her throat as she groped towards him. He put his arms around her, strained her to him as if he would never be able to find any other way to say goodbye.

Only the muffled breathing of his companions told him that he and Linden were not alone. Even that quiet sound echoed like the awakening of something fatal.

He looked upward. At first, he saw no sign of the sky. The well was so deep that its opening was indiscernible. But a moment later light lanced into his eyes as the sun broached the Isle's rim. His friends suddenly appeared beside him as if they had come leaping out of the dark, recreated from the raw cold of the gulf.

The First stood with her determination gripped in both hands. Pitchwife was at her side, grimacing. Supported by Honninscrave, Seadreamer clenched his despair between his teeth and glared whitely around him. Vain looked like an avatar of the gulf's dark. Findail's creamy robe seemed as bright as a torch.

Cail stood near Covenant and Linden with sunlight shining in his eyes. But Brinn was nowhere to be seen. The Guardian of the One Tree had left the cavern, carrying his promise not to interfere to its logical extreme. Or perhaps he did not want to watch what was about to happen to the people he had once served.

Reaching the floor of the well, the sunline moved more slowly; but still it spread by noticeable degrees out from the western wall where the quest stood. Covenant's eyes blurred. The light seemed to vacillate between vagueness and acuity, hope and doom. No one spoke. The atmosphere held them silent and motionless.

Without warning, tips of wood burst into view as the sun touched them. Gleaming like traceries of fire above the heads of the onlookers, twigs ran together to form branches. Boughs intersected and grew downward. In a slow rush like the flow of burning blood, all the boughs joined; and the trunk of the One Tree swept towards its roots in the floor of the gulf.

Limned and distinct against a background of shadow, the great Tree stood before the company like the progenitor of all the world's wood.

It appeared to be enormous. The well had indeed widened as it descended, forming a space as large as a cavern to hold the Tree. The darkness which hid the far walls focused all the sunlight into the centre of the floor, so that the Tree dominated the air with every line and angle of its bright limbs. It was grand and ancient, clad in thick, knaggy bark like a mantle of age, and impossibly powerful.

And yet it had no leaves. Perhaps it had always been leafless. The bare stone was unmarked by any mould or clutter which might have come from the One Tree. Every branch and twig was stark, unwreathed. They would have looked dead if they had not been so vivid with light. The Tree's massive roots had forced their way into the floor with gigantic strength, breaking the surface into jagged hunks which the roots embraced with the intimacy of lovers. The Tree appeared to draw its strength, its leafless endurance, from a subterranean cause that was as passionate as lava and as intractable as gut-rock.

For a long moment, Covenant and his companions simply stood and stared. He did not think he could move. He was too close to the goal which he had desired and loathed across the wide seas. In spite of its light-etched actuality, it seemed unreal. If he touched it, it would evaporate into hallucination and madness.

But the sun was still moving. The configuration of the well made its traversal dangerously swift. The One Tree was fully lit now; the company was falling back into shadow. Soon the sun would reach the eastern wall; and then the Tree would begin to go out. Perhaps it would cease to exist when sunfire no longer burned along its limbs. He was suddenly afraid that he did not have much time.

'Now, Giantfriend,' the First whispered. Her tone was thick with awe. 'It must be done now. While the light endures.'

'Yes – ' Covenant's voice caught in his throat, came out like a flinch. He was appalled by what he meant to do. Linden was the first woman he had met since the ordeal of his illness began who was able to love him. To lose her now – ! But Brinn had said, *Hope and doom. Bear what must be borne.* He would die if he did not, would surely destroy what he loved if he did not.

Abruptly, he raised his right arm, pointed at the Tree. The small twin scars on his forearm shone faintly. 'There.' Above its gnarled trunk, the Tree was wide-boughed and encompassing. From one of the nearest limbs grew a long straight branch as thick as his wrist. It ended in a flat stump as if the rest of it had been cut off. 'I'll take that one.'

Tension squirmed through him. He opened a shutter in his mind, let out a ray of power. A tiny flame appeared on his ring. It intensified until it was as incisive as a blade. There he held it, intending to use it to sever the branch.

Obscurely through the gloom, he saw Vain grinning.

'Wait.' Linden was not looking at him. She was not looking at anything. Her expression resembled the helpless immobility which had rendered her so vulnerable to Joan and Marid and Gibbon. She appeared small and lost, as if she had no right to be here. Her hands made weak pleading movements. Her head shook in denial. 'There's something else.'

'Linden – ' Covenant began.

'Be swift, Chosen,' demanded the First. 'The time flees.'

Linden stared blindly past the company and the Tree and the light. 'Something else here.' She was raw with fear and self-coercion. 'They're connected – but they aren't the same. I don't know what it is. It's too much. Nobody can look at it.' Paralysis or horror made her soft voice wild.

Covenant tried again urgently. '*Linden.*'

Her gaze left the One Tree, touched him and then cringed as if she could not bear the sight of what he meant to do. Her words seemed to congeal towards silence as she spoke them. 'The Tree isn't why nothing lives here. It doesn't make the air smell like the end of the world. It doesn't have that kind of power. There's something else here.' Her vision was focused inward as if like the *Elohim* she were studying herself for answers. 'Resting.'

Covenant faltered. He was torn between too many emotions. His

823

ring burned like venom and potential Desecration. A cry he was unable to utter wrung his heart:

Help me! I don't know what to do!

But he had already made his decision. The only decision of which he was capable. Go forward. Find out what happens. What matters. Who you are. Surely Linden would understand. He could not retreat from the compulsion of his own fear and loss.

When he looked at the First, she made a gesture that urged him towards the Tree.

Jerking himself into motion, he started forward.

At once, Seadreamer left the shadows. Trailed by Honninscrave's soft groan of protest, the mute Giant sprang ahead of Covenant, blocked his way. All the light on his face was gathered around his scar. His head winced refusals from side to side. His fists were poised at his temples as if his brain were about to burst.

'No,' Covenant gritted – a warning of ire and empathy. 'Don't do this.'

The First was already at his side. 'Are you mad?' she barked at Seadreamer. 'The Giantfriend must act now, while the way is open.'

For an instant, Seadreamer burst into an incomprehensible pantomime. Then he took hold of himself. His respiration juddered as he forced himself to move slowly, making his meaning clear. With gestures as poignant as anguish, he indicated that Covenant must not touch the Tree. That would be disaster. He, Seadreamer, would attempt to take the branch.

Covenant started to object. The First stayed him. 'Giantfriend, it is the Earth-Sight.' Pitchwife had joined the Swordmain. He stood as if he were prepared to wrestle Covenant in the name of Seadreamer's wishes. 'In all the long ages of the Giants, no Earth-Sight has ever misled us.'

Out of the dark, Honninscrave cried, 'He is my brother!' Suppressed tears occluded his voice. 'Will you send him to die?'

The tip of the First's sword wavered. Pitchwife watched her with all his attention, waiting for her decision. Covenant's eyes flared back and forth between Honninscrave and Seadreamer. He could not choose between them.

Then Seadreamer hurled himself towards the One Tree.

'No!' The shout tore itself from Covenant's chest. Not again! Not another sacrifice in my place! He started after the Giant with flame pounding in his veins.

Honninscrave exploded past him. Roaring, the Master charged in pursuit of his brother.

But Seadreamer was moving with a desperate precision, as if this also were something he had foreseen exactly. In three strides, he spun to meet Honninscrave. His feet planted themselves on the stone; his fist lashed out.

The blow caught Honninscrave like the kick of a Courser. He staggered backward against Covenant. Only Cail's swift intervention kept the Master from crushing Covenant to the stone. The *Haruchai* deflected Honninscrave's bulk to one side, heaved Covenant to the other.

Covenant saw Seadreamer near the Tree. The First's command and Pitchwife's cry followed him together, but did not stop him. Livid in sudden sunlight, he leaped up the broken rocks which the roots embraced. From that position, the branch Covenant had chosen hung within easy reach of his hands.

For an instant, he did not touch it. His gaze reached towards the company as if he were poised on the verge of immolation. Passions he could not articulate dismayed his face along the line of his scar.

Then he took hold of the branch near its base and strove to snap it from its bough.

26

FRUITION

For a frozen splinter of time, Linden saw everything. Seadreamer's hands were closing on the branch. Covenant yearned forward as if he perceived the death in Seadreamer's eyes as clearly as she did. Cail supported the ur-Lord. The First, Pitchwife, and Honninscrave were in motion; but their running appeared slow and useless, clogged by the cold power in the air. The sunlight made them look at once vivid and futile.

She was alone in the western shadows with Vain and Findail. Percipience and reflected light rendered them meticulously to her. The Demondim-spawn's grin was as feral as a beast's. Waves of fear poured from Findail.

Disaster crouched in the cavern. It was about to strike. She felt it – all Lord Foul's manipulations coming to fruition in front of her. The atmosphere was rife with repercussions. But she could not move.

Then Seadreamer's hands closed.

In that instant, a blast like a shout of rage from the very guts of the Earth staggered the company. The Giants and Covenant were swept from their feet. The stone came up and kicked Linden as she sprawled forward.

Her breathing stopped. She did not remember hitting her head, but the whole inside of her skull was stunned, as if everything had been knocked flat. She wanted to breathe, but the air felt as violent as lightning. It would burn her lungs to cinders.

She had to breathe, had to know what was going on. Inhaling convulsively, she raised her head.

Vain and Findail had remained erect nearby, reflecting each other like antitheses across the gloom.

The well was full of stars.

A swath of the heavens had been superimposed on the cavern and the One Tree. Behind the sunlight, stars flamed with a cold fury. The spaces between them were as black as the fathomless depths of the sky. They were no larger than Linden's hand, no brighter than motes of dizziness. Yet each was as mighty as a sun. Together they transcended every power which life and Time could contain. They swirled like a galaxy in ferment, stirring the air into a brew of utter destruction.

A score of them swept towards Seadreamer. They seemed to strike and explode without impact; but their force lit a conflagration of agony in his flesh. A scream ripped the throat which had released no word since the birth of his Earth-Sight.

And wild magic appeared as if it had been rent free of all restraint by Seadreamer's cry. Covenant stood with his arms spread like a crucifixion, spewing argent fire. Venom and madness scourged forward as he strove to beat back Seadreamer's death. Foamfollower had already died for him.

His fury deflected or consumed the stars, though any one of them should have been too mighty for any mortal power to touch. But he was already too late. Seadreamer's hands fell from the branch. He sagged against the trunk of the Tree. Panting hugely, he took all his life in his hands and wrenched it into the shape of one last cry:

'Do not!'

The next moment, too much force detonated in his chest. He fell as if he had been shattered, thudded brokenly to the floor.

Honninscrave's wail rose among the stars, but it made no difference. They swirled as if they meant to devour all the company.

Covenant's outpouring faltered. Flame flushed up and down his frame like the beating of his pulse, but did not lash out. Horror stretched his visage, a realization of what he had avoided and permitted. In her heart, Linden ran towards him; but her body stayed kneeling, half catatonic, on the stone. She was unable to find the key that would unlock her contradictions. The First and Pitchwife still clung to Honninscrave's arms, holding him back from Seadreamer. Cail stood beside Covenant as if he meant to protect the Unbeliever from the anger of the stars.

And the stars still whirled, imposing themselves on the stone and the air and the retreating sunlight, shooting from side to side closer towards the heads of the companions. Abruptly, Cail knocked Covenant aside to evade a giddy mote. The First and Pitchwife heaved Honninscrave towards the relative safety of the wall, then dived heavily after him. Destruction which no blood or bone might withstand swarmed through the cavern.

Findail tuned himself to a pitch beyond the stars' reach. But Vain made no effort to elude the danger. His eyes were focused on nothing. He smiled ambiguously as one of the stars struck and burst against his right forearm.

Another concussion shocked the cavern. Ebony fire spat like excruciation from the Demondim-spawn's flesh.

When it ended, his forearm had been changed. From elbow to wrist, the skin and muscle and bone were gone, transformed into rough-barked wood. Deprived of every nerve or ligature, his hand dangled useless from his iron-bound wrist.

And still the stars swirled, seeking ruin. The power which had been at rest in the roots of the Isle was rousing. All Linden's nerves screamed at the taste of a world-riving puissance.

Desperately, the First shouted, 'We will be slain!'

While that cry echoed, Covenant reeled to look at her, at Linden. For an instant, he appeared manic with indecision, as if he believed that the peril came from the One Tree itself, that he would have to destroy the Tree in order to save his friends. Linden tried to shout at him. No! That isn't it! But he would not have been able to hear her. When he saw her kneeling stricken on the stone, the danger rose up in him. His fire re-erupted.

The sun was already leaving the One Tree. The light seemed to creep towards the east wall, then rush upward as if it were being expelled by violence. But wild magic burned away all the darkness. Covenant blazed as if he were trying to set fire to the very rock of the Isle.

Extreme argent half blinded Linden. Reeling stars filled her eyes like blots of dazzlement. Potent as suns, they should have surpassed every flame that Covenant's flesh could raise. But he was powerful now in a way that transgressed mortal limits. Avid and fiery, he shone as if he were capable of detonating the sheer foundations of the Earth.

The force of his conflagration struck his companions like the hand of a gale, thrust all of them except Vain and Findail helplessly against the walls. Cail was torn from his side. Pitchwife and the First lay atop Honninscrave, determined to protect him at any hazard. Linden was shoved upright to the stone and held there as if she were still gripped by fetters in Kasreyn's dungeon. Venom as savage as ghouls raged in Covenant. It ignited him, transported him out of all restraint or choice. The stars were swept into him and seemed to vanish as if they were being consumed. Vivid and carious flames came from his scars, the marks of Marid's fangs. They raved through the mounting holocaust like glee.

He was trying to move forward, fighting towards the One Tree. Every vestige of his will and consciousness appeared to be focused on the branch which Seadreamer had touched.

Too deadly –

Alone and indomitable, he stood against the heavens and flailed wild magic at them like ecstasy or madness.

Yet the stars were not defeated. New motes of puissance were born to replace those his fury devoured. If he did not fail soon, he would be driven to the point of cataclysm. Around the roots of the Tree, the stone had begun to ripple and flow. In moments, the lives of his companions would be snuffed out by the unutterable wind of his power. Exalted and damned by fire, he raged against the stars as if his lust for might, mastery, triumph had eaten away every other part of him. He had become nothing except the vessel and personification of his venom.

Too deadly to go on living.

Still Linden could not move. Nothing in her life had prepared her for this. Stars gyred around the Tree, around Covenant. The stone boiled as if it were about to leap upward, take shape in its own defence. Wild magic lacerated her frail flesh, afflicting her with fire as Gibbon-Raver had once filled her with evil. She did not know how to move.

Then hands took hold of her, shook her. They were as compulsory as anguish. She looked away from Covenant and met Findail's frantic yellow eyes.

'You must stop him!' The *Elohim*'s lips did not move. His voice rang directly into her brain. 'He will not hear me!'

She gaped back at the Appointed. There were no words in all the cavern to articulate her panic.

'Do you not comprehend!' he knelled at her. 'He has encountered the Worm of the World's End! Its aura defends the One Tree! Already he has brought it nigh rousing!

'Are you blind at last?' His voice rang like a carillon in agony. 'Employ your sight! You must *see*! For this has the Despiser wrought his ill against you! For *this*! The Worm defends the One Tree! Have you learned nothing? Here the Despiser cannot fail! If the Worm is roused, the Earth will end, freeing Despite to wreak its vengeance upon the cosmos. And if the ring-wielder attempts to match his might against the Worm, he will destroy the Arch of Time. It cannot contain such a battle! It is founded upon white gold, and white gold will rive it to rubble.

'For this was he afflicted with the Despiser's venom!' Findail's clamour tormented every part of her being. 'To enhance his might, enabling him to rend the Arch! This is the helplessness of power! *You must stop him!'*

Still Linden did not respond, could not move. But her senses flared as if he had torn aside a veil, and she caught a glimpse of the truth. The boiling of the stone around the Tree was not caused by Covenant's heat. It came from the same source as the stars. A source buried among the deepest bones of the Earth – a source which had been at rest.

This was the crux of her life, this failure to rise above herself. This was why Lord Foul had chosen her. This paralysis was simply flight in another form. Unable to resolve the paradox of her lust for power and her hatred of evil, her desire and loathing for the dark might of Ravers, she was caught, immobilized. Gibbon-Raver had touched her, taught her the truth. *Are you not evil?* Behind all her strivings and determination lay that denunciation, rejecting life and love. If she remained frozen now, the denial of her humanity would be complete.

And it was Covenant who would pay the price – Covenant who was being duped into destroying what he loved. The unanswerable perfection of Lord Foul's machinations appalled her. In his power, Covenant had become, not the Earth's redeemer, but its doom. He, Thomas Covenant – the man to whom she had surrendered her loneliness. The man who had smiled for Joan.

His peril erased every other consideration.

There was no evil here. She clung to that fact, anchored herself on it. No Ravers. No Despiser. The Worm was inconceivably potent – but it was not evil. Covenant was lunatic with venom and passion – but he was not evil. No ill arose to condition her responses, control what she did. Surely she could afford to unbind her instinct for power? To save Covenant?

With a shout, she thrust away from Findail, began surging through utter and immedicable argent as if it were lava towards the Unbeliever.

At every new lash and eruption of wild magic, every added flurry of stars, she felt that the skin was being flayed from her bones; but she did not stop. The gale howled in her ears. She did not let it impede her. A Giantish voice wailed after her, 'Chosen!' and went unheeded. The cavern had become a chaos of echoes and violence; but she traversed the cacophony as if her will outshone every other sound. The presence of so much power elevated her. Instinctively, she used that force for protection, took hold of it with her percipience so that the stars did not burn her, the gale did not hurl her back.

Power.

Impossibly upright amid conflagrations which threatened to break the Isle, she placed herself between Covenant and the One Tree.

His fire scaled about him in whorls and coruscations. He looked like a white avatar of the father of nightmares. But he saw her. His howl made the roots of the rock shudder as he grabbed at her with wild magic, drew her inside his defences.

She flung her arms around him and forced her face towards his. Mad ecstasy distorted his visage. Kevin must have worn that same look at the Ritual of Desecration. Focusing all the penetration of her senses, she tuned her urgency, her love, her self to a pitch that would touch him.

'You've got to stop!'

He was a figure of pure fire. The radiance of his bones was beyond mortality. But she pierced the blaze.

'It's too much! You're going to break the Arch of Time!'

Through the outpouring, she heard him scream. But she held herself against him. Her senses grappled for his flame, prevented him from striking out.

'This is what Foul wants!'

Driven by the strength she took from him, her voice reached him.

She saw the shock as truth stabbed into him. She saw realization strike panic and horror across his visage. His worst nightmares reared up in front of him, his worst fears were fulfilled. He was poised on the precipice of the Despiser's victory. For one horrendous moment, he went on crying power as if in his despair he meant to tear down the heavens.

Every star he consumed was another light lost to the universe, another place of darkness in the firmament of the sky.

But she had reached him. His face stretched into a wail as if he had just seen everything he loved shatter. Then his features closed like a fist around a new purpose. Desperation burned from him. She felt his power changing. He was pulling it back, channelling it in another direction.

At first, she did not question what he was doing. She saw only that he was regaining control. He had heard her. Clinging to him passionately, she felt his will assert itself against venom and disaster.

But he did not silence his power. He altered it. Suddenly wild magic flooded into her through his embrace. She went rigid with dismay and intuitive comprehension, tried to resist. But she was composed of nothing except flesh and blood and emotion; and he had changed in a moment from unchecked virulence to wild magic incarnate, deliberate mastery. Her grip on his fire was too partial and inexperienced to refuse him.

His might bore her away. It did not touch her physically. It did not unbind her arms from him, did not harm her body. But it translated everything. Rushing through her like a torrent, it swept her out of herself, frayed her as if she were a mound of sand eroded by the

Sea, hurled her out among the stars.

Night burst by her on all sides. The heavens writhed about as if she were the pivot of their fate. Abysms of loneliness stretched out like absolute grief in every direction, contradicting the fact that she still felt Covenant in her arms, still saw the enclosure of the well. And those sensations were fading. She clung to them with frenzy; but wild magic burned them to ash in her grasp and cast her adrift. She floated away into fathomless midnight.

Echoing without sound or hope, Covenant's voice rose after her.

'Save my life!'

She was hurtling towards a fire which became yellow and vicious as she approached it. It defined the night, pulling the dark around it so that it was defended on all sides by blackness.

Then the blaze began to fade as if it had already consumed most of its fuel. As the flames shrank, she sprawled to the ground, lay on her back on a surface of stone. She was in two places at once. The wild magic continued to flow through her, linking her to Covenant, to the cavern of the One Tree. But at the same time she was elsewhere. Her head throbbed as if she had been struck a heavy blow behind one ear. When she tried to rise, the pain almost broke the fragile remnant of her link.

With a fatal slowness, her sight squeezed itself into focus.

She was lying on a rough plane of native rock beside the relict of the bonfire. The rock was in the bottom of a barren and abandoned hollow. Nothing obscured her view of the night sky. The stars were distant and inconceivable. But around the rims of the hollow she saw shrubs, brush, and trees, gaunt and spectral in the dark.

She knew where she was, what Covenant was doing to her. Defying the pain, she heaved upright and faced the body stretched at her side.

His body.

He lay as if he had been crucified on the stone. But the wound was not in his hands or feet or side: it was in his chest. The knife jutted like a plea from the junction of his ribs and sternum. The viscid and dying pool of his life dominated the triangle of blood which had been painted on the rock.

She felt that terrible amounts of time had passed, though she was only three heartbeats away from the cavern of the One Tree. The link was still open. Covenant was still pouring wild magic towards her, still striving to thrust her back into her old world. And that link kept her health-sense alight. When she looked at his body beside her – at the flesh outraged by the approach of death – she knew that he was alive.

The blood oozing from around the knife, the internal bleeding, the loss of fluid were nearly terminal; but not yet, not yet. Somehow, the blade had missed his heart. Flickers of life ached in his lungs, quivered in the failing muscles of his heart, yearned in the passages of his brain. He could be saved. It was still medically feasible to save him.

But before her own heart beat again, another perception altered everything.

Nothing would save him unless he did to himself what he had just done to her – unless he came to reoccupy his dying body. While his spirit, the part of him which desired life, remained absent, his flesh could not rally. He was too far from any other kind of help, too far even from her medical bag. Only his will for life had a chance to sustain him. And his will still burned in the cavern of the One Tree, spending itself to preserve her from doom. He had sent her away as he had once sent Joan, so that his life would be forfeit instead of hers.

First her father.

Then her mother.

Now Covenant.

Thomas Covenant, Unbeliever and white gold wielder, leper and lover, who had taught her to treasure the danger of being human.

Dying here in front of her.

Her heart lurched wildly. The link trembled. She started to protest, *No*! But before the word reached utterance she changed it into something else. As she scrambled to her feet, she clawed at the bond of power connecting her to Covenant. Her senses raced back along the current of wild magic. It was all she had. She had to make it serve her, wrest it from his grasp if necessary, *anything* rather than permit his death. Striving with every fraction of her strength, she cried out across the distance:

'Covenant!'

The sound fell stillborn in the woods. She did not know how to make him hear her. She clung to the link, but it resisted her service. If she had had the entire facilities and staff of a modern emergency room at her immediate disposal, she would not have been able to save him. His grip on the wild magic was too strong. The effort of mastering it had made him strong. Despair made him strong. And she had never wielded power before. In a direct contest for control of his might, she was no match for him.

But her percipience still lived. She knew him in that way more intimately than she had ever known herself. She felt his fierce grief and extremity across the gap between worlds. She knew –

Knew how to reach him.

She did not stop to count the cost. There was not time. Madly, she hurled herself into the bonfire as if it were her personal *caamora*.

For one splintered instant, those yellow flames leaped at her flesh. Harbingers of searing shot along her nerves.

Then Covenant saw her peril. Instinctively, he tried to snatch her back.

At once, she took hold of the link with every finger of her passion. Guided by her senses, she began to fight her way towards the source of the connection.

The woods became as insubstantial as mist, then fell into shreds as the winds between the stars tugged through them. The stone under her feet evaporated into darkness. Covenant's prone form denatured, disappeared. She began to fall, as bright as a comet, into the endless chasm of the heavens.

As she hurtled, she strove to muster words. You've got to come with me! It's the only way I can save you! But suddenly the power was quenched as if Covenant himself had been snuffed out. Her spiritual plummet among the stars seemed to become a physical plunge, a fall from a height which no human body might endure. Her heart wanted to scream, but there was no air, had never been any air, her lungs could not support the ether through which she dropped. She had gone off the edge of her fate. No cry remained which would have made any difference.

Helpless to catch herself, she stumbled forward on to her face on the floor of the cavern. Her pulses raced, chest laboured. Reminders of the bonfire flushed over her skin. A moment passed before she was able to realize that she had suffered no hurt.

Hands came to her aid. She needed the help. Her brain was giddy with transcendent dread. The stone seemed to buck and tremor under her. But the hands lifted her upright. She read the nature of their strength: they were *Haruchai* hands, Cail's hands. She welcomed them.

But she was blind. The floor went on lurching. The Isle had begun to tremble like the presage of a convulsion. There was no light. The stars of the Worm's aura were gone. Covenant's fire was gone. Dazzled by powers and desperation, her eyes refused to adjust to the gloom. All her companions were invisible. They might have been slain –

She fought to see through the Worm's unquiet ambience; but when she looked beyond Cail, she found nothing but Seadreamer's corpse. He lay in Honninscrave's embrace near the base of the One Tree as if his valiant bones had been burned to cinders.

The sight wrung her. Cable Seadreamer, involuntary victim of Earth-Sight and muteness. He had done nothing with his life except give it away in an effort to save the people he most treasured. She had failed him, too.

But then she became aware of Honninscrave himself, realized that the Master was breathing in great, raw hunks of loss. He was alive. That perception seemed to complete her transition, bringing her fully back into the company of her friends. The gloom macerated slowly as her eyes swam into focus.

Softly, Pitchwife said, 'Ah, Chosen, Chosen.' His voice was thick with rue.

A short distance from Honninscrave and Seadreamer, Covenant sat spread-legged on the stone. He appeared unconcious of the violence building in the roots of the Isle. He faced the unattainable Tree with his back bowed as if he had broken his spine.

The First and Pitchwife stood together, trapped between Covenant and Honninscrave by their inability to comfort either pain. She still gripped her sword, but it had become useless to her. Her husband's face was full of silent weeping.

Vain remained a few paces away, wearing his black smile as if the wooden ruin of his right forearm meant nothing to him. Only Findail was nowhere to be seen. He had fled the crisis of Covenant's fire. Linden did not care if he never returned.

Stiffly, she carried her appeal towards Covenant. Kneeling between his legs, she faced him and tried to lift the words into her throat. You've got to go back. But she was unable to speak. It was too late. His power-haunted gaze told her plainly that he already knew what she wanted to say.

'I can't.' His voice sifted into the dark like a falling of ashes. 'Even if I could stand it. Abandon the Land. Let Foul have his way.' His face was only a blur in the gloom, a pale smear from which all hope had been erased. 'It takes too much power. I'd break the Arch.'

Oh, Covenant!

She had nothing else to give him.

27

THE LONG GRIEF

Linden could barely discern her companions through the dimness. Honninscrave and dead Seadreamer; the First and Pitchwife; Vain and Cail. They stood around her like deeper shadows in the pervading dark. But Covenant was the one she watched. The image of him supine on the verge of death with that knife in his chest was as vivid to her as the etchwork of acid. She saw that face — the features acute with agony, the skin waxen and pallid — more clearly than the gaunt visage before her. Its vague shape appeared mortally imprecise, as if its undergirding bones had been broken — as if he were as broken as the Land which Lord Foul had restored to him, as broken as Joan. All the danger had gone out of him.

But the company could not remain where it was. A sharper convulsion shook the stone, as if the Worm were nearly awake. A scattering of pebbles fell from the walls, filling the air with light echoes. There was little time left. Perhaps it would not be enough. Gently, Cail stooped to Covenant. 'Ur-Lord, come. This Isle cannot hold. We must hasten for our lives.'

Linden understood. The Worm was settling back to its rest; and those small movements might tear the Isle apart at any moment. She had failed at everything else; but this exigency was within her grasp. She rose to her feet, extended her hands to help Covenant.

He refused her offer. For a moment, darkness blotted out his mien. When he spoke, his voice was muffled by defeat.

'I should've broken the link. Before you had time to see. But I didn't have the courage to let you go. I can't bear it.'

Yet he moved. In spite of everything, he heeded the company's need. Tortured and leprous, he climbed Cail's support until he was upright.

Another shock staggered the cavern. But Linden kept her balance alone.

The First and Pitchwife went to Honninscrave. With firm care, they urged him erect. He would not release his brother. Bearing Seadreamer in his arms, he permitted himself to be nudged towards the ledge after Covenant and Linden.

In silence, the questers trudged up out of the tomb of their dreams.

Tremors threatened them repeatedly during that hard ascent. The ledge pitched as if it sought to shrug them back into the gulf. Vibrations made the stone quiver like wounded flesh. At intervals, hunks of rock fell, striking out sharp resonations which scaled upward like cries of bereavement. But Linden was not afraid of that. She was hardly aware of the exertion of the climb. She felt that she could count the last drops of blood as they seeped around the knife in Covenant's chest.

When she gained the crest, looked out over the Isle and the wide Sea, she was wanly surprised to see that the sun had fallen no lower than midafternoon. Surely the ruin of the quest had consumed more time than that? But it had not. Such damage was as sudden as an infarction. As abrupt as the collapse of the old man on the roadway into Haven Farm.

Slowly, irresistibly, the violence in the rock continued to build. As she started downward, she saw that the slopes were marked with new scars where boulders and outcroppings had fallen away. The old Sea had swallowed all the rubble without a trace.

The last throes of the Isle were rising. Though she was hardly able to walk without stumbling, she urged the company faster. It was her responsibility. Covenant was so Desecration-ridden, so despair-blind, that he would have plunged headlong if Cail had not supported him. She needed help herself; but Brinn was gone, the First and Pitchwife were occupied with Honninscrave, and Cail's duty was elsewhere. So she carried her own weight and croaked at her companions for haste. As awkwardly as cripples, they raced the Worm's unrest downward.

Vain followed them as if nothing had changed. But his right hand dangled from the dead wood of his transformed forearm. The band of the Staff of Law on his wrist clasped the boundary between flesh and bark.

At last, they reached the longboat. Somehow, it had not been struck by any of the falling boulders. The companions lurched and thudded aboard as if they were in rout.

As the First shoved the craft out into the water, the entire eyot jumped. A large section of the crest crumbled inward. The Sea heaved into deep waves, setting the longboat a-dance. But it rode out the spasms unscathed. Then the First and Pitchwife took the oars and rowed through the sunlight towards Starfare's Gem.

The next tremor toppled more of the Isle's crown. Wide pieces of the engirdling reef sank. After that, the convulsions became almost constant, raising immense exhalations of dust like spume from the island's throat. Impelled by heavy seas, the longboat moved swiftly to the side of the Giantship. In a short time, the company gained the decks. Everyone gathered along the port rail to watch the cairn of the One Tree go down.

It sank in a last tremendous upheaval. Chunks of the Isle jumped like flames as its foundations shattered. Then all the rock settled around the Worm's new resting-place; and the Sea rushed into the gap. The waters rose like a great geyser, spread outward in deep undulations which made the *dromond* roll from side to side. But that was the end. Even the reef was gone. Nothing remained to mark the area except bubbles which broke the surface and then faded, leaving azure silence in their wake.

Slowly, the spectators turned back to their ship. When Linden looked past Vain towards Covenant, she saw Findail standing with him. She wanted to be angry at the *Elohim*, would have welcomed any emotion which might have sustained her. But the time for such things had passed. No expostulation would bring back Covenant's hope. The lines engraving the Appointed's face were as deep as ever; but now, they seemed like scars of pity.

'I cannot ease your sorrow,' he said, speaking so softly that Linden barely heard him. 'That attempt was made, and it failed. But one fear I will spare you. The One Tree is not destroyed. It is a mystery of the Earth. While the Earth endures, it too will endure in its way.

Perhaps your guilts are indeed as many as you deem them – but *that* is one you need not bear.'

Findail's unexpected gentleness made Linden's eyes blur. But the pained slump of Covenant's shoulders, the darkness of his gaze, showed that he had passed beyond the reach of solace. In a voice like the last drops of blood, he replied, 'You could've warned me. I almost – ' The vision of what he had nearly done clogged his throat. He swallowed as if he wanted to curse and no longer had the strength. 'I'm sick of guilt.'

Honninscrave remained huddled over Seadreamer. Sevinhand and Galewrath looked to him for instructions; but he did not respond, did not notice them at all. After a brief pause of respect, the First told the Anchormaster what to do.

Wrapping his old melancholy about him, Sevinhand rallied the crew. The anchors were raised, the sails set. In a short time, Starfare's Gem swung away from the grave of the lost Isle and headed northward into the open Sea.

But Covenant did not stay to watch. Bereft beyond redemption, he left his companions, shambled in the direction of his cabin. He was dying with a knife in his chest and no longer had any way to fight the Despiser. Linden understood. When he turned his back on her, she did not protest.

This was her life after all – as true to herself, to what she was and what she wanted to become, as the existence she had left behind on Haven Farm. The old man whose life she had saved there had said to her, *You will not fail, however he may assail you.* The choices she had made could not be taken from her.

And that was not all. She remembered what Covenant had told her about his Dead in Andelain. His friend, High Lord Mhoram, had said to him, *Do not be deceived by the Land's need. The thing you seek is not what it appears to be.* The same prophecy was true for her as well. Like Brinn, she had found something she had not come seeking. With Covenant after their escape from *Bhrathairealm*, she had let some light into the darkness of her heart. And in the cavern of the One Tree she had found a use for that part of herself – a use which was not evil.

Since Covenant could not bear it now, she accepted from him the burden of hope. *You will not fail* – Not while she still believed in him – and knew how to reach him.

Yet she did not try to keep the tears from her eyes. Too much had been lost. As she went to stand beside Honninscrave, she folded her arms over her heart and let the long grief of the quest settle in her bones.

WHITE GOLD
WIELDER

'To go wherever dreaming goes'

PART I

Retribution

1

THE MASTER'S SCAR

Awkward without its midmast, Starfare's Gem turned heavily toward the north, putting its stern to the water clogged with sand and foam which marked the passing of the One Tree. In the rigging, Giants laboured and fumbled at their tasks, driven from line to line by the hoarse goad of Sevinhand's commands even though Seadreamer lay dead on the deck below them. The Anchormaster stood, lean and rue-bitten, on the wheeldeck and yelled up at them, his voice raw with suppressed pain. If any compliance lagged, the Storesmaster, Galewrath, seconded him, throwing her shout after his like a piece of ragged granite because all the Search had come to ruin and she did not know any other way to bear it. The *dromond* went north simply to put distance between itself and the deep grave of its hope.

But Grimmand Honninscrave, the Giantship's Master, huddled on the afterdeck with his brother in his arms and did not speak. His massive face, so strong against storms and perils, looked like a yielded fortification; his beard tangled the shadows as the sun declined toward setting. And beside him stood the First of the Search and Pitchwife as though they were lost without the Earth-Sight to guide them.

Findail the Appointed stood there also, wearing his old misery like a man who had always known what would happen at the Isle of the One Tree. Vain stood there with one heel of the former Staff of Law bound around his wooden wrist and his useless hand dangling. And Linden Avery stood there as well, torn between bereavements: outrage and sorrow for Seadreamer swimming in her eyes, need for Covenant aching in her limbs.

But Thomas Covenant had withdrawn to his cabin like a crippled animal going to ground; and he stayed there.

He was beaten. He had nothing left.

Harsh with revulsion, he lay in his hammock and stared at the ceiling. His chamber had been made for a Giant: it outsized him, just as his doom and the Despiser's manipulations had outsized him. The red sunset through the open port bloodied the ceiling until dusk came and leeched his sight away. But he had been blind all along, so truncated of perception that he had caught no glimpse of his true fate until Linden had cried it into his face:

This is what Foul wants!

That was how his former strengths and victories had been turned against him. He could not feel Cail standing guard outside his door like a man whose fidelity had been redeemed. Beyond the slow rolling of the Giantship's pace, the salt of futility in the air, the distant creak of rigging and report of canvas, he could not tell the difference between this cabin and the dungeon of the Sandhold or the betrayed depths of Revelstone. All stone was one to him, deaf to appeal or need, senseless. He might have destroyed the Earth in that crisis of power and venom, might have broken the Arch of Time as if he were indeed the Despiser's servant, if Linden had not stopped him.

And then he had failed at his one chance to save himself. Horrified by love and fear for her, he had allowed Linden to return to him, abandoning the stricken and dying body of his other life. Abandoning him to ruin, though she had not intended any ruin.

Brinn had said to him, *That is the grace which has been given to you, to bear what must be borne.* But it was a lie.

In darkness he lay and did not move, sleepless although he coveted slumber, yearned for any oblivion which would bring surcease. He went on staring upward as if he too were graven of dead stone, a reification of folly and broken dreams snared within the eternal ambit of his defeat. Anger and self-despite might have impelled him to seek out his old clothes, might have sent him up to the decks to bear the desolation of his friends. But those garments he had left in Linden's cabin as though for safe-keeping; and he could not go there. His love for her was too corrupt, had been too severely falsified by selfishness. Thus the one lie he had practised against her from the beginning came back to damn him.

He had withheld one important fact from her, hoping like a coward that it would prove unnecessary — that his desire for her would be permissible in the end. But by the lie of withholding he had accomplished nothing except her miscomprehension. Nothing except the Search's destitution and the Despiser's victory. He had let his need for her blind both of them.

No, it was worse than that. He did need her, had needed her so acutely that the poignance of it had shredded his defences. But another need had been at work as well: the need to be the Land's rescuer, to stand at the centre of Lord Foul's evil and impose his own answer upon it; the need to demonstrate his mortal worth against all the bloodshed and pain which condemned him. He had become so wrapped up in his isolation and leprosy, so certain of them and what they meant, that they had grown indistinguishable from Despite.

Now he was beaten. He had nothing left for which he might sanely hope or strive.

He should have known better. The old man on Haven Farm had spoken to Linden rather than to him. The *Elohim* had greeted her as the Sun-Sage, him as the wrongness which imperilled the Earth. Even dead Elena in Andelain had said plainly that the healing of the Land was in Linden's hands rather than his. Yet he had rejected comprehension in favour of self-insistence. His need or arrogance had been too great to allow comprehension.

And still, with the destruction of everything he held precious laid squarely at his door, he would not have done otherwise – would not give up his ring, not surrender the meaning of his life either to Linden or to Findail. It was all that remained to him: to bear the blame if he could not achieve the victory. Failing everything else, he could still at least refuse to be spared.

So he lay in his hammock like a sacrifice, with the stone vessel spread out unreadably around him. Fettered by the iron of his failures, he did not move or try to move. The first night after the dark of the moon filled his eyes. In Andelain, High Lord Mhoram had warned, *He has said that you are his Enemy. Remember that he seeks always to mislead you.* It was true: he was the Despiser's servant rather than Enemy. Even his former victory had been turned against him. Sucking the wounded places of his heart, he returned the sightless stare of the dark and remained where he was.

He had no measure for the passage of time; but the night was not far advanced when he heard a stiff, stretched voice rumble outside his door. It uttered words he was unable to distinguish. Yet Cail's reply was precise. 'The doom of the Earth is upon his head,' the *Haruchai* said. 'Will you not pity him?'

Too weary for indignation or argument, Honninscrave responded, 'Can you believe that I mean him harm?'

Then the door opened, and a lantern led the Master's tall bulk into the cabin.

The light seemed small against the irreducible night of the world; but it lit the chamber brightly enough to sting Covenant's eyes, like tears he had not shed. Still he did not turn his head away or cover his face. He went on staring numbly at the ceiling while Honninscrave set the lantern on the table.

The table was low for the size of the cabin: from the first day of the quest's voyage, the Giantish furniture had been replaced by a table and chairs better suited to Covenant's stature. As a result, the lantern threw the hammock's shadow above him. He seemed to lie in the echo of his own dark.

With a movement that made his sark sigh along the wall, Honninscrave lowered himself to the floor. After long moments of silence, his voice rose out of the wan light.

'My brother is dead.' The knowledge still wrung him. 'Having no other family since the passing of our mother and father, I loved him,

845

and he is dead. The vision of his Earth-Sight gifted us with hope even as it blighted him with anguish, and now that hope is dead, and he will never be released. As did the Dead of The Grieve, he has gone out of life in horror. He will never be released. Cable Seadreamer my brother, bearer of Earth-Sight, voiceless and valiant to his grave.'

Covenant did not turn his head. But he blinked at the sting in his eyes until the shadow above him softened it. *The way of hope and doom*, he thought dumbly, *lies open to you*. Perhaps for him that had been true. Perhaps if he had been honest with Linden, or had heeded the *Elohim*, the path to the One Tree might have held some hope. But what hope had there ever been for Seadreamer? Yet without hope the Giant had tried to take all the doom upon himself. And somehow at the last he had found his voice to shout a warning.

Roughly, Honninscrave said, 'I beseeched of the Chosen that she speak to you, but she would not. When I purposed to come to you myself, she railed at me, demanding that I forbear. "Has he not suffered sufficiently?" she cried. "Have you no mercy?"' He paused briefly, and his voice lowered. 'She bears herself bravely, the Chosen. No longer is she the woman of frailty and fright who quailed so before the lurker of the Sarangrave. But she also was bound to my brother by a kinship which rends her in her way.' In spite of her refusal, he seemed to believe that she deserved his respect.

Then he went on, 'But what have I to do with mercy or forbearance? They are too high for me. I know only that Cable Seadreamer is dead. He will never be released if you do not release him.'

At that, Covenant flinched in surprise and pain. If *I* don't – ? He was sick with venom and protest. How can *I* release him? If revelation and dismay and Linden had not driven restraint so deeply into him during his struggle against the aura of the Worm of the World's End, he would have burned the air for no other reason than because he was hurt and futile with power. How can I bear it?

But his restraint held. And Honninscrave looked preternaturally reduced as he sat on the floor against the wall, hugging his unanswered grief. The Giant was Covenant's friend. In that light, Honninscrave might have been an avatar of lost Saltheart Foamfollower, who had given Covenant everything. He still had enough compassion left to remain silent.

'Giantfriend,' the Master said without lifting his head, 'have you been given the tale of how Cable Seadreamer my brother came by his scar?'

His eyes were hidden beneath his heavy brows. His beard slumped on his chest. The shadow of the table's edge cut him off at the torso; but his hands were visible, gripping each other. The muscles of his forearms and shoulders were corded with fatigue and strain.

'The fault of it was mine,' he breathed into the empty light. 'The exuberance and folly of my youth marked him for all to see that I had been careless of him.

'He was my brother, and the younger by some years, though as the lives of Giants are reckoned the span between us was slight. Surely we were both well beyond the present number of your age, but still were we young, new to our manhood, and but recently prenticed to the seacraft and the ships we loved. The Earth-Sight had not yet come upon him, and so there was naught between us beyond my few years and the foolishness which he outgrew more swiftly than I. He came early to his stature, and I ended his youth before its time.

'In those days, we practised our new crafts in a small vessel which our people name a *tyrscull* – a stone craft near the measure of the longboats you have seen, with one sail, a swinging boom, and oars for use should the wind be lost or misplayed. With skill, a *tyrscull* may be mastered by one Giant alone, but two are customary. Thus Seadreamer and I worked and learned together. Our *tyrscull* we named Foamkite, and it was our hearts' glee.

'Now among prentices it is no great wonder that we revelled in tests against each other, pitting and honing our skills with races and displays of every description. Most common of these was the running of a course within the great harbour of Home – far sufficiently from shore to be truly at sea, and yet within any swimmer's reach of land, should some prentice suffer capsize – a mishap which would have shamed us deeply, young as we were. And when we did not race we trained for races, seeking new means by which we might best our comrades.

'The course was simply marked. One point about which we swung was a buoy fixed for that purpose, but the other was a rimed and hoary rock that we named Salttooth for the sheer, sharp manner in which it rose to bite the air. Once or twice or many times around that course ran our races, testing our ability to use the winds for turning as well as for speed.'

Honninscrave's voice had softened somewhat: remembrance temporarily took him away from his distress. But his head remained bowed. And Covenant could not look away from him. Punctuated by the muffled sounds of the Sea, the plain details of Honninscrave's story transfixed the atmosphere of the cabin.

'This course Seadreamer and I ran as often as any and more than most, for we were eager for the Sea. Thus we came to stand well among those who vied for mastery. With this my brother was content. He had the true Giantish exhilaration and did not require victory for his joy. But in that I was less worthy of my people. Never did I cease to covet victory, or to seek out new means by which it might be attained.

'So it befell that one day I conceived a great thought which caused me to hug my breast in secret, and to hasten Seadreamer to Foamkite, that I might practise my thought and perfect it for racing. But that thought I did not share with him. It was grand, and I desired its wonder for myself. Not questioning what was in me, he came for the simple pleasure of the Sea. Together, we ran Foamkite out to the buoy, then swung with all speed toward upthrust Salttooth

'It was a day as grand as my thought.' He spoke as if it were visible behind the shadows of the cabin. 'Under the faultless sky blew a wind with a whetted edge which offered speed and hazard, cutting the wave-crests to white froth as it bore us ahead. Swiftly before us loomed Salttooth. In such a wind, the turning of a *tyrscull* requires true skill − a jeopardy even to competent prentices − and it was there that a race could be won or lost, for a poor tack might drive a small craft far from the course or overturn it altogether. But my thought was for that turning, and I was not daunted by the wind.

'Leaving Seadreamer to the tiller and the management of the boom, I bid him run in as nigh to Salttooth as he dared. All prentices knew such a course to be folly, for the turning would then bear us beyond our way. But I silenced my brother's protests and went to Foamkite's prow. Still preserving my secret, hiding my hands from his sight, I freed the anchor and readied its line.'

Abruptly, the Master faltered, fell still. One fist lay knotted in his lap: the other twisted roughly into his beard, tugging it for courage. But after a moment, he drew a deep breath, then let the air hiss away through his teeth. He was a Giant and could not leave his story unfinished.

'Such was Seadreamer's skill that we passed hastening within an arm's span of Salttooth, though the wind heeled us sharply from the rock and any sideslip might have done Foamkite great harm. But his hand upon the wind was sure, and an instant later I enacted my intent. As we sped, I arose and cast the anchor upon the rock, snagging us there. Then I lashed the line.

'This was my thought for a turning too swift to be matched by any other *tyrscull*, that our speed and the anchor and Salttooth should do the labour for us − though I was uncertain how the anchor might be unsnared when the turn was done. But I had not told Seadreamer my purpose.' His voice had become a low rasp of bitterness in his throat. 'He was fixed upon the need to pass Salttooth without mishap, and my act surprised him entirely. He half gained his feet, half started toward me as if I had gone mad. Then the line sprang taut, and Foamkite came about with a violence which might have snapped the mast from its holes.'

Again he stopped. The muscles of his shoulders bunched. When he resumed, he spoke so softly that Covenant barely heard him.

'Any child might have informed me what would transpire, but I had given no consideration to it. The boom wrenched across the stern of Foamkite with a force to sliver granite. And Seadreamer my brother had risen into its path.

'In that wind and my folly, I would not have known that he had fallen, had he not cried out as he was struck. But at his cry I turned to see him flung into the Sea.

'Ah, my brother!' A groan twisted his voice. 'I dove for him, but he would have been lost had I not found the path of his blood in the water and followed it. Senseless he hung in my arms as I bore him to the surface.

'With the Sea thus wind-slashed, I saw little of his injury but blood until I had borne him to Foamkite and wrested him aboard. But there his wound seemed so great that I believed his eyes had been crushed in his head, and for a time I became as mad as my intent had been. To this day, I know nothing of our return to the docks of Home. I did not regain myself until a healer spoke to me, compelling me to hear that my brother had not been blinded. Had the boom itself struck him, mayhap he would have been slain outright. But the impact was borne by a cable along the boom, taking him below the eyes and softening the blow somewhat.'

Once more he fell still. His hands covered his face as though to staunch the flow of blood he remembered. Covenant watched him mutely. He had no courage for such stories, could not bear to have them thrust upon him. But Honninscrave was a Giant and a friend; and since the days of Foamfollower, Covenant had not been able to close his heart. Though he was helpless and aggrieved, he remained silent and let Honninscrave do what he willed.

After a moment, the Master dropped his hands. Drawing a breath like a sigh, he said, 'It is not the way of Giants to punish such folly as mine, though I would have found comfort in the justice of punishment. And Cable Seadreamer was a Giant among Giants. He did not blame the carelessness which marked his life forever.' Then his tone stiffened. 'But I do not forget. The fault is mine. Though I too am a Giant in my way, my ears have not found the joy to hear this story. And I have thought often that perhaps my fault is greater than it has appeared. The Earth-Sight is a mystery. None can say why it chooses one Giant rather than another. Perhaps it befell my brother because of some lingering hurt or alteration done him by the puissance of that blow. Even in their youth, Giants are not easily stricken senseless.'

Suddenly Honninscrave looked upward; and his gaze struck foreboding into Covenant's maimed empathy. His eyes under his heavy brows were fierce with extremity, and the new-cut lines around them were as intense as scars. 'Therefore have I come to you,' he said slowly, as if he could not see Covenant quailing. 'I desire a restitution which is not within my power to perform. My fault must be assuaged.

'It is the custom of our people to give our dead to the Sea. But Cable Seadreamer my brother has met his end in horror, and it will not release him. He is like the Dead of The Grieve, damned to his anguish. If his spirit is not given its *caamora*' — for an instant, his voice broke — 'he will haunt me while one stone of the Arch of Time remains standing upon another.'

Then his gaze fell to the floor. 'Yet there is no fire in all the world that I can raise to give him surcease. He is a Giant. Even in death, he is immune to flame.'

At that, Covenant understood; and all his dreads came together in a rush: the apprehension which had crouched in him since Honninscrave had first said, *If you do not release him*; the terror of his doom, to destroy the Earth himself or to surrender it for destruction by ceding his ring to Lord Foul. The Despiser had said, *The ill that you deem most terrible is upon you. Of your own volition you will give the white gold into my hand.* Either that or bring down the Arch of Time. There was no way out. He was beaten. Because he had kept the truth from Linden, seeking to deny it. And Honninscrave asked — !

'You want me to cremate him?' Clenched fear made him harsh. 'With my ring? Are you out of your mind?'

Honninscrave winced. 'The Dead of The Grieve — ' he began.

'No!' Covenant retorted. He had walked into a bonfire to save them from their reiterated hell; but risks like that were too great for him now. He had already caused too much death. 'After I sink the ship, I won't be able to *stop*!'

For a moment, even the sounds of the Sea fell still, shocked by his vehemence. The Giantship seemed to be losing headway. The light of the lantern flickered as if it were going out. Perhaps there were shouts like muffled lamentations in the distance: Covenant could not be sure. His senses were condemned to the surface of what they perceived. The rest of the *dromond* was hidden from him.

If the Master heard anything, he did not react to it. His head remained bowed. Moving heavily, like a man hurt in every limb, he climbed to his feet. Though the hammock hung high above the floor, he stood head and shoulders over the Unbeliever; and still he did not meet Covenant's glare. The light of the lantern was below and behind him as he took one step closer. His face was shadowed, dark and fatal.

In a wan and husky voice, he said, 'Yes, Giantfriend.' The epithet held a tinge of sarcasm. 'I am gone from my mind. You are the ring-wielder, as the *Elohim* have said. Your power threatens the Earth. What import has the anguish of one or two Giants in such a plight? Forgive me.'

Then Covenant wanted to cry out in earnest, torn like dead Kevin

Landwaster between love and defeat. But loud feet had come running down the companionway outside his cabin, had already reached his door. The door sprang open without any protest from Cail: a crewmember thrust her head past the threshold.

'Master, you must come.' Her voice was tight with alarm. 'We are beset by *Nicor*.'

2

LEPER'S GROUND

Honninscrave left the cabin slowly, like a man responding by habit, unconscious of the urgency of the summons. Perhaps he no longer understood what was happening around him. Yet he did respond to the call of his ship.

When the Master reached the companionway, Cail closed the door behind him. The *Haruchai* seemed to know instinctively that Covenant would not follow Honninscrave.

Nicor! Covenant thought, and his heart laboured. Those tremendous serpent-like sea-beasts were said to be the offspring of the Worm of the World's End. Starfare's Gem had passed through a region crowded with them near the Isle of the One Tree. They had been indifferent to the *dromond* then. But now? With the Isle gone and the Worm restive?

And what could one stone vessel do against so many of those prodigious creatures? What could Honninscrave do?

Yet the Unbeliever did not leave his hammock. He stared at the dark ceiling and did not move. He was beaten, defeated. He dared not take the risk of confronting the Giantship's peril. If Linden had not intervened at the One Tree, he would already have become another Kevin, enacting a Ritual of Desecration to surpass every other evil. The threat of the *Nicor* paled beside the danger he himself represented.

Deliberately, he sought to retreat into himself. He did not want to know what transpired outside his cabin. How could he endure the knowledge? He had said, *I'm sick of guilt* – but such protests had no meaning. His very blood had been corrupted by venom and culpability. Only the powerless were truly innocent, and he was not powerless. He was not even honest. The selfishness of his love had brought all this to pass.

Yet the lives at stake were the lives of his friends, and he could not close himself to the *dromond*'s jeopardy. Starfare's Gem rolled slightly in the water as if it had lost all headway. A period of shouts and running had followed Honninscrave's departure, but now the Giantship was silent. With Linden's senses, he would have been able to read what was happening through the stone itself; but he was blind and bereft, cut off from the essential spirit of the world. His numb hands clutched the edges of the hammock.

Time passed. He was a coward, and his dreads swarmed darkly about him as if they were born in the shadows above his head. He gripped himself with thoughts of ruin, held himself still with curses. But Honninscrave's face kept coming back to him: the beard like a growth of pain from his cheeks, the massive brow knuckled with misery, the hands straining. Covenant's friend. Like Foamfollower. *My brother has met his end in horror.* It was intolerable that such needs had to be refused. And now the *Nicor* – !

Even a beaten man could still feel pain. Roughly, he pulled himself into a sitting position. His voice was a croak of coercion and fear as he called out, 'Cail!'

The door opened promptly, and Cail entered the cabin.

The healed wound of a Courser-spur marked his left arm from shoulder to elbow like the outward sign of his fidelity; but his visage remained as impassive as ever. 'Ur-Lord?' he asked flatly. His dispassionate tone gave no hint that he was the last *Haruchai* left in Covenant's service.

Covenant stifled a groan. 'What the hell's going on out there?'

In response, Cail's eyes shifted fractionally. But still his voice held no inflection. 'I know not.'

Until the previous night, when Brinn had left the quest to take up his role as *ak-Haru Kenaustin Ardenol*, Cail had never been alone in his chosen duty; and the mental interconnection of his people had kept him aware of what took place around him. But now he was alone. Brinn's defeat of the former Guardian of the One Tree had been a great victory for him personally, and for the *Haruchai* as a people; but it left Cail isolated in a way that no one who had not experienced such mind-sharing could measure. His blunt *I know not* silenced Covenant like an admission of frailty.

Cail – Covenant tried to say. He did not want to leave the *Haruchai* in that loneliness. But Brinn had said, *Cail will accept my place in your service until the word of the Bloodguard Bannor has been carried to its end.* And no appeal or protest would sway Cail from the path Brinn had marked out for him. Covenant remembered Bannor too poignantly to believe that the *Haruchai* would ever judge themselves by any standards but their own.

Yet his distress remained. Even lepers and murderers were not immune to hurt. He fought down the thickness in his throat and said, 'I want my old clothes. They're in her cabin.'

Cail nodded as if he saw nothing strange in the request. As he left, he closed the door quietly after him.

Covenant lay back again and clenched his teeth. He did not want those clothes, did not want to return to the hungry and unassuaged life he had lived before he had found Linden's love. But how else could he leave his cabin? Those loathed and necessary garments represented the only honesty left to him. Any other apparel would be a lie.

However, when Cail returned he was not alone. Pitchwife entered the chamber ahead of him; and at once Covenant forgot the bundle Cail bore. The deformity which bent Pitchwife's spine, hunching his back and crippling his chest, made him unnaturally short for a Giant: his head did not reach the level of the hammock. But the irrepressibility of his twisted face gave him stature. He was alight with excitement as he limped forward to greet Covenant.

'Have I not said that she is well Chosen?' he began without preamble. 'Never doubt it, Giantfriend! Mayhap this is but one wonder among many, for surely our voyage has been rife with marvels. Yet I do not dream to see it surpassed. Stone and Sea, Giantfriend! She has taught me to hope again.'

Covenant stared in response, stung by an inchoate apprehension. What new role had Linden taken upon herself, when he still had not told her the truth?

Pitchwife's eyes softened. 'But you do not comprehend – as how should you, who have not seen the Sea loom with *Nicor* under the stars, not heard the Chosen sing them to peace.'

Still Covenant did not speak. He had no words for the complex admixture of his pride and relief and bitter loss. The woman he loved had saved the Giantship. And he, who had once defeated the Despiser in direct combat – he no longer signified.

Watching Covenant's face, Pitchwife sighed to himself. In a more subdued manner, he went on, 'It was an act worthy of long telling, but I will briefen it. You have heard that the Giants are able to summon *Nicor* upon occasion. Such a summons we wrought on your behalf, when last the venom-sickness of the Raver possessed you.' Covenant had no memory of the situation: he had been near death in delirium at the time. But he had been told about it. 'Yet to the *Nicor* we do not speak. They lie beyond our gift of tongues. The sounds which may summon them we have learned from our generations upon the Sea. But those sounds we make blindly, uncertain of their meaning. And a Giantship which enters a sea of *Nicor* in their wrath has scant need of summons.'

A small smile quirked his mouth; but he did not stop. 'It was Linden Avery the Chosen who found means to address them for our survival. Lacking the plain might of arm for her purpose, she called Galewrath Storesmaster with her and went below, down to the bottommost hull of the *dromond*. There through the stone she read the ire of the *Nicor* – and gave it answer. With her hands she clapped a rhythm which Galewrath echoed for her, pounding it with hammers upon the hull.'

Then for a moment the Giant's enthusiasm resurged. 'And she was heeded!' he crowed. 'The *Nicor* parted about us, bearing their anger into the south. We have been left without scathe!' His hands gripped the edge of the hammock, rocked it as if to make Covenant hear him. 'There is yet hope in the world. While we endure, and the Chosen and the Giantfriend remain among us, there is hope!'

But Pitchwife's claim was too direct: Covenant flinched from it. He had wronged too many people and had no hope left for himself. A part of him wanted to cry out in protest. Was that what he would have to do in the end? Give Linden his ring, the meaning of his life, when she had never seen the Land without the Sunbane and did not know how to love it? Weakly, he muttered, 'Tell that to Honninscrave. He could use some hope.'

At that, Pitchwife's eyes darkened. But he did not look away. 'The Master has spoken of your refusal. I know not the good or ill of these matters, but the word of my heart is that you have done what you must – and that is well. Do not think me ungrieved by Seadreamer's fall – or the Master's hurt. Yet the hazard of your might is great. And who can say how the *Nicor* would answer such fire, though they have passed us by? None may judge the doom which lies upon you now. You have done well in your way.'

Pitchwife's frank empathy made Covenant's eyes burn: he knew acutely that he had not done well. Pain like Honninscrave's should not be refused, never be refused. But the fear and the despair were still there, blocking everything. He could not even meet Pitchwife's gaze.

'Ah, Giantfriend,' Pitchwife breathed at last. 'You also are grieved beyond bearing. I know not how to solace you.' Abruptly, he stooped, and one hand lifted a leather flask into the hammock. 'If you find no ease in my tale of the Chosen, will you not at the least drink *diamondraught* and grant your flesh rest? Your own story remains to be told. Be not so harsh with yourself.'

His words raised memories of dead Atiaran in Andelain. The mother of the woman he had raped and driven mad had said with severe compassion, *In punishing yourself, you come to merit punishment. This is Despite.* But Covenant did not want to think about Atiaran. *Find no ease* – Belatedly, he pictured Linden in the depths of the *dromond*, holding the survival of the Search in her hands. He could not hear the rhythm of her courage, but he saw her face. Framed by her wheaten hair, it was acute with concentration, knotted between the brows, marked on either side of the mouth by the consequences of severity – and beautiful to him in every bone and line.

Humbled by what she had done to save the ship, he raised the flask to his lips and drank.

When he awoke, the cabin was full of afternoon sunshine, and the pungent taste of *diamondraught* lingered on his tongue. The Giantship was moving again. He remembered no dreams: the impression he bore with him out of slumber was one of blankness, a leper's numbness carried to its logical extreme. He wanted to roll over and never wake up again.

But as he glanced blearily around the sun-sharp cabin, he saw Linden sitting in one of the chairs beside the table.

She sat with her head bowed and her hands open in her lap, as though she had been waiting there for a long time. Her hair gleamed cleanly in the light, giving her the appearance of a woman who had emerged whole from an ordeal — refined, perhaps, but not reduced. With an inward moan, he recollected what the old man on Haven Farm had said to her. *There is also love in the world.* And in Andelain dead Elena, Covenant's daughter, had urged him, *Care for her, beloved, so that in the end she may heal us all.* The sight of her made his chest contract. He had lost her as well. He had nothing left.

Then she seemed to feel his gaze on her. She looked up at him, automatically brushing the tresses back from her face; and he saw that she was not unhurt. Her eyes were hollow and flagrant with fatigue; her cheeks were pallid; and the twinned lines running past her mouth from either side of her delicate nose looked as if they had been left there by tears as well as time. A voiceless protest gathered in him. Had she been sitting here with him ever since the passing of the *Nicor*? When she needed so much rest?

But a moment after he met her gaze she rose to her feet. A knot of anxiety or anger marked her brows. Probing him with her health-sense, she stepped closer to the hammock. What she saw made her mouth severe.

'Is that it?' she demanded. 'You've decided to give up?'

Mutely, Covenant flinched. Was his defeat so obvious?

At once, a look of regret changed her expression. She dropped her eyes, and her hands made an aimless half-gesture as if they were full of remembered failure. 'I didn't mean that,' she said. 'That isn't what I came to say. I wasn't sure I should come at all. You've been so hurt — I wanted to give you more time.'

Then she lifted her face to him again, and he saw her sense of purpose sharpen. She was here because she had her own ideas — about hope as well as about him. 'But the First was going to come, and I thought I should do it for her.' She gazed into him as if she sought a way to draw him down from his lonely bed. 'She wants to know where we're going.'

Where — ? Covenant blinked pain at her. She had not withdrawn her question: she had simply rephrased it. *Where?* A spasm of grief gripped his heart. His doom was summed up in that one grim word. Where *could* he go? He was beaten. All his power had been turned against him. There was nowhere left for him to go – nothing left for him to do. For an instant, he feared he would break down in front of her, bereft even of the bare dignity of solitude.

She was saying, 'We've got to go somewhere. The Sunbane is still there. Lord Foul is still there. We've lost the One Tree, but nothing else has changed. We can't just sail in circles for the rest of our lives.' She might have been pleading with him, trying to make him see something that was already plain to her.

But he did not heed her. Almost without transition, his hurt became resentment. She was being cruel, whether she realized it or not. He had already betrayed everything he loved with his mistakes and failures and lies. How much more responsibility did she wish him to assume? Bitterly, he replied, 'I hear you saved us from the *Nicor*. You don't need me.'

His tone made her wince. 'Don't say that!' she responded intensely. Her eyes were wide with awareness of what was happening to him. She could read every outcry of his racked spirit. 'I need you.'

In the pit of his need, he felt his despair plunging toward hysteria. It sounded like the glee of the Despiser, laughing in triumph. Perhaps he had gone so far down this road now that he *was* the Despiser, the perfect tool or avatar of Lord Foul's will. But Linden's expostulation jerked him back from the brink. It made her suddenly vivid to him – too vivid to be treated this way. She was his love, and he had already hurt her too much.

For a moment, the fall he had nearly taken left him reeling. Everything in the cabin seemed imprecise, overburdened with sunlight: he needed shadows and darkness in which to hide from all the things that surpassed him. But Linden still stood there as if she were the centre around which his head whirled. Whether she spoke or remained silent, she was the one demand he could not refuse. Yet he was altogether unready to tell her the truth he had withheld. Her reaction would be the culmination of all his dismay. Instinctively, he groped for some way to anchor himself, some point of simple guilt or passion to which he might cling. Squinting into the sunshine, he asked thickly, 'What did they do about Seadreamer?'

At that, Linden sagged in relief as though a crisis had been averted. Wanly, she answered, 'Honninscrave wanted to cremate him. As if that was possible.' Memories of suffering seemed to fray the words as she uttered them. 'But the First ordered the Giants to bury him at sea. For a minute there, I thought Honninscrave was going to attack her. But then something inside him broke. It wasn't physical – but I felt it snap.' Her tone said that she had sensed that parting like a rupture in her own heart. 'He bowed to her as if he didn't know what else to do with all that hurt. Then he went back to the wheeldeck. Back to doing his job.' Her shoulders lifted in a pained shrug. 'If you didn't look at his eyes, you wouldn't know he isn't as good as new. But he refused to help them give Seadreamer to the Sea.'

As she spoke, his eyes blurred: he was unable to see her clearly in all that light. Seadreamer should have been burned, should have been freed from his horror in a *caamora* of white fire. Yet the mere thought made Covenant's flesh itch darkly. He had become the thing he hated. Because of a lie. He had known – or should have known – what was going to happen to him. But his selfish love had kept the truth from her. He could not look at her. Through his teeth, he protested, 'Why did you have to do that?'

'Do – ?' Her health-sense did not make her prescient. How could she possibly know what he was talking about?

'You threw yourself in the fire.' The explanation came arduously, squeezed out by grief and self-recrimination. It was not her fault. No one had the right to blame her. 'I sent you away to try to save my life. I didn't know what else to do. For all I knew, it was already too late for anything else – the Worm was already awake, I'd already destroyed – ' A clench of anguish closed his throat. For a moment, he could not say, I didn't know how else to save you. Then he swallowed convulsively and went on. 'So I sent you away. And you threw yourself in the fire. I was linked to you. The wild magic tied us together. For the first time, my senses were open. And all I saw was you throwing yourself in the fire.

'Why did you force me to bring you back?'

In response, she flared as if he had struck a ragged nerve. 'Because I couldn't help you the way you were!' Suddenly, she was shouting at him. 'Your body was there, but *you* weren't! Without you, it was just so much dying meat! Even if I'd had you in a hospital – even if I could've given you transfusions and surgery right then – I could not have saved you!

'I needed you to come back with me. How else was I supposed to get your attention?'

Her pain made him look at her again; and the sight went through him like a crack through stone, following its flaws to the heart. She stood below him with her face hot and vivid in the light and her fists clenched, as intense and uncompromising as any woman he had ever dreamed. The fault was not hers, though surely she blamed herself. Therefore he could not shirk telling her the truth.

At one time, he had believed that he was sparing her by not speaking, that he was withholding information so that she would not be overwhelmed. Now he knew better. He had kept the truth to himself for the simple reason that he did not want it to be true. And by so doing he had falsified their relationship profoundly.

'I should've told you,' he murmured in shame. 'I tried to tell you everything else. But it hurt too much.'

She glared at him as if she felt the presence of something horrible between them; but he did not look away.

'It's always been this way. Nothing here interrupts the physical continuity of the world we came from. What happens here is self-contained. It's always the same. I go into the Land hurt – possibly dying. A leper. And I'm healed. Twice my leprosy disappeared. I could feel again, as if my nerves – ' His heart twisted at the memory – and at the poignant distress of Linden's stare. 'But before I left the Land, something always happened to duplicate the shape I was in earlier. Sometimes my body was moved. I stopped bleeding – or got worse. But my physical condition was always exactly what it would've been if I'd never been to the Land. And I'm still a leper. Leprosy doesn't heal.

'So this time that knife hit me – and when we got to the Land I healed it with wild magic. The same way I healed those cuts the Clave gave me.' They had slashed his wrists to gain blood for their soothtell; yet already the scars had faded, were nearly invisible. 'But it doesn't make any difference. What happens here doesn't change what's going on there. All it does is change the way we feel about it.'

After that, his shame was too great to hold her gaze. 'That's why I didn't tell you about it. At first – right at the beginning – I thought you had enough to worry about. You'd learn the truth soon enough. But after a while I changed. Then I didn't want you to know. I didn't think I had the right to ask you to love a dead man.'

As he spoke, her shock boiled into anger. The moment he stopped, she demanded, 'Do you mean to say that you've been planning to die all along?' Her voice was abruptly livid against the quiet background of the ship and the Sea. 'That you haven't even been *trying* to find a way to survive?'

'No!' In despair, he sought to defend himself. 'Why do you think I wanted a new Staff of Law – needed it so badly? It was my only hope. To fight for the Land without risking wild magic. And to send you back. You're a doctor, aren't you? I wanted you to save me.' But the anguish of her stare did not waver; and he could not meet it, could not pretend that what he had done was justified. 'I've been trying,' he pleaded. But no appeal was enough. 'I didn't tell you because I wanted to love you for a while. That's all.'

He heard her moving; and the fear that she would walk out of the cabin, turn her back on him forever, wrenched at him. But she was not leaving. She retreated to the chair, seated herself there as if something in her had broken. Her hands covered her face as she hunched forward, and her shoulders jerked. Yet she made no sound. At her mother's death-bed, she had learned to keep her weeping to herself. When she spoke, her voice shook.

'Why do I end up killing everybody I care about?'

Her grief hurt him like the raw acid of his guilt. This, too, was on his head. He wanted to descend from the hammock, go to her, take her in his arms; but he had forfeited that privilege. There was nothing he could do except fight back his own rue and protest, 'It's not your fault. You tried. I should've told you. You would've saved me if you could.'

The vehemence of her reaction took him by surprise. '*Stop* that!' she spat. 'I've got eyes! A mind of my own! I'm not some innocent kid you can protect.' The sun flashed on her face. 'You've been lying down here ever since we came back aboard as if you were to blame for everything. But you're not. Foul set this up. He manipulated you into it. What're you trying to do now? Prove him right?'

'I can't help it!' he retorted, stung by the salt she rubbed into his futility. 'Of course he's right. Who do you think he is? He's me. He's just an externalization of the part of me that despises. The part that – '

'No.' Her contradiction cut him off, though she did not shout. She had become too clenched and furious for shouting, too extreme to be denied. 'He's not you. He's not the one who's going to die.' She might have said, I'm the one who kills – The words were plain in every line of her visage. But her passion carried her past that recognition as if she could not bear it in any other way. 'Everybody makes mistakes. But all you've done is try to fight for what you love. You have an answer. I don't.' The heat of her assertion contained no self-pity. 'I haven't had one since this thing started. I don't know the Land the way you do. I haven't got any power. All I've been able to do is follow you around.' Her hands rose into fists. 'If you're going to die, do something to make it count!'

Then like a quick touch of ice he realized that she had not come here to question him simply because the First desired a destination. *She wants to know where we're going.* Her father had killed himself and blamed her for it; and she had killed her mother with her own hands; and now his, Covenant's, death seemed as certain as the Desecration of the Earth. But those things served only to give her the purpose he had lost. She was wearing her old severity now – the same rigid self-punishment and determination with which she had defied him from the moment of their first meeting. Yet the fierce fire in her eyes was new. And he recognized it. It was the unanswered anger of her grief, and it swept all costs aside in its desire for battle.

You've decided to give up?

Her demand made his failure as acute as agony. He could have shouted, I don't have any choice! He *beat* me! There's nothing I can do!

But he knew better. He was a leper and knew better. Leprosy itself was defeat, complete and incurable. Yet even lepers had reasons to go on living. Atiaran had told him that it was the task of the living to give meaning to the sacrifices of the dead; but now he saw that the truth went further: to give meaning to his own death. And to the prices the people he loved had already paid.

In the name of Linden's harsh insistence, he sat up in the hammock and asked hoarsely, 'What do you want?'

His response seemed to steady her. The bitter pressure of her loss eased somewhat. In a hard voice, she said, 'I want you to go back to the Land. To Revelstone. And stop the Clave. Put out the Banefire.' He drew a hissing breath at the sheer audacity of what she required; but she went on without heeding him, 'If you do that, the Sunbane'll slow down. Maybe it'll even recede. That'll give us time to look for a better answer.'

Then she surprised him again by faltering. She did not face him as she concluded, 'Maybe I don't care about the Land the way you do. I was too scared to go into Andelain. I've never seen what it used to be like. But I know sickness when I see it. Even if I weren't a doctor, I'd have the Sunbane carved on me in places where I'll never be able to forget it. I want to do something about that. I don't have anything else. The only way I can fight is through you.'

As she spoke, echoes of power capered in Covenant's veins. He heard what she was saying; but his fear took him back to the beginning. Stop the Clave? Put out the Banefire? In blunt alarm, he replied, 'That'll be a lot of fun. What in hell makes you believe I can even think about things like that without endangering the Arch?'

She met him with a sour smile, humourless and certain. 'Because you know how to restrain yourself now. I felt it – when you called back all that wild magic and used it to send me away. You're more dangerous now than you've ever been. To Lord Foul.'

For a moment, he held the look she gave him. But then his eyes fell. No. It was still too much: he was not ready. The ruin of his life was hardly a day old. How was it possible to talk about fighting, when the Despiser had already defeated him? He had only one power, and it had been transformed by venom and falsehood into a graver threat than any Sunbane. What she wanted was madness. He did not have it in him.

Yet he had to make some reply. She had borne too many burdens for him. And he loved her. She had the right to place demands upon him.

So he groped in bitter shame for a way out, for something he might say or do which would at least postpone the necessity of decision. Still without meeting Linden's stare, he muttered sourly, 'There are too many things I don't understand. I need to talk to Findail.'

He thought that would deflect her. From the moment when the Appointed of the *Elohim* had first attached himself to the Search, he had never come or gone at any behest but that of his own secret wisdom or cunning. Yet if anyone possessed the knowledge to win free of this defeat, surely his people did. And surely also he would not come here simply because the Unbeliever asked for him? Covenant would gain at least that much respite while Linden tried to persuade Findail.

But she did not hesitate – and did not leave the cabin. Turning to face the prow, she rasped the name of the Appointed stridently, as if she expected to be obeyed.

Almost at once, the sunlight seemed to condense against the wall; and Findail came flowing out of the stone into human form as though he had been waiting there for her call.

His appearance was unchanged: behind his creamy mantle and unkempt silver hair, within his bruised yellow eyes, he looked like an incarnation of all the world's misery, an image of every hurt and stress that did not touch his tranquil and self-absorbed people. Where they were deliberately graceful and comely, he was haggard and pain-carved. He appeared to be their antithesis and contradiction – a role which appalled him.

Yet something must have changed for him: before the crisis of the One Tree, he would not have answered any summons. But his manner remained as distant and disapproving as ever. Though he nodded an acknowledgment to Linden, his voice held a note of reproof. 'I hear you. Vehemence is not needful.'

His tone made no impression on Linden. Bracing her fists on her hips, she addressed him as if he had not spoken. 'This has gone on long enough,' she said stiffly. 'Now we need answers.'

Findail did not glance at Covenant. In *Elemesnedene*, the *Elohim* had treated Covenant as if he were of no personal importance; and now the Appointed seemed to take that stance again. He asked Linden, 'Is it the ring-wielder's intent to surrender his ring?'

At once, Covenant snapped, 'No!' Refusals ran in him like echoes of old delirium. Never give him the ring. Never. It was all that remained to him.

'Then,' Findail sighed, 'I must answer as I may, hoping to persuade him from his folly.'

Linden glanced up at Covenant, looking for his questions. But he was too close to his internal precipice: he could not think clearly. Too many people wanted him to surrender his ring. It was the only thing which still wedded him to life, made his choices matter. He did not respond to Linden's gaze.

Her eyes narrowed as she studied him, gauged his condition. Then, as if she were wrenching herself back from a desire to comfort him, she turned away, faced Findail again.

'Why – ?' She spoke with difficulty, wrestling words past a knot in her chest. 'I hardly know where to begin. There's so much – Why did you people do it?' Abruptly, her voice became stronger, full of indignation she had never been able to forget. 'What in God's name did you think you were doing? All he wanted was the location of the One Tree. You could've given him a straight answer. But instead you locked him in that silence of yours.' They had imposed a stasis upon his mind. If Linden had not risked herself to rescue him, he would have remained an empty husk until he died, blank of thought or desire. And the price she had paid for that rescue – ! Her outrage pulled him into focus with her as she concluded, 'You're responsible for this. How can you stand to live with yourself?'

Findail's expression turned into a glower. As soon as she stopped, he replied, 'Does it appear to you that I am made glad by the outcome of my Appointment? Is not my life at hazard as much as yours? Yes, as much and more, for you will depart when your time is ended, but I must remain and bear the cost. The fault is not mine.'

Linden started to protest; but the gathering sadness in his tone halted her. 'No, do not rail against me. I am the Appointed, and the burden of what you do falls to me.

'I do not deny that the path we chose was harsh to the ring-wielder. But are you truly unable to see in this matter? You are the Sun-Sage. He is not. Yet the wild magic which is the crux of the Arch of Time is his to wield, not yours. There lies the hand of evil upon the Earth – and also upon the *Elohim*, who are the Earth's Würd.

'You have said that we serve the evil which you name Lord Foul the Despiser. That is untrue. If you mislike my word, consider other knowledge. Would this Despiser have sent his servant the Raver against you in the storm, when already a servant such as myself stood among you? No. You cannot credit it. Yet I must say to you openly that there is a shadow upon the hearts of the *Elohim*. It is seen in this, that we were able to conceive no path of salvation which would spare you.

'You have not forgotten that there were those among us who did not wish to spare you.

'Surely it is plain that for us the easiest path lay in the simple wresting from him of the ring. With wild magic could we bid any Despite defiance. Then for beings such as we are it would be no great task to achieve the perfection of the Earth. Yet that we did not do. Some among us feared the arrogance of such power, when a shadow plainly lay upon our hearts. And some saw that the entire price of such an act would fall upon you alone. You would be lost to

862

yourselves, deprived of meaning and value. Perhaps the meaning and value of the Earth would be diminished as well.

'Therefore we chose a harder path – to share with you the burden of redemption and the risk of doom. The ring-wielder we silenced, not to harm him, but to spare the Earth the ill of power without sight. As that silence preserved him from the malice of Kasreyn of the Gyre, so also would it have preserved him from the Despiser's intent at the One Tree. Thus the choice would have fallen to you in the end. His ring you might have taken unto yourself, thereby healing the breach between sight and power. Or perhaps you might have ceded the ring to me, empowering the *Elohim* to save the Earth after their fashion. Then would we have had no need to fear ourselves, for a power given is altogether different from one wrested away. But whatever your choice, there would have been hope. To accomplish such hope, the price of the ring-wielder's silence – and of my Appointment – appeared to be neither too great nor too ill.

'That you took from us. In the dungeon of the Sandhold, you chose the wrong which you name possession above the responsibility of sight, and the hope we strove to nurture was lost.

'Now I say to you that he must be persuaded to surrender his ring. If he does not, it is certain that he will destroy the Earth.'

For a moment, Covenant reeled down the path of Findail's explanation. His balance was gone. To hear his own dread expressed so starkly, like a verdict! But when he turned toward Linden, he saw that she had been hit harder than he. Her face had gone pale: her hands made small, fugitive movements at her sides. Her mouth tried to form a denial, but she had no strength for it. Confronted by the logic of her actions as Findail saw it, she was horrified. Once again, he placed her at the centre, at the cusp of responsibility and blame. And Covenant's earlier revelation was still too recent: she had not had time to absorb it. She had claimed fault for herself – but had not understood the extent to which she might be accused.

Ire for her stabilized him. Findail had no right to drop the whole weight of the Earth on her in this way. 'It's not that simple,' he began. He did not know the true name of his objection. But Linden faced him in mute appeal; and he did not let himself falter. 'If Foul planned this all along, why did he go to the trouble?' That was not what he needed to ask. Yet he pursued it, hoping it would lead him to the right place. 'Why didn't he just wake up the Worm himself?'

Findail's gaze held Linden. When her wide eyes went back to his, he replied, 'This Despiser is not mad. Should he rouse the Worm himself, without the wild magic in his hand, would he not also be consumed in the destruction of the world?'

Covenant shrugged the argument aside, went on searching for the question he needed, the flaw in Findail's rationalizations. 'Then why didn't you tell us sooner? Naturally you couldn't condescend to explain anything before she freed me.' With all the sarcasm he could muster, he tried to force the Appointed to look at him, release Linden. 'After what you people did, you knew she'd never give you my ring if she understood how much you want it. But later – before we got to the One Tree. Why didn't you tell us what kind of danger we were in?'

The *Elohim* sighed; but still he did not relinquish Linden. 'Perhaps in that I erred,' he said softly. 'Yet I could not turn aside from hope. It was my hope that some access of wisdom or courage would inspire the ring-wielder to step back from the precipice of his intent.'

Covenant continued groping. But now he saw that Linden had begun to rally. She shook her head, struggled internally for some way to refute or withstand Findail's accusation. Her mouth tightened: she looked as if she was chewing curses. The sight lit a spark of encouragement in him, made him lean forward to aim his next challenge at the *Elohim*.

'That doesn't justify you,' he grated. 'You talk about silencing me as if that was the only decent alternative you had. But you know goddamn well it wasn't. For one thing, you could've done something about the venom that makes me so bloody dangerous.'

Then Findail did look at Covenant. His yellow gaze snapped upward with a fierceness which jolted Covenant. *'We dared not.'* His quiet passion left trails of fire across Covenant's brain. 'The doom of this age lies also upon me, but I dare not. Are we not the *Elohim*, the Würd of the Earth? Do we not read the truth in the very roots of the Rawedge Rim, in the shape of the mountainsides and in the snows which gild the winter peaks? You mock me at your peril. By means of his venom this Despiser attempts the destruction of the Arch of Time, and that is no little thing. But it pales beside the fate which would befall the Earth and all life upon the Earth, were there no venom within you. You conceive yourself to be a figure of power, but in the scale of worlds you are not. Had this Despiser's lust for the Illearth Stone not betrayed him, enhancing you beyond your mortal stature, you would not have stood against him so much as once. And he is wiser now, with the wisdom of old frustration, which some name madness.

'Lacking the venom, you would be too small to threaten him. If he did not seek you out for his own pleasure, you would wander the world without purpose, powerless against him. And the Sunbane would grow. It would grow, devouring every land and sea in turn until even *Elemesnedene* itself had fallen, and still it would grow, and there would be no halt to it. Seeing no blame for yourself, you would not surrender your ring. Therefore he would remain trapped within the Arch. But no other stricture would limit his victory. Even we, the *Elohim*, would in time be reduced to mere playthings for his mirth. While Time endured, the Desecration of the world would not end at all.

'Therefore,' the Appointed articulated with careful intensity, 'we bless the frustration or madness which inspired the gambit of this venom. Discontented in the prison of the Earth, the Despiser has risked his hope of freedom in the venom which gives you such might. It is our hope also. For now the blame is plain. Since you are blind in other ways, we must pray that guilt will drive you to the surrender which may save us.'

The words went through Covenant like a shot. His arguments were punctured, made irrelevant. Findail admitted no alternative to submission except the Ritual of Desecration – the outright destruction of the Earth to spare it from Lord Foul's power. This was Kevin Landwaster's plight on a scale which staggered Covenant, appalled him to the marrow of his bones. If he did not give up his ring, how could he bear to do anything but ruin the world himself in order to foil the eternal Sunbane of the Despiser?

Yet he could not surrender his ring. The simple thought was immediately and intimately terrible to him. That metal circle meant too much: it contained every hard affirmation of life and love that he had ever wrested from the special cruelty of his loneliness, his leper's fate. The alternative was better. *Yes*. To destroy – Or to risk destroying in any kind of search for a different outcome –

His dilemma silenced him. In his previous confrontation with Lord Foul, he had found and used the quiet centre of his vertigo, the still point of strength between the contradictions of his plight; but now there seemed to be no centre, no place on which he could stand to affirm both the Earth and himself. And the necessity of choice was dreadful.

But Linden had taken hold of herself again. The conceptions which hurt her most were not the ones which pierced Covenant; and he had given her a chance to recover. The look she cast at him was brittle with stress; but it was alert once more, capable of reading his dismay. For an instant, empathy focused her gaze. Then she swung back toward the Appointed, and her voice bristled dangerously.

'That's just speculation. You're afraid you might lose your precious freedom, so you're trying to make him responsible for it. You still haven't told us the truth.'

Findail faced her; and Covenant saw her flinch as if the *Elohim*'s eyes had burned her. But she did not stop.

'If you want us to believe you, tell us about Vain.'

At that, Findail recoiled.

Immediately, she went after him. 'First you imprisoned him, as if he was some kind of crime against you. And you tried to trick us

865

about it, so we wouldn't know what you were doing. When he escaped, you tried to kill him. Then, when he and Seadreamer found you aboard the ship, you spoke to him.' Her expression was a glower of memory. 'You said, "Whatever else you may do, *that* I will not suffer."'

The Appointed started to reply; but she overrode him. 'Later, you said, "Only he whom you name Vain has it within him to expel me. I would give my soul that he should do so." And since then you've hardly been out of his sight – except when you decide to run away instead of helping us.' She was unmistakably a woman who had learned something about courage. 'You've been more interested in him than us from the beginning. Why don't you try explaining *that* for a change?'

She brandished her anger at the *Elohim*; and for a moment Covenant thought Findail would answer. But then his grief-ensnared visage tightened. In spite of its misery, his expression resembled the hauteur of Chant and Infelice as he said grimly, 'Of the Demondim-spawn I will not speak.'

'That's right,' she shot back at him at once. 'Of course you won't. If you did, you might give us a reason to do some hoping of our own. Then we might not roll over and play dead the way you want.' She matched his glare; and in spite of all his power and knowledge she made him appear diminished and judged. Sourly, she muttered, 'Oh, go on. Get out of here. You make my stomach hurt.'

With a stiff shrug, Findail turned away. But before he could depart, Covenant interposed, 'Just a minute.' He felt half mad with fear and impossible decisions; but a fragment of lucidity had come to him, and he thought he saw another way in which he had been betrayed. Lena had told him that he was Berek Halfhand reborn. And the Lords he had known had believed that. What had gone wrong? 'We couldn't get a branch of the One Tree. There was no way. But it's been done before. How did Berek do it?'

Findail paused at the wall, answered over his shoulder. 'The Worm was not made restive by his approach, for he did not win his way with combat. In that age, the One Tree had no Guardian. It was he himself who gave the Tree its ward, setting the Guardian in place so that the vital wood of the world's life would not again be touched or broken.'

Berek? Covenant was too astonished to watch the *Elohim* melt out of the cabin. Berek had set the Guardian? Why? The Lord-Fatherer had been described as both seer and prophet. Had he been short-sighted enough to believe that no one else would ever need to touch the One Tree? Or had he had some reason to ensure that there would never be a second Staff of Law?

Dizzy with implications, Covenant was momentarily unaware of the way Linden regarded him. But gradually he felt her eyes on him.

Her face was sharp with the demand she had brought with her into his cabin – the demand of her need. When he met her gaze, she said distinctly, 'Your friends in Andelain didn't think you were doomed. They gave you Vain for a reason. What else did they do?'

'They talked to me,' he replied as if she had invoked the words out of him. 'Mhoram said, "When you have understood the Land's need, you must depart the Land, for the thing you seek is not within it. The one word of truth cannot be found otherwise. But I give you this caution: do not be deceived by the Land's need. The thing you seek is not what it appears to be. In the end, you must return to the Land."'

He had also said, *When you have come to the crux, and have no other recourse, remember the paradox of white gold. There is hope in contradiction.* But that Covenant did not comprehend.

Linden nodded severely. 'So what's it going to be? Are you just going to lie here until your heart breaks? Or are you going to fight?'

Distraught by fear and despair, he could not find his way. Perhaps an answer was possible, but he did not have it. Yet what she wanted of him was certain; and because he loved her he gave it to her as well as he was able.

'I don't know. But anything is better than this. Tell the First we'll give it a try.'

She nodded again. For a moment, her mouth moved as if she wished to thank him in some way. But then the pressure of her own bare grasp on resolution impelled her toward the door.

'What about you?' he asked after her. He had sent her away and did not know how to recall her. He had no right. 'What're you going to do?'

At the door, she looked back at him, and her eyes were openly full of tears. 'I'm going to wait.' Her voice sounded as forlorn as the cry of a kestrel – and as determined as an act of valour. 'My turn's coming.'

As she left, her words seemed to remain in the sunlit cabin like a verdict. Or a prophecy.

After she was gone, Covenant got out of the hammock and dressed himself completely in his old clothes.

3

THE PATH TO PAIN

When he went up on deck, the sun was setting beyond the western sea, and its light turned the water crimson – the colour of disaster. Honninscrave had raised every span of canvas the spars could hold; and every sail was belly-full of wind as Starfare's Gem pounded forward a few points west of north. It should have been a brave sight. But the specific red of that sunset covered the canvas with fatality, gilded the lines until they looked as if they were slick with blood. And the wind carried a precursive chill, hinting at the bitter cold of winter.

Yet Honninscrave strode the wheeldeck as though he could no longer be daunted by anything the Sea brought to him. The air riffled his beard, and his eyes reflected occasional glints of fire from the west; but his commands were as precise as his mastery of the Giantship, and the rawness of his voice might have been caused by the strain of shouting over the wind rather than by the stress of the past two days. He was not Foamfollower after all: he had not been granted the *caamora* his spirit craved. But he was a Giant still, the Master of Starfare's Gem; and he had risen to his responsibilities.

With Cail beside him, Covenant went up to the wheeldeck. He wanted to find some way to apologize for having proven himself inadequate to the Master's need. But when he approached Honninscrave and the other two Giants with him, Sevinhand Anchormaster and a steersman holding Shipsheartthew, the caution in their eyes stopped Covenant. At first, he thought that they had become wary of him – that the danger he represented made them fearful in his presence. But then Sevinhand said simply, 'Giantfriend,' and it was plain even to Covenant's superficial hearing that the Anchormaster's tone was one of shared sorrow rather than misgiving. Instead of apologizing, Covenant bowed his head in tacit recognition of his own unworth.

He wanted to stand there in silence until he had shored up enough self-respect to take another step back into the life of the Giantship. But after a moment Cail spoke. In spite of his characteristic *Haruchai* dispassion, his manner suggested that what he meant to say made him uncomfortable. Involuntarily, Covenant reflected that none of the *Haruchai* who had left the Land with him had come this far unscathed. Covenant did not know how the uncompromising extravagance of the *Haruchai* endured the role Brinn had assigned to Cail. What promise lay hidden in Brinn's statement that Cail would eventually be permitted to follow his heart?

But Cail did not speak of that. He did not address Covenant. Without preamble, he said, 'Grimmand Honninscrave, in the name of my people I desire your pardon. When Brinn assayed himself against *ak-Haru Kenaustin Ardenol* – he who is the sovereign legend and dream of all the *Haruchai* among the mountains – it was not his intent to bring about the death of Cable Seadreamer your brother.'

The Master winced: his cavernous eyes shot splinters of red at Cail. But almost at once he regained his deliberate poise. He glanced around the Giantship as if to assure himself that all was still well with it. Then he turned over his command to Sevinhand, drew Cail and Covenant with him to the port rail.

The setting sun gave his visage a tinge of sacrificial glory. Watching him, Covenant thought obscurely that the sun always set in the west – that a man who faced west would never see anything except decline, things going down, the last beauty before light and life went out.

After a moment, Honninscrave lifted his voice over the wet splashing of the shipside. 'The Earth-Sight is not a thing which any Giant selects for himself. No choice is given. But we do not therefore seek to gainsay or eschew it. We believe – or have believed – ' he said with a touch of bitterness, 'that there is life as well as death in such mysteries. How then should there be any blame in what has happened?' Honninscrave spoke more to himself than to Covenant or Cail. 'The Earth-Sight came upon Cable Seadreamer my brother, and the hurt of his vision was plain to all. But the content of that hurt he could not tell. Mayhap his muteness was made necessary by the vision itself. Mayhap for him no denial of death was possible which would not also have been a denial of life. I know nothing of that. I know only that he could not speak his plight – and so he could not be saved. There is no blame for us in this.' He spoke as though he believed what he was saying; but the loss knotted around his eyes contradicted him.

'His death places no burden upon us but the burden of hope.' The sunset was fading from the west and from his face, translating his mien from crimson to the pallor of ashes. 'We must hope that in the end we will find means to vindicate his passing. To vindicate,' he repeated faintly, 'and to comprehend.' He did not look at his auditors. The dying of the light echoed out of his eyes. 'I am grieved that I can conceive no hope.'

He had earned the right to be left alone. But Covenant needed an answer. He and Foamfollower had talked about hope. Striving to keep his voice gentle in spite of his own stiff hurt, he asked. 'Then why do you go on?'

For a long moment, Honninscrave remained still against the mounting dark as if he had not heard, could not be reached. But at last he said simply, 'I am a Giant. The Master of Starfare's Gem, and sworn to the service of the First of the Search. That is preferable.'

Preferable, Covenant thought with a mute pang. Mhoram might have said something like that. But Findail obviously did not believe it.

Yet Cail nodded as if Honninscrave's words were ones which even the extravagant *Haruchai* could accept. After all, Cail's people did not put much faith in hope. They staked themselves on success or failure – and accepted the outcome.

Covenant turned from the darkling Sea, left the rail. He had no place among such people. He did not know what was preferable – and could not see enough success anywhere to make failure endurable. The decision he had made in Linden's name was just another kind of lie. Well, she had earned that pretence of conviction from him. But at some point any leper needed something more than discipline or even stubbornness to keep him alive. And he had too sorely falsified his relationship with her. He did not know what to do.

Around Starfare's Gem, the Giants had begun to light lanterns against the night. They illuminated the great wheel, the stairs down from the wheeldeck, the doorways to the underdecks and the galley: they hung from the fore- and aftermasts like instances of bravado, both emphasizing and disregarding the gap where the midmast should have been. They were nothing more than small oil lamps under the vast heavens, and yet they made the Giantship beautiful on the face of the deep. After a moment, Covenant found that he could bear to go looking for Linden.

But when he started forward from the wheeldeck, his attention was caught by Vain. The Demondim-spawn stood beyond the direct reach of the lanterns, on the precise spot where his feet had first touched stone after he had come aboard from the Isle of the One Tree; but his black silhouette was distinct against the fading horizon. As always, he remained blank to scrutiny, as though he knew that nothing could touch him.

Yet he had been touched. One iron heel of the old Staff of Law still clamped him where his wrist had been; but that hand dangled useless from the wooden limb which grew like a branch from his elbow. Covenant had no idea why Foamfollower had given him this product of the dark and historically malefic ur-viles. But now he was sure that Linden had been right – that no explanation which did not include the secret of the Demondim-spawn was complete enough to be trusted. When he moved on past Vain, he knew more clearly why he wanted to find her.

He came upon her near the foremast, some distance down the deck from the prow where Findail stood confronting the future like a figurehead. With her were the First, Pitchwife, and another Giant: as Covenant neared them, he recognized Mistweave, whose life Linden had saved at the risk of his own during his most recent venom-relapse. The three Giants greeted him with the same gentle caution Honninscrave and Sevinhand had evinced – the wariness of people who believed they were in the presence of a pain which transcended their own. But Linden seemed almost unconscious of his appearance. In the wan lantern-light, her face looked pallid, nearly haggard; and Covenant thought suddenly that she had not rested at all since before the quest had arrived at the Isle of the One Tree. The energy which had sustained her earlier had eroded away: her manner was febrile with exhaustion. For a moment, he was so conscious of her nearness to collapse that he failed to notice the fact that she, too, was wearing her old clothes – the checked flannel shirt, tough jeans, and sturdy shoes in which she had first entered the Land.

Though her choice was no different from his, the sight of it gave him an unexpected pang. Once again, he had been betrayed by his preterite instinct for hope: unconsciously, he had dreamed that all the shocks and revelations of the past days would not alter her, not impel her to resume their former distance from each other. Fool! he snarled at himself. He could not escape her percipience. Down in his cabin, she had read what he was going to do before he had known it himself.

The First greeted him in a tone made brusque by the sternness of her own emotions; but her words showed that she also was sensitive to his plight. 'Thomas Covenant, I believe that you have chosen well.' If anything, the losses of the past days and the darkness of the evening seemed to augment her iron beauty. She was a Swordmain, trained to give battle to the peril of the world. As she spoke, one hand gripped her sword's hilt as if the blade were a vital part of what she was saying. 'I have named you Giantfriend, and I am proud that I did so. Pitchwife my husband is wont to say that it is the meaning of our lives to hope. But I know not how to measure such things. I know only that battle is better than surrender. It is not for me to judge your paths in this matter – yet am I gladdened that you have chosen a path of combat.' In the way of a warrior, she was trying to comfort him.

Her attempt touched him – and frightened him as well, for it suggested that once again he had committed himself to more than he could gauge. But he was given no chance to reply. For once, Pitchwife seemed impatient with what his wife was saying. As soon as she finished, he interposed, 'Aye, and Linden Avery also is well

Chosen, as I have said. But in this she does not choose well. Giantfriend, she will not rest.' His exasperation was plain in his voice.

Linden grimaced. Covenant started to say, 'Linden, you need – ' But when she looked at him he stopped. Her gaze gathered up the darkness and held it against him.

'I don't have anywhere to go.'

The stark bereavement of Linden's answer went through him like a cry. It meant too much: that her former world had been ruined for her by what she had learned; that like him she could not bear to return to her cabin – the cabin they had shared.

Somewhere in the distance, Pitchwife was saying, 'To her have been offered the chambers of the *Haruchai*. But she replies that she fears to dream in such places. And Starfare's Gem holds no other private quarters.'

Covenant understood that also without heeding it. Brinn had blamed her for Hergrom's death. And she had tried to kill Ceer. 'Leave her alone,' he said dully, as deaf to himself as to Pitchwife. 'She'll rest when she's ready.'

That was not what he wanted to say. He wanted to say, Forgive me. I don't know how to forgive myself. But the words were locked in his chest. They were impossible.

Because he had nothing else to offer her, he swallowed thickly and said, 'You're right. My friends didn't expect me to be doomed. Foamfollower gave me Vain for a reason.' Even that affirmation was difficult for him; but he forced it out. 'What happened to his arm?'

She went on staring darkness at him as if he were the linchpin of her exhaustion. She sounded as misled as a sleep-walker as she responded, 'Mistweave won't go away. He says he wants to take Cail's place.'

Covenant peered at her, momentarily unable to comprehend. But then he remembered his own dismay when Brinn had insisted on serving him; and his heart twisted. 'Linden,' he demanded, forlorn and harsh in his inability to help her, 'tell me about Vain's arm.' If he had dared, he would have taken hold of her. If he had had the right.

She shook her head; and lantern-light glanced like supplication out of her dry eyes. 'I can't.' She might have protested like a child, It hurts. 'His arm's empty. When I close my eyes, it isn't even there. If you took all the life out of the One Tree – took it away so completely that the Tree never had any – never had any meaning at all – it would look like that. If he was actually alive – if he wasn't just a thing the ur-viles made – he'd be in terrible pain.'

Slowly, she turned away as though she could no longer support his presence. When she moved off down the deck with Mistweave walking, deferential and stubborn, behind her, he understood that she also did not know how to forgive.

He thought then that surely his loss and need had become too much for him, that surely he was about to break down. But the First and Pitchwife were watching him with their concern poignant in their faces. They were his friends. And they needed him. Somehow, he held himself together.

Later, Mistweave sent word that Linden had found a place to sleep at last, huddled in a corner of the galley near the warmth of one of the great stoves. With that Covenant had to be content. Moving stiffly, he went back to his hammock and took the risk of nightmares. Dreams seemed to be the lesser danger.

But the next morning the wind was stronger.

It might have been a true sailor's wind – enough to shake the *dromond* out of its normal routine and make it stretch, not enough to pose any threat to the seacraft of the crew. It kicked the crests of the waves into spume and spray, sent water crashing off the Giantship's granite prow, made the lines hum and the sails strain. The sides of the vessel moved so swiftly that their moire markings looked like flames crackling from the Sea. In the rigging, some of the Giants laughed as they fisted the canvas from position to position, seeking the *dromond*'s best stance for speed. If its midmast had not been lost, Starfare's Gem would have flown like exuberance before the blow.

However, the day was dull with clouds and felt unnaturally cold: a south wind should have been warmer than this. It came straight from the place where the Isle had gone down, and it was as chill as the cavern of the One Tree. Without the sun to light it, the Sea had a grey and viscid hue. Though he wore a robe over his clothes, Covenant hunched his shoulders and could not stop shivering.

Seeking reassurance, he went up to the wheeldeck, where Heft Galewrath commanded the *dromond*. But she greeted him with only a blunt nod. Her normally stolid demeanour held a kind of alert watchfulness that he had not seen in her before: for the first time since they had met, she seemed accessible to misgiving. Rather than trouble her with his trepidations, he returned to the afterdeck and moved forward, looking for someone who could be more easily questioned.

It's not that cold, he told himself. It's just wind. But still the chill cut at him. No matter how he hugged the robe about him, the wind found its way to his skin.

Instinctively, he went to the galley, looking for warmth and Linden.

He found her there, seated at one wall near the cheery bustle of the *dromond*'s two cooks, a husband and wife aptly named Seasauce and Hearthcoal. They had spent so much of their lives working over

873

the great stoves that their faces had become perpetually ruddy: they looked like images of each other as they blustered about their tasks, moving with a disingenuous air of confusion which concealed the ease of their teamwork. When they went out on deck, heat overflowed from them; and in their constricted demesne they radiated like ovens. Yet Covenant's chill persisted.

Linden was awake, but still glazed with sleep. She had paid only a part of the debt of her weariness. Though she acknowledged Covenant, behind her eyes everything was masked in somnolence. He thought at once that he should not bother her with questions until she had rested more. But he was too cold for good intentions.

Hunkering down beside her, he asked, 'What do you think of this wind?'

She yawned. 'I think,' she said distantly, 'that Foul's in a hurry to get us back.'

However, after another day's rest, Linden was able to look at the weather more percipiently. By then, Covenant had worn himself petulant with aimless anxiety. He felt repeatedly that he had lost the centre of his life, that he could no longer hold himself from flying outward in all directions when the vertigo of his fear arose. Nothing had happened to suggest that the *dromond* was in danger: yet his inchoate conviction of peril remained. Snappishly, he asked Linden his question a second time.

But long sleep had brought her back to herself, and the gaze she turned toward him was capable of knowledge. She seemed to see without effort that his irritation was not directed at her. She placed a brief touch on his forearm like a promise that she would not forsake him. Then she went out to look at the wind.

After a moment's assessment, she declared that this blow was not unnatural or ill, not something which the Despiser had whipped up for his own ends. Instead, it was a reaction to the fundamental convulsion which had pulled down the Isle of the One Tree. By that violence, the balances of the weather had been disturbed, outraged.

It was conceivable that Lord Foul had known this would happen. But she felt no evidence of his influence on the wind.

When Covenant relayed her verdict to Honninscrave, the Master shrugged, his thoughts hidden behind the buttress of his brows. 'No matter,' he muttered as if he were not listening to himself. 'Should it worsen, Starfare's Gem must run before it. Part-masted as we are, I will not hazard resistance to the wind's path. There is no need. At present, we are borne but a scant span from our true way.'

That should have satisfied Covenant. His experience of the Sea was trivial compared to Honninscrave's. Yet the alarm in his guts refused to be eased. Like Galewrath, the Master conveyed an impression of concealed worry.

During the next two days, the wind became more serious.

Blowing with incessant vehemence a few points west of north, it cut into the Sea like the blade of a plough, whined across the decks of the *dromond* like the ache of its own chill. In spite of its speed, Starfare's Gem no longer appeared to be moving swiftly: the wind bore the water itself northward, and what little bowwave the prow raised was torn away at once. Clouds hugged the world from horizon to horizon. The sails looked grey and brittle as they heaved the heavy stone along.

And that night the cold began in earnest.

When Covenant scrambled shivering out of his hammock the next morning, he found a scum of ice in the washbasin which Cail had set out for him. Faint patches of frost licked the moire-granite as though they had soaked in through the walls. Passing Vain on his way to the warmth of the galley, he saw that the Demondim-spawn's black form was mottled with rime like leprosy.

Yet the Giants were busy about their tasks as always. Impervious to fire if not to pain, they were also proof against cold. Most of them laboured in the rigging, fighting the frozen stiffness of the lines. For a moment while his eyes watered, Covenant saw them imprecisely and thought they were furling the sails. But then he saw clouds blowing off the canvas like steam, and he realized that the Giants were beating the sails to prevent the frost on them building into ice. Ice might have torn the canvas from the spars, crippling Starfare's Gem when the *dromond*'s life depended upon its headway.

His breathing crusted in his beard as he let the wind thrust him forward. Without Cail's help, he would have been unable to wrestle open the galley door: slivers of ice sprang from the cracks and vanished inward as the *Haruchai* broke the seal caused by the moisture of cooking. Riding a gust that swirled stiffly through the galley, Covenant jumped the storm-sill and nearly staggered at the concussion as the door slammed behind him.

'Stone and Sea!' Hearthcoal barked in red-faced and harmless ire. 'Are you fools, that you enter aft rather than forward in this gale?' With a dripping ladle, she gestured fiercely at the other seadoor. Behind her, Seasauce clanged shut his stove's firebox indignantly. But a moment later, all vexation forgotten, he handed Covenant a steaming flagon of diluted *diamondraught*, and Hearthcoal scooped out a bowl of broth for him from the immense stone pot she tended. Awkward with self-consciousness, he sat down beside Linden against one wall out of the way of the cooks and tried to draw some warmth back into his bones.

In the days that followed, he spent most of his time there, sharing with her the bearable clangour and heat of the galley. In spite of his numbness, the cold was too fierce for him; and for her it was worse because her senses were so vulnerable to it. He made one more attempt to sleep in his cabin; but after that he accepted a pallet like hers in the galley. The wind mounted incrementally every day, and with it the air grew steadily more frigid: Starfare's Gem was being hurled like a jerid toward the ice-gnawed heart of the north. When Giants entered the galley seeking food or warmth, their clothing was stiff with grey rime which left puddles of slush on the floor as it melted. Ice clogged their beards and hair, and their eyes were haggard. Covenant made occasional forays out on deck to observe the state of the ship; but what he saw – the thick, dire Sea, the lowering wrack, the frozen knurrs of spume which were allowed to chew at the railings because the crew was too hard-pressed to clear them away – always drove him back to the galley with a gelid knot in his chest.

Once he went far enough forward to look at Findail. When he returned, his lips were raw with cold and curses. 'That bastard doesn't even feel it,' he muttered to no one in particular, although Pitchwife was there with Linden, Mistweave, the two cooks, and a few other Giants. 'It goes right through him.' He could not explain his indignation. It simply seemed unjust that the Appointed should be untouched by the plight of the *dromond*.

But Linden was not looking at him: her attention was fixed on Pitchwife as if she wanted to ask him something important. At first, however, she had no opportunity to interpose her question. Pitchwife was teasing Hearthcoal and Seasauce like a merry child and laughing at the concealed humour of their rebuffs. He had a Giant's tall spirit in his bent frame, and more than a Giant's capacity for mirth. His japing dissipated some of Covenant's acid mood.

At last Pitchwife wrung an involuntary laugh from the cooks; and with that he subsided near Covenant and Linden, the heat of the stoves gleaming on his forehead. Covenant was conscious of Linden's tautness as she mustered her inquiry. 'Pitchwife, what are we getting into?'

The Giant looked at her with an air of surprise which might have been feigned.

'Nobody wants to talk about it,' she pursued. 'I've asked Galewrath and Sevinhand, but all they say is that Starfare's Gem can go on like this indefinitely. Even Mistweave thinks he can serve me by keeping his mouth shut.' Mistweave peered studiously at the ceiling, pretending he did not hear what was said. 'So I'm asking you. You've never held anything back from me.' Her voice conveyed a complex vibration of strain. 'What're we getting into?'

Outside the galley, the wind made a peculiar keening sound as it swept through the anchor-holes. Frost snapped in the cracks of the doors. Pitchwife did not want to meet her gaze; but she held him. By degrees, his good cheer sloughed away; and the contrast made him appear older, eroded by an unuttered fear. For no clear reason,

Covenant was reminded of a story Linden had told him in the days before the quest had reached *Elemesnedene* – the story of the role Pitchwife had played in the death of the First's father. He looked now like a man who had too many memories.

'Ah, Chosen,' he sighed, 'it is my apprehension that we have been snared by the Dolewind which leads to the Soulbiter.'

The Soulbiter.

Pitchwife called it an imprecise sea, not only because every ship that found it did so in a different part of the world, but also because every ship that won free of it again told a different tale. Some vessels met gales and reefs in the south; others, stifling calms in the east; still others, rank and impenetrable beds of sargasso in the west. In spite of this, however, the Soulbiter was known for what it was; for no craft or crew ever came back from it unscathed. And each of those ships had been driven there by a Dolewind that blew too long without let or variance.

Linden argued for a while, vexed by the conflicting vagueness and certainty of Pitchwife's explanations. But Covenant paid no heed to either of them. He had a name now for his chill anxiety, and the knowledge gave him a queer comfort. The Soulbiter. It was not Lord Foul's doing. Neither could it be avoided. And the outcome of that sea might make all other fears unnecessary. Very well. The galley was too warm; but outside cried and groaned a cold which only Giants could endure for any length of time. Eventually, even the din of the cooks became soothing to him, and he passed out of trepidation into a kind of waking somnolence – a stupefied inner silence like an echo of the emptiness which the *Elohim* had imposed upon him in *Elemesnedene*.

That silence comprised the only safety he had known in this world. It was a leper's answer to despair, a state of detachment and passivity made complete by the deadness of every nerve which should have conveyed import. The *Elohim* had not invented it: they had simply incarnated it into the special nature of his doom. To feel nothing and die.

Linden had once redeemed him from that fate. But now he was beaten. He made decisions, not because he believed in them, but because they were expected of him. He did not have the heart to face the Soulbiter.

In the days that followed, he went through the ordinary motions of being alive. He drank enough *diamondraught* to account for his mute distance to the people who watched him. He slept in the galley, took brief walks, acknowledged greetings and conversations like a living man. But inwardly he was becoming untouchable. After years of discipline and defiance, of stubborn argument against the seduction of his illness, he gave the effort up.

And still Starfare's Gem ploughed a straight furrow across the grey and gravid Sea while the wind blew arctic outrage. Except for a few worn paths here and there, the decks were now clenched with ice, overgrown like an old ruin. Its sheer weight was enough to make the Giants nervous; but they could not spare time or strength to clear the crust away. There was too much water in the wind: the blow sheared too much spray off the battered waves. And that damp collected in the sails faster than it could be beaten clear. At intervals, one stretch of canvas or another became too heavy to hold. The wind rent it out of its shrouds: a hail of ice-slivers swept the decks: tattered scraps of sail were left flapping like broken hands from the spars. Then the Giants were forced to clew new canvas up the yards. Bereft of its midmast, the granite *dromond* needed all its sails or none.

Day after day, the shrill whine of the rigging and the groans of the stone became louder, more distressed. The Sea looked like fluid ice, and Starfare's Gem was dragged forward against ever-increasing resistance. Yet the Giantship was stubborn. Its masts flexed and shivered, but did not shatter. Grinding its teeth against the gale, Starfare's Gem endured.

When the change came, it took everyone by surprise. Rest had restored the combative smoulder to Linden's eyes, and she had been fretting for days against the maddening pressure of the blast and the constriction of the galley; but even she did not see what was coming. And the Giants had no warning at all.

At one moment, Starfare's Gem was riding the howl of the wind through the embittered heart of a cloud-dark night. At the next, the *dromond* pitched forward like a destrier with locked forelegs; and the gale was gone. The suddenness of the silence staggered the vessel like a detonation. There was no sound except the faint clink and crash of ice falling from the slack sails. Linden jerked her percipience from side to side, probing the ship: then she muttered in astonishment, 'We've stopped. Just like that.'

For an instant, no one moved. Then Mistweave strode to the forward door, kicked it out of its frost. Cold as pure as absolute winter came flowing inward; but it had no wind behind it. The air across the Giantship was still.

Shouts sprang along the decks. In spite of his inward silence, Covenant followed Mistweave and Linden out into the night.

The clouds were gone: the dark was as clear and sharp as a knife-edge. Spots of light marked out the Giantship as the crew lit more lanterns. Near the eastern horizon stood the moon, yellow and doleful. It was nearly full, but appeared to shed no illumination, cast no reflection onto the black and secret face of the water. The stars littered the sky in every direction, all their portents lost. Linden muttered to herself, 'What in hell – ?' But she seemed unable to complete the question.

Honninscrave and Pitchwife approached from opposite ends of the ship. When the First joined them, Pitchwife said with unconvincing nonchalance, 'It appears that we are here.'

Covenant felt too numb to be cold. But Linden was shivering violently beside him. In a bitten voice, she asked, 'What do we do now?'

'Do?' replied Honninscrave distantly. His visage was benighted, devoid of content. 'This is the Soulbiter. We must await its will.' Plumes of steam came from his mouth as though his spirit escaped him at every word.

Its will, Covenant thought dumbly. My will. Foul's will. Nothing made any difference. Silence was safety. If he could not have hope, he would accept numbness. Returning to the galley, he curled up on his pallet and fell immediately asleep.

But the next morning he was awakened by the cold and the quiet. The stoves put out no heat. Except for Cail, the galley was deserted. Abandoned. Starfare's Gem lay as still as if he and the *Haruchai* were the only people left aboard.

A pang went through him, threatening his defences. Stiff with sleep and chill, he fumbled erect. 'Where – ?' he asked weakly. 'Where did they go?'

Cail's reply was flat and pitiless. 'They have gone to behold the Soulbiter.'

Covenant winced. He did not want to leave the confines of the galley: he feared the return of sensation and pain and responsibility. But Cail's expressionless stare was insistent. Cail was one of the *Haruchai*, kindred to Brinn and Bannor. His comrades Ceer and Hergrom had given their lives. He had the right to make demands. And his gaze was as plain as words.

It is enough. Now you must resume yourself.

Covenant did not want to go. But he adjusted his rumpled attire, made an effort to secure the silence closely about him. When Cail opened the door for him, he took a step over the storm-sill and walked blinking out into the bright, frigid morning.

After so many days hidden behind the glower of the clouds, the sun alone would have been enough to blind him. But it was not alone. White cold glared around the ship. Light sprang at him from all sides: dazzles as piercing as spears volleyed about his head. His tears froze on his cheeks. When he raised his hands to rub the beads away, small patches of skin were torn from his face.

But slowly his sight cleared. He saw Giants lining the rails, their backs to him. Everyone on board stood at the forward railings somewhere, facing outward.

They were still, as quiet as the Sea and the sails hanging empty in their gear. But no hush could silence their expectant suspense. They were watching the Soulbiter. Waiting for it.

Then he recovered enough vision to discern the source of all the dazzling.

Motionless in the water, Starfare's Gem lay surrounded by a flotilla of icebergs.

Hundreds of them in every size and configuration. Some were mere small humps on the flat sea. Others raised jagged crests to the level of the *dromond*'s spars. And they were all formed of the same impeccable ice: ice as translucent and complete as glass, as hard-faced as diamonds; ice on which the morning broke, shattering light in all directions.

They were moving. Singly or in squadrons, they bore slowly down on the ship as they floated southward. A few came so close that a Giant could have reached them in one leap. Yet none of them struck the *dromond*.

Along the deep the flotilla drifted with a wondrous majesty, as bewitching as the cold. Most of the Giants stood as if they had been carved from a muddier ice: they scarcely breathed while their hands froze to the rails and the gleaming burned into their eyes. Covenant joined Linden near the First, Pitchwife, and Mistweave. Behind the raw red of cold in her face lay a blue pallor as though her blood had become as milky as frost; but she had stopped shivering, paid no heed to the drops of ice which formed on her parted lips. Pitchwife's constant murmur did not interrupt the trance: like everyone else, he watched the ice pass stately by as if he were waiting for someone to speak. As if the sun-sharp wonder of this passage were merely a prelude.

Covenant found that he, too, could not look away. Commanded by so much eye-piercing glister and beauty, he braced his hands on one of the crossbeams of the railing and at once lost the power of movement. He was calm now, prepared to wait forever if necessary to hear what the cold was going to utter.

Cail's voice reached him distantly. The *Haruchai* was saying, 'Ur-Lord, this is not well. Chosen, hear me. It is not well. You must come away.' But his protest slowly ran out of strength. He moved to stand beside Covenant and did not speak again.

Covenant had no sense of time. Eventually the waiting ended. A berg drifted past the line of spectators, showing everyone a flat space like a platform in its side. And from that space rose cries.

'A ship at last!'

'Help us!'

'In the name of pity!'

'We have been marooned!'

He seemed to hear the same shouts behind him also, from the

other side of the Giantship. But that strange detail made no impression on him.

His eyes were the only part of him that moved. As the iceberg floated southward amid the slow procession, its flat side passed directly below the watchers. And he saw figures emerge from the pellucid ice – human figures. Three or four of them, he could not be sure: the number was oddly imprecise. But numbers did not matter. They were men, and their destitution made his heart twist against its shackles.

They were hollow-eyed, gaunt, and piteous. Their hands, maimed by frostbite, were wrapped in shreds torn from their ragged clothing. Emaciation and hopelessness lined their faces. Their cracked and splintered voices were hoarse with despair.

'Marooned!' they cried like a memory of the wind.

'Mercy!'

But no one on the *dromond* moved.

'Help them.' Linden's voice issued like a moan between her beaded lips. 'Throw them a line. Somebody.'

No one responded. Gripped by cold, volitionless, the watchers only stared as the iceberg drifted slowly by, bearing its frantic victims away. Gradually, the current took the marooned men out of hearing.

'In the name of God.' Her tears formed a gleaming fan of ice under each eye.

Again Covenant's heart twisted. But he could not break free. His silence covered the sea.

Then another berg drew near. It lay like a plate on the unwavering face of the water. Beneath the surface, its bulk lightly touched the ship, scraped a groan from the hushed hull. For a moment, the plate caught the sun squarely, and its reflection rang like a knell. Yet Covenant was able to see through the glare.

Poised in the sun's image were people that he knew.

Hergrom. Ceer.

They stood braced as if they had their backs to the Sandwall. At first, they were unaware of the Giantship. But then they saw it. Ceer shouted a hail which fell without echo onto the decks of the *dromond*. Leaving Hergrom, he sprinted to the edge of the ice, waved his arms for assistance.

Then out of the light came a Sandgorgon. White against the untrammelled background of the ice, the beast charged toward Hergrom with murder outstretched in its mighty arms.

Tremors shook Cail. Strain made steam puff between his teeth. But the cold held him.

For an instant, the implacable structure of Ceer's face registered the fact that the Giantship was not going to help him. His gaze shivered in Covenant's chest like an accusation that could never be answered. Then he sped to Hergrom's defence.

The Sandgorgon struck with the force of a juggernaut. Cracks sprang through the ice. A flurry of blows scattered Hergrom's blood across the floe. Ceer's strength meant nothing to the beast.

And still no one moved. The Giants were ice themselves now, as frigid and brittle as the wilderland of the Sea. Linden's weeping gasped in her throat. Droplets of blood ran from Covenant's palms as he tried to rip his hands from the railing. But the grasp of the cold could not be broken.

Ceer. Hergrom.

But the plate of ice slowly drifted away, and no one moved.

After that, the waiting seemed long for the first time since Covenant had fallen under the spell of the Soulbiter.

At last another hunk of ice floated near the Giantship. It was small, hardly a yard wide, its face barely above the water: it seemed too small to be the bringer of so much fear.

For a moment, his vision was smeared with light. He could see nothing past the bright assault of the sun's reflections. But then his eyes cleared.

On that little floe stood Cable Seadreamer. He faced the *dromond*, stared up at the watchers. His posture was erect: his arms were folded sternly over the gaping wound in the centre of his chest. Above his scar, his eyes were full of terrible knowledge.

Stiffly, he nodded a greeting. 'My people,' he said in a voice as quiet and extreme as the cold, 'you must succour me. This is the Soulbiter. Here suffer all the damned who have died in a false cause, unaided by those they sought to serve. If you will not reach out to me, I must stand here forever in my anguish, and the ice will not release me. Hear me, you whom I have loved to this cost. Is there no love left in you for me?'

'*Seadreamer*,' Linden groaned. Honninscrave gave a cry that tore the frozen flesh around his mouth, sent brief drops of blood into his beard. The First panted faintly, 'No. I am the First of the Search. I will not endure it.' But none of them moved. The cold had become irrefragable. Its victory was accomplished. Already Seadreamer was almost directly opposite Covenant's position. Soon he would pass amidships, and then he would be gone, and the people of Starfare's Gem would be left with nothing except abomination and rue and cold.

It was intolerable. Seadreamer had given his life to save Covenant from destroying the Earth. Prevented by muteness from sharing the Earth-Sight, he had placed his own flesh in the path of the world's doom, purchasing a reprieve for the people he loved. And Covenant had refused to grant him the simple decency of a *caamora*. It was too much.

In pain and dismay, Covenant moved. With a curse that splintered the silence, he burned his hands off the rail. Wild magic pulsed through him like the hot ichor of grief: white fire burst out of his ring like rage. 'We're going to lose him!' he howled at the Giants. 'Get a rope!'

An instant later, the First wrenched herself free. Her iron voice rang across the Giantship: 'No!'

Jerking toward the mooring of a nearby ratline, she snatched up one of the belaying-pins. 'Avaunt, demon!' she yelled. 'We will not hear you!'

Fierce with fury and revulsion, she hurled the pin straight at Seadreamer.

The Giants gaped as her projectile flashed through him.

It struck a chip from the edge of the ice and skipped away into the Sea, splashing distinctly. At once, his form wavered. He tried to speak again; but already he had dissolved into mirage. The floe drifted emptily away toward the south.

While Covenant stared, the fire rushed out of him, quenched again by the cold.

But an instant later the spell broke with an audible crackle and shatter of ice. Linden lifted raw hands to her face, blinked her cold-gouged eyes. Coughing and cursing, Honninscrave reeled back from the rail. 'Move, sluggards!' His shout scattered flecks of blood. 'Ware the wind!' Relief and dismay were etched in frost on different parts of Pitchwife's face.

Numbly, the other Giants turned from the vista of the sea. Some seemed unable to understand what had happened: others struggled in mounting haste toward their stations. Seasauce and Hearthcoal bustled back to the galley as if they were ashamed of their prolonged absence. The First and Galewrath moved among the slower crew-members, shaking or manhandling them into a semblance of alert-ness. Honninscrave strode grimly in the direction of the wheeldeck.

A moment later, one of the sails rattled in its gear, sending down a shower of frozen dust; and the first Giant to ascend the ratlines gave a hoarse call:

'The south!'

A dark moil of clouds was already visible above the *dromond*'s taffrail. The gale was coming back.

Covenant wondered momentarily how Starfare's Gem would be able to navigate through the flotilla of icebergs in such a wind – or how the ice-laden sails would survive if the blast hit too suddenly, too hard. But then he forgot everything else because Linden was fainting and he was too far away to reach her. Mistweave barely caught her in time to keep her from cracking her head open on the stone deck.

4

SEA OF ICE

The first gusts hit the Giantship at an angle, heeling it heavily to port. But then the main force of the wind came up against the stern, and Starfare's Gem righted with a wrench as the sails snapped and bellied and the blast tried to claw them away. The *dromond* lay so massively in the viscid Sea that for a moment it seemed unable to move. The upper spars screamed. Abruptly, Dawngreeter split from top to bottom, and wind tore shrilling through the rent.

But then Starfare's Gem gathered its legs under it, thrust forward; and the pressure eased. As the clouds came boiling overhead, the Giantship took hold of itself and began to run.

In the first moments, Honninscrave and the steerswoman were tested to their limits by the need to avoid collision with the nearest bergs. Under these frigid conditions, any contact might have burst the granite of the *dromond*'s flanks like dry wood. But soon the flotilla began to thin ahead of the ship. Starfare's Gem was coming to the end of the Soulbiter. The wind continued to scale upward; but now the immediate danger receded. The *dromond* had been fashioned to withstand such blasts.

But Covenant was oblivious to the ship and the wind: he was fighting for Linden's life. Mistweave had carried her into the galley, where the cooks laboured to bring back the heat of their stoves; but once the Giant had laid her down on her pallet, Covenant shouldered him aside. Pitchwife followed Cail into the galley and offered his help: Covenant ignored him. Cursing with methodical vehemence under his breath, he chafed her wrists, rubbed her cheeks, and waited for the cooks to warm some water.

She was too pale – The movement of her chest was so slight that he could hardly believe it. Her skin had the texture of wax: it looked as if it would peel away if he rubbed it too hard. He slapped and massaged her forearms, her shoulders, the sides of her neck with giddy desperation pounding in his temples. Between curses, he reiterated his demand for water.

'It will come,' muttered Seasauce. His own impatience made him sound irate. 'The stoves are cold. I have no theurgy to hasten fire.'

'She isn't a Giant,' Covenant responded without looking away from Linden. 'It doesn't have to boil.'

Pitchwife squatted at Linden's head, thrust a leather flask into

Covenant's view. 'Here is *diamondraught*.'

Covenant did not pause; but he shifted his efforts down to her hips and legs, making room for Pitchwife.

Cupping one huge palm under her head, the Giant lifted her into a half-sitting posture. Carefully, he raised the mouth of his flask to her lips.

Liquid dribbled from the corners of her mouth. In dismay, Covenant saw that she was not swallowing. Her chest rose as she inhaled; but no gag-reflex prevented her from breathing the potent liquor.

At the sight, his mind went white with fire. The hysteria of venom and power coursed through his muscles – keen argent, fretted with reminders of midnight and murder. He thrust Pitchwife away as if the Giant were a child.

But he dared not try to reach heat into Linden. Without any health-sense to guide him, he would be more likely to kill than warm her. Swallowing flame, he wrenched her onto her side, hit her once between the shoulder blades, twice, hoping to dislodge the fluid from her lungs. Then he pressed her to her back again, tilted her head as he had been taught, clasped shut her nose, and with his mouth over hers started breathing urgently down her throat.

Almost at once, effort and restraint made him dizzy. He no longer knew how to find the still point of strength in the centre of his whirling fears. He had no power to save her life except the one he could not use.

'Giantfriend.' Hearthcoal's voice came from a great distance. 'Here is a stewpot able to hold her.'

Covenant's head jerked up. For an instant, he gaped incomprehension at the cook. Then he rapped out, 'Fill it!' and clamped his mouth back over Linden's.

A muffled thunder of water poured into the huge stone pot. Wind shrieked in the hawseholes, plucked juddering ululations from the shrouds. Around Covenant, the galley began to spin. Head up: inhale. Head down: exhale. He had no way to keep his balance except with fire. In another moment, he was going to erupt or lose consciousness, he did not know which.

Then Seasauce said, 'It is ready.' Pitchwife touched Covenant's shoulder. Scooping his arms under Linden, Covenant tried to unknot his cramped muscles, stand erect.

Starfare's Gem brunted through the crest of a wave and dove for the trough. Unable to steady himself, he pitched headlong toward the wall.

Hands caught him. Mistweave held him while Pitchwife pulled Linden from his embrace.

He was giddy and irresistible with fire. He jerked away from Mistweave, followed Pitchwife toward the stove on which sat the oblong stewpot. The floor seemed to yaw viciously, but he kept moving.

The stovetop was as high as his chin: he could see nothing of Linden past the pot's rim except a crown of hair as Seasauce held her head above water. But he no longer needed to see her. Pressing his forehead against the base of the stewpot, he spread his arms as far as possible along its sides. The guts of the stove were aflame; but that heat would take too long to warm so much stone and water. Closing his eyes against the ghoul-whirl of his vertigo, he let wild magic pour down his arms.

This he could do safely. He had learned enough control to keep his power from tearing havoc through the galley. And Linden was buffered from his imprecise touch. With white passion he girdled the pot. Then he narrowed his mind until nothing else impinged upon it and let the fire flow.

In that way, he turned his back on silence and numbness.

For a time, he was conscious only of the current of his power, squeezing heat into the stone but not breaking it, not tearing the fragile granite into rubble. Then suddenly he realized that he could hear Linden coughing. He looked up. She was invisible to him, hidden by the sides of the pot and the steam pluming thickly into the air. But she was coughing, clearing her lungs more strongly with every spasm. And a moment later one of her hands came out of the vapour to clutch at the lip of the pot.

'It is enough,' Pitchwife was saying. 'Giantfriend, it is enough. More heat will harm her.'

Covenant nodded dumbly. With a deliberate effort, he released his power.

At once, he recoiled, struck by the vertigo and fear he had been holding at bay. But Pitchwife put an arm around him, kept him on his feet. As the spinning slowed, he was able to watch Seasauce lift Linden dripping from the water. She still looked as pallid and frail as a battered child; but her eyes were open, and her limbs reacted to the people around her. When Mistweave took her from the cook, she instinctively hugged his neck while he wrapped her in a blanket. Then Cail offered her Pitchwife's flask of *diamondraught*. Still shivering fiercely, she pulled the flask to her mouth. Gradually, two faint spots of colour appeared on her cheeks.

Covenant turned away and hid his face against Pitchwife's mal-formed chest until his relief eased enough to be borne.

For a few moments while the *diamondraught* spread out within her, Linden remained conscious. Though she was so weak that she tottered, she got down from Mistweave's arms. With the blanket swaddled around her, she stripped off her wet clothing. Then her gaze hunted for Covenant's.

He met it as bravely as he could.

'Why – ?' she asked huskily. Her voice quivered. 'Why couldn't we help them?'

'It was the Soulbiter.' Her question made his eyes blur. His heart was still torn by what she had seen. 'They were illusions. We were damned if we refused to help. Because of how we would've felt about ourselves. And damned if we tried. If we brought one of those things aboard.' The Soulbiter, he thought as he strove to clear his vision. It was aptly named. 'The only way out was to break the illusion.'

She nodded faintly: she was fading into the embrace of the *diamondraught*. 'It was like watching my parents.' Her eyes closed. 'If they were as brave as I wanted them to be.' Her voice trailed toward silence. 'If I let myself love them.'

Then her knees folded. Mistweave lowered her gently to her pallet, tucked more blankets around her. She was already asleep.

By increments, the galley recovered its accustomed warmth. Seasauce and Hearthcoal laboured like titans to produce hot food for the hard-pressed crew. As Honninscrave became more confident of the *dromond*'s stance against the gale, he began sending Giants in small groups for aliment and rest: a steady stream of them passed through the galley. They entered with hoar in their hair and strain in their eyes. The same gaunt look of memory marked every face. But the taste of hot food and the comradely bluster of the cooks solaced them; and when they returned to their tasks they bore themselves with more of their wonted jaunty sea-love and courage. They had survived the Soulbiter. Valiantly, they went back to their battle with the bitter grue of the Sea.

Covenant remained in the galley for a while to watch over Linden. Her slumber was so profound that he distrusted it instinctively: he expected her to slip back into the tallow pallor of frostbite. She looked so small, frail, and desirable lying there nearly under the feet of the Giants. But her form curled beneath the blankets brought back other memories as well; and eventually he found himself falling from relief and warmth into bereavement. She was the only woman he knew who understood his illness and still accepted him. Already, her stubborn commitment to him – and to the Land – had proved itself stronger than his despair. He yearned to put his arms around her, clasp her to him. But he did not have the right. And in her sleep she did not need the loyalty of his attendance. To escape the ache of what he had lost, he sashed his robe tightly about him and went out into the keening wind.

Instantly, he stumbled into the swirl of a snowfall as thick as fog. It flurried against his face. Ice crunched under his boots. When he blinked his eyes clear, he saw pinpricks of light around the decks and up in the rigging: the snow veiled the day so completely that the Giants were compelled to use lanterns. The sight dismayed him.

How could Honninscrave keep the Giantship running, headlong and blind in such a sea, when his crew was unable to tend the sails without lamps?

But the Master had no choice. While this wind held, the *dromond* could do nothing but grit its teeth and endure.

The matter was out of Covenant's hands. Braving the flung snow and the ice-knurled decks with Cail's support, he went looking for the First.

But when he found her in the cabin she shared with Pitchwife, he discovered that he did not know what to say. She was polishing her longsword, and her slow stroking movements had a quality of deliberate grimness which suggested that the survival of Starfare's Gem was out of her hands as well. She had broken the spell of the Soulbiter: she could do nothing now. For a long moment, they shared a hard stare of determination and helplessness. Then he turned away.

The snowfall continued. It clung to the air, and the wind whipped it forward, darkening the day as if the sky were clogged with ashes.

It brought with it a slight moderation of the temperature; and the fierceness of the blast was softened somewhat. But in reaction the seas grew more tempestuous. And they no longer followed the thrust of the gale. Other forces bent them out of the grasp of the storm, forcing Starfare's Gem to slog and claw its way across the grain of the current. Honninscrave shifted course as much as he dared to accommodate the seas; but the wind did not give him much latitude. As a result, the massive vessel pounded forward with a wild gait, a slewing pitch-and-yaw with a sickening pause on the seatops while the *dromond* hung momentarily out of control, followed by a plunge which buried the stern to its taffrail in black water. Only the unfrightened demeanour of the Giants convinced Covenant that Starfare's Gem was not about to founder.

Shortly before sunset, the snow lifted, letting a little dirty yellow light lick briefly across the battered seas. At once, Honninscrave sent Giants into the tops to scan the horizons before the illumination failed. They reported no landfall in sight. Then a night blinded by clouds closed down over the Giantship, and Starfare's Gem went running into the pit of an unreadable dark.

In the galley, Covenant rode the storm with his back braced between one wall and the side of a stove and his gaze fixed on Linden. Blank to the vessel's staggering, she slept so peacefully that she reminded him of the Land before the onset of the Sunbane. She was a terrain which should never have been violated by bloodshed and hate, a place that deserved better. But the Land had men and women – however few – who had fought and would fight for its healing. And Linden was among them. Yet in the struggle against her own inner Sunbane she had no one but herself.

The night stretched out ahead of Starfare's Gem. After a meal and a cup of thinned *diamondraught*, Covenant tried to rest. Recumbent on his pallet, he let the seas flop him from side to side and strove to imagine that he was being cradled. Fitfully, he dozed his way into true sleep.

But almost at once he began to flounder. He was back in the Sandhold, in Kemper's Pitch, strapped motionless for torture. He had passed, untouched, through knives and fire; but now he was being hurled down into himself, thrown with the violence of greed toward the hard wall of his fate. Then, however, he had been saved by Hergrom; and now Hergrom was dead. There was no one to save him from the impact that broke everything, filled the air with the splintering thunder of a mountain being riven.

His skin slick with sweat, he awakened – and the sound went on. Starfare's Gem was shattering. Concussions yelled through the hull. His face pressed the wall. A chaos of crockery and untensils burst across the galley. He tried to thrust himself back; but the ship's momentum pinned him. Stone screams answered the wind – the sound of masts and spars splitting under the strain. The *dromond* had been driven into some kind of collision.

The next instant, Starfare's Gem heaved to a halt. Covenant rolled out into the broken litter dancing across the floor. Bruising his knees and hands on the shards, he lurched to his feet. Then a tremendous weight hammered down on the prow of the ship; and the floor tilted as if the Giantship were on its way to the depths. The afterdoor of the galley jumped from its mounts. Until Starfare's Gem stumbled back into a semblance of trim, Covenant had to cling to Cail and let the *Haruchai* uphold him.

The *dromond* seemed to be settling. Cries of breakage retorted along the wind. Outside the galley, the air was frantic with shouts; but over them all rose Honninscrave's stentorian howl:

'*Pitchwife!*'

Then Hearthcoal stirred in one corner; Seasauce shrugged the remains of a broken shelf off his back; and Covenant started to move. His first thought was for Linden; but a swift glance showed him that she was safe: still clasped in the sopor of *diamondraught*, she lay on her pallet with Mistweave braced protectively over her. Seeing Covenant's look, Mistweave gave a quick nod of reassurance. Without hesitation, Covenant surged to the ruptured door and charged out into the teeth of the wind.

He could see nothing: the night was as black as Vain. All the lanterns seemed to have been blown out. When he located a point of light hanging near Shipsheartthew, it showed him only that the wheeldeck had been abandoned. But shouts of command and desperation came from the direction of the prow. Gripping Cail's shoulder because he could not keep his footing on the ice, Covenant laboured forward.

At first, he followed the sound of Honninscrave's bellow, the First's iron orders. Then lanterns began to appear as Giants called for light so that they could see their way amid the snarled wreckage which crowded the vessel's forepeak.

In a prodigious tangle of sundered canvas and gear, pulleys and lines, sprawled several thick stone beams – the two upper spars and a section of the foremast. The great trunk of the mast had been broken in half. One of the fallen spars was intact: the other lay in three jagged pieces. At every step, the Giants kicked through slivers of granite.

Four crewmembers were crumpled in the wreckage.

The lantern-light was so wan, cast so many shadows, that Covenant could not see if any of them were still alive.

The First had her sword in her fist. Wielding it as deftly as a dagger, she cut through shrouds and sails toward the nearest of the fallen Giants. Galewrath and several others attacked the same task with their knives.

Sevinhand started into the wreckage: Honninscrave called him back, sent him instead to muster hands at the pumps. Covenant felt the *dromond* settling dangerously; but he had no time for that fear. Through the din, he shouted at Cail, 'Get Linden!'

'She has consumed much *diamondraught*,' the *Haruchai* replied. 'She will not be lightly roused.' His tone was impersonal.

'I don't care!' snapped Covenant. 'We're going to need her!'

Whirling away, he flung himself in the wake of the First.

She was crouched beside a limp form. As Covenant reached her, she surged erect again. Her eyes echoed the lanterns hotly: darkness lay along her blade like blood. 'Come!' she rasped. 'We can do nothing here.' Her sword sliced into the piled canvas with a sound like a cry.

Covenant glanced at the Giant she had left. The crewmember was a young woman he remembered – a grinning sailor with a cheerful determination to be always in the forefront of any work or hazard. He recognized half her face: the rest had been crushed by the broken butt of the mast.

For a moment, the dark overcame him. Bereft of light, he blundered into the wreckage and could not fight free. But then he felt venom rise like bile in his throat, felt worms of fire begin to crawl down his forearm; and the shock steadied him. He had nearly let the wild destruction slip. Cursing, he stumbled after the First again.

A stolid shout reported that Galewrath had found another of the injured Giants dead. Covenant forced himself to go faster, as if his haste might keep the other crewmembers alive. But the First had already left behind a third corpse, a man with an arm-long splinter of stone driven through the base of his throat. In a fever of suppressed fire, Covenant thrashed onward.

Galewrath and the First converged on the last Giant with Honninscrave and Covenant following closely.

The face of this Giant was less familiar to him: she had never been brought specifically to his notice. But that did not matter. He cared only that she was alive.

Her breath came in hoarse wet heaves: black fluid ran from the corner of her mouth, formed a pool under her head. The bulk of the one unsnapped spar lay across her chest, crushing her to the hard deck. Both her forearms were broken.

The First slapped her longsword into its scabbard. Together, she and Galewrath bent to the beam, tried to lift it. But the huge spar was far too heavy for them. Its ends were trapped: one stretched under the fallen mast; the other was snared in a mountain of gear and canvas.

Galewrath went on straining at the beam as if she did not know how to admit defeat. But the First swung upright, and her voice rang out over the deck, demanding help.

Giants were already on their way. Several of them veered toward the mast, fought to clear it so that they could roll it off the spar; others slashed into the wreckage at the far end with their knives.

There was little time. The life was being squeezed out of the pinned Giant: it panted from her mouth in damp shallow gasps. Her face was intense with pain.

No! Covenant panted in response. *No.* Thrusting himself forward, he cried through the clamour, 'Get back! I'm going to break this thing off her!'

He did not wait to see whether he was obeyed. Wrapping his arms as far as he could around the bole of the spar, he brought up white fire to tear the stone apart.

With a fierce yell, Honninscrave wrenched Covenant from the spar, shoved him away.

'Honninscrave – !' the First began.

'I must have this spar whole!' roared the Master. His beard jutted fury and aggrievement along his jaw. 'Starfare's Gem cannot endure any sea with but one mast!' The plight of his ship consumed him. 'If Pitchwife can mend this shaft by any amount, then I must have a spar to hold sail! He cannot remake the Giantship entire!'

For an instant, he and the First confronted each other furiously. Covenant fought to keep himself from howling.

Then a groan and thud of granite shook the deck as four or five Giants rolled the mast off the end of the spar.

At once, the First and Honninscrave sprang to work. With Galewrath and every Giant who could lay hand to the beam, they pitted their strength against the spar.

The long stone shaft lifted like an ordinary timber in their arms.

As the weight left her, the crushed crewmember let out a shredded moan and lost consciousness.

Immediately, Galewrath crouched under the yard to her. Clamping one hand under the woman's chin, the other at the back of her head to minimize the risk of further injuring a broken spine, the Storesmaster drew her comrade from beneath the spar to a small clear space in the middle of the wreckage.

Covenant gaped at them half-wittedly, trembling as if he had been snatched from the brink of an act of desecration.

Swiftly, Galewrath examined the crushed woman. But the fragmentary light of the lanterns made her appear tentative, hampered by hesitation and uncertainty. She was the *dromond's* healer and knew how to treat any hurt that she could see; but she had no way to correct or even evaluate such severe internal damage. And while she faltered, the woman was slipping out of reach.

Covenant tried to say Linden's name. But at that moment a group of Giants came through the shambles carrying lanterns. Mistweave and Cail were among them. Mistweave bore Linden.

She lay in his arms as if she were still asleep — as if the *diamondraught's* hold over her could not be breached by any desperation.

But when he set her on her feet, her eyes fluttered open. Groggily, she ran her fingers through her hair, pulled it back from her face. Shadows glazed her eyes: she looked like a woman who was walking in her dreams. A yawn stretched her mouth. She appeared unaware of the pain sprawling at her feet.

Then abruptly she sank down beside the dying Giant as though her knees had failed. She bowed her head, and her hair swung forward to hide her face again.

Rigid with useless impatience, the First clenched her fists on her hips. Galewrath glared back at the lamps. Honninscrave turned away as if he could not bear the sight, began whispering commands. His tone made the crew obey with alacrity.

Linden remained bowed over the Giant as though she were praying. The noise of the crew in the wreckage, the creaking of the *dromond's* granite, the muffled crackle of ice made what she was saying inaudible. Then her voice came into clearer focus.

' – but the spinal cord is all right. If you splint her back, strap her down, the bones should mend.'

Galewrath nodded stiffly, glowering as if she knew there was more to be said.

The next moment, a tremor ran through Linden. Her head jerked up.

'Her heart's bleeding. A broken rib – ' Her eyes cast a white blind stare into the dark.

Through her teeth, the First breathed, 'Succour her, Chosen. She must not die. Three others have lost life this night. There must not be a fourth.'

Linden went on staring. Her voice had a leaden sound, as though she were almost asleep again. 'How? I could open her up, but she'd lose too much blood. And I don't have any sutures.'

'*Chosen.*' The First knelt opposite Linden, took hold of her shoulders. 'I know nothing of these "sutures". Your healing surpasses me altogether. I know only that she must die if you do not aid her swiftly.'

In response, Linden gazed dully across the deck like a woman who had lost interest.

'Linden!' Covenant croaked at last. '*Try.*'

Her sight swam into focus on him, and he saw glints of light pass like motes of vision across the dark background of her eyes. 'Come,' she said faintly. 'Come here.'

All his muscles were wooden with suppressed dismay; but he forced himself to obey. Beside the dying Giant, he faced Linden. 'What do you – ?'

Her expression stopped him. Her features wore the look of dreams. Without a word, she reached out, caught his halfhand by the wrist, stretched his arm like a rod over the Giant's pain.

Before he could react, she frowned sharply; and a blare of violation ripped across his mind.

In a rush, fire poured from his ring. Wild magic threw back the night, washing the foredeck with incandescence.

He recoiled in shock rather than pain: her hold did not hurt him. Yet it bereft him of choice. Without warning, all his preconceptions were snatched apart. Everything changed. Once before, in the cavern of the One Tree, she had exerted his power for herself; but he had hardly dared consider the implications. Now her percipience had grown so acute that she could wield his ring without his bare volition. And it *was* a violation. Mhoram had said to him, *You are the white gold.* Wild magic had become a crucial part of his identity, and no one else had the right to use it, control it.

Yet he did not know how to resist her. Her grasp on what she was doing was impenetrable. Already she had set fire to the Giant's chest as if she intended to burn out the woman's heart.

Around the Giantship, every sound fell away, absorbed by fire. The First and Galewrath shaded their eyes against the blaze, watched the Chosen with mute astonishment. Linden's mouth formed mumbling shapes as she worked, but no words came. Her gaze was buried deep in the flames. Covenant could feel himself dying.

For one moment, the Giant writhed against his thighs. Then she took a heavy, shuddering breath; and the trickle of blood at the corner of her mouth stopped. Her chest rose more freely. In a short time, her eyes opened and stared at the sensation of being healed.

Linden dropped Covenant's wrist. At once, the fire vanished. Night clapped back over the *dromond*: for an instant, even the lanterns appeared to have gone out. He flinched back against a pile of ruined gear, his face full of darkness. He hardly heard the First muttering, 'Stone and Sea!' over and over again, unable to voice her amazement in any other way. He was completely blind. His eyes adjusted quickly enough, picking shapes and shadows out of the lantern-glow; but that was only sight, not vision: it had no power or capacity for healing.

Before him, Linden lay across the torso of the Giant she had called back from death. She was already asleep.

From his position in the *dromond*'s prow, Findail studied her as if he expected a transformation to begin at any moment.

Blinking fiercely, Covenant fought to keep the hot grief down. After a moment, he descried Pitchwife near the First. The lamps made the malformed Giant's face haggard, his eyes red: he was breathing heavily, nearly exhausted. But his voice was calm as he said, 'It is done. Starfare's Gem will not run with its wonted ease until it has been granted restoration by the shipwrights of Home. But I have wived the breaches. We will not go down.'

'Run?' Honninscrave growled through his beard. 'Have you beheld the foremast? Starfare's Gem will never run. In such hurt, I know not how to make it walk.'

The First said something Covenant did not hear. Cail came toward him, offered a hand to help him to his feet. But he did not react to any of them. He was being torn out of himself by the roots.

Linden had a better right to his ring than he did.

When the cold seeped so far into him that he almost stopped shivering, he made his preterite way to the oven-thick atmosphere of the galley. Seated there with his back to one wall, he stared at nothing as if he were stupefied, unable to register what he beheld. All he saw was the gaunt, compulsory visage of his doom.

Outside, the Giants laboured at the needs of the ship. For a long time, the muffled thud of the pumps rose from belowdecks. The sails of the aftermast were clewed up to their yards to protect them from any resurgence of the now-diminished Dolewind. The stone of the foremast and its spars was cleared out of the wreckage and set aside: anything that remained intact in the fallen gear and rigging was salvaged. Either Seasauce or Hearthcoal was away from the stoves constantly, carrying huge buckets of broth to the Giants to sustain them while they worked.

But nothing the crew could do changed the essential fact: the *dromond* was stuck and crippled. When dawn came, and Covenant went, hollow-eyed and spectral, to look at the Giantship's condition, he was dismayed by the severity of the damage. Aft of the midship housing, nothing had been hurt: the aftermast raised its arms like a tall tree to the blue depths and broken clouds of the sky. But forward Starfare's Gem looked as maimed as a derelict. Scant feet above the first yards, which had been stripped to the bone by the collapse of the upper members, the foremast ended in a ragged stump.

Covenant had no sea-craft, but he recognized that Honninscrave was right: without sails forward to balance the canvas aft, Starfare's Gem would never be able to navigate.

Aching within himself, he turned to find out what the vessel had struck.

At first, what he saw seemed incomprehensible. Starfare's Gem lay surrounded to the horizons by a vast flat wilderland of ice. Jagged hunks were crushed against the *dromond*'s sides; but the rest of the ice was unbroken: its snow-blown surface appeared free of any channel which could have brought the Giantship to this place.

But when he shaded his gaze and peered southward, he discerned a narrow band of grey water beyond the ice. And, squinting so hard that his temples throbbed, he traced a line between the *dromond*'s stern and the open sea. There the ice was thinner: it was freezing back over the long furrow which Starfare's Gem had ploughed into the floe.

The Giantship was trapped – locked here and helpless. With all three masts intact and a favouring wind, it could not have moved. It was stuck where it sat until spring came to its rescue. If this part of the world ever felt the touch of spring.

Damnation!

The ship's plight stung him like the gusts which came skirling off the ice. In the Land, the Clave was feeding the Banefire, stoking it with innocent blood to increase the Sunbane. No one remained to fight the na-Mhoram's depredations except Sunder and Hollian and perhaps a handful of *Haruchai* – if any of them were still alive. The quest for the One Tree had failed, extinguishing Covenant's sole hope. And now – !

Have mercy on me.

But he was a leper, and there was never any mercy for lepers. Despite did not forbear. He had reached the point where everything he did was wrong. Even his stubborn determination to cling to his ring, to bear the cost of his doom himself, was wrong. But he could not endure the alternative. The simple thought wrung a mute howl from the pit of his heart.

He had to do something, find some way to reaffirm himself. Passivity and silence were no longer viable. His despair itself compelled him. He had to – Linden had proved the *Elohim* right. With his ring she was able to heal. But he could not forget the taste of eager fire when he had warmed the stewpot to save her. *Had* to! He could not give it up.

His ring was all he had left.

He had become the most fundamental threat to everything he loved. But suddenly that was no longer enough to stop him. Deliberately, he set aside Linden's reasons – her wish to see him do what she believed she would do in his place, her desire to fight Lord Foul through him – and chose his own.

To show himself and his companions and the Despiser if necessary that he had the right.

Without looking away from the ice, he said to Cail, 'Tell Honninscrave I want to talk to him. I want to talk to everybody – the First, Linden, Pitchwife. In his cabin.'

When the *Haruchai* moved soundlessly away, Covenant hugged the scant protection of his robe and set himself to wait.

The idea of what he meant to do made his pulse beat like venom in his veins.

There was blue in the sky, the first blue he had seen for days. A crusty glitter reflected the sun. But the ice was not as smooth as the sunlight made it appear. Its surface was marked with sharp spines and ridges, mounds where floe-plates rubbed and depressions which ran from nowhere to nowhere. The ice was a wasteland, its desolation grieving in the cold, and it held his gaze like the outcome of his life. Once in winter he had fought his way through long leagues of snow and despair to confront the Despiser – and he had prevailed. But he knew now that he would never prevail in that way again.

He shrugged against the chill. So what? He would find some other way. Even if the attempt drove him mad. Madness was just a less predictable and scrupulous form of power. And he did not believe that either Lord Foul or Findail had told him the whole truth.

Yet he did not intend to surrender his scruples or go mad. His leprosy had trained him well for survival and affirmation against an impossible future. And Foamfollower had once said to him, *Service enables service*. Hope came from the power and value of what was served, not from the one who served it.

When Cail returned, Covenant felt that he was ready. Slowly, carefully, he turned from the Sea and picked his way across the clogged stone toward one of the entryways to the underdecks.

Below, the door to Honninscrave's cabin was open; and beside it stood Mistweave. His face wore a conflicted expression: Covenant guessed that the Giant had undertaken more than he realized when he had assigned himself to Cail's former responsibility for Linden. How could he have foreseen that his dedication to her would require him to ignore the needs of the *dromond* and the labours of the crew? The dilemma made him look unsure of himself.

But Covenant did not have any relief to offer the Giant, and the door was open. Frowning at the pain all the people around him had to bear, he went into the Master's cabin, leaving Cail outside.

Honninscrave's quarters were austere: except for a few chairs sized for Giants, a huge seachest, and a deep bunk, its only furnishings were a long table cluttered with nautical instruments and charts and two lamps hanging in stone gimbals. Honninscrave stood at the far end of the table as if Covenant's arrival had interrupted him in the act of pacing. Sevinhand sat on the edge of the bunk, more melancholy than ever in his weariness. Near him was the Storesmaster, her shoulders touching the wall, no expression on her blunt features. The First and Pitchwife occupied two of the chairs. She held her back straight, her scabbarded blade across her thighs, as though refusing to admit how tired she was; but her husband was slumped with fatigue, emphasizing the deformation of his spine.

In one corner of the chamber, Linden sat cross-legged on the floor. Sleep made her eyes bleary: when she raised them to acknowledge Covenant, she seemed hardly able to see him. In the company of these Giants, she appeared tiny and misplaced. But the hue of her skin and the steadiness of her respiration showed that she had been essentially restored to health.

The air of the cabin felt tense, as if Covenant had entered in the middle of an argument. None of the Giants except Pitchwife and Sevinhand were looking at him. But when he turned his unspoken question toward Pitchwife, the First's husband bowed his head and did not answer. And the lines of Sevinhand's old rue were too deep to be challenged.

Covenant was stretched taut beyond gentleness. In a raw, brusque voice, he demanded, 'So what do you think we should do about it?'

Linden frowned as if his tone hurt her. Or perhaps she had already read the nature of his intent. Without lifting her head, she murmured, 'That's what they've been arguing about.'

Her explanation eased him somewhat. He had gone so far down the road of his fate that he instinctively expected every hostile or painful or simply difficult emotion to be directed at himself. But his question remained. 'What choice have we got?'

At that, the muscles at the corners of Honninscrave's jaw clenched. Sevinhand rubbed his cheeks with his palms as if he sought to push back the sorrow. The First let a sigh breathe softly through her teeth. But no one answered.

Covenant pulled air into his lungs, gripped his courage in the insensate cold of his fists. 'If you don't have any better ideas, I'm going to break us out of this ice.'

Then every eye was on him, and a shock of apprehension recoiled through the cabin. Honninscrave's face gaped like a reopened wound. All the sleep vanished from Linden's orbs. The First surged to her feet. As harsh as iron, she demanded, 'Will you hazard the Earth to no purpose?'

'Do you think your restraint is that good?' Linden added instantly. She, too, had come to her feet as if she wanted to meet Covenant's folly standing. 'Or are you just looking for an excuse to throw power around?'

'Hell and blood!' Covenant barked. Had Findail taught everyone aboard the *dromond* to distrust him? 'If you don't like it' – his scarred forearm itched avidly – 'give me an alternative! Do you think I *like* being this dangerous?'

His outburst sent a grimace of chagrin across the First's face. Linden dropped her eyes. For a moment, Pitchwife's difficult breathing punctuated the silence. Then his wife said softly, 'Your pardon, Giantfriend. I did not intend affront. But we are not without choice in this strait.' She turned, and her gaze went like the point of a blade toward Honninscrave. 'You will speak now, Master.'

Honninscrave glared at her. But she was the First of the Search: no Giant would have refused to obey her when she used that tone. He complied slowly, uttering each word like a flat piece of stone. Yet as he answered his hands made truncated, fumbling movements among the charts and implements on the table, contradicting him.

'I am uncertain of our position. I have been granted scant opportunity for sightings since the cloud-wrack cleared. And this sea has been little frequented by our people. Our charts and knowledge are likewise uncertain.' The First frowned a reprimand at his digression; but he did not falter. 'Where knowledge is insufficient, all choices are hazardous.

'Yet it would appear that we lie now some four or five score leagues north and east of the coast which you name Seareach, home of the Unhomed and site of their destitute city and grave, *Coercri*, The Grieve.' He articulated that name with a special distinctness, as if he would prefer to hear it sung. Then he outlined the alternative which the First had in mind: that Covenant and the leaders of the Search leave Starfare's Gem and strike westward across the ice until they found land, after which they could follow the coast into Seareach.

'Or,' Linden interposed warily, studying Covenant as she spoke, 'we could forget Seareach and head straight for Revelstone. I don't know the terrain, but it's bound to be quicker than detouring that far south.'

'Aye.' Honninscrave permitted himself a growl of disgust or trepidation. 'Should this littoral lie within hope of our charts.' Emotion rose in his voice, slipping out of his rigid grasp. 'And should the ice remain intact and traversable to that coast. And should this winter hold – for we are somewhat southerly to have encountered such ice in the natural course of the seas, and it may thaw beneath us unseasonably.' To keep himself from shouting, he ground out the words like shards of rock. 'And should the northward reaches of the Land be not rugged or mountainous beyond all possibility of travel. *Then* – ' He grabbed a mouthful of air, held it between his teeth. 'Then, I say, our way is clear before us.'

His distress was acute in the confinement of the cabin. But the First did not relent. 'We hear you,' she said sternly. 'The choice is jeopardous. Complete your tale, Master.'

Honninscrave could not look at her. 'Ah, my tale,' he grated. 'It is no tale of mine. My brother is dead, and the *dromond* I cherish lies locked in the ice and crippled. It is no tale of mine.' Yet the First's authority held him. Clutching a chart in each fist like a weightless and insufficient cudgel, he directed his voice at Covenant.

'You have offered to sunder the ice. Very good. To Cable Seadreamer my brother who gave his life, you refused the fire of release. But in the name of your mad desire for battle you will attempt a league of ice. Very good. But I say to you that Starfare's Gem cannot sail. In this maimed state, no. And were the time taken to do what mending lies within our power – time which is so precious to you – and were a channel opened to the Sea, then still would our plight remain, for the *dromond* is no longer proof against the stress of the seas. With a kind wind, perchance, we might make way toward Seareach. But any storm would hold us in its mercy. A score of days – or ten score – might find us yet farther from our goal. Starfare's Gem' – he had to swallow heavily to force out the words – 'is no longer fit to bear the Search.'

'But – ' Covenant began, then halted. For an instant, he was confused. Honninscrave's grief covered an anger which he could not utter and Covenant could not decipher. Why was the Master so bitter?

But suddenly the implications of Honninscrave's speech swept over Covenant like a breaker; and his comprehension tumbled down the riptide. Starfare's Gem could not sail. And the First wanted the Search to leave the Giantship, set out afoot toward the Land. He found himself facing her with a knot of cold clenched around his heart. Dismay was all that kept him from fury.

'Nearly forty Giants.' Foamfollower's people, the kindred of the Unhomed. 'You're talking about leaving them here to die.'

She was a Swordmain, trained to battle and difficult choices: her sternness as she returned Covenant's gaze looked as careless of costs as a weapon. But behind her eyes moved shadows like spectres of pain.

'Aye.' Honninscrave's voice scraped the air. 'They must be left to die. Or they must accompany us, and Starfare's Gem itself must be left to die. And from that day forward, no one of us shall ever again set gaze upon the crags and harbourage of Home. We have no means for the making of a new *dromond*. And our people know not where we are.' He spoke softly, but every word left a weal across Covenant's mind.

It was intolerable. He was no sailor: he could bear to abandon the Giantship. But to leave nearly forty Giants behind without hope – or to strand them in the Land as the Unhomed had been stranded – !

The First did not waver: she knew her duty and would not shirk it. Covenant swung away from her, confronted Honninscrave down the length of the table. Its height made the Master appear tall and hurt beyond any mitigation. But Covenant could not accept that outcome.

'If we leave the crew here. With the ship.' He drove his gaze up at the Giant until Honninscrave met it. 'What will they need? In order to have any chance at all?'

Honninscrave's head jerked in surprise. For a moment, his mouth parted his beard incredulously, as though he half believed he was being taunted. But then with a wrench he mastered himself. 'Stores we have in plenty.' His eyes clung to Covenant like an appeal: *Be not false to me in this*. 'But the plight of the Giantship remains. It must have all the mending which Pitchwife may contrive. It must have time.'

Time, Covenant thought. He had already been away from the Land for more than sixty days – away from Revelstone for closer to ninety. How many more people had the Clave killed? But the only alternative was to leave Pitchwife behind with the ship. And he would surely refuse. The First herself might refuse. Stiffly, Covenant asked, 'How much time?'

'Two days,' replied Honninscrave. 'Perhaps three. Much pitch will be required. And the labour itself will be awkward and arduous.'

Damnation! Covenant breathed. Three days. But he did not back down. He was a leper: he knew the folly of trying to purchase the future by selling the present. Grimly, he turned to Pitchwife.

Fatigue seemed to emphasize the Giant's deformities. His back bent as if it had been damaged by the weight of his limbs and head. But his eyes glittered, and his expression had lifted. He looked at Covenant as though he knew what the Unbeliever was about to say – and approved of it.

Covenant felt wooden with failure. He had come here primed for fire; but all he had been able to offer his companions was a patience he did not possess. 'Try to do it in one,' he muttered. Then he left the cabin so that he would not have to endure the reactions of the Giants.

Pitchwife's voice followed him. 'Stone and Sea!' the Giant chuckled. 'It is a small matter. What need have I of an entire day?'

Glaring at nothing, Covenant quickened his pace.

But as he reached the ladder leading to the afterdeck, Linden caught up with him. She gripped his arm as if something had changed between them. Her intent seriousness bore no resemblance to her old severity, and her eyes were damp. Her soft mouth, which he had kissed with such longing, wore the shape of a plea.

Yet he had not forgiven himself; and after a moment she dropped her hand. Her gaze retreated somewhat. When she spoke, she sounded like a woman who did not know the words she needed.

'You keep surprising me. I never know what to expect from you. Just when I think you're too far gone to be reached, you do something like that. Like what you did for Sunder and Hollian.' Abruptly, she stopped as if she were hurt by the inadequacy of what she was saying.

Covenant wanted to cry out. His desire for her was too acute to be suffered. He had already perverted whatever authenticity he might have had with her. And she was a healer. She had more right to his ring than he did. Self-loathing made him harsh.

'Do you really think I just want to throw power around? It that your opinion of me?'

At that, she winced. Her expression turned inward like a baffled wail. 'No,' she murmured. 'No. I was just trying to get your attention.' Then her eyes reached toward him again. 'But you scared me. If you could see yourself – '

'If I could see myself,' he rasped so that he would not put his arms around her, 'I'd probably puke.'

Savagely, he flung himself up the ladder away from her.

But when he gained the open air and brittle cold of the afterdeck, he had to knot his arms across his chest to hold in the hurt.

While he ate his breakfast in the galley, trying to absorb some of the stoves' warmth, he could hear the sounds of work outside. At first, Sevinhand's voice and Galewrath's commanded alternately. He supervised the preparation of the foredeck: she led the breaking of the ice and the ritual songs for the burial of the three fallen crewmembers. But after a while Pitchwife made himself heard over the scuffle of feet and clatter of gear, the stiff hiss and thud of half-frozen cable. When Covenant had collected what little courage he had left, he went out to watch.

During the night, the crew had cleared and organized the wreckage: now they were busy readying the truncated foremast. Pitchwife was hunched over a large stone vat of his special pitch; but his eyes and voice followed the sailors as they rigged lines between the intact yard and the splintered end of the mast. Except for the necessary questions and instructions, the Giants were unusually quiet, dispirited. The Dolewind had held them for a long time; and since their encounter with the Soulbiter they had had no rest at all. Now their future had become as fragile and arduous as ice. Even Giants could not carry so much strain indefinitely.

But Covenant had never seen Pitchwife at work before. Grateful for any distraction, he studied Pitchwife with fascination as the First's husband completed his preparations. Consigning his vat to another Giant, he hoisted a slab of setrock in a sling over his shoulder, then went to the ropes and began pulling himself slowly up the foremast.

Below him, the crew set his vat of pitch into a net that they had rigged from a pulley fixed as high as possible on the mast. When he reached that height himself, supported now by a line lashed under his arms and around the mast, two Giants hauled the vat up to him. His breath plumed crisply in the cold.

At once, he began his work. Scooping up gouts of pitch, he larded them into the jagged crown of the mast. The pitch seemed viscid, but he handled it deftly, fingering it down into the cracks and smoothing it on all sides until he had fashioned a flat butt for the broken stone. Then he reached back to his setrock, snapped a chip from one edge, and tapped the piece into the pitch.

Almost without transition, the pitch became stone, indistinguishable from the mast's granite.

Muttering his satisfaction, he followed his vat back down to the deck.

Sevinhand sent several Giants swarming up to the yard to undo everything which had been rigged to the mast. At the same time, other crewmembers began binding ropes around the ends of the intact spar and preparing new gear up on the yard.

Pitchwife ignored them, turned his attention to the fallen portion of the mast. It had broken into several pieces; but one section was as long as all the rest combined. With pitch and setrock, he formed both ends of this section into flat butts like the new cap of the foremast.

Covenant could not see what all this would accomplish. And his need for haste made him restless. After a time, he realized that he had not seen Galewrath since he had come out on deck. When the dead had been given to the Sea, she had gone to some other task. In an effort to keep himself occupied — and to generate some warmth — he tugged his robe tighter and went looking for the Storesmaster.

He found her in her particular demesne, a warren of holds, watercests, and storage-lockers, belowdecks amidships. The *dromond* carried a surprising amount of wood for use both as fuel for the stoves and as raw material for repairs or replacements which could not be readily achieved with stone at sea. Galewrath and three other Giants were at work in a square hold which served as the ship's carpentry.

They were making two large sleds.

These were rough constructs with high rails and rude planking. But they looked sturdy. And each was big enough to carry a Giant.

Two crewmembers glued and pegged the shells together while Galewrath and the other Giant laboured at the more difficult chore of carving runners. With files, knives, and hand-adzes, they stripped the bark from beams as thick as Covenant's thigh, then slowly shaped the wood to carry weight over ice and snow as easily as possible. The floor was already thick with bark and curlings, and the air smelled of clean resin; but the task was far from finished.

In response to Covenant's question, Galewrath replied that to reach Revelstone Covenant and his company would need more supplies than they could bear on their backs. And the sleds would also transport Covenant and Linden when the terrain permitted the Giants to set a pace the humans could not match.

Once again, Covenant was abashed by the providence of the people who sought to serve him. He had not been able to think farther ahead than the moment when he would leave Starfare's Gem; but the Giants were concerned about more than the stark question of their ship's survival. He would have died long ago if other people had not taken such care of him.

His route back toward the upper decks passed the Master's cabin. The door was shut; but from within he heard the First's voice, raised in vexation. She was urging Honninscrave to stay with the *dromond*.

The Master's answering silence was eloquent. As ashamed as an eavesdropper, Covenant hastened away to see what progress Pitchwife and Sevinhand had made.

When he gained the foredeck, the sun stood above the gap where the midmast should have been, and the deformed Giant's plans were taking shape: Covenant was almost able to guess his intent. Pitchwife had finished the long stone shaft on the deck; and he and Sevinhand were watching as the crew wrestled the one unbroken spar up onto the yard. There they stood the spar against the truncated mast and secured it with loop after loop of cable. For two-thirds of its length, the spar reached above the end of the mast. To the upraised tip had been affixed the pulley of a massive block-and-tackle.

Covenant eyed the lashings and the spar distrustfully. 'Is that going to hold?'

Pitchwife shrugged as if his arms had become too heavy for him. His voice was husky with fatigue. 'If it does not, the task cannot be accomplished in one day. The spar I can mend. But the mast we hope to raise must then be broken to smaller fragments which I may bear aloft and wive whole again.' He sighed without looking at Covenant. 'Pray this will hold. The prospect of that labour I do not relish.'

Wearily, he fell silent.

When the tackle had been attached to one flat end of the mast-shaft Pitchwife had prepared, eight or ten Giants lifted the shaft and positioned it below the yard so that the lines hung as straight as possible in order to minimize the sideward stress on the spar. Creaking in its pulleys, the tackle tightened.

Covenant held his breath unconsciously. That spar looked too slender to sustain the granite shaft. But as the ropes strained tighter and the end of the mast-piece lifted, nothing broke.

Then the shaft hung straight from the spar, brushing against the bole of the mast. As the Giants pulled slowly on the tow-line of the tackle, the shaft continued to rise.

When its butt reached the level of Covenant's head, Pitchwife coughed, 'Hold!'

The Giants on the tow-line froze. The tackle groaned: the shaft settled slightly as the ropes stretched. But still nothing broke.

His hands full of pitch, the deformed Giant moved to the shaft and gently covered the butt with an even and heavy layer. Then he retreated to the other side of the mast. A rope dangled near him: when he had carefully cleaned his hands, he gripped it and let the Giants on the yard haul him upward.

Bracing himself once again within a loop of rope passed around the mast and his back, he laboured foot by foot up toward the maimed stump. Alone above the yard, he looked strangely vulnerable; yet he forced himself upward by main strength. Finally he hung at the rim of the mast.

For a long moment, he did not move; and Covenant found himself panting as if he sought to breathe for the Giant, send Pitchwife strength. The First had come to the foredeck: her gaze was clenched on her husband. If the spar snapped, only a miracle could save him from being ripped down by falling stone and flying tackle.

Then he signalled to the Giants below. Sevinhand whispered a command: the crew began to raise the shaft again.

Now the bowing of the spar was unmistakable. Covenant could hardly believe that it was still intact.

By wary degrees, the shaft was drawn upward. Soon its flat crown ascended above Pitchwife's head. Then its butt reached the level of his chest.

He looked too weak to support his own weight; but somehow he braced himself, reached out his arms to prevent the shaft from swinging over the end of the mast – from scraping off its layer of pitch or mating crookedly. The Giants fisted the lines tighter, raised the shaft another foot; then Sevinhand stopped them. Slowly, Pitchwife shifted his position, aligned the stone with the mast.

He gave an urgent gasp of readiness. Fervently careful, the Giants began to lower the shaft. Alone, he guided it downward.

The flat ends met. At once, he thumbed a sliver of setrock into place; and the line separating stone from stone vanished as if it had never existed. The First let relief hiss through her teeth. A raw cheer sprang from the Giants as they let the tackle go.

The mast stood. It was not as tall as the aftermast – but it was tall enough now to carry a second spar. And two spans of canvas forward might give the *dromond* the balance it needed to survive.

The task was not yet done: the spar had to be attached to the new foremast. But most of the afternoon remained, and the necessary repairs were clearly possible now. Two Giants swarmed upward and helped Pitchwife down to the yard, then lowered him to his jubilant comrades. The First greeted him with a hug which looked urgent enough to crack his spine. A jug of *diamondraught* appeared from somewhere and was pressed into his hands. He drank hugely, and another cheer was raised around him.

Weak with relief, Covenant watched them and let his gratitude for Pitchwife's safety and success wash over him.

A moment later, Pitchwife emerged from the crowd of Giants. He was made unsteady on his feet by exhaustion and sudden *diamondraught*; but he moved purposefully toward Covenant. He gave the Unbeliever a florid bow which nearly cost him his balance. Then he said, 'I will rest now. But ere nightfall I will set the spar. That will complete the labour I can do for Starfare's Gem.' The raw rims of his eyes and the sway of his stance were acute reminders that he had saved the *dromond* from sinking before this day's work began.

But he was not done. His voice softened as he added, 'Giantfriend, I thank you that you accorded to me this opportunity to be of service to the Giantship.'

Bright in the sunshine and the reflections of the ice, he turned away. Chuckling at the murmured jests and praise of the crew, he linked arms with the First and left the foredeck like a drunken hero. In spite of his deformed stature, he seemed as tall as any Giant.

The sight eased Covenant in a way that made his eyes burn. Gratitude loosened his tension: Pitchwife had proved his fear and anger unnecessary. As Sevinhand and his crew went back to work, stringing new tackle so that they could hoist the spar into place against the foremast, Covenant moved away in search of Linden. He wanted to show her what the Giant had accomplished. And to apologize for his earlier harshness.

He found her almost at once: she was in the galley, asleep like a waif on her pallet. Her dreams made her frown with the solemn concentration of a child; but she showed no sign of awakening. She was still recuperating from the abrasive cold of the Soulbiter. He let her sleep.

The warmth of the galley reminded him of his own chilled weariness. He stretched out on his pallet, intending to rest for a while and then go back to watch the Giants. But as soon as he closed his eyes, his fatigue arose and carried him away.

Later, in a period of half-consciousness, he thought he heard singing. At first, the songs were ones of gladness and praise, of endurance against exigent seas and safe arrival Home. But after a while the melodies began to grieve, and the songs became ones of parting, of ships lost and kindred sundered; and through them ran a sound like the crackle of flames, the anguish of a *caamora*, auguring doom. Covenant had attempted a *caamora* once, on the headrock of *Coercri*. But that bonfire had not been violent enough to touch him: in the night of the Unhomed's dismay, he had succoured everyone but himself. Now as he sank back into dreams he thought perhaps a more absolute blaze was needed, a more searching and destructive conflagration. And he knew where to find that fire. He slept like a man who feared to face what was coming.

But when he awakened at last, the idea was gone.

The way Seasauce and Hearthcoal bustled about their work suggested that a new day had dawned. Abashed by sleep, he fumbled himself into a sitting position, looked across at Linden's pallet and saw that it was empty. She and Mistweave were not in the galley. But Cail stood nearby, as impassive as if impatience were unknown to him.

When Covenant looked at him, the *Haruchai* said, 'You are timely roused, ur-Lord. The night is past. Those who will sojourn with you ready themselves for departure.'

A pang went through Covenant. Ready, he thought. The people around him did everything possible on his behalf; but he was never ready. Struggling to his feet, he accepted the bowl of porridge Hearthcoal offered him, ate as much as his haste could stomach. Then he went to the door Cail held open for him and stepped out into the sharp morning.

Again, ice-glare and sunlight stung his eyes, but he fought them into focus. After a glance at the new foremast, he picked his way across the frozen afterdeck toward the Giants thronging near the port rail.

Hails greeted him: the crew parted, admitted him to their midst. In a moment, he found himself at the edge of the deck with Linden and Mistweave, the First and Pitchwife, and Honninscrave.

Both Linden and Pitchwife looked stronger than they had the previous day, although she avoided Covenant's gaze as if she did not trust him. The First eyed the west with the keenness of a hawk. But Honninscrave appeared painfully unsolaced, as though he had spent the long night haunted by his conflicting duties.

A glance past the railing showed Covenant that Galewrath's sleds had already been set down on the ice. Both were heavily laden; but the sacks and bundles of supplies had been arranged to accommodate at least one passenger in each sled.

When she had acknowledged Covenant, the First turned to Sevinhand, Galewrath, and the rest of the Giants. 'Now has the time of parting come upon us once more.' Her voice rang crisply across the frigid air. 'The hazard is great, for no longer stands Cable Seadreamer's Earth-Sight at the helm of the Search. Yet do we pursue our sworn purpose – and for that reason I do not fear. We are mortal, and the visage of failure is heinous to us. But we are not required to succeed. It is required of us only that we hold fast in every gale and let come what may. On all the seas of the world, there are none better for this work than you who remain with Starfare's Gem. How then should I be afraid?

'This only do I charge you: when the ice uncloses, come after us. Sail to that littoral which you know, to Seareach and brave *Coercri*, The Grieve. If there we fail to meet you or send word, then the Search falls to you. Do what you must – and do not fear. While one valiant heart yet defends the Earth, evil can never triumph utterly.'

Then she stopped, looked down at Pitchwife as if she were surprised by her own words. For answer, he gave her a gleam of pure pleasure. Sevinhand's eyes reflected hints of the cunning skill which had saved Starfare's Gem from the warships of the *Bhrathair*. Galewrath glowered stolidly at the future as though it had no power to daunt her. Weary and imperilled though they were, the crew-members held up their heads and let their pride shine. Covenant suddenly did not know how he could bear to leave them.

But he had to. The First started down the ladder with Pitchwife behind her; and Covenant had no choice. They were not responsible for the Earth's peril; but their lives were at stake as much as his. When Cail offered him the ladder, he gestured the *Haruchai* ahead to catch him if he fell: then he stooped through the railing, set his numb feet into the rungs, and fought his vertigo and his cold bones downward.

The ice felt as dead as the nerves of his soles, and in the shadow of the Giantship the breeze was as sharp as the Sea; but he strode and slipped across the treacherous surface to one of the sleds. Linden followed him, her hair fluttering like the banner of her determination. Then came Mistweave, still stubborn in his resolve to serve the Chosen.

Honninscrave was last. He seemed hardly able to refrain from giving Galewrath and Sevinhand a host of unnecessary final instructions. But after a moment of silence like a mute cry he wrenched himself away from his ship and joined the company.

Abruptly, several Giants scrambled out of Vain's way as he approached the rail. He vaulted over the side, landed lightly on the ice, and at once resumed his characteristic immobility, his black orbs gazing at nothing.

A shadow glided out of the air: Findail melted back into his human form near Vain as if he and the Demondim-spawn belonged to each other.

Obeying the First's murmured instructions, Covenant climbed into one of the sleds, sat down among the supplies. Linden settled herself in the other sled. Honninscrave and Mistweave picked up the leads, harnessed themselves into the lines. The First and Pitchwife went to the fore: Cail stood between the sleds: Vain and Findail brought up the rear.

Runners crunched against the ice as Covenant and his companions left the Giantship in search of hope.

Sixty-three days had passed since they had said farewell to Sunder and Hollian and Seareach. They were at least eighteen-score leagues from Revelstone.

5

LANDWARD

The First set a rapid pace. Steam panted from Honninscrave's and Mistweave's lungs as they hauled the sleds along; but they did not hang back. All the Giants were eager to get out of sight of the *dromond*, to put behind them their crippled vessel and imperilled people. The runners of the sleds pounded through hollows in the ice, hit and slewed across pressure-ridges: Covenant and Linden were tossed ungently from side to side among the supplies. But Linden clung to the rails, made no protest. And Covenant wanted every stride of speed the Giants could attain. The Land and Lord Foul had taught him many things; but he had never learned how to leave behind friends who needed him. Hunching down into the heavy robes and blankets he had been given, he kept his face turned blear-eyed and cold-bitten toward the west and let Honninscrave draw him at a hungry trot into the white wilderland.

Yet at last the thought of what he was doing impelled him to look back toward the *dromond*. Stark in the distance beyond Vain and Findail, the vessel shrank as if it were being slowly swallowed by the bleak floe; and the sight of its abandonment stuck in his throat. But then he descried the pennon flying from the aftermast. Sevinhand must have raised it as a salute to the departing company. Vivid with colour and jaunty in the wind, it captured for a moment the spirit of Starfare's Gem like a promise of valour and endurance. When

Covenant's vision became too blurred to make out the Giantship any longer, he was able to face forward again and let the stone vessel go.

Linden studied him across the gap between their sleds; but he had nothing to say to her which would support being shouted over the hard scrunching of the runners, the rhythmic thud of the Giants' feet and the gasp of their breathing. Once again he was being borne toward his goal and his fear, not by any effort of his own, but by the exertions of people who cared about him. At every crisis along his way, it was the same: for all his passion and power, he would have come to nothing without help. And what recompense did he make for that help? Only pain and peril and at least one lie: nothing more. But that was not something which his sore heart could cry out under these conditions, under the bitter blue of the sky and the gaze of his companions.

They were travelling due west. When they had left the vantage of Starfare's Gem, a strip of open water had still been visible against the southern horizon; and they could be certain that the closer they went to the Sea the less reliable the floe would become. Under the circumstances, Covenant only hoped that they would not be forced northward to find a safe passage.

The First had pushed several paces ahead of her companions to watch for flaws and fissures in the frozen expanse. Behind her trotted Pitchwife. Though he bore no burden except his own deformity, his gait betrayed that he was already being pressed to his limits. By comparison, Mistweave and Honninscrave appeared able to sustain this speed for days, dragging the heavy sleds behind them and never faltering. And Cail was one of the *Haruchai*, born to ice and arduous survival: only the vapour that plumed from his nostrils and the white crystals which formed along his cheeks showed that he was breathing more deeply than usual.

As for Vain and Findail, they moved as though the long trek ahead meant nothing to them. Vain's wooden forearm dangled uselessly from his elbow, but in every other way he remained the structurally immaculate enigma which the ur-viles had created for their own secret reasons. And the Appointed had long since demonstrated his conclusive immunity to any physical peril or stress.

Around them, the plain of ice seemed featureless and devoid of any content except cold to the edges of the world. The sun came down hard on the white floe, making the ice glare, forcing Covenant to squint until his temples throbbed. And the cold soaked into him through every fold and clasp of his coverings. The beat of the Giants' feet and the expulsion of their breath marked out the frigid silence. The sled jostled him incessantly against a bundle of firewood packed beside him. Grimly, he hugged his blankets and huddled into himself.

The First's fall took him by surprise. She was nothing more than a grey blur across his disfocused stare as she stepped into a fissure.

Scattering snow, she plunged heavily forward. Her chest struck the rim of the break. For an instant, she scrabbled frantically at the edge, then dropped out of sight.

Pitchwife was four or five strides behind her; but immediately he dove after her, skidding headlong to snatch at her disappearing arms.

He was too late. And he could not stop himself. In a flurry of limbs and snow, he toppled after his wife.

Slewing over the slick surface, Honninscrave and Mistweave wheeled the sleds to a halt. The one bearing Linden was nearly overturned; but Cail caught it, slammed it back onto its runners.

Covenant pitched out of his sled, landed on the ice, lurched to his feet. Ahead of him, the Master and Mistweave wrestled at the bindings which harnessed them to their burdens. Findail and Vain had stopped; but Cail was already halfway to the fissure.

Covenant and the Giants reached the rim together, with Linden a scant step behind them. Cail stood there gazing downward as if he had forgotten urgency.

The First and Pitchwife hung a few feet below the edge. The fissure was only a little wider than her shoulders, and she had clamped herself between the walls, holding her position by main strength. Pitchwife's arms clasped her hips: he dangled awkwardly between her thighs.

Below his feet, the snow which had fallen into the fissure became grey slush as the sea absorbed it.

He jerked a glance upward. 'Stone and Sea!' he gasped. 'Make haste!'

But the Master and Mistweave were not slow. Honninscrave threw himself flat on the ice with his head and shoulders over the rim. Mistweave braced the Master's legs; and Honninscrave reached down to take hold of the First.

In a moment, she scrambled out of the fissure, towing Pitchwife after her.

Her stern visage showed no reaction; but he was breathing hard, and his gnarled hands trembled. 'Stone and Sea!' he panted again. 'I am a Giant and love an eventful journey. But such happenings are not altogether to my taste.' Then a chuckle of relief came steaming between his bared teeth. 'Also I am somewhat abashed. I sought to rescue my wife, yet it was she who caught my own fall.'

The First rested a hand lightly on his shoulder. 'Mayhap if you were less impetuous in your rescuing – ' But as she turned to Honninscrave, her voice stiffened. 'Master, it is my thought that we must bend our way somewhat northward. This ice is not safe.'

'Aye,' he growled. Ever since he had been forced to the realization that the company would have to leave Starfare's Gem, he had not been able to stifle the undertone of bitterness in his voice. 'But that way is longer, and we are in haste. Northward the ice will be not so easily travelled. And this north is perilous, as you know.'

The First nodded reluctantly. After a moment, she let out a long sigh and straightened her back. 'Very well,' she said. 'Let us attempt the west again.'

When no one moved, she gestured Covenant and Linden back to the sleds.

Linden turned to walk beside Covenant. Her face was red with cold and severe with concentration. In a flat, quiet voice, she asked, 'Why is this north perilous?'

He shook his head. 'I don't know.' The scars on his right forearm itched in reaction to the First's fall and the suggestion of other hazards. 'I've never been north of Revelstone and *Coercri*.' He did not want to think about nameless dangers. The cold was already too much for him. And he could not figure out how the company was going to get across the fissure.

But that problem was simply solved. While he and Linden climbed into their sleds, the First and Pitchwife leaped the gap. Then Honninscrave and Mistweave drew the sleds to the rim of the crack. There Covenant saw that the sleds were long enough to span the fissure. Honninscrave and Mistweave pushed them out over the gap: the First and Pitchwife pulled them across. When the rest of the company had passed the crack, Honninscrave and Mistweave slipped their arms into the harnesses again, and the First went on her way westward.

Now she set a slower pace, in part for caution and in part to accommodate Pitchwife's weariness. Still her speed was greater than any Covenant could have matched afoot: the ice seemed to rush jolting and skidding under the runners of the sled. But whenever she saw something she distrusted, she dropped to a walk and probed ahead with her longsword until she was sure that the ground was safe.

For the rest of the morning, her care proved unnecessary. But shortly after the company had paused for a brief meal and a few warming swallows of *diamondraught*, the point of her sword bit into the crust, and several hundred feet of packed snow along a thin line to the north and south fell from sight. This fissure also was easily crossed; but when the companions gained the far side, the First faced Honninscrave again and said, 'It is too much. This ice grows fragile beneath us.'

The Master breathed a curse through his frosted beard. Yet he did not demur when the leader of the Search turned toward the north-west and thicker ice.

* * *

911

For most of the afternoon, the floe remained flat, snow-brushed, and unreliable. From time to time, Covenant sensed that the surface was sloping upward; but the brightness of the sun on the white landscape made him unsure of what he saw. Although he sipped *diamondraught* at intervals, the cold sank deeper into his bones. His face felt like beaten metal. Gradually, he drifted into reveries of conflagration. Whenever he became drowsy with liquor and chill, he found himself half dreaming wild magic as if it were lovely and desirable – flame sufficient to tear down Kemper's Pitch; passion powerful enough to contend with the Worm of the World's End; venom capable of subsuming everything in its delirium. That fire was vital and seductive – and as necessary as blood. He would never be able to give it up.

But such dreams led him to places where he did not want to go. To the scream which had nearly torn out his heart when Linden had told him the truth of the venom and the Worm, And to that other fire which lay hidden at the roots of his need – to the *caamora* which he had always failed to find, though his soul depended on it.

Urgent with alarm, he repeatedly fought his way back from the brink of true sleep. And the last time his did so, he was surprised to see that the north was no longer blank. The First's path angled toward a ridge of tremendous ice-chunks: piled into the sky, they reached out for the horizons, east and west. Although the sun was near setting, it was far down in the south and did not blind him, but rather shone full and faintly pink on the ridge, making the ice appear as unbreachable as a glacier.

Here the First turned toward the west again, keeping as close to the base of the ridge as possible without sacrificing a clear route for the sleds. But in her way boulders and monoliths lay like menhirs where they had rolled or fallen from the violence which had riven the ice. She was forced to slow her pace again as the difficulty of the terrain increased. Nevertheless her goal had been achieved. The surface which supported that ridge was unlikely to crack or crumble under the pressure of the company's passage.

As the sun sank, vermilion and fatal, into the west, the travellers halted for the night. Pitchwife slumped to the ice and sat there with his head in his hands, too tired even to talk. Covenant and Linden climbed stiffly from their sleds and walked back and forth, rubbing their arms and stamping their feet, while Mistweave and Honninscrave made camp. Honninscrave unpacked sections of heavily-tarred canvas to use as ground-sheets, then laid more blankets. Mistweave unloaded Linden's sled until he had uncovered a large flat rectangle of stone. This he set out as a base on which to build a fire, so that melting ice would not wet the wood. To no one in particular, the First announced her estimate that the company had come more than twenty leagues. Then she fell silent.

When Mistweave had a crisp blaze going, Pitchwife struggled to his feet, rubbed the frost from his face, and went to do the cooking. As he worked, he muttered indistinctly to himself as if the sound of some voice – his own if no one else's – were necessary to his courage. Shortly, he had produced a thick stew for his companions. But still the pall of the waste hung over them, and no one spoke.

After supper, Pitchwife went to sleep almost at once, hugging his ground-sheet about him. The First sat sternly beside the fire and toyed with the faggots as though she did not want to reconsider her decisions. As determined as ever to emulate the devotion of the *Haruchai*, Mistweave joined Cail standing watch over the company. And Honninscrave stared at nothing, met no one's eyes: his orbs were hidden under the weight of his brows, and his face looked drawn and gaunt.

Linden paced tensely near the fire as if she wanted to talk to someone. But Covenant was absorbed by his visceral yearning for the heat of white flame: the effort of denial left him nothing to say. The silence became as cold and lonely as the ice. After a time, he gathered his blankets and followed Pitchwife's example, wrapping himself tightly in his ground-sheet.

He thought he would be able to sleep, if only because the cold was so persuasive. But Linden made her bed near his, and soon he felt her watching him as if she sought to fathom his isolation. When he opened his eyes, he saw the look of intention in her fire-lit face.

Her gaze was focused on him like an appeal; but the words she murmured softly took him by surprise.

'I never even learned her name.'

Covenant raised his head, blinked his incomprehension at her.

'That Giant,' she explained, 'the one who was hurt when the foremast broke.' The one she had healed with his ring. 'I never found out who she was. I've been doing that all my life. Treating people as if they were pieces of sick or damaged meat instead of actual individuals. I thought I was a doctor, but it was only the disease or the hurt I cared about. Only the fight against death. Not the person.'

He gave her the best answer he had. 'Is that bad?' He recognized the attitude she described. 'You aren't God. You can't help people because of who they are. You can only help them because they're hurt and they need you.' Deliberately, he concluded, 'Otherwise you would've let Mistweave die.'

'Covenant.' Now her tone was aimed at him as squarely as her gaze. 'At some point, you're going to have to deal with me. With who I am. We've been lovers. I've never stopped loving you. It hurts that you lied to me – that you let me believe something that wasn't true. Let me believe we had a future together. But I haven't stopped loving you.' Low flames from the campfire glistened out of the dampness in her eyes. Yet she was resolutely unemotional, sparing him her recrimination or sorrow. 'I think the only reason you loved me was because I was hurt. You loved me because of my parents. Not because of who I am.'

Abruptly, she rolled onto her back, covered her face with her hands. Need muffled the self-control of her whisper. 'Maybe that kind of love is wonderful and altruistic. I don't know. But it isn't enough.'

Covenant looked at her, at the hands clasped over her pain and the hair curling around her ear, and thought, Have to deal with you. Have to. But he could not. He did not know how. Since the loss of the One Tree, their positions had been reversed. Now it was she who knew what she wanted, he who was lost.

Above him, the stars glittered out their long bereavement. But for them also he did not know what to do.

When he awakened in the early dawn, he discovered that Honninscrave was gone.

A wind had come up. Accumulated snow gusted away over the half-buried remains of the campfire as Covenant thrashed out of his blankets and ground-sheet. The First, Pitchwife, and Linden were still asleep. Mistweave lay felled in his canvas cover as if during the night his desire to match Cail had suffered a defeat. Only Cail, the Demondim-spawn, and Findail were on their feet.

Covenant turned to Cail. 'Where – ?'

In response, Cail nodded upward.

Quickly, Covenant scanned the massive chaos of the ridge. For a moment, he missed the place Cail had indicated. But then his gaze leaped to the highest point above the camp; and there he saw Honninscrave.

The Master sat atop a small tor of ice with his back to the south and the company. The wind tumbled down off the crest into Covenant's face, bearing with it a faint smell of smoke.

Blood and damnation! Grimly, Covenant demanded, 'What in hell does he think he's doing?' But he already knew the answer. Cail's reply only confirmed it.

'Some while since, he arose and assayed the ice, promising a prompt return. With him he bore wood and a fire-pot such as the Giants use.'

Caamora. Honninscrave was trying to burn away his grief.

At the sound of Cail's voice, the First looked up from her bed, an inquiry in her eyes. Covenant found suddenly that he could not open his throat. Mutely, he directed the First's gaze up at Honninscrave.

When she saw the Master, she rasped a curse and sprang to her feet. Awakening Pitchwife with a slap of her hand, she asked Covenant and Cail how long Honninscrave had been gone.

Inflexibly, the *Haruchai* repeated what he had told Covenant.

'Stone and Sea!' she snarled as Pitchwife and then Linden arose to join her. 'Has he forgotten his own words? This north is perilous.'

Pitchwife squinted apprehensively up at Honninscrave; but his words were reassuring. 'The Master is a Giant. He is equal to the peril. And his heart has found no relief from Cable Seadreamer's end. Perchance in this way he will gain peace.'

The First glared at him. But she did not call Honninscrave down from his perch.

Eyes glazed with sleep and vision, Linden gazed up at the Master and said nothing.

Shortly, he rose to his feet. Passing beyond the crest, he found his way downward. Soon he emerged from a nearby valley and came woodenly toward the company.

His hands swung at his sides. As he neared the camp, Covenant saw that they had been scoured raw by fire.

When he reached his companions, he stopped, raised his hands before him like a gesture of a futility. His gaze was shrouded. His fingers were essentially undamaged; but the after-effects of his pain were vivid. Linden hugged her own hands under her arms in instinctive empathy.

The First's voice was uncharacteristically gentle. 'Is it well with you, Grimmand Honninscrave?'

He shook his head in simple bafflement. 'It does not suffice. Naught suffices. It burns in my breast – and will not burn out.'

Then as if the will which held him upright had broken he dropped to his knees and thrust his hands into a drift of snow. Tattered wisps of steam arose around his wrists.

Dumb with helpless concern, the Giants stood around him. Linden bit her lips. The wind drew a cold scud across the ice, and the air was sharp with rue. Covenant's eyes blurred and ran. In self-defence there were many things for which he could claim he was not culpable; but Seadreamer's death was not among them.

At last, the First spoke. 'Come, Master,' she breathed thickly. 'Arise and be about your work. We must hope or die.'

Hope or die. Kneeling on the frozen waste, Honninscrave looked like he had lost his way between those choices. But then slowly he gathered his legs under him, stretched his tall frame erect. His eyes had hardened, and his visage was rigid and ominous. For a moment, he stood still, let all the company witness the manner in which he bore himself. Then without a word he went and began to break camp.

Covenant caught a glimpse of the distress in Linden's gaze. But when she met his look of inquiry, she shook her head, unable to articulate what she had perceived in Honninscrave.

Together, they followed the Master's example.

While Honninscrave packed the canvas and bedding, Mistweave set out a cold breakfast. His red-rimmed eyes and weary demeanour held a cast of abashment: he was a Giant and had not expected Cail's endurance to be greater than his. Now he appeared determined to work harder in compensation – and in support of Honninscrave. While Covenant, Linden, and the other Giants ate, Mistweave toiled about the camp, readying everything for departure.

As Covenant and Linden settled into their sleds, bundled themselves against the mounting edge of the wind, the First addressed Honninscrave once more. She spoke softly, and the wind frayed away the sound of her voice.

'From the vantage of your *caamora*, saw you any sign?'

His new hardness made his reply sound oddly brutal:

'None.'

He and Mistweave shrugged themselves into the lines of the sleds. The First and Pitchwife went ahead. With Cail between the sleds and Vain and Findail in the rear, the company set off.

Their progress was not as swift as it had been the previous day. The increased difficulty of the terrain was complicated by the air pouring and gusting down from the ridge. Fistfuls of ice-crystals rattled against the wood of the sleds, stung the faces of the travellers. White plumes and devils danced among the company. The edges of the landscape ached in the wind. *Diamondraught* and food formed a core of sustenance within Covenant, but failed to spread any warmth into his limbs. He did not know how long he could hold out against the alluring and fatal somnolence of the cold.

The next time he rubbed the ice from his lashes and raised his head, he found that he had not held out. Half the morning was gone. Unwittingly, he had drifted into the passive stupor by which winter and leprosy snared their victims.

Linden was sitting upright in her sled. Her head shifted tensely from side to side as if she were searching. For a groggy instant, Covenant thought that she was using her senses to probe the safety of the ice. But then she wrenched forward, and her voice snapped over the waste.

'Stop!'

Echoes rode eerily back along the wind: Stop! Stop! But ice and cold changed the tone of her shout, made it sound as forlorn as a cry raised from the Soulbiter.

At once, the First turned to meet the sleds.

They halted immediately below a pile of broken ice like the rubble of a tremendous fortress reduced by siege. Megalithic blocks and shards towered and loomed as if they were leaning to fall on the company.

Linden scrambled out of her sled. Before anyone could ask her what she wanted, she coughed, 'It's getting colder.'

The First and Pitchwife glanced at each other. Covenant moved to stand beside Linden, though he did not comprehend her. After a moment, the First said, 'Colder, Chosen? We do not feel it.'

'I don't mean the winter,' Linden began at once, urgent to be understood. 'It's not the same.' Then she caught herself, straightened her shoulders. Slowly and sharply, she said, 'You don't feel it – but I tell you it's there. It's making the air colder. Not ice. Not wind. Not winter. Something else.' Her lips were blue and trembling. 'Something dangerous.'

And this north is perilous, Covenant thought dully, as if the chill made him stupid. What kind of peril? But when he opened his mouth, no words came.

Honninscrave's head jerked up. Pitchwife's eyes glared white in his misshaped face.

At the same instant, the First barked, '*Arghule!*' and sprang at Covenant and Linden.

Thrusting them towards the sleds, she shouted, 'We must flee!' Then she wheeled to scan the region.

Covenant lost his footing, skidded into Cail's grasp. The *Haruchai* flipped him unceremoniously into his sled. Linden vaulted to her place. At once, Honninscrave and Mistweave heaved the sleds forward as quickly as the slick surface allowed.

Before they had taken three strides, the ice a stone's throw ahead rose up and came toward them.

The moving shape was as wide as the height of a Giant, as thick as the reach of Covenant's arms. Short legs bore it forward with deceptive speed. Dark gaps around its edge looked like maws.

Cold radiated from it like a shout.

The First slid to a halt, planted herself in the path of the creature. '*Arghule!*' she cried again. 'Avoid!'

Pitchwife's answering yell snatched her around. His arm flailed a gesture toward the ridge. '*Arghuleh!*'

Two more creatures like the first had detached themselves from the rubble and were rushing toward the company.

In the south appeared a fourth.

Together, they emitted cold as fierce as the cruel heart of winter.

For an instant, the First froze. Her protest carried lornly across the wind. 'But the *arguleh* do not act thus.'

Abruptly, Findail melted into a hawk and flew away.

Honninscrave roared a command: 'Westward!' He was the Master of Starfare's Gem, trained for emergencies. With a wrench that threw Covenant backward, he hauled his sled into motion. 'We must break past!'

Mistweave followed. As he laboured for speed, he called over his shoulder to Linden, 'Do not fear! We are Giants, proof against cold!'

The next moment, the *arghuleh* attacked.

The creature approaching the First stopped. At Pitchwife's warning shout, she whirled to face the *arghule*. But it did not advance. Instead, it waved one of its legs.

From the arc of the gesture, the air suddenly condensed into a web of ice.

Expanding and thickening as it moved, the web sailed toward the First like a hunter's net. Before it reached her, it grew huge and heavy enough to snare even a Giant.

At the same time, the *arghule* coming from the south halted, settled itself as though it were burrowing into the waste. Then violence boomed beneath it: ice shattered in all directions. And a crack sprang through the surface, ran like lightning toward the company. In the space between one heart-beat and another, the crack became as wide as the sleds.

It passed directly under Vain. The Demondim-spawn disappeared so quickly that Covenant did not see him fall.

Instinctively, Covenant turned to look toward the other two *arghuleh*.

They were almost close enough to launch their assaults.

The sled lurched as Honninscrave accelerated. Covenant faced again toward the First.

The web of ice was dropping over her head.

Pitchwife struggled toward her. But his feet could not hold the treacherous surface. Cail sped lightly past him as if the *Haruchai* were as sure-footed as a Ranyhyn.

The First defended herself without her sword. As the web descended, she chopped at it with her left arm.

It broke in a blizzard of splinters that caught the light in instant chiaroscuro and then rattled faintly away along the wind.

But her arm came down encased by translucent ice. It covered her limb halfway to the shoulder, immobilized her elbow and hand. Fiercely, she hammered at the sheath with her right fist. But the ice clung to her like iron.

The sleds gained momentum. Nearing the First, Honninscrave and Mistweave veered to the side in an effort to bypass the *arghule*. The crack which had swallowed Vain faded toward the north. Findail was nowhere to be seen. Linden clutched the rail of her sled, a soundless cry stretched over her face.

Cail dashed past the First to challenge her assailant.

As one, she and Pitchwife shouted after him, '*No!*'

He ignored them. Straight at the creature he aimed his *Haruchai* strength.

Before he could strike, the *arghule* bobbed as if it were bowing. Instantly, a great hand of ice slapped down on him out of the empty air. It pounded him flat, snatched him under the bulk of the creature.

Covenant fought to stand in the slewing sled. Cail's fall went through him like an auger. The landscape was as white and ruined as wild magic. When his heart beat again, he was translated into fire. Power drove down through him, anchored him. Flame as hot as a furnace, as vicious as venom, cocked back his half-fist to hurl destruction at the *arghule*.

Then a web flung by one of the trailing creatures caught him. The two *arghuleh* from the north had changed direction to pursue the company; then one of them had stopped to attack. The snare did not entirely reach him. But its leading edge struck the right side of his head, licked for an instant over his shoulder, snapped on his upraised fist.

Wild magic pulverized the ice: nothing was left to encase him. But an immense force of cold slammed straight into his brain.

Instantly, paralysis locked itself around him.

He saw what was happening: every event registered on him. But he was stunned and helpless, lost in a feral chill.

While Honninscrave and Mistweave fought the sleds sideward to avoid the *arghule*, the First sprang to Cail's aid with Pitchwife behind her. The creature sought to retreat; but she moved too swiftly. Bracing itself, it repeated the bow which had captured Cail.

Her left arm was useless to her, but she ignored the handicap. Fury and need impelled her. As the *arghule* raised its ice, she put her whole body into one blow and struck the creature squarely with all the Giantish might of her good fist.

The *arghule* shattered under the impact. The boom of its destruction echoed off the towering ridge.

Amid volleying thunder, the sleds rushed past the First. She whirled to face the pursuing *arghuleh*. Pitchwife dove wildly into the remains of the creature. For an instant, he threw chunks and chips aside. Then he emerged, wearing frost and ice-powder as though even in death the *arghule* nearly had the capacity to freeze him. In his arms, he bore Cail.

From head to foot, the *Haruchai* was sheathed like the First's left arm in pure ice, bound rigid as if he were frozen past all redemption. Carrying him urgently, Pitchwife sped after the sleds.

The First snatched up a white shard, hurled it at the *arghuleh* to make them hesitate. Then she followed the company.

In response, the creatures squatted against the ice; and cracks like cries of frustration and hunger shot through the floe, gaping jaggedly after the travellers. For a moment, the First had to skid and dodge across a ground that was falling apart under her: then she missed her footing, fell and rolled out of the path of the attack. The cracks searched on for the company; but the sleds were nearly out of range.

The First regained her feet. Soon she, too, was beyond the reach of the *arghuleh*.

Covenant saw her come running up behind Pitchwife, clap him

encouragingly on the shoulder. Pitchwife panted in great raw gasps as he strove to sustain his pace. The misshaping of his back made him appear to huddle protectively over Cail. Cail's scar was unnaturally distinct, amplified by the translucence of his casing. He was the last of the *Haruchai* who had promised themselves to Covenant. And Covenant still could not break the cold which clenched his mind. All hope of fire was gone.

Linden was shouting to the First, 'We've got to stop! Cail needs help! *You* need help!'

Honninscrave and Mistweave did not slacken their pace. The First returned, 'Should the *arguleh* again draw nigh, will you perceive them?'

'Yes!' Linden shot back. 'Now that I know what they are!' Her tone was hard, certain. 'We've got to stop! I don't know how long he can stay alive like that!'

The First nodded. 'Master!' she barked. 'We must halt!'

At once, Honninscrave and Mistweave shortened their strides, let the sleds drag themselves to a standstill.

Pitchwife managed a few more steps, then stumbled to his knees in a low bowl of snow. The wind whipped flurries around him. His breathing rattled hoarsely as he hunched over Cail, hugging the *Haruchai* as if he sought to warm Cail with his own life.

Linden leaped from her sled before it stopped moving, caught her balance and hastened to Pitchwife's side. But Covenant remained frozen while Honninscrave and Mistweave drew the sleds around to Pitchwife, Cail, Linden and the First.

Vain stood there as well. Covenant had not seen the Demondim-spawn arrive, did not know how he had escaped. Bits of ice clung to his tattered apparel, but his black form was unscathed. He did not breathe, and his midnight eyes were focused on nothing.

Pitchwife set Cail down. Linden knelt beside the *Haruchai*, searched him with her eyes, then touched her fingers to his case. At once, pain hissed between her teeth. When she snatched back her hands, her fingertips left small patches of skin on the ice. Bright in the sunlight, red droplets oozed from her torn flesh. 'Damn it!' she rasped, more frightened and angry than hurt, 'that's *cold*.' Raising her head to the First, she shivered, 'You obviously know something about these *arghuleh*. Do you know how to treat this?'

In reply, the First drew her falchion. Gripping it above her head, she brought its hilt down hard on the crust which locked her left arm. The ice broke and fell away, leaving her limb free, the skin undamaged. Stiffly, she flexed her hand and wrist. A wince touched her face, but she changed it to a scowl.

'See you? We are Giants — proof against cold as against fire. Requiring no other unction, we have learned none.' Her glare suggested that she deemed this ignorance to be a kind of failure.

But Linden had no time for failure. 'We can't do that to him,' she muttered, thinking aloud. 'We'd break half his bones.' She peered closely at Cail to confirm her perceptions. 'He's still alive — but he won't last long.' Red-tipped, her fingers moved as if she had already forgotten their hurt. 'We need fire.'

Then she looked toward Covenant.

At the sight of him, her eyes went wide with shock and fear. She had not realized that he had been hit by the cold of the *arghuleh*.

It felt like a numb nail driven through the side of his head, impaling his mind painlessly. And it was slowly working its way deeper. His left eye had gone blind: most of the nerves of his left side were as dead as leprosy. He wanted to cry out for help, but no longer knew how.

From out of nowhere, Findail appeared. Regaining his abused human shape, he placed himself at the fringes of the company and fixed his attention on Linden.

Ice muffled whatever she was saying. Covenant could not bear it: he did not want to die like this. Mad protests surged through him. All winter was his enemy: every league and ridge of the floe was an attack against him. From the pit of his dismay, he brought up flame and venom as if he meant to rid the Earth of all cold forever, tear Time from its foundations in order to shear away the gelid death which locked his brain.

But then there was another presence in him. It was alien and severe, desperate with alarm — and yet he found it strangely comforting. He struggled instinctively when it took his flame from him; but the cold and his impercipience made his strivings pointless. And the intrusion — an external identity which somehow inhabited his mind as if he had let down all his defences — gave him warmth in return: the warmth of its own strict desire for him and the heat of his fire combined. For a moment, he thought he knew that other presence, recognized it intimately. Then the world turned into white magic and passion; and the cold fled.

A few heart-beats later, his eyes squeezed back into focus, and he found himself on his hands and knees. Linden had withdrawn from him, leaving behind an ache of absence as though she had opened a door which enabled him to see how empty his heart was without her. Dull bereavement throbbed in his right forearm; but his ring still hung on the last finger of his halfhand. The wind sent chills ruffling through his clothes: the sun shone as if the desecration of the Sunbane would never be healed. He had failed again. And proved once more that she —

This time she had simply reached into him and taken possession.

There was no difference between that and what Lord Foul had done to Joan. What he was doing to the Land. No difference except the difference between Linden herself and the Despiser. And

921

Gibbon-Raver had promised that she would destroy the Earth.

She had the power to fulfil that prophecy now. She could take it whenever she wanted it.

Urgent grief came over him – grief for both of them, for himself in his doomed inefficacy, for her in her dire plight. He feared he would weep aloud. But then the wind's flat rush was punctuated by hoarse, hard breathing; and that sound restored his awareness of his companions.

The ice which had held the *Haruchai* was gone, and Cail was coming back to life the hard way – fighting for every breath, wresting each inhalation with bared teeth from the near-death of cold. Even the *merewives* had not so nearly slain him. But Linden had restored him to the verge of survival. As Covenant watched, Cail carried himself the rest of the distance.

Honninscrave, Mistweave, and the First studied Cail and Linden and Covenant with concern and appreciation mixed together in their faces. Pitchwife had mastered his own gasping enough to grin like a grimace. But Linden had eyes only for Covenant.

She was wan with dismay at what she had done. From the first, her loathing for possession had been greater than his; yet the necessity of it was thrust upon her time and again. She was forced to evil by the fundamental commitments which had made her a physician. And how was she forced? he asked himself. By her lack of power. If she were given his ring, as the *Elohim* desired, she would be saved the peril of this damnation.

He could not do it. Anything else: he would do anything else. But not this. More than once, she had challenged his protective instincts, protested his desire to spare her. But how could he have explained that everything else – every other attempt at protection or preservation – was nothing more than an effort to pay for this one refusal? To give her something in compensation for what he would not give.

Now he did it again. Ice-gnawed and frost-burned though he was – leprous, poisoned, and beaten – he wrenched his courage to its feet and faced her squarely. Swallowing grief, he said thickly, 'I hope I didn't hurt anybody.'

It was not much. But for the time being it was enough. Her distress softened as if he had made a gesture of forgiveness. A crooked smile took the severity from her lips. Blinking at sudden tears, she murmured, 'You're hard to handle. The first time I saw you' – he remembered the moment as well as she did: he had slammed his door in her face – 'I knew you were going to give me trouble.'

The love in her voice made him groan because he could not go to her and put his arms around her. Not as long as he refused to make the one sacrifice she truly needed.

At her back, Mistweave had unpacked a pouch of *diamondraught*. When he handed it to her, she forced her attention away from Covenant and knelt to Cail. Between heaving respirations, the *Haruchai* took several sips of the tonic liquor.

After that his condition improved rapidly. While his companions shared the pouch, he recovered enough strength to sit up, then to regain his feet. In spite of its flatness, his expression seemed oddly abashed: his pride did not know how to sustain the fact of defeat. But after his experience with the seduction of the *merewives*, he appeared to place less importance on his self-esteem. Or perhaps Brinn's promise – that Cail would eventually be free to follow his heart – had somehow altered the characteristic *Haruchai* determination to succeed or die. In a moment, Cail's visage was as devoid of inflection as ever. When he indicated that he was ready to travel again, his word carried conviction.

No one demurred. At a wry glance from Pitchwife, however, the First announced that the company would eat a meal before going on. Cail appeared to think that such a delay was unnecessary; yet he accepted the opportunity for more rest.

While the companions ate, Linden remained tense: she consumed her rations as if she were chewing fears and speculations, trying to find her way through them. But when she spoke, her question showed that she had found, not an answer, but a distraction. She asked the First, 'How much do you know about those *arghuleh*?'

'Our knowledge is scant,' replied the Swordmain. She seemed unsure of the direction of Linden's inquiry. 'Upon rare occasion, Giants have encountered *arghuleh*. And there are tales which concern them. But together such stories and encounters yield little.'

'Then why did you risk it?' Linden pursued. 'Why did we come this far north?'

Now the First understood. 'Mayhap I erred,' she said in an uncompromising tone. 'The southern ice was uncertain, and I sought safer passage. The hazard of the *arghuleh* I accepted because we are Giants, not readily slain or harmed by cold. It was my thought that four Giants would suffice to ward you.

'Moreover,' she went on more harshly, 'I was misled in my knowledge.

'Folly,' she muttered to herself. 'Knowledge is chimera, for beyond it ever lies other knowledge, and the incompleteness of what is known renders the knowing false. It was our knowledge that *arghuleh* do not act thus.

'They are savage creatures, as dire of hate as the winter in which they thrive. And their hate is not solely for the beasts and beings of blood and warmth which form their prey. It is also for their own kind. In the tales we have heard and the experience of our people,

923

it is plain that the surest defence against the assault of one *arghule* is the assault of a second, for they will prefer each other's deaths above any other.

'Therefore,' the First growled, 'did I believe this north to be the lesser peril. Against any *arghule* four Giants must surely be counted a sufficient company. I did not know,' she concluded, 'that despite all likelihood and nature they had set aside their confirmed animosity to act in concert.'

Linden stared across the waste. Honninscrave watched the knot of his hands as if he feared it would not hold. After a moment, Covenant cleared his throat and asked, 'Why?' In the Land, the Law of nature was being steadily corrupted by the Sunbane. Had Lord Foul's influence reached this far? 'Why would they change?'

'I know not,' the First said sourly. 'I would have believed the substance of Stone and Sea to be more easily altered than the hate of the *arghuleh*.'

Covenant groaned inwardly. He was still hundreds of leagues from Revelstone; and yet his fears were harrying him forward as if he and his companions had already entered the ambit of the Despiser's malice.

Abruptly, Linden leapt to her feet, faced the east. She gauged the distance, then rasped, 'They're coming. I thought they'd give up. Apparently co-operation isn't the only new trick they've learned.'

Honninscrave spat a Giantish obscenity. The First gestured him and Mistweave toward the sleds, then helped Pitchwife upright. Quickly, the Master and Mistweave packed and reloaded the supplies. Covenant was cursing to himself. He wanted a chance to talk to Linden privately. But he followed her tense example, and climbed back into his sled.

The First took the lead. In an effort to outdistance the pursuit, she set the best pace Pitchwife could maintain, pushing him to his already-worn limits. Yet Cail trotted between Covenant and Linden as if he were fully recovered.

Vain and Findail brought up the rear together, shadowing each other across the wind-cut wilderness.

That night, the company obtained little rest, though Pitchwife needed it urgently. Shortly after moonrise, Cail's native caution impelled him to rouse Linden; and when she had tasted the air, she sent the company scrambling for the sleds.

The moon was only three days past its full, and the sky remained clear: the First was able to find a path with relative ease. But she was held back by Pitchwife's exhaustion. He could not move faster than a walk without her support. And in an effort to shore up his strength, he had consumed so much *diamondraught* that he was not entirely sober. At intervals, he began to sing lugubriously under his breath, as though he were lunatic with fatigue. Somehow, the companions kept a safe distance between themselves and the *arghuleh*. But they were unable to increase their lead.

And when the sun rose over the wasted ice, they found themselves in worse trouble. They were coming to the end of the floe. During the night, they had entered a region where the ice to the south became progressively more broken as hunks snapped off and drifted away. Ahead of the First, the west became impassable. And beyond a wide area where icebergs were being spawned lay open water. She had no choice but to force her way up into the ragged ridge which separated the arctic glacier from the crumbling sheet of the floe.

There Covenant thought that she would abandon the sleds. He and Linden climbed out to make their way on foot; but that did not sufficiently lighten the loads Honninscrave and Mistweave were pulling. Yet none of the Giants faltered. Forging into a narrow valley which breached the ridge, they began to struggle toward the north and west as if in spite of the exhaustion they now shared with Pitchwife they had not begun to be daunted. Covenant marvelled at their hardiness; but he could do nothing to help them except strive to follow without needing help himself.

That task threatened to surpass him. Cold and lack of sleep sapped his strength. His numb feet were as clumsy as cripples. Several times, he had to catch himself on a sled so that he would not fall back down the valley. But Honninscrave or Mistweave bore the added burden without complaint until Covenant could regain his footing.

For some distance, the First's route seemed inspired or fortuitous. As the valley rose into the glacier, bending crookedly back and forth between north and west, its bottom remained passable. The companions were able to keep moving.

Then they gained the upper face of the glacier and their path grew easier. Here the ice was as rugged as a battleground – pressure-splintered and wind-tooled into high fantastic shapes, riddled with fissures, marked by strange channels and hollows of erosion – and the company had to wend still farther north to find a path. Yet with care, the First was able to pick a passage which did not require much strength. And as the companions left the area of the glacier's rim, they were able to head once again almost directly westward.

Giddy with weariness and cold and the ice-glare of the sun, Covenant stumbled on after the sleds. A pace or two to his side, Linden was in little better condition. *Diamondraught* and exertion could not keep the faint, fatal hint of blue from her lips; and her face looked as pallid as bone. But her clenched alertness and the stubborn thrust of her strides showed that she was not yet ready to fall.

For more than a league, with the air rasping his lungs and fear at his back, Covenant followed the lead of the Giants. Somehow, he did not collapse.

But then everything changed. The First's route was neither inspired nor fortuitous: it was impossible. Balanced unsteadily on locked knees, his heart trembling, Covenant looked out from the edge of the cliff where the company had stopped. There was nothing below him but the bare, black Sea.

Without forewarning, the company had reached the western edge of the glacier.

Off to the left was the jagged ridge which separated the main ice-mass from the lower floe. But elsewhere lay nothing but the endless north and the cliff and the grue-bitten Sea.

Covenant did not know how to bear it. Vertigo blew up at him like a wind from the precipice, and his knees folded.

Pitchwife caught him. 'No,' the deformed Giant coughed. His voice seemed to snag and strangle deep in his throat. 'Do not despair. Has this winter made you blind?' Rough with fatigue, he jerked Covenant upright. 'Look before you. It needs not the eyes of a Giant to behold this hope.'

Hope, Covenant sighed into the silence of his whirling head. Ah, God. I'd hope if I knew how.

But Pitchwife's stiff grasp compelled him. Groping for balance, he opened his eyes to the cold.

For a moment, they would not focus. But then he found the will to force his gaze clear.

There he saw it: distinct and unattainable across half a league of the fatal Sea, a thin strip of land.

It stretched out of sight to north and south.

'As I have said,' Honninscrave muttered, 'our charts hold no certain knowledge of this region. But mayhap it is the coast of the Land which lies before us.'

Something like a madman's laughter rose in Covenant's chest. 'Well, good for us.' The Despiser would certainly be laughing. 'At least now we can look at where we want to go while we're freezing to death or being eaten by *arghuleh*.' He held the mirth back because he feared it would turn to weeping.

'Covenant!' Linden said sharply — a protest of empathy or apprehension.

He did not look at her. He did not look at any of them. He hardly listened to himself. 'Do you call this hope?'

'We are Giants,' the First responded. Her voice held an odd note of brisk purpose. 'Dire though this strait appears, we will wrest life from it.'

Mutely, Honninscrave stripped off his sark, packed it into one of the bundles on his sled. Mistweave dug out a long coil of heavy rope, then followed the Master's example.

Covenant stared at them. Linden panted, 'Do you mean – ?' Her eyes flared wildly. 'We won't last eight seconds in water that cold!'

The First cast a gauging look down the cliff. As she studied the drop, she responded, 'Then our care must suffice to ward you.'

Abruptly, she turned back to the company. Indicating Honninscrave's sled, she asked Cail, 'Does this weight and the Giantfriend's surpass your strength?'

Cail's flat mien suggested disdain for the question as he shook his head.

'The ice affords scant footing,' she warned.

He regarded her expressionlessly. 'I will be secure.'

She gave him a firm nod. She had learned to trust the *Haruchai*. Returning to the rim, she said, 'Then let us not delay. The *arghuleh* must not come upon us here.'

A prescient nausea knotting his guts, Covenant watched Honninscrave tie one end of the rope to the rear of his sled. The Giant's bare back and shoulders steamed in the sharp air, but he did not appear to feel the cold.

Before Covenant could try to stop her, the First sat down on the edge, braced herself, and dropped out of sight. Linden's gasp followed her away.

Fighting dizziness, he crouched on the ice and crept forward until he could look downward.

He arrived in time to see the First hit heavily into the sea. For an instant, white froth marked the water as if she were gone for good: then she splashed back to the surface, waved a salute up at the company.

Now he noticed that the cliff was not sheer. Though it was too smooth to be climbed, it angled slightly outward from rim to base. And it was no more than two hundred feet high. Honninscrave's rope looked long enough to reach the water.

From the edge, Pitchwife grimaced down as his wife. 'Desire me good fortune,' he murmured. Weariness ached in his tone. 'I am ill made for such valours.' Yet he did not falter. In a moment, he was at the First's side, and she held him strongly above the surface.

No one spoke. Covenant locked his teeth as if any word might unleash the panic crowding through him. Linden hugged herself and stared at nothing. Honninscrave and Mistweave were busy lashing their supplies more securely to the sleds. When they were done, the Master went straight to the cliff; but Mistweave paused beside Linden to reassure her. Gently, he touched her shoulder, smiled like a reminder of the way she had saved his life. Then he followed Honninscrave.

Covenant and Linden were left on the glacier with Cail, Vain, and the Appointed.

Gripping the rope, Cail nodded Covenant toward the sled.

Covenant groaned. Vertigo squirmed through him. What if his hold failed? And what made the Giants think these sleds would float? But he had no choice. The *arghuleh* must be drawing nearer. And he had to reach the Land somehow, had to get to Revelstone. There was no other way. The Giants had already committed themselves. For a moment, he turned toward Linden. But she had drawn down into herself, was striving to master her own trepidation.

Woodenly, he climbed into the sled.

As Covenant settled himself, tried to seal his numb fingers to the rails, brace his legs among the bundles, Cail looped his rope around Vain's ankles. Then he knotted the heavy line in both fists and set his back to the sled, began pushing it toward the cliff.

When the sled nosed over the edge, Linden panted, 'Hold on,' as though she had just noticed what was happening. Covenant bit down on the inside of his cheek so hard that blood smeared his lips, stained the frost in his beard.

Slowly, Cail let the weight at the end of the rope pull him toward Vain again.

Vain had not moved a muscle: he seemed oblivious to the line hauling across the backs of his ankles. Reaching the Demondim-spawn, Cail stopped himself against Vain's black shins.

Without a tremor, the *Haruchai* lowered Covenant and the sled hand over hand down the face of the cliff.

Covenant chewed blood for a moment to control his fear; but soon the worst was over. His dizziness receded. Wedged among the supplies, he was in no danger of falling. Cail paid out the line with steady care. The rope cut small chunks out of the lip of the cliff; but Covenant hardly felt them hit. A shout of encouragement rose from Pitchwife. The dark Sea looked as viscid as a malign chrism, but the four Giants swam in it as if it were only water. Pitchwife needed the First's support, but Honninscrave and Mistweave sculled themselves easily.

Honninscrave had placed himself in the path of the sled.

As its tip entered the water, he dodged below it and took the runners onto his shoulders. Rocking while he groped for a point of balance, the sled gradually became level. Then he steadied the runners, and Covenant found that the Master was carrying him.

Mistweave untied the rope so that Cail could draw it back up. Then Honninscrave started away from the wall of ice. The First said something to Covenant, but the lapping of the low waves muffled her voice.

Covenant hardly dared turn his head for fear of upsetting Honninscrave's balance: but peripherally he watched Linden's descent. The thought that Vain might move hurt his chest. He felt faint with relief as the second sled came safely onto Mistweave's shoulders.

At a shout from the First, Cail dropped the rope, then slid down the ice-face to join the company.

Instinctively, Covenant fixed his attention like yearning on the low line of shore half a league away. The distance seemed too great. He did not know where Honninscrave and Mistweave would get the strength to bear the sleds so far. At any moment, the frigid hunger of the Sea would surely drag them down.

Yet they struggled onward, though that crossing appeared cruel and interminable beyond endurance. The First upheld Pitchwife and did not weaken. Cail swam between the sleds, steadied them whenever Honninscrave or Mistweave wavered. If the seas had risen against them, they would have died. But the water and the current remained indifferent, too cold to notice such stark effrontery. In the name of the Search and Covenant Giantfriend and Linden Avery the Chosen, the Giants endured.

And they prevailed.

That night, the company camped on the hard shingle of the shore as if it were a haven.

6

WINTER IN COMBAT

For the first time since he had left the galley of Starfare's Gem, Covenant thought his bones might thaw. On this coast, the warmer currents which kept the Sea free of ice moderated the winter's severity. The shingle was hard but not glacial. Clouds muffled the heavens, obscuring the lonely chill of the stars. Mistweave's fire – tended by Cail because all the Giants were too weary to fend off sleep – spread a benison around the camp. Wrapped in his blankets, Covenant slept as if he were at peace. And when he began to awaken in the stiff gloom of the northern dawn, he would have been content to simply eat a meal and then go back to sleep. The company deserved at least one day of rest. The Giants had a right to it.

But as the dawn brightened, he forgot about rest. The sunrise was hidden behind ranks of clouds, but it gave enough light to reveal the broad mass of the glacier the company had left behind. For a moment, the grey air made him uncertain of what he was seeing. Then he became sure.

In the water, a spit of ice was growing out from the cliff – from

929

the same point at which the quest had left the glacier. It was wide enough to be solid. And it was aimed like a spear at the company's camp.

With an inward groan, he called the First. She joined him, stood staring out at the ice for a long moment. Uselessly, he hoped that her Giantish sight would contradict his unspoken explanation. But it did not. 'It appears,' she said slowly, 'that the *arghuleh* remain intent upon us.'

Damnation! Splinters of ice stuck in Covenant's memory. Harshly, he asked, 'How much time have we got?'

'I know not when they commenced this span,' she replied. 'To gauge their speed is difficult. But I will be surprised to behold them gain this shore ere the morrow.'

He went on cursing for a while. But anger was as pointless as hope. None of the companions objected as they repacked the sleds for departure: the necessity was obvious. Linden looked worn by the continuing strain of this journey, uncertain of her courage. But the Giants had shed the worst of their exhaustion. The light of attention and humour in Pitchwife's eyes showed that he had begun to recover his essential spirit. In spite of his repeated failures to match Cail, Mistweave bore himself with an air of pride, as if he were looking forward to the songs his people would sing about the feats of the company. And the Master appeared to welcome the prospect of the trek ahead as an anodyne for the immedicable gall of his thoughts.

Covenant did not know how Vain and Findail had crossed the water. But Vain's black blankness and the *Elohim's* Appointed pain remained unaltered, dismissing the need for any explanation.

The company was still intact as it left the shore, and started south-west up the low sloping shingle to the uneven line of hills which edged the coast.

While the ground remained bare, Covenant and Linden walked beside Cail and the sleds. Though he was not in good shape, Covenant was glad for the chance to carry his own weight without having to fight the terrain. And he wanted to talk to Linden: he hoped she would tell him how she was doing. He had no ability to evaluate her condition for himself.

But beyond the hills lay a long, low plain; and there heavy snow began to fall. In moments, it obscured the horizons, wrapped isolation around the travellers, collected quickly at their feet: soon it was thick enough to bear the sleds. The First urged Covenant and Linden to ride so that she would be free to amend her pace. Aided by her keen eyesight and her instinctive sense of terrain, she led her companions through the thick snowfall as if the way were familiar to her.

Toward midafternoon, the snow stopped, leaving the travellers alone in a featureless white expanse. Again, the First increased her pace, thrusting herself through the drifts at a speed which no other people could have matched afoot. Only the Ranyhyn – Covenant mused. Only the Ranyhyn could have borne him with comparable alacrity to meet his doom. But the thought of the great horses gave him a pang. He remembered them as beasts of beautiful fidelity, one of the treasures of the Land. But they had been forced to flee the malison of the Sunbane. Perhaps they would never return. They might never get the chance.

That possibility brought him back to anger, reminded him that he was on his way to put an end to the Clave and the Banefire which served the Sunbane. He began to think about his purpose more clearly. He could not hope to take Revelstone by surprise: Lord Foul surely knew that the Unbeliever would come back to the Land, counted on Covenant's return for the fulfilment of his designs. But it was possible that neither the Despiser nor his Ravers understood how much damage Covenant intended to do along the way to his last crisis.

That had been Linden's idea. *Stop the Clave. Put out the Banefire. Some infections have to be cut out.* But he accepted it now, accepted it deep in the venom and marrow of his power. It gave him a use for his anger. And it offered him a chance to make the arduous and unfaltering service of the Giants mean something.

When he thought about such things, his right forearm itched avidly, and darkness rose in his gorge. For the first time since he had agreed to make the attempt, he was eager to reach Revelstone.

Two days later, the company still had not come to the end of the snow-cloaked plain.

Neither Linden's health-sense nor the Giants' sight had caught any glimpse of the *arghuleh*. Yet none of the companions doubted that they were being hunted. A nameless foreboding seemed to harry the sleds. Perhaps it arose from the sheer wide desolation of the plain, empty and barren. Or perhaps the whole company was infected by the rawness of Linden's nerves. She studied the winter – scented the air, scrutinized the clouds, tasted the snow – as though it had been given birth by strange forces, some of them unnatural; and yet she could not put words to the uneasiness of what she perceived. Somewhere in this wasteland, an obscure disaster fore-gathered. But she had no idea what it was.

The next day, however, mountains became visible to the east and south. And the day after that, the company rose up out of the plain, winding through low, rumpled foothills and valleys toward the ice-gnawed heights above them.

This range was not especially tall or harsh. Its peaks were old, and millennia of winter had worn them down. By sunset, the companions had gained a thousand feet of elevation, and the foothills and the plain were hidden behind them.

The following day, they were slowed to a crawl. While Covenant and Linden struggled through the snow on foot, the company worked from side to side up a rough, steep slope which disappeared into the gravid clouds and seemed to go on without end. But that ascent gave them another two thousand feet of altitude; and when it was over, they found themselves in a region which resembled rolling hills rather than true mountains. Time and cold had crumbled the crests which had once dominated this land: erosion had filled in the valleys. The First let the company camp early that night; but the next morning she was brisk with hope for good progress.

'Unless we're completely lost,' Covenant announced, 'this should be the Northron Climbs.' The simple familiarity of that name lifted his heart: he hardly dared believe he was right. 'If it is, then eventually we're going to hit Landsdrop.' Running generally north-westward through the Northron Climbs, the great cliff of Landsdrop formed the boundary between the Lower Land and the Upper.

But it also marked the border of the Sunbane; for the Sunbane arose and went west across the Upper Land from Lord Foul's covert in the depths of Mount Thunder, which straddled the mid-point of Landsdrop. When the company reached the cliff, they would cross back into the Despiser's power. Unless the Sunbane had not yet spread so far north.

However, Linden was not listening to Covenant. Her eyes studied the west as if she were obsessed with thoughts of disaster. Her voice conveyed an odd echo of memory as she murmured, 'It's getting colder.'

He felt a pang of fear. 'It's the elevation,' he argued. 'We're a lot higher up than we were.'

'Maybe.' She seemed deaf to his apprehension. 'I can't tell.' She ran her fingers through her hair, tried to shake her perceptions into some semblance of clarity. 'We're too far south for so much winter.'

Remembering the way Lord Foul had once imposed winter on the Land in defiance of all natural Law, Covenant gritted his teeth and thought about fire.

For Linden was right: even his truncated senses could not mistake the deepening chill. Though there was no wind, the temperature seemed to plummet around him. During the course of the day, the snow became crusted and glazed. The air had a whetted edge that cut at his lungs. Whenever snow fell, it came down like thrown sand.

Once the surface had hardened enough to bear the Giants, their work became easier: they no longer needed to force a path through the thigh-deep freeze. As a consequence, their pace improved markedly. Yet the cold was bitter and penetrating. Covenant felt brittle with frost and incapacity, caught between ice and fire. When the company stopped for the night, he found that his blankets had frozen about him like cerements. He had to squirm out of them as if he were emerging from a cocoon in which nothing had been transformed.

Pitchwife gave him a wry grin. 'You are well protected, Giant-friend.' The words came in gouts of steam as if the very sound of his voice had begun to freeze. 'Ice itself is also a ward from the cold.'

But Covenant was looking at Linden. Her visage was raw, and her lips trembled. 'It's not possible,' she said faintly. 'There can't be that many of them in the whole world.'

No one had to ask her what she meant. After a moment, the First breathed, 'Is your perception of them certain, Chosen?'

Linden nodded. The corners of her eyes were marked with frost. 'They're bringing this winter down with them.'

In spite of the fire Mistweave built, Covenant felt that his heart itself was freezing.

After that, the weather became too cold for snow. For a day and a night, heavily-laden clouds glowered overhead, clogging the sky and the horizons. And then the sky turned clear. The sleds bounced and slewed over the frozen surface as though it were a new form of granite.

The First and Pitchwife no longer led the company. Instead, they ranged away to the north to watch for *arghuleh*. The previous night, she had suggested that they turn southward in order to flee the peril. But Covenant had refused. His imprecise knowledge of the Land's geography indicated that if the company went south they might not be able to avoid Sarangrave Flat. So the travellers continued toward Revelstone; and the First and Pitchwife kept what watch they could.

Shortly after noon, with the sun glaring balefully off the packed white landscape and the still air as keen as a scourge, the company entered a region where ragged heads and splintered torsos of rock thrust thickly through the snow-pack, raising their white-crowned caps and bitter sides like menhirs in all directions. Honninscrave and Mistweave had to pick a twisting way between the cromlechs, some of which stood within a Giant's arm-span of each other; and the First and Pitchwife were forced to draw closer to the company so that they would not lose sight of the sleds.

Among the companions, Linden sat as tense as a scream and muttered over and over again, 'They're here. Jesus God. They're here.'

But when the attack came, they had no warning of it. Linden's senses were foundering, overwhelmed by the sheer numbers and intensity of the cold: she was unable to pick specific dangers out of the general peril. And Pitchwife and the First were watching the north. The assault came from the south.

The company had entered a region which the *arghuleh* already controlled.

Honninscrave and Mistweave were striding through the centre of a rude ring of tall stones, Mistweave on the Master's left, when two low hillocks across the circle rose to their feet. Maws clacking hungrily, the creatures shot forward a short distance, then stopped. One spun an instant web of ice which sprang at Mistweave's head: the other waited to give pursuit when the companions broke and ran.

Covenant's shout and Honninscrave's call rang out together. Impossibly sure-footed on the iced snow, Mistweave and the Master leaped into a sprint. The jerk threw Covenant back in the sled. He grappled for the left railing, fought to pull himself upright. The First's answer echoed back; but she and Pitchwife were out of reach beyond the menhirs.

Then Linden's sled crashed against Covenant's. The impact almost pitched him out onto the snow.

Mistweave's burst of speed had taken him out from under the ice-web. But Linden was directly in its path. Heaving on the ropes, he tried to swing her aside. But Covenant's sled was in the way.

The next instant, the net came down on the lines and front of Linden's sled. Immediately, it froze. The lines became ice. When Mistweave hauled on them again, they snapped like icicles. Linden's head cracked forward, and she crumpled.

Cail had been between the sleds in his accustomed position. As the Giants had started into a run, he had run also, keeping himself between Covenant and the *arghuleh*. So even his *Haruchai* reflexes had not been enough to protect him as Mistweave had slewed Linden's sled to the side. Leaping to avoid the collision, he had come down squarely under the web.

His speed saved him from the full grasp of that ice. But the net caught his left arm, binding him by the elbow to the sled.

Honninscrave had already pulled Covenant past Linden. Covenant had no time to shout for the Master to stop: the *arghule* was poised to launch another web. Venom seemed to slam through his forearm. With wild magic clenched in his half-fist, he swung to hurl power in Linden's defence.

In that instant, another *arghule* leaped from atop the nearest boulder and landed on Honninscrave. It bore him to the ground, buried him under sudden ice. Covenant's sled overturned. He sprawled to the crust practically within reach of the beast.

But his fear was fixed on Linden: he hardly comprehended his own peril. His head reeled. Shedding frost and snow in a flurry like a small explosion, a precursor of the blast within him, he surged to his feet.

Stark and lorn against the bare white, she still sat in her trapped sled. She was not moving: the rapacious cold of the *arghuleh* overloaded her nerves, cast her back into her atavistic, immobilizing panic. For an instant, she bore no resemblance to the woman he had learned to love. Rather, she looked like Joan. At once, the inextricable venom/passion of his power thronged through him, and he became ready to tear down the very cromlechs and rive the whole region if necessary to protect her.

But Mistweave was in his way.

The Giant had not moved from the spot where he had stumbled to a halt. His head jerked from side to side as his attention snapped frantically between Linden's plight and Honninscrave's. Linden had once saved his life: he had left Starfare's Gem to take Cail's place at her side. Yet Honninscrave was the Master. Caught between irreconcilable exigencies, Mistweave could not choose. Helplessly, he blocked Covenant from the *arghuleh* behind him.

'Move!' Fury and cold ripped the cry from Covenant's throat.

But Mistweave was aware of nothing except the choice he was unable to make. He did not move.

Over his right shoulder arced a second web. Gaining size and thickness as it sailed, it spread toward Linden. Its chill left a trail of frost across Covenant's sight.

Cail had not been able to free his left arm. But he saw the net coming like all the failures of the *Haruchai* – Hergrom's slaughter and Ceer's death and the siren-song of the *merewives* encapsulated in one peril – and he drew himself up as though he were the last of his people left alive, the last man sworn to succeed or die. His thews bunched, strained, stood out like bone – and his arm broke loose, still encased in a hunk of ice as big as a Giant's head.

Swinging that chunk like a mace, he leaped above Linden and shattered the web before it reached her.

She gaped through the spray of splinters as if she had gone blind.

Before Covenant could react, the second *arghule* behind Mistweave reared up and ripped the Giant down under its frigid bulk.

Then the First landed like the plunge of a hawk on the beast holding Honninscrave. Pitchwife dashed around one of the boulders toward Linden and Cail. And Covenant let out a tearing howl of power that blasted the first *arghule* to pieces in one sharp bolt like a rave of lightning.

From somewhere nearby, Findail gave a thin cry: 'Fool!'

Over her shoulder, the Swordmain panted, 'We are hunted!' Hammering and heaving at the ice, she fought to pull Honninscrave free. 'The *arghuleh* are many! A great many!' Honninscrave lay among the ruins of the beast as if it had succeeded in smothering him. But as the First manhandled him upright, a harsh shudder ran through him. All at once, he took his own weight, staggered to his feet.

'We must flee!' she cried.

Covenant was too far gone to heed her. Linden was safe, at least momentarily: Pitchwife had already snapped the ice from Cail's arm; and the two of them could ward her for a little while. Tall and bright with fire, he stalked toward the beast still struggling to subdue Mistweave. Whatever force or change had overcome the native hate of the *arghuleh* had also left them blind to fear or self-preservation. The creature did not cease its attack on Mistweave until Covenant burned its life to water.

In his passion, he wanted to turn and shout until the menhirs trembled, Come on! Come and get me! The scars on his forearm shone like fangs. I'll kill you all! They had dared to assail Linden.

But she had come back to herself now, had found her way out of her old paralysis. She was running toward him; and she was saying, crying, 'No! That's enough! You've done enough. Don't let go!'

He tried to hear her. Her face was sharp with urgency; and she came toward him as if she meant to throw herself into his arms. He had to hear her. There was too much at stake.

But he could not. Behind her were more *arghuleh*.

Pitchwife had rushed to help Mistweave. Cail was at Linden's side. Fighting to draw the sleds after them, the First and a dazed Honninscrave scrambled to form a cordon around Covenant and Linden. Findail had disappeared. Only Vain stood motionless.

And from every side at once charged the vicious ice-beasts, crowding between the monoliths, a score of them, two score, as if each of them wanted to be the first to feast on warm flesh. As if they had come in answer to Covenant's call. Enough of them to devour even Giants. Without wild magic, none of the company except Vain had any chance to survive.

Something like an avid chuckle spattered across the background of Covenant's mind. In his own way, he was hungry for violence, fervid for a chance to stuff his helplessness back down the Despiser's throat. Thrusting Linden behind him, he went out to meet his attackers.

His companions did not protest. They had no other hope.

Bastards! he panted at the *arghuleh*. They were all around him, but he could barely see them: his brain had gone black with venom. Come and get me!

Abruptly, the First shouted something — a call of warning or surprise. Covenant did not hear the words; but the iron in her voice made him turn to see what she had seen.

Then plain shock stopped him.

From the south side of the ring, grey shapes smaller than he was appeared among the *arghuleh*. They were roughly human in form, although their arms and legs were oddly proportioned. But their unclad bodies were hairless: their pointed ears sat high on the sides of their bald skulls. And they had no eyes. Wide flat nostrils marked their faces above their slitted mouths.

Barking in a strange tongue, they danced swiftly around the *arghuleh*. Each of them carried a short, slim piece of black metal like a wand which splashed a vitriolic fluid at the ice-beasts.

That liquid threw the *arghuleh* into confusion. It burned them, broke sections off their backs, chewed down into their bodies. Clattering in pain, they forgot their prey, thrashed and writhed blindly in all directions. Some of them collided with the cromlechs, lost larger sections of themselves, died. But others, reacting with desperate instinct, covered themselves with their own ice and were able to staunch their wounds.

Softly, as though at last even he had become capable of surprise, Cail murmured, 'Waynhim. The old tellers speak of such creatures.'

Covenant recognized them. Like the ur-viles, they were the artificial creations of the Demondim. But they had dedicated themselves and their weird lore to pursuits which did not serve the Despiser. During Covenant's trek toward Revelstone, a band of Waynhim had saved him from a venom-relapse and death. But that had occurred hundreds of leagues to the south.

Swiftly, the creatures girdled the company, dashing the fluid of their power at the *arghuleh*.

Then Covenant heard his name called by an unexpected voice. Turning, he saw a man emerge between the southward rocks. 'Thomas Covenant!' the man shouted once more. 'Come! Flee! We are unready for this battle!'

A man whose soft brown eyes, human face, and loss-learned kindness had once given Covenant a taste of both mercy and hope. A man who had been rescued by the Waynhim when the na-Mhoram's *Grim* had destroyed his home, During Stonedown. A man who served these creatures and understood them and loved them.

Hamako.

Covenant tried to shout, run forward. But he failed. The first instant of recognition was followed by a hot rush of pain as the implications of this encounter reached him. There was no reason why Hamako and this Waynhim *rhysh* should be so far from home — no reason which was not terrible.

But the plight of the company demanded speed, decision. More *arghuleh* were arriving from the north. And more of those which had been damaged were discovering the expedient of using their ice to heal themselves. When Cail caught him by the arm, Covenant allowed himself to be impelled toward Hamako.

Linden trotted at his side. Her face was set with purpose now. Perhaps she had identified Hamako and the Waynhim from Covenant's descriptions of them. Or perhaps her percipience told her all she needed to know. When Covenant seemed to lag, she grasped his other arm and helped Cail draw him forward.

The Giants followed, pulling the sleds. Vain broke into a run to catch up with the company. Behind them, the Waynhim retreated from the greater numbers of the *arghuleh*.

In a moment, they reached Hamako. He greeted Covenant with a quick smile. 'Well met, ring-wielder,' he said. 'You are an unlooked-for benison in this waste.' Then at once he added, 'Come!' and swung away from the ring. Flanked by Waynhim, he ran into the maze of the menhirs.

Covenant's numb feet and heavy boots found no purchase on the snow-pack: repeatedly, he slipped and stumbled as he tried to dodge after Hamako among the rocks. But Cail gripped his arm, upheld him. Linden moved with small quick strides which enabled her to keep her footing.

At the rear of the company, several Waynhim fought a delaying action against the *arghuleh*. But abruptly the ice-beasts gave up the chase as if they had been called back – as if whatever force commanded them did not want to risk sending them into ambush. Shortly, one of the grey, Demondim-made creatures spoke to Hamako; and he slowed his pace.

Covenant pushed forward to the man's side. Burning with memory and dread, he wanted to shout, Well met like hell! What in blood and damnation are you doing here? But he owed Hamako too much past and present gratitude. Instead, he panted, 'Your timing's getting better. How did you know we needed you?'

Hamako grimaced at Covenant's reference to their previous meeting, when this *rhysh* had arrived too late to aid the ring-wielder. But he replied as if he understood the spirit of Covenant's gibe, 'We did not.

'The tale of your departure from the Land is told among the Waynhim.' He grinned momentarily. 'To such cunning watchers as they are, your passage from Revelstone to the Lower Land and Seareach was a plain as fire.' Swinging around another boulder into a broad avenue among the stones, he continued, 'But we knew naught of your return. Our watch was set rather upon these *arghuleh*, that come massed from the north in defiance of all Law, seeking ruin. Witnessing them gather here, we sought to discover their purpose. Thus at last we saw you. The mustering-place of the *rhysh* is not greatly distant' – he gestured ahead – 'but distant enough to leave you unsuccoured in your need.'

Listening hard, Covenant grappled with his questions. But there were too many of them. And the cold bit into his lungs at every breath. With an effort of will, he concentrated on keeping his legs moving and schooled himself to wait.

938

Then the group left the region of jumbled monoliths and entered a wide, white plain that ended half a league away in an escarpment which cut directly across the vista of the south. Eddies of wind skirled up and down the base of the escarpment, raising loose snow like dervishes; and Hamako headed toward them as if they were the sign-posts of a sanctuary.

When Covenant arrived, weak-kneed and gasping for air, at the rock-strewn foot of the sheer rise, he was too tired to be surprised by the discovery that the snow-devils were indeed markers or sentinels of an eldritch kind. The Waynhim called out in their barking tongue; and the eddies obeyed, moving to stand like hallucinated columns on either side of a line that led right into the face of the escarpment. There without transition an entrance appeared. It was wide enough to admit the company, but too low to let the Giants enter upright; and it opened into a tunnel warmly lit by flaming iron censers.

Smiling a welcome, Hamako said, 'This is the mustering-place of the Waynhim, their *rhyshyshim*. Enter without fear, for here the ring-wielder is acknowledged, and the foes of the Land are withheld. In these times, there is no true safety anywhere. But here you will find reliable sanctuary for one more day – until the gathered *rhysh* come finally to their purpose. To me it has been granted to speak for all Waynhim that share this Weird. Enter and be welcome.'

In response, the First bowed formally. 'We do so gladly. Already your aid has been a boon which we are baffled to repay. In sharing counsel and stories and safety, we hope to make what return we may.'

Hamako bowed in turn: his eyes gleamed pleasure at her courtesy. Then he led the company down into the tunnel.

When Vain and the last of the Waynhim had passed inward, the entrance disappeared, again without transition, leaving in its place blunt, raw rock that sealed the company into the firelight and blissful warmth of the *rhyshyshim*.

At first, Covenant hardly noticed that Findail had rejoined them. But the Appointed was there as though Vain's side were a post he had never deserted. His appearance drew a brief, muted chittering from the Waynhim; but then they ignored him as if he were simply a shadow of the black Demondim-spawn.

For a few moments, the tunnel was full of the wooden scraping of the sleds' runners. But when the companions reached a bulge in the passage like a rude antechamber, Hamako instructed the Giants to leave the sleds there.

As the warmth healed Covenant's sore respiration, he thought that now Hamako would begin to ask the expected questions. But the man and the Waynhim bore themselves as if they had come to the end of all questions. Looking at Hamako more closely, Covenant saw things which had been absent or less pronounced during their previous encounter – resignation, resolve, a kind of peace. Hamako looked like a man who had passed through a long grief and been annealed.

With a small jolt, Covenant realized that Hamako was not dressed for winter. Only the worn swathe of leather around his hips made him less naked than the Waynhim. In vague fear, Covenant wondered if the Stonedownor had truly become Waynhim himself? What did such a transformation mean?

And what in hell was this *rhysh* doing here?

His companions had less reason for apprehension. Pitchwife moved as though the Waynhim had restored his sense of adventure, his capacity for excitement: his eyes watched everything, eager for marvels. Warm air and the prospect of safety softened the First's iron sternness, and she walked with her hand lightly on her husband's shoulder, willing to accept whatever she saw. Honninscrave's thoughts were hidden beneath the concealment of his brows. And Mistweave –

At the sight of Mistweave's face, Covenant winced. Too much had happened too swiftly: he had nearly forgotten the tormented moment of Mistweave's indecision. But the Giant's visage bore the marks of that failure like toolwork at the corners of his eyes, down the sides of his mouth – marks cut into the bone of his self-esteem. His gaze turned away from Covenant's in shame.

Damn it to hell! Covenant rasped to himself. Is every one of us doomed?

Perhaps they all were. Linden walked at his side without looking at him, her mien pale and strict with the characteristic severity which he had learned to interpret as fear. Fear of herself – of her inherited capacity for panic and horror which had proved once again that it could paralyse her despite every commitment or affirmation she made. Perhaps her reaction to the ambush of the *arghuleh* had restored her belief that she, too, was doomed.

It was unjust. She judged that her whole life had been a form of flight, an expression of moral panic. But in that she was wrong. Her past sins did not invalidate her present desire for good. If they did, then Covenant himself was damned as well as doomed, and Lord Foul's triumph was already assured.

Covenant was familiar with despair. He accepted it in himself. But he could not bear it in the people he loved. They deserved better.

Then Hamako's branching way through the rock turned a corner to enter a sizeable cavern like a meeting-hall; and Covenant's attention was pulled out of its galled channel.

The space was large and high enough to have held the entire crew of Starfare's Gem; but its rough walls and surfaces testified that the Waynhim had not been using it long. Yet it was comfortably well-lit: many braziers flamed around the walls, shedding kind heat as well as illumination. For a moment, Covenant found himself wondering obliquely why the Waynhim bothered to provide light at all, since they had no eyes. Did the fires aid their lore in some fashion? Or did they draw a simple solace from the heat or scent of the flames? Certainly the former habitation of Hamako's *rhysh* had been bright with warmth and firelight.

But Covenant could not remember that place and remain calm. And he had never seen so many Waynhim before: at least three score of them slept on the bare stone, worked together around black metal pots as if they were preparing *vitrim* or invocations, or quietly waited for what they might learn about the people Hamako had brought. *Rhysh* was the Waynhim word for a community; and Covenant had been told that each community usually numbered between one and two score Waynhim who shared a specific interpretation of their racial Weird, their native definition of identity and reason for existence. (This Weird, he remembered, belonged to both the Waynhim and the ur-viles, but was read in vastly different ways.) So he was looking at at least two *rhysh*. And Hamako had implied that there were more. More communities which had been ripped from home and service by the same terrible necessity that had brought Hamako's *rhysh* here?

Covenant groaned as he accompanied Hamako into the centre of the cavern.

There the Stonedownor addressed the company again. 'I know that the purpose which impels you toward the Land is urgent,' he said in his gentle and pain-familiar voice. 'But some little time you can spare among us. The horde of the *arghuleh* is unruly and advances with no great speed. We offer you sustenance, safety, and rest as well as inquiries' – he looked squarely at Covenant – 'and perhaps also answers.' That suggestion gave another twist to Covenant's tension. He remembered clearly the question Hamako had refused to answer for him. But Hamako had not paused. He was asking, 'Will you consent to delay your way a while?'

The First glanced at Covenant. But Covenant had no intention of leaving until he knew more. 'Hamako,' he said grimly, 'why are you here?'

The loss and resolution behind Hamako's eyes showed that he understood. But he postponed his reply by inviting the company to sit with him on the floor. Then he offered around bowls of the dark, musty *vitrim* liquid which looked like vitriol and yet gave nourishment like a distillation of *aliantha*. And when the companions had satisfied their initial hunger and weariness, he spoke as if he had deliberately missed Covenant's meaning.

'Ring-wielder,' he said, 'with four other *rhysh* we have come to give battle to the *arghuleh*.'

'Battle?' Covenant demanded sharply. He had always known Waynhim as creatures of peace.

'Yes.' Hamako had travelled a journey to this place which could not be measured in leagues. 'That is our intent.'

Covenant started to expostulate: Hamako stopped him with a firm gesture. 'Though the Waynhim serve peace,' he said carefully, 'they have risen to combat when their Weird required it of them. Thomas Covenant, I have spoken to you concerning that Weird. The Waynhim are made creatures. They have not the justification of birth for their existence, but only the imperfect lores and choices of the Demondim. And from this trunk grow no boughs but two – the way of the ur-viles, who loathe what they are not, and the way of the Waynhim, who strive to give value to what they are through service to what they are not, to the birth by Law and beauty of the life of the Land. This you know.'

Yes. I know. But Covenant's throat closed as he recalled the manner in which Hamako's *rhysh* had formerly served its Weird.

'Also you know,' the Stonedownor went on, 'that in the time of the great High Lord Mhoram, and of your own last battle against the Despiser, Waynhim saw and accepted the need to wage violence in defence of the Land. It was their foray which opened the path by which the High Lord procured the survival of Revelstone.' His gaze held Covenant's though Covenant could hardly match him. 'Therefore do not accuse us that we have risen to violence again. It is not fault in the Waynhim. It is grief.'

And still he forestalled Covenant's protest, did not answer Covenant's fundamental question. 'The Sunbane and the Despiser's malign intent rouse the dark forces of the Earth. Though they act by their own will, they serve his design of destruction. And such a force has come among the *arghuleh*, mastering their native savagery and sending them like the hand of winter against the Land. We know not the name of that might. It is hidden from the insight of the Waynhim. But we see it. And we have gathered in this *rhyshyshim* to oppose it.'

'How?' the First interposed. 'How will you oppose it?' When Hamako turned toward her, she said, 'I ask pardon if I intrude on that which does not concern me. But you have given us the gift of our lives, and we have not returned the bare courtesy of our names and knowledge.' Briefly, she introduced her companions. Then she continued, 'I am the First of the Search – a Swordmain of the Giants. Battle is my craft and my purpose.' Her countenance was sharp in the firelight. 'I would share counsel with you concerning this combat.'

Hamako nodded. But his reply suggested politeness rather than any hope for help or guidance – the politeness of a man who had looked at his fate and approved of it.

'In the name of these *rhysh*, I thank you. Our intent is simple. Many of the Waynhim are now abroad, harrying the *arghuleh* to lure them hither. In this they succeed. That massed horde we will meet on the outer plain upon the morrow. There the Waynhim will concert their might and strike inward among the ice-beasts, seeking the dark heart of the force which rules them. If we discover that heart – and are equal to its destruction – then will the *arghuleh* be scattered, becoming once more their own prey.

'If we fail – ' The Stonedownor shrugged. There was no fear in his face. 'We will at least weaken that horde sorely ere we die.'

The First was faster than Covenant. 'Hamako,' she said, 'I like this not. It is a tactic of desperation. It offers no second hope in event of first failure.'

But Hamako did not waver. 'Giant, we are desperate. At our backs lies naught but the Sunbane, and against that ill we are powerless. Wherefore should we desire any second hope? All else has been rent from us. It is enough to strike this blow as best we may.'

The First had no answer for him. Slowly, his gaze left her, returned to Covenant. His brown eyes seemed as soft as weeping – and yet too hard to be daunted. 'Because I have been twice bereft,' he said in that kind and unbreachable voice, 'I have been granted to stand at the forefront, forging the puissance of five *rhysh* with my mortal hands.'

Then Covenant saw that now at last he would be allowed to ask his true question; and for an instant his courage failed. How could he bear to hear what had happened to Hamako? Such extravagant human valour came from several sources – and one of them was despair.

But Hamako's eyes held no flinch of self-pity. Covenant's companions were watching him, sensitive to the importance of what lay between him and Hamako. Even Mistweave and Honninscrave showed concern; and Linden's visage ached as if Hamako's rue were poignant to her. With a wrench of will, Covenant denied his fear.

'You still haven't told me.' Strain made his tone harsh. 'All this is fine. I even understand it.' He was intimately familiar with desperation. In the warmth of the cavern, he had begun to sweat. 'But why in the name of every good and beautiful thing you've ever done in your life are you here at all? Even the threat of that many *arghuleh* can't compare with what you were doing before.'

The bare memory filled his throat with inextricable wonder and sorrow.

Lord Foul had already destroyed virtually all the natural life of the Land. Only Andelain remained, preserved against corruption by Caer-Caveral's power: everything else that grew by Law or love from seed or egg or birth had been perverted.

Everything except that which Hamako's *rhysh* had kept alive.

In a cavern which was huge on the scale of lone human beings, but still paltry when measured by the destitution of the Land, the Waynhim had nurtured a garden that contained every kind of grass, shrub, flower and tree, vine, grain, and vegetable they had been able to find and sustain. And in another cave, in a warren of pens and dens, they had saved as many species of animal as their lore and skill allowed.

It was an incomparable expression of faith in the future, of hope for the time when the Sunbane would be healed and the Land might be dependent upon this one tiny pocket of natural life for its renewal.

And it was gone. From the moment when he had recognized Hamako, Covenant had known the truth. Why else were the Waynhim here, instead of tending to their chosen work?

Useless rage filled his chest like weeping, and his courage felt as brittle as dead bone, as he waited for Hamako's response.

It was slow in coming; but even now the Stonedownor did not waver. 'It is as you have feared,' he said softly. 'We were driven from our place, and the work of our lives was destroyed.' Then for the first time his voice gave a hint of anger. 'Yet you have not feared enough. That ruin did not befall us alone. Across all the Land, every *rhysh* was beaten from its place and its work. The Waynhim gathered here are all that remain of their race. There will be no more.'

At that, Covenant wanted to cry out, plead, protest, No! Not again! Was not the genocide of the Unhomed enough? How could the Land sustain another such loss?

But Hamako seemed to see Covenant's thoughts in his aghast face. 'You err, ring-wielder,' said the Stonedownor grimly. 'Against Ravers and the Despiser, we were forewarned and defended. And Lord Foul had no cause to fear us. We were too paltry to give him threat. No. It was the ur-viles, the black and birthless kindred of the Waynhim, that wrought our ruin from *rhysh* to *rhysh* across the Land.'

Wrought our ruin. Our ruin across the Land. Covenant was no longer looking at Hamako. He could not. All that beauty. Gone to grief, where all dreams go. If he met those soft, brown, irreparable eyes, he would surely begin to weep.

'Their assault was enabled to succeed because we did not expect it – for had not ur-vile and Waynhim lived in truce during all the millennia of their existence? – and because they have studied destruction as the Waynhim have not.' Slowly, the edge of his tone was blunted. 'We were fortunate in our way. Many of us were slain – among them some that you have known. *Vraith, dhurng, ghramin.*' He spoke the names as if he knew how they would strike Covenant; for those were Waynhim who had given their blood so that he could reach Revelstone in time to rescue Linden, Sunder, and Hollian. 'But many escaped. Other *rhysh* were butchered entirely.

'Those Waynhim that survived wandered without purpose until they encountered others to form new *rhysh*, for a Waynhim without community is a lorn thing, deprived of meaning. And therefore,' he concluded, 'we are desperate in all sooth. We are the last. After us there will be no more.'

'But why?' Covenant asked his knotted hands and the blurred light, his voice as thick as blood in his throat. 'Why did they attack – ? After all those centuries?'

'Because – ' Hamako replied; and now he did falter, caught by the pain behind his resolve. 'Because we gave you shelter – and with you that making of the ur-viles which they name Vain.'

Covenant's head jerked up, eyes afire with protests. This crime at least should not be laid to his charge, though instinctively he believed it: he had never learned how to repudiate any accusation. But at once Hamako said, 'Ah, no, Thomas Covenant. Your pardon. I have led you to miscomprehend me.' His voice resumed the impenetrable gentleness of a man who had lost too much. 'The fault was neither yours nor ours. Even at Lord Foul's command the ur-viles would not have wrought such harm upon us for merely sheltering you and any companion. Do not think it. Their rage had another source.'

'What was it?' Covenant breathed. 'What in hell happened?'

Hamako shrugged at the sheer simplicity of the answer. 'It was their conviction that you gained from us an explanation of Vain Demondim-spawn's purpose.'

'But I didn't!' objected Covenant. 'You wouldn't tell me.'

The Waynhim had commanded Hamako to silence. He had only replied, *Were I to reveal the purpose of this Demondim-spawn, that revelation could well prevent the accomplishment of his purpose.* And, *That purpose is greatly desirable.*

Now he sighed. 'Yes. But how could our refusal be conveyed to the ur-viles? Their loathing permitted them no understanding of our Weird. And they did not inquire of us what we had done. In our place, they would not have scrupled to utter falsehood. Therefore they could not have believed any reply we gave. So they brought down retribution upon us, compelled by the passion of their desire that the secret of this Vain not be untimely revealed.'

And Vain stood behind the seated company as if he were deaf or impervious. The dead wood of his right forearm dangled from his elbow; but his useless hand was still undamaged, immaculate. As beautifully sculpted as a mockery of Covenant's flawed being.

But Hamako did not flinch or quail again, though his sombre gaze now held a dusky hue of fear.

'Thomas Covenant,' he said, his voice so soft that it barely carried across the circle of the company. 'Ring-wielder.' His home, During Stonedown, had been destroyed by the na-Mhoram's *Grim*; but the

Waynhim had given him a new home with them. And then that new home had been destroyed, ravaged for something the *rhysh* had not done. *Twice bereft.* 'Will you ask once more? Will you inquire of me here the purpose of this black Demondim-spawn?'

At that, Linden sat up straighter, bit her lips to hold back the question. The First tensed, anticipating explanations. Pitchwife's eyes sparkled like hope: even Mistweave stirred from his gloom. Cail cocked one dispassionate eyebrow.

But Covenant sat like Honninscrave, his emotions tangled by Hamako's apprehension. He understood the Stonedownor, knew what Hamako's indirect offer meant. The Waynhim no longer trusted their former refusal – were no longer able to credit the unmalice of the ur-viles' intent. The violence of their ruin had shaken them fundamentally. And yet their basic perceptions remained. The trepidation in Hamako's visage showed that he had learned to dread the implications of both speaking and not speaking.

He was asking Covenant to take the responsibility of decision from him.

He and his *rhysh* had come here to die. Fiercely, with all the attention of the company on him, Covenant forced himself to say, 'No.'

His gaze burned as he confronted Hamako across the rude stone. 'You've already refused once.' Within himself, he swore bitterly at the necessity which compelled him to reject everything that might help or ease or guide him. But he did not shrink from it. 'I trust you.'

Linden gave him a glare of exasperation. Pitchwife's face widened in surprise. But Hamako's rue-worn features softened with undisguised relief.

Later, while Covenant's companions rested or slept in the warmth of the cavern, Hamako took the Unbeliever aside for a private conversation. Gently, Hamako urged Covenant to depart before the coming battle. Night was upon the Northron Climbs, the night before the dark of the moon; but a Waynhim could be spared to guide the company up the escarpment toward the relative safety of Landsdrop. The quest would be able to travel without any immediate fear of the *arghuleh.*

Covenant refused brusquely. 'You've done too much for me already. I'm not going to leave you like this.'

Hamako peered into Covenant's clenched glower. After a moment, the Stonedownor breathed, 'Ah, Thomas Covenant. Will you hazard the wild magic to aid us?'

Covenant's reply was blunt. 'Not if I can help it.' If he had heeded the venom coursing in him, the itch of his scarred forearm, he would already have gone out to meet the *arghuleh* alone. 'But my friends aren't exactly useless.' And I don't intend to watch you die for nothing.

He knew he had no right to make such promises: the meaning of Hamako's life, of the lives of the gathered Waynhim, was not his to preserve or sacrifice. But he was who he was. How could he refuse to aid the people who needed him?

Scowling at unresolved contradictions, he studied the creatures. With their eyeless faces, gaping nostrils, and limbs made for running on all fours, they looked more like beasts or monsters than members of a noble race that had given its entire history to the service of the Land. But long ago one of them had been indirectly responsible for his second summons to the Land. Savagely maimed and in hideous pain, that Waynhim had been released from the Despiser's clutches to bait a trap. It had reached the Lords and told them that Lord Foul's armies were ready to march. Therefore High Lord Elena had made the decision to call Covenant. Thus the Despiser had arranged for Covenant's return. And the logic of that return had led ineluctably to Elena's end, the breaking of the Law of Death, and the destruction of the Staff of Law.

Now the last of the Waynhim people stood on the verge of ruin.

A long time passed before Covenant was able to sleep. He saw all too clearly what Lord Foul might hope to gain from the plight of the Waynhim.

But when his grasp on consciousness frayed away, the *vitrim* he had consumed carried him into deep rest; and he slept until the activity around him became constant and exigent. Raising his head, he found that the cavern was full of Waynhim – at least twice as many as he had seen earlier. The bleary look in Linden's face showed that she had just awakened; but the four Giants were up and moving tensely among the Waynhim.

Pitchwife came over to Linden and Covenant. 'You have slept well, my friends,' he said, chuckling as if he were inured to the expectancy which filled the air. 'Stone and Sea! this *vitrim* is a hale beverage. A touch of its savour commingled with our *diamondraught* would gladden even the dullest palate. Life be praised, I have at last found the role which will make my name forever sung among the Giants. Behold!' With a flourish, he indicated his belt, which was behung on all sides with leather *vitrim*-skins. 'It will be my dear task to bear this roborant to my people, that they may profit from its potency in the blending of a new liquor. And that unsurpassable draught will be named *pitchbrew* for all the Earth to adore. Then,' he laughed, 'will my fame outmeasure even that of great Bahgoon himself!'

The misshapen Giant's banter drew a smile from Linden. But Covenant had climbed out of sleep into the same mood with which the peril of the Waynhim had first afflicted him. Frowning at Pitchwife's humour, he demanded, 'What's going on?'

The Giant sobered rapidly. 'Ah, Giantfriend,' he sighed, 'you have slept long and long. Noon has come to the wasteland, and the Waynhim are gathered to prepare for battle. Although the *arghuleh* advance slowly, they are now within sight of this covert. I conceive that the outcome of their conflict will be determined ere sunset.'

Covenant swore to himself. He did not want the crisis to be so near at hand.

Linden was facing him. In her controlled, professional voice, she said, 'There's still time.'

'Time to get out of here?' he returned sourly. 'Let them go out there and probably get butchered as a race without so much as one sympathetic witness to at least grieve? Forget it.'

Her eyes flared. 'That isn't what I meant.' Anger sharpened the lines of her face. 'I don't like deserting people any more than you do. Maybe I don't have your background' – she snarled the word – 'but I can still see what Hamako and the Waynhim are worth. You know me better than that.' Then she took a deep breath, steadied herself. Still glaring at him, she said, 'What I meant was, there's still time to ask them about Vain.'

Covenant felt like a knotted thunderhead, livid and incapable of release. Her pointed jibe about his background underscored the extent to which he had falsified their relationship. From the time of their first meeting on Haven Farm, he had withheld things from her, arguing that she did not have the background to understand them. And this was the result. Everything he said to or heard from the woman he loved became gall.

But he could not afford release. Lord Foul was probably already gloating at the possibility that he, Covenant, might unleash wild magic to aid the Waynhim. Grimly, he stifled his desire to make some acerbic retort. Instead, he replied, 'No. I don't want to hear it from Hamako. I don't want to let Findail off the hook.'

Deliberately, he turned toward the Appointed. But Findail met him with the same trammelled and impenetrable rue with which he had rebuffed every challenge or appeal. More to answer Linden than to attack Findail, Covenant concluded, 'I'm waiting for this bloody *Elohim* to discover the honesty, if not the simple decency, to start telling the truth.'

Findail's yellow eyes darkened; but he said nothing.

Linden looked back and forth between Covenant and the Appointed. Then she nodded. Speaking as if Findail were not present, she said, 'I hope he makes up his mind soon. I don't like the idea of having to face the Clave when they still know more about Vain than we do.'

Grateful for at least that much acceptance from her, Covenant tried to smile. But he achieved only a grimace.

The Waynhim were milling around the cavern, moving as if each of them wanted to speak to everyone else before the crisis; and their low, barking voices thickened the atmosphere. But the Giants were no longer among them. Honninscrave leaned against one wall, detached and lonely, his head bowed. Pitchwife had remained with Covenant, Linden and Cail. And the First and Mistweave stood together near the opposite side of the space. Mistweave's stance was one of pleading; but the First met whatever he said angrily. When he beseeched her further, her reply cracked over the noise of the Waynhim.

'You are mortal, Giant. Such choices are harsh to any who must make them. But failure is only failure. It is not unworth. You are sworn and dedicate to the Search, if not to the Chosen, and I will not release you.'

Sternly, she left his plain dismay, marched through the throng toward the rest of her companions. When she reached them, she answered their mute questions by saying, 'He is shamed.' She looked at Linden. 'His life you saved when Covenant Giantfriend's was at risk. Now he deems that his indecision in your need is unpardonable. He asks to be given to the Waynhim, that he may seek expiation in their battle.' Unnecessarily, she added, 'I have refused him.'

Linden muttered a curse. 'I didn't ask him to serve me. He doesn't need – '

Abruptly, she cried, 'Honninscrave! Don't!' But the Master did not heed her. Fury clenched in his fists, he strode toward Mistweave as though he meant to punish the Giant's distress.

Linden started after him: the First stopped her. In silence, they watched as Honninscrave stalked up to his crewmember. Confronting Mistweave, the Master stabbed one massive finger at the Giant's sore heart as if he knew the exact location of Mistweave's bafflement. His jaws chewed excoriations; but the interchanges of the Waynhim covered his voice.

Softly, the First said, 'He is the Master. It is enough for me that he has found room in his own pain for Mistweave. He will do no true harm to one who has served him aboard Starfare's Gem.'

Linden nodded. But her mouth was tight with frustration and empathy, and she did not take her eyes off Mistweave.

At first, Mistweave flinched from what Honninscrave was saying. Then a hot belligerence rose up in him, and he raised one fist like a threat. But Honninscrave caught hold of Mistweave's arm and snatched it down, thrust his jutting beard into Mistweave's face. After a moment, Mistweave acquiesced. His eyes did not lose their heat; but he accepted the stricture Honninscrave placed upon him. Slowly, the ire faded from the Master's stance.

Covenant let a sigh through his teeth.

Then Hamako appeared among the Waynhim, came toward the

company. His gaze was bright in the light of the braziers: his movements hinted at fever or anticipation. In his hands he bore a long scimitar that looked as if it had been fashioned of old bone. Without preamble, he said, 'The time has come. The *arghuleh* draw nigh. We must issue forth to give combat. What will you do? You must not remain here. There is no other egress, and if the entrance is sealed you will be ensnared.'

The First started to reply; but Covenant forestalled her. Venom nagged at the skin of his forearm. 'We'll follow you out,' he said roughly. 'We're going to watch until we figure out the best way to help.' To the protest in Hamako's mien, he added, 'Stop worrying about us. We've survived worse. If everything else goes to hell and damnation, we'll find some way to escape.'

A grin momentarily softened Hamako's tension. 'Thomas Covenant,' he said in a voice like a salute, 'I would that we had met in kinder times.' Then he raised his scimitar, turned on his heel, and started toward the throat of the cavern.

Bearing curved, bony daggers like smaller versions of his blade, all the Waynhim followed him as if they had chosen him to lead them to their doom.

They numbered nearly two hundred, but they needed only a few moments to march out of the cavern, leaving the company behind in the undiminished firelight.

Honninscrave and Mistweave came to join their companions. The First looked at Covenant and Linden, then at the other Giants. None of them demurred. Linden's face was pale, but she held herself firm. Pitchwife's features worked as if he could not find the right jest to ease his tension. In their separate ways, the First, Mistweave, and Honninscrave looked as unbreachable as Cail.

Covenant nodded bitterly. Together, he and his friends turned their backs on warmth and safety, went out to meet the winter.

In the tunnel, he felt the temperature begin to drop almost immediately. The change made no difference to his numb fingers and feet; but he sashed his robe tight as though in that way he might be able to protect his courage. Past the branchings of the passage he followed the Waynhim until the company reached the rude antechamber where the sleds were. Mutely, Honninscrave and Mistweave took the lines. Their breath had begun to steam. Firelight transmuted the wisps of vapour to gold.

The entrance to the *rhyshyshim* was open; and cold came streaming inward, hungry to extinguish this hidden pocket of comfort. Deep in Covenant's guts, shivers mounted. His robe had previously kept him alive, if not warm; but now it seemed an insignificant defence against the frozen winter. When he looked at Linden, she answered as if his thoughts were palpable to her:

'I don't know how many. Enough.'

Then the entrance loomed ahead. Now the air blew keenly into Covenant's face, tugging at his beard, drawing tears from his eyes. A dark pressure gathered in his veins. But he ducked his head and went on. With his companions, he strode through the opening onto the rocky ground at the foot of the escarpment.

The plain was sharp with sunlight: from a fathomless sky, the midafternoon sun burned across the white waste. The air felt strangely brittle, as though it were about to break under its own weight. Stiff snow crunched beneath Covenant's boots. For a moment, the cold seemed as bright as fire. He had to fight to keep wild magic from leaking past his restraint.

When his sight cleared, he saw that the whirling snow-devils which had marked and guarded the *rhyshyshim* were gone. The Waynhim had no more need of them.

Barking softly to each other, the creatures surged together into the compact and characteristic wedge which both they and the ur-viles used to concentrate and wield their combined force. Hamako stood at the apex of the formation. When it was complete and the invocations had been made, he would hold the lore and power of five *rhysh* in the blade of his scimitar. As long as they did not break ranks, the Waynhim along the sides of the wedge would be able to strike individual blows; but Hamako's might would be two hundred strong.

Every moment, the battle drew closer. Looking northward, Covenant found that he could barely see the region of monoliths beyond the massed advance of the *arghuleh*.

Ponderous and fatal, they came forward – a slow rush of white gleaming over the snow and ice. Already, their feral clatter was audible above the voices of the Waynhim. It echoed like shattering ice off the face of the escarpment. The horde did not appear to greatly outnumber the Waynhim; but the far larger bulk and savagery of the *arghuleh* made their force seem overwhelming.

The company still had time to flee. But no one suggested flight. The First stood, stern and ready, with one hand resting on the hilt of her longsword. Glints reflected out of Honninscrave's eyes as if he were eager to strike any blow which might make his grief useful. Pitchwife's expression was more wary and uncertain: he was no warrior. But Mistweave bore himself as though he saw his chance for restitution coming and had been commanded to ignore it. Only Cail watched the advancing horde with dispassion, unmoved alike by the valour of the Waynhim and the peril of the company. Perhaps he saw nothing especially courageous in what the *rhysh* were doing. Perhaps to his *Haruchai* mind such extravagant risk was simply reasonable.

Covenant struggled to speak. The cold seemed to freeze the words in his throat. 'I want to help them. If they need it. But I don't know how.' To the First, he said, 'Don't go out there unless the wedge starts to break. I've seen this kind of fighting before.' He had seen ur-viles slash into the Celebration of Spring to devour the Wraiths of Andelain – and had been powerless against that black wedge. 'As long as their formation holds, they aren't beaten.' Then he turned to Linden.

Her expression stopped him. Her face was fixed, pale with cold, toward the *arghuleh*, and her eyes looked as livid as injuries. For one dire moment, he feared she had fallen again into her particular panic. But then her gaze snapped toward him. It was battered but not cowed. 'I don't know,' she said tightly. 'He's right. There's some force out there. Something that keeps them together. But I can't tell what it is.'

Covenant swallowed a knot of dread. 'Keep trying,' he murmured. 'I don't want these Waynhim to end up like the Unhomed.' Damned as well as doomed.

She did not reply; but her nod conveyed a fierce resolve as she turned back to the *arghuleh*.

They were dangerously close now. A score of them led the advance, and their mass was nearly that many deep. Though they were beasts of hate that preyed on everything, they had become as organized as a conscious army. Steadily, they gathered speed to hurl themselves upon the Waynhim.

In response, the Waynhim raised a chant into the chill. Together, they barked a raw, irrhythmic invocation which sprang back at them from the escarpment and resounded across the flat. And a moment later a black light shone from the apex of the wedge. Hamako flourished his scimitar. Its blade had become as ebon as Demondim vitriol: it emitted midnight as if it were ablaze with death.

At the same time, all the smaller blades of the Waynhim turned black and began to drip a hot fluid which steamed and sizzled in the snow.

Without knowing what he was doing, Covenant retreated. The frigid air had become a thrumming shout of power, soundless in spite of the chant which summoned it; and that puissance called out to him. His yearning for fire battered at the walls he had built around it: the scars on his forearm burned poisonously. He took a few steps backward. But he could not put any distance between himself and his desire to strike. Instinctively, he fumbled his way to the only protection he could find: a jagged rock that stood half his height near the entrance to the *rhyshyshim*. Yet he did not crouch or cower there. His numb hands gripped the argute stone in the same way that his eyes clung to the Waynhim and the *arghuleh*; and within himself he pleaded, No. Not again.

He had not been required to watch the destruction of the Unhomed.

Then Hamako gave a shout like a huzzah; and the wedge started forward. Moving as one, the Waynhim went out to the foe they had chosen for their last service.

Hushed amid the vicious advance of the ice-beasts, the long hoarse chant of the Waynhim, the echoes breaking up and down the escarpment, Covenant and his companions watched as the wedge drove in among the *arghuleh*.

For a moment, its thrust was so successful that the outcome appeared foregone. The *rhysh* poured their power into Hamako: he cut an irresistible swathe for the wedge to follow. And as individuals the Waynhim slashed their ice-corroding fluid in all directions. *Arghuleh* snapped apart, fell back, blundered against each other.

Screaming from their many maws, they swarmed around the wedge, trying to engulf it, crush it among them. But that only brought the third side of the wedge into the fray. And Hamako's scimitar rang like a hammer on the ice, sent shards and limbs flying from side to side with every blow. He had aimed the wedge toward an especially large beast at the rear of the mass, an *arghule* that seemed to have been formed by one creature crouching atop another; and with each step he drew closer to that target.

The *arghuleh* were savage, impervious to fear. Webs and snares were flung across the wedge. Booming cracks riddled the snow-pack. But black liquid burned the nets to tatters. Falling chunks bruised the Waynhim, but did not weaken their formation. And the hard ground under the snow rendered the cracks ineffective.

Covenant leaned against his braced hands, half frozen there, hardly daring to credit what he saw. Low shouts of encouragement broke from the First; and her sword was in her hands. Avid with hope, Pitchwife peered into the fray as if he expected victory at any moment, expected the very winter to break and flee.

Then, without warning, everything changed.

The *arghuleh* were virtually mindless, but the force which ruled them was not. It was sentient and cunning. And it had learned a lesson from the way the Waynhim had rescued the company earlier.

Abruptly, the horde altered its tactics. In a sudden flurry like an explosion of white which almost obscured the battle, all the beasts raised their ice at once. But now that ice was not directed at the wedge. Intead, it covered every *arghule* that had been hurt, broken, or even killed by the Waynhim.

Ice slapped against every gout of vitriol, smothered the black fluid, effaced it, healed the wounds.

Ice bandaged every limb and body that Hamako had hacked or shattered, restoring crippled creatures to wholeness with terrible celerity.

Ice gathered together the fragments of the slain, fused them anew, poured life back into them.

The Waynhim had not stopped fighting for an instant. But already half their work had been undone. The *arghuleh* revitalized each other faster than they were damaged.

More and more of them were freed to attack in other ways.

Unable to rend the wedge with their webs, they began to form a wall of ice around it as if they meant to encyst it until its power gave out through sheer weariness.

Covenant stared in horror. The Waynhim were clearly unprepared for this counterattack. Hamako whirled his blade, flaring desperation around him. Three times he pounded an *arghule* into pieces no larger than his fist; and each time a web snatched the pieces together, restored them, sent the beast at him again. Wildly he sprang forward to assail the web itself. But in so doing he broke contact with the wedge. Instantly, his scimitar relapsed to bone: it splintered when he struck. He would have fallen himself; but hands reached out from the wedge and jerked him back into position.

And there was nothing Covenant could do. The Giants were calling to him, beseeching him for some command: the First shouted imprecations he did not hear. But there was nothing he could do.

Except unleash the wild magic.

Venom thudded in his temples. The wild magic, unquenchable and argent. Every thought of it, every memory, every ache of hunger and yearning was as shrill and frantic as Linden's fervid cry: *You're going to break the Arch of Time! This is what Foul wants!* Desecration filled each pulse and wail of his heart. He could not call up that much power and still pretend to control it.

But Hamako would be killed. It was as distinct as the declining sunlight on the white plain. The Waynhim would be slaughtered like the people of the Land to feed the lust of evil. That same man and those Waynhim had brought Covenant back from delirium once – and had shown him that there was still beauty in the world. The winter of their destruction would never end.

Because of the venom. Its scars still burned, as bright as Lord Foul's eyes, in the flesh of his right forearm, impelling him to power. The Sunbane warped Law, birthed abominations; but Covenant might bring Time itself to chaos.

At no great distance from him, the wedge no longer battled offensively: it struggled simply to stay alive. Several Waynhim had fallen in bonds of ice they could not break. More would die soon as the *arghuleh* raised their wall. Hamako remained on his feet, but had no weapon, no way to wield the might of the wedge: he was thrust into the centre of the formation, and a Waynhim took his place, fighting with all the fluid force its small blade could channel.

'Giantfriend!' the First yelled. 'Covenant!'

The wedge was dying; and the Giants dared not act, for fear that they would place themselves in the way of Covenant's fire.

Because of the venom: sick fury pounding like desire between the bones of his forearm. He had been made so powerful that he was powerless. His desperation demanded blood.

Slipping back his sleeve, he gripped his right wrist with his left hand to increase his leverage, then hacked his scarred forearm at the sharpest edges of the rock. His flesh ground against the jagged projections. Red slicked the stone, spattered the snow, froze in the cold. He ignored it. The Clave had cut his wrists to gain power for the soothtell which had guided and misled him. Deliberately, he mangled his forearm, striving by pain to conceive an alternative to venom, struggling to cut the fang-marks out of his soul.

Then Linden hit him. The blow knocked him back. Flagrant with urgency and concern, she caught her fists in his robe, shook him like a child, raged at him.

'Listen to me!' she flamed as if she knew he could hardly hear her, could not see anything except the blood he had left on the rock. 'It's like the Kemper! Like Kasreyn!' Back and forth she heaved him, trying to wrestle him into focus on her. 'Like his son! The *arghuleh* have something like his *son*!'

At that, clarity hit Covenant so hard that he nearly fell.

The Kemper's son. Oh my God.

The *croyel*.

Before the thought was finished, he had broken Linden's grasp and was running toward the Giants.

The *croyel*! – the succubus from the dark places of the Earth which Kasreyn had borne on his back, and with which he had bargained for his arts and his preternaturally prolonged life. And out there was an *arghule* which looked like one ice-beast crouched on another. That creature had contracted with the *croyel* for the power to unite its kind and wage winter wherever it willed.

Findail must have known. He must have understood what force opposed the Waynhim. Yet he had said nothing.

But Covenant had no time to spend on the mendacity of the *Elohim*. Reaching the First, he shouted, 'Call them back! Make them retreat! They can't win this way!' His arm scattered blood. 'We've got to tell them about the *croyel*!'

She reacted as if he had unleashed her. Whirling, she gave one command that snatched the Giants to her side; and together they charged into the fray.

Covenant watched them go in fear and hope. Still furious for him, Linden came to his side: taking rough hold of his right wrist, she forced him to bend his elbow and clamp it tightly to slow the bleeding. Then she watched with him in silence.

With momentum, weight, and muscle, the four Giants crashed in among the *arghuleh*. The First swung her longsword like a bludgeon, risking its metal against the gelid beasts. Honninscrave and Mistweave fought as hugely as titans. Pitchwife scrambled after them, doing everything he could to guard their backs. And as they battled, they shouted Covenant's call in the roynish tongue of the Waynhim.

The reaction of the wedge was almost immediate. Suddenly, all the Waynhim pivoted to the left; and that corner of the formation became their apex. Sweeping Hamako along, they drove for the breach the Giants had made in the attack.

The *arghuleh* were slow to understand what was happening. The wedge was half free of the fray before the ice-beasts turned to try to prevent the retreat.

Pitchwife went down under two *arghuleh*. Honninscrave and Mistweave sprang to his aid like sledgehammers, yanked him out of the wreckage. A net took hold of the First. The leader of the wedge scored it to shreds. Frenetically, the Waynhim and the Giants struggled toward Covenant.

They were not swift enough to outrun the *arghuleh*. In moments, they would be engulfed again.

But the Waynhim had understood the Giants. Abruptly, the wedge parted, spilling Hamako and a score of companions in Covenant's direction. Then the *rhysh* reclosed their formation and attacked again.

With the help of the Giants, the wedge held back the *arghuleh* while Hamako and his comrades sped toward Covenant and Linden.

Covenant started shouting at Hamako before the Stonedownor neared him; but Hamako stopped a short distance away, silenced Covenant with a gesture. 'You have done your part, ring-wielder,' he panted as his people gathered about him. 'The name of the *croyel* is known among the Waynhim.' He had to raise his voice: the creatures were chanting a new invocation. 'We lacked only the knowledge that the force confronting us was indeed *croyel*.' An invocation Covenant had heard before. 'What must be done is clear. Come no closer.'

As if to enforce his warning, Hamako drew a stone dirk from his belt.

Recognition stung through Covenant. He was familiar with that knife. Or one just like it. It went with the invocation. He tried to call out, Don't! But the protest failed in his mouth. Perhaps Hamako was right. Perhaps only such desperate measures could hope to save the embattled *rhysh*.

With one swift movement, the Stonedownor drew a long incision across the veins on the back of his hand.

The cut did not bleed. At once, he handed the dirk to a Waynhim. Quickly, it sliced the length of its palm, then passed the knife to its neighbour. Taking hold of Hamako's hand, the Waynhim pressed its cut to his. While the invocation swelled, the two of them stood there, joined by blood.

When the Waynhim stepped back, Hamako's eyes were acute with power.

In this same way, his *rhysh* had given Covenant the strength to run without rest across the whole expanse of the Centre Plains in pursuit of Linden, Sunder, and Hollian. But that great feat had been accomplished with the vitality of only eight Waynhim; and Covenant had barely been able to contain so much might. There were twenty creatures ranged around Hamako.

The second had already completed its gift.

One by one, his adopted people cut themselves for him, pressed their blood into him. And each infusion gave him a surge of energy which threatened to burst his mortal bounds.

It was too much. How could one human being hope to hold that much power within the vessel of ordinary thew and tissue? Watching, Covenant feared that Hamako would not survive.

Then he remembered the annealed grief and determination he had seen in Hamako's eyes; and he knew the Stonedownor did not mean to survive.

Ten Waynhim had given their gift. Hamako's skin had begun to burn like tinder in the freezing air. But he did not pull back, and his companions did not stop.

At his back, the battle was going badly. Covenant's attention had been fixed on Hamako: he had not seen how the *arghuleh* had contrived to split the wedge. But the formation was in two pieces now, each struggling to focus its halved strength, each unable to break through the ice to rejoin the other. More Waynhim had fallen: more were falling. Ice crusted the Giants so heavily that they seemed hardly able to move. They fought heroically; but they were no match for beasts which could be brought back from death. Soon sheer fatigue would overcome them, and they would be lost for good and all.

'Go!' Covenant panted to Cail. Icicles of blood splintered from his elbow when he moved his arm. 'Help them!'

But the *Haruchai* did not obey. In spite of the ancient friendship between the Giants and his people, his face betrayed no flicker of concern. His promise of service had been made to Covenant rather than to the First; and Brinn had commanded him to his place.

Hellfire! Covenant raged. But his ire was directed at himself. He could tear his flesh until it fell from the bones; but he could not find his way out of the snare Lord Foul had set for him.

Fifteen Waynhim had given blood to Hamako. Sixteen. Now the Stonedownor's radiance was so bright that it seemed to tug involuntary fire from Covenant's ring. The effort of withholding it reft him of balance and vision. Pieces of midnight wheeled through him. He did not see the end of the Waynhim gift, could not witness the manner in which Hamako bore it.

But as that power withdrew toward the *arghuleh*, Covenant straightened his legs, pushed himself out of Cail's grasp, and sent his gaze like a cry after the Stonedownor.

Half naked in the low sunlight and the tremendous cold, Hamako shone like a cynosure as he flashed through the ice-beasts. The sheer intensity of his form melted the nearest attackers as if a furnace had come among them. From place to place within the fray he sped, clearing a space around the Giants, opening the way for the Waynhim to reform their wedge; and behind him billowed dense clouds of vapour which obscured him and the battle, made everything uncertain.

Then Linden shouted, 'There!'

All the steam burned away, denaturing so fiercely that the ice seemed to become air without transition and the scene of the combat was as vivid as the waste. Scores of *arghuleh* still threw themselves madly against the wedge. But they had stopped using their ice to support each other. And some of them were attacking their fellows, tearing into each other as if the purpose which had united them a moment ago had been forgotten.

Beyond the chaos, Hamako stood atop the leader of the *arghuleh*. He had vaulted up onto the high back of the strangely doubled beast and planted himself there, pitting his power squarely against the creature and its *croyel*.

The beast did not attempt to topple him, bring him within reach of it limbs and maws. And he struck no blows. Their struggle was simple: fire against ice, white heat against white cold. He shone like a piece of the clean sun: the *arghule* glared bitter chill. Motionless, they aimed what they had become at each other; and the entire plain rang and blazed to the pitch of their contest.

The strain of so much quintessential force was too much for Hamako's mortal flesh to sustain. In desperate pain, he began to melt like a tree under the desert avatar of the Sunbane. His legs slumped: the skin of his limbs spilled away: his features blurred. A cry that had no shape stretched his mouth.

But while his heart beat he was still alive – tempered to his purpose and indomitable. The focus of his given heat did not waver for an instant. All the losses he had suffered, all the loves which had been taken from him came together here; and he refused defeat. In spite of the ruin which sloughed away his flesh, he raised his arms, brandished them like sodden sticks at the wide sky.

And the double creature under him melted as well. Both *arghule* and *croyel* collapsed into water and slush until their deaths were inseparable from his – one stained pool slowly freezing on the faceless plain.

With an almost audible snap, the unnatural cold broke. Most of the *arghuleh* went on trying to kill each other until the *rhysh* drove them away; but the power they had brought with them was gone.

Linden was sobbing openly, though all her life she had taught herself to keep her grief silent. 'Why?' she protested through her tears. 'Why did they let him do it?'

Covenant knew why. Because Hamako had been twice bereft when no man or woman or Waynhim should have had to endure such loss so much as once.

As the sun went down in red and rue beyond the western line of the escarpment, Covenant closed his eyes, hugged his bloody arm to his chest, and listened to the lamentation of the Waynhim rising into the dusk.

7

PHYSICIAN'S PLIGHT

Though the night was moonless, the company resumed its journey shortly after the Waynhim had finished caring for their dead. The Giants were unwilling to submit to their weariness; and the pain Covenant shared with Linden made him loath to remain anywhere near the place of Hamako's end. While Mistweave prepared a meal, Linden treated Covenant's arm, washing it with *vitrim,* wrapping it in firm bandages: then she required him to drink more *diamondraught* than he wanted. As a result, he could hardly keep himself awake as the company left the region of the last *rhyshyshim.* While several Waynhim guided the Giants up the escarpment, he strove against sleep. He knew what his dreams were going to be.

For a time, the hurt in his forearm helped him. But once the Giants had said their long, heart-felt farewells to the Waynhim, and had settled into a steady gait, striding southwestward as swiftly as the dim starlight permitted, he found that even pain was not enough to preserve him from nightmares.

In the middle of the night, he wrenched himself out of a vision of Hamako which had made him sweat anguish. With renewed fervour, he fought the effect of the *diamondraught.*

'I was wrong,' he said to the empty dark. Perhaps no one heard him over the muffled sound of the runners in the snow: he did not want anyone to hear him. He was not speaking to be heard. He only wanted to fight off sleep, stay away from dreams. 'I should've listened to Mhoram.'

The memory was like a dream: it had the strange immanence of dreaming. But he clung to it because it was more tolerable than Hamako's death.

When High Lord Mhoram had tried to summon him to the Land for the last battle against Lord Foul, he, Covenant, had resisted the call. In his own world, a small girl had just been bitten by a timber-rattler – a lost child who needed his help. He had refused Mhoram and the Land in order to aid that girl.

And Mhoram had replied, *Unbeliever, I release you. You turn from us to save life in your own world. We will not be undone by such motives. And if darkness should fall upon us, still the beauty of the Land endures – for you will not forget. Go in peace.*

'I should've understood,' Covenant went on, addressing no one but the cold stars. 'I should've given Seadreamer some kind of *caamora*. Should've found some way to save Hamako. Forget the risk. Mhoram took a terrible risk when he let me go. But anything worth saving won't be destroyed by choices like that.'

He did not blame himself: he was simply trying to hold back nightmares of fire. But he was human and weary, and only the blankets wrapped around him held any warmth at all. Eventually, his dreams returned.

He could not shake the image of Hamako's strange immolation.

Without hope, he slept until sunrise. When he opened his eyes, he found that he was stretched out, not in the sled, but in blankets on the snow-packed ground. His companions were with him, though only Cail, Pitchwife, Vain, and Findail were awake. Pitchwife stirred the faggots of a small fire, watching the flames as though his heart were somewhere else.

Above him loomed a ragged cliff, perhaps two hundred feet high. The sun had not yet reached him; but it shone squarely on the bouldered wall, giving the stones a faint red hue like a reminder that beyond them lay the Sunbane.

While Covenant slept, the company had camped at the foot of Landsdrop.

Still groggy with *diamondraught*, he climbed out of his blankets, cradling his pain-stiff arm inside his robe next to the scar in the centre of his chest. Pitchwife glanced at him absently, then returned his gaze to the fire. For the first time in many long days, no ice crusted the twisting lines of his visage. Though Covenant's breath steamed as if his life were escaping from him, he was conscious that the winter had become oddly bearable – preferable to what lay ahead. The small fire was enough to steady him.

Left dumb by dreams and memories, Covenant stood beside the deformed Giant. He found an oblique comfort in Pitchwife's morose silence. Surely Cail's flat mien contained no comfort. The *Haruchai* were capable of grief and admiration and remorse; but Cail kept whatever he felt hidden. And in their opposite ways Vain and Findail represented the antithesis of comfort. Vain's makers had nearly exterminated the Waynhim. And Findail's yellow eyes were miserable with the knowledge he refused to share.

He could have told Hamako's *rhysh* about the *croyel*. Perhaps that would not have altered Covenant's plight — or Hamako's. But it would have saved lives.

Yet when Covenant looked at the *Elohim*, he felt no desire to demand explanations. He understood Findail's refusal to do anything which might relieve the pressure of his, Covenant's, culpability. The pressure to surrender his ring.

He did not need explanations. Not yet. He needed vision, percipience. He wanted to ask the Appointed, Do you think she's up to it? Is she that strong?

However, he already knew the answer. She was not that strong. But she was growing toward strength as if it were her birthright. Only her preterite self-contradictions held her back — that paralysis which gripped her when she was caught between the horror of what her father had done to her and the horror of what she had done to her mother, between her fundamental passions for and against death. And she had a better right to the wild magic than he did. Because she could see.

Around him, his companions began to stir. The First sat up suddenly, her sword in her hands: she had been dreaming of battle. As he rose stiffly to his feet, Honninscrave's eyes looked strangely like Hamako's, as if he had learned something grim and sustaining from the example of the Stonedownor. Mistweave shambled upright like an image of confusion, a man baffled by his own emotions: the release and clarity of fighting the *arghuleh* had met some of his needs, but had not restored his sense of himself.

When Linden awoke, her gaze was raw and aggrieved, as if she had spent half the night unable to staunch her tears.

Covenant's heart went out to her, but he did not know how to say so. The previous evening, she had tended his mangled arm with a ferocity which he recognized as love. But the intensity of his self-repudiation had isolated them from each other. And now he could not forget that her right was better than his. That his accumulating falseness corrupted everything he did or wanted to do.

He had never learned how to give up.

His nightmares insisted that he needed the fire he feared.

Mistweave moved woodenly about the task of preparing breakfast; but abruptly Pitchwife stopped him. Without a word, the crippled Giant rose to his feet. His manner commanded the attention of the company. For a moment, he remained motionless and rigid, his eyes damp in the sunrise. Then, hoarsely, he began to sing. His melody was a Giantish plainsong, and his stretched and fraying voice drew a faint echo from the cliff of Landsdrop, an added resonance, so that he seemed to be singing for all his companions as well as for himself.

'My heart has rooms that sigh with dust
  And ashes in the hearth.
They must be cleaned and blown away
  By daylight's breath.
But I cannot essay the task,
For even dust to me is dear;
For dust and ashes still recall,
  My love was here.

'I know not how to say Farewell,
  When Farewell is the word
That stays alone for me to say
  Or will be heard.
But I cannot speak out that word
Or ever let my loved one go:
How can I bear it that these rooms
  Are empty so?'

'I sit among the dust and hope
  That dust will cover me.
I stir the ashes in the hearth,
  Though cold they be.
I cannot bear to close the door,
To seal my loneliness away
While dust and ashes yet remain
  Of my love's day.'

When he was done, the First hugged him hard; and Mistweave looked as if he had been eased. Linden glanced at Covenant, bit her lips to keep them from trembling. But Honninscrave's eyes remained shrouded, and his jaws chewed gall as though Farewell were not the only word he could not bring himself to utter.

Covenant understood. Seadreamer had given his life as bravely as Hamako, but no victory had been gained to make his death endurable. And no *caamora* had been granted to accord him peace.

The Unbeliever was bitterly afraid that his own death would have more in common with Seadreamer's than with Hamako's.

While the companions ate a meal and repacked the sleds, Covenant tried to imagine how they would be able to find their way up the harsh cliff. Here Landsdrop was not as imposing as it was nearer the centre of the Land, where a thousand feet and more of steep rock separated the Lower Land from the Upper, Sarangrave Flat from Andelain – and where Mount Thunder crouched like a titan, presiding darkly over the rift. But still the cliff appeared impassable.

But the eyesight of the Giants had already discovered an answer. They towed the sleds southward; and in less than a league they reached a place where the rim of the precipice had collapsed, sending a wide scallop of earth down fan-like across its base. This slope was manageable, though Covenant and Linden had to ascend on foot while the Giants carried the sleds. Before the morning was half gone, the company stood among the snows of the Upper Land.

Covenant scanned the terrain apprehensively, expecting at any moment to hear Linden announce that she could see the Sunbane rising before them. But beyond Landsdrop lay only more winter and a high ridge of mountains which blocked the west and south.

These appeared to be as tall and arduous as the Westron Mountains. However, the Giants were undaunted, wise in the ways of peaks and valleys. Though the rest of the day was spent winding up into the thin air of the heights, Covenant and Linden were able to remain in their sleds, and the company made good progress.

But the next day the way was harder, steeper, cramped with boulders and old ice; and wind came slashing off the crags to blind the eyes, confuse the path. Covenant clung to the back of the sled and trudged after Honninscrave. His right arm throbbed as if the cold were gnawing at it: his numb hands had no strength. Yet *vitrim* and *diamondraught* were healing him faster than he would have believed possible; and the desire not to burden his companions kept him on his feet.

He lost all sense of progress: the ridge seemed to tower above him. Whenever he tried to breathe deeply, the air sawed at his lungs. He felt frail and useless – and immeasurably far from Revelstone. Still he endured. The specific disciplines of his leprosy had been lost long ago; but their spirit remained to him – the dogged and meticulous insistence on survival which took no account of the distance ahead or the pain already suffered. When the onset of evening finally forced the company to halt, he was still on his feet.

The following day was worse. The air became as cold as the malice of the *arghuleh*: wind flayed like outrage down the narrow coombs which gave the company passage. Time and again, Cail had to help either Covenant or Linden, and was needed to assist the sleds. But he seemed to flourish in this thin air. The Giants fought and hauled their way upward as if they were prepared to measure themselves against any terrain. And Linden stayed with them somehow – as stubborn as Covenant, and in an odd way tougher. Her face was as pale as the snow among the protruding rocks: cold glazed her eyes like frost. Yet she persevered.

And that night the company camped in the lower end of a pass between peaks ranging dramatically toward the heavens. Beyond the far mouth of the pass were no more mountains high enough to catch the sunset.

The companions had to struggle to keep their fire alight long enough to prepare a meal: the wind keening through the pass tore at the brands. Without a makeshift windbreak of blankets, no fire would have been possible at all. But the Giants did their best, contrived both to warm some food and to heat the water Linden needed for Covenant's arm. When she unwrapped his bandages, he was surprised to see that his self-inflicted wounds were nearly well. After she had washed the slight infection which remained, she applied another light bandage to protect his arm from being chafed.

Grateful for her touch, her concern, her endurance – for more things than he could name in that wind – he tried to thank her with his eyes. But she kept her gaze averted, and her movements were abrupt and troubled. When she spoke, she sounded as forlorn as the peaks.

'We're getting close to it. This – ' She made a gesture that seemed to indicate the wind. 'It's unnatural. A reaction to something on the other side.' The lines of her face stiffened into a scowl. 'If you want my guess, I'd say there's been a desert sun for two days now.'

She stopped. Tensely, Covenant waited for her to go on. From the first, the Sunbane had been a torment to her: the added dimension of her senses exposed her unmercifully to the outrage of that evil, to the alternating drought and suppuration of the world, the burning of the deserts and the screaming of the trees. Gibbon had prophesied that the true destruction of the Earth would be on her head rather than Covenant's – that she would be driven by her very health-sense to commit every desecration the Despiser required. And then the Raver had touched her, poured his malice like distilled corruption into her vulnerable flesh; and the horror of that violation had reduced her to a paralysis as deep as catatonia for two days.

When she had come out of it, after Covenant had rescued her from the hold of Revelstone, she had turned her back entirely on the resource of her percipience. She had begged him to spare her, as he had tried to spare Joan. And she had not begun to recover until she had been taught that her health-sense was also open to beauty, that when it exposed her to ill it also empowered her to heal.

She was a different woman now: he was humbled by the thought of how far she had come. But the test of the Sunbane remained before her. He did not know what was in her heart; but he knew as well as she did that she would soon be compelled to carry a burden which had already proved too heavy for her once.

A burden which would never have befallen her a second time if he had not allowed her to believe the lie that they had a future together.

Firelight and the day's exertions made her face ruddy against the background of the night. Her long-untended hair fluttered on either side of her head: in her eyes, the reflection of the wind-whipped flames capered. She looked like a woman whose features would not obey her, refused to resume the particular severity which had marked her life. She was returning to the place and the peril that had taught her to think of herself as evil.

Evil and doomed.

'I never told you,' she murmured at last. 'I just wanted to forget about it. We got so far away from the Land – even Gibbon's threats started to seem unreal. But now – ' For a moment, her gaze followed the wind. 'I can't stop thinking about it.'

After the extremity of the things she had already related to him, Covenant was dismayed that more remained to be told. But he held himself as steady as he could, did not let his regard for her waver.

'That night.' An ache crept into her voice. 'The first night we were on Starfare's Gem. Before I finally figured out we had a Raver aboard. And that rat bit you.' He remembered: that bite had triggered a venom-relapse which had nearly destroyed the quest and the Search and the *dromond* before she found a way to penetrate it and treat him. 'I had the most terrible nightmare.'

Softly, she described the dream. They had been in the woods behind Haven Farm; and he had taken Joan's place at the mercy of Lord Foul's misled band of fanatics; and she, Linden, had gone running down the hillside to save him. But never in all her life had she been able to stop the violence which had driven the knife into his chest. And from the wound had gushed more blood than she had ever seen. It had welled out of him as if a world had been slain with that one blow. As if the thrust of the knife had stabbed the very heart of the Land.

She had been altogether unable to staunch it. She had nearly drowned in the attempt.

The memory left her aghast in the unsteady light; but now she did not stop. She had been gnawing her questions for a long time and knew with frightening precision what she wanted to ask. Looking straight into Covenant's consternation, she said, 'On Kevin's Watch, you told me there were two different explanations. External and internal. Like the difference between surgery and medicine. The internal one was that we're sharing a dream. "Tied into the same unconscious process," you said.

'That fits. If we're dreaming, then naturally any healing that happens here is just an illusion. It couldn't have any effect on the bodies we left behind – on our physical continuity back where we came from.

'But what does it mean when you have a nightmare in a dream? Isn't that some kind of prophecy?'

Her directness surprised him. She had surpassed him: he could not follow without groping. His own dreams – Quickly, he scrambled to protest, 'Nothing's that simple.' But then he had to pause. An awkward moment passed before he found a countering argument.

'You had that dream under the influence of a Raver. You dreamed what it made you feel. Lord Foul's prophecy – not yours. It doesn't change anything.'

Linden was no longer looking at him. She had bowed her head, braced her forehead in her palms; but her hands did not hide the silent tears streaming down her cheeks. 'That was before I knew anything about power.' With an honesty that dismayed him, she exposed the root of her distress. 'I could've saved Hamako. I could've saved them all. You were so close to erupting – I could've taken your wild magic and torn out that *croyel*'s heart. *I'm* no danger to the Arch of Time. None of them had to die.'

Dread burned like shame across his face. He knew she spoke the truth. Her health-sense was still growing. Soon she would become capable of anything. He swallowed a groan. 'Why didn't you?'

'I was watching *you*!' she flung back at him in sudden anguish. 'Watching you tear your arm apart. I couldn't think about anything else.'

The sight of her pain enabled him to take hold of himself, fight down his instinctive panic. He could not afford to be afraid: she needed something better from him.

'I'm glad you didn't,' he said. 'Never mind what it would've done to me. I'm glad you didn't for his sake.' Thinking of her mother, he added deliberately, 'You let him achieve the meaning of his own life.'

At that, her head jerked up: her gaze knifed at him. 'He *died*!' she hissed like an imprecation too fierce and personal to be shouted. 'He saved your life at least twice, and he spent his own life serving the Land you claim to care so much about, and the people that adopted him were nearly wiped off the face of the Earth, and he *died*!'

Covenant did not flinch. He was ready now for anything she might hurl at him. His own nightmares were worse than this. And he would have given his soul for the ability to match Hamako. 'I'm not glad he died. I'm glad he found an answer.'

For a long moment, her glare held. But then slowly the anger frayed out of her face. At last, her eyes fell. Thickly, she murmured, 'I'm sorry. I just don't understand. Killing people is wrong.' The memory of her mother was present to her as it was to Covenant. 'But dear Christ! Saving them has got to be better than letting them die.'

'Linden.' She clearly did not want him to say anything else: she had raised the fundamental question of her life and needed to answer it herself. But he could not let the matter drop. With all the gentleness he had in him, he said, 'Hamako didn't want to be saved. For the opposite reason that your father didn't want to be saved. And he won.'

'I know,' she muttered. 'I know. I just don't understand it.' As if to keep him from speaking again, she left the fire, went to get her blankets.

He looked around at the mute, attentive faces of the Giants. But they had no other wisdom to offer him. He wanted intensely to be saved himself; but no one would be able to do that for him unless he surrendered his ring. He was beginning to think that his death would be welcome when it came.

A short time later, the fire blew out. Mistweave tried to light it again and failed. But when Covenant finally went to sleep, he dreamed that the blaze had become violent enough to consume him.

During the night, the wind died. The dawn was as crisp as crystal; and the crags shone in the high, thin air as if no taint could reach them. A mood of impossible hope came over the companions as they laboured toward the far end of the pass.

Under other circumstances, the view from that eminence would have delighted them. Sunlight flashed through the pass to illumine the range as it tumbled downward in a dramatic succession of snow-bright crests and saw-backed aretes, mighty heads fronting the heavens and spines sprawling toward lower ground. And beyond the bare foothills all the way to the south-western horizon lay the high North Plains which led to Revelstone.

But where the sun hit the Plains they looked as brown and battered as a desert.

That in itself would not have wrenched the Giants to silence, raised Linden's hands to her mouth, stifled Covenant's breathing; for at this time of year the region below them might be naturally dry. But as soon as the sun touched the denuded waste, a green fur began to spread across it. Distance made teeming shoots and sprouts look like an unconscionably rapid pelt.

With a curse, Covenant wheeled to scan the sun. But he could see no sign of the corona which should have accompanied the sudden verdure.

'We're under the fringe,' said Linden tonelessly. 'I told you about that – the last time we crossed Landsdrop. We won't see the aura until later.'

Covenant had not forgotten her explanation. The Sunbane was a corruption of Earthpower, and it arose from the ground, from the deep roots of Mount Thunder where Lord Foul now made his home. But it was focused or triggered by the sun and manifested itself visibly there, in the characteristic penumbra of its phases and the power for perversion of its initial contact.

Thickly, he grated to his companions, 'We'll need stone for protection. It's the first touch that does the damage.' He and Linden had been preserved by the alien leather of their footwear. The *Haruchai* and Vain had already shown that they were immune. Findail needed no advice on how to care for himself. But the Giants – Covenant could not bear that they might be at risk. 'From now on – every day. We've got to have stone under us when the sun comes up.'

The First nodded mutely. She and her people were still staring at the green mantle which thickened at every moment across the distant Plains.

That sight made Covenant long for Sunder and Hollian. The Graveller of Mithil Stonedown had left his home and people to serve as Covenant's guide through the perils of the Sunbane; and his obdurate skill and providence, his self-doubting courage, had kept Covenant and Linden alive. And Hollian's eh-Brand ability to foretell the phases of the Sunbane had been invaluable. Though he had Giants with him now, and Linden's strength, Covenant felt entirely unready to face the Sunbane without the support of his former companions.

And he wanted to know what had happened to them. He had sent them from Seareach because they had believed that they had no clear role in the quest for the One Tree, no place among such mighty beings as Giants – and because he had loathed to leave the Clave uncontested during the unpredictable period of his absence. So he had given them the *krill* of Loric, the powerful blade which he had raised from Glimmermere. And he had laid upon them the charge of mustering resistance among the villages against the bloody requirements of the Clave. Accompanied only by Stell and Harn, armed with nothing more than their own knives, the *krill*, Sunder's *orcrest* stone and Hollian's *lianar* wand, and encouraged by the thin hope that they might eventually gain the aid of more *Haruchai*, the two lone Stonedownors had gone in sunlight and poignant valour to hazard their lives against the forces which ruled the Land.

That memory outweighed any amount of unreadiness. The distant preternatural green swelling below him brought back the past with renewed vividness. Sunder and Hollian were his friends. He had come this far in the name of Revelstone and the Clave; but now he wanted keenly to rejoin the two Stonedownors.

Rejoin or avenge.

'Come on,' he rasped to his companions. 'Let's get down there.'

The First gave him a measuring glance, as though she half distrusted the constant hardening of his attitude. But she was not a woman who hung back. With a stern nod, she sent him and Linden to the sleds. Then she turned and started down the steep, snow-bound slope as if she, too, could not wait to confront the ill that had brought the Search here.

Heaving Covenant's sled into motion, Honninscrave let out a cry like a challenge and went plunging after the Swordmain.

In the course of that one day, the company passed down out of the mountains, came to the foothills and the end of the snow. Careening at a mad pace which could only have been controlled by Giants, they sped from slope to slope, pausing only when the First needed to consider her best route. She seemed determined to regain the time lost by the arduous ascent of the range. Before noon, a band of green – the colour of chrysoprase and Daphin's eyes – closed around the sun like a garrotte. But Covenant could not look at it. He was nearly blind with vertigo. He was barely able to cling to the rails of the sled and hold the contents of his stomach down.

Then the ice and snow of the heights failed on the verge of a moiling chaos of vegetation which had already grown high enough to appear impenetrable. His head still reeling, Covenant considered himself fortunate that dusk prevented the First from tackling the verdure immediately. But the Swordmain was not insensitive to the nausea in his face – or the aggravated ache in Linden's. While Mistweave and Honninscrave prepared a camp, she passed a flask of *diamondraught* to the two humans, then left them alone to try to recover themselves.

The liquor settled Covenant's guts, but could not soften the wide, white outrage and dread of Linden's stare. At intervals during the evening, Pitchwife and the First addressed comments to her; but her replies were monosyllabic and distant. The crouching vegetation spoke a language that only she could hear, consuming her attention. Unconscious of being watched, she chewed her lips as if she had lost her old severity and did not know how to recapture it.

Her huddled posture – thighs pressed against her chest, arms hugged around her shins, chin braced on her knees – reminded him of a time many days ago, a time when they had begun travelling together, and she had nearly broken under the pressure of her first fertile sun. She had quailed into herself, protesting, *I can't shut it out. It's too personal. I don't believe in evil.*

She believed in evil now; but that only made the sensory assault of the Sunbane more intimate and unanswerable – as heinous as murder and as immedicable as leprosy.

He tried to stay awake with her, offering her the support of his silent companionship. But she was still taut and unslumberous when the mortal pull of his dreams took him away. He went to sleep thinking that if he had possessed anything akin to her percipience the Land would not be in such danger – and she would not be so alone.

Visions he could neither face nor shun seemed to protract the night; yet dawn and Cail's rousing touch came too early. He awoke with a jerk and found himself staring at the dense growth. His companions were already up. While Pitchwife and Mistweave prepared a meal, and Honninscrave dismantled the sleds, the First studied the choked terrain, clenching a tuneless hum between her teeth. A gap among the peaks sent an early shaft of light onto the vegetation directly in front of the camp. The sun would touch the company soon.

Covenant's skin crawled as he watched the verdure writhe and grow. The contrast between the places where the sun hit and where it did not only made the effect more eerie and ominous. In the stony soil among the foothills, there were no trees. But the hardy, twisted shrubs were already as tall as trees; thistles and other weeds crowded the ground between the trunks; huge slabs of lichen clung to the rocks like scabs. And everything the sun touched grew so rapidly that it seemed animate – a form of helpless flesh tortured mercilessly toward the sky. He had forgotten how horrific the Sunbane truly was. He dreaded the moment when he would have to descend into that lush green anguish.

Then the sunlight fell through the gap onto the company.

At the last moment, the First, Honninscrave, and Pitchwife had found rocks on which to stand. Under Mistweave's feet lay the stone with which he had formerly shielded his campfires from ice and snow.

Distantly, Linden nodded at the caution of the Giants. 'Cail's got something you don't have,' she murmured. 'You need the protection.' But Vain and Findail required no defence; and Covenant and Linden had their footwear. Together, they faced the onset of the sun.

As it first crested the gap, the sun appeared normal. For that reason, at least this much of the foothills remained free of vegetation. Yet the company stayed motionless, suspended and silent in an anticipation like dread. And before their eyes the sun changed. A green aura closed around it, altering the light. Even the strip of bare ground between the end of the snow and the beginning of the vegetation took on an emerald timbre.

Because of the winter which still held the mountains, the air was not warm. But Covenant found that he was sweating.

Grimly, Linden turned her back on the sun. The Giants went to their tasks. Vain's constant, black, ambiguous smile betrayed no reaction. But Findail's pain-marked face looked more aggrieved than ever. Covenant thought he saw the *Elohim*'s hands trembling.

Shortly after the company had eaten, Honninscrave finished reducing the sleds to firewood. He and Mistweave packed their supplies into huge bundles for themselves and smaller ones for

Pitchwife and the First. Soon Covenant's companions were prepared to commence the day's journey.

'Giantfriend,' the First asked sternly, 'is there peril for us here other than that which we have all witnessed?'

Peril, he thought dumbly. If the Riders of the Clave don't come this far north. And nothing else has changed. 'Not under this sun,' he replied with sweat in his voice. 'But if we stand still too long, we'll have trouble moving again.'

The Swordmain nodded. 'That is plain.'

Drawing her blade, she took two long steps down the hillside and began hacking tall thistles out of her way.

Honninscrave followed her. With his bulk and muscle, he widened her path for the rest of the company.

Covenant compelled himself to take his position at Pitchwife's back. Cail followed between the Unbeliever and Linden. Then came Mistweave, with Vain and Findail inseparably behind him.

In that formation, the failed quest for the One Tree met the atrocity of the Sunbane.

For the morning and part of the afternoon, they managed a surprising pace. Monstrous scrub-brush and weeds gave way to stands of immense, raw bracken clotted with clumps of grass; and every added degree of the sun's arc made each frond and leaf and stem yearn more desperately upward, as frantic as the damned. Yet the First and Honninscrave forged ahead as fast as Covenant and Linden could comfortably walk. The air became warmer, noticeably more humid, as the snows and elevation of the mountains were left behind. Although Covenant had added his robe to Pitchwife's bundle, he perspired constantly. But his days in the range had toughened him somewhat: he was able to keep the pace.

But toward midafternoon the company entered a region like a surreal madland. Juniper trees as contorted as ghouls sprawled thickly against each other, strangled by the prodigious vines which festooned them like the web of a gargantuan and insane spider. And between the vine-stems and tree-trunks the ground was profuse with lurid orchids that smelled like poison. The First struck one fierce blow against the nearest vine, then snatched back her green-slick blade to see if she had damaged it: the stem was as hard as ironwood. Around her, the trees and vines rustled like execration. In order to advance at all, the companions had to clamber and squirm awkwardly among the hindrances.

Night caught them in the middle of the region, with no stone in sight and scarcely enough space for them to lay their blankets between the trunks. But when Cail roused the company the next morning, they found that he had somehow contrived to collect sufficient small rocks to protect two of the Giants. And the stone which Mistweave still carried could hold two more. Thus warded, they braced themselves to meet the sun.

When its first touch filtered insidiously down through the choked trees, Covenant flinched; and Linden jerked a hand to her mouth to stifle a gasp.

They could see only pieces of the sun's aura. But those pieces were red. The colour of pestilence.

'Two days!' Covenant spat to keep himself from groaning. 'It's getting worse.'

The First stared at him. Bitterly, he explained that the Sunbane had formerly moved in a cycle of three days. Any foreshortening of that period meant that its power was increasing. And *that* meant – But he could not say such things aloud: the hurt of them went too deep. It meant that Sunder and Hollian had failed. Or that the na-Mhoram had found a source of blood as large as his malice. Or that Lord Foul was now confident of victory, and therefore the Clave no longer made any pretence of holding back the Sunbane.

Glowering, the First absorbed Covenant's answer. After a moment, she asked carefully, 'May it be that this is but a variation – that the essential period remains unaltered?'

That was possible. He remembered one sun of two days. But when he turned to Linden for her opinion, she was not looking at him. Her hand had not come down from her mouth. Her teeth were closed on the knuckle of her index finger, and a drop of blood marked her chin.

'*Linden.*' He grabbed at her wrist, yanked her hand away.

Her dismay slapped at him. 'The sun of pestilence.' Her voice came twisted and harsh from her knotted throat. 'Have you forgotten what it's like? We don't have any *voure.*'

At that, a new fear stung Covenant. *Voure* was the pungent sap of a certain plant – a sap that warded off the insects which thrived under a red sun. And more: it was also an antidote for the Sunbane-sickness. That pestilential disease could attack through any kind of exposed cut or injury. 'Hellfire,' he breathed. Then snapped, 'Get a bandage on that finger!' His arm was healed enough to be safe; but this sun might prove the small marks on her knuckle fatal.

Around him, steam rose like a miasma. Wherever the light touched the vines and trunks, their bark opened and began to ooze. The steam stank of decomposition.

Nameless insects started to whine like augers through the mounting stench. Suddenly, Covenant caught up with Linden's apprehension. In addition to everything else, she had realized before he did that even a Giant might sicken and fail from breathing too much of that vapour – or from being bitten by too many of those insects.

She had not moved. Her eyes appeared glazed and inward, as if she could not move. Small red beads formed around her knuckle and dropped to the dirt.

Fierce with exasperation and alarm, Covenant snarled at her, 'By hell! I said, get a bandage on that *finger*. And *think* of something. We're in big trouble.'

She flinched. 'No,' she whispered. The delicacy of her features seemed to crumple. 'No. You don't understand. You don't feel it. It was never this – I can't remember – ' She swallowed heavily to keep herself from crying out. Then her tone became flat and dead. 'You don't feel it. It's hideous. You can't fight it.'

Wisps of steam passed in front of her face as if she, too, had begun to rot.

Urgently, Covenant grabbed her shoulders, ground his numb fingers into her. 'Maybe I can't. But you can. You're the Sun-Sage. What do you think you're here for?'

The Sun-Sage. The *Elohim* had given her that title. For an instant, her gaze became wild; and he feared he had torn the thin fabric of her sanity. But then her eyes focused on him with an emotional impact that made him wince. Abruptly, she was alabaster and adamantine in his grasp. 'Let go of me,' she articulated distinctly. 'You don't give enough to have the right.'

He pleaded with her mutely, but she did not relent. When he dropped his arms and stepped back, she turned away as if she were dismissing him from her life.

To the First, she said, 'Get some green wood. Branches or whatever you can find.' She sounded oddly hard and brittle, not to be touched. 'Soak the ends in *vitrim* and light them. The smoke should give us some protection.'

The First cocked an eyebrow at the tension between Covenant and Linden. But the Giants did not hesitate: they were acquainted with Linden's health-sense. In moments, they had wrenched several boughs the size of brands from nearby trees. Pitchwife muttered mournfully at the idea of using his precious *vitrim* for such a purpose, but he handed one of his pouches to the First readily enough. Shortly, the four Giants and Cail held flaming branches that guttered and spat with enough smoke to palliate the reek of rot. Outsize flying insects hummed angrily around the area, then shot off in search of other prey.

When the supplies had been repacked, the First turned to Linden for instructions, tacitly recognizing the change which had taken place in the Chosen. Covenant was Giantfriend and ring-wielder; but it was Linden's percipience upon which the company depended now for its survival.

Without a glance at Covenant, Linden nodded. Then she took Pitchwife's place behind the First and Honninscrave; and the company started moving.

Beclouded with smoke and rot, the company struggled on through the wild region. Under the particular corruption of the sun's scarlet aura, vines which had been too hard for the First's sword were now marked with swellings that burst and sores that ran. Fetor and borers took hold of some of the trees, ate out their hearts: others lost wide strips of bark, exposing bald wood fatally veined with termites. The narcoleptic sweetness of the orchids penetrated the acrid smoke from time to time. Covenant felt that he was labouring through the fruition of what Lord Foul had striven to achieve ten years and three and a half millennia ago – the desecration of all the Land's health to leprosy. Here the Despiser emerged in the throes of victory. The beauty of Land and Law had been broken. With smoke in his eyes and revulsion in his guts, images of gangrene and pain on all sides, Covenant found himself praying for a sun of only two days.

Yet the red sun produced one benefit: the rotting of the wood allowed the First to begin cutting a path once more. The company was able to improve its pace. And finally the juniper wilderness opened into an area of tall, thick grass as corrupt and cloying as a tar pit. The First called a halt for a brief meal and a few swallows of *diamondraught*.

Covenant needed the liquor, but he could hardly eat. His gaze refused to leave the swelling of Linden's bitten finger.

Sunbane-sickness, he thought miserably. She had suffered from it once before. Sunder and Hollian, who were familiar with such illnesses, had believed she would die. He would never forget the look of her as she had lain helpless in the grip of convulsions as flagrant as his nightmares. Only her health-sense and *voure* had saved her.

That memory compelled him to risk her ire. More harshly than he intended, he began, 'I thought I told you – '

'And I told you,' she retorted, 'to leave me alone. I don't need you to mother me.'

But he faced her squarely, forced her to recognize his concern. After a moment, her belligerence failed. Frowning, she turned her head away. 'You don't have to worry about it,' she sighed. 'I know what I'm doing. It helps me concentrate.'

'Helps – ?' He did not know how to understand her.

'Sunder was right,' she responded. 'This is the worst – the sun of pestilence. It sucks at me – or soaks into me – I don't know how to describe it. I become it. It becomes me.' The simple act of putting her plight into words made her shudder. Deliberately, she raised her hand, studied her hurt finger. 'The pain. The way it scares me. It helps make the distinction. It keeps me separate.'

Covenant nodded. What else could he do? Her vulnerability had become terrible to him. Huskily, he said, 'Don't let it get too bad.'

Then he made another attempt to force food down into his knotted stomach.

The rest of the day was atrocious. And the next day was worse. But early in the evening, amid the screaming of numberless cicadas and the piercing frustration of huge, smoke-daunted mosquitoes, the company reached a region of hills where wide boulders still protruded from the surrounding morass of moss and ground-ivy. That proved to be a fortuitous camping-place; for when the sun rose again, it was wreathed in dusty brown.

After only two days.

The elevation of the rocks protected the travellers from the effect of the desert sun on the putrefying vegetation.

Everything that the fertile sun had produced and the sun of pestilence had blighted might as well have been made of wax. The brown-clad sun melted it all, reduced every form of plant fibre, every kind of sap or juice, every monstrous insect to a necrotic grey sludge. The few bushes in the area slumped like over-heated candles: moss and ivy sprawled into spilth that formed turbid pools in the low places of the terrain: the bugs of dawn fell like clotted drops of rain. Then the sludge denatured as if the desert sun drank it away.

Long before midmorning, every slope and hollow and span of ground had been burned to naked ruin and dust.

For the Giants, that process was more horrible than anything else they had seen. Until now, only the scale of the Sunbane's power had been staggering: verdure grew naturally, and insects and rot could be included in the normal range of experience. But nothing had prepared Covenant's companions for the quick and entire destruction of so much prodigious vegetation and pestilence.

Staring about her, the First breathed, 'Ah, Cable Seadreamer! There is no cause for wonder that you lacked voice to utter such visions. The wonder is that you endured to bear them at all – and that you bore them in loneliness.'

Pitchwife clung to her as if he were reeling inwardly. Open nausea showed in Mistweave's face: he had learned to doubt himself, and now the things he could no longer trust covered all the world. But Honninscrave's deep eyes flamed hotly – the eyes of a man who knew now beyond question that he was on the right path.

Grimly, Linden demanded a knife from Pitchwife. For a moment, he could not answer her. But at last the First stirred, turned from the harsh vista of the waste; and her husband turned with her.

Dazedly, he gave Linden his blade. She used its tip to lance her infected finger. With *vitrim*, she cleansed the wound thoroughly, then bound it in a light bandage. When she was done, she lifted her head; and her gaze was as intense as Honninscrave's. Like him, she now appeared eager to go forward.

Or like High Lord Elena, who had been driven by inextricable abhorrence and love, and by lust for power, to the mad act of breaking the Law of Death. After only three days under the Sunbane, Linden appeared capable of such things.

Soon the company started southwestward again across a wasteland which had become little more than an anvil for the fierce brutality of the sun.

It brought back more of the past to Covenant: heat-haze as thick as hallucination and dust bleached to the colour of dismay made his memories vivid. He and Linden had been summoned to Kevin's Watch during a day of rain; but that night Sunder's father, Nassic, had been murdered, and the next day had arisen a desert sun – and Covenant and Linden had encountered a Raver amid the hostility of Mithil Stonedown.

Many of the consequences had fallen squarely upon Sunder's shoulders. As the Stonedown's Graveller, he had already been required to shed the lives of his own wife and son so that their blood would serve the village. And then the Raver's action had cost him his father, had compelled him to sacrifice his friend, Marid, to the Sunbane, and had faced him with the necessity of bleeding his mother to death. Such things had driven him to flee his duty for the sake of the Unbeliever and the Chosen – and for his own sake, so that he would be spared the responsibility of more killing.

Yet during that same desert sun Covenant's life had also been changed radically. The corruption of that sun had made Marid monstrous enough to inflict the Despiser's malice. Out in the wasteland of the South Plains, Marid had nailed venom between the bones of Covenant's forearm, crucifying him to the fate Lord Foul had prepared for him.

The fate of fire. In a nightmare of wild magic, his own terrible love and grief tore down the world.

The sun would not let him think of anything else. The company had adequate supplies of water, *diamondraught*, and food; and when the haze took on the attributes of vertigo, leeched the strength out of Covenant's legs, Honninscrave carried him. Foamfollower had done the same for him more than once, bearing him along the way of hope and doom. But now there was only haze and vertigo and despair – and the remorseless hammer-blow of the sun.

That phase of the Sunbane also lasted for only two days. But it was succeeded by another manifestation of pestilence.

The red-tinged heat was less severe. The stricken Plains contained nothing which could rot. And here the insect-life was confined to creatures that made their homes in the ground. Yet this sun was arduous and bitter after its own fashion. It brought neither moisture nor shade up out of the waste. And before it ended, the travellers began to encounter stag-beetles and scorpions as big as wolves among the low hills. But the First's sword kept such threats at bay. And whenever Honninscrave and Mistweave took on the added weight of Covenant and Linden, the company made good speed.

In spite of their native hardness, the Giants were growing weary, worn down by dust and heat and distance. But after the second day of pestilence came a sun of rain. Standing on stone to meet the dawn, the companions felt a new coolness against their faces as the sun rose ringed in blue like a concentration of the sky's deep azure. Then, almost immediately, black clouds began to pile westward.

Covenant's heart lifted at the thought of rain. But as the wind stiffened, plucking insistently at his unclean hair and beard, he remembered how difficult it was to travel under such a sun. He turned to the First. 'We're going to need rope.' The wind hummed in his ears. 'So we don't lose each other.'

Linden was staring toward the south-west as if the idea of Revelstone consumed all her thoughts. Distantly, she said, 'The rain isn't dangerous. But there's going to be so much of it.'

The First glared at the clouds, nodded. Mistweave unslung his bundles and dug out a length of line.

The rope was too heavy to be tied around Covenant and Linden without hampering them. As the first rain-drops hit, heavy as pebbles, the Swordmain knotted the line to her own waist, then strung it back through the formation of the company to Mistweave, who anchored it.

For a moment, she scanned the terrain to fix her bearings in her mind. Then she started into the darkening storm.

As loud as a rabble, the rain rushed out of the east. The clouds spanned the horizons, blocking the last light. Gloom fell like water into Covenant's eyes. Already, he could barely discern the First at the head of the company. Pitchwife's misshapen outlines were blurred. The wind leaned against Covenant's left shoulder. His boots began to slip under him: without transition, soil as desiccated as centuries of desert changed to mud and clay. Instant pools spread across the ground. The downpour became as heavy as cudgels. Blindly, he clung to the rope.

It led into a blank abyss of rain. The world was reduced to this mad drenching lash and roar, this battering cold. He should have retrieved his robe before the rain started: his scant T-shirt was meaningless against the torrents. How could there be so much water, when for days the North Plains and all the Land had been desperately athirst? Only Pitchwife's shape remained before him, badly smudged but still solid – the only solid thing left except the rope. When he tried to look around toward Cail, Mistweave, Vain, and Findail, the storm hit him full in the face. It was a doomland he wandered in because he had failed to find any answer to his dreams.

Eventually, even Pitchwife was gone. The staggering downpour dragged every vestige of light and vision out of the air. His hands numb with leprosy and cold, Covenant could only be sure of the rope by clamping it under his elbow, leaning his weight on it. Long after he had begun to believe that the ordeal should be given up, that the company should find some shelter and simply huddle there while the storm lasted, the line went on drawing him forward.

But then, as suddenly as the summons which had changed his life, a pressure jerked back on the rope, hauled it to a stop; and he nearly fell. While he stumbled for balance, the line went slack.

Before he recovered, something heavy blundered against him, knocked him into the mire.

The storm had a strange timbre, as if people were shouting around him.

Almost at once, huge hands took hold of him, heaved him to his feet. A Giant: Pitchwife. He was pushed a few steps toward the rear of the formation, then gripped to a halt.

The rain was at his back. He saw three people in front of him. They all looked like Cail.

One of them caught his arm, put a mouth to his ear. Cail's voice reached him dimly through the roar.

'Here are Durris and Fole of the *Haruchai*! They have come with others of our people to oppose the Clave!'

Rain pounded at Covenant: wind reeled through him. 'Where's Sunder?' he cried. 'Where's Hollian?'

Blurred in the fury of the torrents, two more figures became discernible. One of them seemed to hold out an object toward Covenant.

From it, a white light sprang through the storm, piercing the darkness. Incandescence shone from a clear gem which had been forged into a long dagger, at the cross where blade and hilt came together. Its heat sizzled the rain; but the light itself burned as if no rain could touch it.

The *krill* of Loric.

It illumined all the faces around Covenant: Cail and his kinfolk, Durris and Fole; Mistweave flanked by Vain and Findail; Pitchwife; the First and Honninscrave crowding forward with Linden between them. And the two people who had brought the *krill*.

Sunder son of Nassic, Graveller from Mithil Stonedown.

Hollian Amith-daughter, eh-Brand.

8

THE DEFENDERS OF THE LAND

The torrents came down like thunder. The rain was full of voices Covenant could not hear. Sunder's lips moved, made no sound: Hollian blinked at the water streaming down her face as if she did not know whether to laugh or weep. Covenant wanted to go to them, throw his arms around them in sheer relief that they were alive; but the light of the *krill* held him back. He did not know what it meant. The venom in his forearm ached to take hold of it and burn –

Cail spoke directly into Covenant's ear again. 'The Graveller asks if your quest has succeeded!'

At that, Covenant covered his face, pressed the ring's immanent heat against the bones of his skull. The rain was too much for him: suppressed weeping knotted his chest. He had been so eager to find Sunder and Hollian safe that he had never considered what the ruin of the quest would mean to them.

The First's hearing was keener than his: Sunder's query had reached her. She focused her voice to answer him through the roar. 'The quest has failed!' The words were raw with strain. 'Cable Seadreamer is slain! We have come seeking another hope!'

The full shout of Sunder's reply was barely audible. 'You will find none here!'

Then the light receded: the Graveller had turned away. Holding the *krill* high to guide the company, he moved off into the storm.

Covenant dropped his hands like a cry he could not utter.

For an instant, no one followed Sunder. Silhouetted against the *krill*'s shining, Hollian stood before Covenant and Linden. He hardly saw what she was doing as she came to him, gave him a tight hug of welcome. Before he was able to respond, she left him to embrace Linden.

Yet her brief gesture helped him pull himself together. It felt like an act of forgiveness – or an affirmation that his return and Linden's were more important than hope. When Cail urged him after the light, he pushed his numb limbs into motion.

They were in a low place between hills: gathered water reached almost to his knees. But its current ran in the direction he was going, and Cail bore him up. The *Haruchai* seemed more certain than ever. It must have been the mental communion of his people which had

979

drawn Durris and Fole, with the Stonedownors behind them, toward the company. And now Cail was no longer alone. Mud and streams and rain could not make him miss his footing. He supported Covenant like a figure of granite.

Covenant had lost all sense of his companions; but he was not concerned: he trusted the other *Haruchai* as he trusted Cail. Directing his attention to the struggle for movement, he followed Sunder as quickly as his imbalance and fatigue allowed.

The way seemed long and harsh in the clutches of the storm. At last, however, he and Cail neared an impression of rock and saw Sunder's *krill*-light reflecting wetly off the edges of a wide entrance to a cave. Sunder went directly inward, used the argent heat of the *krill* to set a ready pile of wood afire. Then he rewrapped the blade and tucked it away within his leather jerkin.

The flames were dimmer than the *krill*, but they spread illumination around a larger area, revealing bundles of wood and bedding stacked against the walls. The Stonedownors and *Haruchai* had already established a camp here.

The cave was high but shallow, hardly more than a depression in the side of a hill. The angle of the ceiling's overhang let rainwater run inward and drizzle to the floor, with the result that the cave was damp and the fire not easily kept alight. But even that relative shelter was a balm to Covenant's battered nerves. He stood over the flames and tried to rub the dead chill out of his skin, watching Sunder while the company arrived to join him.

Durris brought the four Giants. Fole guided Linden as if he had already arrogated to himself Mistweave's chosen place at her side. Vain and Findail came of their own accord, though they did not move far enough into the cave to avoid the lashing rain. And Hollian was accompanied by Harn, the *Haruchai* who had taken the eh-Brand under his care in the days when Covenant had rescued them from the hold of Revelstone and the Banefire.

Covenant stared at him. When Sunder and Hollian had left Seareach to begin their mission against the Clave, Harn had gone with them. But not alone: they had also been accompanied by Stell, the *Haruchai* who had watched over Sunder.

Where was Stell?

No, more than that: worse than that. Where were the men and women of the Land, the villagers Sunder and Hollian had gone to muster? And where were the rest of the *Haruchai*? After the heinous slaughter which the Clave had wrought upon that people, why had only Durris and Fole been sent to give battle?

You will find none here.

Had the na-Mhoram already won?

Gaping at Sunder across the guttering fire, Covenant moved his jaw, but no words came. In the cover of the cave, the storm was muffled but incessant – fierce and hungry as a great beast.

And Sunder was changed. In spite of all the blood his role as the Graveller of Mithil Stonedown had forced him to shed, he had never looked like a man who knew how to kill. But he did now.

When Covenant had first met him, the Stonedownor's youthful features had been strangely confused and conflicted by the unresolved demands of his duty. His father had taught him that the world was not what the Riders claimed it to be – a punishment for human offence – and so he had never learned to accept or forgive the acts which the rule of the Clave and the stricture of the Sunbane required him to commit. Unacknowledged revulsion had marked his forehead: his eyes had been worn dull by accumulated remorse: his teeth had ground together, chewing the bitter gristle of his irreconciliation. But now he appeared as honed and whetted as the poniard he had once used to take the lives of the people he loved. His eyes gleamed like daggers in the firelight. And all his movements were tense with coiled anger – a savage and baffled rage that he could no longer utter.

His visage held no welcome. The First had told him that the quest had failed. Yet his manner suggested that his tautness was not directed at the Unbeliever – that even bare relief and pleasure had become impossible to articulate.

In dismay, Covenant looked to Hollian for an explanation.

The eh-Brand also showed the marks of her recent life. Her leather shift was tattered in places, poorly mended: her arms and legs exposed the thinness of scant rations and constant danger. Yet she formed a particular contrast to Sunder.

They were both of sturdy Stonedownor stock, dark-haired and short, though she was younger than he. But her background had been entirely different than his. Until the shock which had cost her her home in Crystal Stonedown – the crisis of the Rider's demand for her life, and of her rescue by Covenant, Linden, and Sunder – she had been the most prized member of her community: as an eh-Brand, able to foretell the phases of the Sunbane, she had given her people a precious advantage. Her past had contained little of the self-doubt and bereavement which had filled Sunder's days. And that difference was more striking now. She was luminous rather than angry – as warm of welcome as he was rigid. If the glances she cast at the Graveller had not been so full of endearment, Covenant might have thought that the two Stonedownors had become strangers to each other.

But the black hair that flew like raven wings about her shoulders when she moved had not changed. It still gave her an aspect of fatality, a suggestion of doom.

In shame, Covenant found that he did not know what to say to her either. She and Sunder were too vivid to him: they mattered too much. *You will find none here.* With a perception as acute as intuition, he saw that they were not at all strangers to each other. Sunder was so tight and bitter precisely because of the way Hollian glowed; and her luminescence came from the same root as his pain. But that insight did not give Covenant any words he could bear to say.

Where was Stell?

Where were the people of the Land? And the *Haruchai*?

And what had happened to the Stonedownors?

The First tried to bridge the awkward silence with Giantish courtesy. In the past, the role of spokesman in such situations had belonged to Honninscrave; but he had lost heart for it.

'Stone and Sea!' she began, 'it gladdens me to greet you again, Sunder Graveller and Hollian eh-Brand. When we parted, I hardly dared dream that we would meet again. It is – '

Linden's abrupt whisper stopped the First. She had been staring intensely at Hollian; and her exclamation stilled the gathering, bore clearly through the thick barrage of the rain.

'Covenant. She's pregnant.'

Oh my God.

Hollian's slim shape showed nothing. But hardly ninety days had passed since the Stonedownors had left Seareach. Linden's assertion carried instant conviction: her percipience would not be mistaken about such a thing.

The sudden weight of understanding forced him to the floor. His legs refused to support the revelation. *Pregnant.*

That was why Hollian glowed and Sunder raged. She was glad of it because she loved him. And because he loved her, he was appalled. The quest for the One Tree had failed. The purpose for which Covenant had sent the Stonedownors back to the Upper Land had failed. And Sunder had already been compelled to kill one wife and child. He had nowhere left to turn.

'Oh, Sunder.' Covenant was not certain that he spoke aloud. Eyes streaming, he bowed his head. It should have been covered with ashes and execration. 'Forgive me. I'm so sorry.'

'Is the fault yours then that the quest has failed?' asked Sunder. He sounded as severe as hate. 'Have you brought us to this pass, that my own failure has opened the last door of doom?'

Yes, Covenant replied – aloud or silent, it made no difference.

'Then hear me, ur-Lord.' Sunder's voice came closer. Now it was occluded with grief. 'Unbeliever and white gold wielder, Illender and Prover of Life.' His hands gripped Covenant's shoulders. 'Hear me.'

Covenant looked up, fighting for self-control. The Graveller crouched before him. Sunder's eyes were blurred: beads of wet firelight coursed his hard jaws.

'When first you persuaded me from my home and duty in Mithil

982

Stonedown,' he said thickly, 'I demanded of you that you should not betray me. You impelled me on a mad search of the desert sun for my friend Marid, whom you could not save – and you refused me the use of my blood to aid you – and you required of me that I eat *aliantha* which I knew to be poison – and so I beseeched of you something greater than fidelity. I pleaded of you meaning for my life – and for the death of Nassic my father. And still you were not done, for you wrested Hollian Amith-daughter from her peril in Crystal Stonedown as though it were your desire that I should love her. And when we fell together into the hands of the Clave, you redeemed us from that hold, restored our lives.

'And *still* you were not done. When you had taught us to behold the Clave's evil, you turned your back on that crime, though it cried out for retribution in the face of all the Land. There you betrayed me, ur-Lord. The meaning of which I was in such need you set aside. In its place, you gave me only a task that surpassed my strength.'

That was true. In blood-loss and folly and passion, Covenant had made himself responsible for the truth he had required Sunder to accept. And then he had failed. What was that, if not betrayal? Sunder's accusations made him bleed rue and tears.

But Sunder also was not done. 'Therefore,' he went on hoarsely, 'it is my right that you should hear me. Ur-Lord and Unbeliever, white gold wielder,' he said as if he were addressing the hot streaks that stained Covenant's face, 'you have betrayed me – and I am glad that you have come. Though you come without hope, you are the one hope that I have known. You have it in your hands to create or deny whatever truth you will, and I desire to serve you. While you remain, I will accept neither despair or doom. There is neither betrayal nor failure while you endure to me. And if the truth you teach must be lost at last, I will be consoled that my love and I were not asked to bear that loss alone.

'Covenant, hear me,' he insisted. 'No words suffice. I am glad that you have come.'

Mutely, Covenant put his arms around Sunder's neck and hugged him.

The crying of his heart was also a promise. This time I won't turn my back. I'm going to tear those bastards down.

He remained there until the Graveller's answering clasp had comforted him.

Then Pitchwife broke the silence by clearing his throat; and Linden said in a voice husky with empathy, 'It's about time. I thought you two were *never* going to start talking to each other.' She was standing beside Hollian as if they had momentarily become sisters.

Covenant loosened his hold; but for a moment longer he did not release the Graveller. Swallowing heavily, he murmured, 'Mhoram used to say things like that. You're starting to resemble him. As long as the Land can still produce people like you. And Hollian.' Recollections of the long-dead Lord made him blink fiercely to clear his sight. 'Foul thinks all he has to do is break the Arch of Time and rip the world apart. But he's wrong. Beauty isn't that easily destroyed.' Recalling a song that Lena had sung to him when she was still a girl and he was new to the Land, he quoted softly, '"The soul in which the flower grows survives."'

With a crooked smile, Sunder rose to his feet. Covenant joined him, and the two of them faced their companions. To the First, Sunder said, 'Pardon my unwelcome. The news of your quest smote me sorely. But you have come far across the unknown places of the Earth in pain and peril, and we are well met. The Land has need of you – and to you we may be of use.' Formally, he introduced Durris and Fole in case the Giants had not caught their names earlier. Then he concluded, 'Our food is scanty, but we ask that you share it with us.'

The First replied by presenting Mistweave to the Stonedownors. They already knew Vain; and Findail she ignored as if he had ceased to impinge upon her awareness. After a glance around the shallow, wet cave, she said, 'It would appear that we are better supplied for sharing. Graveller, how great is our distance from this Revelstone the Giantfriend seeks?'

'A journey of five days,' Sunder responded, 'or of three, if we require no stealth to ward us from the notice of the Clave.'

'Then,' stated the First, 'we are stocked to the verge of bounty. And you are in need of bounty.' She looked deliberately at Hollian's thinness. 'Let us celebrate this meeting and this shelter with sustenance.'

She unslung her pack; and the other Giants followed her example. Honninscrave and Mistweave started to prepare a meal; Pitchwife tried to stretch some of the kinks out of his back. The rain continued to hammer relentlessly onto the hillside, and water ran down the slanted ceiling, formed puddles and rivulets on the floor. Yet the relative dryness and warmth of the shelter were a consolation. Covenant had heard somewhere that exposure to an incessant rain could drive people mad. Rubbing his numb fingers through his beard, he watched his companions and tried to muster the courage for questions.

The First and Pitchwife remained stubbornly themselves in spite of rain and weariness and discouragement. While she waited for food, she took out her huge longsword, began to dry it meticulously; and he went to reminisce with Sunder, describing their previous meeting and adventures in Sarangrave Flat with irrepressible humour. Mistweave, however, was still doubtful, hesitant: at one point, he appeared unable to choose which pouch of staples he should open, confused by that simple decision until Honninscrave growled at him. Neither time nor the blows he had struck against the *arghuleh* had healed his self-distrust, and its cracks were spreading.

And the Master seemed to grow increasingly un-Giant-like. He showed a startling lack of enthusiasm for his reunion with the Stonedownors, for the company of more *Haruchai* – even for the prospect of food. His movements were duties he performed simply to pass the time until he reached his goal, had a chance to achieve his purpose. Covenant did not know what that purpose was; but the thought of what it might be sent a chill through him. Honninscrave looked like a man who was determined to rejoin his brother at any cost.

Covenant wanted to demand some explanation; but there was no privacy available. Setting the matter aside, he looked around the rest of the gathering.

Linden had taken Hollian to a drier place against one wall and was examining the eh-Brand with her senses, testing the health and growth of the child Hollian carried. The noise of the rain covered their quiet voices. But then Linden announced firmly, 'It's a boy.' Hollian's dark eyes turned toward Sunder and shone.

Vain and Findail had not moved. Vain appeared insensate to the water that beaded on his black skin, dripped from his tattered tunic. And even direct rain could not touch the Appointed: it passed through him as if his reality were of a different kind altogether.

Near the edge of the cave, the *Haruchai* stood in a loose group. Durris and Fole watched the storm: Cail and Harn faced inward. If they were mentally sharing their separate stories, their flat expressions gave no sign of the exchange.

Like Bloodguard, Covenant thought. Each of them seemed to know by direct inspiration what any of the others knew. The only difference was that these *Haruchai* were not immune to time. But perhaps that only made them less willing to compromise.

He was suddenly sure that he did not want to be served by them anymore. He did not want to be served at all. The commitments people made to him were too costly. He was on his way to doom: he should have been travelling alone. Yet here were five more people whose lives would be hazarded with his. Six, counting Hollian's child, who had no say in the matter.

And what had happened to the other *Haruchai* – to those that had surely come like Fole and Durris to oppose the Clave?

And why had Sunder and Hollian failed?

When the food was ready, he sat down among his companions near the fire with his back to the cave-wall and his guts tight. The act of eating both postponed and brought closer the time for questions.

Shortly, Hollian passed around a leather pouch. When Covenant drank from it, he tasted *metheglin*, the thick, cloying mead brewed by the villages of the Land.

Implications snapped at him. His head jerked up. 'Then you *didn't* fail.'

Sunder scowled as if Covenant's expostulation pained him; but Hollian met the statement squarely. 'Not altogether.' Her mouth smiled, but her eyes were sombre. 'In no Stonedown or Woodhelven did we fail altogether – in no village but one.'

Covenant set the pouch down carefully in front of him. His shoulders were trembling: he had to concentrate severely to keep his hands and voice steady. 'Tell me.' All the eyes of the travellers were on Sunder and Hollian. 'Tell me what happened.'

Sunder threw down the hunk of bread he had been chewing. 'Failure is not a word to be trusted,' he began harshly. His gaze avoided Covenant, Linden, the Giants, nailed itself to the embers of the fire. 'It may mean one thing or another. We have failed – and we have not.'

'Graveller,' Pitchwife interposed softly. 'It is said among our people that joy is in the ears that hear, not in the mouth that speaks. The quest for the One Tree has brought to us many aghast and heart-cruel tales, and we have not always heard them well. Yet are we here – sorely scathed, it may be' – he glanced at Honninscrave – 'but not wholly daunted. Do not scruple to grant us a part in your hurt.'

For a moment, Sunder covered his face as if he were weeping again. But when he dropped his hands, his fundamental gall was bright in his eyes.

'Hear me, then,' he said stiffly. 'Departing Seareach, we bore with us the *krill* of Loric and the ur-Lord's trust. In my heart were hope and purpose, and I had learned a new love when all the old were dead.' All slain: his father by murder, his mother by necessity, his wife and son by his own hand. 'Therefore I believed that we would be believed when we spoke our message of defiance among the villages.

'From The Grieve, we wended north as well as west, seeking a way to the Upper Land which would not expose us to the lurker-bourne of Sarangrave Flat.' And that part of the journey had been a pleasure, for they were alone together except for Stell and Harn; and Seareach from its coast to its high hills and the surviving remnant of Giant Woods had never been touched by the Sunbane. Uncertainty had clouded their earlier traversal of this region; but now they saw it as a beautiful land in the height of its autumn glory, tasted the transforming savour of woodlands and animals, birds and flowers. The Clave taught that the Land had been created as a place of punishment, a gallow-fells, for human evil. But Covenant had repudiated that teaching; and in Seareach for the first time Sunder and Hollian began to comprehend what the Unbeliever meant.

So their purpose against the Clave grew clearer; and at last they dared the northern reaches of the Sarangrave in order to begin their work without more delay.

Climbing Landsdrop, they re-entered the pale of the Sunbane.

The task of finding villages was not easy: they had no maps and were unacquainted with the scope of the Land. But eventually the far-sighted *Haruchai* spotted a Rider; and that red-robed woman unwittingly led the travellers to their first destination – a small Woodhelven crouched in a gully among old hills.

'Far Woodhelven did not entirely welcome us,' muttered the Graveller sourly.

'The Rider took from them their youngest and their best,' Hollian explained. 'And not in the former manner. Always the Clave has exercised caution in its demands, for if the people were decimated where would the Riders turn for blood? But with the foreshortening of the Sunbane such husbandry was set aside. Riders accosted each village with doubled and trebled frequency, requiring every life that their Coursers might bear.'

'Deprived of the *Haruchai* which you redeemed,' Sunder added to Covenant, 'the Riders turned from their accustomed harvestry to outright ravage. If the tales we have heard do not mislead us, this ravage commenced at the time of our seaward passage from the Upper Land into Sarangrave Flat. The na-Mhoram read us in the *rukh* which I then bore, and he knew you were gone into a peril from which you could not strike back at him.' The Graveller spoke as if he knew how Covenant would take this news – how Covenant would blame himself for not giving battle to the Clave earlier. 'Therefore what need had he for any caution?'

Covenant flinched inwardly; but he clung to what the Stonedownors were saying, forced himself to hear it.

'When we entered Far Woodhelven,' the eh-Brand went on, 'they were reduced to elders and invalids and bitterness. How should they have welcomed us? They saw us only as blood with which they might purchase a period of survival.'

Sunder glared into the fire, his eyes as hard as polished stone. 'That violence I forestalled. Using the *krill* of Loric and the *orcrest* Sunstone, I raised water and *ussusimiel* without bloodshed under a desert sun. Such power was an astonishment to them. Thus when I had done they were ready to hear whatever words we might speak against the Clave. But what meaning could our speech have to them? What opposition remained possible to the remnant of their village? They were too much reduced to do aught but huddle in their homes and strive for bare life. We did not altogether fail,' he rasped, 'but I know no other name for that which we accomplished.'

Hollian put a gentle hand on his arm. The rain roared on outside the cave. Water trickled constantly past Covenant's legs. But he ignored the wet, closed his mind to the fierce and useless regret rising like venom from the pit of his stomach. Later he would let himself feel the sheer dismay of what he had unleashed upon the Land: right now he needed to listen.

'One thing we gained from Far Woodhelven,' the eh-Brand continued. 'They gave us knowledge of a Stonedown lying to the west. We were not required to make search for the opportunity to attempt our purpose for a second time.'

'Oh, forsooth!' Sunder snarled. Bafflement and rage mounted within him. 'That knowledge they gave us. Such knowledge is easily ceded. From that day to this, we have not been required to make any search. The failure of each village has led us onward. As we passed ever westward, nearer to Revelstone, each Woodhelven and Stonedown became more arduous of suasion, for the greater proximity of the na-Mhoram's Keep taught a greater fear. Yet always the gifts of *krill* and Sunstone and *lianar* obtained for us some measure of welcome. But those folk no longer possessed blood enough to sustain their fear – and so also they lacked blood for resistance. Their only answer to our gifts and words was their knowledge of other villages.

'Thomas Covenant,' he said suddenly, 'this is bile to me – but I would not be misheard. Betimes from village to village we happened upon a man or a woman young and hale enough to have offered other aid – and yet unwilling. We encountered folk for whom it was inconceivable that any man or woman might love the Land. Upon occasion our lives were attempted, for what dying people would not covet the powers we bore? Then only the prowess of the *Haruchai* preserved us. Yet in the main we were given no other gift because no other gift was possible. I have learned a great bitterness which I know not how to sweet – but the blame of it does not fall upon the people of the Land. I would not have believed that the bare life of any village could suffer so much loss and still endure.'

For a moment, he fell silent; and the battering sound of the rain rang through the cave. He had placed his hand over Hollian's: the force of his grip corded the backs of his knuckles. He was no taller than Linden, but his stature could not be measured by size: to Covenant, he appeared as thwarted and dangerous as Berek Half-hand had been on the slopes of Mount Thunder, when the ancient hero and Lord-Fatherer had at last set his hand to the Earthpower.

The silence was like the muffled barrage of the storm. The Clave had already shed a heinous amount of blood – yet too many lives remained at stake, and Covenant did not know how to protect them. Needing support, he looked toward Linden. But she did not notice his gaze. Her head was up, her eyes keen, as if she were scenting the air, tracing a tension or peril he could not discern.

He glanced at the Giants. But Honninscrave's orbs were hidden beneath the clenched fist of his brows; and those of Mistweave,

Pitchwife, and the First were fixed on the Stonedownors.

At the mouth of the cave, Cail raised one arm as though in spite of his native dispassion he wished to make a gesture of protest. But then he lowered his hand back to his side.

Abruptly, Sunder began speaking again. 'Only one village did not accord to us even that chimera of a gift – and it was the last.' His voice was knotted and rough. 'From it we have lately come, retracing our way because we had no more hope.

'Our path from village to village led us westward in a crescent-line, so that we passed to the east of Revelstone wending toward the north – toward a place which named itself Landsverge Stonedown. The Woodhelven giving us that knowledge lay perilously nigh the Keep of the na-Mhoram, but Landsverge Stonedown was nigher – and therefore we feared its fear of the Clave would be too great to be countered. Yet when we gained the village, we learned that it would never suffer such fear again.'

He paused, then growled, 'It was altogether empty of life. The Riders had gutted it entirely, borne every beating heart away to feed the Banefire. Not one child or cripple remained to be consumed by the Sunbane.'

After that, he stopped – gripped himself still as if he would not be able to say another word without howling.

Hollian gave him a sad hug. 'We knew not where to turn,' she said, 'so we returned eastward. It was our thought that we must avoid the grasp of the Clave and await you – for surely the Unbeliever and white gold wielder would not fail of his quest' – her tone was candid, but free of sarcasm or accusation – 'and when he came he would come from the east. In that, at least, we were blessed. Far sooner than we had dared desire, the *Haruchai* became cognizant of your presence and guided us together.' A moment later, she added, 'We have been blessed also in the *Haruchai*.'

Linden was no longer facing the loose circle of her companions: she had turned toward Cail and his people; and the lines of her back were tight, insistent. But still she said nothing.

Covenant forced himself to ignore her. The Stonedownors were not done. Apprehension made his tone as trenchant as anger. 'How did you meet Durris and Fole?' He could no longer suppress his quivering. 'What happened to Stell?'

At that, a spasm passed across Sunder's face. When the answer came, it came from the eh-Brand.

'Thomas Covenant,' she said, speaking directly to him as if at that moment nothing else mattered, 'you have twice redeemed me from the malice of the Clave. And though you reft me of my home in Crystal Stonedown, where I was acknowledged and desired, you have given me a purpose and a love to repair that loss. I do not wish to cause you hurt.'

She glanced at Sunder, then continued, 'But this tale also must be told. It is needful.' Stiffening herself to the necessity, she said, 'When we passed to the east of Revelstone – tending toward the north – we encountered a band of some score *Haruchai*. With four score more of their people, they had come to make answer to the depredations of the Clave. And when they had heard our story, they understood why the people of the Land had not arisen in resistance. Therefore they set themselves a task – to form a cordon around Revelstone, a barrier that would prevent the passage of any Rider. Thus they thought to oppose the Clave – and to starve the Banefire – while they also awaited your return.

'Yet four of them elected to join the purpose of our search. Durris and Fole, whom you see, and also Bern and Toril' – her throat closed momentarily – 'who are gone – as Stell is gone. For our ignorance betrayed us.

'It was known to all that the Clave possesses power to dominate minds. By that means were the *Haruchai* ensnared in the past. But none among us knew how great the power had grown. As we traversed the proximity of Revelstone, Bern, Toril, and Stell·scouted some distance westward to ensure our safety. We were yet a day's journey from the Keep, and not Harn, Durris, nor Fole met any harm. But the slightly greater nearness of the others bared them to the Clave's touch – and to its dominion. Setting aside all caution, they left us to answer the Clave's coercion.

'Sensing what had transpired – the utter loss of mind and will – Harn, Durris, and Fole could not give chase, lest they also fall under the na-Mhoram's sway. But Sunder and I –' The memory made her falter, but she did not permit herself to stop. 'We gave pursuit. And we gave battle, striving with *krill*-fire and force to break the hold of the Clave – though in so doing we surely made our presence known to the na-Mhoram, forewarning him of us – and perhaps also of you. Mayhap we would have opposed Stell and his companions to the very gates of Revelstone. We were desperate and fevered – But at the last we halted.' She swallowed convulsively. 'For we saw that Bern, Stell, and Toril were not alone. From around the region came a score and more of the *Haruchai* – all ensnared, all walking mindless and deaf toward the knife and the Banefire.' Tears filled her eyes. 'And at that sight,' she went on as if she were ashamed, 'we were broken. We fled because naught else remained for us to do.

'During the night,' she finished softly, 'Gibbon na-Mhoram reached out to us and attempted mastery of the *krill*'s white gem. But Sunder, my love, kept the light clean.' Then her tone hardened. 'If the na-Mhoram remains in any way accessible to fear, I conceive he has been somewhat daunted – for surely Sunder gave him to believe that the ur-Lord was already returned.'

But Covenant hardly heard her conclusion. He was foundering in the visions her words evoked: the immedicable stupor of the *Haruchai*; the frenzy of the Stonedownors as they had pleaded, opposed, struggled, driving themselves almost into the jaws of the Clave and still failing to save their comrades; the glee or apprehension implicit in Gibbon's efforts to conquer the *krill*. His brain reeled with images of the enormous consequences of his earlier refusal to fight the Clave. Among the Dead in Andelain, Bannor had said to him, *Redeem my people. Their plight is an abomination.* And he had thought himself successful when he had broken open the hold of Revelstone, set the *Haruchai* free. But he had not succeeded. He had let the Riders and the na-Mhoram live to do again every evil thing they had ever done before; and the Sunbane had risen to a period of two days on the blood of ravaged villages and the helpless *Haruchai*.

Yet Linden's sharp protest pierced him, snatched him out of himself: an instinct deeper than panic or shame wrenched him to his feet and sent him after her as she scrambled toward Cail and Harn.

But she was too slow, had divined the meaning of their tension too late. With appalling suddenness, Harn struck Cail a blow that knocked him out into the force of the rain.

Sunder, Hollian, and the Giants sprang upright behind Covenant. One running stride ahead of him, Linden was caught by Fole and heaved aside. An instant later, Durris's arm slammed like an iron bar across Covenant's chest. He stumbled back against the First.

She held him. He hung in her grasp, gaping for breath while small suns of pain staggered around his sight.

Veiled by torrents, Cail and Harn were barely visible. In mud that should have made footing impossible, rain that should have blinded them, they battled with the precise abandon of madmen.

Furiously, Linden yelled, 'Stop it! Are you out of your minds?'

Without inflection, Durris replied, 'You miscomprehend.' He and Fole stood poised to block any intervention. 'This must be done. It is the way of our people.'

Covenant strove for air. Stiffly, the First demanded an explanation.

Durris's dispassion was implacable. He did not even glance at the fierce struggle being waged through the rain. 'In this fashion, we test each other and resolve doubt.'

Cail appeared to be at a disadvantage, unable to match the sheer conviction of Harn's attack. He kept his feet, countered Harn's blows with a skill which seemed inconceivable in that downpour; but he was always on the defensive.

'Cail has spoken to us concerning *ak-Haru Kenaustin Ardenol*. He was companion to the victor, and we desire to measure our worth against his.'

A sudden feint unbalanced Cail, enabling Harn to slash his feet from under him; but he recovered with a tumbling roll-and-kick.

'Also it has been said that Brinn and Cail betrayed their chosen fidelity to the seduction of the *merewives*. Cail seeks to demonstrate that the lure of their seduction would have surpassed any *Haruchai* in his place.'

Cail and Harn were evenly matched in ability and strength. But Harn had watched his kindred lose their wills and walk into the jaws of the Clave: he struck with the force of repudiation. And Cail had succumbed to the *merewives*, learned to judge himself. Brinn's victory over the Guardian of the One Tree had led to Cable Seadreamer's death. A flurry of punches staggered Cail. As he reeled, a heavy two-fisted blow drove his face into the mire.

Cail!

Covenant grabbed a shuddering breath and twisted out of the First's hands. Fire flashed in his mind, alternately white and black: flames spread up his right forearm as if his flesh were tinder. He gathered a shout that would stop the *Haruchai*, stun them where they stood.

But Durris went on inflexibly, 'Also we desire to grieve for Hergrom and Ceer – and for those whose blood has gone to the Banefire.'

Without warning, he spun away from the company, leaped lithe and feral into the rain toward Cail and Harn. Fole was at his side. Together, they attacked.

Then Sunder cried at Covenant, 'Do not!' He caught Covenant's arm, braved fire to halt the imminent eruption. 'If the na-Mhoram is conscious of the *krill* in my hands, how much more clearly will your power call out to him?'

Covenant started to yell, *I don't care! Let him try to stop me!* But Fole and Durris had not hurled themselves solely upon Cail. They were assailing each other and Harn as well; and Cail had risen from the mud to plunge into the general mêlée. Blows hammered impartially in all directions.

We desire to grieve – Slowly, the fire ran out of Covenant. *Ah, hell,* he sighed. *Have mercy on me.* He had no right to question what the *Haruchai* were doing. He had too much experience with the violence of his own grief.

Linden studied the combatants intently; her face showed a physician's alarm at the possibility of injury. But Sunder met Covenant's gaze and nodded mute comprehension.

As abruptly as it had begun, the fighting stopped. The four *Haruchai* returned stoically to the shelter of the cave. They were all bruised and hurt, though none as sorely as Cail. But his visage concealed defeat, and his people wore no aspect of triumph.

He faced Covenant squarely. 'It is agreed that I am unworthy.' Slow blood trickled from a cut on his lip, a gash over one cheekbone. 'My place at your side is not taken from me, for it was accorded by

992

ak-Haru Kenaustin Ardenol. But I am required to acknowledge that the honour of such a place does not become me. Fole will ward the Chosen.' After a fraction of hesitation, he added, 'Other matters have not been resolved.'

'Oh, Cail!' Linden groaned. Covenant spat a curse that was covered by the First's swearing and Pitchwife's expostulation. But there was nothing any of them could do. The *Haruchai* had passed judgment, and they were as untouchable as Bloodguard.

Muttering direly to himself, Covenant hugged his arms over his heart and retreated to the simple comfort of the fire.

After a moment, Sunder and Hollian joined him. They stood nearby in silence until he raised his head. Then, in a softer voice, as if his own plight had been humbled by astonishment, Sunder said, 'You have much to tell us, ur-Lord.'

'Stop calling me that,' Covenant growled. His mouth was full of gall. Ur-Lord was the title the *Haruchai* typically used for him. 'There haven't been any Lords worth mentioning for three thousand years.'

But he could not refuse to give the Stonedownors the story of his failed quest.

The task of narration was shared by Linden, the First, and Pitchwife. Sunder and Hollian gaped at the tale of the *Elohim* and Findail, of the way in which Covenant had been silenced; but they had no words for their incomprehension. When the companions began to speak of Cable Seadreamer, Honninscrave rose abruptly and stalked out into the rain; but he returned shortly, looking as sharp and doomed as a boulder gnawed by the sempiternal hunger of the sea. His voice rising in grief at loss and celebration of valour, Pitchwife described the crisis of the One Tree. Then the First related the sailing of Starfare's Gem into the bitter cold of the north. She explained the company's harsh decision to abandon the *dromond*; and the stern iron of her voice made the things she said seem more bearable.

It fell to Covenant to speak of Hamako and the Waynhim, of the company's re-entry into the Sunbane. And when he was finished, the violence of the storm had become less.

The rain was fading toward sunset. As the downpour receded to a drizzle, the clouds broke open in the east and followed the sun away, exposing the Land to a night as clear and cold as the stars. A moon with a look of rue on its face swelled toward its full.

The fire seemed brighter now as dark deepened outside the cave. Sunder stirred the embers while he considered what he had heard. Then he addressed Covenant again, and the flames glinted like eagerness in his eyes. 'Is it truly your intent to assail the Clave? To bring the Banefire to an end?'

Covenant nodded, scowling.

Sunder glanced at Hollian, then back to Covenant. 'I need not say that we will accompany you. We have been thwarted beyond endurance. Even Hollian's child – ' For a moment, he faltered in confusion, murmured, 'My son,' as if he had just realized the truth. But then he resumed firmly, 'Even he is not too precious to be hazarded in such a cause.'

Covenant started to retort, No, you're wrong. You're all too precious. You're the future of the Land. If it has a future. But the Graveller had come too far to be denied. And Covenant had lost the right or the arrogance to try to withhold the consequences of their own lives from the people he loved.

He took a deep breath, held it to steady himself. The force of Durris's arm had left a pain in his chest that would not go away. But Sunder did not ask the question he feared, did not say, How can you think to confront the might of Revelstone, when your power threatens the very foundation of the Earth? Instead, the Graveller inquired, 'What will become of the *Haruchai*?'

That question, too, was severe; but Covenant could face it. Slowly, he let the pent air out of his lungs. 'If I succeed, they'll be all right.' Nightmares of fire had annealed him to his purpose. 'If I fail, there won't be much left to worry about.'

Sunder nodded, looked away. Carefully, he asked, 'Thomas Covenant, will you accept the *krill* from me?'

More abruptly than he intended, Covenant snapped, 'No.' When he had first given away Loric's blade, Linden had asked him why he no longer needed it. He had replied, *I'm already too dangerous*. But he had not known then how deep the danger ran. 'You're going to need it.' To fight with if he failed.

Or if he succeeded.

That was the worst gall, the true root of despair – that even a complete victory over the Clave would accomplish nothing. It would not restore the Law, not heal the Land, not renew the people of the Land. And beyond all question it would not cast down the Despiser. The best Covenant could hope for was a postponement of his doom. And that was as good as no hope at all.

Yet he had been living with despair for so long now that it only confirmed his resolve. He had become like Kevin Landwaster, incapable of turning back, of reconsidering what he meant to do. The sole difference was that Covenant already knew he was going to die.

He preferred that to the death of the Land.

But he did not say such things to his companions. He did not want to give the impression that he blamed Linden for her inability to aid his dying body in the woods behind Haven Farm. And he did not wish to quench the Stonedownors' nascent belief that they had one more chance to make what they had undergone meaningful. Despair belonged to the lone heart, and he kept it to himself. Lord Foul had corrupted everything else – had turned to ill even the affirmative rejection of hate which had once led Covenant to withhold his hand from the Clave. But Sunder and Hollian had been restored to him. Some of the *Haruchai* and the Giants could still be saved. Linden might yet be returned safely to her natural world. He had become ready to bear it.

When Honninscrave left the cave again to pace out his tension under the unpitying stars, Covenant followed him.

The night was cold and poignant, the warmth of the earth drenched away by the long rain. Apparently unconscious of Covenant, Honninscrave climbed the nearest hillside until he gained a vantage from which he could study the south-western horizon. His lonely bulk was silhouetted against the impenetrable sky. He held himself as rigid as the fetters in Kasreyn's dungeon; but the manacles on him now were more irrefragable than iron. From far back in his throat came small whimpering noises like flakes of grief.

Yet he must have known that Covenant was there. After a moment, he began to speak.

'This is the world which my brother purchased with his soul.' His voice sounded like cold, numb hands rubbing each other to no avail. 'Seeing that the touch of your power upon the One Tree would surely rouse the Worm, he went to his death to prevent you. And this is the result. The Sunbane waxes, perpetrating atrocity. The human valour of the Stonedownors is baffled. The certainty of the *Haruchai* is thwarted. And against such evils you are rendered futile, bound by the newborn doom to which Cable Seadreamer served as midwife. Do you consider such a world worthy of life? I do not.'

For a time, Covenant remained silent. He was thinking that he was not the right person to hear Honninscrave's hurt. His own despair was too complete. His plight was constricted by madness and fire on all sides; and the noose was growing tighter. Yet he could not let the need in Honninscrave's question pass without attempting an answer. The Giant was his friend. And he had his own losses to consider. He needed a reply as sorely as Honninscrave did.

Slowly, he said, 'I talked to Foamfollower about hope once.' That memory was as vivid as healthy sunshine. 'He said it doesn't come from us. It doesn't depend on us. It comes from the worth and power of what we serve.' Without flinching, Foamfollower had claimed that his service was to Covenant. When Covenant had protested, *It's all a mistake*, Foamfollower had responded, *Then are you so surprised to learn that I have been thinking about hope?*

But Honninscrave had a different objection. 'Aye, verily?' he growled. He did not glance at Covenant. 'And where now under all the Sunbane lies the "worth and power" that you serve?'

'In you,' Covenant snapped back, too vexed by pain to be gentle. 'In Sunder and Hollian. In the *Haruchai*.' He did not add, In Andelain.

Honninscrave had never seen that last flower of the Land's loveliness. And he could not bring himself to say, In me. Instead, he continued, 'When Foamfollower and I were together, I didn't have any power. I had the ring – but I didn't know how to use it. And I was trying to do exactly what Foul wanted. I was going to Foul's Creche. Walking right into the trap. Foamfollower helped me anyway.' The Giant had surrendered himself to agony in order to carry Covenant across the fierce lava of Hotash Slay. 'Not because there was anything special or worthy or powerful about me, but simply because I was human and Foul was breaking my heart. That gave Foamfollower all the hope he needed.'

In the process, Covenant had caused the Giant's death. Only the restraint he had learned in the cavern of the One Tree kept him from crying, Don't talk to me about despair! I'm going to destroy the world and there's nothing I can do about it! I need something better from you! Only that restraint – and the tall dark shape of the Master as he stood against the stars, torn by loss and as dear as life.

But then Honninscrave turned as if he had heard the words Covenant had not uttered. His moon-gilt stance took on a curious kindness. Softly, he said, 'You are the Giantfriend, and I thank you that there is yet room in your heart for me. No just blame attaches to you for Seadreamer's death – nor for the refusal of *caamora* with which by necessity you sealed his end. But I do not desire hope. I desire to *see*. I covet the vision which taught my brother to accept damnation in the name of what he witnessed.'

Quietly, he walked down from the hilltop, leaving Covenant exposed to the emptiness of the night.

In the cold silence, Covenant tried to confront his plight, wrestled for an escape from the logic of Lord Foul's manipulations. Revelstone was perhaps only three days away. But the wild magic had been poisoned, and venom coloured all his dreams. He contained no more hope than the black gulf of the heavens, where the Worm of the World's End had already fed. Honninscrave's difficult grace did not feel like forgiveness. It felt as arduous as a grindstone, whetting the dark to a new sharpness. And he was alone.

Not because he lacked friends. In spite of the Land's destitution, it had blessed him with more friendship than he had ever known. No, he was alone because of his ring. Because no one else possessed this extreme power to ruin the Earth. And because he no longer had any right to it at all.

That was the crux, the conflict he could not resolve or avoid; and it seemed to cripple his sense of himself, take his identity away. What did he have to offer the Land except wild magic and his stubborn passion? What else was he worth to his friends? – or to Linden, who would have to carry the burden as soon as he set it down? From the beginning, his life here had been one of folly and pain, sin and ill; and only wild magic had enabled him to make expiation. And now the Clave had reduced the villages to relics. It had ensnared the *Haruchai* once more. The Sunbane had attained a period of two days. Seadreamer and Hergrom and Ceer and Memla and Hamako were dead. If he surrendered his ring now, as Findail and doom urged, how would he ever again be able to bear the weight of his own actions?

We are foemen, you and I, enemies to the end. But the end will be yours, Unbeliever, not mine. At the last there will be but one choice for you, and you will make it in all despair. Of your own volition you will give the white gold into my hand.

Covenant had no answer. In Andelain among the Dead, Mhoram had warned, *He has said to you that you are his Enemy. Remember that he seeks always to mislead you.* But Covenant had no idea what the former High Lord meant.

Around him, a dismay which no amount of moonlight could palliate gripped the hills. Unconsciously, he had sunk to the ground under the glinting accusation of the stars. Findail had said like the Despiser, *He must be persuaded to surrender his ring. If he does not, it is certain that he will destroy the Earth.* Covenant huddled into himself. He needed desperately to cry out and could not – needed to hurl outrage and frenzy at the blind sky and was blocked from any release by the staggering peril of his power. He had fallen into the Despiser's trap, and there was no way out.

When he heard feet ascending the hill behind him, he covered his face to keep himself from pleading abjectly for help.

He could not read the particular emanations of his companions: he did not know who was approaching him. Vaguely, he expected Sunder or Pitchwife. But the voice which sighed his name like an ache of pity or appeal was Linden's.

He lurched erect to meet her, though he had no courage for her concern, which he had not earned.

The moon sheened her hair as if it were clean and lovely. But her features were in shadow: only the tone of her voice revealed her mood. She spoke as if she knew how close he was to breaking.

As softly as a prayer, she breathed, 'Let me try.'

At that, something in him did break. '*Let* you?' he fumed suddenly. He had no other way to hold back his grief. 'I can hardly *prevent* you. If you're so all-fired bloody eager to be responsible for the world, you don't need *my* permission. You don't even need the physical ring. You can use it from there. All you have to do is *possess* me.'

'Stop,' she murmured like an echo of supplication, 'stop.' But his love for her had become anguish, and he could not call it back.

'It won't even be a new experience for you. It'll be just like what you did to your mother. The only difference is that I'll still be alive when you're done.'

Then he wrenched himself to a halt, gasping with the force of his desire to retract his jibe, silence it before it reached her.

She raised her fists in the moonlight, and he thought she was going to start railing at him. But she did not. Her percipience must have made the nature of his distress painfully clear to her. For a long moment, she held up her arms as if she were measuring the distance a blow would have to travel to strike him. Then she lowered her hands. In a flat, impersonal tone that she had not used toward him for a long time, she said, 'That isn't what I meant.'

'I know.' Her detachment hurt him more than rage. He was certain now that she would be able to make him weep if she wished. 'I'm sorry.' His contrition sounded paltry in the sharp night, but he had nothing else to offer her. 'I've come all this way, but I might as well have stayed in the cavern of the One Tree. I don't know how to face it.'

'Then let somebody try to help you.' She did not soften; but she refrained from attacking him. 'If not for yourself, do it for me. I'm right on the edge already. It is all I can do,' she articulated carefully, 'to just look at the Sunbane and stay sane. When I see you suffering, I can't keep my grip.

'As long as I don't have any power, there's nothing I can do about Lord Foul. Or the Sunbane. So you're the only reason I've got. Like it or not. I'm here because of you. I'm fighting to stay in one piece because of you. I want to *do* something' – her fists rose again like a shout, but her voice remained flat – 'for this world – or against Foul – because of you. If you go on like this, I'll crack.' Abruptly, her control frayed, and pain welled up in her words like blood in a wound. 'I need you to at least stop looking so much like my goddamn father.'

Her father, Covenant thought mutely. A man of such self-pity that he had cut his wrists and blamed her for it. *You never loved me anyway*. And from that atrocity had come the darkness which had maimed her life – the black moods, the violence she had enacted against her mother, the susceptibility to evil. Her instances of paralysis. Her attempt on Ceer's life.

Her protest wrung Covenant's heart. It showed him with stunning vividness how little he could afford to fail her. Any other hurt or dread was preferable. Instinctively, he made a new promise – another commitment to match all the others he had broken or kept.

'I don't know the answer,' he said, keeping himself quiet in fear that she would perceive how his life depended on what he was saying. 'I don't know what I need. But I know what to do about the Clave.' He did not tell her what his nightmares had taught him. He did not dare. 'When we're done there, I'll know more. One way or the other.'

She took him at his word. She had a severe need to trust him: if she did not, she would be forced to treat him as if he were as lost as her parents; and that alternative was plainly appalling to her. Nodding to herself, she folded her arms under her breasts and left the hilltop, went back to the shelter and scant warmth of the cave.

Covenant stayed out in the dark alone for a while longer. But he did not break.

9

MARCH TO CRISIS

Before dawn, the new company ate breakfast, repacked their supplies, and climbed the nearest hillside to await the sun with stone underfoot. Covenant watched the east gauntly, half fearing that the Sunbane might already have accelerated to a cycle of only one day. But as the sun crested the horizon, the air set blue about it like a coronal, giving the still sodden and grey landscape a touch of azure like a hint of glory – as if, Covenant thought dourly, the Sunbane in any hands but Foul's would have been a thing of beauty. But then blackness began to seethe westward; and the light on the hills dimmed. The first fingers of the wind teased at Covenant's beard, mocking him.

Sunder turned to him. The Graveller's eyes were as hard as pebbles as he took out the wrapped bundle of the *krill*: his voice carried harshly across the wind. 'Unbeliever, what is your will? When first you gave the *krill* into my hand, you counselled that I make use of it as I would a *rukh* – that I attune myself to it and bend its power to my purpose. This I have done. It was my love who taught me' – he glanced at Hollian – 'but I have learned the lesson with all my strength.' He had come a long way and was determined not to be found wanting. 'Therefore I am able to ease our way – to hasten our journey. But in so doing I will restore us unquestionably to the Clave's knowledge, and Gibbon na-Mhoram will be forewarned against us.' Stiffly, he repeated, 'What is your will?'

Covenant debated momentarily with himself. If Gibbon were forewarned, he might kill more of his prisoners to stoke the Banefire. But it was possible that he was already aware of the danger. Sunder had suggested as much the previous day. If Covenant travelled cautiously, he might simply give the na-Mhoram more time for preparation.

Covenant's shoulders hunched to strangle his trepidation. 'Use the *krill,*' he muttered. 'I've already lost too much time.'

The Graveller nodded as if he had expected no other reply.

From his jerkin, he took out his Sunstone.

It was a type of rock which the Land's former masters of stone-lore had named *orcrest.* It was half the size of his fist, irregularly shaped but smooth; and its surface gave a strange impression of translucence without transparency, opening into a dimension where nothing but itself existed.

Deftly, Sunder flipped the cloth from the *krill's* gem, letting bright argent blaze into the rain-thick gloom. Then he brought the Sunstone and that gem into contact with each other.

At once, a shaft of vermeil power from the *orcrest* shot straight toward the hidden heart of the sun. Sizzling furiously, the beam pierced the drizzle and the thunderheads to tap the force of the Sunbane directly. And the *krill* shone forth as if its light could cast back the rain.

In a snarl of torrents and heavy thunder, the storm swept over the hilltop. The strait red shaft of the *orcrest* seemed to call down lightning like an affront to the heavens. But Sunder stood without flinching, unscathed by any fire.

On the company, no rain fell. Wind slashed the region: thunder crashed: lightning ran like streams across the dark. But Sunder's power formed a pocket in the storm, a zone free of violence.

He was doing what the Clave had always done, using the Sunbane to serve his own ends. But his exertion cost no blood. No one had been shed to make him strong.

That difference sufficed for Covenant. With a grim gesture, he urged his companions into motion.

Quickly, they ranged themselves around Sunder. With Hollian to guide him, the Graveller turned toward the south-west. Holding his *orcrest* and the *krill* clasped together so that they flamed like a challenge, he started in the direction of Revelstone. His protection moved with him, covering all the company.

By slow degrees, a crimson hue crept into the brightness of the *krill,* tinging the light as if the core of the gem had begun to bleed; and long glints of silver streaked the shaft of Sunbane-fire. But Sunder shifted his hands, separated the two powers slightly to keep them pure. As he did so, his zone contracted somewhat, but not enough to hamper the company's progress.

They were scourged by wind. Mud clogged their strides, made every step treacherous. Streams frothing down the hillsides beat against their legs, joined each other to form small rivers and tried to sweep the travellers away. Time and again, Covenant would have fallen without Cail's support. Linden clung severely to Fole's shoulder. All the world had been reduced to a thunderous wall of water – an impenetrable downpour lit by vermeil and argent, scored by lightning. No one tried to speak: only the Giants would have been able to make themselves heard. Yet Sunder's protection enabled the company to move faster than the Sunbane had ever permitted.

Sometime during the day, two grey, blurred shapes appeared like incarnations of the storm and entered the rainless pocket, presented themselves to Covenant. They were *Haruchai*. When he had acknowledged them, they joined his companions without a word.

The intensity with which Linden regarded Sunder told Covenant something he already knew: the Graveller's mastery of two such disparate periapts was a horrendous strain on him. Yet he was a Stonedownor. The native toughness of his people had been conditioned by generations of survival under the ordeal of the Sunbane. And his sense of purpose was clear. When the day's journey finally ended, and he let his fires fall, he appeared so weary that he could hardly stand – but he was no more defeated by fatigue than Covenant, who had done nothing except labour through nearly ten leagues of mire and water. Not for the first time, Covenant thought that the Graveller was more than he deserved.

As the wind whipped the clouds away to the west, the company made camp in an open plain which reminded Covenant of the strict terrain near Revelstone. In a bygone age, that region had been made fruitful by the diligence of its farmers and cattleherds – and by the beneficent power of the Lords. Now everything was painfully altered. He felt that he was on the verge of the Clave's immediate demesne – that the company was about to enter the ambit of the na-Mhoram's Keep.

Nervously, he asked Hollian what the next day's sun would be. In response, she took out her slim *lianar* wand. Its polished surface gleamed like the ancient woods of the Land as she held it up in the light of the campfire.

Like Sunder's left forearm, her right palm was laced with old scars – the cuts from which she had drawn blood for her foretellings. But she no longer had any need of blood. Sunder smiled and handed her the wrapped *krill*: she uncovered it only enough to let one white beam into the night. Then, reverently, like a woman who had never learned anything but respect for her own abilities, she touched her *lianar* to the light.

And flame grew like a plant from the wood. Delicate shoots waved into the air: buds of filigree fire bloomed: leaves curled and opened. Without harming her or the wood, flame spread around her like a growth of mystery.

It was as green and tangy as springtime and new apples.

At the sight, Covenant's nerves tightened involuntarily.

Hollian did not need to explain to him and Linden what her fire meant: they had witnessed it several times in the past. But for the benefit of the watching, wide-eyed Giants, she said quietly, 'The morrow will bring a fertile sun.'

Covenant glanced at Linden. But she was studying the *Haruchai*, scrutinizing them for any sign of peril. However, Sunder had said that Gibbon's grasp extended only a day's journey beyond the gates of Revelstone; and when Linden at last met Covenant's gaze she shook her head mutely.

Two more days, he thought. One until that Raver can reach us. Unless he decides to try his *Grim* again. *The ill that you deem most terrible* – That night, nightmares stretched him until he believed he would surely snap. They had all become one virulent vision, and in it his fire was as black as venom.

In the pre-green gloom of dawn, another pair of *Haruchai* arrived to join the company. Their faces were as stony and magisterial as the mountains where they lived; and yet Covenant received the dismaying impression that they had come to him in fear. Not fear of death, but of what the Clave could make them do.

Their plight is an abomination. He accepted them. But that was not enough. Bannor had commanded him to redeem them.

When the sun rose, it tinged the stark bare landscape a sick hue that reminded him of the Illearth Stone.

Six days had passed since the desert sun had melted every vestige of vegetation off the Upper Land. As a result, all the plain was a wilderness. But the ground was so water-soaked that it steamed wherever the sun touched it; and the steam seemed to raise fine sprouts of heather and bracken with the suddenness of panic. Where the dirt lay in shadow, it remained as barren as naked bones; but elsewhere the uncoiling green stems grew desperately, flogged by the Sunbane and fed by two days of rain. In moments, the brush had reached the height of Covenant's shins. If he stood still much longer, he might not be able to move at all.

But ahead of him, the Westron Mountains thrust their ragged snowcaps above the horizon. And one promontory of the range lay in a direct line with Sunder's path. Perhaps Revelstone was already visible to the greater sight of the Giants.

If it were, they said nothing about it. Pitchwife watched the preternatural heath with a look of nausea. Mistweave's doubt had assumed an aspect of belligerence, as if he resented the way Fole had supplanted him at Linden's side – and yet believed that he could not justify himself. The First hefted her longsword, estimating her strength against the vegetation. Only Honninscrave studied the south-west eagerly; but his clenched visage revealed nothing except an echo of his earlier judgment: *This is the world which my brother purchased with his soul. Do you consider such a world worthy of life?*

However, the First was not required to cut the company's way.

Sunder used his Sunstone and the *krill* as the Riders used their *rukhs*, employing the Sunbane to force open a path. With vermeil fire and white light, the Graveller crushed flat the growth ahead of the company, ploughed a way through it. Unhindered by torrents and streams and mire, the travellers were able to increase the previous day's pace.

Before the heather and bracken grew so tall that they blocked Covenant's view of the mountains, he glimpsed a red beam like Sunder's standing from the promontory toward the sun. With an inward shiver, he recognized it. To be visible from that distance, it would have to be tremendous.

The shaft of the Banefire.

Then the writhing brush effaced all the south-west from sight.

For a time, the tight apprehension of that glimpse occupied all his attention. The Banefire. It seemed to dwarf him. He had seen it once, devouring blood with a staggering heat and ferocity that had filled the high cavity of the sacred enclosure. Even at the level where the Readers had tended the *master-rukh*, that conflagration had hit him with an incinerating force, burning his thoughts to ashes. The simple memory of it made him flinch. He could hardly believe that even rampant wild magic would be a match for it: the conflict between such powers would be fierce enough to shatter mountains. And the Arch of Time? He did not know the answer.

But by midmorning Sunder began to stumble; and Covenant's attention was wrenched outward. The Graveller used his periapts as if together they formed a special kind of *rukh*; but they did not. The *rukhs* of the Riders drew their true strength straight from the *master-rukh* and the Banefire, and so each Rider needed only enough personal exertion to keep open a channel of power to Revelstone: the Banefire did the rest. But Sunder wielded the Sunbane and the *krill* directly.

The effort was exhausting him.

Linden read his condition at a glance. 'Give him *diamondraught*,' she muttered stiffly. Her rigid resistance to the ill of the vegetation made her sound distant, impersonal. 'And carry him. He'll be all right, if we take care of him.' After a moment, she added, 'He's stubborn enough to stand it.'

Sunder smiled at her wanly. Pallor lay beneath the shade of his skin; but as he sipped the Giantish liquor he grew markedly stronger. Yet he did not protest when Honninscrave hoisted him into the air. Sitting with his back against the Master's chest, his legs bent over the Giant's arms, he raised his powers again; and the company resumed its trek.

Shortly after noon, two more *Haruchai* joined Covenant, bringing to ten the number of their people ranged protectively on either side of him and his companions.

He saluted them strictly; but their presence only made him more afraid. He did not know how to defend them from Gibbon.

And his fear increased as Sunder grew weaker. Even with Sunstone and *krill*, the Graveller was only one lone man. While the obstacles swarming in front of him were simply bracken and heather, he was able to furrow them as effectively as any Rider. But then the soil changed: the terrain became a jungle of mad rhododendron, jacaranda, and honeysuckle. Through that tangle he could not force his way with anything like the direct accuracy which the Banefire made possible. He had to grope for the line of least resistance; and the jungle closed behind the travellers as if they were lost.

The sun had fallen near the Westron Mountains, and the light had become little more than a filtered gloom, when Linden and Hollian gasped simultaneously, 'Sunder!'

Honninscrave jerked to a halt. The First wheeled to stare at the Graveller. Covenant's throat constricted with panic as he scrambled forward at Linden's back.

The Master set Sunder down as the company crowded around them. At once, Sunder's knees buckled. His arms shook with a wild ague.

Covenant squeezed between the First and Pitchwife to confront the Graveller. Recognition whitened Hollian's face, made her raven hair look as stark as a dirge. Linden's eyes flicked back and forth between the Sunstone and the *krill*.

The vermeil shaft springing from his *orcrest* toward the setting sun had a frayed and charred appearance, as if it were being consumed by a hotter fire. And in the core of the *krill*'s clear gem burned a hard knot of blackness like a canker.

'The na-Mhoram attempts to take him!' Hollian panted desperately. 'How can he save himself, when he is so sorely weary?'

Sunder's eyes were fixed on something he could no longer see. New lines marked his ashen face, cut by the acid sweat that slicked his skin. Tremors knotted in his muscles. His expression was as naked and appalled as a seizure.

'Put them down!' Linden snapped at him, pitching her voice to pierce his fixation. 'Let go! Don't let him do this to you!'

The corners of Sunder's jaw bulged dangerously. With a groan as if he were breaking his own arm, he forced down the Sunstone, dropped it to the ground. Instantly, its crimson beam vanished: the *orcrest* relapsed to elusive translucence.

But the blackness at the centre of the *krill* swelled and became stronger.

Grimly, Sunder clinched his free hand around the blade's wrappings. Heat shone from the metal. Bowing his head, he held the *krill* in a grip like fever and fought to throw off the Clave's touch — fought with the same human and indefeasible abandon by which he had once nearly convinced Gibbon that Covenant was dead.

Linden was shouting, 'Sunder! Stop! It's killing you!' But the Graveller did not heed her.

Covenant put out his halfhand. Fire spattered from his ring as though the simple proximity of Gibbon's power made the silver-white band unquenchable.

Findail's protest rang across the jungle. Covenant ignored it. Sunder was his friend, and he had already failed too often. Perhaps he was not ready to test himself against the Clave and the Banefire. Perhaps he would never be ready. But he did not hesitate. Deliberately, he took hold of the *krill*. With the strength of fire, he lifted the blade from Sunder's grasp as if the Graveller's muscles had become sand.

But when he closed wild magic around the *krill*, all his flame went black.

Midnight conflagration as hungry a hate burst among the company, tore through the trees. A rage of darkness raved out of him as if at last the venom had triumphed, had become the whole truth of his power.

For an instant, he quailed. Then Linden's wild cry reached him.

Savage with extremity, he ripped his fire out of the air, flung it down like a tapestry from the walls of his mind. The *krill* slipped between his numb fingers, stuck point first in the desecrated soil.

Before he could move, react, breathe, try to contain the horror clanging in his heart like the carillon of despair, a heavy blow was struck behind him; and Cail reeled through the brush.

Another blow: a fist like stone. Covenant pitched forward, slammed against the rough trunk of a rhododendron, and sprawled on his back, gaping as if all the air had been taken out of the world. Glints of sunset came through the leaves like emerald stars, spun dizzily across his vision.

Around him, fighting pounded among the trees. But it made no sound. His hearing was gone. Linden's stretched shout was mute: the First's anger had no voice.

Galvanized by frenzy, Hollian dragged Sunder bodily out of the way of the battle. She passed in front of Covenant, blocked his view for a moment. But nothing could block the bright, breathless vertigo that wheeled through him, as compulsory and damning as the aura of the Worm.

Cail and the Giants were locked in combat with Harn, Durris, and the rest of the *Haruchai*.

The movements of the attackers were curiously sluggish, imprecise: they did not appear to be in control of themselves. But they struck with the full force of their native strength – blows so hard that even the Giants were staggered. Pitchwife went down under the weighty might of Fole and another *Haruchai*. Swinging the flat of her falchion, the First struggled to her husband's aid. Honnin-scrave levelled one of the *Haruchai* with each fist: Cail's people no longer had the balance or alertness to avoid his massive punches. But the attackers came back to their feet as if they were inured to pain and assailed him again. Mistweave bearhugged one *Haruchai*, knocked another away with a kick. But the *Haruchai* struck him a blow in the face that made his head crack backward, loosened his grasp.

Moving as stiffly as a man in a *geas*, Harn pursued Cail through the battle. Cail eluded him easily; but Harn did not relent. He looked as mindless as Durris, Fole, and the others.

They had been mastered by the Clave.

Slowly, the vertigo spinning across Covenant's sight came into focus; and he found himself staring at the *krill*. It stood in the dirt like a small cross scant feet from his face. Though fighting hit and tumbled everywhere, no one touched Loric's eldritch blade.

Its gem shone with a clear, clean argence: no taint marred the pure depths of the jewel.

Gibbon's attempt on it had been a feint – a way of distracting the company until he could take hold of all the *Haruchai*.

All except Cail.

With the dreamy detachment of anoxia, Covenant wondered why Cail was immune.

Abruptly, the knotting of his muscles eased. He jerked air into his lungs, biting raw hunks of it past the stunned paroxysm which had kept him from breathing; and sound began to leech back into the jungle – the slash of foliage, the grunt and impact of effort. For a moment, there were no voices: the battle was fought in bitter muteness. But then, as if from a great distance, he heard Linden call out, 'Cail! The *merewives*! You got away from them!'

Covenant heaved himself up from the ground in time to see Cail's reaction.

With the suddenness of a panther, Cail pounced on Harn. Harn was too torpid to counter effectively. Ducking under Harn's blunt blows, Cail knocked him off balance, then grabbed him by the shoulder and hip, snatched him into the air. Harn lacked the bare self-command to twist aside as Cail plunged him toward a knee raised and braced to break his back.

Yet at the last instant Harn did twist aside. When Brinn and Cail had been caught in the trance of the *merewives*, Linden had threatened to snap Brinn's arm; and that particular peril had restored him to himself. Harn wrenched out of Cail's grasp, came to his feet facing his kinsman.

For a moment, they gazed at each other impassively, as if nothing had happened. Then Harn nodded. He and Cail sprang to the aid of the Giants.

Still coughing for air, Covenant propped himself against a tree and watched the rest of the fight.

It did not last long. When Cail and Harn had broken Fole and Durris free of Gibbon's hold, the four of them were soon able to rescue the remaining six.

Pitchwife and Mistweave picked their battered bodies out of the brush. The First glared sharply about her, holding her sword ready. Honninscrave folded his arms over his chest to contain the startling force of his own rage. But the *Haruchai* ignored the Giants. They turned away to face each other, speaking mind-to-mind with the silent dispassion of their people. In spite of what had just happened, they did not appear daunted or dismayed.

When their converse was over, Cail looked at the Giants and Linden, then met Covenant squarely. He did not apologize. His people were *Haruchai*, and the offence to their rectitude went too deep for mere contrition. In a voice entirely devoid of inflection, free of any hint of justification or regret, he said, 'It is agreed that such unworth as mine has its uses. Whatever restitution you command we will undertake. But we will not again fall from ourselves in this way.'

Covenant did not know what to say. He had known the *Haruchai* for a long time, and the Bloodguard before them; yet he was still astonished by the extravagance of their judgments. And he was certain that he would not be able to bear being served by such people much longer. The simple desire to be deserving of them would make him wild.

How was it possible that his white fire had become so black in so little time?

Pitchwife murmured something like a jest under his breath, then grimaced when no one responded. Honninscrave had become too bleak for mirth. In his frustrated desire to prove himself to himself, Mistweave had forgotten laughter. And the First was not mollified by Cail's speech. The *Haruchai* had aroused her battle-instinct; and her face was like her blade, whetted for fighting.

Because the sun was setting and Sunder was exhausted, she commanded the Master and Mistweave to prepare a camp and a meal. Yet the decision to rest did not abate her tension. Dourly, she stalked around the area, hacking back the brush to form a relatively clear space for the camp.

Covenant stood and watched her. The blow he had received made everything inside him fragile. Even his truncated senses were not blind to her sore, stern vexation.

Linden would not come near him. She stayed as far away from him as the First's clearing permitted, avoiding him as if to lessen as much as possible his impact on her percipience.

The glances that Hollian cast toward him over Sunder's shoulder were replete with fright and uncertainty in the deepening twilight. Only Vain, Findail, and the *Haruchai* behaved as if they did not care.

Covenant started to cover his face, then lowered his hands again. Their numbness had become repugnant to him. His features felt stiff and breakable. His beard smelled of sweat: his whole body smelled, he was unclean and rank from head to foot. He feared that his voice would crack; but he forced himself to use it.

'All right. Say it. Somebody.'

The First delivered a fierce cut that severed a honeysuckle stem as thick as her forearm, then wheeled toward him. The tip of her blade pointed accusations at him.

Linden winced at the First's anger, but did not intervene.

'Giantfriend,' the leader of the Search rasped as if the name hurt her mouth. 'We have beheld a great ill. Is it truly your intent to utter this dark fire against the Clave?'

She towered over Covenant, and the light of Mistweave's campfire made her appear dominant and necessary. He felt too brittle to reply. Once he had tried to cut the venom out of his forearm on a ragged edge of rock. Those faint scars spread like fretwork around the fundamental marks of Marid's fangs. But now he knew better. Carefully, he said, 'He will not do that to me and get away with it.'

The First did not waver. 'And what of the Earth?'

Her tone made his eyes burn, but not with tears. Every word of his answer was as distinct as a coal. 'A long time ago,' with the blood of half-mindless Cavewights on his head, 'I swore I was never going to kill again. But that hasn't stopped me.' With both hands, he had driven a knife into the chest of the man who had slain Lena; and that blow had come back to damn him. He had no idea how many *Bhrathair* had died in the collapse of Kemper's Pitch. 'The last time I was there, I killed twenty-one of them.' Twenty-one men and women, most of whom did not know that their lives were evil. 'I'm sick of guilt. If you think I'm going to do anything that will destroy the Arch of Time, you had better try to stop me now.'

At that, her eyes narrowed as if she were considering the implications of running her blade through his throat. Hollian and Linden stared; and Sunder tried to brace himself to go to Covenant's aid. But the First, too, was the Unbeliever's friend. She had given him the title he valued most. Abruptly, the challenge of her sword dropped. 'No, Giantfriend,' she sighed. 'We have come too far. I trust you or nothing.'

Roughly, she sheathed her longsword and turned away.

Firelight gleamed in the wet streaks of Linden's concern and relief. After a moment, she came over to Covenant. She did not meet his gaze. But she put one hand briefly on his right forearm like a recognition that he was not like her father.

While that touch lasted, he ached to take hold of her hand and raise it to his lips. But he did not move. He believed that if he did he would surely shatter. And every promise he had made would be lost.

The next day, the fruits of the verdant sun were worse: they clogged the ground with the teeming, intractable frenzy of a sea in storm. And Sunder's weariness went too deep to be cured by one night of *diamondraught*-induced sleep, one swallow of the rare and potent roborant Pitchwife created by combining his liquor with *vitrim*. But the Clave made no more efforts to take control of the *krill* or the *Haruchai*. The shade of the trees held some of the underbrush to bearable proportions. No *Grim* or other attack came riding out of Revelstone to bar the way. And the travellers had made such good progress during the past two days that they did not need to hurry now. None of them doubted that the Keep of the na-Mhoram was within reach. At infrequent intervals, the distortion of the jungle provided a glimpse of the south-western sky; and then all the companions could see the hot, feral shaft of the Banefire burning toward the sun like an immedicable scald in the green-hued air.

Every glimpse turned Linden's taut, delicate features a shade paler: memory and emanations of power assaulted her vulnerable senses. She had once been Gibbon-Raver's prisoner in Revelstone, and his touch had raised the darkness coiled around the roots of her soul to the stature of all night. Yet she did not falter. She had aimed the company to this place by the strength of her own will, had wrested this promise from Covenant when he had been immobile with despair. In spite of her unresolved hunger and loathing for power, she did not let herself hang back.

The Stonedownors also held themselves firm. They had a score to settle with the Clave, a tally that stretched from the hold of Revelstone and the ruin of the villages down to the Sunbane-shaped foundations of their lives. Whenever Sunder's need for rest became severe, Hollian took the *orcrest* and *krill* herself, though she was unskilled at that work and the path she made was not as clear as his. The silent caterwaul and torment of the vegetation blocked the ground at every step; but the company found a way through it.

And as the sun began to sag toward the high ridge of the Westron Mountains – still distant to the south and west beyond the region which had once been named Trothgard, but near at hand in the east-jutting promontory of the range – the companions reached the verge of the jungle below the rocky and barren foothills of the high Keep.

Halting in the last shelter of the trees, they looked up at their destination.

Revelstone: once the proud bastion and bourne of the ancient, Land-serving Lords; now the home of the na-Mhoram and the Clave.

Here, at the apex of the promontory, the peaks dropped to form an upland plateau pointing east and sweeping north. All the walls of the plateau were sheer, as effective as battlements; and in the centre of the upland lay Glimmermere, the eldritch tarn with its waters untouched by the Sunbane until they cascaded down Furl Falls in the long south face of the promontory and passed beyond the sources of their potency. But the Keep itself stood to the east of Glimmermere and Furl Falls. The Unhomed had wrought the city of the Lords into the eastward wedge of the plateau, filling that outcrop of the Earth's hard gut-rock with habitations and defences.

Directly above the company stood the watchtower, the tip of the wedge. Shorter than the plateau, its upper shaft rose free of the main Keep bulking behind it; but its lower half was sealed by walls of native stone to the rest of the wedge. In that way, Revelstone's sole entrance was guarded. Long ago, massive gates in the south-east curve of the watchtower's base had protected a passage under the tower – a tunnel which gave admittance only to the closed courtyard between the tower and the main Keep, where stood a second set of gates. During the last war, the siege of Revelstone had broken the outer gates, leaving them in rubble. But Covenant knew from experience that the inner gates still held, warding the Clave with their imponderable thickness and weight.

Above the abutment over its opening, the round shaft of the watchtower was marked with battlements and embrasures to the crenellated rim of its crown. They were irregular and unpredictable, shaped to suit the tower's internal convolutions. Yet the face of the watchtower was as simple as child-work compared to the dramatic complexity of the walls of the main Keep. For a surprising distance into the plateau, the sheer cliffs had been crafted by the Unhomed – written with balconies and buttresses, parapets and walkways, and punctuated with windows of every description, embrasures on the lower levels, oriels and shaded coigns higher up – a prolific and apparently spontaneous multiplication of detail that always gave Covenant an impression of underlying structure, the meaning of which only Giants could read. The faint green sunset danced and sheened on the south face, confusing his human ability to grasp the organization of something so tall, grand, and timeless.

But even his superficial senses felt the tremendous power of the Banefire's beam as it struck sunward from athwart the great Keep. With one stroke, that red force transgressed all his memories of grandeur and glory, changed the proud habitation of the Lords to a place of malefic peril. When he had approached Revelstone so many days ago to rescue Linden, Sunder, and Hollian, he had been haunted by grief for the Giants and Lords and beauty the Land had lost. But now the knot of his chosen rage was pulled too tight to admit sorrow.

He intended to tear that place down if necessary to root out the Clave — and the bare thought that he might be forced to damage Revelstone made him savage.

Yet when he looked at his companions, saw the rapt faces of the Giants, his anger loosened slightly. The Keep had the power to entrance them. Pitchwife's mien was wide with the glee of appreciation: the First's eyes shone pride at the handiwork of her long-dead people: Mistweave gazed upward hungrily, all dismay forgotten for a time. Even Honninscrave had momentarily lost his air of doom, as though he knew intuitively that Revelstone would give him a chance to make restitution.

Conflicting passions rose in Covenant's throat. Thickly, he asked, 'Can you read it? Do you know what it means? I've been here three times' — four counting the brief translation during which he had refused Mhoram's summons — 'but no one's ever been able to tell me what it means.'

For a moment, none of the Giants answered. They could not step back from the wonder of the Keep. They had seen *Coercri* in Seasearch and marvelled at it; but for them Revelstone was transcendent. Watching them, Covenant knew with a sudden pang that now they would never turn back — that no conceivable suasion would induce them to set their Search and their private purposes aside, to leave the Sunbane and Lord Foul to him. The Sunbane had eroded them in fundamental ways, gnawing at their ability to believe that their Search might actually succeed. What could Giants do to aid a Land in which nature itself had become the source of horror? But the sight of Revelstone restored them to themselves. They would never give up their determination to fight.

Unless Covenant found his own answer soon, he would not be able to save them.

Swallowing heavily, Pitchwife murmured, 'No words — There are none. Your scant human tongue is void — ' Tears spread through the creases of his face, mapping his emotion.

But the First said for him, 'All tongues, Giantfriend. All tongues lack such language. There is that in the granite glory of the world's heart which may not be uttered with words. All other expression must be dumb when the pure stone speaks. And here that speech has been made manifest — Ah, my heart!' Her voice rose as if she wanted to both sing and keen. But for her also no words were adequate. Softly, she concluded, 'The Giants of the Land were taught much by their loss of Home. I am humbled before them.'

For a moment, Covenant could not respond. But then a memory came back to him — a recollection of the formal salutation that the people of Revelstone had formerly given to the Giants. *Hail and welcome, inheritor of Land's loyalty. Welcome whole or hurt, in boon or bane – ask or give. To any requiring name we will not fail –* In a husky voice, he breathed:

> 'Giant-troth Revelstone, ancient ward –
> Heart and door of Earthfriend's main:
> Preserve the true with Power's sword,
> Thou ages-Keeper, mountain-reign.'

At that, the First turned toward him; and for an instant her face was concentrated with weeping as if he had touched her deep Giantish love of stone. Almost immediately she recovered her sternness – but not before he had seen how absolutely she was ready now to serve him. Gruffly, she said, 'Thomas Covenant, I have titled you Giant-friend, but it is not enough. You are the Earthfriend. No other name suffices.'

Then she went and put her arms around her husband.

But Covenant groaned to himself, Earthfriend. God help me! That title belonged to Berek Halfhand, who had fashioned the Staff of Law and founded the Council of Lords. It did not become a man who carried the destruction of the Arch of Time in his envenomed hands. The man who had brought to ruin all Berek's accomplishments.

He glared back up at the Keep. The sun had begun to set behind the Westron Mountains, and its light in his eyes hampered his sight; but he discerned no sign that the watchtower was occupied. He had received the same impression the last time he had been here – and had distrusted it then as he did now. Though the outer gates were broken, the tower could still serve as a vital part of the Keep's defences. He would have to be prepared for battle the moment he set foot in that tunnel. If the Clave did not seek to attack him before then.

His shoulders hunched like anticipations of brutality, he turned away from the Keep and retreated a short distance into the vegetation to an area of rocks where the company could camp for the night.

Shortly, his companions gathered around him. The Giants left their delighted study of Revelstone to clear the ground, start a fire, and prepare food. Sunder and Hollian cast repeated glances like wincing toward the Keep, where the ill of their lives had its centre, and where they had once nearly been slain; but they sat with Covenant as if he were a source of courage. The *Haruchai* arranged themselves protectively around the region. Findail stood like a shadow at the edge of the growing firelight.

Linden's disquiet was palpable. Vexation creased her brows: her

1012

gaze searched the twilight warily. Covenant guessed that she was feeling the nearness of the Raver; and he did not know how to comfort her. During all the Land's struggles against Despite, no one had ever found a way to slay a Raver. While Lord Foul endured, his servants clung to life. The Forestal of Garroting Deep, Caer-Caveral's creator and former master, had demonstrated that Herem or Sheol or Jehannum might be sorely hurt or reduced if the bodies they occupied were killed and they were not allowed to flee. But only the body died: the Raver's spirit survived. Covenant could not believe that the Land would ever be free of Gibbon's possessor. And he did not know what else to offer that might ease Linden.

But then she named the immediate cause of her unease; and it was not the na-Mhoram. Turning to Covenant, she said unexpectedly, 'Vain's gone.'

Taken aback, he blinked at her for a moment. Then he surged to his feet, scanned the camp and the surrounding jungle.

The Demondim-spawn was nowhere in sight.

Covenant wheeled toward Cail. Flatly, the *Haruchai* said, 'He has halted a stone's throw distant.' He nodded back the way the company had come. 'At intervals we have watched him, but he does not move. Is it your wish that he should be warded?'

Covenant shook his head, groping for comprehension. When he and Vain had approached Revelstone looking for Linden, Sunder, and Hollian, the Clave had tried to keep Vain out – and had hurt him in the process. Yet he had contrived his way into the Keep, found the heels of the Staff of Law. But after that he had obeyed the Riders as if he feared what they could do to him. Was that it? Having obtained what he wanted from Revelstone, he now kept his distance so that the Clave would not be able to damage him again?

But how was it possible that the Demondim-spawn could be harmed at all, when the Sunbane did not affect him and even *Grim*-fire simply rolled off his black skin?

'It's because of what he is,' Linden murmured as though Covenant's question were tangible in the air. They had discussed the matter at other times; and she had suggested that perhaps the Clave knew more about Vain than the company did. But now she had a different answer. 'He's a being of pure structure. Nothing but structure – like a skeleton without any muscle or blood or life. Rigidity personified. Anything that isn't focused straight at him can't touch him.' Slowly, as if she were unconscious of what she was doing, she turned toward Revelstone, lifted her face to the lightless Keep. 'But that's what the Sunbane does. What the Clave does. They corrupt Law – disrupt structure. Desecrate order. If they tried hard enough' – she was glowering as if she could see Gibbon waiting in his malice and his glee – 'they could take him apart completely, and there wouldn't be enough of him left to so much as remember why he was made in the first place. No wonder he doesn't want to come any closer.'

Covenant held his breath, hoping that she would go on – that in this mood of perception or prophecy she would name the purpose for which Vain had been created. But she did not. By degrees, she lowered her gaze. 'Damn that bastard anyway,' she muttered softly. 'Damn him to hell.'

He echoed her in silence. Vain was such an enigma that Covenant continually forgot him – forgot how vital he was, to the hidden machinations of the *Elohim* if not to the safety of the Earth. But here Findail had not hesitated to leave the Demondim-spawn's side; and his anguished yellow eyes showed no interest in anything except the hazard of Covenant's fire. Covenant felt a prescient itch run through his forearm. Wincing, he addressed Cail.

'Don't bother. He'll take care of himself. He always has.'

Then he went sourly back to his seat near the fire.

The companions remained still as they ate supper, chewing their separate thoughts with their food. But when they were done, the First faced Covenant across the smoking blaze and made a gesture of readiness. 'Now, Earthfriend.' Her tone reminded him of a polished blade, eager for use. 'Let us speak of this proud and dire Keep.'

Covenant met her gaze and grimaced in an effort to hold his personal extremity beyond the range of Linden's percipience.

'It is a doughty work,' the First said firmly. 'In it the Unhomed wrought surpassingly well. Its gates have been broken by a puissance that challenges conception – but if I have not been misled, there are gates again beyond the tower. And surely you have seen that the walls will not be scaled. We would be slain in the attempt. The Clave is potent, and we are few. Earthfriend,' she concluded as if she were prepared to trust whatever explanation he gave, 'how do you purpose to assail this donjon?'

In response, he scowled grimly. He had been expecting that question – and dreading it. If he tried to answer it as if he were sane, his resolve might snap like a rotten bone. His friends would be appalled. And perhaps they would try to stop him. Even if they did not, he felt as certain as death that their dismay would be too much for him.

Yet some reply was required of him. Too many lives depended on what he meant to do. Stalling for courage, he looked toward Hollian. His voice caught in his throat as he asked, 'What kind of sun are we going to have tomorrow?'

Dark hair framed her mien, and her face itself was smudged with the dirt of long travel; yet by some trick of the firelight – or of her nature – she appeared impossibly clear, her countenance unmuddied by doubt or despair. Her movements were deft and untroubled as she accepted the *krill* from Sunder, took out her *lianar*, and invoked the delicate flame of her foretelling.

After a moment, fire bloomed from her wand. Its colour was the dusty hue of the desert sun.

Covenant nodded to himself. A desert sun. By chance or design, he had been granted the phase of the Sunbane he would have chosen for his purpose. On the strength of that small grace, he was able to face the First again.

'Before we risk anything else, I'm going to challenge Gibbon. Try to get him to fight me personally. I don't think he'll do it,' though surely the Raver would covet the white ring for itself and might therefore be willing to defy its master's will, 'but if he does, I can break the Clave's back without hurting anybody else.' Even though Gibbon held the whole force of the Banefire: Covenant was ready for that as well.

But the First was not content. 'And if he does not?' she asked promptly. 'If he remains within his fastness and dares us to harm him?'

Abruptly, Covenant lurched to his feet. Linden's gaze followed him with a flare of alarm as she caught a hint of what drove him; but he did not let her speak. Pieces of moonlight filtered through the dense leaves; and beyond the trees the moon was full — stretched to bursting with promises he could not keep. Above him, the walls and battlements of Revelstone held the silver light as if they were still beautiful. He could not bear it.

Though he was choking, he rasped out, 'I'll think of something.' Then he fled the camp, went blundering through the brush until he reached its verge on the foothills.

The great Keep towered there, as silent and moon-ridden as a cairn for all the dreams it had once contained. No illumination of life showed from it anywhere. He wanted to cry out at it, What have they done to you? But he knew the stone would not hear him. It was deaf to him, blind to its own desecration — as helpless against evil as the Earth itself. The thought that he might hurt it made him tremble.

Cail attended him like an avatar of the night's stillness. Because he had passed the limit of what he could endure, he turned to the *Haruchai* and whispered hoarsely, 'I'm going to sleep here. I want to be alone. Don't let any of them near me.'

He did not sleep: he spent the night staring up at the city as though it were the last barrier between his hot grief and Lord Foul's triumph. Several times, he heard his friends approach him through the brush. Each time, Cail turned them away. Linden protested his refusal, but could not breach it.

1015

That solitary and intimate fidelity enabled Covenant to hang on until dawn.

He saw the light first on the main Keep's rim beyond the parapets of the watchtower, while the shaft of the Banefire shot toward the east. This daybreak had the hue of deserts, and the sun gave the high grey stone a brown tinge. Once again, Hollian had foretold the Sunbane accurately. As he levered his strain-sore and weary bones upright, he thought of the eh-Brand with an odd pang. Married by the child she bore, she and Sunder had grown steadily closer to each other – and Covenant did not know how to heal the wound between himself and Linden.

Behind him, he heard Linden accost Cail a second time. When the *Haruchai* denied her again, she snapped in exasperation, 'He's got to eat. He's still at least that human.' Her voice sounded ragged, as if she also had not slept. Perhaps the air around Revelstone was too full of the taste of Ravers to permit her to sleep. Gibbon had shown her the part of herself which had arisen in hunger to take her mother's life. Yet now, in this fatal place, she was thinking of Covenant rather than of herself. She would have forgiven him long ago – if he had ever given her the chance.

Stiffly, as if all his muscles had been calcified by the night and his long despair, he started up the hill toward Revelstone.

He could not face Linden now, feared to let her look at him almost as much as he feared the massive granite threat of the Keep. Concealment was no longer possible for him; and he dreaded how she would react to what she saw.

The light was on the watchtower, colouring it like a wilderland and dropping rapidly toward the foothills. At the edges of his vision on either side, he saw the treetops start to melt; but the centre of his sight was filled by the tower. Its embrasures and abutments were empty, and the darkness behind them made them look like eyes from which the light of life had been extinguished. Light of life and desecration, he thought vaguely, as if he were too weak with inanition and fear to be troubled by contradictions. He knew how to deal with them: he had found that answer in the thronehall of Foul's Creche, when the impossibility of believing the Land true and the impossibility of believing it false had forced him to take his stand on the still point of strength at the centre of his vertiginous plight. But such comprehension was of no use to him now. All the anger had gone out of him during the night; and he ascended toward the gaping mouth of Revelstone like a husk for burning.

Yet the apparent desertion of the city made him uneasy. Was it possible that the Clave had fled – that his mere approach had driven the Riders into hiding? No. The virulence of the Banefire's beam gave no indication that it had been left untended. And Lord Foul would not have permitted any withdrawal. What better victory for the Despiser than that Covenant should bring down the Arch in conflict with the Clave?

Lord Foul had said, *At the last there will be but one choice for you, and you will make it in all despair.* He had promised that, and he had laughed.

Something that might have been power stirred in Covenant. His hands curled into fists, and he went on upward.

The sun laid his shadow on the bare dirt in front of him. Its heat gripped the back of his neck, searching for the fibre of his will in the same way that it would reduce all the Upper Land's monstrous verdure to grey sludge and desert. He seemed to see himself spread out for sacrifice on the ground – exposed for the second time to a glow as murderous as the knife which had pierced his chest, stabbed the hope out of his life. An itch like a faint scurry of vermin spread up his right forearm. Unconsciously, he quickened his pace.

Then he reached the level ground at the base of the tower, and the tunnel stood open before him among its ruined gates. The passage was as dark as a grave until it met the dim illumination reflecting into the courtyard from the face of the main Keep. Dimly, he saw the inner gates at the far side of the court. They were sealed against him.

Involuntarily, he looked back down toward the place where his companions had camped. At first the sun was in his eyes, and he could descry nothing except the eviscerated grey muck which stretched out to the horizons like a sea as the Sunbane denatured life from the terrain. But when he shaded his sight, he saw the company.

His friends stood in a cluster just beyond the edge of the sludge. The First and two *Haruchai* were restraining Honninscrave. Pitchwife held Linden back.

Covenant swung around in pain to face the tunnel again.

He did not enter it. He was familiar with the windows in its ceiling which allowed the Keep's defenders to attack anyone who walked that throat. And he did not raise his voice. He was instinctively certain now that Revelstone was listening acutely, in stealth and covert fear. He sounded small against the dusty air of the great city and the growing desert as he spoke.

'I've come for you, Gibbon. For you. If you come out, I'll let the rest of the Riders live.' Echoes mocked him from the tunnel, then subsided. 'If you don't, I'll take this place apart to find you.

'You know I can do it. I could've done it the last time – and I'm stronger now.' *You are more dangerous now than you've ever been.* 'Foul doesn't think you can beat me. He's using you to make me beat myself. But I don't care about that anymore. Either way, you're going to die. Come out and get it over with.'

The words seemed to die before they reached the end of the passage. Revelstone loomed above him like the corpse of a city which had been slain ages ago. The pressure of the sun drew a line of bitter sweat down his spine.

And a figure appeared in the tunnel. Black against the reflection of the courtyard, it moved outward. Its feet struck soft echoes of crepitation from the stone.

Covenant tried to swallow – and could not. The desert sun had him by the throat.

A pair of hot pains transfixed his forearm. The scars gleamed like fangs. An invisible darkness flowed out of the passage toward him, covering his fire with the pall of venom. The sound of steps swelled.

Then sandalled feet and the fringe of a red robe broached the sunshine; and Covenant went momentarily faint with the knowledge that his first gambit had failed. Light ran swiftly up the lines of the stark scarlet fabric to the black chasuble which formalized the robe. Hands appeared, empty of the characteristic *rukh*, the black iron rod like a sceptre with an open triangle fixed atop it, which a Rider should have held. Yet this was surely a Rider. Not Gibbon; the na-Mhoram wore black. He carried a crozier as tall as himself. The habitual beatitude or boredom of his round visage was punctured only by the red bale of his eyes. The man who came out to meet Covenant was not Gibbon.

A Rider, then. He appeared thick of torso, though his ankles and wrists were thin, and his bearded cheeks had been worn almost to gauntness by audacity or fear. Wisps of wild hair clung like fanaticism to his balding skull. His eyes had a glazed aspect.

He held his palms open before him as if to demonstrate that he had come unarmed.

Covenant wrestled down his weakness, fought a little moisture into his throat so that he could speak. In a tone that should have warned the Rider, he said, 'Don't waste my time. I want Gibbon.'

'Halfhand, I greet you,' the man replied. His voice was steady, but it suggested the shrillness of panic. 'Gibbon na-Mhoram is entirely cognizant of you and will waste neither time nor life in your name. What is your purpose here?'

Impressions of danger crawled between Covenant's shoulder-blades. His mouth was full of the copper taste of fear. The Rider's trunk appeared unnaturally thick; and his robe seemed to move slightly of its own accord as if the cloth were seething. Covenant's scars began to burn like rats gnawing at his flesh. He hardly heard himself reply, 'This has gone on too long. You make the whole world stink. I'm going to put a stop to it.'

The Rider bared his teeth – a grin that failed. His gaze did not focus on Covenant. 'Then I must tell you that the na-Mhoram does not desire speech with you. His word has been given to me to speak, if you will hear it.'

Covenant started to ask, What word is that? But the question never reached utterance. With both hands, the Rider unbelted the sash of his robe. In prescient dread, Covenant watched the Rider open his raiment to the sun.

From the line of his shoulders to the flex of his knees, his entire body was covered with wasps.

Great yellow wasps, as big as Covenant's thumb.

When the light touched them, they began to snarl.

For one hideous moment, they writhed where they were; and the Rider wore them as if he were one of the Sunbane-warped, made savage and abominable by corruption. Then the swarm launched itself at Covenant.

In that instant, the world went black. Venom crashed against his heart like the blow of a sledgehammer.

Black fire: black poison: black ruin. The flame raging from his ring should have been as pure and argent as the metal from which it sprang; but it was not *was not*. It was an abyss that yawned around him, a gulf striding through the air and the ground and the Keep to consume them, swallow the world and leave no trace. And every effort he made to turn the dark fire white, force it back to the clean pitch of its true nature, only raised the blaze higher, widened the void. Swiftly, it became as huge as the hillside, hungry for ruin.

Linden was not shouting at him. If she had torn her heart with screams, he would not have been able to hear her: she was too far away, and the gathering cataclysms of his power filled all his senses. Yet he heard her in his mind – heard her as she had once cried to him across the Worm's aura and the white ring's eruption, *This is what Foul wants!* – felt the remembered grasp of her arms as she had striven to wrest him back from doom. If he let his conflagration swell, they would all die, she and the others he loved and the Land he treasured, all of them ripped out of life and meaning by blackness.

The strain of self-mastery pushed him far beyond himself. He was driven to a stretched and tenuous desperation from which he would never be able to turn back – a hard, wild exigency that he would have to see through to its conclusion for good or ill, ravage or restitution. But the simple knowledge that he would not be able to turn back and did not mean to try enabled him to strangle the destruction pouring from him.

Abruptly, his vision cleared – and he had not been stung. Thousands of small, charred bodies still smoked on the bare ground. Not one of the wasps was left to threaten him.

The Rider remained standing with his mouth open and his eyes white, miraculously unscathed and astonished.

Covenant felt no triumph: he had gone too far for triumph. But he was certain of himself now, at least for the moment. To the Rider, he said, 'Tell Gibbon he had his chance.' His voice held neither doubt nor mercy. 'Now I'm coming in after him.'

Slowly, the astonishment drained from the man's face. His frenzy and glee seemed to collapse as if he had suffered a relapse of mortality. Yet he remained a Rider of the Clave, and he knew his enemy. All the Land had been taught to believe that Covenant was a betrayer. The man looked human and frail, reduced by failure; but he did not recant his faith.

'You surpass me, Halfhand.' His voice shook. 'You have learned to wield – and to restrain. But you have come to havoc the long service of our lives, and we will not permit you. Look to your power, for it will not aid you against us.'

Turning as if he were still able to dismiss Covenant from consideration, he followed the echoes of his feet back into the tunnel under the watchtower.

Covenant watched him go and cursed the mendacity which enabled Lord Foul to take such men and women, people of native courage and dedication, and convince them that the depredations of the Clave were virtuous. Revelstone was full of individuals who believed themselves responsible for the survival of the Land. And they would be the first to die: the Despiser would sacrifice them before hazarding his truer servants.

Yet even for them Covenant could not stop now. The fire still raved within him. He had not quenched it: he had only internalized it, sealed its fury inside himself. If he did not act on it, it would break out with redoubled vehemence, and he would never be able to contain it again.

Violence taut in his muscles, he started stiffly down the hillside toward his friends.

They began the ascent to meet him. Anxiously, they studied the way he moved as if they had seen him emerge from the teeth of hell and could hardly believe it.

Before he reached them, he heard the flat thunder of hooves.

He did not stop: he was wound to his purpose and unbreachable. But he looked back up at Revelstone over his shoulder.

Between the broken gates came Riders mounted on Coursers, half a dozen of them pounding in full career down the slope. The Sunbane-bred Coursers were large enough to carry four or five ordinary men and women, would have been large enough to support Giants. They had malicious eyes, the faces and fangs of sabretooths, shaggy pelts, and poisoned spurs at the back of each ankle. And the Riders held their *rukhs* high and bright with flame as they charged. Together they rushed downward as if they believed they could sweep the company off the hillside.

Yet for all their fury and speed they looked more like a charade than a true assault. The Banefire made them dangerous; but they were only six, and they were hurling themselves against ten *Haruchai*, four Giants, the Appointed of the *Elohim*, and four humans whose strength had not yet been fully measured. Covenant himself had already killed. Deliberately, he left the charge to his companions and walked on.

Behind him, the Coursers suddenly went wild.

Sunder had snatched out his Sunstone and the *krill*; but now he did not draw his power from the sun. Instead, he tapped the huge beam of the Banefire. And he was acquainted with Coursers. At one time, he had learned to use a *rukh* in order to master a group of the beasts: he knew how to command them. Fierce red flarings shot back and forth through the *krill*'s white light as he threw his force at the attack; but he did not falter.

The impact of his countervailing instructions struck chaos into the Coursers. Two of them fell trying to lunge in several directions simultaneously. A third stumbled over them. The others attacked the fallen, tried to kill them.

Reft of control, the Riders sprawled to the hard ground. One was crushed under the massive body of a Courser. Another received a dangerous spur slash. She cried out to her comrades for help; but they were already in flight back toward the Keep, bearing the broken Rider for his blood. Weakly, she struggled after them.

Sunder ordered the Coursers out into the desert so that the Clave would not be able to use them again. But two of them squealed with pain when they tried to obey: they had broken legs. Gripping her falchion in both fists, the First stalked up to the maimed beasts and slew them.

Then Sunder, Linden, and Pitchwife approached Covenant.

The Graveller was panting heavily. 'Gibbon does not put forth his full strength. I am not the equal of six Riders.' Yet there was a grim pride in his tone. At last he had struck an effective blow against the Clave.

'He's trying to provoke you,' Linden warned. 'You almost didn't pull back in time. You've got to be careful.' Fear of Ravers twisted her face into a scowl.

'Earthfriend,' breathed Pitchwife, 'what will you do? There is a madness upon Grimmand Honninscrave. We will not be long able to withhold him.'

But Covenant made no reply. His legs were trembling now, and he could not stop what he was doing or turn aside. He headed toward a blunt boulder jutting from the lower slope of the foothill. When he reached it, he struggled up onto its crown, defying the way the wide landscape below and about him sucked at his balance. All his limbs felt leaden with suppressed devastation. From horizon to horizon, the desert sun had almost finished its work: in the low places of the terrain lay ponds of sludge which had once been trees and brush and vines, but every slope and rise was burned to dust and death. The thought that he would have to damage Revelstone was intolerable. Sheer grief and self-loathing would break him if he set his hand to that stone. Yet the necessity was inescapable. The Clave and the Banefire could not be permitted to go on. His heart quivered at the conflict of his fears – fear of harming the Keep and of not harming it, fear of himself, of the risk he meant to take; his desire to avoid killing and his need to protect his friends. But he had already chosen his path. Now he started down it.

Trembling as if he were on the verge of deflagration, he spoke the name he had been hoarding to himself ever since he had begun to understand the implications of what he meant to do.

The name of a Sandgorgon.

'Nom.'

10

THE BANEFIRE

Clearly through the sudden shock of the company, he heard Linden gasp. There was no wind, nothing to soften the arid pressure of the sun. Below him, the terrain was falling into the paradoxical purity of desecration. The cleanliness of extermination. No wonder fire was so hard to resist. His balance seemed to spin out of him into the flat brown sky. He had not eaten or slept since the previous day: perhaps it was inanition which made the horizons cant to one side as if they were about to sail away. Inanition or despair.

But Pitchwife and Cail caught him, lowered him from the boulder; and Linden came to him in a blur of vertigo. He had never been good at heights. He knew that she was saying his name, yet he felt unable to hear her. Her face was impossible to focus. She should have been protesting, A Sandgorgon? Are you out of your mind? What makes you think you can control it? But she was not. Her hands gripped his shoulders roughly, then flinched away: this time, her gasp was like a cry. 'You – !' she began. But the words would not come. 'Oh, Covenant!'

The First's voice cut through the wild reel of the hills. 'What harms him?' All his friends were crowded around him and spinning. He saw Mhoram and Foamfollower, Bannor and Elena – and Caer-

Caveral — all there as if they deserved better from him. 'What has transpired to harm him?' They had met him in Andelain and given him everything they dared; and this was the result. He was caught on a wheel that had no centre. 'Chosen, you must speak!'

'He's on fire.' Linden's tone was wet with tears. 'The venom's on fire. We'd already be dead, but he's holding it inside. As long as he can. Until it eats its way out.'

The First cursed, then snapped a command that Covenant failed to hear. A moment later, Pitchwife's heat-impervious hands lifted a bowl of *diamondraught* to Covenant's mouth.

Its potent smell stung his nostrils with panic. *Diamondraught* would restore him. Perhaps it would restore his self-mastery as well. Or it might fuel the blaze of his suppressed power. He could not take the chance.

Somehow, he slowed the spin. Clarity was possible. He could not afford to fail. And he would not have to hang on long: only until he reached the culmination of his nightmares. It was possible. When he was certain of the faces hovering around him, he said as if he were suffocating, 'Not *diamondraught*. *Metheglin*.'

The First glared doubt at him; but Linden nodded. 'He's right,' she said in a rush. 'He has to keep his balance. Between strength and weakness. *Diamondraught* is too strong.'

People were moving: Hollian and Mistweave went away, came back at once with a pouch of the Land's thick mead. That Covenant drank, sparingly at first, then more deeply as he felt his grasp on the conflagration hold. By degrees, the vertigo frayed out of him. His friends were present and stable. The ground became solid again. The sun rang in his eyes, clanged against his temples, like Lord Foul's silent laughter; and his face streamed with the sweat of desperation. But as the *metheglin* steadied him, he found that he was at least able to bear the heat.

With Pitchwife's help, he gained his feet. Squinting, he turned to the east and thrust his gaze out into the shimmering desert.

'Will it come?' the First asked no one in particular. 'The wide seas intervene, and they are no slight barrier.'

'Kasreyn said it would.' Linden bit her lips to control her apprehension, then continued, 'He said, "Distance has no meaning to such power."' Covenant remembered that. *The Sandgorgons answer their release swiftly.* That was how Hergrom had been killed. But Covenant had already summoned Nom once at Linden's instigation; and he had not been slain. And Nom had gone back to Sandgorgons Doom. Therefore why should the beast answer him now? He had no reason for such a wild hope — no reason at all except the fact that Nom had bowed to him when he had refrained from killing it.

But the east was empty, and the haze closed against him like a curtain. Even the eyes of the Giants discerned no sign of an answer.

Abruptly, Cail's uninflected voice broke the silence.

'Ur-Lord, behold.'

With one arm, he pointed up the hillside toward Revelstone.

For an instant, Covenant believed that the *Haruchai* wanted him to observe the immense hot vermeil shaft of the Banefire. With sun-echoes burning white and brown across his sight, he thought the sizzling beam looked stronger now, as though Gibbon-Raver were feeding it furiously to arm the Clave for combat. Killing the captured villagers and *Haruchai* as fast as their blood could be poured onto the floor of the sacred enclosure where the Banefire burned.

At the idea, the spots flaring against the backs of his eyes turned black. His restraint slipped. The fang-marks on his forearm hurt as if they had been reopened.

But then he saw the Riders at the base of the tower. Four of them: two holding up their *rukhs* to master the *Haruchai* they had brought with them; two equipped with knives and buckets.

They intended to shed their mind-bound prisoner in full view of Covenant and the company.

Covenant let out a shout that made the air throb. But at the same time he fought for control, thinking, No. No. He's trying to provoke me. The blackness in him writhed. He refused it until it subsided.

'Honninscrave.' The First sounded almost casual, as if the sight of atrocities made her calm. 'Mistweave. It is my thought that we need not permit this.'

Half the *Haruchai* had started upward at a sprint. She made no effort to call them back. Stooping to the dirt, she picked up a rock larger than her palm; and in the same motion she hurled it at the Riders.

Striking the wall behind them, it burst in a shower of splinters that slashed at them like knives.

Instantly, Honninscrave and Mistweave followed the First's example. Their casts were so accurate that one of the Riders had a leg smashed, another was ripped by a hail of rebounding fragments. Their companions were compelled to release the *Haruchai* so that they could use their *rukhs* to defend themselves.

While the four Riders retreated into the tunnel, their captive turned on them. Suddenly free of their coercion, he slew the injured men. Then he pivoted disdainfully on his heel and strode down the slope to meet his people. He was bleeding from several cuts inflicted by sharp pieces of stone, but he bore himself as if he were unscathed.

Covenant hated killing. He had chosen his path in an effort to spare as many lives as possible. But as he watched the released *Haruchai* walking toward him like pure and utter dispassion, a dire grin twisted the corners of his mouth. In that moment, he became more dangerous to Gibbon and the Clave than any host of warriors or powers.

When he looked toward the east again, he saw a plume of dust rising through the haze.

He did not doubt what it was. Nothing but a Sandgorgon could travel with enough swift strength to raise that much dust.

Mutely, Linden moved to his side as if she wanted to take his arm and cling to it for support. But the dark peril he radiated kept her from touching him.

Mistweave watched the dust with growing amazement. Pitchwife muttered inanely to himself, making pointless jests that seemed to ease his trepidation. The First grinned like a scimitar. Of the Giants, only Honninscrave did not study the beast's approach. He stood with his head bowed and his arms manacled across his chest as if throwing stones at the Riders had whetted his hunger for violence.

Unexpectedly, Findail spoke. He sounded weary, worn thin by the prolonged burden of his responsibility; but some of the bitterness was gone from his voice. 'Ring-wielder,' he said, 'your purpose here is abominable and should be set aside. Those who hold the Earth in their hands have no justification for vengeance. Yet you have found a wise way to the accomplishment of your ends. I implore that you entrust them to this beast. You little comprehend what you have summoned.'

Covenant ignored the *Elohim*. Linden glanced at the Appointed. Sunder and Hollian gazed at him in confusion. But none of the companions spoke.

Nom had become visible at the arrow-point of the advancing dust.

Albino against the desiccated waste, the beast approached at a startling pace. Its size was not commensurate with its might: it was only a few hands taller than Covenant, only a little more thickly built than the *Haruchai*; yet given time and concentrated attention and freedom it was capable of reducing the entire gut-rock wedge of Revelstone to wreckage. It had a strange gait, suited to deserts: its knees were back-bent like a bird's to utilize the full thrust of the wide pads of its feet. Lacking hands, its arms were formed like battering-rams.

And it had no face. Nothing defined its hairless head except the faint ridges of its skull under its hide and two covered slits like gills on either side.

Even to Covenant's unpenetrating sight, the Sandgorgon looked as pure and uncontestable as a force of nature – a hurricane bound into one savage form and avid for a place to strike.

It came running as if it meant to hurl itself at him. ·

But at the last it stopped in a thick nimbus of dust, confronted him across a scant stretch of bare dirt. For a moment, it trembled as it had trembled when he had defeated it in direct combat and it had not known how to hold back its elemental fury even to save its own life. Service was an alien concept to its brute mind: violence made more sense. Sweat blurred the edges of his vision as he watched the beast quiver for decision: involuntarily, he held his breath. A few small flames slipped past his control and licked at his forearm until he beat them back.

Nom's trembling mounted – and abruptly subsided. Lowering itself to the ground, the beast placed its forehead in the dirt at Covenant's feet.

Slowly, he let pent air leak away through his teeth. A muffled sigh of relief passed through the company. Linden covered her face momentarily, then thrust her fingers through her hair as if she were trying to pull courage up out of her alarm.

'Nom,' he said, and his voice shook. 'Thanks for coming.'

He did not know to what extent the beast was able to understand him; but it surged erect by unfolding its knees and stood waiting before him.

He did not let himself hesitate. The bond which held Nom was fragile. And he could feel venom gnawing in him like acid. His purpose was as clear to him as the soothtell which had sent him on his futile quest for the One Tree. Turning to his companions, he addressed them as a group.

'I want you to stay here.' Gritting his will, he strove to suppress the tremors which made his tone harsh. 'Leave it to Nom and me. Between us, we're already too much for the job.' And I can't bear to lose any of you.

He had no right to say such things. Every member of the company had earned a place in this hazard. But when he considered what might happen to them, he burned to spare them.

'I'll need Linden,' he went on before anyone could protest. 'Gibbon's going to try to hide from me. I won't be able to locate the Raver without her.' The mere thought hurt him: he knew how deeply she dreaded Ravers. 'And I'll take Cail and Fole. To guard our backs.' Even that concession made him want to rage. But Linden might need the protection. 'The rest of you just wait. If I fail, you'll have to do it for me.'

Unable to face what his friends wanted to say, the pained indignation in their eyes, the expostulations rising from their hearts, he impelled Linden into motion with his hand on the small of her back. A gesture called Nom to his side. Striding stiffly past the people who had served him with their lives and deserved better than this, he started up the slope toward Revelstone.

Then for a moment he came so close to tears that his courage nearly broke. Not one of his companions obeyed. Without a word, they arranged themselves for battle and followed him.

Under her breath, Linden murmured, 'I understand. You think it all depends on you. Why should people as good as they are have to suffer and maybe get killed for it? And I'm so scared – ' Her face was pale and drawn and urgent. 'But you have got to stop trying to make other people's decisions for them.'

He did not reply. Keeping his attention fixed on the open tunnel under the watchtower, he forced his power-clogged muscles to bear him steadily upward. But now he feared that he was already defeated. He had too much to lose. His friends were accompanying him into his nightmares as if he were worthy of them. Because he had to do something, no matter how insufficient or useless it might be, he moved closer to Cail and whispered, 'This is enough. Bannor said you'd serve me. Brinn told you to take his place. But I don't need this kind of service anymore. I'm too far gone. What I need is hope.'

'Ur-Lord?' the *Haruchai* responded softly.

'The Land needs a future. Even if I win. The Giants'll go Home. You'll go about your business. But if anything happens to Sunder or Hollian – ' The idea appalled him. 'I want you to take care of them. All of you. No matter what.' He was prepared to endanger even Linden for this. 'The Land has got to have a future.'

'We hear you.' Cail's tone did not betray whether he was relieved, moved, or offended. 'If the need arises, we will remember your words.'

With that Covenant had to be content.

Nom had moved somewhat ahead of him, thrusting toward the great Keep as if it triggered a racial memory of the Sandwall which the *Bhrathair* had raised to oppose the Sandgorgons in the years before Kasreyn had bound them to their Doom. The beast's arms swung in anticipation. Grimly, Covenant quickened his pace.

In that way, with Linden beside him, two Stonedownors and four Giants behind him, and eleven *Haruchai* nearby, Thomas Covenant went to pit himself against the Clave and the Banefire.

There was no reaction from Revelstone. Perhaps the na-Mhoram did not know what a Sandgorgon was, wanted to see what it would do before he attempted to provoke Covenant again. Or perhaps he had given up provocation in order to prepare his defences. Perhaps the Raver had found a small worm of fear at the bottom of his malice. Covenant liked that idea. What the Clave and the Banefire had done to the Land could not be forgiven. The way in which this Raver had transformed to ill the ancient and honourable Council of Lords could not be forgiven. And for Gibbon's attack on Linden, Covenant would accept no atonement except the cleansing of the Keep.

Those who hold the Earth in their hands have no justification for vengeance.

Like hell, Covenant gritted. Like hell they don't.

But when he reached the base of the watchtower, he commanded Nom to halt and paused to consider the tunnel. The sun was high enough now to make the inner courtyard bright; but that only deepened the obscurity of the passage. The windows of the tower gaped as if the rooms behind them were abandoned. A silence like the cryptic stillness of the dead hung over the city. There was no wind – no sign of life except the stark hot shaft of the Banefire. Between the two slain Coursers, dead wasps littered the ground. The Riders had taken their own fallen with them for the sake of the blood. But red splotches marked the rocks in front of the tower as though to tell Covenant that he had come to the right place.

He turned to Linden. Her taut pallor frightened him, but he could no longer afford to spare her. 'The tower,' he said as the company stood behind him. 'I need to know if it's empty.'

The movement of her head as she looked upward seemed fatally slow, as if her old paralysis had its hand on her again. The last time she was here, Gibbon's touch had reduced her to near catatonia. *The principal doom of the Land is upon your shoulders. Through eyes and ears and touch, you are made to be what the Despiser requires.* Once she had pleaded with Covenant, *You've got to get me out of here. Before they make me kill you.*

But she did not plead now or seek to shirk the consequences of her choice. Her voice sounded dull and stunned: yet she accepted Covenant's demands. 'It's hard,' she murmured. 'Hard to see past the Banefire. It wants me – wants to throw me at the sun. Throw me at the sun forever.' Fear glazed her eyes as if that cast had already begun. 'It's hard to see anything else.' However, a moment later she frowned. Her gaze sharpened. 'But Gibbon isn't there. Not there. He's still in the main Keep. And I don't feel anything else.' When she looked at Covenant again, she appeared as severe as she had at their first meeting. 'I don't think they've ever used the tower.'

A surge of relief started up in Covenant, but he fought it down. He could not afford that either. It blunted his control, let hints of blackness leak through his mind. Striving to match her, he muttered, 'Then let's go.'

With Nom and Linden, Cail and Fole, he walked into the tunnel; and his companions followed him like echoes.

As he traversed the passage, he instinctively hunched his shoulders, bracing himself against the attack he still expected from the ceiling of the tunnel. But no attack came. Linden had read the tower accurately. Soon he stood in the courtyard. The sun shone before him on the high, buttressed face of the Keep and on the massive inner gates.

Those stone slabs were notched and bevelled and balanced so that they could open outward smoothly and marry exactly when they closed. They were heavy enough to rebuff any force of which their makers had been able to conceive. And they were shut, interlocking with each other like teeth. The lines where they hinged and met were barely distinguishable.

'I have said it,' the First breathed behind Covenant. 'The Unhomed wrought surpassingly well in this place.'

She was right: the gates looked ready to stand forever.

Suddenly, Covenant became urgent for haste. If he did not find an answer soon, he would go up like tinder and oil. The sun had not yet reached midmorning; and the shaft of the Banefire stood poised above him like a scythe titanic and bloody enough to reap all the life of the world. Sunder's hands clutched the *krill* and his *orcrest*, holding them ready; but he looked strangely daunted by the great Keep, by what it meant and contained. For the first time in the ordeal of the Search, Pitchwife seemed vulnerable to panic, capable of flight. Linden's skin was the colour of ashes. But Honninscrave held his fists clinched at his sides as if he knew he was close to the reasons for Seadreamer's death and did not mean to wait for them much longer.

Covenant groaned to himself. He should have begun his attack last night, while most of his friends slept. He was sick of guilt.

With a fervid sweep of his arm, he sent Nom at the gates.

The Sandgorgon seemed to understand instinctively. In three strides, it reached full speed.

Hurtling forward like a juggernaut, it crashed headlong against the juncture of the clenched slabs.

The impact boomed across the courtyard, thudded in Covenant's lungs, rebounded like a cannonade from the tower. The stones underfoot shivered: a vibration like a wail ran through the abutments. The spot Nom struck was crushed and dented as if it were formed of wood.

But the gates stood.

The beast stepped back as though it were astonished. It turned its head like a question toward Covenant. But an instant later it rose up in the native savagery of all Sandgorgons and began to beat at the gates with the staggering might of its arms.

Slowly at first, then more and more rapidly, the beast struck, one sledgehammer arm and then the other in accelerating sequence, harder and faster, harder and faster, until the courtyard was full of thunder and the stone yowled distress. He was responsible for this — and still the gates held, bore the battery. Chips and splinters spat in all directions: granite teeth screamed against each other: the flagstones of the court seemed to ripple and dance. Still the gates held.

To herself, Linden whimpered as though she could feel every blow in her frangible bones.

Covenant started to shout for Nom to stop. He did not understand what the Sandgorgon was doing. The sight of such an attack would have rent Mhoram's heart.

But an instant later he heard the rhythm of Nom's blows more clearly, heard how that pulse meshed with the gut-rock's protesting retorts and cries; and he understood. The Sandgorgon had set up a resonance in the gates, and each impact increased the frequency and amplitude of the vibrations. If the beast did not falter, the slabs might be driven to tear themselves apart.

Abruptly, red fire poured down off the abutment immediately above the gates. Riders appeared brandishing their *rukhs*: four of five of them. Wielding the Banefire together, they were more mighty than an equal number of individuals; and they shaped a concerted blast to thrust Nom back from the gates.

But Covenant was ready for them. He had been expecting something like this, and his power was hungry for utterance, for any release that would ease the strain within him. Meticulous with desperation, he put out wild magic to defend the Sandgorgon.

His force was a sickening mixture of blackness and argence, mottled and leprous. But it was force nonetheless, fire capable of riving the heavens. It covered the Riders, melted their *rukhs* to slag, then pitched them back into the Keep with their robes aflame.

Nom went on hammering at the gates in a transport of destructive ecstasy as if it had finally met an obstacle worthy of itself.

Honninscrave quivered to hurl himself forward; but the First restrained him. He obeyed her like a man who would soon be beyond reach of any command.

Then Nom struck a final blow – struck so swiftly that Covenant did not see how the blow was delivered. He saw only the small still fraction of time as the gates passed from endurance to rupture. They stood – and the change came upon them like the last inward suck of air before the blast of a hurricane – and then they were gone, ripped apart in a wrench of detonation with fragments whining like agony in all directions and stone-powder billowing so thickly that Nom disappeared and the broken mouth of Revelstone was obscured.

Slowly, the high, wide portal became visible through the dust. It was large enough for Coursers, suitable for Giants. But the Sandgorgon did not reappear. Covenant's stunned ears were unable to pick out the slap of Nom's feet as the beast charged alone into the stone city.

'Oh my God,' Linden muttered over and over again, 'oh my God,' and Pitchwife breathed, 'Stone and Sea!' as if he had never seen a Sandgorgon at work before. Hollian's eyes were full of fear. But Sunder had been taught violence and killing by the Clave, had never learned to love Revelstone: his face was bright with eagerness.

Half deafened by the pain of the stone, Covenant entered the Keep because now he had no choice left but to go forward or die. And he did not know what Nom would do to the city. At a wooden run, he crossed the courtyard and passed through the dust into

Revelstone as if he were casting the die of his fate.

Instantly, his companions arranged themselves for battle and followed him. He was only one stride ahead of Cail, two ahead of the First, Linden, and Honninscrave, as he broached the huge forehall of the na-Mhoram's Keep.

It was as dark as a pit.

He knew that hall: it was the size of a cavern. It had been formed by Giants to provide a mustering-space for the forces of the former Lords. But the sun angled only a short distance into the broken entrance; and some trick of the high stone seemed to absorb the light; and there was no other illumination.

Too late, he understood that the forehall had been prepared to meet him.

With a crash, heavy wooden barriers slammed shut across the entryway. Sudden midnight echoed around the company.

Instinctively, Covenant started to release a blaze from his ring. Then he yanked it back. His fire was entirely black now, as corrupt as poison: it shed no more light than the scream that swelled against his self-control, threatening to tear his throat and split Revelstone asunder.

For an instant like a seizure, no one moved or spoke. The things they could not see seemed to paralyse even the First and the *Haruchai*. Then Linden panted, 'Sunder.' Her voice shook wildly: she sounded like a madwoman. 'Use the *krill*. Use it now.'

Covenant tried to swing toward her. What is it? What do you see? But his imprecise ears missed her position in the dark. He was peering straight at Sunder when the *krill* sent a peal of vivid white ringing across the cavern.

He had no defence as Hollian's shrill cry echoed after the light:

'The na-Mhoram's *Grim*!'

Argent dazzled him. The *Grim*! He could not think or see. Such a sending had attacked the company once before; and under an open sky it had killed Memla na-Mhoram-in, had nearly slain Linden and Cail. In the enclosed space of the forehall – !

And it would damage Revelstone severely. He had seen the remains of a village which had fallen under the *Grim*. During Stonedown, Hamako's birthplace. The acid force of the na-Mhoram's curse had eaten the entire habitation to rubble.

Covenant wheeled to face the peril; but still he could not see. His companions scrambled around him like panic. For one mad instant, he believed they were fleeing. But then Cail took hold of his arm, ignoring the pain of suppressed fire; and he heard the First's stern voice. 'Mistweave, we must have more light. Chosen, instruct us. How may this force be combated?'

From somewhere beyond his blindness, Covenant heard Linden reply, 'Not with your sword.' The ague in her voice blurred the words: she had to fight to make them comprehensible. 'We've got to quench it. Or give it something else to burn.'

Covenant's vision cleared in time to see the black hot thunderhead of the *Grim* rolling toward the company just below the cavern's ceiling.

Confined by the forehall, it appeared monstrously powerful.

Nom was nowhere to be seen; but Covenant's knees felt vibrations through the floor as if the Sandgorgon were attacking the Keep's inner chambers. Or as if Revelstone itself feared what Gibbon had unleashed.

From the entryway came the noise of belaboured wood as Mistweave sought to break down the barrier which sealed the hall. But it had been fashioned with all the stoutness the Clave could devise: it creaked and cracked at Mistweave's blows, but did not break.

When the boiling thunderhead was directly over the company, it shattered with a tremendous and silent concussion that would have flattened Covenant if Cail had not upheld him.

In that instant, the *Grim* became stark black flakes that floated muderously downward, bitter as chips of stone and corrosive as vitriol. The thick *Grim*-fall spanned the company.

Covenant wanted to raise fire to defend his friends. He believed he had no choice: venom and fear urged him to believe he had no choice. But he knew with a terrible certainty that if he unleashed the wild magic now he might never be able to call it back. All his other desperate needs would be lost. Loathing himself, he watched and did nothing as the dire flakes settled toward him and the people he loved.

Fole and another *Haruchai* impelled Linden to the nearest wall, as far as possible from the centre of the *Grim*-fall. Harn tugged at Hollian, but she refused to leave Sunder. Cail was ready to dodge – ready to carry Covenant if necessary. The First and Honninscrave braced themselves to pit their Giantish immunity to fire against the flakes. Findail had disappeared as if he could sense Covenant's restraint and cared about nothing else.

Glaring in the *krill*-light, the flakes wafted slowly downward.

And Sunder stood to meet them.

From his *orcrest* he drew a red shaft of Sunbane-fire and started burning the black bits out of the air.

His beam consumed every flake it touched. With astonishing courage or abandon, he faced the entire *Grim* himself. But the bits were falling by the thousands. They were too much for him. He could not even clear the air above his own head to protect himself and Hollian.

Then Pitchwife joined him. Incongruously crippled and valiant, the Giant also attacked the *Grim*, using as his only weapon the pouches of *vitrim* he had borne with him from Hamako's *rhyshyshim*. One after another, he emptied them by spraying *vitrim* at the flakes.

Each flake the liquid touched became ash and drifted harmlessly away.

His visage wore a grimace of grief at the loss of his carefully-hoarded Waynhim roborant; but while it lasted he used it with deliberate extravagance.

Honninscrave slapped at the first flake which neared his head, then gave an involuntary cry as the black corrosive ate into his palm. The *Grim* had been conceived to destroy stone, and no mortal flesh was proof against it.

Around Covenant, the cavern started to reel. The irreconcilable desperation of his plight was driving him mad.

But at that instant a huge splintering crashed through the air; and the wooden barricade went down under Mistweave's attack. More light washed into the forehall, improving the ability of the *Haruchai* to dodge the *Grim*. And wood followed the light: fiercely, Mistweave tore the barrier beam from timber and flung the pieces toward the company.

Haruchai intercepted the smaller fragments, used them as cudgels to batter *Grim*-flakes from the air. But the First, Honninscrave, and then Pitchwife snatched up the main timbers. At once, wood whirled around the company. The First swung a beam as tall as herself as if it were a flail: Honninscrave swept flakes away from Sunder and Hollian: Pitchwife pounced to Linden's defence with an enormous club in each fist.

The *Grim* destroyed the wood almost instantly: each flake tore the weapon which touched it to charcoal. But the broken barricade had been huge; and Mistweave attacked it with the fury of a demon, sending a constant rush of fragments skidding across the floor to the hands of the company.

Honninscrave took another flake on his shoulder and nearly screamed; yet he went on fighting as if he were back in the cave of the One Tree and still had a chance to save his brother.

Three of the *Haruchai* threw Linden from place to place like a child. In that way they were able to keep her out of the path of the *Grim*-fall more effectively than if one of them had tried to carry her. But their own movements were hampered. Two of them had already suffered burns; and as Covenant watched a black bit seemed to shatter Fole's left leg. He balanced himself on his right as if pain had no meaning and caught Linden when she was tossed to him.

Around the cavern, flakes began to strike the floor and detonate, ripping holes the size of Giant-hands in the smooth stone. Acrid smoke intensified the air as if the granite were smouldering.

Durris, Harn, and two more *Haruchai* whipped brands and staves around the Stonedownors. Sunder lashed a frenzy of red power at the *Grim*. The First and Honninscrave laboured like berserkers, spending wood as rapidly as Mistweave fed it to them. Pitchwife followed his wife's example, protected her back with boards and timbers. He still had one pouch of *vitrim* left.

And Cail bounded and ducked through the drifting peril with Covenant slung over his shoulder like a sack of grain.

Covenant could not catch his breath to shout: Cail's shoulder forced the air from his lungs. But he had to make himself heard somehow. 'Sunder,' he gasped. 'Sunder.'

By intuition or inspiration, the *Haruchai* understood him. With a strength and agility that defied the thickening *Grim*-fall, he bore Covenant toward the Graveller.

An instant later, Covenant was whirled to his feet beside Sunder. Vertigo squalled around him: he had no balance. His hands were too numb to feel the fire mounting in him at every moment. If he could have seen Sunder's face, he would have cried out, for it was stretched and frantic with exhaustion. But the light of the *krill* blazed at Covenant's eyes. In the chaos of the cavern, that untrammelled brightness was the only point on which he could anchor himself.

The company had already survived miraculously long. But the *Grim* seemed to have no end, and soon even Giants and *Haruchai* would have to fall. This sending was far worse than the other one Covenant had experienced because it was enclosed – and because it was being fed directly by the Banefire. Through the stamp of feet and the burst of fires, he heard Linden cursing the pain of the people who kept her alive – people she could not help even though she suffered their hurts like acid in her own flesh. He had nowhere else to turn except to the *krill*.

Plunging toward Sunder, he got both hands on Loric's blade. He did not feel the edges cut into his fingers, did not see the blood. He feared that his weight would topple Sunder; but somehow Sunder braced himself against the collision, managed to hold Covenant upright for a moment.

That moment was long enough. Before he fell tangled in the Graveller's arms, Covenant sent one heart-rending blast of wild magic and risk through the gem of the *krill*.

His power was as black as the *Grim* now. But his desire was pure; and it struck the *krill* with such suddenness that the gem was not tainted by it. And from that gem, light rang like a piece of the clean sun. Its brightness seemed to tear asunder the veil of Revelstone's gloom, lay bare the essential skeleton of the granite. Light shone through both flesh and stone, swept all shadow and obscurity away, made clear the farthest corners of the forehall, the heights of the vaulted ceiling. If his eyes had been equal to the argence, in that instant he would have seen the deep heart of the great Keep and Gibbon already fleeing to the place where he had chosen to hide himself. But Covenant was blind to such things. His forehead was butted against Sunder's shoulder and he was falling.

When he rolled himself off Sunder's panting chest, groped through dizziness to regain his feet, the moment of his power had passed. The cavern was lit only by the sun's reflection from the entrance and the *krill*'s normal shining. His companions stood at various distances from him; but while his head spun he seemed to have no idea who they were.

But the *Grim* was gone. The black flakes had been swept away. And still he retained his grip on the wild magic.

He could not make the stone under him stop whirling. Helplessly, he clung to the first *Haruchai* who came to him. The numbness of his hands and feet had spread to his other senses. His mind had gone deaf. He heard nothing but the rumble of distant thunder, as if the sun outside Revelstone had become a sun of rain.

His thoughts spun. Where was Nom? There were villagers in the hold – and *Haruchai*. Unless the Clave had killed them already? Gibbon had to be somewhere. What would he do next? The venom made Covenant vicious, and the sheer effort of containing so much ignited violence took his sanity away. He thought he was speaking aloud, but his teeth were clenched and immobile. Why doesn't somebody tell that damn thunder to shut up so I can hear myself?

But the thunder did not stop; and the people around him fought their weariness and injuries to ready themselves. Dimly, he heard the First's battlecry as she swept out her sword.

Then the darkness at the end of the forehall came toward him, and he saw that the Riders had unleashed their Coursers at the company.

Need cleared his head a little. The *Haruchai* holding him pushed him away, and other hands took him. He found himself near Linden at the rear of the company, with only Mistweave between them and the entrance. All the *Haruchai* around them were injured: those who were not had gone with the First and Honninscrave to meet the charge of the Coursers. Sunder and Hollian stood alone in the centre of the hall. She supported him while he strove urgently to interfere with the Clave's command over the beasts. But exhaustion weakened him and the Banefire was too near: he could not blunt the assault.

At least a score of the fierce Coursers rushed forward, borne by the stone thunder of their hooves.

The *Haruchai* protecting Covenant and Linden were severely wounded. Fole stood with his left foot resting in a pool of his own blood. Harn had a deep burn on one hip. The other four *Haruchai* there were nearly maimed by various hurts. The air still reeked of *Grim*-flakes and pain.

The beasts struck with a scream of animal fury; and Covenant wanted to shriek with them because it was too much and he was no closer to his goal and the fingers of his will were slipping moment by moment from their hold on the world's ruin.

One heart-beat later, the scream arose again behind him like an echo. Riding his vertigo, he turned in time to see Mistweave go down under the hooves of four more Coursers.

The Giant had remained at the entrance to guard the company's rear. But he had been watching the battle, the plight of his companions: the return of the beasts which Sunder had scattered earlier took him by surprise. They reared behind him, pounded him to the stone. Then they thudded past him inward, their feral red eyes flaming like sparks of the Banefire.

Covenant could not resist as Harn and two more *Haruchai* thrust him toward one wall, interposed themselves between him and the Coursers. Fole and the rest bore Linden to the opposite wall so that the attack would be divided. Wounded and extravagant *Haruchai* faced the huge savagery of the Sunbane-shaped mounts.

You bastard! Covenant cried at Gibbon as if he were weeping. You bloody bastard! Because he had nothing else left, he braced himself on venom and readied his fire so that no more *Haruchai* would have to die for him.

But once again he had underestimated them. Two of the Coursers veered toward Linden: two came for him. And Harn hobbled out to meet them. He was between Covenant and the beasts: Covenant could not strike at them. He had to watch as Harn pitched headlong to the stone directly under the hooves of the leading Courser.

Pitched and rolled, and came up under the beast's belly with its left fetlock gripped in both hands.

Unable to halt, the Courser plunged to the stone. The fall simultaneously crushed its knee and drove its poisonous spur up into its barrel.

Squealing, it thrashed away from him. Its fangs slashed the air. But it could not rise with its leg broken, and the poison was already at work.

Near the entrance, Mistweave struggled to lever himself to his feet. But one of his arms sprawled at an unconscionable angle, and the other seemed too weak to lift him.

As the first Courser fell, the second charged toward Covenant. Then it braked with all four legs to keep itself from crashing into the wall. It looked as immense as thunder as it reared to bring its hooves and spurs down on Covenant and his defenders.

The Ranyhyn also had reared to him, and he felt unable to move. Instinctively, he submitted himself to his dizziness. It unbalanced him, so that he stumbled away to the right.

Each forehoof as it hammered down was caught by one of the *Haruchai*.

Covenant did not know their names; but they stood under the

1036

impact of the hooves as if their flesh was granite. One of them had been burned on the arm and could not keep his grip; he was forced to slip the hoof past his shoulder to avoid the spur. But his comrade held and twisted until the other spur snapped off in his hands.

Instantly, he drove the spur like a spike into the base of the Courser's neck.

Then the floor came up and kicked Covenant in the chest. At once, he was able to see everything. But there was no air in his lungs, and he had forgotten how to control his limbs. Even the fire within him was momentarily stunned.

The uninjured *Haruchai* were taking their toll on the beasts pounding in the far end of the hall. Honninscrave swung his fists like bludgeons, matching his bulk and extremity against the size and strength of the Coursers. Pitchwife struck and struck as though he had temporarily become a warrior like his wife. But the First surpassed them all. She had been trained for combat, and her longsword leaped from thrust to thrust as if it were weightless in her iron hands, slaying Coursers on all sides.

Only one of the beasts got past her and her companions to hurl itself at Sunder and Hollian.

The Graveller tried to step forward; but Hollian stopped him. She took the *orcrest* and *krill* from him, held them high as she faced the Courser. Red fire and white light blazed out of her hands, daunting the beast so that it turned aside.

There Cail caught up with it and dispatched it as if it were not many times larger than he.

But the *Haruchai* guarding Linden were not so successful. Hampered by their wounds, they could not match the feats of their people. Fole attempted what Harn had done; but his leg failed him, and the Courser pulled from his grasp. It ploughed into another *Haruchai*, slammed the man against the wall with such force that Covenant seemed to see Hergrom being crushed by a Sandgorgon in the impact. The third *Haruchai* thrust Linden away an instant before a hoof clipped the side of his head. His knees folded, and he sagged to the floor. Covenant had never seen one of the *Haruchai* fall like that.

Fole started after Linden; but a kick caught him by the shoulder, knocked him aside.

Then both Coursers reared over Linden.

Her face was clear in the reflected light from the courtyard. Covenant expected to see panic, paralysis, horror; and he gulped for air, struggled to put out power fast enough to aid her. But her visage showed no fear. It was argute with concentration: her eyes stabbed up at the beasts. Every line of her features was as precise as a command.

And the Coursers faltered. For an instant, they did not plunge at her. Somehow with no power to support her she drove her percipience into their minds, confused them.

Their minds were brutish, and the Banefire was strong: she could not hold them for more than an instant. But that was enough.

Before they recovered, Mistweave crashed into them like a battering-ram.

He had once left Linden in peril of her life because he had not been able to choose between her and Honninscrave; and that failure had haunted him ever since. But now he saw his chance to make restitution – and did not mean to let any mortal pain or weakness stop him. Ignoring his hurts, he threw himself to Linden's rescue.

His right arm flopped at his side, but his left was still strong. His initial charge knocked both Coursers back. One of them fell onto its side; and he followed it at once, struck it a blow which made its head rebound with a sickening thud from the hard stone, its body quiver and lie still.

Wheeling, he met the second Courser as it rose to pound down on him. His good hand caught it by the gullet: his fingers ground inward to strangle the beast.

Its fangs gaped for his face. Its eyes flared insanely. Its forehooves slashed at his shoulders, tearing him with its spurs: blood streamed down his sides. But Linden had saved his life when he had been more deeply injured than this – and he had failed her. He would not do so again.

He held the beast until Fole and the other *Haruchai* came to his aid. They grabbed its forelegs, turned its spurs against itself. In a moment, the Courser was dead. Mistweave dropped it heavily to the floor.

His muscles began to tremble as the poison worked its way into him.

Then the fighting was over. Gasps and silence echoed from the far end of the forehall. Grimly, Covenant gained his feet to stumble desperately toward Linden and Mistweave.

She had not been harmed: Mistweave and the *Haruchai* had taken all the hurt onto themselves. Her eyes ran as if the wounds of her friends had been etched on her heart. Yet the shape of her mouth and the angles of her cheeks were sharp with wrath. She looked like a woman who would never be paralysed again. If she had spoken, she might have said, Just let him try. Just let that butchering sonofabitch try.

Before Covenant could summon any words, the First reached his side.

She was panting with exultation. Her eyes were bright, and her blade dripped thick blood. But she did not talk of such things. When she addressed him, she took him by surprise.

'The Master is gone,' she said through her teeth. 'He pursues his purpose inward. I know not what he seeks – but I fear that he will find it.'

Behind her, Pitchwife retched for air as if his exertions had torn the tissues of his cramped lungs. Mistweave shivered toward convulsions as Courser-poison spread into him. Sunder's face was grey with exhaustion: Hollian had to hold him to keep him on his feet. Six of the *Haruchai* had been burned by the *Grim* and nearly crippled: one was in Mistweave's plight, gouged by a spur during the battle. Findail had vanished. Linden looked as bitter as acid.

And Honninscrave was gone. Nom was gone. Seeking their individual conceptions of ruin in the heart of Revelstone.

Too many lives. Too much pain. And Covenant was no closer to his goal than the entrance-hall of the na-Mhoram's Keep.

That tears it, he thought dumbly. That is absolutely enough. I will not take any more of this.

'Linden,' he said thickly. His voice was hoarse with fire. 'Tell Pitchwife how to treat these people.'

For an instant, her eyes widened. He feared that she would demur. She was a physician: seven *Haruchai* and Mistweave needed her sorely. But then she seemed to understand him. The Land also required healing. And she had wounds of her own which demanded care.

Turning to Pitchwife, she said, 'You've got some *vitrim* left.' In spite of the Banefire, her senses had become explicit, immune to bafflement. 'Use it on the burns. Give *diamondraught* to everybody who's hurt.' Then she gazed squarely back at Covenant. 'Mistweave's arm can wait. But *voure* is the only thing I know of that'll help against the poison.'

He did not hesitate: he had no hesitation left. 'Cail,' he said, 'you know Revelstone. And you know *voure*.' The distilled sap which the Clave used to ward off the effects of the sun of pestilence had once saved Cail's life. 'Tell your people to find some.' There were only four *Haruchai* uninjured. 'And tell them to take Sunder and Hollian with them.' Hollian was experienced with *voure*. 'For God's sake, keep them safe.'

Without waiting for a response, he swung toward the First.

'What you ought to do is secure our retreat.' His tone thickened like blood. He had told all his companions to stay out of Revelstone, and none of them obeyed. But they would obey him now. He would not accept refusal. 'But it's too late for that. I want you to go after Honninscrave. Find him somehow. Don't let him do it – whatever it is.'

Then he faced Cail again. 'I don't need to be protected. Not anymore. But if there's anybody left in the hold,' any villagers or *Haruchai* the Clave had not yet shed, 'they need help. Break in there somehow. Get them out. Before they're fed to the Banefire.

1039

'Linden and I are going after Gibbon.'

None of his companions protested. He was impossible to refuse. He held the world in his hands, and his skin seemed to be wearing thinner, so that the black power gnawing in him showed more and more clearly. His cut fingers dripped blood; but the wound gave him no pain. When Linden indicated the far end of the forehall, he went in that direction with her, leaving behind him all the needs and problems for which he lacked both strength and time. Leaving behind especially Sunder and Hollian, on whom the future depended; but also the First and Pitchwife, who were dear to him; Mistweave on the verge of convulsions; the proven *Haruchai*: leaving them behind, not as encumbrances, but as people who were too precious to be risked. Linden also he would have left behind, but he needed her to guide him and to support him. He was hag-ridden by vertigo. The reports of their steps rustled like dry leaves as they moved; and he felt that he was going to the place where all things withered. But he did not look back or turn aside.

When they passed out of the cavern into the mazing, Giant-planned ways of the great Keep, they were suddenly attacked by a small band of Riders. But the proximity of *rukh*-fire triggered his ring. The Riders were swept away in a wash of midnight.

The dark was complete for a short distance. Ahead, however, the normal lights of the city burned, torches smoking in sconces along the walls. No fires of the Lords had ever smoked: their flames had not harmed the essential wood. The Clave kept its passages lit so that Gibbon could move his forces from place to place; but these halls were empty. They echoed like crypts. Much beauty had died here, been undone by time or malice.

Behind him, Covenant heard the sounds of renewed combat; and his shoulders flinched.

'They can take care of themselves,' Linden gritted, holding her fear for her friends between her teeth. 'This way.'

Covenant stayed with her as she turned toward a side-passage and started down a long sequence of stairs toward the roots of Revelstone.

Her perception of the Raver made no mistakes. Not uncertainty, but only her ignorance of the Keep, caused her to take occasional corridors or turnings which did not lead toward her goal. At intervals, Riders appeared from nowhere to attack and retreat again as if they raised their fire for no other reason than to mark Covenant's progress through the Keep. They posed no danger in themselves: his defences were instantaneous and thorough. But each onslaught accentuated his dizziness, weakened his control. His ability to suppress the black raving frayed. He had to lean on Linden as if she were one of the *Haruchai*.

Always the path she chose tended downward; and after a while he felt a sick conviction that he knew where she was going – where Gibbon had decided to hazard his fate. The place where any violence would do the most damage. His forearm throbbed as if it had been freshly bitten. Then Linden opened a small, heavy door in a chamber which had once been a meeting hall, with curtains on its walls; and a long, twisting stairwell gaped below them. Now he was sure. Night gyred up out of the depths like a plummet from a precipice. He thought that he would fall. But he did not. She upheld him. Only his nightmares gathered around him as they made the long descent toward the place where Gibbon meant to break him.

Abruptly, she stopped, wheeled to look upward. A man came down the stairs, as noiseless as wings. In a moment, the *Haruchai* reached them.

Cail.

He faced Covenant. Haste did not heighten his respiration: disobedience did not abash him. 'Ur-Lord,' he said, 'I bring word of what transpires above.'

Covenant blinked at the *Haruchai*; but the nauseous whirl of his vision blurred everything.

'It is fortunate that *voure* was readily found, for the company is now sorely beleaguered. That battle is one to wring the heart' – he spoke as if he had no heart – 'for it is fought in large part by those who should not give battle. Among the few Riders are many others who merely serve the Clave and Revelstone. They are cooks and herders, artisans and scullions, tenders of hearth and Courser. They have no skill for this work, and it is a shameful thing to slay them. Yet they will not be halted or daunted. A possession is upon them. They accept naught but their own slaughter. Felling them, Pitchwife weeps as no *Haruchai* has ever wept.' Cail spoke flatly; but Linden's grasp on Covenant's arm conveyed a visceral tremor of the emotion Cail projected.

'*Voure* and *vitrim* enable the company for defence,' he went on. 'And the hold has been opened. There were found Stell and some few other *Haruchai*, though no villagers. They have gone to the support of the company. The Graveller and the eh-Brand are well. But of neither the First nor the Master have we seen sign.'

Then he stopped. He did not ask permission to remain with Covenant: his stance showed that he had no intention of leaving.

Because Covenant said nothing, Linden breathed for him, 'Thanks. Thanks for coming.' Her voice ached on behalf of the innocent men and women who were Gibbon's victims – and of her companions, who had no choice –

But Covenant had passed beyond the details of pain and loss into a state of utter purpose, of unanodyned grief and quintessential fury. *Felling them, Pitchwife weeps as no* Haruchai *has ever wept.* That must be true: Cail would not lie. But it was only one more drop in an

1041

ocean eating away the very shores of Time. The ocean of Lord Foul's cruelty. Such things could not be permitted to continue.

Lifting himself out of vertigo and Linden's grasp, the Unbeliever started downward again.

She called his name, but he did not answer. With Cail at her side, she came hastening after him.

The way was not long now: soon he reached the bottom of the stairwell, halted in front of a blank wall that he remembered – a wall with an invisible door which he had seen only once before and never been asked to open. He did not know how to open it. But that did not matter. What mattered was that Gibbon had chosen this place, *this place*, for his battleground. Simple dismay added a twist which nearly snapped the knot of Covenant's self-command.

But he was not required to breach the door for himself. It opened inward at Gibbon's word, admitting Covenant, Linden, and Cail to one of the greatest treasures of the old Lords.

To the Hall of Gifts.

After all these centuries, it was still intact. The air was tanged with smoke because the torches Gibbon had set for himself created light by destruction. And that kind of light could not do justice to the wonder of the high cavern. But everything Covenant saw was still intact.

The legacy of the Lords to a future which despised them.

The makers of Revelstone had wrought little in this spacious cave: they had given it a smooth floor, but had not touched the native stone of its walls, the rough columns which rose tremendously to support the ceiling and the rest of the Keep. Yet that lack of finish suited the purpose for which the Hall had been conceived. The rude surfaces everywhere displayed the best work of the finest artists and craftspeople of the ancient Land.

Tapestries and paintings behung the walls, defying the decay of centuries – preserved by some skill of the artists or quality of the Hall's atmosphere. Stands between the columns held large sculptures and carvings. Small pieces rested on wooden shelves cunningly attached to the stone. Many different fabrics were displayed; but all the other works were made of either wood or stone, the two fundamental materials which the Land had once revered: the Hall contained no metal of any description.

Covenant had not forgotten this place, never forgotten it; but he thought now that he had forgotten its pricelessness. It seemed to bring everything back to him in a rush, every treasured or abhorred memory: Lena and Atiaran, love and rape; Mhoram's hazardous and indefeasible compassion; the unscrupulous lore of ur-viles; Kevin in his despair; Ranyhyn as proud as wind, Ramen as stubborn as earth. And Giants, Giants on all sides, Giants wondrously depicted with their fealty and grief and grandeur wreathed about them as if the tapestries and stone-works and carvings were numinous with eternity. Here the people of the Land had shown what they could do when they were given peace.

And it was here, in this place of destructible beauty and heritage, that Gibbon-Raver had chosen to challenge Covenant for the survival of the Earth.

Moving unconsciously inward, as if he were blind to the brink of madness gaping at his feet, Covenant went to meet the na-Mhoram.

Stark in his black robe and scarlet chasuble, with his iron crozier held ready and his red eyes bright, Gibbon stood on a mosaic which swirled through the centre of the floor. Covenant had not seen that mosaic before: it must have been set at a later time. It was formed of small stone chips the colour of *aliantha* and agony; and it portrayed Kevin Landwaster at the Ritual of Desecration. Unlike most of the works around it, it conveyed no sense of underlying affirmation. Instead, it expressed Kevin's lurid and extreme pain as if that were a source of satisfaction.

Gibbon had taken his position over the Landwaster's heart.

At the edge of the mosaic, Honninscrave knelt in the stone.

Covenant's entrance into the Hall of Gifts did not make the Giant look up, though his head was the only part of himself he could have moved. By some cunning of Gibbon-Raver's power, Honninscrave had been fused into the floor. Kneeling, he had sunk into it to the middle of his thighs and forearms as though it were quicksand: then it had solidified around him, imprisoning him absolutely.

His eyes stared in despair at the failure of his life. Loss scarred his face with memories of Seadreamer and Starfare's Gem.

And the na-Mhoram laughed.

'See you, Unbeliever?' His voice was crimson and eager. 'No Unbelief will redeem you now. I will spare you only if you grovel.'

In response, Cail sprang past Covenant toward Gibbon as if he thought he could shatter the Raver.

But Gibbon was ready. His fist tightened on his crozier: fire spread from the open triangle at its tip.

An involuntary scream tore through Honninscrave.

Cail leaped to a halt, stood almost trembling a few feet from the na-Mhoram.

'I know you, *Haruchai*,' the Raver breathed softly, savagely. 'The groveller you serve will not assail me – he values the relics of his dead past and fears to harm them. He values the lost Earth. But you have not the folly of that scruple. Yet you remain a fool. You will not require me to crush the life of this mad Giant who sought to confront me, deeming me as paltry as himself.'

Cail turned on his heel, strode back to Covenant's side. His visage held no expression. But sweat beaded on his temples, and the muscles at the corners of his eyes squeezed and released like the labour of his heart.

Linden tried to curse, but the words came out like wincing. Instinctively, she had placed herself half behind Covenant.

'Hear you?' Gibbon went on, raising his voice so that it contaminated every corner of the great Hall. 'You are all fools, and you will not lift finger or flame against me. You will do naught but grovel at my whim or die. You are beaten, Unbeliever. You fear to destroy that which you love. Your love is cowardice, and you are beaten.'

Covenant's throat closed as if he were choking on smoke.

'And *you*, Linden Avery.' His raw contempt filled the air. 'Knowing my touch, you have yet dared me again. And this you name victory to yourself, thinking that such folly expiates your rooted evil. You conceive that we have misesteemed you, that you have put aside Despite. But your belief is anile. You have not yet tasted the depths of your Desecration.'

'Hear you all?' he cried suddenly, exalted by malice. 'You are damned beyond description, and I will feast upon your souls!'

Torn between outrage and visceral horror, Linden made whimpering noises between her teeth. She had come this far because she loved Covenant and loathed evil; but Gibbon appalled her in every nerve and fibre of her being. Her face was as pale as a gravestone: her eyes stared like wounds. Covenant had gone numb to everything else; but he was still aware of her: he knew what was happening to her. She was being ripped apart by her desire for the power to crush Gibbon – to extirpate him as if he were the part of herself she most hated.

If she did that, if she took hold of Covenant's fire and wielded it for herself, she would be lost. The inheritance of her parents would overcome her. Destroying Gibbon, she would shape herself in his image, affirm the blackness which had twisted her life.

That at least Covenant could spare her. And the moment had come. He was caught in the throes of a rupture so fundamental and puissant that it might tear Time asunder. If he did not act now, his control would be gone.

Deliberately, desperately, he started forward as if he did not realize that he had gone past the brink.

At once, Gibbon lifted his crozier higher, gripped it more tightly. His eyes spat red. 'Bethink you, Unbeliever!' he snapped. 'You know not what you do! Consider your hands.'

Involuntarily, Covenant looked down at them, at the *krill*-cuts across the insides of his fingers.

His severed flesh gaped, exposing bone. But the cuts were not bleeding. Instead, they oozed an essence of leprosy and venom. The very fluid in his veins had become corruption.

Yet he was prepared for this. His chosen path had brought him here. It was foretold by dreams. And he had already caused the shattering of Revelstone's gates, already brought immeasurable damage into the Keep: more harm would not alter his doom.

The scars on his forearm shone black fury. Like poison and flame, he strode onto the mosaic toward Gibbon.

'Fool!' the na-Mhoram cried. A grimace of fear betrayed his face. 'You cannot oppose me! The Banefire surpasses you! And if it does not, I will possess your Linden Avery. Will you slay her also?'

Covenant heard Gibbon. He understood the threat. But he did not stop.

Suddenly, the Raver sent a blast of fire toward Honninscrave; and Covenant erupted to protect the Master.

Erupted as if his heart could no longer contain the magma of his power.

Flame as dark and fathomless as an abyss shouted across the glittering surface of the mosaic, rebounded among the pillars, echoed off the high ceiling. Soulless force ripped Gibbon's blast from the air, scattered it in tatters, rose on and on with a deafening vehemence, trumpeting for the Raver's life. His hands lifted in front of him with the palms outward like an appeal for peace; but from his sliced fingers wild magic streamed, venomous and fatal. All his flesh had turned black: his bones were ebon and diseased. The only pure things about him were the stark circle of his ring and the quality of his passion.

The na-Mhoram retreated a step or two, held up his crozier with vermeil frenzy wailing from its triangle. Fire hot enough to incinerate stone crashed at Covenant: the concentrated ferocity of the Banefire seemed to scorch straight into his vitals. But he went forward through it.

That Gibbon had slaughtered the people of the Land to feed the Banefire and the Sunbane. That he had taught rites of bloodshed to those who survived, so that they slew each other in order to live. That he had filled Revelstone itself with such pollution. *Blast and counter-blast, Honninscrave struggling uselessly again, Cail hauling Linden out of the terrible concussion of powers with screams in her eyes too acute for paralysis and precious artefacts falling like faggots.* That he had torn the forehall with *Grim*-fire and had sent his innocent servants to compel their own butchery from the company. That he had so appalled Linden that she believed the legacy of her parents. That he had brought his violence *here*, requiring Covenant to spend the Land's treasured past as tinder.

Gibbon's crozier channelled so much might from the Banefire, so much force and rage, that Covenant nearly wept at the ruin it wrought, the price it exacted from him. Under his boots, the coloured pieces of the mosaic caught fire, became as brilliant and incandescent as prophecy. He trod an image of the Landwaster's heart as if that were where his own path led.

Erect and benighted in the core of his infernal power, he tried to advance on the na-Mhoram.

And failed.

Air and light ceased to exist. Every precious thing near his blaze burned away. The nearby columns began to melt: the floor of the Hall rippled on the verge of dissolution. More force than ever before in his life coursed from him and slammed at Gibbon. The essential fabric of the Earth's existence trembled as if the last wind had begun to blow.

Yet he failed.

Lord Foul had planned well, prepared well. Gibbon-Raver was cornered and could not flee, and so he did not falter. And the Banefire was too strong. Centuries of bloodshed had produced their intended fruit; and Gibbon fed it to Covenant, thrust it morsel by bitter morsel between his unwilling teeth. The Banefire was not stronger than he was: it was simply stronger than he dared to be. Strong enough to withstand any assault which did not also crumble the Arch of Time.

At the taste of that knowledge, Covenant felt his death closing around him, and his despair grew wild. For a long moment with red fury blazing at him like the sun, he wanted to cry out, scream, howl so that the heavens would hear him, *No! NO!*

Hear him and fall.

But before the weaving of the world could tear, he found he knew that answer also. *To bear what must be borne.* After all, it was endurable – if he chose to go that far, and the choice was not taken from him. Certainly it would be expensive. It would cost him everything. But was that not preferable to a Ritual of Desecration which would make Kevin's look like an act of petty spite? Was it not?

After a time, he said softly, Yes. And again, Yes. Accepting it fully for the first time. *You are the wild magic.* Yes.

With the last ragged fragments of his will, he pulled himself back from the brink of cataclysm. He could not quench the blackness – and if he did not quench it soon, it would kill him. The venom was eating away his life. But not yet. His face was stretched and mortal with unutterable pain; but he had accepted it. Turning away from Gibbon, he walked off the mosaic.

As he looked toward Linden and Cail to beg their forgiveness, Nom burst into the Hall of Gifts with the First in fierce pursuit.

She wrenched to a halt when she saw the wreckage of the Hall, the extent of Covenant's desperation; then she went swiftly to join Cail and Linden. But the Sandgorgon shot toward the na-Mhoram as if the beast at last had located its perfect prey.

Flashing past Covenant, pounding across the mosaic, Nom crashed into the red heart of Gibbon's power.

And was catapulted away over Honninscrave's head like a flung child. Even a Sandgorgon was a small thing to pit against the force of the Banefire.

But Nom understood frustration and fury, effort and destruction: it did not understand fear or defeat. Surely the beast recognized the sheer transcendence of Gibbon's might. But Nom did not therefore desist or flee. Instead, it attacked in another way.

With both arms, it hit the floor so hard that the entire centre of the Hall bucked and spattered like a sheet of water.

The mosaic cracked across its face, lifted in pieces, fell apart.

Shrieking rage, Gibbon staggered to regain his balance, then cocked back his crozier to deliver a blast which would fry Nom's flesh from its bones.

But he was maddened by strain and death-lust, and his blow required a moment's preparation: he did not see the chief result of Nom's attack.

That blow sent a fracture from wall to wall – a split which passed directly through the place where Honninscrave knelt in the stone. His bonds were shattered as if that had been Nom's intent.

With a roar, Honninscrave charged the na-Mhoram.

Gibbon was too intensely focused on Nom, too precariously poised: he could not react in time. His human flesh had no defence as Honninscrave struck him a blow which seemed to crush his bones. His crozier clattered across the floor, rang against the base of a column, and lay still, deprived of fire.

The First cried Honninscrave's name; but her voice appeared to make no sound in the stunned Hall.

For a moment, Honninscrave remained hunched and panting over Gibbon's corpse. Covenant had time for one clear thought: You can't kill a Raver that way. You can only kill the body –

Then the Master turned toward his companions; and Covenant nearly broke. He did not need Linden's percipience to see what had happened, did not need to hear her anguished whisper. He had witnessed such horrors before. And Honninscrave's plight was plain.

He stood as if he were still himself. His fists clenched as if he knew what he was doing. But his face was flowing like a hallucination, melting back and forth between savage glee and settled grim resolve. He was Grimmand Honninscrave, the Master of Starfare's Gem. And he was *samadhi* Sheol, the Raver that had led the Clave in Gibbon's body.

At war with each other.

The entire battle was internal. Red flared into his eyes and glazed away. Grins bared his teeth, were fought back. Snarling laughter choked in his throat. When he spoke, his voice cracked and seized under the strain.

'Thomas Covenant.'

At once, his voice scaled upward out of control, crying, 'Madman! Madman!'

He forced it down again. 'Earthfriend. Hear me.' The effort seemed to tear the muscles of his face. Helpless with power, Covenant watched in fever as Honninscrave wrestled for possession of his soul. Through his teeth, the Giant articulated like a death gasp, 'Heed the bidding of your despair. It must be done.'

At once, several piercing shrieks burst from him – the Raver's staccato anguish, or Honninscrave's. 'Help him,' Linden panted. 'Help him. Dear God.' But there was nothing anybody could do. She alone had the capacity to interfere in such a struggle – and if she made the attempt, Covenant meant to stop her. If *samadhi* Sheol sprang from Honninscrave to her, it would have access to the wild magic through her.

Retching for air, Honninscrave gained the mastery.

'You must slay me.' The words bled from his lips, but they were distinct and certain. His face turned murderous, then regained its familiar lines. 'I will contain this Raver while you slay me. In that way, it also will be slain. And I will be at peace.'

Sheol writhed for freedom; but Honninscrave held.

'I beg of you.'

Covenant let out a groan of fire, but it went nowhere near the Giant. The First gripped her sword in both fists until her arms trembled; but her tears blinded her, and she could not move. Cail folded his arms across his chest as if he were deaf.

Linden was savage with suppressed weeping. 'Give me a knife. Somebody give me a knife. Oh God damn you all to hell. *Honninscrave.*' But she had no knife, and her revulsion would not let her go any closer to the Raver.

Yet Honninscrave was answered.

By Nom, the Sandgorgon of the Great Desert.

The beast waited a moment for the others to act, as if it understood that they all had to pass through this crisis and be changed. Then it padded over to Honninscrave, its strange knees tense with strength. He watched it come while the Raver in him gibbered and yowled. But he was the Master now in a way which surpassed *samadhi* Sheol, and his control did not slip.

Slowly, almost gently, Nom placed its arms around his waist. For an instant, his eyes gazed toward his companions and yearned as if he wished to say farewell – wished poignantly at the last that he had found some way to go on living. Then, with a wrench as unexpected as an act of kindness, the Sandgorgon crumpled him to the floor.

As though he were not in tears, Covenant thought dumbly, You can't kill a Raver that way. But he was not sure anymore. There were mysteries in the world which even Lord Foul could not corrupt.

Linden gave a gasp as if her own bones had broken. When she raised her head, her eyes were bright and hungry for the power to exact retribution.

Stiffly, the First started toward the body of her friend.

Before she reached him, Nom turned; and Cail said as though even his native dispassion were not proof against surprise, 'The Sandgorgon speaks.'

Covenant could not clear his sight. All his peripheral vision was gone, blackened by imminent combustion.

'It speaks in the manner of the *Haruchai*.' Faint lines of perplexity marked the space between Cail's brows. 'Its speech is alien – yet comprehensible.'

His companions stared at him.

'It says that it has rent the Raver. It does not say slain. The word is "to rend". The Raver has been rent. And the shreds of its being Nom has consumed.' With an effort, Cail smoothed the frown from his forehead. 'Thus has the Sandgorgon gained the capacity for such speech.'

Then the *Haruchai* faced Covenant. 'Nom gives you thanks, ur-Lord.'

Thanks, Covenant grieved. He had let Honninscrave die. Had failed to defeat Gibbon. He did not deserve thanks. And he had no time. All his time had been used up. It was too late for sorrow. His skin had a dark, sick underhue: his sense of himself was fraying away. A gale of blackness rose in him, and it demanded an answer. The answer he had learned in nightmares. From Linden and the First and Cail and Nom and fallen Honninscrave he turned away as if he were alone and walked like a mounting flicker of fire out of the Hall of Gifts.

But when he put his feet to the stairs, a hand closed around his mind, and he stopped. Another will imposed itself on his, taking his choices from him.

Please, it said. *Please don't.*

Though he had no health-sense and was hardly sane, he recognized Linden's grasp. She was possessing him with her percipience.

Don't do this to yourself.

Through the link between them, he knew that she was weeping wildly. But behind her pain shone a fervid passion. She would not permit him to end in this way. Not allow him to go willingly out of her life.

I can't let you.

He understood her. How could he not? She was too vulnerable to everything. She saw that his control was almost gone. And his purpose must have been transparent to her: his desperation was too extreme to elude her discernment. She was trying to save him.

You mean too much.

But this was not salvation: it was doom. She had misinterpreted his need for her. What could she hope to do with him when his madness had become irremediable? And how would she be able to face the Despiser with the consequences of possession chained about her soul?

He did not try to fight her with fire. He refused to risk harming her. Instead, he remembered the imposed silence of the *Elohim* — and the delirium of venom. In the past, either defence had sufficed to daunt her. Now he raised them together, sought deliberately to close the doors of his mind, shut her out.

She was stronger than ever. She had learned much, accepted much: she was acquainted with him in ways too intimate to be measured: she was crying hotly for him, and her desire sprang from the roots of her life. She clinched her will to his with a white grip and would not let him go.

To shut her out was hard, atrociously hard. He had to seal off half of himself as well as all of her, silence his own deep yearning. But she still did not comprehend him. She still feared that he was driven by the same self-pity grown to malice which had corrupted her father. And she had been too badly hurt by the horror of Gibbon's power and Honninscrave's death to be clear about what she was doing. At last he was able to close the door, to leave her behind as he started up the stairs again.

Lorn and aggrieved, her cry rose after him:

'I love you!'

It made him waver for a moment. But then he steadied himself and went on.

Borne by a swelling flood of black fire, he made his way toward the sacred enclosure. Twice he encountered bands of Riders who opposed him frenetically, as if they could sense his purpose. But he had become untouchable and was able to ignore them. Instinct and memory guided him to the base of the huge cavity in the heart of Revelstone where the Banefire burned.

It was here that the former inhabitants of the city had come together to share their communal dedication to the Land. Within its sheer cylinder were balconies where the people had stood to hear the Lords speak from the dais below them. But that dais was gone now, replaced by a pit from which the Banefire licked blood for food.

At the nearest doorway he stopped. Findail stood there waiting for him.

The yellow anguish of the Appointed's eyes had not changed: his face was a wasteland of fear and old pain. But the anger with which he had so often denounced Covenant was gone. In its place, the *Elohim* emitted simple rue. Softly, he said, 'You are going to your death, ring-wielder. I comprehend you now. It is a valiant hazard. I

1050

cannot answer for its outcome – and I know not how I will prove worthy of you. But I will not leave you.'

That touched Covenant as the *rukhs* of the Riders had not. It gave him the strength to go on into the sacred enclosure.

There the Banefire met him, howling like the furnace of the sun. Its flames raged as high as the upper balconies where the immense iron triangle of the *master-rukh* now rested, channelling the power of the Sunbane to the Clave. Its heat seemed to char his face instantly, sear his lungs, cinder the frail life of his flesh and rave through him into the last foundation of his will. The fang-marks on his forearm burned like glee. Yet he did not halt or hesitate. He had set his feet to this path of his own volition: he accepted it completely. Pausing only to bring down the *master-rukh* in molten rain so that the surviving Riders would be cut off from their strength, he moved into the inferno.

That is the grace which has been given to you.

A small clear space like hope opened in his heart as he followed his dreams into the Banefire.

To bear what must be borne.

After a time, the blackness in him burned white.

PART II

Apotheosis

11

AFTERMATH

Held upright and active only by the fierce pressure of her need, Linden Avery walked numbly down through the ways of Revelstone, following the mounting stream of water inward. She had just left Nom on the upland plateau, where the Sandgorgon tended the channel it had brunted through sheer rock and dead soil from the outflow of Glimmermere to the upper entrance of the Keep; and the tarn's untainted waters now ran past her along a path prepared for it by the First, Pitchwife, and a few *Haruchai*.

Pure in spite of the harsh ages of the Sunbane, those waters shone blue against the desert of the late afternoon sun until they began to tumble like rapids into Revelstone: then torchlight glinted across their splashing rush so that they looked like the glee of mountains as they washed passages, turned at closed doors and new barricades, rolled whitely down stairways. The Giants were adept at stone, and they read the inner language of the Keep: the route they had designed led with surprising convolution and efficiency to Linden's goal.

It was an open door at the base of the sacred enclosure, where the Banefire still burned as though Thomas Covenant had never stood within its heart and screamed against the heavens.

In rage and despair she had conceived this means of quenching the Clave's power. When Covenant had turned away from the Hall of Gifts and his friends, she had seen where he was going; and she had understood him – or thought she understood. He meant to put an end to his life, so that he would no longer be a threat to what he loved. Like her father, possessed by self-pity. But, standing so near to Gibbon-Raver, she had learned that her own former visceral desire for death was in truth a black passion for power, for immunity from all death forever. And the way that blackness worked upon her and grew showed her that no one could submit to such hunger without becoming a servant of the Despiser. Covenant's intended immolation would only seal his soul to Lord Foul.

Therefore she had tried to stop him.

Yet somehow he had remained strong enough to deny her. In spite of his apparently suicidal abjection, he had refused her completely. It made her wild.

In the Hall, the First had fallen deep into the grief of Giants. Nom had begun to belabour a great grave for Honninscrave, as if the gift the Master had given Revelstone and the Land belonged there. Cail had looked at Linden, expecting her to go now to aid the rest of the company, care for the wounded. But she had left them all in order to pursue Covenant to his doom. Perhaps she had believed that she would yet find a way to make him heed her. Or perhaps she had simply been unable to give him up.

His agony within the Banefire had nearly broken her. But it had also given her a focus for her despair. She had sent out a mental cry which had brought Nom and Cail running to her with the First between them. At the sight of what Covenant was doing, the First's visage had turned grey with defeat. But when Linden had explained how the Banefire could be extinguished, the First had come instantly back to herself. Sending Cail to rally their companions, she had sped away with Nom to find the upland plateau and Glimmermere.

Linden had stayed with Covenant.

Stayed with him and felt the excoriation of his soul until at last his envenomed power burned clean, and he came walking back out of the Banefire as if he were deaf and blind and newborn, unable in the aftermath of his anguish to acknowledge her presence or even know that she was there, that through her vulnerable senses she had now shared everything with him except his death.

And as he had moved sightlessly past her toward some place or fate which she could no longer guess, her heart had turned to bitterness and dust, leaving her as desolate as the demesne of the Sunbane. She had thought that her passion was directed at him, at his rejection of her, his folly, his desperate doom; but when she saw him emerge from the Banefire and pass by her, she knew better. She had been appalled at herself – at the immedicable wrong of what she had tried to do to him. Despite her horror of possession, her revulsion for the dark ill which Lord Foul had practised on Joan and the Land, her clear conviction that no one had the right to master others, suppress them, rule them in that way, she had reacted to Covenant's need and determination as if she were a Raver. She had tried to save him by taking away his identity.

There was no excuse. Even if he had died in the Banefire, or brought down the Arch of Time, her attempt would have been fundamentally evil – a crime of the spirit beside which her physical murder of her mother paled.

Then for a moment she had believed that she had no choice but to take his place in the Banefire – to let that savage blaze rip away her offences so that Covenant and her friends and the Land would no longer be in danger from her. Gibbon-Raver had said, *The principal doom of the Land is upon your shoulders.* And, *You have not yet tasted the depths of your Desecration.* If her life had been shaped by a miscomprehended lust for power, then let it end now, as it deserved. There was no one nearby to stop her.

But then she had become aware of Findail. She had not seen him earlier: he seemed to have appeared in answer to her need. He had stood there before her, his face a hatchment of rue and strain; and his yellow eyes had ached as if they were familiar with the heart of the Banefire.

'Sun-Sage,' he had breathed softly, 'I know not how to dissuade you. I do not desire your death – though mayhap I would be spared much thereby. Yet consider the ring-wielder. What hope will remain for him if you are gone? How will he then refuse the recourse of the Earth's ruin?'

Hope? she had thought. I almost took away his ability to even know what hope is. Yet she had not protested. Bowing her head as if Findail had reprimanded her, she had turned away from the sacred enclosure. After all, she had no right to go where Covenant had gone. Instead, she had begun trying to find her way through the unfamiliar passages of Revelstone toward the upland plateau.

Before long, Durris had joined her. Reporting that the resistance of the Clave had ended, and that the *Haruchai* had already set about fulfilling her commands, he had guided her up to the afternoon sunlight and the stream of Glimmermere.

She had found the First and Nom together. Following the First's instructions, Nom was bludgeoning a channel out of the raw rock: the beast obeyed her as if it knew what she wanted, understood everything she said – as if it had been tamed. Yet the Sandgorgon did not appear tame as it tore into the ground, shaping a watercourse with swift, exuberant ferocity. Soon the channel would be ready, and the clear waters of Glimmermere could be diverted from Furl Falls.

Leaving Nom to Linden, the First went back into Revelstone to help the rest of the company. Shortly she sent another *Haruchai* upland to say that the hurts of *Grim*-fire and Courser-poison were responding to *voure*, *vitrim*, and *diamondraught*. Even Mistweave was out of danger. Yet there were many injured men and women who required Linden's personal attention.

But Linden did not leave the Sandgorgon until the channel was open and water ran eagerly down into the city and Nom had convinced her that it could be trusted not to attack the Keep once more. That trust came slowly: she did not know to what extent the rending of the Raver had changed Nom's essential wildness. But Nom came to her when she spoke. It obeyed her as if it both understood and approved of her orders. Finally she lifted herself out of her desert enough to ask the Sandgorgon what it would do if she left it alone. At once, it went and began improving the channel so that the water flowed more freely.

Then she was satisfied. And she did not like the openness of the plateau. The wasted landscape on all sides was too much for her: she seemed to feel the desert sun shining straight into her, confirming her as a place of perpetual dust. She needed constriction, limitation – walls and requirements of a more human scale – specific tasks that would help her hold herself together. Leaving the Sandgorgon to go about its work in its own way, she followed the water back into Revelstone.

Now the rapid chattering torchlight-spangled current drew her in the direction of the Banefire.

Durris remained beside her; but she was hardly aware of him. She sensed all the *Haruchai* as if they were simply a part of Revelstone, a manifestation of the Keep's old granite. With the little strength she still possessed, she focused her percipience forward, toward the fierce moil of steam where the Banefire fought against extinction. For a time, the elemental passion of that conflict was so intense that she could not see the outcome. But then she heard more clearly the chuckling eagerness with which Glimmermere's stream sped along its stone route; and she knew the Banefire would eventually fail.

In that way, the upland tarn proved itself a thing of hope.

But hope seemed to have no meaning any more. Linden had never deluded herself with the belief that the quenching of the Banefire would alter or weaken the Sunbane. Ages of bloodshed had only fed the Sunbane, only accelerated its possession of the Land, not caused it or controlled it.

When Covenant had fallen into despair after the loss of the One Tree, she had virtually coerced him to accept the end of the Clave's power as an important and necessary goal. She had demanded commitments from him, ignoring the foreknowledge of his death as if it signified nothing and could be set aside, crying at him, *If you're going to die, do something to make it count!* But even then she had known that the Sunbane would still go on gnawing its way inexorably into the heart of the Earth. Yet she had required this decision of him because she needed a concrete purpose, a discipline as tangible as surgery on which she could anchor herself against the dark. And because anything had been preferable to his despair.

But when she had wrested that promise from him, he had asked, *What're you going to do?* And she had replied, *I'm going to wait,* as if she had known what she was saying. *My turn's coming.* But she had not known how truly she spoke – not until Gibbon had said to her, *You have not yet tasted the depths of your Desecration,* and she had reacted by trying to possess the one decent love of her life.

Her turn was coming, all right. She could see it before her as vividly as the savage red steam venting like shrieks from all the doors of the sacred enclosure. *Driven to commit all destruction.* The desert sun lay within her as it lay upon the Land: soon the Sunbane would have its way with her altogether. Then she would indeed be a kind of Sun-Sage, as the *Elohim* avowed – but not in the way they meant.

An old habit which might once have been a form of self-respect caused her to thrust her hands into her hair to straighten it. But its uncleanness made her wince. Randomly, she thought that she should have gone to Glimmermere for a bath, made at least that much effort to cleanse – or perhaps merely disguise – the grime of her sins. But the idea was foolish, and she dismissed it. Her sins were not ones which could be washed away, even by water as quintessentially pure as Glimmermere's. And while the Banefire still burned, and the company still needed care, she could not waste time on herself.

Then she reached the wet fringes of the steam. The Banefire's heat seemed to condense on her face, muffling her perceptions; but after a moment she located the First and Pitchwife. They were not far away. Soon they emerged from the crimson vapour as if Glimmermere's effect upon the Banefire restored them to life.

Pitchwife bore the marks of battle and killing. His grotesque face was twisted with weariness and remembered hurt: it looked like the visage of a man who had forgotten the possibility of mirth. Yet he stood at his wife's side; and the sight tightened Linden's throat. *Weeps as no* Haruchai *has ever wept.* Oh, Pitchwife, she breathed to him mutely. I'm sorry.

The First was in better shape. The grief of Honninscrave's end remained in her eyes; but with Pitchwife beside her she knew how to bear it. And she was a Swordmain, trained for combat. The company had achieved a significant victory. To that extent, the Search she led had already been vindicated.

Somehow, they managed to greet Linden with smiles. They were Giants, and she was important to them. But a dry desert wind blew through her because she could not match them. She did not deserve such friends.

Without preamble, the First gestured toward the sacred enclosure. 'It is a bold conception, Chosen, and worthy of pride. With mounting swiftness it accomplishes that which even the Earthfriend in his power – ' But then she stopped, looked more closely at Linden. Abruptly, her own rue rose up in her, and her eyes welled tears. 'Ah, Chosen,' she breathed. 'The fault is not yours. You are mortal, as I am – and our foe is malign beyond endurance. You must not – '

Linden interrupted the First bitterly, 'I tried to possess him. Like a Raver. I almost destroyed both of us.'

At that, the Giant hardened. 'No.' Her tone became incisive. 'It skills nothing to impugn yourself. There is need of you. The wounded are gathered in the forehall. They must be tended.' She swallowed a memory of pain, then went on, 'Mistweave labours among them, though he is not less hurt. He will not rest.' Facing Linden squarely, the First concluded, 'It is your work he does.'

I know, Linden sighed. I know. Her eyes blurred and ran as if they had no connection to the arid loss in her heart.

With that for recognition and thanks, she let Durris guide her toward the forehall.

The sheer carnage there smote her as she entered the great hall. The *Grim* had done severe damage to the floor, tearing chunks from it like lumps of flesh. Dead Coursers sprawled in pools of their own blood. A number of the *Haruchai* had been hurt as badly as Mistweave: one of them was dead. Riders lay here and there across the floor, scarlet-robed and contorted, frantic with death. But worse than anything else were the hacked and broken bodies of those who should never have been sent into battle: cooks and cleaners, herders and gatherers, the innocent servants of the Clave. Among the litter of their inadequate weapons, their cleavers, pitchforks, scythes, clubs, they were scattered like the wreckage which their masters had already wrought upon the villages of the Land.

Now Linden could not staunch her tears – and did not try. Through the blur, she spoke to Durris, sent him and several other *Haruchai* in search of splints, bindings, a sharp knife, hot water, and all the *metheglin* they could find to augment the company's scant *vitrim* and dwindling *diamondraught*. Then, using percipience instead of sight to direct her, she went looking for Mistweave.

He was at work among the fallen of the Clave as if he were a physician – or could become one by simply refusing to let so much hurt and need lie untended. First he separated the dead from those who might yet be saved. Then he made the living as comfortable as possible, covered their wounds with bandages torn from the raiment of the dead. His aura reached out to her as though he, too, were weeping; and she seemed to hear his very thoughts: This one also I slew. Her I broke. Him I crippled. These I took from life in the name of service.

She felt his distress keenly. Self-distrust had driven him to a kind of hunger for violence, for any exertion or blow which might earn back his own esteem. Now he found himself in the place to which such logic led – a place that stank like an abattoir.

In response, something fierce came unexpectedly out of the wilderness of Linden's heart. He had not halted his labour to greet her. She caught him by the arm, by the sark, pulled at him until he bent over her and she was able to clinch her frail strength around his neck. Instinctively, he lifted her from the floor in spite of his broken arm; and she whispered at him as if she were gasping, 'You saved my life. When I couldn't save myself. And no *Haruchai* could save me. You're not responsible for this. The Clave made them attack you. You didn't have any choice.' Mistweave. 'You couldn't just let them kill you.' Mistweave, help me. All you did was fight. I tried to *possess* him.

He's gone, and I'll never get him back.

For a moment, Mistweave's muscles knotted with grief. But then slowly his grip loosened, and he lowered her gently to her feet. 'Chosen,' he said as if he had understood her, 'it will be a benison to me if you will tend my arm. The pain is considerable.'

Considerable, Linden thought. Sweet Christ, have mercy. Mistweave's admission was an appalling understatement. His right elbow had been crushed, and whenever he moved the splinters ground against each other. Yet he had spent the entire day in motion, first fighting for the company, then doing everything he could to help the injured. And the only claim he made for himself was that the pain was considerable.

He gave her more help than she deserved.

When Durris and his people brought her the things she had requested, she told him to build a fire to clean the knife and keep the water hot. Then while the sun set outside and night grew deep over the city, she opened up Mistweave's elbow and put the bones back together.

That intricate and demanding task made her feel frayed to the snapping point, worn thin by shared pain. But she did not stop when it was finished. Her work was just beginning. After she had splinted and strapped Mistweave's arm, she turned to the injuries of the *Haruchai*, to Fole's leg and Harn's hip and all the other wounds dealt out by the *Grim* and the Coursers, the Riders and the people of Revelstone. Fole's hurt reminded her of Ceer's – the leg crushed by a Sandgorgon and never decently treated – and so she immersed herself in the damage as if restitution could be made in that way, by taking the cost of broken bones and torn flesh upon herself. And after that she began to tend as best she could the Riders and servants of the Clave.

Later, through the riven gates at the end of the forehall, she felt midnight rise like the moon above the Keep. The reek of spilled and drying blood filled the air. Men and women cried out as if they expected retribution when she touched them. But still she went weary and unappeased about her chosen work. It was the only answer she had ever found for herself until she had met Covenant. Now it was the only answer she had left.

Yes. It was specific and clean: it had meaning, value: the pain of it was worth bearing. Yes. And it held her in one piece.

As if for the first time: Yes.

She had never faced so many wounds at once, so much bloodshed. But after all the number of men and women, old and young, who had been able to survive their hurts this long was finite. The

1061

consequences of the battle were not like the Sunbane, endless and immedicable. She had nearly finished everything she knew how to ask of herself when Cail came to her and announced that the ur-Lord wished to see her.

She was too tired to feel the true shock of the summons. Even now she could see Covenant standing in the Banefire until his blackness burned away as if he had taken hold of that evil blaze and somehow made it holy. His image filled all the back of her mind. But she was exhausted and had no more fear.

Carefully, she completed what she was doing. As she worked, she spoke to Durris. 'When the Banefire goes out, tell Nom to turn the stream back where it belongs. Then I want the dead cleaned out of here. Tell Nom to bury them outside the gates.' They deserved at least that decency. 'You and your people take care of these – ' She gestured toward the people arrayed around her in their sufferings and bandages. 'The Land's going to need them.' She understood poignantly Covenant's assertion that Sunder and Hollian were the Land's future. Freed from the rule of the Clave, these wounded men and women might help serve the same purpose.

Durris and Cail blinked at her, their faces flat in the incomplete torchlight. They were *Haruchai*, disdainful of injury and failure – not healers. And what reason did they have to obey her? Their commitment was to Covenant, not to her. With Brinn, Cail had once denounced her as a minion of Corruption.

But the *Haruchai* were not unaffected by their part in the Land's plight. The *merewives* and the Clave had taught them their limitations. And Brinn's victory over the Guardian of the One Tree had done much to open the way for Cable Seadreamer's death and the Despiser's manipulations. In a strange way, the *Haruchai* had been humbled. When Linden looked up at Cail, he said as if he were still unmoved, 'It will be done. You are Linden Avery the Chosen. It will be done.'

Sighing to herself, she did what she could for the last of the wounded – watched him die because she was only one woman and had not reached him in time. Then she straightened her stiff knees and went with Cail out of the forehall.

As she turned, she glimpsed a perfect ebony figure standing at the verge of the light near the gates. Vain had returned. Somehow, he had recognized the end of the Clave and known that he could safely rejoin the company. But Linden was past questioning anything the Demondim-spawn did. She lost sight of him as she entered the passages beyond the forehall; and at once she forgot him.

Cail guided her deep into a part of Revelstone which was new to her. The movement and confusion of the past day had left her sense of direction so bewildered that she had no idea where she was in relation to the Hall of Gifts; and she could barely discern the sacred enclosure in the distance as the Banefire declined toward extinction. But when she and Cail reached a hall that led like a tunnel toward the source of a weird silver illumination, she guessed their destination.

The hall ended in a wide, round court. Around the walls were doorways at intervals, most of them shut. Above the doors up to the high ceiling of the cavity were coigns which allowed other levels of the Keep to communicate with this place. But she recognized the court because the polished granite of its floor was split from wall to wall with one sharp crack, and the floor itself shone with an essential argence like Covenant's ring. He had damaged and lit that stone in the excess of his power when he had emerged from the soothtell of the Clave. Here had been revealed to him enough of the truth to send him on his quest for the One Tree – but only enough to ensure the outcome Lord Foul intended. In spite of her exhaustion, Linden shivered, wondering how much more had been revealed to him now.

But then she saw him standing in one of the doorways; and all other questions vanished. Her eyes were full of silver: she felt she could hardly see him as he dismissed Cail, came out into the light to meet her.

Mute with shame and longing, she fought the inadequacy of her vision and strove to anele her sore heart with the simple sight of him.

Luminous in silver and tears, he stood before her. All the details were gone, blinded by the pure glow of the floor, his pure presence: she saw only that he carried himself as if he had not come to berate her. She wanted to say in a rush before she lost her sight altogether, Oh, Covenant, I'm so sorry, I was wrong, I didn't understand, forgive me, hold me, *Covenant*. But the words would not come. Even now, she read him with the nerves of her body: her percipience tasted the timbre of his emanations. And the astonishment of what she perceived stopped her throat.

He was there before her, clean in every limb and line, and strong with the same stubborn will and affirmation which had made him irrefusable to her from the beginning. Alive in spite of the Banefire: gentle toward her regardless of what she had tried to do to him. But something was gone from him. Something was changed. For a moment while she tried to comprehend the difference, she believed that he was no longer a leper.

Blinking furiously, she cleared her vision.

His cheeks and neck were bare, free of the unruly beard which had made him look as hieratic and driven as a prophet. The particular scraped hue of his skin told her that he had not used wild magic to burn his whiskers away: he had shaved himself with some kind of blade. With a blade instead of fire, as if the gesture had a special meaning for him. An act of preparation or acquiescence. But physically that change was only superficial.

The fundamental alteration was internal. Her first guess had been wrong: she saw now that his leprosy persisted. His fingers and palms and the soles of his feet were numb. The disease still rested, quiescent, in his tissues. Yet something was gone from him. Something important had been transformed or eradicated.

'Linden.' He spoke as if her name sufficed for him – as if he had called her here simply so that he could say her name to her.

But he was not simple in any way. His contradictions remained, defining him beneath the surface. Yet he had become new and pure and cleanly. It was as if his doubt were gone – as if the self-judgments and repudiation which had tormented him had been reborn as certainty, clarity, acceptance in the Banefire.

It was as if he had managed to rid himself of the Despiser's venom.

'Is it – ?' she began amazedly. 'How did you – ?' But the light around him seemed to throng with staggering implications, and she could not complete the question.

In response, he smiled at her – and for one stunned instant his smile seemed to be the same one he had given Joan when he had exchanged his life for hers, giving himself up to Lord Foul's malice so that she would be free. A smile of such valour and rue that Linden had nearly cried out at the sight of it.

But then the angles of his face shifted, and his expression became bearable again. Quietly, he said, 'Do you mind if we get out of this light? I'm not exactly proud of it.' With his halfhand, he gestured toward the doorway from which he had emerged.

The cuts on his fingers had been healed.

And there were no scars on his forearm. The marks of Marid's fangs and of the injuries he had inflicted on himself had become whole flesh.

Dumbly, she went where he pointed. She did not know what had happened to him.

Beyond the door, she found herself in a small suite of rooms clearly designed to be someone's private living quarters. They were illuminated on a more human scale by several oil lamps and furnished with stone chairs and a table in the forechamber, a bare bed in one back room and empty pantry-shelves in another. The suite had been unused for an inestimably long time, but the ventilation and granite of Revelstone had kept it clean. Covenant must have set the lamps himself – or asked the *Haruchai* to provide them for her.

The centre of the table had been strangely gouged, as though a knife had been driven into it like a sharp stick into clay.

'Mhoram lived here,' Covenant explained. 'This is where I talked to him when I finally started to believe that he was my friend – that he was capable of being my friend after everything I'd done.' He spoke without gall, as if he had reconciled himself to the memory. 'He told me about the necessity of freedom.'

Those words seemed to have a new resonance for him; but almost immediately he shrugged them aside. Indicating the wound in the tabletop, he said, 'I did that. With the *krill*. Elena tried to give it to me. She wanted me to use it against Lord Foul. So I stabbed it into the table and left it there where nobody else could take it out. Like a promise that I was going to do the same thing to the Land.' He tried to smile again; but this time the effort twisted his face like a grimace. 'I did that even before I knew Elena was my daughter. But he was still able to be my friend.' For a moment, his voice sounded chipped and battered; yet he stood tall and straight with his back to the open door and the silver lumination as if he had become unbreakable. 'He must've removed the *krill* when he came into his power.'

Across the table, he faced her. His eyes were gaunt with knowledge, but they remained clear. 'It's not gone,' he said softly. 'I tried to get rid of it, but I couldn't.'

'Then what – ?' She was lost before him, astonished by what he had become. He was more than ever the man she loved – and yet she did not know him, could not put one plain question into words.

He sighed, dropped his gaze briefly, then looked up at her again. 'I guess you could say it's been fused. I don't know how else to describe it. It's been burned into me so deeply that there's no distinction. I'm like an alloy – venom and wild magic and ordinary skin and bones melted together until they're all one. All the same. I'll never be free of it.'

As he spoke, she saw that he was right: he gave her the words to see that he was right. Fused. An alloy. Like white gold itself, a blend of metals. And her heart gave a leap of elation within her.

'Then you can control it!' she said rapidly, so rapidly that she did not know what she was about to say until she said it. 'You're not at Foul's mercy anymore!' Oh, *beloved*. 'You can beat him!'

At that, sudden pain darkened his visage. She jerked to a halt, unable to grasp how she had hurt him. When he did not reply, she took hold of her confusion, forced it to be still. As carefully as she could, she said, 'I don't understand. I can't. You've got to tell me what's going on.'

'I know,' he breathed. 'I know.' But now his attention was fixed on the gouged centre of the table as if no power had ever been able to lift the knife out of his own heart; and she feared that she had lost him.

After a moment, he said, 'I used to say I was sick of guilt. But not any more.' He took a deep breath to steady himself. 'It's not a sickness any more. I *am* guilt. I'll never use power again.'

She started to protest; but his certainty stopped her. With an effort, she held herself mute as he began to quote an old song.

>'There is wild magic graven in every rock,
>contained for white gold to unleash or control –
>gold, rare metal, not born of the Land,
>nor ruled, limited, subdued
>by the Law with which the Land was created –
>but keystone rather, pivot, crux
>for the anarchy out of which Time was made:
>wild magic restrained in every particle of life,
>and unleashed or controlled by gold
>because that power is the anchor of the arch of life
>that spans and masters Time.'

She listened to him intently, striving for comprehension. But at the same time her mind bifurcated, and she found herself remembering Dr Berenford. He had tried to tell her about Covenant by describing one of Covenant's novels. According to the older doctor, the book argued *that innocence is a wonderful thing except for the fact that it's impotent. Guilt is power. Only the damned can be saved.* The memory seemed to hint at the nature of Covenant's new certainty.

Was that it? Did he no longer doubt that he was damned?

He paused, then repeated, 'Keystone. The Arch of Time is held together at the apex by wild magic. And the Arch is what gives the Earth a place in which to exist. It's what imprisons Foul. That's why he wants my ring. To break Time so he can escape.

'But nothing's that simple anymore. The wild magic has been fused into me. I *am* wild magic. In a sense, I've become the keystone of the Arch. Or I will be – if I let what I am loose. If I ever try to use power.

'But that's not all. If it were, I could stand it. I'd be willing to be the Arch forever, if Foul could be beaten that way. But I'm not just wild magic. I'm venom, too. Lord Foul's venom. Can you imagine what the Earth would be like if venom was the keystone? If everything in the world, every particle of life, was founded on venom as well as wild magic? That would be as bad as the Sunbane.' Slowly, he lifted his head, met Linden with a glance that seemed to pierce her. 'I won't do it.'

She felt helpless to reach him; but she could not stop trying. She heard the truth as he described it: he had named the change in himself for her. In the Banefire he had made himself as impotent as innocence. The power to resist Despite, the *reason* of his life, had been burned out of him. Aching for him, she asked, 'Then what? What will you do?'

His lips drew taut, baring his teeth: for an instant, he appeared starkly afraid. But no fear marked his voice. 'When I saw Elena in Andelain, she told me where to find Foul. In Mount Thunder – a place inside the Wightwarrens called Kiril Threndor. I'm going to pay him a little visit.'

'He'll kill you!' Linden cried, immediately aghast. 'If you can't defend yourself, he'll just kill you and it'll be wasted.' Everything he had suffered, venom-relapses, the loss of Seadreamer and Honninscrave, of Ceer, Hergrom, and Brinn, the silence of the *Elohim*, his *caamora* for the Unhomed of Seareach, the tearing agony and fusion of the Banefire. '*Wasted!* What kind of answer is *that?*'

But his certainty was unshaken. To her horror, he smiled at her again. Until it softened, his expression wrung her out of herself, made her want to scream at him as if he had become a Raver. Yet it did soften. When he spoke, he sounded neither desperate nor doomed, but only gentle and indefeasibly resigned.

'There are a few things Foul doesn't understand. I'm going to explain them to him.'

Gentle, yes, and resigned; but also annealed, fused to the hard metal of his purpose. *Explain* them to him? she thought wildly. But in his mouth the words did not sound like folly. They sounded as settled and necessary as the fundament of the Earth.

However, he was not untouched by her consternation. More urgently, as though he also wanted to bridge the gulf between them, he said, 'Linden, think about it. Foul can't break the Arch without breaking me first. Do you really think he can do that? After what I've been through?'

She could not reply. She was sinking in a vision of his death – of his body back in the woods behind Haven Farm pulsing its last weak life onto the indifferent stone. The old man whose life she had saved before she had ever met Covenant had said to her like a promise, *You will not fail, however he may assail you. There is also love in the world.* But she had already failed when she had let Covenant be stricken by that knife, let him go on dying. All love was gone.

But he was not done with her. He was leaning on the table now, supporting himself with his locked arms to look at her more closely; and the silver glow of the floor behind him limned his intent posture, made him luminous. Yet the yellow lamplight seemed human and needy as it shone on his face, features she must have loved from the beginning – the mouth as strict as a commandment, the cheeks lined with difficulties, the hair greying as if its colour were the ash left by his hot mind. The kindness he conveyed was the conflicted empathy and desire of a man who was never gentle with himself. And he still wanted something from her. In spite of what she had tried to do to him. Before he spoke, she knew that he had come to his reason for summoning her here – and for selecting this particular place, the room of a compassionate, dangerous, and perhaps wise man who had once been his friend.

In a husky voice, he asked, 'What about you? What're you going to do?'

He had asked her that once before. But her previous response now seemed hopelessly inadequate. She raised her hands to her hair, then pushed them back down to her sides: the touch of her unclean tresses felt so unlovely, impossible to love, that it brought her close to tears. 'I don't know,' she said. 'I don't know what my choices are.'

For a moment, his certitude faded. He faced her, not because he was sure, but because he was afraid. 'You could stay here,' he said as if the words hurt him. 'The lore of the old Lords is still here. Most of it, anyway. Maybe the Giants could translate it for you. You might find a way out of this mess for yourself. A way back.' He swallowed at an emotion that leaked like panic past his resolve. Almost whispering, he added, 'Or you could come with me.'

Come with – ? Her percipience flared toward him, trying to read the spirit behind what he said. What was he afraid of? Did he dread her companionship, fear the responsibility and grief of having her with him? Or was he dismayed to go on without her?

Her legs were weak with exhaustion and desire, but she did not let herself sit down. A helpless tremor ran through her. 'What do you want me to do?'

He looked as if he would have given anything to be able to turn his head away; yet his gaze held. Even now, he did not quail from what he feared.

'I want what you want. I want you to find something that gives you hope. I want you to come into your power. I want you to stop believing that you're evil – that your mother and father are the whole truth about you. I want you to understand why you were chosen to be here.' His visage pleaded at her through the lamplight. 'I want you to have *reasons*.'

She still did not comprehend his apprehension. But he had given her an opportunity she coveted fervidly, and she was determined to take it at any cost. Her voice was thick with a kind of weeping she had suppressed for most of her life; but she no longer cared how much frailty or need she exposed. All the severity and detachment to which she had trained herself had fled, and she did not try to hail them back. Trembling fiercely to herself, she uttered her avowal.

'I don't want hope. I don't want power. I don't care if I never go back. Let Foul do his worst – and to hell with him. I don't even care if you're going to die.' That was true. Death was later: he was now. 'I'm a doctor, not a magician. I can't save you unless you go back with me – and if you offered me that, I wouldn't take it. What's happening here is too important. It's too important to *me*.' And that also was true: she had learned it among the wounded in the forehall of the Keep. 'All I want is a living love. For as long as I can get it.'

Defying her weakness, she stood erect before him in the lamplight as if she were ablaze. 'I want you.'

At that, he bowed his head at last; and the relief which flooded from him was so palpable that she could practically embrace it. When he looked up again, he was smiling with love – a smile which belonged to her and no one else. Tears streaked his face as he went to the door and closed it, shutting out the consequences of wild magic and venom. Then from the doorway he said thickly, 'I wish I could've believed you were going to say that. I would've told Cail to bring us some blankets.'

But the safe gut-rock of Revelstone enclosed them with solace, and they did not need blankets.

12

THOSE WHO PART

They did not sleep at all that night. Linden knew that Covenant had not slept the previous night, on the verge of the jungle outside Revelstone, because she had been awake herself, watching the stretched desperation of his aura with her percipience because Cail had refused to let her approach the ur-Lord. But the memory no longer troubled her: in Covenant's place, she might have done the same thing. Yet that exigent loneliness only made this night more precious – too precious to be spent in sleep. She had not been in his arms since the crisis of the One Tree; and now she sought to impress every touch and line of him onto her hungry nerves.

If he had wanted sleep himself, she would have been loath to let him go. But he had resumed his certainty as if it could take the place of rest; and his desire for her was as poignant as an act of grace. From time to time, she felt him smiling the smile that belonged solely to her; and once he wept as if his tears were the same as hers. But they did not sleep.

At the fringes of her health-sense, she was aware of the great Keep around her. She felt Cail's protective presence outside the door. She knew when the Banefire went out at last, quenched by the sovereign waters of Glimmermere. And as the abused stone of the sacred enclosure cooled, the entire city let out a long granite sigh which seemed to breathe like relief through every wall and floor. Finally she felt the distant flow of the lake stop as Nom restored the stream to its original channel. For the remainder of this one night, at least, Revelstone had become a place of peace.

Before dawn, however, Covenant arose from Mhoram's intimate bed. As he dressed, he urged Linden to do the same. She complied without question: the communion between them was more important than questions. And she read him clearly, knew that what he had in mind pleased him. That was enough for her. Shrugging her limbs back into the vague discomfort of her grimy clothes, she accepted the clasp of his numb hand and climbed with him through the quiet Keep to the upland plateau.

At Revelstone's egress, they left Cail behind to watch over their privacy. Then, with a happy haste in his strides, Covenant led her west and north around the curve of the plateau toward the eldritch tarn which she had used against the Banefire without ever having seen it.

Toward Glimmermere, where Mhoram had hidden the *krill* of Loric for the Land's future. Where sprang the only water outside Andelain Earthpowerful enough to resist the Sunbane. And where, Linden now remembered, Covenant had once gone to be told that his dreams were true.

She felt he was taking her to the source of his most personal hope.

From the east, a wash of grey spread out to veil the stars, the harbinger of dawn. A league or two away in the west, the Mountains strode off toward the heavens; but the hills of the upland were not rugged. In ages past, their grasses and fields had been rich enough to feed all the city at need. Now, however, the ground was barren under Linden's sensitive feet; and some of her weariness, a hint of her wastelanded mood, returned to her, leeching through her soles. The sound of the water, running unseen past her toward Furl Falls, seemed to have a hushed and uncertain note, as if in some way the outcome of the Earth were precariously balanced and fragile about her. While the Sunbane stalked the Land, she remembered that Covenant's explanation of his new purpose made no sense.

There are a few things Foul doesn't understand. I'm going to explain them to him.

No one but a man who had survived an immersion in the Banefire could have said those words as if they were not insane.

But the dry coolness of the night still lingered on the plateau; and his plain anticipation made doubt seem irrelevant, at least for the present. Northward among the hills he led her, angling away from the cliffs and toward the stream. Moments before the sun broached the horizon, he took her past the crest of a high hill; and she found herself looking down at the pure tarn of Glimmermere.

It lay as if it were polished with its face open to the wide sky. In spite of the current flowing from it, its surface was unruffled, as flat and smooth as burnished metal: it was fed by deep springs which did not stir or disturb it. Most of the water reflected the fading grey of the heavens; but around the rims of the tarn were imaged the hills which held it, and to the west could be seen the Westron Mountains, blurred by dusk and yet somehow precise, as faithfully displayed as in a mirror. She felt that if she watched those waters long enough she would see all the world rendered in them.

All the world except herself. To her surprise, the lake held no echo of her. It reflected Covenant at her side; but her it did not heed. The sky showed through her as if she were too mortal or insignificant to attract Glimmermere's attention.

'Covenant — ?' she began in vague dismay. 'What — ?' But he gestured her to silence, smiled at her as if the imminent morning made her beautiful. Half running, he went down the slope to the tarn's edge. There he pulled off his T-shirt, removed his boots and pants. For an instant, he looked back up at her, waved his arm to call her after him. Then he dove out into Glimmermere. His pale flesh pierced the water like a flash of joy as he swam toward the centre of the lake.

She followed half involuntarily, both moved and frightened by what she saw. But then her heart lifted, and she began to hurry. The ripples of his dive spread across the surface like promises. The lake took hold of her senses as if it were potent enough to transform her: her whole body ached with a sudden longing for cleanliness. Out in the lake, Covenant broke water and gave a holla of pleasure that carried back from the hills. Quickly, she unbuttoned her shirt, kicked her shoes away, stripped off her pants, and went after him.

Instantly, a cold shock flamed across her skin as if the water meant to burn the grime and pain from her. She burst back to the surface, gasping with a hurt that felt like ecstasy. Glimmermere's chill purity lit all her nerves.

Her hair straggled across her face. She thrust the tresses aside and saw Covenant swimming underwater toward her. The clarity of the lake made him appear at once close enough to touch and too far away to ever be equalled.

The sight burned her like the water's chill. She could see him — but not herself. Looking down at her body, she saw only the reflection of the sky and the hills. Her physical substance seemed to terminate at the waterline. When she raised her hand, it was plainly visible — yet her forearm and elbow beneath the surface were invisible. She saw only Covenant as he took hold of her legs and tugged her down to him.

Yet when her head was underwater and she opened her eyes, her limbs and torso reappeared as if she had crossed a plane of translation into another kind of existence.

His face rose before her. He kissed her happily, then swung around behind her as they bobbed back upward. Breaking water, he took a deep breath before he bore her down again. But this time as they

1071

sank he gripped her head in his hands, began to scrub her scalp and hair. And the keen cold water washed the dirt and oil away like an atonement.

She twisted in his grasp, returned his kiss. Then she pushed him away and regained the surface to gulp air as if it were the concentrated elixir of pleasure.

At once, he appeared before her, cleared his face with a jerk of his head, and gazed at her with a light like laughter in his eyes.

'You – !' she panted, almost laughing herself. 'You've got to tell me.' She wanted to put her arms around him; but then she would not be able to speak. 'It's wonderful!' Above her, the tops of the western hills were lit by the desert sun, and that shining danced across the tarn. 'How come I disappear and you don't?'

'I already told you!' he replied, splashing water at her. 'Wild magic and venom. The keystone of the Arch.' Swimming in this lake, he could say even those words without diminishing her gladness. 'The first time I was here, I couldn't see myself either. You're *normal*!' His voice rose exuberantly. 'Glimmermere *recognizes* me!'

Then she did fling her arms about his neck; and they sank together into the embrace of the tarn. Intuitively, for the first time, she understood his hope. She did not know what it meant, had no way to estimate its implications. But she felt it shining in him like the fiery water; and she saw that his certainty was not the confidence of despair. Or not entirely. Venom and wild magic: despair and hope. The Banefire had fused them together in him and made them clean.

No, it was not true to say that she understood it. But she recognized it, as Glimmermere did. And she hugged and kissed him fervently – splashed water at him and giggled like a girl – shared the eldritch lake with him until at last the cold required her to climb out onto a sheet of rock along one edge and accept the warmth of the desert sun.

That heat sobered her rapidly. As Glimmermere evaporated from her sensitive skin, she felt the Sunbane again. Its touch sank into her like Gibbon's, drawing trails of desecration along her bones. After all, the quenching of the Banefire had not significantly weakened or even hampered Lord Foul's corruption. The Land's plight remained, unaltered by Covenant's certitude or her own grateful cleansing. Viscerally unwilling to lie naked under the desert sun, she retrieved her clothes and Covenant's, dressed herself while he watched as if he were still hungry for her. But slowly his own high spirits faded. When he had resumed his clothes, she saw that he was ready for the questions he must have known she would ask.

'Covenant,' she said softly, striving for a tone that would make him sure of her, 'I don't understand. After what I tried to do to you, I don't exactly have the right to make demands.' But he dismissed her attempted possession with a shrug and a grimace; so she let it go. 'And anyway I trust you. But I just don't understand why you want to go face Foul. Even if he can't break you, he'll hurt you terribly. If you can't use your power, how can you possibly fight him?'

He did not flinch. But she saw him take a few mental steps backward as though his answer required an inordinate amount of care. His emanations became studied, complex: he might have been searching for the best way to tell her a lie. Yet when he began to speak, she heard no falsehood in him: her percipience would have screamed at the sound of falsehood. His care was the caution of a man who did not want to cause any more pain.

'I'm not sure. I don't think I can fight him at all. But I keep asking myself, how can he fight me?

'You remember Kasreyn.' A wry quirk twisted the corner of his mouth. 'How could you forget? Well, he talked quite a bit while he was trying to break me out of that silence. He told me that he used pure materials and pure arts, but he couldn't create anything pure. "In a flawed world purity cannot endure. Thus within each of my works I must perforce place one small flaw, else there would be no work at all." That was why he wanted my ring. He said, "Its imperfection is the very paradox of which the Earth is made, and with it a master may form perfect works and fear nothing." If you look at it that way, an alloy is an imperfect metal.'

As he spoke, he turned from her slowly, not to avoid her gaze, but to look at the fundamental reassurance of his reflection in the tarn. 'Well, I'm a kind of alloy. Foul has made me exactly what he wants – what he needs. A tool he can use to perfect his freedom. And destroy the Earth in the process.

'But the question is my freedom, not his. We've talked about the necessity of freedom. I've said over and over again that he can't use a tool to get what he wants. If he's going to win, he has to do it through the choices of his victims. I've said that.' He glanced at her as if he feared how she might react. 'I believed it. But I'm not sure it's true anymore. I think alloys transcend the normal strictures. If I really am nothing more than a tool now, Foul can use me any way he wants, and there won't be anything we can do about it.'

Then he faced her again, cocked his fists on his hips. 'But *that* I don't believe. I don't believe I'm anybody's tool. And I don't think Foul can win through the kinds of choices any of us has been making. The *kind* of choice is crucial. The Land wasn't destroyed when I refused Mhoram's summons for the sake of a snake-bitten kid. It isn't going to be destroyed just because Foul forced me to choose between my own safety and Joan's. And the opposite is true, too. If I'm the perfect tool to bring down the Arch of Time, then I'm also the perfect tool to preserve it. Foul can't win unless I choose to let him.'

His surety was so clear that Linden almost believed him. Yet within herself she winced because she knew he might be wrong. He had indeed spoken often of the importance of freedom. But the *Elohim* did not see the world's peril in those terms. They feared for the Earth because Sun-Sage and ring-wielder were not one – because he had no percipience to guide his choices and she had no power to make her choices count. And if he had not yet seen the full truth of Lord Foul's machinations, he might choose wrongly despite his lucid determination.

But she did not tell him what she was thinking. She would have to find her own answer to the trepidation of the *Elohim*. And her fear was for him rather than for herself. As long as he loved her, she would be able to remain with him. And as long as she was with him, she would have the chance to use her health-sense on his behalf. That was all she asked: the opportunity to try to help him, redeem the harm of her past mistakes and failures. Then if he and the Land and the Earth were lost, she would have no one to blame but herself.

The responsibility frightened her. It implied an acknowledgment of the role the *Elohim* had assigned to her, an acceptance of the risk of Gibbon's malign promise, *You are being forged* – But there had been other promises also. Covenant had avowed that he would never cede his ring to the Despiser. And the old man on Haven Farm had said, *You will not fail, however he may assail you.* For the first time, she took comfort in those words.

Covenant was looking at her intently, waiting for her response. After a moment, she pursued the thread of his explanation.

'So he can't break you. And you can't fight him. What good is a stalemate?'

At that, he smiled harshly. But his reply took a different direction from that she had expected. 'When I saw him in Andelain,' – his tone was as direct as courage – 'Mhoram tried to warn me. He said, "It boots nothing to avoid his snares, for they are ever beset with other snares, and life and death are too intimately intergrown to be severed from each other. When you have come to the crux, and have no other recourse, remember the paradox of white gold. There is hope in contradiction."' By degrees, his expression softened, became more like the one for which she was insatiable. 'I don't think there's going to be any stalemate.'

She returned his smile as best she could, trying to emulate him in the same way that he strove to match the ancient Lord who had befriended him.

She hoped he would take her in his arms again. She wanted that, regardless of the Sunbane: she could bear the violation of the desert sun for the sake of his embrace. But as they gazed at each other, she heard a faint, strange sound wafting over the upland hills – a high run of notes, as poignant as the tone of a flute. But it conveyed no discernible melody. It might have been the wind singing among the barren rocks.

Covenant jerked up his head, scanned the hillsides. 'The last time I heard a flute up here – ' He had been with Elena; and the music of a flute had presaged the coming of the man who had told him that his dreams were true.

But this sound was not music. It cracked on a shrill note and fell silent. When it began again, it was clearly a flute – and clearly being played by someone who did not know how. Its lack of melody was caused by simple ineptitude.

It came from the direction of Revelstone.

The tone cracked again; and Covenant winced humorously. 'Whoever's playing that thing needs help,' he muttered. 'And we ought to go back anyway. I want to settle things and get started today.'

Linden nodded. She would have been content to spend a few days resting in Revelstone; but she was willing to do whatever he wanted. And she would be able to enjoy her scrubbed skin and clean hair better in the Keep, protected from the Sunbane. She took his hand, and together they climbed out of the basin of the tarn.

From the hilltop, they heard the flute more accurately. It sounded like its music had been warped by the desert sun.

The plains beyond the plateau looked flat and ruined to the horizons, all life hammered out of them: nothing green or bearable lifted its head from the upland dirt. Yet Glimmermere's water and the shape of the hills seemed to insist that life was still possible here, that in some stubborn way the ground was not entirely wasted.

However, the lower plains gave no such impression. Most of the river evaporated before it reached the bottom of Furl Falls: the rest disappeared within a stone's throw of the cliff. The sun flamed down at Linden as if it were calling her to itself. Before they reached the flat wedge of the plateau which contained Revelstone, she knew that her determination to stand by him would not prove easy. In the bottom of her heart lurked a black desire for the power to master the Sunbane, make it serve her. Every moment of the sun's touch reminded her that she was still vulnerable to desecration.

But by the time they rejoined Cail at the city's entrance, they could hear that the fluting came from the tip of the promontory overlooking the watchtower. By mute agreement, they walked on down the wedge; and at the Keep's apex they found Pitchwife. He sat with his legs over the edge, facing eastward. The deformation of his spine bent him forward: he appeared to be leaning toward a fall.

His huge hands held a flute to his mouth as if he were wrestling with it – as if he thought that by sheer obstinate effort he would be able to wring a dirge from the tiny instrument.

At their approach, he lowered the flute to his lap, gave them a wan smile of habit rather than conviction. 'Earthfriend,' he said; and his voice sounded as frayed and uncertain as the notes he had been playing. 'It boons me to behold you again and whole. The Chosen has proven and reproven her worth for all to see – and yet has survived to bring her beauty like gladness before me.' He did not glance at Linden. 'But I had thought that you were gone from us altogether.'

Then his moist gaze wandered back to the dry, dead terrain below him. 'Pardon me that I have feared for you. Fear is born in doubt, and you have not merited my doubt.' With an awkward movement, like suppressed violence, he indicated the flute. 'The fault is mine. I can find no music in this instrument.'

Instinctively, Linden went to stand behind the Giant, placed her hands on his shoulders. In spite of his sitting posture and crooked back, his shoulders were only a little below hers; and his muscles were so oaken that she could hardly massage them. Yet she rubbed at his distress because she did not know how else to comfort him.

'Everybody doubts,' Covenant breathed. He did not go near the Giant: he remained rigidly where he was, holding his vertigo back from the precipice. But his voice reached out through the sun's arid heat. 'We're all scared. You have the right.' Then his tone changed as if he were remembering what Pitchwife had undergone. Softly, he asked, 'What can I do for you?'

Pitchwife's muscles knotted under Linden's hands. After a moment, he said simply, 'Earthfriend, I desire a better outcome.'

At once, he added, 'Do not mistake me. That which has been done here has been well done. Mortal though you are, Earthfriend and Chosen, you surpass all estimation.' He let out a quiet sigh. 'But I am not content. I have shed such blood – The lives of the innocent I have taken from them by the score, though I am no Swordmain and loathe such work. And as I did so, my doubt was terrible to me. It is a dire thing to commit butchery when hope has been consumed by fear. As you have said, Chosen, there must be a reason. The world's grief should unite those who live, not sunder them in slaughter and malice.

'My friends, there is a great need in my heart for song, but no song comes. I am a Giant. Often have I vaunted myself in music. "We are Giants, born to sail, and bold to go wherever dreaming goes." But such songs have become folly and arrogance to me. In the face of doom, I have not the courage of my dreams. Ah, my heart must have song. I find no music in it.

'I desire a better outcome.'

His voice trailed away over the cliff-edge and was gone. Linden felt the ache in him as if she had wrapped her arms around it. She wanted to protest the way he seemed to blame himself; yet she sensed that his need went deeper than blame. He had tasted the

Despiser's malice and was appalled. She understood that. But she had no answer to it.

Covenant was more certain. He sounded as strict as a vow as he asked, 'What're you going to do?'

Pitchwife responded with a shrug that shifted Linden's hands from his shoulders. He did not look away from the destitution sprawling below him. 'The First has spoken of this,' he said distantly. The thought of his wife gave him no ease. 'We will accompany you to the end. The Search requires no less of us. But when you have made your purpose known, Mistweave will bear word of it to Seareach. There Starfare's Gem will come if the ice and the seas permit. Should you fail, and those with you fall, the Search must yet continue. The knowledge which Mistweave will bear to Seareach will enable Sevinhand Anchormaster to choose the path of his service.'

Linden looked at Covenant sharply to keep him from saying that if he failed there would be no Earth left for the Search to serve. Perhaps the journey the First had conceived for Mistweave was pointless: still Linden coveted it for him. It was clear and specific, and it might help him find his way back to himself. Also she approved the First's insistence on behaving as if hope would always endure.

But she saw at once that Covenant had no intention of denying the possibility of hope. No bitterness showed beyond his empathy for Pitchwife: his alloyed despair and determination were clean of gall. Nor did he suggest that Pitchwife and the First should join Mistweave. Instead, he said as if he were content, 'That's good. Meet us in the forehall at noon, and we'll get started.'

Then he met Linden's gaze. 'I want to go look at Honninscrave's grave.' His tone thickened momentarily. 'Say goodbye to him. Will you come with me?'

In response, she went to him and hugged him so that he would understand her silence.

Together they left Pitchwife sitting on the rim of the city. As they neared the entrance to Revelstone, they heard the cry of his flute again. It sounded as lorn as the call of a kestrel against the dust-trammelled sky.

Gratefully, Linden entered the great Keep, where she was shielded from the desert sun. Relief filled her nerves as she and Covenant moved down into the depths of Revelstone, back to the Hall of Gifts.

Cail accompanied them. Beneath his impassivity she sensed a strange irresolution, as if he wanted to ask a question or boon and did not believe he had the right. But when they reached their goal, she forgot his unexplained emanations.

During Covenant's battle with Gibbon, and the rending of the

Raver, she had taken scant notice of the cavern itself: all her attention had been focused on what was happening – and on the blackness which Gibbon had called up in her. As a result, she had not registered the extent to which the Hall and its contents had been damaged. But she saw the havoc now, felt its impact.

Around the walls, behind the columns, in the corners and distant reaches, much of the Land's ancient artwork remained intact. But the centre of the cavern was a shambles. Tapestries had been cindered, sculptures split, paintings shredded. Cracks marked two of the columns from crown to pediment: hunks of stone had been ripped from the ceiling, the floor: the mosaic on which Gibbon had stood was a ruin. Centuries of human effort and aspiration were wrecked by the uncontainable forces Covenant and the Raver had unleashed.

For a moment, Covenant's gaze appeared as ravaged as the Hall. No amount of certainty could heal the consequences of what he had done – and had failed to do.

While she stood there, caught between his pain and the Hall's hurt, she did not immediately recognize that most of the breakage had already been cleared away. But then she saw Nom at work, realized what the Sandgorgon was doing.

It was collecting pieces of rock, splinters of sculpture, shards of pottery, any debris it was able to lift between the stumps of its forearms, and it was using those fragments meticulously to raise a cairn for Honninscrave.

That funerary pile was already taller than Linden; but Nom was not yet satisfied with it. With swift care, the beast continued adding broken art to the mound. The rubble was too crude to have any particular shape. Nevertheless Nom moved around and around it to build it up as if it were an icon of the distant gyre of Sandgorgons Doom.

This was Nom's homage to the Giant who had enabled it to rend Gibbon-Raver. Honninscrave had contained and controlled *samadhi* Sheol so that the Raver could not possess Nom, not take advantage of Nom's purpose and power. In that way, he had made it possible for Nom to become something new, a Sandgorgon of active mind and knowledge and volition. With this cairn, Nom acknowledged the Master's sacrifice as if it had been a gift.

The sight softened Covenant's pain. Remembering Hergrom and Ceer, Linden would not have believed that she might ever feel anything akin to gratitude toward a Sandgorgon. But she had no other name for what she felt as she watched Nom work.

Though it lacked ordinary sight or hearing, the beast appeared to be aware of its onlookers. But it did not stop until it had augmented Honninscrave's mound with the last rubble large enough for its arms to lift. Then, however, it turned abruptly and strode toward Covenant.

A few paces in front of him, it stopped. With its back-bent knees, it lowered itself to the floor, touched its forehead to the stone.

He was abashed by the beast's obeisance. 'Get up,' he muttered. 'Get up. You've earned better than this.' But Nom remained prostrate before him as though it deemed him worthy of worship.

Unexpectedly, Cail spoke for the Sandgorgon. He had recovered his *Haruchai* capacity for unsurprise: he reported the beast's thoughts as if he were accustomed to them.

'Nom desires you to comprehend that it acknowledges you. It will obey any command. But it asks that you do not command it. It wishes to be free. It wishes to return to its home in the Great Desert and its bound kindred. From the rending of the Raver, Nom has gained knowledge to unmake Sandgorgons Doom — to release its kind from pent fury and anguish. It seeks your permission to depart.'

Linden felt that she was smiling foolishly; but she could not stop herself. Fearsome though the Sandgorgons were, she had hated the idea of their plight from the moment when Pitchwife had told her about it. 'Let it go,' she murmured to Covenant. 'Kasreyn had no right to trap them like that in the first place.'

He nodded slowly, debating with himself. Then he made his decision. Facing the Sandgorgon, he said to Cail, 'Tell it, it can go. I understand it's willing to obey me, and I say it can go. It's free. But,' he added sharply, 'I want it to leave the *Bhrathair* alone. Those people have the right to live, too. And God knows I've already done them enough damage. I don't want them to suffer any more because of me.'

Faceless, devoid of expression, the albino beast raised itself erect again. 'Nom hears you,' Cail replied. To Linden's percipience, his tone seemed to hint that he envied Nom's freedom. 'It will obey. It will teach its folk obedience also. The Great Desert is wide, and the *Bhrathair* will be spared.'

Before he finished, the Sandgorgon burst into a run toward the doorway of the Hall. Eager for its future, it vanished up the stairs, speeding in the direction of the open sky. For a few moments, Linden felt its wide feet on the steps: their force seemed to make the stone Keep jangle. But then Nom passed beyond her range, and she turned from it as if it were a healed memory — as if in some unexpected way the deaths of Hergrom and Ceer and Honninscrave had been made bearable at last.

She was still smiling when Covenant addressed Cail. 'We've got some time before noon.' He strove to sound casual; but the embers in his eyes were alight for her. 'Why don't you find us something to eat? We'll be in Mhoram's room.'

Cail nodded and left at once, moving with swift unhaste. His manner convinced Linden that she was reading him accurately: something had changed for him. He seemed willing, almost eager, to be apart from the man he had promised to protect.

But she had no immediate desire to question the *Haruchai*. Covenant had put his arm around her waist, and time was precious. Her wants would have appeared selfish to her if he had not shared them.

However, when they reached the court with the bright silver floor and the cracked stone, they found Sunder and Hollian waiting for them.

The Stonedownors had rested since Linden had last seen them, and they looked better for it. Sunder was no longer slack-kneed and febrile with exhaustion: Hollian had regained much of her young clarity. They greeted Covenant and Linden shyly, as if they were uncertain how far the Unbeliever and the Chosen had transcended them. But behind their shared mood, their differences were palpable to Linden.

Unlike Sunder's former life, Hollian's had been one of acceptance rather than sacrifice. The delicate scars which laced her right palm were similar to the pale pain-lattice on his left forearm, but she had never taken anyone else's blood. Yet since that time her role had been primarily one of support, aiding Sunder when he had first attuned himself to Memla's *rukh* during the company's journey toward Seareach as well as in his later use of the *krill*. It was he, guilt-sore and vehement, who hated the Clave, fought it – and had been vindicated. He had struck necessary blows on behalf of the Land, showing himself a fit companion for Giants and *Haruchai*, Covenant and Linden. Now he bore himself with a new confidence; and the silver light seemed to shine bravely in his eyes, as though he knew that his father would have been proud of him.

Hollian herself was proud of him. Her open gaze and gentle smile showed that she regretted nothing. The child she carried was a joy to her. Yet Linden saw something plainly unfinished in the eh-Brand. Her emanations were now more complex than Sunder's. She looked like a woman who knew that she had not yet been tested. And she wanted that test, wanted to find the destiny which she wore about her like the raven-wings of her lustrous hair. She was an eh-Brand, rare in the Land: she wished to learn what such rareness meant.

Covenant gave Linden a glance of wry rue; but he accepted the untimely presence of the Stonedownors without protest. They were his friends, and his surety included them.

In response to Covenant's greeting, Sunder said with abrupt awkwardness, 'Thomas Covenant, what is your purpose now?' His recent accomplishments had not given him an easy manner. 'Forgive us that we intrude upon you. Your need for rest is plain.' His regard told Linden that her fatigue was more obvious than Covenant's. 'Should you elect to remain here for any number of days, the choice would become you. In times past' – his scowl was a mix of self-mockery and regret – 'I have questioned you, accusing you of every madness and all pain.' Covenant made a gesture of dismissal; but Sunder hastened to continue, 'I do not question you now. You are the Earthfriend, Illender and Prover of Life – and my friend. My doubt is gone.

'Yet,' he went on at once, 'we have considered the Sunbane. The eh-Brand foretells its course. With Sunstone and *krill*, I have felt its power. The quenching of Banefire and Clave is a great work – but the Sunbane is not diminished. The morrow's sun will be a sun of pestilence. It reigns still upon the Land, and its evil is clear.'

His voice gathered strength and determination as he spoke. 'Thomas Covenant, you have taught me the falsehood of the Clave. I had believed the Land a gallow-fells, a punishing place conceived by a harsh Master. But I have learned that we are born for beauty rather than ill – that it is the Sunbane which is evil, not the life which the Sunbane torments.' His gaze glinted keenly. 'Therefore I find that I am not content. The true battle is yet before us.' He was not as tall as Covenant; but he was broader and more muscular: he looked as solid as the stone of his home. 'Thus I ask, what is your purpose now?'

The question distressed Covenant. His certainty could not protect him from his own empathy. He concealed his pain; but Linden saw it with her health-sense, heard it in the gruffness of his reply. 'You're not content,' he muttered. 'Nobody's content. Well, you ought to be.' Beneath the surface, he was as taut as a fraying bowstring. 'You've done enough. You can leave the Sunbane to me – to me and Linden. I want you to stay here.'

'Stay – ?' the Graveller was momentarily too surprised to understand. 'Do you mean to depart from us?' Hollian placed a hand on his arm, not to restrain him, but to add her concern to his.

'Yes!' Covenant snapped more strongly than necessary. But at once he steadied himself. 'Yes. That's what I want. You're the future of the Land. There's nobody else. The people the Clave let live are all too old or sick to do much, or too young to understand. You two are the only ones left who know what's happened, what it means. What the life of the Land should be like. If anything happens to you, most of the survivors won't even know the Clave was wrong. They'll go on believing those lies because there won't be anybody around to contradict them. I need you to tell them the truth. I can't risk you.'

Linden thought he would say, Please. *Please*. But Sunder's indignation was vivid in the sharp light. 'Risk, ur-Lord?' he rasped as soon as Covenant stopped. 'Is it risk you fear? Or do you deem us unworthy to partake of your high purpose? Do you forget who we are?' His hand gripped at the *krill* wrapped and hidden within his jerkin. 'Your world is otherwhere, and to it you will return when your task is done. But we are the Land. We are the life which remains. We will not sit in safety while the outcome of that life is determined!'

Covenant stood still under Sunder's outburst; but the small muscles around his eyes flinched as if he wanted to shout, What's the matter with you? We're going to face Lord Foul! I'm trying to spare you! Yet his quietness held.

'You're right,' he said softly – more softly than Linden's desire to defend him. 'You are the life of the Land. And I've already taken everything else away from you. Your homes, your families, your identities – I've spent them all and let you bear the cost. Don't you understand? I want to give something back. I want you to have a *future*.' The one thing he and Linden did not possess. 'So your son will have at least that much chance to be born and grow up healthy.' The passion underlying his tone reminded her that he had a son whom he had not seen for eleven years. He might have been crying, Let me do this for you! 'Is safety such a terrible price to pay?'

Hollian appeared to waver, persuaded by Covenant's unmistakable concern. But Sunder did not. His anger was swept out of him: his resolution remained. Thickly, he said, 'Pardon my unseemly ire. Thomas Covenant, you are my friend in all ways. Will you grant to me your white ring, that I may ward you from the extremity of the Land's plight?' He did not need to wait for Covenant's answer. 'Neither will I cede to you the meaning of my life. You have taught me to value that meaning too highly.'

Abruptly, he dropped his gaze. 'If it is her wish, Hollian will abide here. The son she bears is ours together, but that choice must be hers.' Then his eyes fixed Covenant squarely again. 'I will not part from you until I am content.'

For a moment, the Graveller and Covenant glared at each other; and Linden held her breath. But then Hollian broke the intensity. Leaning close to Sunder, grinning as if she meant to bite his ear, she breathed, 'Son of Nassic, you have fallen far into folly if you credit that I will be divided from you in the name of simple safety.'

Covenant threw up his hands. 'Oh, hell,' he muttered. 'God preserve me from stubborn people.' He sounded vexed; but his frown had lost its seriousness.

Linden gave a sigh of relief. She caught Hollian's glance, and a secret gleam passed between them. With feigned brusqueness, she said, 'We're going to leave at noon. You might as well go get ready. We'll meet you in the forehall.'

Allowing Covenant no opportunity to demur, she drew him into Mhoram's quarters and closed the door.

But later through Revelstone's vital rock she felt the midday of the desert sun approaching; and her heart shrank from it. Sunder was right: the Sunbane had not been diminished. And she did not know how much more of it she could bear. She had stood up to it across the expanse of the North Plains. She had faced Gibbon-Raver, although his mere proximity had made the darkness in her writhe for release. But those exertions had pushed her to her limits. And she had had no sleep. The comfort of Covenant's love did many things for her, but it could not make her immune to weariness. In spite of the shielding Keep, a visceral dread seeped slowly into her.

Covenant himself was not impervious to apprehension. The mood in which he hugged her was complicated by a tension that felt like grief. When Cail called them to the forehall, Covenant did not hesitate. But his eyes seemed to avoid hers, and his hands fumbled as he buckled his belt, laced up his boots.

For a moment, she did not join him. She sat naked on Mhoram's bed and watched him, unwilling to cover his place against her breasts with the less intimate touch of her shirt. Yet she knew that she had to go with him, that everything she had striven for would be wasted if she faltered now. She said his name to make him look at her; and when he did so, she faced her fear as directly as she could.

'I don't really understand what you think you're going to do — but I suppose that doesn't matter. Not right now, anyway. I'll go with you — anywhere. But I still haven't answered my own question. Why me?' Perhaps what she meant was, Why do you love me? What am I, that you should love me? But she knew that if she asked her question in those terms she might not comprehend the reply. 'Why was I chosen? Why did Gibbon keep insisting I'm the one — ?' She swallowed a lump of darkness. 'The one who's going to desecrate the Earth.' Even if I give in — even if I go crazy and decide I want to be like him after all. Where would I get that kind of power?

Covenant met her gaze through the dim lantern-light. He stood straight and dear before her, a figure of dread and love and contradiction; and he seemed to know what she sought. Yet the timbre of his voice told her he was not certain of it.

'Questions like that are hard. You have to create your own answer. The last time I was here, I didn't know I was going to beat Foul until I did it. Then I could look back and say that was the reason. I was chosen because I had the capacity to do what I did — even though I didn't know it.' He spoke quietly, but his manner could not conceal the implications of severity and hope which ran through his words. 'I think you were chosen because you're like me. We're the kind of people who just naturally feel responsible for each other. Foul thinks he can use that to manipulate us. And the Creator – ' For an instant, he reminded her strangely of the old man who had said to her, *You will not fail, however he may assail you. There is also love in the world.* 'He hopes that together we'll become something greater than we would alone.'

Severity and hope. Hope and despair. She did not know what would happen – but she knew how important it had become. Arising from the bed, she went to Covenant and kissed him hard. Then she donned her clothes quickly so that she would be ready to accompany him wherever he wanted to go.

In the name of his smile, she accepted everything.

While she hurried, Cail repeated his announcement that the Giants, *Haruchai*, and Stonedownors were waiting in the forehall. 'We're coming!' Covenant responded. When she nodded, he opened the door and ushered her outward with a half humorous flourish, as if she were regal in his eyes.

Cail bowed to them, looking as much as his dispassion allowed like a man who wanted to say something and had almost made up his mind to say it. But Linden saw at a glance that he still had not found the right moment. She returned his bow because he, too, had become someone she could trust. She had never doubted his fidelity, but the native extravagance of his judgment had always made him appear dangerous and unpredictable. Now, however, she saw him as a man who had passed through repudiation and unworth to reach a crucial decision – a decision she hoped she would be able to comprehend.

Together, Covenant, Cail, and Linden left behind the bright silver aftermath of the Unbeliever's first encounter with the Clave. That radiance shining against her back gave her a pang of regret: it represented a part of him which had been lost. But he was frowning to himself as he strode forward, concentrating on what lay ahead. That was his answer to loss. And he did not need Cail's guidance to find his way through the involute Keep. For a sharp moment, she let the rue wash through her, experiencing it for both of them. Then she shrugged her attention back to his side and tried to brace herself for the Sunbane.

The forehall hardly resembled her memory of it. Its floor remained permanently pocked and gouged, awkward to walk; but the space was bright with torches, and sunlight reflected through the broken gates. The bodies of the dead had been cleared away: the blood of battle had been sluiced from the stone. And the wounded had been moved to more comfortable quarters. The improvement suggested that Revelstone might yet become habitable again.

Near the gates were gathered the people who had accompanied or fought for the Unbeliever and survived: the First of the Search with Pitchwife and Mistweave; Sunder and Hollian; Durris and Fole, Harn, Stell, and the rest of the *Haruchai*; the black Demondim-spawn; Findail the Appointed. Pitchwife hailed Covenant and Linden as if the prospect of leaving Revelstone had restored some portion of his good cheer; but the rest of the company stood silent: they seemed to wait for Covenant as if he were the turning point of their lives. Even the *Haruchai* — Linden sensed with a touch of quiet wonder. In spite of their mountain-bred intransigence, they were balanced on a personal cusp and could be swayed. As Covenant drew near, each of them dropped to one knee in mute homage.

The others had fewer questions to ask. Neither Vain nor Findail had any use for questions. And Covenant had already accepted the companionship of the First and Pitchwife, Hollian and Sunder. They only needed to know where they were going. The issues which had yet to be resolved belonged to the *Haruchai*.

But when Covenant had urged Cail's people back to their feet, it was the First who addressed him. In spite of battle and grief, she looked refreshed: unlike her husband, she had found exigencies and purposes she understood, was trained for, in the test of combat. 'Earthfriend,' she said formally, a gleam in her hair and her voice, 'you are well come. The quenching of Clave and Banefire and the freeing of Revelstone merit high pride, and they will be honoured in song from sea to sea wherever our people still hold music in their hearts. None would gainsay you, should you choose to bide here in rest and restoration. It is fitting that the craft and vision of this Giant-wrought bourne should serve as accolade to that which you and the Chosen have accomplished.

'Yet,' she went on without pausing, 'I applaud the purpose which draws you away. From peril to loss across the world I have followed in your wake, and at last have been granted to strike a blow against evil. But our losses have been dire and sore, and one blow does not suffice. I desire to strike again, if I am able. And the Stonedownors have shown to us that the Sunbane remains, seeking the rapine of the Earth. The Search has not reached its end. Earthfriend, where do you go?'

Linden looked at Covenant. He was an upright self-contradiction, at once fearful and intrepid. He held his head high as if he knew that he was worthy of the Giants and *Haruchai*, the Graveller and the eh-Brand; and sunlight reflecting from the washed stone lit his clean face, so that he looked like the pure bone of the Earth. And yet his shoulders were rigid, knotted in the act of strangling his own weakness, his desire to be spared. Too much depended on him, and he had no health-sense for guidance.

Frail, invincible, and human, he met the First's gaze, looked past her to Cail and Durris and the injured *Haruchai*. Then he answered.

'When I was in Andelain, I met some of my old friends — the people who had faith in me, took care of me, loved me long before I could do any of those things for myself. Mhoram reminded me of a few lessons I should've already learned. Foamfollower gave me Vain. Bannor promised his people would serve me. And Elena,' Elena his daughter, who had loved him in the same unbalanced way that she had hated Lord Foul, 'told me what I'd have to do in the end. She said, "When the time is upon you, and you must confront the Despiser, he is to be found in Mount Thunder — in Kiril Threndor, where he has taken up his abode."' He swallowed thickly. 'That's where I'm going. One way or another, I'm going to put an end to it.'

Though he spoke quietly, his words seemed to ring and echo in the high hall.

The First gave a nod of grim, eager approval.

She started to ask him where Mount Thunder was, then stopped. Durris had taken a step forward. He faced Covenant with an unwonted intensity gleaming from his flat eyes.

'Ur-Lord, we will accompany you.'

Covenant did not hesitate. In a voice as unshakable as the *Haruchai*'s, he said, 'No, you won't.'

Durris lifted an eyebrow, but permitted himself no other sign of surprise. For an instant, his attention shifted as he conferred silently with his people. Then he said, 'It is as you have claimed. A promise of service was given to you by Bannor of the Bloodguard among the Dead. And that service you have earned in our redemption from the compulsion and sacrifice of the Clave. Ur-Lord, we will accompany you to the last.'

Pain twisted Covenant's mouth. But he did not waver. His hands were closed into fists, pressed against his thighs. 'I said, no.'

Again, Durris paused. The air was tight with suspense: issues Linden did not know how to estimate had come to a crisis. She did not truly comprehend Covenant's intent. The First moved as though she wanted to interpose some appeal or protest. But the *Haruchai* did not need her to speak for them. Durris leaned slightly closer to Covenant, and his look took on a hint of urgency: his people knew better than anyone else what was at stake.

'Thomas Covenant, bethink you.' Obliquely, Linden wondered why it was Durris who spoke and not Cail. 'The *Haruchai* are known to you. The tale of the Bloodguard is known to you. You have witnessed that proud, deathless Vow — and you have beheld its ending. Do not believe that we forget. In all the ages of that service, it was the grief of the Bloodguard that they gave no direct battle to Corruption. And yet when the chance came to Bannor — when he stood at your side upon Landsdrop with Saltheart Foamfollower and knew your purpose – he turned aside from it. You had need of him, and he turned aside.

'We do not judge him. The Vow was broken. But I say to you that we have tasted failure, and it is not to our liking. We must restore our faith. We will not turn aside again.'

Shifting still closer to Covenant, he went on as if he wanted no one else to hear him, 'Ur-Lord, has it become with you as it was with Kevin Landwaster? Is it your intent to be parted from those who would prevent you from the Ritual of Desecration?'

At that, Linden expected Covenant to flare out. She wanted to protest herself, deny hotly Durris's unwarranted accusation. But Covenant did not raise his voice. Instead, he lifted his halfhand between himself and Durris, turned it palm outward, spread his fingers. His ring clung like a manacle to what had once been his middle finger.

'You remember,' he said, allowing himself neither sarcasm nor bitterness. 'Have you forgotten why the Vow was broken?

'I'll tell you why. Three Bloodguard got their hands on a piece of the Illearth Stone, and they thought that made them powerful enough to do what they always wanted. So they went to Foul's Creche, challenged Corruption. But they were wrong. No flesh and blood is immune. Foul mastered them – the same way he mastered Kevin when Elena broke the Law of Death. He maimed them to look like me – like *this*' – he waved his halfhand stiffly – 'and sent them back to Revelstone to mock the Bloodguard.'

An outcry rose in him; but he held it down. 'Are you surprised the Vow was broken? I thought it was going to break their hearts.

'Bannor didn't turn aside. He gave me exactly what I needed. He showed me it was still possible to go on living.'

He paused to steady himself; and now Linden felt the meld of his certainty and power growing, felt him become palpably stronger.

'The fact is,' he said, without accusation, 'you've been wrong all along. You've misunderstood your own doubt from the beginning. What it means. Why it matters. First Kevin, then the other Lords, then me – ever since your people first came to the Land, you've been swearing yourselves in service to ordinary men and women who simply can't be worthy of what you offer. Kevin was a good man who broke down when the pressure got to be worse than he could stand – and the Bloodguard were never able to forgive him because they pinned their faith on him and when he failed they thought it was their fault for not making him worthy, not preventing him from being human. Over and over again, you put yourselves in the position of serving someone who *has* to fail you for the mere reason that he's human and all humans fail at one time or another – and then you can't forgive him because his failure casts doubt on your service. And you can't forgive yourselves either. You want to serve perfectly, and that means you're responsible for everything. And whenever something comes along to remind you you're mortal – like the *merewives* – that's unforgivable too, and you decide you aren't worthy to go on serving. Or else you want to do something crazy, like fighting Foul in person.'

Slowly, he lowered his hand; but the gaze he fixed on Durris did not falter, and his clarity burned from his eyes. 'You can do better than that. Nobody questions your worth. You've demonstrated it a thousand times. And if that's not enough for you, remember Brinn faced the Guardian of the One Tree and won. *Ak-Haru Kenaustin Ardenol*. Any one of you would've done the same in his place. You don't need to serve me anymore.'

'And,' he added carefully, 'I don't need you. Not in the way you think. I don't want you to come with me.'

Durris did not retreat. But Linden sensed that he wished to draw back, that Covenant's certain strength abashed him. He seemed unable to deny the image Covenant painted – and unwilling to accept its implications.

'Ur-Lord, what would you have us do?' he asked as if he felt no distress. 'You have given our lives to us. We must make recompense. That is necessary.' In spite of its inflexibility, his voice put the weight of *Haruchai* history into the word, *necessary*. The extravagance and loyalty of his people required an outlet. 'The Vow of the Bloodguard was sworn to meet the bounty and grandeur of High Lord Kevin and Revelstone. It was not regretted. Do you ask such an oath from us again, that we may preserve the meaning of our lives?'

'No.' Covenant's eyes softened and blurred, and he put his hand on Durris's shoulder as if he wanted to hug the *Haruchai*. Linden felt pouring from him the ache of his appreciation. Bloodguard and *Haruchai* had given themselves to him without question; and he had never believed that he deserved them. 'There's something else I want you to do.'

At that, Durris's stance sharpened. He stood before the Unbeliever like a salute.

'I want you to stay here. In Revelstone. With as many of your people as you can get. For two reasons. To take care of the wounded. The Land's going to need them. It's going to need every man or woman who can possibly be persuaded to face the future. And to protect the city. This is Revelstone, Lord's Keep. It belongs to the Land – not to Corruption or Ravers. I want it safe. So the future will have a place to centre. A place where people can come to learn about the past – and see what the Land means – and make plans. A place of defence. A place of hope. You've already given me everything Bannor promised and more. But I want you to do this, too.

For me. And for yourselves. Here you can serve something that isn't going to fail you.'

For a long moment, Durris was silent while his mind addressed his people. Then he spoke, and his dispassionate voice thrilled Linden's hearing like a distant tantara of horns.

'Ur-Lord, we will do it.'

In response, Covenant squeezed Durris's shoulder and tried to blink the gratitude out of his eyes. Instinctively, Linden put her arms around him, marvelling at what he had become.

But when Durris withdrew to stand among the other *Haruchai*, Cail came forward. His old scar showed plainly on one arm; but he bore other hurts as well. With Brinn, he had once demanded retribution against Linden, believing her a servant of Corruption. And with Brinn, he had succumbed to the song of the *merewives*. But Brinn had gone alone to meet the Guardian of the One Tree: Cail had been left behind to pay the price of memory and loss.

'Thomas Covenant,' he said softly. 'Earthfriend. Permit me.'

Covenant stared at him. A strange bleakness showed in Cail's eyes.

'I have heard your words,' said the *Haruchai*, 'but they are not mine to acknowledge or eschew. Since that time when the white beauty and delusion of the *merewives* took me from myself, I have not stood in your service. Rather have I followed the command placed upon me by *ak-Haru Kenaustin Ardenol*. You have not forgotten.' Covenant nodded, wary of grief; but still Cail quoted, ' "Cail will accept my place at your side until the word of the Bloodguard Bannor has been carried to its end." ' Then he went on, 'That I have done. But it was not I who was proven against the Guardian of the One Tree. In the stead of victory, I have met only the deaths of Giants and the doubt of my people. And this I have done, not solely because I was commanded, but also because I was promised. It was given to me that when the word of Bannor was fulfilled I would be permitted to follow my heart.

'Earthfriend, you have proclaimed that fulfilment. And I have served you to my best strength. I ask now that you permit me.

'Permit me to depart.'

'Depart?' Covenant breathed. His open face showed that this was not what he had expected. He made an effort to pull himself out of his surprise. 'Of course you can go. You can do whatever you want. I wouldn't stop you if I could. You've earned – ' Swallowing roughly, he changed direction. 'But you're needed here. Are you going home – back to your family?'

Without expression, Cail replied, 'I will return to the *merewives*.'

Covenant and the First reacted in simultaneous protest, but her hard voice covered his. 'That is madness! Have you forgotten that you were scant moments from death? Almost Galewrath and I failed of your rescue. I will not see the life which I brought up from the deep cast away!'

But surprise and apprehension seemed to tighten Linden's percipience to a higher pitch, a keener penetration; and she saw Cail with sudden acuity, felt parts of him which had been hidden until now. She knew with the instantaneous certainty of vision that he did not intend to throw his life away, did not want death from the Dancers of the Sea: he wanted a different kind of life. A resolution for the inextricable desire and bereavement of his extreme nature.

She cut Covenant off, stopped the First. They glared at her; but she ignored their vehemence. They did not understand. Brinn had said, *The limbs of our women are brown from sun and birth. But there is also a whiteness as acute as the ice which bleeds from the rock of mountains, and it burns as the purest snow burns in the most high tor, the most wind-flogged col.* And from it grew a yearning which Cail could no longer bear to deny. Panting with the force of her wish to support him, give him something in return for his faithfulness, she rushed to utter the first words that came to her.

'Brinn gave his *permission*. Don't you see that? He knew what he was saying – he knew what Cail would want to do. He heard the same song himself. Cail isn't going to die.'

But then she had to halt. She did not know how to explain her conviction that Brinn and Cail could be trusted.

'Thomas Covenant,' Cail said, 'I comprehend the value of that which you have granted to the *Haruchai* – a service of purity and worth. And I have witnessed Brinn's encounter with *ak-Haru Kenaustin Ardenol*, the great victory of our people. But the cost of that victory was the life of Cable Seadreamer. For myself I do not desire such worth.

'The song of the *merewives* has been named delusion. But is not all life a manner of dreaming? Have you not said that the Land itself is a dream? Dream or delusion, the music I have heard has altered me. But I have not learned the meaning of this change. Ur-Lord, I wish to prove what I have dreamed to its heart. Permit me.'

Linden looked at Covenant, imploring him with her eyes; but he did not meet her gaze. He faced Cail, and conflicting emotions wrestled each other visibly across his mien: recognition of what Cail was saying; grief over Seadreamer; fear for the *Haruchai*. But after a moment he fought his way through the moil. 'Cail – ' he began. His throat closed as though he dreaded what he meant to say. When he found his voice, he sounded unexpectedly small and lonely, like a man who could not afford to let even one friend go.

'I heard the same song you did. The *merewives* are dangerous. Be very careful with them.'

Cail did not thank the Unbeliever. He did not smile or nod or speak. But for an instant the glance he gave Covenant was as plain as a paean.

Then he turned on his heel, strode out of the forehall into the sunlight, and was gone.

Covenant watched the *Haruchai* go as if even now he wanted to call Cail back; but he did not do so. And none of the other *Haruchai* made any move to challenge Cail's decision. Slowly, a rustle like a sigh passed through the hall, and the tension eased. Hollian blinked the dampness out of her eyes. Sunder gazed bemusement and awe at the implications of Cail's choice. Linden wanted to show Covenant the gratitude Cail had neglected; but it was unnecessary. She saw that he understood now, and his expression had softened. Behind his sorrow over all the people he had lost lurked a wry smile which seemed to suggest that he would have made Cail's choice if she had been a Dancer of the Sea.

The First cleared her throat. 'Earthfriend, I am no equal for you. These determinations surpass me. In your place, my word would have been that our need for the accompaniment of the *Haruchai* is certain and immediate. But I do not question you. I am a Giant like any other, and such bravado pleases me.

'Only declare swiftly where this Mount Thunder and Kiril Threndor may be found, that Mistweave may bear the knowledge eastward to Seareach. It may be that his path and Cail's will lie together – and they will have need of each other.'

Covenant nodded at once. 'Good idea.' Quickly, he described as well as he could Mount Thunder's location astride the centre of Landsdrop, where the Soulsease River passed through the Wightwarrens and became the main source for Sarangrave Flat and the Great Swamp. 'Unfortunately,' he added, 'I can't tell you how to find Kiril Threndor. I've been there once – it's in the chest of the mountain somewhere – but the whole bloody place is a maze.'

'That must suffice,' the First said. Then she turned to Mistweave. 'Hear you? If skill and courage may achieve it, Sevinhand Anchormaster will bring Starfare's Gem to Seareach and The Grieve. There you must meet him. If we fail, the fate of the Earth falls to you. And if we do not,' she continued less grimly, 'you will provide for our restoration Homeward.' In a softer voice, she asked, 'Mistweave, are you content?'

Linden looked at Mistweave closely and was reassured. The Giant who had sought to serve her and believed that he had failed was injured and weary, his arm in a sling, bruises on his broad face; but much of his distress had faded. Perhaps he would never entirely forget his self-doubt. But he had redeemed most of it. The spirit within him was capable of peace.

She went to him because she wanted to thank him – and wanted to see him smile. He towered over her; but she was accustomed to that. Taking one of his huge hands in her small grasp, she said up to him, 'Sevinhand's going to be the Master now. Galewrath'll be the Anchormaster.' Deliberately she risked this reference to Honninscrave's end. 'Starfare's Gem will need a new Storesmaster. Someone who knows something about healing. Tell them I said you should have the job.'

Abruptly, he loomed over her, and she was swept into the embrace of his uninjured arm. For an instant, she feared that he was hurt and weeping; but then his emotions came into better focus, and she returned his clasp as hard as she could.

When he set her down again, he was grinning like a Giant.

'Begone, Mistweave,' the First muttered in a tone of gruff kindness. 'Cail *Haruchai* will outdistance you entirely.'

In response, he shouted a laugh. 'Outdistance a Giant? Not while I live!' With a holla to Pitchwife and a salute to Covenant and Linden, he snatched up his sack of supplies and dashed for the tunnel under the watchtower as if he intended to run all the way to Landsdrop rather than let Cail surpass him.

After that, nothing remained to delay the company. The First and Pitchwife shouldered their packs. Sunder and Hollian lifted the bundles they had prepared for themselves. For a moment, Covenant looked around the stone of the forehall as though he feared to leave it, dreaded the consequences of the path he had chosen; but then his certitude returned. After saying a brief farewell to the *Haruchai*, and accepting their bows with as much grace as his embarrassment allowed, he turned his feet toward the sunlight beyond the broken gates. Vain and Findail took their familiar positions behind him – or behind Linden – as the company moved outward.

Gritting her teeth against the shock of the Sunbane on her bare nerves, Linden went back out into the desert sun.

13

THE EH-BRAND

It was worse than she had expected. It seemed worse than it had been that morning. Glimmermere's cleansing and Revelstone's protection appeared to have sharpened her health-sense, making her more vulnerable than ever to the palpable ill of the Sunbane. The sun's heat felt as hard and heavy as stone. She knew it was not literally gnawing the flesh from her bones, not charring her bones to the malign blackness which she had inherited from her father. Yet she felt that she was being eaten away – that the Sunbane had found its likeness in her heart and was feeding on her.

During the long days when she and the quest had been away from the sun's corruption, she had groped toward a new kind of life. She had heard intimations of affirmation and had followed them urgently, striving to be healed. At one time, with the tale of her mother told for the first time and Covenant's arms about her, she had believed that she could say no forever to her own dark hungers. *There is also love in the world.* But now the desert sun flamed at her with the force of an execration, and she knew better.

In some ways, she was unable to share Covenant's love for the Land. She had never seen it healthy: she could only guess at the loveliness he ascribed to it. And to that extent he was alone in his dismay. *There's only one way to hurt a man who's lost everything. Give him back something broken.* Yet she was like the Land herself. The power tormenting it was the same might which demonstrated to her undefended nerves that she was not whole.

And she and her companions were on their way to confront Lord Foul, the source and progenitor of the Sunbane.

And they were only eight. In effect, they were only six: two Giants, two Stonedownors, Covenant and Linden. Vain and Findail could be trusted to serve no purposes but their own. With the sun burning against her face as it started its afternoon decline, she lost what little understanding she had ever had of Covenant's reasons for refusing the aid of the *Haruchai*. Their intransigent integrity at her side might have helped to keep the Sunbane out of her soul.

Mount Thunder lay to the east; but Covenant was leading the company west and south down through the dead foothills below the intricately-wrought face of the Keep. His intent, he explained, was to join the watercourse which had once been the White River and follow it toward Andelain. That was not the most direct path, but it would enable the company to do what Sunder, Linden, and he had done previously – to ride the river during a sun of rain. Recollections of cold and distress made Linden shiver, but she did not demur: she favoured any plan which might reduce the amount of time she had to spend exposed to the sun.

Above her rose the sheer, hard face of Revelstone. But some distance ahead Furl Falls came tumbling down the side of the plateau; and its implications were comforting. Already, much of the potent water springing from the roots of Glimmermere had been denatured: Furl Falls was only a wisp of what it should have been. Yet it remained. Centuries of the Sunbane had not ruined or harmed the upland tarn. Through the brown heat and light of the sun, Furl Falls struck hints of blue like sparks from the rough rock of the cliff.

To the south, the hills spread away like a frown of pain in the ground, becoming slowly less rugged – or perhaps less able to care what happened to them – as they receded from the promontory of the Westron Mountains. And between them wound the watercourse Covenant sought. Following what might once have been a road, he brought the company to an ancient stone bridge across the broad channel where the White River had stopped running. A trickle of water still stretched thinly down the centre of the riverbed; but even that moisture soon vanished into a damp, sandy stain. The sight of it made Linden thirsty with empathy, although she had eaten and drunk well before leaving Mhoram's quarters.

Covenant did not cross the bridge. For a moment, he glared at the small stream as if he were remembering the White River in full spate. Then, controlling his fear of heights with a visible effort, he found a way down into the riverbed. The last sun of rain had not left the channel smooth or clear, but its bottom offered an easier path than the hills on either side.

Linden, Sunder and Hollian followed him. Pitchwife came muttering after them. Vain leaped downward with a lightness which belied his impenetrability: on his wooden wrist and left ankle, the heels of the Staff of Law caught the sun dully. Findail changed shape and glided to the river bottom as gracefully as an albatross. But the First did not join the rest of the company. When Covenant looked back up at her, she said, 'I will watch over you.' She gestured along the higher ground of the east bank. 'Though you have mastered the Clave, some caution is needful. And the exertion will ease me. I am a Giant and eager, and your pace gives me impatience.'

Covenant shrugged: he seemed to think that he had become immune to ordinary forms of peril. But he waved his acceptance; and the First strode away at a brisk gait.

Pitchwife shook his head, bemused by his wife's sources of strength. Linden saw a continuing disquiet in the unwonted tension of his countenance; but most of his unhappiness had sunk beneath the surface, restoring his familiar capacity for humour. 'Stone an Sea!' he said to Covenant and Linden, 'is she not a wonder? Should ever we encounter that which can daunt her, then will I truly credit that the Earth is lost. But then only. For the while, I will study the beauty of her and be glad.' Turning, he started down the watercourse as if he wished his friends to think he had left his crisis behind.

Hollian smiled after them. Softly, Sunder said, 'We are fortunate in these Giants. Had Nassic my father spoken to me of such beings, mayhap I would have laughed – or mayhap wept. But I would not have believed.'

'Me neither,' Covenant murmured. Doubt and fear cast their shadows across the background of his gaze; but he appeared to take no hurt from them. 'Mhoram was my friend. Bannor saved my life. Lena loved me. But Foamfollower made the difference.'

Linden reached out to him, touched her palm briefly to his clean cheek to tell him that she understood. The ache of the Sunbane was so strong in her that she could not speak.

Together, they started after Pitchwife.

The riverbed was a jumble of small stones and large boulders, flat swathes of sand, jutting banks, long pits. But it was a relatively easy road. And by midafternoon the west rim began casting deep shade into the channel.

That shade was a balm to Linden's abraded nerves – but for some reason it did not make her any better able to put one foot in front of another. The alteration of shadow and acid heat seemed to numb her mind, and the consequences of two days without rest or sleep came to her as if they had been waiting in the bends and hollows of the watercourse. Eventually, she found herself thinking that of all the phases of the Sunbane the desert sun was the most gentle. Which was absurd: this sun was inherently murderous. Perhaps it was killing her now. Yet it gave less affront to her health-sense than did the other suns. She insisted on this as if someone had tried to contradict her. The desert was simply dead. The dead could inspire grief, but they felt no pain. The sun of rain had the force of incarnate violence: the malign creatures of the sun of pestilence were a pang of revulsion: the fertile sun seemed to wring screams from the whole world. But the desert sun only made her want to weep.

Then she was weeping. Her face was pressed into the sand, and her hand scrubbed at the ground on either side of her head because they did not have the strength to lift her. But at the same time she was far away from her fallen body, detached and separate from Covenant and Hollian as they called her name, rushed to help her. She was thinking with the precision of a necessary belief, This can't go on. It has got to be stopped. Every time the sun comes up, the Land dies a little deeper. It has got to be stopped.

Covenant's hands took hold of her, rolled her onto her back, shifted her fully into the shadows. She knew they were his hands because they were urgent and numb. When he propped her into a sitting position, she tried to blink her eyes clear. But her tears would not stop.

'Linden,' he breathed. 'Are you all right? Damn it to hell! I should've given you a chance to rest.'

She wanted to say, This has got to be stopped. Give me your ring. But that was wrong. She knew it was wrong because the darkness in her leaped up at the idea, avid for power. She could not hold back her grief.

Hugging her hard, he rocked her in his arms and murmured words which meant nothing except that he loved her.

Gradually, the helplessness faded from her muscles, and she was able to raise her head. Around her stood Sunder, Hollian, the First, and Pitchwife. Even Findail was there; and his yellow eyes yearned with conflicts, as if he knew how close she had come – but did not know whether he was relieved or saddened by it. Only Vain ignored her.

She tried to say, I'm sorry. Don't worry. But the desert was in her throat, and no sound came.

Pitchwife knelt beside her, lifted a bowl to her lips. She smelled *diamondraught*, took a small swallow. The potent liquor gave her back her voice.

'Sorry I scared you. I'm not hurt. Just tired. I didn't realize I was this tired.' The shadow of the west bank enabled her to say such things.

Covenant was not looking at her. To the watercourse and the wide sky he muttered, 'I ought to have my head examined. We should've stayed in Revelstone. One day wouldn't have killed me.' Then he addressed his companions. 'We'll camp here. Maybe tomorrow she'll feel better.'

Linden started to smile reassurance at him. But she was already asleep.

That night, she dreamed repeatedly of power. Over and over again, she possessed Covenant, took his ring, and used it to rip the Sunbane out of the Earth. The sheer violence of what she did was astounding: it filled her with glee and horror. Her father laughed blackness at her. It killed Covenant, left him as betrayed as her mother. She thought she would go mad.

You have committed murder. Are you not evil?

No. Yes. Not unless I choose to be. I can't help it.

This has got to be stopped. Got to be stopped. *You are being forged as iron is forged* – Got to be stopped.

But sometime during the middle of the night she awoke and found herself enfolded by Covenant's sleeping arms. For a while, she clung to him; but he was too weary to waken. When she went back to sleep, the dreams were gone.

And when dawn came she felt stronger: stronger and calmer, as if during the night she had somehow made up her mind. She kissed Covenant, nodded soberly in response to the questioning looks of her friends. Then, while the Stonedownors and Giants defended themselves against the sun's first touch by standing on rock, she climbed a slope in the west bank to get an early view of the Sunbane. She wanted to understand it.

It was red and baleful, the colour of pestilence. Its light felt like disease crawling across her nerves.

But she knew its ill did not in fact arise from the sun. Sunlight acted as a catalyst for it, a source of energy, but did not cause the Sunbane. Rather, it was an emanation from the ground, corrupted

Earthpower radiating into the heavens. And that corruption sank deeper every day, working its way into the marrow of the Earth's bones.

She bore it without flinching. She intended to do something about it.

Her companions continued to study her as she descended the slope to rejoin them. But when she met their scrutiny, they were reassured. Pitchwife relaxed visibly. Some of the tension flowed out of the muscles of Covenant's shoulders, though he clearly did not trust his superficial vision. And Sunder, who remembered Marid, gazed at her as if she had come back from the brink of something as fatal as venom.

'Chosen, you are well restored,' said the First with gruff pleasure. 'The sight gladdens me.'

Together, Hollian and Pitchwife prepared a meal which Linden ate ravenously. Then the company set itself to go on down the watercourse.

For the first part of the morning, the walking was almost easy. This sun was considerably cooler than the previous one; and while the east bank shaded the river bottom, it remained free of vermin. The ragged edges and arid lines of the landscape took on a tinge of the crimson light which made them appear acute and wild, etched with desiccation like the dreams of a Sandgorgon. Pitchwife joined the First as she ascended the hillsides again to keep watch over the company. Although Hollian shared Sunder's visceral abhorrence of the sun of pestilence, they were comfortable with each other: in the shade's protection, they walked and talked, arguing companionably about a name for their son. Initially, Sunder claimed that the child would grow up to be an eh-Brand and should therefore be given an eh-Brand's name; but Hollian insisted that the boy would take after his father. Then for no apparent reason they switched positions and continued contradicting each other.

By unspoken agreement, Linden and Covenant left the Stonedownors to themselves as much as possible. She listened to them in a mood of detached affection for a time; but gradually their argument sent her musing on matters that had nothing to do with the Sunbane – or with what Covenant hoped to accomplish by confronting the Despiser. In the middle of her reverie, she surprised herself by asking without preamble, 'What was Joan like? When you were married?'

He looked at her sharply; and she caught a glimpse of the unanswerable pain which lay at the roots of his certainty. Once before, when she had appealed to him, he had said of Joan, *She's my ex-wife*, as if that simple fact were an affirmation. Yet some kind of guilt or commitment toward Joan had endured in him for years after their divorce, compelling him to accept responsibility for her when she had come to him in madness and possession, seeking his blood.

Now he hesitated momentarily as though he were searching for a reply which would give Linden what she wanted without weakening his grasp on himself. Then he indicated Sunder and Hollian with a twitch of his head. 'When Roger was born,' he said, overriding a catch in his throat, 'she didn't ask me what I thought. She just named him after her father. And her grandfather. A whole series of Rogers on her side of the family. When he grows up, he probably won't even know who I am.'

His bitterness was plain. But other, more important feelings lay behind it. He had smiled for Joan when he had exchanged his life for hers.

And he was smiling now — the same terrible smile that Linden remembered with such dismay. While it lasted, she was on the verge of whispering at him in stark anguish, Is *that* what you're going to do? Again? *Again?*

But almost at once his expression softened; and the thing she feared seemed suddenly impossible. Her protest faded. He appeared almost unnaturally sure of what he meant to do; but, whatever it was, it did not reek of suicide. Inwardly shaken, she said, 'Don't worry. He won't forget you.' Her attempt to console him sounded inane, but she had nothing else to offer. 'It's not that easy for kids to forget their parents.'

In response, he slipped an arm around her waist, hugged her. They walked on together in silence.

But by midmorning sunlight covered most of the riverbed, and the channel became increasingly hazardous. The rock-gnarled and twisted course, with its secret shadows and occasionally overhanging banks, was an apt breeding-place for pestilential creatures which lurked and struck. From Revelstone Hollian had brought an ample store of *voure*; but some of the crawling, scuttling life that now teemed in the river bottom seemed to be angered by the scent or immune to it altogether. Warped and feral sensations scraped across Linden's nerves: every time she saw something move, a pang of alarm went through her. Sunder and Hollian had to be more and more careful where they put their bare feet. Covenant began to study the slopes where the Giants walked: he was considering the advantages of leaving the channel.

When a scorpion as large as Linden's two fists shot out from under a rock and lashed its stinger at the side of Covenant's boot, he growled a curse and made his decision. Kicking the scorpion away, he muttered, 'That does it. Let's get out of here.'

No one objected. Followed mutely by Vain and Findail, the four companions went to a pile of boulders leaning against the east bank and climbed upward to join the First and Pitchwife.

They spent the rest of the day winding through the hills beside the empty River. Periodically, the First strode up to a crest that gave her a wider view over the region; and her fingers rubbed the hilt of her longsword as if she were looking for a chance to use it. But she saw nothing that threatened the company except the waterless waste.

Whenever the hills opened westward, Linden could see the Westron Mountains sinking toward the horizon as they curved away to the south. And from the top of a rocky spine she was able to make out the distant rim of Revelstone, barely visible now above the crumpled terrain. Part of her yearned for the security it represented, for stone walls and the guardianship of *Haruchai*. Red limned the edges of the land, made the desert hills as distinct as the work of a knife. Overhead, the sky seemed strangely depthless: considered directly, it remained a pale blue occluded with fine dust; but the corners of her vision caught a hue of crimson like a hint of the Despiser's bloody-mindedness; and that colour made the heavens look flat, closed.

Though she was defended by *voure*, she flinched internally at the vibrating ricochet of sandflies as big as starlings, the squirming haste of oversized centipedes. But when the First and Covenant started on down the far side of the spine, she wiped the sweat from her forehead, combed her hair back from her temples with her fingers, and followed.

Late in the afternoon, as shadows returned the sun's vermin to quiescence, the company descended to the watercourse again so that they could travel more easily until sunset. Then, when the light faded, they stopped for the night on a wide stretch of sand. There they ate supper, drank *metheglin* lightly flavoured with *diamondraught*, hollowed beds for themselves. And Hollian took out her *lianar* wand to discover what the morrow's sun would be.

Without a word, Sunder handed her the wrapped *krill*. Carefully, as if Loric's blade still awed her, she parted the cloth until a clear shaft of argent pierced the twilight. Sitting cross-legged with the knife in her lap, she began to chant her invocation; and as she did so, she raised her *lianar* into the *krill*-gem's light.

From the wood grew shoots and tendrils of fine fire: they spread about her on the ground like creepers, climbed into the argence like vines. They burned without heat, without harming the wand; and their radiant filigree made the night eldritch and strange.

Her flame was the precise incarnadine of the present sun.

Linden thought then that Hollian would cease her invocation. A second day of pestilence was not a surprise. But the eh-Brand kept her power alight, and a new note of intensity entered her chant. With a start, Linden realized that Hollian was stretching herself, reaching beyond her accustomed limits.

After a moment, a quiet flare of blue like a gentle coruscation appeared at the tips of the fire-fronds.

For an instant, azure rushed inward along the vines, transforming the flames, altering the crimson ambience of the dark. Then it was quenched: all the fire vanished. Hollian sat with the *lianar* cradled in her fingers and the light of the *krill* on her face. She was smiling faintly.

'The morrow's sun will be a sun of pestilence.' Her voice revealed strain and weariness, but they were not serious. 'But the sun of the day following will be a sun of rain.'

'Good!' said Covenant. 'Two days of rain, and we'll practically be in Andelain.' He turned to the First. 'It looks like we're not going to be able to build rafts. Can you and Pitchwife support the four of us when the River starts to run?'

In answer, the First snorted as if the question were unworthy of her.

Gleaming with pride, Sunder put his arms around Hollian. But her attention was fixed on Covenant. She took a deep breath for strength, then asked, 'Ur-Lord, is it truly your intent to enter Andelain once again?'

Covenant faced her sharply. A grimace twisted his mouth. 'You asked me that the last time.' He seemed to expect her to renew her former refusal. 'You know I want to go there. I never get enough of it. It's the only place where there's any Law left alive.'

The *krill*-light emphasized the darkness of her hair; but its reflection in her eyes was clear. 'You have told that tale. And I have spoken of the acquaintance of my people with the peril of Andelain. To us its name was one of proven madness. No man or woman known to us entered that land where the Sunbane does not reign and returned whole of mind. Yet you have entered and emerged, defying that truth as you defy all others. Thus the truth is altered. The life of the Land is not what it was. And in my turn I am changed. I have conceived a desire to do that which I have not done — to sojourn among my fears and strengths and learn the new truth of them.

'Thomas Covenant, do not turn aside from Andelain. It is my wish to accompany you.'

For a long moment, no one spoke. Then Covenant said in a husky voice, 'Thanks. That helps.'

Softly, Hollian re-covered the *krill*, let darkness wash back over the company. The night was the colour of her hair, and it spread its wings out to the stars.

The next day, the red sun asserted its hold over the Land more swiftly, building on what it had already done. The company was forced out of the watercourse well before midmorning. Still they made steady progress. Every southward league softened the hills slightly, and by slow degrees the going became easier. The valleys between the rises grew wider; the slopes, less rugged. And Hollian had said that the next day would bring a sun of rain. Severely, Linden tried to tell herself that she had no reason to feel so beaten, so vulnerable to the recurring blackness of her life.

But the Sunbane shone full upon her: it soaked into her as if she had become a sponge for the world's ill. The stink of pestilence ran through her blood. Hidden somewhere among the secrets of her bones was a madwoman who believed that she deserved such desecration. She wanted power in order to extirpate the evil from herself.

Her percipience was growing keener – and so her distress was keener.

She could not inure herself to what she felt. No amount of determination or decision was enough. Long before noon, she began to stumble as if she were exhausted. A red haze covered her mind, blinding her to the superficial details of the terrain, the concern of her friends. She was like the Land, powerless to heal herself. But when Covenant asked her if she wanted to rest, she made no answer and went on walking. She had chosen her path and did not mean to stop.

Yet she heard the First's warning. Unsteady on her feet, her knees locked, she halted with Covenant as the Giants came back at a tense trot from a low ridge ahead of the company. Distress aggravated Pitchwife's crooked features. The First looked apprehensive, like iron fretted with rust. But in spite of their palpable urgency, they did not speak for a moment. They were too full of what they had seen.

Then Pitchwife groaned far back in his throat. 'Ah, Earthfriend.' His voice shuddered. 'You have forewarned us of the consequences of this Sunbane – but now I perceive that I did not altogether credit your words. It is heinous beyond speech.'

The First gripped her sword as an anchor for her emotions. 'We are blocked from our way,' she said, articulating the words like chewed metal. 'Perchance we have come blindly upon an army of another purpose – but I do not believe it. I believe that the Despiser has reached out his hand against us.'

Trepidation beat the haze from Linden's mind. Her mouth shaped a question. But she did not ask it aloud. The Giants stood rigid before her; and she could see as clearly as language that they had no answer.

'Beyond that ridge?' asked Covenant. 'How far?'

'A stone's throw for a Giant,' the First replied grimly. 'No more. And they advance toward us.'

He glanced at Linden to gauge her condition, then said to the First, 'Let's go take a look.'

She nodded, turned on her heel and strode away.

He hurried after her. Linden, Sunder, and Hollian followed. Pitchwife placed himself protectively at Linden's side. Vain and Findail quickened their steps to keep up with the company.

At the ridgecrest, Covenant squatted behind a boulder and peered down the southward slope. Linden joined him. The Giants crouched below the line of sight of what lay ahead. Findail also stopped. Careful to avoid exposing themselves, Sunder and Hollian crept forward. But Vain moved up to the rim as if he wanted a clear view and feared nothing.

Covenant spat a low curse under his breath; but it was not directed at the Demondim-spawn. It was aimed at the black seethe of bodies moving toward the ridge on both sides of the watercourse.

As black as Vain himself.

The sight of them sucked the strength from Linden's limbs.

She knew what they were because Covenant had described them to her – and because she had met the Waynhim of Hamako's *rhysh*. But they had been changed. Their emanations rose to her like a shout, telling her precisely what had happened to them. They had fallen victim to the desecration of the Sunbane.

'Ur-viles,' Covenant whispered fiercely. 'Hell and blood!'

Warped ur-viles.

Hundreds of them.

Once they had resembled the Waynhim: larger, black instead of grey; but with the same hairless bodies, the same limbs formed for running on all fours as well as for walking erect, the same eyeless faces and wide, questing nostrils. But no longer. The Sunbane had made them monstrous.

Over the sickness in her stomach, Linden thought bleakly that Lord Foul must have done this to them. Like the Waynhim, the ur-viles were too lore-wise to have exposed themselves accidentally to the sun's first touch. They had been corrupted deliberately and sent here to block the company's way.

'Why?' she breathed, aghast. *'Why?'*

'Same reason as always,' Covenant growled without looking away from the grotesque horde. 'Force me to use too much power.' Then suddenly his gaze flashed toward her. 'Or to keep us out of Andelain. Exposed to the Sunbane. He knows how much it hurts you. Maybe he thinks it'll make you do what he wants.'

Linden felt the truth of his words. She knew she could not stay sane forever under the pressure of the Sunbane. But a bifurcated part of her replied, Or maybe he did it to punish them. For doing something he didn't like.

Her heart skipped a beat.

For making Vain?

The Demondim-spawn stood atop the ridge as if he sought to attract the notice of the horde.

'Damnation!' Covenant muttered. Creeping back a short way from the rim, he turned to the Giants. 'What're we going to do?'

The First did not hesitate. She gestured eastward along the valley below the ridge. 'There lies our way. Passing their flank unseen, we may hope to outrun them toward Andelain.'

Covenant shook his head. 'That won't work. This isn't exactly the direct route to Andelain – or Mount Thunder, for that matter – but Foul still knew where to find us. He has some way of locating us. It's been done before.' He glared at his memories, then thrust the past aside. 'If we try to get around them, they'll know it.'

The First scowled and said nothing, momentarily at a loss for alternatives. Linden put her back to the boulder, braced her dread on the hard stone. 'We can retreat,' she said. 'Back the way we came.' Covenant started to protest; but she overrode him. 'Until tomorrow. When the rain starts. I don't care how well they know where we are. They're going to have trouble finding us in the rain.' She was sure of that: she knew from experience that the Sunbane's torrents were as effective as a wall. 'Once the rain starts, we can ride the River right through the middle of them.'

Covenant frowned. His jaws chewed a lump of bitterness. After a moment, he asked, 'Can you do it? Those ur-viles aren't likely to rest at night. We'll have to keep going until dawn. And we'll have to stay right in front of them. So they won't have time to react when we try to get past them.' He faltered out of consideration for her, then forced himself to say, 'You're already having trouble just staying on your feet.'

She gave him a glare of vexation, started to say, What choice have we got? I can do whatever I have to. But a black movement caught the edge of her sight. She turned her head in time to see Vain go striding down the slope to meet the ur-viles.

Covenant snapped the Demondim-spawn's name. Pitchwife started after Vain: the First snatched him back. Sunder scooted to the rim to see what would happen, leaving Hollian with a taut concentration on her face.

Linden ignored them. For the first time, she felt an emotion radiating from Vain's impenetrable form.

It was anger.

The horde reacted as if it could smell his presence even from this range. Perhaps that was how they knew where to find the company. A spatter of barking burst from the ur-viles: they quickened their pace. Their wide mass converged toward him.

At the foot of the slope, he halted. The ur-viles were no great distance from him now. In a few moments, they would reach him. As they moved, their barking resolved into one word:

'*Nekhrimah!*'

The word of command, by which Covenant had once compelled

1103

Vain to save his life. But Foamfollower had said that the Demondim-spawn would not obey it a second time.

For a moment, he remained still, as though he had forgotten motion. His right hand dangled, useless, from his wooden forearm. Nothing else marred his passive perfection: the scraps of his raiment only emphasized how beautifully he had been made.

'Nekhrimah!'

Then he raised his left arm. His fingers curved into claws: his hand made a feral, clutching gesture.

The leading ur-vile was snatched to the ground as if Vain had taken hold of its heart and ripped the organ apart.

Snarling furiously, the horde broke into a run.

Vain did not hurry. His good arm struck a sideward blow through the air: two ur-viles went down with crushed skulls. His fingers knotted and twisted: one of the approaching faces turned to pulp. Another was split open by a punching movement that did not touch his assailant.

Then they were on him, a tide of black, monstrous flesh breaking against his ebon hardness. They seemed to have no interest in the company. Perhaps Vain had always been their target. All of them tried to hurl themselves at him. Even the ur-viles on the far bank of the River surged toward him.

'Now!' breathed the First eagerly. 'Now is our opportunity! While they are thus engaged, we may pass them by.'

Linden swung toward the Giant. The fury she had felt from Vain whipped through her. 'We can do that,' she grated. 'As long as we leave him to die. Those are ur-viles. They know how he was made. As soon as he kills enough of them to get their attention, they're going to remember how to unmake him.' She rose to her feet, knotted her fists at her sides. 'We've got to make him stop.'

Behind her, she felt the violence of Vain's struggle, sensed the blood of ur-viles spurting and flowing. They would never kill him by physical force: he would reduce them one at a time to crushed, raw meat. All that butchery – ! Even the abominable products of the Sunbane did not deserve to be slaughtered. But she knew she was right. Before long, the frenzy of the horde would pass: the ur-viles would begin to think. They had shown that they were still capable of recognition and thought when they had used the word of command. Then Vain would die.

Covenant appeared to accept her assertion. But he responded bitterly, 'You stop him. He doesn't listen to me.'

'Earthfriend!' the First snapped. 'Chosen! Will you remain here and be slain because you can neither redeem nor command this Vain? We must flee!'

That's right. Linden was thinking something different; but it led to the same conclusion. Findail had moved to the ridgecrest: he stood watching the bloody fray with a particular hunger or hope in his eyes. In *Elemesnedene*, the *Elohim* had imprisoned Vain to prevent him from the purpose for which he had been designed. But they had been thwarted because Linden had insisted on leaving the area – and Vain's instinct to follow her or Covenant had proved stronger than his bonds. Now Findail seemed to see before him another means by which the Demondim-spawn could be stopped. And the answer was unchanged: flee so that Vain would follow.

But how? The company could not hope to outrun the ur-viles now.

'Perhaps it may be done,' said Hollian, speaking so quietly that she could barely be heard over the savage din. 'Assuredly it is conceivable. The way of it is plain. Is it not then possible?'

Sunder turned back from the rim to gape at her. Inchoate protests tumbled together in him, fell voiceless.

'Conceivable?' Covenant demanded. 'What're you talking about?'

Hollian's pale face was intense with exaltation or vision. Her meaning was so clear to her that she seemed beyond question.

'Sunder and I have spoken of it. In Crystal Stonedown Sivit na-Mhoram-wist titled me Sun-Sage – and that naming was false. But does not his very fear argue that such work is possible?'

Linden flinched. She had never done anything to earn the epithet the *Elohim* had given her: she feared even to consider its implications. Did Hollian think that she, Linden, could change the Sunbane?

But Sunder strode toward Hollian urgently, then stopped and stood trembling a few steps away. 'No,' he murmured. 'We are mortal, you and I. The attempt would reave us to the marrow. Such power must not be touched.'

She shook her head. 'The need is absolute. Do you wish to lose the lives of the ur-Lord and the Chosen – the hope of the Land – because we dare not hazard our own?' He started to expostulate: suddenly, her voice rose like flame. 'Sunder, I have not been tested! I am unknown to myself. No measure has been taken of that which I may accomplish.' Then she grew gentle again. 'But your strength is known to me. I have no doubt of it. I have given my heart into your hands, and I say to you, it is possible. It may be done.'

From beyond the ridge came harsh screams as Vain ripped and mangled the ur-viles. But the pace of their cries had diminished: he was killing fewer of them. Linden's senses registered a rippling of power in the horde. Some of the clamour had taken on a chanting cadence. The monsters were summoning their lore against the Demondim-spawn.

'Hellfire!' Covenant ejaculated. 'Make sense! We've got to do something!'

Hollian looked toward him. 'I speak of the alteration of the Sunbane.'

Surprise leaped in his face. At once, she went on, 'Not of its power or its ill. But of its course, in the way that the shifting of a stone may alter the course of a river.'

His incomprehension was plain. Patiently, she said, 'The morrow's sun will be a sun of rain. And the pace of the Sunbane increases as its power grows, ever shortening the space of days between the suns. It is my thought that perhaps the morrow's sun may be brought forward, so that its rain will fall upon us now.'

At that, Linden's apprehension jerked into clarity, and she understood Sunder's protest. The strength required would be enormous! And Hollian was pregnant, doubly vulnerable. If the attempt ran out of control, she might rip the life out of more than one heart.

The idea appalled Linden. And yet she could think of no other way to save the company.

Covenant was already speaking. His eyes were gaunt with the helplessness of his alloyed puissance: thoughts of warped black flesh and bloodshed tormented him. 'Try it,' he whispered. 'Please.'

His appeal was directed at Sunder.

For a long moment, the Graveller's eyes went dull, and his stature seemed to shrink. He looked like the man who had faced Linden and Covenant in the prison-hut of Mithil Stonedown and told them that he would be required to kill his own mother. If she had been able to think of any alternative at all – any alternative other than the one which horrified her – Linden would have cried out, You don't have to do this!

But then the passion that Covenant had inspired in Sunder's life came back to him. The muscles at the corners of his jaw bunched whitely, straining for courage. He was the same man who had once lied to Gibbon-Raver under extreme pain and coercion in an effort to protect the Unbeliever. Through his teeth, he gritted, 'We will do it. If it can be done.'

'Praise the Earth!' the First exhaled sharply. Her sword leaped into her hands. 'Be swift. I must do what I may to aid the Demondim-spawn.' Swinging into motion, she passed the rim and vanished in the direction of Vain's struggle.

Almost immediately, a roynish, guttural chorus greeted her. Linden felt the mounting power of the ur-viles fragment as they were thrown into frenzy and confusion by the First's onset.

But Sunder and Hollian had room in their concentration for nothing else. Slowly, woodenly, he placed himself before her. She gave him a smile of secret eagerness, trying to reassure him: he scowled in reply. Fear and determination stretched the skin of his forehead across the bones. He and Hollian did not touch each other. As formally as strangers, they sat down cross-legged, facing each other with their knees aligned.

Covenant came to Linden's side. 'Watch them,' he breathed.

'Watch them hard. If they get into trouble, we've got to stop them. I can't stand — ' He muttered a curse at himself. 'Can't afford to lose them.'

She nodded mutely. The clangour of battle frayed her attention, urged it away from the Stonedownors. Gritting her teeth, she forced herself into focus on Sunder and Hollian. Around her, the edges of the landscape throbbed with the sun's lambence, the hue of blood.

Sunder bowed his head for a moment, then reached into his jerkin and drew out his Sunstone and the wrapped *krill*. The *orcrest* he set down squarely between himself and Hollian. It lay like a hollow space in the dead dirt: its strange translucence revealed nothing.

Hollian produced her *lianar*, placed it across her ankles. A soft invocation began to sough between her lips as she raised her palms to Sunder. She was the eh-Brand: she would have to guide the power to its purpose.

Dread twisted Sunder's visage. His hands shook as he exposed the *krill*, let its light shine into his eyes. Using the cloth to protect his grip from the *krill*'s heat, he directed its tip at Hollian's palms.

Covenant winced as the Graveller drew a cut down the centre of each of her hands.

Blood streaked her wrists. Her face was pale with pain, but she did not flinch. Lowering her arms, she let thick drops fall onto the *orcrest* until all its surface was wet. Then she took up her wand.

Sunder sat before her as if he wanted to scream; but somehow he forced his passion to serve him. With both fists, he gripped the handle of the *krill*, its tip aimed upward in front of his chest. The eh-Brand held her *lianar* likewise, echoing his posture.

The sun was almost directly above them.

Faintly, Linden heard the First cursing, felt an emanation of Giantish pain. Pieces of the ur-viles' power gathered together, became more effective. With a groan like a sob, Pitchwife tore himself from the Stonedownors and ran past the ridge to help his wife.

Sweating under the sun of pestilence, Linden watched as Sunder and the eh-Brand reached *krill* and *lianar* toward each other.

His arms shook slightly: hers were precise. Her knuckles touched his, wand rested against *krill*-gem, along a line between the bloodied *orcrest* and the sun.

And hot force stung through Linden as a vermeil shaft sprang from the Sunstone. It encompassed the hands of the Stonedownors, the blade and the wand, and shot away into the heart of the sun.

Power as savage as lightning: the keen might of the Sunbane. Sunder's lips pulled back from his teeth. Hollian's eyes widened as if the sheer size of what she was attempting suddenly appalled her. But neither she nor the Graveller withdrew.

Covenant's halfhand had taken hold of Linden's arm. Three

points of pain dug into her flesh. On the Sandwall, for entirely different reasons, Cail had gripped her in that same way. She thought she could hear the First's sword hacking against distorted limbs, hideous torsos. Vain's anger did not relent. The strain of Pitchwife's breathing came clearly through the blood-fury of the urviles.

Their lore grew sharper.

But the scalding shaft of Sunbane-force had a white core. Argent blazed within the beam, reaching like the will of the stonedownors to pierce the sun. It came from the gem of the *krill* and the clenched strength of Sunder's determination.

It pulled him so far out of himself that Linden feared he was already lost.

She started forward, wildly intending to hurl herself upon him, call him back. But then the eh-Brand put forth her purpose; and Linden froze in astonishment.

In the heart of the gem appeared a frail, blue glimmer.

Sensations of power howled silently against Linden's nerves, scaled upward out of comprehension, as the blue gleam steadied, became stronger. Flickers of it bled into the beam and flashed toward the sun; still it became stronger, fed by the eh-Brand's resolve. At first, it appeared molten and limited, torn from itself drop after drop by a force more compelling than gravity. But Hollian renewed it faster than it bled. Soon it was running up the beam in bursts so rapid that the shaft seemed to flicker.

Yet the aura around the sun showed no sign of alteration.

The Stonedownors chanted desperately, driving their exertion higher; but their voices made no sound: the incandescent beam absorbed their invocations directly into itself. Soundless force screamed across Linden's hearing. Something inside her gibbered, Stop them, stop, they'll kill themselves, *stop!* But she could not. She could not tell the difference between their agony and the wailing in her mind.

The *krill*'s jewel shone blue. Constant azure filled the core of the shaft, hurled itself upward. Still the aura around the sun did not change.

The next instant, the power became too great.

The *lianar* caught fire: it burst in Hollian's hands, shedding a bright vehemence that nearly blinded Linden. The wood flared to cinders, burned the eh-Brand's palms to the bone. A cry ripped through her. The shaft wavered, faltered.

But she did not fall back. Leaning into the power, she closed her naked hands around the blade of the *krill*.

At her touch, the shaft erupted, shattering the Sunstone, shattering the heavens. The ground wrenched itself aside in a convulsion

1108

of pain, sent Linden and Covenant sprawling. She landed on him while the hills reeled. The air was driven from his lungs. She rolled off him, fought to get her feet under her. The earth quivered like outraged flesh.

Another concussion seemed to wipe everything else out of the world. It rent the sky as if the sun had exploded. She fell again, writhed on the heaving dirt. Before her face, the dust danced like shocked water, leaving fine whorls in the wake of the blast. The light faded as if the fist of the heavens had begun to close.

When she raised her head, she saw tremendous thunderheads teeming toward her from all the horizons, rushing to seal themselves over the sun's blue corona.

For an instant, she could not think, had forgotten how to move. There was no sound at all except the on-coming passion of the rain. Perhaps the battle beyond the ridge was over. But then awareness recoiled through her like a thunderclap. Surging in panic to her hands and knees, she flung her percipience toward the Stonedownors.

Sunder sat as though the detonation of earth and sky had not touched him. His head was bowed. The *krill* lay on the ground in front of him, its handle still partially covered. The fringes of the cloth were charred. His breathing was shallow, almost indiscernible. In his chest, his heart limped like a mauled thing from beat to beat. To Linden's first alarm, his life looked like the fading smoke of a snuffed wick. Then her health-sense reached deeper, and she saw that he would live.

But Hollian lay twisted on her back, her cut and heat-mangled palms open to the mounting dark. Her black hair framed the pale vulnerability of her face, pillowed her head like the cupped hand of death. Between her lost lips trickled a delicate trail of blood.

Scrambling wildly across the dirt, Linden dove for the eh-Brand, plunged her touch into Hollian and tried to call back her spirit before it fled altogether. But it was going fast: Linden could not hold it. Hollian had been damaged too severely. Linden's fingers clutched at the slack shoulders, tried to shake breath back into the lungs; but there was nothing she could do. Her hands were useless. She was just an ordinary woman, incapable of miracles – able to see nothing clearly except the extent of her failure.

As she watched, the life ran out of the eh-Brand. The red rivulet from her mouth slowed and stopped.

Power: Linden had to have power. But grief closed her off from everything. She could not reach the sun. The Earth was desecrated and dying. And Covenant had changed. At times in the past, she had tapped wild magic from him without his volition; but that was no longer possible. He was a new being, an alloy of fire and person:

his might was inaccessible without possession. And if she had been capable of doing that to him, it would have taken time – time which Hollian had already lost.

The eh-Brand looked pitifully small in death, valiant and fragile beyond endurance. And her son also, gone without so much as a single chance at life. Linden stared blindly at the failure of her hands. The *krill*-gem glared into her face.

From all directions at once, the rain ran forward, hissing like flame across the dirt.

Drops of water splashed around her as Covenant took hold of her, yanked her toward him. Unwillingly, she felt the feral thrust of his pain. 'I told you to watch!' he raged, yelling at her because he had asked the Stonedownors to take this risk in spite of his inability to protect them from the consequences. 'I told you to *watch*!'

Through the approaching clamour of the rain, she heard Sunder groan.

He took an unsteady breath, raised his head. His eyes were glazed, unseeing, empty of mind. For an instant, she thought he was lost as well. But then his hands opened, stretching the cramps from his fingers and forearms, and he blinked several times. His eyes focused on the *krill*. He reached out to it stiffly, wrapped it back in its cloth, tucked it away under his jerkin.

Then the drizzle caught his attention. He looked toward Hollian.

At once, he lurched to his feet. Fighting the knots in his muscles, the ravages of power, he started toward her.

Linden shoved herself in front of him. 'Sunder!' she tried to say. 'It's my fault. I'm so sorry.' From the beginning, failure had dogged her steps as if it could never be redeemed.

He did not heed her. With one arm, he swept her out of his way so forcefully that she stumbled. A blood-ridden intensity glared from his orbs. He had lost one wife and son before he had met Linden and Covenant. Now they had cost him another. He bent over Hollian for a moment as if he feared to touch her: his arms hugged the anguish in his chest. Then, fiercely, he stooped to her and rose again, lifting her out of the new mud, cradling her like a child. His howl rang through the rain, transforming the downpour to grief:

'*Hollian!*'

Abruptly, the First hove out of the thickening dark with Pitchwife behind her. She was panting hugely: blood squeezed from the wide wound in her side where the lore of the ur-viles had burned her. Pitchwife's face was aghast at the things he had done.

Neither of them seemed to see Hollian. 'Come!' called the First. 'We must make our way now! Vain yet withholds the ur-viles from us. If we flee, we may hope that he will follow and be saved!'

No one moved. The rain belaboured Linden's head and shoulders. Covenant had covered his face with his hands: he stood immobile in the storm as though he could no longer bear the cost of what he had become. Sunder breathed in great, raw hunks of hurt, but did not weep. He remained hunched over Hollian, concentrating on her as if the sheer strength of his desire might bring her back.

The First gave a snarl of exasperation. Still she appeared unaware of what had happened. Aggravated by her injury, she brooked no refusal. 'Come, I say!' Roughly, she took hold of Covenant and Linden, dragged them toward the watercourse.

Pitchwife followed, tugging Sunder.

They scrambled down into the riverbed. The water racing there frothed against the thick limbs of the Giants. Linden could hardly keep her feet. She clung to the First. Soon the River rose high enough to carry the company away.

Rain hammered at them as if it were outraged by its untimely birth. The riverbanks were invisible. Linden saw no sign of the ur-viles or Vain. She did not know whether she and her friends had escaped.

But the lightning that tore the heavens gave her sudden glimpses around her. One of them revealed Sunder. He swam ahead of Pitchwife. The Giant braced him with one hand from behind.

He still bore Hollian in his arms. Carefully, he kept her head above water as if she were alive.

At intervals through the loud rain and the thunder, Linden heard him keening.

14

THE LAST BOURNE

At first, the water was so muddy that it sickened Linden. Every involuntary mouthful left sand in her throat, grit on her teeth. Rain and thunder fragmented her hearing. At one moment, she felt totally deaf: the next, sound went through her like a slap. Dragged down by her clothes and heavy shoes, she would have been exhausted in a short time without the First's support. The Swordmain's wound was a throbbing pain that reached Linden in spite of the chaos of water, the exertion of swimming. Yet the Giant bore both Covenant and the Chosen through the turmoil.

But as the water rose it became clearer, less conflicted – and colder. Linden had forgotten how cold a fast river could be with no sunlight on it anywhere. The chill leeched into her, sucking at her bones: it whispered to her sore nerves that she would be warmer if she lowered herself beneath the surface, out of the air and the battering rain. Only for a moment, it suggested kindly. Until you feel warmer. You've already failed. It doesn't matter anymore. You deserve to feel warmer.

She knew what she deserved. But she ignored the seduction, clung instead to the First – concentrated on the hurt in the Giant's side. The cleaner water washed most of the sand and blood from the burn; and the First was hardy: Linden was not worried about infection. Yet she poured her percipience toward that wound, put herself into it until her own side wailed as if she had been gored. Then, deliberately, she numbed the sensation, reducing the First's pain to a dull ache.

The cold frayed her senses, sapped her courage. Lightning and thunder blared above her, and she was too small to endure them. Rain flailed the face of the River. But she clinched herself to her chosen use and did not let go while the current bore the company hurtling down the length of the long afternoon.

At last the day ended. The torrents thinned: the clouds rolled back. Legs scissoring, the First laboured across to the west bank, then struggled out of the water and stood trembling on the sodden ground. In a moment, Pitchwife joined her. Linden seemed to feel his bones rattling in an ague of weariness.

Covenant looked as pale as a weathered tombstone, his lips blue with cold, gall heavy on his features. 'We need a fire,' he said as if that, too, were his fault.

Sunder walked up the wet slope without a glance at his companions. He was hunched over Hollian as though his chest were full of broken glass. Beyond the reach of the River, he stumbled to his knees, lowered Hollian gently to the ground. He settled her limbs to make her comfortable. His blunt fingers caressed the black strands of hair from her face, tenderly combed her tresses out around her head. Then he seated himself beside her and wrapped his arms over his heart, huddling there as if his sanity had snapped.

Pitchwife unshouldered his pack, took out a Giantish firepot which had somehow remained sealed against the water. Next he produced a few faggots from his scant supply of firewood. They were soaked, and he was exhausted; but he bent over them and blew raggedly until they took flame from the firepot. Nursing the blaze, he made it hot enough to sustain itself. Though it was small and pitiable, it gave enough heat to soften the chill in Linden's joints, the gaunt misery in Covenant's eyes.

Then Pitchwife offered them *diamondraught*. But they refused it until he and the First had each swallowed a quantity of the potent liquor: because of his cramped lungs and her injury, the Giants were in sore need of sustenance. After that, however, Linden took a few

1112

sips which ran true warmth at last into her stomach.

Bitterly, as if he were punishing himself, Covenant accepted the pouch of *diamondraught* from her; but he did not drink. Instead, he forced his stiff muscles and brittle bones toward Sunder.

His offer produced no reaction from the Graveller. In a burned and gutted voice, Covenant urged, pleaded: Sunder did not raise his head. He remained focused on Hollian as if his world had shrunk to that frail compass and his companions no longer impinged upon him. After a while, Covenant shambled back to the fire, sat down, and covered his face with his hands.

A moment later, Vain appeared.

He emerged from the night into the campfire's small illumination and resumed at once his familiar blank stance. An ambiguous smile curved his mouth. The passion Linden had felt from him was gone: he appeared as insentient and unreachable as ever. His wooden forearm had been darkened and charred, but the damage was only superficial.

His left arm was withered and useless, like a congenital deformity. Pain oozed from several deep sores. Mottled streaks the colour of ash marred his ebony flesh.

Instinctively, Linden started toward him, though she knew that she could not help him, that his wounds were as imponderable as his essential nature. She sensed that he had attacked the ur-viles for his own reasons, not to aid or even acknowledge the company; yet she felt viscerally that the wrong his sculptured perfection had suffered was intolerable. Once he had bowed to her. And more than once he had saved her life. Someone had to at least try to help him.

But before she reached him, a wide, winged shape came out of the stars like the plunge of a condor. Changing shapes as it descended, it landed lightly beside the Demondim-spawn in human form.

Findail.

He did not look at Covenant or Linden, ignored Sunder's hunched and single-minded grief. Instead, he addressed Vain for the first time since the Appointed had joined the company.

'Do not believe that you will win my heart with bravery.' His voice was congested with old dismay, covert and unmistakable fear. His eyes seemed to search the Demondim-spawn's inscrutable soul. 'I desire your death. If it lay within the permit of my Würd, I would slay you. But these comrades for whom you care nothing have again contrived to redeem you.' He paused as if he were groping for courage, then concluded softly, 'Though I abhor your purpose, the Earth must not suffer the cost of your pain.'

Suddenly lambent, his right hand reached out to Vain's left shoulder. An instant of fire blazed from the touch, cast startling implications which only Linden could hear into the fathomless night. Then it was gone. Findail left Vain, went to stand like a sentinel confronting the moonlit prospect of the east.

The First breathed a soft oath of surprise. Pitchwife gaped in wonder. Covenant murmured curses as if he could not believe what he had seen.

Vain's left arm was whole, completely restored to its original beauty and function.

Linden thought she caught a gleam of relief from the Demondim-spawn's black eyes.

Astonishment stunned her. Findail's demonstration gave her a reason to understand for the first time why the *Elohim* believed that the healing of the Earth should be left to them, that the best choice she or Covenant could make would be to give Findail the ring and simply step aside from the doom Lord Foul was preparing for them. The restoration of Vain's arm seemed almost miraculous to her. With all the medical resources she could imagine, she would not have been able to match Findail's feat.

Drawn by the power he represented, she turned toward him with Sunder's name on her lips. Help him. He doesn't know how to bear it.

But the silhouette of the Appointed against the moon refused her before she spoke. In some unexplained way, he had aggravated his own plight by healing Vain. Like Sunder, he was in need of solace. His stance told her that he would deny any other appeal.

Pitchwife sighed. Muttering aimlessly to himself, he began to prepare a meal while the fire lasted.

Later that night, Linden huddled near Covenant and the fading embers of the fire with a damp blanket hugged around her in an effort to ward off the sky-deep cold and tried to explain her failure. 'It was too sudden. I didn't see the danger in time.'

'It wasn't your fault,' he replied gruffly. 'I had no right to blame you.' His voice seemed to issue from an injury hidden within the clenched mound of his blanket – hidden and fatal. 'I should've made them stay in Revelstone.'

She wanted to protest his arrogation of responsibility. Without them, we'd all be dead. How else were we going to get away from those ur-viles? But he went on, 'I used to be afraid of power. I thought it made me what I hate – another Landwaster. A source of Despite for the people I care about. But I don't need power. I can do the same thing by just standing there.'

She sat up and peered at him through the moon-edged night. He lay with his back to her, the blanket shivering slightly on his shoulders. She ached to put her arms around him, find some safe warmth in the contact of their bodies. But that was not what he needed. Softly, harshly, she said, 'That's wonderful. You're to blame for everything. Next I suppose you're going to tell me you bit yourself with that venom, just to prove you deserve it.'

He jerked over onto his back as if she had hit him between the shoulder-blades: his face came, pale and wincing, out of the blanket. For a moment, he appeared to glare at her. But then his emanations lost their fierce edge. 'I know,' he breathed to the wide sky. 'Atiaran tried to tell me the same thing. After all I did to her.' Quietly, he quoted, '"Castigation is a doom which achieves itself. In punishing yourself, you come to merit punishment." All Foul has to do is laugh.' His dark features concentrated toward her. 'The same thing's true for you. You tried to save her. It wasn't your fault.'

Linden nodded. Mutely, she leaned toward him until he took her into his embrace.

When she awoke in the early grey of dawn, she looked toward Sunder and saw that he had not moved during the night.

Hollian was rigid with death now, her delicate face pallid and aggrieved in the gloom; but he appeared unaware of any change, uncognizant of night or day – numb to anything except the shards of pain in his chest and her supine form. He was chilled to the bone, but the cold had no power to make him shiver.

Covenant roused with a flinch, yanked himself roughly out of his dreams. For no apparent reason, he said distinctly, 'Those ur-viles should've caught up with us by now.' Then he, too, saw Sunder. Softly, he groaned.

The First and Pitchwife were both awake. Her injury was still sore; but *diamondraught* had quickened her native toughness, and the damage was no longer serious. She glanced at the Graveller, then faced Covenant and Linden and shook her head. Her training had not prepared her to deal with Sunder's stricken condition.

Her husband levered himself off the ground with his elbows and crawled toward the sacks of supplies. Taking up a pouch of *diamondraught*, he forced his cramped muscles to lift him upright, carry him to the Graveller's side. Without a word, he opened the pouch and held it under Sunder's nose.

Its scent drew a sound like a muffled sob from the Stonedownor. But he did not raise his head.

Helpless with pity, Pitchwife withdrew.

No one spoke. Linden, Covenant, and the Giants ate a cheerless meal before the sun rose: then the First and Pitchwife went to find stone on which to meet the day. In shared apprehension, Linden and Covenant started toward Sunder. But, by chance or design, he had seated himself upon an exposed face of rock: he needed no protection.

Gleaming azure, the sun crested the horizon, then disappeared as black clouds began to host westward.

Spasms of wind kicked across the gravid surface of the White River. Pitchwife hastened to secure the supplies. By the time he was finished, the first drizzle had begun to fall. It mounted toward downpour with a sound like frying meat.

Linden eyed the quick current of the White and shuddered. Its cold ran past her senses like the edge of a rasp. But she had already survived similar immersions without *diamondraught* or *metheglin* to sustain her. She was determined to endure as long as necessary. Grimly, she turned back to the problem of Sunder.

He had risen to his feet. Head bowed, eyes focused on nothing, he faced his companions and the River.

He held Hollian upright in his arms, hugging her to his sore breast so that her soles did not touch the ground.

Covenant met Linden's gaze: then he moved to stand in front of Sunder. The muscles of his shoulders bunched and throttled; but his voice was gentle, husky with rue. 'Sunder,' he said, 'put her down.' His hands clenched at his sides. 'You'll drown yourself if you try to take her with you. I can't lose you too.' In the background of his words blew a wind of grief like the rising of the rain. 'We'll help you bury her.'

Sunder gave no response, did not look at Covenant. He appeared to be waiting for the Unbeliever to get out of his way.

Covenant's tone hardened. 'Don't make us take her away from you.'

In reply, Sunder lowered Hollian's feet to the ground. Linden felt no shift in his emanations, no warning. With his right hand, he drew the *krill* from his jerkin.

The covering of the blade fell away, flapped out of reach along the wind. He gripped the hot handle in his bare fingers. Pain crossed his face like a snarl, but he did not flinch. White light shone from the gem, as clear as a threat.

Lifting Hollian with his left arm, he started down toward the River.

Covenant let him pass. Linden and the Giants let him pass. Then the First sent Pitchwife after him, so that he would not be alone in the swift, cold hazard of the current.

'He's going to Andelain,' Covenant grated. 'He's going to carry her all the way to Andelain. Who do you think he wants to find?'

Without waiting for an answer, he followed Pitchwife and the Graveller.

Linden stared after them and groaned, His Dead! The Dead in Andelain. Nassic his father. Kalina his mother. The wife and son he had shed in the name of Mithil Stonedown.

Or Hollian herself?

Sweet Christ! How will he stand it? He'll go mad and never come back.

Diving into the current, Linden went downriver in a wild rush with the First swimming strongly at her side.

She was not prepared for the acute power of the cold. As her health-sense grew in range and discernment, it made her more and more vulnerable to what she felt. The days she had spent in the Mithil River with Covenant and Sunder had not been this bad. The chill cudgelled her flesh, pounded her raw nerves. Time and again, she believed that surely *now* she would begin to wail, that at last the Sunbane would master her. Yet the undaunted muscle of the First's shoulder supported her. And Covenant stayed with her. Through the bludgeoning rain, the thunder that shattered the air, the lightning that ripped the heavens, his stubborn sense of purpose remained within reach of her percipience. In spite of numbing misery and desperation, she wanted to live – wanted to survive every ill Lord Foul hurled against her. Until her chance came to put a stop to it.

Visible by lightning-burst, Pitchwife rode the River a stroke or two ahead of the First. With one hand, he held up the Graveller. And Sunder bore Hollian as if she were merely sleeping.

Sometime during the middle of the day, the White dashed frothing and tumbling into a confluence that tore the travellers down the new channel like dead leaves in the wind. Joined by the Grey, the White River had become the Soulsease; and for the rest of the day – and all the next – it carried the company along. The rains blinded Linden's sense of direction. But at night, when the skies were clear and the waning moon rose over the pummelled wasteland, she was able to see that the River's course had turned toward the east.

The second evening after the confluence, the First asked Covenant when they would reach Andelain. He and Linden sat as close as possible to the small heat of their campfire; and Pitchwife and the First crouched there also as if even they needed something more than *diamondraught* to restore their courage. But Sunder remained a short distance away in the same posture he had assumed the two previous nights – hunched over his pain on the sheetrock of the campsite with Hollian outstretched rigidly in front of him as though at any moment she might begin to breathe again.

Side by side, Vain and Findail stood at the fringes of the light. Linden had not seen them enter the River, did not know how they travelled the rain-scoured waste. But each evening they appeared together shortly after sunset and waited without speaking for the night to pass.

Covenant mused into the flames for a moment, then replied, 'I'm a bad judge of distances. I don't know how far we've come.' His face appeared waxen with the consequences of cold. 'But this is the Soulsease. It goes almost straight to Mount Thunder from here. We ought – ' He extended his hands toward the fire, put them too close to the flames, as if he had forgotten the reason for their numbness. But then his leper's instincts caused him to draw back. 'It depends on the sun. It's due to change. Unless we get a desert sun, the River'll keep running. We ought to reach Andelain sometime tomorrow.'

The First nodded and went back to her private thoughts. Behind her Giantish strength and the healing of her injury, she was deeply tired. After a moment, she drew her longsword, began to clean and dry it with the slow, methodical movements of a woman who did not know what else to do.

As if to emulate her, Pitchwife took his flute from his pack, shook the water out of it, and tried to play. But his hands or his lips were too weary to hold any music. Soon he gave up the attempt.

For a while, Linden thought about the sun and let herself feel a touch of relief. A fertile sun or a sun of pestilence would warm the water. They would allow her to see the sky, open up the world around her. And a desert sun would certainly not be cold.

But gradually she became aware that Covenant was still shivering. A quick glance showed her he was not ill. After his passage through the Banefire, she doubted that he would ever be ill again. But he was clenched around himself, knotted so tightly that he seemed feverish.

She put her hand over his right forearm, drew his attention toward her. With her eyes, she asked what troubled him.

He looked at her gauntly, then returned his gaze to the fire as if among the coals he might find the words he needed. When he spoke, he surprised her by inquiring, 'Are you sure you want to go to Andelain? The last time you had the chance, you turned it down.'

That was true. Poised at the south-west verge of the Hills with Sunder and Hollian, she had refused to go with Covenant, even though the radiance of health from across the Mithil River had been vivid to her bruised nerves. She had feared the sheer power of that region. Some of her fear she had learned from Hollian's dread, Hollian's belief that Andelain was a place where people lost their minds. But most of it had arisen from an encompassing distrust of everything to which her percipience made her vulnerable. The Sunbane had bored into her like a sickness, as acute and anguished as any disease; but as a disease she had understood it. And it had suited her: it had been appropriate to the structure of her life. But for that very reason Andelain had threatened her more intimately. It had endangered her difficult self-possession. She had not believed that any good could come of anything which had such strength over her.

And later Covenant had relayed to her the words of Elena among the Dead. The former High Lord had said, *I rue that the woman your companion lacked heart to accompany you, for you have much to bear. But she must come to meet herself in her own time. Care for her, beloved, so that in the end she may heal us all.* In addition, the Forestal had said, *It is well that your companions did not accompany you. The woman of your world would raise grim shades here.* The simple recollection of such things brought back Linden's fear.

A fear which had made its meaning clear in lust and darkness when Gibbon-Raver had touched her and affirmed that she was evil.

But she was another woman now. She had found the curative use of her health-sense, the access to beauty. She had told Covenant the stories of her parents, drawn some of their sting from her heart. She had learned to call her hunger for power by its true name. And she knew what she wanted. Covenant's love. And the end of the Sunbane.

Smiling grimly, she replied, 'Try to stop me.'

She expected her answer to relieve him. But he only nodded, and she saw that he still had not said what was in him. Several false starts passed like shadows across the background of his expression. In an effort to reach him, she added, 'I need the relief. The sooner I get out of the Sunbane, the saner I'll be.'

'Linden – ' He said her name as if she were not making his way easier. 'When we were in Mithil Stonedown – and Sunder told us he might have to kill his mother – ' He swallowed roughly. 'You said he should be allowed to put her out of her misery. If that was what he wanted.' He looked at her now with the death of her mother written plainly in his gaze. 'Do you still believe that?'

She winced involuntarily. She would have preferred to put his question aside until she knew why he asked it. But his frank need was insistent. Carefully, she said, 'She was in terrible pain. I think people who're suffering like that have the right to die. But mercy killing isn't exactly merciful to the people who have to do it. I don't like what it does to them.' She strove to sound detached, impersonal; but the hurt of the question was too acute. 'I don't like what it did to me. If you can call what I did mercy instead of murder.'

He made a gesture that faltered and fell like a failed assuagement. His voice was soft; but it betrayed a strange ague. 'What're you going to do if something's happened to Andelain? If you can't get out of the Sunbane? Caer-Caveral knew he wasn't going to last. Foul's corrupted everything else. What'll we do?' His larynx jerked up and down like a presage of panic. 'I can stand whatever I have to. But not that. Not that.'

He looked so belorn and defenceless that she could not bear it. Tears welled in her eyes. 'Maybe it'll be all right,' she breathed. 'You can hope. It's held out this long. It can last a little longer.'

But down in the cold, dark roots of her mind she was thinking, *If it doesn't, I don't care what happens. I'll tear that bastard's heart* out. I'll get the power somewhere, and I'll tear his heart out.

She kept her thoughts to herself. Yet Covenant seemed to sense the violence inside her. Instead of reaching out to her for comfort, he withdrew into his certainty. Wrapped in decisions and perceptions she did not understand and could not share, he remained apart from her throughout the night.

A long time passed before she grasped that he did not mean to reject her. He was trying to prepare himself for the day ahead.

But the truth was plain in the sharp, grey dawn, when he rolled, bleak and tense, out of his blankets to kiss her. He was standing on an inner precipice, and his balance was fragile. The part of him which had been fused in the Banefire did not waver; but the vessel bearing that sure alloy looked as brittle as an old bone. Yet in spite of his trepidation he made the effort to smile at her.

She replied with a grimace because she did not know how to protect him.

While Pitchwife prepared a meal for the company, Covenant went over to Sunder. Kneeling behind the Graveller, he massaged Sunder's locked shoulders and neck with his numb fingers.

Sunder did not react to the gesture. He was aware of nothing except Hollian's pallid form and his own fixed purpose. To Linden's health-sense, his body ached with the weakness of inanition. And she felt the hot blade of the *krill* scalding his unshielded belly under his jerkin. But he seemed to draw strength from that pain as if it were the promise that kept him alive.

After a while, Covenant rejoined the two Giants and Linden. 'Maybe he'll meet her in Andelain,' he sighed. 'Maybe she'll be able to get through to him.'

'Let us pray for that outcome,' muttered the First. 'His endurance must fail soon.'

Covenant nodded. As he chewed bread and dried fruit for breakfast, he went on nodding to himself like a man who had no other hope.

A short time later, the sun rose beyond the rim of the world; and the companions stood on the rain-swept sheetrock to meet the daybreak.

It crested the horizon in a flaring of emerald, cast green spangles up the swift, broken surface of the River.

At the sight, Linden went momentarily weak with relief. She had not realized how much she had feared another sun of rain.

Warmth: the fertile sun gave warmth. It eased the vehemence of the current, softened the chill of the water. And it shone on her nerves like the solace of dry, fire-warmed blankets. Supported by the First, with Covenant beside her and Pitchwife and Sunder only a few short strokes away, she rode the Soulsease and thought for

1120

the first time that perhaps the River had not been gratuitously named.

Yet relief did not blind her to what was happening to the earth on either side of the watercourse. The kindness of the fertile sun was an illusion, a trick performed by the River's protection. On the banks, vegetation squirmed out of the ground like a ghoul-ridden host. Flailed up from their roots, vines and grasses sprawled over the rims of the channel. Shrubs raised their branches as if they were on fire; trees clawed their way into the air, as frantic as the damned. And she found that her own relative safety only accentuated the sensations pouring at her from the wild, unwilling growth. She was floating through a wilderness of voiceless anguish: the torment around her was as loud as shrieks. Tortured out of all Law, the trees and plants had no defence, could do nothing for themselves except grow and grow – and hurl their dumb hurt into the sky.

Perhaps after all the Forestal of Andelain was gone. How long could he bear to hear these cries and be helpless?

Between rising walls of agony, the River ran on toward the east and Mount Thunder after a long southeastward stretch. Slowly, Linden fell into a strange, bifurcated musing. She held to the First's shoulder, kept her head above water, watched the riverbanks pass, the verdure teem. But on another level she was not aware of such things. Within her, the darkness which had germinated at Gibbon's touch also grew: fed by the Sunbane, it twined through her and yearned. She remembered now as if she had never forgotten that behind the superficial grief and pain and abhorrence had lurked a secret glee at the act of strangling her mother – a wild joy at the taste of power.

In a detached way, she knew what was happening to her. She had been too long exposed to Lord Foul's corruption. Her command over herself, her sense of who she wanted to be, was fraying.

She giggled harshly to herself – a snapping of mirth like the sound of a Raver. The idea was bitterly amusing. Until now it had been the sheer difficulty and pain of travelling under the Sunbane which had enabled her to remember who she was. The Despiser could have mastered her long ago by simply allowing her to relax.

Fierce humour rose in her throat. Fertility seemed to caper along her blood, frothing and chuckling luridly. Her percipience sent out sneaky fingers to touch Covenant's latent fire as if at any moment she would muster the courage to take hold of it for herself.

With an effort of will, she pulled at the First's shoulder. The Giant turned her head, murmured over the wet mutter of the River, 'Chosen?'

So that Covenant would not hear her, Linden whispered, 'If I start to laugh, hit me. Hold me under until I stop.'

1121

The First returned a glance of piercing incomprehension. Then she nodded.

Somehow, Linden locked her teeth against the madness and did not let it out.

Noon rose above her and passed by. From the truncated perspective of the water-line, she could see only a short distance ahead. The Soulsease appeared to have no future. The world contained nothing except tortured vegetation and despair. She should have been able to heal that. She was a doctor. But she could not. She had no power.

But then without transition the terrain toward which the company was borne changed. Beyond an interdict as precise as a line drawn in the Earth, the wild fertility ended; and a natural woodland began on both sides of the Soulsease.

The shock of it against her senses told her what it was. She had seen it once before, when she had not been ready for it. It rushed into her even from this distance like a distillation of all *vitrim* and *diamondraught*, a cure for all darkness.

The First nudged Covenant, nodded ahead. Thrashing his legs, he surged up in the water; and his crow split the air:

'Andelain!'

As he fell back, he pounded at the current like a boy, sent sunglistered streams of spray arcing across the Soulsease.

In silence, Linden breathed, Andelain, Andelain, as if by repeating that name she might cleanse herself enough to enter among the Hills. Hope washed through her in spite of everything she had to fear. *Andelain.*

Brisk between its banks, the River ran swiftly toward the Forestal's demesne, the last bastion of Law.

As they neared the demarcation, Linden saw it more acutely. Here thronging, tormented brush and bracken, mimosas cracked by their own weight, junipers as grotesque as the dancing of demons, all stopped as if they had met a wall: there a greensward as lush as springtime and punctuated with peonies like music swept up the graceful hillslopes to the stately poplars and red-fruited elders that crowned the crests. At the boundary of the Forestal's reign, mute hurt gave way to *aliantha*, and the Sunbane was gone from the pristine sky.

Gratitude and gladness and relief made the world new around her as the Soulsease carried the company out of the Land's brokenness into Andelain.

When she looked behind her, she could no longer see the Sunbane's green aura. The sun shone out of the cerulean heavens with the yellow warmth of loveliness.

Covenant indicated the south bank: the First and Pitchwife turned in that direction, angling across the current. Covenant swam with all his strength; and Linden followed. The water had already changed from ordinary free-flowing cleanness to crystal purity, as special and renewing as dew. And when she placed her hands on the grass-rich ground to boost herself out of the River, she received a new thrill, a sensation of vibrancy as keen as the clear air. She had been exposed to the Sunbane for so long that she had forgotten what the Earth's health felt like.

But then she stood on the turf with all her nerves open and realized that what she felt was more than simple health. It was Law quintessenced and personified, a reification of the vitality which made life precious and the Land desirable. It was an avatar of spring, the revel of summer: it was autumn glory and winter peace. The grass under her feet sprang and gleamed, seemed to lift her to a taller stature. The sap in the trees rose like fire, beneficent and alive. Flowers scattered colour everywhere. Every breath and scent and sensation was sapid beyond bearing – and yet they urged her to bear them. Each new exquisite perception led her onward instead of daunting her, carried her out of herself like a current of ecstasy.

Laughter and weeping rose in her together and could not be uttered. This was Andelain, the heart of the Land Covenant loved. He lay on his face in the grass, arms outspread as if to hug the ground; and she knew that the Hills had changed everything. Not in him, but in her. There were many things she did not understand; but this she did: the bale of the Sunbane had no power here. She was free of it here. And the Law which brought such health to life was worth the price any heart was willing to pay.

That affirmation came to her like a clean sunrise. It was the positive conviction for which she had been so much in need. Any price. To preserve the last beauty of the Land. Any price at all.

Pitchwife sat on the grass and stared hungrily up the hillsides, his face wide with astonishment. 'I would not have credited – ' he breathed to himself. 'Not have believed – ' The First stood behind him, her fingertips resting on his shoulders. Her eyes beamed like the sun-flashes dancing on the gay surface of the Soulsease. Vain and Findail had appeared while Linden's back had been turned. The Demondim-spawn betrayed no reaction to Andelain; but Findail's habitual distress had lightened, and he took the crisp air deep into his lungs as if, like Linden, he knew what it meant.

Free of the Sunbane and exalted, she wanted to run – wanted to stretch and bound up the Hills and tumble down them, sport like a child, see everything, taste everything, race her bruised nerves and tired bones as far as they would go into the luxuriant anodyne of this region, the sovereign solace of Andelain's health. She skipped a few steps away from the River, turned to call Covenant after her.

He had risen to his feet, but was not looking at her. And there was no joy in his face.

His attention was fixed on Sunder.

Sunder! Linden groaned, instantly ashamed that she had forgotten him in her personal transport.

He stood on the bank and hugged Hollian upright against his chest, seeing nothing, comprehending no part of the beauty around him. For a time, he did not move. Then some kind of focus came into his eyes, and he stumbled forward. Too weak now to entirely lift the eh-Brand's death-heavy form, he half dragged her awkwardly in front of him across the grass.

Ashen with hunger and exhaustion and loss, he bore her to the nearest *aliantha*. There he laid her down. Under its hollylike leaves, the bush was thick with viridian treasure-berries. The Clave had proclaimed them poison; but after Marid had bitten Covenant, *aliantha* had brought the Unbeliever back from delirium. And that experience had not been lost on Sunder. He picked some of the fruit.

Linden held her breath, hoping he would eat.

He did not. Squatting beside Hollian, he tried to feed the berries between her rigid lips.

'Eat, love.' His voice was hoarse, veined and cracked like crumbling marble. 'You have not eaten. You must eat.'

But the fruit only broke on her teeth.

Slowly, he hunched over the pain of his fractured heart and began to cry.

Pain twisted Covenant's face like a snarl as he moved to the Graveller's side. But when he said, 'Come on,' his voice was gentle. 'We're still too close to the Sunbane. We need to go farther in.'

For a long moment, Sunder shook with silent grief as if at last his mad will had failed. But then he scooped his arms under Hollian and lurched, trembling, to his feet. Tears streamed down his grey cheeks, but he paid them no heed.

Covenant gestured to the Giants and Linden. They joined him promptly. Together, they turned to the south-east and started away from the River across the first hillsides.

Sunder followed them, walking like a mute wail of woe.

His need conflicted with Linden's reactions to the rich atmosphere of Andelain. As she and her friends moved among the Hills, sunshine lay like immanence on the slopes: balm filled the shade of the trees. With Covenant and the Giants, she ate *aliantha* from the bushes along their way; and the savour of the berries seemed to add a rare spice to her blood. The grass gave a blessing back to the pressure of her shoes, lifting her from stride to stride as if the very ground sought to encourage her forward. And beneath the turf, the soil and skeleton of Andelain were resonant with well-being, the good slumber of peace.

And birds, soaring like melody above the treetops, squabbling amicably among the branches. And small woodland animals, cautious of the company's intrusion, but not afraid. And flowers everywhere, flowers without number – poppy, amaryllis, and lark-spur – snapdragon, honeysuckle, and violet – as precise and numinous as poetry. Seeing them, Linden thought that surely her heart would burst with pleasure.

Yet behind her Sunder bore his lost love inward as if he meant to lay her at the feet of Andelain itself and demand restitution. Carrying death into the arduously defended region, he violated its ambience as starkly as an act of murder.

Though Linden's companions had no health-sense, they shared her feelings. Covenant's visage worked unselfconsciously back and forth between leaping eagerness and clenched distress. Pitchwife's eyes devoured each new vista, every added benison – and flicked repeatedly toward Sunder as if he were flinching. The First held an expression of stern acceptance and approval on her countenance; but her hand closed and unclosed around the handle of her sword. Only Vain and the Appointed cared nothing for Sunder.

Nevertheless the afternoon passed swiftly. Sustained by treasure-berries and gladness, and by rills that sparkled like liquid gem-fire across their path, Linden and her companions moved at Sunder's pace among the copses and hillcrests. And then evening drew near. Beyond the western sky-line, the sun set in grandeur, painting orange and gold across the heavens.

Still the travellers kept on walking. None of them wanted to stop.

When the last blazon of sunset had faded, and stars began to wink and smile through the deepening velvet of the sky, and the twittering communal clamour of the birds subsided, Linden heard music.

At first it was music for her alone, melody sung on a pitch of significance which only her hearing could reach. It sharpened the star-limned profiles of the trees, gave the light of the low, waning moon on the slopes and trunks a quality of etched and lovely evanescence. Both plaintive and lustrous, it wafted over the Hills as if it were singing them to beauty. Rapt with eagerness, Linden held her breath to listen.

Then the music became as bright as phosphorescence; and the company heard it. Covenant drew a soft gasp of recognition between his teeth.

Swelling and aching, the melody advanced. It was the song of the Hills, the incarnate essence of Andelain's health. Every leaf, every petal, every blade of grass was a note in the harmony: every bough and branch, a strand of singing. Power ran through it – the strength which held back the Sunbane. But at the same time it was mournful, as stern as a dirge; and it caught in Linden's throat like a sob.

'Oh, Andelain! forgive! for I am doomed to fail this war.
  I cannot bear to see you die – and live,
Foredoomed to bitterness and all the grey Despiser's lore.

But while I can I heed the call
Of green and tree; and for their worth,
I hold the glaive of Law against the Earth.'

While the words measured out their sorrow and determination, the singer appeared on a rise ahead of the company — became visible like a translation of song.

He was tall and strong, wrapped in a robe as fine and white as the music which streamed from the lines of his form. In his right hand, he gripped a long, gnarled tree-limb as though it were the staff of his might. For he was mighty – oh, he was mighty! The sheer potency of him shouted to Linden's senses as he approached, stunning her not with fear but with awe. A long moment passed before she was able to see him clearly.

'Caer-Caveral,' whispered Covenant. 'Hile Troy.' Linden felt his legs tremble as if he ached to kneel, wanted to stretch himself prostrate in front of the eldritch puissance of the Forestal. 'Dear God, I'm glad to see you.' Memories poured from him, pain and rescue and bittersweet meeting.

Then at last Linden discerned through the phosphorescence and the music that the tall man had no eyes. The skin of his face spread straight and smooth from forehead to cheek over the sockets in which orbs should have been.

Yet he did not appear to need sight. His music was the only sense he required. It lit the Giants, entrancing them where they stood, leaving them with a glamour in their faces and a cessation of all hurt in their hearts. It trilled and swirled through Linden, carrying her care away, humbling her to silence. And it met Covenant as squarely as any gaze.

'You have come,' the man sang, drawing glimmers of melody from the greensward, spangled wreaths of accompaniment from the trees. 'And the woman of your world with you. That is well.' Then his singing concentrated more personally on Covenant; and Covenant's eyes burned with grief. Hile Troy had once commanded the armies of the Land against Lord Foul. But he had sold himself to the Forestal of Garroting Deep to purchase a vital victory – and the price had been more than three millennia of service.

'Thomas Covenant, you have become that which I may no longer command. But I ask this of you, that you must grant it.' Melody flowed from him down the hillside, curling about Covenant's feet and passing on. The music tuned itself to a pitch of authority. 'Ur-Lord and Illender, Unbeliever and Earthfriend. You have earned the valour of those names. Stand aside.'

Covenant stared at the Forestal, his whole stance pleading for comprehension.

'You must not intervene. The Land's need is harsh, and its rigour

1126

falls upon other heads as well as yours. No taking of life is gentle, but in this there is a necessity upon me, which you are craved to honour. This Law also must be broken.' The moon was poised above the Hills, as acute as a sickle; but its light was only a pale echo of the music that gleamed like droplets of bright dew up and down the slope. Within the trunks of the trees rose the same song which glittered on their leaves. 'Thomas Covenant,' the Forestal repeated, 'stand aside.'

Now the rue of the melody could not be mistaken. And behind it shimmered a note of fear.

'Covenant, please,' Caer-Caveral concluded in a completely different voice – the voice of the man he had once been. 'Do this for me. No matter what happens. Don't interfere.'

Covenant's throat worked. 'I don't – ' he started to say. I don't understand. Then, with a wrench of will, he stepped out of the Forestal's way.

Stately and grave, Caer-Caveral went down the hillside toward Sunder.

The Graveller stood as if he did not see the tall, white figure, heard no song. Hollian he held upright against his heart, her face pressed to his chest. But his head was up: his eyes watched the slope down which Caer-Caveral had come. A cry that had no voice stretched his visage.

Slowly, like an action in a dream, Linden turned to look in the direction of Sunder's gaze.

As Covenant did the same, a sharp pang sprang from him.

Above the company, moonshine and Forestal-fire condensed to form a human shape. Pale silver, momentarily transparent, then more solid, like an incarnation of evanescence and yearning, a woman walked toward the onlookers. A smile curved her delicate mouth; and her hair swept a suggestion of dark wings and destiny past her shoulders; and she shone like loss and hope.

Hollian eh-Brand. Sunder's Dead, come to greet him.

The sight of her made him breathe in fierce, shuddering gasps, as if she had set a goad to his heart.

She passed by Covenant, Linden, and the Giants without acknowledging them. Prehaps, for her, they did not exist. Erect with the dignity of her calling, the importance of her purpose, she moved to the Forestal's side and stopped, facing Sunder and her own dead body.

'Ah, Sunder, my dear one,' she murmured. 'Forgive my death. It was my flesh that failed you, not my love.'

Helpless to reply, Sunder went on gasping as though his life were being ripped out of him.

Hollian started to speak again; but the Forestal raised his staff, silencing her. He did not appear to move, to take any action. Yet music leaped around Sunder like a swirl of moonsparks, and the Graveller staggered. Somehow, Hollian was taken from him. She was enfolded tenderly in the crook of the Forestal's left arm: Caer-Caveral claimed her stiff death for himself. The song became keener, whetted by loss and trepidation.

Wildly, Sunder snatched the *krill* from its resting place against his burned belly. Its argent passion pierced the music. All reason was gone from him. Racked for air, he brandished Loric's blade at the Forestal, mutely demanding that Hollian be given back to him.

The restraint Hile Troy had asked of Covenant made him shudder.

'Now it ends,' fluted Caer-Caveral. The singing which conveyed his words was at once exquisitely beautiful and unbearable. 'Do not fear me. Though it is severe, this must be done. I am weary, eager of release and called to rest. Your love supplies the power, and none other may take the burden from you. Son of Nassic' – the music contained no command now, but only sorrow – 'you must strike me.'

Covenant flinched as if he expected Sunder to obey. The Graveller was desperate enough for anything. But Linden watched him with all her senses and saw his inchoate violence founder in dismay. He lowered the *krill*. His eyes were wide with supplication. Behind the mad obsession which had ruled him since Hollian's death still lived a man who loathed killing – who had shed too much blood and never forgiven himself for it. His soul seemed to collapse inward. After days of endurance, he was dying.

The Forestal struck the turf with his staff, and the Hills rang. 'Strike!'

His demand was so potent that Linden raised her hands involuntarily, though it was not directed at her. Yet some part of Sunder remained unbroken, clear. The corners of his jaw knotted with the old obduracy which had once enabled him to defy Gibbon. Deliberately, he unbent his elbow, let the *krill* dangle from his weak hand. His head slumped forward until his chin rested on his chest. He no longer made any effort to breathe.

Caer-Caveral sent a glare of phosphorescence at the Graveller. 'Very well,' he trilled angrily. 'Withhold – and be lost. The Land is ill served by those who will not pay the price of love.' Turning sharply away, he strode back through the company in the direction from which he had come. He still bore Hollian's physical form clasped in his left arm.

And the Dead eh-Brand went with him as if she approved. Her eyes were silver and grieving.

It was too much. A strangled cry tore Sunder's refusal. He could not let Hollian go: his desire for her was too strong. Raising the *krill* above his head in both fists, he ran at the Forestal's back.

Too late, Covenant shouted, 'No!' and leaped after Sunder.

The Giants could not move. The music held them fascinated and motionless. Linden was not certain that they were truly able to see what was happening.

She could have moved. She felt the same stasis which enclosed the First and Pitchwife; but it was not strong enough to stop her. Her percipience could grasp the melody and make it serve her. With the slow instantaneousness of visions or nightmares, she knew she was able to do it. The music would carry her after Sunder so swiftly that he might never reach the Forestal.

Yet she did not. She had no way to measure the implications of this crisis. But she had seen the pain shining in Hollian's eyes, the eh-Brand's recognition of necessity. And she trusted the slim, brave woman. She made no effort to stop Sunder as he hammered the point of the *krill* between Caer-Caveral's shoulder-blades with the last force of his life.

From the blow burst a deflagration of pearl flame which rent away immobility, sent Linden and the Giants sprawling, hurled Covenant to the grass. At once, all the music became fire and raced toward the Forestal, sweeping around him – and Sunder and Hollian with him – so that they were effaced from sight, consumed in an incandescent whirlwind that spouted into the heavens, reached like the ruin of every song toward the bereft stars. A cacophony of fear clashed and wept around the flame; but the flame did not hear it. In a rush of ascension, the blaze burned its hot, mute agony against the night as if it fed on the pure heart of Andelain, bore that spirit writhing and appalled through the high dark.

And as it rose, Linden seemed to hear the fundamental fabric of the world tearing.

Then, before the sight became unendurable, the fire began to subside. By slow stages, the conflagration changed to an ordinary fire, yellow with heat and eaten wood, and she saw it burning from the black and blasted stump of a tree trunk which had not been there when Caer-Caveral was struck.

Stabbed deep into the charred wood beyond any hope of removal was the *krill*. Only the flames that licked the stump made it visible: the light of its gem was gone.

Now the fire failed swiftly, falling away from the stricken trunk. Soon the blaze was extinguished altogether. Smoke curled upward to mark the place where the Forestal had been slain.

Yet the night was not dark. Other illuminations gathered around the stunned companions.

From beyond the stump, Sunder and Hollian came walking hand-in-hand. They were limned with silver like the Dead; but they were alive in the flesh – human and whole. Caer-Caveral's mysterious purpose had been accomplished. Empowered and catalysed by the Forestal's spirit, Sunder's passion had found its object; and the *krill* had severed the boundary which separated him from Hollian. In that way, the Graveller, who was trained for bloodshed and whose work was killing, had brought his love back into life.

Around the two of them bobbed a circle of Wraiths, dancing a bright cavort of welcome. Their warm loveliness seemed to promise the end of all pain.

But in Andelain there was no more music.

15

ENACTORS OF DESECRATION

In the lush, untrammelled dawn of the Hills, Sunder and Hollian came to say farewell to Covenant and Linden.

Linden greeted them as if the past night had been one of the best of her life. She could not have named the reasons for this: it defied expectation. With Caer-Caveral's passing, important things had come to an end. She should have lamented instead of rejoicing. Yet on a level too deep for language she had recognized the necessity of which the Forestal had spoken. *This Law also* – Andelain had been bereft of music, but not of beauty or consolation. And the restoration of the Stonedownors made her too glad for sorrow. In a paradoxical way, Caer-Caveral's self-sacrifice felt like a promise of hope.

But Covenant's mien was clouded by conflicting emotions. With his companions, he had spent the night watching Sunder and Hollian revel among the Wraiths of Andelain – and Linden sensed that the sight gave him both joy and rue. The healing of his friends lightened his heart: the price of that healing did not. And surely he was hurt by his lack of any health-sense which would have enabled him to evaluate what the loss of the Forestal meant to Andelain.

However, there were no clouds upon the Graveller and the eh-Brand. They walked buoyantly to the place where Linden and Covenant sat; and Linden thought that some of the night's silver still clung to them, giving them a numinous cast even in daylight, like a new dimension added to their existence. Smiles gleamed from Sunder's eyes. And Hollian bore herself with an air of poised loveliness. Linden was not surprised to perceive that the child in the eh-Brand's womb shared her elusive, mystical glow.

For a moment, the Stonedownors gazed at Covenant and Linden and smiled and did not speak. Then Sunder cleared his throat. 'I crave your pardon that we will no longer accompany you.' His voice held a special resonance that Linden had never heard before in him, a suggestion of fire. 'You have said that we are the future of the Land. It has become our wish to discover that future here. And to bear our son in Andelain.

'I know you will not gainsay us. But we pray that you find no rue in this parting. We do not – though you are precious to us. The outcome of the Earth is in your hands. Therefore we are unafraid.'

He might have gone on; but Covenant stopped him with a brusque gesture, a scowl of gruff affection. 'Are you kidding?' he muttered. 'I'm the one who wanted you to stay behind. I was going to ask you – ' He sighed, and his gaze wandered the hillside. 'Spend as much time here as you can,' he breathed. 'Stay as long as possible. That's something I've always wanted to do.'

His voice trailed away; but Linden was not listening to its resigned sadness. She was staring at Sunder. The faint silver quality of his aura was clear – and yet undefinable. It ran out of her grasp like water. Intuition tingled along her nerves, and she started speaking before she knew what she would say.

'The last time Covenant was here, Caer-Caveral gave him the location of the One Tree.' Each word surprised her like a hint of revelation. 'But he hid it so Covenant couldn't reach it himself. That's why he had to expose himself to the *Elohim*, let them work their plots – ' The bare memory brought a tremor of anger into her voice. 'We should never have had to go there in the first place. Why did Caer-Caveral give him that gift – and then make it such a secret?'

Sunder looked at her. He was no longer smiling. A weird intensity filled his gaze like a swirl of sparks. Abruptly, he said, 'Are you not now companioned by the Appointed of the *Elohim*? How otherwise could that end have been achieved?'

The strangeness of the Graveller's tone snatched back Covenant's attention. Linden felt him scrambling after inferences: a blaze of hope shot up in him. 'Are you – ?' he asked. 'Is that it? Are you the new Forestal?'

Instead of answering, Sunder looked to Hollian, giving her the opportunity to tell him what he was.

She met his gaze with a soft smile. But she answered quietly, kindly, 'No.' She had spent time among the Dead and appeared certain of her knowledge. 'In such a transferral of power, the Law which Caer-Caveral sought to rend would have been preserved. Yet we are not altogether what we were. We will do what we may for the sustenance of Andelain – and for the future of the Land.'

Questions thronged in Linden. She wanted a name for the alteration she perceived. But Covenant was already speaking.

'The Law of Life.' His eyes were hot and gaunt on the Stone-downors. 'Elena broke the Law of Death – the barrier that kept the living and the dead from reaching out to each other. The Law Caer-

Caveral broke was the one that kept the dead from crossing back into life.'

'That is sooth,' replied Hollian. 'Yet it is a fragile crossing withal, and uncertain. We are sustained, and in some manner defined, by the sovereign Earthpower of the Andelainian Hills. Should we depart this region, we would not long endure among the living.'

Linden saw that this was true. The strange gleam upon the Stonedownors was the same magic which had given Caer-Caveral's music its lambent strength. Sunder and Hollian were solid, physical, and whole. Yet in a special sense they had become beings of Earthpower – and they might easily die if they were cut off from their source.

Covenant must have understood the eh-Brand's words also. But he heard them with different ears from Linden's. As their implications penetrated him, his sudden hope went out.

That loss sent a pang through Linden. She had been concentrating too hard on Sunder and Hollian: she had not realized that Covenant had been looking for an answer to his own death.

At once, she reached out a hand to his shoulder, felt the effort he made to suppress his dismay. But the exertion was over in an instant. Braced on his certainty, he faced the Stonedownors. His tone belied the struggle he made to keep it firm.

'I'll do everything I can,' he said. 'But my time's almost over. Yours is just beginning. Don't waste it.'

Sunder returned a smile that seemed to make him young. 'Thomas Covenant,' he promised, 'we will not.'

No goodbyes were said. This farewell could not be expressed with words or embraces. Arm in arm, the Graveller and the eh-Brand simply turned and walked away across the bedewed grass. After a moment, they passed the crest of the hill and were gone.

Behind them, they left a silence that ached as if nothing would be able to take their place.

Linden stretched her arm over Covenant's shoulders and hugged him, trying to tell him that she understood.

He kissed her hand, then rose to his feet. As he scanned the bright morning, the untainted sun, the flower-bedizened landscape, he sighed, 'At least there's still Earthpower.'

'Yes,' Linden averred, climbing erect to join him. 'The Hills haven't changed.' She did not know how else to comfort him. 'Losing the Forestal is going to make a difference. But not yet.' She was sure of that. Andelain's health still surged around her in every blade and leaf, every bird and rock. No disease or weakness was visible anywhere. And the shining sun had no aura. She thought that the tangible world had never held so much condensed and treasurable beauty. Like a prayer for Andelain's endurance, she repeated, 'Not yet.'

A grin of grim relish bared Covenant's teeth. 'Then he can't hurt us. For a while, anyway. I hope it drives him crazy.'

Linden breathed a secret relief, hoping that he had weathered the crisis.

But all his moods seemed to change as soon as he felt them. An old bleakness dulled his gaze: haggard lines marked his mien. Abruptly, he started toward the charred stump which had once been the Forestal of Andelain.

At once, she followed him. But she stopped when she understood that he had gone to say farewell.

He touched the inert gem of the *krill* with his numb fingers, tested the handle's coldness with the back of his hand. Then he leaned his palms and forehead against the blackened wood. Linden could hardly hear him.

'From fire to fire,' he whispered. 'After all this time. First Hamako. Then Honninscrave. Now you. I hope you've found a little peace.'

There was no answer. When at last he withdrew, his hands and brow were smudged with soot like an obscure and contradictory anointment. Roughly, he scrubbed his palms on his pants; but he seemed unaware of the stain on his forehead.

For a moment, he studied Linden as if he sought to measure her against the Forestal's example. Again she was reminded of the way he had once cared for Joan. But Linden was not his ex-wife: she faced him squarely. The encompassing health of the Hills made her strong. And what he saw appeared to reassure him. Gradually his features softened. Half to himself, he murmured, 'Thank God you're still here.' Then he raised his voice. 'We should get going. Where are the Giants?'

She gave him a long gaze which Hollian would have understood before she turned to look for the First and Pitchwife.

They were not in sight. Vain and Findail stood near the foot of the slope exactly as they had remained all night; but the Giants were elsewhere. However, when she ascended to the hillcrest, she saw them emerge from a copse on the far side of a low valley, where they had gone to find privacy.

They responded to her wave with a hail and a gesture eastward, indicating that they would rejoin her and Covenant in that direction. Perhaps their keen eyes were able to descry the smile she gave them, glad to see that they felt safe enough in Andelain to leave their companions unguarded.

Covenant came to her wearily, worn by strain and lack of sleep. But at the sight of the Giants — or of the Hills unfurled before him like pleasure rolling along the kind breeze — he, too, smiled. Even from this distance, the restoration of Pitchwife's spirit was visible in the way he hobbled at his wife's side with a gait like a mummer's capriole. And her swinging stride bespoke eagerness and a fondly remembered night. They were Giants in Andelain: the pure expanse of the Hills suited them.

Softly, Covenant mused, 'They aren't people of the Land. Maybe *Coercri* was enough. Maybe they won't meet any Dead here.' As he remembered the slain Unhomed – and the *caamora* of release he had given them in The Grieve – the timbre of his voice conveyed pride and pain. But then his gaze darkened; and Linden saw that he was thinking of Saltheart Foamfollower, who had lost his life in Covenant's former victory over the Despiser.

She wanted to tell him not to worry. Perhaps the battle for Revelstone had made Pitchwife familiar with despair and doom. Yet she believed that eventually he would find the song he needed. And the First was a Swordmain, as true as her blade: she would not lightly submit to death.

But Covenant had his own strange sources of surety and did not wait for Linden's answer. With his resolve stiffening, he placed his halfhand firmly in her clasp and drew her toward the east along a way among the Hills which would intersect the path of the Giants.

After a moment, Findail and Vain appeared behind them, following them as always in the direction of their fate.

For a while, Covenant walked briskly, his smudged forehead raised to the sun and the savoury atmosphere. But at the first brook they encountered, he stopped. From under his belt, he drew a knife which he had brought with him from Revelstone. Stooping to the crisp water, he drank deeply, then soaked his ragged beard and set himself to shave.

Linden held her breath as she watched him. His grasp on the blade was numb; and fatigue made his muscles awkward. But she did not try to intervene. She sensed that this risk was necessary to him.

When he had finished, however, and his cheeks and neck were scraped clean, she could not conceal her relief. She knelt beside him, cupped water into her hands, and washed the soot from his forehead, seeking to remove the innominate implications of that mark.

An oak with a tremendous trunk spread its wide leaves over that part of the brook. Satisfied with Covenant's face, she pulled him after her and leaned back into the shade and the grass. The breeze played down the length of her legs like the sport of a lover; and she was in no hurry to rejoin the Giants.

But suddenly she felt a mute cry from the tree, a burst of pain which shivered through the ground, seemed to violate the very air. She whirled from Covenant's side and surged to her feet, trembling to find the cause of the oak's hurt.

The cry rose. For an instant, she saw no reason for it. Harm shook the boughs: the leaves wailed: muffled rivings ran through the heartwood. Around the oak, the Hills seemed to concentrate as if they were appalled. But she saw nothing except that Vain and Findail were gone.

Then, too swift for surmise, the Appointed came flowing out of the wood's anguish.

As he transformed himself from oak to flesh, his care-cut visage wore an unwonted shame. Vexed and defensive, he faced Linden and Covenant. 'Is he not Demondim-spawn?' he demanded as if they had accused him unjustly. 'Are not his makers ur-viles, that have ever served the Despiser with their self-abhorrence? And will you trust him to my cost? He must be slain.'

At his back, the oak's hurt sharpened to screaming.

'You bastard!' Linden spat, half guessing what Findail had done – and afraid to believe it. 'You're killing it! Don't you even care that this is Andelain? – the only place left that at least ought to be safe?'

'Linden?' Covenant asked urgently. 'What – ?' He lacked her percipience, had no knowledge of the tree's agony.

But he did not have to wait for an answer. A sundering pain like the blow of an axe split Linden's nerves; and the trunk of the oak sprang apart in a flail of splinters.

From the core of the wood, Vain stepped free. Unscathed, he left the still quivering tree in ruins. He did not glance at Findail or anyone else. His black eyes held nothing but darkness.

Linden stumbled to her knees in the grass and wrapped her arms around the hurt.

For a stunned moment, grief held the Hills. Then Covenant rasped, 'That's terrific.' He sounded as shaken as the dying boughs. 'I hope you're proud of yourself.'

Findail's reply seemed to come from a great distance. 'Do you value him so highly? Then I am indeed lost.'

'I don't give a good goddamn!' Covenant was at Linden's side: his hands gripped her shoulders, supporting her against the empathic force of the rupture. 'I don't trust either of you. Don't you *ever* try anything like that again!'

The *Elohim* hardened. 'I will do what I must. From the first, I have avowed that I will not suffer his purpose. The curse of Kastenessen will not impel me to that doom.'

Swirling into the form of a hawk, he flapped away through the treetops. Linden and Covenant were left amid the wreckage.

Vain stood before them as if nothing had happened.

For a moment longer, the ache of the tree kept Linden motionless. But by degrees Andelain closed around the destruction, pouring health back into the air she breathed, spreading green vitality up from the grass, loosening the knotted echo of pain. Slowly, her head cleared. Sweet Christ, she mumbled to herself. I wasn't ready for that.

Covenant repeated her name: his concern reached her through

his numb fingers. She steadied herself on the undergirding bones of the Hills and nodded to him. 'I'm all right.' She sounded wan; but Andelain continued to lave her in its balm. Drawing a deep breath, she pulled herself back to her feet.

Across the greensward, the sunshine lay like sorrow among the trees and shrubs, *aliantha* and flowers. But the shock of violence was over: already, the distant hillsides had begun to smile again. The brook resumed its damp chuckle as though the interruption had been forgotten. Only the riven trunk went on weeping while the tree died, too sorely hurt to keep itself alive.

'The old Lords – ' Covenant murmured, more to himself than to her. 'Some of them could've healed this.'

So could I, Linden nearly replied aloud. If I had your ring. I could save it all. But she bit down the thought, hoped it did not show in her face. She did not trust her intense desire for power. The power to put a stop to evil.

However, he lacked the sight to read her emotions. His own grief and outrage blinded him. When he touched her arm and gestured onward, she leaped the brook with him; and together they continued among the Hills.

Unmarred except by the dead wood of his right forearm, Vain followed them. His midnight countenance held no expression other than the habitual ambiguity of his slight grin.

The day would have been one of untrammelled loveliness for Linden if she could have forgotten Findail and the Demondim-spawn. As she and Covenant left the vicinity of the shattered oak, Andelain reasserted all its beneficent mansuetude, the gay opulence of its verdure, the tuneful sweep and soar and flash of its birds, the endearing caution and abundance of its wildlife. Nourished by treasure-berries and rill-water, and blandished from stride to stride by the springy turf, she felt crowded with life, as piquant as the scents of the flowers, and keen for each new vista of the Andelainian Hills. After a time, the First and Pitchwife rejoined Linden and Covenant, appearing from the covert of an antique willow with leaves in their hair and secrets in their eyes. For greeting, Pitchwife gave a roistering laugh that sounded like his old humour; and it was seconded by one of his wife's rare, beautiful smiles.

'Look at you,' Linden replied in mock censure, teasing the Giants. 'For shame. If you keep that up, you're going to become parents whether you're ready for it or not.'

A shade like a blush touched the First's mien; but Pitchwife responded with a crow. Then he assumed an air of dismay. 'Stone and Sea forfend! The child of this woman would surely emerge bladed and buckered from the very womb. Such a prodigy must not be blithely conceived.'

The First frowned to conceal her mirth. 'Hush, husband,' she murmured. 'Provoke me not. Does it not suffice you that one of us is entirely mad?'

'Suffice me?' he riposted. 'How should it suffice me? I have no wish for loneliness.'

'Aye, and none for wisdom or decorum,' she growled in feigned vexation. 'You are indeed shameful.'

When Covenant grinned at the jesting of the Giants, Linden nearly laughed aloud for pleasure.

Yet she did not know where Findail had gone or what he would do next. And the death of the oak remained aching in the back of her mind. Ballasted by such things, her mood did not altogether lose itself in the analystic atmosphere. There was a price yet to be paid for the passing of the Forestal, and the destination of the company had not changed. In addition, she had no clear sense of what Covenant hoped to achieve by confronting the Despiser. Caer-Caveral had once said of her, *The woman of your world would raise grim shades here.* She relished Pitchwife's return to glee, enjoyed the new lightness which the badinage of the Giants produced in Covenant. But she did not forget.

As evening settled around Andelain, she experienced a faint shiver of trepidation. At night the Dead walked the Hills. All of Covenant's olden friends, lambent with meanings and memories she could not share. The woman he had raped. And the daughter of that rape, who had loved him – and had broken the Law of Death in his name, trying as madly as hate to spare him from his harsh doom. She was loath to meet those potent revenants. They were the men and women who had shaped the past, and she had no place among them.

Under a stately Gilden, the company halted. A nearby stream with a bed of fine sand provided water for washing. *Aliantha* were plentiful. The deep grass cushioned the ground comfortably. And Pitchwife was a wellspring of good cheer, of *diamondraught* and tales. While the satin gloaming slowly folded itself away, leaving Linden and her companions uncovered to the darkness and the hushed stars, he described the long Giantclave and testing by which the Giants of Home had determined to send out the Search and had selected his wife to lead it. He related her feats as though they were stupendous, teasing her with her prowess. But now his voice held a hidden touch of fever, a suggestion of effort which hinted at his more fundamental distress. Andelain restored his heart; but it could not heal his recollection of Revelstone and gratuitous bloodshed, could not cure his need for a better outcome. After a time, he lapsed into silence; and Linden felt the air of the camp growing tense with anticipation.

Across the turf, fireflies winked and wandered uncertainly, as if they-were searching for the Forestal's music. But eventually they went away. The company settled into a vigil. The mood Covenant emitted was raw with fatigue and hunger: he, too, appeared to fear his Dead as much as he desired them.

Then the First broke the silence. 'These Dead,' she began thoughtfully. 'I comprehend that they are held apart from their deserved rest by the breaking of the Law of Death. But why do they gather here, where all other Law endures? And what impels them to accost the living?'

'Companionship,' murmured Covenant, his thoughts elsewhere. 'Or maybe the health of Andelain gives them something as good as rest.' His voice carried a distant pang: he also had been left forlorn by the loss of Caer-Caveral's song. 'Maybe they just haven't been able to stop loving.'

Linden roused herself to ask, 'Then why are they so cryptic? They haven't given you anything except hints and mystification. Why don't they come right out and tell you what you need to know?'

'Ah, that is plain to me,' Pitchwife replied on Covenant's behalf. 'Unearned knowledge is perilous. Only by the seeking and gaining of it may its uses be understood, its true worth measured. Had Gossamer Glowlimn my wife been mystically granted the skill and power of her blade without training or test or experience, by what means could she then choose where to strike her blows, how extremely to put forth her strength? Unearned knowledge rules its wielder, to the cost of both.'

But Covenant had his own answer. When Pitchwife finished, the Unbeliever said quietly, 'They can't tell us what they know. We'd be terrified.' He was sitting with his back to the Gilden; and his fused resolve gave him no peace. 'That's the worst part. They know how much we're going to be hurt. But if they tell us, where will we ever get the courage to face it? Sometimes ignorance is the only kind of bravery or at least willingness that does any good.'

He spoke as if he believed what he was saying. But the hardness of his tone seemed to imply that he had no ignorances left to relieve the prospect of his immedicable intent.

The Giants fell still, unable to deny his assertion or respond to it. The stars shone bleak rue around the scant sliver of the moon. The night grew intense among the Hills. Behind the comforting glow of its health and wholeness, Andelain grieved for the Forestal.

Terrified? Linden asked herself. Was Covenant's purpose as bad as that?

Yet she found it impossible to question him: not here, with the Giants listening. His need for privacy was palpable to her. And she was too restless to concentrate. She remained charged with the energy and abundance of the Hills; and the night seemed to breathe her name, urging her to walk off her nervous anticipation. Covenant's Dead were nowhere in evidence. Within the range of her percipience lay only the fine slumber and beauty of the region.

A strange glee rose in her: she wanted to run and caracole under the slight moon, tumble and roll and tumble again down the lush hillsides, immerse herself in Andelain's immaculate dark. Perhaps a solitary gambol would act as an anodyne for the other blackness which the Sunbane had nourished in her veins.

Abruptly, she sprang to her feet. 'I'll be back,' she said without meeting the eyes of her companions. 'Andelain is too exciting. I need to see more of it.'

The Hills murmured to her, and she answered, sprinting away from the Gilden southward with all the gay speed of her legs.

Behind her, Pitchwife had taken up his flute. At once broken, piercing and sweet, its awkward tones followed her as she ran. They carried around her like the ghost-limbs of the trees, the crouching midnight of the bushes, the unmoonlit loom and pause of the shadows. He was trying to play the song which had streamed so richly from Caer-Caveral.

For a moment, he caught it – or almost caught it – and it went through her like loss and exaltation. Then she seemed to outrun it as she passed over a rise and sped downward again, deeper into the occult night of the Andelainian Hills.

The Forestal had said that she would raise grim shades here; and she thought of her father and mother. Unintentionally, without knowing what they were doing, they had bred her for suicide and murder. But now she defied them. Come on! she panted up at the stars. I dare you! For good or ill, healing or destruction, she had become stronger than her parents. The passion surging in her could not be named or confined by the harsh terms of her inheritance. She taunted her memories, challenging them to appear before her. But they did not.

And because they did not, she ran on, as heedless as a child – altogether unready for the door of might which opened suddenly against her, slapping her to the ground as if she were not strong or real enough to be noticed by the old puissance emerging from it.

A door like a gap in the first substance of the night, as abrupt and stunning as a detonation, and as tall as the heavens. It opened so that the man could stride through it. Then it closed behind him.

Her face was thrust into the grass. She fought for breath, strove to raise her head. But the sheer force of the presence towering over her crushed her prostrate. His bitter outrage seemed to fall on her like the wreckage of a mountain. Beneath his ire, he was so poignant with ruin, so extreme in the ancient and undiminished apotheosis of his despair, that she would have wept for him if she had been able. But his tremendous wrath daunted her, turned her vulnerability against herself. She could not lever her face out of the turf to look at him.

He felt transcendently tall and powerful: for an instant, she believed that he could not be aware of her, that she was too small for his notice. Surely he would pass by her and go about his fell business. But almost immediately her hope failed. His regard lit between her shoulder-blades like the point of a spear.

Then he spoke. His voice was as desolate as the Land under a desert sun, as twisted and lorn as the ravages of a sun of pestilence. But anger gave it strength.

'Slayer of your own Dead, do you know me?'

No, she panted. *No*. Her fingers gouged into the loam as she struggled to shift her abject posture. He had no right to do this to her. Yet his glare impaled her, and she could not move.

He replied as if her resistance had no meaning:

'I am Kevin. Son of Loric. High Lord of the Council. Founder of the Seven Wards. And enactor of the Land's Desecration by my own hand. I am Kevin Landwaster.'

In response, she was able to do nothing except groan, Dear God. Oh, dear God.

Kevin.

She knew who he was.

He had been the last High Lord of Berek's lineage, the last direct inheritor of the Staff of Law. The wonder and munificence of his reign in Revelstone had won the service of the Bloodguard, confirmed the friendship of the Giants, advanced the Council's dedication to the Earthpower, given beauty and purpose to all the Land. And he had failed. Tricked and defeated by the Despiser, he had proved himself unequal to the Land's defence. By his own mistakes, the object of his love and service had been doomed. And because he had understood that doom, he had fallen into despair.

Madly, he had conceived the ploy of the Ritual of Desecration, believing that Lord Foul would thereby be undone – that the price of centuries of devastation for the Land would purchase the Despiser's downfall. Therefore they had met in Kiril Threndor within the heart of Mount Thunder, mad Lord and malign foe. Together, they had set in motion the dire Ritual.

But in the end it was Kevin who fell while Lord Foul laughed. Desecration had no power to rid the world of Despite.

Yet that was not the whole tale of his woe. Misled by the confusion of her love and hate, the later High Lord, Elena daughter of Lena and Covenant, had thought that the Landwaster's despair would be a source of irrefusable might; and so she had selected him for her breaking of the Law of Death, had rent him from his natural grave to hurl him in combat against the Despiser. But Lord Foul had turned the attempt against her. Both she and the Staff of Law had been lost; and Dead Kevin had been forced to serve his foe.

The only taste of relief he had been granted had come when Thomas Covenant and Saltheart Foamfollower had defeated the Despiser.

But that victory was now three millennia past. The Sunbane was rampant upon the Land, and Lord Foul had found the path to triumph. Kevin's dismay and wrath poured from him in floods. His voice was as hard as a cable under terrific stress.

'We are kindred in our way – the victims and enactors of Despite. You must heed me. Do not credit that you may exercise choice here. The Land's need admits no choice. You must heed me. *Must!*'

The word hammered and echoed and pleaded through her. *Must*. He had not come to appal her, meant her no harm. Rather, he approached her because he had no other way to reach out among the living, exert himself against the Despiser's machinations.

Must.

She understood that. Her fingers relaxed their grasp on the grass: her senses submitted to his vehemence. Tell me what it is, she said as if she had no more need to choose. Tell me what I should do.

'You will not wish to heed me. The truth is harsh. You will seek to deny it. But it will not be denied. I have borne horror upon my head and am not blinded by the hope which refuses truth. You must heed me.'

Must.

Yes.

Tell me.

'Linden Avery, you must halt the Unbeliever's mad intent. His purpose is the work of Despite. As I have done before him, he seeks to destroy that which he loves. He must not be permitted.

'If no other means suffice, you must slay him.'

No! In a rush of trepidation, she strove against his power – and still she had no strength to raise her head. Slay him? Goaded by his gaze, her heart laboured. No! You don't understand. He wouldn't do that.

But his voice came down on her back like a fall of stone.

'No. It is you who do not understand. You have not yet learned to comprehend the cunning of despair. Can you think that I allowed my fellow Lords to guess my purpose when I had set my heart to the Ritual? Have you been granted the gift of such sight, and are you yet unable to see? When evil rises in its full power, it surpasses truth and may wear the guise of good without fear of discovery. In that way was I brought to my own doom.

'He walks the path which his friends among the Dead have conceived for him. But they also do not comprehend despair. They were redeemed from it by his brave mastery of the Despiser – and so

1141

they see hope where there is only Desecration. Their vision of evil is incomplete and false.'

He gathered force in the night, became as shattering as a shout of disaster.

'It is his intent to place the white ring into Lord Foul's hand.

'If you suffer him to succeed, the term of our grief will be slight, for all Earth and Time will be lost.

'You must halt him.'

Repeating until all the Hills replied, *Must. Must.*

After a moment, he left her. The door of his power closed behind him. But she did not notice his departure. For a long time, she went on staring blindly into the grass.

16

'ANDELAIN! FORGIVE!'

Later, it started to rain.

Drizzling lightly, clouds covered the stars and the moon. The rain was as gentle as the touch of springtime, as clean and kind and sad as the spirit of the Hills. It fed the grass, blessed the flowers, garlanded the trees with droplets. In no way did it resemble the hysterical fury of the sun of rain.

Yet it closed the last light out of the world, leaving Linden in darkness.

She lay outstretched on the turf. All will and movement were gone from her. She had no wish to lift her head, to stir from her prostration. The crushing weight of what she had learned deprived her of the bare desire to breathe. Her eyes accepted the rain without blinking.

The drizzle made a quiet stippling noise on the leaves and grass, a delicate elegy. She thought that it would carry her away, that she would never be asked to move again. But then she heard another sound through the spatter of drops: a sound like the chime of a small, perfect crystal. Its fine note conveyed mourning and pity.

When she looked up, she saw that Andelain was not altogether dark. A yellow light shed streaks of rain to the grass. It came like the chiming from a flame the size of her palm which bobbed in the air as it burned from an invisible wick. And the dancing fire sang to her, offering her the gift of its sorrow.

One of the Wraiths of Andelain.

At the sight, pain seized her heart, brought her to her feet. That such things would be destroyed! That Covenant meant to sacrifice even Wraiths and Andelain on the altar of his despair, let so much lorn and fragile beauty be ripped out of life! Instinctively, she knew why the flame had come to her.

'I'm lost in this rain,' she said. Outrage rose behind her clenched teeth. 'Take me back to my people.'

The Wraith bobbed like a bow: perhaps it understood her. Dancing and guttering, it moved away through the drizzle. Droplets crossed its light like falling stars.

She followed it without hesitation. Darkness crowded around her and through her; but the flame remained clear.

It did not mislead her. In a short time, it guided her to the place where she had left her companions.

Under the Gilden, the Wraith played for a moment above the huge, sleeping forms of the First and Pitchwife. They were not natives of the Land: unappalled by personal revenants, they slumbered as though they had been unable to refuse the peace of the Hills.

The flitting flame limned Vain briefly, sparked the rain beading on his black perfection so that he seemed to wear an intaglio of glisters. His ebon orbs watched nothing, admitted nothing. His slight smile appeared to have no meaning.

But Covenant was not there.

The Wraith left her then as if it feared to go farther with her: it chimed away into the dark like a fading hope. Yet when her sight adjusted to the cloud-closed night, she caught a glimpse of what she sought. In a low hollow to the east lay a soft glow of pearl.

She moved in that direction, and the light became brighter.

It revealed Thomas Covenant standing among his Dead.

His wet shirt clung to his torso. Rain-dark hair straggled across his forehead. But he was oblivious to such things. And he did not see Linden coming. All of him was concentrated on the spectres of his past.

She knew them by the stories and descriptions she had heard of them. The Bloodguard Bannor resembled Brinn too closely to be mistaken. The man in the grave and simple robe had dangerous eyes balanced by a crooked, humane mouth: High Lord Mhoram. The woman was similarly attired because she also was a former High Lord; and her lucid beauty was marred – or accentuated – by a prophetic wildness that echoed Covenant's: she was Elena, daughter of Lena. And the Giant with laughter and certainty and grief shining from his gaze was surely Saltheart Foamfollower.

The power they emanated should have abashed Covenant, though it was not on the same scale as Kevin's. But he had no percipience with which to taste their peril. Or perhaps his ruinous intent called that danger by another name. His whole body seemed to yearn toward them as if they had come to comfort him.

To shore up his resolve, so that he would not falter from the destruction of the Earth.

And why not? In that way they would be granted rest from the weary millennia of their vigil.

Must, Linden thought. The alternative was altogether terrible. Yes. Her clothes soaked, her hair damp and heavy against her neck, she strode down into the gathering; and her rage shaped the night.

Covenant's Dead were potent and determined. At one time, she would have been at their mercy. But now her passion dominated them all. They turned toward her and fell silent in mingled surprise, pain, refusal. Bannor's face closed against her: Elena's was sharp with consternation. Mhoram and Foamfollower looked at her as if she cast their dreams into confusion.

But only Covenant spoke. 'Linden!' he breathed thickly, like a man who had just been weeping. 'You look awful. What's happened to you?'

She ignored him. Stalking through the drizzle, she went to confront his friends.

They shone a ghostly silver that transcended moonlight. The rain fell through their incorporeal forms. Yet their eyes were keen with the life which Andelain's Earthpower and the breaking of the Law of Death made possible for them. They stood in a loose arc before her. None of them quailed.

Behind her, Covenant's loss and love and incomprehension poured into the night. But they did not touch her. Kevin had finally opened her eyes, enabled her to see what the man she loved had become.

She met the eyes of the Dead one by one. The flat blade of Mhoram's nose steered him between the extremes of his vulnerability and strength. Elena's eyes were wide with speculation, as if she were wondering what Covenant saw in Linden. Bannor's visage wore the same dispassion with which Brinn had denounced her after the company's escape from *Bhrathairealm*. The soft smile that showed through Foamfollower's jutting beard underscored his concern and regret.

For a fraction of a moment, Linden nearly faltered. Foamfollower was the Pure One who had redeemed the *jheherrin*. He had once walked into lava to aid Covenant. Elena had been driven into folly at least in part by her love for the man who had raped her mother. Bannor had served the Unbeliever as faithfully as Brinn or Cail. And Mhoram – Linden and Covenant had embraced in his bed as though it were a haven.

But it had not been a haven. She had been wrong about that, and the truth appalled her. In her arms, in Mhoram's bed, Covenant had already decided on desecration – had already become certain of it. *It is his intent to place the white ring into Lord Foul's hand.* After he had sworn that he would not. Anguish surged up in her. Her cry ripped fiercely across the rain.

'Why aren't you *ashamed*?'

Then her passion began to blow like a high wind. She fanned it willingly, wanted to snuff out, punish, eradicate if she could the faces silver-lit and aghast in front of her.

'Have you been dead so long that you don't know what you're doing any more? Can't you remember from one minute to the next what matters here? This is *Andelain*! He's saved your souls at least once. And you want him to destroy it!

'*You.*' She jabbed accusations at Elena's mixed disdain and compassion. 'Do you still think you love him? Are you that arrogant? What good have you ever done him? None of this would've happened if you hadn't been so eager to rule the dead as well as the living.'

Her denunciation pierced the former High Lord. Elena tried to reply, tried to defend herself; but no words came. She had broken the Law of Death. The blame of the Sunbane was as much hers as Covenant's. Stricken and grieving, she wavered, lost force, and went out, leaving a momentary afterglow of silver in the rain.

But Linden had already turned on Bannor.

'And *you*. You with your bloody self-righteousness. You promised him service. Is that what you call *this*? Your people are sitting on their hands in Revelstone when they should be *here*! Hollian was killed because they didn't come with us to fight those ur-viles. Caer-Caveral is dead and it's only a matter of time before Andelain starts to rot. But never mind that. Aren't you satisfied with letting Kevin ruin the Land once? She flung the back of her hand in Covenant's direction. 'They should be here to stop him!'

Bannor had no answer. He cast a glance like an appeal at Covenant: then he, too, faded away. Around the hollow, the darkness deepened.

Fuming, Linden swung toward Foamfollower.

'Linden, no,' Covenant grated. 'Stop this.' He was close to fire. She could feel the burning in his veins. But his demand did not make her pause. He had no right to speak to her. His Dead had betrayed him – and now he meant to betray the Land.

'And *you*. Pure One! You at least I would've expected to care about him more than this. Didn't you learn anything from watching your people die, seeing that Raver rip their brains out? Do you think desecration is *desirable*?' The Giant flinched. Savagely, she went on, 'You could've prevented this. If you hadn't given him Vain. If you hadn't tried to make him think you were giving him hope, when what you were really doing was teaching him to surrender. You've got him believing he can afford to give in because Vain or some other miracle is going to save the world anyway. Oh, you're Pure all right. Foul himself isn't that Pure.'

'Chosen – ' Foamfollower murmured, 'Linden Avery – ' as if he wanted to plead with her and did not know how. 'Ah, forgive – The Landwaster has afflicted you with this pain. He does not comprehend. The vision which he lacked in life is not supplied in death. The path before you is the way of hope and doom, but he perceives only the outcome of his own despair. You must remember that he has been made to serve the Despiser. The ill of such service darkens his spirit. Covenant, hear me. Chosen, forgive!'

Shedding gleams in fragments, he disappeared into the dark.

'Damnation!' Covenant rasped. 'Damnation!' But now his curses were not directed at Linden. He seemed to be swearing at himself. Or at Kevin.

Transported out of all restraint, Linden turned at last to Mhoram.

'And you,' she said, as quiet as venom. '*You*. They called you "seer and oracle". That's what I've heard. Every time I turn around, he tells me he wishes you were with him. He values you more than anyone.' Her anger and grief were one, and she could not contain them: fury that Covenant had been so misled; tearing rue that he trusted her too little to share his burdens, that he preferred despair and destruction to any love or companionship which might ease his responsibilities. 'You should have told him the truth.'

The Dead High Lord's eyes shone with silver tears – yet he did not falter or vanish. The regret he emitted was not for himself: it was for her. And perhaps also for Covenant. An aching smile twisted his mouth. 'Linden Avery' – he made her name sound curiously rough and gentle – 'you gladden me. You are worthy of him. Never doubt that you may justly stand with him in the trial of all things. You have given sorrow to the Dead. But when they have bethought themselves of who you are, they will be likewise gladdened. Only this I urge of you: strive to remember that he also is worthy of you.'

Formally, he touched his palms to his forehead, then spread his arms wide in a bow that seemed to bare his heart. 'My friends!' he said in a voice that rang, 'I believe that you will prevail!'

Still bowing, he dissolved into the rain and was gone.

Linden stared after him dumbly. Under the cool touch of the drizzle, she was suddenly hot with shame.

But then Covenant spoke. 'You shouldn't have done that.' The effort he made to keep himself from howling constricted his voice. 'They don't deserve it.'

In response, Kevin's *Must!* shouted through her, leaving no room for remorse. Mhoram and the others belonged to Covenant's past, not hers. They had dedicated themselves to the ruin of everything for which she had ever learned to care. From the beginning, the breaking of the Law of Death had served only the Despiser. And it served him still.

She did not turn to Covenant. She feared that the mere shape of him, barely discernible through the dark, would make her weep like the Hills. Harshly, she replied, 'That's why you did it, isn't it? Why you made the *Haruchai* stay behind. After what Kevin did to the Bloodguard, you knew they would try to stop you.'

She felt him strive for self-mastery and fail. He had met his Dead with an acute and inextricable confusion of pain and joy which made him vulnerable now to the cut of her passion. 'You know better than that,' he returned. 'What in hell did Kevin say to you?'

Bitter as the breath of winter, she rasped, ' "I'll never give him the ring. Never." How many times do you think you said that? How many times did you promise – ?' Abruptly, she swung around, her arms raised to strike out at him – or to ward him away. 'You incredible bastard!' She could not see him, but her senses picked him precisely out of the dark. He was as rigid and obdurate as an icon of purpose carved of raw granite hurt. She had to rage at him in order to keep herself from crying out in anguish. 'Next to you, my father was a hero. At least he didn't *plan* to kill anybody but himself.' Black echoes hosted around her, making the night heinous. 'Haven't you even got the guts to go on living?'

'Linden.' She felt intensely how she pained him, how every word she spat hit him like a gout of vitriol. Yet instead of fighting her he strove for some comprehension of what had happened to her. 'What did Kevin say to you?'

But she took no account of his distress. He meant to betray her. Well, that was condign: what had she ever done to deserve otherwise? But his purpose would also destroy the Earth – a world which in spite of all corruption and malice still nurtured Andelain at its heart, still treasured Earthpower and beauty. Because he had given up. He had walked into the Banefire as if he knew what he was doing – and he had let the towering evil burn the last love out of him. Only pretence and mockery were left.

'You've been listening to Findail,' she flung at him. 'He's convinced you it's better to put the Land out of its misery than to go on fighting. I was terrified to tell you about my mother because I thought you were going to hate me. But this is worse. If you hated me, I could at least hope you might go on fighting.'

Then sobs thronged up in her. She barely held them back. 'You mean everything to me. You made me live again when I might as well have been dead. You convinced me to keep trying. But you've decided to give up.' The truth was as plain as the apprehension which etched him out of the wet dark. 'You're going to give Foul your ring.'

At that, a stinging pang burst from him. But it was not denial. She read it exactly. It was fear. Fear of her recognition. Fear of what she might do with the knowledge.

'Don't say it like that,' he whispered. 'You don't understand.' He appeared to be groping for some name with which to conjure her, to compel acquiescence – or at least an abeyance of judgment. 'You said you trusted me.'

'You're right,' she answered, grieving and weeping and raging all at once. 'I don't understand.'

She could not bear any more. Whirling from him, she fled into the rain. He cried after her as if something within him were being torn apart; but she did not stop.

Sometime in the middle of the night, the drizzle took on the full force of a summer storm. A cold, hard downpour pelted the Hills: wind sawed at the boughs and brush. But Linden did not seek shelter. She did not want to be protected. Covenant had already taken her too far down that road, warded her too much from the truth. Perhaps he feared her – was ashamed of what he meant to do and so sought to conceal it. But during the dark night of Andelain she did him the justice of acknowledging that he had also tried to protect her for her own sake – first from involvement in Joan's distress and the Land's need, then from the impact of Lord Foul's evil, then from the necessary logic of his death. And now from the implications of his despair. So that she would be free of blame for the loss of the Earth.

She did him that justice. But she hated it. He was a classic case: people who had decided on suicide and had no wish to be saved typically became calm and certain before taking their lives. Sheer pity for him would have broken her heart if she had been less angry.

Her own position would have been simpler if she could have believed him evil. Or if she had been sure that he had lost his mind. Then her only responsibility would have been to stop him at whatever cost. But the most terrible aspect of her dilemma was that his fused certainty betrayed neither madness nor malice at her health-sense. In the grip of an intent which was clearly insane or malign, he appeared more than ever to be the same strong, dangerous, and indomitable man with whom she had first fallen in love. She had never been able to refuse him.

Yet Kevin had loved the Land as much as anyone, and his protest beat at her like the storm. *When evil rises in its full power, it surpasses truth and may wear the guise of good without fear –*

Evil or crazy. Unless she fought her way into him, wrestled his deepest self-conceptions away from him and looked at them, she had no way to tell the difference.

But once before when she had entered him, trying to bring him back from the silence imposed on his spirit by the *Elohim*, he had appeared to her in the form of Marid – an innocent man made monstrous by a Raver and the Sunbane. A tool for the Despiser.

Therefore she fled him, hastened shivering and desperate among the Hills. She could not learn the truth without possessing him. And possession itself was evil. It was a kind of killing, a form of death. She had already sacrificed her mother to the darkness of her unhealed avarice for the power of death.

She did not seek shelter because she did not want it. She fled from Covenant because she feared what a confrontation with him would entail. And she kept on walking while the storm blew and rushed around her because she had no alternative. She was travelling eastward, toward the place where the sun would rise – toward the high crouched shoulders and crown of Mount Thunder.

Toward Lord Foul.

Her aim was as grim as lunacy – yet what else could she do? What else but strive to meet and outface the Despiser before Covenant arrived at his crisis? There was no other way to save him without possessing him – without exposing herself and him and the Land to the hot ache of her capacity for blackness.

That's right, she thought. I can do it. I've earned it.

She knew she was lying to herself. The Despiser would be hideously stronger than any Raver; and she had barely survived the simple proximity of *samadhi* Sheol. Yet she persisted. In spite of the night, and of the storm which sealed away the moon and the stars, she saw as clearly as vision that her past life was like the Land, a terrain possessed by corruption. She had let the legacy of her parents denude her of ordinary health and growth, had allowed a dark desire to rule her days like a Raver. In a sense, she had been possessed by hate from the moment when her father had said to her, *You never loved me anyway* – a hatred of life as well as of death. But then Covenant had come into her existence as he had into the Land, changing everything. He did not deserve despair. And she had the right to confront the Despite which had warped her, quenched her capacity for love, cut her off from the vitality of living. The right and the necessity.

Throughout the night, she went on eastward. Gradually, the storm abated, sank back to a drizzle and then blew away, unveiling a sky so star-bedizened and poignant that it seemed to have been washed clean. The slim curve of the moon setting almost directly behind her told her that her path was true. The air was cold on her sodden clothes and wet skin: her hair shed water like shivers down her back. But Andelain sustained her. Opulent under the unfathomable heavens, it made all things possible. Her heart lifted against its burdens. She kept on walking.

But when she crossed a ridge and met the first clear sight of the sunrise, she stopped – frozen in horror. The slopes and trees were heavy with raindrops; and each bead caught the light in its core, echoing back a tiny piece of daybreak to the sun, so that all the grass and woods were laced with gleams.

Yellow gleams fatally tinged by vermilion.

The sun wore a halo of pestilence as the Sunbane rose over the Hills.

It was so faint that only her sight could have discerned it. But it was there. The rapine of the Land's last beauty had begun.

For a long moment she remained still, surprised into her old paralysis by the unexpected swiftness with which the Sunbane attacked Andelain's residual Law. She had no power. There was nothing she could do. But her heart scrambled for defences – and found one. Her friends lacked her Land-bred senses. They would not see the Sunbane rising toward them; and so the Giants would not seek stone to protect themselves. They would be transformed like Marid into creatures of destruction and self-loathing.

She had left them leagues behind, could not possibly return to warn them in time. But she had to try. They needed her.

Abandoning all other intents, she launched herself in a desperate run back the way she had come.

The valley below the ridge was still deep in shadow. She was racing frenetically, and her eyes were slow to adjust. Before she was halfway down the hillside, she nearly collided with Vain.

He seemed to loom out of the crepuscular air without transition, translated instantly across the leagues. But as she reeled away from him, staggered for balance, she realized that he must have been trailing her all night. Her attention had been so focused on her thoughts and Andelain that she had not felt his presence.

Behind him in the bottom of the valley were Covenant, the First, and Pitchwife. They were following the Demondim-spawn.

After two nights without rest, Covenant looked haggard and febrile. But determination glared from his strides. He would not have stopped to save his life – not with Linden travelling ahead of him into peril. He did not look like the kind of man who could submit to despair.

But she had no time to consider his contradictions. The sun was rising above the ridge. 'The Sunbane!' she cried. 'It's here! Find stone!'

Covenant did not react: he appeared too weary to grasp anything except that he had found her again. Pitchwife stared dismay at the ridgecrest. But the First immediately began to scan the valley for any kind of rock.

Linden pointed, and the First saw it: a small, hoary outcropping of boulders near the base of the slope some distance away. At once, she grabbed her husband by the arm and pulled him at a run in that direction.

Linden glanced toward the sun, saw that the Giants would reach the stones with a few minutes to spare.

In reaction, all her strength seemed to wash out of her. Covenant was coming toward her, and she did not know how to face him. Wearily, she slumped to the grass. Everything she had tried to define for herself during the night had been lost. Now she would have to bear his company again, would have to live in the constant presence of his wild purpose. The Sunbane was rising in Andelain for the first time – She covered her face to conceal her tears.

He halted in front of her. For a moment, she feared that he would be foolish enough to sit down. But he remained standing so that his boots would ward him against the sun. He radiated fatigue, lamentation, and obduracy.

Stiffly, he said, 'Kevin doesn't understand. I have no intention of doing what he did. He raised his own hand against the Land. Foul didn't enact the Ritual of Desecration alone. He only shared it. I've already told you I'm never going to use power again. Whatever happens, I'm not going to be the one who destroys what I love.'

'What difference does that make?' Her bitterness was of no use to her. All the severity with which she had once endured the world was gone and refused to be conjured back. 'You're giving up. Never mind the Land. There're still three of us left who want to save it. We'll think of something. But you're abandoning yourself.' Do you expect me to forgive you for that?

'No.' Protest made his tone ragged. 'I'm not. There's just nothing left I can do for you any more. And I can't help the Land. Foul took care of that long before I ever got here.' His gall was something she could understand. But the conclusion he drew from it made no sense. 'I'm doing this for myself. He thinks the ring will give him what he wants. I know better. After what I've been through, I *know* better. He's wrong.'

His certainty made him impossible to refute. The only arguments she knew were the ones she had once used to her father, and they had always failed. They had been swallowed in darkness – in self-pity grown to malice and hosting forth to devour her spirit. No argument would suffice.

Vaguely, she wondered what account of her flight he had given the Giants.

But to herself she swore, I'm going to stop you. Somehow. No evil was as great as the ill of his surrender. The Sunbane had risen into Andelain. It could never be forgiven.

Somehow.

Later that day, as the company wended eastward among the Hills, Linden took an opportunity to drift away from Covenant and the First with Pitchwife. The malformed Giant was deeply troubled: his grotesque features appeared aggrieved, as if he had lost the essential cheer which preserved his visage from ugliness. Yet he was plainly reluctant to speak of his distress. At first, she thought that this reluctance arose from a new distrust of her. But as she studied him, she saw that his mood was not so simple.

She did not want to aggravate his unhappiness. But he had often shown himself willing to be pained on behalf of his friends. And her need was exigent. Covenant meant to give the Despiser his ring.

Softly, so that she would not be overheard, she breathed, 'Pitchwife, help me. Please.'

She was prepared for the dismal tone of his reply, but not for its import. 'There is no help,' he answered. 'She will not question him.'

'She – ?' Linden began, then caught herself. Carefully, she asked, 'What did he say to you?'

For an aching moment, Pitchwife was still. Linden forced herself to give him time. He would not look at her. His gaze wandered the Hills morosely, as if already they had lost their lustre: without her senses, he could not see that Andelain had not yet been damaged by the Sunbane. Then, sighing, he mustered words out of his gloom.

'Rousing us from sleep to hasten in your pursuit, he announced your belief that it is now his intent to destroy the Land. And Gossamer Glowlimn my wife will not question him.

'I acknowledge that he is the Earthfriend – worthy of all trust. But have you not again and again proven yourself alike deserving? You are the Chosen, and for the mystery of your place among us we have been accorded no insight. Yet the *Elohim* have named you Sun-Sage. You alone possess the sight which proffers hope of healing. Repeatedly the burdens of our Search have fallen to you – and you have borne them well. I will not believe that you who have wrought so much restoration among the Giants and the victims of the Clave have become in the space of one night mad or cruel. And you have withdrawn trust from him. This is grave in all sooth. It must be questioned. But she is the First of the Search. She forbids.

'Chosen – ' His voice was full of innominate pleading, as if he wanted something from her and did not know what it was. 'It is her word that we have no other hope than him. If he has become untrue, then all is lost. Does he not hold the white ring? Therefore we must preserve our faith in him – and be still. Should he find himself poised on the blade-edge of his doom, we must not overpush him with our doubt.

'But if he must not be called to an accounting, what decency or justice will permit you to be questioned? I will not do it though the lack of this story is grievous. If you are not to be equally trusted, you must at least be equally left in silence.'

Linden did not know how to respond. She was distressed by his troubled condition, gratified by his fairness, and incensed by the

First's attitude. Yet would she not have taken the same position in the Swordmain's place? If Kevin Landwaster had spoken to someone else, would she not have been proud to repose her confidence in the Unbeliever? But that recognition only left her all the more alone. She had no right to try to persuade Pitchwife to her cause: both he and his wife deserved better than that she should attempt to turn them against each other — or against Covenant. And yet she had no way to test or affirm her own sanity except by direct opposition to him.

Even in his fixed weariness and determination, he was so dear to her that she could hardly endure the acuity of her desire for him.

A fatigue and defeat of her own made her stumble over the uneven turf. But she refused the solace of Pitchwife's support. Wanly, she asked him, 'What are you going to do?'

'Naught,' he replied. 'I am capable of naught.' His empathy for her made him acidulous. 'I have no sight to equal yours. Before the truth becomes plain to me, the time for all necessary doing will have come and gone. That which requires to be done, you must do.' He paused; and she thought that he was finished, that their comradeship had come to an end. But then he gritted softly through his teeth, 'Yet I say this, Chosen. You it was who obtained Vain Demondim-spawn's escape from the snares of *Elemesnedene*. You it was who made possible our deliverance from the Sandhold. You it was who procured safety for all but Cable Seadreamer from the Worm of the World's End, when the Earthfriend himself had fallen nigh to ruin. And you it was who found means to extinguish the Banefire. Your worth is manifold and certain.

'The First will choose as she wishes. I will give you my life, if you ask it of me.'

Linden heard him. After a while, she said simply, 'Thanks.' No words were adequate. In spite of his own baffled distress he had given her what she needed.

They walked on together in silence.

The next morning, the sun's red aura was distinct enough for all the company to see.

Linden's open nerves searched the Hills, probing Andelain's reaction to the Sunbane. At first, she found none. The air had its same piquant savour, commingled of flowers and dew and treesap. *Aliantha* abounded on the hillsides. No discernible ill gnawed at the wood of the nearby Gildens and willows. And the birds and animals that flitted or scurried into view and away again were not suffering from any wrong. The Earthpower treasured in the heart of the region still withstood the pressure of corruption.

But by noon that was no longer true. Pangs of pain began to run up the tree trunks, aching in the veins of the leaves. The birds seemed to become frantic as the numbers of insects increased; but the woodland creatures had grown frightened and gone into hiding. The tips of the grass-blades turned brown: some of the shrubs showed signs of blight. A distant fetor came slowly along the breeze. And the ground began to give off faint, emotional tremors – an intangible quivering which no one but Linden felt. It made the soles of her feet hurt in her shoes.

Muttering curses, Covenant stalked on angrily eastward. In spite of her distrust, Linden saw that his rage for Andelain was genuine. He pushed himself past the limits of his strength to hasten his traversal of the Hills, his progress toward the crisis of the Despiser. The Sunbane welded him to his purpose.

Linden kept up with him doggedly, determined not to let him get ahead of her. She understood his fury, shared it: in this place, the red sun was atrocious, intolerable. But his ire made him appear capable of any madness which might put an end to Andelain's hurt, for good or ill.

Dourly, the Giants accompanied their friends. Covenant's best pace was not arduous for Pitchwife: the First could have travelled much faster. And her features were sharp with desire for more speed, for a termination to the Search, so that the question which had come between her and her husband would be answered and finished. The difficulty of restraining herself to Covenant's short strides was obvious in her. While the company paced through the day, she held herself grimly silent. Her mother had died in childbirth; her father, in the Soulbiter. She bore herself as if she did not want to admit how important Pitchwife's warmth had become to her.

For that reason, Linden felt a strange, unspoken kinship towards the First. She found it impossible to resent the Swordmain's attitude. And she swore to herself that she would never ask Pitchwife to keep his promise.

Vain strode blankly behind the companions. But of Findail there was no sign. She watched for him at intervals, but he did not reappear.

That evening, Covenant slept for barely half the night: then he went on his way again as if he were trying to steal ahead of his friends. But somehow through her weary slumber Linden felt him leave. She roused herself, called the Giants up from the faintly throbbing turf, and went after him.

Sunrise brought an aura of fertility to the dawn and a soughing rustle like a whisper of dread to the trees and brush. Linden felt the leaves whimpering on their boughs, the greensward aching plaintively. Soon the Hills would be reduced to the victimized helplessness of the rest of the Land: they would be scourged to wild growth, desiccated to ruin, afflicted with rot, pummelled by torrents. And that thought made her as fierce as Covenant, enabled her to keep up with him while he exhausted himself. Yet the mute pain of green and tree was not the worst effect of the Sunbane. Her senses had been scoured to raw sensitivity: she knew that beneath the sod, under the roots of the woods, the fever of Andelain's bones had become so argute that it was almost physical. A nausea of revulsion was rising into the Earthpower of the Hills. It made her guts tremble as if she were walking across an open wound.

By degrees, Covenant's pace became laboured. Andelain no longer sustained him. More and more of is waning strength went to ward off the corruption of the Sunbane. As a result, the fertile sun had little superficial effect. A few trees groaned taller, grew twisted with hurt: some of the shrubs raised their branches like limbs of desecration. All the birds and animals seemed to have fled. But most of the woods and grass were preserved by the power of the soil in which they grew. *Aliantha* clung stubbornly to themselves, as they had for centuries. Only the analystic refulgence of the Hills was gone – only the emanation of superb and concentrated health – only the exquisite vitality.

However, the sickness in the underlying rock and dirt mounted without cessation. That night, Covenant slept the sleep of exhaustion and *diamondraught*. But for a long time Linden could not rest, despite her own fatigue. Whenever she laid her head to the grass, she heard the ground grinding its teeth against a backdrop of slow moans and futile outrage.

Well before dawn, she and her companions arose and went on. She felt now that they were racing the dissolution of the Hills.

That morning, they caught their first glimpse of Mount Thunder.

It was still at least a day away. But it stood stark and fearsome above Andelain, with the sun leering past its shoulder and a furze of unnatural vegetation darkening its slopes. From this distance, it looked like a titan that had been beaten to its knees.

Somewhere inside that mountain, Covenant intended to find Lord Foul.

He turned to Linden and the Giants, his eyes red-rimmed and flagrant. Words yearned in him, but he seemed unable to utter them. She had thought him uncognizant of the Giants' disconsolation, offended by her own intransigent refusal; but she saw now that he was not. He understood her only too well. A fierce and recalcitrant part of him felt as she did, fought like loathing against his annealed purpose. He did not want to die, did not want to lose her or the Land. And he had withheld any explanation of himself from the Giants so that they would not side with him against her. So that she would not be altogether alone.

He wished to say all those things. They were palpable to her aggrieved senses. But his throat closed on them like a fist, would not let them out.

She might have reached out to him then. Without altering any of her promises, she could have put her love around him. But horror swelled in the ground on which they stood, and it snatched her attention away from him.

Abhorrence. Execration. Sunbane and Earthpower locked in mortal combat beneath her feet. And the Earthpower could not win. No Law defended it. Corruption was going to tear the heart out of the Hills. The ground had become so unstable that the Giants and Covenant felt its tremors.

'Dear Christ!' Linden gasped. She grabbed Covenant's arm. 'Come on!' With all her strength, she pulled him away from the focus of Andelain's horror.

The Giants were aghast with incomprehension; but they followed her. Together, the companions began to run.

A moment later, the grass where they had been standing erupted.

Buried boulders shattered. A large section of the greensward was shredded: stone-shards and dirt slashed into the sky. The violence which broke the Earthpower in that place sent a shock throughout the region, gouged a pit in the body of the ground. Remnants of ruined beauty rained everywhere.

And from the naked walls of the pit came squirming and clawing the sick, wild verdure of the fertile sun. Monstrous as murder, a throng of ivy teemed upward to spread its pall over the ravaged turf.

In the distance, another eruption boomed. Linden felt it like a wail through the ground. Piece by piece, the life of Andelain was being torn up by the roots.

'Bastard!' Covenant raged. 'Oh, you bastard! You've crippled everything else. Aren't you content.'

Turning, he plunged eastward as if he meant to launch himself at the Despiser's throat.

Linden kept up with him. Pain belaboured her senses. She could not speak because she was weeping.

17

INTO THE WIGHTWARRENS

Early the next morning, the company climbed into the foothills of Mount Thunder near the constricted rush of the Soulsease River. Covenant was gaunt with fatigue, his gaze as grey as ash. Linden's eyes burned like fever in their sockets: strain throbbed through the bones of her skull. Even the Giants were tired. They had only stopped to rest in snatches during the night. The First's lips were the colour of her fingers clinching the hilt of her sword. Pitchwife's visage looked like it was being torn apart. Yet the four of them were united by their urgency. They attacked the lower slopes as if they were racing the sun which rose behind the fatal bulk of the mountain.

A desert sun.

Parts of Andelain had already become as blasted and ruinous as a battlefield.

The Hills still clung to the life which had made them lovely. While it lasted, Caer-Caveral's nurture had been complete and fundamental. The Sunbane could not simply flush all Earthpower from the ground in so few days. But the dusty sunlight reaching past the shoulders of Mount Thunder revealed that around the fringes of Andelain – and in places across its heart – the damage was already severe.

The vegetation of those regions had been ripped up, riven, effaced by hideous eruptions. Their ground was cratered and pitted like the ravages of an immedicable disease. The previous day, the remnants of those woods had been overgrown and strangled by the Sunbane's feral fecundity. But now, as the sun advanced on that verdure, every green and living thing slumped into viscid sludge which the desert drank away.

Linden gazed toward the Hills as if she, too, were dying. Nothing would ever remove the sting of that devastation from her heart. The sickness of the world soaked into her from the landscape outstretched and tormented before her. Andelain still fought for its life and survived. Much of it had not yet been hurt. Leagues of soft slopes and natural growth separated the craters, stood against the sun's arid rapine. But where the Sunbane had done its work the harm was as keen as anguish. If she had been granted the chance to save Andelain's health with her own life, she would have taken it as promptly as Covenant. Perhaps she, too, would have smiled.

She sat on a rock in a field of boulders that cluttered the slope too thickly to admit vegetation. Panting as if his lungs were raw with ineffective outrage, Covenant had stopped there to catch his breath. The Giants stood nearby. The First studied the west as though that scene of destruction would give her strength when the time came to wield her blade. But Pitchwife could not bear it. He perched himself on a boulder with his back to the Andelainian Hills. His hands toyed with his flute, but he made no attempt to play it.

After a while, Covenant rasped, 'Broken – ' There was a slain sound in his voice, as if within him also something vital were perishing. 'All that beauty – ' Perhaps during the night he had lost his mind. '"Your very presence here empowers me to master you. The ill that you deem most terrible is upon you."' He was quoting

Lord Foul; but he spoke as if the words were his. '"There is despair laid up for you here – "'

At once, the First turned to him. 'Do not speak thus. It is false.'

He gave no sign that he had heard her. 'It's not my fault,' he went on harshly. 'I didn't do any of this. None of it. But I'm the cause. Even when I don't do anything. It's all being done because of me. So I won't have any choice. Just by being alive, I break everything I love.' He scraped his numb fingers through the stubble of his beard; but his eyes continued staring at the waste of Andelain, haunted by it. 'You'd think I wanted this to happen.'

'No!' the First protested. 'We hold no such conception. You must not doubt. It is doubt which weakens – doubt which corrupts. Therefore is this Despiser powerful. *He* does not doubt. While you are certain, there is hope.' Her iron voice betrayed a note of fear. 'This price will be exacted from him if you do not doubt!'

Covenant looked at her for a moment. Then he rose stiffly to his feet. His muscles and his heart were knotted so tightly that Linden could not read him.

'That's wrong.' He spoke softly, in threat or appeal. 'You need to doubt. Certainty is terrible. Let Foul have it. Doubt makes you human.' His gaze shifted toward Linden: it reached out to her like flame or beggary, the culmination and defeat of all his power in the Banefire. 'You need every doubt you can find. I want you to doubt. I'm hardly human any more.'

Each flare and wince of his eyes contradicted itself. Stop me. Don't touch me. Doubt me. Doubt Kevin. Yes. No. Please.

Please.

His inchoate supplication drew her to him. He did not appear strong or dangerous now, but only needy, appalled by himself. Yet he was as irrefusable as ever. She touched her hand to his scruffy cheek: her arms hurt with the tenderness of her wish to hold him.

But she would not retreat from the commitments she had made, whatever their cost. Perhaps her years of medical training and self-abnegation had been nothing more than a way of running away from death; but the simple logic of that flight had taken her in the direction of life, for others if not for herself. And in the marrow of her bones she had experienced both the Sunbane and Andelain. The choice between them was as clear as Covenant's pain.

She had no answer for his appeal. Instead, she gave him one of her own. 'Don't force me to do that.' Her love was naked in her eyes. 'Don't give up.'

A spasm of grief or anger flinched across his face. His voice sank to a desert scraping in the back of his throat. 'I wish I could make you understand.' He spoke flatly, all inflection burned away. 'He's gone too far. He can't get away with this. Maybe he isn't really sane any more. He isn't going to get what he wants.'

But his manner and his words held no comfort for her. He might as well have announced to the Giants and Vain and the ravaged world that he still intended to surrender his ring.

Yet he remained strong enough for his purpose, in spite of little food, less rest, and the suffering of Andelain. Dourly, he faced the First and Pitchwife again as if he expected questions or protests. But the Swordmain held herself stern. Her husband did not look up from his flute.

To their silence, Covenant replied, 'We need to go north for a while. Until we get to the River. That's our way into Mount Thunder.'

Sighing, Pitchwife gained his feet. He held his flute in both hands. His gaze was focused on nothing as he snapped the small instrument in half.

With all his strength, he hurled the pieces toward the Hills.

Linden winced. An expostulation died on the First's lips. Covenant's shoulders hunched.

As grim as a cripple, Pitchwife raised his eyes to the Unbeliever. 'Heed me well,' he murmured clearly. 'I doubt.'

'Good!' Covenant rasped like a snarl. Then he started moving again, picking a path for himself among the boulders.

Linden followed with old cries beating against her heart. *Haven't you even got the guts to go on living? You never loved me anyway*. But she knew as surely as vision that he did love her. She had no means by which to measure what had happened to him in the Banefire. And Gibbon's voice answered her, taunting her with the truth. *Are you not evil?*

The foothills of Mount Thunder, ancient Gravin Threndor, were too rugged to bear much vegetation. And the light of the desert sun advanced rapidly past the peak now, wreaking dissolution on the ground's residual fertility. The company was hampered by strewn boulders and knuckled slopes, but not by the effects of the previous sun. Still the short journey toward the Soulsease was arduous. The sun's loathsome corruption seemed to parch away the last of Linden's strength: heatwaves like precursors of hallucination tugged at the edges of her mind. A confrontation with the Despiser would at least put an end to this horror and rapine. One way or the other. As she panted at the hillsides, she found herself repeating the promise she had once made in Revelstone – the promise she had made and broken. *Never. Never again*. Whatever happened, she would not return to the Sunbane.

Because of her weakness, Covenant's exhaustion, and the difficulty of the terrain, the company did not reach the vicinity of the River until midmorning.

The way the hills baffled sound enabled her to catch a glimpse of the swift water before she heard it. Then she and her companions topped the last rise between them and the Soulsease; and the loud howl of its rush slapped at her. Narrowed by its stubborn granite channel, the River raced below her, white and writhing as if it had abandoned itself to its doom. And its doom towered over it, so massive and dire that the mountain filled all the east. Perhaps a league to Linden's right, the River flumed into the gullet of Mount Thunder and was swallowed away – ingested by the catacombs which mazed the hidden depths of the peak. When that water emerged again, on the Lower Land behind Gravin Threndor, it would be so polluted by the vileness of the Wightwarrens, so rank with the waste of charnels and breeding dens, the spillage of forges and laboratories, the effluvium of corruption, that it would be called the Defiles Course – the source of Sarangrave Flat's peril and perversion.

For a crazy moment, Linden thought Covenant meant to ride that extreme current into the mountain. But then he pointed toward the bank directly below him; and she saw that a roadway had been cut into the foothills at some height above the River. The River itself was declining: six days had passed since the last sun of rain; and the desert sun was rapidly drinking away the water which Andelain still provided. But the markings on the channel's sheer walls showed that the Soulsease virtually never reached as high as the roadway.

Along this road in ages past, armies had marched out of Mount Thunder to attack the Land. Much of the surface was ruinous, cracked and gouged by time and the severe alternation of the Sunbane, slick with spray; but it was still traversable. And it led straight into the dark belly of the mountain.

Covenant gestured toward the place where the walls rose like cliffs to meet the sides of Mount Thunder. He had to shout to make himself heard, and his voice was veined with stress. 'That's Treacher's Gorge! Where Foul betrayed Kevin and the Council openly for the first time! Before they knew what he was! The war that broke Kevin's heart started there!'

The First scanned the thrashing River, the increasing constriction of the precipitate walls, then raised her voice through the roar. 'Earthfriend, you have said that the passages of this mountain are a maze! How then may we discover the lurking place of the Despiser?'

'We won't have to!' His shout sounded feverish. He looked as tense and strict and avid as he had when Linden had first met him – when he had slammed the door of his house against her. 'Once we get in there, all we have to do is wander around until we run into his defences. He'll take care of the rest. The only trick is to stay alive until we get to him!'

Abruptly, he turned to his companions. 'You don't have to come! I'll be safe. He won't do anything to me until he has me right in front of him.' To Linden, he seemed to be saying the same things he had said on Haven Farm. *You don't know what's going on here. You couldn't possibly understand it. Go away. I don't need you.* 'You don't need to risk it.'

But the First was not troubled by such memories. She replied promptly, 'Of what worth is safety to us here? The Earth itself is at risk. Hazard is our chosen work. How will we bear the songs which our people will sing of us, if we do not hold true to the Search? We will not part from you.'

Covenant ducked his head as though he were ashamed or afraid. Perhaps he was remembering Saltheart Foamfollower. Yet his refusal or inability to meet Linden's gaze indicated to her that she had not misread him. He was still vainly trying to protect her, spare her the consequences of her choices – consequences she did not know how to measure. And striving also to prevent her from interfering with what he meant to do.

But he did not expose himself to what she would say if he addressed her directly. Instead, he muttered, 'Then let's get going.' The words were barely audible. 'I don't know how much longer I can stand this.'

Nodding readily, the First at once moved ahead of him toward an erosion gully which angled down to the roadway. With one hand, she gripped the hilt of her longsword. Like her companions, she had lost too much in this quest. She was a warrior and wanted to measure out the price in blows.

Covenant followed her stiffly. The only strength left in his limbs was the stubbornness of his will.

Linden started after him, then turned back to Pitchwife. He still stood on the rim of the hill, gazing down into the River's rush as if it would carry his heart away. Though he was half again as tall as Linden, his deformed spine and grotesque features made him appear old and frail. His mute aching was as tangible as tears. Because of it, she put everything else aside for a moment.

'He was telling the truth about that, anyway. He doesn't need you to fight for him. Not anymore.' Pitchwife lifted his eyes like pleading to her. Fiercely, she went on, 'And if he's wrong, I can stop him.' That also was true: the Sunbane and Ravers and Andelain's hurt had made her capable of it. 'The First is the one who needs you. She can't beat Foul with just a sword – but she's likely to try. Don't let her get herself killed.' *Don't do that to yourself. Don't sacrifice her for me.*

His visage sharpened like a cry. His hands opened at his sides to show her and the desert sky that they were empty. Moisture blurred his gaze. For a moment, she feared he would say farewell to her; and hard grief clenched her throat. But then a fragmentary smile changed the meaning of his face.

'Linden Avery,' he said clearly, 'have I not affirmed and averred to all who would hear that you are well Chosen?'

Stooping toward her, he kissed her forehead. Then he hurried after the First and Covenant.

When she had wiped the tears from her cheeks, she followed him.

Vain trailed her with his habitual blankness. Yet she seemed to feel a hint of anticipation from him – an elusive tightening which he had not conveyed since the company had entered *Elemesnedene*.

Picking her way down the gully, she gained the rude shelf of the roadway and found her companions waiting for her. Pitchwife stood beside the First, reclaiming his place there; but both she and Covenant watched Linden. The First's regard was a compound of glad relief and uncertainty: she welcomed anything that eased her husband's unhappiness – but was unsure of its implications. Covenant's attitude was simpler. Leaning close to Linden, he whispered against the background of the throttled River, 'I don't know what you said to him. But thanks.'

She had no answer. Constantly, he foiled her expectations. When he appeared most destructive and unreachable, locked away in his deadly certainty, he showed flashes of poignant kindness, clear concern. Yet behind his empathy and courage lay his intended surrender, as indefeasible as despair. He contradicted himself at every turn. And how could she reply without telling him what she had promised?

But he did not appear to want an answer. Perhaps he understood her, knew that in her place he would have felt as she did. Or perhaps he was too weary and haunted to suffer questions or reconsider his purpose. He was starving for an end to his pain. Almost immediately, he signalled his readiness to go on.

At once, the First started along the crude road toward the gullet of Mount Thunder.

With Pitchwife and then Vain behind her, Linden followed, stalking the stone as if she were pursuing the Unbeliever to his crisis.

Below her, the Soulsease continued to shrink between its walls, consumed by the power of the Sunbane. The pitch of the rush changed, as its roar softened toward sobbing. But she did not take her gaze from the backs of the First and Covenant, the rising sides of the Gorge, the dark bulk of the mountain. Off that sun-ravaged crown had once come creatures of fire to rescue Thomas Covenant and the Lords from the armies of Drool Rockworm, the mad Cavewight. But those creatures had been called down by Law; and there was no more Law.

She had to concentrate to avoid the treachery of the road's surface. It was cracked and dangerous. Sections of the ledge were so tenuously held in place that her percipience felt them shift under her weight. Others had fallen into the Gorge long ago, leaving bitter scars where the road should have been: only narrow rims remained to bear the company past the gaps. Linden feared them more on Covenant's behalf than on her own: his vertigo might make him fall. But he negotiated them without help, as if his fear of heights were just one more part of himself that he had already given up. Only the strain burning in his muscles betrayed how close he came to panic.

Mount Thunder loomed into the sky. The desert sun scorched over the rocks, scouring them bare of spray. The noise of the Soulsease sounded increasingly like grief. In spite of her fatigue, Linden wanted to run — wanted to pitch herself into the mountain's darkness for no other reason than to get out from under the Sunbane. Out of daylight into the black catacombs, where so much power lurked and hungered.

Where no one else would be able to see what happened when the outer dark met the blackness within her and took possession.

She fought the logic of that outcome, wrestled to believe that she would find some other answer. But Covenant intended to give Lord Foul his ring. Where else could she find the force to stop him?

She had done the same thing once before, in a different way. Faced with her dying mother, the nightmare blackness had leaped up in her, taking command of her hand while her brain had detached itself to watch and wail. And the darkness had laughed like lust.

She had spent every day of every year of her adulthood fighting to suppress that avarice for death. But she knew of no other source from which she might obtain the sheer strength she would need to prevent Covenant from destruction.

And she had promised —

Treacher's Gorge narrowed and rose on either side. Mount Thunder vaulted above her like a tremendous cairn that marked the site of buried banes, immedicable despair. As the River's lamentation sank to a mere shout, the mountain opened its gullet in front of the company.

The First stopped there, glowering distrust into the tunnel that swallowed the Soulsease and the roadway. But she did not speak. Pitchwife unslung his diminished pack, took out his firepot and the last two faggots he had borne from Revelstone. One he slipped under his belt: the other he stirred into the firepot until the wood caught flame. The First took it from him, held it up as a torch. She drew her sword. Covenant's visage wore a look of nausea or dread; but he did not hesitate. When the First nodded, he started forward.

Pitchwife quickly repacked his supplies. Together, he and Linden followed his wife and Covenant out of the Gorge and the desert sun.

Vain came after them like a piece of whetted midnight, acute and imminent.

Linden's immediate reaction was one of relief. The First's torch hardly lit the wall on her right, the curved ceiling above her: it shed no light into the chasm beside the roadway. But to her any dark felt kinder than the sunlight. The peak's clenched granite reduced the number of directions from which peril could come. And as Mount Thunder cut off the sky, she heard the sound of the Soulsease more precisely. The crevice drank the River like a plunge into the bowels of the mountain, carrying the water down to its defilement. Such things steadied her by requiring her to concentrate on them.

In a voice that echoed hoarsely, she warned her companions away from the increasing depth of the chasm. She sounded close to hysteria; but she believed she was not. The Giants had only two torches. The company would need her special senses for guidance. She would be able to be of use again.

But her relief was shortlived. She had gone no more than fifty paces down the tunnel when she felt the ledge behind her heave itself into rubble.

Pitchwife barked a warning. One of his long arms swept her against the wall. The impact knocked the air from her lungs. For an instant while her head reeled, she saw Vain silhouetted against the daylight of the Gorge. He made no effort to save himself.

Thundering like havoc, the fragments of the roadway bore him down into the crevice.

Long tremors ran through the road, up the wall. Small stones rained from the ceiling, pelted after the Demondim-spawn like a scattering of hail. Linden's chest did not contain enough air to cry out his name.

Torchlight splayed across her and Pitchwife. He tugged her backward, kept her pressed to the wall. The First barred Covenant's way. Sternness locked her face. Sputtering flames reflected from his eyes. 'Damnation,' he muttered. 'Damnation!' Little breaths like gasps slipped past Linden's teeth.

The torch and the glow of day beyond the tunnel lit Findail as he melted out of the roadway, transforming himself from stone to flesh as easily as thought.

He appeared to have become leaner, worn away by pain. His cheeks were hollow. His yellow eyes had sunk into his skull: their sockets were as livid as bruises. He was rife with mortification or grief.

'You did that,' Linden panted. 'You're still trying to kill him.'

He did not meet her gaze. The arrogance of his people was gone from him. 'The Würd of the *Elohim* is strict and costly.' If he had raised his eyes to Linden's, she might have thought he was asking for understanding or acceptance. 'How should it be otherwise? Are we not the heart of the Earth in all things? Yet those who remain in the bliss and blessing of *Elemesnedene* have been misled by their comfort. Because the *clachan* is our home, we have considered that all questions may be answered there. Yet it is not in *Elemesnedene* that the truth lies, but rather in we who people that place. And we have mistaken our Würd. Because we are the heart, we have conceived that whatever we will must perforce transcend all else.

'Therefore we do not question our withdrawal from the wide Earth. We contemplate all else, yet give no name to what we fear.'

Then he did look up; and his voice took on the anger of self-justification. 'But I have witnessed that fear. Chant and others have fallen to it. Infelice herself knows its touch. And I have participated in the binding to doom of the Appointed. I have felt the curse of Kastenessen upon my head.' He was ashamed of what he had done to Vain — and determined not to regret it. 'You have taught me to esteem you. You bear the outcome of the Earth well. But my peril is thereby increased.

'I will not suffer that cost.'

Folding his arms across his chest, he closed himself off from interrogation.

In bafflement, Covenant turned to Linden. But she had no explanation to offer. Her percipience had never been a match for the *Elohim*. She had caught no glimpse of Findail until he emerged from the roadway, still knew nothing about him except that he was Earthpower incarnate, capable of taking any form of life he wished. Altogether flexible. And dangerously unbound by scruple. His people had not hesitated to efface Covenant's mind for their own inhuman reasons. More than once, he had abandoned her and her companions to death when he could have aided them.

His refusals seemed innumerable; and the memory of them made her bitter. The pain of the tree he had slaughtered in his last attempt on Vain's life came back to her. To Covenant, she replied, 'He's never told the truth before. Why should he start now?'

Covenant frowned darkly. Although he had no cause to trust Findail's people, he appeared strangely reluctant to judge them, as if instinctively he wanted to do them more justice than they had ever done him.

But there was nothing any of the company could do about Vain. The River-cleft was deep now — and growing sharply deeper as it advanced into the mountain. The sound of the water diminished steadily.

The First gestured with her torch. 'We must hasten. Our light grows brief.' The faggot she held was dry and brittle: already half of it had burned away. And Pitchwife had only one other brand.

Swearing under his breath, Covenant started on down the tunnel.

Linden was shivering. The stone piled imponderably around her felt cold and dire. Vain's fall repeated itself across her mind. Her breathing scraped in her throat. No one deserved to fall like that. In spite of Mount Thunder's chill atmosphere, sweat trickled uncertainly between her breasts.

But she followed Covenant and the First. Bracing herself on Pitchwife's bulky companionship, she moved along the roadway after the wavering torch. She stayed so close to the wall that it brushed her shoulder. Its hardness raised reminders of the hold of Revelstone and the dungeon of the Sandhold.

Findail walked behind her. His bare feet made no sound.

As the reflected light from the mouth of the gullet faded, the darkness thickened. Concentrated midnight seemed to flow up out of the crevice. Then a gradual bend in the wall cut off the outer world altogether. She felt that the doors of hope and possibility were being closed on all sides. The First's torch would not last much longer.

Yet her senses clung to the granite facts of the road and the tunnel. She could not see the rim of the chasm; but she knew where it was exactly. Pitchwife and Findail were also explicit in spite of the dark. When she focused her attention, she was able to read the surface of the ledge so clearly that she did not need to stumble. If she had possessed the power to repulse attack, she could have wandered the Wightwarrens in relative safety.

That realization steadied her. The inchoate dread gnawing at the edges of her courage receded.

The First's brand started to gutter.

Beyond it, Linden seemed to see an indefinable softening of the midnight. For a few moments, she stared past the First and Covenant. But her percipience did not extend so far. Then, however, the Swordmain halted, lowered her torch; and the glow ahead became more certain.

The First addressed Covenant or Linden. 'What is the cause of that light?'

'Warrenbridge,' Covenant replied tightly. 'The only way into the Wightwarrens.' His tone was complex with memories. 'Be careful. The last time I was here, it was guarded.'

The leader of the Search nodded. Placing her feet softly, she moved forward again. Covenant went with her.

Linden gripped her health-sense harder and followed.

Gradually, the light grew clear. It was a stiff, red-orange colour; and it shone along the ceiling, down the wall of the tunnel. Soon Linden was able to see that the roadway took a sharp turn to the right near the glow. At the same time, the overhanging stone vaulted upward as if the tunnel opened into a vast cavern. But the direct light was blocked by a tremendous boulder which stood like a door ajar across the ledge. The chasm of the River vanished under that boulder.

Cautiously, the First crept to the edge of the stone and peered beyond it.

For an instant, she went rigid with surprise. Then she breathed a

Giantish oath and strode out into the light.

Advancing behind Covenant, Linden found herself in a high, bright cavity like an entryhall to the catacombs.

The floor was flat, worn smooth by millennia of use. Yet it was impassable. The cleft passed behind the boulder, then turned to cut directly through the cavern, disappearing finally into the far wall. It was at least fifty feet wide, and there were no other entrances to the cavity on this side. The only egress lay beyond the crevice.

But in the centre of the vault, a massive bridge of native stone spanned the gulf. Warrenbridge. Covenant's memory had not misled him.

The light came from the crown of the span. On either side of it stood a tall stone pillar like a sentinel; and they shone as if their essential rock were afire. They made the entire cavern bright – too bright for any interloper to approach Warrenbridge unseen.

For an instant, the light held Linden's attention. It reminded her of the hot lake of gravelling in which she and the company had once almost lost their lives. But these emanations were redder, angrier. They lit the entrance to the Wightwarrens as if no one could pass between them in hope or peace.

But the chasm and the bridge and the light were not what had surprised the First. With a wrench, Linden forced herself to look across the vault.

Vain stood there, at the foot of Warrenbridge. He seemed to be waiting for Covenant or Linden.

Near him on the stone sprawled two long-limbed forms. They were dead. But they had not been dead long. The blood in which they lay was still warm.

A clench of pain passed across Findail's visage and was gone.

The First's torch sputtered close to her hand. She tossed its useless butt into the chasm. Gripping her longsword in both fists, she started onto the span.

'Wait!' Covenant's call was hoarse and urgent. At once, the First froze. The tip of her blade searched the air for perils she could not see.

Covenant wheeled toward Linden, his gaze as dark as bloodshed. Trepidation came from him in fragments.

'The last time – It nearly killed me. Drool used those pillars – that rocklight – I thought I was going to lose my mind.'

Drool Rockworm was the Cavewight who had recovered the Staff of Law after the Ritual of Desecration. He had used it to delve up the Illearth Stone from the roots of Mount Thunder. And when Covenant and the Lords had wrested the Staff from Drool, they had succeeded only in giving the Illearth Stone into Lord Foul's hold.

Linden's percipience scrambled into focus on the pillars. She scrutinized them for implications of danger, studied the air between them, the ancient stone of Warrenbridge. That stone had been made as smooth as mendacity by centuries of time, the pressure of numberless feet. But it posed no threat. Rocklight shone like ire from the pillars, concealing nothing.

Slowly, she shook her head. 'There's nothing there.'

Covenant started to ask, 'Are you – ?' then bit down his apprehension. Waving the First ahead, he ascended the span as if Warrenbridge were crowded with vertigo.

At the apex, he flinched involuntarily: his arms flailed, grasping for balance. But Linden caught hold of him. Pitchwife put his arms around the two of them. By degrees, Covenant found his way back to the still centre of his certitude, the place where dizziness and panic whirled around him but did not touch him. In a moment, he was able to descend toward the First and Vain.

With the tip of her sword, the First prodded the bodies near the Demondim-spawn. Linden had never seen such creatures before. They had hands as wide and heavy as shovels, heads like battering rams, eyes without pupil or iris, glazed by death. The thinness of their trunks and limbs belied their evident strength. Yet they had not been strong enough to contend with Vain. He had broken both of them like dry wood.

'Cavewights,' Covenant breathed. His voice rattled in his throat. 'Foul must be using them for sentries. When Vain showed up, they probably tried to attack him.'

'Is it possible' – the First's eyes glared in the rocklight – 'that they contrived to send alarm of us ere they fell?'

'Possible?' growled Covenant. 'The way our luck's going, can you think of any reason to believe they didn't?'

'It is certain.' Findail's unexpected interpolation sent a strange shiver down Linden's spine. Covenant jerked his gaze to the Appointed. The First swallowed a jibe. But Findail did not hesitate. His grieving features were set. 'Even now,' he went on, 'forewarning reaches the ears of the Despiser. He savours the fruition of his malign dreams.' He spoke quietly; yet his voice made the air of the high vault ache. 'Follow me. I will guide you along ways where his minions will not discover you. In that, at least, his intent will be foiled.'

Passing through the company, he strode into the dark maze of the Wightwarrens. And as he walked the midnight stepped back from him. Beyond the reach of the rocklight, his outlines shone like the featureless lumination of *Elemesnedene*..

'*Damn* it!' Covenant spat. 'Now he wants us to trust him.'

The First gave a stern shrug. 'What choice remains to us?' Her gaze trailed Findail down the tunnel. 'One brand we have. Will you rather trust the mercy of this merciless bourne?'

At once, Linden said, 'We don't need him. I can lead us. I don't need light.'

Covenant scowled at her. 'That's terrific. Where're you going to lead us? You don't have any idea where Foul is.'

She started to retort, I can find him. The same way I found Gibbon. All I need is a taste of him. But then she read him more clearly. His anger was not directed at her. He was angry because he knew he had no choice. And he was right. Until she felt the Despiser's emanations and could fix her health-sense on them, she had no effective guidance to offer.

Swallowing her vexation, she sighed, 'I know. It was a bad idea.' Findail was receding from view: soon he would be out of sight altogether. 'Let's get going.'

For a moment, Covenant faced her as though he wanted to apologize and did not know how because he was unable to gauge the spirit of her acquiescence. But his purpose still drove him. Turning roughly, he started down the tunnel after the Appointed.

The First joined him. Pitchwife gave Linden's shoulder a quick clasp of comradeship, then urged her into motion.

Vain followed them as if he were in no danger at all.

The tunnel went straight for some distance: then side-passages began to mark its walls. Glowing like an avatar of moonlight, Findail took the first leftward way, moved into a narrow corridor which had been cut so long ago that the rock no longer seemed to remember the violence of formation. The ceiling was low, forcing the Giants to stoop as the corridor angled upward. Findail's illumination glimmered and sheened on the walls. A vague sense of peril rose behind Linden like a miasma: she guessed that more of the Despiser's creatures had entered the tunnel which the company had just left. But soon she reached a high, musty space like a disused mustering-hall; and when she and her companions had crossed it to a larger passage, her impression of danger faded.

More tunnels followed, most of them tending sharply downward. She did not know how the Appointed chose his route; but he was sure of it. Perhaps he gained all the information he needed from the mountain itself, as his people were said to read the events of the outer Earth in the peaks and cols of the Rawedge Rim which enclosed *Elemesnedene*. Whatever his sources of knowledge, however, Linden sensed that he was leading the company through delvings which were no longer inhabited or active. They all smelled of abandonment, forgotten death — and somehow, obscurely, of ur-viles, as if this section of the catacombs had once been set apart for the products of the Demondim. But they were gone now, perhaps forever: Linden caught no scent or sound of any life here.

1169

No life except the breathing, dire existence of the mountain, the sentience too slow to be discerned, the intent so immemorially occluded and rigid that it was hidden from mortal perception. Linden felt she was wandering the vitals of an organism which surpassed her on every scale – and yet was too time-spanning and ponderous to defend itself against quick evil. Mount Thunder loathed the banes which inhabited it, the use to which its depths were put. Why else was there so much anger compressed in the gut-rock? But the day when the mountain might react for its own cleansing was still centuries or millennia away.

The First's bulk blocked most of Findail's glow. But Linden did not need light to know that Vain was still behind her, or that Covenant was nearly prostrate on his feet, frail with exhaustion. Yet he appeared determined to continue until he dropped. For his sake, she called Findail to a halt. 'We're killing ourselves like this.' Her own knees trembled with strain: weariness throbbed in her temples. 'We've got to rest.'

Findail acceded with a shrug. They were in a rude chamber empty of everything except stale air and darkness. She half expected Covenant to protest; but he did not. Numbly, he dropped to the floor and leaned his fatigue against one wall.

Sighing to himself, Pitchwife rummaged through the packs for *diamondraught* and a meal. Liquor and food he doled out to his companions, sparing little for the future: the future of the Search would not be long, for good or ill.

Linden ate as much as she could stomach, but only took a sip of the *diamondraught* so that she would not be put to sleep. Then she turned her attention to Covenant.

He was shivering slightly. Findail's light made him look pallid and spectral, ashen-eyed, doomed. His body seemed to draw no sustenance from the food he had consumed. Even *diamondraught* had little effect on him. He looked like a man who was bleeding internally. On Kevin's Watch, he had healed the wound in his chest with wild magic. But no power could undo the blow which had pierced him back in the woods behind Haven Farm. Now his physical condition appeared to be merging with that of the body he had left behind, the lorn flesh with the knife still protruding from its ribs.

He had told her this would happen.

But other signs were missing. He had no bruises to match the ones he had received when Joan had been wrested from him. And he still had his beard. She clung to those things because they seemed to mean that he was not yet about to die.

She nearly cried out when he raised the knife he had brought from Revelstone and asked Pitchwife for water.

Without question, Pitchwife poured the last of the company's water into a bowl and handed it to the Unbeliever.

Awkwardly, Covenant wet his beard, then set the knife to his throat. His hands trembled as if he were appalled. Yet by his own choice he conformed himself to the image of his death.

Linden struggled to keep herself from railing at his self-abnegation, the surrender it implied. He behaved as though he had indeed given himself up to despair. It was unbearable. But the sight of him was too poignant: she could not accuse or blame him. Wrestling down her grief, she said in a voice that still sounded like bereavement, 'You know, that beard doesn't look so bad on you. I'm starting to like it.' Pleading with him.

His eyes were closed as if in fear of the moment when the blade would slice into his skin, mishandled by his numb fingers. Yet with every stroke of the knife his hands grew calmer.

'I did this the last time I was here. An ur-vile knocked me off a ledge. Away from everyone else. I was alone. So scared I couldn't even scream. But shaving helped. If you'd seen me, you would've thought I was trying to cut my throat in simple terror. But it helps.' Somehow, he avoided nicking himself. The blade he used was so sharp that it left his skin clean. 'It takes the place of courage.'

Then he was done. Putting the knife back under his belt, he looked at Linden as if he knew exactly what she had been trying to say to him. 'I don't like it.' His purpose was in his voice, as hard and certain as his ring. 'But it's better to choose your own risks. Instead of just trying to survive the ones you can't get out of.'

Linden hugged her head and made no attempt to answer him. His face was raw – but it was still free of bruises. She could still hope.

Gradually, he recovered a little strength. He needed far more rest than he allowed himself; but he was noticeably more stable as he climbed erect and announced his readiness.

The First joined him without hesitation. But Pitchwife looked toward Linden as if he wanted confirmation from her. She saw in his gaze that he was prepared to find some way to delay the company on Covenant's behalf if she believed it necessary.

The question searched her; but she met it by rising to her feet. If Covenant were exhausted, he would be more easily prevented from destruction.

At once, her thoughts shamed her. Even now – when he had just given her a demonstration of his deliberate acquiescence to death, as if he wanted her to be sure that Kevin had told her the truth – she felt he deserved something better than the promises she had made against him.

Mutely, Findail bore his light into the next passage. The First shouldered her share of the company's small supplies, drew her longsword. Muttering to himself, Pitchwife joined her. Vain gazed absently into the unmitigated dark of the catacombs. In single-file, the questers followed the Appointed of the *Elohim* onward.

Still his route tended generally downward, deeper by irregular stages and increments toward the clenched roots of Mount Thunder; and as the company descended, the character of the tunnels changed. They became more ragged and ruinous. Broken gaps appeared in the walls, and from the voids beyond them came dank exhalations, distant groaning, cold sweat. Unseen denizens slithered away to their barrows. Water oozed through cracks in the gut-rock and dripped like slow corrosion. Strange boiling sounds rose and then receded.

With a Giant's fearlessness of stone and mountains, Pitchwife took a rock as large as his fist and tossed it into one of the gaps. For a long time, echoes replied like the distant labour of anvils.

The strain of the descent made Linden's thighs ache and quiver.

Later, she did hear anvils, the faint, metallic clatter of hammers. And the thud of bellows – the warm, dry gusts of exhaust from forges. The company was nearing the working heart of the Wight-warrens. Sourceless sounds made her skin crawl. But Findail did not hesitate or waver; and gradually the noise and effort in the air lessened. Moiling and sulphur filled the tunnel as if it were a ventilation shaft for a pit of brimstone. Then they, too, faded.

The tremendous weight of the mountain impending over her made Linden stoop. It was too heavy for her. Everywhere around her was knuckled stone and darkness. Findail's light was ghostly, not to be trusted. Somewhere outside Mount Thunder, the day was ending – or had already ended, already given the Land its only relief from the Sunbane. But the things which soughed and whined through the catacombs knew no relief. She felt the old protestations of the rock like the far-off moaning of the damned. The air felt as cold, worn, and dead as a gravestone. Lord Foul had chosen an apt demesne: only mad creatures and evil could live in the Wightwarrens.

Then, abruptly, the wrought passages through which Findail had been travelling changed. The tunnel narrowed, became a rough crevice with a roof beyond the reach of Linden's percipience. After some distance, the crevice ended at the rim of a wide, deep pit. And from the pit arose the fetor of a charnel.

The stench made Linden gag. Covenant could barely stand it. But Findail went right to the edge of the pit, to a cut stair which ascended the wall directly above the rank abysm. Covenant fought himself to follow; but before he had climbed a dozen steps he slumped against the wall. Linden felt nausea and vertigo gibbering in his muscles.

Sheathing her blade, the First lifted him in her arms, bore him upward as swiftly as Findail was willing to go.

Cramps knotted Linden's guts. The stench heaved in her. The stair stretched beyond comprehension above her: she did not know how to attempt it. But the gap between her and the light – between her and Covenant – was increasing at every moment. Fiercely, she turned her percipience on herself, pulled the cramps out of her muscles. Then she forced herself upward.

The fetor called out to her like the Sunbane, urged her to surrender to it – surrender to the darkness which lurked hungrily within her and everywhere else as well, unanswerable and growing toward completion with every intaken breath. If she let go now, she would be as strong as a Raver before she hit bottom; and then no ordinary death could touch her. Yet she clung to the rough treads with her hands, thrust at them with her legs. Covenant was above her. Perhaps he was already safe. And she had learned how to be stubborn. The mouth of the old man whose life she had saved on Haven Farm had been as foul as this; but she had borne that putrid halitus in order to fight for his survival. Though her guts squirmed, her throat retched, she fought her way to the top of the stair and the wall.

There she found Findail, the First, and Covenant. And light – a different light than the Appointed emitted. Reflecting faintly from the passage behind him, it was the orange-red colour of rocklight. And it was full of soft, hot, boiling, slow splashes. A sulphurous exudation took the stench from the air.

Pitchwife finished the ascent with Vain behind him. Linden looked at Covenant. His face was waxen, slick with sweat: vertigo and sickness glazed his eyes. She turned to the First and Findail to demand another rest.

The *Elohim* forestalled her. His gaze was shrouded, concealing his thoughts. 'Now for a space we must travel a common roadway of the Wightwarrens.' Rocklight limned his shoulders. 'It is open to us at present – but shortly it will be peopled again, and our way closed. We must not halt here.'

Linden wanted to protest in simple frustration and helplessness. Roughly, she asked the First, 'How much more do you think he can take?'

The Giant shrugged. She did not meet Linden's glare: her efforts to refuse doubt left little room for compromise. 'If he falters, I will carry him.'

At once, Findail turned and started down the passage.

Before Linden could object, Covenant shambled after the Appointed. The First moved protectively ahead of the Unbeliever.

Pitchwife faced Linden with a grimace of wry fatigue. 'She is my wife,' he murmured, 'and I love her sorely. Yet she surpasses me. Were I formed as other Giants, I would belabour her insensate rather than suffer this extremity.' He clearly did not mean what he was saying: he spoke only to comfort Linden.

But she was beyond comfort. Fetor and brimstone, exhaustion and peril pushed her to the fringes of her self-control. Fuming futilely, she coerced her unsteady limbs into motion.

The passage soon became a warren of corridors; but Findail threaded them unerringly toward the source of the light. The air grew noticeably warmer: it was becoming hot. The boiling sounds increased, took on a subterranean force which throbbed irrhythmically in Linden's lungs.

Then the company gained a tunnel as broad as a road; and the rocklight flared brighter. The stone thrummed with bottomless seething. Ahead of Findail, the left wall dropped away: acrid heat rose from that side. It seemed to suck the air out of Linden's chest, tug her forward. Findail led the company briskly into the light.

The road passed along the rim of a huge abyss. Its sheer walls were stark with rocklight: it blazed heat and sulphur.

At the bottom of the gulf burned a lake of magma.

Its boiling made the gut-rock shiver. Tremendous spouts reached massively toward the ceiling, then collapsed under their own weight, spattering the walls with a violence that melted and reformed the sides.

Findail strode down the roadway as if the abyss did not concern him. But Covenant moved slowly, crouching close to the outer wall. The rocklight shone garishly across his raw face, made him appear lunatic with fear and yearning for immolation. Linden followed almost on his heels so that she would be near if he needed her. They were halfway around the mouth of the gulf before she felt his emanations clearly enough to realize that his apprehension was not the simple dread of vertigo and heat. He recognized this place: memories beat about his head like dark wings. He knew that this road led to the Despiser.

Linden dogged his steps and raged uselessly to herself. He was in no shape to confront Lord Foul. No condition. She no longer cared that his weakness might lessen the difficulty of her own responsibilities. She did not want her lot eased: she wanted him whole and strong and victorious, as he deserved to be. This exhausting rush to doom was folly, madness.

Gasping at the heat, he reached the far side of the abyss, moved two steps into the passage, and sagged to the floor. Linden put her arms around him, trying to steady herself as well as him. The molten passion of the lake burned at her back. Pitchwife was nearly past the rim. Vain was several paces behind.

'You must now be swift,' Findail said. He sounded strangely urgent. 'There are Cavewights nigh.'

Without warning, he sped past the companions, flashed back into the rocklight like a striking condor.

As he hurtled down the roadway, his form melted out of humanness and assumed the shape of a Sandgorgon.

Fatal as a bludgeon, he crashed headlong against the Demondim-spawn.

Vain made no effort to evade the impact. Yet he could not withstand it. Findail was Earthpower incarnate. The shock of collision made the road lurch, sent tremors like wailing through the stone. Vain had proved himself stronger than Giants or storms, impervious to spears and the na-Mhoram's *Grim*. He had felt the power of the Worm of the World's End and had survived, though that touch had cost him the use of one arm. He had escaped alone from *Elemesnedene* and all the Elohim. But Findail hit him with such concentrated might that he was driven backward.

Two steps. Three. To the last edge of the rim.

'Vain!' Covenant thrashed in Linden's grasp. Frenzy almost made him strong enough to break away from her. 'Vain!'

Instinctively, Linden fought him, held him.

Impelled by Covenant's fear, the First charged past Pitchwife after the Appointed.

Vain caught his balance on the lip of the abyss. His black eyes were vivid with intensity. A grin of relish sharpened his immaculate features. The iron heels of the Staff of Law gleamed dully in the hot rocklight.

He did not glance away from Findail. But his good arm made a warding gesture that knocked the First backward, stretched her at her husband's feet, out of danger.

'Fall!' the Appointed raged. His fists hammered the air. The rock under Vain's feet ruptured in splinters. 'Fall and die!'

The Demondim-spawn fell. With the slowness of nightmare, he dropped straight into the abyss.

At the same instant, his dead arm lashed out, struck like a snake. His right hand closed on Findail's forearm. The Appointed was pulled after him over the edge.

Rebounding from the wall, they tumbled together toward the centre of the lake. Covenant's cry echoed after them, inarticulate and wild.

Findail could not break Vain's grip.

He was *Elohim*, capable of taking any form of the living Earth. He dissolved himself and became an eagle, pounded the air with his wings to escape the spouting magma. But Vain clung to one of his legs and was borne upward.

Instantly, Findail transformed himself to water. The heat threw him in vapour and agony toward the ceiling. But Vain clutched a handful of essential moisture and drew the Appointed back to him.

Swifter than panic, Findail became a Giant with a greatsword in both fists. He hacked savagely at Vain's wrist. But Vain only clenched his grip and let the blade glance off his iron band.

They were so close to the lava that Linden could barely see them through the blaze. In desperation, Findail took the shape of a sail and rode the heat upward again. But Vain still held him in an unbreakable grasp.

And before he rose high enough, a spout climbed like a tower toward him. He tried to evade it by veering; but he was too late. Magma took both *Elohim* and Demondim-spawn and snatched them down into the lake.

Linden hugged Covenant as if she shared his cries.

He was no longer struggling. 'You don't understand!' he gasped. All the strength had gone out of him. 'That's the place. Where the ur-viles got rid of their failures. When something they made didn't work, they threw it down there. That's why Findail – ' The words seized in his throat.

Why Findail had made his final attempt upon the Demondim-spawn here. Even Vain could not hope to come back from that fall.

Dear Christ! She did not understand how the *Elohim* saw such an extravagant threat in one lone creation of the ur-viles. Vain had bowed to her once – and had never acknowledged her again. He had saved her life – and had refused to save it. And after all this time and distance and peril, he was lost before he found what he sought. Before she understood –

He had gripped Findail with the hand that hung from his wooden forearm.

Other perceptions demanded her attention, but she was slow to notice them. She had not heeded the Appointed's warning. Too late, she sensed movement in the passage which had led the company to this abyss.

Along the rim of the pit, a party of Cavewights charged into the rocklight.

At least a score of them. Upright on their long limbs, they were almost as tall as Pitchwife. They ran with an exaggerated, jerky awkwardness, like stick-figures; but their strength was unmistakable: they were the delvers of the Wightwarrens. The red heat of lava burned in their eyes. Most of them were armed with truncheons: the rest carried battleaxes with wicked blades.

Still half stunned by the force of Vain's blow, the First reeled to her feet. For an instant, she wavered. But the company's need galvanized her. Her longsword flashed in readiness. Roaring, 'Flee!' she faced the onset of the Cavewights.

Covenant made no effort to move. The people he loved were in danger, and he had the power to protect them – power he dared not use. Linden read his plight immediately. The exertion of will which held back the wild magic took all his strength.

She fought herself into motion. Summoning her resolve, she began to wrestle him down the tunnel.

He seemed weightless, almost abject. Yet his very slackness hampered her. Her progress was fatally slow.

Then Pitchwife caught up with her. He started to take Covenant from her.

The clangour of battle echoed along the passage. Linden spun and saw the First fighting for her life.

She was a Swordmain, an artist of combat. Her glaive flayed about her, at once feral and precise: rocklight flared in splinters off the swift iron. Blood spattered from her attackers as if by incantation rather than violence, her blade the wand or sceptre by which she wrought her theurgy.

But the roadway was too wide to constrict the Cavewights. Their reach was as great as hers. And they were born to contend with stone: their blows had the force of granite. Most of her effort went to parry clubs which would have shattered her arms. Step by step, she was driven backward.

She stumbled slightly on the uneven surface, and a truncheon flicked past her. On her left temple, a bloody welt seemed to appear without transition. The Cavewight that hit her pitched into the abyss, clutching his slashed chest. But more creatures crowded after her.

Linden looked at Pitchwife. He was being torn apart by conflicting needs. His eyes ached whitely, desperate and suppliant. He had offered her his life. Like Mistweave.

She could not bear it. He deserved better. 'Help the First!' she barked at him. 'I'll take care of Covenant.'

Pitchwife was too frantic to hesitate. Releasing the Unbeliever, he sped to the aid of his wife.

Linden grabbed Covenant by the shoulders, shook him fiercely. 'Come on!' she raged into his raw visage. 'For God's sake!'

His struggle was terrible to behold. He could have effaced the Cavewights with a simple thought – and brought down the Arch of Time, or desecrated it with venom. He was willing to sacrifice himself. But his friends! Their peril rent at him. For the space of one heart-beat, she thought he would destroy everything to save the First and Pitchwife. So that they would not die like Foamfollower for him.

Yet he withheld – clamped his ripped and wailing spirit in a restraint as inhuman as his purpose. His features hardened: his gaze became bleak and desolate, like the Land under the scourge of the Sunbane. 'You're right,' he muttered softly. 'This is pathetic.'

Straightening his back, he started down the tunnel.

She clenched his numb halfhand and fled with him into darkness. Cries and blows shouted after them, echoed and were swallowed by the Wightwarrens.

As the reflected rocklight faded, they reached an intersection.

Covenant veered instinctively to the right; but she took the leftward turning because it felt less travelled. Almost at once, she regretted her choice. It did not lead away from the light. Instead, it opened into a wide chamber with fissures along one side that admitted the shining of the molten lake. Sulphur and heat clogged the air. Two more tunnels gave access to the chamber; but they did not draw off the accumulated reek.

The roadway along the rim of the abyss was visible through the fissures. This chamber had probably been intended to allow Mount Thunder's denizens to watch the road without being seen.

The First and Pitchwife were no longer upon the rim. They had retreated into the tunnel after Linden and Covenant. Or they had fallen –

Linden's senses shrilled an alarm. Too late: always too late. Bitterly, she wheeled to face the Cavewights that thronged into the chamber from all three entrances.

She and her companions must have been spotted from this covert when they first made their way past the abyss. And the brief time they had spent watching Vain and Findail had given the Cavewights opportunity to spring this trap.

In the tunnel Linden and Covenant had used, the First and Pitchwife appeared, battling tremendously to reach their friends. But most of the Cavewights hurried to block the Giants' way. The Swordmain and her husband were beaten back.

Pitchwife's inchoate cry wrung Linden's heart. Then he and the First were forced out of sight. Cavewights rushed in pursuit.

Brandishing cudgels and axes, the rest of the creatures advanced on Covenant and Linden.

He thrust her behind him, took a step forward. Rocklight limned his desperate shoulders. 'I'm the one you want.' His voice was taut with suppression and wild magic. 'I'll go with you. Leave her alone.'

Rapt and grim, the Cavewights gave no sign that they heard him. Their eyes smouldered.

'If you hurt her,' he gritted, 'I'll tear you apart.'

One of them grabbed him, manacled both his wrists in a huge fist. Another raised his club and levelled a crushing blow at Linden's head.

She ducked. The truncheon whipped through her hair, almost touched her skull. Launching herself from the wall, she dodged toward Covenant.

The Cavewights seemed slow, awkward: for a moment, they did not catch her.

Somehow, Covenant twisted his wrists free. He snatched his knife from his belt, began slashing frantically about him. A Cavewight howled, hopped back. But the blade was deep in the creature's ribs, and Covenant's halfhand failed of its grip: the knife was ripped from him.

Weaponless, he spun toward Linden. His face stretched as if he wanted to cry out, *Forgive!*

The Cavewights surrounded him. They did not use their cudgels or axes: apparently, they wanted him alive. With their fists, they beat him until he fell.

Linden tried to reach him. She was avid for power, futile without it. Her arms and legs were useless against the Cavewights. They laughed coarsely at her struggles. Wildly, she groped for Covenant's ring with her health-sense, tried to take hold of it. The infernal air choked her lungs. Bottomless and hungry through the fissures came the boiling of the molten lake. Vain and Findail had fallen. The First and Pitchwife were lost. Covenant lay like a sacrifice on the stone. She had nothing left –

She was still groping when a blow came down gleefully on the bone behind her left ear. At once, the world turned over and sprawled into darkness.

18

NO OTHER WAY

Thomas Covenant lay face down on the floor. It pressed like flat stone against his battered cheek. Bruises malformed the bones of his visage. Though he wanted nothing but peace and salvation, he had become what he was by violence – the consequences of his own acts. From somewhere in the distance arose a throaty murmuring, incessant and dire, like a litany of invocation, dozens of voices repeating the same word or name softly, but with different cadences, at varying speeds. They were still around him, the people who had come to bereave him. They were taunting his failure.

Joan was gone.

Perhaps he should have moved, rolled over, done something to soften the pain. But the effort was beyond him. All his strength was sand and ashes. And he had never been physically strong. They had taken her from him without any trouble at all. It was strange, he reflected abstractly, that someone who had as little to brag of as he did spent so much time trying to pretend he was immortal. He should have known better. God knew he had been given every conceivable opportunity to outgrow his arrogance.

Real heroes were not arrogant. Who could have called Berek arrogant? Or Mhoram? Foamfollower? The list went on and on, all of them humble. Even Hile Troy had finally given up his pride. Only people like Covenant himself were arrogant enough to believe that the outcome of the Earth depended on their purblind and fallible choices. Only people like himself. And Lord Foul. Those who were capable of Despite and chose to refuse it. And those who did not. Linden had told him any number of times that he was arrogant.

That was why he had to defeat Lord Foul – why the task devolved on him alone.

Any minute now, he told himself. Any minute now he was going to get up from the floor of his house and go exchange himself for Joan. He had put it off long enough. She was not arrogant – not really. She did not deserve what had happened to her. She had simply never been able to forgive herself for her weaknesses, her limitations.

Then he wanted to laugh. It would have done him a world of good to laugh. He was not so different from Joan after all. The only real difference was that he had been summoned to the Land while it was still able to heal him – and while he was still able to know what that meant. He was sane – if he *was* sane – by grace, not by virtue.

In a sense, she actually was arrogant. She placed too much importance on her own faults and failures. She had never learned to let them go.

He had never learned that lesson either. But he was trying. Dear God, he was trying. Any minute now, he was going to take her place in Lord Foul's fire. He was going to let everything go.

But somehow the floor did not feel right. The murmurous invocation that filled his ears and his lungs and his bones called on a name that did not sound like the Despiser's. It perplexed him, seemed to make breathing difficult. He had forgotten something.

Wearily, he opened his eyes, blinked at the blurring of his vision, and remembered where he was.

Then he thought that surely his heart would fail. His bruises throbbed in his skull. He had received them from Cavewights, not from Joan's captors. He did not have long to live.

He lay near the centre of a large cave with rough walls and a ragged ceiling. The air smelled thickly of rocklight, which burned from special stones set into the walls at careless intervals. The cave was crudely oval in shape: it narrowed at both ends to dark, unattainable tunnels. The odour of the rocklight was tinged with a scent of ancient mouldering – rot so old that it had become almost clean again.

It came from a large, high mound nearby. The heap looked like a barrow, as if something revered had been buried there. But it was composed entirely of bones. Thousands of skeletons piled in one place. Most of them had been set there so long ago that they had decomposed to fine grey dust, no longer of interest even to maggots. But the top of the mound was more recent. None of the skeletons were whole: all had been either broken in death or dismembered afterward. Even the newer ones had been cleaned of flesh. However, a few of them still oozed from the marrow.

They were not human bones, or ur-vile. Cavewight, then. Apparently, the creatures that the First and Pitchwife had slain had already been added to the mound.

The murmuring went on without let, as if dozens or hundreds of predators were growling to themselves. He felt that sound like the touch of panic in his vitals. Some name was being repeated continuously, whispered or muttered at every pitch and pace: but he could not distinguish it. Heat and sound and rocklight squeezed sweat from the sore bones of his head.

He was surrounded by Cavewights. Most of them squatted near the walls, their knees jutting at their ears, their hot eyes glowing. Others appeared to be dancing about the mound, stork-like and graceless on their long legs. Their hands attacked the air like spades. They all murmured and murmured, incantatory and hypnotic. He had no idea what they were saying, or how much longer he would be lulled, snared.

He was afraid – so afraid that his fear became a kind of lucidity. Not afraid for himself: he had met that particular terror in the Banefire and burned it to purity. These creatures were only Cavewights, the weak-minded and malleable children of Mount Thunder's gut-rock, and Lord Foul had mastered them long ago. They could hardly hope to come between Covenant and the Despiser. Though the way to it was hard, his purpose was safe.

But in a small clear space against one wall sat Linden. He saw her with the precision of his fear. Her right shoulder leaned on the stone. With her arms, she hugged her knees to her chest like a lorn child. Her head was bowed: her hair had fallen forward, hiding her face. But the side of her neck was bare. It gleamed, pale and vulnerable, in the red-orange illumination.

Black against the pallor, dried blood marked her skin. It led in a crusted trail from behind her left ear down to the collar of her shirt.

She, too – ! A tremor of grief went through him. She, too, had been made to match the physical condition of the body she had left behind in the woods behind Haven Farm.

They did not have much time left.

He would have cried out, if he had possessed the strength. Not much time – and to spend it like this! He wanted to hold her in his arms, make her understand that he loved her – that no death or risk of ruin could desecrate what she meant to him. Lena had once tried

to comfort him by singing, *The soul in which the flower grows survives.*
He wanted –

But perhaps the blow she had been struck had been harder than either of them had realized, and she also was about to die. Killed like Seadreamer because she had tried to save him. And even if she did not die, she would believe that she had lost him in despair. In Andelain, Elena had told him to *Care for her. So that in the end she may heal us all.* He had failed at that as at so many other things.

Linden. He tried to say her name, but no sound came. A spasm of remorse twisted his face, made his bruises throb. Ignoring the pain, the fathomless ache of his exhaustion, he levered his elbows under him and strove to pry his weakness off the stone.

A rough kick pitched him onto his back, closer to the mound of bones. Gasping, he looked up into the leer of a Cavewight.

'Be still, accursed!' the creature spat. 'Punishment comes. Punishment and apocalypse! Do not hasten it.'

Cavorting grotesquely on his gangly limbs, he resumed his muttering and danced away.

Covenant wrestled for breath and squirmed onto his side to look toward Linden again.

She was facing him now, had turned toward him when the Cavewight spoke. Her visage was empty of blood, of hope. The gaze she cast at him was stark with abuse and dumb pleading. Her hands clasped each other uselessly. Her eyes seemed as dark and hollow as wounds.

She must have looked like that when she was a child, locked in the attic with her father while he died.

He fought for his voice, croaked her name through the manifold invocation of the Cavewights. But she did not appear to hear him. Slowly, she dropped her head, lowered her gaze to the failure of her hands.

He could not go to her. He hardly knew where he might find enough strength to stand. And the Cavewights would not let him move. He had no way to combat them except with his ring – the wild magic he could not use. He and she were prisoners completely. And there was no name that either of them might call upon for rescue.

No name except the Despiser's.

Covenant hoped like madness that Lord Foul would act quickly.

But perhaps Lord Foul would not act. Perhaps he permitted the Cavewights to work their will, hoping that Covenant would once again be forced to power. Perhaps he did not understand – was incapable of understanding – the certainty of Covenant's refusal.

The throaty chant of the Cavewights was changing: the incessant various repetitions were shifting toward unison. One creature started a slightly sharper inflection, a more specific cadence; and his immediate neighbours fell into rhythm with him. Cavewight by Cavewight, the unison spread until the invoked name took Covenant by surprise, jolted alarm through him.

He knew that name.

Drool Rockworm.

More than three millennia ago, Drool Rockworm of the Cavewights had recovered the lost Staff of Law – and had conceived a desire to rule the Earth. But he had been too unskilled in lore to master what he had found. In seduction or folly, he had turned to the Despiser for knowledge. And Lord Foul had used the Cavewight for his own purposes.

Drool Rockworm.

First he had persuaded Drool to summon Covenant, luring the Cavewight with promises of white gold. Then he had snatched Covenant away, sent the Unbeliever instead to the Council of Lords. And the Lords had responded by challenging Drool's power. Sneaking into the Wightwarrens, they had taken the Staff from him, had called down the Fire-Lions of Mount Thunder to destroy him.

Thus armed, they had thought themselves victorious. But they had only played into the Despiser's hands. They had rid him of Drool, thereby giving him access to the terrible bane he desired – the Illearth Stone. And from that time forward the Cavewights had been forced to serve him like puppets.

Drool Rockworm.

The name vibrated like acid in the air. The rocklight throbbed. All the Cavewights held themselves still. Their laval eyes focused on what they were invoking.

Beside Covenant, an eerie glow began to leak from the mound of bones. Sick red flames licked like swamp-fire around the pile. Fragments of bone seemed to waver and melt as if they were passing into hallucination.

Suddenly, he no longer believed that these creatures served the Despiser.

Drool Rockworm!

'Covenant.' Linden's voice reached between the beats of the name. She had come out of herself, drawn by what the Cavewights were doing. 'There's something – ' Fiercely, she struggled to master her despair. 'They're bringing it to life.'

Covenant winced in dismay. But he did not doubt her. The Law that protected the living had been broken. Any horror might now be summoned past the barrier of death, given the will – and the power. The mound squirmed with fires and gleamings like a monstrous cocoon, decay and dust in the throes of birth.

Then one of the Cavewights moved. He strode across the chant toward Covenant. 'Rise, accursed,' he demanded. His eyes were as feral as his grin. 'Rise for blood and torment.'

Covenant stared whitely up at him, did not obey.

'Rise!' the creature raged. With one spatulate hand, he grabbed Covenant's arm and nearly dislocated it yanking him to his feet.

Covenant bit down panic and pain. 'You're going to regret this!' He had to shout to make himself heard. The invocation pounded in his chest. 'Foul wants me! Do you think you can defy him and get away with it?'

'Ha!' barked the Cavewight as if he were close to ecstasy. 'We are too wily! He does not know us. We have learned. Learned! Him so wise.' For an instant, all the voices shared his contempt. *Drool Rockworm!* 'He is blind. Believes we have not found you.' The creature spat wildness instead of laughter.

Then he wrenched Covenant around to face the mound. Linden groaned Covenant's name: he heard a thud as one of the creatures silenced her. His arm was gripped by fingers that knew how to break stone.

Flames began to writhe like ghouls across the mound, casting anguish toward the roof of the cave.

'Witness!' the Cavewight grated. 'The Wightbarrow!'

The invocation took on a timbre of lust.

'We have served and served. Forever we have served. Chattel. Fodder. Sacrifice. And no reward. Do this. Do that. Dig. Run. Die. No reward. None!

'Now he pays. Punishment and *apocalypse*!'

The Cavewights' virulence staggered Covenant. The muscles of his arm were being crushed. But he shut his mind to everything else. Groping for a way to save Linden's life if not his own, he protested hoarsely, 'How? He's the Despiser! He'll tear your hearts out!'

But the Cavewights were beyond fear. 'Witness!' Covenant's captor repeated. 'See it. Fire. Life! The Wightbarrow of Drool Rockworm!'

Drool Rockworm, hammered the chant. *Drool Rockworm!*

'From the dead. We have learned. Bloodshed. Sunbane. Law broken. The blood of the accursed!' He almost capered in his exultation. 'You!'

His free hand clasped a long spike of rock like a dagger.

In litany, he shouted, 'Blood brings power! Power brings life! Drool Rockworm rises! Drool takes ring! Ring crushes Despiser! Cavewights are free! Punishment and apocalypse!'

Brandishing his spike at Covenant's face, he added, 'Soon. You are the accursed. Bringer of ruin. Your blood shed upon the Wightbarrow.' The side of the spike stroked Covenant's stiff cheek. 'Soon.'

Covenant heard Linden pant as she struggled for breath. 'Bones – ' He winced, expecting her to be hit again. But still she tried to make him hear her. 'The bones – '

Her voice was congested with effort and intention; but he had no idea what she meant.

The flames worming through the mound made his skin crawl; yet he could not look away from them. Perhaps everything he had decided or understood was false, Foul-begotten: perhaps the Banefire had been too essentially corrupt to give him any kind of trustworthy *caamora*. How could he tell? He could not see.

The pain in his arm made his head reel. The rocklight seemed to yell orange-red heat, stoking the fire in the Wightbarrow. He had lost the First and Pitchwife and Vain, had lost Andelain itself: now he was about to lose his life and Linden and everything because there was no middle ground, no wild magic without ruin. She was whispering his name, but it no longer made any difference.

His balance drifted, and he found himself staring emptily at the stone on which he barely stood. It was the only part of the floor that had been purposefully shaped. The Cavewight had placed him in the centre of a round depression like a basin. Its shallow sides had been rubbed smooth and polished until they reflected rocklight around him like burnished metal.

From between his feet, a narrow trough led straight under the mound. A trough to channel his blood toward what remained of Drool Rockworm's bones. Fire rose hungrily toward the ceiling.

Abruptly the invocation was cut off, slashed out of the air as if by the stroke of a blade. Its sudden cessation seemed to leave him deaf. He jerked up his head.

The spike was poised to strike like a fang at the middle of his chest. He planted his feet, braced himself to try to twist away, make one last effort for life.

But the blow did not fall. The Cavewight was not looking at him. None of the creatures were looking at him. Around the cave, they surged upright in outrage and fear.

An instant later, he recovered his hearing as the clamour of battle resounded past the Wightbarrow.

Into the cave charged the First and Pitchwife.

They were alone; but they attacked as if they were as potent as an army.

Surprise made them momentarily irresistible. She was battered and weary; but her longsword flashed in her hands like red lightning, hit with the force of thunder: the Cavewights went down before her like wheat in a storm. He followed at her back with a battleaxe in each hand and fought as if he were not wounded and scarcely able to draw breath. Bright galls scored her sark where the mail had deflected blows: his dripped blood where cudgels had crushed it into his flesh. Exertion sheened their faces and limbs.

The Cavewights moiled against them in frenzy.

The creatures were too frantic to fight effectively. They hampered each other, blocked their own efforts. The First and Pitchwife were halfway to the Wightbarrow before the sheer pressure of numbers stopped them.

But there the impetus of combat shifted. Desperation rallied the Cavewights. And the widening of the cave allowed the Giants to be surrounded, assailed from all sides. Their attempted rescue was valiant and doomed. In moments, they would be overwhelmed.

Sensing their opportunity, the creatures became less wild. Their mountain-delving strength dealt out blows which forced the First and Pitchwife back-to-back, drove them to fight defensively, for bare survival.

Covenant's captor faced him again. The Cavewight's laval eyes burned flame and fury. Rocklight gleamed on his spike as he cocked his arm to stab out Covenant's life.

Hoarse with panic and insight, Linden yelled, 'The bones! Get the bones!'

At once, one of the creatures hit her so hard that she sprawled into the basin at Covenant's feet. She lay there, stunned and twisted. He feared her back had been broken.

But the Cavewights understood her if he did not. A sound like a wail shrilled across the combat. They fought with redoubled fever. The spike aimed at Covenant wavered as the Cavewight looked fearfully toward the fray.

Covenant could not see the First or Pitchwife through the fierce press. But suddenly her shout sprang at the ceiling – the tantara of a Swordmain summoning her last resources:

'Stone and Sea!'

And the throng of Cavewights seemed to rupture as if she had become a detonation. Abandoning Pitchwife, she crashed past the creatures, shed them from her arms and shoulders like rubble. In a spray of blood, she hacked her way toward the Wightbarrow.

Pitchwife could have been slain then. But he was not. His assailants hurled themselves after the First. His axes bit into their backs as he followed her.

The wailing scaled into a shriek when she reached the mound.

Snatching up a bone, she whirled to face her attackers. The bone shed flame like a faggot; but her Giantish fingers bore the pain and did not flinch.

Instantly, all the creatures froze. Silence seized their cries: horror locked their limbs.

Pitchwife wrenched one axe out of the spine of a Cavewight, raised his weapons to parry blows. But none came. He was ignored. Retching for air, he thrust through the crowd toward the First. No one moved.

He limped to her side, dropped one axe, and grasped another

burning bone. The paralysis of the Cavewights tightened involuntarily. Their eyes pleaded. Some of them began to shiver in chill panic.

By threatening the mound, the First and Pitchwife endangered the only thing which had given these creatures the courage to defy Lord Foul.

Covenant struggled against his captor, tried to reach Linden. But the Cavewight did not release him, seemed oblivious to his efforts – entranced by fear.

Stooping, the First wiped the blood from the glaive on the nearest body. Then she sheathed the longsword and took up a second bone. Fire spilled over her hands, but she paid it no heed. 'Now,' she panted through her teeth. 'Now you will release the Earthfriend.'

The Cavewight locked his fingers around Covenant's arm and did not move. A few creatures at the fringes of the press shifted slightly, moaned in protest.

Abruptly, Linden twitched. With a jerk, she thrust herself out of the basin. When she got her feet under her, she staggered and stumbled as if the floor were tilting. Yet somehow she kept her balance. Her eyes were glazed with anger and extremity. She had been pushed too far. Half lurching, she passed behind Covenant.

Among the Cavewights crouching there, she found a loose truncheon. It was almost too heavy for her to lift. Gripping its handle in both hands, she heaved it from the floor, raised it above her head, and brought it down on the wrist of the creature holding Covenant.

He heard a dull snapping noise. The Cavewight's fingers were torn from his arm.

The creature yowled. Madly, he cocked the spike to stab it down at Linden's face.

'Hold!' The First's command rang through the cave. She thrust one foot into the mound, braced herself to kick dust and fragments across the floor.

The Cavewight froze in renewed terror.

Slowly, she withdrew her foot. A faint sigh of relief soughed around the walls of the cave.

Pain lanced through Covenant's elbow, knifed into his shoulder. For a moment, he feared that he would not be able to stand. The clutch of the Cavewight had damaged his arm: the blood pounding back into it felt like acid. The cave seemed to roar in his ears. He heard no other sound except Pitchwife's harsh respiration.

But he had to stand, had to move. The Giants deserved better than this from him. Linden and the Land deserved better. He could not afford such weakness. It was only pain and vertigo, as familiar to him as an old friend. It had no power over him unless he was afraid – unless he let himself be afraid. If he held up his heart, even despair was as good as courage or strength.

That was the centre, the point of stillness and certainty, Briefly, he rested. Then he let the excruciation in his arm lift him out of the basin.

Linden came to him. Her touch made his body totter; but inwardly he did not lose his balance. She would stop him if he proved himself wrong. But he was not wrong. Together, they moved towards the Giants.

Pitchwife did not look up from his gasping. His lips were flecked with red spittle: his exertions had torn something in his chest. But the First gave Covenant and Linden a nod of greeting. Her gaze was as grim as a hawk's. 'You gladden me!' she muttered. 'I had not thought to behold you again alive. It is well that these simple creatures do not glance often behind them. Thus we were able to follow when we had foiled our pursuers. What dire rite do they seek to practise against you?'

Linden answered for Covenant, 'They're trying to bring an old leader back from the dead. He's buried under there somewhere.' She grimaced at the Wightbarrow. 'They want Covenant's blood and the ring. They think this dead leader'll free them from Foul. We've got to get out of here.'

'Aye,' growled the First. Her eyes assayed the Cavewights. 'But they are too many. We cannot win free by combat. We must entrust ourselves to the sanctity of these bones.'

Covenant thought he smelled the faint reek of charring flesh. But he had no health-sense, could not tell how seriously the Giants' hands were being burned.

'My husband,' the First gritted, 'will you lead us?'

Pitchwife nodded. A moment of coughing brought more blood to his lips. Yet he rallied. When he raised his head, the look in his eyes was as fierce as hers.

With a bone flaming like a brand in one hand, an axe in the other, he started toward the nearer mouth of the cave.

At once, a snarl sharpened the air, throbbing from many throats. A shiver ran through the Cavewights. The ones farthest from the Wightbarrow advanced slightly, placed themselves to block Pitchwife's path. Others tightened their hands on their weapons.

'No!' Linden snapped at Pitchwife. 'Come back!'

He retreated. When he reached the mound, the Cavewights froze again.

Covenant blinked at Linden. He felt too dizzy to think. He knew he ought to understand what was happening. But it did not make sense.

'What means this, Chosen?' the First asked like iron. 'Are we snared in this place for good and all?'

Linden replied with a look toward Covenant as if she were begging him for courage. Then, abruptly, she wrapped her arms around her chest and strode away from the mound.

The First breathed a sharp warning. Linden's head flinched from side to side. But she did not stop. Deliberately, she moved among the Cavewights.

She was alone and small and vulnerable in their midst. Her difficult bravery was no defence: any one of them could have felled her with one blow. But none of them reacted. She squeezed between two of them, passed behind a poised cluster, walked halfway to the cavemouth. Their eyes remained fixed on the First and Pitchwife – on the bones and the Wightbarrow.

As she moved, she raised her head, grew bolder. The vindication of her percipience fortified her. Less timorously, she made her way back to her companions.

Rocklight burned in Covenant's eyes. The First and Pitchwife stared at Linden. Grimly, she explained, 'They won't move while you threaten the mound. They need it. It's their reason – the only answer they've got.' Then she faltered; and her gaze darkened at the implications of what she was saying. 'That's why they won't let us take any of the bones out of here.'

For one moment – a piece of time as acute as anguish – the First looked beaten, overcome by everything she had already lost and would still be required to lose. Honninscrave and Seadreamer had been dear to her. Pitchwife was her husband. Covenant and Linden and life were precious. Her sternness broke down, exposing a naked hurt. Both her parents had given their lives for her, and she had become what she was by grief.

Yet she was the First of the Search, chosen for her ability to bear hard decisions. Almost at once, her visage closed around itself. Her hands knotted as if they were hungry for the fire of the bones.

'Then,' she responded stiffly, 'I must remain to menace this mound, so that you may depart.' She swallowed a lump of sorrow. 'Pitchwife, you must accompany them. They will have need of your strength. And I must believe that you live.'

At that, Pitchwife burst into a spasm of coughing. A moment passed before Covenant realized that the malformed Giant was trying to laugh.

'My wife, you jest,' he said at last. 'I have found my own reply to doubt. The Chosen has assigned me to your side. Do not credit that the song which the Giants will sing of this day will be sung of you alone.

'I am the First of the Search!' she retorted. 'I command – '

'You are Gossamer Glowlimn, the spouse of my heart.' His mouth was bloody; but his eyes gleamed. 'I am proud of you beyond all endurance. Demean not your high courage with foolishness. Neither

1189

Earthfriend nor Chosen has any need of my accompaniment. They are who they are – and will not fail. I am sworn to you in love and fealty, and I will remain.'

She glared at him as though she were in danger of weeping openly. 'You will *die*. I have borne all else until my heart breaks. Must I bear *that* also?'

'No.' Around Covenant, the rock seemed to spin and fade as if Mount Thunder itself were on the verge of dissolution; but he clung to the centre of his mortality and stood certain, an alloy in human flesh and bone of wild magic and venom, life and death. 'No,' he repeated when the First and Pitchwife met his gaze. 'There's no reason for either of you to die. It won't take long. Kiril Threndor can't be very far from here. All I have to do is get there. Then it'll be over, one way or the other. All you have to do is hang on until I get there.'

Then Pitchwife did laugh, and his face lifted with gladness. 'There, my wife!' he chortled. 'Have I not said that they are who they are? Accept that I am with you, and be content.' Abruptly, he dropped his axe, drew out his last faggot and lit it from the Wightbarrow, handed the sputtering wood to Linden. 'Begone!' he gleamed, 'ere I become maudlin at the witnessing of such valour. Fear nothing for us. We will hold and hold until the mountain itself is astonished, and still we will hold. Begone, I say!'

'Aye, begone,' growled the First as if she were angry; but her tears belied her tone. 'I must have opportunity to instruct this Pitchwife in the obedience which is his debt to the First of the Search.'

Covenant wanted words, but none came to him. What could he have said? He had made his promises long ago, and they covered everything. He rubbed the heels of his hands into his eyes to clear his sight. Then he turned toward Linden.

If he had spoken, he would have asked her to stay with the Giants. He had never forgotten the shock of her intervention in the woods behind Haven Farm. And he had not loved her then. Now everything was multiplied to the acuteness of panic. He did not know how he might preserve the bare shreds and tatters of dignity – not to mention clear courage or conviction – if she accompanied him.

But the look of her silenced him. She was baffled and perceptive, frightened and brave; terrified of Cavewights and Lord Foul, and yet avid for a chance to stand against them; mortal, precious, and irrefusable. Her face had lost its imposed severity, had become in spite of wear and strain as soft as her mouth and eyes. Yet its underlying structure remained precise, indomitable. The sad legacy of her parents had led her to what she was – but the saddest thing about her was that she did not understand how completely she had transformed that legacy, had made of herself something necessary and admirable. She deserved a better outcome than this. But he had nothing else to offer her.

She held his gaze as if she wanted to match him – and feared she could not. Then she tightened her grip on her torch and stepped out among the clenched Cavewights.

She had read them accurately: any threat to the Wightbarrow outweighed all other considerations. When Covenant left the First and Pitchwife, a raw muttering aggravated the rocklight. Several Cavewights shifted their positions, raised their weapons. But the First poised one foot to begin scattering the mound; and the creatures went rigid again. Covenant let weakness and fear and pain carry him like hope toward the mouth of the cave.

'Go well, Earthfriend,' the First breathed after them, 'hold faith, Chosen,' as if she had become impervious to doubt. Pitchwife's faint chuckling was torn and frayed; but it followed Covenant and Linden like an affirmation of contentment.

Barely upright on his feet, Covenant made his way past the Cavewights. Their eyes flamed outrage and loss at him; but they did not take the risk of striking out. The cave narrowed to a tunnel at its end, and Linden began to hurry. He did his best to keep up with her. The vulnerable place between his shoulder-blades seemed to feel the Cavewights turning to hurl their truncheons; but he entrusted himself to the Giants, did not look back. In a moment, he left the rocklight behind. Linden's torch led him back into the darkness of the catacombs.

At the first intersection, she turned as if she knew where she was going. Covenant caught up with her, put his hand on her arm to slow her somewhat. She acceded, but continued to bear herself as though she were being harried by unseen wings in Mount Thunder's immeasurable midnight. As her senses hunted the way ahead for peril or guidance, she began to mutter – to herself or to him, he could not tell which.

'They're wrong. They don't know enough. Whatever they brought back from the dead, it wasn't going to be Drool Rockworm. Not just another Cavewight. Something monstrous.

'Blood brings power. They had to kill someone. But what Caer-Caveral did for Hollian can't be done here. It only worked because they were in Andelain. And Andelain was intact. All that concentrated Earthpower – Concentrated and clean. Whatever those Cavewights resurrected, it was going to be abominable.'

When he understood that she was not talking about the Cavewights and Drool – that she was trying to say something else entirely – Covenant stumbled. His throbbing arm struck the wall of the passage, and he nearly lost his balance. Pain made his arm dangle as if it were being dragged down by the inconceivable weight of his ring. She was talking about the hope which he had never admitted to himself – the hope that if he died he, too, might be brought back.

'Linden – ' He did not wish to speak, to argue with her. They had so little time left. Fire gnawed up in his arm. He needed to husband his determination. But she had already gone too far in his name. Swallowing his weakness, he said, 'I don't want to be resurrected.'

She did not look at him. Roughly, he went on, 'You're going to go back to your own life. Sometime soon. And I won't get to go with you. You know it's too late to save me. Not back there. Where we come from, that kind of thing doesn't happen. Even if I'm resurrected, I won't get to go with you.

'If I can't go with you' – he told her the truth as well as he could – 'I'd rather stay with my friends.' Mhoram and Foamfollower. Elena and Bannor. Honninscrave. And the wait for Sunder and Hollian would not seem long to him.

She refused to hear him. 'Maybe not,' she rasped. 'Maybe we can still get back in time. I couldn't save you before because your spirit wasn't there – your will to live. If you would just stop giving up, we might still have a chance.' Her voice was husky with thwarted yearning. 'You're bruised and exhausted. I don't know how you stay on your feet. But you haven't been *stabbed* yet.' Her gaze flashed toward the faint scar in the centre of his chest. 'You don't have to die.'

But he saw the grief in her eyes and knew that she did not believe her own protestation.

He drew her to a halt. With his good hand, he wrested his wedding band from its finger. His touch was cold and numb, as if he had no idea what he was doing. Fervent and silent as a prayer, he extended the ring toward her. Its unmarred argent cast glints of the wavering torchlight.

At once, tears welled in her eyes. Streaks of reflected fire flowed down the lines which severity and loss had left on either side of her mouth. But she gave the ring no more than a glance. Her gaze clung to his countenance. 'No,' she whispered. 'Not while I can still hope.'

Abruptly, she moved on down the passage.

Sighing rue and relief like a man who had been reprieved or damned and did not know the difference – did not care if there were no difference – he thrust the ring back into place and followed her.

The tunnel became as narrow as a mere crack in the rock, then widened into a complex of junctions and chambers. The torch barely lit the walls and ceiling; it revealed nothing of what lay ahead. But from one passage came a breeze like a scent of evil that made Linden wince; and she turned that way. Covenant's hearing ached as he struggled to discern the sounds of pursuit or danger. But he lacked her percipience: he had to trust her.

The tunnel she had chosen angled downward until he thought that even vertigo would not be strong enough to keep him upright. Darkness and stone piled tremendously around him. The torch continued to burn down: it was half consumed already. Somewhere beyond the mountain, the Land lay in day or night; but he had lost all conception of time. Time had no meaning here, in the lightless unpity of Lord Foul's demesne. Only the torch mattered – and Linden's pale-knuckled grasp on the brand – and the fact that he was not alone. For good or ill, redemption or ruin, he was not alone. There was no other way.

Without warning, the walls withdrew, and a vast impression of space opened above his head. Linden stopped, searched the dark. When she lifted the torch, he saw that the tunnel had emerged from the stone, left them at the foot of a blunt gut-rock cliff. Chill air tingled against his cheek. The cliff seemed to go straight up forever. She looked at him as if she were lost. The scant fire made her eyes appear hollow and brutalized.

A short distance from the tunnel's opening rose a steep slope of shale, loam, and refuse – too steep and yielding to be climbed. He and Linden were in the bottom of a wide crevice. Something high up in the dark had collapsed any number of millennia ago, filling half the floor of the chasm with debris.

Memories flocked at him out of the enclosed night: recognitions ran like cold sweat down his spine. All his skin felt clammy and diseased. This looked like the place – The place where he had once fallen, with an ur-vile struggling to bite off his ring and no light anywhere, nothing to defend him from the ambush of madness except his stubborn insistence on himself. But that defence was no longer of any use. Kiril Threndor was not far away. Lord Foul was close –

'This way.' Linden gestured toward the left, along the sheer wall. Her voice sounded dull, half stupefied by the effort of holding onto her courage. Her senses told her things that appalled her. Though his own perceptions were fatally truncated, he felt the potential for hysteria creep upward in her. But instead of screaming she became scarcely able to move. How virulent would Lord Foul be to nerves as vulnerable as hers? Covenant was at least protected by his numbness. But she had no protection, might as well have been naked. She had known too much death. She hated it – and ached to share its sovereign power. She believed that she was evil.

In the unsteady torchlight, he seemed to see her already falling into paralysis under the pressure of Lord Foul's emanations.

Yet she still moved. Or perhaps the Despiser's will coerced her. Kiril Threndor was not far away. Dully, she walked in the direction she had indicated.

He joined her. All his joints were stiff with pleading. Hang on. You have the right to choose. You don't have to be trapped like this. Nobody can take away your right to choose. But he could not work the words into his locked throat. They were stifled by the accumulation of his own dread.

Dread which ate at the rims of his certainty, eroded the place of stillness and conviction where he stood. Dread that he was wrong—

The air was as damp and dank as compressed sweat. Shivering in the chill atmosphere, he accompanied Linden along the bottom of the chasm and watched the volition leak out of her until she was barely moving.

Then she stopped. Her head slumped forward: the torch hung at her side, nearly burning her hand. He prayed her name, but she did not respond. Her voice trickled like blood between her lips:

'Ravers.'

And the steep slope beside them arose as if she had called it to life.

Two of them: creatures of scree and detritus from the roots of the mountain. They were nearly as tall as Giants, but much broader: they looked strong enough to crush boulders in their massive arms. One of them struck Covenant a stone blow that scattered him to the floor. The other impelled Linden to the wall.

Her torch fell, guttered and went out. But the creatures did not need that light. They emitted a ghastly lumination that made their actions as vivid as atrocities.

One stood over Covenant to prevent him from rising. The other confronted Linden. It reached for her. Her face stretched to scream, but even her screams were paralysed. She made no effort to defend herself.

With a gentleness worse than any violence, the creature began to unbutton her shirt.

Covenant gagged for breath. Her extremity was more than he could bear. Every inch of him burned for power. Suddenly, he no longer cared whether his attacker would strike him again. He rolled onto his chest, wedged his knees under him, tottered to his feet. His attacker raised a threatening arm. He was battered and frail, barely able to stand: yet the passion raging from him halted the creature in mid-blow, forced it to retreat a step. It was a Raver, sentient and accessible to fear. It understood what his wild magic would do, if he willed.

His halfhand trembling, he pointed at the creature in front of Linden. It stopped at the last buttons. But it did not turn away.

'I'm warning you.' His voice spattered and scorched like hot acid. 'Foul's right about this. If you touch her, I don't care what else I destroy. I'll rip your soul to atoms. You won't live long enough to know whether I break the Arch or not.'

The creature did not move. It seemed to be daring him to unleash his white gold.

'Try me,' he breathed on the verge of eruption. 'Just try me.'

Slowly, the creature lowered its arms. Backing carefully, it retreated to stand beside its fellow.

A spasm went through Linden. All her muscles convulsed in torment or ecstasy. Then her head snapped up. The dire glow of the creatures flamed from her eyes.

She looked straight at Covenant and began to laugh.

The laughter of a ghoul, mirthless and cruel.

'Slay me then, groveller!' she cried. Her voice was as shrill as a shriek. It echoed hideously along the crevice. 'Rip my soul to atoms! Perchance it will pleasure you to savage the woman you love as well!'

The Raver had taken possession of her, and there was nothing in all the world that he could do about it.

He nearly fell then. The supreme evil had come upon her, and he was helpless. *The ill that you deem most terrible* – Even if he had grovelled entirely, abject and suppliant, begging the Ravers to release her, they would only have laughed at him. Now in all horor and anguish there was no other way – could be no other way. He cried out at himself, at his head to rise, his legs to uphold him, his back to straighten. Seadreamer! he panted as if that were the liturgy of his conviction, his fused belief. Honninscrave. Hamako. Hile Troy. All of them had given themselves. There was no other way.

'All right,' he grated. The sound of his voice in the chasm almost betrayed him to rage; but he clamped down his wild magic, refused it for the last time. 'Take me to Foul. I'll give him the ring.'

No way except surrender.

The Raver in Linden went on laughing wildly.

19

HOLD POSSESSION

She was not laughing.

Laughter came out of her mouth. It sprang from her corded throat to scale like gibbering up into the black abyss. Her lungs drew in the air which became malice and glee. Her face was contorted like the vizard of a demon – or the rictus of her mother's asphyxiation.

But she was not laughing. It was not Linden Avery who laughed. It was the Raver.

It held possession of her as completely as if she had been born for its use, formed and nurtured for no other purpose than to provide flesh for its housing, limbs for its actions, lungs and throat for its malign joy. It bereft her of will and choice, voice and protest. At one time, she had believed that her hands were trained and ready, capable of healing – a physician's hands. But now she had no hands with which to grasp her possessor and fight it. She was a prisoner in her own body and the Raver's evil.

And that evil excoriated every niche and nerve of her being. It was heinous and absolute beyond bearing. It consumed her with its memories and purposes, crushed her independent existence with the force of its ancient strength. It was the corruption of the Sunbane mapped and explicit in her personal veins and sinews. It was the revulsion and desire which had secretly ruled her life, the passion for and against death. It was the fetid halitus of the most diseased mortality condensed to its essence and elevated to the transcendence of prophecy, promise, suzerain truth – the definitive commandment of darkness.

All her life, she had been vulnerable to this. It had thronged into her from her father's stretched laughter, and she had confirmed it by stuffing it down her mother's abject throat. Once, she had flattered herself that she was like the Land under the Sunbane, helplessly exposed to desecration. But that was false. The Land was innocent.

She was *evil*.

Its name was *moksha* Jehannum, and it brought its past with it. She remembered now as if all its actions were her own the covert ecstasy with which it had mastered Marid – the triumph of the blow that had driven hot iron into Nassic's human back (and the rich blood frothing at the heat of the blade) – the cunning which had led *moksha* to betray its possession of Marid to her new percipience, so that she and Covenant would be condemned and Marid would be exposed to the perverting sun. She remembered bees – Remembered the apt mimesis of madness in the warped man who had set a spider to Covenant's neck. She might as well have done those things herself.

But behind them lay deeper crimes. Empowered by a piece of the Illearth Stone, she had mastered a Giant. She had named herself Fleshharrower and had led the Despiser's armies against the Lords. And she had tasted victory when she had trapped the defenders of the Land between her own forces and the savage forest of Garroting Deep – the forest which she hated, had hated for all the long centuries, hated in every green leaf and drop of sap from tree to tree – the forest which should have been helpless against ravage and fire, would have been helpless if some outer knowledge had not intervened, making possible the interdict of the Colossus of the Fall, the protection of the Forestals.

Yet she had been tricked into entering the deep, and so she had fallen victim to the Deep's guardian, Caerroil Wildwood. Unable to free herself, she had been slain in torment and ferocity on Gallows Howe, and her spirit had been sorely pressed to keep itself alive.

For that reason among many others, *moksha* Jehannum was avid to exact retribution. Linden was only one small morsel to the Raver's appetite. Yet her possessor savoured the pleasure her futile anguish afforded. Her body it left unharmed for its own use. But it violated her spirit as fundamentally as rape. And it went on laughing.

Her father's laughter pouring like a flood of midnight from the old desuetude of the attic: a throng of nightmares in which she foundered: triumph hosting out of the dire cavern and plunge which had once been his frail mouth. *You never loved me anyway.* Never loved him – or anyone else. She had not mustered the bare decency to cry aloud as she strangled her mother, drove that poor sick woman terrified and alone into the last dark.

This was what Joan had felt, this appalled and desperate horror which made no difference of any kind, could not so much as muffle the sound of malice. Buried somewhere within herself, Joan had watched her own fury for Covenant's blood, for the taste of his pain. And now Linden looked out at him as if through *moksha* Jehannum's eyes, heard him with ears that belonged to the Raver. Lit only by the ghoulish emanations of the creatures, he stood in the bottom of the crevice like a man who had just been maimed. His damaged arm dangled at his side. Every line of his body was abused with need and near-prostration. The bruises on his face made his visage appear misshapen, deformed by the pressures building inside him, where the wild magic was manacled. Yet his eyes gleamed like teeth, focused such menace toward the Ravers that *moksha* Jehannum's brother had not dared to strike him again.

'Take me to Foul,' he said. He had lost his mind. This was not despair: it was too fierce for despair. It was madness. The Banefire had cost him his sanity. 'I'll give him the ring.'

His gaze lanced straight into Linden. If she had owned a voice, she would have cried out.

He was smiling like a sacrifice.

Then she found that she did not have to watch him. The Raver could not require consciousness of her. Its memories told her that most of its victims had simply fled into mindlessness. The moral paralysis which had made her so accessible to *moksha* Jehannum would protect her now, not from use but from awareness. All she had to do was let go her final hold upon her identity. Then she would be spared from witnessing the outcome of Covenant's surrender.

With glee and hunger, the Raver urged her to let go. Her consciousness fed it, pleased it, sharpened its enjoyment of her

1197

violation. But if she lapsed, it would not need exertion to master her. And she would be safe at last – as safe as she had once been in the hospital during the blank weeks after her father's suicide – relieved from excruciation, inured to pain – as safe as death.

There were no other choices left for her to make.

She refused it. With the only passion and strength that remained to her, she refused it.

She had already failed in the face of Joan's need – been stricken helpless by the mere sight of Marid's desecration. Gibbon's touch had reft her of mind and will. But since then she had learned to fight.

In the cavern of the One Tree, she had grasped power for the first time and had used it, daring herself against forces so tremendous – though amoral – that terror of them had immobilized her until Findail had told her what was at stake. And in the Hall of Gifts – There *samadhi* Sheol's nearness had daunted her, misled her, tossed her in a whirlwind of palpable ill: she had hardly known where she stood or what she was doing. But she had not been stripped of choice.

Not, she insisted, careless of whether the Raver heard her. Because she had been needed. By all her friends. By Covenant before the One Tree, if not in the Hall of Gifts. And because she had experienced the flavour of efficacy, had gripped it to her heart and recognized it for what it was. Power: the ability to make choices that mattered. Power which came from no external source, but only from her own intense self.

She would not give it up. Covenant needed her still, though the Raver's mastery of her was complete and she had no way to reach him. *I'll give him the ring.* She could not stop him. But if she let herself go on down the blind road of paralysis, there would be no one left to so much as wish him stopped. Therefore she bore the pain. *Moksha* Jehannum crowded every nerve with nausea, filled every heart-beat with vitriol and dismay, shredded her with every word and movement. Yet she heeded the call of Covenant's fierce eyes and flagrant intent. Consciously, she clung to herself and refused oblivion, remained where the Raver could hurt her and hurt her, so that she would be able to watch.

And try.

'Will you?' chortled her throat and mouth. 'You are belatedly come to wisdom, groveller.' She raged at that epithet: he did not deserve it. But *moksha* only mocked him more trenchantly. 'Yet your abasement has been perfectly prophesied. Did you fear for your life among the Cavewights? Your fear was apt. Anile as the Dead, they would have slain you – and blithely would the ring have been seduced from them. From the moment of your summoning, all hope has been folly! All roads have led to the Despiser's triumph, and all struggles have been vain. Your petty – '

'I'm sick of this,' rasped Covenant. He was hardly able to stay on his feet – and yet the sheer force of his determination commanded the Ravers, sent an inward quailing through them. 'Don't flatter yourselves that I'm going to break down here.' Linden felt *moksha*'s trepidation and shouted at it, Coward! then gritted her teeth and gagged for bare life as its fury crashed down on her. But Covenant could not see what was happening to her, the price she paid for defiance. Grimly, he went on, 'You aren't going to get my ring. You'll be lucky if he even lets you live when he's finished with me.' His eyes flashed, as hard as hot marble. 'Take me to him.'

'Most assuredly, groveller,' *moksha* Jehannum riposted. 'I tremble at your will.'

Tearing savagery across the grain of Linden's clinched consciousness, the Raver turned her, sent her forward along the clear spine of the chasm.

Behind her, the two creatures – both ruled now by *moksha*'s brother – set themselves at Covenant's back. But she saw with the senses of the Raver that they did not hazard touching him.

He followed her as if he were too weak to do more than place one foot in front of the other – and too strong to be beaten.

The way seemed long: every step, each throb of her heart was interminable and exquisite agony. The Raver relished her violation and multiplied it cunningly. From her helpless brain, *moksha* drew images and hurled them at her, made them appear more real than Mount Thunder's imponderable gut-rock. Marid with his fangs. Joan screaming like a predator for Covenant's blood, racked by a Sunbane of the soul. Her mother's mouth, mucus drooping at the corners – phlegm as rank as putrefaction from the rot in her lungs. The incisions across her father's wrists, agape with death and glee. There was no end to the ways she could be tortured, if she refused to let go. Her possessor savoured them all.

Yet she held. Stubbornly, uselessly, almost without reason, she clung to who she was, to the Linden Avery who had made promises. And in the secret recesses of her heart she plotted *moksha* Jehannum's downfall.

Oh, the way seemed long to her! But she knew, had no defence against knowing, that for the Raver the distance was short and eager, little more than a stone's throw along the black gulf. Then the dank light of Covenant's guards picked out a stairway cut into the left wall. It was a rude ascent, roughly hacked from the sheer stone immemorially long ago and worn blunt by use; but it was wide and safe. The Raver went upward with strong strides, almost jaunty in its anticipation. But Linden watched Covenant for signs of vertigo or collapse.

His plight was awful. She felt his bruises aching in the bones of his skull, read the weary limp of his pulse. Sweat like fever or failure beaded on his forehead. An ague of exhaustion made all his movements awkward and imprecise. Yet he kept going, as rigid of intent as he had been on Haven Farm when he had walked into the woods to redeem his ex-wife. His very weakness and imbalance seemed to support him.

He was entirely out of his mind; and Linden bled for him while *moksha* Jehannum raked her with scorn.

The stairway was long and short: it ascended for several hundred feet and hurt as if it would go on forever without surcease. The Raver gave her not one fragment or splinter of respite while it used her body as if she had never been so healthy and vital. But at last she reached an opening in the wall, a narrow passage-mouth with rocklight reflecting from its end. The stairs continued upward; but she entered the tunnel. Covenant followed her, his guards behind him in single-file.

Heat mounted against her face until she seemed to be walking into fire; but it meant nothing to *moksha*: the Raver was at home in dire passages and brimstone. For a while, all the patients she had failed to help, all the medical mistakes she had made beat about her mind, accusing her like furies. In the false name of life, she was responsible for so much death. Perhaps she had employed it for her own ends. Perhaps she had introduced pain and loss to her victims, needing them to suffer so that she would have power and life.

Then the passage ended, and she found herself in the place where Lord Foul had chosen to wield his machinations.

Kiril Threndor. Heart of Thunder.

Here Kevin Landwaster had come to enact the Ritual of Desecration. Here Drool Rockworm had recovered the lost Staff of Law. It was the dark centre of all Mount Thunder's ancient and fatal puissance.

The place where the outcome of the Earth would be decided.

She knew it with *moksha* Jehannum's knowledge. The Raver's whole spirit seemed to quiver in lust and expectation.

The cave was large, a round, high chamber. Entrances gaped like mute cries, stretched in eternal pain, around its circumference. The walls glared rocklight in all directions. They were shaped entirely into smooth, irregular facets which cast their illumination like splinters at Linden's eyes. And that sharp assault was whetted and multiplied by a myriad keen reflections from the chamber's ceiling. There the stone gathered a dense cluster of stalactites, as bright and ponderous as melting metal. Among them swarmed a chiaroscuro of orange-red gleamings.

But no light seemed to touch the figure that stood on a low dais in the middle of the time-burnished floor. It rose there like a pillar, motionless and immune to revelation. It might have been the back of a statue or a man: perhaps it was as tall as a Giant. Even the senses of the Raver saw nothing certainly. It appeared to have no colour and no clear shape or size. Its outlines were blurred as if they transcended recognition. But it radiated power like a shriek through the echoing rocklight.

The air reeked of sulphur – a stench so acrid that it would have brought tears to her eyes if it had not given such pleasure to her possessor. But under the rank odour lay a different scent, a smell more subtle, insidious, and consuming than any brimstone. A smell on which *moksha* fed like an addict.

A smell of attar. The sweetness of the grave.

Linden was forced to devour it as if she were revelling.

The force of the figure screamed into her like a shout poised to bring down the mountain, rip the vulnerable heart of the Land to rubble and chaos.

Covenant stood a short distance away from her now, dissociating his light from hers so that she would not suffer the consequences of his company. He had no health-sense. And even if his eyes had been like hers, he might not have been able to discern what was left of her – might not have seen the way she cried out to have him beside her. She knew everything to which he was blind, everything that could have made a difference to him. Everything except how in his battered weakness he had become strong enough to stand there as though he were indefeasible.

With *moksha*'s perceptions, she saw the two creatures and the Raver which controlled them leave the chamber: they were no longer needed. She saw Covenant look at her and form her name, trying mutely to tell her something that he could not say and she could not hear. The light flared at her like a shattered thing, stone trapped in the throes of fragmentation, the onset of the last collapse. The stalactites shed gleams and imminence as if they were about to plunge down on her. Her unbuttoned shirt seemed to let attar crawl across her breasts, teasing them with anguish. Heat closed around her faint thoughts like a fist.

And the figure on the dais turned.

Even *moksha* Jehannum's senses failed her: they were a blurred lens through which she saw only outlines that dripped and ran, features smeared out of focus. She might have been trying to gauge the figure past the high, hot intervention of a bonfire. But it resembled a man. Parts of him suggested a broad chest and muscular arms, a patriarchal beard, a flowing robe. Tall as a Giant, puissant as a mountain, and more exigent than any conflagration of bloodshed and corruption, he turned; and his gaze swept Kiril Threndor – swept her and Covenant as if with a blink he could have brushed them out of existence.

His eyes were the only precise part of him.

She had seen them before.

Eyes as bitter as fangs, carious and cruel: eyes of deliberate force, rabid desire: eyes wet with venom and insatiation. In the woods behind Haven Farm, they had shone out of the blaze and pierced her to the pit of her soul, measuring and disdaining every aspect of her as she had crouched in fright. They had required paralysis of her as though it were the first law of her existence. When she had unlocked her weakness, run down the hillside to try to save Covenant, they had fixed her like a promise that she would never be so brave again, never rise above her mortal contradictions. And now with infinitely multiplied and flagrant virulence they repeated that promise and made it true. Reaching past *moksha* Jehannum to the clinched relic of her consciousness, they confirmed their absolute commandment.

Never again.

Never.

In response, her voice said, 'He has come to cede his ring. I have brought him to your will,' and chortled like a burst of involuntary fear: even the Raver could not bear its master's direct gaze and sought to turn that baleful regard aside.

But for a moment Lord Foul did not look away. His eyes searched her for signs of defiance or courage. Then he said, 'To you I do not speak.' His voice came from the rocklight and the heat, from the reek of attar and the chiaroscuro of the stalactites – a voice as deep as Mount Thunder's bones and veined with savagery. Orange-red facets glittered and glared in every word. 'I have not spoken to you. There was no need – is none. I speak to set the feet of my hearers upon the paths I design for them, but your path has been mine from the first. You have been well bred to serve me, and all your choices conduce to my ends. To attain that which I have desired from you has been a paltry exercise, scarce requiring effort. When I am free' – she heard a grin in the swarming reflections – 'you will accompany me, so that your present torment may be prolonged forever. I will gladly mark myself upon such flesh as yours.'

With her mouth, the Raver giggled tense and sweating approval. The Despiser's gaze nailed dismay into her. She was as abject as she had ever been, and she tried to wail: but no sound came.

Then she would have let go. But Covenant did not. His eyes were midnight with rage for her: his passion refused to be crushed. He looked hardly capable of taking another step – yet he came to her aid.

'Don't kid yourself,' he snapped like a jibe. 'You're already beaten, and you don't even know it. All these threats are just pathetic.'

Assuredly he was out of his mind. But his sarcasm shifted the Despiser toward him: Linden was left to the cunning tortures of her possessor. They slashed and flayed at her, showed her in long whipcuts all the atrocities an immortal could commit against her. But when Lord Foul's gaze left her, she found that she was still able to cling. She was stubborn enough for that.

'Ah,' the Despiser rumbled like the sigh of an avalanche, 'at last my foeman stands before me. He does not grovel – but grovelling has become needless. He has spoken words which may not be recalled. Indeed, his abasement is complete, though he is blind to it. He does not see that he has sold himself to a servitude more demeaning than prostration. He has become the tool of my Enemy, no longer free to act against me. Therefore he submits himself, deeming in his cowardice that here the burden of havoc and ruin will pass from him.' Soft laughter made the rocklight throb: mute shrieks volleyed from the walls. 'He is the Unbeliever in all sooth. He does not believe that the Earth's doom will at last be laid to his charge.

'Thomas Covenant' – he took an avid step forward – 'the spectacle of your puerile strivings gives me glee to repay my long patience, for your defeat has ever been as certain as my will. Were I to be foiled, the opportunity belonged to your companion, not to you – and you see how she has availed herself of it.' With one strong, blurred arm, he made a gesture toward Linden that nearly unseated her reason. Again, he laughed; but his laughter was devoid of mirth. 'Had she seduced you of the ring – ah, then would I have been tested. But therefore did I choose her, a woman altogether unable to turn aside from my desires.

'You are a fool,' he went on, 'for you have known yourself doomed, and yet you have come to me. Now I require your soul.' The heat of his voice filled Linden's lungs with suffocation. *Moksha* Jehannum shivered, hungry for violence and ravage. The Despiser sounded unquestionably sane – but that only made him more terrible. One of his hands – a bare smear across the Raver's sight – seemed to curl into a fist; and Covenant was jerked forward, within Lord Foul's reach. The walls spattered light like sobs, as if Mount Thunder itself were appalled.

As soft as the whisper of death, the Despiser said, 'Give the ring to me.'

Linden believed that she would have obeyed in Covenant's place. The command of that voice was absolute. But he did not move. His right arm hung at his side: the ring dangled as if it were empty of import – as if his numb finger within the band had no significance. His left fist closed and unclosed like the aggrieved labour of his heart. His eyes looked as dark as the loneliness of stars. Somehow, he held his head up, his back straight – upright in conviction or madness.

'Talk's cheap. You can say anything you want. But you're wrong, and you ought to know it. This time you've gone too far. What you did to Andelain. What you're doing to Linden – ' He swallowed acid.

'We aren't enemies. That's just another lie. Maybe you believe it — but it's still a lie. You should see yourself. You're even starting to look like me.' The special gleam of his gaze reached Linden like a gift. He was irremediably insane — or utterly indomitable. 'You're just another part of me. Just one side of what it means to be human. The side that hates lepers. The poisonous side.' His certainty did not waver at all. 'We are one.'

His assertion made Linden gape at what he had become. But it only drew another laugh from the Despiser — a short, gruff bark of dismissal. 'Do not seek to bandy truth and falsehood with *me*,' he replied. 'You are too inane for the task. Lies would better serve the trivial yearning which you style love. The truth damns you here. For three and a half millennia I have muttered my will against the Earth *in your absence*, groveller. I am the truth. *I*. And I have no use for the sophistry of your Unbelief.' He levelled his voice at Covenant like the blade of an axe. Fragments of rocklight shot everywhere but could not bring his intense form into any kind of focus. 'Give the ring to me.'

Covenant's visage slackened as if he were made ill by the necessity of his plight. But still he withheld submission. Instead, he changed his ground.

'At least let Linden go.' His stance took on an angle of pleading. 'You don't need her anymore. Even you should be satisfied with how much she's been hurt. I've already offered her my ring once. She refused it. Let her go.'

In spite of everything, he was still trying to spare her.

Lord Foul's response filled Kiril Threndor. 'Have done, groveller.' Attar made the Raver ecstatic, racked Linden. 'You weary my long patience. She is forfeit to me by her own acts. Are you deaf to yourself? You have spoken words which can never be recalled.' Concentrated venom dripped from his outlines. As distinct as the breaking of boulders, he demanded a third time. 'Give the ring to me.'

And Covenant went on sagging as though he had begun to crumble. All his strength was gone. He could no longer pretend to hold himself upright. One by one, his loves had been stripped from him: he had nothing left. After all, he was only one ordinary man, small and human. Without wild magic, he was no match for the Despiser.

When he weakly lifted his halfhand, began tugging the ring from his finger, Linden forgave him. *No choice but to surrender it.* He had done everything possible, everything conceivable, had surpassed himself again and again in his efforts to save the Land. That he failed now was cause for grief, but not for blame.

Only his eyes showed no collapse. They burned like the final dark, the last deep midnight where no Sunbane shone.

His surrender took no more than three heart-beats. One to raise his hand, take hold of the ring. Another to pull the band from his finger as if in voluntary riddance of marriage, love, humanity. A third to extend the immaculate white gold toward the Despiser.

But extremity and striving made those three moments as long as agony. During them, Linden Avery pitted her ultimate will against her possessor.

She forgave Covenant. He was too poignant and dear to be blamed. He had given everything that her heart could ask of him.

But she did not submit.

Gibbon had said, *The principal doom of the Land is upon your shoulders.* Because no one else had this chance to come between Covenant and his defeat. *You are being forged as iron is forged to achieve the ruin of the Earth.* Forged to fail here. *Because you can see.*

Now she meant to determine what kind of metal had been made of her.

Gibbon-Raver had also told her she was evil. Perhaps that was true. But evil itself was a form of power.

And she had become intimately familiar with her possessor. From the furthest roots of its past, she felt springing its contempt for all things that had flesh and could be mastered — a contempt born of fear. Fear of any form of life able to refuse it. The Forests. Giants. The *Haruchai*. It was unquenchably hungry for immortal control, for the safety of sovereignty. All refusals terrified it. The logic of its failures led inexorably to death. If it could be refused, then it could also be slain.

She had no way to understand the lost communal mind of the Forests. But Giants and Haruchai were another question. Though *moksha* Jehannum ripped and shrieked at her, she picked up the strands of what she knew and wove them to her purpose.

The Giants and *Haruchai* had always been able to refuse. Perhaps because they had not suffered the Land's long history of Ravers, they had not learned to doubt their autonomy. Or perhaps because they used little or no outward expressions of power, they comprehended more fully that true choice was internal. But whatever the explanation, they were proof against possession where the people of the Land were not. They believed in their capacity to make choices which mattered.

That belief was all she needed.

Moksha was frantic now, savage and brutal. It assailed every part of her that was able to feel pain. It desecrated her as if she were Andelain. It made every horrifying memory of her life incandescent before her: Nassic's murder and Gibbon's touch; the lurker of the Sarangrave; Kasreyn's malign cunning; Covenant bleeding irretrievably to death in the woods behind Haven Farm. It poured acid into every wound which futility had ever inflicted upon her.

And it argued with her. She could not choose: she had already made the only choice that signified. When she had accepted the legacy of her father and stuffed it in handfuls of tissue down her mother's throat, she had declared her crucial allegiance, her definitive passion – a passion in no way different from her possessor's. Despite had made her what she was, a lost woman as ravaged as the Land, and the Sunbane dawning in her now would never set.

But the sheer intensity of her hurt made her lucid. She saw the Raver's lie. Only once had she tried to master death by destroying life. After that, all her striving had gone to heal those who suffered. Though she had been haunted and afraid, she had not been cruel. Suicide and murder and flight were not the whole story. When the old man on Haven Farm had collapsed in front of her, the stink issuing from his mouth had sickened her like the foretaste of Despite; but she had willingly breathed and breathed that fetor in her efforts to save him.

She was evil. Her visceral response to the dark might of her tormentors gave her the stature of a Raver. And yet her instinct for healing falsified *moksha*.

That contradiction no longer paralysed her. She accepted it.

It gave her the power to choose.

Squalling like a butchered thing, the Raver fought her. But she had entered at last into her true estate. *Moksha* Jehannum was afraid of her. Her will rose up in its shackles. Tested the iron of her possessor's malice. Took hold of the chains.

And broke free.

Lord Foul had not yet grasped the ring. There was still an instant of space between his hand and Covenant's. Rocklight yowled desire and triumph from the walls.

Linden did not move. She had no time to think of that. Motionless as if she were still frozen, she hurled herself forward. With her Land-born health-sense, she sprang into Covenant, scrambled toward the fiery potential of his wedding band.

Empowered by wild magic, she drew back his hand.

At that, rage swelled Lord Foul: he sent out a flood of fury which should have washed her away. But she ignored him. She was sure that he would not touch her now – not now, while she held possession of Covenant and the ring. She was suddenly strong enough to turn her back upon the Despiser himself. The necessity of freedom protected her. The choice of surrender or defiance was hers to make.

In the silent privacy of his mind, she faced the man she loved and took all his burdens upon herself.

He could not resist her. Once before, he had beaten back her efforts to control him. But now he had no defence. With his own strength, she mastered him as completely as ever the *Elohim* or Kasreyn had mastered him.

Not evil! she breathed at him. *Not this time.* Her previous attempt to possess him had been wrong, inexcusable. She had read in him his intent to risk the Banefire, and she had reacted as if he meant to commit suicide: instinctively, she had tried to stop him. But then his life and the risk had been his alone. She had had no right to interfere.

Now, however, he surrendered the Earth as well as himself. He was not simply risking his own life: he was submitting all life to certain destruction. Therefore she had the responsibility to intervene. The responsibility and the right.

The right! she cried. But he made no answer. Her will occupied him completely.

She seemed to meet him where they had met once before, when she had surrendered herself to save him from the silence of the *Elohim* – in a field of flowers, under an inviolate sky, a clean sun. But now she recognized that field as one of the rich leas of Andelain, bordered by hills and woods. And he was no longer young. He stood before her exactly as he stood before the Despiser – altogether untouchable, his face misshaped by bruises he did not deserve, his body nearly prostrate with exhaustion, the old knife-cut in the centre of his shirt gaping. His eyes were fixed on her, and they flamed hot midnight, the final extremity of the heavens.

No smile in the world could have softened his gaze. ·

He stood there as if he were waiting for her to search him, catechize him, learn the truth. But she failed to close the gulf between them. She ran and ran toward him, aching to fling her arms around him at last; but the field lay as still as the sunlight, and his eyes shone darkness at her, and all her strength brought her no nearer. She knew that if she reached him she would understand – that the vision or despair which he had found in the Banefire would be communicated to her – that his certainty would become comprehensible. He was certain, as sure as white gold. But she could not approach him. He met her appeal with the indefeasible *Don't touch me* of leprosy or ascension, apotheosis.

His refusal made grief well up in her like the wail of a lost child.

Then she wanted to turn and hurl all her new-found force at the Despiser, wanted to call up white fire and scourge him from the face of the Earth. *Some infections have to be cut out. Why else do you have all that power?* She could do it. He had hurt Covenant so deeply that she was no longer able to reach him. In her anguish she was greedy for fire. She possessed him heart and limb – and his left hand held the ring, gripped it on the brink of detonation. She was capable of that. If no other hope remained, and she could not touch her love, then

1207

let it be she who fought, she who ravaged, she who ruled. Let Lord Foul learn the nature of what he had forged!

Yet Covenant's gaze held her as if she were sobbing, too weak to do anything except weep. He said nothing, offered her nothing. But the purity of his regard did not let her turn. How could he speak, do anything other than repudiate her? She had taken his will from him – had dehumanized him as thoroughly as if she were a Raver and relished his helplessness. And yet he remained human and desirable and stubborn, as dear as life to her. Perhaps he was mad. But was she not something worse?

Are you not evil?

Yes. Beyond question.

But the black flame in his eyes did not accuse her of evil. He did not despise her in any way. He only refused to be swayed.

You said you trusted me.

And who was she to believe him wrong? If doubt was necessary, why should it be doubt of him rather than of herself? Kevin Landwaster had warned her, and she had felt his honesty. But perhaps after all he did not understand, was blinded by the consequences of his own despair. And Covenant remained before her in sunshine and flowers as if the beauty of Andelain were the ground on which he took his stand. His darkness was as lonely as hers. But hers was like the lightless cunning and violence of the Wightwarrens: his resembled the heart of the true night, where the Sunbane never shone.

Yes, she said again. She had known all along that possession in every guise was evil; but she had tried to believe otherwise, both because she wanted power and because she wanted to save the Land. Destruction and healing: death and life. She could have argued that even evil was justified to keep the white ring out of Lord Foul's grasp. But now she was truly weeping. Covenant had said, *I'm going to find some other answer.* That was the only promise which mattered.

Deliberately, she let him go – let love and hope and power go as if they were all one, too pure to be possessed or desecrated. Locking her cries in her throat, she turned and walked away across the lea. Out of sunshine into attar and rocklight.

With her own eyes, she saw Covenant lift the ring once more as though his last fears were gone. With her own ears, she heard the savage relief of Lord Foul's laughter as he claimed his triumph. Heat and despair seemed to close over her like the lid of a coffin.

Moksha Jehannum tried to enter her again, cast her down. But the Raver could not touch her now. Grief crowded upward in her, thronged for utterance. She was hardly aware of *moksha*'s failure.

The Despiser made Kiril Threndor shudder:

'Fool!'

He was crowing over Linden, not Covenant. His eyes bit a trail of venom through her mind.

'Have I not said that all your choices conduce to my ends? You serve me absolutely!' The stalactites threw shards of malice at her head. 'It is you who have accorded the ring to me!'

He raised one hand like a smear across her sight. In his grasp, the band began to blaze. His shout gathered force until she feared it would shatter the mountain.

'Here at last I hold possession of all life and Time forever! Let my Enemy look to his survival and be daunted! Freed of my gaol and torment, I will rule the cosmos!'

She could not remain upright under the weight of his exaltation. His voice split her hearing, hampered the rhythm of her heart. Kneeling on the tremorous stone, she gritted her teeth, swore to herself that even though she had failed at everything else she would at least breathe no more of this damnable attar. The walls threw argent in carillon from all their facets. The Despiser's power scaled toward apocalypse.

Yet she heard Covenant. Somehow, he kept his feet. He did not shout; but every word he said was as distinct as augury.

'Big deal. I could do the same thing – if I were as crazy as you.' His certainty was unmatched. 'It doesn't take power. Just delusion. You're out of your mind.'

The Despiser swung toward Covenant. Wild magic effaced the rocklight, made Kiril Threndor scream white fire. 'Groveller, I will teach you the meaning of my suzerainty!' His whole form rippled and blurred with ecstasy, violence. Only his carious eyes remained explicit, as cruel as fangs. They seemed to shred the substance from Covenant's bones. 'I am your *Master*!'

He towered over Covenant: his arms rose in transport or imprecation. In one fist, he held the prize for which he had craved and plotted. The searing light he drew from the ring should have blinded Linden entirely, scorched her eyes out of their sockets. But from *moksha* Jehannum she had learned how to protect her senses. She felt that she was peering into the furnace of the desecrated sun; but she was still able to see.

Able to see the blow which Lord Foul hammered down on Covenant as if the wild magic were a dagger.

It made Mount Thunder lurch, snapped stalactites from the ceiling like a rain of spears which narrowly missed Linden: it slapped Covenant to the floor as if all his limbs had been broken. For an instant, a convulsion of lightning writhed over him. Power and coruscation like the immaculate silver-white of the ring clamoured through him, shrilled along the lines of his form. She tried to yell; but the air in her lungs had given out.

When the blow passed, it left white flame spouting from the centre of his chest.

The wound bled argent: all his blood was ablaze. Fire fountained from his gaping hurt, spat gouts and plumes of numinous and incandescent deflagration, untainted by any darkness or venom. During that moment, he looked like he was still alive.

But it was transitory. The fire faded rapidly. Soon it flickered and failed. His blasted husk lay on the floor and did not move again.

Too stunned to cry out, Linden hugged her arms around herself and keened in the marrow of her bones.

But Lord Foul went on laughing.

Like a ghoul he laughed, a demon of torment and triumph. His lust riddled the mountain: more stalactites fell. From wall to wall, a crack sprang through the chamber; and shattered stones burst like cries from the fissure. Kiril Threndor shrieked argent. The Despiser became titanic with white fire.

'Ware of me, my Enemy!' His shout deafened Linden in spite of her instinctive self-protection. She heard him, not with her overwhelmed ears, but with the tissues and vessels of her lungs. 'I hold the keystone of Time, and I will reave it to rubble! Oppose me if you dare!'

Fire mounted around him, whipped higher and higher by his fierce arms. The ring raged like a growing sun in his fist. Already, his power dwarfed the Banefire, outsized every puissance she had ever witnessed, surpassed even the haunted faces of her nightmares.

Yet she moved. Crawling across the agonized lurch and shudder of the stone, she wrestled her weak body toward Covenant. She could not help him. She could not help herself. But she wanted to hold him in her embrace one more time. To ask his forgiveness, though he would never be able to hear her. Lord Foul had become so tremendous that only the edges of his gathering cataclysm were still discernible. She crept past him as if she were ignoring him. Battered and aggrieved of body and soul, she reached Covenant, sat beside him, lifted his head into her lap, and let her hair fall around his face.

In death, his visage wore a strange grimace of relief and pain. He looked like a man who was about to laugh and weep at the same time.

At least I trusted you, she replied. Whatever else I did wrong. I trusted you in the end.

Then anguish seized her heart.

You didn't even say goodbye.

None of the people who had died while she loved them had ever said goodbye.

She did not know how it was possible to continue breathing. Lord

Foul's attar had become as intense as the light. The destruction he purposed tore a howl through the stone: Kiril Threndor became the stretched mouth of the mountain's hurt. Her mere flesh seemed to fray and dissolve in the proximity of such power. His blast was nearly ready.

Instinctively, almost involuntarily, she looked up from Covenant's guilt and innocence, impelled by an inchoate belief that there should be at least one witness to the riving of Time. While her mind lasted, she could still watch what the Despiser did, still send her protest to hound him into the heavens.

A maelstrom swept around him and grew as if he meant to break the Earth by consuming it alive. His fire was so extreme that it pulsed through the mountain, made all of Mount Thunder pound. But gradually he pulled the flame into himself, focused it in the hand that held the ring. Too bright to be beheld, his fist throbbed like the absolute heart of the world.

With a terrible cry, he hurled his globe-splitting power upward.

An instant later, his exaltation changed to astonishment and rage.

Somewhere in the rock which enclosed Kiril Threndor, his blast shattered. Because it was aimed at the Arch of Time, it was not an essentially physical force, though the concussion of its delivery nearly reft Linden of consciousness: it did no physical damage. Instead, it burst as if it had struck a midnight sky and snapped. In a fathomless abyss, ruptured fragments of fire shot and blazed.

And the hot lines of light spread like etchwork, merged and multiplied swiftly, took shape within the bulk of the mountain. From wild magic and nothingness, they created a sketch of a man.

A man who had placed himself between Lord Foul and the Arch of Time.

The outlines gained substance and feature as they absorbed the Despiser's attack.

Thomas Covenant.

He stood there inside Mount Thunder's gut-rock, a spectre altogether different from the ponderous stone. All which remained of his mortal being was the grimace of power and grief that marked his countenance.

'No!' the Despiser howled. '*No!*'

But Covenant replied, 'Yes.' He had no earthly voice, made no human sound. Yet he could be heard through the clamour of tormented stone, the constant repercussions of Lord Foul's fury. Linden listened to him as if he were as clear as a trumpet. 'Brinn showed me the way. He beat the Guardian of the One Tree by sacrificing himself, letting himself fall. And Mhoram told me to "Remember the paradox of white gold". But for a long time I didn't understand. I'm the paradox. You can't take the wild magic away from me.' Then he seemed to move forward, concentrating more intensely on the Despiser. His command was as pure as white fire. 'Put down the ring.'

'Never!' Lord Foul shouted instantly. Might leaped in him, wild for use. 'I know not what chicane or madness has brought you before me from the Dead – but it will not avail! You have once cast me down! I will not suffer a second debasement! *Never!* The white gold is mine, freely given! If you combat me, Death itself will not ward you from my wrath!'

Something like a smile sharpened the spectre's acute face. 'I keep telling you you're wrong. I wouldn't dream of fighting you.'

Lord Foul's retort was a bolt that sizzled the air like frying meat. Power fierce enough to blow off the crown of the peak sprang at Covenant, raging for his immolation.

He did not oppose it, made no effort to resist or evade the attack. He simply accepted it. The clench of pain between his brows showed that he was hurt; but he did not flinch. The blast raved and scourged into him until Linden feared that even a dead soul could not survive it. Yet when it ended he had taken it all upon himself. Bravely, he stood forth from the fire.

'I'm not going to fight you.' Even now, he seemed to pity his slayer. 'All you can do is hurt me. But pain doesn't last. It just makes me stronger.' His voice held a note of sorrow for the Despiser. 'Put down the ring.'

But Lord Foul was so far gone in fury and frustration that he might have been deaf. 'No!' he roared again. No fear hampered him: he was transported to the verge of absolute violence.

'*No!*'

'NO!'

And with every cry he flung his utterest force against the Unbeliever.

Blast after blast, faster and faster. Enough white power to bring Mount Thunder down in rubble, cast it off Landsdrop into the ruinous embrace of Sarangrave Flat. Enough to leave the One Tree itself in ash and cinders. Enough to shatter the Arch of Time. All Lord Foul's ancient puissance was multiplied and channelled by the argent ring: he struck and struck, the unanswerable knell of his hunger adumbrating through Kiril Threndor until Linden's mind reeled and her life almost stopped, unable to support the magnitude of his rage. She clung to Covenant's body as if it were her last anchor and fought to endure and stay sane while Lord Foul strove to rip down the essential definition of the Earth.

But each assault hit nothing except the spectre, hurt nothing except Covenant. Blast after blast, he absorbed the power of Despite and fire and became stronger: surrendering to their savagery, he transcended them. Every blow elevated him from the mere grieving spectation of the Dead in Andelain, the ritualized helplessness of the Unhomed in *Coercri*, to the stature of pure wild magic. He became an unbreakable bulwark raised like glory against destruction.

At the same time, each attack made Lord Foul weaker. Covenant was a barrier the Despiser could not pierce because it did not resist him; and he could not stop. After so many millennia of yearning, defeat was intolerable to him. In accelerating frenzy, he flung rage and defiance and immitigable hate at Covenant. Yet each failed blow cost him more of himself. His substance frayed and thinned, denatured moment by moment, as his attacks grew more reckless and extravagant. Soon he had reduced himself to such evanescence that he was barely visible.

And still he did not stop. Surrender was impossible for him. If he had not been limited and confined by the mortal Time of his prison, he would have gone on forever, seeking Covenant's eradication. For a while, his form guttered and wailed as complete fury drove him to the threshold of banishment. Then he failed and went out.

Though she was stunned and stricken, Linden heard the faint metallic clink of the ring when it fell to the dais and rolled to a stop.

20

THE SUN-SAGE

Slowly, silence settled like dust back into Kiril Threndor. Most of the rocklight had been extinguished, but pieces still flared along the facets of the walls, giving the chamber an obscure illumination. Without the cloying scent of attar, the brimstone atmosphere smelled almost clean. Holes gaped in the ceiling where many of the stalactites had hung. Long tremors still rumbled into the distance, but they were no longer dangerous. They subsided like sighs as they passed beyond Linden's percipience.

She sat cross-legged near the dais, with Covenant's head in her lap. No breath stirred his chest. He was already growing cold. The capacity for peril which had made him so dear to her had gone out. But she did not let him go. His face wore a grimace of defeat and victory – a strange fusion of commandment and grace – that was as close as he would ever come to peace.

She did not look up to meet the argent gaze of his revenant. She did not need to see him bending over her as though his heart bled to comfort her. The simple sense of his presence was enough. In silence, she bowed over his body. Her eyes streamed at the beauty of what he had become.

For a long moment, his empathy breathed about her, clearing the last reek from the air, the taste of ruin from her lungs. Then he said her name softly. His voice was tender, almost human, as if he had not passed beyond the normal strictures of life and death. 'I'm sorry.' He seemed to feel that it was he who needed her forgiveness, rather than she who ached for his. 'I didn't know what else to do. I had to stop him.'

I understand, she answered. You were right. Nobody else could've done it. If she had possessed half his comprehension, a fraction of his courage, she might have tried to help him. There had been no other way. But she would have failed. She was too tainted by her own darkness for such pure sacrifices.

Nobody else, she repeated. But any moment now she was going to begin sobbing. She had lost him at last. When the true grief started, it might never stop.

Yet he had already passed beyond compassion into necessity. Or perhaps he felt the hurt rising in her and sought to answer it. As gentle as love, he said, 'Now it's your turn. Pick up the ring.'

The ring. It lay at the edge of the dais perhaps ten feet from her. And it was empty — devoid of light or power — an endless silver-white band with no more meaning than an unused manacle. Without Covenant or Lord Foul to wield it, it had lost all significance.

She was too weak and lorn to wonder why Covenant wanted her to do something about his ring. If she had been given some reason to hope that his spirit and his flesh might be brought back to each other, she would have obeyed him. No frailty or incomprehension would have prevented her from obeying him. But those questions had already been answered. And she had no desire to let his body out of her embrace.

'Linden.' His emanations were soft and kind; but she felt their ugency growing. 'Try to think. I know it's hard — after what you've been through. But try. I need you to save the Land.'

She could not look up at him. His dead face was all that remained to her, all that held her together: if she raised her head to his unbearable beauty, she would be lost as well. With her fingertips, she stroked the gaunt lines of his cheek. In silence, she said, I don't need to. You've already done it.

'No,' he returned at once. 'I haven't.' Every word made his tension clearer. 'All I did was stop him. I haven't healed anything. The Sunbane is still there. It has a life of its own. And the Earthpower's been too badly corrupted. It can't recover by itself.' His tone went straight into her heart. 'Linden, please. Pick up the ring.'

Into her heart, where a storm of lamentation brewed. Instinctively, she feared it. It seemed to rise from the same source which had given birth to her old hunger for darkness.

I can't, she said. Gusts and rue tugged through her. You know what power does to me. I can't stop hurting the people I want to help. I'll just turn into another Raver.

His spirit shone with comprehension. But he did not try to answer her dread, to deny or comfort it. Instead, his voice took on a note of harsh exigency.

'I can't do it myself. I don't have your hands – can't touch that kind of power any more. I'm not physically alive. And I can be dismissed. I'm like the Dead. They can be invoked – and they can be sent away. Anybody who knows how can make me leave.' He appeared to believe he was in that danger. 'Even Foul could've done it, if he hadn't tried to use wild magic against me.

'Linden, think.' His sense of peril burned in the cave. 'Foul isn't dead. You can't kill Despite. And the Sunbane will bring him back. It'll restore him. He can't get past me to break the Arch. But he'll be able to do anything he wants to the Land – to the whole Earth.

'Linden!' The appeal broke from him. But at once he coerced himself to quietness again. 'I don't mean to hurt you. I don't want to demand more than you can do. You've already done so much. But you've got to understand. You're starting to fade.'

That was true: she recognized it with a dim startlement like the foretaste of a gale. His body had become harder and heavier, more real – or else her own flesh was losing definition. She heard winds blowing like the ancient respiration of the mountain. Everything around her – the rocklight, the blunt stone, the atmosphere of Kiril Threndor – sharpened as her perceptions thinned. She was dwindling. Slowly, inexorably, the world grew more quintessential and necessary than anything her trivial mortality could equal. Soon she would go out like a snuffed candle.

'This is the way it usually works,' Covenant went on. 'The power that called you here recoils when whoever summoned you dies. You're going back to your own life. Foul isn't dead – but as far as your summons goes, he might as well be. You'll lose your last chance.' His demand focused on her like anger. Or perhaps it was her own diminishment that made him sound so fiercely grieved. 'Pick up the ring!'

She sighed faintly. She did not want to move: the prospect of dissolution struck her as a promise of peace. Perhaps she would die from it – would be spared the storm of her pain. That hurt cut at her, presaging the wind which blew between the worlds. She had lost him. Whatever happened now, she had lost him absolutely.

Yet she did not refuse him. She had sworn that she would put a stop to the Sunbane. And her love for him would not let her go. She had failed at everything else.

She was in no hurry. There was still time. The process leeching her away was slow, and she retained enough percipience to measure it. Groaning at the ache in her bones, she unbowed her back, lowered his head tenderly to her thighs. Her fingers fumbled stiffly, as if they were no longer good for anything; but she forced them to serve her – to rebutton her shirt, closing at least that much protection over her bare heart. In her nightmare, she had used her shirt to try to staunch the bleeding. But she had failed then as well.

At that moment, a voice as precise as a bell rang in her mind. She seemed to recognize it, though it could not be him, that was impossible. Nothing had prepared her for his desperation.

– Avaunt, shade! Your work is done! Urge me no more dismay!

Commands clamoured through the chamber: revocations thronged against Covenant. Instantly, his spectre frayed and faded like blown mist. His power was gone: he had no way to refuse the dismissal.

Crying Linden's name in supplication or anguish, he dissolved and was effaced. His passing left trails of argent across her vision. Then they, too, were gone. There was nothing left of him to which she might cling.

At once, the bell rang again, clarion and compulsory. It was so close to frenzy that it nearly deafened her.

– Chosen, withhold! Do not dare the ring!

In the wake of the clangour, Findail and Vain entered Kiril Threndor, came struggling forward as if they were locked in mortal combat.

But the battle was all on one side. Findail thrashed and twisted, fought wildly: Vain simply ignored him. The *Elohim* was Earthpower incarnate, so fluid of essence that he could turn himself to any conceivable form. Yet he was unable to break the Demondim-spawn's grip. Vain still clasped his wrist. The black creation of the ur-viles remained adamantine and undaunted.

Together, they moved toward the ring. Findail's free hand clawed in that direction. His mute voice was a tuneless clatter of distress.

– He has compelled me to preserve him! But he must not be suffered! Chosen, withhold!

Now Vain resisted Findail, exerted himself to hold the *Elohim* back. But in this Findail was too strong for him. Fighting like hawks, they strove closer and closer to the dais.

Then Linden thought that she would surely move. She would go to the ring and take it, if for no other reason than because she trusted neither the Appointed nor his ebon counterpart. Vain was either unreachable or utterly violent. Findail showed alternate compassion and disdain as if both were simply facets of his mendacity. And Covenant had tried to warn her. The abrupt brutality of his dismissal drew anger from her waning heart.

But she had waited too long. The mounting winds blew through her as if she were a shadow. Covenant's head had become far more real than her legs: she could not shift them. The ceiling leaned over her like a distillation of itself, stone condensed past the obduracy of diamond. The snapped fragments of the stalactites were as irreducible as grief. This world was too much for her. In the end, it surpassed all her conceptions of herself. Flashes of rocklight seemed to leave lacerations across her sight. Findail and Vain struggled and struggled toward the ring; and every one of their movements was as acute as a catastrophe. Vain wore the heels of the Staff of Law like strictures. She was fading to extinction. Covenant's dead weight held her helpless.

She tried to cry out. But she was too insubstantial to make any sound which Mount Thunder might have heard.

Yet she was answered. When she believed that she had wasted all hope, she was answered.

Two figures burst from the same tunnel which had brought her to Kiril Threndor. They entered the chamber, stumbled to a halt. They were desperate and bleeding, exhausted beyond endurance, nearly dead on their feet. Her longsword was notched and gory: blood dripped from her arms and mail. His breathing retched as if he were haemorrhaging. But their valour was unquenchable. Somewhere, Pitchwife found the strength to gasp urgently, 'Chosen! The ring!'

The sudden appearance of the Giants defied comprehension. How could they have escaped the Cavewights? But they were *here*, alive and half prostrate and willing. And the sight of them lifted Linden's spirit like an act of grace. They brought her back to herself in spite of the gale pulling her away.

Findail was scarcely a step from the ring. Vain could not hold him back.

But the Appointed did not reach it.

Linden grasped Covenant's wedding band with the thin remains of her health-sense, drew fire spouting like an affirmation out of the metal. It was her ring now, granted to her in love and necessity; and the first touch of its flame restored her with a shock at once exquisitely painful and glad, ferocious and blessed. Suddenly, she was as real as the stone and the light, as substantial as Findail's frenzy. Vain's intransigence, the Giants' courage. The pressure thrusting her out of existence did not subside; but now she was a match for it. Her lungs took and released the sulphur-tinged air as if she had a right to it.

With white fire, she repelled the *Elohim*. Then, as kindly as if he were alive, she slid her legs from under Covenant's head.

Leaving him alone there, she went to take the ring.

For an instant, she feared to touch it, thinking its flame might burn her. But she knew better. Her senses were explicit: this blaze was hers and would not harm her. Deliberately, she closed her right fist around the fiery band.

At once, argent flame ran up her forearm as if her flesh were afire. It danced and spewed to the beat of her pulse. But it did not consume her, took nothing away from her: the price of power would be paid later, when the wild magic was gone. Instead, it seemed to flow into her veins, infusing vitality. The fire was silver and lovely, and it filled her with stability and strength and the capacity for choice as if it were a feast.

She wanted to shout aloud for simple joy. This was power, and it was not evil if she were not. The hunger which had dogged her days was only dark because she had feared it, denied it: it had two names and one of them was life.

Her first impulse was to turn to the Giants, heal the First and Pitchwife of their hurts, share her relief and vindication with them. But Vain and Findail stood before her – the Appointed held by the clench of Vain's hand – and they demanded her attention.

The Demondim-spawn was looking at her: a feral grin shaped his mouth. Rough bark unmarked by lava or strain enclosed his wooden forearm. But Findail could not meet her gaze. The misery of his countenance was now complete. His eyes were blurred with tears: his silver hair straggled to his shoulders in strands of pain. He sagged against Vain as if all his strength had failed. His free hand clutched at his companion's black shoulder like pleading.

Linden had no more anger for them. She did not need it. But the focus of Vain's midnight eyes baffled her. She knew intuitively that he had come to the cusp of his secret purpose – and that somehow its outcome depended on her. But even white gold did not make her senses sharp enough to read him. She was sure of nothing except Findail's fear.

Clinging to Vain's shoulder, the Appointed murmured like a child, 'I am *Elohim*. Kastenessen cursed me with death – but I am not made for death. I must not die.'

The Demondim-spawn's reply was so unexpected that Linden recoiled a step. 'You will not die.' His voice was mellifluous and clean, as perfect as his sculpted flesh – and entirely devoid of compassion. He neither dismissed nor acknowledged Findail's fear. 'It is not death. It is purpose. We will redeem the Earth from corruption.'

Then he addressed Linden. Neither deference nor command flawed his tone. 'Sun-Sage, you must embrace us.'

She stared at him. 'Embrace – ?'

He did not respond: his voice seemed to lapse as if he had uttered all the words he had been given and would never speak again. But his gaze and his grin met her like expectation, an unwavering and inexplicable certainty that she would comply.

For a moment, she hesitated. She knew she had little time. The pressure which sought to recant her summoning continued to grow: before long, it would become too potent to be resisted. But the decision Vain required of her was crucial. Everything came together here – the purpose of the ur-viles, the plotting of the *Elohim*, the survival of the Land – and she had already made too many bad choices.

She glanced toward the Giants. But Pitchwife had no more help to give her. He sat against the wall and wrestled with the huge pain in his chest. Crusted blood rimmed his mouth. And the First stood beside him, leaning on her sword and watching Linden: she held herself like a mute statement that she would support with her last strength whatever the Chosen did.

Linden turned back to the Demondim-spawn.

For no sufficient reason, she found that she was sure of him. Or perhaps she had become sure of herself. White fire curled up and down her right arm, plumed toward her shoulder, accentuated the strong rush of her life. He was rigid and murderous, blind to any concerns but his own. But because he had been given to Covenant by Foamfollower – because he had bowed to her once – because he had saved her life – and because he had met with anger the warping of his makers – she did what he asked.

When she put her arms around his neck and Findail's, the *Elohim* flinched. But his people had Appointed him to this peril, and their will held. At the last instant, he raised his head to meet his personal Würd.

In that instant, Linden became a staggering concussion of power which she had not intended and could not control.

But the blast had no outward force: it cast no light or fire, flung no fury. It might have been invisible to the Giants. All its energy was directed inward.

At the two strange beings hugged in her arms.

> *Wild magic graven in every rock,*
> *contained for white gold to unleash or control –*
> *gold, rare metal, not born of the Land,*
> *nor ruled, limited, subdued*
> *by the Law with which the Land was created –*
> *and white – white gold –*
> *because white is the hue of bone:*
> *structure of flesh,*
> *discipline of life.*

Filled with white passion, her embrace became the crucible in which Vain and Findail melted and were made new.

Findail, the tormented *Elohim*: Earthpower incarnate. Amoral, arrogant, and self-complete, capable of anything. Sent by his people to redeem the Earth at any cost. To obtain the ring for himself if he could. And if he could not, to pay the price of failure.

This price.

And Vain, the Demondim-spawn: artificially manufactured by ur-viles. More rigid than gut-rock, less tractable than bone. Alive to his inbred purpose and cruelly insensate to every other need or value or belief.

In Linden's clasp, empowered by wild magic, their opposite bodies bled together. While she held them, they began to merge.

Findail's fluid Earthpower. Vain's hard, perfect structure. And between them, the old definition forged into the heels of the Staff of Law. The *Elohim* lost shape, seemed to flow through the Demondim-spawn. Vain changed and stretched toward the iron bands which held his right wrist and left ankle.

His forearm shed its bark, gleamed like new wood. And the wood grew, spread out across the transformation, imposed its form upon the merging.

When she understood what was happening, Linden poured herself into the apotheosis. Wild magic supplied the power, but that was not enough: Vain and Findail needed more from her. Vain had been so perfectly made that he attained the stature of natural Law, brought to beauty all the long self-loathing of the ur-viles. But he had no ethical imperative, no sense of purpose beyond this climax. Findail's essence supplied the capacity for use, the strength which made Law effective. But he could not give it meaning: the *Elohim* were too self-absorbed. The transformation required something which only the human holder of the ring could provide.

She gave the best answer she had. Fear and distrust and anger she set aside: they had no place here. Exalted by white fire, she shone forth her passion for health and healing, her Land-born percipience, the love she had learned for Andelain and Earthpower. By herself, she chose the meaning she desired and made it true.

In her hands, the new Staff began to live.

Living Law filled the bands of lore: living power shone in every fibre of the wood. The old Staff had been rune-carved to define its purpose. But this Staff was alive, almost sentient: it did not need runes.

As her fingers closed around the wood, she was swept away in a flood of possibility.

Almost without transition, her health-sense became as huge as the mountain. She tasted Mount Thunder's tremendous weight and ancientness, felt the slow, racked breathing of the stone. Cavewights scurried like moles through the unmeasured catacombs. Far below her, two Ravers cowered among the banes and creatures of the depths. Somewhere above them, the few surviving ur-viles watched Kiril Threndor in a reflective pool of acid and barked vindication at Vain's success. Spouting lava cast its heat onto her bare cheek. A myriad passages, dens, offal-pits, and charnels ached emptily and stank because the River which should have run through Treacher's Gorge was dry, supplied no water to wash the Wightwarrens. At the peak, Fire-Lions crouched, waiting in eternal immobility for the invocation to life.

And still her range increased. Wild magic and Law carried her outward. Before she could clarify half her perceptions, they reached beyond the mountain, went out to the Land.

The sun was rising. Though she stood in Kiril Threndor as if she were entranced, she felt the Sunbane dawn over her.

It was insanely intense. She had become too vulnerable: it stabbed along her nerves like the life-thrust of a hot knife, pierced her heart with venom like a keen fang. At once, she snatched herself back toward shelter – recoiled as if she were reeling to the cave where the Giants watched her in wide astonishment and Covenant lay dead upon the floor.

A fertile sun. Visceral fever gripped her. Sunder and Hollian had abhorred the sun of pestilence more than any other. But for Linden the fertile sun was the worst. It was ill beyond bearing, and everything it touched became a sob of anguish.

Echoes of her fire licked the walls. One long crack marked the floor: something precious had been broken here. The First and Pitchwife stared at her as if she had become wonderful.

She had so little time left. She needed time, needed peace and rest and solace in which to muster courage. But the pressure of her dismissal continued to build. And the Staff of Law multiplied that force. Summons and return acted by rules which the Staff affirmed. Only her fist on the ring and her grip on the clean wood – only her clenched will – held her where she was.

She knew what she would have to do.

The prospect appalled her.

But she had already borne so much, and it would all be rendered meaningless if she faltered now. She did not have to fail. This was why she had been chosen. Because she was fit to fulfil Covenant's last appeal. It was too much – and yet it was hardly enough to repay her debts. Why should she fail? The mere thought that she would have to let the Sunbane touch her and touch her made her guts writhe, sent nausea beating down her veins. Horror raised mute cries of protest. In a sense, she would have to become the Land – to expose herself as fully as the Land to the Sunbane's desecration. It would be like being locked again in the attic with her dying father while dark glee came hosting against her – like enduring again her mother's abject blame until she was driven to the point of murder.

But she had survived those things. She had found her way through them to a life worthy of more respect than she had ever given it. And the old man whose life she had saved on Haven Farm had given her a promise to sustain her.

Ah, my daughter, do not fear. You will not fail, however he may assail you. There is also love in the world.

Because she needed at least one small comfort for herself, she turned to the Giants.

They had not moved. They had no eyes to see what was happening. But indomitability still shone in the First's face. No grime or bloodshed could mar her iron beauty. She looked as acute as an eagle. And when he met Linden's gaze, Pitchwife grinned as if she were the last benison he would ever need.

With the Staff of Law and the white ring, Linden caressed the fatigue out of the First's limbs, restored her Giantish strength. The rupture in Pitchwife's lungs Linden effaced, healing his respiration. Then, so that she would be able to trust herself later, she unbent his spine, restructured the bones in a way that allowed him to stand straight, breathe normally.

But after that she had no more time. The wind between the worlds keened constantly across the background of her thoughts, calling her away. She could not refuse it much longer.

Be true.

Deliberately, she opened her senses and went by her own choice back out into the Sunbane.

Its power was atrocious beyond belief; and the Land lay broken under it – broken and dying, a helpless body slain like Covenant in her worst nightmare, the knife driven by an astonishing violence which had brought up more blood than she had ever seen in her life. And from that wound corruption welled upward.

Nothing could stop it. It ate at the ground like venom. The wound grew wider with every sunrise. The Land had been stabbed to its vitals. Murder spewed across the sodden hillsides, clogged the dry riverbeds, gathered and reeked in every hollow and valley. Only the heart of Andelain remained unruined; but even there the sway of slaughter grew. The very Earth was bleeding to death. Linden had no way to save herself from drowning.

That was the truth of the Sunbane. It could never be staunched. She was a fool to make the attempt.

But she held wild magic clenched like bright passion in her right fist; and her left hand gripped the living Staff. Both were hers to wield. Guided by her health-sense – by the same vulnerability which let the Sunbane run through her like a riptide, desecrating every thew of her body, every ligament of her will – she stood within her mind on the high slopes of Mount Thunder and set herself to do battle with perversion.

It was a strange battle, weird and terrible. She had no opponent. Her foe was the rot Lord Foul had afflicted upon the Earthpower; and without him the Sunbane had neither mind nor purpose. It was simply a hunger which fed on every form of nature and health and life. She could have fired her huge forces blast after blast and struck nothing except the ravaged ground, done no hurt to anything not already lost. Only scant moments after dawn, green sprouts of vegetation stretched like screams from the soil.

And beyond this fertility lurked rain and pestilence and desert in erratic sequence, waiting to repeat themselves over and over again, always harder and faster, until the foundations of the Land crumbled. Then the Sunbane would be free to spread.

Out to the rest of the Earth.

But she had learned from Covenant – and from the Raver's possession. She did not attempt to attack the Sunbane. Instead, she called it to herself, accepted it into her personal flesh.

With white fire she absorbed the Land's corruption.

At first, the sheer pain and horror of it excruciated her hideously. One shrill cry as hoarse as terror ripped her throat, rang like Kevin's despair over the wide landscape below her, echoed and echoed in Kiril Threndor until the Giants were frantic, unable to help her. But then her own need drove her to more power.

The Staff flamed so intensely that her body should have been burned away. Yet she was not hurt. Rather, the pain she had taken upon herself was swept from her – cured and cleansed, and sent spilling outward as pure Earthpower. With Law she healed herself.

She hardly understood what she was doing: it was an act of exaltation, chosen by intuition rather than conscious thought. But she saw her way now with the reasonless clarity of joy. It could be done: the Land could be redeemed. With all the passion of her thwarted heart, all the love she had learned and been given, she plunged into her chosen work.

She was a storm upon the mountain, a barrage of determination and fire which no eyes but hers could have witnessed. From every league and hill and gully and plain of the Land, every slope of Andelain and cliff of the peaks, every southern escarpment and northern rise, she drew ruin into herself and restored it to wholeness, then sent it back like silent rain, analystic and invisible.

Her spirit became the medicament that cured. She was the Sun-Sage, the healer, Linden Avery the Chosen, altering the Sunbane with her own life.

It fired green at her like the sickness of emeralds. But she understood intimately the natural growth and decay of plants. They found their Law in her, their lush or hardy order, their native abundance or rarity; and then the green was gone.

Blue volleyed thunderously at her head, then lost the Land as she accepted every drop of water and flash of violence.

The brown of deserts came blistering around her, scorched her skin. But she knew the necessity of heat – and the restriction of climate. She felt in her bones the rhythm of rise and fall, the strict and vital alternation of seasons, summer and winter. The desert fire was cooled to a caress by the Staff and emitted gently outward again.

And last, the red of pestilence, as scarlet as disease, as stark as adders: it swarmed against her like a world full of bees, shot streaks of blood across her vision. In spite of herself, she was fading, could not keep from being hurt. But even pestilence was only a distortion of the truth. It had its clear place and purpose. When it was reduced, it fit within the new Law which she set forth.

Sun-Sage and ring-wielder, she restored the Earthpower and released it upon the racked body of the Land.

She could not do everything. Already, she had made herself faint with self-expenditure, and the ground sprawling below her to the horizons reeled. She had nothing left with which she might bring back the Land's trees and meadows and crops, its creatures and birds. But she had done enough. She knew without questioning the knowledge that seeds remained in the soil – that even among the wrecked treasures of the Waynhim were things which might yet produce fruit and young – that the weather would be able to find its own patterns again. She saw birds and animals still flourishing in the mountains to the west and south, where the Sunbane had not reached: they would eventually return. The people who stayed alive in their small villages would be able to endure.

And she saw one more reason for hope, one more fact that made the future possible. Much of Andelain had been preserved. Around its heart, it had mustered its resistance – and had prevailed.

Because Sunder and Hollian were there.

In their human way, they contained as much Earthpower as the Hills; and they had fought – Linden saw how they had fought. The loveliness of what they were – and of what they served – was lambent about them. Already, it had begun to regain the lost region.

Yes, she breathed to herself. Yes.

Across the wide leagues, she spoke a word to them that they would understand. Then she withdrew.

She feared the dismissal would take her while she was still too far from her body to bear the strain. As keen as a gale, the wind reached toward her. Too weary even to smile at what she had accomplished, she went wanly back through the rock toward Kiril Threndor and dissolution.

When she gained the cave, she saw in the faces of the Giants that she had already faded beyond their perceptions. Grief twisted Pitchwife's visage: the First's eyes streamed. They had no way of knowing what had happened – and would not know it until they found their way out of the Wightwarrens to gaze upon the free Land. But Linden could not bear to leave them hurt. They had given her too much. With her last power, she reached out and placed a silent touch of victory in their minds. It was the only gift she had left.

But it, too, was enough. The First started in wonder: unexpected gladness softened her face. And Pitchwife threw back his head to crow like a clean dawn, 'Linden Avery! Have I not said that you are well Chosen?'

The long wind pulled through Linden. In moments, she would lose the Giants forever. Yet she clung to them. Somehow, she lasted long enough to see the First pick up the Staff of Law.

Linden still held the ring; but at the last moment she must have dropped the Staff beside the dais. The First lifted it like a promise. 'This must not fall to ill hands,' she murmured. Her voice was as solid as granite: it nearly surpassed Linden's hearing. 'I will ward it in the name of the future which Earthfriend and Chosen have procured with their lives. If Sunder or Hollian yet live, they will have need of it.'

Pitchwife laughed and cried and kissed her. Then he bent, lifted Covenant into his arms. His back was strong and straight. Together, he and the First left Kiril Threndor. She strode like a Swordmain, ready for the world. But he moved at her side with a gay hop and caper, as if he were dancing.

There Linden let go. The mountain towered over her, as imponderable as the gaps between the stars. It was heavier than sorrow, greater than loss. Nothing would ever heal what it had endured. She was only mortal; but Mount Thunder's grief would go on without let or surcease, unambergrised for all time.

Then the wind took her, and she felt herself go out.

Out into the dark.

EPILOGUE

Restoration

21

'TO SAY FAREWELL'

But when she was fully in the grip of the wind, she no longer felt its
force. It reft her from the Land as if she were mist; but like mist she
could not be hurt now. She had been battered numb. When the
numbness passed, her pain would find its voice again and cry out.
But that prospect had lost its power to frighten her. Pain was only
the other side of love; and she did not regret it.

Yet for the present she was quiet, and the wind bore her gently
across the illimitable dark. Her percipience was already gone, lost
like the Land: she had no way to measure the spans of loneliness
she traversed. But the ring – Covenant's ring, *her* ring – lay in her
hand, and she held it for comfort.

And while she was swept through the midnight between worlds,
she remembered music – little snatches of a song Pitchwife had once
sung. For a time, they were only snatches. Then their ache brought
them together.

> My heart has rooms that sigh with dust
> And ashes in the hearth.
> They must be cleaned and blown away
> By daylight's breath.
> But I cannot essay the task,
> For even dust to me is dear;
> For dust and ashes still recall,
> My love was here.
>
> I know not how to say Farewell,
> When Farewell is the word
> That stays alone for me to say
> Or will be heard.
> But I cannot speak out that word
> Or ever let my loved one go:
> How can I bear it that these rooms
> Are empty so?
>
> I sit among the dust and hope
> That dust will cover me.
> I stir the ashes in the hearth,

> Though cold they be,
> I cannot bear to close the door,
> To seal my loneliness away
> While dust and ashes yet remain
> Of my love's day.

The song made her think of her father.

He came back to her like Pitchwife's voice, sprawling there in the old rocker while his last life bled away — driven to self-murder by the possession of Despite. His loathing of himself had grown so great that it had become a loathing of life. It had been like her mother's religion, only able to prove itself true by imposing itself upon the people around it. But it had been false; and she thought of him now with regret and pity which she had never before been able to afford. He had been wrong about her: she had loved him dearly. She had loved both her parents, although she had been badly misled by her own bitterness.

In a curious way, that recognition made her ready. She was not startled or bereft when Covenant spoke to her out of the void.

'Thank you,' he said gruffly, husky with emotion. 'There aren't enough words for it anywhere. But thanks.'

The sound of his voice made tears stream down her face. They stung like sorrow on her cheeks. But she welcomed them and him.

'I know it's been terrible,' he went on. 'Are you all right?'

She nodded along the wind that seemed to rush without motion around her as if it had no meaning except loss. I think so. Maybe. It doesn't matter. She only wanted to hear his voice while the chance lasted. She knew it would not last long. To make him speak again, she said the first words that occurred to her.

'You were wonderful. But how did you do it? I don't have any idea how you did it.'

In response, he sighed — an exhalation of weariness and remembered pain, not of rue. 'I don't think I did it at all. All I did was *want*. The rest of it —

'Caer-Caveral made it possible. Hile Troy.' An old longing suffused his tone. 'That was the "necessity" he talked about. Why he had to give his life. It was the only way to open that particular door. So that Hollian could be brought back. And so that I wouldn't be like the rest of the Dead — unable to act. He broke the Law that would've kept me from opposing Foul. Otherwise I would've been just a spectator.

'And Foul didn't understand. Maybe he was too far gone. Or maybe he just refused to believe it. But he tried to ignore the paradox. The paradox of white gold. And the paradox of himself. He wanted the white gold — the ring. But I'm the white gold too. He couldn't change that by killing me. When he hit me with my own fire, he did the one thing I couldn't do for myself. He burned the venom away. After that, I was free.'

He paused for a moment, turned inward. 'I didn't know what was going to happen. I was just terrified that he would let me live until after he attacked the Arch.' Dimly, she remembered the way Covenant had jibed at Lord Foul as if he were asking for death.

'We aren't enemies, no matter what he says. He and I are one. But he doesn't seem to know that. Or maybe he hates it too much to admit it. Evil can't exist unless the capacity to stand against it also exists. And you and I are the Land – in a manner of speaking, anyway. He's just one side of us. That's his paradox. He's one side of us. We're one side of him. When he killed me, he was really trying to kill the other half of himself. He just made me stronger. As long as I accepted him – or accepted myself, my own power, didn't try to do to him what he wanted to do to me – he couldn't get past me.'

There he fell silent. But she had not been listening to him with any urgency. She had her own answers, and they sufficed. She listened chiefly to the sound of his voice, cared only that he was with her still. When he stopped, she groped for another question. After a moment, she asked him how the First and Pitchwife had been able to escape the Cavewights.

At that, a note like a chuckle gleamed along the wind. 'Ah, that.' His humour was tinged with grimness; but she treasured it because she had never heard him come so close to laughter. 'That I'll take credit for.

'Foul gave me so much power – And it made me crazy to stand there and not be able to touch you. I had to do something. Foul knew what the Cavewights were doing all along. He let them do it to put more pressure on us. So I made something rise out of the Wightbarrow. I don't know what it was – it didn't last long. But while the Cavewights were bowing, the First and Pitchwife had a chance to get away. Then I showed them how to reach you.'

She liked his voice. Perhaps guilt as well as venom had been burned out of it. They shared a moment of companionship. Thinking about what he had done for her, she almost forgot that she would never see him alive again.

But then some visceral instinct warned her that the darkness was shifting – that her time with him was almost over. She made an effort to articulate her appreciation.

'You gave me what I needed. I should be thanking you. For all of it. Even the parts that hurt. I've never been given so many gifts. I just wish – '

Shifting and growing lighter. On all sides, the void modulated toward definition. She knew where she was going, what she would find when she got there; and the thought of it brought all her hurts and weaknesses together into one lorn outcry. Yet that cry went unuttered back into the dark. In mute surprise, she realized that the future was something she would be able to bear.

Just wish I didn't have to lose you.

Oh, Covenant!

For the last time, she lifted her voice toward him, spoke to him as if she were a woman of the Land.

'Farewell, beloved.'

His response came softly, receding along the wind. 'There's no need for that. I'm part of you now. You'll always remember.'

At the edge of her heart, he stopped. She was barely able to hear him.

'I'll be with you as long as you live.'

Then he was gone. Slowly, the gulf became stone against her face.

Light swelled beyond her eyelids. She knew before she raised her head that she had come back to herself in the ordinary dawn of a new day.

The air was cool. She smelled dew and springtime and cold ash and budding trees. And blood that was already dry.

For a long moment, she lay still and let the translation complete itself. Then she levered her arms under her.

At once, a forgotten pain laboured in the bones behind her left ear. She groaned involuntarily, slumped again to the stone.

She would have been willing to lie still while she persuaded herself that the hurt did not matter. She was in no hurry to look at her surroundings. But as she slumped, unexpected hands came to her shoulders. They were not strong in the way she had learned to measure strength; but they gripped her with enough determination to lift her to her knees. 'Linden,' a man's care-aged voice breathed. 'Thank God.'

Her eyes were slow to focus: her sight seemed to come back from a great distance. She was conscious of the dawn, the blurred grey stone, the barren hollow set like a bowl of death into the heart of the green woods. But gradually she made out Covenant's form. He was stretched on the rock nearby, within the painted triangle of blood. The light stroked his dear face like a touch of annunciation.

From the centre of his chest jutted the knife which had made everything else necessary.

The man holding her repeated her name. 'I'm so sorry,' he murmured. 'I never should've got you into this. We shouldn't have let him keep her. But we didn't know he was in this much danger.'

Slowly, she turned her head and met the alarmed and wearied gaze of Dr Berenford.

His eyes seemed to wince in their sockets, making the heavy pouches under them quiver. His old moustache drooped over his mouth. The characteristic wry dyspepsia of his tone was gone: it failed him here. Almost fearfully, he asked her the same question

1232

Covenant had asked. 'Are you all right?'

She nodded as well as the pain in her skull allowed. Her voice scraped like rust in her throat. 'They killed him.' But no words were adequate to her grief.

'I know.' He urged her into a sitting position. Then he turned away to snap open his medical bag. A moment later, she smelled the pungence of antiseptic. With reassuring gentleness, he parted her hair, probed her injury, began to cleanse the wound. But he did not stop talking.

'Mrs Jason and her three kids came to my house. You probably saw her outside the courthouse the first day you were here. Carrying a sign that said, "Repent". She's one of those people who think doctors and writers just naturally go to hell. But this time she needed me. Got me out of bed a few hours ago. All four of them − ' He swallowed convulsively. 'Their right hands were terribly burned. Even the kids.'

He finished tending her hurt, but did not move to face her. For a while, she stared sightlessly at the dead ash of the bonfire. But then her gaze returned to Covenant. He lay there in his worn T-shirt and old jeans as if no cerements in all the world could give his death dignity. His features were frozen in fear and pain − and in a kind of intensity that looked like hope. If Dr Berenford had not been with her, she would have taken Covenant into her arms for solace. He deserved better than to lie so untended.

'At first she wouldn't talk to me,' the older man went on. 'But while I drove them to the hospital, she broke down. Somewhere inside her, she had enough decency left to be horrified. Her kids were wailing, and she couldn't bear it. I guess none of them knew what they were doing. They thought God had finally recognized their righteousness. They all had the same vision, and they just obeyed it. They whipped themselves into a tizzy killing a horse to get the blood they used to mark his house. They weren't sane anymore.

'Why they picked on him I don't know.' His voice shook. 'Maybe because he wrote "un-Christian" books. She kept talking about "the maker of desecration". When he was forced to offer himself for sacrifice, the world would be purged of sin. Retribution and apocalypse. And Joan was his victim. She couldn't be rescued any other way.' His bitterness mounted. 'What a wonderful idea. How could they resist it? They thought they were saving the world when they put their hands in that fire.

'They didn't snap out of it until you interrupted them.'

Linden understood his dismay, his anger. But she had passed the crisis. Without turning, she said, 'They were like Joan. They hated themselves − their lives, their poverty, their ineffectuality.' Like my parents. 'It made them crazy.' She yearned with pity for the people who had done this to Covenant.

'I suppose so,' Dr Berenford sighed. 'It wouldn't be the first time.' Then he resumed, 'Anyway, I left Mrs Jason in Emergency and got the Sheriff. He didn't exactly believe me – but he came out to Haven Farm anyway. We found Joan. She was asleep in the house. When we woke her up, she didn't remember a thing. But she looked like she had her mind back. I couldn't tell. At least she wasn't violent anymore.

'I made the Sheriff take her to the hospital. Then I came looking for you.'

Again he swallowed at his distress. 'I didn't want him with me. I didn't want him to think you were responsible for this.'

At that, she looked toward him in wonder. His concern for her – his desire to spare her the conclusions which the Sheriff might draw from finding her alone with Covenant's body – touched the spring of something new in her; and it opened as if it were blossoming. His face had sagged under the weight of his baffled care: he appeared reluctant to meet her gaze. But he was a good man; and when she looked at him she saw that Covenant's spirit was not dead. Without knowing it, he showed her the one true way to say Farewell.

She placed her hand on his shoulder. Softly, she said, 'Don't blame yourself. You couldn't have known what would happen. And he got what he wanted most. He made himself innocent.' Then she leaned on him so that she could rise to her feet.

The sunlight felt warm and kind to her weariness. Above the bare slopes of the hollow stood trees wreathed in the new green of spring, buoyant, ineffable, and clean. In this world also there was health to be served, hurts to be healed.

When the older man joined her, she said, 'Come on. We've got work to do. Mrs Jason and her kids weren't the only ones. We have a lot more burned hands to take care of.'

After a moment, Dr Berenford nodded. 'I'll tell the Sheriff where to find him. At least we can make sure he gets a decent burial.'

'Yes,' she answered. The sun filled her eyes with brightness. Together, she and her companion started up the barren hillside toward the trees.

With her right hand, Linden Avery kept a sure hold on her wedding ring.

GLOSSARY

Aimil: daughter of Anest; wife of Sunder

a-Jeroth of the Seven Hells: Lord of wickedness; Clave-name for Lord Foul the Despiser

Akkasri na-Mhoram-cro: a member of the Clave

ak-Haru: a supreme *Haruchai* honorific

aliantha: treasure-berries

Alif, the Lady: a woman Favoured of the *gaddhi*

Amith: a woman of Crystal Stonedown

Anchormaster: second-in-command aboard a Giantship

Andelain, the Hills of: a region of the Land free of the Sunbane

Andelainscion: a region in the Centre Plains

Anest: woman of Mithil Stonedown; sister of Kalina

Annoy: a Courser

Appointed, the: an *Elohim* chosen to bear a particular burden; Findail

Arch of Time, the: symbol of the existence and structure of time

arghule/arghuleh: ferocious ice-beasts

Atiaran Trell-mate: former woman of Mithil Stonedown; mother of Lena

Aumbrie of the Clave: storeroom for former Lore

Auspice, the: throne of the *gaddhi*

Bahgoon: character in a Giantish tale

Bandsoil Bounds: region north of Soulsease River

Banefire, the: the fire by which the Clave wields the Sunbane

Bannor: former Bloodguard

Bareisle: island off the coast of *Elemesnedene*

Benj, the Lady: a woman Favoured of the *gaddhi*

Berek Halfhand: ancient hero; the Lord-Fatherer

Bern: *Haruchai* lost to the Clave

Bhrathair, the: a people who live on the verge of the Great Desert

Bhrathairain: the town of the *Bhrathair*

Bhrathairain Harbour: the port of the *Bhrathair*

Bhrathairealm: the land of the *Bhrathair*

Bloodguard: former servants of the Council of Lords

Boulder Fash: a region in the Centre Plains

Brannil: man of Stonemight Woodhelven

Brinn: a leader of the *Haruchai*; protector of Covenant
Brow Gnarlfist: a Giant; father of the First of the Search

caamora: Giantish ordeal of grief by fire
Cable Seadreamer: a Giant; member of the Search; brother of Honninscrave; possessed of the Earth-Sight
Caer-Caveral: Forestal of Andelain; formerly Hile Troy
Caerroil Wildwood: former Forestal of Garroting Deep
Cail: *Haruchai*; protector of Linden Avery
Caitiffin: a captain of the armed forces of *Bhrathairealm*
Callowwail, the River: stream arising from *Elemesnedene*
Cavewights: evil earth-delving creatures
Ceer: one of the *Haruchai*
Celebration of Spring, the: the Dance of the Wraiths of Andelain on the dark of the moon in the middle night of Spring
Centrepith Barrens: a region in the Centre Plains
Centre Plains, the: a region of the Land
Chant: one of the *Elohim*
Chatelaine, the: courtiers of the *gaddhi*
Chosen, the: title given to Linden Avery
clachan, the: demesne of the *Elohim*
Clang: a Courser
Clangor: a Courser
Clash: a Courser
Clave, the: the rulers of the Land
Coercri: The Grieve; former home of the Giants in Seareach
Colossus of the Fall, the: ancient stone figure formerly guarding the Upper Land
Consecear Redoin: a region north of the Soulsease River
Corruption: *Haruchai* name for Lord Foul
Council of Lords: former rulers of the Land
Courser: beast of transport made by the Clave by the power of the Sunbane
Creator, the: the maker of the Earth
Croft: Graveller of Crystal Stonedown
croyel, the: mysterious creatures which bargain for power
Crystal Stonedown: village of the Land; home of Hollian

Damelon Giantfriend: son of Berek; former Lord
Dancers of the Sea, the: *merewives*
Daphin: one of the *Elohim*
Dawngreeter: highest sail on the foremast of a Giantship
Dead, the: spectres of those who have died
Defiles Course: a river in the Lower Land
Demondim, the: spawners of ur-viles and Waynhim
Demondim-spawn: Vain

Despiser, the: Lord Foul
Despite: evil; a name given to the designs of Lord Foul
dhraga: a Waynhim
dhubha: a Waynhim
dhurng: a Waynhim
diamondraught: Giantish liquor
Din: a Courser
Dolewind, the: wind blowing to the Soulbiter
drhami: a Waynhim
dromond: a Giantship
Drool Rockworm: former Cavewight
durhisitar: a Waynhim
During Stonedown: home of Hamako
Durris: *Haruchai*

Earthfriend: title given to Berek Halfhand, then to Covenant
Earthpower, the: source of all power in the Land
Earthroot: lake under *Melenkurion* Skyweir
Earth-Sight: Giantish ability to perceive distant dangers and needs
eftmound: gathering-place of the *Elohim*
eh-Brand: one who can use wood to read the Sunbane; Hollian
Elemesnedene: home of the *Elohim*
Elena: former High Lord; daughter of Lena and Covenant
Elohim, the: a faery people first met by the wandering Giants
Elohimfest: a gathering of the *Elohim*
Emacrimma's maw: a region in the Centre Plains
Enemy: Lord Foul's term of reference for the Creator

Far Woodhelven: a village of the Land
Favoured, the: courtesan of the *gaddhi*
Fields of Richloam: a region in the Centre Plains
Findail: one of the *Elohim*; the Appointed
Fire-Lions: fire-flow of Mount Thunder
First Betrayer: Clave-name for Berek Halfhand
First Circinate: first level of the Sandhold
First Mark: former leader of the Bloodguard
First of the Search, the: leader of the Giants who follow the Earth-Sight
First Ward: primary knowledge left by Kevin
Fleshharrower: former Giant-Raver; *moksha* Jehannum
Foamkite: *tyrscull* belonging to Honninscrave and Seadreamer
Fole: *Haruchai*
Foodfendhall: eating-hall and galley aboard a Giantship
Forestal: a protector of the forests of the Land
Foul's Creche: the Despiser's former home; destroyed by Covenant
Furl Falls: waterfall at Revelstone

gaddhi, the: sovereign of *Bhrathairealm*

Gallows Howe: place of execution in Garroting Deep

Garroting Deep: a former forest of the Land

ghohritsar: a Waynhim

ghramin: a Waynhim

Giants: a seafaring people of the Earth

Giantclave: Giantish conference

Giantfriend: title given first to Damelon, later to Covenant

Giantship: stone sailing vessel made by Giants

Giantway: path made by Giants

Giant Woods: a forest of the Land

Gibbon: the na-Mhoram; leader of the Clave

Gilden: a maplelike tree with golden leaves

Glimmermere: a lake on the upland above Revelstone

Gossamer Glowlimn: a Giant; the First of the Search

Graveller: one who uses stone to wield the Sunbane; Sunder

gravelling: fire-stones

Gravelingas: former master of stone-lore

Gravin Threndor: Mount Thunder

Great Desert, the: a region of the Earth; home of the *Bhrathair* and the Sandgorgons

Great Swamp, the: Lifeswallower; a region of the Land

Greshas Slant: a region in the Centre Plains

Grey Desert, the: a region south of the Land

Grey River, the: a river of the Land

Grey Slayer: Lord Foul the Despiser

Greywightswath: a region north of the Soulsease River

Grieve, The: *Coercri*

Grim, the: destructive storm sent as a curse by the Clave

Grimmand Honninscrave: a Giant; Master of Starfare's Gem; member of the Search; brother of Cable Seadreamer

Grimmerdhore: former forest of the Land

Guardian of the One Tree, the: mystical figure warding the approach of the One Tree; also *ak-Haru Kenaustin Ardenol*

Halfhand: title given to Covenant as well as to Berek

Hall of Gifts, the: large chamber in Revelstone devoted to artworks of the Land

Hamako: former Stonedownor adopted by Waynhim

Harbour Captain: chief official of the port of *Bhrathairealm*

Harn: *Haruchai*; protector of Hollian

Haruchai, the: a people who live in the Westron Mountains

Hearthcoal: a Giant; cook of Starfare's Gem; wife of Seasauce

Heartthew: a title given to Berek Halfhand

Heft Galewrath: a Giant; Storesmaster of Starfare's Gem

Herem: a Raver; also known as *turiya*

Hergrom: one of the *Haruchai*

High Lord: former leader of the Council of Lords

Hile Troy: a man formerly from Covenant's world who became a Forestal

Hollian: daughter of Amith; eh-Brand of Crystal Stonedown

Home: homeland of the Giants

Horizonscan: lookout atop the midmast of a Giantship

Horse, the: human soldiery of the *gaddhi*

Hotash Slay: flow of lava which protected Foul's Creche

hurtloam: a healing mud

husta hustin: partly human soldiers bred by Kasreyn to be the *gaddhi*'s Guard

Hyrim: a former Lord of the Council

Illearth Stone, the: green stone; a source of evil power

Illender: title given to Covenant

Infelice: reigning leader of the *Elohim*

Isle of the One Tree, the: location of the One Tree

Jehannum: a Raver; also known as *moksha*

jheherrin: soft ones; living by-products of Lord Foul's misshaping

Jous: a man of Mithil Stonedown; son of Prassan; father of Nassic; inheritor of the Unfettered One's mission

Kalina: wife of Nassic; mother of Sunder; daughter of Alloma

Kasreyn of the Gyre: a thaumaturge; the *gaddhi*'s Kemper

Kastenessen: one of the *Elohim*; former Appointed

Keep of the na-Mhoram: Revelstone

Kemper, the: chief minister of the *gaddhi*

Kemper's Pitch: highest level of the Sandhold

Kenaustin Ardenol: a figure of *Haruchai* legend; paragon and measure of all *Haruchai* virtues

Kevin Landwaster: son of Loric; former Lord; enactor of the Ritual of Desecration

Kevin's Watch: mountain lookout near Mithil Stonedown

Kiril Threndor: Heart of Thunder; chamber of power within Mount Thunder

Korik: former Bloodguard

krill, the: knife of power formed by Loric Vilesilencer

Kurash Festillin: a region in the Centre Plains

Lake Pelluce: a lake in Andelainscion

Land, the: a focal region of the Earth

Landsdrop: great cliff separating the Upper and Lower Lands

Landsverge Stonedown: a village of the Land

Landwaster: title given to Kevin

Law, the: the natural order
Law of Death, the: separation of the living from the dead
Law of Life, the: separation of the dead from the living
Lena: daughter of Atiaran; mother of Elena
lianar: wood of power used by an eh-Brand
Lifeswallower: the Great Swamp; a region of the Land
Lord-Fatherer, the: title given to Berek
Lord Foul: the Despiser
Lord of Wickedness: a-Jeroth
Lords, the: former rulers of the Land
Lord's Keep: Revelstone
loremaster: ur-vile leader
Loric Vilesilencer: son of Damelon; father of Kevin; former Lord
Lost, the: Giantish name for the Unhomed
Lower Land, the: region east of Landsdrop
lucubrium: laboratory of a thaumaturge
lurker of the Sarangrave: a swamp-monster

maidan: open land around *Elemesnedene*
Majesty, The: throne-room; fourth level of the Sandhold
Marid: a man of Mithil Stonedown; Sunbane victim
Master: Clave-name for the Creator
Master, the: captain of a Giantship
master-rukh: iron triangle in Revelstone which feeds and reads all other *rukhs*
Melenkurion Skyweir: a mountain in the Westron Mountains
Memla: a former Rider of the Clave
merewives: the Dancers of the Sea
metheglin: a beverage; mead
Mhoram: former High Lord of the Council
mirkfruit: papaya-like fruit with narcoleptic pulp
Mistweave: a Giant
Mithil River: a river of the Land
Mithil Stonedown: a village in the South Plains of the Land
moksha: a Raver; also known as Jehannum
Morin: a former First Mark of the Bloodguard
Morinmoss: a former forest of the Land
Morninglight: one of the *Elohim*
Mount Thunder: a peak at the centre of Landsdrop

na-Mhoram, the: leader of the Clave
na-Mhoram-cro: lowest rank of the Clave
na-Mhoram-in: highest rank of the Clave
na-Mhoram-wist: middle rank of the Clave
Nassic: father of Sunder; son of Jous; inheritor of the Unfettered One's mission to welcome Covenant

Nelbrin: son of Sunder; 'heart's child'

Nicor: great sea-monsters; said to be offspring of the Worm of the World's End

Nom: a Sandgorgon

North Plains, the: a region of the Land

Northron Climbs, the: a region of the Land

Oath of Peace: former oath by the people of the Land against needless violence

Offin: a former na-Mhoram

One Forest, the: ancient sentient forest which once covered most of the Land

One Tree, the: mystic tree from which the Staff of Law was made

Old Lords, the: the Lords of the Land prior to the Ritual of Desecration

orcrest: Sunstone; a stone of power, used by a Graveller

pitchbrew: a beverage combining *diamondraught* and *vitrim*, conceived by Pitchwife

Pitchwife: a Giant; member of the Search; husband of Gossamer Glowlimn

Prothall: a former High Lord

Prover of Life: title given to Covenant

Pure One, the: redemptive figure of *jheherrin* legend; Saltheart Foamfollower

Quest for the Staff of Law: former quest which recovered the Staff of Law from Drool Rockworm

Questsimoon, the: the Roveheartswind

Ramen: a people of the Land; tenders of the Ranyhyn

Rant Absolain: the *gaddhi*

Ranyhyn: the great horses; formerly inhabited the Plains of Ra

Ravers: Lord Foul's three ancient servants

Raw, the: fjord into the demesne of the *Elohim*

Rawedge Rim, the: mountains around *Elemesnedene*

Reader: a member of the Clave who tends and uses the *master-rukh*

Rede, the: knowledge of history and survival promulgated by the Clave

Revelstone: mountain-city of the Clave

rhysh: a community of Waynhim; 'stead'

rhyshyshim: a gathering of *rhysh*; a place in which such a gathering occurs

Riddenstretch: a region north of the Soulsease River

Rider: a member of the Clave

ring-wielder: *Elohim* term of reference for Covenant

Rire Grist: a Caitiffin of the *gaddhi*'s Horse

Ritual of Desecration: act of despair by which Kevin Landwaster destroyed much of the Land

Riversward: a region north of the Soulsease River

rocklight: light emitted by glowing stone

Roveheartswind, the: the *Questsimoon*

rukh: iron talisman by which a Rider wields power

Runnik: former Bloodguard

sacred enclosure: former Vespers hall in Revelstone; now site of the Banefire and the *master-rukh*

Saltheart Foamfollower: former Giant

Saltroamrest: bunkhold for the crew in a Giantship

Salttooth: jutting rock in the harbour of Home

samadhi: a Raver; also known as Sheol

Sandgorgon: a monster of the Great Desert

Sandgorgons Doom: imprisoning storm created by Kasreyn to trap the Sandgorgons

Sandhold, the: castle of the rulers of *Bhrathairealm*

Sandwall, the: great wall defending *Bhrathairealm*

Santonin: a Rider of the Clave

Sarangrave Flat: a region of the Lower Land

Scroll the Appalling: character in a Giantish tale

Search, the: quest of the Giants for the wound in the Earth seen by the Earth-Sight

Seareach: a region of the Land; formerly inhabited by the Giants

Seasauce: a Giant; cook of Starfare's Gem; husband of Hearthcoal

Seatheme: dead wife of Sevinhand

Second Circinate: second level of the Sandhold

Second Ward: second unit of Kevin's hidden knowledge

Setrock: a type of stone used with pitch to repair stone

Seven Hells, the: a-Jeroth's demesne; desert, rain, pestilence; fertility, war, savagery, darkness

Seven Wards, the: collection of knowledge hidden by Kevin

Sevinhand: a Giant; Anchormaster of Starfare's Gem

Shattered Hills: a region of the Land near Foul's Creche

Sheol: a Raver; also known as *samadhi*

Shetra: a former Lord of the Council

Shipsheartthew: the wheel of a Giantship

Sivit: a Rider of the Clave

skest: acid-creatures serving the lurker of the Sarangrave

soft ones: the *jheherrin*

soothreader: a seer

soothtell: ritual of prophecy practised by the Clave

Soulbiter, the: dangerous ocean of Giantish legend

Soulbiter's Teeth: reefs in the Soulbiter

Soulcrusher: former Giantish name for Lord Foul

Soulsease River, the: a river of the Land

South Plains, the: a region of the Land

Spikes, the: guard-towers at the mouth of *Bhrathairain* Harbour

Spray Frothsurge: a Giant; mother of the First of the Search

Staff of Law, the: a tool of power formed by Berek from the One Tree

Starfare's Gem: Giantship used by the Search

Starkin: one of the *Elohim*

Stell: *Haruchai*; former protector of Sunder

Stonedown: a village of the Land

Stonedownor: inhabitant of a Stonedown

Stonemight, the: name for a fragment of the Illearth Stone

Stonemight Woodhelven: a village of the Land in the South Plains

Storesmaster: third-in-command aboard a Giantship

Sunbane, the: a power arising from the corruption of nature by Lord Foul

Sunbirth Sea: ocean east of the Land

Sunder: son of Nassic; former Graveller of Mithil Stonedown

Sun-Sage, the: title given to Linden Avery by the *Elohim*; one who can affect the progress of the Sunbane

Sunstone: *orcrest*

***sur-jheherrin*:** descendants of the *jheherrin*; inhabitants of Sarangrave Flat

Swarte: a Rider of the Clave

Swordmain/Swordmainnir: Giant trained as a warrior

test of silence: interrogation technique used by the people of the Land

Third Ward: third unit of Kevin's hidden knowledge

Three Corners of Truth: basic formulation of beliefs promulgated by the Clave

thronehall, the: the Despiser's former seat in Foul's Creche

Tier of Riches, the: showroom of the *gaddhi*'s wealth; third level of the Sandhold

Toril: *Haruchai* lost to the Clave

Treacher's Gorge: river-opening into Mount Thunder

treasure-berries: *aliantha*; a nourishing fruit

Trell: father of Lena; former Gravelingas of Mithil Stonedown

Triock: former inhabitant of Mithil Stonedown who loved Lena

Trothgard: a region of the Land

***turiya*:** a Raver; also named Herem

***tyrscull*:** a Giantish training vessel for apprentice sailors

Unbeliever, the: title given to Covenant

Unfettered, the: formerly, lore-students freed from conventional responsibilities

Unfettered One, the: founder of a line of men waiting to greet Thomas Covenant's return to the Land

Unhomed, the: former Giants of Seareach

upland: plateau above Revelstone

Upper Land, the: region west of Landsdrop

ur-Lord: title given to Covenant

ur-viles: Demondim-spawn; evil creatures of power; creators of Vain

ussusimiel: nourishing melon grown by the people of the Land

Vain: Demondim-spawn; bred by the ur-viles for a secret purpose

Vespers: former self-consecration ritual of the Lords

Victuallin Tayne: a region in the Centre Plains

vitrim: nourishing fluid created by Waynhim

voure: a plant-sap which wards off insects; a medicine for Sunbane-sickness

Vow, the: Bloodguard oath of service to the Lords

vraith: a Waynhim

Warrenbridge: bridge leading to the catacombs under Mount Thunder

Wavedancer: Giantship commanded by Brow Gnarlfist

Waynhim: Demondim-spawn; opposed to ur-viles

Weird of the Waynhim, the: Waynhim concept of doom, destiny, or duty

Westron Mountains: mountains bordering the Land

white gold: a metal of power not found in the Land

White River, the: a river of the Land

Wightbarrow, the: cairn under which Drool Rockworm is buried

Wightwarrens: catacombs; home of the Cavewights under Mount Thunder

wild magic: the power of white gold; considered the keystone of the Arch of Time

Windscour: region in the Centre Plains

Winshorn Stonedown: a village in the South Plains

Woodenwold: region of trees surrounding the *maidan* of *Elemesnedene*

Woodhelven: a village of the Land

Woodhelvennin: inhabitants of a Woodhelven

Worm of the World's End, the: mystic creature believed by the *Elohim* to have formed the foundation of the Earth

Wraiths of Andelain: creatures of living light which inhabit Andelain

Würd of the Earth, the: term used by the *Elohim* to suggest variously their own nature, the nature of the Earth, and their ethical compulsions; could be read as Word, Worm, or Weird

STEPHEN DONALDSON

REAVE THE JUST
and Other Tales

The world-renowned author of the *Thomas Covenant* trilogies
returns to mainstream fantasy after more than ten years – with a
brand-new collection of stories.

Here are tales rich with exotic atmosphere, mysticism
and menace, including 'The Djinn Who Watches Over the
Accursed', an unnerving fable about a reckless adulterer;
'The Killing Stroke', in which martial-arts masters fight as
champions in a great mind-battle between mages; 'Penance', a
haunting story of a vampire who roams a battlefield, searching
for the dying; and 'Reave the Just', which demonstrates that
neither brute force nor alchemy can contend with the power of
suggestion.

Spellbinding, unpredictable and always entertaining, this
new collection displays the remarkable imagination and extraor-
dinary range of a writer at the height of his powers, and
confirms Stephen Donaldson's position as a master of modern
fantasy.

'If there is any justice in the literary world, Donaldson will earn
the right to stand shoulder to shoulder with Tolkien.'   *Time Out*

'A writer of central significance as an author of demanding and
exploratory fantasy.'   JOHN CLUTE

'The most individual of the Tolkien successors.'   *Guardian*

'Comparable to Tolkien at his best.'   *Washington Post*

ISBN 0 00 651171 6

Assassin's Apprentice

Book One of The Farseer Trilogy

Robin Hobb

A glorious classic fantasy combining the magic of Le Guin with the epic mastery of Tolkien

Fitz is a royal bastard, cast out into the world with only his magical link with animals for solace and companionship.

But when Fitz is adopted into the royal household, he must give up his old ways and learn a new life: weaponry, scribing, courtly manners; and how to kill a man secretly. Meanwhile, raiders ravage the coasts, leaving the people Forged and soulless. As Fitz grows towards manhood, he will have to face his first terrifying mission, a task that poses as much risk to himself as it does to his target: for Fitz is a threat to the throne . . . but he may also be the key to the future of the kingdom.

'Refreshingly original'   JANNY WURTS

'I couldn't put this novel down'   *Starburst*

ISBN: 0-00-648009-8

Curse of the Mistwraith

The Wars of Light and Shadows: Volume 1

Janny Wurts

TWO BROTHERS WORLDS APART,
THEIR FATES INTERLOCKED IN ENMITY
BY THE CURSE OF MISTWRAITH . . .

The world of Althera lives in eternal fog, its skies obscured
by the malevolent Mistwraith. Only the combined powers
of two half-brothers can challenge the Mistwraith's stran-
glehold:

Arithon – Master of Shadows
Lysaer – Lord of Light

Arithon and Lysaer will find that they are inescapably
bound inside a pattern of events dictated by their deepest
convictions. Yet there is much more at stake than one
battle with the Mistwraith – as the sorcerers of the
Fellowship of Seven know well. For between them the
half-brothers hold the balance of the world, its harmony
and its future in their hands.

It ought to be illegal for one person to have so much talent
STEPHEN DONALDSON

Astonishingly original and compelling
RAYMOND E. FEIST

ISBN: 0-586-21069-5